CRAIG THOMAS

CRAIG THOMAS

FIREFOX

FIREFOX DOWN

SEA LEOPARD

Firefox first published in Great Britain in 1977
by Michael Joseph Ltd
Sea Leopard first published in Great Britain in 1981
by Michael Joseph Ltd
Firefox Down first published in Great Britain in 1983
by Michael Joseph Ltd

This omnibus edition first published in Great Britain in 1987
exclusively for Marks and Spencers Plc
by Michael Joseph Ltd,
27 Wrights Lane,
London W8

Firefox © Craig Thomas 1977
Sea Leopard © Craig Thomas 1981
Firefox Down © Craig Thomas 1983

ISBN 014–087–268–X

Typeset by Cambrian Typesetters, Frimley, Surrey
Printed in Great Britain by
Richard Clay Ltd, Bungay, Suffolk

CONTENTS

FIREFOX

for TERRY
who built the Firefox,
and made her fly

Acknowledgements

I wish to acknowledge the invaluable help given to me, in time and expertise, by T. R. Jones, with all the technical matters connected with the experimental aircraft that features so prominently in the book.

I am indebted also for their assistance with matters geographical to Miss Audrey Simmonds and Mr Graham Simms; I would also like to thank Mr. Peter Payne, whose enthusiastic scepticism kept me alert, but hopeful, during the writing of the book.

I am indebted finally to various publications, particularly to John Barron's highly informative and invaluable book, *KGB*, and to the admirable series of Jane's publications – particularly to current editions of *All the World's Aircraft*, *Fighting Ships*, and *Weapons Systems*, from each of which I gleaned much valuable technical information.

Craig Thomas
Lichfield

Nor law, nor duty bade me fight,
Nor public men nor cheering crowds,
A lonely impulse of delight
Drove to this tumult in the clouds;
I balanced all, brought all to mind,
The years to come seemed waste of breath,
A waste of breath the years behind
In balance with this life, this death.

W. B. Yeats

The man lay on the bed in his hotel room, his hands raised like claws above his chest, as if reaching for his eyes. His body was stretched out, rigid with tension. A heavy perspiration shone on his brow and darkened the shirt beneath his arms. His eyes were wide open, and he was dreaming.

The nightmare did not come often now; it was like a fading malaria. He had made it that way – he had, not Buckholz or the psychiatrists at Langley. He despised them. He had done it himself. Yet, when the dream did come, it returned with all its old force, the fossilisation of all memory and all conscience. It was all that was left of Vietnam. Even as he suffered, sweated within its toils, a cold part of his mind observed its images and effects – charting the ravages of the disease.

In his dream he had become a Vietnamese, Viet-Cong or peasant – it did not matter – and he was burning to death, slowly and horribly; the napalm that the searching Phantom had dropped was devouring him. The roar of the retreating jets was drowned in the roar of the flames as he singed, burned, began to melt . . .

In the flames, too, other times and other images flickered; flying sparks. Even as his muscles withered, shrivelled in the appalling heat, he saw himself, as if from a point far at the back of his brain, flying the old Mig-21 and frozen in the moment of catching the USAF Phantom in his sights . . . then the drugs in Saigon, the dope that had led to the time when he had been caught in the sights of a Mig . . . then there was the breakdown, the months in the Veterans' Hospital and the crying, bleeding minds all around him until he teetered on the verge of madness and wanted to sink into the new darkness where he would not hear the cries of other minds or the new shrieks of his own brain.

Then there was the work in the hospital, the classic atonement that had turned to a vile taste at the back of his throat. Then there was the Mig, and learning to fly Russian, think Russian, be Russian . . . Lebedev, the defector with the Georgian accent, they had brought in to coach him, thoroughly – because he had to be fluent . . .

Then the training on the American-copied Mig-25, and the study of Belenko's debriefing, Belenko who had flown a Foxbat to Japan years before . . . and the days and weeks in the simulator, flying a plane he had never seen, that did not exist.

The napalm and the flames and Saigon . . .

The smell of his own burning was heavy in his nostrils, vividly clear, the bluish flame from the melting fat . . . Mitchell Grant, in his hotel room, burned to death in agony.

LUNCH WITH SAMMY ?
— THURS. 1245

Call H.S. 2136 / Ext 74.

ESTIMATES 76/77
Check with Geoffrey

KNOWN FACTS 22 AUG 75

① The A/c 10-15 years ahead of M.R.C.A and USAF's Y16.

② It will be flying by 1980 - Operational by ?

③ Performance - projected Mach 5 plus etc !

④ Designed around Adv. Tech. Engines and possesses Thought Guided Weapons System.
— Nato does not. — NOR IS IT LIKELY !

⑤ Nato codenamed - without euphemism —
"FIREFOX"

⑥ We do not have —— a) the budget b) technology.
.... so — we must have the firefox !

(SOLUTION ?) ← « Simple really

STEAL ONE

Talk to Plessey
Ferranti
etc .

Dear Prime Minister,

   You asked for fuller information concerning the Mikoyan
project at Bilyarsk. I therefore enclose the report I received last
Autumn from Aubrey, who is controller of the espionage effort
there. You will see he has a rather radical suggestion to make! Your
comments would be illuminating.

               Sincerely,
               Richard Cunningham

                 *   *   *   *

EYES ONLY – HEAD OF SIS   18/9/75

My dear Cunningham,

   You have received the usual digests of my full reports with
regard to the espionage effort being made against the secret
Mikoyan project at Bilyarsk, which has received the NATO
codename "Firefox". In asking for my recommendations, I wonder
whether you are sufficiently prepared for what I propose.
   You do not need me to outline Soviet hopes of this new aircraft.
Something amounting to a defence contingency fund has been set
aside, we believe, to cope with eventual mass-production of this
aircraft. Work on the two scheduled successors to the current Mig-
25, the "Foxbat", has or is being run down; the Foxbat will remain
the principal strike plane of the Soviet Air Force until that service is
re-equipped with the Mig-31, the "Firefox". At least three new
factory-complexes are planned or under construction in European
Russia solely, one suspects, to facilitate the production of the
Mig-31.
   As to the aircraft itself, I do not need to reiterate its potency. If it
fulfils Soviet hopes, then we will have nothing like it before the end
of the eighties, if at all. Air supremacy will pass entirely to the Soviet
Union. We all know the reasons for SALT talks and defence cuts,
and it is too late for recriminations. Suffice it to say that an
unacceptable balance of power would result from Russian possession
of the production interceptor and strike versions of this aircraft.
   With regard to our own espionage effort, we are fortunate in
having acquired the services of Pyotr Baranovich, who is engaged

on the design and development of the weapons-system itself. He has recruited, as you are aware, two other highly-qualified technicians, and David Edgecliffe has supplied the Moscow end of the pipeline – Pavel Upenskoy, his best native Russian agent. However impressive it all sounds – and we both know that it is – it is not sufficient! What we have learned, or are likely to learn will be insufficient to reproduce or neutralise the threat of the Mig-31. Baranovich and his team know little of the aircraft outside their own specialisations, so compartmented is the secrecy of the research.

Therefore, we must mount, or be preparing to mount within the next five years, an operation against the Bilyarsk project. I am suggesting nothing less than that we should *steal* one of the aircraft, preferably a full production prototype around the time of its final trials.

I can conceive your surprise! However, I think it feasible, providing a pilot can be found. I would think it necessary to employ an American, since our own RAF pilots no longer train in aerial combat (I am considering *all* the possibilities), and an American with combat experience in Vietnam might be best of all. We have the network in Moscow and Bilyarsk which could place pilot and plane in successful proximity.

Your thoughts on the above should prove enlightening. I look forward to receiving them.

> Sincerely,
> Kenneth Aubrey

*   *   *   *

EYES ONLY – PM/"C"   11/2/76

My dear Sir Richard,

I am grateful for your prompt reply to my request. I really wished to know more about the aircraft itself – perhaps you could forward a digest of Aubrey's reports over the past three years? As to his suggestion – I presume he is not in earnest? It is, of course, ridiculous to talk of piracy against the Soviet Union!

> My regards to your wife.

> Sincerely,
> Andrew Gresham

*   *   *   *

Kenneth —

I enclose a copy of the P.M.'s letter of yesterday. You will see what he thinks of your budding criminality! At least as far as aircraft are concerned. His opinion is also mine – officially. Privately, I'll admit this Bilyarsk thing is scaring the pants off me! Therefore, do what you can to find a pilot, and work up a scenario for this proposed operation – just in case! You might try making enquiries of our friend Buckholz in the CIA, who has just got himself promoted Head of the Covert Action Staff – or is his title Director over there? Anyway, the Americans have as much to lose as Europe in this, and are just as interested in Bilyarsk.

Good hunting. On this, don't call me, I'll call you – if and when!

Sincerely,
Richard

*   *   *   *

EYES ONLY – PRIME MINISTER   29/6/76

My dear Prime Minister,

You requested Sir Richard Cunningham to supply you with clarification of certain technical matters arising in connection with the aircraft we have codenamed the "Firefox" (Mikoyan Mig-31). I suppose that this letter is an opportunity to further plead my cause, but I think it important that you understand the gravity of Russian development in certain fields of military aviation, all of which are to meet in the focal point of this aircraft.

Our information comes principally from the man Baranovich, who has been responsible for the electronics that make practical the theoretical work of others on a thought-guided weapons-system for use in high-technology aircraft. Baranovich cannot supply us with all the information we require even on this area of the Bilyarsk project, and we would be unlikely to successfully remove him from Russia, guarded as they all are in Bilyarsk. Hence my suggestion that we steal one of the later series of production prototypes, which will contain everything the Russians intend to put in the front-line versions.

Perhaps I should cite at this point an interesting civil development of the idea of thought guidance – the latest type of invalid chair being studied in the United States. This is intended to enable a completely paralysed and/or immobilised person to control the movements of an invalid carriage by positive thought activity. The chair would be electronically rigged so that sensors attached to the brain (via a "cap" or headrest of some kind) would transmit the commands of the brain, as electronic impulses, to the mechanics of the wheelchair or invalid carriage. A mental command to move ahead, turn round, to move left or right, shall we say, would come direct from the brain – instead of the command being transmitted to wasted or useless muscles, it would go into the artificial "limbs" of the wheelchair. There is no projected military development of any such system; whereas the Soviets, it would appear, are close to perfecting just such a system for military use. (And the West has not yet built the wheelchair.)

The system which we are convinced Baranovich is developing seems designed to couple radar and infra-red, those two standard forms of detection and guidance in modern aircraft – with a thought-guided and -controlled arsenal aboard the plane. Radar, as you are aware, bounces a signal off a solid object, and a screen reveals what is actually there: infra-red reveals on a screen what heat-sources are in the vicinity of the detection equipment. For guidance purposes, either or both these methods can be used to direct missiles and to aim them. The missiles themselves contain one or both of these systems themselves. However, the principal advantage of the thought-guided system is that the pilot retains command of his missiles after firing, as well as having a speeded-up command of their actual release, because his mental commands become translated directly to the firing-system, without his physical interference.

It must be said that we do not have, nor do the Russians we understand, weapons that will exploit such a sophisticated system – such as new kinds of missile or cannon. However, unless we quickly nullify the time advantage of the Russian programme, we will be left too far behind by the undoubted acceleration of missile and cannon technology ever to catch up.

Therefore, we must possess the system. We must steal a Mig-31, at some time.

Sincerely,
Kenneth Aubrey

*   *   *   *

PM TO KA   24/9/76

My dear Aubrey,

   My thanks for your communication. I appreciate your anxiety,
though I reject your solution. And, in view of the recent "present"
brought to the West by Lt. Belenko, namely the "Foxbat", are you
not perhaps worrying unduly? It will take the Russians years,
surely, to recover from the loss of the Foxbat's secrets?

                 Sincerely,
                 Andrew Gresham

                 *   *   *   *

KA TO PM   30/9/76

My dear Prime Minister,

   In reply to your query, I am convinced that the Foxbat, the Mig-
25, is little more than a toy compared with the projected aircraft
which NATO has codenamed the Firefox. We must not be lulled
into a false sense of security by the recent accident in Japan – a piece
of good fortune we hardly deserve, and which may not prove to our
final advantage.
   I should also add that information coming back to our technical
experts here from Japan suggests that the Mig-25 is not all that it
might be. It is constructed in large part of steel rather than titanium,
it has difficulty in obtaining its maximum speed and holding it, and
its electronics are by no means as sophisticated as we were led to
believe.
   However, we have the opinion of Baranovich in Bilyarsk that the
proposed MIG-31 *will* live up to even extravagant expectations. He
is aware of the shortcomings of the Mig-25, by means of scientific
gossip – but no one is carping at Bilyarsk about the Firefox.

                 Sincerely,
                 Kenneth Aubrey

                 *   *   *   *

                       15

Richard,

    Have you seen the S.A.C. Radar reports on the initial trials of FIREFOX?

    The Americans had everything, including the Breakfast bar in the air, monitoring the performance trials, based on Baranovichs INFO. ref times, flight path etc.

— she flew and — NOTHING.!

② <u>IF</u> it's what I think it is — — then the Soviets have developed Anti-Radar for FIREFOX and the DEW. Line can be put away along with the longbow and cutlass!

③ Advise the P.M.! —— <u>NOW</u>

In haste

Kenneth

My dear Prime Minister,

   I do not know what anti-radar is, nor how it works, in the case of
the Russian system. Reports from Bilyarsk, from our sources who are
not privy to its secrets, indicate that it is not mechanical or electronic
at all — and therefore cannot be adversely affected by any counter-
measures. It is therefore totally unlike our own "Chaff" which is used
to confuse radars, or any American developments in terms of
electronic confusion of radar. Neither the USAF nor the RAF have
anything in mind such as the Russian system would appear to be.
   It is evident now that the Firefox is the most serious threat to the
security of the West since the development of nuclear weapons by
the Soviet Union and China.

          Sincerely,
          Kenneth Aubrey

               *   *   *   *

"C"/KA   30/7/79

Kenneth —

   You have the go-ahead from the P.M. and from Washington. You
will liaise with Buckholz. Your scenario, including pilot (an odd
bird, wouldn't you say?), refuelling point, and method of getting
pilot to Bilyarsk, are approved. It is understood that the pilot should
have some kind of homing-device which he can use to find the
refuelling point — one which the Russians will not be aware of, and
will therefore be unable to trace. The P.M. realises the urgency, and
Farnborough have started work. See a man there called Davies.
   Good luck to you. The ball is now firmly in your court.
   Richard

               *   *   *   *

Alone in his office, the smell of fresh paint still strong in his nostrils, KGB Colonel Mihail Yurievich Kontarsky, Head of the "M" Department assigned to security of the Mikoyan project at Bilyarsk, was again a prey to lurid doubts. He had been left alone by his assistant, Dmitri Priabin, and the sense of reassurance he had drawn from the work they had done that afternoon had dissipated in the large room. He sat behind the big, new desk, and willed himself to remain calm.

It had been going on too long, he realised – this need for the sedative of work. He had lost, he knew, the sense of perspective, now that the date for the final weapons-trials on the Mig-31 was so close. It was nothing, it seemed, but a last-minute panic – grabbing up the bits and pieces of his job like scattered baggage. All the time afraid that he had forgotten something.

He was afraid to leave his office at that moment, because he knew his body could not yet assume its characteristic arrogance of posture. He would be recognised in the corridors of the Centre as a worried man; and that might prove an irretrievable error on his part.

He had known about the security leaks at Bilyarsk for years – about Baranovich, Kreshin and Semelovsky – and their courier, Dherkov the grocer. Over such a period of time as the Mig had taken to be developed and built, it was impossible that he should not have known.

But, he and his department had done nothing about them, nothing more than reduce the flow of information to a trickle by tightening surveillance, preventing meetings, drops, and the like. Because – he suddenly dropped his head into his hands, pressing his palms against his closed eyelids – he had gambled, out of fear. He had been afraid to recommend the removal of vital human components from the project, and afraid that even if he did then the British or the CIA would suborn others whose existence would be unknown to him, or put in new agents and contacts he did not know. Better the devil you know, he had told Priabin when he made the decision, trying to smile; and the young man had gone along with him. Now it seemed an eminently foolish remark.

The price of failure had been absolute, even then. Disgrace, even execution. He tried to comfort himself by thinking that whatever the British and Americans knew, it was far less than they might have known . . .

His narrow, dark features were wan and tired, his grey eyes fearful. He had had to let them continue working, even if they were spies. The words sounded hollowly, as if he were already reciting them to an unbelieving audience, even to Andropov himself . . .

PART ONE

THE THEFT

ONE:

The Murder

The walk from the British Airways BAC-111 across the tarmac of Cheremetievo Airport seemed interminable to the slightly-built man at the end of the file of passengers. The wind whipped at his trilby, which he held in place, jamming it firmly down with one hand while in the other he held a travel bag bearing the legend of the airline. He was an undistinguished individual – he wore spectacles, heavy-rimmed, and his top lip was decorated with a feeble growth of moustache. His nose was reddened, and his cheeks blanched, by the chill wind. He wore a dark topcoat and dark trousers, and anonymous shoes. Only the churning of his stomach, the bilious fear, placed and defined him.

It was only because it was the express practice of the KGB to photograph all passengers arriving on foreign flights at Moscow's principal airport that he, too, was photographed with a camera equipped with a telephoto lens. He guessed that it had happened, though he could not have said at what point in his walk across the tarmac, his head bent in an attempt to keep the flying dust from his face and eyes.

The sudden warmth of the disembarkation lounge struck him, tempted him to turn down the collar of his coat, remove his hat, and brush at the brown hair. He slicked it away from his forehead, so that with its evident white seam of a parting it belonged to a man unconscious of fashion. At that point, he was photographed again. In fact, it was as if he had posed for such a study. He looked about him, and then moved towards the customs desk. Around him, the human tide of any international terminal flowed, attracted his attention. Delegations filed through, and his eyes picked out the flamingo colours of African national costume. There were others – Orientals, Europeans. He became an item in that vast congress, and the cosmopolitan familiarity of an airport lounge settled his stomach. If anything, he appeared very cold, and more than a little airsick.

He knew that the men who stood behind the customs officials were probably security men – KGB. He placed his airline bag

21

between the screens of the detector, and his other luggage came sliding towards him on the conveyor belt. The man did not move – he had already anticipated what would happen next. One of the two men standing with apparent indifference behind the customs men, stepped forward and lifted the two suitcases clear of the belt.

The man watched the customs officer fixedly, seeming to ignore the security man as he opened each of the suitcases, and ungently, thoroughly, ruffled through the clothing they contained. The customs official checked his papers, and then passed them to the controller at the end of the long counter. The ruffling of the clothes became more urgent, and the smile on the face of the KGB man disappeared, replaced by an intent, baffled stare into the well of each suitcase.

The official said: "Mr. Alexander Thomas Orton? What is your business in Moscow?"

The man coughed, and replied: "As you can see from my papers, I am an export agent of the Excelsior Plastics Company, of Welwyn Garden City."

"Yes, indeed." The man's eyes kept flickering to the frustrated mime of the security officer. "You – have been to the Soviet Union several times during the past two years, Mr. Orton?"

"Again, yes – and nothing like this has happened to me before!" The man was not annoyed, merely surprised. He seemed determined to be pleasant, a seasoned, knowledgeable visitor to Russia, and not to regard the insults being levied at his possessions.

"I apologise," the official said. The KGB man was now in muttered conversation with the customs officer. The remainder of the passengers had already passed through the gate, and spilled into the concourse of the passenger lounge. They were gone, and Mr. Alexander Thomas Orton was feeling rather alone.

"I have all the correct papers, you know," he said. "Signed by your Trade Attaché at the Soviet Embassy in London." There was a trace of nervousness in his voice, as if some practical joke which he did not understand were being perpetrated against him. "As you say, I've been here a number of times – there's never been any trouble of this kind before. Does he really have to make such a mess of my belongings – what is he looking for?"

The KGB man approached. Alexander Thomas Orton brushed a hand across his oiled hair, and tried to smile. The Russian was a big man, with flattened Mongol features and an unpleasant aura of minor, frustrated, power about him. He took the passport and the visas from the official, and made a business of their scrutiny.

When he appeared satisfied, he stared hard into Orton's face and said: "Why do you come to Moscow, Mr. – Orton?"

22

"Orton – yes. I am a businessman, an exporter, to be exact."

"What do you hope to export to the Soviet Union, from your country?" There was a sneer in the Russian's voice, a curl of the lip to emphasise it. There was something unreal about the whole business. The man brushed his oiled hair again, and seemed more nervous than previously, as if caught in some prank.

"Plastic goods – toys, games, that sort of thing."

"Where are your samples – the rubbish you sell, Mr. Orton?"

"Rubbish? Look here!"

"You are English, Mr. Orton? Your voice . . . it does not sound very English."

"I am Canadian by birth."

"You do not look Canadian, Mr. Orton."

"I – try to appear as English as possible. It helps, in sales abroad, you understand?" Suddenly, he remembered the vocal training, with a flick of irritation like the sting of a wet towel; it had seemed amidst his other tasks absurd in its slightness. Now, he was thankful for it.

"I do not understand."

"Why did you search my luggage?"

The KGB man was baffled for a moment. "There – is no need for you to know that. You are a visitor to the Soviet Union. Remember that, Mr. Orton!" As if to express his anger, he held up the small transistor radio as a last resort, looked into Orton's face, then tugged open the back of the set. Orton clenched his hands in his pockets, and waited.

The Russian, evidently disappointed, closed the back and said: "Why do you bring this? You cannot receive your ridiculous programmes in Moscow!" The man shrugged, and the set and the passport were thrust at him. He took them, trying to control the shaking of his hands.

Then he stooped, picked up his hand grip, and waited as the KGB man closed his suitcases, and then dropped them at his feet. The locks of one burst, and shirts and socks brimmed over. The KGB man laughed as Orton scrabbled after two pairs of rolling grey socks, on his knees. When he finally closed the lid, his hair was hanging limply over his brow, interfering with his vision. He flicked the lock away, adjusted his spectacles, and hoisted his cases at his sides. Then, mustering as much offended dignity as he could, he walked slowly away, into the concourse, towards the huge glass doors which would let him into the air, and relief. He did not need to look behind him to understand that the KGB man was already consulting with his colleague who had not moved from his slouched, assured stance against the wall behind the customs desk, and who had obviously been the superior in rank. That second man had watched him intently throughout his time at the desk – customs, passport and KGB.

Gant knew that they would be 2nd Chief Directorate personnel – probably from the 1st section, 7th department, which directed security with regard to American, British, and Canadian tourists. And, Gant reflected, his stomach relaxing for the first time since he had left the aircraft, in a way he was all three, and therefore, very properly, their concern.

He called for a taxi from the rank outside the main doors of the passenger lounge, setting down his suitcases, and cramming his trilby on his head once more against the fierce wind, little abated by the shelter of the terminal building.

A black taxi drew up, and he said: "Hotel Moskva, please," in as pleasant, innocuous a voice as he could muster.

The driver opened the door for him, loaded his suitcases, jumped back in the cab, and then waited, engine idling. Gant knew he was waiting for the KGB tail-car to collect him. Gant had seen the signal from the KGB man who had bullied him, a shadowy, bulking figure. He took off his hat and leaned sideways, so that he saw the long, sleek, vividly-chromed saloon in the driver's mirror. Then the driver of the taxi engaged the gears and they pulled out of the airport, onto the motorway that would take him south-east into the centre of Moscow – the wide, prestigious Leningrad Avenue. He settled back in his seat, being careful not to glance behind him through the tinted rear window. The black saloon would be behind him, he knew.

So, he thought, feeling the tension drift down and vanish, Alexander Thomas Orton had passed his first inspection. He was not sweating – the taxi had an inefficient heater, and the temperature inside was low. Yet, he admitted, he had been nervous. It had been a test he had to pass. He had had to play a part already familiar to his audience, so familiar that they would have noticed any false note. He had had to become totally self-effacing, not merely behind the mask of Orton's greasy hair, spectacles, and weak jaw, but in his movements, his voice. At the same time, he had had to carry with him, like the scent of a distinctive after-shave, an air of suspicion, of seediness. Thirdly, and perhaps most difficult for him, he had had to possess a certain, ill-fitting, acquired Englishness of manner and accent.

As he considered his success, and was thankful for the solid lack of imagination and insight of his interrogator, he acknowledged the brilliance of Aubrey's mind. The little plump Englishman had been developing Gant's cover as Orton, a cover merely to get him

24

unobtrusively into Russia, for a long time. For almost two years, a man looking very much as Gant did now, had been passing through customs at Cheremetievo. An exporter, touting with some success a range of plastic toys. Apparently, they sold rather well in GUM, in Red Square. A fact that had amused Aubrey a great deal.

There was, naturally, more; Alexander Thomas Orton was a smuggler. The KGB's suspicions had been carefully aroused concerning Orton's possible activities in the drug-smuggling line a little more than a year before. Orton had been watched carefully, closely – yet never harried so openly before. Gant wondered whether Aubrey had not turned the screw on him. The big, dumb KGB man had expected to find something in his luggage, that was certain. And, now that his suspicions, aroused and then frustrated, had remained unfulfilled, Gant was being tailed to his hotel.

The taxi passed the Khimky Reservoir on the right, the expanse of grey water looking cold and final under the cloudy, rushing sky. Soon, they were into the built-up, urban mass of the city, and Gant watched the Dynamo Stadium sliding past the window to his left.

Aubrey, Gant knew, had been unimpressed by him. Not that he cared. Gant, for all his involvement in the part he was playing, had never intended to impress. He was at the beginning of his journey and, if he felt any emotion at all, it was one of impatience. Only one thing had mattered to him, ever since Buckholz had found him, in that dead-beat pizza palace in Los Angeles during his lunch-break, when he had been working as a garage-hand – it had been the first, and only time, he had left the Apache group, the tame Mig-squadron belonging to the USAF, and only one thing had ever mattered. He would get to fly the greatest airplane in history. If Gant possessed a soul any longer, which he doubted, it would be in that idea, enshrined perhaps, even embalmed therein. Buckholz had got him to fly again, on the Mig-21, and then the Foxbat; then he had left, tried to run away. Then Buckholz had found him again, and the idea had been broached . . . the Firefox.

His playing at being Orton amused Aubrey – was necessary. With true and utter single-mindedness, however, Gant viewed it merely as a prelude. It got him nearer to the Firefox.

Gant had always possessed a self-belief that amounted almost to illness. He had never lost that belief. Not in the nightmares, in the drugs, in the hospital, in the breakdown, in the attempted atonement. He had never ceased to think of himself in any other way than as a flyer – and as the best. Buckholz had known that, the bastard, Gant reflected – and he had used that because it was the lever that would work, the only one . . . He couldn't run away. The job in Los Angeles – that had been a fake, a drop-out as real as putting on a disguise. Before that, the hospital, and the white uniform he had adopted – they had been disguises, too. He had tried to hide from the truth, the truth that the best could be afraid, that he could overtax himself, that he could, might fail.

That had been the real nightmare. Gant's precarious world, the whole person that he was, was threatened, by stretched nerves, by too many missions, by too much danger and tension.

Gant rubbed a hand across his brow, and looked down at his damp fingertips. He wore an expression of distaste, almost disgust, on his face. He was sweating now. It was not reaction from the goddam stupid games he was beginning to have to play with the KGB, on their home field – not that; rather the memory of his attempts to escape.

Gant came from a family of nonentities. By the time he entered his teens, he despised his parents, and his brother, the insurance salesman who was a conspicuous failure. He despised, though he could not help loving, the elder sister who was an untidy slut with four kids, and a drunk for a husband. He had come from a dirt town in the vast, featureless expanse of the Mid-West – Clarkville, pop. 2763, the signposts had read – together with the legend "A Great Little Town". Gant had hated Clarkville. Every moment he spent within its confines, or locked within the rolling, flat corn-belt that buried it, he had been nothing, had felt himself nothing. He had left Clarkville behind him long ago, and he had never been back, not even for the funeral of his mother, or the comfort of his ageing father. His sister had written to him, once, berating and pleading in turns. He had not replied. The letter had reached him in Saigon. Gant had never escaped from Clarkville. He carried it with him, wherever he went. It had shaped him.

He wiped the sweat from his forehead on the leg of his dark trousers. He closed his eyes, and tried not to think about the past. It had been the dream, he thought. That damned dream had started this. That, and his nettled, irritated pride because smug, patronising Aubrey had looked down his nose at him. Gant's hands bunched into fists on the plastic seat. Like a child, all he wanted to do now was to show them, show them all, just as he had wanted to show them in Clarkville, that dead town of dead people. There was only one way to show Aubrey. He had to bring back his airplane – the Firefox.

Kontarsky was on the telephone, the extension that linked him with his superior officer within the Industrial Security Section of the 2nd Chief Directorate, of which the "M" Department formed a small, but vital, part. Dmitri Priabin watched his chief carefully, almost like a prompter following an actor, script open on his knees. Kontarsky seemed much more at ease than during their interview the previous day, as if action had soothed him during the last twenty-four hours.

During that elapsed period, Kontarsky had received an up-to-date report from the KGB unit at Bilyarsk, and surveillance of the underground cell had been increased. There had been no unaccountable arrivals at Bilyarsk during the past forty-eight hours, and only the courier, Dherkov, had left the small town. His grocery van had been thoroughly searched on his return from Moscow. Kontarsky had ordered searches of all vehicles arriving in the town, and a thorough scrutiny of all personnel passing inside the security fence of the factory. Dog patrols had been intensified around the perimeter fence, and the number of armed guards in the hangars had been trebled.

Once those things had been done, Kontarsky and Priabin had both begun to feel more at ease. Priabin himself was to leave for Bilyarsk that night by KGB helicopter, and take over effective command of the security forces from the officer on the spot. Effectively, within hours, he could seal Bilyarsk tight. Kontarsky had decided not to travel with the First Secretary and his party, but to impress by being on the spot himself twenty-four hours before the test-flight. They would arrest the members of the underground only a matter of hours before the flight, and at the time of arrival of the First Secretary, they would already be undergoing interrogation. It would, he calculated, be sure to impress the First Secretary and Andropov who would be part of the entourage. Both Priabin and Kontarsky anticipated extracting the maximum satisfaction from the interrogations. Baranovich, Kreshin, Semelovsky, Dherkov and his wife, would be snatched out of their false sense of security in a theatrical, and impressive, display of ruthless KGB efficiency.

Kontarsky put down the telephone receiver. He smiled broadly at his aide, and at the third person in his office – Viktor Lanyev, assistant KGB security chief at Bilyarsk. Lanyev had been flown to Moscow to make a report, thereby doubling Kontarsky's sense of security after having received a written report from Tsernik, the chief security officer at Bilyarsk. After listening to Lanyev's meticulous diary of the movements and contacts of the three men under observation, Kontarsky had been relieved, had set himself on a course of optimism, at the end of which journey he could already envisage a successful conclusion.

The security arrangements at Bilyarsk were a minor classic, entirely orthodox, without imagination – a policy of overkill. There were the resident, declared hierarchy of KGB officers, and their select squad from the 2nd Directorate; as a support group, there

27

were personnel of the GRU, Soviet Military Intelligence, who performed as guards and patrols both at the airstrip and in the town; thirdly, there were the "unofficial" members of the KGB, the informants and civilian spies closest to the research and development teams. All three groups were focusing their attention on four men and a woman. They watched everything, saw and knew everything.

Kontarsky, prematurely luxuriating in the congratulations of his superior, said, after a while, steepling his fingers as he leaned back in his chair: "We will make doubly sure, my friends. We must take no risks at this point – this late point in time. Therefore, I suggest we commandeer a special detachment from the 5th Chief Directorate, one of their Security Support Units. You agree?"

Lanyev, the man on the spot, seemed somewhat insulted. "There is no need, Comrade Colonel."

"I say there is – *every* need!" Kontarsky's eyes were angry, commanding. "I must have the most complete assurances that nothing will, or can, go wrong at Bilyarsk. Are you prepared to guarantee – in the most definite, unequivocal way – that nothing can go wrong?"

Kontarsky was smiling at Lanyev. The middle-aged man, who had risen as high in the ranks of the KGB as he would ever achieve, looked down, and shook his head.

"No, Comrade Colonel, I would not wish to do that," he said quietly.

"Naturally – and we are not asking that you should, Viktor Alexeivich, no." He beamed at his two subordinates. Priabin sensed the swing of Kontarsky's mood. At times, his chief struck him as portraying many of the symptoms of the manic-depressive in miniature. Now the doubts of the previous day were deeply buried. Kontarsky would, almost, not have recognised himself had he confronted the frightened man of yesterday.

"How many men, Colonel?" he asked.

"Perhaps a hundred – discreetly, of course – but a hundred. We may run the risk of frightening them off, but that will be better than failing to catch them at whatever they have planned."

"Comrade Tsernik does not believe that anything is planned, Comrade Colonel," Lanyev interpolated.

"Mm. Perhaps not. But we must act as if they intend to sabotage the test-flight – something wrong with one of the missiles, or with the cannon . . . a mid-air explosion. I do not have to draw pictures for either of you. Production of the Mig-31 would be put back, perhaps reconsidered. Either that, or we should all, *all* of us, be – heavily disgraced?" Kontarsky was still smiling. For a moment, there was a worried drawing together of the eyebrows, and then he shook off the doubts. He could face his fear now, because he could not see or envisage how he might fail. Mere multiplication gave him confidence. Almost two hundred men at Bilyarsk – not to mention the informers . . .

"I must check with the Political Security Service as to which of the informers we have been – *loaned* – are most reliable," Kontarsky went on briskly. "We should not need them – but they will be inside the factory complex, and therefore closest to the dissidents. They will be armed, under your direction, Viktor Alexeivich." Lanyev nodded. "And issued with communicators. Now, where will our three traitors be in the hours before the flight, when the aircraft is being armed?"

Lanyev consulted his notes.

"All three of them will be inside the hangar itself, Comrade Colonel – unfortunately."

"Yes, indeed. Three times as dangerous as they might otherwise be. Give me details."

"Baranovich has worked on the weapons-system itself, Comrade Colonel – as you know."

"He will be working on the aircraft during the night, until it takes off?"

"Yes, Comrade Colonel."

"He cannot be replaced?"

"Not possibly."

"Very well! What of the others?"

"Kreshin and Semelovsky are both little more than highly-favoured mechanics, Comrade Colonel," Lanyev supplied. "They will be concerned with the fuelling, and the loading of the missiles and the other weapons. Also, the Rearward Defence Pod. But they are most familiar with the systems, and not easy to replace."

"They can be watched?"

"Very closely. Our informers will be shoulder-to-shoulder with them throughout the night."

"As long as our informers know enough to recognise attempted sabotage when they see it!"

"They do, Comrade Colonel."

"Good. For that, I can take your word. Dherkov, naturally, will be at home, sleeping with that fat wife of his." Kontarsky smiled. His mood was being sustained by what he was hearing, by the action he appeared to be taking, the decisiveness of his manner, his voice . . . "Yes. May I sum up, gentlemen? Our GRU colleagues will throw a ring around Bilyarsk that will be impregnable; our borrowed Security Support Unit will arrive tomorrow, and will assist the guards on the perimeter fence, the hangars, the factory, and the boundaries of the town itself. Our three dissidents will be very closely watched – especially Baranovich. Have I left anything out, Dmitri?"

"I have everything here, in my notes," Priabin said.

Kontarsky stretched behind his desk, arms above his head. The smile that was beginning to irritate Priabin was fixed on his thin, dark features. His uniform collar was open at the neck, showing his prominent Adam's apple, and the thin, bird-like throat, the skin stretched, yet loose, like a turkey . . . Priabin dismissed the irritation from his mind.

"I think, as a further precaution, we will go and collect the Moscow end of the chain. No, not tonight. If they disappear with almost forty-eight hours to go, then Lansing may discover that fact, and warn off our friends at Bilyarsk. No! Tomorrow will do, giving us perhaps twenty-four hours to find out what they know! You will take care of that, Dmitri?"

"Yes, Colonel. I shall have the warehouse they use as a cover watched from tonight – and move in on your orders."

"Good. I would like to see them before – before I myself fly down to Bilyarsk tomorrow. Yes. Ask for surveillance by the 7th Directorate, Dmitri, on the warehouse. We – need not spare too many of our own men, and they are in business to watch people. They can be replaced by our team when I give the word."

"Very well, Colonel."

"Very well? Yes, Dmitri – I begin to feel that it may indeed be very well!" Kontarsky laughed. Priabin watched the Adam's apple bob up and down in the turkey-throat, hating his superior's overconfidence more than he feared his lapses of nerve.

The black saloon had eased itself into a convenient parking-place opposite the portico of the Moskva Hotel. As Gant had passed into the hotel foyer, and had patted his pockets as if to ensure he still had his papers, he had observed that the two men inside the saloon had made no move to follow him. One was already reading a newspaper, while the other, the driver, had just lit a cigarette. Warned by their inactivity, Gant surveyed the foyer from the vantage point of the hotel desk, and picked out the man who was waiting to identify him. His picture must have been transmitted via wireprint from Cheremetievo to Dzerzhinsky Street.

Had he not been thoroughly briefed by Aubrey as to what to expect, Gant might have been left breathless by such efficiency; the intrusive, dogged pursuit of himself. As it was, the realisation of the degree and intensity of the security with regard to himself, merely as a suspected "economic criminal", though deadened, still caused him a momentary feeling of wateriness in the pit of his stomach.

The man watching for him, masked by his copy of *Pravda*, showed no sign of interest. He was seated in one of the many alcoves off the central foyer, overcoat thrown over a chair, apparently at his ease. If, and when, Gant left the Moskva, that man would follow him. Probably already, the car outside had been relieved by another, operating under the auspices of the same Directorate of the KGB as the man behind the newspaper.

Once in his room, Gant removed the clear-glass spectacles, ruffled his hair deliberately, and pulled off his tie. It was as if he had released himself from a strait-jacket. He opened his suitcases, then slipped off his shoes. The room was a small suite, with the tall windows looking out over the windswept expanse of Red Square. Gant ignored the window, and helped himself to a Scotch from the drinks trolley placed in one corner of the room. He seated himself on a low sofa, put his feet up, and tried to relax. He had begun to realise that his attempted indifference would not work, not even in the apparent, luxurious safety of his centrally-heated, double-glazed hotel room. He had been instructed not to look for bugs, since he couldn't be sure he was not being observed through some two-way mirror device.

He glanced in the direction of the huge mirror on one wall, and then dragged his eyes away from it. He began to experience the hypnotic effect of KGB surveillance. It was so easy – it required a real effort of mind to avoid doing so – to imagine himself pinned on a card, naked and exposed, with a bright white light beating down upon him. He shivered involuntarily, and swallowed at the Scotch. The liquor, to which he had become used merely as a part of his general training to assume the mask of Orton, warmed his throat and stomach. He inhabited a landscape of eyes.

It was difficult to consider, coldly, objectively, the Russian defence system, the hours of the flight in the Firefox, the training on the Foxbat and the simulator constructed from the photographs and descriptions supplied by the man at Bilyarsk – Baranovich. With an effort, he decided to postpone such considerations.

He lapsed into thoughtless inactivity. Getting up, he moved to the window and looked down from the twelfth floor over Red Square. He had no interest in the rank of cars parked directly below. Under the lowering sky, in the gathering gloom of the late afternoon, he stared, for a long time, down the vast length of the square, over the roof of the History Museum, towards the towers and domes of the Kremlin. He could just pick out the guards before the bronze doors of the Lenin Mausoleum, and the tiny figures moving in and out of the glass doors of the grey edifice of GUM. At the far end of the square, huge, incredible, was St. Basil's Cathedral – garish, irreligious. His eyes continued to rove over the desert of Red Square, barely focused.

The Scotch, as he swallowed another mouthful, no longer warmed him. Already his thoughts were reaching into the immediate future, towards the meeting with three men he did not know on the embankment of the Moskva, near the Krasnoknlinski Bridge. He was to leave the hotel after dinner, and behave as a tourist, no matter who tailed him. All he had to do was to be certain to arrive at ten-thirty. He was to be sure to take his hat and overcoat – no, to wear them – and he had to take the transistor radio. That told him that he would not be returning to the hotel; it would be the beginning of his journey to Bilyarsk.

Alexander Thomas Orton left the bar of the Moskva Hotel a little before ten that evening, having taken dinner in the hotel dining-room. Throughout his meal he had been observed by a KGB man from the Surveillance Directorate – a short, obese man who had dined at a single table placed advantageously so that he could observe everyone in the huge room. The man had followed him into the bar, and had sat blatantly watching him, a large vodka before him on the table. Gant suspected that his room would be thoroughly searched during the meal, which was why the small transistor radio sat in the pocket of his overcoat, as it had done throughout dinner – he had hung the coat where he could see it, and where he could be seen to be able to see it. The pockets had not been searched.

Throughout dinner, he had studied his *Nagel Guide to Moscow*, following the text on a large map which he folded ostentatiously out over the table cloth during his dessert. He had continued to study map and text during the hour he had spent in the bar. When he left, he was followed almost immediately.

As he went down the steps of the hotel, into Red Square, the short fat man paused, and overtly lit a cigarette, the gas lighter flaring in the darkness. Gant did not see the signal, but he saw the dark figure detach itself from a large car parked near the spot where the tail-car had pulled in that afternoon. Only one man there, he thought – and the short fat man coming down the steps behind him. Two.

The headlights of the car flared in the darkness, flickered in time with the coughing engine, then blazed as the engine roared. It had seemed quiet until that moment, that the noise of the engine was exaggerated. Gant had a momentary fear that he was about to be arrested, prevented from leaving the vicinity of the hotel – but there was no attempt to overhaul him, even though he paused to check, turning up his collar against the wind that was blowing down the square into his face. He had to hold the unfamiliar, irritating trilby on his head, and bend forward into the wind.

He chose the left-hand pavement as he came out of Manezhnaya Square and into the Red Square proper. This would take him past the façade of GUM. There were many Muscovites in the square – the queue outside the Lenin Mausoleum had dispersed, but many people window-shopped in the glass of the great store, cold faces lit by the white lighting. Gant did not bother to check his tail – its distance, or persistence. He knew they would stay with him, and that some kind of general alert would go out the moment they lost him, and he would be hunted. Which was precisely what he did not want. These men had to stay close to him. Hence, he spent some time looking at the fashion displays, the often inadequate replicas of Western fashions that GUM offered, the grey monster that was the largest department store in the world, before he passed out of Red Square, again taking his time, strolling, staring across the windy space at the towers of the Kremlin.

By the time he reached the Moskva river, and the Moskvoretski Bridge, he was thoroughly cold. His hat was jammed on his head, and his hands thrust in his pockets. He did not appear to be a man going anywhere in particular, but he could no longer be taken for a sightseer, enjoying Moscow by lamplight. The wind coming off the river seemed icy, and he now reluctantly held on to his hat, because it was a signpost, it informed the men tailing him where he was, even though he would have rather kept his numb, white hand in his overcoat pocket. He bent over the parapet of the road bridge, looking down into the black, lamp-flecked water, its surface rippled by the wind. Someone paused further back down the bridge, immediately highlighted by his lack of movement since all the other figures on the bridge moved swiftly, tugged and pushed by the wind. Gant smiled to himself.

He turned his back to the river, and pulled his collar tight around his neck. Casually, he inspected the road across the bridge. The car had stopped, headlights switched off, seemingly empty, parked well away from the street lamps. And there was a second pedestrian, leaning with his back against the bridge, on the other side of the road, slightly ahead of him.

Gant began to walk again. Despite what he had been told, despite the tail-spotting in which he had engaged in New York and Washington as part of his training under Buckholz, a small knot of tension had begun to form in his stomach. He did not know what would happen when he reached the Krasnoknlinski Bridge, downriver of where he was now, but he had been instructed not to lose his tail. Aubrey had made that clear in the smoke-filled room of his hotel in London the previous night. The KGB was to be kept with him.

As he crossed the Drainage Canal that ran beside the Moskva and turned onto the Ozerkovskaia Quay, descending a flight of stone steps down to the embankment, he wanted to stop and be violently sick. He realised that the artificial calm he had felt until that moment had deserted him finally. He could no longer pretend to himself that this was only a tiresome preliminary, to be gone through before he came face-to-face with his part in the total proceedings. *This was real.* The cold and the wind had now been abated slightly by the level of the bridge; the men on his tail – he could hear them now, footsteps softly clattering, unhurried and assured, down the flight of steps to the embankment, forty or so yards behind him. He was frightened. One hand came out of his pocket and he gripped his coat where it sat across his stomach, twisting the material in his hand.

He wondered about the car and its occupants. He could not turn round now, to count heads. He knew, with a sickening certainty, that there were three, perhaps four men behind him now, and that the car would be driving along the Ozerkovskaia Quay above him, waiting for him to regain the street.

He passed the Oustinski Bridge, and glanced at his watch. Ten-twenty. It would take him no more than another ten minutes to reach the next bridge, where he was to make his rendezvous with . . . with whom? In the shadow of the bridge there was a strange silence. The Sadovisheskaya Embankment, where he stood, was empty except for one or two couples strolling towards him, arm-in-arm, idling by the canal as if miles from the centre of the city.

He breathed deeply three or four times, in the way he had done when settling his flying-helmet on his head, and glancing, for the first time, across the instrument panel of the aircraft he was about to fly. The memory, inspired by the physical control he asserted, seemed to calm him. He had to think that he was doing something of which he was a master – flying. If he could think that, then he could go on. The footsteps had stopped behind him, like patient guardians, waiting until he might be strong enough to continue.

He walked on, passed a young couple absorbed in each other without even a glance in their direction, and measured the pace of his footsteps. He could hear footsteps behind him, a little clatter rebounding from the embankment wall, then the stronger, over-lapping signals from the following KGB men. The footsteps of the couple, slower it seemed and less purposeful, faded away behind

34

him. He wanted to run – he could not believe that they would let him reach the bridge. He wanted to run . . . It was a question of easing back the speed, not to overfly: he imagined the aerial situation, of having overflown a target, pulling back, waiting patiently, even though he had lost sight of the Mig, lost sight of the Phantom, when he himself had been flying the Foxbat . . . the terrible moments before re-contact. He calmed himself. It wasn't the same, this situation, it was *less* dangerous.

He walked on, having regained an hallucinatory equilibrium. He *was* the best there was . . . he was flying.

He climbed up the steps of the embankment to the Krasnoknlinski Bridge, crossed the canal without seeming to hurry, and descended the flight of steps down to the narrow embankment of the Moskva, on the south side of the river. The black water stretched away to the line of yellow lights along the Kotelnitcheskaia Quay on the other bank. There were no footsteps behind him for seconds after he ended his descent, yet his refined, nervous hearing picked up the muffled sound of the engine from the bridge above. The car had rejoined the tail. Now, the KGB would be predicting his movements and purposes. He looked at his watch. Ten-thirty. They, too, would probably see some significance in the exactitude of the time. He heard footsteps come cautiously down the stone steps, as he stared out into the river. Two pairs. Then only one. One of the KGB men had paused half-way down the steps.

He stared into the darkness under the bridge. No figures detached themselves from the shadows. He turned his back, and began to walk along the embankment.

It was only a few hundred yards to the first flight of steps down from the Gorovskaia Quay and, as he approached, three shadows appeared on the steps and moved towards him. For a moment, he wondered whether they were not KGB men – then one of the men spoke softly in English.

"Mr. Orton?" the voice said.

"Yes." There had been no trace of a foreign accent.

The three men joined him swiftly, and a torch flared in his face. The English voice said: "Yes, it's him."

The tallest of the three men, young, square-featured, blond, took up the dialogue.

"How many followed you?" His accent was Russian, though he spoke in English.

Gant replied in Russian, testing his pronunciation: "Three on foot, I think – and a car. It's up on the bridge."

"Good," the Russian replied. Gant was watching the first man, the Englishman he assumed was from the Embassy security staff. He was the same build as Gant, and his hair was brushed back from his forehead. He smiled at Gant, as if in encouragement, or conspiracy. Gant returned the smile.

"What are they doing, Pavel?" the Englishman asked, keeping his eyes on Gant.

"The one on the steps has returned to the car – the short fat one is wondering what to do, since there are four of us here now." The Russian laughed softly. "I think he is frightened!"

"Then help is on the way – we'd better get Mr. Orton away from here right away, while they're still in two minds."

Gant was on edge, ready for sudden movement, for flight . . . They had been standing in a tight group and the material of the Englishman's coat, so like Gant's own, was pressed against him. The big Russian, Pavel, drew a heavy wooden truncheon from beneath his own dark coat. They were a circle of dark coats, Gant thought irrelevantly, and the Englishman was wearing his hair in the same out-of-date style as he was . . .

Fenton, the Englishman who had played the part of Orton many times in the last two years, cried out in surprise – then the surprise became pain. Pavel brought the heavy club down across the Englishman's forehead – once, twice. Then the Englishman was on the ground, moaning, and the club descended another three sickening times. Even as his stomach revolted, as his mind screamed that he was in a pit of snakes, like the Veterans' Hospital, Gant realised that the big Russian was rendering the Englishman's face unrecognisable.

The police whistle scratched across his awareness, then seemed to accelerate and to slide up the scale, as if it were on record and the turntable had speeded up to make the sound recognisable. The KGB man was calling for reinforcements.

"Your papers – quickly!" Pavel snapped, bending over the battered features of the Englishman. The sight of the face seemed to hypnotise Gant. "Your papers!"

He reached into his breast pocket and handed over his passport, his movement visas, his identification from the Soviet Embassy, in a trance-like state. They were stuffed into Fenton's pockets, and the Englishman's own papers removed. The third man snatched the trilby from Gant's head, and then helped the big Russian to lift the body and roll it the few yards to the edge of the embankment. They released it and it slid into the black ruffled waters of the Moskva. The dark topcoat billowed, and the man's arms became the arms of a crucifix – he floated slowly away, drawn by the current.

"Quickly! Follow us – to the Pavolets station, the metro," Pavel growled in his ear, shaking him out of immobility. Other whistles were answering the summons from the KGB man fifty yards away.

Gant's feet began to move, a hundred miles away beneath him. He stumbled up the steps onto the Gorovskaia Quay, following Pavel and the other Russian. Whistles shrilled behind him, and feet galloped echoingly along the embankment. Pavel and the other man were running ahead of him, drawing away. He saw the flash of white as Pavel turned his face to him.

"Quickly!" he yelled.

Gant began to run, faster, faster, leaving the whistles behind, leaving the floating body . . .

The short, fat man, and the taller figure who had detached himself from the car in front of the Moskva Hotel, were up to their waists in the chill waters of the Moskva, dragging the body to the embankment. The fat man was grunting and cursing with the effort.

When they had tugged the corpse up onto the flagstones, the fat man bent over it, wracked by coughing, fishing in the breast pocket as he did so. He pulled out a British passport, soggily closed around other papers. The taller man flashed a torch onto the picture of the man with the greasy hair, then at the ruined face at the edge of the circle of torchlight.

"Mm," the fat man said after a while. "I warned them at the Centre about this." There was a note of self-satisfaction in his voice. "He didn't have any drugs on him at Cheremetievo. It was obvious that he was unable to meet demands. They have killed him, Stechko. His smuggling friends have killed Mr. Alexander Thomas Orton."

TWO:

The Journey

Gant had a hurried impression of a huge façade, ornamental, almost oriental, that was the main-line railway station, and then their pace slowed, they were descending the elevator to the level of the Pavolets metro station. Gant tried to disguise his breathing from the few incurious Russians and his eyes wandered over the brightly lit, sombre marble walls of the descent. Nothing he had seen in New York, or London, or Paris, was like this. The Pavolets station was like the grandiose architecture of a museum in which the actual vehicles that rushed with a sigh of air from the dark tunnel holes seemed almost out of place.

The platform was uncrowded, but they remained apart so as to be inconspicuous as they waited for the train. Pavel stood next to Gant for no more than a moment and deftly slipped a bundle of documents, inside a blue British passport, into Gant's hands.

He murmured, "Study these before you leave the train. Your name is Michael Grant, almost your own name. You are a tourist staying at the Warsaw Hotel. They are not looking for an Englishman, remember. Just stay calm."

Pavel wandered further along the platform. Gant glanced at the passport photograph, registered the image of himself there, and took off the trilby and the spectacles and shoved them into the pockets of the overcoat. Then he removed his overcoat, and held it casually over his arm. His dark, formal suit still seemed to betray him; its cut was so obviously foreign. One or two Russians appeared to stare at him.

The train swooped into the bright strip of station and he moved forward, tugging his overcoat back onto his shoulders. He knew he had made a mistake, that the overcoat was more anonymous. He turned in his seat as the train pulled out, and saw Pavel unconcernedly reading a newspaper, his long legs stretched out into the aisle. The other man was not in the same compartment.

Gant began to scrutinise the faces in the compartment. There were only faces of travellers – tired, bored, introverted, eyes avoiding contact with fellow passengers. The faces of the world's

38

subways, he thought. He had seen them a million times before. Yet the feeling of nakedness would not go away. The train sighed into another brightly lit strip of platform, and he saw the name slide past his gaze – Taganskaia. They were heading north-east, away from the centre of Moscow. The doors of the compartment whispered open, and Gant watched those who left, and stared at those who came. No one even so much as glanced in his direction. He felt sweat beading on his forehead, and glanced once more in the direction of Pavel. The big Russian glared silently at him, his whole manner of body and the force of his expression displaying a command to behave normally.

Gant nodded, and attempted to relax. He was moving, but it appeared too much like drifting to comfort him. He did not know where he was going, and he had no idea how far he could trust his companions – except that he had Aubrey's assurance. But Gant could not relax. A man had been murdered in the centre of Moscow, and they were making their getaway on public transport. The whole thing had a faint atmosphere of the ridiculous about it – and, Gant acknowledged, anonymity. Aubrey again.

Aubrey had told him nothing about the manner of his disappearance from Moscow, nor of the manner of his transportation to Bilyarsk. He was luggage, freight, until they reached the factory and the hangar. And that was how, he admitted, he had tried to regard the whole operation – yet, the shock to his system, to his reserves of calm and indifference, administered by the death on the embankment, made it increasingly difficult to remain freight, or luggage. He was scared.

When the train stopped briefly in the Kourskaia station, he managed not to look out of the window, except in the most bored manner, and he managed not to inspect the passengers boarding the train. When he looked back at Pavel, however, as the doors sighed shut and the train surged forward, the big Russian was looking back down the platform. Gant followed the direction of his gaze. At the gateway to the moving-staircase, passengers who had just descended from the train were being questioned by two men in overcoats and hats.

Gant, fear dry in his throat, waited for Pavel to turn his gaze back into the carriage. When he did so, and saw Gant staring at him, he merely nodded, once. Gant understood him. KGB. They were covering their bets. Even if they had not yet begun the massive operation of boarding every metro train, they were already sealing up their bolt-holes. They knew how good an escape route the metro was – they had a map of the system and a timetable, just as Aubrey had done when he planned the escape route. And the murder had been done conveniently near the Pavolets station.

Swiftly, almost as a distraction, he studied the papers Pavel had given him. When he had finished, he put them away, and his eyes were drawn hypnotically to the window again.

The dark tunnel rushed past the window, and Gant felt the knot of tension harden in his stomach, and tasted the bile at the back of his throat. He stared, helplessly, at the door connecting his carriage with the one ahead, waiting for it to open, to admit an overcoated figure whose manner would betray his authority, whose eyes would scorch across his features.

The train slowed, the darkness beyond the grimy windows becoming the harsh lighting of the Komsomolskaia station. Involuntarily, he looked at Pavel. The big man had got casually to his feet, and was hanging idly onto a handrail near the sliding doors. Gant got up unsteadily – he knew that his face must be pale and sweating – and stood squarely at the second set of doors in the carriage.

As the train stopped and the doors slid open, he realised that he knew nothing of what the papers in his pocket contained. In sudden panic, he had forgotten. He stepped shakily down onto the platform, was pushed from behind by another passenger and the movement was a grateful trigger. Grant . . . like his own name. He remembered. His eyes sought the exit flight. Yes, there were two KGB men there.

Pavel pushed close to him, as if as a reassuring presence. A small crowd of people seemed to have left the train at that station, and he and the big man were at its heart. It moved slowly, as if with communal wariness, towards the exit. The station's opulence glanced across his awareness. Even here there were no hoardings, no advertisements of women in underclothes or huge bottles of Scotch or cinema posters – only frescoes of the great and praise-worthy victories of the Russian people since 1917, in the bold, awkward, cartoon style of Soviet realism.

He sensed Pavel fade back into the crowd again, but did not turn his head. The crocodile drifted towards the waiting men at the foot of the exit stairs. They were inspecting papers, and he reached into his pocket for Michael Grant's documents. He pulled them from his pocket and re-inspected them as swiftly as he could. Michael Grant – passport, entry visa, hotel reservation, Intourist information brochure.

The KGB man's face loomed in front of him, a white, high-boned, thin face, with a large, aquiline nose, and sharp, powerful eyes. He was inspecting Gant's papers thoroughly, and glancing from photograph to face, and back again. Then he looked at the documents issued to Michael Grant since his arrival in Moscow, three days before. Gant wondered whether such a man had booked

40

into the Warsaw Hotel on that day – and he knew it wouldn't have been overlooked. Michael Grant would be a bona fide tourist, whose papers had been borrowed and duplicated.

"You do not appear to be in the best of health, Mr. – Grant?" the KGB man said in English. He was smiling, and seemed without suspicion.

"No." Gant faltered. "I – a little tummy trouble. The food, you know . . ." He smiled weakly.

"In your photograph you are wearing glasses, Mr. Grant?"

Gant patted his pockets, and continued to smile, a smile that was wan, and remarkably stupid. "In my pocket . . ."

"The food at the Warsaw – it is not good?"

"Yes, fine – just a little too rich for me."

"Ah. Thank you, Mr. Grant."

The man had taken the number of the passport, and the numbers of the documents that he had handed back. Gant had walked a dozen steps before he realised that he had bluffed his way through, that his feet had automatically stepped onto the ascending flight of stairs, and he was being moved up and out of sight of the two KGB officers. His stomach felt watery and he belched. He wanted to be sick with relief. He forced himself not to turn round to look for Pavel and the other man, to stifle the growing panic of the thought that they might have been picked up, and he was now alone . . .

He stepped off the staircase, and moved over to study a large map of the Moscow metro system. He did not dare to turn his attention from the map, his hands thrust deep into the pockets of the topcoat, his shoulders slightly bowed, as he fought against the tide of nausea. He told himself, over and over, that the tension was the same as flying – the sudden, violent twists of time which moved from calm and boredom, to terror, were things that he had experienced many times before. But it did not seem to work, the sedative of familiarity. Perhaps, in the huge, ornate foyer of the metro station, with its gigantic statuary, marbles and bronzes, and the mosaic floor and frescoed walls – perhaps he was unable to transpose himself to the cockpit, and calm his growing panic. All he knew that moment was that he was alone, stranded – they would have picked up Pavel, and the other man. What could he do?

A hand fell on his shoulder, and he jumped away as if stung by some electric charge within him. He turned round, and Pavel saw the damp, frightened face, and doubt flickered in his eyes.

"Thank God," Gant breathed.

"You look terrible," Pavel said, without humour. "Mr. Grant – I watched your performance . . . it was not very convincing."

"Jesus! I was shit-scared, man!" Gant burst out.

41

Pavel looked at him, towering over him. Gant seemed smaller, slighter, less impressive than even his disguise would normally have made him. Pavel, remembering what Edgecliffe, the SIS Head of Station in Moscow, had said of the American, agreed. This man was a risk. Edgecliffe had said – if he causes serious trouble on the journey, get rid of him – don't risk the whole network, just for him. And Gant looked as if he might be big trouble.

"Go and make yourself sick," Pavel said, with distaste in his voice. "Go, and hide yourself in the toilets. There will be more KGB men on the way. We shall leave the station *after* they feel they are sufficiently reinforced – when they are confident that, if we reach the main entrance, then we must have been searched at least three or four times. Go!" He spat out the last word and Gant, after staring at him for a long moment, turned his back and walked away. Pavel watched him go, shook his head, and then set himself to watch, from the cover of his newspaper, the arrivals at the Komsomolskaia metro station.

David Edgecliffe, ostensibly Trade Attaché to the British Embassy, was in the bar of the Moskva Hotel. From his position near the door, he could look out into the foyer of the hotel. He saw the KGB men arrive, together with at least two people from the Political Security Service. If his diagnosis was correct, then Fenton, poor lad, had not died in vain. He shook his head, sadly, over his Scotch, and swallowed the last of it. The appearance of those particular KGB officers would mean that the bluff of Orton's murder at the hands of his supposed Moscow pushers because of the failure of supplies to reach them, would have been swallowed. Orton was dead – long live Gant.

He smiled sadly to himself and a waiter, at his signal, came over with another Scotch on a tray, together with a small jug of water. He paid for his drink, and appeared to return to his book. Covertly, he watched the KGB men as they carried away Gant's luggage. They would have searched the room, he knew, and would have removed everything. Orton, the mysterious Englishman who looked so harmless, but who had infected the youth of Moscow with the terrible affliction of heroin, would be thoroughly investigated. Edgecliffe was smiling. In his signal to Aubrey, that night at least, he could report a state of satisfactory progress.

Besides the false papers he had shown to the KGB searching the metro, to protect himself from identification as a suspected drug-trafficker, Pavel had in his pocket, among other things, something that would have caused Gant to become far more ill than he had thus far seemed to be: it was a red card, such as was only carried by members of the KGB. It was a card which he sincerely hoped not to have to use since it was a fake, but which he knew he might have to employ if there was no other way out of the station.

He had watched them arrive. As yet there were few, but they were thorough. He had already shifted his ground a dozen times in less than fifteen minutes, straining his nerves and patience to make his movements appear casual, unobtrusive. There were KGB men at the main entrance, where a hastily erected barrier had been thrown across the gap into the square and the night, and all departing and arriving passengers were having their papers inspected. They were a motley collection of duty and off-duty personnel from the various departments of the 2nd Chief Directorate, and some faces he knew from Edgecliffe's files on the Political Security Service. They were looking for the murderers of Orton, the "economic criminals" that formed one of their main interests in life.

He had seen Vassily, the third man on the embankment, only once, sitting in a station restaurant, eating a huge, doughy cake, and sipping coffee. The coffee was good, and the pastries and cakes cheap and filling for a man like Vassily, whose papers proclaimed him to be a nightwatchman. Vassily could stay in the restaurant for a couple of hours yet, and be searched and questioned, without arousing suspicion. So might he – but not Gant.

The remainder of the KGB personnel, who had not dropped out of sight to the lower levels and platforms of the metro station, were engaged in searching all possible places of concealment in the station foyer. A small team was busy opening all the left-luggage boxes, set against the far wall. Others checked papers, questioned ascending passengers, bullied and threatened. Pavel watched, with a degree of fascination, a typical and very thorough KGB operation against the citizens of Moscow.

He tried to keep in his line of sight the entrance to the gents' where Gant had retreated. The man was having a bad time. He could not comprehend how Gant had ever been selected for this mission. Pavel himself was only a link in the chain, one of Edgecliffe's small Russian force in Moscow, but he knew more than perhaps he should have done, since Edgecliffe respected all those native Russians who worked for him, Jew or non-Jew, with a more than ordinary respect. He, unlike Aubrey, appreciated the risk they took – and, if he could avoid it, he wouldn't let them walk in the dark: in the case of Pavel, not even for the Firefox.

Pavel almost missed the KGB man heading down the steps to the gents', because he was watching the furore as someone was arrested at the entrance to the station. Some irregularity in the man's papers, in his travel visas or work permit, perhaps — it had been sufficient. As soon as he saw the KGB man, head bobbingly descending the steps, he moved away from his position near the restaurant, coming casually off the wall like a hoarding unstuck by the weather. It still wasn't sufficient to prevent another KGB man coming from the restaurant, wiping his lips with a dark blue handkerchief, from asking him for his papers. For a moment, but only for a moment, Pavel considered ignoring the order. Then, he turned his head and tried to smile nervously, reaching slowly, innocently, into his breast-pocket.

Gant was still in one of the closets, seated on the lavatory, his coat pulled around him, one hand gripping the lapels tightly across his throat, the other clenched in a pocket in an attempt to disguise its shaking. He knew he was close to the condition he had found himself in in Saigon. He was close to having the dream again.

He hadn't needed to make himself sick. He had only just made it to the sanctuary of the closet before he had heaved up his dinner. The bout of nausea, continuing until he was retching drily and gathering bile at the back of his throat to make the retching less painful, had left him weak and unable to move. He had settled wearily, agedly, onto the seat, trying to control his racing heartbeat, and the flickering, fearful images in his head. He listened to the footsteps, the muttered talk, the whistling, the splashing of water and the tugged clicks of roller-towels. A dozen times, the washroom had been empty, but he had not moved. He did not think he could.

He felt like a man beginning a ten-thousand-mile journey who breaks his leg, slipping on his own doorstep. The cold part of his mind which continued to function, though merely as an impotent observer, found his situation ridiculous, and shameful. He could not explain why he should feel so shot to hell, but he suspected that he simply had not prepared himself for what he had encountered. Gant had no resistance to fear. His brittle, overwhelming arrogance left him vulnerable to situations he could not control — and, however much he tried to persuade himself that his situation was controllable, the fiction would not take root in his imagination, calm him.

He heard footsteps on the tiled floor outside the cubicle. He promised himself he would leave as soon as the washroom was empty again. Then a fist banged on the door.

"In there," he heard, in Russian. "Your papers. Quickly."

"I — I . . ." he forced the words out. "I'm on the loo," he said, recollecting the English vernacular that had been drummed into him.

"English?" the man called out, in a thick accent. "State Security," he added. "Your papers, please."

44

"Can you – wait a minute?"

"Very well," the man replied in irritation.

Gant tore paper from the roll, crushed it noisily, then flushed the lavatory. He undid and rattled the buckle on his belt, and the loose change in his pocket, and then slid back the bolt and stepped out of the cubicle.

The KGB man was thick-waisted but heavily-muscled, and displeased. He was, Gant guessed, low in status within the service, but did not intend to let an English tourist see that. He puffed his chest, and glared theatrically.

"Your papers – please." He held out his hand, staring at Gant's face. "You are ill – or, maybe, frightened?"

"No – stomach," Gant said weakly, patting his overcoat.

The KGB man went through the papers carefully, without imagination or haste. Then he looked up. He offered them to Gant, and said: "Your papers are not in order!"

Buckholz had told Gant repeatedly that such a trick was a stock tactic in preliminary investigation. The accusation, of something, anything – just to gauge the reaction. Yet he was unable to respond innocently. He panicked. Fear showed in his eyes, in the furtive darting of his gaze – the animal seeking a bolt-hole. The KGB man reached for his pocket, and Gant knew the man was about to draw a gun. Reacting instinctively, he bulled against the man, hand reaching for the hand in the Russian's pocket, driving him off balance, even as he sought the gun.

The KGB man was driven up against the roller-towel cabinet before he could regain his balance. He was still trying to reach the gun in his pocket, the one reassuring factor, as Gant tugged frantically at the towel. The hand that had closed upon the gun wriggled in his grasp – he found it difficult to hold the thick wrist. He brought his knee up into the Russian's groin, and the man's breath exploded and he groaned, sagging against the wall. Then Gant had a huge loop of towel free and he wound the loop around the man's head. Then he pulled. The Russian's free hand struggled with the tightening folds – his eyes seemed to enlarge, become totally bulbous. Gant's own vision clouded, and he continued twisting and tugging the towel. He seemed to hear a voice, distant and high, and feel a hand on his shoulder, pulling at him . . . he held on. Then, he was turned bodily, and something exploded across his face.

He was staring at Pavel, his hand raised to slap him a second time. His face expressed a cold, ruthless fury.

"You – stupid animal! He was KGB – don't you understand what that means? And – you've killed him!" Gant turned to stare dumbly at the pop-eyed, discoloured features of the Russian on the floor. The man's tongue was hanging out fatly. He turned back to Pavel.

"I – I thought he'd – guessed who I was . . ." he said in a feeble voice.

"You're a menace, Gant!" Pavel said. "You could get us all killed, do you realise that?" He stared at the body for a moment, as if mesmerised, then he bent swiftly, galvanised by a cold fear, and unwound the towel. Taking the body under the armpits, he dragged it across the floor of the washroom and into an empty cubicle. He tucked the legs inside the door, rummaged in the pockets, and then locked himself in the cubicle.

"Is it clear?" Gant heard him ask.

"Yes," Gant replied in the voice of a zombie.

He looked up, and watched as the big man climbed over the door of the cubicle and dropped beside him. He was wiping his hands which were dusty from the top of the door. He patted a pocket. "I have tried to – disguise your stupidity by making it appear that the man was robbed." He sniffed at Gant. "Now," he added, "quickly go up the stairs, and make your way slowly to the entrance. If anyone – *anyone* – calls on you to stop, obey them. Show your papers, and pretend you're ill, as before – understand?"

"Yes. He – he said my papers were not in order."

"You damned fool – you killed him for that? They *are* in order. He was only trying to put you up."

"I – I didn't know where you were . . ."

"I was stopped, by the KGB. But my papers also were in order." He pushed Gant ahead of him. "Now – quickly, up to the entrance. This fat officer could become the object of a search at any moment, and then no one would be allowed to leave this station!"

Gant was stopped twice crossing the station concourse by minor KGB officers who glanced at his papers, asked after his health and his movements, and then let him go. Slowly he approached the temporary barrier thrown across the entrance of the station.

He had no idea how far behind him Pavel was. He would have to wait for him – if he got through the barrier.

The men at the barrier, at least a tall, grey-haired figure with the side of the face that had, at some time, received very poor plastic surgery – Gant assumed it to have been a war-wound – appeared to possess more authority than the big man he had strangled. Gant passed his papers across to a younger man standing in front of the grey-haired, expressionless senior officer, and waited. He tried not to look at the scarred, half-repaired face, but found his gaze drawn to it. The tall man smiled thinly, and rubbed his artificially smooth cheek with one long-fingered hand.

46

"English?" the younger man asked.

"Uh – oh, yes."

"Mm. Mr. Grant – we must ask you to wait at one of the tables here for a moment, until we check with your hotel."

"I have the papers . . ."

"Yes, and your passport and papers have received a Security Service stamp – nevertheless, we must ask you to wait."

The young man lifted up the barrier, so that a hinged section stood on end, and Gant was ushered through. Other tables besides the one at which he was directed to sit, were occupied. About half-a-dozen people in all. Not all of them Russians. He heard an American voice, belonging to an elderly man, saying:

"There's no right on earth makes you question that passport and those papers, sonny!" A young KGB man, crop-haired, waved the remark aside, and continued with a telephone conversation.

Gant sat down, heavily, at the table. It was a rickety affair, erected for the express purpose of providing a semblance of the KGB's normal interrogation facilities. He swallowed hard. He turned his eyes to the barrier, and saw Pavel repossessing his papers and passing out of the entrance to the station, without a backward glance. Suddenly, he felt deserted, alone. He was once more no longer in control of the situation. He stared at the black telephone isolated on the table.

Then the young man slid into the chair opposite him, and smiled, "This won't take very long, let us hope, Mr. Grant," he said.

As he dialled the number of the Warsaw Hotel, Gant saw, clearly, and for the first time, the odds against him. He was taking on the largest, the most ruthless, the most thorough security service the world had ever seen. It was small comfort to recollect that Aubrey had described the KGB as notoriously inefficient because of its very size. To Gant, sitting at that table, in the cold foyer of the metro station, it was no comfort at all, the smooth platitudes of a man in an hotel room in the middle of London.

"Hotel Warsaw?" the young man asked in Russian. Gant kept his eyes on the table, so that he did not betray any sign that he followed the conversation. "Ah – State Security here. Let me talk to Prodkov, please." Prodkov would be the name of the KGB man who worked on the staff of the hotel – he might have been a waiter, desk-clerk, dishwasher, but he possessed far more power than the hotel manager.

There was a considerable wait, then: "Prodkov – I have a tourist here, Michael Grant. He is registered in room 308 . . . Yes, you know him. Tell me, what does he look like? Would you look at me for a moment, Mr. Grant, please? Thank you – go ahead, Prodkov . . .

Mm. Yes . . . yes – I see. And he is not there now?" There was another, longer pause. Gant waited, in disbelief. Aubrey could never have anticipated what was happening to him now – now it would emerge that Grant looked different, or was already tucked up in his bed. "Good. Thank you, Prodkov. Goodbye."

The young man was smiling affably to deny what had just occurred. There had been no suspicion, no force – merely a very ordinary, routine check on a tourist's papers. He handed back the sheaf of papers, tucked neatly into the cover of the passport bearing the name of Michael Grant.

"Thank you, Mr. Grant – I apologise for any delay. We – are engaged in a search for – criminals, shall we say? Of course, we wished merely to eliminate you from our enquiries. You are now free to resume your nocturnal sightseeing tour of our city." The young man was obviously proud of his English. He stood up, gravely shook hands with Gant, and then waved him through the barrier. The grey-haired man smiled crookedly as Gant passed him, only one side of his face wrinkling with the expression.

Gant nodded to him, and then he was outside the barrier and walking as steadily as he could towards the entrance. Outside the ornate entrance, beneath its elaborate, decorated portico, the wind was suddenly cold. Gant realised that his body was bathed in a sweat of relief. He looked around him and saw Pavel detach himself from the shadows.

"Good," he said. "Now, we have wasted far too much time already. Soon, it will be dangerous to be on the streets, impeccable papers or otherwise. Come – we have a short distance to walk. You go ahead of me, down the Kirov Street. When we are away from the station, I will catch you up, and show where we are heading. Good? Very well, begin walking."

They picked up two of the known associates of Pavel Upenskoy and Vassily Levin just before six in the morning. Both were family men, living in the same tower block of Soviet Workers' flats on the wide Mira Prospekt, overlooking the vast permanent site of the Exhibition of Economic Achievements in the northern suburbs of Moscow. The black saloons of Kontarsky's team parked in the forecourt of the block, while it was hardly light, and the men moved in swiftly. The whole operation took hardly more than three minutes, including the ascent of the lift to the fourteenth and sixteenth floors. When the team returned, the two additional human beings appearing satisfactorily disturbed, barely awake, and deeply frightened, Priabin knew that his chief would be satisfied.

Priabin grinned into the frightened, wan faces of the two men taken from their beds as they passed him with nervous side-glances. They knew, he sensed, why he had come for them – and they knew what to expect when they were returned to the Centre, to Dzerzhinsky Street. He watched them being loaded into two of the black cars, and then glanced up at the block of flats. On the sixteenth floor, he could make out the smudge of a white face at a dark window – the wife, or perhaps a child. It did not matter.

His breath smoked round him in the cold dawn air as he returned to his car. Dipping his head at the passenger window, he said to the driver: "Very well – give the order for the surveillance-team to move in on the warehouse. Let's get Upenskoy as well, while we're about it!"

Gant woke from a fitful, dream-filled sleep as the doors of the removal van were opened noisily by Pavel Upenskoy. Shaking his head, muttering, he pulled himself into a sitting position on the mattress which had been laid just behind the driver's cab. Gant had boarded it in the warehouse of the Sanitary Manufacturing Company of Moscow.

The light of cold, high bulbs filtered into the interior of the truck, but Upenskoy was hidden from Gant's view by the stacked lavatory bowls and cisterns that he was to drive that day to Kuybyshev, a town lying more than a hundred miles south of Bilyarsk, and more than seven hundred road miles from Moscow. A new hotel being constructed in Kuybyshev awaited the toilet fittings.

"Gant – are you awake?"

"Yes," Gant replied sullenly, trying to moisten his dry, stale mouth with saliva. "What time is it?"

"Nearly five-thirty. We leave for Bilyarsk just before six. If you want, the old man has made some coffee – come and get it."

Gant heard the heavy footsteps retreat across the concrete floor of the warehouse, and ascend some steps. A flimsy door banged shut. Then, the only sounds were those of his hands rubbing at the stubble on his chin, and the sucking of his lips as he tried to rid himself of the dry, evil taste in his mouth. He brushed a hand across his forehead and examined the thin film of sweat on his fingertips carefully, as if it were something alien, or something familiar the appearance and nature of which he had long forgotten. Then he wiped his hand on the trouser-leg of his faded blue overalls into which he had changed when he arrived at the warehouse.

He had not slept well. He had not been allowed to sleep for more than two hours after being brought by Pavel to the warehouse, in a narrow commercial street that ran off the Kirov Street. They were only a quarter of a mile from the Komsomolskaia metro station.

Pavel had not allowed him to sleep as he had hammered home to him the facts and nuances of his new, and third, identity – that of Boris Glazunov, driver's mate, who lived in a block of flats on the Mira Prospekt, who was married with two children and who, in reality, Pavel had explained, would be staying home and out of sight, while Gant accompanied him in the delivery truck as far as Bilyarsk. The briefing had been conducted entirely in Russian – Gant had been forcibly reminded more than once of his language training with the defector, Lebedev, at Langley, Virginia.

At last, after a recital of his assumed life history, and a repeated account of what papers he carried, and what they represented, he had been allowed to sleep – to sleep as soundly as his own mind would allow him. He had relived the strangulation of the KGB man in the washroom, in a grotesque, balletic slow-motion in endless repetition – relived the reaction that had caused him to sag against a shop window in the Kirov Street, so that Pavel had hurried to catch him up, and hold his shaking body until the epilepsy of reaction passed.

Gant climbed to his feet, and tried to put the vivid images from his mind. As he clambered and squeezed his way out of the back of the truck, he tried to consider the future, the hours ahead, to help drive away the past. He knew now that he could rely completely on Pavel Upenskoy.

In any and every word that the big man had spoken, Gant had sensed the contempt in which he was held by the Russian. It was as if, Gant admitted, he had been insulted with the company of a weekend flyer in the cockpit of the Firefox, Pavel having to tag him along until he could dump him outside Bilyarsk. Gant understood the ruthless professionalism of the big Russian. Where and how British Intelligence had recruited him, he did not know, but the old man, the nightwatchman at the warehouse, had muttered through his gums something about Pavel having had a Jewish wife, who was still in prison or labour camp for having demonstrated against the Russian invasion of Czechoslovakia, twelve years before. That had been when Pavel had left him briefly alone with the old man who had tried to soften Pavel's harsh treatment of the American. Apart from that fact, Gant knew nothing about Pavel Upenskoy. Yet, strangely, he accepted the big man's contempt, and brusque manner with equanimity. The man was good.

Pavel and the old man were sitting at a small, bare table in the despatch-office of the warehouse. As yet, none of the day-staff had reported for work. Pavel intended to be long gone before they arrived. He looked up as Gant shut the flimsy door behind him, as if inspecting the American critically in the light of the naked bulb suspended from the ceiling. The room, like the warehouse, was cold and Gant rubbed his hands together for warmth. Pavel indicated the coffee pot on the ancient electric ring plugged into the wall, and Gant collected a chipped mug from the table and poured himself some black coffee. Without sugar, the drink was bitter, but it was hot. Uneasily, as if uninvited, he settled himself at the table. The old man, as if at a signal, finished his coffee, and left the room.

"He goes to see if we are under surveillance here," Pavel explained without looking at Gant.

"You mean they . . .?" Gant began quickly.

"No — I do not mean they know where you are," the Russian replied. "These will not be the men who followed you last night, or that gang at the station — but the department of the KGB that is concerned with the security of the airplane knows who I am, and who the others are — they will be watching, no doubt, since the weapons-trials are in," he looked at his watch, "less than thirty hours' time!"

"Then — they'll know I'm on my way?"

"Not necessarily. They will merely be watching us."

"If they stop us?" Gant persisted. "It'll all be blown to hell, before I can leave Moscow!"

"No! If we are stopped, there are other arrangements." Pavel seemed to be battling with some doubt in himself.

"What other arrangements?" Gant said scornfully. "I've got to get six hundred miles today, man! How do I do it — *fly*?" Gant laughed, a high-pitched sound. Pavel looked at him in contempt.

"I am ordered to — die, if necessary, to ensure that you get away free," Pavel said softly. "It is not what I would consider a willing or worthwhile sacrifice . . . However, if we get out of here safely, then we shall not be stopped again until we reach the circular motorway, where another vehicle will be waiting, in the event of trouble, to collect you. If there is any trouble, then you continue with me. Understood?"

Gant was silent for a time, then he said: "Yes."

"Good. Now, go and shave, in the next room — clean yourself up, a little, yes?" Gant nodded, and crossed the room. Just as he was about to close the door behind him, he heard Pavel say: "Gant — can you fly that plane — really fly it?"

Gant poked his head back round the door. Pavel was staring into the bottom of his mug, hands clasped round it, elbows on the bare wooden table. His big frame seemed somehow shrunken in the blue overalls.

"Yes," Gant said. "I can fly it. I'm the best there is."

Pavel looked up into Gant's eyes, stared at him for a long moment in silence, then nodded, and said: "Good. I would not want to die to deliver faulty goods to Bilyarsk."

He returned his gaze to the coffee mug, and Gant closed the door behind him. He switched on the weak, naked bulb, ran the water until it was lukewarm, and inspected himself in the speckled mirror. Pavel had cut his hair the previous night, and then he had washed it. It was short now, flat on his head, without hair oil. He looked younger, perhaps a little like he had done as a teenager in Clarkville – except for the ridiculous moustache that survived from his personae as Orton and then as Grant. He soaped his face with a stubby brush and tugged at the bristles of the moustache until it had become hairs floating in the grey shaving water. Then he began, methodically, to shave the rest of his face.

When he returned to the office, Pavel was obviously ready to leave. The old man had returned, and vanished again, presumably to keep watch.

"They are here," Pavel said softly. Gant sensed a new tension about the man, his ordinariness showing through.

"How many?" Gant asked, keeping his voice steady with an effort.

"Three – in one car. The old man has seen them before. They are part of the team appointed to the security of the Bilyarsk project. They follow Mr. Lansing about Moscow, and Dherkov, the courier who comes from Bilyarsk. The old man thinks they are only watching – if they had come to make arrests, there would be more of them."

Gant nodded when the Russian had finished. Then, his expression turned to one of surprise when Pavel drew an automatic from his overall pocket.

"What – ?"

"You can use this?"

Gant took the gun, and turned it over in his hand. It was a type he had not met before, a Makarov, but it seemed close enough to the Walther P-38 that he had used more than once, if only on the range. He nodded.

"Good. *Don't* – unless it's absolutely necessary!"

"Yes."

"Are you ready?"

"Yes."

"Then let us be gone from here. It is a little before six – soon it will be light, and we have six hundred miles to go." He opened the door, and followed Gant through.

Once they were in the big cab of the truck, whose nose pointed at the double-doors of the warehouse, Pavel started the engine and flickered the headlights. Gant spotted the old nightwatchman by the doors, and they began to swing open; Pavel eased the truck into gear and they rolled forward towards the widening gap of grey light. He caught a glimpse of the old man's face, smiling grimly, and then they were out into the side street, with Pavel heaving on the wheel of the truck to straighten it. Gant caught a glimpse of a black saloon further down the street, in the opposite direction to the one they had taken, and then they were turning into the Kirov Street, sodium-lit, grey, and deserted.

Behind them, the KGB car was quiet. No one had panicked, started the engine. Instead, one of the three men, the oldest and largest, had picked up the car telephone, and was in direct contact with KGB Colonel Mihail Kontarsky within seconds.

"They have just left – two of them, in the sanitary ware delivery truck. What do you wish us to do, Colonel?"

There was a pause, then: "I will check with Priabin at the Mira Prospekt. For the moment, you may follow them – but do *not* close up!"

"Yes, Colonel." He nodded to the driver, who fired the engine. The car pulled out from the kerb, past the now-closed doors of the warehouse, and stopped at the junction with the Kirov Street. The truck was a distant black lump on the road, heading north-east towards the Sadovaya, the inner road around the city.

"Close up," the man in charge said to the driver. "But not too close. Just enough not to lose him on the Sadovaya."

"Right!" The driver pressed his foot on the accelerator, and the saloon shot forward, narrowing the distance between itself and the truck. By the time they were a hundred metres in the rear, the truck was slowing at the junction of the Kirov Street and the Sadovaya. The saloon idled into the kerb, waiting until the truck pulled out into the heavier traffic of the ring road. The indicator showed that the driver, the man Upenskoy, intended to turn right, to the south-east.

The truck pulled out, then the man in the passenger seat said: "Colonel – Colonel, they're on the Sadovaya now, heading south-east. We're pulling out – now." The car skittered across the road, and was hooted at by an oncoming lorry, straightened, and the truck was more than five hundred metres away. "Close up again," the man said, and the driver nodded. He skipped the saloon out into the outside lane, and accelerated. Kontarsky's voice came over the radio receiver.

"Priabin has just requested you pick up the man Upenskoy – he has the other two, Glazunov and Riassin. Who is that in the truck with him, Borkh?"

"I do not know, Colonel – it should be – "

"Exactly! It should be Glazunov, should it not, if Upenskoy is making a real delivery somewhere . . . should it not?"

"Yes, Colonel. The truck has turned onto Karl Marx Street now, Colonel – it looks as if they're heading out of the city, all right."

"Where is Upenskoy scheduled to deliver?"

"I don't know, Colonel – we can find out."

"He will have to report to the travel control on the motorway, Borkh, we can find out then. You follow them until they reach the checkpoint, then we shall decide what to do. Priabin is bringing in Glazunov and Riassin – perhaps they will be able to tell us?"

The men in the car heard Kontarsky's laughter, and then the click of the receiver. Borkh replaced the telephone, and studied the truck, now only a hundred metres ahead of them on Bakouninskaia Street, headed like an arrow north-east out of the city, towards the Gorky road.

"Our Colonel seems to be in a merry mood this morning," the driver observed. "Then, he hasn't spent the night in a freezing car!"

"Disrespect, Ilya?" Borkh said with a smile.

"Who – me? No chance! Hello, our friend is taking a left turn," he added. The car was crossing the Yaouza, the tributary of the Moskva, flowing south at that point to join the river at the Oustinski Bridge. The truck ahead of them had turned left directly after the bridge over the sluggish tributary. The car followed, keeping its required distance. "Think he's spotted us?"

"Not necessarily – he's picking up the Gorky road, maybe – see, I thought so – right onto the Chtcholkovskoie Way, and heading east," Borkh said. "He's on his way to Gorky, all right."

"And to Kazan – and then to . . .?" the driver asked, smiling.

"Maybe – maybe. That's for our Colonel to worry about."

"And worry he will," the third man added from beneath his hat in the back seat, where he was stretched out comfortably.

"Oh, you're awake then, are you?" Borkh asked with heavy sarcasm.

"Just about – it must be the boring life I lead, and the boring company," the man replied, settling himself back again.

"You will have your photograph taken at this checkpoint," Pavel was saying as he pulled the truck into the side of the road, along the narrowing line of bollards that signified the lane for heavy goods vehicles. Gant, looking ahead, saw that they were approaching what, to all intents and purposes, was a customs post, as if the motorway ringing the outskirts of Moscow marked some kind of territorial boundary.

"Are they KGB on guard here?" he asked, as the face of a soldier in drab brown uniform slid past the cab window.

"No – Red Army. But they're commanded by a KGB man – he'll be sitting in that hut over there." Gant followed the nod of Pavel's head, and observed a young man in civilian clothes lounging in the doorway of a wooden hut, smoking a long cigarette. Gant could not see through the window into the interior – the newly-risen sun reflected in a sheet of yellow-orange from the glass.

"What happens – just a check on papers?" he asked.

"Usually, and your photograph is taken, from the smaller hut next to the office, but don't smile – they'll wonder what you're trying to hide!" Pavel smiled grimly, and tugged on the handbrake loudly. "Now, get out," he said.

Gant opened the door, and climbed down. The tension in his stomach was returning, but not severely – it seemed just to be moving up a gear from the slightly unsettled feeling that had been with him ever since Pavel had told him that the saloon had followed them all the way from the Kirov Street out to the motorway. He resisted an itching desire to look behind, to see the faces behind the windscreen of the KGB car.

Pavel stood beside him, casually smoking a cigarette. Gant tried not to look about him with too obvious an interest. His cover presumed him to have undergone this formality a number of times before.

A military guard collected their papers, and took them away and into the office. Gant idly watched the cars and lorries that drew up in the three lanes that were used by outbound traffic. The circular motorway swept above them on huge concrete piles, and he could hear the thrumming of the traffic from overhead.

"One of the men from the car has just gone into the office," Pavel said levelly. "You know where the car is, if you have to run for it . . ."

"You think it might come . . .?"

"No. At the moment, you are unremarkable as far as they are concerned. Ah, here come our papers."

The same guard crossed from the office, his boots clattering distinctly on the concrete, and handed them their papers, which had been stamped with the necessary permit for travel as far as Gorky on the main road. At Gorky, they would need another permit to travel as far east as Kazan, and then another from Kazan to Kuybyshev. Pavel nodded, stubbed out the remainder of his cigarette, and climbed back aboard the truck. Gant, careful not to watch the door of the office, rounded the front of the truck and regained his seat.

Pavel switched on, slid the engine into gear, and drew away. A red-and-white barrier slid up in front of them, to allow them to pass beneath the motorway out onto the Gorky road.

Pavel looked across at Gant, and said, "Gorky by lunchtime, and Kazan in time for tea – or don't you Americans take tea?" He laughed, encouraging Gant to smile.

Gant said, "Are they tailing us?'

Pavel looked into the wing-mirror, and said: "No, not yet – but they'll have someone pick us up later on. Don't worry! The KGB aren't worried, just curious. They want to know who you are!"

"You mean they don't believe I'm this guy Glazunov?"

"If they do now, they won't do before long. Your picture will be at the records office of the State Highway Militia by this afternoon, and checked against existing photographs of Glazunov, then they'll *really* want to know who you are!"

"And they'll stop us, and ask me?" Gant persisted.

"Perhaps. But – they are very confident, at Bilyarsk. Let us hope they want to play a waiting game. There are alternatives for you at each of our scheduled stops, so don't worry. If they stopped us on the road, they would be asking for trouble, wouldn't they?" He smiled. "We shall hope that they leave us alone, until they come to be just a little bit afraid – and that takes a long time for the KGB!"

It was early in the afternoon when David Edgecliffe, looking immensely regretful, grave and dignified, identified the body of his agent, Fenton, as the mortal remains of Alexander Thomas Orton. He stood with Inspector Tortyev of the Moscow police in the mortuary, a cold and depressing room, and gazed down at the battered, barely recognisable face and nodded after a suitable pause and catch in the throat. The wounds did not take him by surprise. Fenton looked now as Gant might have looked, in his persona as Orton. There was not sufficient left of the features for anyone to be able to distinguish between the American and the Englishman – especially since Gant had gone through two further transformations since he left the Moskva the previous night.

"Yes," he said softly. "Insofar as I can judge, that is the body of Mr. Orton." He looked up at Tortyev, who dropped the cloth back over Fenton's ruined features.

"You could not be mistaken, Mr. Edgecliffe?" he asked.

"I – don't think so, Inspector," Edgecliffe said levelly, with a tiny shrug. "There was a – lot of damage, of course."

"Yes, indeed. Almost as if his former associates did not want him to be recognised?"

"Quite. Why, though?"

Edgecliffe's eyes appeared a little baffled, but he was watching

Tortyev keenly. He did not know the man, but he was aware that, though he posed as an ordinary civil policeman, Tortyev was KGB.

"I don't know, Mr. Edgecliffe – nor do you know, I suppose?" Tortyev was smiling. He was young, ruthless, charming, and tough. His grey eyes were piercing and intelligent. He was one of the university graduates increasingly appearing in the front-line of the KGB, Edgecliffe reflected. A man to be watched.

"Mm. Wish I could help you, Inspector – devil of a fuss this'll cause at home."

"It will cause a devil of a fuss, Mr. Edgecliffe, here in Moscow," Tortyev snapped, "until we find the men who killed him!" Then he relaxed, and said: "But come, Mr. Edgecliffe, I am sure you could do with a drink. This is not a pleasant task. Shall we go?"

He ushered Edgecliffe from the room with a winning smile.

"Then who is this man?" Kontarsky was saying, holding the photograph of Gant standing by the truck at the checkpoint under the noses of Borkh and Priabin. "Have either of you any idea?"

The light was on in his office as the day outside the window darkened. It had been a fine April day. Kontarsky had walked in the Alexandrovski Gardens after lunch and the air had been mild. Now, with something of a satisfied mood about him still, he looked at his two subordinates. He was hardly worried, merely concerned that the driver's mate with Upenskoy had not yet been identified. He was unknown to the "M" Department. The truck, naturally, was being tailed, always in sight of the tail-car. Lanyev had returned alone to Bilyarsk, with new orders for Tsernik, and advance information concerning the movements of Upenskoy and the truck.

"We do not know, Colonel," Priabin said.

Kontarsky, despite his confidence, was adroit at displaying anger with his subordinates. He said: "Do not know – we have had this photograph for hours!"

"We are checking, Colonel. The Computer and Records Directorate is giving it priority, sir," Borkh felt called upon to say.

"Is it? Is it, indeed? And why them?"

"We are assuming that this man is a foreign agent, sir," Priabin said. "British, perhaps?"

"Mm. Is that likely?"

"Why don't we stop the truck and ask him, Colonel?" Borkh blurted out.

Kontarsky turned his angry stare upon him. "Idiot!" was all he said.

Priabin understood. Kontarsky was looking for a spectacular triumph. He sensed that the man in the truck with Upenskoy was important, but he reacted by assuming that Bilyarsk was impregnable – which it was, Priabin had to admit – and that he therefore had leisure to play this man on a line, hoping that he would lead him to others, tie in with some big SIS or CIA operation. Priabin was irritated – but he, too, could not consider the threat of a single individual, even if he was travelling towards Bilyarsk, as anything to be taken seriously.

Kontarsky, seeing the keenness of his assistant's study of him, said: "What of your interrogation?"

"Nothing – so far. They're holding out, so far."

"Holding out, Dmitri?"

"Yes, sir."

"You showed the man Glazunov this photograph of someone who was pretending to be him – was he not outraged?"

Priabin did not feel called upon to smile. He said: "Colonel – I don't think he knows who is in the truck with Upenskoy."

"But – you and I agree the truck is heading for Bilyarsk?"

"Yes, Colonel – it must be."

"Then this man, whoever he is, and from wherever he comes – must be a saboteur?"

"Probably, Colonel."

"Undoubtedly, Dmitri." Kontarsky rubbed his blue jowl. "But, what can one man do to the Mig-31 that cannot be done by Baranovich and the others already on the spot – eh?" He was thoughtful for a moment, then he added: "What kind of operation could it be? If we knew *who* he was, then we might net ourselves something very useful." He smiled, and Priabin wondered again at his motives. Kontarsky was enjoying himself, of that there was no doubt. He expected some kind of additional success, connected with this man – but what? Priabin would have stopped the truck by now.

Kontarsky went on: "I shall delay my flight to Bilyarsk by a few hours. Meanwhile, alert the security there concerning this truck . . . Borkh, get me Colonel Leprov in Records – I want this man identified as soon as possible. Meanwhile, Dmitri, get back to our friends and ask them once more who he is!"

Kontarsky's finger tapped the photograph of Gant as Borkh dialled the number and Priabin left the room.

Gant was tired, cramped with travel, his mind numbed by the endlessness of the Russian steppe, that great sweep of plain stretching as far as the Urals, two hundred miles beyond Bilyarsk. His mind had plumbed his own past, prompted by the similarity of the country to his own Mid-West. It had not been a pleasant experience, and he was sick with the memories and the petrol fumes that seeped into the cab.

It was dark now, and Upenskoy had switched on the headlights. The tail-car was a steady five hundred metres behind. It had picked them up on the outskirts of Kazan, taking over from its predecessor as they had crossed the vast new Lenin Bridge over the Volga which had replaced the ferry. The tail-car was not using its lights – but both he and Pavel knew it was there.

"How far now?" he asked, breaking a long silence.

"The turn-off is about four miles further on – then Bilyarsk is fourteen miles up the road."

"And I have to meet the pick-up on that road – at the point you showed me on the map?"

"Yes."

"Then it's time for me to leave you . . ." Gant said.

"Not yet."

"Yes. The first copse up ahead, and I'm going to jump for it," Gant said decisively.

Pavel looked across at him, then said, "Very well. I will try not to let them overtake me for as long past the guard-post as possible. Then, with luck, I shall leave them behind when I abandon my trusty vehicle, which is bringing the benefits of modern plumbing to the Volga Hotel at Kuybyshev!" Pavel, curiously to Gant, roared with laughter.

Gant said, "Don't get yourself caught."

"Not if I can help it," Pavel replied. "Semelovsky will have passed through the guardpost less than fifteen minutes ago."

"How do you know?"

"He was at the petrol station in Kazan. I didn't speak to him, but he was there."

"How – did he get out of Bilyarsk? I thought it was sealed up tight until after tomorrow's show."

"It is. He's from Kazan – his mother is dying, so they let him out – in company with a KGB man, of course. No, don't worry. The KGB man saw him on his way. They're not worried about him. They know he's one of us, and they expect him to return to Bilyarsk."

"His mother is – really dying?"

"It would appear so – to the doctor, that is. However, she is a very tough old lady . . ." He smiled. "Semelovsky will be waiting for you on the road."

It seemed to Gant that every man he had come into contact with was under sentence of death. A sentence they all accepted as their lot. He wanted to say something to Pavel, in the selflessness of the moment.

Pavel's voice cut across the mood. "Trees coming up, and a few bends in the road, just to keep truck drivers from falling asleep!" He looked at Gant, and added: "Don't say anything – your words would be useless, maybe even insulting. Just fly that damn aeroplane out of Russia!"

THREE:

The Suspicions

A pair of men's shoes were placed on Police Inspector Tortyev's desk, under the hard strip-lighting, and the young man's attention seemed to be riveted upon them. He leaned back in his chair, one foot pushing against the desk, steepled fingers tapping insistently at his pursed lips. At that moment, he was alone in his office and had been for half-an-hour, because he had wanted to think. He had still not decided what to do about the shoes.

The chair creaked as he regained an upright position, and reached out a hand. He picked up the white label tied to one of the shoes, and read again that it was the property of Alexander Thomas Orton. Shaking his head, as if in puzzled amusement, he shunted the left and right shoes, which were not a pair – one being black, the other brown – together. One shoe was a size-and-a-half bigger than the other. The black shoe from Orton's body was still damp from its ducking in the Moskva. The other shoe, still shining and barely worn, though the heel was showing signs of wear already – the other shoe had been taken from Orton's room at the Moskva Hotel.

He shunted the shoes apart, then together again, his lips pursing as he did so. He whistled softly, tunelessly, his eyes staring at the shoes, as if willing them to inform him of the cause of their discrepancy in size. The hat size had been the same, the collar size the same, the overcoat at the hotel had fitted the dead man, the suits had fitted, the socks . . . but not the shoes. Why not? Did any man have shoes that varied so much in size? Why?

He pushed back his chair again, assuming his former position. It was, indeed, mysterious. The answer, of course, forming itself in his mind all the time he had been alone in his office, was that the man in the river was not the man who had booked into the Moskva Hotel, the man who had passed through security at Cheremetievo, who had taken that walk from the hotel along the embankment, only to be murdered.

Why was it not the same man? The question was more important than the discovery, the solution to the problem of the shoes. One of the three men who had met Mr. Orton had – taken his place in the river? Why?

The question might not have interested an ordinary policeman, not as directly, or as insistently as it interested Tortyev. But then, Tortyev was not an ordinary member of the Moscow police. He held a police rank, and his offices were situated in the Police Headquarters but, like many of his colleagues, he was a member of the KGB 2nd Chief Directorate. His only superiors, the only people to whom he was answerable, were KGB officers in the Political Security Service.

Tortyev had been in charge of the Orton case since the first addiction cases had come to the attention of the Moscow police and, naturally and inevitably, to the attention of his section of the KGB. His rank in the police had been made up to Inspector, at thirty-three, and he was given authority to co-opt suitable resources in order to unearth, and smash, the ring creating the addiction.

Tortyev had a hatred of drugs, and of pushers. It was as burning a hatred as belonged to any member of any drugs squad anywhere in the world. Tortyev would have done equally valuable work in New York, or London, or Amsterdam. He hated Orton. When Holokov, fat, efficient Holokov, had informed him of the Englishman's death, he had been pleased, though, in another way, frustrated. He had wanted to confront Orton, see him sentenced. Yet his death had not mattered – they knew the others, the ones Orton had supplied.

Yet now, Orton was not dead at all, he admitted. His teeth ground together audibly in the silence of the room. He picked up the telephone. An operator at a special switchboard divorced from the switchboard that served the rest of the police building, answered.

"Get me the Seventh Directorate – the office of Colonel Ossipov," he said, and waited for his call to be answered. When it was, he swiftly requested assistance, in the form of men and time, from the KGB Colonel responsible for the surveillance of English tourists. The call took less than a minute. Tortyev had priority with the Seventh Directorate.

When he had put the telephone down again, he went back to studying the shoes, pushing them together, pulling them apart, as if making them perform some simple dance. Now that he had requested more men, to begin checking on Orton's movements, he would need Stechko, Holokov, and possibly the sergeant, Filipov, even if the man was a Jew, to begin checking through their records of the previous visits of Orton to Moscow, their records of his contacts, behaviour-pattern, habits . . .

As he pressed the intercom switch to summon his subordinates, he was still staring at the odd shoes. He was smiling, as if they represented a challenge to him.

At the moment he was about to speak, he suddenly wondered what had become of the transistor-radio that had been itemised at the airport – and had been inspected for drugs. It had not been in his hotel room, nor on the body. Of course, it might be at the bottom of the river.

"Stechko – get Holokov and Filipov right away – I've got some important paperwork for you," he said, his smile becoming puzzlement once more. Where was that radio?

Semelovsky was waiting for him, the small Moskvitch saloon pulled into the side of the narrow road leading to Bilyarsk, the bonnet open. Gant could see the faint outline of Semelovsky hunched into the open jaws of the car, as if in the process of being swallowed. He settled down at the peak of the bank which bordered the road, and waited. The man went on working, or appearing to work, on the engine of the small car. Gant spent ten minutes checking that the figure was alone, and that the road was empty. When the man stood up, stretched his back, and cursed in Russian, Gant ducked back out of sight. Semelovsky was small – Gant saw light glint from the two moons of his spectacles. The man looked around him, and up and down the road, then returned his head beneath the bonnet. Gant heard muffled tinkering, and a tuneless whistle, then slowly got to his feet, and eased himself down the slope of the bank. The man's back was to him, and if he were not Semelovsky, then . . .

"How long have you been watching me?" the little man asked in Russian, in an irritated voice, without lifting his head from beneath the bonnet. Gant stopped in his tracks, one foot raised from the ground in a half-made step.

"Semelovsky?" he asked as the shock dissipated in his system.

The man emerged from beneath the bonnet, wiping his hands on an oily rag. He studied Gant by the light of the moon, low on the horizon still, nodded to himself as if in satisfaction, and closed the bonnet loudly. Gant moved closer to him. The man was in his late forties, possibly fifties. The remainder of his frizzy grey hair clung to his ears, but the top of his head was bald. He was dressed in a drab suit, and wore a raincoat. He was barely more than five feet in height. He looked up at Gant, the light glinting from his spectacles as he studied the American.

"You're late," he said at last.

"I'm sorry," Gant snapped back, irritated by the man.

"It's a question of the guards," Semelovsky explained, as if to a child. "A little longer, and one of the guard-posts, either at the junction or the other end of the road, would have sent someone to discover where I was. It is almost an hour since I checked through the first guard-post – which is why my car has, to all intents and purposes, broken down."

Gant nodded, and then said: "How do I get into Bilyarsk?"

"A good question. In the boot of the car, of course."

"Won't they search it?"

"Probably not. It was searched at the other end. Thoroughly. The KGB work very mindlessly, most of the time," he added, as if lecturing on the subject of an inefficient mechanism. "If the one guard-post is detailed to search all incoming vehicles, and the other all outgoing traffic, then they do not, as a rule, change functions – despite the recent draft of extra guards into the town. Do you know, there were more than a dozen jammed into the guard-post at the highway junction." Semelovsky smiled suddenly, brilliantly. "They must be expecting trouble, of one kind or another!"

He walked round Gant to the rear of the car, and opened the boot. He gestured to the American, sharply, as if accusing himself of having wasted valuable time, and Gant joined him. The boot was empty, and small. Pocketing the gun he had held all the time in his right hand, Gant climbed into the small space, hunched himself into a foetal position, and nodded. The Russian stood watching him for a moment, and then nodded back. The light disappeared, and Gant was in a confined, cramped darkness. He accepted that Semelovsky would have prepared the boot so that he would not asphyxiate. The darkness held no terrors for him. The boot was not as cramped as his own thoughts had proved, those months in the hospital. He heard the tinny roar of the engine, realised that Semelovsky, with careful attention to detail, was firing on only three cylinders, and then was heaved against the cold metal of the boot-door as the Russian pulled onto the road.

Semelovsky gave little thought to his passenger as he negotiated the remaining miles to the outskirts of Bilyarsk, where the quarters for the technical and scientific staff had been constructed. The road was narrow and deeply rutted by the passage of numerous heavy vehicles, bringing equipment to the project site. Semelovsky thought only of his function within the total operation that was intended to bring Gant and the Mig-31 into successful proximity. He had been recruited into the underground cell by Baranovich, for whom, and for whose sufferings at the hands of the NKVD and later the KGB, he had an almost religious respect. Semelovsky was himself a Jew, but had spent most of his adult life working successfully on various technical and military projects for the regime that despised and harried, in large numbers, the people of his race. But, Baranovich was sufficiently his hero to shake him out of the political cowardice of years; like all converts, he was zealous to an extreme.

The second guard-post lay in a gap in the high wire fence that surrounded the whole project area, including the airstrip. The original farming village of Bilyarsk lay outside the wire, a separate, and separated, community of wooden houses, communal agriculture, and poverty. The project-town had been grafted on to it, a hybrid growth surrounded by trees, ordered, secret.

Semelovsky slowed the car as he approached the gates in the wire, and he saw the increased size of the guard, a pattern he already expected from the junction guard-post fourteen miles down the road. Two guards, rather than the usual one, approached the vehicle, and he was almost blinded by the new, powerful searchlight mounted on the back of a truck. The beam of a searchlight mounted on one of the guard-towers, fifty yards away, swung to pick him up, and he was bathed in cold, white light. He wound down the window, and stuck out his head. He recognised the guard.

"Ah, Feodor — I see you have some new toys to play with, eh?" He laughed naturally, smiling inwardly at his own bravado.

"Dr Semelovsky — where have you been? You were checked through the guard-post more than an hour ago." The guard was frowning, more, Semelovsky suspected, because an officer he did not recognise was watching the little scene, than because he was suspicious or angry.

Semelovsky held out his hands, and the oily stains were clearly visible in the searchlight's glare.

"Damn car broke down!" he said. "Much as the latest Five-Year Plan has achieved, it has not solved the problem of the Moskvitch — eh?" He laughed again, inviting the guard to join him. The guard smiled.

The second guard joined him, and said: "Turn on the engine, please." Semelovsky did not recognise this guard, looked at Feodor for a time, then shrugged and did as he was ordered. He revved loudly, and the missing cylinder could be plainly detected. The guard motioned him to release the bonnet-catch, and lifted the bonnet, his head disappearing. Semelovsky spared a momentary glance at the officer, who appeared to be persuaded of the normality of the situation. He was smoking, and appeared bored.

Leaning out of the window, he called: "Any idea what it is?"

The second guard slammed down the bonnet suddenly, as if caught at some forbidden prank, and replied gruffly: "That engine's filthy. You're a scientist — you should take more care." Then he seemed to realise that his mask of deference had slipped. Semelovsky, surprised by his unguarded tone, realised that the man

65

had to be KGB or GRU, whatever his uniform said. He nodded in reply.

"They keep us too busy . . ." he began.

The second guard turned away, and shook his head in the direction of the officer lounging against the wall of the guard-hut. The officer waved a hand nonchalantly, and the gates swung apart. The guard Feodor waved Semelovsky through.

He eased the car into gear, and pulled forward. He passed through the gates, and they closed behind him. At that point, and at that point only, a wave of fear swept over him. The incident was more fraught in retrospect than it had been as he experienced it. He had smuggled Gant into the complex, and his job was done.

He steered the car through the straight streets of the living quarters. Each *dacha*-like dwelling, wooden and one-storeyed, was identical, set back from the road behind a strip of lawn. It was, he thought, more of a camp than a town. Not a camp like the ones Baranovich knew from personal experience, on what they called the Gulag Archipelago, but it was a camp, nevertheless. It did not have walls like Mavrino, where Baranovich had spent years of his creative adult life – but there were electric fences, and guard-towers, and the KGB.

He turned the wheel of the car, and drove it up the slightly-sloping drive and into the opened garage of a house half-way down Tupolev Avenue. It was near the middle of the fenced-in township, identical to almost every other street, except those which contained the shops, the bars, and the cinema and dance-hall.

Semelovsky glimpsed the watcher in the black car parked across the street from the house. He was suddenly afraid again. It did not matter that Baranovich had told him, and that he knew himself perfectly well, that they would not arrest them until after the weapons-trials – otherwise, who would complete the arming of the plane, the rest of the work . . . ? It was only by recalling Baranovich's face, and by hearing his voice, that he was able to calm himself. Then the bumper of the car bounced gently away from the car-tyre at the end of the garage, and he tugged on the handbrake and switched off the engine. As if forgetting Gant, locked in the boot, he sat for some moments, breathing regularly and deeply. He had seen too much, too quickly.

Then he opened the door, took the key from the ignition, and closed the garage door before he opened the boot.

"And you have learned nothing from either of them, Dmitri – *still* nothing?" The silkiness that had earlier invested it was gone from Kontarsky's voice. Instead, it was querulous, impatient. He was pacing his office, while Priabin sat in a chair before his desk, maintaining a ceaseless patrol. It was ten past seven. Priabin had left the cellar-room in Dzerzhinsky Street only minutes earlier, after Riassin, the man who seemed most likely to break of the two they had collected from the Mira Prospekt flats that morning, had slipped again into unconsciousness. Priabin tasted the ashes of an unsuccessful interrogation. There had been no time for the more refined, slower processes he preferred – this had been a brutal softening-up, and the massive misuse of pentathol on both men. Yet, they had learned nothing. Priabin was of the opinion that there was nothing to learn, other than the fact that the two men knew Pavel Upenskoy, and that one of them, Glazunov, worked with him, as driver's mate on his delivery truck. Glazunov had been instructed to remain at home that day, despite the fact that Upenskoy was leaving for a delivery to Kuybyshev, a long trip but, so he claimed under drugs, he had not been told why.

However, Kontarsky was in no mood to believe that Priabin had tried as hard as he could, pushed as hard as he dare, without killing Glazunov and the other man – he was prepared to believe only that his aide had failed. Kontarsky, it was obvious, still believed that the two men possessed the information.

Priabin's eyes followed Kontarsky as he paced the carpet. He, like his chief, had a sense that there was a mounting urgency about the circumstances of the second man in the truck. The problem was the inability to understand what these agents of British and American intelligence could hope to gain by smuggling one man into Bilyarsk . . . for that must be where the impostor was heading. What could he do, that one man, that could not be done by Baranovich, the brilliant original mind, or Semelovsky, or even Kreshin – all of whom would be working on the actual aircraft during the night? A stranger would not be able to get anywhere near the Mig. And to consider that he had come merely to spy, to photograph, was ridiculous, Priabin concluded once more.

He realised that Kontarsky had halted in front of him. He looked up into the colonel's strained face. The man was already hours late in departing for Bilyarsk, since he wanted to go with positive information concerning the man travelling in the same direction in Upenskoy's truck. A KGB helicopter had been waiting for him on the outskirts of the city since early afternoon.

"Very well," Kontarsky said, appearing to have come to some decision. "Pick up the phone, Dmitri. Get in touch with the tail-car, and have Upenskoy and the other man pulled in – at once!"

"Sir."

Priabin picked up the telephone. A simple instruction would be relayed via radio to the KGB office in Kazan, whence it would be passed on to the tail-car.

"Tell them to request what help they need from the guard-post at the Bilyarsk junction," Kontarsky added. "How many men in that car?"

"Three," Priabin replied. Then he said: "The last position of the truck showed it to have passed the junction to Bilyarsk – it didn't slow down, and it didn't stop . . ." He held the phone loosely in his hand.

Kontarsky whirled round, and snapped: "Then they must stop it now – I want to know if that second man is still aboard!"

As soon as he passed the Bilyarsk junction, glancing at the guard-post as he did so in the deepening dusk, Pavel Upenskoy knew that his time was limited. Without slowing, taking one hand from the wheel, he unzipped his jacket, and tugged an old service automatic from his waistband. He laid it gently on the passenger seat which Gant had occupied.

The tail-car had abandoned the idea of following him without lights. He could see the spreading stains of its headlights on the road behind. He wondered whether it would stop to consult the guards on the road to Bilyarsk, but it did not – probably, they were in conversation with them by radio. They would learn that he had not stopped, or slowed – and they would wonder why.

Upenskoy reckoned on having perhaps ten miles of road before they would become suspicious, or whoever they were answerable to ordered them to investigate his mysterious passenger. Then they would overtake, and order him to slow down. He knew the road between Kazan and Kuybyshev fairly well. It was farming country, isolated villages miles apart, some farms, but no town on the road before Krasny Yar, itself only ten or fifteen miles from Kuybyshev. He would not be allowed to get that far.

He had accepted the risks. He knew how important the Bilyarsk project was to the Soviets, how vital it was to NATO. He understood the desperation behind the plan to steal the aircraft. And the desperation that had induced Edgecliffe to sacrifice himself, and poor Fenton, and the others. He prided himself that Edgecliffe knew his worth, and would not lightly throw him away. Now, however, he was on his own, expendable – he was to avoid capture, if possible, for at least twelve hours, until Gant . . . There was no time to wonder about Gant, or to retrace the uncomfortable, depressing feeling the man exuded, like body odour.

He decided that he would run for it – there would be no road-blocks, in all probability, before Krasny Yar. He had to make sure he could get close enough to stand a chance of hiding there. He knew no one in the town, but that thought didn't worry him. He needed only shelter, which he could find, and food, which he could steal – then . . . He sensed that it did not do to consider the future. No, he would not think about it, merely react when the car behind him made its move.

He thought about Marya, his wife. It was time, he considered, to allow himself that luxury. How old was she now? Thirty-seven, three years older than himself. Twelve years in prison – for demonstrating against the invasion of Czechoslovakia in 1968. Her original sentence had been for three years, but she had smuggled out pamphlets and writings describing her treatment in prison, had been discovered, and her sentence had been increased by ten years. Pavel knew, with a sick certainty, that she would never be released – that she would not take that much favour from a regime she hated and despised.

Marya was Jewish, and highly educated. She had once been a school-teacher, before her political activities had got her dismissed, then locked away. He had never understood how she came to marry him, simple, uneducated as he was. Yet he worshipped her for having done so, and he had spent the last twelve years trying to be worthy of her. Whatever had been asked of him by Edgecliffe and Lansing, and those who had preceded them at the British Embassy, he had done.

He was not sure, because one could never be sure of such things, but he thought it probable that his wife had been given forcible mental treatment, such as was concomitant with Kremlin and KGB thinking. Anyone who dissented must be a lunatic, thus ran the official line. Yet the worst thought of all was not that, but the fact that, because of the way the years in prison would have aged her, he might have passed her in the street without recognising her. He was almost afraid, should that impossibility ever come to pass.

He checked the driving-mirror, and saw that the car had pulled up on him. He glanced to his side, checking that the gun had not shifted. The butt still lay towards him so that he could snatch it up. He checked the mirror again. The car was flashing its lights now, as if to overtake. Pavel smiled grimly. They knew that he knew who they were, and they assumed, in semi-divine arrogance, that now they had decided the little game was played out, he would fold like a house of cards. He pressed his foot down on the accelerator, and the lights of the car dropped away behind, then spurted nearer as the car realised he was attempting to escape.

They were on a straight stretch of road, but a stretch that had not yet been converted and widened to dual carriageway. To overtake him, the car would have to pass close to him, in the northbound lane. It was that for which he hoped. If he attempted to outrun the car for long enough, he reckoned on insulted KGB arrogance to make that attempt to pass him. He watched, the smile set on his features, as the car attempted to stop him by flashing its lights. He accelerated up to seventy miles an hour.

Again, the lights fell away behind, and then neared suddenly. Pavel knew that the men in the car would be angry by this time – they were unused to being defied, in any way at all. He tensed himself, and studied the road ahead. There were no trees on this stretch, merely the road itself bordered by low banks which separated it from the wheat-growing countryside through which it passed. The bank would have to do, would do for his purposes.

The car began to nose out into the other lane, cautiously, as if suspecting some trick. The driver was hanging back, still flashing his lights. Then the car seemed to leap forward, as the driver's foot went hard down and, almost taking Pavel by surprise, was all but level with his cab before he reacted. Viciously he swung the wheel, and the truck swerved across the road. He heard, and felt, the tearing impact as the two vehicles collided, then he straightened the wheel, and the lights of the car wavered crazily before ploughing into the bank. He took his foot from the accelerator, and braked sharply. The truck screeched to a halt. He rolled down the window and listened. There was silence. The engine of the car had stalled as it collided with the bank. He picked up the gun and climbed down from the cab. The car was more than a hundred yards away, its nose buried in the bank. As he walked towards it, he could see the body of the front-seat passenger lying across the bonnet, thrown at seventy miles an hour through the windscreen.

He was surprised when the rear door fell open and a dark shape slumped onto the road. He stopped, tense for movement. The flash from the gun and the noise of the shots, two sharp, flat cracks shocked him as if they were entirely out of place in the scene. One bullet missed him, the other tore through his shoulder. Raising the gun, as if oblivious of his wound, he fired twice in return. The dark figure slowly, balletically, extended itself on the road.

He did not have to inspect his wound to know that it would make steering the heavy truck almost impossible. Holding the wounded arm at his side, he turned back to the truck and, with great difficulty, a mist of pain before his eyes, sweat cold on his brow, he hauled himself aboard. With a supreme effort, his whole frame shaking, he shoved the truck into gear and pulled away from the scene of the accident, his body leaning heavily on the steering wheel, his eyes clouded with the pain and the loss of blood. He had only two thoughts in his mind – to get to Krasny Yar before he passed out, and the face of his wife, Marya, as he remembered her . . .

Pavel Upenskoy died when the truck failed to negotiate a bend in the road ten miles from the scene of the accident with the KGB car, overturned, and he was flung unconscious from the cab into the road. The truck half-mounted the bank, then fell back on top of his body.

Pyotr Vassilyevich Baranovich was no longer puzzled by the American, Gant. At first, and during the first hour or more of his presence in the house in Tupolev Avenue, he had been increasingly puzzled by his behaviour. He had watched the man eat his meal, served by the woman who lived with Kreshin, a secretary from the finance office of the Bilyarsk project. He had watched the American, and had not understood him. He had studied him while they talked of his journey, and of Pavel – who was God knew where by now on the road to Kuybyshev, or in the hands of the KGB – and still been puzzled. Then they had begun to talk of the Mikoyan Mig-31, the Firefox as NATO called it, and he had seen the eager, dry hunger, like lust, in the man's eyes and he no longer was dubious about Buckholz's choice of pilot.

Gant, he understood, *needed*, for some deep reason of his own, to fly the airplane. This man seated before him had been bundled from America to England, then to Russia, from Moscow to Bilyarsk, like so much washing – and he had allowed it to happen to him because at the end of the journey, like a monstrous child's prize for good behaviour, was the shiny toy of the Mig.

Semelovsky had left them almost as soon as he had delivered the American, to return to his own quarters. They would not meet again until they reported to the hangar to prepare the aircraft for the weapons-trials the following day. Kreshin and he, on the other hand, would pass through the security net into the factory complex together at two in the morning.

Baranovich was aware that the KGB would keep a careful watch upon himself and Kreshin and Semelovsky throughout the night. Without doubt, they would have orders to arrest them hours before the flight. That was only to be expected. But, until the work was done on the weapons-system they would not touch him. All they could do was watch from a car across the street. This was why Gant's presence in the house, so apparent a security risk, was in reality a safety precaution. It was safer than trying to hide him anywhere else in Bilyarsk. It was the last place they would look.

Baranovich had no intention of dwelling on his personal future.

Like Gant himself, and like Aubrey in London, Baranovich accepted the slivers of time that were given to him, and did not seek to understand what might occur in the future hours and days. He had learned to live like that in Mavrino, and before that in the labour camps. He had known what he was doing when he had accepted the order to work at Bilyarsk, to develop the purely theoretical work that had already been done on a thought-controlled weapons-system, by a man now dead. The KGB had been aware of what they were doing when they released him to take up the appointment. Baranovich had lived on borrowed time for many years, almost since the end of the war – no, before that, he corrected himself, since a soldier lives on borrowed time, especially on the Russian front in winter. Because he had done so for the greater part of his life, it came as no special occasion now to understand that he was living on borrowed time.

"How well have you been briefed?" he asked, settling himself to throw off the useless speculations about himself and the character of the American.

They were seated in Kreshin's living-room, small, warm and comfortable. The younger man had left them alone – Baranovich suspected that he and the woman were making love in the next room, perhaps with the desperation of the young to whom time, borrowed or otherwise, is precious. Kreshin would, perhaps, be trying to forget the hours ahead in the illusion of passion. Baranovich had told Gant that he could speak without being overheard. The house was indeed bugged – but for that evening the electronics expert had rigged pre-recorded tapes to supply innocuous talk and the noise of the television a background mutter, for the KGB listeners.

"I told you – I flew some of the Mig-25 copies we built in the States for a couple of years, then I spent months on the simulator flying the Mig-31," Gant replied. In his turn, he was impressed by Baranovich. The man's patriarchal appearance, white hair and goatee beard, clear blue eyes, and unlined brow, demanded respect.

"No doubt your training, then, was thorough," Baranovich said, smiling, puffing at his pipe, seemingly relaxed as if he and Gant were happily theorising in a university common-room. It had been a very long time, perhaps forty years, since Baranovich had been in such a room.

"It was," Gant agreed. He paused, then said: "The weapons-system . . . you need to tell me about that."

Baranovich seemed unaffected by Gant's directness. In fact, he respected it. This was the time and place for such directness.

"Yes. It is not, I must say, my own development, though I have done most of the work on the electronics involved, the miniaturisation, and so forth." He puffed at his pipe. "You are literally plugged into the weapons-system. The sensors which respond to your thought-processes and your eye movements are built into the helmet you wear, into the shell and the visor. A single lead carries the brain-impulses to the firing mechanisms, which you manually plug into the console – you know where that is located on the panel?" Gant nodded. "Good. What happens is not important as a process, only, for you, as an end product, a result. The radar system in the aircraft is specially developed to work in conjunction with the weapons-control – basically, it speeds up the firing-time. You receive an impulse quicker than the eye can respond, from the radar, which causes a reaction in your brain to which the weapons-system reacts. It makes the launching of air-to-air missiles, or the firing of the cannons, that much quicker . . . and, of course, for visual contact as opposed to radar contact, it places you seconds ahead of any other airplane or pilot. When your eyes *see* the target, the impulse is transmitted from the brain to the weapons-control – and whatever weapon you *decide* to launch *is* launched and it allows your brain to guide the missile in flight to its target."

Baranovich smiled at Gant's staring eyes. "Don't worry, my friend – some of our Red Air Force pilots are very unintelligent. This system works only as long as you are wearing the helmet, and are plugged in. Besides," he added with a smile, "I cannot tell you more – it is top-secret, eh?" Baranovich took his pipe from his mouth, and roared with laughter. Still smiling, he added: "There *is* a master lock-out switch, by the way, which prevents you from blowing friends out of the sky with evil thoughts!"

After a pause, Baranovich sighed. His eyes seemed to be directed inwards, and when he spoke next, it was as if he were summarising a problem for his own satisfaction alone.

"Your government realises the importance of the weapons-system. It is the logical next step, and it has endless possibilities. I could tell them much, of course, except that they know they can never get me out of the Soviet Union. To steal the Mig is easier . . ." He sucked at the dead pipe, and continued, "The United States has hardly begun to develop such a system. If it does not have one soon, then it will never be able to catch up with the flood of refinements and applications that will follow from what is, at present, still a crude electronic implement. So, they have to have the Mig, since they cannot have me. The applications could be endless, infinite, as the system is refined. You, naturally, are interested only as a pilot, not as a scientist. At the moment, it employs conventional weaponry – who knows? Soon, the weaponry may leap ahead to match the thought-guided system . . ."

He looked sharply at Gant, who wiped the lack of interest from his face. There was a look sharp with pain in Baranovich's eyes as he said: "Of course, I bore you. Perhaps it is self-pity. I would like to go on living, perhaps in the United States . . ."

Gant said gently: "The – anti-radar . . .?"

"Ah." Baranovich shook his head. "About that, I know nothing. It is the most secret aspect of the whole project – a Jew with a long record of dissidence would not be allowed to become familiar with it." Gant nodded.

"I have to know," he said, "whether the Russians can switch it off by remote control when I'm airborne – or if I could switch it off by accident?"

Baranovich looked thoughtful for a moment, puffing stolidly at his pipe. Once again, Gant was forcibly reminded of a university seminar, rather than a vital intelligence briefing.

"No," the Russian said, shaking his head, then rubbing his nose with thumb and forefinger. "As far as I have heard from rumours – and those rumours have been few and uncertain – I understand that the anti-radar capacity is not mechanical at all."

"What in the hell . . .?"

"As far as I understand it, that is so," Baranovich repeated levelly. "It is something – perhaps a skin, even a paint, of some kind, like the low-friction finish developed for certain American airplane projects?" Gant's eyes widened. "Mm. Even we know of it – American security is not as good as the Pentagon would like to think . . . However, as I was saying, it would appear that the anti-radar stems from some such system, so that the radar-beam flows over the surface of the aircraft, and passes on, nothing having registered on the screens. I do know that the system can be neutralised for safety requirements, such as landing at your own airfield in the worst weather, by the pilot, but I can't tell you how it is done." His face darkened. "You won't be able to use it." He shook his head. "I am dubious myself, Mr. Gant. I only repeat what I have heard. And we both know it works. That part of the project has been developed elsewhere, not in Bilyarsk."

There was a silence, then Gant said, "How long can you give me inside the cockpit?"

"No time at all, I think. The security is tighter than ever. You know that the First Secretary is flying down here tomorrow to witness this triumph of Soviet technology? Accompanied by Andropov, the Chairman of the KGB, and other Party notables, of course. Well, because of that – or, even, because of us, Semelovsky,

74

Kreshin and myself – the security is massive, more than ever before." He paused and puffed at his pipe in silence. Then he added: "A special detachment of GRU troopers was flown in yesterday. They will be under the command of the KGB, of course, but there are more than one hundred of them, in addition to the considerable garrison already here." He spread his hands in front of him. "Which is why we have been forced to the extremity we have in order to get you into the hangar area . . ." Baranovich's eyes twinkled, and he smiled. "You will need to have your hair cut even shorter, of course, so that the helmet and sensors can work efficiently, and your photograph taken for a very special set of papers – but nothing more will need to be done to you."

Gant shrugged. There was no resistance whatever to the idea of disguise, of assumed identity. His indifference to his own identity, a quality that Buckholz had understood from the first, made him successful as a chameleon. Most agents attempt, subconsciously, to retain something of themselves – an item of clothing, a mannerism, an inflection – as if they were swimmers, fearing to leave their personalities heaped like clothes until they should come back, fearing they might not be there when they returned. Gant had no such qualms, conscious or subconscious. Orton, Grant, Glazunov – and the man he was shortly to portray, whoever he was – they were shadows, as he was.

"What about my route – what's the lay-out of the hangar area?" he said bluntly.

Baranovich watched the American's face for a moment with keen eyes, then nodded as if satisfied, and stood up, gesturing Gant to where a large-scale drawing hung like the edge of a white tablecloth from the small dining-table. Kreshin had left it there after Gant had finished eating.

Baranovich fussily straightened and smoothed the pencil-drawn map of the huge compound, and began to point out its features to Gant.

"We are here," he said, "almost in the centre of the living-area – and all technical and scientific staff enter the hangar and factory complex through this gate . . ." His finger traced a route along the streets until it stopped at a line marked in red, further marked by red crosses at intervals. "Yes," Baranovich continued, "there is another fence, electric, and guarded by these watch-towers . . ." his finger tapped at the red crosses, "inside the perimeter fence, which keeps us and the project divided from the village. There is only one other gate in this fence – over here, on the other side of the airstrip." Again his finger tapped at the stiff paper. "That is used only by se urity personnel – it is the one *you* will use."

"How, for God's sake?"

Baranovich smiled.

"With bravado, naturally – and a little help from myself and the others. Don't worry about it." The Russian returned to his pipe, sucked at it energetically, and spilled a thick cloud of smoke from his lips. Gant wrinkled his nose, as if in disapproval. "Do you smoke?" Baranovich asked.

"No. Not any more."

Nodding, Baranovich reached into a pocket of his worn, leather-elbowed jacket, and pulled out a packet of American cigarettes.

"Learn again – now," he said simply.

"Uh?"

"Learn to smoke in the next hour, before you rest."

Gant pulled a face. "They're not Russian," he said.

"A status-symbol? Foreign cigarettes, in the mouth of the person you will be, will prove as convincing as anything else – even your papers." Baranovich smiled, then returned his attention to the map. Gant picked up the pack of cigarettes from the map, and slipped it into the breast-pocket of his overalls. "From this gate, you will make your way to this area here, on the far side of the runway." The long finger tapped. Gant watched, as if fascinated, the mottled, thick-veined hand as it lay on the white background of the map. "This building is the main hangar, where both prototypes are stored. We will be working here through the night, preparing the airplane that is to take part in the trials. Attached to the hangar are the security offices, right on the spot, and also the pilots' rooms. You see that?" Gant nodded. "Good. You have to go upstairs, and along this corridor . . ." Baranovich's finger was now tracing the direction on a second-storey plan of the buildings attached to the huge main hangar. "The other buildings – they are merely the laboratories, wind-tunnels, test-houses, and the like. Waste no time with them. Get yourself to the pilots' dressing-room as soon as you can. Red Air Force Lieutenant-Colonel Yuri Voskov will arrive some hours before the flight. You must be ready for him."

"What about visitors?" Gant asked. "I could be there for three, four hours."

Baranovich explained patiently, as if to a child: "Conceal the body – there are a number of lockers, metal ones, all with good locks." He smiled. "The pilots complained of a great deal of pilfering of the Western luxury items supplied them for being well-behaved and well-adjusted . . . the locks are good. As for yourself, since you do not appear to be very much like Voskov, except in general build – you will be taking a shower."

"For three hours?"

76

"You will appear to be taking a shower. Once it nears the time for our little – *diversion* to occur, you will dress and the visor of the helmet will conceal your features. We on the weapons-guidance system request the pilots to wear the helmets until removed in the laboratory. It will not seem strange that you are wearing it even an hour or more before the flight."

Gant nodded. "What about this diversion?"

"You need not worry. I have a very small radio device which will tell you when to come down from your room to the hangar-area. What you will see there will enable you to enter the cockpit and roll the aircraft out of the hangar, without anyone being in the least suspicious."

Gant's eyes widened again. He was thoughtful for a moment, and then he said: "What happens to you guys, after I lift out of there?" His voice was quiet, breathy, as if he already knew the answer.

"It does not matter," Baranovich said softly. His expression betrayed a sympathy for his visitor that the American could not comprehend.

"The hell it doesn't!" Gant said, stepping back, his arms raised at his sides. "Hell!" He turned away from the Russian, his shoulders hunched, then turned back and said, waving his arm before him: "You guys, all of you – you're so damn *willing* to die, I don't understand! Don't you resent those guys in London, ordering your deaths?"

Baranovich was silent for a long time, then he said: "It is easy for you to feel indignant, Mr. Gant. You are an American. *Any* order that you are given is a source of resentment, is that not so? You are a free man . . ." Gant smiled cynically, and Baranovich seemed angered by his expression. "You *are* free! I am not. There is a difference. If I resent the men in London who are ordering me to die, then it is a small thing when compared with my – *resentment* of the KGB!" Baranovich was staring down at the map with unseeing eyes, his features strained, his hands knuckled on the table, so that the heavy blue veins stood out like ropes. It was a long time before he straightened, and was able to smile at Gant.

"I'm sorry . . ." Gant began.

"Nonsense. Why should you be aware of – our little problems? Now, shall we go over the armament of the plane again. Luckily, for your purposes at least, they will be concerned to use air-to-air missiles in the first trial, not ground-attack weapons."

He waved Gant back to his chair. "Please smoke," he said. "We don't want you coughing amateurishly at the gate, do we?" His eyes had recovered their smile.

* * *

The beat of the rotors over his head had become almost inaudible to Kontarsky during the flight from Moscow. Now, at ten o'clock, they were more than half-way to Bilyarsk, flowing over the moonlit, silvered country below, marked by the lights of the scattered villages and collective farms, sliced by the beams of the occasional truck or car on the road between Gorky and Kazan, which they were, at that point, paralleling. The helicopter seat was comfortable in the interior of the MIL MI-8. Behind Kontarsky as he sat behind the pilot and co-pilot, were seats for twenty-eight more passengers. Only four of the seats were occupied, by Kontarsky's personal guard, a male secretary and a classified radio operator – all of them were KGB staff.

Kontarsky was sleepy, despite the tension within him. He had delayed leaving for as long as possible, in order that he could arrive in Bilyarsk with at least some information concerning the identity, and therefore the mission, of the man who had passed through traffic controls at Moscow, Gorky, and Kazan as Glazunov. The result of Priabin's investigations was – nothing. True, they had found the tail-car, a few miles beyond the turn-off to Bilyarsk; true, also, that they had found the overturned truck and the crushed body of Pavel Upenskoy ten miles further down the road to Kuybyshev. There was no sign of the second man. Therefore, with a nauseous, logical certainty, Kontarsky and Priabin had been faced with the knowledge that the second man was on his way, on foot, or by some alternative transport, to Bilyarsk. The old man at the warehouse had died almost as soon as they began to beat his knowledge out of him. Frail, weak heart. Kontarsky was still angry at such unfastidious waste.

The man's photograph had been transmitted to Bilyarsk, and the security-guard alerted. Kontarsky had panicked himself into flying at once to Bilyarsk, to take personal charge of the counter-measures.

He lit yet another cigarette, having glanced over his shoulder, at the radio-operator sitting before his console. The man, as if telepathically aware that his chief's eyes were on him, shook his head mournfully. Kontarsky turned back, facing forward in the helicopter again, staring at the helmeted heads in front of him, as if they might provide some inspiration. There was the taste of fear in the back of his throat. He brushed a hand across his eyebrows nervously. He knew there would be no sleep for him until the trials were successfully completed. He felt the common KGB impotence of having to rely upon computers, upon the whole huge unwieldy apparatus of the Security Service for results.

At that moment, Priabin was gaining access to the central records computer in Dzerzhinsky Street, a priority request for computer time. He was searching for a man, British or American without doubt, who had entered the Soviet Union recently, under a false name and passport, who could be identified as an intelligence agent. He was using the electronic mind of a huge machine to run to earth the second man in the truck. An electronic hunt, he summarised bitterly. Like Priabin, Kontarsky's faith lay in what people could tell him, what they could extract from individual minds and tongues. Yet the two they had picked up knew nothing, that much was obvious, except their own speculations that the man was an intelligence agent whose destination was Bilyarsk and the Mikoyan project; and Upenskoy, who would have known for certain, was dead, crushed to pulp beneath the weight of the truck.

Kontarsky's thought processes were defensive, even at the moment when he most needed daring, and imagination. Mentally, he was already preparing a defence for the officers of the Special Investigations Department who would be calling on him in the event of his failure. He writhed at the thought of having to depend upon a computer's master index of files in the Registry and Archives Department of the KGB. Yet, rely upon that machine he had to. There was no other alternative now. There was no one living to ask.

There was a further problem, of course. Unless he allowed the three dissident agents of the CIA and the British SIS to complete their vital work on the aircraft, there would be no trial the following day.

He cleared his throat, cleared his mind. He was terrified of espionage, of an attempt to sabotage the trial in front of Andropov and the First Secretary . . .

He would, he decided, allow himself at least two hours before the arrival of the official aircraft, to question the dissidents. He looked at his watch. Ten-fifteen. He was anxious now, to arrive, to be on the spot, to become active.

Police Inspector Tortyev was scrutinising a dossier of photographs of Alexander Thomas Orton. He had spread the snapshots across his desk regardless of date or place, and picked up samples at random. For half an hour, he had been picking up and discarding, and comparing samples from the heap. It had taken his small team three hours to collect the full dossier, from various sources within the KGB 2nd Chief Directorate. He had been denied computer time, which would have immensely simplified and speeded-up his enquiries. He gathered there was some kind of priority-search being mounted, and his team had been lucky to obtain the number of photographs they had done by manual extraction from the files, to supplement his own dossier on Orton.

Again, as with the man's shoes, Tortyev recognised the significance of the photographs. Almost casually, he selected two, one of Orton taken at Cheremetievo two days ago, and one of the man taken eighteen months before, in a Moscow street, just leaving a tourist shop. It had been taken as part of a routine surveillance, before Tortyev had become interested in the activities of the businessman from England. Holding them together between thumb and forefinger, he passed them across his desk to Holokov and Filipov, who had sat silently awaiting the outcome of his deliberations.

"What do you think?" he said, offering the two pictures to Holokov. Filipov leaned across, almost touching Holokov's shoulder.

The fat man studied the pictures for some time, then shook his head. "What is it you want me to say, Inspector?" he asked.

Tortyev smiled. "What you *really* think – even if that is a rather unusual request for me to make."

"Mm." Holokov glanced at Filipov, flashed the pictures at him, and then added: "It's not the same man."

"Good, Holokov – good." Without interest, he added: "You agree, Filipov?"

Filipov looked dubious, and then said: "I – I'm not sure, Inspector."

"Naturally. *I* am – you, too, Holokov?" The fat man nodded. "Which poses a question – eh? Which of these two is the dead man?"

"How can we tell? They're very alike," Filipov said.

"Their common disguise makes them alike, Filipov!" Tortyev snapped. "The face was ruined so that we would not discover that there were two men involved in this deception. Why were there two of them?"

Holokov looked bemused, and Filipov remained silent. Tortyev left his desk and began to pace the room. Suddenly, a sense of urgency had come over him, though he could not explain its origin. He felt a nervous energy, a sense of being trapped by the walls of his office. He looked up at the clock. It was ten-thirty. He turned to Holokov.

"What of that KGB man killed at the Komsomolskaia metro station yesterday evening – who killed him?"

"One of Orton's associates?" It was Filipov who spoke.

"Why not Orton – he's not dead, after all!" Tortyev replied, bending over Filipov as he sat in his hard upright chair before the desk. "Why not Orton himself?" Filipov shrugged, as if he had no answer to the question. "*Who* are Orton's associates? We have men you have pulled in, the usual crowd, the ones in Orton's file – you have searched their homes, their storeplaces. What have you found – eh? Nothing – nothing at all!"

He moved away from Filipov and Holokov, and began to reason aloud. "Where is Orton – where have they hidden him? Why did he want it to appear that he had been killed? To throw us off the scent? Why not die in London, if that was the case, where we could not check so thoroughly, where we would not have the evidence of the body itself?" He paused, turned, paced the length of the room once in silence, and then continued. Holokov and Filipov sat mutely, digesting their inspector's ruminations. "No. The answer does not lie there. Orton had to disappear here, inside the Soviet Union, inside Moscow. Why?"

He paused again in his stride, in the middle of his office, and said, calmly, but with a catch of excitement in his voice that both his subordinates felt: "If we had not been persuaded that Mr. Alexander Thomas Orton was a drug-smuggler, what would we think he was? Eh? Based on what has happened – including the killing of a KGB man, which must have had something to do with this, and which shows the desperate extent of what has been happening – two deaths, a fake Orton and one of ourselves . . . based on that, what would we think?"

He stood staring at them, willing them to arrive at his own conclusion, nervous of the leap his mind had made, hoping that theirs would leap in the same way.

Holokov cleared his throat, fussily, apologetically, infuriatingly, and said: "He is an agent?"

"Exactly!" Tortyev was smiling. "He is an espionage agent, of the British, or the Americans – the drugs blinded us to the truth! Now, now he has disappeared – for what reason? Where is he – what is he up to – eh?"

Neither of his subordinates appeared to be possessed of further ideas. Gathering up the sheaf of photographs, Tortyev bundled them into his arms, and made for the door.

"Holokov – come with me. I want this face processed by the central computer – now! This man is dangerous, and I want to know who he is. The central registry of known or suspected agents may give us some clue as to his real identity." He turned to Filipov. "Get in touch with our people in the British Embassy, Filipov. Give them my authority for your enquiries, and tell them it's urgent. I want to know who Orton's contact is – and I want to know now!"

Filipov nodded, but the door had already closed behind the inspector and his fat assistant trailing in his wake. Filipov picked up one photograph that Tortyev's sweeping arms had failed to gather, and looked down at it. By chance, it was a photograph of Gant in the persona of Orton, rather than Fenton. He seemed to study it for a moment, turning it in his fingers, letting the face catch the light from the strip-light overhead. Filipov's dark, swarthy features were harassed, his shoulders bowed with concern.

Filipov knew that it would take only a little time if Tortyev began to ask questions of the KGB informants who worked in the kitchens, the corridors and the typing-pool of the British Embassy, a little time before he began to realise that there were a multitude of connections between Edgecliffe and Lansing at the Embassy and the man Fenton in his persona as Orton. Fenton was SIS, based in London. He had come to Moscow this time undisguised, an ordinary tourist with a package holiday, and had gone to ground in the Embassy only an hour or so before his death – re-emerging briefly as Orton. Someone might have seen him, made the connection. They might even discover that the substitute for Fenton on the package holiday, now moved on to Leningrad, was not the man who arrived at Cheremetievo from London.

He realised that Edgecliffe had to be told, and quickly. He got up from the chair, in a quick, nervous bound. He could not call from Tortyev's office, the line would be monitored. Yet he could not leave the building – Tortyev would be back within ten minutes, perhaps a little more. As far as he knew, the telephones – the "social lines", as they were called – in the off-duty rest-rooms on the second floor would not be monitored at that time of night. He would have to risk it. He had to call Edgecliffe before Tortyev received any information from the informants in the British Embassy. He closed the door of the office noiselessly behind him.

At the direct order of the Head of Intelligence, "C", Kenneth de Vere Aubrey had condescended to temporarily vacate the usual offices of SO-4, his own section of the SIS's Special Operations Function, and to take up residence in a specially prepared and utterly secure room within the complex of the Ministry of Defence. Aubrey did not like M.O.D. He and his number two, Shelley, had occupied the room with its wireprint and secure telephones for most of the day and evening, preparing it with the maps that now covered the walls – European Russia, the Barents Sea and north into the Arctic Ocean, the Moscow metro system, a Moscow street plan. All the necessary landscapes and seascapes of his operation. Now the room had acquired two other occupants, the Americans Buckholz and Anders, his aide. They had commandeered two of the small desks that had been moved in, scorning, apparently, the trestle-tables that Aubrey had drafted in with the original furniture. Shelley, returning to the room from a journey to the kitchens, saw Buckholz talking on one red telephone, and Anders up the step-ladder, pinning a satellite weather photograph of the Arctic region on the wall, next to the map of the same region. That map, like the others of European Russia and the North Sea, was ringed by satellite weather-pictures. It was not those, however, that especially caught Shelley's eye. His gaze was drawn to the map of European Russia that Buckholz had begun working on when he had left with the supper dishes for the kitchens. Aubrey had allowed no one inside the room except himself, Shelley, and the two Americans who had arrived a little after eight. It was now one o'clock in the morning in London, two hours ahead of Moscow time.

Shelley walked over to Aubrey and stood beneath the huge map, looking up. Facing him now, instead of the clean unmarked map, was something that made him, thousands of miles away, frightened and dubious. He had a sudden image of Gant standing belligerently before him in his hotel room – and he regretted his stupid, petty dislike of the American. What Shelley was staring at was Buckholz's breakdown, in graphic form, of the Russian defence system which Gant would have to penetrate, even if he got the Firefox off the ground at Bilyarsk. Much of what was on the map Shelley already knew, but to see it, indicated in coloured pins and ribbons, shocked him thoroughly.

Near the top of the map, extending deep into the polar pack at the neck of the conical orthomorphic projection map, was a yellow ribbon, in great loops reaching upwards. This signified the effective extent of the Russian DEW-line, the least of Gant's worries. What really attracted his gaze, riveted his attention, were the sweeps of small pins that marked the fighter bases, those known or guessed, and the missile sites. The fighter stations, all of which would be manned in a twenty-four-hour readiness manner, would possess at least a dozen aircraft that could be scrambled within minutes. These bases were marked in blue and extended along the northern coast of the Soviet Union from Murmansk and Archangelsk in the west to the Taimyr Peninsula fifteen hundred miles to the east. The bases were a little more than one hundred miles apart.

Below these pins were two sweeps of red circles, showing the missile sites. These were slightly less than a hundred miles apart, and extended over the same area of the map, its total east–west projection. Each missile site was semi-fixed, and possessed perhaps a dozen or more surface-to-air proximity and infra-red missiles, launched from concrete pads. Between each pair in both chains, though unmarked, Shelley nevertheless knew there would be mobile, truck-borne missiles, perhaps half-a-dozen to each convoy.

83

The radar system would be located at each of the missile bases, linked to the central radar-control which processed the information supplied by the DEW-line.

Shelley felt mesmerised by the two sweeps of red circles, one along the coast, the second another three hundred miles or more inland, following the same path. It looked like a plan of a classic battle, an army drawn up in two parallel lines – an army of missiles, in this case, linked to radar that scanned every cubic foot of air over the Soviet Union. Gant would have to cross each line, and avoid the fighter-scramble that would follow hard upon his theft of the Firefox.

And, thought Shelley, Buckholz hasn't yet filled in the positions of Soviet spy trawlers, missile cruisers of the Red Banner Northern Fleet, and submarine activity in the Arctic Ocean and the Barents Sea.

He saw that Aubrey was looking at him, quizzically, perhaps even vulnerably. "There are a lot of them – eh, Shelley?" he said softly.

"Too many," Shelley blurted out. "Too bloody many by half! He hasn't got a chance!" He dropped his eyes, seeing Aubrey's anger at his impolitic display of emotion. "Poor sod," he muttered.

FOUR:

The Concealment

Gant was tired, yet his mind refused to stop racing. Baranovich and the woman, Kreshin's mistress, fussed around him fitting his disguise. Kreshin himself sat in one of the room's low, inexpensive armchairs, watching intently, as if studying the American, expecting to learn something from the way he moved, the way he stood still. Gant despised the building tension and excitement within himself. It was the wrong way to be, he knew. Yet however he strove to control his feelings, he could not avoid hanging over the edge, staring into the abyss of the hours ahead.

The disguise was, when he considered it, inevitable. There was only one way to walk through a tight security net which was on the look-out for the least unfamiliar thing – to be a part of that net. Baranovich got up from his knees and stood back, hands on hips, in the posture of a couturier inspecting his creation. Gant self-consciously pulled the uniform jacket straight at the hips, adjusted the belt, and looked across at himself in the mirror. The cap he now wore hid his newly-cropped hair, cut close to his head, so that the contacts inside his flying helmet that would control the weapons-system would function, picking up his brain patterns, transmitting them to radar, missiles, or cannon.

Underneath the dark peak, the face that stared at him was cold, narrow, lined and tired. It was the face of a stranger, despite the fact that nothing in the way of disguise had been done to it. In the wall mirror, all he could see of himself besides was the collar of the brown shirt, the dark uniform tie, and the bright tabs on the lapels of his uniform jacket.

"That is – good," Baranovich pronounced at last. "It is a good fit now that Natalia has made the little alterations." He smiled over Gant's shoulder at the woman, who was sitting on the arm of Kreshin's chair, her arm about his neck, as if seeking warmth. Something about the uniform seemed to disturb her, make her seek physical contact with her lover.

"Captain Grigory Chekhov, attached to the Security Support Unit of the GRU, at present assigned under the command of . . ."

"Major Tsernik, KGB officer responsible for security of the Mikoyan project, Bilyarsk," Gant finished for Baranovich, a slight smile at the corner of his mouth.

Baranovich nodded. "What do you think of him, Ilya?"

"Very – convincing," Ilya Kreshin offered, holding the girl's hand at his shoulder. "At least, he frightens Natalia – doesn't he?" He was smiling at the girl as he looked into her face, and she tried to smile back. "You see?" he added, turning back to Gant and Baranovich. "She takes you for the real thing, and she helped you into the disguise!" He laughed loudly, reassuringly, patting the girl's hand as he did so.

"You recall the rest of your operational background?" Baranovich asked. Gant nodded. "Good. Now, sit down, or walk about – let that uniform become comfortable – strut a little!" There was an almost malicious humour in Baranovich's blue eyes. Gant smiled, and began to walk up and down the room. Baranovich watched him, and then said: "No – with the thumbs tucked into the belt – so . . ." He demonstrated by hooking his thumbs into his trousers. Gant copied him. "That is good. You must always remember – you will only give yourself away if you fail to be what the guards at the gate expect. And they will expect to see a captain who is arrogant, detached – who means business. If you get the chance, reprimand at least one or two of them, for minor things – their uniform, for example, or anyone who is smoking." Again Gant nodded. This was an expert talking, one who knew the *look* of the KGB, or the GRU, intimately, through long and bitter experience. Gant surrendered his own ego, accepted the expertise he was being offered. "Now – sit down. You stand rather well, eh, Ilya?"

Gant sat down, first wiping the seat of the vacant armchair, and inspecting his fingertips for dust. Then he sat in the chair, completely relaxed, one booted leg crossed over the other. Without looking at them, he drew a silver cigarette case from his pocket, and a rolled-gold lighter – items he could only have purchased in the KGB luxury shop across the square from the Centre itself in Dzerzhinsky Street – extracted an American cigarette, lit it, exhaled noisily, picked tobacco from the tip of his tongue, and then turned his head and looked stonily towards Kreshin in the armchair. The young man clapped loudly.

"It is amazing," Baranovich observed. "How melodramatic it all was – and how *correct!*" His face clouded, as if he were assailed at that moment by a bad memory, then he smiled, his eyes clearing, and added: "That was very good – you have the gift, Mr. Gant. You can be, without trying, someone else . . ."

Gant nodded his head politely, frostily.

86

"Tell me about the observations you made on your lovers' walk earlier," he said to Kreshin, his eyes hard. It was not a request, but an order. Gant had found that he could channel the useless, wasted adrenalin pumping into his system into his characterisation of Chekhov, whose fictitious papers he had in his pocket, complete with the all-important yellow GRU ID card, transit papers, and the rest. His fake dog-tags were on a thin chain around his neck. He had not asked how the forgery, the disguise, had been accomplished. Baranovich was an expert, driven by hate, and by ego. The results were good.

Kreshin smiled, and said: "The guard on that gate has been reinforced – there are troops of the usual KGB guard, but more of them. The Security Support Group has not been used there – probably because Tsernik feels insulted that the GRU have been called in . . . it's always happening."

"What about the perimeter fence?"

"The watch-towers are full to overflowing – and there are dog patrols inside the fence, every ten minutes or so. It's a double fence, by the way, and the dogs will be loose by the time you arrive – no one in their right mind would try cutting the wire. The watch-towers are a hundred yards apart – you'll have to pass at least four of them."

"You must look as if you are inspecting the wire itself – don't forget to challenge the guards in the towers, wake them up," Baranovich interrupted. "Go on, Ilya."

"There is a lot of light at the gate itself – you will be seen from some distance as you approach. The outer gate is merely a barrier with its accompanying guard-post. You will be required to show your papers here. The guards will be curious, because they will not recognise you, but the GRU tabs on your uniform will allay any suspicions they might have. When you are allowed to pass inside the outer barrier, you will encounter a mesh-gate, which will be locked. The guard will be *inside* this gate, and they will require you to show your papers again before they will open up."

"They will open up?" Gant asked softly.

"There is no need to worry – we have checked the current papers and identification of GRU officers of the Special Groups, and yours are in order," Baranovich explained. Gant merely nodded. Baranovich took up the narrative, Kreshin returning to an idle, thoughtful patting of Natalia's hand as it lay on his shoulder. "Once inside, you should make as directly as possible across the airfield. You may ignore any helicopter activity overhead – the uniform will be enough to satisfy them. When you arrive at the security guard outside the administrative building which, as I mentioned earlier, is physically linked to the hangar containing the Firefox, you will need to show your papers but, since you will be walking into the KGB head-quarters at Bilyarsk, no one is likely to assume that you do not, in fact, belong there!" Baranovich smiled. "Once inside, make for the pilots' rest-room on the floor above. It will not be occupied at that time."

"Where is the pilot – Voskov?" Gant asked sharply.

"At this moment?" Kreshin asked, exaggeratedly looking at his watch. "He will be in bed."

"He has quarters in a special compound – where the KGB and other *reliable* members of the team here are housed." Baranovich's contempt showed for a moment, as if he had lifted a veil and shown a corner of his soul. "It is where they keep those who work on the anti-radar, which is why we have picked up nothing in scientists' gossip during the last months."

"But, he *will* come to the rest-room?" Gant persisted.

"Yes. He will change there, and perhaps have a meal – though Voskov is not a good eater before one of these flights . . . Are you, Mr. Gant?" Baranovich's eyes twinkled.

"No, but I can usually sleep," Gant replied.

"Yes, of course. We will be leaving at two-thirty. You will have perhaps only a couple of hours."

"Never mind," Gant said, stifling a yawn and forcing himself into wakefulness. "I want to go over it all again."

"The security?"

"No. The airplane. The weapons-system, the Rearward Defence Pod. Tell me again – everything."

Gant felt himself as two layers of response, suddenly. At the surface of his mind was the growing excitement, now that he had put aside his masquerade as a GRU officer, the tension connected with the Firefox, burning hot as a lust in him; he had a curious reluctance to stay awake, an unformed desire to be in darkness, with an empty mind. It was the first time he had ever wished back the void of the Veterans' Hospital since the day he had left it. It was a feeling he avoided examining.

Dmitri Priabin and Alexei Tortyev knew each other – not as close friends, but as graduates of the KGB training school. They had been contemporaries, and as junior officers had worked within the same department. This was before Priabin, who was regarded as the more promising, was promoted as aide to Kontarsky in Department "M", and Tortyev, whose brilliant mind was officially mistrusted by such a degree which would ensure his rotting at his present rank until he retired, had moved into the KGB section of the Moscow Police, into the Political Security Service.

It was not unnatural, then, that having met in the cold, metallic room which housed the programmers for the central records computer, below ground level in Dzerzhinsky Street, and having enquired after each other's recent careers, and complained about their own and each other's superior officers, they began to discuss the cases on which they were working.

It was a remarkable coincidence that had brought them to the central computer at the same time. Such discussion was the privilege of young officers, safe from their superiors, each alive to the possibilities of their separate cases. The senior echelons of the KGB, like its predecessors, have always discouraged the professional gossip associated with police forces in other countries, other societies, in a further attempt to enforce the absolute security seemingly demanded by a secret police force. However, the present generation of KGB officers, among whom were Tortyev and Priabin, both highly intelligent graduates of the Lenin University of Moscow, possessed, in the eyes of many of their seniors, a remarkable degree of scepticism towards some of the cherished aims of the service – notably in the matter of gossip. They realised, unlike their hidebound seniors, that the cross-fertilisation of such gossip more than outweighs its detraction from absolute security. Priabin, seated in one of the armchairs in the waiting-room next to the metallic, sterile room with its banks of lights and spools and controls, was saying as much to Tortyev.

"They don't realise, Alexei, how much they lose by being so rigidly compartmentalised. One hand never knows what the other is doing."

Tortyev, who had shoved his file of photographs into the hands of one of the white-coated operators, and was merely waiting for an estimate of how long the computer-run would take after the features of the man Orton had been broken down into computer-language, nodded his head sagely, a smile of complicity playing around his mouth.

"Quite true," he replied. "Take us, for instance."

"True – we are, after all, both looking for foreign agents, are we not?"

There was a silence. Priabin lit a long cigarette, of British manufacture, while Tortyev was content to pick at his fingernails. Priabin had revisited the computer room throughout the afternoon and evening, almost as a kind of obsessive, childhood habit, as if he could, by appearing before the officers with irritation plainly written on his features, prompt the operators into jogging the computer into more rapid activity. Thus far, the computer had failed to answer his question – who was the man in the truck with Upenskoy? This was

89

despite the fact that it had at its disposal the files, descriptions, possible disguises – a whole identifit library of each face in every file, and suggestions as to how those faces might be disguised successfully – and present whereabouts, if known, of thousands of known or suspected agents – American, European, Israeli; even Warsaw Pact countries and developing African nations had their places in the computer-banks as possible enemies of the KGB.

Priabin was angry with the computer – he had presented the machine with a simple problem, the sort of problem it would take a large team of men a week to complete, and he wondered what machines were for if they couldn't come up with the answers he required. He puffed angrily at his cigarette now that the conversation had idled, and wished that, indeed, Tortyev could help with his problem – what was it he was worrying about, some body in the Moskva, with its face beaten in?

"Who is this man you're after?" he asked, as much for the sake of distracting himself as for the sake of conversation, or interest in what Tortyev was doing. Kontarsky would already be at Bilyarsk, strutting like a turkey-cock, attempting to drive doubt from his mind by an over-zealous inspection of security there. While he left his assistant holding the damned baby! Priabin concluded. What was it Kontarsky had said to him, just before leaving, and for perhaps the twentieth time since he had seen that bloody photograph of the man who called himself Glazunov, and who had popped up out of nowhere like the devil himself? What was it? Find out, Dmitri – for your sake, and for mine. Find out tonight. Yes – that was it.

Priabin grimaced at his thoughts. Dmitri Priabin was doing it for Dmitri Priabin's sake – he would find out, if that damned computer didn't break down – for his own sake.

"Ah," said Tortyev meditatively in reply. "That is what I want our noble machine to discover – I know him as Orton . . ."

Priabin creased his brow in thought, and said: "What's he supposed to have done?"

Tortyev looked slighted for a moment, and then replied: "He came to my attention as a drug-smuggler." Priabin nodded, and appeared to lose interest. Tortyev continued, nettled that a man with whom he was at training school should regard his problems as unimportant: "But, the strange thing is – this Orton, who died by the hand of one of his associates – or so we believed – is not the man who arrived at Cheremetievo two days ago."

Priabin sat bolt upright in the comfortable armchair. "When?" he snapped.

"Two days ago . . ."

"When did he – die?" Priabin asked, his voice shaky with

excitement. Even as the surface of his thoughts leapt at the impossible proximity, he was telling himself that he was being merely foolish.

"The same night."

"You – caught the men?"

"We rounded up all of Orton's known associates – and found nothing to connect his death with them," Tortyev explained, gratified that he seemed to have stung Priabin into interest, though he was puzzled at the man's upright, attentive posture.

"Who killed him, Alexei?"

"We – don't know, in fact, we don't even know who died."

"What?"

"As I said – the man who died was not the Orton who arrived at the airport, complete with passport and papers from the London Embassy . . ."

"Then who the hell was he – who were they *both*?"

Tortyev spread his hands in a gesture of ignorance. "I have enlisted the aid of our glorious revolutionary computer to discover that very fact."

Priabin nodded, then said, a tone of suppressed excitement in his voice: "All right – you think there was a substitution – yes?"

Tortyev nodded. "Why?" asked Priabin.

"One reason only – the one who arrived two days ago – is an agent, covering his tracks with this dead body."

Priabin slapped his forehead. His face was flushed with excitement – then paled, momentarily with doubt, then he smiled at Tortyev.

"What – happened to the men who – left the body?"

"They ran off."

"Where?"

"To the nearest metro station – the Pavolets."

"And then?"

"Nowhere. They were lost – by the people from here, and the police – they weren't looking for Orton then."

Priabin said, "We're looking for a man – an agent, we are sure – who appeared suddenly driving out of Moscow in a truck early yesterday morning . . ." His face drained of all colour. "Stop . . ." he breathed, as if realising for the first time with the whole of his mind what he had stumbled upon. "Stop . . ."

Tortyev leapt in the same direction as Priabin, a fact which pleased, and comforted, Kontarsky's lieutenant.

"You think – ?"

"There's no record of a man of his appearance arriving in the Soviet Union during the past two weeks. He could have been here

91

longer but, even then, how did he get in? I'm having the computer run down all known or suspected American or British agents, trying to match the photograph."

"And I'm looking for Orton . . ." Tortyev added. "Where is this agent of yours now?"

"In Bilyarsk."

"God! You mean he's . . ."

"Probably he's inside the complex by now – in another disguise."

"To do what?"

"Who knows? Anything – blow up the bloody plane, perhaps?"

Tortyev stared at Priabin, seeing the fear, the recurrent fear, that had replaced the earlier fiery enthusiasm.

There was a knock at the door. "Come in," Priabin said abstractedly.

A young, crumpled individual in a dirty white coat entered, a sheaf of photographs in his hands. He stood before Priabin, evidently pleased with his work, but nervous of its reception by the KGB lieutenant.

"We haven't run down your man . . ." he began.

"You haven't?"

"No. Nothing in the files on him, under American or British."

"Then start with the . . ." Priabin began.

"What we've done meanwhile," the young man pressed on, keeping his eyes behind their horn-rimmed spectacles on the sheaf of photographs, "is to draw up for you a series of identifit pictures of what he might look like in various disguises – without detectable make-up or surgery. We're running these through the computer, to see whether he appears in any guise. It'll be a long job, I'm afraid."

Priabin looked up at the young man, scowled, and said: "You'd better bloody well get on with it, then – hadn't you?"

The young man, considering himself let off lightly, turned on his heel and scuttled from the room, leaving the sheaf of pictures in Priabin's lap. Priabin glanced down at them, shuffled them disconsolately.

"Well?" Tortyev asked, on the edge of his chair.

"Well what?"

"Look at the bloody pictures, man!" Tortyev said angrily.

"What's the point?"

Tortyev crossed the space of dark carpet that separated them, snatched up the sheaf and flipped through them. Once or twice, he stopped, or looked back at a previous identifit mock-up, then he threw the sheaf away from him. Priabin smiled at his irritation, until he saw his face and the fact that he retained one picture still in his hand.

"It's him – Orton," he said softly, turning the picture of a seedy, tired, moustached individual with spectacles in Priabin's direction. "It's him . . ."

Priabin stared at him. The knock on the door caused him to leap to his feet, as if guiltily surprised. The door opened to reveal Holokov, out of breath, his overcoat badly tugged on, collar up, his face red with exertion. Tortyev had left him in the restaurant at the Centre, upstairs, where the food was as good as any of Moscow's principal hotels, and cheaper. Holokov had spilled tea on his tie, which was askew, Tortyev noticed.

"What is it?" he said sharply, rising to his feet.

"Stechko . . ." Holokov said wheezingly. "Phone call from headquarters – that bloody little Jew, Filipov, has been in contact with the British Embassy."

"*What?*"

"True. They were monitoring the phones in the rest-room, and he placed a call from there. Stechko's got him in your office now."

Tortyev continued staring at Holokov for a moment, digesting this information. Then he turned to Priabin, and said: "All our problems solved in one fell swoop, Dmitri – eh? This bloody little traitor must know who Orton is, and why he's gone to Bilyarsk! He's warned the British that we're close to finding out who he is – we have the answer in the palm of our hands."

Priabin's face broke into a slow smile. "Come on," he said. "Your car still waiting for you?" Tortyev nodded. "Then I'll come, too – with your permission?"

Tortyev smiled. "Naturally, Dmitri."

As they passed through the door, and fat Holokov closed it behind them, Priabin said: "The value of gossip, eh, Alexei – the value of gossip!" He slapped Tortyev on the shoulder, and he and the detective laughed loudly in unison.

Priabin stood at Tortyev's desk, the telephone receiver in his hand, waiting for the Centre's code-room to answer him. He looked across the room, to where the unconscious, bloody form of Filipov was collapsed into a chair, held there only by the straps on his wrists. The man's dark, ascetic features were bruised and swollen. Blood had run over his chin from broken teeth and a damaged lip, and the skin was split and discoloured around his closed eyes. His nose had bled freely when Holokov's huge fist had broken it. Stechko and Holokov hovered in that same corner of the room, silenced machines awaiting fresh commands, while Tortyev paced the room. The time was after one in the morning.

Priabin was indifferent to the damage done by Tortyev's apes.

They had had to work swiftly – too crudely for his taste but, surprisingly, not for Tortyev. Perhaps Alexei Tortyev was angry with Filipov, especially angry because he had trusted him – or merely because he was a Jew. Such anti-Semitism was by no means unusual in the KGB.

Priabin had communicated with Kontarsky, as his first priority, reporting that the man in the truck was obviously an agent, and that he expected swift results from the interrogation of the traitor, Filipov. At twelve-fifty, he had to call his chief again, to report that Filipov had not talked, even though he had confessed himself an agent of the British, had spilled the whole story of his recruitment by the Cultural Attaché, Lansing. Filipov had talked, but he had not told them what he ought to have been able to tell them.

Kontarsky was thus left suddenly in the dark as to the present appearance of the man known to Filipov as Orton, despite the fact that Priabin had wire-printed the pictures of Orton. Kontarsky already had with him the photographs of Upenskoy's companion from the security checks at Moscow, Gorky and Kazan, wire-printed to him from the local KGB offices as a matter of urgency.

Kontarsky, Priabin now had to admit to himself, was panicky. He knew that a human bomb was in Bilyarsk, somewhere, but he had no idea of the time-mechanism, the extent, the force . . . He was hamstrung. He had requested all the identifit pictures of Orton supplied by the computer to be wire-printed, a task which had just been completed.

What concerned him now, as the code-room answered Priabin's call, was sending coded instructions to the Russian Embassies in London and Washington, in order to request the senior KGB Resident at each of them to supply information, descriptions, and whereabouts of all recent arrivals at the CIA headquarters in Langley, Virginia, or at the Ministry of Defence in London, or any of the various SIS offices in the city. It might be, he knew, a forlorn gamble, but it was one he had to take. At best, such records of arrivals and departures at the security headquarters of the two organisations were patchy and incomplete; nevertheless, unlike Tortyev, who seemed unable to ignore, or leave alone, the beaten, bloody policeman in the chair, he had doubts that Filipov even knew the real identity of the man who had been Orton, and then had posed as Glazunov. His only real hope was to obtain a lead which would enable them to discover just what kind of agent the man was, and thereby to forestall his purpose at Bilyarsk.

"Hello – Priabin, Department 'M', 2nd Directorate here," he said into the mouthpiece. Tortyev looked up at him for a moment, and then looked away. "I want the following coded messages transmitted, on the authority of Colonel Kontarsky, to the Washington and London Residents, as soon as possible . . ."

The call took only a couple of minutes. When he had finished, he put down the telephone thoughtfully. He looked in the direction of Filipov, and saw Tortyev attempting to revive the man for further questioning.

"Not for the moment, Alexei," he said. "I've an idea – I may want to make another call."

Tortyev turned away from Filipov, as if with reluctance, and said: "What is it?"

"Let's review what's been done thus far," he said. "We've checked on known or suspected agents of most of the Western intelligence services, who might be interested in the Bilyarsk project, and capable of mounting this sort of operation." Tortyev nodded. "Because the man's been clever, we've assumed that he's a very good agent, one of their top men – which means we ought to have found him by now – eh?"

"Agreed. He's obviously new, or been kept back for this one job – it's big enough to warrant that."

"Too bloody true," Priabin commented gruffly.

"Exactly. So – why haven't we found him – and where do we look?"

"Just my own thought. As I was saying – he's either a top agent or, he's not an agent at all."

"He *has* to be – with this kind of cover-operation going on." Tortyev nodded over his shoulder at the slumped form of the Jew. "They've used Filipov knowing they might be expending him. They expended another top man, the truck-driver. That's two down. The British are always careful of their operatives, Dmitri, they don't throw them away!"

"No – I don't mean he's not working for the British, or the Americans . . . just that he's been recruited from some other field. Look at it this way. What if he's not there to damage the project? After all, what would be the point? As far as we know, the Americans are so far behind, they'd need ten years to catch up with the Mig-31 despite being handed a Mig-25 by Belenko four years ago." Priabin's voice had sunk to a confidential whisper, and he glanced sideways at Stechko and Holokov who, politically, seemed to be occupied with the limp form of Filipov, minutely inspecting him in a grotesque form of damage-report.

"I agree – from what you've told me."

"So – our security has been able to intercept most of what has been passed to London and Washington by the underground at Bilyarsk, via the Embassy here. Therefore, the Americans and

British want to know more. They want a first-hand report of what's going on, perhaps even photographs, and an eye-witness account . . ."

"You mean – an expert?"

"Yes!" Priabin's voice was suddenly louder. "What if they've sent an aeronautics expert, who knows what to look for, what questions to ask?"

"God – it could be anyone – someone we don't even know!" There was a silence.

"I don't think he knows," Priabin said, nodding towards Filipov, who groaned with returning consciousness as he did so.

"He *could* do." Tortyev replied. "Besides," he added in a menacing tone, "I haven't finished with him yet, the little Jewish shit!"

Priabin shrugged. "Suit yourself," he said. "But don't start on him again until I've made another call. I want a check run through the computer on the entire American and British aerospace industries."

"It'll take hours . . .!" Tortyev protested.

"No longer than it will take your gorillas to beat it out of Filipov. There won't be many names – not capable of making the most of this elaborate subterfuge to smuggle him into Bilyarsk. Let me make the call – then you can resort to the physical stuff!"

Tortyev hesitated for a moment, shrugged in his turn, and Priabin picked up the receiver.

The searchlight picked him up early, with fifty yards still to go, fixed on him, and he walked into the tunnel of its white, blinding light. He tried to appear casual, yet irritated, and shaded his eyes studiously. Each footstep threatened to become reluctant, to stutter to a halt, his frame and motive power running down, like a machine dying. He forced his legs to work. The cramp was coming back to his stomach. He knew the sweat was standing out on his forehead, and his hands were shaking. Gant was suddenly threatened. It was as if his ego had been stripped and he knew he could not carry it through. This was worse than the flying – this was the struggle of the stranded fish.

"Identify yourself," the voice said and he realised, with a shock, that he was close to the gate. A guard was pointing a rifle in his direction. "Identify yourself."

His voice sounded old and weak, winding up hoarsely like an ancient clock to strike. "Identify yourself – *sir*!" he snapped. "Soldier!"

The guard reacted. It was what he expected from a GRU officer, even though he did not know the face, and he replied as expected.

"Identity, please – sir."

Gant fished in his papers and passed them across, the yellow ID card on the top. The guard took it, and inspected it. Gant knew he had to light a cigarette now, to calm himself, to occupy the hands that threatened to betray him. He reached as casually as he could into the hip-pocket of his jacket, and pulled out the cigarette case. He lit the cigarette and inhaled, almost choking on the raw smoke. He exhaled thankfully, stifling a cough. He began to inspect the arrangements at the gate.

There were six guards, frozen into unreal postures in the harsh light that bathed the wire and the open space before it. The red-and-white barrier remained firmly lowered, and two uniformed KGB guards stood woodenly behind it, rifles casually pointed in his direction. There was a guard-hut at either side of the barrier, giving it the appearance of a customs-post, and in the doorway of each another soldier was visible. The sixth man stood behind the guard inspecting his papers. Gant checked the piping and the tabs on each of the uniforms. Each guard was KGB, not part of the GRU Security Support Group to which he was supposed to belong. That, at least, would explain his unfamiliar face.

"Why were you outside the wire – sir?"

There was a silence, and then Gant said: "You have your orders, soldier – I have mine. You *know* that a suspected agent is in the vicinity." He leaned forward, staring into the soldier's face, and smiled. "Or perhaps you don't?"

The soldier was silent for a moment, then he said: "Yes, sir – we've been alerted."

"Good. Then I suggest you get a dog out here, and look at that clump of trees regularly during the next few hours."

Gant watched the soldier's eyes. His whole consciousness focused on them. Slowly, infinitely slowly, he watched the moment turn over, like a world orbiting. It retreated. The soldier snapped to attention, and nodded.

"Yes, sir. Good idea, sir."

Gant touched his cap ironically, still smiling. The barrier swung up at a signal from the guard, and Gant saw one of the figures in a hut-doorway turn inside, presumably to inform the guards at the second gate that the officer had been cleared for entry. Nodding, he stepped forward, feeling the sudden weakness of his legs, as if they were somewhere far away from the rest of his body.

The rotors of a chopper buzzed suddenly loud, as if his hearing had become suddenly acute. He looked up, forcing himself to act casually; then he had reached the gate, which remained closed against him. He saw the guard, gun at the ready, then saw a second guard emerge from the guard-hut, and signal that the gate could be safely opened. Gant drew his ID card from his pocket, dropped his cigarette in the dirt and ground his heel on it. He appeared irritated at the delay, standing with his hands on his hips, his lips pursed. He saw, comfortingly, that the guard was beginning to fall back into his routine pattern of behaviour. He had been confronted with a uniform, superior in rank to his own, and he had accepted it.

The gate opened, not the huge double gate but a small personnel door set into the gates. Gant, nodding irritatedly, stepped through, and it clattered shut behind him. He didn't bother to study the guards, but headed down the track which skirted the runway, towards the hangar. It was all he could do to prevent the surge of adrenalin through his system from driving his body at a run. Probably, the guards at the gate had already forgotten him. Yet, their eyes bored into his back. His shirt was sticky with sweat across the small of his back. His heart pumped loudly in his ears, drumming him into activity, into a run . . .

He stepped across the runway, turning off the road. He glanced swiftly along its length, then gazed ahead of him. The hangar was nearer now. He followed the taxi-way that led to it from the runway proper.

A chopper buzzed overhead, the downdraught plucking at his cap and jacket, flapping his trousers. He held onto his cap, and looked up. He saw a face at the open door of the chopper and he waved, the abrupt wave of an officer with every right to be where he was. The chopper pulled round in a tight circle, and the face grinned at him, a hand waved, and the chopper pulled away. Settling his cap firmly on his head, Gant walked on.

It was less than a hundred yards now, he estimated. He could see the guards stationed at the hangar doors, see the spillage of warm light on the concrete, hear the sounds of echoed metal dimly. The hangar door, as the taxi-way curved and straightened, opened before him, and he felt a quickening of his pulse, the surge of adrenalin in his system – but not as before, not because fear was gripping his stomach, crawling up his spine. This was an elation, an excitement. He could not pause, to stare open-mouthed into the hangar, but he possessed all the sudden wonder and response of the child at an exhibition. Gant was a single-minded individual. There was no real complexity to his character. The only thing he had been able to do supremely well, ever, was to fly airplanes. Now, in the hangar spilling its raw, warm light, echoing with voices and noise, he glimpsed the Firefox. Its elongated nose was tilted up and towards him, and he saw the attendant, insect figures busy about the gleaming silver fuselage. Two huge intakes glared blackly at him, and there was the fleeting impression of wings edge-on . . .

Then he had turned aside. His momentary pause would not have been out of character for a man new to the project and who had flown in the previous night.

There was activity of a different kind at the door of the KGB building, the security headquarters attached to the hangar. It was, Gant reflected, with an unusual poetry, a symbol – wherever Soviet achievements went, the KGB was sure to go, linked by an umbilical cord. As he approached, guards on the door snapped to attention, and for a moment he wondered whether he had not attracted this respect – then the door opened, held by a guard from inside, and he was face to face with KGB Colonel Mihail Kontarsky, head of security for the Mikoyan project. He snapped to attention, fingers at his peak, as he confronted the short, slim, busy-looking man, and noticed the edge of worry in the eyes, the nervous movement they possessed.

Kontarsky stared at Gant. "Yes, Captain?" he snapped nervously.

Gant realised his mistake. He had made it appear that he wished to report to Kontarsky. Behind Kontarsky was Tsernik, looking at him in puzzlement. He was a strange face, and Gant knew that to Tsernik he should not have been a strange face. Tsernik would have met him, had he really arrived with the GRU detachment the previous day, or would have seen his file and photograph.

The moment hit him in the stomach, bunching it, twisting it in its grip. He was less than a hundred yards from his objective, the airplane, and he had walked straight into the arms of the security chief.

"Sir – I have, without your permission, ordered a dog for the guards on the security entrance . . . to search the belt of trees, thoroughly," Gant said, his voice level, controlled by a supreme effort; his mind screaming at him to break and run.

Kontarsky seemed to take a moment to realise what was being said to him, as if he were concentrating on something else, then he nodded.

"Good thinking, Captain – my thanks." Kontarsky touched the peak of his cap with his glove and passed on. Gant dropped his hand, then raised it again to salute as Tsernik passed him. With a sweeping relief, Gant realised that his report had been accepted by the second-in-command. He merely nodded, no longer looking puzzled, and passed on behind Gant.

As they moved away, he heard Kontarsky say: "Now is the time to pick up Dherkov – now that the others are safely inside. You agree, Tsernik?"

"Yes, Colonel, of course. I will get onto that right away – and his wife."

Gant heard no more. He passed inside the door, the guards remaining at attention until he was inside. Once there, he leaned against the wall in a narrow corridor, hardly noticing the guard posted there in his sudden, overwhelming relief, until the guard said: "Are you all right, Captain?"

Gant looked at him, startled. The guard saw a white face, sweaty and strained, and a hand gripping the stomach – and the uniform.

"I – just indigestion. Think I've got an ulcer," he added, for the sake of veracity.

"Would you like a drink, Captain?" the guard was solicitous.

Gant shook his head. He had to move away now. The incident was already becoming too memorable, his face too familiar; the story would be recounted in the other ranks' mess when the guard went off-duty. He smiled, a poor imitation of the real thing, and straightened himself.

"No – thanks, soldier. No. Just comes in spasms . . ." Then he realised he was being far too human, he was responding as if he did have an ulcer. He brushed his jacket straight, and jammed his cap on his head. He glared at the soldier, as if he had in some way offended rank by noticing his officer's difficulties, then strode off down the corridor, his boots clicking loudly along the linoleum. In front of him were the stairs up to the officers' mess, and to the pilots' rest-room.

As he mounted the stairs, the images of the last minutes dying in his mind, the feverish pulse slowing, he hoped to his God that Dherkov, the courier, did not know what he looked like. He glanced at his watch. Still not three o'clock. More than three hours. He wondered how brave a man the grocer was.

There were five of them now in Aubrey's secluded operations room: the two CIA men and the two representatives of the SIS had been joined by a man wearing the uniform of a Captain in the U.S. Navy – Captain Eugene Curtin, from the office of the Chief of Naval Operations, USN. Curtin it was who had been responsible for the arrangements for the refuelling of the Firefox, presuming Gant to be able to steal it on schedule, and head in the right direction – north, towards the Barents Sea.

Curtin was in his forties, square-built, the uniform stretched across his broad shoulders and back. His hair was clipped so short it seemed he had recently survived an internment in some POW camp. His face was large, square, chiselled, and his eyes were piercingly blue. He had just completed some amendments to the huge projection of the Arctic seas, marking the latest reported positions of Russian surface and sub-surface vessels. To Aubrey's eye, there appeared a great many of them – too bloody many, he reflect wryly, as Shelley might have said. Also, Curtin had brought with him a new set of satellite weather photographs, as well as sheets of more local weather reports, and some of the numerous SAC radar and weather planes flying over the seas to the north of Soviet Russia.

Curtin saw Aubrey regarding his amendments to the wall-map, and grinned at him.

"Looks bad – uh?" he said.

Aubrey said nothing, but continued to regard the wall. He disliked the disconcerting honesty that Curtin shared with Buckholz, and other Americans he had encountered in the field of intelligence, whether operational, or merely analytical. The Americans, he considered, had a penchant for being disconcertingly blunt about things. It simply did not do to assume that Gant had no chance of success – the only way to prevent such gloomy reflections was not to think too far ahead – one step at a time.

Aubrey sipped at the cup of tea that Shelley had poured for him, and continued to study the map without any apparent reaction on his features.

Curtin joined Buckholz and his aide, Anders, at their desk where they were analysing the weather reports, linking them with the latest positions of the Soviet trawler fleets supplied by the office of Rear-Admiral Philipson over the telephone.

"Well?" Curtin asked softly, his eye on Aubrey.

Buckholz looked up at him. "It looks good," he said, adopting the same conspiratorial whisper. He picked up his coffee and swallowed the last of it. He pulled a face. He had let the coffee get cold in the bottom of the cup. He handed the empty cup to Anders, who went away to refill it.

"The weather up there can change like – that," Curtin said amiably, clicking his thumb and forefinger.

"It's been good for the last four days," Buckholz pointed out.

"Means nothing," Curtin observed unhelpfully. "That means there's four days less of good weather left to play with."

Buckholz scowled at him. "How bad can it get?" he said.

"Too bad for Hotshot ever to find the fuel he's going to need," Curtin replied, "*if* he ever gets off the ground at Bilyarsk. What about the information Aubrey received?"

"I don't know. Our British friend plays it very close to his chest."

Curtin nodded. "Yeah. I don't understand why. But, if they're onto Hotshot – what chance has he got?"

"Some," Buckholz admitted reluctantly. "These guys at Bilyarsk on Aubrey's payroll are no fools, Curtin."

"I never said they were. But I heard the KGB were pretty good at their job, too. If they find out we sent a flyer to Bilyarsk, Hotshot will never get near that damn plane."

"I know that." Buckholz appeared suddenly irritated with Curtin. He was being too honest, too objective – breezing in late, like a cold wind, disrupting the close, confined, suppressed subjectivity of the mood of the four intelligence operatives. Sometimes, Buckholz considered, there was a right time for a little deceptive hope. And now was the right time.

"Sorry," Curtin said with a shrug. "I'm only the Navy's messenger boy – I just bring you the facts."

"Yeah, I know that, too."

Curtin looked down at the mass of papers on Buckholz's desk, and observed: "Jesus, but this is a half-cock operation."

"Yeah?"

"Uh-huh. I wonder why you let the British do all the planning, Buckholz, I really do."

"They had the men on the ground, brother – that's why."

"But – so much depends on – so many people."

"It's called the element of surprise, Curtin."

"You mean – it's a surprise if it works?" Curtin said, his eyebrow raised ironically.

"Maybe – maybe." Buckholz looked down at the papers before him, as if to signal the end of the conversation. Curtin continued to regard him curiously.

Buckholz, he knew, had survived, even benefited from, the purges which had followed the Congressional enquiry into the activities of the CIA, following Watergate. In fact, it had placed him as Head of the Covert Action Staff within the coterie of top advisers that surrounded the Director himself. It was he, seemingly fired by Aubrey's crack-brained scheme to steal the new Mig, who had pushed through the arrangements for the theft, laid on, in his own bulldozing, dogged fashion, the refuelling arrangements, the radar-watch, the coordination of SAC and USN assistance he required. He had persuaded the Chief of Naval Operations to second Curtin to his staff until the completion of "Operation Rip-Off", a fact for which Curtin was only dubiously grateful. It had handed him immense, if temporary, power, but it was an operation that could write *finis* to Curtin's naval career. And that was something he did not like to contemplate.

The details of Russian surface and sub-surface strength in the Barents Sea and the Arctic Ocean that he had transferred to the wall-map filled Curtin with doubt. He, better than anyone there, knew the current strength of the Red Banner Northern Fleet of the

Red Navy, and how swiftly and thoroughly it could be brought to operate against any discovered intruder into what were considered by the Kremlin to be Soviet waters. So far, the refuelling vessel had not been detected – at least, no moves had been made against her, which ought to have meant the same thing. But, in the upheaval which would follow the theft of the aircraft, in the comprehensive radar and sonar searches by missile cruisers, spy trawlers and submarines – who could say?

As he headed for the coffee percolator on a trolley in one corner of the room, he said to Buckholz, who continued studiously to ignore him: "He hasn't got a hope in hell, brother – not a hope in hell!"

It was after three-thirty when Lieutenant-Colonel Yuri Voskov arrived in the pilots' rest-room on the second floor of the security building attached to the Firefox's hangar at Bilyarsk. He paused inside the door, and his hand reached for the light switch. When that hand encountered another guarding the light switch, his surprise had insufficient time to become shock and alarm before he was struck behind the ear by a terrible, killing blow. He never saw the face of his assassin – the floor rushed up, unseen, as he keeled over from the force of the blow which flung him half-way across the room.

Gant flicked on the light, and crossed to the inert body, rubbing the fist that had delivered the blow. Then, like some great exhalation, the nerves exploded in him, shaking his body like a wind. He had been able to kill Voskov, coldly and mechanically and with his hands, when even Buckholz had sometimes wondered about it. But the reaction continued to shake him, and it was what seemed like minutes before he could kneel steadily by the dead man. Then, gently, as if a medical expert, he felt for the pulse he knew would not be evident. Voskov was dead.

Gant rolled the body onto its back and looked down at the dead face of Voskov. The man was older than Gant, in his early forties, perhaps. He felt no remorse. He had removed a necessary piece from the board, that was all. He merely wondered how good Voskov had been.

Suddenly galvanised into action, he tugged the body across the carpet towards the tall steep lockers ranged against one wall. Dumping Voskov in a heap, he fished in his jacket pocket for the master key that Baranovich had supplied, and opened one of the lockers. It was, as he had expected, and had been told to expect, empty. Holding the door ajar with his foot, he pushed the head and shoulders of the body into the locker. Then, as if engaged in some grotesque, energetic dance in slow-motion, he heaved at the body, until it stood as if alive, upright in the locker. Swiftly, he closed the door and locked it, hearing the soft concussion of Voskov's body as it leaned forward against the door. Then he pocketed the key.

Opening another of the lockers, he inspected the pressure-suit that hung there – Voskov's. Voskov was about his own build. At least, they were sufficiently alike for Gant to be able to use the Russian's pressure-suit. Fortunately, it was merely an adaptation of the normal aircraft pressure-suit, not something tailor-made like a NASA space-suit. Had that been the case, the slightest difference in form, height, build, would have made the wearing of Voskov's suit impossible.

Having completed his inspection, Gant began to remove his GRU uniform. It was three-forty-six in the morning. Gant felt his nerves beating his stomach, a fist. As he removed his shirt, he looked at the bleeper device taped beneath his arm that would summon him to the hangar.

He had two-and-a-half hours to go.

FIVE:

The Rip-Off

Kontarsky glanced at his gold wrist-watch. It was four o'clock. From where he was standing in the open doorway of the main hangar, he could survey the scene of quiet, intense activity within. He had seen the guards become aware of him, not only those on the doors, but those at their stations close to the aircraft became suddenly more aware, more intent in their scrutiny. Many of the scientists and technicians took no notice of him – though he had seen Kreshin look up and then mutter something to Semelovsky, who stood next to him. Baranovich he could see as a hunched figure, swallowed to the waist by the open cockpit, giving instructions to the technician seated in the pilot's couch of the Mig-31.

Kontarsky had no aesthetic or military feelings concerning the aircraft. Its aerodynamic lines, its potency, the huge gaping mouths of its air intakes, were nothing to him but a problem in security. And with that problem, he had taken every precaution he possibly could.

He ought to have felt a comfortable self-pride, he realised. Such a feeling, however, eluded him. The night had remained mild, but he felt cold. He was chewing on an indigestion tablet now as he stood outside the hangar. It seemed to be having no effect whatsoever.

The Production Prototype One was less than a hundred feet from him; behind it, ignored by the team of patient, hardly moving technicians, a second aircraft – the PP Two – stood near the rear of the giant hangar.

Kontarsky wondered whether to speak to the guards near the aircraft, but decided against it. They were all picked men, and he had briefed them thoroughly before they went on duty. To have inspected them now at close quarters would have been an error of leadership, a sign of absent confidence, and he knew it. Reluctantly, he crossed the strip of light spilling from the open doors, and rejoined his personal bodyguard who was in conversation with one of the door-guards. Nodding to him to fall in behind him, he headed for the second hangar, the one in which the Mig-31 had been built – it was locked and in darkness, but it would not hurt to have the guards who ringed it make one more interior search.

Priabin was, at that moment, he knew, running the agent to earth. As the hours of the night had limped by, he had become more and more open to his aide's suggestion that the man must be some kind of technical expert, sent to talk to Baranovich and the others before they were arrested, as would be inevitable as soon as the trials were successfully completed, and to observe as much as he could of the trials themselves. What kind of equipment, other than his eyes, he had brought with him, Kontarsky had no idea. As he crossed the bright, stark space between the hangars, he looked out beyond the fence, seeking some vantage-point from which such an observer might consider he had a good view of the runway. There was no hillock, no rising ground.

When he had completed his inspection of the production hangar, he told himself, it would be as well to send out dog patrols beyond the fence -- just in case.

Despite his decision, he still felt that the man was inside the fence, a part of the complex, in some disguise or other. He would have the whole area searched again.

Baranovich watched the form that he recognised as belonging to Kontarsky as it crossed the black hole of the night, and vanished in the direction of the production hangar. When he looked down again from his perch on top of a pilot's ladder wheeled against the fuselage of the Firefox, he saw the squat, flattened features of the mechanic in the pilot's couch looking up at him, grinning. Baranovich, with as much aplomb as he could muster, smiled back and the mechanic, who had expected and wished to see fear, or unsettlement at the least, on Baranovich's face, scowled and turned back to his work. He was in the process of checking the circuits within the weapons-guidance system. Part of the instrument panel on the left-hand side was removed, and the intricate wiring and miniature circuits of the system were exposed. Under Baranovich's direction, the final check proceeded slowly.

Baranovich knew that the mechanic was KGB. For months now, as he had installed and perfected the system on which he had been forced to work originally while still in the scientific prison of Mavrino, he had had assigned to his technical team this man, Grosch, an electronics technician of high capability. Grosch was the child of a German scientist captured by the Red Army early in 1945; there was no more loyal member of the Party.

Baranovich felt no anger at the man – not because his father was a Nazi, or because he himself was a secret policeman. If Gant had been able to see the look on his face as he gazed down at the top of Grosch's cropped head, he would have recognised that look of painful wisdom, of detached pity, which he had seen at Kreshin's quarters. Baranovich looked unobtrusively at his watch. Four minutes after four. He looked round him at the security within the hangar as Grosch absorbed himself in checking a printed circuit. He had decided already on the method of diversion he would use.

He looked back over the tail-unit of the Firefox, to where the second production prototype stood, rather shunted into a corner. The aircraft, seemingly in shadow, unglamorous, lacking the pristine deadliness of the model atop which he stood, was fully fuelled, in a state of readiness for take-off against some kind, any kind, of airborne attack upon the factory. All Soviet aircraft, whether prototype, production model, or service aircraft, as long as they were military, remained in a maximum twenty-four-hour condition of readiness while on the ground.

Therefore, Baranovich concluded, there was only one thing that could be done when Gant escaped at the controls of the first aircraft. They would send the second one after him. There would be a delay, of course, while it was fully-weaponed – perhaps an hour, including a quickest possible check of systems and controls. And the second aircraft would be refuelled in mid-air, unlike Gant, who would have to refuel on the ground, wherever that ground was. Unless he, Kreshin and Semelovsky could put that second aircraft out of action, Gant could be caught, and destroyed, by the only plane capable of doing both to him – PP Two.

Fire: he knew the answer. A hangar fire would create a panic, and allow Gant to climb aboard as the pilot, and taxi the aircraft onto the taxi-way outside without suspicion. Two birds with one stone, he remarked to himself. Gant away, and the pursuit of him prevented at the same time. There was so much fuel, oil, timber and other inflammables in the hangar that causing the fire would be no problem. Fire was one of the plans he had outlined to the others – now he would tell them of his final decision in its favour.

Baranovich spent no time wondering whether Gant would survive the flight. He would show up on no radar, which meant the Russians would need a visual sighting before they could loose off infra-red or proximity missiles, or send aircraft after him. He glanced towards the tail where Semelovsky was supervising the fitting of the special tail-unit, his own project from first to last, on which Kreshin had worked as his assistant – the tail-assembly that provided Gant's most effective anti-missile system and ECM gear. Semelovsky said it would work, but it had only been tried on an RPV – that day, it would be a part of the weapons-trials and a man would have to use it. Gant would need it, he knew.

It was a question of timing, he decided. The First Secretary's aircraft was scheduled to arrive at nine. Before that, he knew, he and the others would be placed under arrest. Their work would be completed by six-thirty at the latest. This meant that six-thirty was the latest time for the diversion, and the take-off. He would have to arrange the time-table with the others at their next coffee-break, which was at five.

The security was so tight that when he had visited the toilets at the other end of the hangar an hour earlier, a guard had detached himself from the wall, and followed him inside, making no effort to relieve himself, but merely contenting himself with observing Baranovich. Grosch should find that damaged power transistor within the next few minutes, he thought, which would helpfully lengthen the final checks.

He was suddenly, oddly, assailed by memory, a memory that was akin to his present situation, but removed from self-concern. He was in the same overalls as now, but those in his memory were oil-stained, uncleaned. The temperature was well below zero, and his hands were numb. He was bending forward into the cockpit of a Mig, an old, wartime Mig. He was in a hangar at the Red Army air base outside Stalingrad. Because he was a Jew, he was an army mechanic, nothing more glorified than that.

He shrugged off the memory. The past was an intrusion, an interference in what he had to do, had to plan. He thought of the gun beneath his armpit. He had not been searched on entering the gates. The gun, he realised, with the kind of shock of cold water on drowsy skin, meant that he had accepted that this was the end. He did not expect to live through the day.

Baranovich smiled as Grosch found the malfunctioning circuit-board, and looked up into his face. Grosch held up the extracted plastic square, with its thirty-seven gold-plated tags, into his face.

"Looks like the power transistor, Comrade Director Baranovich," he said. Baranovich smiled. Grosch was being obsequiously civil. He, too, then understood that it was the end.

"Mm." Baranovich turned the square of plastic over in his hand, nodding. Then he handed it back to Grosch. "Scrap it, then. I'll get another."

"From the experimental technical stores, Director?" Grosch queried with a smile.

"Yes, Grosch. But you won't have to get out of that comfortable seat to accompany me. The guard will take me."

Before Grosch could reply, he began to descend the ladder, with a light, youthful, untroubled step.

"You incompetent bloody fool, Stechko – he's dead! You've killed him!" Tortyev exploded. He rounded on Stechko, and the big man

108

stepped back, a look of confused, abashed defeat on his face. Tortyev rose from his haunches where he had squatted before the sagging, lifeless form of Filipov, and glared at his subordinate. The beatings had been too regular, too vicious, too hurried – he knew that now. In his desperate effort to make the man talk, he had allowed Stechko and Holokov to kill him. He ground his teeth and clenched and unclenched his fists in the fury of impotence.

When he turned to Priabin, the KGB lieutenant was already on the telephone. His indifference seemed to anger Tortyev further. He crossed the room to confront Holokov who was sitting on a hard chair, astride, watching the body intently as if for some sign of life. Tortyev stood before him, and Holokov's intensity of expression became transformed to doubt.

"You stupid fat shit," Tortyev breathed, his eyes blazing. "You incompetent lump of dogshit!"

"You pressed us . . ." Holokov began, and then recoiled as Tortyev slapped him across the cheek with the back of his hand. He reached for his cut lip, in surprise, inspected his fingers, and the smear of blood on them in some state of shock.

"He knew nothing." Tortyev heard Priabin speak quietly, and turned on him. Priabin was holding one hand over the receiver, and smiling. His smile irritated Tortyev.

"What the hell do you mean by that?" he said.

"He knew nothing – hell, he'd have told you long ago if he had anything to tell."

"You clever bastard – what's the answer, then? Your precious bloody aircraft is still in danger, or had you forgotten that?" Tortyev wiped the saliva from his lip.

Priabin continued to smile irritatingly, and waggled the receiver in Tortyev's direction.

"Why do you think I want to talk to the computer?" he said mildly.

Tortyev looked at the clock, and said: "You'd better get a bloody move-on! It's four-thirty, or hadn't you noticed?" There was a sneer in his voice, a returning self-confidence. He had done his part. Now it was up to Priabin.

"Hello?" Priabin said into the receiver. "Priabin. What news?" He listened for a while, and then said: "How quickly are you checking out the whereabouts of these people?" Irritation crossed his face. "I don't care – the information's in that machine's guts somewhere, and I want it!" He slammed the telephone down, and saw Tortyev smiling at him.

"What's the matter – less than miraculous, is it, that machine?" he said.

109

Priabin ignored him, thought for a moment, and then said: "We couldn't do it any faster – a lot slower, in fact." He looked across at the body and said: "Get that out of here, you two – now." Holokov looked at Tortyev, and the policeman nodded. The two detectives hoisted the body to its dragging feet, and took it through the door.

The break seemed to calm both men. When they were alone, Tortyev said: "What are they checking out?"

"They've got a list of less than a dozen top aeronautics experts in America and Europe, young enough and fit enough to be our man. But they're checking current whereabouts of all of them, and it's taking time . . . too much time," he added quietly, his voice strained. "They've linked into the First Directorate's computer, whose banks have constant monitor-records, as you know, on thousands of useful or important public and scientific figures in the West. The answers are coming . . ."

"But they might be too late."

"Too true."

Priabin left his desk and began to pace the room, his hand cupping his chin, or pulling at his lower lip. It was minutes before he spoke again. Then he said: "I can't speed up the process. We'll either get the information in time, or we won't. In which case, I prefer not to think about it. But, what *else* can I do – what else can I ask that bloody machine to do at the same time as it's processing these people?" He was standing before Tortyev, a look of appeal on his face.

Tortyev was silent for a moment, then he said: "Anything to do with aircraft. Check everyone and everything, Dmitri."

"How?"

"Check on every file of every person we know to be connected with the American or European aerospace programmes, or who ever has been connected . . ." Tortyev's face seemed to illuminate from within. "They sent a young, fit man – with brains. Why not an astronaut? One of our own cosmonauts would know what to look for, know how to analyse information received from someone like this Baranovich, wouldn't he?"

Priabin was silent for a moment. "It seems unlikely, doesn't it?" he said, wanting to be convinced.

"Well – is it, though? Think of it. You're looking for a man in his thirties, fit, intelligent, elusive . . . you thought he was an agent, at first. He has to possess some of the qualities of a commando, and of a scientist. The NASA astronauts are the mostly highly-trained people in the world. Why not?"

Priabin seemed still reluctant. "Mm. I wonder?"

110

"You don't have too much time in which to wonder, Dmitri," Tortyev reminded him.

"I know! Let me think . . . I wonder how many files there are relating to astronauts and to air force pilots, and the like?"

"Hundreds – perhaps thousands. Why?"

"In that case, because our service collects anything and everything and, like the careful housewife, never throws anything away, we have to have an order of preference. We'll have to look at the computer-index."

"Very well," said Tortyev, seemingly glad of action. "I'll help you."

"Thanks."

"Besides which – this place is beginning to smell of Jews – and death," Tortyev added.

"Very well, then – I'll ring for a car."

"Don't bother – at this time in the morning, it'll be quicker to walk."

It was four-forty when the two men left the room together.

Gant had moved a chair into the shower-cubicle and arranged a fold of the shower-curtain to shield him from the spray. The cubicle was full of steam.

He was in no doubt that Pavel was dead by now, or in some local KGB cellar, having his name and mission beaten out of him. It troubled Gant to know for certain that Pavel would take a lot of punishment before he would tell, if he ever told. Again, he was forced to feel responsible.

More than Pavel, however, who might well have died neatly and quickly in a gunfight of some kind, he was troubled by Baranovich and the others. He had never encountered dumb, accepting courage such as that before, and it puzzled him.

Gant had removed his uniform, and was sitting in the cubicle in his shorts. The GRU uniform, now an encumbrance, had gone into the same locker as Voskov. He had had to hold the body with one hand, to stop it toppling outwards, while he flung the creased bundle that had been Captain Chekhov into the corner of the locker. He had not looked into Voskov's face and thankfully he had locked the body out of sight once more. Then he had turned on the shower. The steam, though it made his breathing unpleasant, kept him warm. He sat astride the chair, his arms folded across the back, chin resting on his arms, letting the constant stream of hot water lull him, closing his eyes. He could not sleep, and knew he must not, but he tried to reduce the activity of his thoughts by the semblance of sleep.

111

At first he didn't hear the voice from the room beyond, from the rest-room. The second call alerted him and he sprang to his feet, unconsciously being careful not to scrape the chair on the floor of the shower.

"Yes?" he called.

"Security check, Colonel – important."

It had to be the KGB – it had to be Kontarsky's last fling, his final attempt to trace the agent he must suspect was already inside Bilyarsk.

"What do you want?"

"Your identification."

Gant panicked. He had left Voskov's papers in his pockets, bundling the body quickly and thankfully into the locker. Now they wanted to see his papers – if they didn't see them, then they would want to see him . . .

He wondered how he might bluff his way out. The nervous reaction had jolted him awake, and his pulse was hammering in his head, and he found it hard to catch his breath. Though he only half-suspected it, this latest, unexpected jolt was drawing vastly on his reserves of control. Clearly, above the levels of the blood's panic, he thought that Voskov would be a pampered individual, one likely to take unkindly to such an intrusion.

Loudly, irritatedly, he called out: "I am having a shower, whoever you are. What do you mean by disturbing me with your stupid questions?" To him, his voice sounded, in the steam-filled curtained hole, to be weak, high-pitched, unconvincing. He heard a cough, deferential, abashed, from the man in the rest-room. He peered through the steam and the shower-curtain. There was a shadow, against the light from the door into the bathroom. It was two or three steps across the space of tiles between himself and that shadow.

"Sorry, Colonel, but . . ."

"This is your idea, of course – soldier? It is not Colonel Kontarsky's direct order that the rest-room should be searched, and myself questioned?" He felt his voice gaining power, arrogance. He could play the part of Voskov – it was a part close to his own professional arrogance, expressing his own contempt.

"I – orders, sir," he heard, and knew that the man was lying.

Gant hesitated, until he thought the moment was almost past and he was too late, then he barked: "Get out, before you find yourself reported!"

He waited. No doubt the man could see his shadow, as the shower-curtain wafted against his skin, drawn in by the heat. He wondered whether the man would dare cross that space of cold tiles,

112

just to be sure. He had left the gun, Chekhov's regulation Makarov automatic, in the pocket of Voskov's bathrobe, hanging behind the bathroom door. He cursed himself for that lapse, and wondered, at the same moment, whether he could kill the man with his hands before a shot was fired.

The moment passed. Again, Gant had the sense of something massive, a whole world in orbit, turning over, leaving him spent, tired, drained.

"Sorry, sir – of course. But – be careful, sir. The Colonel issued us with instructions to kill – the man's dangerous. Good luck with the flight, sir," he added ingratiatingly. Gant felt his blood pumping like a migraine in his temples.

He hardly heard the bathroom door close behind the man who had been only a voice, and a shadow against the light. When he realised that the patch of light which had outlined the KGB man was no longer there, he stepped from behind the shower-curtain, and fumbled in the pocket of Voskov's bathrobe. He clutched the gun in both hands, then pressed the cold metal of the barrel against his temple. Then he held his left hand in front of his face. He saw the tremor, faint, but increasing. His face registered the fear, as if he were looking at something outside himself, something inevitable that he could not prevent. He sagged, dripping wet, onto the seat of the lavatory, head hanging, gun held limply between his knees.

Gant was terrified. He knew he was about to have the dream again, that the last minutes had drained him of his last reserves of bravado, self-deception, and nerve. He was a limp rag, an empty vessel into which the dream would pour. He could not stop it now.

He felt his muscles tightening behind his knees, in his calves. He knew he had to get dry, get into Voskov's pressure-suit while he could still move, before the paralysis that inevitably accompanied the images trapped him where he sat. He tried to get up, but his legs were a long, long way from his brain, and were rubbery and weak. He sagged back onto the seat. He punched at his thighs, as if punishing them for a rebellion – he struck himself across the thigh with the barrel of the gun, but he felt little. The hysterical paralysis had returned, taken over . . .

He was trapped, he knew. He could only hope that the dream, and the fit, would pass in time.

He could smell burning in his nostrils, and the noise of the shower crackled like wood on a fire. He could smell burning flesh . . .

There was a kind of grotesque, mocking courtesy about the way in which Baranovich, Kreshin, and Semelovsky were served with their coffee and sandwiches at the side of the aircraft itself. While the technicians, including the still-grinning, obsequious, ironical Grosch, left the hangar for the restaurant in the adjoining security building, the three suspected men were ordered to remain by the junior KGB officer in command of hangar security. Guards stood with apparent indifference ten yards from them.

Baranovich, as he sipped the hot, sweet liquid, was grateful that the KGB, as yet, seemed to have little idea of what to do with them. It would seem, he thought, that they had taken the easiest path, making sure that a number of eyes were upon them, at every moment. Baranovich smiled at Kreshin, whose lip trembled as he attempted to imitate the gesture.

Baranovich said: "I know, Ilya, that it looks very much like a firing-squad, with the three of us with our backs to the plane, and the guards with their rifles at the ready." Kreshin nodded, and swallowed, still trying to smile. "Don't be afraid," Baranovich added softly.

"I — can't help it, Pyotr," Kreshin replied.

Baranovich nodded. "I gave up being afraid many years ago — but then, it was when the flesh no longer seemed to call so very strongly to me." He placed his hand on Kreshin's shoulder as the young man stood next to him. He felt Kreshin's frame trembling beneath his strong grip. Kreshin looked up at him, wanting to face the truth, and wanting to be told comfortable lies. Baranovich shook his head sadly. "You love her very much then?"

"Yes . . ." Kreshin's eyes were bright with moisture, and his tongue licked at his lower lip.

"I — am sorry for that," Baranovich murmured. "That will make it very hard for you."

Kreshin seemed to come to a decision. Baranovich's hand was still on his shoulder, and the older man could feel the muscular effort the man was making, to control the tremor.

"If — *you*, you can do this — then, so can I . . ." he said.

"Good. Drink your coffee now, and warm yourself. That guard over there thinks you are afraid. Don't give him the satisfaction." Unable to complete the heroic fiction, he added: "Even if such ideas are nonsense, to an intelligent man . . ."

"What do we do?" snapped Semelovsky, as if eager to complete the whole process, including his own demise. "We have little time left. Kreshin and I have slowed the work on the tail-assembly as much as possible — but it is nearly complete."

Baranovich nodded. "I understand. Grosch, my *bête noire*, my devil — he, too, will become suspicious if we do not finish within half-an-hour, or a little more." He sipped at his coffee, and then took a bite from a hefty ham sandwich that had been brought down to him. "Of course, you realise that our friends over there are indicating in no uncertain manner that – the game is up?" He looked at Semelovsky.

"Of course – we knew that. The weapons-trials would be our deadline."

"And – you don't mind?"

"Do *you*?" Semelovksy asked pointedly.

Baranovich looked at the muttering guards for a moment – at each of the four faces turned to him. He wanted to answer in the affirmative, to explain that life becomes harder to throw away, the older one gets, not easier. That it is the young who make glad sacrifices, for good causes or for bad. He wanted to explain that the old are tenacious of life, on any terms. Instead, feeling a heaviness of responsibility, and of guilt, he gave the answer he knew they both needed, and wished to hear.

"No," he said.

Semelovsky nodded. "There you are, then," he said.

Baranovich swallowed the bile of guilt at the back of his throat. He, it was, who had led them here, to this place, and who would lead them, in time, to the cellars, and the questions, and the pain.

Baranovich was ruthless, with others, as with himself. He shrugged the guilt away and decided that he would, at least, grant them a quick death.

"It has to be the fire we talked about – over there. *No*, don't look about like that . . . by the second prototype. One of us has to be over there for some reason at the time we decide the operation will start. What do you think – what time shall we decide?"

"Six-thirty is the latest possible!" Semelovsky snapped in his habitual fussy, irritated manner. "I guessed it would come to that," he added.

"It is the only sensible place," Baranovich said. "Right in the area around the second prototype. As I said, it may damage the second plane, which will be to our American friend's advantage. Certainly, it will mean that this aircraft . . ." He tapped his hand on the cool metal of the fuselage at his side. "This one will be ordered out of the hangar. If Gant appears at the right moment and climbs into the pilot's couch, no one will ask to see his papers, or his face." He studied their reactions, saw the inevitability of death looking out from their eyes.

Semelovsky nodded, his features softening. He said: "I, for one, have no great relish at the thought of Colonel Kontarsky taking out on my skin the anger and frustration of his ruined career."

"You understand what I'm saying, Ilya – also?" Baranovich asked.

The young man was silent for some moments, then he said: "Yes, Pyotr Vassilyeivich – I understand."

"Good. You have your gun?" Kreshin nodded. "Good. That means that you, Maxim Ilyich, will have to start the fire. Besides," he added, smiling, "you look the least dangerous."

"Mm. Very well. At — six-ten, I shall excuse myself, and make for the toilets. If a guard accompanies me, so much the worse for him!" The little, balding man seemed ridiculous as he puffed out his narrow chest, and squared his stooping shoulders. Yet Baranovich knew that Semelovsky was capable of killing, if necessary. In some ways, he was the most desperate of the three of them, the newly converted zeal never having seemed to cool. He was a crusader.

"Only if necessary are you to kill the guard," Baranovich warned. "We don't want you hurt."

"Not *before* I start the fire — eh?" Semelovsky's eyes twinkled. Baranovich could sense the challenge that the little man felt, the same kind of bravado, though Baranovich did not know it, that he had revealed at the gate when Gant was in the boot of his car.

"No, not before." Baranovich relaxed into the partial honesty of the moment. "When you come out from the toilet, you will find the necessary materials stacked against the wall of the hangar, behind Prototype Two — some drums of fuel."

"I don't need to be told how to start a fire, Pyotr Vassilyeivich," Semelovsky said, bridling.

"I agree. Just make it big, and bright."

"It will be done."

"At six-twelve," Baranovich said. "Then you and I, Ilya, will have to cover the path to the second aircraft until the blaze is sufficient to distract *all* the security-guards — all of them. Understand?"

"Yes. We — are part of the distraction?"

Baranovich nodded. He looked beneath the fuselage of the aircraft as he heard the sound of returning voices in the echoing hangar. "Time to get back to work," he said. He looked at his watch. "Start counting the seconds now," he said. "It is five-twenty-three now. Synchronise your watches when you can do it without being observed."

He looked at his two companions. Suddenly his eyes felt misty. "Good luck, my friends," he said, and turned to the pilot's ladder and began to ascend. Kreshin watched his back for a moment, and then he followed Semelovsky towards the tail of the Firefox. He glanced once in the direction of the guards, now being relieved and reporting back to their officer.

Concentrate your hate on them, he told himself. Hate them, and what they represent, and what they do. Hate them . . .

Kontarsky looked at his watch. The time was seven minutes past six.

116

He had just received a directive from the Centre that the Tupolev TU-144 airliner carrying the First Secretary, the Chairman of the KGB, and the Marshal of the Soviet Air Force had left Moscow, and was expected to land at Bilyarsk at six-thirty. Kontarsky had been profoundly shaken by the news. The plane was not scheduled to arrive until after nine. He could do little but wonder why the First Secretary should be precipitate in his arrival. He suspected that it was some kind of pressure put upon him, a calculated insult. The Tower had been put on stand-by, to land the aircraft. There was nothing else he could do, except what he was engaged in at the moment, futile recriminations, coupled with the more practical step of once more contacting Priabin and, through him, receiving a progress report on the foreign agent who had penetrated Bilyarsk, and who was still at large.

A team of men sat at rickety tables in the bare duty-room in the security building, each analysing the reports of the teams who had combed the project area thoroughly. The final search had just been completed. Like the others, it had drawn a blank.

Below them, in a smaller room, with white walls and powerful lights, Dherkov and his wife were being questioned. Each had been made to watch the other's suffering – and neither of them had told him what he wished to know. He was unable to admit the possibility that they knew nothing of importance. There had been too many frustrations, too many blind alleys. To him, and to the interrogators, they were merely stubborn.

The doctor had used drugs. He had ruined the man's mind almost immediately, sending him into deep unconsciousness from which he had emerged incoherent. The woman, despite the massive jolt to her resistance that such damage to her husband must have been, still refused to betray the whereabouts of the agent, or his identity. Kontarsky had ordered the doctor to use the pentathol again, on her, but the doctor had been unwilling. Kontarsky had raged at him, but he suspected that the dosages were too small.

Kontarsky's fingers drummed on the desk as he waited for his connection to his office at the Centre. Priabin could not be found, for the moment. Kontarsky's call was being transferred to the computer-room. As he waited, his eyes roved the team of men bent at their tables, in shirt-sleeves for the most part, intent, driven. No face turned up to him with an answer, with a possible line of enquiry. Kontarsky felt the bitter, selfish anger of a man who sees a fortune turn to ashes in his hands. He had felt, throughout the night, that he had only to reach out and he would grasp the answer. Each answer, each source of knowledge, had crumbled between his fingers. He felt trapped.

Priabin was out of breath when he answered his superior's call. Kontarsky heard his voice clearly, though there was some quality of distance about it that might have been elation. His own stomach jumped at the proximity of a solution.

"Colonel – we've got him. He's been identified!" he heard Priabin say. "Colonel, are you there?"

"Quickly, Priabin – tell me?" One or two of the nearest heads looked up, at the sound of Kontarsky's choked, quiet whisper. They sensed that the breakthrough had come.

"He's a pilot . . . Mitchell Gant, an American . . ."

"American?" Kontarsky repeated mechanically.

"Yes. A member of their Mig squadron, the one they built to train their pilots in combat with Russian machines, the Apache group, they call it, designated by the Red Air Force and ourselves as the Mirror-squadron."

"Go on, Priabin. Why him?"

"Obviously, sir, he knows our aircraft as well as anyone. He'd be a good choice for sabotage, or for analysis of information. Perhaps he intends a – close inspection of the Mig-31?" There was a silence at the other end of the line. The truth, huge and appalling, struck both men at the same moment. In the silence, Kontarsky's voice dropped like a feeble stone.

"He – he *can't* be here for that . . .?"

"No, sir, surely not. They couldn't hope to get away with it!"

Kontarsky's voice trembled as he said: "Thank you, Dmitri – thank you. Well done." The receiver clanged clumsily into its rest as he replaced it. Kontarsky looked out over the team for a few moments, then he picked up the receiver again. He dialled the number of the guard-post at the hangar, and drummed his fingers as he waited.

"Tsernik – is that you? Arrest Baranovich and the others – now!"

"You've had news, sir?"

"Yes – dammit, yes! I want to know from them where this agent is – at once. And let no one near that aircraft – no one, understand?"

"Sir." Tsernik replaced his receiver. Kontarsky looked around the room again, at the men at their futile paperwork. Then he looked at his watch. Eleven minutes past six. "Some of you – all of you!" he shouted. "Get down to that hangar now – no, half of you there, the rest search this building – quickly!"

The room moved before him, as men gathered their coats, checked their weapons.

One voice, distant, said: "Who are we looking for, sir?"

"A pilot – dammit, a *pilot*!" Kontarsky's voice was high, piercing, almost hysterical.

Baranovich watched the slight figure of Semelovsky as he emerged from the laboratory at the end of the hangar. The little man stepped away from the door and began crossing the hangar, unconcernedly it appeared at that distance: Baranovich waited. A guard had followed Semelovsky to the lavatory. Baranovich wondered whether he would emerge.

Semelovsky reached the shadow of the PP Two, and the guard had still not appeared. Baranovich smiled, a smile of fierce success. Semelovsky, probably with a spanner or wrench, had killed the guard. He loosened the white coat which he wore on top of his overalls, not against the temperature, but to conceal the automatic thrust into the waistband of his trousers. Then he nodded, without looking in Kreshin's direction. He knew he would be watching for his signal.

The work on the aircraft had been completed a little after six. Grosch, suspecting that Baranovich was delaying completion of the work, but misconstruing the motive as simple fear, had returned to the restaurant, together with most of the other technicians and scientific team-leaders. One man, Pilac, an electronics expert like himself, had deliberately passed him as he left, nodding rather helplessly in his direction. Baranovich had been touched by the gesture, despite its futility.

He reached into the pocket of his coat, and flipped over the switch on a tiny transmitter. Inaudibly, it transmitted to the bleeper taped to Gant's arm, a one-to-the-second noise that would alert him to the fact that the diversion had begun. When Baranovich turned the switch over, the signal would become a continuous bleep, Gant's signal that he was to make his way to the hangar as quickly as possible. He turned his head to survey the distance between himself and the nearest guard. He estimated it at about twelve yards. The guards were still much in evidence – he counted four within twenty-five yards and, despite the hour of the morning, they did not seem tired, or inattentive. They had been changed too frequently to become thoroughly bored or fatigued.

He looked to the far end of the hangar. He thought, as his heart leapt in anticipation, he detected the flare of Semelovsky's lighter or matches. Almost immediately, burning across his gaze, a column of flame shot up. He could not any longer see Semelovsky's bending figure, and had no way of knowing whether the man had immolated himself in the sudden blaze.

He turned, drawing the gun from his waistband. Already, the moment before the column of flame had shot up, to roll out under the roof of the hangar, there had been cries from the booth, away behind him. Holding the gun across his stiffened forearm, he shot the nearest guard through the stomach, and then moved swiftly towards Kreshin and the other end of the hangar. A bullet plucked at the fuselage above his head as he ran in a ducking crouch, and then someone screamed for the firing to stop, because it was endangering the Mig. He smiled to himself as he pushed at the immobile, frozen form of Kreshin, caught as if in a spotlight, so that the two of them were running towards the fire, together with other forms.

The alarm bell began to clatter its hysterical note and, despite the fire drills that had been endlessly practised, Baranovich got the impression of a surge of people in the direction of the gouting flames. He had a confused, jolting image of a small figure in a white coat, burning like a torch, and he knew it had to be Semelovsky. He thrust the automatic back in his pocket and, shoulder to shoulder with Kreshin, he paused, in a shifting, purposeless group, the heat from the flames like a desert wind striking his face. He flipped over the switch on the transmitter in his pocket, praying that his now continuous signal was reaching Gant. Pushed aside by an unseeing guard tugging a hose behind him, then another, he glanced down at his watch. Six-thirteen. He looked over his shoulder. Over the heads of the crowd pressing behind him, he could see the guard's body near the Firefox and saw, too, the ring of security men surrounding the aircraft. He knew they had discovered, or guessed, what was intended by the diversion, who the agent in Bilyarsk was, and what he intended.

Somehow the distraction was understood for what it was, and the Mig had not been left temporarily unguarded. He could see the squat form of Tsernik directing the formation of the ring of guards, and the junior officer in charge of hangar-security detailing men to fight the fire. A voice crackled over the loudspeaker system, above the noise of the flames, which seemed to have made the watchers oblivious to their danger. Flame spilled across the hangar floor beneath the second aircraft, like swift lava, and the pall of smoke was beginning to engulf them, masking the most forward of the guards with their hoses and extinguishers.

The loudspeaker ordered them to clear the area, clamouring for their attention above the racket of the alarm and the new, added note of the fire-tender, rushing into the chaos of the hangar from its station near the development-hangar.

There was only one thing to do, he realised, the flames at his back now as he watched the fire-tender and the movements of a second group of hurrying guards, the off-duty squad hastily recalled. They were looking for him, and for Kreshin. There was only one thing to

120

do – he had to show himself, draw their fire, draw away, if possible, the ring around the Mig. He began to move in the direction of the retreating tide of spectators as the bulk of the fire-tender edged its way through them. He glanced towards the door through which he knew Gant must enter the hangar. There was no sign of him.

At first, the signal from the bleeper was a muscular tic, not even a sound to Gant as he was consumed by the flames of his dream. He was still in the posture of defeat, sagging stiffly, immobile, on the lavatory seat, his body damp with sweat. Something pulsed in his arm, he was aware of it, but he could not move his hand to scratch it, to rub the spot. The dream was drawing towards an end, and he was patiently waiting for his release. There was no need to move, no need to fight. It had been bad, but it was ebbing now, the separate images flung off like frozen sparks, photographs of his past in a flickering album.

The noise ate down into his mind, the one-to-the-second bleeping of the receiver. A part of Gant's mind, the part that always coldly observed the progress of the dream, powerless to prevent or still, recognised that it was some kind of signal and fumbled, as with frozen fingers, to decipher its significance. Something to do with an alert – not an alert like others, not a scramble . . .

With sudden, frightening clarity he knew what it was, so that the image of the Firefox, in one of the photographs he had studied, was before him – then the memory of the cockpit simulator they had built for him, on which he had learned . . . He knew what it was. Baranovich. He saw the wise face, peering kindly, in Olympian pity, through the flames.

Tic and noise coordinated. The bleeper on his arm, taped there by Baranovich. The instructions filtered through, like pebbles dropped irregularly into dark water. The bleep was the alert – wait for the continuous sound, which is the summons.

He tried to move, felt that he was moving against a great wave, which pinned him where he was, struggled, tried again to raise himself – and did so.

The bathroom came into a kind of focus, and he shook his head, rubbed both stiff hands down his cheeks. It was like coming back from the dead, far worse than coming back from a narcotic trip, far worse than that. The water, still running, filtered through his mind as a distant sound, nothing to do with the crackling of flames. He had always been afraid of moving like this, before the dream had played itself out. Now he knew he had to.

He opened the bathroom door, his hand like a frozen claw gripping the door handle clumsily. He slammed the door behind him. He felt an ache, dull and distant, in his thigh. He looked down. There was a bruise across his muscle. He presumed it was some self-inflicted blow, performed an age before.

He walked stiffly, like a man on new limbs, across to the locker which he remembered contained Voskov's pressure-suit. He had to dress himself . . .

The bleep is the alert, wait for the continuous noise, which is the summons. Baranovich smiled down on him, the memory of that moment in Kreshin's bedroom, the white-haired man holding the cup of sweet coffee. He saw the face from that angle, as he had lain on the bed.

He spilled the suit onto the floor and bent wearily, a long way down, to pick it up. He untaped the bleeper, then stuck it to the locker door. Then he began to struggle into the legs, fitting his clumsy limbs into the stiff, unyielding garment. He was running freely with sweat.

Another sound clamoured for the attention of his fogged awareness – an alarm, a fire-alarm, he decided. He knew then what the diversion was, responding to stimuli as he was. He knew that it signalled an increase in the urgency of his efforts. It marked another stage passed, a new tempo introduced. He began to struggle with the lacing, the all-important lacing that was his only protection against the disastrous effects of the G-forces he would encounter in the Firefox. It was a skilled job, it required more of him than he was able to give. Yet it had to be right – it might kill him, as surely as any mechanical malfunction in the aircraft, more surely. He tried to concentrate.

It was not easy, but it was familiar. He knew what he was doing. He forced himself to pay attention, his own harsh breathing roaring in his ears.

The bleep is the alert; wait for the continuous noise, which is the summons, Baranovich told him, above the panic of the blood.

At last he had finished. The suit was hot, choking, sticky with his frantic efforts. He had no time to put on dry underclothes. He picked the pilot's helmet from its shelf, glanced inside it, and could make nothing of the contacts and sensors of the thought-system. They had been checked by Baranovich the previous day.

He tugged on the helmet, snapped down the visor, and the image of flame roared up in his imagination, the dying effort of the dream to swallow his consciousness.

Wait for the continuous noise, which is the summons, Baranovich whispered above the noise of the flames.

He realised that the bleep had vanished. There was a continuous, penetrating cry from the receiver on the locker. He reached into the locker, and picked from the shelf the innards of the transistor radio. He looked at the small black object, like a cigarette case now its disguise of transistors and batteries had gone. In the radio it had appeared nothing more sinister than a circuit-board.

The continuous noise is the summons.

He moved stiffly towards the door.

The crowd simply seemed, as if by a communal awareness and command, to disappear, to drift to either side of the two Jews. They were alone, and marked. There was nowhere to hide, no shelter for them. A group of guards in a semi-circle was advancing slowly towards them, through the smoke that was filling the hangar, rolling like a pall towards the open doors. Tsernik's head was hidden by the loud-hailer he had raised to his lips, and they heard his amplified, mechanical voice call to them.

"Put down your weapons – now, or I will order them to open fire! Put down your weapons – immediately!"

There seemed little else to do. The fire-tender had been joined, raucously, by its twin, and the fire-fighting units were soaking the aircraft and the hangar floor with foam, choking out Semelovsky's fire, Semelovsky's funeral pyre. There were people all around them now, backing away, as from something diseased or deformed – men in white coats, others in overalls, the technicians and scientists who had rushed towards the fire, then retreated from it like an ebbing wave. Baranovich and Kreshin were between the crescent of the approaching guards, and the crescent of the fire-fighters behind them. Baranovich felt the drop in temperature as the foam choked the life from the fire beneath the second Mig. Around the first one, around Gant's plane, the circle of guards had thinned, though they had not disappeared, not all left their posts.

Where was Gant? He had turned over the switch. The summons should have brought him by now. If he did not appear within seconds at the door leading to the security-building and the pilots' rest-room, the guards would have arrested them, and re-formed around the aircraft. The gleaming silver flanks of the plane reflected the light of the dying flames. The fuel tanks of the second Mig had not caught fire as Baranovich had hoped. With luck, for the Soviets, it would still fly.

There seemed noise like a wall behind him, pushing against him with an almost physical force. In front of him, there was a cone of silence, with Kreshin and himself at the point, and the semi-circle of closing guards embraced within it as they moved slowly forward. It was one of the most powerful visual images of his life, the approaching guards and then, beating at his ears, a palpable silence.

A gun roared at his side and its sound, too, seemed to come from far away, as if muffled. He saw a guard drop, and a second one lurch sideways. It was too easy, he thought, they are too close together, as he had once seen advancing Germans in the defence of Stalingrad – too close . . . His mind did not tell him to open fire. His own gun lay uselessly in his pocket.

"Drop your weapons, or I shall order them to open fire!" he heard the distant, mechanical voice say.

He did not hear the command, but he saw the flames from the rifles, sensed, rather than saw, Kreshin plucked away from his side. Then, with growing agony and the terrible revulsion of the awareness of death, he felt his own body plucked by bullets, his coat ripped as if by small detonations. He felt odd. He staggered, no longer sure of his balance. He stumbled back a couple of paces, then sat untidily down on the ground, like a child failing a lesson in walking. Then it seemed as if the hangar lights had been turned off, he rolled sideways from the waist, like an insecure doll flopping onto its side. His eyes were tightly closed, squeezed shut, to avoid the terrible moment of death and, as his face slapped dully against the concrete floor, he didn't see Gant, a dim shadow in the dull green pressure-suit, standing at the entrance to the hangar from the security-building. Baranovich died believing that Gant would not come.

Gant could see from where he stood something in a white coat on the ground, and the closing, cautious semi-circle of guards approaching it. He saw Kreshin's blond head, and his limbs flung in the careless attitude of violent death. The aircraft was thirty yards from him, no more.

There had been a fire at the other end of the hangar. He could see the two fire-tenders, and the foam-soaked frame of the second prototype now being rolled clear of the smouldering materials that had begun, and sustained, the fire. Already, he realised, the occupants of the hangar were in a position to begin to turn their attention back to the Firefox. He was almost too late – he might, in fact, be too late. The excuse for rolling the plane out of the hangar was almost over, the fire out. He saw a spurt of flame near the wall of the hangar, and an asbestos-suited fireman rear back from it. He heard the dull concussion of a fuel-drum explode. The second prototype was clear of the flame, but the men towing it with a small tractor hurried to get it further off. It was his chance.

His legs were still stiff, rebellious, from the hysterical paralysis of the dream, but he forced them to stride out, to cross the thirty yards of concrete to the Firefox.

The pilot's ladder that Baranovich had used for his supervision of

Grosch's work was still in place, and he began to climb it. As he bent over the cockpit, a voice at the bottom of the ladder called up to him.

"Colonel Voskov?"

He looked round, and nodded down at the young, distraught, sweating face below him. The man was in the uniform of a junior officer in the KGB. His gun was in his hand.

"Yes?" he said.

"What are you doing, Colonel?"

"What the devil do you think I'm doing, you idiot? Do you want this plane to be damaged like the other one? I'm taking it out of here, that's what I'm doing." He swung his legs over the sill, and dropped into the pilot's couch. While he still looked down at the young KGB man, his hands sought for the parachute straps, and he buckled himself in, following this by strapping himself to the couch itself.

The young man had stepped back a couple of paces, so that he could still see Gant clearly. The tinted face-mask of the helmet, combined with the integral oxygen-mask, made it impossible for him to tell that it wasn't Colonel Voskov in the pilot's position. He was at a loss what action to take. He glanced swiftly down the hangar. It was true that the second Mig-31 was being towed towards him from the far end of the hangar and, although it appeared under control, there was still smoke and flame from the fire there. He had been told by Tsernik that no one, on the express orders of Colonel Kontarsky, was to be allowed near the plane. But did that apply to the pilot?

Gant ignored the KGB man and went through his pre-start checks as swiftly as he could. He plugged in his radio and communications equipment, finding the location of the socket instinctively, as if he had always flown that aircraft. The simulator which had been built in Langley, Virginia, at CIA headquarters, from Baranovich's smuggled descriptions and photographs and from computer projections, now proved its worth. Then, he plugged in the connection from his helmet to the weapons-system, a single jack-plug similar to the radio. He pushed the jack-plug home into the side of the ejector seat itself. It was the final sophistication of the weapons-system of the Mig: if he were forced to eject, then he could control the destruct mechanism of the system to prevent any part or fragment of the plane's weaponry and its control-system from falling into enemy hands.

He glanced down at the KGB man, swiftly, as if taking in the reading from one of his gauges. The junior officer still seemed perplexed, reluctant. Gant connected up his oxygen supply, then coupled in the emergency oxygen. Next, he switched in the anti-G device, a lead which plugged into the pressure-suit just below the left knee. It was this which would bleed air into the suit to counteract the effects of increased G-forces on his blood, forcing it round his system against the effect of sudden turns, dives or accelerations. Cautiously, he tested it, felt the air bleed in rapidly, and checked the gauges which confirmed his bodily reaction. It was working.

He knew he was stripping the pre-flight routine to the bone, but there weren't even seconds to spare. His eyes read the gauges; flaps, brakes and fuel. The fuel-tanks were full, and they would need to be since, as he sat there, he did not even know the nature or position of his refuelling-point.

There was one more thing. He extracted the innards of the transistor radio from a pouch-pocket on the thigh of the suit, bared an adhesive strip, and then fixed the anonymous collection of circuits in their wafer-thin black case developed at Farnborough exclusively for his use to the corner of the instrument panel, with a silent prayer that it had not been damaged during the past three days. If it had been, he would never know.

He was ready. His routine had taken mere seconds to complete. The second Firefox was only yards away as it trailed behind the small tractor. He had a single moment in which to convince the man below him. He leaned down, and waved his hand for him to move, yelling as he did so.

"You'll get your head knocked off if you stand there any longer!" He swept a finger across his throat, and pointed to the wing and engine-intake behind the Russian. The young man looked, understood, and self-preservation made him move clear, tugging the ladder obligingly after him.

Gant smiled, relaxed, and turned his attention to the aircraft. As he did so, his gaze swept across the door into the hangar through which he had entered perhaps a minute earlier. He saw Kontarsky, his face white, his arm extended, finger pointing in his direction. There were other men at his side, perhaps half-a-dozen, filling the doorway behind him. In a purely reflex action, he pressed the hood control, and automatically the hood swung down, locked electronically. Then he locked it manually as a standard double-check. He was isolated in the machine. A part of it.

The fogginess, the lethargy, the nausea of the dream, all had left him now. There was, curiously, no elation either. There was only the functioning of smooth machinery – a mechanism within a larger mechanism. Elation would come later perhaps.

He checked the cockpit air-pressure; then, reaching forward, he gang-loaded the ignition switches, switched on the starter-motors, turned on the high-pressure cock and, without hesitation, even for self-drama, pressed the starter button.

Half-way down the fuselage, there was the sound of a double explosion, like the noise of a twelve-bore against his ears, as the cartridge start functioned. Two puffs of sooty smoke rolled away from the engines. There was a rapid, mounting whirring as the huge turbines built up; he checked gyro instruments erect. He saw the flashing light which indicated that he had forgotten the fuel-booster pump, switched it in, and the light disappeared on the panel. He eased up the throttles, and watched the rpm gauges as they mounted to twenty-seven per cent, and he steadied them there. He glanced out of his side-window. Kontarsky and two of his men, as if galvanised by the explosions of the starter-cartridges, were moving forward but, by comparison with the speed of his actions and responses, as if they were moving underwater, slowly – too slowly to stop him now. He saw a gun raised, and something whined away off the cockpit, harmlessly.

With one eye on the JPT (jet-pipe temperature) gauge, he opened the throttles until the rpm gauges were at fifty-five per cent and the whine had increased comfortingly. He released the brakes.

The Firefox had been tugging against the brakes' restraint and now that they were released, skipped rather than rolled forward, towards the hangar doors through which Gant could see the dawn streaking and lighting the sky. He saw men rushing to the doors, in an attempt to close them against him – but they, too, moved with a painful, ludicrous slowness and they were too late, far too late. He checked the gauges and booster-pumps and then he was through the hangar doors and out onto the taxi-way. In his mirror he could see running figures, left ridiculously behind him as the Firefox rolled towards the runway.

Using the rudder and differential braking, he turned onto the runway. As he straightened the airplane, he ran through the checks again.

He breathed deeply, once, then he opened the throttles to full. He pushed the throttles straight through the detent, and brought the reheat of the massive engines into play. He felt their power as a huge shove in the back, an almost sexual surge forward. There was a moment of elation, fierce, pure. The plane gathered speed. At 160 knots, it was skipping on the ridges in the runway-slabs. At 165 knots, he brought the elevator-controls into play, and the Firefox left the ground. There was a further surge of acceleration as the drag induced by contact with the runway vanished. He retracted the undercarriage.

The Firefox wobbled its wings as he over-controlled, unused to the quality and finesse of the power-control system. He was lifting away steeply now, within seconds.

In the rising sun he saw, off to the right of the nose, a glint of sun on metal. He pulled back, and hauled the stick to the right. He felt the pressure of the anti-G as he went into the turn, almost rolled the plane completely through his over-control, then levelled the wings. He looked out to his left, and below and behind him. A Tupolev TU-144, carrying, he knew, the First Secretary, was turning to make its final approach to the runway at Bilyarsk. He looked at his altimeter. He was already at almost eight thousand feet.

It was fifteen seconds since the undercarriage had left contact with the runway. He was a thousand miles from the Russian border – any Russian border. As the sweat of reaction from his near-collision ran down his sides, beneath his arms, he grinned to himself. He had done it. He had stolen the Firefox.

PART TWO

THE FLIGHT

SIX:

Counter-Measures

By the time Kontarsky came aboard the First Secretary's Tupolev Tu-144, the moment after the giant supersonic airliner had rolled to a halt on the runway at Bilyarsk, dashing up the mobile passenger-gangway in which he had ridden from the hangar, the First Secretary of the Soviet Communist Party had already been told of the theft of the Mig-31 over the flight-deck UHF. As he was ushered into the military command section of the aircraft, aft of the passenger accommodation, the equivalent of the war command officer on board the U.S. President's aircraft, he was confronted by what was, in fact, a council of war. The room was already filled with heavy cigar smoke.

Kontarsky saluted rigidly, and kept his eyes straight ahead. Only the back of a radio-operator's head at the far end of the cigar-shaped room filled his vision. Yet he knew that the eyes of the room's principal occupants were on him. An awareness that seemed to seep through the skin like damp told him where each of those powerful men sat. He knew that each was regarding him intently. He understood the details of the expression on each face. Directly in front of him, round the command table, circular in shape and fitted with projection equipment which would throw onto the table a relief map of any part of the Soviet Union, any part of the world, sat the First Secretary himself; on his right sat Kutuzov, Marshal of the Soviet Air Force, a world war ace, and a hardline Communist of the Stalinist school; to the left of the Soviet First Secretary sat Andropov, Chairman of the KGB and his ultimate superior. It was that trinity which so frightened him, which made the moments since he had stepped through the guarded door into this sanctum seem like minutes, hours . . . endless.

It was the First Secretary who spoke. Kontarsky, still rigidly to attention, and not requested to be at ease or to sit, saw from the corner of his eye the restraining hand of the First Secretary fall on the sleeve of Andropov's suit, and he caught the glint of an overhead strip-light reflected from the gold-rimmed spectacles worn by the Chairman of the KGB.

"Colonel Kontarsky – you will explain what has happened," the First Secretary said, his voice soft, authoritative. He seemed unhurried. There was no other sound in the room except the steady hiss from a radio. It was nearly three minutes since Gant had taken off in the Mig, yet nothing seemed to have been done.

Now that he had failed, Kontarsky was almost hysterically eager to encourage and exhort the efforts to reclaim – or destroy, he presumed – the stolen aircraft.

He swallowed. "An American . . ." he began, and coughed. He kept his eyes looking directly ahead, at the scrubbed neck of the radio-operator. "An American pilot called Gant is responsible for the theft of the Mig-31, sir."

"On the contrary, Colonel, it is you who are responsible," the First Secretary replied, in a voice bereft of menace, bereft of humanity. "Proceed."

"He infiltrated the compound here with the aid of various dissident Jews, who are now dead."

"Mm. But not before they told you what you wished to know, I presume?"

Kontarsky looked down into the broad, lined face. It was a strong face. He had always thought so. The eyes were like chips of grey stone.

"We – learned nothing . . ." he managed to say.

There was a silence. He noticed that the radio-operator was sitting more upright in his chair, as if tense. When his eyes returned to the circular table, he could see the First Secretary's strong, veined hand tapping at the sleeve of the Chairman's dark, sober business suit, as if restraining him.

"You – do not know what the destination of the Mig-31 will be?" he heard the First Secretary ask.

"You know nothing?" Kutuzov interposed, shocked. Kontarsky saw the First Secretary glance swiftly at the ageing Marshal who was in full uniform, the sombre blue tinselled with insignia and overlapping decorations. The old pilot fell silent.

"No," Kontarsky said, and his voice was small and flat, as if the room were deadened, without reverberation.

"Very well," the First Secretary intoned after a moment of heavy, oppressive silence. At that moment, Kontarsky saw his ruin. For the First Secretary, and for the others, military personnel and KGB, gathered round the circular table, he had ceased to exist. "You will place yourself under close guard, Colonel." Kontarsky's lip trembled, and he looked once into the First Secretary's eyes. It was like looking in a mirror that refused to reflect his physical presence. "You are dismissed."

When Kontarsky had left the room, the door closing behind him softly, the First Secretary glanced in the direction of the Marshal. He nodded, once, and then turned his head to look at Andropov. He said:

"There is no time now for recriminations. That will come later. It appears obvious to me that this is a CIA venture, a desperate attempt to cancel the huge advantage in air superiority that the aircraft would have given to the Soviet Union. We know nothing else than the man's name, and his official file. It would tell us nothing of use. As each moment passes now, the Mig-31 moves further and further away from us, towards . . . where, Mihail Ilyich?"

The Marshal of the Soviet Air Force glanced over his shoulder at the back of an operator at a small console.

"Give us the 'Wolfpack' map of the U.S.S.R., quickly!" he said.

The operator punched buttons in instant obedience and, as the men seated at the table withdrew their hands, and packets of cigarettes and cigar-cases, the surface of the table registered a projection-map of the Soviet Union, clustered with tiny dots of varying colours. There before them on the screen of the table lay the diagram of the immense outer defences of the Soviet Union. The First Secretary leaned forward across the table, and tapped at the map.

"Bilyarsk," he said. His finger traced a circle round the area he had indicated. "Now, in which direction has he gone?"

"We do not know, First Secretary," Kutuzov said, his voice gruff. He had had an operation for cancer of the throat two years earlier, and it had left his voice a tired, dry whisper.

He looked across the table, across the glowing projection of the map, at Vladimirov, the tall, lean-faced officer with grey hair and watery blue eyes who sat opposite him. The ruthlessness, the confidence, of that face helped him to regain a little of his calm, after the blow of the theft of the Mig. He had been winded, temporarily paralysed, by what had happened. It had been even more of a body blow than Belenko's defection in a Foxbat four years before. He could still see, in his mind, the bright, swift glint of the fuselage as the aircraft had pulled away from the Tupolev, climbing swiftly. A glimpse, that had been all he had.

Over the UHF, then, had come the information that an un-authorised aircraft had taken off from the single main runway below them in the strengthening light. He had known, with a sudden, sick realisation, what aircraft it had been; before confirmation had flowed in, even as they touched down and the big plane had skipped once and then settled on the runway. Someone, an

American, had stolen the greatest aircraft the Soviet Union had ever produced – *stolen* it.

"What do you think, Vladimirov?" he said.

The tall, lean-faced man glanced down at the map, then looked up, addressing his remarks to the First Secretary. General Med Vladimirov, commandant of the tactical strike arm of the Soviet Air Force, the "Wolfpack", as it was designated, was worried. He, too, understood the problem – how to trace an untraceable aircraft – but he did not intend to allow the First Secretary to see his doubts. Then, as lethargy seemed to have left him, he spoke.

"I suggest a staggered sector scramble, First Secretary," he said directly, "in two areas. We must put up as many planes as we can, along our southern and northern borders."

"Why there?"

"Because, First Secretary," he said, looking down at the map, "this lunatic must refuel if he is to fly the aircraft to a place of complete safety. He will not refuel in the air – we would know if some mother-plane were waiting for him over neutral or hostile sky."

"What is the range of this aircraft?" General Leonid Borov asked, seated next to Vladimirov. Borov was commandant of the ECM (Electronic Counter-Measures) section of the Soviet Air Force. He, it would be, in the event of a pre-emptive strike by the West, who would coordinate the radar and missile defences with the air defences.

"It would be fully fuelled," Kutuzov said. "Almost three thousand miles maximum, depending on what this American knows, and how he handles the aircraft."

"Which would put him here – or here," Vladimirov said, his hand sweeping the Arctic Ocean, then drifting across the expanse of the table to indicate the Iranian border, and then the Mediterranean.

"Why would he go either north or south, Vladimirov?" the First Secretary asked. His voice had become impatient now, and his body seemed eager for activity, as if the blood were tinglingly returning to his limbs after cramp.

"Because, First Secretary, any pilot who ran the risk of the Moscow defences would be committing suicide – even in a plane that allows no radar trace!"

There was a brief silence. All of them there, the five men round the circular table, and the team of guards, ciphermen, radio-operators and aides to the ranking officers, all of them understood that the unvoiceable had been uttered. Now that the American had stolen the Mig he had turned that unique fact to his advantage, the fact that the airplane's defences incorporated an anti-radar system.

"It works too well!" Kutuzov growled in his characteristic whisper. "It works too damn well!"

"The American knows of it?" Andropov said, speaking for the first time. Heads turned in the direction of the bland, urbane Chairman of the KGB. He seemed unabashed by the failure sustained by one of his officers, the monumental failure. Vladimirov smiled thinly. Perhaps, he thought, with a hardline pro-Stalinist First Secretary, the Chairman considered himself untouchable. He continued looking at the man across the table from him, who looked like nothing so much as a prosperous, efficient Western businessman, rather than the head of the most powerful police and intelligence force in the world.

"He must know," Vladimirov said, ice in his voice. "Your man's security must have been *full* of holes, Chairman, for the CIA to have got him this far."

The First Secretary's hand slapped the table once, the projection-map jiggling momentarily under the impact.

"No recriminations! None. I want action, Vladimirov – and quickly! How much time do we have?"

Vladimirov looked at his watch. The time was six-twenty-two. The Mig had been airborne for seven minutes.

"He has more than a thousand miles to go before he crosses any Soviet border, First Secretary. He will travel at sub-sonic speed for the most part, because he will want to conserve fuel, and because he will not want to betray his flight-path with a supersonic footprint – we have more than an hour, even should he fly directly . . ."

"One hour?" The First Secretary realised he was in a foreign element, that Vladimirov and the other military experts would possess a time-scale where minutes stretched, were elastic – in which all things could be accomplished. He added: "It is enough. What do you propose – Kutuzov?"

"As 'Wolfpack' Commandant suggests, First Secretary, a staggered sector scramble. We must institute a search for this aircraft, a visual search. We must put in the air a *blanket* of aircraft, a *net* in which he will be caught. All our 'Wolfpack' and 'Bearhunt' squadrons know this sequence clearly. It leaves no holes, no gaps. We merely have to institute it in reverse order. 'Bearhunt' will begin, seeking the American within the area three hundred miles within our borders – 'Wolfpack' can be scrambled at the same time, patrolling the borders themselves."

"I see." The First Secretary was thoughtful, silent for a moment, then he said: "I agree."

There was a relaxation of suspense in the War Command Centre of the Tupolev. It was from that room that the First Secretary, if ever

135

the need arose, would order Armageddon to commence – a replica, except for its size, of the War Command Centre in the heart of the Kremlin. For the Soviet leader, and those members of the High Command who were present, it was the only stroke of fortune that early morning, that they possessed, in portable form, the nerve-centre of the Soviet defence system. The suspense that vanished was replaced by the heady whiff of tension, the tension of the runner on his blocks, the tension that precedes violent activity.

"Thank you, First Secretary," Vladimirov said. He got to his feet, his thin figure stooping over the table, studying the coloured zones overlying the topography of the map, picking out the spots of colour that indicated his squadron bases, and their linked missile bases.

"Bleed in the 'Bearhunt' status map," he ordered.

As he watched, the numbers of coloured dots increased, filling the inland spaces of the map at regular intervals. He brushed his hand across the table, smiled grimly to himself, and said: "Scramble, with Seek-briefing, and in SSS sequence, squadrons in White through Red sectors, and Green through Brown sectors. Put up 'Bearhunt' squadrons, same briefing, G through N." He rubbed his chin, and listened to the chatter of the cipher machines, waited for the transmission of the coded signals to the Communications Officer, a young colonel seated before a console behind him, with his team of three ranged beside him.

When the high-speed transmission had begun, Vladimir looked at the First Secretary, and said: "What do you wish done when they sight the Mig?"

The First Secretary glared at him, and replied: "I wish to talk to this American who has stolen the Soviet Air Force's latest toy – obtain the frequency – if he will not land the aircraft as directed, then it must be destroyed – completely!"

The inertial navigator that had been fitted into the Firefox was represented on the control panel by a small display similar to the face of a pocket calculator. It also possessed a series of buttons marked, for example, "Track", "Heading", "Ground Speed", and "Coordinates". He could feed into it known navigational information and the on-board computer would calculate and display such information as distance to travel, time for distance. By starting the programmes in the computer at a known time and position, the computer could measure changes in speed and direction, and keep track of the aircraft's position. Standard procedure required the data displayed to be confirmed by more conventional means – such as visual sightings of landmarks.

Gant had an appointment to keep in the airspace north-west of

Volgograd, with the early morning civilian flight from Moscow, a rendezvous which would establish him as travelling towards the southern border of the Soviet Union – a fact he very much wanted to establish in the minds of those who would be controlling the search for him.

He throttled back slightly, keeping his speed at little more than six hundred and fifty knots. He had not pushed the Firefox to its supersonic speeds because, travelling at his present height of almost 15,000 feet, the supersonic footprint he would leave behind him would act like a giant arrow as to his direction for those with eyes to see and ears to hear. There were another twenty-three minutes to his rendezvous.

He had made a minute inspection of the equipment packed into the Firefox. Most of it, communications and radar especially, had been built into the simulator at Langley, and was of a type which closely paralleled U.S. developments in the same fields. They weren't the reason why he was stealing the Firefox. One reason lay in the two mighty Turmansky turbojets which produced in excess of 50,000 lbs of thrust each, giving the plane its incredible speed in excess of Mach 5. Another reason was in the magic of its anti-radar system which, as dead Baranovich had suggested, was non-mechanical, but rather some kind of treatment of, or application to, the skin of the aircraft, and a further reason lay in the thought-guided missiles and cannon the Firefox carried.

The sky ahead of him was clear, pale blue, the rising sun to port of him dazzling off the perspex, the glare diffused and deadened by the tinted mask of the flying helmet. There was nothing to see.

Gant had no interest in the stretching, endless steppe below him. His eyes hardly left the instrument panel, especially the radar which would warn him of the approach of aircraft, or of missiles. One of his ECM devices, which Baranovich had explained in his final briefing, was a constant monitor of the radar-emissions from the terrain over which he passed. Effectively, the "Nose", as Baranovich had called it, sniffed out radar signals directed at him. The "Nose" seemed unnecessary to Gant, since he could not be picked up on any radar screen on the ground or in the air but, Baranovich explained and he had seen, a visual sighting of him would lead to intense radar activity on the ground, using the sighting plane as the guide to his whereabouts. In addition, as long as he went on monitoring the read-out on the tiny screen of the "Nose", he would know where, and in what pattern, missile radars on the ground below him were.

Gant knew what form the search for him would take. The Russians would guess he would head either direct north or direct south – that to the east was only, eventually, and long after he ran out of fuel, the People's Republic of China, while to the west, between himself and a friendly country, lay the massive defences that surrounded Moscow. He knew that "Bearhunt" squadrons would be up looking for him, and he also suspected the Russians would be using their sound-detection system – NATO-designated, with inappropriate levity, "Big Ears" – which in the unpopulated interior of the Russian heartland was designed to detect low-flying aircraft that might have eluded the radar net. Gant had no idea of how numerous might be such installations, nor how efficient they were in obtaining accurate bearings on machines moving at more than six hundred miles an hour – nor did he know at what altitude the system ceased to be effective.

One other thing, he reminded himself. Satellite photography, high-speed and infra-red. He didn't know whether it would be effective within the tiny time-scale of his flight. But it was something else to worry about. He was fighting an electronic war. He was like an asthmatic man with heavy, creaking boots trying to move through a room of insomniacs without disturbing them.

Gant had no idea of the nature, or precise location, of his refuelling point. In his memory were a sequence of different coordinates which he was to feed into the inertial navigator.

He had left the UHF channel open, knowing that they would attempt to contact him from Bilyarsk. In fact, he hoped and expected that they would do so. As soon as he spoke, anybody within a range of two hundred miles of him, using UDF equipment, would not only pick up the broadcast, but would be able to obtain, with the assistance of two other fix lines, an almost instant fix on his position. In his case, it would only help to confirm the decoy of his journey south.

He suspected that the silence since his take-off was caused by the take-over of command by the War Command Centre on board the First Secretary's Tupolev. He waited with impatience, a surge of vanity in him wanting, above the desire of being assumed to be heading towards the southern borders of the U.S.S.R., to hear from the First Secretary, or the Marshal of the Soviet Air Force, at the least. He wanted to feed upon their anger, their threats.

The radio crackled into life. The voice was one he recognised from newsreels, from interviews – that of the First Secretary of the Soviet Communist Party. Involuntarily, his eyes flicked to the instruments, checking his heading and speed, checking the conformity of the dials and readouts.

"I am speaking to the individual who has stolen the property of the U.S.S.R.," the voice said, levelly, without inflection, almost as if on purpose to disappoint him. "Can you hear me, Mr. Gant? I presume you have discarded your military rank since you became employed by – shall we say, *other persons*?" Gant smiled at the man's emphasis, and his caution.

Ever since the U-2 incident, he thought. Softly, softly. It was not to be admitted, not yet, that he was working for the CIA, even that he was an American.

He said: "Go ahead – I'm listening."

"Are you enjoying your ride, Mr. Gant – you like our new toy?"

"It could be improved," Gant said laconically.

"Ah – your expert opinion, Mr. Gant."

Gant could almost see the big man, with the strong, square face, sitting before the transmitter in the War Command Centre, while the frenzy of activity around him went almost unnoticed. Already, no doubt, someone had pushed beneath his gaze the details of the fix they had obtained on him. At that moment, however, it was between the two of them, between one man in an airplane, and another man with the powers of a god at his disposal. Yet Gant held all the cards, the voice seemed to say. Gant remained unfooled. He understood the fury of the search for him. He was being played like a fish, lulled, until they found him.

"You could say that," he said. "Don't you want to threaten me, or something?"

"I will do so, if that is what you wish," was the level reply. "But first, I will merely ask you to bring back what does not belong to you."

"And then you'll forget the whole thing, uh?"

There was what sounded like soft laughter at the other end of the UHF. Then: "I don't think you would believe that, Mr. Gant – would you? No, of course not. The CIA will have filled your head with nonsense about the Lubyanka, and the security services of the Soviet Union. No. All I will say is that you will live, if you return immediately. It is calculated that no more than forty flying minutes would be required before we would be able to sight you back over Bilyarsk. It has been a nice try, Mr. Gant, as you would say – but now, the game is most definitely over!"

Gant waited before replying, then said: "And the alternatives . . . ?"

"You will be obliterated, Mr. Gant – simply that. You will not be allowed to hand over the Mig-31 to the security services of your country. We could not allow that to happen."

"I understand. Well, let me tell you, sir – I *like* this plane. It fits me. I think I'll just keep it, for the moment . . ."

"I see. Mr. Gant, as you will be aware, I am not interested in the life of one rogue pilot with a poor health record – I was hoping to save the millions of roubles that have been poured into the development of this project. I see that you won't allow that to happen. Very well. You will not, of course, make it to wherever you are heading. Goodbye, Mr. Gant."

Gant flicked off the UHF and smiled to himself behind the anonymity of the flying mask. All he really had to worry about, he told himself – the one factor in the game which would cancel out all his advantages – was burning in the hangar at Bilyarsk: the second Firefox. If they could continue to trace him, and put that up against him . . . He shrugged.

The civilian flight from Moscow to Volgograd took him by surprise. Suddenly, there was a glint of sunlight off duralumin, and he was on top of it. The vapour trail, at that hour of the morning in those air conditions, had become visible very late. He had intended to cross the nose of the Tupolev, but there was the short contrail away to port. He switched off the auto-pilot.

He rolled the Firefox onto a wingtip, felt the pressure-suit perform its anti-G function, tightening then loosening round his thighs and upper body, and he pulled the aircraft round. The bright, hard glint of the Tupolev Tu-134 was almost directly ahead of him now. He had to give its flight-crew the opportunity to make a positive visual identification, and he had to be heading south as he crossed the nose.

He banked away to port, accelerating into a dive. He moved away from the airliner, losing sight of it. It registered as a bright green blip near the centre of the radar screen. When he had decided that he had slid across and behind it, and accelerated sufficiently to overtake it again, he straightened onto his original course, watching the blip attempt to regain its position to one side of the screen's centre line. He steadied the Firefox like an eager horse as the airliner moved into visual range to starboard, and he could see the contrail and the tiny glint of sunlight. He eased open the throttles, and the Firefox surged forward on what would appear a collision course to the pilot of the airliner.

There was never a moment when he considered he might have misjudged the distance, the heading. He rolled the plane onto a wingtip, and dived away from the oncoming Tupolev, now filling his starboard window. They would have seen him, and panicked, since their radar screens would be stupefyingly empty. The slim fuselage, and the huge engines of an unknown aircraft, suddenly appearing, would be imprinted on their minds by fear. He rolled the plane into a Mach descent, a thousand feet below the airliner, and listened to the chatter of the pilot over the Russian airline frequency, smiling in satisfaction.

The ground rushed at the Firefox as he screamed down from 15,000 feet. He trimmed slightly nose-up, then pulled out of the suicidal dive, levelling at little more than two hundred feet above the flat terrain of the steppes. The pressure on the G-suit was evident, uncomfortable, as he was thrust back into the pilot's couch. His vision blurred, reddened, and then cleared, and he read off the instruments before him.

He switched in the auto-pilot and fed in the next coordinates that he had memorised so exactly, and the inertial navigator took over, settling the Firefox onto its new course. He had been seen, and the sighting would confirm the UDF fix they must have. They would have confirmed the fact that he was heading south, beyond Volgograd, towards perhaps the border with Iran, and some kind of rendezvous in Israel, or over the Mediterranean. The search would fatten in that sector of the Soviet defence system. Now he had need of at least some fair proportion of the Firefox's speed capability. He opened the throttles and watched the rpm gauges swing over, and the Mach-counter which was his only intimation, other than his ground speed read-out, that he was travelling faster than the speed of sound. He was heading east, towards the mountain chain of the Urals, seeking the shelter, he hoped, of their eastern slopes before turning due north. He could not employ the real cruising capability of the plane. Nevertheless, it was with satisfaction that he watched the numbers slipping through the Mach-counter . . . Mach 1, 1.1, 1.2, 1.3, 1.4, 1.5 . . .

Just below him, the flat, empty, silent expanse of the steppes fled past, receded. The buoyancy he had felt, the clearness and pleasure of the first moments of the flight, returned to him. He was flying the greatest warplane ever built. It was a meeting of that aircraft, and the only human being good enough to fly it. His egotism, cold, unruffled, calculating, was fulfilled. A visual sighting at the height he was travelling became less and less likely. The supersonic footprint of his passage was narrow at two hundred feet, and there was little below him of human manufacture or human residence to record it. All he needed to avoid was the "Big Ears" sound-detection network. He had no idea of its capability, or location. In the Urals, however, the echoes set up by his passage would confuse any such equipment.

Suddenly, in a violent alteration of mood, he felt naked and his equilibrium seemed threatened. He was running for cover. Despite his better judgement, he pushed the throttles forward and watched, with satisfaction, as the Mach-counter reeled off the mounting numbers. Mach 1.8, 1.9, Mach 2, 2.1, 2.2 . . .

He knew he was wasting fuel, precious fuel, yet he did not pull back the throttles. He watched the numbers mount until he had reached Mach 2.6, and then he steadied the speed. Now, the terrain below him was merely a blur. He was a soundless cocoon, removed from the world. He began to feel safe as he switched in the TFR (Terrain Following Radar) which was his eyes and his reactions, operating as it did via the autopilot. He had not expected to need it until he entered the foothills of the Urals, but at his present speed of almost two thousand mph, he had to switch them in. He was no longer flying the aircraft. The Urals were only minutes away now and there, safe, he would regain control of the Firefox. His sense of well-being began to return. The sheer speed of the aircraft deadened the ends of nerves. The steadied figure of Mach 2.6 on the Mach-counter was brilliantly clear in his vision. At this speed, despite the draining-away of the irreplaceable kerosene, a visual sighting was as good as impossible. He was safe, running and safe . . .

"Give the alert to the contingency refuelling locations at once, would you?" Aubrey said blandly. He was speaking via a scrambler to Air Commodore Latchford at Strike Command, High Wycombe. He had, that moment, received a report from Latchford which indicated a definite lift-off by Gant from Bilyarsk. The AEWR (Airborne Early Warning Radar) had recorded signs of a staggered sector scramble amongst border squadrons of the Red Air Force and this, in conjunction with radio- and code-monitoring which had shown signs of furious code-communication between sections of the Red Air Force, and between the First Secretary and the Admiral of the Red Banner Northern Fleet, as well as Russian ships in the Mediterranean – all of this evidence amounted to a sighting of Gant lifting clear of the runway at Bilyarsk.

Latchford affirmed an immediate alert for both contingency refuelling points to begin transmission of the homing-signal which operated on the very special frequency of Gant's transistor-innards which would lead him home.

"Mother Two and Mother Three will go on alert now," the Air Commodore said. "You'll take care of Mother One yourself – at least, I presume you will, since I have no idea where to find her?" There was a chuckle at the other end of the line. Latchford had had to know about the two contingency refuelling points, but had been kept in the dark concerning the one Gant was expected to use. Aubrey sensed a communion of tension, of suppressed excitement.

"Yes, Captain Curtin will take care of Mother One," Aubrey assured him, and then added: "Thank you, Air Commodore – your news comes, if I may say, like a ray of pure sunshine. Many thanks." He listened to Latchford's throaty chuckle for a moment, seeming to

142

draw comfort from the sound, and then replaced the receiver.

Buckholz, elbows on his desk, was watching him intently as he looked up. "They confirm? All that activity isn't just because they caught our boy?" he enquired.

Aubrey shook his head. "No, my dear Buckholz," Aubrey said blandly. "AEW Radar confirms the predicted air activity on the part of the Red Air Force, northern and southern borders – Gant is in the air."

Buckholz breathed deeply, his breath exhaling loudly. He turned to Anders, almost asleep next to him, and grinned with the pure self-satisfaction of a child.

"Thank God," he whispered.

There was a silence, broken by Curtin's creaking descent from the step-ladder. When he regained the floor, he said to Aubrey: "I didn't reckon on doing the office-boy's job when I volunteered for this!" He grinned as he said it. "You want me to tell Washington to alert Mother One, Mr. Aubrey?"

Aubrey nodded. "Yes, my boy – do that now, would you? If the weather's still holding, that is."

Curtin walked back to the map, picked up a pointer and tapped at a satellite weather-photograph pinned high on the wall. "That's the latest – two a.m., your time. All clear."

"And the track of Mother One?"

"Constant – moving slowly south, in an area of loosened pack. Temperature low enough. She's holding."

"Good. Then put through your call, Captain. Mother One it is."

Before Curtin could place the call, they were startled by the chatter of a teletype from the Code Room. Aubrey watched Shelley as the younger man ripped the sheet of flimsy from the machine.

"Communications picked this up only minutes ago," he said, a slight smile on his tired face. "Plain language. Picked up by the operator listening in on the Soviet airline frequency."

"Ah," Aubrey remarked. "And . . .?"

"He was spotted north-west of Volgograd – almost tore the nose off the airliner, before they lost sight of him. The pilot was screaming his head off, before someone told him to keep quiet!"

"Good."

Aubrey inspected the sheet of paper, and then offered it to Buckholz who had crossed to perch on the table.

Buckholz stared at it, as if needing to be convinced, and then said: "Good. Damn good." He looked into Aubrey's face, and added: "So far, so good?"

"I agree, my dear Buckholz. Hopefully, the Russians are now scrambling everything, including the mess bar, to the south of Gant." He rubbed his chin, and said: "I still worry about 'Big Ears', you know. Gant must be making a frightful amount of noise, heading east to the Urals."

"It is not, my dear Kutuzov, a war situation," the First Secretary said, seated in his chair before the round table. His eyes disregarded the map of European Russia, from the Polish border to the Urals, from the Arctic Ocean to the Black Sea, despite its glowing squares of colour, despite the winking strings of tiny lights that signalled the interceptor stations with fighters in the air, despite the other lights forming links in the glowing chain which signalled the missile sites on full war alert. Kutuzov seemed, on the other side of the table, unable to remove his fixed stare from the hypnotic projection before him. Reluctantly, it seemed, he lifted his eyes, and gazed at the First Secretary.

"You have considered that this might be some kind of supreme bluff by the Americans, First Secretary. To distract us from looking northward, while this single aircraft attempts to escape to the south." It was not a question. Marshal Kutuzov was evidently serious in his supposition.

The First Secretary sighed and said: "No, Kutuzov. This is a CIA venture – with the backing of the office of the President, and the Pentagon, no doubt." His palms were raised from the desk to prevent interruption. "But it is no more than a wildcat affair. Elaborate, yes. Far-sighted, yes. Well-planned and executed, yes. All of those things. But it is not war! No. The CIA will have arranged a refuelling point for this madman, somewhere – our computers will, no doubt, tell us the most likely places. But, if we shoot down the Mig-31, and even if we destroy the refuelling-vehicle, the Americans will act dumb, as they say. They will do nothing. And that – all of you . . ." His voice was suddenly raised, so that the background chatter of the Command Centre stilled, and all eyes turned to him. "All of you understand this. If we can destroy, or recover, the aircraft, then we will hear no more of the matter."

"You are sure?" Kutuzov said. His face expressed a desire to be convinced. He had been staring at the edge of a void from the moment the idea had occurred to him, that he was witnessing the opening move in the end-game for the world.

"I am – certain. The Americans, and the British, both want this aircraft, because they are aware of its potential. They both have made massive cuts in their defence budgets during the past few years, especially in the area of development and research. Therefore, despite the *free gift* of the Mig-25 some years ago, they have, as we know, nothing on the drawing-board remotely capable of matching the Mig-31."

He turned a suddenly baleful glare upon Andropov, standing at his shoulder. "Chairman Andropov — the security for this project was — unforgiveable!"

Andropov nodded slowly. The strip-lighting of the room glinted from his spectacles. Vladimirov, standing near Kutuzov, sensed the man's anger. Also, he understood the suppressed anger of the First Secretary which had prompted the icy remark.

"Yes — unfortunately, First Secretary." He looked across at the two military men on the other side of the table. "I remember that Marshall Kutuzov and General Vladimirov both wished the security to be strengthened, after the initial trials." He smiled, coldly. "It would appear they were right."

"The Americans knew far too much," Kutuzov growled, in a voice hardly more than a throaty whisper.

The First Secretary raised his hand. He realised that he had initiated yet another internecine squabble between the military and the KGB.

"Leave it at that," he said levelly. "It will be examined thoroughly. It would appear, from the Chairman's initial enquiries, that Colonel Kontarsky gambled — and failed." Behind the First Secretary, Andropov nodded slowly, then looked across the table.

Neither Kutuzov nor Vladimirov said anything. Kontarsky had played a lone hand. He had attempted to use the security of the Bilyarsk project to enhance his promotion, and his reputation. It had happened before. The KGB officer at the head of KGB observation-security in the Middle East, in 1967, had held back information vital to the Kremlin and to the Kremlin's satellite, Egypt, concerning the Israeli preparations for war, until they had taken him by surprise. Department V of the KGB, the assassination department, had liquidated him soon afterwards. Kontarsky would not survive his failure.

There was a knock at the door. The First Secretary's KGB bodyguard opened it and accepted the sheaf of papers that were handed to him by someone in a white coat. Then the door was closed.

"Thank you," the First Secretary said. He studied the papers for a moment, then looked up, and passed them to Kutuzov. "Tell me what they mean."

The old Marshal studied them intently, after plucking a pair of battered, wire-rimmed spectacles from the breast-pocket of his tunic. The background chatter of the code and communications operators was hardly sufficient to drown the noise of the papers as he shuffled through them. When he had finished, he pulled his glasses from his face, and handed the papers to Vladimirov.

Coughing, he said: "It is a damage report on the second Mig, First Secretary, as you are aware. It would appear that the dissidents failed to put the aircraft out of commission."

It suddenly became clear to Vladimirov, looking across the table to the First Secretary and Andropov, that the War Command Centre was a venue of desperation. To those two pre-eminently powerful men, who did not understand the air or aircraft, this was some kind of panacea; this was what they were hoping for, what they had been anticipating with an almost virginal excitement. They truly believed that, if they could only put up the second prototype, they would be able to bring down the running American. He dismissed the beginnings of a smile from his face.

"How soon – how soon can it be ready to fly – armed?" the First Secretary asked, his voice unsettled with excitement.

"Perhaps an hour, perhaps less," Vladimirov put in, consulting the papers in his hand. "It was, of course in a condition of flight readiness as a back-up to the PP1, but it has to be cleared of foam, pre-flighted and armed, First Secretary."

"But we need to know where he is, *exactly*!" growled Kutuzov in his familiar whisper. Vladimirov realised that his superior was less alive to the political niceties of the atmosphere in the War Command Centre. All that the First Secretary wanted was to get the second plane airborne. He would not welcome reminders of the practical difficulties of a seek and destroy mission for the aircraft.

"I *know* that, Kutuzov!" the First Secretary snapped, silencing the old Marshal. He looked round the walls of the room, as if the bent backs of the operators would inspire him, supply him with the answers he required.

Vladimirov sensed his desperation beneath the icy calm, beneath the strength of the man's personality. For him, the staggered sector scramble provided the only hope, slim though it was. Something nagged at the back of his mind, something he had first thought of in the early years of the Mig-31 project, something that he had raised as a possible objection to the anti-radar system that had been developed, and thrust upon the Bilyarsk development. It had been a cool voice, a sprinkling of water on a burning enthusiasm.

Vladimirov was, by nature, a cool, rational man, a strategist. As O.C. "Wolfpack", commandant of the Russian interceptor force, he had found his fulfilment as a military man. He, with Kutuzov, had pressed for the delay in defence spending that would ensure the rapid production of hundreds of Mig-31s, to replace the Foxbats that at present formed the strongest card in the Russian suit. The thought-guided weapons-system developed for the aircraft was, he

146

recognised, its real trump, together with its huge range and frightening speed. It would put the Red Air Force into a different league, beyond the present or immediately future capabilities of the RAF and the USAF.

He wandered away from the tense, electric atmosphere surrounding the circular table in the middle of the War Command Centre, and listened with half an ear to the flow of decoded reports issuing from the teams of operators. Everything was being recorded, ready for instant playback if there was need to consult the reports.

The sighting north-west of Volgograd filled him with suspicion. A former ace, he suspected the obvious. He had been forced to respect Gant, the American pilot. Studying the KGB file on him, transmitted by wire-print from the Centre in Moscow, he appreciated the selection of the man by the CIA. Gant was a rogue pilot, a Vietnam ace. Vladimirov hoped that, had the roles been reversed, he would have had the foresight and the daring to select such a man.

He felt he knew Gant, felt the *need* of the man to steal the Mig, to prove it could be done. Gant would want to complete the mission. He would be determined to take the Mig home.

From the pilot's report, it had been made to appear that the American had been surprised by the sudden appearance of the airliner to starboard of him, right on a collision course. Vladimirov knew that Gant's radar would have warned him of the airliner's presence in plenty of time to avoid such a sighting. And Gant was a fine pilot, perhaps the best if his record told no lies. Even in an unfamiliar aircraft, he would not have made such an error of airmanship. Vladimirov was sure that a simulator had been built at Langley, Virginia, to assist Gant in his training. He mentally cursed Kontarsky who, in the harsh glare of failure, appeared a gross fool. A great deal of information must have passed to the Americans over the past years, a great deal.

He dismissed Gant from his mind. To think of him was to dwell on the unchangeable past. No, there was something more important, something that might circumvent Gant's supreme advantage of the radar immunity of the Mig-31. What the devil was it?

He rubbed at his chin as he walked, a continuous, harsh motion of the hand. The voice of an operator repeating a communication struck him clearly. The words slid across his consciousness, without resonating.

"Positive sound-trace, installation at Orsk . . ." the voice at his side was saying. He was unaware of the stillness suddenly around him, unaware that the operator had turned to look up at him. No, he thought, it had nothing to do with sound. It was – was . . . Then he had it, elusive, yet brilliantly clear, even as his mind registered

147

the silence around him and he saw the expectant face of the radio-operator from the corner of his eye.

He had said clearly, a lone voice amid the atmosphere of military and political euphoria, that radar-immunity by and of itself did not render any aircraft, however advanced, completely safe from detection. Infra-red detection equipment, designed not to bounce a signal off a solid object but to detect heat-sources on the ground or in the air, might be used to detect the presence of an aircraft immune to radar. The heat emission from a jet engine would show up on an infra-red screen as an orange blip. It would be a poor substitute in tracking and fixing a target, but it would, even without its limitations, cancel some of the total advantage of the Mig-31's anti-radar system. It might prove sufficiently accurate for heat-seeking missiles to be launched in the direction of the prospective target. They would then, with their own sensors, seek out the heat-source that would have shown up on the infra-red screens on the ground. That was it! He looked at his hand in front of his face, and saw that it was quivering.

It was the answer. His staggered sector scramble did not have to rely upon the faint possibility of a clear visual sighting. Every fighter could train its infra-red weapons-aiming system ahead of the plane, in a cone. Anything with a jet engine passing through that cone, in whatever atmospheric conditions, at whatever altitude, would show up as a bright orange heat-spot on the pilot's infra-red detection screen.

He saw the face of the operator, holding one hand to his head like a man with toothache, saw the smile of puzzlement on the face.

"Yes?" he said. "What did you say?"

"General — there has been an unidentified sound-trace from a low-flying aircraft travelling at more than Mach 2, picked up on the mobile unit west of Orsk."

"Where is Orsk?" Vladimirov snapped, the excitement in the young face in front of him seeming to become infectious. Without waiting for an answer, the General turned to the man at the map-console, who computed the patterns and details to be fed onto the projection on the table. "Orsk! Blow up that region for me." He remembered. "It's at the southern tip of the Urals . . ."

He slapped his hand against his forehead, not noticing the silence of the entire War Command Centre as the truth of his suspicions came home to him. Gant had *deliberately* been sighted travelling south!

"What is the matter, General Vladimirov?" he heard the First Secretary ask. Unconsciously, he waved his hand dismissively in the direction of the voice.

148

"Get me a confirmation of that report – quickly!" he snapped. "Call it out to me."

Swiftly, he crossed to the map beneath the screen of the table, oblivious to the rising anger displayed on the face of the First Secretary. Eagerly, he studied the enlargement of the southern tip of the Urals mountain chain, realised that the area was too small and said: "Replace this – give me a projection of the Urals, and of as much to the north and south as you can – now."

His fingers tapped at the table edges as he waited. The map dissolved, and then re-formed. The Urals spread like a livid scar down the centre of the projection. To the south was the brown, dusty-coloured expanse of Iran, and to the north the deepening blue of the Barents Sea and the Arctic Ocean. Still ignoring the First Secretary, who sat at the table like a carved figure, Vladimirov traced his finger across the map, first southwards, towards the Middle East and the Mediterranean; then, more slowly and thoughtfully, the slender, long-nailed finger tracked northward across the map, up the chain of the Urals. It paused over Novaya Zemlya, then pushed on north, then curved in an arc to the north-west into the Arctic Ocean.

When he looked up, it was only to hear the radio-operator who had informed him of the sound trace, saying: "Trace confirmed, sir. Aircraft, which refused to answer a demand for identification, heading north-east into the mountains. They lost the trace within thirty seconds, but they confirm heading and speed."

Vladimirov realised that Gant had made his first mistake, had made what might be promoted into a fatal error. He had ignored the demand for identification, and that made him suspicious. Also, he was travelling far too fast, running for shelter . . . his fuel could not last as long as he must have hoped at first, at that speed. He studied the map again, realising that Gant was seeking the shelter, from visual and sound detection, of the eastern foothills of the Urals.

Which could only mean . . . yes, he realised with a mounting excitement, could only mean that his refuelling point lay to the north of the Soviet Union, in the Barents Sea, or above it. He looked up.

The First Secretary had not moved. "Well?" he said softly.

"If you will look at the map, First Secretary," Vladimirov said, sensing Kutuzov at his shoulder, "I will try to explain my deductions." Swiftly, he outlined Gant's probable course. When he had finished, he added: "We can track him, despite his radar-immunity, First Secretary."

There was a silence and then Andropov, arms folded across his

149

chest and standing behind the First Secretary, said in a soft, ironical voice: "How?"

Vladimirov explained, as simply as he could, the manner in which the infra-red weapons-aiming system could be used as a directional search-beam. Kutuzov clapped him on the shoulder, and Vladimirov sensed the quiver of excitement in the old man's frame. More distantly, he sensed that he had somehow sealed the succession, that he would be the next Marshal of the Air Force. The prospect did not affect him. At that moment, he was concerned only with the elimination of Gant as a military threat.

"Good – that is good, General Vladimirov," the First Secretary said. "You agree, Mihail Ilyich?" Kutuzov nodded. "This needs no mechanical adjustment?" Vladimirov shook his head.

"No – merely a coded instruction to that effect from you, or from Marshal Kutuzov."

The First Secretary nodded. "What, then, do you suggest, Vladimirov?"

"You must alert units of the Red Banner Northern Fleet, First Secretary. They must begin looking for a surface, or subsurface . . ." He paused. No, it had to be a surface craft, and even that was unlikely. "More probably, an aircraft, waiting to refuel the Mig in mid-air, First Secretary." The Soviet leader nodded. "Then, we must put up 'Wolfpack' squadrons nearest to our northern coastline, to seek out the mother-plane." He glanced round into Kutuzov's keen eyes. The old man nodded. "And, we alert *all* missile sites along the First Firechain to expect Gant. They, too, must use their infra-red aiming-systems to search for him, in concert with the 'Wolfpack' units."

Suddenly, his finger stabbed at the map, almost immediately in front of the First Secretary. "There," he said. "Just there. If he follows the Urals to their northernmost point, then he will use the Gulf of Ob, or the gulf to the west of the Yamal Peninsula as a visual sighting, before altering course for his rendezvous with the mother-aircraft. As you can see, First Secretary, there are two fixed units in the First Firechain within range, as well as the mobile link between them, and our 'Wolfpack' squadrons based on the peninsula." He looked up, and there was a smile on his face. "It will take only minutes to organise, First Secretary – and the American will walk into the most powerful trap ever sprung." He was still smiling when he said: "Will you give permission for any Soviet aircraft who gains a visual sighting to act as a target for the missiles – if it becomes necessary?"

Vladimirov heard Kutuzov's indrawn breath, but kept his eyes on the First Secretary. In the man's grey, flinty eyes he could see the succession confirmed. This time, it moved him with a distinct, though momentary, pleasure. The First Secretary merely nodded. "Of course," he said.

"Very well, First Secretary – then Gant is dead."

The journey through the Urals had taken Gant little more than two hours, since in covering the sixteen or more hundred miles from Orsk to Vorkuta through the eastern foothills, he had never exceeded six hundred knots, keeping his speed sub-sonic in order to conserve the fuel he now wished he had not burned in his panic-dash to the cover of the mountains. The lower speed would also stop his presence being betrayed by a supersonic footprint across the sparsely-populated ground below. The foothills had been wreathed in mist, which made visual detection almost impossible, either from the ground or from the air.

Knowledge concerning military installations in the Urals chain was sketchy. Buckholz and Aubrey had been able to provide him with very little in the way of fact. It had been assumed, dubiously, that the eastern slopes of the mountain chain would be the less heavily armed and surveyed. Once he had taken a visual sighting on Orsk, to obtain a bearing, he had fed the coordinates of his northward flight into the inertial navigator, and slotted the aircraft into its flight-path. Then he had again switched in the TFR and the auto-pilot, and passed like a ghost into a grey world of terrain-hugging mist, chill to the eye, featureless as the moon, or the landscape of his memory.

He had feared a return of the dream or, at least, of some of the physical symptoms of the hysterical paralysis – even the nausea. Yet, it had not happened. It was as though he had passed from shadow into light, as if the person he had been before the take-off had been shed like skin. He spent no time in marvelling at his new, recovered integrity of mind, calmness of thought. It wasn't unfamiliar to him. Even in Vietnam, towards the end, he had been able to fly almost perfectly, leaving behind him, like the uniform in his locker, the wreck of an individual sliding towards the edge.

His ECM instrument for picking up radar-emissions from the terrain below had recorded nothing since the beginning of his flight through the mountains. He had moved in a world cut off, entirely separate, the kind of isolation he had heard NASA men talk about after orbiting the earth in one of the Skylabs, or returning from testing the newest re-entry vehicles. Once he had met Collins, one of the lunar astronauts. He had said the same. In his own way, Gant had always felt that removed when his aircraft was on auto-pilot. There was nothing, except a cabin, pressurised, stable, warm – and the human multitude and their planet fled by formlessly as the mist through which he had travelled. That utter isolation was something he had never rid himself of on the ground, not even in violent drinking-jags, or in the relief of Saigon prostitutes. And the reason he sought that lonely superiority of the skies was because the ground had never offered him more than an inferior copy of the same empty isolation.

It was just after nine, and the mist was clearing at his height, shredding away from the cockpit, so that sunlight glanced from the perspex, and the faded blue of the morning sky was revealed. On his present heading, he knew he would pass over the Gulf of Kara, the sharp intrusion of the Kara Sea to the west of the Yamal Peninsula within minutes, at this present speed. With the cross-check of a visual bearing on the neck of the gulf, he would be able to feed in the next set of coordinates to the inertial navigator.

He looked ahead. Visibility was not good. There was no sign of water, only the hazy, grey absence of a horizon. He knew he would have to drop down as low as he could, risking visual sighting from the ground, risking the gauntlet of the Firechain which looped across this northern coast. Nevertheless, he had to do it.

The last northern strand of the mountains, limping towards the sea, neared again as he changed altitude, sliding down towards the pockets of mist not yet dispersed by the strengthening sun. He saw the small town of Vorkuta away to port, and knew that his heading was correct and that the sea lay only minutes ahead of him.

Suddenly then, the edge of his radar screen showed the presence of an aircraft, higher and away to starboard; big, probably a Badger long-range reconnaissance plane no doubt returning from a routine patrol out over the Kara Sea and the Arctic Ocean.

Moments passed in which he seemed content just with the knowledge that he was closing on the Badger, judging he would pass well behind it. He assumed that, with a minimum of luck, most of the electronic detection equipment on board the Badger would be shut down that close to its home base. Then, almost with disbelief, three bright orange spots registered on the screen, glowing, climbing, nearing. An infra-red source. Someone on the ground had loosed a bracket of missiles from a Firechain station.

They knew where he was. He realised this, his mind crying out at the jolt its apparent immunity from attack and detection had been given, the sudden draining of confidence.

He could not believe it. The missiles had to be heat-seeking, homing on the exhaust gases of the sky's hottest point. Somehow he was visible to them. And he knew how. The Firechain station had to be using its infra-red equipment to search for the imprint of his exhaust. He was invisible on radar; on an infra-red screen, he would be revealed as a point of orange light. Radar immunity of something which yet gave off hot exhaust gases – it would have to be him. They would have been told that much on the ground. The removing of his immunity stunned him. He watched in paralysed fascination as the cluster of three glowing orange spots on his own screen enlarged as the missiles closed on the Firefox.

SEVEN:

Search and Destroy

Contact time, seven seconds. The moment of Gant's stunned failure to respond passed. He pulled his gaze from the three orange spots on the screen. Also registering on the screen was the bright green blip of the Badger, now no more than a few short miles away and moving away below him now and to port. The single screen which constituted the detection "eye" of the Firefox's electronics was built to register infra-red emissions of heat as orange spots, while radar images appeared as green blips. The missiles behind him were in the lower half of the screen, while the Badger ahead was in the upper half. He was still heading towards it, and it lay along the central ranging bar of the screen.

The Badger was the key to his safety, he realised. Here was a way he could misdirect the seeking missiles. He had to create a hotter spot than his own engines in the sky on to which they would home. He had to destroy the Badger, let it burn like a bonfire.

He pulled the Firefox onto a collision course with the Russian plane. He ignored, with every effort his mind could make, the three orange blips closing towards the centre of the screen. Contact time, five seconds. He pushed open the throttles; he had to be closer to the Badger before he loosed one of his own missiles. The anti-G suit tightened round him, then relaxed as it countered the increased pressure of his speed and dive. The three orange blips slipped across his screen, then centred again as they followed him. The green spot of the Badger enlarged. Gant flicked the "Weapon Arming" switch on the console to his left. His thumb then flicked the switches to activate the thought-trigger and -guidance systems. These switches safeguarded against the inadvertent firing and guiding of the weapons-system at any time. Gant could guide his missiles visually by direct observations of missile and target, or on the screen. What he saw with his eyes, and required the missile to perform, was converted in the brain into electrical impulses, detected by the electrodes in his helmet, and fed into the weapons-system which transmitted a steering signal to the missile. As the distance-to-target read-out indicated the optimum moment for a hit, the thought-guided system automatically launched one of the missiles under the wing. The missile left its bracket, then pulled up and away from the track he had been following. For a moment, light flicked at the corner of his eye as he caught the firing of its motor.

Three seconds to contact time. He began to hope. He saw the outline of the Badger clearly for a moment, directly ahead of him, an enlarging, slim grey shape. He pulled the Firefox into a sudden turn to the right, away as acutely as possible from the Badger. Two seconds. On the screen the orange spot almost seemed to be merging with, overflying, the single green blip.

The Badger was in the centre of the screen: it was like a flower opening, a huge flower, orange, the hottest part of the sky as his own missile detonated. Contact time, zero seconds. The flower bloomed even brighter, just below the centre of the screen as he left the maelstrom behind – full bloom as the missile detonated amid the inferno of the Badger's destruction.

He realised he was sweating freely inside the pressure-suit, and he felt a wave of relief, sharp as nausea, pass through him. Below him on the ground, the infra-red screens which had picked him up would now be confused, filled with light from the massive detonation. When it cleared, he would be out of range. He hoped they would draw the conclusion that he had himself perished in the explosion.

He checked his speed. Just below seven hundred mph. He could not go supersonic as he neared the coast. Too many trained ears, listening for the supersonic wake of his passage.

Now that he had survived, he began to take stock of the Firefox. The thought-guided weapons-system worked, as he had been certain it would. It had been Baranovich's project and, despite the fact that it was difficult to recall his face and the sound of his voice, as though a gulf of time separated them, there had been an unconscious, deep assurance that had been associated with the Russian Jew. He had seen only the tip of the iceberg. He had not needed to react at the speed of thought, but had had to make a conscious decision. But, when he had formed the thought, regarding the port wingtip missile, the advanced Anab-type of AAM, it had fired. All he had felt was the slight roll as the missile had detached itself.

He glanced again at the TFR. He was crossing the coastal strip. The mist that had clung to the coastal mountains had now become what he guessed must be a sea-fog – light, threatening to dissipate, but concealing. Best of all, it provided a sound-muffler, dispersing the noise of his engines so that a sound-trace such as the Russians were known to possess would be confused by echoes.

Then he saw the coast as an uneven line across the TFR screen. The narrow neck of sea formed the furthest inland penetration of the Gulf of Kara. His memory supplied the next set of coordinates as the Firefox passed out over the water, even as he pushed the nose down and lost more height, keeping within the slim belt of fog which slipped past the cabin, grey and formless, removing him from the world. The read-out supplied him with the required heading, and he obeyed the inertial navigator, turning onto the heading that would take him towards the twin islands of Novaya Zemlya, north-west of his present position.

He registered that the altimeter stated two hundred feet, checked the TFR, and eased back the throttles. The engine revolutions dropped, and he saw it register on the airspeed indicator. He levelled the aircraft, keeping it at a steady height of two hundred feet, and still eased back the throttles. While in the fog, he had the opportunity to conserve fuel, and thus make less engine noise. If he was heard, he wanted to sound as little like a fleeing thief as possible, and as much like an authorised search-plane as he could. At 250 mph, he steadied.

He reached up and his hand closed upon the transistor radio's innards, the special device developed for him at Farnborough, solely for the task which he now hoped it would perform. It was a homer pick-up, working on an incredibly complex pre-set pattern, searching for a beacon set on the same alternating pattern of signal frequencies. The signal remained on one frequency only long enough to be dismissed by anyone picking it up as static, or as unimportant. Gant could not tell, but the machine could, at what point it entered the sequence when switched on. The device had to be as complicated as it was because voice communication of any kind, however brief or cryptic, was open to being monitored by the Russians. He flicked the switch on the face of the apparently purposeless piece of hardware. Nothing, but at that moment he was unsurprised.

He knew the machine was searching the frequency band for a signal, and that there was a limit to its range when operational – yet he began to worry at the moment his hand flipped the switch. Only when the machine was functioning did he become truly aware of how much he depended upon it. Unless he picked up the signal transmitted by the refuelling craft, and unless his receiver co-ordinated with the transmitter to make the homing signal a continuous directional impulse, then he was lost, and he would run out of fuel somewhere over the Arctic Ocean and die.

The "Deaf-Aid", as Aubrey had called it with one of the bastard's sardonic smiles, was required because no one, not even Buckholz, with Baranovich's inside knowledge, could be certain that the Russians might not be able to jam every transmitter and receiver aboard the Firefox when it was in the air – in which case Gant would never find the fuel he needed. Even if the Soviets could only track every transmitter and receiver, then Gant would lead them straight to "Mother".

And, Gant thought, noticing that the sea fog was thinning, and that the oppressive greyness, the uniformity, of his visual world was lightening, they had not told him where to find "Mother", just in case he got caught. What he himself did not know, lunatic though the logic was, he could not tell anyone, whatever they did to him.

He looked at the fuel-gauges. Less than a quarter full. He had no idea how far he had to go. If, and when, he picked up the signal, he would know he was no more than three hundred miles away from the refuel point. The Farnborough gimmick remained silent.

He had switched in the auto-pilot, coupled with the TFR. The longest part of his journey was beginning, the part of the journey to stretch the nerves, to test him as no other part of his mission had done – flying by faith, and a single box of tricks never operationally tested before. Guinea-pig. Pigeon. That was what he was.

Gant was an electronic pilot. He had relied on instruments all his flying life. Yet he had never depended on just one, one totally detached from his flying skill, one totally unaffected by anything he could do as the plane's pilot.

The featureless contours of the sea flowed across the TFR screen, endless, empty of vessels. He pushed up the plane's nose, rising above the still thinning fog, into the brief glare of sunlight and an impression of blue sky at four hundred feet. Nothing. He ducked the Firefox back into the mist. All his instruments told him that Novaya Zemlya was too far ahead to register – yet, he had wanted the comfort of a visual check, as if his contemplation of his dependence upon a single piece of electronic hardware had made him revert to an earlier age of flying.

He looked again at the fuel-gauges. The refuelling point would be hundreds of miles beyond the Russian coastline, had to be, for safety. Less than a quarter full, the huge wing tanks, the skin of the fuselage itself that acted as a fuel tank.

Gant had no relish for the equation of fuel against distance, and again cursed his panic-dash for the Urals. What had given him a sense of escape then, of life, might well have killed him.

"What is the matter, General Vladimirov?" the First Secretary asked conversationally. Vladimirov stopped in mid-stride and turned to face the Soviet leader. "You must learn to accept success with more aplomb, my dear Vladimirov!" The First Secretary laughed.

Vladimirov smiled a wintry smile, and said: "I wish I could be certain, First Secretary – much as I fear my mood must displease you, I am *not* certain . . ."

"You're not happy that we have lost the Mig-31?"

"No. I'm not happy that we *have* lost it – I wonder whether we could kill this man Gant quite so easily."

"But it was your plan we followed, Vladimirov – you have doubts about it now?" Andropov asked from behind the First Secretary, a thin smile on his lips.

"I never was certain of its success, Chairman," Vladimirov replied.

"Come," the First Secretary said softly. "What would make you happy, Vladimirov? I am in a generous mood." The man smiled, broadly, beatifically.

"To continue, and intensify, the search for Gant." Vladimirov's tone was blunt, direct.

"Why?"

"Because – *if* he's alive, our self-congratulation might be just the help he needs. Find the refuelling aircraft, or ship, or whatever it is, that must be waiting for him."

The First Secretary seemed to be looking into Vladimirov's mind as he debated the argument. After a long silence, he looked not at Vladimirov with his refocused gaze, but at Kutuzov.

"Well, Mihail Ilyich – what do you say?"

Kutuzov, his throat apparently rusty with disuse, said: "I would agree to every precaution being taken, First Secretary."

"Very well." The First Secretary's bonhomie had disappeared, and he seemed displeased that the euphoric mood of the room that had existed since the report from Firechain One-24 had been dispelled. He was brusque, efficient, cold. "What do you need, apart from the *massive* forces you have already called upon . . .?" There was an almost sinister emphasis on the word, and he left the sentence hanging uncomfortably in the air.

"Give me the Barents Sea map, and bleed in current naval dispositions in the area, together with trawler activity and Elint vessels," Vladimirov called over his shoulder, standing himself squarely in front of the circular table, his hand plucking at his chin thoughtfully. The projection of the northern coastline of the USSR faded, taking with it the pricks of light that had been the Firechain stations and the "Wolfpack" bases, and was replaced by a projection of the Barents Sea.

Vladimirov waited, as the map operator punched out his demands on the computer-console. Slowly, one by one, like stars winking in as dusk fell, lights began to appear on the map, the stations of ships in the Barents Sea and the southern Arctic Ocean. Vladimirov stared at them for a long time in silence. "Where is the print-out?" he asked after a while. The map operator detached himself from his console, and handed Vladimirov a printed sheet of flimsy which registered the identification and exact last reported position and course of each of the dots on the projection glowing on the table. Vladimirov studied the sheet, glancing occasionally at the map.

North of Koluyev Island and west of Novaya Zemlya, the clustered dots of a trawler-fleet registered in white. The neutral colour signified their non-military purpose. They were a large and genuine fishing fleet. However, slightly apart from the close cluster were two deep-blue dots, which signified Elint vessels, spy trawlers, overfitted with the latest and most powerful aerial, surface and sub-surface detection equipment. They flanked the fishing fleet like sheepdogs but, as Vladimirov knew, their interest lay elsewhere. At that moment, they would be sweeping the skies with infra-red detectors, checking traces with the search-pattern they would have received from the "Wolfpack" sector commander the coast of whose area they were sailing. It was early in the year for Elint vessels to be operating in the Barents Sea, but Deputy Defence Minister, Admiral of the Soviet Fleet Gorshkov, liked his spy ships in action as soon in the Arctic year as was feasible. Because of the southward drift of the ice in the Arctic spring, at the moment they did little more than supplement the coastal radars.

Vladimirov's eye wandered north across the projection of the Barents Sea, picking up the scarlet dot of a naval vessel. From the list in front of him, he knew it was the helicopter and missile cruiser, "Moskva" class, the *Riga*, and the pride of the Red Banner Northern Fleet: 18,000 tons displacement, armed with two surface-to-air missile-launchers, and two surface or anti-submarine launchers, four sixty-millimetre guns, mortars, four torpedo-tubes, and four hunter-killer helicopters of the Kamov Ka-25 type. She was proceeding at that moment on an easterly course, at the express command of the First Secretary, through Gorshkov in Leningrad, which would, within little more than an hour, bring her close to Novaya Zemlya.

Elsewhere on the living map, Vladimirov registered the presence of two missile-destroyers, smaller, less powerfully armed replicas of the missile cruiser, without that ship's complement of helicopters. One of them was well to the north of Novaya Zemlya, near Franz Josef Land on the edge of the permanent ice-sheet, and the other was steaming rapidly south and east from the Spitzbergen area. The majority

159

of the Red Banner Fleet's surface vessels were in Kronstadt, the huge island naval base in the estuary of the Neva, near Leningrad; it was too early for operations, too early for exercises, in the Barents Sea.

There were, however, Vladimirov saw with some relief, a number of yellow dots glowing on the surface of the map, signifying the presence of Soviet submarines. He glanced down at the list, identifying the types available to him, mentally recalling their armament and their search-capability. Soviet naval policy in the Barents Sea was to keep the surface vessels in dock during the bitter winter months and during the early spring onslaught of the southward drift of the impermanent pack-ice, and to use a single weapon in the arsenal of the Red Banner Fleet for patrol duties – the huge submarine fleet at the disposal of the Kremlin and the Admiral of the Soviet Fleet. The policy explained why the Soviet Union had concentrated for so long, and so successfully, on the development of the Soviet submarine fleet, and why they had even returned to the commissioning of new, cheaper, conventional diesel-powered submarines, instead of an exclusive concentration, as had been U.S. policy, on the hideously expensive nuclear subs.

He ignored, for the moment, the three nuclear-powered "V" type anti-submarine subs, and the two ballistic-missile subs returning to Kronstadt after their routine strike-patrol along the eastern sea-board of the United States. They would be of no use to him. What he required were submarines with the requisite search-capability for spotting an aircraft, and for bringing it down.

"What are the reports of the search for wreckage of the plane?" he asked aloud at last, tired suddenly of the lights on the map. It was impossible for Gant to escape, and yet . . . he should already be dead.

"Nothing so far, sir – air-reconnaissance reports no indications of wreckage other than that of the Badger . . . the ground search parties have not yet arrived at the site of the crash."

"Give me a report on the search for the refuelling-craft," Vladimirov said in the wake of the report.

A second voice sang out: "Negative, sir. No unidentified surface vessels or aircraft in the area the computer predicts to be the limit of the Mig's flight."

Vladimirov looked angry, and puzzled. It was what he wanted to hear, from one point of view. No planes or ships of the West anywhere near the area. It was, frankly, impossible. There *had* to be a refuelling-point. But the nearest neutral or friendly territory had to be somewhere in Scandinavia. It was, of course, possible to suppose that Gant was scheduled to make another alteration of course, to head west and follow the Russian coastline to the North Cape, or Finnish Lapland . . .

160

He did not believe it, even though he had taken the necessary precautions already. He believed that the CIA and the British SIS would not have been able to persuade any of the Scandinavian governments to risk what the landing of the Mig on their territory would mean, in their delicate relations with the Soviet Union on their doorsteps. No, the refuelling had to be out at sea, or at low altitude somehow. It could not be a carrier, there wasn't one in the area, not remotely in the area. Apart from which, the Mig-31 was not equipped for a deck landing. But could the base be an American weather-station on the permanent ice-sheet of the Pole?

Vladimirov disliked having to confront the problem of the refuelling. Until final confirmation that Gant had crossed the coast, and the evidence that there was no refuelling-station apparent, he had concentrated on stopping him over Soviet territory. But, now . . .

"Where is it?" he said aloud.

"Where is what?" the First Secretary asked. His face was creased with thought, with his approaching decision.

"The refuelling ship . . . or aircraft, whatever it is!" Vladimirov snapped in reply, without looking up from the map.

"Why?"

A thought struck Vladimirov. Without replying to the First Secretary, he said, over his shoulder: "Any trace of infra-red or sound-detectors further west, either from Firechain bases, or from coastal patrols?"

There was a silence for a moment, and then the non-committal voice replied: "Negative, sir. Nothing except the staggered sector scramble in operation."

"Nothing at all?" Vladimirov said with a kind of desperation in his voice.

"No, sir. Completely negative."

Vladimirov was at a loss. It was like staring at a jigsaw puzzle that didn't make sense, or a game of chess where unauthorised moves had been suddenly introduced, to leave him baffled and losing. He realised he had operated too rigidly as a tactician, and that the people who had planned the theft of the Mig had been experts in the unexpected – security men like Andropov. He glanced quickly in the Chairman's direction. He decided not to involve him. Realising that he was perhaps committing Kontarsky's crime, he decided to handle it himself.

There had to be an answer, but he could not see it. The more he thought about the problem of Gant's refuelling, the more he became convinced that it was the key to the problem.

But, how?

He glared at the map as though commanding it to give up its secrets. On it, every single light represented a Soviet vessel, except for a British trawler-fleet on the very edge of the map, in the Greenland Sea, west of Bear Island.

He wondered, and decided that it was too far. Gant would not have sufficient fuel to make it – and how did the British navy expect to conceal an aircraft carrier inside a trawler-fleet? The idea was ludicrous.

No. The map didn't hold the answer. It told him nothing.

His hand thumped the map, and the lights jiggled, faded and then strengthened. "Where is he?" he said aloud.

After a moment, the First Secretary said: "You are *convinced* that he is still alive?"

Vladimirov looked up, and nodded.

"Yes, First Secretary. I am."

There it was, Aubrey thought, a single orange pinhead on the huge wall map. Mother One. An unarmed submarine, hiding beneath an ice-floe which was drifting slowly south in its normal spring perambulation, its torpedo room and forward crew's quarters flooded with precious paraffin to feed the greedy and empty tanks of Gant's plane.

He coughed. Curtin turned slowly round, then the spell that had seemed to hold them rigidly in front of the map was broken by the entry of Shelley, preceded by a food trolley. Aubrey smelt the aroma of coffee. With a start, he realised that he was hungry. Despite being envious of Shelley who was shaved and washed and had changed his shirt, Aubrey was not displeased by the sight of the covered dishes on the trolley.

"Breakfast, sir!" the younger man called out, his smile broadening as he watched his chief's surprise grow, and then become replaced by obvious pleasure. "Bacon and eggs, I'm afraid," he added to the Americans. "I couldn't find anyone in the canteen who could make flapjacks or waffles!"

Curtin grinned at him, and said: "Mr. Shelley – a real English breakfast is the first thing we Americans order when we book into one of your hotels!" Shelley, absurdly pleased with himself, Aubrey thought, was unable to grasp the irony of Curtin's remark. Not that it mattered.

"Thanks," Buckholz said, lifting one of the covers. Aubrey deeply inhaled the aroma of fried bacon, left his chair and joined them at the trolley.

They ate in silence for a little time, then Aubrey said, his knife scraping butter onto a thin slice of toast, his voice full of a satisfied

162

bonhomie: "Tell me, Captain Curtin, what is the present *condition* of the ice-floe beneath which our fuel tanker is hiding?"

Curtin, eating with his fork alone in the American style, leaned an elbow on the table around which they sat, and replied: "The latest report on the depth of the ice, and its surface condition, indicates all systems go for the landing, sir."

Aubrey smiled at his excessive politeness, and said: "You are *sure* of this?"

"Sir." As he explained, his fork jabbed the air in emphasis. "As you know, sir, all signals from Mother One come via the closest permanent weather-station, and are disguised to sound, if anyone picked them up, just like ordinary weather reports or ice-soundings. So we don't know what Frank Seerbacker in his ship really thinks, only what he sends. But the conditions are good, sir. The ice surface hasn't been changed or distorted by wind, and the floe still hasn't really begun to diminish in size – take it perhaps another three or four days to get south enough to begin melting."

"And – it's thick enough?" Aubrey persisted. Shelley smiled behind another mouthful of bacon and egg poised on his fork. He recognised the signs. Whenever Aubrey was at a loss in the matter of expertise, as he plainly was in the area of polar ice and its nature and behaviour, he repeated questions, sought firmer and firmer assurances from those who posed as experts.

"Sir," Curtin nodded with unfailing courtesy. "And it's long enough and wide enough," he added, with the hint of a smile on his lips. "Gant, if he's anything of a pilot, can land that bird on it."

"And the weather?" Aubrey continued.

Buckholz looked up, grinned and said: "What's the matter, Aubrey? Indigestion, or something?"

"And the weather?" Aubrey persisted, not looking at Buckholz.

"The weather is, at the moment, fine – sir," Curtin informed him. He was silent for a moment, then he said: "It's abnormally fine for the time of year, in that sort of latitude . . ."

"Abnormal?"

"Yes, sir. It could change – like that." Curtin snapped the fingers of his disengaged hand.

"Will it?" Aubrey asked, his eyes narrowing, as if he suspected some massive joke at his expense. "Will it?"

"I can't say, sir. Nothing large is showing up, not on the last batch of satellite pictures."

"What of the reports from the submarine itself?"

"Nothing yet, sir. The weather's perfect. The sensors are being thrust up through the floe from the submarine's sail every hour, on the hour. The local weather's fine, sir – just fine." Curtin ended with a visible shrug, as if to indicate that Aubrey had bled him dry, both of information and reassurance.

Aubrey seemed dissatisfied. He turned his attention to Buckholz. "It's a lunatic scheme — you must admit that, Buckholz, eh?"

Buckholz glowered at him across his empty plate. He said: "I'm admitting no such thing, Aubrey. It's my end of the business, this refuelling. You got him there, I admit that — a great piece of work, if that's what you want me to say — but I have to get him home, and you just better trust me, Aubrey, because I'm not about to change my plans because of your second thoughts."

"My dear chap," Aubrey said, spreading his hands on the table in front of him, "nothing was further from my thoughts, I assure you." He smiled disarmingly. "I just — like to be in the picture, so to speak, just like to be in the picture. Nothing more."

Buckholz seemed mollified. "Sure, it's a crazy scheme, landing a plane on a floating ice-floe, refuelling it from a submarine — I admit that. But it'll work, Aubrey. There's just no trace of that sub, not at the moment, because it's under the floe, and showing up on no sonar screen anywhere, except as part of the floe. It comes up out of the water, fills up the tanks, and our boy's away." He smiled at Aubrey. "We can't use disguises, not like you, Aubrey. Out there, on the sea, you can't disguise a ship to look like a pregnant seal!"

There was a moment of silence, and then Aubrey said: "Very well, Buckholz. I accept your rationale for using this submarine. However, I shall be a great deal happier when the refuelling is over and done with."

"Amen to that," Buckholz said, pouring himself a cup of coffee from the percolator. "Amen to that."

Almost as soon as the last of the coastal fog vanished and the bitter grey surface of the Barents Sea was sliding beneath him, strangely unreflective of the pale blueness of the sky, Gant was on top of the trawler. He was travelling at a fraction more than 200 mph, idling by the standards of the Firefox, heading for the twin islands of Novaya Zemlya, his next visual coordinate checkpoint, and the trawler was suddenly almost directly beneath him. As he flashed over the deck, at a height of less than a hundred feet, he saw, in the briefest glimpse, a white upturned face. A man had been emptying slops over the side. Then the trawler was gone, become a point of green light on the radar screen, and he cursed the fact that he had confidently switched off his forward-looking radar when he crossed the coast. Now, too late, he switched it on again. In the moment of success against the Badger, he had been careless, excited. In the moment he had glimpsed the white, upturned face, he had seen something else, something much more deadly. As if to confirm his sighting, the ECM register of radar activity indicated powerful emissions from a source directly behind him, and close. What he had the vicious bad luck to pass over was an Elint ship, a spy trawler. Even now, they could be following his flight-path on infra-red.

He pushed the stick forward and the nose of the Firefox dipped, and the grey, wrinkled sea lifted up at him, threateningly. He levelled off at fifty feet, knowing that, with luck, he was already out of electronic view, at his present height. The Elint ship's infra-red operators would have seen him disappear from their screens, even as they informed the captain of their trace, even as the man with the empty slop-bucket raced towards the bridge, mouth agape at what he had seen. They would have some kind of fix on him, a direction in which he had been travelling. He was heading for Novaya Zemlya – a blind man could pass that information back to whoever was coordinating the search for him.

He glanced at the fuel-gauge, and once more cursed the panic that had made him run for the Urals after visual sighting by the Soviet airliner north-west of Volgograd. If only . . .

He had no time, he realised, to concern himself with the futile. He could, he decided, do nothing except follow the course outlined, and to make the next, and final, course adjustment when he reached Novaya Zemlya.

His hand closed over the throttles. There were missile sites on Novaya Zemlya, abandoned as a testing-ground for Russia's nuclear weapons and now serving as the most northerly extension of the Russian DEW-line, and its first Firechain links. The Firefox was capable, he had proven, of Mach 2.6 at sea-level. How fast it could really travel he had no idea; he suspected at height its speed might well touch Mach 6, not the Mach 5 he had been briefed to expect. In excess of four-and-a-half thousand miles per hour. And perhaps two-point-two-thousand miles per hour at sea-level. The Firefox was a staggering warplane.

He pushed the throttles open. He *had* to use precious, diminishing fuel. Almost with anguish, he watched the Mach-counter slide upwards, clocking off the figures . . . Mach 1.3, 1.4, 1.5 . . . The Firefox was a pelican, devouring itself.

The Firefox was nothing more than a blur towing a hideous booming noise in its wake to the spotters above the missile site at Matochkin Shar, at the south-eastern end of the narrow channel between the two long islands of Novaya Zemlya. On the infra-red screens, he was a sudden blur of heat, nearing, then just as suddenly, a receding trace as he flashed through the channel at less than two hundred feet. Gant was flying by the auto-pilot and the TFR – if a ship was in the narrow channel, he would have no time to avoid it in the split-second between his sighting it and his collision with it; but the TFR would cope. His eyes were glued to his own screen, waiting for the glow that would tell him of a missile-launch. None came.

As the cliffs of the channel, a grey curtain of insubstantial rock, vanished and the sea opened out again, he felt a huge, shaking relief, and punched in the coordinates the Firefox was to fly. Automatically, the aircraft swung onto its new course and, slowly, he eased off the throttles, claiming manual control of the aircraft again, desperate to halt the madness of his fuel consumption.

As the aircraft slowed to a sub-sonic speed, like the return of sanity after a fever, Gant realised why no missiles had been launched in his wake. Any missile launched at a target at his height might well have simply driven itself into the opposite cliff, without ever aligning itself on a course to pursue him.

Now he was flying on a north-westerly course, a course which would eventually, long after his fuel ran out, take him into the polar ice-pack at a point between Spitzbergen and Franz Josef Land. Long before he reached it, he would be dead. The bitter grey sea flowed beneath him like a carpet, looking almost solid. The sky above him was pale blue, deceptively empty.

The loneliness ate at him, ravenous. He shivered. The "Deaf Aid" gave him no comfort. It remained silent. He began to wonder whether it worked. He began to wonder whether there was something, somebody, up ahead of him, waiting to refuel the Firefox. The screen was empty, the sky above empty, the sea devoid of vessels. The Firefox moved on, over a flowing, grey desert, eating the last reserves of its fuel.

The report from the Elint ship, followed by the confirmatory information from Matochkin Shar, had angered the First Secretary. It was suddenly as if he had accepted Vladimirov's doubts and precautions purely in the nature of an academic exercise; now he knew that they had been necessary, that Gant had not been destroyed in the explosion of the Badger.

It was perhaps the fact that he had been taken in that caused him to be so furiously angry that he turned on Vladimirov, and berated him, in a voice high, gasping with anger, for not having destroyed the Mig-31.

When his anger had subsided, and he had returned shaking and silent to his chair before the Arctic map on the circular table, Vladimirov at last spoke. His voice was subdued, chastened. He had been badly frightened by the outburst of the First Secretary. Vladimirov now knew he was playing with his own future, professional and personal. Gant had to die. It was as simple, and as difficult, as that.

He moved swiftly now, without fuss, without consultation with the First Secretary or with Marshal Kutuzov; the former appeared to have relapsed into silence, and the latter, the old airman, appeared embarrassed and shaken by the politician's outburst against a military man trying to attain the near-impossible.

Vladimirov briefly studied the map on the table's glowing surface. If Gant's course had been accurately charted after he left Novaya Zemlya, then he was heading, though he could not yet know it, directly towards the missile-cruiser, the *Riga*, and her two attendant hunter-killer submarines. Out of that fact, if it was a fact, he could manufacture another trap.

Swiftly, he ordered search planes into the area of permanent pack towards which Gant was heading to make a possible landfall. It was possible to stop Gant. His finger unconsciously tapped the map at the point which registered as the present location of the *Riga*. At that moment, her two attendant protectors, the missile-carrying, diesel-powered "F" class anti-submarine submarines, were still submerged. Because of the importance of their role in protecting the missile-cruiser, they had been adapted to carry sub-surface-to-air missiles, to supplement the hideous fire-power of the *Riga* against aerial attack.

"Instruct the *Riga* to hold her present position," he called out, "and inform her two escorts to surface immediately."

"Sir," the code-operator replied, confirming the order.

"Send a general alert to all ships of the Red Banner Fleet," he said. "Prepare them for an alteration of Gant's suspected course. Give them that course."

"Sir."

"What is the prediction on Gant's fuel supply?" he said.

Another voice answered him promptly. "The computer predicts less than two hundred miles left, sir."

"How accurate is that forecast?"

"An error factor of thirty per cent, sir."

This meant that Gant might have fuel for another hundred and forty miles, or for nearly three hundred. Vladimirov rubbed his chin. Even the most generous estimate would leave him well short of the polar-pack. He ignored the inference, behaving as Buckholz's advisers had predicted. Vladimirov, since the days of his flying, had become a cautious man, unimaginative: daring by the standards of the Soviet high command, in reality safe, unimaginative. He could

167

not make the mental jump required. If Gant's fuel would not last him to the pack, then the inference was that he would crash into the sea. There could not be another answer. He checked.

"Any unidentified aerial activity in the area?"

"None, sir. Still clear."

"Very well." He returned to his contemplation of the map. Gant would not take the aircraft up, not now, without fuel to make use of its speed. Therefore, as he had been doing when sighted, he would be travelling as close to the surface of the sea as he could. That meant, with luck, visual fire-control from the cruiser, at close range. Otherwise, there would be need to depend on infra-red weapons-aiming, which was not the most efficient of the fire-control systems aboard the *Riga*. However, it would do. It would have to do . . .

A voice interrupted his train of thought. "Report from the Tower, sir – Major Tsernik. PP2 is ready for take-off, sir."

Vladimirov's head turned in the direction of the voice, then, as his gaze returned to the map, he saw the First Secretary staring at him. He realised that something was expected of him, but he could not immediately understand what it was. There was no need to despatch the second Mig, not now, with Gant more than three thousand miles away, and running out of fuel. He was not going to be able to refuel now, therefore the intercept role designed for the second plane was irrelevant.

"Who is the pilot?" the First Secretary asked bluntly.

"I – I don't believe I know his . . ." Vladimirov said, surprised at the question.

"Tretsov," Kutuzov whispered. "Major Alexander Tretsov."

"Good. I realise there is little time, but I will speak with him before he takes off." The First Secretary appeared to be on the point of rising.

Vladimirov realised, with a flash, that the First Secretary expected him to order the second prototype to take off and to pursue, at maximum speed, the wake of the first.

Vladimirov knew it would take Tretsov less than an hour to reach Novaya Zemlya on Gant's trail. As far as he was concerned, it was a waste of time. He looked at the First Secretary.

"Of course, First Secretary," he said politically, judging the man's mood correctly. The First Secretary nodded in satisfaction. With an inward relief, Vladimirov called over his shoulder: "Summon Major Tretsov at once. And tell the Tower and inform all forces to stand by for take-off of the second Mig within the next few minutes."

The refuelling planes would need to be alerted. At a point somewhere on the coast west of Gant's crossing point, the Mig-31 would be refuelled in the air from a tanker. He ordered the alert. He realised that he had to play the farce to its conclusion. It would be impolitic, more than that, to voice his feeling that Gant was not going to reach his fuel supply, or that he was confident that the *Riga* would bring him down.

The latter, he knew, would be a very unwise thing to say, at this juncture.

He looked down at the map again. There was nothing more to do. Now, it was up to the *Riga*, and her attendant submarines. It was most certainly not, he thought, up to Tretsov haring off into the blue in pursuit.

There was still no signal from the "Deaf Aid". Gant's fuel-gauge registered in the red, and he was flying on what he presumed was the last of the reserve supply. He had switched in the reserve tanks minutes before. He had no idea of their capacity, but he knew he was dead anyway unless he heard the signal from his fuel supply within the next couple of minutes, and unless that signal was being transmitted from close at hand.

The sea was empty. The radar told him the sky was empty of aircraft. He was dead, merely moving through the stages of decomposition while still breathing. That was all.

It occurred to Gant that Buckholz's refuelling point had been an aircraft, one that had attempted to sneak in under the DEW-line – one that had been picked up, challenged, and destroyed. There *had* been a refuelling tanker, but it no longer existed.

He did not think of death, not in its probable actuality, drowning, freezing to death, at the same time as the plane slid beneath the wrinkled waves. Despite what one of Buckholz's experts had described as a tenuous hold on life, Gant was reluctant to die. It was not, he discovered, necessary to have a great deal to live for to be utterly opposed to dying. Death was still a word, not a reality – but the word was growing in his mind, in letters of fire.

The radar screen registered the presence ahead of a surface vessel of large proportions. Even as he moved automatically to take evasive action, and his mind moved more slowly than his arm to question the necessity of such action, the screen revealed two more blips, one on either side of the surface vessel. He knew what he was looking at. Nothing less than a missile cruiser would merit an escort of two submarines. He was moving directly on a contact-course towards them.

The read-off gave him a time of one minute at his present speed to the target. He grinned behind his face-mask at the word that formed in his mind. Target. A missile cruiser. He, Gant, was the target. No doubt, the ship's infra-red had already spotted him, closed his height and range, tracked his course and fed the information into the fire-control computer. There was, already, no effective evasive action he could take.

If he was to die, he thought, then he wanted to see what the Firefox could really do. He made no conscious decision to commit suicide by remaining on his present course. He would have been incapable of understanding what he was doing in the light of self-immolation. He was a flyer, and the enemy target was ahead of him – a minute ahead.

It was then that the "Deaf-Aid" shrieked at him. He was frozen in his couch. He could not look at the visual read-out on the face of the "Deaf-Aid". He did not want to know by how little he had missed, how little the time was between living and dying. The missile cruiser and the submarines closed on the radar screen even as he watched them. Distance-to-target read-out was thirty seconds. Because of his near-zero height, he had been on top of them before he knew. Now it was too late.

The "Deaf-Aid" signal was a continuous, maddening noise in his headset, like a frantic cry, a blinding light. He stared ahead of him, waiting for the visual contact with the missile cruiser, waiting to die.

EIGHT:

Mother One

It could have been no more than a fraction of a second, that pause between fear and activity, that tiny void of time before the training that had become instinct flooded in to occupy the blank depth of his defeat, his numb, stunned emptiness. Nevertheless, in that fraction of time, Gant might have broken – the resolution of despair, suddenly shattered by the clamour of the homing signal, and the read-out which told him that the distance was less than one hundred and forty-six miles to his refuelling point, to fuel and life – but he did not break. The huge blow to his system was somehow absorbed by some quality of personality that Buckholz or his psychologists at Langley must have recognised in his dossier, must have assumed to be still present in him. Perhaps it had only been the assumption by Buckholz that an empty man cannot break.

There was a fierce thrill that ran through him. A cold anger. A restrained, violent delight. He was going against the Russian missile cruiser. He clung to that idea.

Swiftly, coolly, he analysed the situation. The homing device indicated that the source of the signal-emission, whatever it was, lay in an almost-direct line beyond the cruiser. His fuel-gauge told him he could not take avoiding action. The shortest distance between two points . . . and he was looking for the shortest distance. He had to. He had to commit himself. Even if he wanted to live – and he realised, with a cold surprise, as if suddenly finding something he had lost for years, that he *did* want to live – he still had to go against the missile cruiser and its horrendous firepower. Now that there was no alternative, it was the path to life and not to death, and the thought gave him a grim satisfaction.

Radar analysis indicated that the two submarines were approximately three miles to port and starboard of the cruiser, providing a sonar and weapons screen for the big ship. Now they had surfaced, and would be training their own infra-red systems in his direction. If he remained at zero feet, they would be on his horizon, making an accurate fix by their fire-control difficult – with luck, he would have only the cruiser to worry about. The submarine closest to him, depending on which side he passed the cruiser, would not dare to loose off infra-red missiles in close proximity to the cruiser and its huge turbines.

Swiftly he analysed the capability of the cruiser's weapons against the Firefox. At his speed, any visual weapons control was out of the question. The torpedo-tubes were for submarines only, as were the mortars, four in twin mountings. The hunter-killer helicopters might be in the air, but they might not have yet been armed with air-to-air weapons to do him any damage – though they were there, he acknowledged, and their fire control was linked into the central ECM control aboard the cruiser. The guns, 60 mm mounted forward of the bridge, would be controlled by the same electronic computerised fire-control system, linked to the search radar, which operated also in infra-red. Yet they were not important. At speed, at zero feet, they would, in all probability, not be sufficiently depressed to bear on him if he flew close enough to the ship.

He stripped the cruiser of its armaments, one by one. There was one only left – the four surface-to-air missile launchers of the advanced SA-N-3 type. Neither the surface-to-surface, nor the anti-sub missiles, had any terrors for him. But the SA missiles would be infra-red, heat seeking, armed and ready to go.

He remembered the Rearward Defence Pod and prayed that it would work. The SA missile twin-launchers were located forward of the bridge superstructure, leaving the fattened, widened aft quarter of the ship for the four Kamov helicopters. Hoping to present the smallest target possible to him, the ship would be directly head-on to his course. There was no time now for any attack on the cruiser itself. Gant abandoned the idea without regret of any kind. He was part of the machine he flew, now; cold, calculating, printing-out the information recovered from his memory of his briefing.

He wondered how good the cruiser captain's briefing had been. Had he been told of the tail-unit, of the armament of the Firefox, or its speed? He assumed not. The Soviet passion for secrecy, for operating the most compartmentalised security service in the world, would operate like a vast inertia, the inertia of sheer habit, against the Red Navy officer being told more than was necessary. He would have received an order – stop the unidentified aircraft, by any means possible.

The read-out gave the time-to-target as twenty-one seconds, distance-to-target as two point two miles. Soon, within seconds, he would see the low shape ahead of him. It was the Firefox against the . . . He wished he knew the name of the cruiser.

A long, low ice-floe slipped beneath the belly of the Firefox, dazzlingly white against the bitter, unreflecting grey of the Barents

Sea. He had passed over other floes during the past few minutes, the southernmost harbingers of the spring drift of the impermanent pack. Then he saw the cruiser, a low shape on the edge of the horizon which neared with frightening rapidity. He felt that moment of tension, as the adrenalin pumped into his system, and the heart hammered at the blood, the precursor of action.

He wondered whether the cruiser would wait like a complacent animal, to swallow him in its fire, or whether it would launch a brace of missiles while he was still more than a mile away. Infra-red was imprecise – technology had been unable to narrow the inevitable spread of a heat-source as it registered on the screen. It was not a good way to obtain an accurate fix. Nevertheless, fire-control aboard the cruiser, using infra-red missiles, did not need to be precise.

He knew he was now visible to the men on the bridge, a grey petrel seemingly suspended just above the surface of the icy water. He watched the screen, waiting for the sudden bloom of missile-exhausts to emerge from the bulk of the cruiser. At the moment of launch, any SA missile would show up as a bright orange pinprick.

On the radar screen, he picked up what he guessed was one of the cruiser's Kamov helicopters, and his ECM read-out calculated height and range. He decided to launch one of his own AA missiles, as a diversion, let the electronic adrenalin of the information flood the cruiser's fire-control computer, let the physical diversion of a hit on the chopper add another dimension to the chessboard across which he moved towards the cruiser.

He launched. The missile pulled away, and whisked up and out of his view. He watched it tracking across the screen, homing on the helicopter which, he knew, would have picked up the missile, and would be scuttling to take avoiding action. Gant bared his teeth behind his facemask. The electronic war that was all he had ever known thrilled him to the bone, every nerve and muscle fulfilled. War was reduced to a game of chess, to an elaboration upon elaboration of move and counter-move. And he was the best.

The deck of the cruiser bloomed with pale fire, brighter spots on the screen. They had waited, anticipating that he would pull away from the threat of the submarines and the helicopters. Yet he had maintained the same course, heading directly towards them. The fire-control on the bridge, as he had hoped, had been triggered by his own attack upon the Kamov – the helicopter burst into flames in the sky above him, but he saw it only peripherally as a sudden orange flower, petals falling . . .

They had wanted to drive him between the cruiser and one of the submarines, expected him to pull up and away from them. But he had kept coming at them. Whatever the Soviet captain knew or did not know, he would have been told of the perilous estimate of the Firefox's fuel supply. That would have driven him to action. The Soviet captain had jumped the gun, triggered by Gant into a reflex action.

The ship was only hundreds of yards ahead of him as the SA missiles leapt from the twin launcher forward of the bridge. Gant pulled away, sliding with exposed underbelly to port, to pass the cruiser. On the screen in front of him, he saw the missiles deviate from their original track, to close on him with frightening speed. Then, at his silent command as he reached the optimum moment, the thought-guided weapons-system triggered the tail-unit. Behind him, suddenly, there was an incandescent flare that paled the sun. He shoved the throttles forward, and the Firefox leapt across the water like a spun stone, skipping the tops of the wrinkled waves, the bows of the cruiser looming above the cockpit in one brief, momentary glance, and then he could see nothing but the grey water as he passed no more than fifty yards from the ship's plates.

Behind him, the tail-units, releasing a heat-source which, for four seconds, burned far hotter than his two Turmansky turbo-jets at low speed, attracted the pair of heat-seeking missiles, and the ball of fire on the screen brightened until it seemed to hurt his eyes, even behind his tinted facemask. Then the bloom died suddenly. On the screen, the cruiser was more than a mile behind him as he went supersonic.

His fuel-gauge registered empty. The Mach-counter showed him steadied at Mach 1.6. The altimeter showed him skipping over the sea at less than fifty feet, still, he hoped, out of sight of the submarines and their infra-red, though by now they would have a transmitted bearing and range from the cruiser.

He watched the screen, saw the two patches of dull orange from the exhausts of a second pair of SA infra-red missiles overhauling him. The Soviet captain had been premature. He had been waiting for the better target, the optimum moment, but the trick of the tail-unit must have taken him by surprise. However, he had responded by ordering the release of two more missiles – and . . .

Gant saw the patch of light at the port edge of the screen as another two remotely launched SA missiles from the submarine nearest to him began to converge on his exhaust.

He checked the read-out on the "Deaf Aid". The bearing of the transmitter remained dead ahead of his present course, right on the last course he had fed into the aircraft after leaving the Novaya Zemlya channel. The distance was still one hundred and sixteen miles to its location. The homing signal began to clamour at his brain in the silent aftermath of the split seconds of violent action. He knew it was imperative to slow down.

Easing the throttles back he slowed, so that on the screen the four distant dots of dull orange seemed to draw swiftly nearer. The tail-unit had worked. Gant knew he was gambling, but this time he had an alternative, whereas before he had had none. He could attempt to outrun the pursuing missiles until his fuel ran out.

It was a curious sensation of helplessness, with not even a button to press, as his only link with reality seemed to be the four closing points of orange light. He felt, since he was not looking up from the screen, as if he were a still, helpless point, a kind of sacrifice. He could feel the sweat beneath his arms, running down his sides, chill inside the pressure-suit. He knew that under the weight of the grip he was exerting on the throttles, his hand was shaking fiercely. He waited . . .

He threw the throttles forward, and the Firefox leapt like a startled animal, flew like a terrified bird. The tail-unit released again and the explosion was almost instantaneous, huge and audible; then the shock-wave rocked the Firefox and he fought to steady the plane. It was like an extra thrust of engine-power. Quickly, he eased back the throttles and the speed dropped to below 170 knots once more.

He ignored the fuel-gauge. His eyes turned to the "Deaf-Aid", his whole attention being on the noise of the homing signal. Less than a hundred miles. In the sudden, almost sexual release after his escape from the coordinated missiles from cruiser and submarine, he didn't see how he could make it.

Ice-floes, larger, more frequent now, passed beneath the belly of the Firefox as he headed north.

The First Secretary's conversation was brief, and to the point. He wasted no time on an appeal to Major Alexander Tretsov's loyalty as a Russian and as a member of the Party, or on specious inspiration. Rather he used the other weapon which had become synonymous with his name – fear. He told Tretsov what was at stake, and he impressed upon him the price of failure. Tretsov was to head northwards, at top speed, using the phenomenal power of the Mig-31, and to rendezvous with a tanker-aircraft over the northern coastline of Russia. From there, he would head for the current position of the *Riga*, from which vessel there had, as yet, been no report; here another tanker would be waiting in the event that he required a further refuelling. The tankers were already en route to their contact coordinates.

Tretsov had been visibly nervous of the weight being thrust upon his shoulders. For a senior test pilot in the Red Air Force, he was young, in his early thirties, and he looked younger than that. Vladimirov had felt for him as the whole crushing weight of the First Secretary's personality acted upon him, and the silent presence of Andropov struck coldly. Yet he was good, his record was a fine one, Vladimirov was forced to admit. Whether, in the unlikely event of his being able to locate Gant, he was good enough to destroy the American, was another matter. Vladimirov was almost sorry for Tretsov that he was to be put to the test. He was technically the junior test pilot on the Bilyarsk project, and had flown fewer hours than his senior, Voskov – but Voskov was dead, killed by Gant. The KGB had found his body in the locker. Rather grotesquely, it had fallen comically out of the locker like a mummy from a sarcophagus.

The atmosphere in the War Command Centre after the departure of the chastened, grim-mouthed Tretsov was, for the First Secretary, more congenial. The exercise of power, and the gratifying obedience tinged with fear that had shown itself in the pilot's eyes, soothed him, reinforced his sense of the overwhelming odds ranged against Gant, the American who had dared . . . The First Secretary felt his anger rising again, and fought to calm himself. The second Mig-31, cleansed of the foam sprayed on it following the attempted sabotage, and armed to the teeth with AA missiles and cannon-shells, sat at the end of the main runway, waiting for the final clearance from the Tower. In moments, it would pass close to the First Secretary's Tupolev. The Soviet leader positioned himself at one of the small portholes let into the room to observe the take-off.

For Vladimirov, the situation was neither so simple, nor so gratifying. For the Commandant of "Wolfpack", the period of the conversation of the First Secretary with the almost silent Tretsov had been a period of anxiety. The First Secretary appeared to wish to ignore the minutes ticking away, the time approaching of Gant's expected interception with the course of the missile cruiser and her two subs. The Soviet leader listened, perhaps, to other voices, in other rooms. But Vladimirov knew that the cruiser *had* to stop Gant, that it was the last chance; last, because he still didn't know how Gant expected to refuel, but knew that he must. He churned the possibilities in his mind, in an attempt of his own to ignore the clock with its red second-hand sliding round the face.

Carrier . . . carrier-sub . . . polar-pack . . . aircraft . . . ditch, to be collected by sub?

None of them made any sense. It was almost impossible for a sub to hide itself in the Barents Sea and he had nothing but a wild theory that the Americans could have produced a carrier-sub, especially since the Mig was not adapted for a carrier-landing of any

176

kind. No, it had to be an aircraft. And there wasn't one. Unpalatable though it was, it was the truth. There was no unidentified aircraft in the area, nor likely to be at the time one would be required by Gant.

He considered the possibility of Gant ditching the Mig at sea, hoping for collection by a submarine. The plane would be submerged, and could then be towed behind the submarine back to wherever the CIA had arranged. It was fantastic, but it might be made to work. The plane would be damaged by sea water, but the Americans would learn sufficient from it to remove the Mig-31 completely as a threat to air superiority.

Yet there was no submarine in the area either, and no surface vessel capable of reaching Gant's last position for hours.

Which meant it had to be the polar-pack. Gant must be hoping to use the last of his fuel in as steep a climb as he could muster, and to glide the remainder of the way. It was a desperate idea, but no more desperate than sending one man in the first place to take on the KGB, in order to get out of Moscow and arrive at Bilyarsk. And Gant had done that at the bidding of his masters — why not this? The theory was that an aircraft like the Mig could gain perhaps as much as two miles in a glide for every thousand feet it climbed. Gant could climb high enough, if he had the fuel, to glide to the edge of the permanent pack.

He was on the point of requesting the puzzle be fed to the computer for analysis when he heard the voice of the code-operator. The computer-conceived code in which the message had been transmitted from the *Riga* had been broken down and it was this that the operator read from his print-out.

"Sir," he said. "Message from the *Riga* . . ." It was as if the operator were unwilling to proceed with it, feeling the attention of the room drawn to him in an instant.

"What is it?" Vladimirov snapped.

"Contact made with unidentified aircraft. Missiles fired, infra-red type, from cruiser in two groups of two, and from submarine escort in one group of two . . ."

"Well?"

"The aircraft appeared to be carrying some kind of drone tail-unit which detached and ignited." There was a pause, then: "The Mig-31, sir, wasn't destroyed as far as they can tell. It was already over all radar horizons before the contact time of the missiles, but the captain is not prepared to verify positive contact." The code-operator looked directly at Vladimirov. "He would like clarification of the type and capability of the aircraft that he attempted to destroy, sir."

Vladimirov's head spun round, so that his eyes stared into the grey, slaty surfaces of those of the Soviet leader. The words of challenge and contempt which were rising to his lips died in his mind. He said nothing. The face that confronted him was implacable, and all the righteous indignation that O.C. "Wolfpack" felt was squashed, buried. He could not throw his career away, not so lightly as that, in heaping his recriminations upon the First Secretary. Instead, he snapped at the code-operator:

"Secrecy must be maintained. Thank him for the job he — *attempted* to do, and order him to stand by for further instructions."

"Sir!"

The keys of the encoding-console clicked almost at once. The disguised mimicry of the First Secretary's maxim concerning security was the furthest Vladimirov felt he could allow himself to go. The recognition made him ashamed. Then he dismissed the feeling.

"What do you intend to do now, Vladimirov?" the First Secretary asked him, his mouth a straight line, his eyes completely without expression. In that face, in that moment, Vladimirov saw the truth of power in the Soviet Union, saw the heart of the cadres and coteries that were contained within the Kremlin. Because the First Secretary was able to put the blame for failure upon others, then the failure itself was no longer important. If Vladimirov were dismissed, disgraced for the loss of Mig-31, that would be all that would matter. This man before him cared nothing for the realities of the situation, only for the personal politics of his own survival.

Vladimirov was sickened, rather than frightened. With selflessness in extremity taught as one of the virtues of the military caste to which his family had belonged for generations, he gave no thought to his own survival or success. Yet the Mig-31 must not be lost to the Americans, thrown away.

"I — I shall order all available units into the area of the *Riga*, First Secretary," he managed to say in a level voice, from which he carefully excluded any trace of anger, or bitterness.

"And — what will *they* do?" Andropov asked with contempt.

Kutuzov came to his rescue. Perhaps he, too, had been sickened by what he had silently witnessed in the War Command Centre, or perhaps he sensed the tension in Vladimirov and intended to help save his career for him. Whatever, the old man's bravery as he spoke with contempt to the Chairman of the Committee for State Security made Vladimirov warm towards him.

"*They*, as you put it, Chairman, will make every effort to recover the Mig-31 that your poor security in Moscow and at Bilyarsk allowed to be successfully stolen by one man — one single American!" The whisper from the ruined throat carried clearly to

178

every ear in the room, the tone of the voice imprinting itself on every consciousness. The Chairman of the KGB flushed, two points of colour on the parchment-toned skin over the cheekbones. The smile, cynical and aloof, disappeared from his face.

Vladimirov transferred his gaze to the First Secretary's face. The Soviet leader appeared disconcerted, as if reminded of painful realities. He said, as if somehow to make amends without actual apology:

"Mihail Ilyich – I know that you will do all you can. But – what is it that you propose to do, with the whole of the Red Banner Northern Fleet and most of 'Wolfpack', northern sector, at your disposal?" The voice was calm, almost gentle – mollifying.

Kutuzov turned his gaze to Vladimirov, nodded, as if at some secret understanding, and then Vladimirov said: "The first priority, First Secretary, is to order the take-off of the Mig." The First Secretary turned back to the small window, as if prompted by the calculated priority the O.C. "Wolfpack" had placed on his own pet surmise.

"Of course," he said. "Pass the order to the Tower." The order was transmitted by one of the radio-operators. Still keeping his gaze on the runway through the window, he said: "And – next?"

Vladimirov looked down at the map in front of him, revealing the bright, isolated points of light in the wastes of the Barents Sea, north to the permanent pack.

"Order the *Riga* and her submarine escorts to alter course, and head north in the wake of the Mig at all possible speed."

Over the clicks of the encoding-console, Vladimirov heard the First Secretary mutter: "Good." Already, it appeared, the man's huge complacency was returning. Vladimirov had noted it often before, in his dealings with those who governed his country, the anodyne that could be found in action.

He looked down at the map, ignoring the broad back of the First Secretary in the grey suit, the fabric stretched across the powerful shoulders. Were he a less elevated individual, he thought, it might be possible to draw comfort from that rigid stance, that overbearing impression of strength.

"Scramble the Polar Search squadrons immediately," he ordered. He watched the leonine head nod in approval, saw the shoulders settle comfortably. Surface craft, he thought. "Order the missile destroyers *Otlitnyi* and *Slavny* to proceed with all possible speed to the predicted landfall of the Mig on the permanent pack."

"Sir."

"The three 'V'-type submarines to proceeed at once on courses to the same landfall reference."

"Sir."

Vladimirov paused. Faintly through the fuselage of the Tupolev, he heard the whine of engines running up. The Mig, cleared from the Tower, was preparing for take-off. He did not cross to the tiny window as he heard the engines increase in volume as the Mig raced down the runway. Instead, he watched the shoulders of the First Secretary and the slight, hopeful tilt of the head. There was a blur from the runway beyond the window, and then the unmistakeable sound of a jet aircraft pulling away from the field in a steep climb. For a moment, the First Secretary remained at the window, as if deep in contemplation, then he turned back into the room, and Vladimirov noticed the slight smile on his face.

The distance to the transmitter of the homing-signal still crying from the "Deaf Aid" registered as ninety-two miles. The fuel-gauges registered empty. Gant was flying on little more than fresh air, and he knew it. It was time – and it might already be too late – to go into a zoom climb and begin the long glide to the contact-point with the refuelling-tanker.

The more he considered the problem, the more Gant became convinced that such a glide was his only chance. He had to go as high as possible, and then hope that he would leave himself enough fuel for the tricky and delicate task of matching speeds with the tanker-aircraft, and coupling to the fuel-umbilical trailing behind the tanker. Not once had he considered that the tanker might be some kind of surface craft. It could not be a carrier – the USN would not dare put a huge and vulnerable target like that into the Barents Sea. Unlike Vladimirov, he knew that the Americans had developed no carrier-sub.

Therefore, he was going to have to refuel in the air. He knew the Firefox's predecessor, the Mig-25 Foxbat, had established an absolute altitude record of almost 119,000 feet, and that the Firefox was intended as being capable of a greater performance. And, in the present atmospheric conditions, at two-and-a-half miles for every thousand feet of height, he could easily reach the tanker, if he could only pull the Firefox up to an altitude of perhaps forty or more thousand feet.

Yet he had to take a terrible risk. He still had to have plenty of height when he made the rendezvous, and sufficient fuel left for the final manoeuvres.

The fuel-tanks of the Firefox had to be almost empty – had to be, he told himself. It was one aspect of the aircraft with which he was not familiar. Though he had asked Baranovich, the electronics engineer had been unable to help him.

180

The engines, at his crawling speed across the grey, ice-littered sea, still operated without hesitation. Yet he could take no further risk. The automatic emergency tanks must have cut in by that time, and he had no idea of the extra range they would give him but he suspected it wouldn't be sufficient to take him to the contact-point.

He pushed the throttles forward, and pulled back on the column. The nose of the Firefox lifted and he accelerated, watching the altimeter begin to climb, steadily at first, and then more and more rapidly as he increased the thrust of the two huge turbojets. He seemed not to breathe, not once during the minute-and-a-half of climb. The pale, spring blue of the sky began to deepen as he climbed.

He levelled out at sixty-two thousand feet, throttling back the engines until there was just sufficient power to maintain the function of the generators. At that height, he would be at about twenty-seven thousand feet when he arrived at the tanker's location. It would be enough. He checked the screen. Nothing.

There was only one thing to hope – that it remained as clean of activity as it was at that moment.

The bearing of the signal remained dead ahead of him. The distance read-out gave him eighty-eight miles to target. He still wondered how much fuel remained, and the thought nagged at him. He began to think that he might have overplayed the safety margin, with regard to his zoom climb. It must have drained the emergency tanks.

Ahead of him, far ahead, he saw the grey heaviness of cloud building up. The screen remained empty of activity. The Firefox glided silently through an empty sky, the dark blue canopy of the thin upper layers of the atmosphere above, the tiny, silent greyness of the northern limits of the Barents Sea below. Ahead of him, far ahead, beyond where the cloud seemed to be building, there was an edge of whiteness in sight – the polar-pack.

United States Navy Captain Frank Delano Seerbacker lay on his cramped bunk in his cramped quarters aboard the USS *Pequod*, a nuclear-powered "Sturgeon" class submarine, as it drifted beneath the ice-floe whose southward path it had imitated for the past five days. Seerbacker's submarine had passed beneath the polar-pack near the western coast of Greenland and, rigged for silent running, had slithered out into the Barents Sea after fourteen days at sea.

The journey had possessed three distinct phases for the captain, his officers and the crew. There had been the top-speed dash from the submarine's concealed base on the Connecticut coast, then the claustrophobic passage beneath the polar ice – and since then, the captain thought again with irritation, they had been drifting without engines, averaging three-point-one miles a day beneath the floe.

The *Pequod* was unarmed, another fact which Seerbacker bitterly resented. The submarine's torpedo room and forward crew's quarters were flooded with high-octane paraffin, fuel for the super-plane that the CIA was stealing for the good old US of A.

Seerbacker's craggy, lined face creased in a frown of contempt. His long nose flared. He disliked, he decided, the CIA – especially when that crud organisation told him to sit under a damn ice-floe and wait for a superjet to land on it!

He stirred on his cot, raising his knees merely for the sake of altering the position of his limbs. His hands were behind his head, and he was staring sightlessly at the ceiling. He and his men were sick, he decided, of the whole monotonous routine of the mission; sick to death, following the ice-floe's unvarying, snail-like course southward.

It wasn't, he thought grimly, as if they'd even had the change of routine involved in looking for a suitable floe. The floe – the so-called runway, he thought with contempt – had been selected from the study of hundreds of satellite photographs, in the first instance, the findings of which had been checked and confirmed by a Lockheed Orion which had collected both photographs and visual findings. Proven statistical data from oceanographic surveys allowed experts at Langley to make a firm prediction about the floe's ability to take the weight of the Firefox. Seerbacker had merely been told where to find it. He realised he was being merely bloody-minded in cursing the domination of machinery, but he went on doing so anyway. There was after all, he told himself, damn all else to do except to curse the temporal powers and their crazy ideas, who had got him into this mess, who had messed up his boat with their paraffin!

There was a soft knock at his door.

"What?" he said, irritated rather than thankful at being roused from his fruitless reverie. A crewman handed him a sheaf of flimsy. On it, in the hand of his Exec., who was acting as weather-officer, he read the information that he had been expecting, but which was doubly unwelcome when it came. The temperature of the air above the floe was dropping much too rapidly. Cloud was building up in the area, cloud that would mask from Gant the position and dimensions of the floe.

Seerbacker tossed his head at the information. It was his bloody luck, just his godawful luck! He dismissed the crewman. He needed no further information. If there was anything else, then the Exec. would send it to him. He had no need to go to the control room, not yet. He cursed again the constant trimming of the tanks, the regular, futile checks to be made on the paraffin that flooded the tubes and the forward quarters, and on the weather, the surface temperature of the floe, the condition of the ice surface . . . It was, he decided, no job for a man with twenty years in the service, and with one of the best crews in the Navy.

He considered the information concerning the air temperature. It was dropping rapidly, which could, and probably would, mean a change in the weather conditions which had been unusually settled and mild for those latitudes and the time of year. The change, when it came, could so easily become freezing fog, localised in their area, spreading perhaps as little as a few square miles. In freezing fog, Seerbacker did not have to know anything about aircraft and pilots to know that there was no way Gant could land on the floe. They had no navigational aids aboard that could help him, allow him to make an automatic landing – nothing except the transmitter that would tell Gant where they were. Already, as the message had told him, there was a local build-up of cloud. Perhaps Gant might not be able to get down, even in that . . .

The introduction of doubt prompted his mind to review the emergency procedures. In the final event, he was to avoid capture at all costs. It could never be admitted by Washington that a submarine of the U.S. Navy had been a part of the scheme to steal the Firefox – he was to destroy the *Pequod*, if necessary, to prevent its capture by the Russians.

His mind winced away from the secret orders he had opened at sea; if Gant failed to land on the floe, or if he crashed onto the ice, or into the sea in the vicinity of the *Pequod*, then he was to make every effort to rescue the pilot – and an even greater effort to capture the plane, and tow it home beneath the ice-pack. The havoc that would cause with his crew, and his navigation, he was not prepared to consider. It was, he knew, theoretically feasible, but he hoped that none of this would be necessary and that Gant was good enough to set the Firefox down like a feather.

The trouble was, Seerbacker admitted to himself finally – Gant was late. He had been briefed as to the performance and range of the Firefox, and the ETA for the plane over the floe had already passed – was minutes past. And with that plane, he knew, minutes were really huge gaps of time – a big enough gap for a man's death. He would not know whether Gant had even stolen the plane until it appeared, or failed to appear, on the submarine's infra-red. Up through the ice was thrust a single metal spike, camouflaged in white, carrying the transmitter of the homing-signal tuned to Gant's "Deaf Aid", the complex, changing signal that he should be picking up. It was his one and only link with the American pilot.

Seerbacker cursed the British designer for not including a facility, built-in, so that Gant could identify himself – but it was strictly one-way. The *Pequod* transmitted, and the Firefox received – at least, until the aircraft was close enough for the transponder in the homing device to emit an identification signal, and that distance was within visual range anyway. As his Exec. had commented – if General Dynamics had fitted it as standard equipment in "Sturgeon" class subs, it would dispense Coca-Cola, along with doing the laundry and playing canned music. Seerbacker's lips twisted in a reflective smile.

When Gant appeared over the floe, the frequency of the signal he received would change, and he would hear the equivalent of an instantaneous echo, as on sonar. Then, no doubt, to his appalled mind it would become clear that he would have to land on an ice-floe – in cloud, Seerbacker added vitriolically, perhaps in freezing fog. This would probably mean scraping the pilot off the ice, sinking the remains of the plane, and towing it thousands of miles back to Connecticut. It didn't bear thinking about.

Gant was late. The thought nagged at him. Minutes only – but late. His fuel must be shot to hell by now, Seerbacker thought savagely. Must be. He thought about going down to the control-room, almost swung his long, thin legs off the cot, and then decided against it. After five days, he couldn't start showing a yellow flag as soon as the guy was a couple of minutes overdue. He reflected that there was very little aerial activity in the area – even if that lack of activity included Gant.

There was no comfort to be found, he decided. None at all . . .

Surprisingly, it was Buckholz, massive, self-confident, almost silent Buckholz, who cracked first. Aubrey had been aware of the tension rising in the room as the morning wore on, after Shelley had cleared the breakfast remains, and they had finished with the coffee. Then, suddenly, there had been nothing to do. The tension in the room had been palpable, lifting the hair at the nape of the neck like static electricity. A profound silence had descended on the five occupants, broken only by the creaking of the stepladder whenever Curtin ascended or descended, pinning his satellite weather photographs to the wall, or altering and supplementing the coloured pins in the map of the Barents Sea.

Buckholz had ceased to take notice of the map. For more than half an hour he had not looked once in its direction. It was as if he

184

were listening to some inner voice, seeing some mental image, and did not need the confirmation of pictures and pins.

Aubrey knew why he was silent, grim-faced, tense. He shared that tension because he, too, understood how perilous Gant's fuel state must be. The last report from the *Pequod*, from Mother One and Seerbacker, was a routine weather report which contained no coded reference to sighting Gant by infra-red and contained, moreover, some discouraging news concerning the weather in the area of the floe, news that would make it difficult for Gant to land. Aubrey did not want his neat, carefully conceived, methodically executed operation to end with the humiliation of a crash-landing on the floe, and the ignominy of a Firefox damaged and affected by the corrosive sea-water from being towed home behind the *Pequod*.

But, it was the fuel state that worried him, more than the weather. To Buckholz, Aubrey guessed, it signified that Gant had already failed. Aubrey glanced up at the clock, and then again at Buckholz. It was the wrong thing to do, he realised, to remind Buckholz of what he had evidently forgotten but, nevertheless, he said, his voice carefully deferential:

"Is it not time we released the decoy submarine into the arena, Buckholz?"

There was a moment of silence, then Buckholz, his lips working, snapped: "What in hell's name for?" His eyes glared at Aubrey, as if the latter had interrupted some kind of ritual, solemn and awful, proceeding within the American.

Aubrey spread his arms. "It is time, by the clock," he said blandly.

"Why waste it?" Buckholz asked.

"What?"

"The decoy — decoy for what, man?" Buckholz seemed to half-rise from his seat, as if to browbeat the small, rotund Aubrey.

"We don't *know* he's lost . . ." Aubrey began.

"What in the hell was all that coded stuff we picked up, between Bilyarsk and the *Riga*, then?" Buckholz snapped. "They got him, Aubrey — blew the ass from under him!"

Aubrey tried to retain a smile of encouragement on his face, and said: "I don't know — it could have meant they *didn't* get him."

There was a silence. Buckholz seemed to sink back into his chair. Anders, standing behind him, a plastic cup clutched in his big hand, looked down at Buckholz's cropped head, then looked across the room at Aubrey. His gaze seemed quizzical. Aubrey nodded, and mouthed the single word: "Decoy." Anders crossed to a telephone in the corner, dialled a number, and spoke. Hearing his voice, Buckholz turned incuriously to watch him, then glanced across at Aubrey, and shook his head.

185

Buckholz had returned to his sightless contemplation of the papers in front of him. By this time Anders had completed his telephone call to an operations room in the M.O.D. which would alert the decoy submarine at that moment lying to the west of Spitzbergen and the decoy aircraft waiting to take off from Greenland, or already in the air to the east of that frozen land-mass.

Aubrey nodded to Anders in acknowledgement of his call, then proceeded to gaze across the room at the map. The decoy planes would be picked up by Russian landborne and seaborne radar within minutes, and be seen to be heading towards the vicinity of North Cape, while the submarine would entice Russian surface vessels and submarines to investigate, drawing them away from the *Pequod* while she was on the surface, refuelling the Firefox.

A doubt suddenly struck him, cold in the pit of his stomach, clutching with a hot, burning sensation in his chest, like indigestion or a heart murmur. Would the *Pequod* ever need to surface? Looking again at Buckholz, it was evident that he didn't think so. Aubrey rubbed his smooth, cherubic cheeks, and wondered.

At twenty-two thousand feet, the Firefox dropped into the top of the cloud-stack that Gant had watched inexorably approaching. The silent, gliding aircraft slid through the ruffled, innocuous edges of the cloud, into the grey silence, with the helplessness of a stone. He had been unable to estimate the depth of the stack — it could, he knew, reach down to the surface of the pewter-coloured sea. He was four minutes to target, descending at a steady rate of three-and-a-half thousand feet per minute, moving ahead at 180 knots, three miles a minute. When he reached the target location, he would still be eight thousand feet above sea-level. It would have to be enough. There was nothing on the screen. Only the TFR reflected the monotonous pattern of ice-floes slipping past him, below the cloud. There was nothing that looked remotely like a ship, anywhere within the limits of the target area. There was no aircraft. There was merely the incessant, monotonous signal, emanating from some unknown source, beckoning.

In the cloud, Gant felt cold. The signal was his only contact with reality, and yet it seemed to possess no other reality than that of sound. He was unable to believe in his physical source. Gant had always been an electronic pilot, always relied on instruments. Stories older men told him, of flying bombers over Germany in the last days of the last war, were tales that might have come from ancient Greece — mythological. Therefore, he did not panic, was not really afraid. The signal did have a source, however distant, however ghostly. It was no illusion. He trusted it.

Nevertheless, it began, subtly but certainly, to feel cold in the cabin of the Firefox, a chill, arctic cold, salt like the sea.

Seerbacker was swinging his legs off the bunk even as his Exec. — who in his excitement had come in person — peered round the door to his quarters and said, almost breathless with sudden, renewed tension: "Aircraft contact, sir — heading this way."

"Range?" Seerbacker snapped, tugging his cap on his head, and pressing past the younger man, who followed his captain's rapid progress towards the control-room.

"Less than four miles, sir — height about twelve thousand — she's on the bearing, sir. And there's no radar contact, only a very faint infra-red. She's either on lowest power or not using her engines at all."

Without looking behind him, Seerbacker said: "Then it's him." Then he added: "What's the surface temperature of the floe?"

"Still dropping, sir. Dewpoint's still a couple of degrees away."

Seerbacker suddenly stopped, and turned on his Exec. "A couple of degrees?" he repeated.

"Yes, sir."

"Wind?"

"Five to ten knots, variable."

"Insufficient turbulence, then?" he said mysteriously, and the younger man, Lt. Commander Dick Fleischer, nodded, understanding his drift. "But, what about *his* turbulence, when he comes into land — uh? What happens then?"

"It shouldn't . . ." the younger man began.

"With this old tub's luck, Dick — what d'you think'll happen? He'll put the wheels down, stick back — and phut! The lights'll go out!" He tried to smile, but the effect was unconvincing. Both he and Fleischer knew that, however he said it, the content of his statement was deadly serious. Two degrees drop in the temperature would mean that the air above the surface of the floe would achieve dewpoint, that point on the scale where freezing fog would begin to form. The effect of the turbulence of the Firefox attempting to land could trigger the drop in temperature.

Seerbacker, as if prompted by his own lurid imaginings, clattered off down the companionway. As soon as he thrust his thin, lanky form into the control-room of the sub, he said:

"Where is he?"

"Three miles — a little over eleven thousand feet, sir!" the radar-operator sang out.

"Is he still on the same bearing?"

"Sir."

"Can he see the floe?"

"Yes, sir. Cloudbase is thirteen-and-one-half thousand."

"Then let's surprise him, gentlemen," Seerbacker said with a grim smile. "Blow all tanks — hit it!"

The floe was the only thing down there that Gant really saw. He had dropped out of the cloud at thirteen thousand feet, only three minutes or a little more away from the target — and there it was. Big, perhaps two miles north-south, and almost the same across. It lay directly in his path. On the radar-screen, there was no craft of any kind. Yet the target lay less than six miles ahead of him. That floe was the right distance away. Only its distance from him had made him regard it at all.

He knew it had to be the floe. For a long time, he had suspected that he had never been intended to reach the polar-pack, nor had he ever been intended to rendezvous with a tanker-aircraft — that would have been too risky, too dangerous by half. It had to be the floe — and a landing. His eyes searched ahead, saw nothing. For a moment, then, he felt close to panic. A fat floe, like a dirty white water-lily on the surface of the bitter arctic water. It was surrounded by others, smaller for the most part. There was no sign of life! He felt the bile of fear at the back of his throat, and his mind refused to function, analyse the information — then it happened. The signal changed, the homing-signal began to emit a broken, bleeping call, two to the second. He recognised its similarity to a sonar-contact, instantaneous echo. Even as the seconds passed, the bleep became more and more insistent, urgent. He *was* closing on the target. He studied the condition of the sea, estimating the windspeed again — yes, five to ten knots, no more. Even before the questions had been answered, even before the shock of the changing signal had dispersed, he began the routines required if he were to land on the floe. The last of the ice-crystals starred on the windscreen dispersed under the effects of the de-mister. Again, more urgently now, he studied the surface of the floe, but only a small part of him was looking for signs of life. Principally he looked at the flatness, the length of possible runways, looked for markings, judged the direction of the wind . . .

When it came, it came with the sudden shock of freezing water, or a physical blow. At the western edge of the floe, away to port, and still ahead of him, the ice buckled, curled at the edge before cracking. The reinforced sail of a nuclear submarine came into view, and Gant saw the bulk of the ship beneath; ice spun away from it, sliding from its hull.

A bright orange balloon was released from the sail, and then an orange streamer of smoke which spurted vertically before the wind tugged it flat downwind of the submarine. Gant knew as soon as he saw the emerging sail that he was looking at an American submarine.

Automatically, he checked the radar. Negative. He eased on power, felt the aircraft shove forward, and dropped the nose. As he touched on the air-brakes, and stabilised his speed at 260 knots, the smoke was passing beneath his wingtip. He noticed, with almost idle curiosity, that the sonar-like pinging of the homing-device had changed to a continuous signal – instantaneous echo. The target was below him, a submarine full of paraffin; it would be a matter of less than an hour before he was refuelled, and ready to take off. He hauled the aircraft to the left, in a rate one turn that would line him up in the direction of the wind-flattened smoke from the sail.

The wind direction was such that he would land along the north-south axis of the floe, which gave him almost two miles of snow-covered ice in which to stop. He knew the snow, unless it was utterly frozen, would act as an efficient braking-system – it would be, he told himself with a grim smile, the relief at finding the sub still warming him, like landing on a carrier – something else he had learned to do in Vietnam.

He dropped the undercarriage, and the lights glowed, registered the wheels "locked". He slowed his speed to 220 knots, and levelled the wings. The floe was ahead, with the dark cigar of the submarine embedded in it, a lizard half-emerged from its shell, its streamer of orange smoke in line with his course.

He checked back on the stick, and read his altitude as one thousand feet. He dropped his speed to 180 knots, and stabilised there. His rate of descent was now 350 feet per minute. The grey, wrinkled waves seemed to speed up, to reach up at him hungrily. He eased back the throttle, and the speed dropped to 175 knots. He was almost dazzled now by the glare of the ice-floe, yet through the dazzle, the surface still looked good.

He chopped the throttle, and the Firefox suddenly seemed to sag tiredly in the air, began to sink. He checked back on the stick into the flare-out position. On full flap, the Firefox seemed to drop for a moment, then the plane jolted viciously as the wheels bit into the surface snow, and the nose-wheel slammed down. Visibility disappeared for a moment as the snow spewed around the nose, and it was a second or more before the de-mister coped. The forward screen cleared.

Even as Gant wondered whether the engine would flame out because of snow in the air-intakes, he saw that his visibility had disappeared. He was rushing across a surface of ice and snow, enveloped in a thick, rolling grey fog.

NINE:

Pressure

Gant understood what had happened – dewpoint; the formation of a thick, rolling blanket of fog along his rushing track had been almost instantaneous. The knowledge did not lessen the rising unease he felt, could not counteract the explosion of adrenalin in his system. The engines had not flamed out, and the snow flung up around the cockpit by the nose-wheel had slid from the screen – yet he could see nothing. He was helpless – the snow on the surface of the floe was slowing the aircraft as swiftly as any reverse thrust from the engines and yet he was slipping across an ice surface, down the north-south axis of the floe, towards the icy grey waters of the Barents Sea. If the size of the floe were too small, inadequate, if he had miscalculated, if . . .

The Firefox slowed to walking pace, trundling more unevenly now, jolted by the indentations and scabs of the surface ice beneath the thin blanket of snow. And the fog was already thinning, as the turbulence of his passage became less; it was spreading, thinning to a grey, damp mist. He looked over his shoulder, shifting in the couch for perhaps the first time in an hour. He could not see the orange balloon, nor could he see the line of the streamer of smoke, which would give him some indication of the direction of the sub. He turned the aircraft to port, through one hundred and eighty degrees, and taxied back up the line of his landing, crawling forward, his eyes searching for figures moving in the mist, lights or signals which might direct him. He felt the unease and the adrenalin drain from him. He was down.

He thought he saw a lumping, shapeless figure moving to port of him, but could not be sure. The mist seemed to have thickened again. The figure had not been carrying a light. He pressed the button, and raised the cockpit cover. The sudden change of temperature as the heated air of the cabin rushed out and was replaced by the arctic air above the floe seemed to knife through the protection of the anti-G suit as if it had been made of thin summerweight cotton. He was chilled to the bone in a moment, his teeth chattering uncontrollably behind the tinted facemask of his flying helmet. His hands on the controls seemed to tremble, as if registering the groundshock of an explosion. He unlocked the helmet and tugged it up and away from his head. His cropped head seemed to prickle with a cold fire. Ignoring the noise of his teeth, he craned his head, listening and looking in the direction from which he had glimpsed the figure in the mist.

He thought, twice, in swift succession, that he heard voices away to his left, that he was paralleling the path of men searching for him – but he couldn't be certain. The voices, like the cries of alien birds, seemed to distort in the thick mist, and he couldn't be sure of the direction from which they came. Then he realised that the men would be heading to what they would have assumed was the point of his halt, behind him now – they would not, perhaps, have expected him automatically to make a 180-degree turn, and cover his tracks.

Then he saw a dull glow, lighting a misshapen, lumbering figure, a lamp held low in a swinging hand. He heard his own name being called, loudly, yet seeming faint, insubstantial. He did not reply, and the figure called again. Gant felt a curious reluctance to speak, despite the cold, despite the sudden, rushing sense of loneliness, of the interminable time of his journey from Bilyarsk – and before that, from London. The voice was American. He smiled, in spite of his detachment – that was it, he recognised, it was detachment he felt, a sense of *removal* from this figure cautiously approaching. It was so, so *ordinary*, a lumping shadow with a New York accent – nothing really to do with him, and the Firefox, and what he had done.

He shrugged off the feeling. The wind gusted to perhaps twelve knots, and the blast of it struck him in the face, reviving him to the present, to his physical cold and discomfort. He raised his hand to his face, cupped it and yelled. His own voice sounded thin, almost unreal. "Over here – the plane's over here, man!"

"That you, Gant?" the voice replied. Gant realised only as he began to cast about that his own eyesight was vastly superior to that of the figure to his left. He turned the Firefox in the mist, very slowly, and saw the figure straighten, and become certain of his whereabouts. "Jesus – I must need glasses, for Chrissake!" the figure said.

Gant had no need to apply the brakes; slowed by the surface snow, the aircraft rolled to a halt. The great turbojets made only an impatient murmur behind him. He could hear the figure, which now seemed tall and thin, only given a tent-like shape by the parka it was wearing, talking into an R/T handset.

"O.K., you men – I found him. Get over here, on the double!"

191

Then the figure moved forward. A mittened hand slapped against the fuselage and Gant, leaning out of the cockpit, stared down into an ascetic, lined face. He could see the gold leafing on the peak of a Navy cap beneath the fur trimming of the parka hood. Gant smiled, foolishly, feeling there was nothing to say. A great wave of relief surged in him, almost nauseous, and he began to shiver with emotion rather than the cold.

"Hi, fella," Seerbacker said.

"Hi," Gant said, in a choking voice. He saw other figures moving in the mist, and the round globes, furred and dim, of lamps.

"Hey, skipper – you want us to line up now?" a voice called.

Seerbacker, seemingly distracted from a perusal of Gant's features, turned his head, and yelled over his shoulder, "Yeah – let's get this bird over to its mother – it's dying of thirst!" He turned back to Gant, and added in a low voice: "You don't look like anything special, mister – but I guess you must be – uh?"

"Right now – you're pretty special yourself, Captain!" Gant said.

Seerbacker nodded, and lifted the handset to his face. He said: "O.K., this is the captain. Call in for me."

He listened intently as men began to call in, as at a roll-call. When there was silence once more, he looked up at Gant, and said: "I've got half of my crew standing on this goddam ice, mister, in two nice straight lines, all the way to the ship. Think you can ride down the middle?"

"Like the freeway," Gant said.

Seerbacker raised his hand, gripped the spring-loaded hand- and toe-holds and hoisted himself clear of the ground.

"Mind if I hitch a ride?"

"They're pretty rough on freeloaders on this railroad."

"I'll take my chances," Seerbacker said with a grin. "O.K., let's roll."

Gant eased off the brakes, and the Firefox slid forward. He saw the first two men, their lights haloed, bright, and then other lights, a tunnel in the mist. He straightened the nose down the centre of the tunnel, and the lights began to roll slowly past on either side, only just visible in the mist. He heard Seerbacker giving an order.

"O.K., you guys, move in, dammit! This bird won't bite – it's one of ours, for Chrissake!"

The lights ahead wobbled, narrowed, became brighter, more helpful to him.

"Thanks," he said to the invisible Seerbacker below him.

"O.K., mister. They're only here to help – even if they don't like it." There was an edge to his voice as he ended his sentence. Gant sensed, beneath the surface, the resentment that had emerged along with relief at his arrival – the resentment of men stuck in the middle of an enemy sea for day after day, tracking the drifting floe.

"I'm sorry," he said, involuntarily.

"What?" Seerbacker began, then added: "Oh, yeah. It's just orders, mister – don't give a mind to it." Gant saw a long low shape, sail atop, ahead of him through the mist. "There she is," Seerbacker said unnecessarily, and Gant felt the pride in his voice. It was the pride of a commanding officer in his ship.

"Yeah – I see it," he said.

"Pull up alongside," Seerbacker said. "You want to eat in the car, or come on inside?" Gant swung the Firefox parallel with the fattened cigar of the ship, half-buried in ice, like something reptilian emerging from a white shell. He cut the motors, and the plane died. In the absolute silence of the next moment, Gant felt a fierce affection for the aircraft. It was not something he had stolen, a *freight* for the CIA – it was what had brought him from the heart of Russia, helped *him* to escape, taken on a missile-cruiser, taken on . . . Seerbacker interrupted the flood of his fierce, cold, mechanical love for another machine.

"Welcome to 'Joe's Diner'. The cabaret isn't much good, but the hamburgers are a delight to the weary traveller! Step down, Mister Gant – step down, and welcome."

Gant unstrapped himself from the webbing of the couch. As he stood up, his muscles and joints protested as he moved. The wind seemed to gust at him, the freezing cold from the Pole search through his suit, eat at him. He shuddered.

"Thanks," he said. "Thanks." He stepped out of the cockpit, no longer reluctant, down onto the ice.

"Call them out," Vladimirov said. "A report from every Polar Search Squadron now!"

It took four minutes for the report to be completed, time which the First Secretary seemed not to consider wasted, wherever Gant was, and whatever he was doing. Vladimirov loathed the political game that was being played and in which he had joined, his silence giving assent, his cowardice dictating his silence. When the last search-plane had reported on its findings in its designated area, it was clear that there had been no attempt by the Americans to establish any kind of fuel-dump on the ice, no attempt to mark out or clear any kind of runway. Vladimirov, his belief shaken but not destroyed, felt his bemusement hum in his head like a maddening insect. He *had* the answer, somewhere at the back of his mind, he was sure of it . . . !

The cold eyes of the First Secretary, and the glint of the strip-light on Andropov's glasses, made him bury his reflections.

"Now," the Soviet leader said, "order all available units into the North Cape area – everything you have!"

Vladimirov nodded.

"Scramble 'Wolfpack' squadrons in the North Cape sector through to Archangelsk sector," he snapped. "Staggered sector scramble for *all* units." He did not glance at the map-table, did not ask for the map to be changed. He was oblivious to it, seeing in his mind with absolute clarity, the dispositions of all surface, sub-surface and aerial units that might be employed.

"Order the *Otlitnyi* and the *Slavny* to alter course at once for North Cape – order them to proceed at utmost speed."

"Sir!"

"Order all submarines on the Barents Sea map to alter course, and to proceed to the Cape area at top speed."

"Sir!"

"Order the *Riga* to alter course, together with her escorts, and to put up her helicopters at once – they are to proceed at top speed to the Cape."

"Sir!"

It was futile, he knew – the bellowing challenge of a coward after the bully is out of earshot, the simulated fury of the defeated. Yet he became caught up in its frenetic, useless energy. He was intoxicated by the power he possessed.

Like a child he had once seen building on the sands at Odessa a long time ago, he made himself oblivious to the sea of truth creeping up behind him, and threw all his energies into the task of making his fragile, impermanent structure of sand. He flung everything into the air, changed the course of every surface and sub-surface vessel in the Barents Sea.

The map on the table was now showing the western sector of the Barents Sea – its operator had bled in the map reflecting Vladimirov's countless orders. Vladimirov realised he was sweating; his legs suddenly weak, unable to support him any longer. He lowered himself into a chair, looked up and found the First Secretary smiling complacently at him.

"Well, my dear Vladimirov – that wasn't so bad, after all – eh?" He laughed. Behind him, like an echo, Andropov smiled thinly. Vladimirov shook his head, smiled foolishly, like a rewarded child. "You seem to enjoy it – eh? Power . . . you understand, eh?" The man was leaning towards him. Vladimirov could do nothing but continue grinning foolishly, and nod his head.

A voice cut into his vacuous confrontation with the Soviet leader.

194

"Tretsov reports the Mig-31 crossing the coast on the line of longitude 50 degrees, near Indiga."

It was like a single stone dropping into the flat silence of a pond. All of them around that table were suddenly reminded of the awesome potentiality, the enormous power, of the thing that had been stolen. It was little more than twenty-five minutes since Tretsov had taken off. The coast was approximately 1250 miles due north from Bilyarsk, and the Mig-31 had already reached it, passed over it, heading for its rendezvous over the Barents Sea with a tanker aircraft.

Vladimirov looked at the First Secretary, saw the momentary hesitation in his eyes.

"Shall I order Tretsov to alter course, First Secretary?" he asked tiredly.

The big man shook his head, still smiling. "Not for the moment — let Tretsov make his rendezvous with the tanker first. When we have a sighting, we will point him like an arrow at the American — eh, like an arrow, Vladimirov?"

The First Secretary laughed. Vladimirov derived no comfort from the sound, from the over-confidence it betrayed.

Twenty minutes after he had landed, Gant was back on the surface of the floe, checking the progress of the refuelling. Despite the bitter, freezing cold, the raw wind that swirled the thick mist around him, whipped the smoking breath away from his numbed lips, Gant stood on the ice near the Firefox, as if unwilling to surrender the aircraft entirely to the attentions of Seerbacker's crew. The frost had already begun to rime the fur of his borrowed parka, which did not seem to warm him, and he stood, a hunched figure, his hands thrust into his pockets, staring into the grey, formless world of the floe, seeing shadowy, labouring figures on the ice. The two hoses, each four inches in diameter, snaked across the floe towards the plane. The crew worked like men at the scene of some desperate, frozen fire. A trolley-pump had been wheeled out across the ice, having been lowered from the forward hatch by a winch, and then a smaller hatch in the forward deck had been opened. Gant's nostrils had been assailed by the sudden, bitter-sweet smell of the paraffin. A heavy-duty hose disappeared into the hatch above the forward crew's quarters.

It would take, Gant knew, perhaps another twenty minutes to refuel. Unlike the huge pressure-pumps available at an airbase in the front line, which could transfer as much as three thousand gallons of paraffin a minute to the thirsty tanks of a warplane, this trolley-pump was an aged, short-breathed thing.

There had been a delay, while Gant devoured a plate of chilli in Seerbacker's quarters, before the pump had begun to operate. The bonding wire running from the sub, which was required to earth the Firefox to prevent the danger of a spark from the static electricity in the fuselage igniting any spillage, had been too short. The sub's crew had spliced in another length of wire, and the huge crocodile clip had been fastened to the nose-wheel strut. Only then had the refuelling begun.

When the two civilians carried by the *Pequod* – an engineer and an electronics expert – had begun working on the plane, Gant agreed to return to Seerbacker's cabin.

Once there, he sat in silence except when, after looking at his watch, he murmured, "Ten minutes."

A minute or two later, there was a knock at the door.

"Yeah?"

The Exec., Fleischer, stuck his head into the room. "Weather report, sir," he said.

Gant suddenly seemed to come awake. His eyes fixed on Fleischer's face, the intensity of the gaze making the young man falter.

"What is it?" Gant said.

"The wind's getting up, sir – gusting to fifteen knots at times." Fleischer spoke to Seerbacker, quite deliberately. "The fog seems to be lifting."

Seerbacker nodded. Gant had relaxed. Fifteen-knot gusts were no real threat to take-off.

"What about the shore-party?"

"Almost through, sir – another seven or eight minutes, by Peck's reckoning." Seerbacker nodded. Peck, the *Pequod*'s chief engineer, would not be much out in his reckoning. He would have bullied the men into utmost effort, whatever his private considerations concerning Gant and the safety of the ship.

Fleischer withdrew his head, and Gant made to rise from his chair. The next thing he knew was the huge jolt of the deck moving beneath him, and he was flung head-first across the table. He had a brief glimpse of Seerbacker catapulting off his bunk, and then his left shoulder struck the bulkhead with a jarring blow. The ship's lights winked out, and then returned, glowing brightly again. He felt the numbness of his shoulder and side, and the weight of Seerbacker's body lying winded across his chest. He heard a clatter from the companionway, presumably Fleischer's body being thrown to the ground. He shifted his body, and saw Seerbacker's stunned, frightened face staring up at him.

"What in hell's name . . .?" he said, his voice small, choking.

"What was it?" Gant said.

Seerbacker struggled to his feet, ungainly, bruised. Blood seeped from the corner of his mouth. He had bitten his tongue. He wiped the blood from his face, and stared at his reddened fingers for a moment. Then he seemed galvanised into action by the sound of running feet outside. He heaved open the door.

"What the hell's going on, sailor?" he bawled.

Gant picked himself off the floor, rubbing his shoulder. Feeling was returning to it, and he reckoned that nothing was dislocated or broken.

"Sir — we don't know."

"What? Then what the hell are you doing here, sailor? Find out!"

"Sir!" The man's footsteps retreated down the companionway.

"The Firefox!" Gant said.

"The hell with that!" Seerbacker exploded. "What about my boat?"

Gant followed him out of the cabin. Fleischer was leaning against the bulkhead, blood oozing from a deep, livid gash on his forehead. Seerbacker ignored him, dazed as he was, and pressed past him towards the control room. Gant stopped briefly to examine the wound, then he patted the young man on the shoulder, and followed in the captain's wake.

The control room gave a confused impression of men picking themselves up, of furniture overturned. Gant headed towards the hatch-ladder up to the bridge.

"Get me a damage-report — and quick!" barked the captain.

The freezing air bit through Gant's parka, and the wind plucked his first raw breath away from him. From the top of the sail, he could see the Firefox in the improved visibility, apparently undamaged. The men who had been working on the ice were scattered, one or two still prone, obviously injured, other men bending over them, others spreading out over the ice.

Gant yelled down to a sailor near the submarine:

"What happened?"

The man looked up, saw the captain standing alongside Gant.

"Don't know, sir. We — heard this cracking sound, like a scream, and then I was trying to push my face into the floe. I thought it was a fish homing on the boat, sir!"

"It was no torpedo. Where's Mr. Peck?"

"He headed off that way, sir," the sailor replied, pointing due north across the floe.

Gant strained his eyes, but the mist still clung to the floe in patches, and visibility was no more than a hundred yards at best. He stared in the direction of Peck's disappearance, and there was an

197

unstable yet formless apprehension watery in his stomach. As the minutes passed, the wind, stronger now it seemed, gusted occasionally into his face, making his eyes water. And he began to be afraid.

Then he saw Peck's figure emerging from the mist. As if prompted by something in his mind, or as if Peck's appearance heralded an answer, he began to run towards the Chief Engineer.

"What is it?" he asked breathlessly, reaching the big man. "What's wrong?"

Peck looked down at him, and said simply: "Pressure-ridge."

"What?" Gant's face was open with shock. "How big?"

"Three, maybe four feet – right across the floe, if my guess is right."

"Where, man – where? Show me!" He dragged at Peck's sleeve, and the big man turned round, following him. Gant's white, desperate face disturbed him, especially the way he kept moving ahead in obvious impatience and then looking round, like a dog hurrying its master. Seerbacker, puzzled, followed in their wake.

The pressure-ridge was almost four feet high and it had emerged from the ice like a low wall stretching right across the floe, as far as Gant could see in either direction.

"You said it – goes all the way?"

"All the way – I walked a fair piece of it, in both directions. I guess it goes right across."

Gant looked as though he disbelieved Peck for a moment but he knew that the engineer would have understood the significance of the ridge, and would have checked its extent for the right reason.

"How – did it happen?" he said stupidly.

"Only one way," the big man said grimly. "Gusting wind drove one of the smaller floes behind us right up our ass – like an automobile smash. Result, one pressure-ridge."

Gant turned on Peck, grabbing the sleeves of his parka in both hands. "You realise what this means?" he said. "I can't damn well get out of here. I can't take off!"

The result of his deliberations, of his self-recriminations and the growing certainty that he was right and the First Secretary was disastrously wrong was, Vladimirov reflected bitterly, nothing more than a hesitation, a glance in the direction of the most powerful man in the Soviet Union. When the bulky figure merely nodded, emphasising his last order, Vladimirov turned back to the console in front of him and spoke.

"Tretsov – Vladimirov." Though he had ignored code, he would not identify the aircraft with which he was communicating, other than by the pilot's name. In that lay a degree of anonymity.

At that moment, Tretsov, the second test-pilot on the Mig-31 project, was at fifty thousand feet, his nose-probe buried in the udder of a refuelling plane, with which the Mig had made rendezvous minutes before.

Static crackled through the console speaker. "Tretsov – over," came the faint voice.

"Vladimirov to Tretsov. Proceed to the North Cape area as soon as refuelling is completed."

"North Cape – repeat your message, please."

Vladimirov's voice betrayed his anger. Of course the pilot wondered at the change of plan!

"I said North Cape – make radio contact with the following units – missile-cruiser *Riga*, 'Wolfpack' ground patrol Murmansk – do you copy?"

After a silence: "Tretsov – I copy. Proceed to North Cape, contact *Riga* and ground control Murmansk – over."

"Good. Await further instructions – over and out."

Vladimirov flicked the switch, and turned away from the transmitter. It did not matter, he thought, that the Americans would undoubtedly pick up the signal, transmitted in clear voice as it had been. It was merely another unit being directed towards the decoy area. He looked once more at the First Secretary but the Soviet leader was in whispered conversation with Andropov. He turned his gaze towards Kutuzov. The old man's rheumy eyes met his, and he shook his head slightly. Vladimirov's eyes thanked him for the gesture of sympathy, of understanding.

Then the thoughts began to nag at him again. If only he could be *sure* in some way . . . He knew how it had been done, what the search-units ought to be looking for. But he was afraid, afraid to risk the shreds of his credibility, the remains of his career, on such a wild idea. He swallowed. He knew the answer – and he knew the First Secretary would not listen.

He despised himself. He was throwing away the Mig-31, handing it to the Americans on a platter! Yet he could do nothing – they would not believe him.

They had checked the floe. As Peck had surmised, the ridge ran the whole east-west axis. It was a little more than half-way down the length of the floe, down the runway for the aircraft. Gant could not possibly, by any mechanical or physical means, take off along the length of snow-covered ice available to him while the ridge remained.

"It will work, sir," Peck was saying, leaning forward, standing taller than the thin figure of Seerbacker. Fleischer, his training and experience inadequate for these particular circumstances, remained silent. Peck's second engineer, Haynes, contributed his assessments of time and effort in support of his chief. With Gant, there were now five of them, standing stiffly in the raw air, wrapped in the mist that still clung to the floe. The wind was still gusting, but less strongly now as if, having achieved its purpose, it had become satisfied, quiescent.

"Hell, Jack – have we enough axes and shovels on board to do the job?" Seerbacker said. His eyes slid for a moment towards Gant, who seemed to be studying the floe intently, taking no notice of the discussion. Seerbacker was irritated by the man's apparent detachment, then dismissed it from his mind.

"Sir, we've got enough – crowbars, heavy screwdrivers, axes – anything!" Peck seemed to take Seerbacker's caution as a personal affront. "And we could place a couple of small charges, maybe?" he added.

"Damn that, Jack!"

"No, sir. You place 'em properly, small ones – you won't damage the ice!"

Seerbacker was silent for a moment, then he said, addressing Gant:

"How wide is the wheel-track on that bird, Gant?"

"Twenty-two feet," Gant replied mechanically.

"You certain?"

Gant merely nodded, without shifting his gaze from the ridge. He kicked at it aimlessly with a boot. Some loose snow flicked away, spattered on the toe – he had not marked the surface of the ridge.

"How much d'you need – how much of this wall you want to come down?" Peck said.

Gant turned his head, recognising the challenge in the big man's voice. He smiled humourlessly, thought for a moment, and then said: "Thirty feet."

There was a leaden silence for a moment, then Seerbacker said:

"Don't bullshit, Gant. You're not going to waste my time and wreck that bird just to prove something to my chief engineer!" His eyes flickered between the two men, sensing the challenge and response, its origins in Gant's earlier momentary panic in front of Peck.

"Thirty feet," Gant said. "That's all I need."

"Then it's thirty fuckin' feet you'll get, mister!" Seerbacker spat back. "Now you pick out the spot, man – and Mr. Peck and his team will get to work for you!"

Gant strolled away from them, and the four men tagged wearily behind him, as if unwilling. Seerbacker regretted the way he had

200

handled Gant, bridling him, making him say something which he would obviously regret. Yet there was no sign of doubt on Gant's face, no fear that a margin for error of four feet on either side of the main undercart in the visibility now available to him was almost like cutting his throat with a blunt knife.

Damn him to hell! Seerbacker thought. He gets right under my skin!

Gant stopped, waited for them, and said: "Here."

He kicked a boot hard into the ice at the crest of the ridge at stomach height, and chipped the crest slightly. Peck reached into the pocket of his parka, pulled out an aerosol can, and sprayed it on the ice. Part of the chipped portion of the crest sagged under the impact of the alcohol-based de-icing fluid. Gant paced out thirty feet, and waited for Peck to mark the ice. Then he nodded. Seerbacker sensed they were almost in the centre of the ridge, near the centre of the floe. Gant had picked the longest north-south axis for his take-off.

"How long to clear thirty feet, Mr. Peck?" Seerbacker asked.

"An hour, sir – if you include the spraying-down."

Gant wanted to tell them it was too long – but there was no point in futile protest.

"An hour?"

Peck nodded. Seerbacker was silent for a moment, then tugged his handset from his pocket. He pressed the button, and said: "Waterson, hook me up to the ship's address system, huh?" He waited until his request was accomplished, and then he said: "This is the captain – hear this. It will take one hour for the pressure-ridge to be cleared, and that means we have to stay on the surface for that length of time. I want utmost vigilance at all times; air, surface, and sub-surface searches to be thorough. If any of you guys misses something, you kill all of us – understand that. You won't just be shitting on yourself or your service record! And you stay rigged for silent running – we're going to be making enough noise up here for all of you, so keep it quiet. You guys on the plane – just keep it de-iced and ready to roll the *minute* you get the word. Mr. Peck is in charge of the shore-party to work on the ridge, and I'll let him tell you who's volunteered, and what equipment he wants out here. Just a minute – Doc?" There was a pause, then:

"Yes, skipper?"

"What about our casualties?"

"Harper's concussed – hit that hard head of his on the deck-plates. Smith lost a couple of teeth fighting the ice, and I'm putting four stitches in the back of Riley's skull. Anything else is less dramatic than that."

"Thanks, Doc. Tell Riley it should improve his brain – and Smith's looks will definitely have improved! O.K., here's Mr. Peck, you guys. Hear him good."

He switched off and pocketed his own handset, and left Peck calling out his list of names, the catalogue of brawn that the *Pequod* was able to muster.

Seerbacker joined Gant. He stared at him for a moment, then said: "You are sure?"

Gant nodded.

"Don't worry – Peck doesn't get to me. I can get out through thirty feet of clear ice."

"In visibility like this?"

"In worse."

"Hell, man – O.K., but it's your funeral."

There was a silence, then Gant said: "Thanks, Seerbacker – for the hour."

Seerbacker felt awkward. Gant, he sensed, was making a real effort, meant what he was saying.

"Yeah – sure. I wouldn't do it for just anybody, though," he said, and grinned.

"I – I'll go take a look at the plane."

"Sure – you do that."

Gant nodded, and walked away. Near the *Pequod*, he could see figures hurrying through the grey curtain of the mist, wrapped in the white breath of their effort. Peck, he thought without rancour, was a taskmaster, and when he said jump, they jumped. It wasn't his business. Peck knew what he was doing.

It had been his suggestion, from the beginning. The crude hacking out of a section of the ridge, then the smoothing process to follow, the former accomplished by brute force and axes, the latter by spraying the broken section of the ridge with the superheated steam that drove the turbines of the submarine, directed onto the ice by pressure hoses.

The Firefox was clear of ice. Alongside, looking as if it had strayed from some gigantic toolshed, was a ten-foot piece of equipment resembling nothing so much as a garden-spray. This was linked by a hose to a fluid tank in the sail of the *Pequod*, and from it, pumped by a small electric motor, gushed a stream of alcohol-based anti-icing fluid – the "booze" as Seerbacker's crew referred to it. This kept the wings and fuselage free of ice. Four men operated the sprayer – two men pushed it on its undercarriage, and two others directed the fine, pressurised spray from two small hoses tucked beneath their arms. They went about their task with a mechanical, unthinking precision, and Gant could see the light indentations of the wheels beneath the sprayer where they had ceaselessly circumnavigated the plane.

Gant stood and watched the Firefox for a long time, as if drawn to the machine, as if feeding through his eyes. He had had no time until now, no moment of being *outside* the plane with time to absorb its lines, its design, its functional wickedness of appearance. The first time – there had only been the confused impression of noise, and light, and the fire at the far end of the hangar, and Baranovich's white-coated figure slumped on the concrete . . . Now he watched in silence, taking in the slim fuselage, the bulging air-intakes in front of the massive engines, larger than anything Turmansky had ever thought of fitting to an interceptor-attack plane, the seemingly impossible stubbiness of the wings, with the advanced Anab missiles slung in position beneath them. He saw the scorch marks where he had fired two of them – one to bring down the Badger, the other to goad the captain of the *Riga* into premature action. He walked closer. The two missiles had been replaced, making up his complement of four.

This didn't really surprise him. A Mig-25 had been captured from the Syrians in the dummy-run for this operation. Presumably, it had been armed and its missiles, Anabs, had been assigned to Seerbacker, for delivery. Buckholz, Gant realised, missed nothing.

The refuelling had been completed even while he, Seerbacker and Peck had discussed the ridge. The hoses had been withdrawn, the bonding wire removed from the nose-wheel strut. Presumably, the refuelling crew were now taking their turn at the ridge.

He walked away with reluctance, then, as the distance increased, and the Firefox became a shadowy, insubstantial bulk in the mist, he lengthened his stride.

It took him almost half-an-hour to walk from the Firefox to the southerly end of the floe and then to traverse the floe from south to north, along the line of his visualised runway. The collision of the floes had not damaged the runway, other than by the ridge. He was returning from the northern edge of the floe when the handset that Fleischer had issued him bleeped in his pocket.

"Yes?"

"Gant?" Seerbacker's voice sounded laboured, out of breath. "Listen to me, mister. We've got three sonar contacts to the south of us, along your flight-path."

Gant was silent for a moment, then he said: "Yes – it has to be the cruiser and her two escorts – hunter-killer subs."

"Jesus – you know how to make trouble for me, Gant – you really, really do!"

"How long before they get here?"

"Forty — maybe forty-five minutes."

"Then that's enough."

"Fuck you, mister! Enough time for you to get the hell out of here — what about my ship? What about its gallant crew who are at this moment working their tails off to get you a runway you can use?"

"I — I'm sorry, Seerbacker — I didn't think . . ."

Almost as if he were winning a point, Seerbacker replied:

"Anyway — it'll take longer than we thought. It seems Mr. Peck was a little optimistic in his estimates. We'll need almost the same time to get you out of here as they'll need to catch up on us!"

Gant was silent. Eventually, Seerbacker said: "You still there, Gant?"

"Uh — yeah. You sure they're heading this way?"

"Maybe, maybe not. They *weren't*, that's for sure."

"Weren't?"

"They were steaming west, across the track of the floe, but sure as hell is hot, Gant, if we can see them, then they can damn well see us!"

TEN:

The Duel

Vladimirov confronted the First Secretary, a renewed sense of purpose doing little to contradict or overcome the tension he felt. He knew, with a sickening certainty, that he did not want to throw his career away, that he wanted Kutuzov's rank and post when the old man was put out to grass. Yet he was contained within a dilemma. Even if he managed to quell the rising doubts and proceed as ordered, there was still the chance that, if Gant succeeded in escaping with the Mig-31 intact, he himself would be blamed for the Soviet failure to recapture or destroy. It was that knowledge finally that persuaded him to demand that action be taken with regard to the sonar-contact reported by the *Riga* a minute before.

"In my estimation, First Secretary," he began, keeping his voice neutral, level, with a vast effort of will, "this contact, though confused by the presence of ice-floes, is worth investigation."

His words seemed to be swallowed in the silence of the War Command Centre. Vladimirov was aware that everybody, from Andropov down to the most junior radio-operator, understood that the room had polarised around the First Secretary and the O.C. "Wolfpack". They were spectators in a power game being played out between the two men. They seemed to the General, tense with anticipation, almost to appreciate the fact that he was at last making his move – his final move.

"In your estimation," the Soviet leader said softly after a while, his voice seeming to blame Vladimirov for speaking.

Vladimirov nodded. Then he said: "I – I am sure that I understand now how they intended to refuel the Mig at sea . . ." He chose the cryptic words with care. He had to play the First Secretary like a recalcitrant, dangerous fish, a shark. Yet he had committed himself. If his assumption proved to be correct, and they still failed, it would be tantamount to professional suicide to have voiced his ideas. The wild idea had grown in him slowly; he had tried to deny it, rid himself of it and the personal perspectives it evoked. Now, however, it possessed him, and he could no longer avoid its communication to the First Secretary. Damnation, he thought, almost grinding his teeth as he envisaged the consequences of his ensuing conflict with the Soviet leader — but it was their last and only chance to prevent the Mig from falling into American hands, delivered by Gant.

His hatred of Gant burnt at the back of his throat like nausea.

"Yes — they have used — *are using* — a large ice-floe as a runway, and the refuelling vessel is undoubtedly a submarine. That is the sonar-contact that the *Riga* has made!" In bald, hurried words, the idea seemed ridiculous, unconvincing. Yet, in his mind, he could visualise the scene so clearly! The parka-clothed figures, the fuel-lines, the aircraft sitting on the ice . . . there were a thousand floes the Americans could have chosen from!

"The aircraft has *landed*, Vladimirov?"

Vladimirov knew he had lost. The voice, dry and calm, told him he had failed to convince. He looked around him. Faces turned away, stares directed aside, or downwards, not meeting his eyes. Even Kutuzov turned away, the eyes of a spectator at a road accident.

"Yes." His voice was too high, he knew it. Damn, he could not even control his voice any more! How was it, he wondered, that the man was able to frighten him from the other side of the map-table, on the surface of which the coloured lights scuttled towards the North Cape? They had accepted Aubrey's decoys — Vladimirov *knew* they were decoys, aircraft and a submarine, bustling to no purpose but to trick them — and the total available Soviet air and sea forces had been ordered to dash for the North Cape. The man in front of him now possessed power that could ruin him, drop him, crush him, imprison him — say that he was mad. And Vladimirov did not want to end up like Grigorenko, in an asylum.

He tried once more.

"The contact is on the flight-path last registered by the *Riga* and her escorts — just before the trace was lost."

Then he subsided into silence. He watched, almost like a spectator himself, as the large, square, grey-suited man stared, apparently idly, at the map-table. The *Riga* and the two escorting submarines were rapidly becoming solitary lights as the scene of Soviet surface and air activity moved further west. Then he looked up into Vladimirov's eyes. The incredulous General saw, for an instant before the eyes became hooded again, naked, stark fear. He could not assimilate the information, until the First Secretary said:

"It would take too long to recall the helicopters, and order them to make a search of the area. Instead, my dear general, because you seem to have this — obsessive concern with ice-floes and tanker-submarines . . ." He paused and Andropov, seated now next to him, smiled thinly. He supplied the expected reaction, even as his humourless eyes behind the steel-framed spectacles indicated that he understood the motives of the Soviet leader. "As I said – to give you peace of mind, my dear Vladimirov – we will despatch *one* of the escorting submarines to investigate this highly dubious sonar-contact that the cruiser claims to have made." He smiled blandly, recovering from the moment of naked understanding he had seen in the Chairman's eyes.

"But, if it is . . ." Vladimirov began.

The First Secretary held up his huge hand. "*One* of the escorts, Vladimirov – how long will it take?"

"Forty minutes, no more."

"Then – if there is anything to report, if the contact turns out to be interesting – the second Mig-31 will be ordered to return from its rendezvous off the North Cape – at top speed."

It was over. Vladimirov felt the tension drain away, leaving him physically weak, exhausted. At least it was something. Yet he could not sense a victory. He was unable to do more than continue to despise himself.

Swiftly, as if to hide the feelings that must show on his face, he turned to the encoding-console to issue orders to the captain of the *Riga*.

Gant had watched the green sonar-screen and the sweep of its tireless arm until his eyes ached. The endless revolution of the arm, dragging the wash of whiteness behind it that left three crystallised points of light in its wake, unnerved him. After silent, tense minutes in the control room of the *Pequod*, leaning over the sailor wearing headphones, listening to the amplified pinging of the contact, it became apparent what was occurring. One of the blips on the screen, one of the escort submarines, had detached itself from its westward course, and was moving along the line of a bearing that would bring it homing on the *Pequod*. The other two blips continued on their westward course.

As yet the blips appeared only on the long-range sonar-screen, the extent of whose survey carried for a thirty-mile radius around the submarine. They were at the top of the screen – and the sonar had been working in a directional sweep, when the three vessels had been picked up. Now, the blip of the escort submarine homing on them was little more than twenty miles away.

After a huge silence filled only with the quick human breathing of the crew and the reiterated pinging of the contact-echo, Seerbacker, at Gant's elbow, said, "How long before it gets here?"

The operator didn't look up, but said: "Can't say, sir. You know what this long-range sonar is like — distortion factor of twenty per cent, sometimes. I can't be sure, sir."

"Hell!"

"How fast can those Russian subs move?" Gant said.

"How the hell do I know?" Seerbacker stormed, turning on him, his long face white with anger, and fear. "I don't even know what *kind* of submarine it is, man! Until it transfers from the long-range screen into close-up, we can't get a 3-D image of it from the computer that'll identify it."

"Contact bearing Red Three-Niner, and closing," the operator called out, apparently undisturbed by the emotions of Seerbacker snarled in his ear.

"What — will you do?" Gant asked.

Seerbacker looked at him for a moment, and then said:

"I have a sealed packet for you — your route, I guess. That's the first thing. Second, I have to get our disguise out the wardrobe, and dust it off!"

Gant looked at him, puzzled.

"Contact still bearing Red Three-Niner and closing."

Seerbacker looked at the operator's neck, as if he wished the man dead, or dumb at least, then he said: "Give me the blower." Fleischer thrust the microphone into his hand, and pressed the alert button at the side of the transmitter, signalling the crew to prepare for a message from the captain.

Seerbacker nodded, and then said into the microphone: "Hear this — this is the captain. It's operate 'Harmless' procedure, on the double. We have about thirty minutes, maybe less, I doubt more. Get the lead out of your asses, and move — move as fast as you've ever moved before."

Having relieved his tension by way of bullying his crew, Seerbacker turned to Gant with a more even countenance. Smiling, he nodded towards the watertight door leading to his cabin, and Gant followed in his wake.

"What is 'Harmless'?" he asked as the footsteps clicked along the companionway.

Seerbacker was silent until he turned into his cabin, Gant still behind him, and had locked the door. Then he went to a wall-safe, cranked the dial, and pulled the small door open. He handed Gant a package inside a cellophane wrapper. Gant nodded, as Seerbacker's two-fingered grip revealed the presence of an acid capsule within the clear plastic, the "auto-destruct" for the sealed orders.

Gant unfolded the single sheet of flimsy within the envelope, studying it carefully.

"What is 'Harmless'?" he repeated.

Seerbacker grinned. "Just our little joke – only it may save our lives," he said. "We'll go up top in a while – you can see for yourself."

Gant nodded, as if the answer to his question did not really interest him. His orders were simple. There was a list of map coordinates, and times, which he knew would take him at first low across the Finnish coast, east of the North Cape decoy area, across the lake-strewn landscape of Finland, towards Stockholm. Once there, where the Gulf of Bothnia encountered the Baltic, he was instructed to rendezvous with the late afternoon British Airways commercial flight from Stockholm to London. He knew why. If he tucked in behind the plane, and below it, not only would he be out of sight of the crew, but all that would show up on an infra-red screen would be the single image of the airliner's heat-source. And the airliner would be expected across the North Sea, on route and on schedule. And he was immune to any sort of detection other than visual – an unlikely possibility. No Elint ship in the North Sea warned to watch for him would guess where he was. When he arrived at a specified coordinate off the English coast, he was to call R.A.F. Scampton in Lincolnshire on a frequency within the general aviation band, assuming the identity of a test-flight for a commercial passenger plane receiving its Certificate of Airworthiness check-up. With luck, if it worked, the Russians would lose him, if they had ever found him, off the eastern coast of Sweden, when he linked infra-red images with the British Airways flight.

He read the coordinates once more, committing them firmly to memory. Then he replaced the sheet in its buff envelope, and the envelope in its wrapper. Seerbacker had already placed a large steel ashtray on the table. Gant placed the packet in the ashtray, then ground the heel of his hand on it. Almost immediately, the fumes of the released acid rose pungently and the packet began to dissolve. Gant watched it until it consisted of no more than a few blackened, treacly specks.

Then he nodded, as if to himself, and said: "O.K. – let's get urgent, Captain. I want to see what progress has been made on my runway." His eyes, surprisingly to Seerbacker, almost twinkled for a moment, and he added: "And I want to see 'Harmless'."

Of course, Aubrey reflected, he could not be certain – no, not by a very long way, not just at present. Nevertheless, he was unable quite to extinguish the small flame of hope that warmed his stomach like good brandy; the heat of success. The code activity from the Russians, combined with the success of the decoy-missions around the North Cape area, and the signal from Seerbacker aboard the *Pequod* that the Firefox was safely down, and refuelled — all added to his barely suppressed sense of satisfaction.

Shelley, too, he could see, could hardly keep a schoolboyish grin from his smooth features. The Americans, having swung down with the graph of Buckholz's doubts, been infected by indecision, now lifted in a rising curve again. Curtin was on the steps, adjusting the positions of Russian planes and vessels as they moved further and further into the decoy area. Aubrey glanced up at the huge map, and saw only the position of the floe, and the coloured pin representing the Firefox alongside it.

Had Seerbacker risked getting off another signal, to confirm the sonar-contact with the approaching Russian submarine, or had Aubrey been aware of Vladimirov's intuition, and partial success in Bilyarsk, his mood might have been less equable, his ego-temperature somewhat lower. But he was still blinded by the brilliance of his own design, and Seerbacker had not informed him of the suspicious escort submarine in his vicinity. For Aubrey, the design had become now only a mechanical matter — as long as Gant followed instructions, it was in the bag.

Aubrey maintained that he was a man who never, absolutely on no occasion, counted his chickens — but now he did. The magnitude of what he had achieved, from inception, through planning, to execution, stunned him, shone like a fierce sun on his vanity, causing it to bloom.

"Hm — gentlemen," he said, clearing his throat. "I realise that perhaps this may be a little premature . . ." He smiled deprecatingly, knowing that they shared his mood. "Nevertheless — perhaps we might permit ourselves a little — a modicum of celebratory alcohol?"

Buckholz grinned openly. "You sure put it tortuously, Aubrey — but yes, I reckon we could open a bottle," he said.

"Good."

Aubrey moved to the drinks trolley that had stood throughout their vigil in the corner of the operations room. Suddenly, the place seemed to be without the stale, almost rancid, smell of old cigar smoke and unchanged clothing. The faces were no longer strained with tension. It was merely that they were a little tired — tired with the satisfying tiredness of a job well done, of something completed.

He broke the seal on the malt whisky, and poured the pale gold liquid into four tumblers in generous measures. Then, deferentially, he handed the drinks round on a small silver tray, brought from his own flat, in readiness.

Aubrey raised his glass, smiled benignly, and said: "Gentlemen — to the Firefox . . . and, of course, to Gant."

"Gant — and the Firefox," the four men chanted in a rough

unison. Aubrey watched, with mild distaste, as Buckholz threw his drink into the back of his throat, swallowed the precious liquid in one. Really, he thought, the man has absolutely no *taste* – none at all.

As he sipped at his own drink, it seemed more than ever merely a matter of time. He glanced at the telephone. In a few minutes, no more, it would be time to order the car to transport them to R.A.F. Scampton – if Gant were not to arrive before themselves, which would not do at all.

He smiled at the thought.

Peck was standing in front of Gant and Seerbacker, looming over them both. Sweat rimmed the fur of his hood in crystals of ice, and ice stood out stiffly on his moustache. His face was pale, drained by effort.

"Well?" Seerbacker said, his hand still on the sail-ladder of the *Pequod*.

"It's done, sir," Peck said. Then he looked at Gant, and his voice hardened. "We've cleared your damn runway, Mr. Gant!"

"Peck!" Seerbacker warned.

For a moment, Gant thought the huge Chief Engineer was intending to strike him, and he flinched physically. Then he said: "I'm sorry, Peck."

Peck seemed nonplussed by his reply. He scrutinised Gant's face, as if suspecting some trick, nodded as he appeared satisfied, and then seemed to feel that some explanation was required of him. He said: "Sorry – Major . . ." Gant's eyes opened in surprise. It was the first time anyone had used his old rank. Peck meant it as a mark of respect. "We – it's just the feeling, sir. Working out there on that damn pressure-ridge, the men and me – well, we just kept thinking how we could have been getting out of this place, instead of breaking our backs." The big man's voice tailed off, and he looked steadily down at his feet.

Gant said: "It's O.K., Peck – and thanks. Now, tell me where we are, what stage you have reached."

Peck became business-like, immediately formal. "We've got a thirty-feet gap hacked out of the ridge. Now we run the hoses from the turbine on a direct-feed – we need a lot of pipe, Major – it'll take time."

Gant nodded.

"Get to it, Peck – the sooner you've done, the sooner you can get going. When you've finished smoothing down the surface of the floe – and make it as smooth as possible, 'cos I don't want to hit a bump at a hundred-and-fifty knots – I want you to spray steam on the ice, down the length of the runway, starting as near the northern edge of the floe as you can, running down to the Firefox – if you have the time."

Peck looked puzzled. "Why, Major?"

"Clear the surface snow, Peck – that's what it'll do. I don't need to be held back by the surface-resistance . . ."

"Get to it, Peck," Seerbacker said. "I've just got to check on the decoy procedure, and then I'm coming to take a look at your night-school efforts!"

Peck grinned, nodded, and moved away down the length of the *Pequod*, forward to the hatch above the turbines, where two members of the engineering crew were feeding down great serpent-loops of hose into the belly of the submarine.

"You want to see 'Harmless'?" Seerbacker said. "Come take a look."

"Harmless" was hurried, crude, and brilliant, Gant was forced to admit. The feverish activity of those members of the sub's crew not working on the pressure-ridge at first seemed to obey no overall strategy, tend towards no definable object. Then he realised what was happening.

The submarine was being transformed into the headquarters of an arctic weather-station. Over the transmitter in his pocket, Seerbacker snapped out orders that the torpedo-tubes and forward crew-quarters were to be flushed out with sea water, the evidence of the paraffin to be removed. This would be followed by faked evidence of hull damage to explain the presence of residual water in both compartments. On the ice, a hut had been assembled from its components, and crude wooden furniture carried inside. Maps and charts covered the newly erected walls, Gant saw as he peered through one of the windows. Impressive lists of figures filled notepads and sheets attached to clipboards. Two masts had been erected, one twenty feet high, the other reaching to thirty feet. The taller of the pair was a radio mast, while an anemometer revolved on the top of the other one, and below this a vane swung, indicating direction of the measured wind.

A white chest, a Stephenson Screen, containing thermometers and hygrometers, stood beneath the smaller mast, and the disguising of the floe as a weather-station was completed by holes drilled into the ice, in some cases through to the sea beneath, into which thermometers had been lowered.

As Gant watched Peck and his men unroll the lengths of hose, clip the sections together, he saw a bright orange weather-balloon float up into the sky. Still clinging to the surface of the floe were shredding, rolling embers of mist, but above it, the cloud base began

212

at thirteen thousand feet. A second balloon hovered a hundred feet above the *Pequod*, attached by a nylon line. The balloons would explain the earlier release of a signal balloon when he landed.

It took a little more than fifteen minutes to transform the surface of the floe into the appearance of a U.S. weather-station studying the movements and characteristics of a large ice-floe in its southward path to immolation. The fact that the *Pequod* was operating in the northern Barents Sea, rather than east of Greenland, was the only weakness as far as Gant could see.

As Seerbacker said, as he joined Gant near the bridge-ladder of the submarine: "They can't prove a thing, Gant – as long as you're long gone from here before that Russian boat climbs all over us!"

Gant glanced reflectively down at the ice, and then said: "What about the exhaust – they'll be keeping infra-red watch on this floe. They must have tumbled something?"

"Hell, Gant – I don't give a cuss for your heat-trail. Just get that bird out of here, and leave me to do the worrying, will you?"

Gant smiled at the mock ferocity of Seerbacker's answer. The man was frightened, knew he was treading a fine edge of ground steel. He nodded. "Sure. I'll get out of here, just as soon as I can."

"Good." Seerbacker plucked the radio-transmitter from the pocket of his parka, pressed it to his cheek, and flicked the switch. "This is the captain – you there, Fleischer?"

"Sir." From the radio, Fleischer's voice had a quality of unreality, one that impressed upon Gant the whole situation – the tiny floe, the bitter wastes of the Barents Sea, the approach of the Russian hunter-killer submarine.

"What's the news on our friend?"

There was a pause, then the Exec. said: "We're getting a computer-prediction now, sir. Subject to a seven-per-cent error in the sonar contact . . ."

"Yeah. Tell me the bad news."

"The ETA for the sub is seventeen minutes."

"Jesus!"

"Course and speed appear to be exactly the same, sir. She's coming straight for us."

Seerbacker wore a strained look on his face for a moment, then he grinned at Gant. "You hear that?" Gant nodded. "O.K., Fleischer – I'm leaving this set on receive from now on – I want you to call it to me every minute, understand?"

"Sir."

"When the sub comes up on close-range sonar, call me the exact speed and distance every thirty seconds."

"Sir."

Seerbacker clipped the handset to the breast pocket of his parka, tugged at it to ensure that it wouldn't come adrift, nodded to Gant, and headed away from the submarine in the direction indicated by the two hoses which trailed like endless black snakes away into the mist. Following him, the ridge still out of sight, the violent hiss of steam hardly audible, Gant was once more possessed by a sense of the precariousness of his position. The hunched, loping figure of Seerbacker seemed slight, almost insubstantial, certainly not a presence capable of supporting the weight of his escape. The firm ice beneath his feet, the glimpse of the Firefox in the mist as he turned his head to glance at it – they did not reassure him. The Russian submarine was homing on the floe and the *Pequod*. They had sixteen minutes, give or take a little.

Two men manned each nozzle, directing a jet of superheated steam onto the ugly, unfinished plasterwork of the hole in the ridge. It was supposed to be thirty feet across. Gant's brain measured it – to his imagination it looked small, too small. The steam played over the rough surface of the floe, over the hacked, torn edges of the gap – smoothing it out. It took them only a couple of minutes to give the gap smooth edges, a smooth, gleaming floor.

Peck had turned once, acknowledged the presence of Gant and the captain, and then ignored them. As soon as the gap was smoothed to his satisfaction, he bawled at his team: "All right, you guys – get this runway smoothed off!"

"What for, chief?"

"Because I'm telling you to do it – you'll enjoy it, Clemens!"

The hoses snaked away into the mist, unwillingly following the men dragging at them. They snaked past Gant's feet, slowly, far too slowly. He looked at his watch, just as Fleischer's voice squawked from near Seerbacker's shoulder.

"The sub's transferred to close-range screen, sir."

Seerbacker leaned his head like a bird attending to ruffled feathers, and said: "Tell me the worst."

"Computer-identification: Russian, type hunter-killer submarine, range four-point-six miles, ETA nine minutes . . ."

"What?" Seerbacker bawled.

"Sorry, sir – the sonar-error must have been larger than we thought . . ."

"Now you tell me!" Seerbacker was silent for an instant, then he said: "Get off the air – Peck!"

"Sir?"

"You heard that, Chief?"

"Yes, sir – we'll never get this runway cleared, not a thirty-yard width all the way down the floe."

Seerbacker looked at Gant. "What the hell do you want?" he said.

"I – a hundred yards this side of the floe," Gant replied, pointing beyond the gap in the ridge, to the north. "Just give me that, and a clear runway this side of the gap." He waved his hand towards the Firefox.

Seerbacker repeated his instructions. Peck sounded dubious that he could complete the work, but affirmed that he would try. Gant stared into the mist, saw the huddled, squat shapes of men moving closer, straining as they dragged the unwilling hoses back on their tracks. He heard the recommencement of the spraying, smoothing out his runway, blasting the loose, powdery surface snow clear. If he was to reach the take-off speed he required, it *had* to be done. And he had to wait until it was done.

Seerbacker was speaking again. "Give me a status report on 'Harmless' – and this is the last time anyone refers to anything except the weather – understand?" He listened intently, almost leaning forward on the balls of his feet. When the voice at the other end had finished, he nodded in apparent satisfaction. Then he looked at Gant. "It's O.K. – we're covered, as long as we get you airborne."

"ETA seven minutes." Fleischer's voice was infected by something that sounded dangerously like panic.

"When he contacts you – give him the low-down, like on the script – O.K., Dick?" Seerbacker's voice was soothing.

"Sir."

Gant watched the steam skid across the snow. Blasts of powder lifted into the misty air. The hoses snaked nearer, the men straining at them, joined now by other, anonymous figures who passed Gant, summoned by Peck's call over the handset. Around the men, the self-inflicted blizzard raged, until Gant himself was enveloped in the blinding white smoke.

"ETA six minutes . . . still no radio contact, sir." Gant heard Fleischer's voice coming squeakily from the settling storm, saw the thin figure of Seerbacker outlined once more as the hoses passed away down the floe towards the plane. He wiped the snow from his stubbled face with the back of a mitten.

Seerbacker remained silent for a long time, his back to Gant as he watched Peck's party clearing the runway. To him, they appeared to be moving slowly, far too slowly. Unable to bear the tension or the silence any longer, he turned to Gant, and said:

"Are they going to make it?"

Gant nodded. "A minute to spare," he said.

"Can you get out of here in that time?"

215

"So far away, you wouldn't believe!" Gant said, with a grim smile.

"You better be right, mister – you just better be!"

"The contact is confirmed, First Secretary!" Vladimirov said, his hand slamming down on the map-table, so that the lights joggled and blurred for a moment.

The man in front of him seemed unmoved, perhaps still even contemptuous of the military man's urgency. Vladimirov knew that he was risking everything now, that there was no time for the niceties of career, and politics. He had *known* that it was an American submarine, and he had known its purpose. The silence had told on him. He was white and strained, and there was sweat on his forehead. He sensed that, alone in the room, only the old man, Kutuzov, supported him. Even he was silent.

"Vladimirov, calm yourself!" the First Secretary growled.

"Calm – calm myself?" Vladimirov's voice was high-pitched, out of control. He had committed himself now, he knew. Yet he could not stand by, even though he had schooled himself to do so, tried to quell the pendular motion of self-interest and duty that had plagued him throughout the morning. He had been unable to eat lunch, there had been such tightness in his stomach, such a knot of fear. Perhaps, he sensed, it was that he was afraid, the appalling knowledge that he was a coward, that had driven him to do his duty.

"Yes – calm yourself!"

"How can I be calm – when your stupidity – *stupidity*, is losing that aircraft to the Americans? You have read the file – you know what this man Gant is. He could land that aircraft on an ice-floe, and take off again. Listen to me – before it's too late!"

Like a frozen hare, Vladimirov watched the emotions chase each other across the face of the First Secretary. The initial hot rage at the insult was controlled in an instant, becoming once more the cold contempt of habit; a sense of sadistic pleasure seemed present to Vladimirov – lastly, however, he saw the emotion for which he searched . . . doubt.

Vladimirov pressed on, knowing that, even as he ruined himself, the First Secretary was afraid to ignore him any longer. The Soviet leader was unable to hold Vladimirov's gaze, and turned to look over his shoulder at Andropov. The Chairman's face was inscrutable.

"You *must* act, First Secretary – it is too *late* for politics."

The big man seemed as if poised to spring at the O.C. "Wolfpack", then he summoned a smile to his face, lightness to his voice: "Very well, Vladimirov, very well, if it means that much to you . . ." The voice hardened. "If you are so ready to − *spoil* things by your behaviour − I can do no more than humour you." He waved his hand in a generous gesture. "What is it you require?"

"The immediate recall of the second Mig from the North Cape rendezvous."

Vladimirov felt his voice tighten in his throat. His energy drained away. Now there was nothing left but fear, the sense of lost honours, of power thrown away. His victory was a bitter, icy moment in time. The First Secretary nodded, once. It did not matter about the remainder of the massive forces misdirected to the Cape. Not now. Only the second Mig-31 and Tretsov could affect the outcome this late. And, as if in recompense for his career sacrifice, he wanted Gant dead now, wanted Tretsov to finish him.

As he crossed to the console to issue orders to Tretsov, he glanced in the direction of Kutuzov. He thought for a moment, that he saw a kindly, even admiring, wisdom in the rheumy eyes, coupled with a profound compassion. Then he received the impression that the old man was detached, unaware of what was going on. He felt very alone, unable to decide which impression was the truth.

He snapped out his orders − possibly the last orders he would issue as O.C. "Wolfpack", he reflected grimly − in a calm, level voice, aware of the eyes behind him, watching him. The room was still with tension.

As Tretsov acknowledged, and the second Mig altered course for the ice-floe using its top speed of over four thousand miles an hour, Vladimirov grasped at this last chance that Tretsov would kill Gant.

"They're calling, sir − want identification immediately, sir," Fleischer's voice creaked out of the handset still clipped to Seerbacker's top pocket.

"The hell they do. You know the routine, it's written down. Do it."

"The Russian wants to speak to you, sir."

"Tell him I'll be along − I'm engaged in goddam experiments at the other end of the floe! Tell him I'll be along."

"Sir. ETA three minutes and fourteen seconds."

The conversation had gone on somewhere outside Gant, at a great distance. He and Seerbacker, waiting now by the aircraft, watching the snail-like approach of the men and the hoses, were miles apart in reality. Gant knew, almost to the second, how much time was left, and how much time they needed. They had precisely one minute to spare.

Seerbacker was visibly on edge. The voice of Fleischer acted on his lanky form like a twitch of the puppeteer's strings, pulling him taut.

He could not, as the Russian closed on the *Pequod*, any longer believe that the crude hut, the bogus charts, and the thermometers and the masts, would save him. Gant, however, was like a passenger whose train has arrived, calmly collecting the luggage of his thoughts prior to departure. He was no longer what Seerbacker had privately thought him, a man without a past on his way to no discernible future. He was in transit, and the figures on the landscape of mist and ice had little or nothing to do with him.

"Hell – they'll never make it!" Seerbacker snapped, unable to bear the tension.

"They will," Gant said calmly, his voice so level, almost a whisper, that Seerbacker looked at him curiously.

"Man, but you're cool . . ."

Gant smiled. "Somebody once told me I was dead – the flying corpse, they called me in Vietnam," Gant said.

"You minded?"

"No," Gant replied, shaking his head slightly. "Most of the guys who used the name were dead before they pulled us out . . . missiles, AA guns, enemy planes."

"Yes," Seerbacker said softly. "Hell of a war . . ."

Peck, sweating, pale, angry and weary, came towards them. There remained only a hundred yards of runway left to clear. He said, towering over Gant: "We won't make it, mister – if you don't get that bird out of here before the Reds arrive, we're all for the Lubyanka!"

Gant shook his head. "You have a minute in hand, Chief," he said. Peck stared at him, his mouth opening and closing, his eyes reflecting baffled incomprehension which changed slowly to conviction.

"If you say so," he muttered and turned away, back towards the hoses, exhorting his men blasphemously.

"You sure impress the hell out of the chief," Seerbacker said with a thin smile. "I just hope you don't have to do it to the Russians."

"ETA two minutes and thirty seconds," Fleischer said. "He keeps asking for you, sir. He wants convincing – I don't think I've done a very good job."

"To hell with that, Dick. Keep stalling him – does he look like surfacing? Has he asked any awkward questions?"

"No, sir. He seems just naturally suspicious – not as if he's looking for anything special."

Powdery snow blew into Gant's face. For a moment, distracted by the voices, he glanced up at the cloudy sky half-hidden by the shreds of mist. Then he realised that it was the vanguard of Peck's blizzard. The hose-men were still on schedule. He smiled to himself, and pulled off the parka. Peck's men were forty yards away from the Firefox. The de-icing team trundled past him, and stopped to look enquiringly in his direction. He nodded at them, at which they seemed vastly relieved, and the giant garden-spray was wheeled speedily towards the *Pequod*, to be hauled aboard and stowed before the arrival of the Russians.

Gant waited, like a guest anxious to be gone, until Seerbacker had finished his conversation with his Exec.

Seerbacker seemed surprised that he was stripped to his anti-G suit once more. He smiled awkwardly. "I – er, of course . . ." he said.

"So long, Seerbacker – and thanks."

"Get out of here, you bum!" Seerbacker said with mock severity.

Gant nodded, and swung his foot to the lowest rung of the pilot's ladder set in the fuselage. He climbed up, and slid feet first into the cockpit. There, he tugged on the integral helmet, plugged in the oxygen, the weapons-control jackplug, and the communications equipment. He needed first of all to taxi gently back to the southern extremity of the floe, where the snow had not, as yet, been cleared – it would be slowing, he knew, but he needed the maximum distance to the ridge. He went through the pre-start checks swiftly. He plugged in the anti-G suit automatically, even as he read off the dials and gauges that informed him of the condition of flaps, brakes and fuel. The fuel-tanks, he saw, smiling grimly, were satisfyingly full. It seemed aeons since there had been so much fuel in his universe. He pressed the hood control and it swung down, locked automatically, then he locked it manually. The handset issued him by Seerbacker was in the breast-pocket of the pressure-suit. He heard Fleischer's voice, from a great distance, saying:

"ETA one minute and thirty seconds."

"You hear that, Gant?" Seerbacker's voice chimed in. He continued, without waiting for a reply: "Good luck, fella. Got to get Mr. Peck's suspicious hoses stowed now, so get out of here!"

Gant gang-loaded the ignition, switched on the starter motors, turned on the high-pressure cock, and pressed the button. He heard, with relief, the sound of a double explosion as the cartridge start functioned. There was the same rapid, mounting whirring that he had heard in the hangar at Bilyarsk, as the huge turbines began to build. He switched in the fuel-booster, and eased open the throttles, until the rpm gauges were steady at twenty-seven per cent. He paused for only a second, then pushed the throttles open, until he reached the fifty-five per cent rpm, then he released the brakes.

The Firefox did not move.

He hauled back the throttles, and applied the brakes again. Even though he knew instantly what it was, and knew that it could be cured, his own failure to anticipate it made him weak and chill with sweat.

He opened the hood, tugged open the face-mask, and yelled into the handset: "Seerbacker – get those hoses over here – on the double!"

"What in the hell is it, Gant – can't you leave us . . ."

"Get over here! The wheels, they've frozen in!"

"You're stuck – with those engines, man?"

Already, even as Seerbacker apparently argued with him, he saw Peck and the others tugging the hoses towards the aircraft.

"If I try and pull myself out, I'll end up on my belly!"

Looking over the side of the cockpit, he saw Seerbacker's face looking up at him. Seerbacker was openly grinning. Steam billowed around him, snow flew up around the cockpit of the Firefox as the superheated steam was played carefully over the embedded wheels. Gant had not needed to warn Peck that if he played too much steam onto the tyres, at too high a pressure, he would, literally, melt them.

Peck had understood. He emerged from beneath the fuselage, looked up at Gant, and said into his handset: "O.K., Major Gant – now, for God's sake, get out of here!"

Gant signalled him with the thumbs-up, closed the hood once more, checked the gauges, and opened the throttles, until the rpm gauge once more showed fifty-five per cent. He released the brakes, the aircraft jolted out of the pits which the wheels and the applied steam had made, and rolled forward. Peck, Seerbacker and the others were moving away swiftly, tugging the thick, snaking hoses after them. Already, men were emerging from the *Pequod*, dressed in civilian parkas, the decoy scientists and technicians who should, by virtue of Seerbacker's ploy, occupy the floe when the Russians arrived. Gant turned the aircraft, and headed down the floe, directly in the line of the runway. He kept the Firefox completely straight on course. He would need his own tracks on his return.

The grey sea was ahead of him. He searched for any sign of the Russian submarine. There was nothing. Probably, the captain had decided not to surface until he arrived and stopped engines at the *Pequod*'s position, something to do with psychological surprise. Whatever it was, Gant was grateful on behalf of Seerbacker and his crew. No one would visually sight the Firefox.

He turned the plane in a semi-circle, lined up on his own tyre tracks in the surface snow, and opened the throttles. Almost immediately, he felt the restraint of the surface snow, the inability of the aircraft with normal take-off power to accelerate sufficiently. He could not use too much power. It would have the effect of digging in the nose, changing the relative airflow over the surfaces of the plane. He would, in fact, slow the plane if he used more power. There was little impression of speed until he passed over the spot on the ice where he had parked, and joined the smoothed, polished surface of the ice-runway blasted out for him by Peck and his men. Only now could he see the ridge, a tiny hump ahead of him. He could not see, in the poor visibility, the gap of thirty feet that had been carved in its face. The undercarriage shook free of the restraining snow, and he felt the plane lurch forward as if freed from glue or treacle. Now he was able to open the throttles, push up the rpm, and gather speed. The only impression of speed was from the crinkled, roughened edge of the runway as it flowed past him at an increasing rate. He had to be right in the centre of the crude runway because he couldn't use the brakes to steer on the ice. They would have no effect. The rudder would not operate effectively until he reached a speed of eighty-five knots. At that moment he was at a little more than fifty.

As his eyes strained into the shredding mist, he heard, coming from a great distance, but with utter clarity, Seerbacker's voice.

"Good luck, man. Can't stop to talk, we've got visitors!" The voice had come from the handset.

His body was chilled, but he sweated. The second it took for him to pass into that region of speed which returned the power of steering to him seemed like an age. Then his speed topped ninety knots, and he centred the Firefox smoothly on the runway. He eased open the throttles, and the rpm needle seemed to leap with a jerk across the face of the dial. He saw the gap rushing at him; now that his eyes had a point of focus in the diffused whiteness of the floe, he was suddenly aware of his speed, transferred from his dials to the landscape. In cold air, he recited to himself, he needed less distance for take-off. He did not believe it, not for a split-second.

The gap leapt at him, the distance it had been from him eaten by the huge engines. He was through the gap at 150 knots, and 170 was his take-off speed. He shoved the throttles into reheat, and pulled back on the stick. He dare not now plough back into the soft surface snow where Peck had had no time to clear the runway.

He could see the snow – he swore that he could see it, the point where the runway of ice ended. It was impossible. It passed under the plane's belly as he hauled back on the stick. He knew the undercarriage was clear of the floe, yet there was no impression of climbing.

In the rear-view mirror, Gant saw a cloud of snow belly out behind him, caused by the sudden downthrust of the jets. The Firefox squatted, it seemed for an instant, nose-high, then, like a limb tearing itself free of restraining, glutinous mud, the aircraft pulled away from the floe. Gant trimmed flaps up, and retracted the undercarriage. The airspeed indicator flicked over, and he pushed the throttles forward. The plane kicked him in the back, and he felt the anti-G suit compensate for the sudden surge of acceleration. He checked the fuel flow, saw that all the needles were in the green, and hauled the aircraft into a vertical climb.

The climb towards the cloud took no more than a few seconds. As he entered the cloud, the Mach-meter crossed the figure 1 – then 1.1, 1.2, 1.3, 1.4 . . .

The Firefox burst out of the cloud at 22,000 feet, into dazzling sunlight, cloudless, vast blue.

He had taken off heading due north. Now he set his course, punching out the coordinates for his crossing-point on the Finnish coast. He banked the plane round to a heading of 210 degrees, still climbing. The maximum altitude of which the Firefox was reputedly capable was in excess of 120,000 feet – more than twenty-five miles high. Gant intended to use as much of that staggering height as he could. It was unlikely, he knew, that he would be able to avoid infra-red detection, even at that height. However, moving as fast as the aircraft was capable, in a vast leap over the Barents Sea, it would be impossible for any interception to take place. A little before he crossed the coast, he would descend to sea-level, and begin his complicated, top-speed dash across Finland to the Gulf of Bothnia, and Stockholm.

There was no aircraft that could touch him, no missile that could home on him, at that height, that speed. He smiled to himself as the altimeter indicated 50,000 feet and still climbing. Now, he thought, now he could put the Firefox through its paces, really *fly* the great plane . . .

There was a fierce, cold joy in him, his closest approximation to an ecstatic emotion. There was nothing to compare, he knew, not with this.

He had read the army psychiatrist's report in Saigon – he had broken into the records office, late at night. An emotional cripple, that's what they had called him, though not in those words – an emotional cripple scarred for life by his early experiences. That Clarkville crap that he had fed the head-shrinker, he'd based his judgement on that, his judgement of a man who had flown more than fifty combat missions, who was the best, the judgement of a fat-assed head-shrinker hundreds of miles from the nearest 'Cong soldier, or missile-launcher.

He calmed the adrenalin that was beginning to course through his system. There was no point, he told himself, no point at all. He was the best. Buckholz knew it, knew it when he picked him. The Firefox climbed through 60,000 feet.

There was no thought for Upenskoy, for Baranovich, and Kreshin, and Semelovsky, and all the others. Since he had left Bilyarsk, they had dropped from his mind, gone more completely than faded, sepia photographs of the dead on wall and mantel.

Tretsov saw him punching through 60,000 feet, the vapour-trail ahead and below him was clear against the grey sea across a gap in the cloud. He knew it was Gant. There was infra-red, but no radar image on his screen. It had to be the stolen Mig-31.

Tretsov's mind worked like surgical steel. He knew what he had to do. He knew Gant's file, knew his experience in combat. His own combat experience, in the old Mig-21, was limited to engagements with Israeli Phantoms in the Middle East as a very young pilot seconded to the Egyptian Air Force, one of a select few reinforcing the inadequate pilots the Red Air Force had trained. Gant was better than he was . . .

On paper.

Gant had flown the Mig-31 for perhaps five hours – less. Tretsov had flown the aircraft for upwards of two hundred hours. Gant wanted to complete his mission. Tretsov had Voskov to avenge. And fear – always, the fear. He would kill Gant. He had to.

He had to get into the tail-cone of the other Mig, so that the missiles would have the best chance of homing on the heat-source of the huge engines – and because Gant's infra-red would only pick him up when it was too late to do anything about it. At that moment, watching the Mig still climbing steadily, he knew that Gant was not aware of him, that crossing his path and being on Gant's starboard flank, the infra-red's blind spot hid him temporarily. He would have to slot in swiftly behind the American, and then . ..

The Mig moved above him now, through his own cruising height of 70,000 feet, still climbing. He changed course, still holding a visual sighting on the contrail, confirming the information of his screen. He eased the Firefox PP 2 in behind the American until the bright orange blip on the screen was directly ahead of him, along the central ranging bar. The thought-guided weapons-system launched two of the Anab missiles and he watched them slide up the ranging bars, homing on the brighter blip of the American's heat-source.

The ECM equipment bleeped horrendously in Gant's earphones, tearing at his memory. He saw the two missiles, sliding up the ranging bars towards him. Impossible, but there . . . The mind deliberated, refused to comprehend, sought the source of the heat-seeking missiles – even as the body responded, seized the electronic means of survival, reaching back into old patterns and grabbing at an old technique.

There was one, he knew, of avoiding infra-red missiles – only one chance. It had been used by Israeli pilots in the Six-Day War, and by Americans in Vietnam. If he could change direction with sufficient suddenness, then the heat-source from his engines would be lost to the tracking sensors in the nose of the missiles and they would be unable to maintain or regain contact with the Firefox.

He chopped the throttles, pulled the stick back and over into a zoom climb, seeking to bend the plane's course at an acute angle to his former course, removing the heat-source of his engines from the sensors of the closing missiles. He rolled the aircraft to the right at the same time, and allowed the nose to drop, following a curve which brought him under the line of the missile's path. His vision tunnelled with the G-effect. He stared at the G-meter, and saw that he was pulling plus 8-G. If his vision narrowed any more, he knew it would be the direct precursor of a black-out. Ten G, and he would black out for certain, and the plane would go out of control. All his vision now showed him was the ominous G-meter, the pressure-suit a distant sensation as it clamped on his legs and stomach. He cursed the fact of finding himself with a lower G-tolerance at that critical moment in time.

The missiles, suddenly and violently altered in position on the screen, slid past him on their original course, past the point in space and time of expected impact. They had lost the scent and would continue, vainly, until their fuel ran out and they dropped into the sea.

He eased back on the stick, and his vision opened, like blinds being drawn in a room. His speed was beginning to fall off, and he found himself sweating desperately. He had almost been taken; like an inexperienced boy. There was nothing on the screen. Tretsov, though Gant did not know it, was still directly behind him and in the blind spot of the infra-red detection. A sense of panic mounted in him. He had to find the enemy visually, or not at all. He was blind, a blind man in the same room as a psychopath. The cold fear trickled down his body, inside the pressure-suit. He suspected the nature of the enemy, but would not admit it yet.

The pilot of the other plane – aircraft it had to be – had obviously climbed to follow him, angry no doubt at his failure to press home the surprise, make the quick kill.

In the rear-view mirror, Gant caught a glint of sunlight off a metal surface. Still nothing on the radar. Now he knew for certain.

Baranovich and Semelovsky had not immobilised the second Firefox by means of the hangar fire. Somehow, whatever damage that had been done had been repaired, and they had sent it after him.

Now he felt very cold. The rivulets of sweat beneath his arms chilled his sides, his waist. Beneath the pressure-suit, he could sense the clammy coldness of his vest. The other plane was the equal of his, the mirror-image – and the pilot was vastly more experienced . . .

The mind proceeded, its infection of imagination unabated, raging in his system while the body calculated that if they continued on their climb turn, the Russian would intercept him. The eyes picked up the glint of light again in the mirror, the hands pushed open the throttles savagely, and the body was comforted by the release of energy from the huge turbines. The body was pressed back into the couch.

The body stopped the climb and pulled the Firefox even more sharply to the left. The Russian kept with him, coming inside him to the left, closing the range. Gant pulled even tighter to the left, then straightened out with a suddenness that caused the inertia of the head to bang the helmet against the cockpit. His hand operated the lever, and the couch dropped into its "battle position", flattening the body almost to the horizontal.

In the mirror, the Russian stayed with him, and the body was only able to hold off the hunter behind from an optimum firing position which the Russian pilot would now be seeking, now that he had wasted two of his four missiles. He might even be closing for a cannon burst, to cripple and slow his quarry.

The man was good, the mind admitted, overheating with its own fever. It was unable to free itself from past and future, the moments before, the moments to come. He had been taken – whatever he did, the Russian would stay with him, behind him, closing the range.

The body registered the appearance of the second Firefox on the screen as an orange blip. It was old information, useless to the body. He already knew what plane it was tucked behind him.

The body tried another stratagem, because the Russian's plane was coming into the "up-sun" position. Gant flicked the aircraft to the left, then continued into a barrel-roll. At the same time, he saw in the mirror the series of ragged puffs of mist from the wings of the Russian plane, the burst of cannon fire they signified. Orange globules drifted with apparent slowness towards him, accelerating as under a great depth of water to overtake him. Tretsov had fired because he, too, was on edge, anxious to end the developing drama, make the fictitious quick kill. The power of his aircraft lulled him into precipitate action.

225

The Russian, now that Gant was in the roll and realising that the cannon burst had gone wide, would expect him to turn into the line of the sun. Instead, he held the roll another ninety degrees, checked and pulled on the stick – the Firefox shuddered through its length, and Gant's stomach muscles cramped up, the vision narrowing again to the long tunnel. He screamed into the face-mask to reduce the effects of the mounting, stunning G-force. The G-meter registered plus 9, he saw with his severely limited vision of the control panel.

As he came out of the roll, he saw the Russian plane ahead of him. The mind shouted with relief, the sudden prospect of an optimal firing position as his vision cleared and he saw the Russian plane emerging from the expanding diaphragm of the lens his vision had become. He was in the Russian's tail-cone, at a range of six hundred yards. He thought, and two Anab missiles were launched. The aircraft shuddered again, straightened, and he watched the missiles slide home. He had aimed via the aiming system, a reflective panel in front of the windscreen, since he had no guidance just as the Russian had possessed none. The thought-guidance system was linked to the radar, not infra-red.

Tretsov had been unable to direct the missiles once he had fired, without the radar image, and Gant now saw, with a stunned sense of defeat, that he was unable to do so either. He saw the Russian pilot use his own trick, chopping the throttles and pulling the aircraft into a climb and roll to the right. The Anabs drove harmlessly past, seeking the heat-source the Russian had whisked away from them.

Gant realised that the mind had interfered with the body, infected it. It was like the last days in Vietnam, before the hospital. A sense of the failure of the past, and a present inadequacy, crushed him for a moment. He was flying badly now, as then – on raw nerves and a draining supply of mental energy. He was afraid again. He could be dead – already the matrix of circumstances which had made his death inevitable might have been established. It might already be too late to initiate an action that would save him.

The body, functioning a split second below its unimpaired best, wrenched the plane to the right. Again, the G-forces momentarily stupefied body and mind. Vision closed in. He followed the Russian. He had been too quick, too eager, squeezing the thought like a firing button, loosing the missiles.

It was too late to calm himself. He was committed now. He was the electronic chessmaster who had lifted his hand from the piece he had elected to move. There was no going back, no reappraisal. He had to fly as he was, the system buckling under the flow of emotion, the adrenalin pumping through him, memory flickering on a screen as if lit by flames.

He eased the controls, and the grey Arctic Ocean swung slowly across his head as his eyes quartered the airspace. The search was frantic because he had lost the Russian again. The sea slid down behind his shoulder. Then his eyes caught a reflection of light in the mirror. He had found the Russian, who had used Gant's own trick of the barrel-roll. He was now behind him, closing the range rapidly, coming for the kill – and making certain that Gant would have no time, no room, in which to wriggle away; small fish from hungry predator. The body recognised that the Russian was good – the mind gibbered that he was dead already.

Gant trod the left rudder, and smacked the stick hard over, pulling the Firefox to the left, seeing as he did so a missile flick away from the Russian plane, bright, mesmeric orange. He wrenched the column back, feeling the G-forces sagging him deep into the couch, the awful pressure for a moment on legs and stomach and the mask pulling at the flesh of his face, his head pinned to his chest . . .

The mind retreated from the sudden pain, leaving the clarity of the body that he needed. Then the plane kicked in response to his hand on the column and there was a wild shuddering through its length.

He was in a flat spin, the nose of the plane pitching fifteen degrees and more above and below the horizon. There was a moment of relief as the Anab was left targetless high above him – then alarm spread as the G-pressure mounted on the meter, through 8½, towards 9-G. His airspeed plummeted towards the 100 knot marker.

There was a clicking in his headphones as the automatic igniters worked madly to prevent a flame-out in the huge turbines behind him. The disturbed airflow of the spin was dousing the engines like a liquid, and they were being relit every half second. His eyes flicked to the rpm gauges, and saw that they were down to sixty per cent and the needles flickering. Before he realised it, he had tumbled through eight thousand feet, the altimeter unwinding madly.

He lost all sight of the Russian aircraft, but Tretsov had watched him, and thrust his own aircraft into a dive. The American was a sitting target.

Gant went through the SOP for a flat-spin, pushing the column forward. Nothing happened. The Firefox did not respond. Now, the Russian above him and no doubt following him down had no existence or reality. Now he was fighting the plane itself as it plunged out of control towards the sea. He moved the column back and forth, jockeyed the throttles to get the nose down and to give him better airflow over the elevators. He was trying to put the plane

227

into a more nose-down attitude in order to pick up speed and regain control.

For perhaps two seconds, nothing happened, except the continued chatter of the auto-ignition and the unwinding of the altimeter. Already he was down to thirty thousand feet and still falling like a leaden leaf. In desperation, he reached his hand for the controls, and dumped the undercarriage to provide a sudden shock of drag on the plane – something the body remembered from a conversation, a story long before. The tail lifted with a twitch, and the nose dipped suddenly and the spin steepened. He applied opposite rudder, and opened the throttles. He was twenty thousand feet up, the altimeter still unwinding, but he was back in control. He exerted pressure on the column to level out, and retracted the undercarriage. He pulled the column steadily towards him, and eased the throttles further open. The plane began to level out. The body breathed, its first dragging inhalation since the spin had begun.

Then he saw with an icy shock that the Russian was a bright glow on the screen. The pilot had followed him down, battening on him as he recovered from the spin. The speed of his approach, Gant calculated, was in excess of Mach 1.6. The Russian knew he could kill, that he could get close enough to finish Gant. There was to be no margin for error, no slight gap through which brilliance or luck might slip.

Gant saw him in the mirror, an image leaping at him. The mind cracked open, gibbering in the moment of its death. The orange globules that sprang out of the puffs of mist at the wing edges chased him at a frightening speed, overhauling him. He flung the plane aside, as if trying to avoid some charging animal, and saw in the mirror the Russian turning to follow him, turning inside Gant's heat-cone, jockeying for the optimum position with one missile left.

There was a false relief that he knew was vapid and unreal even as he felt it; to have escaped the cannon fire was meaningless, a prolongation of seconds.

The body, struggling to master the crying mind, fought to regain control. His hand opened the throttles and he eased the column back and to the right. The mind cried out for something to fire at the tailing Russian, something that would operate on an enemy behind.

The mind's imperative overrode the body. It was a command the body would never have considered. The mind screamed the order to the thought-guidance system, and the last of the decoys in the Rearward Defence Pod was jettisoned. There was a blinding light in the rear mirror that burned eyesight as the decoy heat-source, the incandescent ball, detached itself and hung for a moment in the air. Then the mirror erupted in burning light, brighter than the ball. The

228

body, stunned by its own apparent inactivity, sensed the shock-wave.

Gant held the Firefox in the tight turn. As he steadied the aircraft, there was nothing within the circle he was describing in the air except a pall of black, oily smoke, lit from within by livid, orange flame. Glistening fragments of metal tumbled down from the smoke-pall, like metal leaves turning in the sunlight.

He understood what had happened. While the mind spewed its relief, its incoherent sense of escape and victory, it realised that the incandescent ball of fire released from the tail of the Firefox had been greedily swallowed by one of the huge intakes of the Russian Firefox and it had exploded instantaneously.

Gant wanted to throw up. He choked on his vomit, preventing it from filling the face-mask and suffocating him. The mind invaded the body, and he realised that he was shaking all over.

While he remained capable of effort, he switched in the auto-pilot and then punched in, hesitantly and with a vast effort of memory, the coordinates of his course. The Firefox banked round, steadied, and headed for Finland, while he lay back in the couch, weak, empty, shaking.

Eventually, he knew he would recover. Then he would take over the manual control of the plane. But not yet, not just yet . . .

The Mig-31, NATO codenamed Firefox, and the single, priceless example of its type, cruised at 80,000 feet, at a speed of Mach 3.7, towards the hidden coast of Finland.

FIREFOX DOWN

for CLINT EASTWOOD
— *pilot of the Firefox*

Author's Note

One of the perils of writing a sequel, especially to a novel which I originally completed early in 1975, is the very passage of time. The present novel takes up the story of Mitchell Gant and the MiG-31 at precisely the point where its predecessor left them. One of the principal characters of the earlier novel was Yuri Andropov, then Chairman of the Soviet intelligence service and secret police, the KGB. Events have overtaken me, since that gentleman is now, following the demise of Leonid Brezhnev, the leader of the Soviet Union. For the sake of continuity, I have had to keep him in his former job. However, I shall always think of him, in company, no doubt, with millions of Soviet citizens, as the head of the most powerful and repressive secret police force the modern world has ever experienced.

Acknowledgements

My thanks, especially on this occasion, to my wife, Jill, for her editing of the manuscript, and for bullying and cajoling me through the writing process! Thanks, too, to T. R. Jones, for acting as my technical adviser.

Acknowledgement must also be made to Faber & Faber Ltd for permission to quote from *Hawk Roosting* by Ted Hughes.

The quotation from *Fire and Ice* by Robert Frost is reproduced by kind permission of Jonathan Cape and Holt, Rinehart & Winston, on behalf of the estate of Robert Frost, and comes from the collection of *Poetry* edited by Edward Connery Latham.

PART ONE

THE PILOT

"I think I know enough of hate
To say that for destruction ice
Is also great
And would suffice."

Fire and Ice
– Robert Frost

ONE:

Down

Beginning . . .

The Firefox crossed the Norwegian coast eighty thousand feet above the Tanafjord. The on-board computer issued instructions to the auto-pilot for the first predetermined change of course. The aircraft banked. Mitchell Gant watched the curve of the earth far below him tilt and then reassert itself. Above him, the sky darkened almost to black. It was empty. He was entirely alone.

Beginning to relax . . .

The shower of turning, bright, sun-caught metal leaves, falling out of the tumult of smoke that a moment earlier had been the second Firefox, returned to flash upon a screen at the back of his mind. A white ball of flame, then erupting, boiling black smoke, then the spiralling, falling pieces, then the empty clean sky.

Nausea diminishing, almost gone. Hands almost not shaking now as they rested on his thighs. Left cheek's tic – he waited, counting the seconds – still now.

He had done it. He had won. He was able to form the thoughts with calm, precise, satisfying clarity. He had done it. He had won. And, like an undercurrent, he admitted another idea – he was still alive.

The Firefox banked once more, the scimitar-edge of the earth's surface tilted again, then levelled. The aircraft had begun its complex zig-zag across Finland, en route to its rendezvous with the commercial flight from Stockholm to Heathrow. In the infra-red shadow of the airliner, he would be hidden as he crossed the North Sea to RAF Scampton, where Aubrey the Englishman would be waiting for him with Charlie Buckholz from the CIA. Two men whose orders had placed him in continual danger for the past three days. Two men who had given him . . . ? He let the thought go. He didn't owe them. They owed him.

The congratulations . . . he wanted those. The unconcealable smiles and gestures of satisfaction, even of surprise and relief. They owed him all of those.

The other faces came back, then, as if to lessen and spoil the moment. Baranovich, Pavel, Semelovsky, Kreshin – Fenton's broken face on the wet embankment of the Moskva river. All of them dead. All of them willingly dead, except for Fenton, simply to put him in physical conjunction with the Firefox. *This* . . .

His hands smoothed the controls, like the hands of a man buying his first new car and expressing his awed sense of ownership. He touched the instrument panel in front of him, he read the Machmeter – Mach 0.9. His speed would remain below Mach 1. He had no wish to trail a betraying sonic boom across Finland. The altimeter displayed 60,000 feet. The Firefox was dropping slowly towards its rendezvous altitude through the dark blue empty sky.

He didn't want to entertain the faces, and they slipped from his mind. It was all becoming unreal; hard to understand that it was no more than three days since he had arrived at Moscow's Cheremetievo airport disguised as Orton the Canadian businessman and suspected drug-trafficker. There was, increasingly, only *now*, this moment. He owned the moment as he owned the aircraft. The Firefox was his. In perhaps less than two hours he would have to surrender it to others – to men who could never, in a million years, fly it. It would be examined, tested, dismantled, reduced to a hollow shell; finally shipped in crates in the belly of a Hercules across the Atlantic. But now, it was his airplane. In two hours, also, he would begin his own decline, his return to the anonymity, the emptiness of what he had been before Buckholz had resurrected him.

He wanted to cry out against it, for his sake, for the sake of the airplane. Instead, he squashed the thought like a beetle. Not now, not yet –

In the mirror, the sky was dark blue behind him. The cloud-layer was far below him. The curve of the earth fell away on either side of the aircraft. He was utterly detached from the globe beneath. A stream of sparkling diamonds rushed away like the tail of a comet behind the Firefox, like the wake of a swan he had once seen lifting from a lake at evening. Sparkling water . . .

The aircraft's nose eased round a few degrees as the Firefox automatically altered course once more. The stream of diamond droplets altered with it. Tinker-Bell, he thought, remembering the darkened, whispering, escape-from-his-father movie theatre in Clarkville and the petulant sprite and her Disney trail of gleaming dust. His mother always gave him money for the movies saved from her meagre housekeeping, if she knew his father had been drinking, though there was rarely the extra for popcorn. By the time the main feature ended, his father might have fallen into a drunken sleep.

And then he knew. His heart and stomach seemed stunned by a

physical blow. Fuel droplets, escaping into the thin cold atmosphere. A broken necklace of fuel droplets —

Frantically, he flicked switches, read the gauges and flow-meters, made the calculations with a frozen, horrified sense of urgency. Before he had noticed, before it had dawned on him, the tanks were almost dry. He gripped the control column, but did not move it. It helped to still his shaking hands and forearms. He guessed what must have happened. The fuselage and the tanks had been punctured during the dogfight. Either that or the second Firefox had ruptured one of the fuel-lines with cannon fire. Even one of the falling metal leaves from the exploding aircraft might have done it.

He knew that he would never make landfall in England.

Perhaps not even in Norway. A safe landing? Perhaps nowhere. The calculations were horrifyingly simple. At his present speed, he had less than twenty-five minutes' flying time left. Much less, because of the fuel he was losing. The rate of loss he could not accurately measure. He could not stop it. Twenty five minutes . . .? As little as ten . . .?

The cloud-layer seemed a long, long way beneath him. The Firefox would drop towards and through it into a frozen wilderness. At first, the clouds would be light, gauzy, slipping past the cockpit like curtains brushed aside. Then the light would go. Greyness would thicken until he broke through to the snow that lay beneath. Trees would rush endlessly beneath the Firefox's belly as it glided on empty tanks. Finally, the airplane would run out of supporting air, as if it had gained weight, and the trees would brush against its flanks and belly. They would snap it first, then their strength in succession and combination would snap the wings, pull the Firefox into the ground.

By that time, he would have ejected. In order to die of frostbite and exposure. He would freeze to death in Finnish Lapland. All this he knew, and despite his fierce grip on the control column, his forearms quivered. His body felt weak, helpless. And filled with a self-accusation that burned him. *He should have checked.* After the dogfight he should have checked! He had been caught like a rookie pilot on his first solo flight.

His mistake had killed him. He was almost out of fuel, despite the mockery with which the two huge Turmansky turbo-jets behind him continued to roar as violently as ever. The noise was like their own, last protest —

Fifty-two thousand feet.

What? Where?

He couldn't land the Firefox in neutral Finland, that had been made clear to him from the beginning. Never, under any circumstances . . . Nor Sweden, because of the same neutrality. There was only Norway. But where? Bardufoss was far to the north-west by now – he was well south of Kirkenes. Both of those airfields were, effectively, closed to him by distance.

Oslo was hundreds of miles ahead of him still.

Did he have more than twenty minutes left? He could not believe he did.

The Firefox's nose nudged round as the aircraft altered course once more, mockingly obedient to its computer instructions. A chicken with its head cut off, still running.

What – ?

He glanced down at the map strapped to his knee. He released the control column with his right hand, stilled its quivering, and estimated distances. Kirkenes was less than ten miles from the Soviet border with Norway. Bardufoss was perhaps another hundred miles further from his present position, but it was a NATO base.

How – ?

Climb.

Climb, he thought, climb, climb . . . The sweat ran freely down his arms and sides. His whole body arched in a sigh of relief. His facemask was misty when he finally exhaled. Zoom climb. As he had done before, before he found the ice-floe and the American submarine with its priceless cargo of fuel. Climb.

He hesitated for no more than a moment, then switched off the auto-pilot and cancelled the on-board computer's instructions. Once more, Gant controlled the Firefox. Out over the Arctic Ocean, ignorant of the location and nature of the rendezvous, he had had to glide on over the sea, slowly dropping towards it, the Arctic ice-cap white on his horizon. Now, he knew the distances, he could calculate the length of his glide. He would make it.

He moved the control column and the Firefox banked, altering course for Bardufoss airfield. Altitude, forty-nine thousand feet. He pulled back on the column and eased the throttles forward, wincing as he did so; then he recalculated. Seventeen minutes' flying time left to him. The engines roared steadily. He lifted the nose further. The sky was dark blue almost deepening to black ahead of him. And empty. Gant felt competence return, an almost-calm. Every panic was shorter now. He came out of his helplessness more and more quickly each time. He would make it –

The aircraft began to climb. He had to assume virtually empty tanks by the time he reached Bardufoss. To glide the whole distance, he would require an altitude of more than one hundred and thirty thousand feet. Once he reached the required altitude, he would set up the engines for maximum range. Then all that remained to him was to fly until the engines failed through lack of fuel. Bardufoss was – he tapped at the tiny keyboard of the inertial navigator display, summoning a distance-to-target read-out. Almost at once, the dark green screen declared in glowing red – Bardufoss was two hundred and twenty-four-point-six miles away. He calculated his best speed to be two hundred and sixty knots. Even if the engines suddenly cut at one hundred and thirty-two thousand feet, gliding at that speed he would make it all the way.

He watched, edgy as a feeding bird, as the altimeter needle ascended through the fifties, then the sixties – seventy-two, seventy-four thousand. The sky darkened; deep purple-blue. Almost space. Eighty. He listened to the Turmansky engines. They roared steadily, healthily. Eight-four, eighty-six . . .

Come on, *come on* –

His left hand twitched on the throttles, and he had to restrain himself from pushing them forward. It was an illusion. His speed was OK, all he needed to reach the required altitude.

Ninety-eight thousand feet. Purple-black above and ahead and around. The curve of the earth was evident even in the mirror. One-zero-nine.

The engine note remained steady, comforting. Not quite empty. One hundred and twenty thousand. Almost there, almost . . .

He pulled back the throttles, retaining only sufficient power to keep the generators functioning. He almost heard the thin, upper-atmosphere slipstream outside the cockpit. The Firefox quivered in its flow as he began his glide.

Yes. He'd make it now. They'd need the new Arrestor Barrier at Bardufoss to help him brake. He'd have no reverse thrust by the time he arrived. The last of the fuel was trailing behind him now in a thin crystal stream.

It didn't matter. Then a warning noise bleeped in his headset. He saw that two bright blips of light had appeared on his passive radar screen. Two aircraft, climbing very fast towards him. The power used in the zoom climb must have betrayed his position to infra-red. Two jets, small and fast enough to be nothing else but high-level interceptors. The closest one was already through ninety-five thousand feet and still climbing at more than Mach 2.

Foxbats. Had to be. MiG-25s. And if they were Foxbat-Fs, they had a high enough ceiling to reach him. Two of them. Closing.

He could see them now, far below him. Gleaming.

The read-out confirmed contact time at six seconds.

The windows in the fuselage of the Tupolev Tu-144, the Russian version of the Concorde, were very small, no larger than tiny, oblong portholes. Nevertheless, Soviet Air Force General Med Vladimirov could see, in the clear, windy afternoon sunlight, the crumpled, terrified figure of KGB Colonel Kontarsky being escorted from the main security building towards the small MiL helicopter which would return him to Moscow. In the moment of the destruction of the second prototype Firefox, KGB Chairman Andropov had remembered the subordinate who had failed, and given the order for his transfer to the Lubyanka prison. His dismissive, final tone had been as casual as the whisking away of a noisy insect. Watching the defeated and fearful Kontarsky climbing into the interior of the green helicopter, Vladimirov witnessed an image of his own future; bleak, filled with disgrace and insult, and short.

He turned reluctantly to look back into the cigar-shaped room that was the Soviet War Command Centre. The map-table was unlit and featureless. Already a box of matches, a packet of cigarettes, a full ashtray, an untidy sheaf of decoded signals had invested the smooth grey surface. It was a piece of equipment for which there was no further use. The personnel of the command centre remained at their posts, seated before consoles, encoders, avionics displays, computer terminals. Motionless. Machines no longer of use. Air Marshal Kutuzov leaned his elbows on the map-table. The Soviet First Secretary of the Party stood at attention, strong hands clasped together behind his back, pinching the coat-tail of his grey suit into creases. His head was lifted to the low, curving ceiling of the room, cocked slightly on one side. He listened as if to music.

The only sound in the room, loud enough to mask the hum of radios and encoding consoles, was Tretsov's voice. The First Secretary had ordered the tapes of Tretsov's last moments to be replayed, almost as if he could edit them, alter their message, create victory rather than defeat. Despite himself, Vladimirov listened as Tretsov died in playback. The command centre was hot. He was certain of it. It was not himself nor the rush of anticipation through him, it was the ambient temperature. The air-conditioning must have failed. He was hot.

"I'm behind him . . . I'm on his tail . . . careful, careful . . . he's doing nothing, he's given up . . ." It was the excitement of a boy regaling his parents with the highlights of a school football match in which he had scored the final, winning goal. "Nothing . . . he's beaten and he knows it . . ." Caution, *caution*, Vladimirov's thoughts repeated. He had silently yelled the thought the instant he heard the tone of delight in the young test-pilot's voice. The boy thought he had a kill, had already counted Gant a dead man, had begun to see the hero's reception . . . *caution*! Even had he shouted the word into the

244

microphone, it would have been too late. Tretsov would have been dead before he heard him. *Caution* . . . "I've got – "

That had been the end of it. A crackle of static and then silence. Total and continuing, leaking from the receiver as palpably as sound. Tretsov had not known Gant, had not understood him and the American had fooled him. He had triggered the tail decoy, in all probability, and one of Tretsov's huge air intakes had greedily swallowed the incandescent ball.

"I've got – " the tape repeated. Not quite the end. Only the moment when Vladimirov had known it was the end. He'd sensed the change of tone before the last words. "Oh *God!*" the tape shrieked, making Vladimirov wince once more, hunch into himself. The static scratched like the painful noise of fingernails drawn slowly down a pane of glass, and then the silence began leaking into the hot command centre once more.

Oh *God* – !

"Switch it off – switch it off!" Vladimirov snapped in a high, strained voice. "Damn, do you want to *revel* in it? The boy's *dead!*"

The First Secretary turned slowly to face Vladimirov. His large, square face seemed pinched into narrowness. His wide nostrils were white with anger, his eyes heavily lidded.

"A communications failure," he announced. Even Andropov beyond him seemed surprised and perplexed.

"No," Vladimirov announced tiredly, shaking his head. "The boy is dead. The second Firefox no longer exists."

"How do you *know* that?" Vladimirov could sense the large hands clenching tightly behind the First Secretary's back.

"Because I know the American. Tretsov was . . . too eager. Gant probably killed him by using the tail decoy."

"What?"

"Tretsov's aircraft *ate* a ball of fire and exploded! Couldn't you hear the horror in his voice? There was nothing he could do about it!"

A moment of silence. Andropov's features, especially the pale eyes behind the gold-rimmed spectacles, advised caution, even apology. But Vladimirov experienced the courage of outrage and failure. His own future was not something he could rationally contemplate or protect.

Then, in a calm, steely voice, the First Secretary said, "And you, General Vladimirov? What can *you* do about it?"

Behind the Russian leader, the shoulders of a young radio operator were still with tension. The back of the man's neck and his ears were red. In the distance Vladimirov heard the helicopter bearing the arrested Kontarsky lift into the midday sky and drone away from Bilyarsk. Vladimirov was aware of the awesome, complete power he had held until a few moments before, and which had disappeared with the second Firefox, and then he moved swiftly to the dull surface of the map-table, his hands sweeping the ashtray, the matches, the batch of signals onto the floor. Cigarette butts spilled near the First Secretary's shining black shoes, and the ashtray rolled beneath the chair of an encoding console operator, who flinched.

"Give me North Cape and Norway – quickly!" he snapped. The operator of the map-table's computer terminal was galvanised into frantic typing at his keyboard. The dull grey faded, the blue of the sea, the green and brown of a country – Norway – glowed, flickered, then resolved into sharpness. The operator typed in the dispositions of aircraft and ships and submarines without instruction. The First Secretary and the Chairman of the KGB both remained aloof from the map.

Vladimirov noted the positions of the missile cruiser *Riga*, the Red Banner Northern Fleet hunter-killer submarines, the "Wolf-pack" squadrons aloft. They remained concentrated in the area west of North Cape.

Where? he asked himself. Where now? He's refuelled . . . all he needs is friendly airspace.

The long backbone of Norway stretched from top to bottom of the map, a twisted spine of mountains. Like the Urals, Vladimirov thought. He used the Urals to mask his exit – would he use the mountains again? Perhaps –

"Any reports?" he snapped. He could not be blind again, rush at this. "Any visual sightings, infra-red – ?"

"No, sir – "

"Nothing, Comrade General – "

"No – "

The chorus was infinitely depressing. However, as he glanced up, it seemed to satisfy Andropov in particular. The KGB's failure to protect the prototype Firefox was well in the past; forgotten, avoidable now. Vladimirov had volunteered himself as the ultimate scapegoat.

"Very well." Kutuzov's watery old eyes had warned him. Expressed something akin to pity, too, and admiration for his recklessness. But he could not prevent himself. This contest was as real and immediate as if he were flying a third Firefox himself against the American. He would not surrender. He was challenged by perhaps the best pilot he had ever encountered to fulfil his reputation as the Soviet Air Force's greatest and most innovative strategist. Gant had declared the terms of the encounter, and Vladimirov had accepted them.

He was on the point of suggesting incursions into Norwegian airspace. His voice hesitated just as his hand hovered above the spine of Norway glowing beneath the surface of the map-table. And perhaps the hesitation saved him − at least, prolonged his authority.

"Something, sir . . ." one of the operators murmured, turning in his chair, one hand clutching the earpiece of his headset. His face wore a bright sheen of delight. Vladimirov sensed that the game had begun again. "Yes, sir − visual contact − *visual contact!*" It was the eager, breathless announcement of a miracle. The operator nodded as he listened to the report they could not hear. His right hand scribbled furiously on a pad.

"Cabin speaker!" Vladimirov snapped. The operator flicked a switch. Words poured from the loudspeaker overhead, a brilliant excited bird-chatter. The First Secretary's eyes flicked towards the speaker. Heads lifted slowly, like a choir about to sing. Vladimirov suppressed a grin of almost savage pleasure.

There was surprise, too, of course. And gratitude. He had hesitated for a moment, and the moment had proven fateful. He would have said Norway − even now the country lay under his gaze and his hands like a betrayal − and it would have been an error. Gant was over Finland; neutral innocent Finland. At one hundred and thirty thousand feet − why? And he'd been picked up visually and trailed by two MiG-25 Foxbats, at high altitude themselves. Now he had climbed almost to his maximum ceiling. Why was he at such an extreme altitude? Contact time a matter of seconds . . . orders required . . . Vladimirov blessed the young map operator who had typed in new instructions. The twisted spine of Norway disappeared. The land mass fattened, blurred, then resolved. Finland, Swedish Lapland and northern Norway occupied the area of the map-table. Orders? What − ?

His eyes met the steady, expectant, even amused gaze of the First Secretary. Everyone in the room understood the narrowness of his escape from an irredeemable blunder. Andropov was smiling thinly, in mocking appreciation.

"Sir!"

"Yes?" he answered hoarsely.

"An AWACS Tupolev has picked up the two Foxbats. We − "

"Bleed in the present position − quickly!"

Then he waited. Contact time diminishing, split-seconds now . . . Gant still climbing but he must have seen them by now . . . orders required . . . engage? *What was that?*

247

"Repeat that!" the First Secretary ordered before Vladimirov could utter the same words. The order was transmitted, and the voice of the Foxbat pilot repeated the information. Fuel droplets – a thin stream of fuel! Gant had a serious fuel-leak. He had climbed to that extreme altitude in order to stretch his fuel, and to be able to glide when the fuel ran out. Just as he must have done to find the submarine and the ice-floe. "Engage!"

"No!" Vladimirov shouted. The First Secretary glared at him, his mouth twisted with venom. He took a single step towards the map-table. The positions of the two MiG-25s glowed as a single bright white star on the face of Finnish Lapland. Vladimirov's cupped hand stroked towards the pinpoint of light and beyond it into Russia. "No," he repeated. "We can bring him back – we can bring him back! Don't you see?"

"Explain – hold that order." The two men faced each other across the surface of the map. The colours of the sea and land shone palely on their features, mottling them blue and brown and green. "Explain."

Vladimirov's hands anticipated his tongue. They waved and chopped over the glowing surface of Lapland. Then his right forefinger stabbed at the white star that represented the two MiG-25s.

"There," he said. "They are two seconds away . . ." The First Secretary's face was expressionless as Vladimirov looked up for an instant. Then the Soviet general, one lock of silver hair falling across his intently creased high forehead, spoke directly to the map-table. "It's already beginning . . . they'll peel away and return without a definite order . . . they're good pilots . . ." *They have to be*, he thought – to be in their squadron. The aircraft are advanced Foxbat-Fs, the next best thing to the Firefox itself. "The *border is here* . . ." The finger stabbed, again and again, as if an ant on the surface of the table persisted in maintaining life. "Less than a hundred miles . . . minutes of flying time at the most. They can *shepherd* him – !" He looked up once more. Puzzlement. The Russian leader's thoughts were seconds behind his own. "Look – they can do this with him . . ." Once more, his hand swept across the map, ushering the white star towards the red border, away from dotted blue lakes to more dotted blue lakes – Soviet lakes. For a split second, Vladimirov remembered reading the *samizdat* of Solzhenitsyn's short story of the lake guarded by barbed wire that represented his country, then he shook his head and dismissed the image.

His voice was unchanged as he continued. "It will take clever flying, but I'm certain it can be done. Once he's across the border, then he can be brought down. He's almost out of fuel, I'm sure of that, he will have to land. We can shepherd him straight into an airfield . . . one of ours."

He looked up. The First Secretary was, for the moment, dazzled. He nodded eagerly. Vladimirov listened. Over the speaker, the leading pilot of the two Foxbats was reporting the peel-off and the encroaching return. Contact time, four seconds.

"Shepherd – repeat, *shepherd,* " he snapped. A remote mike had been patched in. They could hear him direct. "You know the procedure – it's . . . ninety miles and no more to the border – bring him home!" He grinned as the second of hesitation passed and the leading pilot acknowledged with a chuckle in his voice. Then he studied the map before ordering: "Patch me into *all* forward border squadron commanders – all of them. And to flight leaders of 'Wolfpack' squadrons already in the air. Every commander and flight leader who can give me a Foxbat-F." He looked up at the Russian leader – beyond his shoulder the light glinted from Andropov's glasses but Vladimirov ignored any signal they might be transmitting – and smiled confidently. "We'll put up everything we have that can reach that altitude," he announced. "The American will feel like the last settler left alive inside the circle of the wagon-train!"

The First Secretary seemed to remember the old cowboy-and-indian films which, as the child of a prominent Party member, he would have been privileged to see, and laughed.

Vladimirov looked down at the map once more, and breathed deeply. It would take constant dialogue with the two pilots, instantaneous communications, if he was to supervise the recapture of the MiG-31. But, he could do it – yes. It would take perhaps eight or ten minutes' flying for any other MiGs to reach Gant. The two Foxbats would be working alone – but they would be sufficient, he assured himself. No other aircraft could achieve that altitude except another Foxbat-F. And there were only the two of them in the area. The map, with its clearly-marked border and the slowly-moving white dot of the routine Early Warning Tupolev Tu-126 "Moss" aircraft travelling southwards along its snaking line, confirmed his optimism.

For a moment, as the two Foxbats at more than Mach 1.5 had peeled away from the Firefox, the single white dot that represented them had become a double sun. Now, the separate lights had once more become a single white star.

They had come sweeping up towards him, then past and above. He had loosed neither of the remaining advanced Anab missiles, slung one beneath each wing; suppressing the mental command to fire with a certain, decisive violence of reaction. The two Foxbats had broken their unity, peeling away in opposite directions and dropping away from the purple-blue towards the globe below like exhausted shuttlecocks. Then, finally, they had begun to climb again, almost touching wings as if joining hands. Aiming at him like darts. Contact time – four seconds. Their speed was slower now, as if they had been advised to the utmost caution. Gant was fiercely aware once more of the two remaining air-to-air missiles. Two MiGs, advanced Foxbat-Fs, two missiles. Fuel – critical.

Unlike the Foxbats, he had the fuel neither to fight nor to run. He had to wait, just as he suspected the two Russian pilots were themselves waiting for orders.

They bobbed up to port and starboard of him like corks on the surface of invisible water, slightly above him at one hundred and twenty-five thousand feet and hanging, like him, apparently suspended from the purple blackness above. On his screen they had converged to a single glow and at the extreme edge the dot of the slow-moving AWACS plane patrolling the Soviet-Finnish border continued its flight. He had been aware of it when he began his climb, and had smiled in the secure knowledge that he was invisible to it. Now, however, it could see the two Foxbats. His position was known – to everyone.

The fear passed quickly, surprising him by its feeble hold; delighting him, too. He accepted his role. He had to wait until they attacked . . . One twenty-two thousand feet. His slow flight north-west had begun, but now he would not be allowed to continue. His hand gripped the throttle-levers, but he did not move them either backward or forward. Slowly, as if tired, the Firefox continued to descend.

He looked to port and starboard. The two Foxbats were sliding gently in towards him. Each of the pilots was engaged in a visual scan. By now they knew he had only two missiles. By now, they knew he had a fuel leak, and they would have guessed at the reason for his altitude. They would be confident . . . Orders and decisions would be crackling and bleeping in their headsets. Not long now. Gant armed the weapons systems, switched on the firing circuits, calculated his remaining flying time. He knew he would have to use the engines, use *all* his remaining fuel, to escape the Foxbats.

The Foxbat to starboard, no more than two hundred yards from him, was now in sharp profile. Gant waited, beginning to sweat, his mind coldly clear. The Foxbat loomed on his right, and yawed slightly towards him. Cannon fire flashed ahead of him as the Russian plane slid across and below the level of the cockpit sill and he lost sight of it. He flung the Firefox to port –

250

Flickers of flame at the wingtips from the cannon, the Foxbat in profile, the savage lurch of the sky, a glimpse of the port Foxbat maintaining its course, then he was below it and levelling out, watching the radar. Two dots. He watched the mirror, the radar, the sky ahead of him, the mirror, the radar, the sky . . .

Bobbing corks. They were on either side of him again as he flew level, the distant dot of the AWACS Tupolev now in the corner of his screen, ahead of him.

He glanced to port and starboard. He could see the pilots. He watched them as they watched him. He understood what they had witnessed. He'd dropped away from the cannon fire rather than dived. He had confirmed his fear of empty tanks as clearly as if he had spoken to them.

Port, starboard, port, starboard . . . Gant's head flicked from side to side. With each movement, his eyes glanced across the instrument panel, registering the dials and screens minutely as if they were small, precise physical sensations on his skin or at his fingertips. He waited for movement. Between them, he knew himself to be safe from their AA-6 missiles. They were too close to one another to be certain of hitting only him. It would be when one of them dropped away suddenly that the other would launch a missile.

Yet they remained level.

Ninety-nine thousand now. They'd followed his slow descent exactly paralleling his course. He could try to stretch them, exceed their ceiling, yet knew he would not . . . he had calculated that he dare not afford the fuel. Ninety-five thousand feet, still descending . . . They remained with him, long slim bodies dropping from the darkening arch of the sky. Twenty miles above the earth.

Ninety-four thousand feet . . . three-fifty . . . three . . .

The port Foxbat-F slid towards him like a huge animal turning lazily to crush him, enlarging alongside and over him, its shadow falling across the cockpit, across the instruments, the sunlight gleaming from its closing flank –

He saw the black visor of the pilot's helmet, and understood the man's hand signals. He was being ordered to follow the Soviet fighter and to land inside Russia. Alter course . . . follow me . . . land, the hand signals read. Gant watched the pilot's turned head. He waved acceptance, his body tensing as he did so. Had he delayed sufficiently? Would his acceptance appear genuine?

He waited.

Then the Foxbat banked to its left and began a shallow descent. Gant saw it gradually accelerate. The second Foxbat remained to starboard of him, as if wary of some trick. He dipped the nose of the Firefox, following the Russian aircraft. Then he gave the command.

The port wing quivered and he saw the flame at the tail of the Anab missile as it sprang ahead of him. It dropped away with terrible quickness, pursuing the descending Foxbat. Its trail quivered like the tail of an eager dog as it sought and found the heat emissions from the Foxbat and locked onto them. Gant banked fiercely to prevent the second Foxbat manoeuvring behind him. He glimpsed the engines of the descending Foxbat flare and the plane flick up and away, standing on its tail. The speed of the tactic shook loose the trailing missile. The aircraft was already perhaps three miles from the Firefox. The missile continued its now-wavering course downwards. It would run out of fuel thousands of feet from the ground.

Gant pulled back on the control column and eased the throttles forward, beginning to climb again. He had, he realised, committed himself. He could not, with the slightest certainty of success, complete his flight to Norway. But he would not be shepherded back to Russia.

The Foxbat was closing again, its white dot moving back swiftly towards the centre of his screen. The second Foxbat had done no more than remain with him, exactly duplicating his fierce bank and levelling out, popping up again to starboard and beginning to climb with him. It remained apparently passive, as if its companion had, like a child, run to play and was now returning to a complacent parent. Evidently, neither pilot had orders to fire, or destroy. Unless, no doubt, he failed to comply with their instructions or attempted to elude them.

Bobbing cork, and the second Foxbat-F had already turned, closed up and resumed its position on his port wing. One hundred and fifteen thousand feet –

The AWACS plane was on the Soviet side of the border. The border was less than seventeen miles away. He understood what they were doing. He had run between them, cautiously and yet with as little choice as a sheep between two dogs. He was almost back in the Soviet Union. He pulled back on the throttles and levelled out, then pushed the control column gently forward, dipping the nose of the Firefox. Like mirror-images, though silver not black, the two Foxbats dipped their noses in unison, beginning to descend with him.

Fifteen miles . . .

One hundred and eight thousand feet . . .

The two Foxbats were like slim, dangerous silver fish swimming downwards with him. Once again, he imagined he could hear the noise of the slipstream against the canopy, much as if he had been hang-gliding. The wingtip of the starboard Foxbat wobbled, re-

252

inforcing the impression of fragility, of slow-motion – of powerless-ness.

He flung the Firefox into a tight roll, the globe and sky exchanging places with wrenching suddenness, and slowed the aircraft. When the horizon re-established itself, he was behind and only slightly to starboard of one of the Foxbats. He glanced around –

The port Foxbat had imitated his roll and drop in speed. He saw it gleam in his rear mirror. He was boxed again, and fear surfaced for a moment as he realised he had made himself a sitting target. Then the Russian aircraft drew level again to starboard. The pilot waved, as if they had been practising for an air display.

Twelve miles . . .

Ninety-seven thousand feet. Cloud lay like a carpet far below; the air was perceptibly bluer. Eleven and a half miles to target. The AWACS plane was still maintaining its border patrol, passing slowly across the screen. Nothing else showed, but Gant knew that the border squadrons would be waiting for the order to scramble. Once airborne, they would be only minutes away. When they came they would buzz around him like flies, hemming him in.

The port Foxbat banked slightly, slipping across the intervening space, casting its shadow on the cockpit of the Firefox. He watched it settle into a position directly above him, no more than a hundred feet above. As they dropped lower, the Foxbat increased the rate of its descent, pressing as palpably as a flat-iron towards him. He increased his own rate of descent, cursing but impotent.

Clever. Good pilots. Armed with eight AA-6 missiles.

Nine miles – eighty thousand feet.

The three aircraft slid downwards . . . seconds passed . . . seventy thousand feet . . . seconds passed . . . seven miles . . .

Clever, the mind behind it, the orders being issued, Gant thought, and the silence of his cockpit pressed upon him like the form of the Russian fighter above. *UHF* –

He switched on the UHF set, his fingers hesitating until he recognised the button for the search facility. A red dot stuttered and flashed, then steadied as the search was completed.

A voice, speaking in Russian, crackled in his ears. Gant pressed the lock-on button. It was one of the two Foxbat pilots replying to an instruction. Gant smiled. It was one of the most secret tactical channels with variable frequencies used by the Soviet Air Force. The red dot stuttered as the frequency altered, perhaps two or three times a second. But the signal was constant.

"Bring him lower," he heard; the voice of the man in Bilyarsk who controlled the situation. "Bring him right down."

The order was acknowledged. Gant watched the form of the

253

Foxbat above him as it inclined its nose more steeply, its speed exactly matched to his own. He dipped the nose of the Firefox obediently, preserving the distance between the two fuselages. Then the Russian aircraft slipped sideways, as if moved by no more than the airflow over it, and dropped suddenly towards him. At the same moment, his headset crackling with the voices of the two Russian pilots, the starboard Foxbat bobbed higher and sideways towards him, banking slightly. Then it, too, settled down towards him, as if the air were too thin to support its weight.

The two Russian fighters lowered gently, inexorably, towards his wingtips, as though applying pressure to snap them off. He waggled the wings, as if warding them off, wiping flies away. The headset gabbled at him, most of the Russian too quick and distorted for him to understand. They were attempting to break his nerve.

Four miles − sixty-one thousand feet . . .

Then he heard the order, over the same frequency: "Scramble designated squadrons."

From the western margin of the Kola Peninsula, where the latest MiG interceptors were based, was no more than a few minutes' flying time at top speed. They had fuel to squander, literally squander.

He had run out of time, almost run out of distance. Two miles. He must be over the border by now, in Russia.

The two Foxbats pressed down upon him. Altitude now forty-nine thousand feet. The three aircraft were in what might have been termed a dive. The two Russian pilots had tilted him forward and down, throwing the Firefox over a cliff of air towards the clouds beneath.

Dive −

Gant thrust the control column forward, then rammed the throttles forward almost to the detent and reheat. The Firefox leapt at the cloud layer, the huge Turmansky jets roaring. He saw the two Foxbats accelerate behind him, closing the gap he had opened. He opened the airbrakes, jolting the aircraft, then flung the Firefox into a roll and pull-through, suddenly changing the direction in which he was moving. It avoided the optimum firing position he had given them on his tail, and increased the time lag between them. He closed the airbrakes and pushed the throttles open as he came out of the pull-through. In his mirror, two abandoned stars gleamed and winked. On his screen, the white dot moved away from him. He forced his left hand to keep the throttles wide open. The silver trail of droplets sprayed out into a mist behind him. The white dot on the screen steadied, altered course by going through his own manoeuvre, and then began to struggle to regain the centre of the screen. The headset babbled in Russian, from the pilots and from Bilyarsk.

He jabbed the airbrakes out again, slowing with wrenching suddenness, rolled and pulled through, closed the brakes, and opened the throttles again. Once more, the two Foxbats were left further behind and away from his tail. He felt the suit around him resist the pressure of the G-forces. He was now travelling directly west, across the neutrality of Finland towards Norway. How much distance the tanks would still give him he did not know because he had no idea how quickly he was losing fuel in that sparkling, dazzling spray of diamonds behind him. But any distance between the Firefox and the border with Russia was good and right and necessary.

The Foxbats altered course and closed once more. Airbrakes, roll, pull-through, close brakes, throttles. He whirled like a falling sycamore pod once again.

Thirty thousand feet . . . twenty-five . . . twenty, nineteen . . . the figures unrolled on the altimeter. The white dot that was the two Foxbats still in close formation was steady in the lower half of his screen. No more than a mile away.

Fourteen thousand, and the sun disappeared and he was blind, the grey cloud slipping past as if his speed were tearing it like rags, but it was still thick enough to exclude the light. Ten thousand feet . . .

Eight, seven, six –

He used the airbrakes and closed the throttles. He pulled back on the column. The Firefox began to level out.

Four . . . three . . . two-point-seven, two-five. The white dot split into two tiny stars, and both moved nearer the centre of the screen. The headset babbled. Bilyarsk ordered the border squadrons at top speed to the last visual sighting, before he entered the cloud.

Cloud, *cloud* –

The Proximity Warning began to bleep again as the Foxbats closed.

Fifteen hundred feet, the glimpse of a sombre, snow-covered landscape, an horizon of low white hills, a uniformly grey sky now above him – he pulled back on the column, and nosed the Firefox back into the cloud. The world contracted, wrapping its shreds tightly around the cockpit. He slowed almost to stalling speed, feeling the adrenalin and nerves and fear and sweat catch up with his decisions. He breathed quickly and heavily enough to begin to cloud the facemask of his helmet. There was a heavy dew of sweat on his brow. The two white dots hurried towards the centre of his screen, blind but somehow confident. They would pass within a mile of him, to starboard of his present flight path. Other, new dots had appeared at the edge of the screen, like spectators spilling onto a football field. He demanded a range-to-target read-out for the approaching squadrons. Then he altered the request — time-to-target. Two minutes seven-point-four, the computer read-out supplied. Then the distance between the two Foxbats increased, and Gant realised that one of them was retreating again above the cloud layer; a tactic designed to catch him by surprise if he suddenly increased altitude. He would pop out of the cloud into bright betraying sunlight, within missile range. He grinned.

He banked the Firefox, moving to intercept the other Foxbat as it continued to rush through the cloud. He armed the only remaining Anab missile, and waited. He cancelled the read-out, replacing it with the information on the closing Foxbat. Range-to-target — two miles, one-point-nine, one-point-seven . . . He activated the thought-guidance systems on the console to his left.

He would have to be right. Optimum moment. The Anabs that had been replaced by the submarine crew on the ice-floe were not equipped with a steering system linked to his thought-control capability. They were an earlier model, captured from a Foxbat in Syria. He had to rely on judgement, on selecting the exact moment. He could not guide the missile once he launched it.

Point-nine . . . point eighty-seven, six, five . . . six, *fire*. He formed the command precisely, in Russian, and felt the Anab drop, then flick forward. It was an orange glow in the cloud, then it disappeared. He watched the screen, the infra-red glow of the missile's exhaust slipping across the small gap of screen between himself and the Foxbat. The Russian fighter, blind in the cloud, continued to descend like a white meteorite, nothing showing on his radar.

Then the white dot suddenly altered course. The pilot's headset had yelled a warning. The orange dot encroached, neared, sidled towards . . . The white dot accelerated, changed course, dipped and weaved. The orange dot, like a faithful dog, ran behind, accelerated, sniffing the radar and other electronic emissions from the Foxbat, closed, closed, dodged with the white dot, closed, closed —

A brief flare on the screen, and then there remained only the white dots of the second Foxbat above the clouds, the slowly-moving AWACS plane, and the more distant interceptors at the edge of the screen. Gant banked the Firefox, easing the throttles forward as he settled on his new heading, and began running west. Altitude three thousand feet, speed two hundred and seventy knots, fuel non-existent.

The crowd of white dots rushed towards the centre of the radar screen, towards the now-fading flare that had a moment before been an aircraft and a pilot. The cloud slipped past him, seemingly lighter and thinner.

He tensed himself for the first visual sighting when he ran out of the cloud.

The ministry car had left the M1 north of Leicester, and they had used the A46 through Newark and Lincoln to reach Scampton by lunchtime. Flat land beneath a cloud-strewn sky, the three honey-coloured towers of Lincoln Cathedral overlooking the red-roofed city, and then they were on a minor road between clipped, weather-strained hedges before arriving at the Guard Room of the RAF station.

Kenneth Aubrey had been voluble during the journey, as excited as a child on an annual holiday. To the two Americans, Buckholz and Curtin, he was tiresome in his complete and impenetrable pleasure at the success of the Firefox operation. Their passes were inspected by the guard, and then they were directed towards the CO's office.

Group Captain Bradnum was on the steps of the main administration building, two stories of red brick, and he hurried to the car as it came to a halt. Aubrey almost bounced out of the rear seat to shake his hand, his smile bordering on something as vulgar and uninhibited as a grin. Bradnum's heavy features reflected the expression he saw on Aubrey's lips. It was all right. Everything was all right.

"Well, Group Captain?" Aubrey asked archly. Buckholz and Curtin left the car with less speed and more dignity, yet with as much pleasurable anticipation.

"He must be safe by now," Bradnum replied.

Aubrey glanced at his watch. "The British Airways flight from Stockholm leaves in thirty minutes, I see. I presume Gant's going to be on time – mm, Charles?" He turned to Buckholz, who shrugged, then nodded. "Oh, my apologies, Group Captain – Charles Buckholz of the CIA, and Captain Eugene Curtin of the USN Office of Naval Intelligence." Hands were shaken. When the formalities were over, Aubrey said, "You said he must be safe by now. Why? Has anything happened?"

Bradnum's face was lugubrious. "The Nimrod – at your request – was monitoring Gant's advised flight path . . ."

"Yes, yes," Aubrey snapped impatiently. "What of it?"

"Only minutes ago there was nothing in the area except a Russian AWACS plane on the Soviet side of the border with Finland."

"And – ?"

"Now there are two Foxbat interceptors in that airspace – and a great deal of coded signal traffic, and – " Bradnum shrugged. His

257

mirroring of Aubrey's smile had been unwarranted, a moment away from the truth. "Eastoe in the Nimrod claims they were climbing very fast, very positively . . ."

"On an interception course?"

"They're close enough to spit at the Firefox, Eastoe said."

"Why weren't we told this?" Buckholz demanded heavily.

"It happened only minutes ago."

"And in those minutes?"

"Eastoe's reported a great deal of manoeuvring . . ."

Aubrey turned away, facing south across the still-wet runways. Beyond the hangars and other buildings, beyond the flagpole and the perimeter fence, a sudden gleam of sunlight displayed the distant towers of Lincoln cathedral on its perch of limestone. Then the towers were dulled as the watery sun disappeared behind a swiftly-moving cloud. He turned back to Bradnum.

The noise of an RAF Vulcan taking off seemed a mocking, unnecessary intrusion into the tense silence.

"I know Eastoe – what's his best guess?" Aubrey asked quietly. "He would have one and he would have offered it, asked or no."

Bradnum nodded. "They've been in the tightest formation and descending very slowly for two minutes or more. He thinks the Firefox is there, too. It's too deliberate to be for no reason."

Aubrey snapped his fingers in an inadequate expression of anger and urgency.

"We must talk to Eastoe," he said, addressing Buckholz. "At once. From your Ops. Room, Group Captain. Lead on, if you please."

At the edge of eyesight, another shaft of sunlight warmly lit the distant cathedral towers. Aubrey shivered with the cold of the wind.

"What now? What now?" the First Secretary demanded. The Tupolev Tu-144 was cruising at fifty thousand feet, almost a hundred miles of the journey from Bilyarsk to Moscow already accomplished.

Vladimirov leaned heavily on the other side of the map-table, his eyes focused upon the dark-haired wrists that protruded from beneath the Russian leader's shirt cuffs. Grey hairs, too . . .

The report from the surviving Foxbat confirmed that visual contact with the Firefox had been lost. Gant was hidden somewhere in the twelve or thirteen thousand feet of the cloud layer. On low power, an infra-red trace would be difficult to establish, almost impossible to pinpoint and attack. Because attack would be the next order. Vladimirov knew that. For him the game was up. Deluded by the apparent passivity of the American and the success of his two Foxbat pilots, Vladimirov had fatally delayed the order to the border

258

squadrons on the Kola Peninsula to scramble. Now, he was once more blind, the Firefox's anti-radar concealing the American. Neither the surviving Foxbat nor the AWACS Tupolev "Moss" could detect his presence.

Vladimirov's own future remained difficult to envisage. His pride was hurt. He had lost to the American once again, and he could not forgive himself. The anger of others failed to interest him.

Eventually, he looked up at the Russian leader. The man's face was dark with habitual anger, habitual power. Threat. The image of the bully. Yet the stupid man had no ideas of his own – had no *conception* – !

The scatter of luminous blips representing the scrambled interceptors, mainly MiG-25s and swing-wing MiG-27 Floggers, moved across the bright map towards the border with Finland. Other dots scurried south-eastwards from the west of North Cape, their contact time still six minutes away. Although no more than a futile gesture, the AWACS Tupolev had changed course to patrol the hundred miles or so of border which contained the point at which Gant would have crossed – *had crossed*, he reminded himself – into Russia. The single remaining Foxbat's white dot buzzed and twisted in tight little circles on the map, like an insect dying.

"In two minutes we will have eighteen, even twenty-four aircraft in the area,' Vladimirov said calmly. "Visual contact will be re-established."

The First Secretary sneered, then compressed his lips above his clenched jaw. When he spoke, all he said was: "And what will you do if and when he is sighted?"

"I – await your orders, Comrade First Secretary . . ." Vladimirov announced in a quiet, restrained voice. Behind the Russian leader, Air Marshal Kutuzov nodded with the wisdom and cowardice of great age, paining Vladimirov by his assent. Andropov smiled thinly, and flicked a little nod in the direction of the general. The gesture acknowledged the acquisition of good sense, proper caution; the priority of survival. The First Secretary appeared suspicious, then mollified.

"Very well." He leant more closely over the surface of the map, the colours of the projected land mottling his features. It was a parody of knowledge, apeing the strategist. The First Secretary had been a Political Commissar during the Great Patriotic War. His reputation suggested, even in the sanitised, history-book version now current, that he had killed many more Russians than he had Nazis. No, no, Vladimirov warned himself, stilling the angry tremor of his hands. You've begun it – play it out. "Very well," the First Secretary repeated. "We – will wait, until our forces are in the area."

He looked to Vladimirov for approval, and the general nodded perfunctorily.

Masterly, Vladimirov announced silently and with irony. Quite masterly. Aloud, he said: "Contact time of closed squadrons – one minute. Warn them to concentrate on infra-red search. Blanket the area. Gant is virtually weaponless, and out of fuel." Even to himself, his optimism sounded remarkably hollow. It appeared, however, to satisfy Andropov and the First Secretary.

The room was filled with the crackles and bleeps of exchanged communications. The Kola squadron flight leaders, the surviving Foxbat pilot, the AWACS captain. An energising electronic chatter. Easy to picture them, translate the moving dots into planes and men and tactics and search-patterns. His fingers circled the area where the Foxbat had been destroyed by Gant's last missile. In there, he's in there . . .

The First Secretary's impatience was evidently growing. To do nothing, to abdicate the display of power, was anathema to him. Vladimirov suspected that the impotence of inactivity had determined the Russian leader's order for the Tupolev to return to Moscow. The physical location of the War Command Centre was a matter of indifference to Vladimirov. The First Secretary studied the map, he glanced from face to face, he listened to the reports. He watched the red second-hand of the largest of the room's many clocks moving like a spider-leg around the white face. He watched time pass without the search locating the MiG-31. One minute . . . a minute and a half . . . two minutes . . . three . . . Vladimirov controlled his features, controlled his sense of rising body temperature.

Gant was out of fuel – he should be hugging the ground – the weather satellite shows broken cloud, he can't run around inside the cloud forever – he should be hugging the ground, making a run . . . when would the American's nerve break, when would he run for cover, skimming across Finland like a flat stone before his engines sighed and surrendered . . .?

Four minutes . . . four and a half . . . five . . . six . . .

Then: "Got him! He's run out of cloud!" The operator had increased the volume so that the Foxbat pilot's ringing, boyish voice was audible above the cheer in the command centre. "He's at zero feet and travelling sub-sonic, perhaps four hundred knots, no more. I'm going down!" Then, more formally, he added: "What are your orders, Comrade General?"

"His exact position and heading!" Vladimirov snapped, then to the room at large: "Alert the search to home in on the MiG-25 – repeat speed and altitude just – "

"Give the order to attack!" the First Secretary announced, glaring at Vladimirov. "No more games – no *strategy*! Tell them to destroy the MiG-31 on sight!"

Ground-clutter, ground-clutter, clutter, ground-clutter, his mind kept repeating as the Firefox leapt at the landscape at an altitude of less than a hundred feet, the automatic pilot and the terrain-following radar preserving it from the snow-softened folds and contours of Finnish Lapland. Invisible, invisible, he chanted almost as a prayer. The clutter of images from the landscape would mask the Firefox from any searching eyes – other than those of the MiG-25F still on his tail, less than two miles behind him.

Two pilots with no more to do than choose the moment for the kill; to select, savour, review, revise, re-select the optimum moment. Two pilots – one with four AA-6 missiles, the other with cannon fire and empty tanks. Effectively, he and the pilot of the Foxbat were alone, skimming across the surface of Finnish Lapland. The squadrons of searching MiGs above them were rendered doubly blind – the anti-radar protected him, the ground-clutter masked his pursuer from assistance. The pilot of the Foxbat was transmitting a steam of positional fixes to his newly-arrived colleagues, but he was offering old news, history. The Firefox flicked, twisted, whipped through the landscape at four hundred knots – a butterfly that refused to be pinned to the card.

Until it ran out of fuel, finally . . .

The threat had hung over him for so long – perhaps fifteen minutes' flying time since he had first noticed his fuel state – that he had begun to disbelieve the gauges. They claimed he could have as much as six minutes' flying time left at his present speed. Yet each evasive manoeuvre squandered fuel, and even more fuel streamed away behind him. And he still could not shake the pursuing Foxbat. It followed him indefatigably. Over his headset, Gant heard the frantic but assured reports of his pursuer. There was a gap of time to be traversed, the optimum moment for the kill still lay in the future, but there was no doubt of the outcome.

He'd heard, too, the strong voice that had first addressed him after the take-off from Bilyarsk. The Soviet First Secretary. This time, he had heard it snapping orders, not addressed to him but to every particle of the pursuit. *Kill, eliminate, obliterate. Destroy the MiG-31.* The First Secretary's voice had cut across that of the strategist, the man who had weighed and watched and planned and guessed. The gambler. The man who, if Gant could outwit him, offered the chance of escape. He had pride and self-confidence and he believed he would win. Therein lay the potential for error, for opening the wrong door just long enough for Gant to take his chance. But the Soviet leader's voice expressed only power, accepted only certainties. He wished to end the game – now.

Landscape, suddenly rushing at him with a new ferocity. Mountains, hills, ridges, folds. Lake Inari, the sacred lake of the Lapps, had been no more than a brief glimpse of ice-blocks, ice-sheets, snowbound wooded silent islets and the occasional glimmer of windows in sudden disappearing villages. Now the land creased and folded as if to battle the terrain-following radar, confuse his eyesight. The Firefox bucked, nose up, then dipped again over the brow of a snow-covered hillock. Gant's stomach settled, and the pressure-suit relaxed its reassuring grip on his frame. Snow flew and boiled in the wake of the Firefox, flung up by the passage of his slipstream across the treetops. It made the rear mirror blind, but he knew that his pursuer remained behind him. Waiting for the moment to launch one of his missiles. The Foxbat would be carrying two infra-red homing missiles, and two which homed on radar. The rocket motors of the missiles were capable of propelling them at speeds far in excess of the Mach 3 that was the MiG-25's top speed. Gant knew that with full tanks he might have outrun a launched missile; but not now. He would have to wait. The range of the missiles was perhaps twelve miles. His pursuer, clear of his rearward-looking radar sensor, was less than two miles behind him.

Gant's course was north-west, towards the nearest point of the Norwegian border.

Wait –

It was all he could do. The two Turmanskys continued to roar but, at ground level, he was wasting the last of his fuel . . .

Wait –

Two narrow frozen lakes, smooth-surfaced, then white-clad forest, then the narrow valley of a frozen river. Snow flew and rumbled down behind him from the sides of the steep, knife-cut valley. He watched the rearward screen. He was travelling in a straight line, it was a moment of calm in the violent changes of course demanded by the landscape.

Optimum moment . . .?

A dot detached itself from the pursuing Foxbat, which had entered the valley. There was nothing in the mirror but rolling clouds of snow. Out of that would spring –

The AA-6 missile leapt up towards the centre of his screen, homing on his exhaust heat. A tenth-of-a-second, a fifth, a quarter . . . Gant's hands were still on the throttles. The right thumb had already armed the tail-decoy system. His left hand twitched on the throttle-levers. The missile moved dementedly, like a virulently-

262

poisoned insect, coming at him at perhaps more than Mach 4. He hesitated ... point-seven of a second, point eight ... point-nine –

He released the tail-decoy. Almost immediately, it ignited and the snow was a dazzling, torn-apart curtain, hurting his eyes. Then it brightened further, and he felt the shock wave of the explosion overtake him and shudder through the airframe. His teeth chattered. There was nothing on the radar except the pursuing Foxbat, which had broken to port to avoid the debris and had then dropped back into the narrow valley. It was already accelerating, too. Less than a mile and closing.

A hillock ahead. Without conscious thought, Gant cancelled the automatic pilot and terrain-following radar. He banked the Firefox to starboard, slowing his speed as he did so. The pursuing Foxbat swung left of the long, white, whale-backed hillock, and Gant knew that the pilot had made an error. He anticipated catching Gant broadside on, an unmissable target for cannon fire or another missile. If he just hadn't slowed enough, however. Gant had time to form the thought in the second he was hidden from the Foxbat, and then he realised that the valley was a closed one. He would have to lift over the ridge, exposing the Firefox's flank to attack – he'd made the mistake, not the Russian. The hillock had tricked him. The valley wall rose in front of them. He pulled back on the control column, sweating with new fear.

The Foxbat leapt the ridge a split-second ahead of him, its pilot similarly surprised by the valley wall ahead, his speed no more than a few mph faster than that of the Firefox.

But he was there. For a moment, he was there – !

Gant banked savagely and pulled tighter, then fired. The Foxbat, caught like an athlete half-way through a jump, seemed to hold, even stagger in the air. As Gant closed on the silver shape, he continued firing. The cannon shells raked through the cockpit and down the spine of the fuselage.

Gant passed beneath the Foxbat, buffeted by its slipstream as it continued to climb. There was a minor explosion – Gant saw it as he pulled round to attack once more – and the cowling of the port engine was breaking up. The Foxbat lurched, staggered, but continued to climb. Gant followed, overtaking it as it reached the apex of some already-dictated parabola. He could see the pilot dead in the cockpit, beneath the cracked and starred canopy. The nose tilted, began to drop . . .

The Foxbat stalled at five thousand feet, dropping back towards the ground with as little weight and independence as a leaf. Gant glanced at his radar. The white dots of searching MiGs were scattered across it like crumbs from a meal untidily eaten. Fire was streaming from the Foxbat's port engine. In a matter of seconds, the aircraft would explode –

And he would, with it . . .

He grinned. He would disappear. The Foxbat fell towards a hillside, spinning. It would bury itself in deep snow. He spiralled down, following it. It was a second from impact and burning like a torch. He loosed a tail-decoy and it ignited, glowing on his infra-red screen, to be matched then surpassed by the explosion of the Foxbat at the base of the hill behind him.

Two fireballs in close succession. Two kills.

The cockpit was silent, except for the jabbering Russian as Bilyarsk and the search squadrons tried to raise the dead Foxbat pilot. He switched off the UHF set. It *was* silent.

Christ –

Then it happened. The sudden sense of the Firefox slowing that he had dreaded. His rpm was falling rapidly. In his headphones, he could hear the chatter of the auto-igniters. Altitude four thousand feet, fuel non-existent . . .

He could see the snowbound landscape beneath. He had no more than minutes in which to decide to eject or to land. Then the engines caught for a moment as the pumps dredged the last of the fuel from the tanks. He pulled back on the column. He needed all the altitude he could muster. Three seconds later the engines died again, the rpm dropped, the gauges presented zero readings. The engines were silent, empty. Again, he had to decide – eject or try to land . . .?

He wouldn't eject, he told himself. Not now, not after everything that had happened.

He banked the Firefox over the wilderness beneath the grey sky, searching for a runway that did not exist.

"AWACS Tupolev reports losing all trace, Comrade General."

"We can't raise the pilot, sir. He's not answering."

"No infra-red trace after the two explosions, sir."

Two explosions, Vladimirov thought, and immediately found himself trapped in the Byzantine labyrinth of his own qualifications and guesses and instincts. It was a maze which was inescapable every time he appeared to be presented with evidence that the American had died, that the Firefox had been destroyed. And again now, when it seemed certain that the second Foxbat, itself shot down, had caused an explosion aboard the MiG-31, he doubted. He hesitated, he would not look up from the map-table, he would not listen to the First Secretary's gruff sense of relief.

264

And yet, he could no longer express his doubts. He had learned that much diplomacy. He had learned silence.

"Very well," he replied to the now-finished chorus of reports, still without looking up. "Very well. Institute a reconnaissance search for wreckage of the two aircraft – and possible survivors . . ." He looked up into the First Secretary's face and at Andropov behind the Soviet leader. "Just to make certain," he added. "Routine." He hated the apologetic tone in his voice. This new role did not suit him, but it was the only one which offered itself. He had, at last, begun to consider his own future. "It should not offend our friends, the Finns – if they ever discover our over-flights."

The Soviet leader laughed. "Come, Vladimirov – the game is over. And to you, yes, it was only a game? Played with the most expensive toys?" His hand slapped the general's shoulder and Vladimirov steeled himself not to wince at the contact. Kutuzov appeared tired and relieved. The operators began to relax. The cabin speaker had been switched off.

Nothing, Vladimirov told himself without hope of conviction, nothing . . . There is nothing there now except wreckage. The American is dead.

"Chairman Andropov – some drinks, surely?" the Soviet leader instructed. Andropov smiled and moved to summon a steward. "No, no – we'll leave this crowded room – come, some comfortable chairs and good drink before we land – mm?"

"Yes, of course, First Secretary," Vladimirov murmured, following the Soviet leader out of the War Command Centre into a narrow, deceptively-spacious lounge filled with well-upholstered, deep chairs, a television screen, a bar. Already, drinks were being poured . . .

Kutuzov appeared at his elbow and whispered, "You've shown good sense, Med – at last." His voice was a dry whisper. He'd been operated on, successfully, for cancer of the throat some years before. "It's over now."

"Do you think so?" Vladimirov asked in an urgent whisper. "Do you?"

Kutuzov indicated Andropov and the First Secretary, backs to them, already at the bar. "It would be foolish – monumentally stupid – for you to think otherwise at this moment," he whispered. Then he smiled. "Come on, drink with them, listen to them – and remember to *smile*!"

"It was – such a beautiful aircraft," Vladimirov announced abstractedly. "And the American showed us how good it really was."

"Perhaps they'll build us some more – but don't count on it."

Kutuzov's laughter clogged and grated in his throat. The First Secretary offered them vodka.

"Come," he said. "A toast."

Two frozen lakes. Silence except for the clicking of the automatic ignition with no fuel with which to work. Gant switched it off. Silence. Two frozen lakes, lying roughly north-south, one larger and more elongated than the other, both surrounded by birch and conifer forest. Snowbound, isolated, uninhabited country in the north of Finnish Lapland.

Little more, according to the map on his knee, than forty miles from the border with the Soviet Union. His escape from the Foxbat had taken him further north than he had wished and turned him unnoticed back towards Russia.

Silence. Wind. Out of time.

He was gliding, the heavy airframe wobbling and quivering in the stormy airflow. Altitude, two thousand five hundred feet. The lakes moved slowly southwards behind him. He banked sharply and glided towards them once again.

He would not eject, would not . . . He'd come this far. The airplane stayed in one piece.

Two thousand feet. The larger of the two lakes was perhaps more than one mile long – long enough to be a runway. The second lake was fatter, rounder, and he would have to land diagonally across it to be certain of stopping the Firefox with room to spare. There appeared to be a lot of surface snow which would effectively slow the aircraft. It would have to be the larger lake.

Pretend it's the floe, he told himself. Just pretend it's the floe. At the end of March, the ice should be thick enough, it should bear the weight of the airframe.

It didn't matter. It was the only available alternative to a crash-landing, or to an ejection which would leave the Firefox to plough into the ground and break up once it ran out of supporting air. He would not let that happen. Instead, he would land the airplane, and wait. When he was certain the search for him had been called off, he could communicate with Bardufoss or Kirkenes – Kirkenes was much the closer – and they could drop him fuel. He checked that the airbrakes were in and the booster pumps off. All the trims he set to zero. He tugged at his straps, checking their security.

He could make it. The conifers grew down to the southern neck of the narrow lake and stretched out drunkenly over it – he could see that clearly – and if he could get in close enough to the frozen shore, he would be sheltered from any chance visual sighting. Excitement coursed through him. He could do it. He could preserve the Firefox.

Altitude, a thousand feet. He had only the one chance.

He nudged the rudder and the Firefox swung as lazily and surely through the chill grey air as a great bird. He lowered the undercarriage as he levelled, and operated the flaps. Four hundred feet, well above the trees which rushed beneath the aircraft's belly. The lake joggled in his vision ahead of the plane's nose. Two hundred feet and out over the ice. He'd got it right. The Firefox sagged now, on full flap, dropping with frightening swiftness, and the wheels skimmed the surface snow for a moment, then dug into it, flinging up a great wake around and behind him. He gripped the control column fiercely, keeping the nose steady. The nosewheel touched, dug in, and Gant saw the surface snow ahead rushing towards him, beneath him. The Firefox began to slow, began to stroll, then walk . . .

The Firefox rolled gently towards the southern neck of the lake, towards the frozen stream that either fed or drained the lake in summer. His speed slowed quickly − too quickly? The aircraft seemed to no more than crawl towards the overhanging shelter of the trees. Would he make it? It had to reach the cover of the trees . . .

It was enough. The airplane had sufficient speed to move in close to the bank at the very end of the lake, where it narrowed almost to a point at its conjunction with the frozen stream. Low-hanging branches deposited their weight of snow on the cockpit canopy as he slowed to a final stop. Branches scraped along the fuselage. The nosewheel stopped just short of the bank.

He'd done it. The Firefox was hidden. In one piece, and safely hidden. He breathed deeply. Then he raised the cockpit canopy. Cold air rushed in, chilling him to the bone, making his teeth chatter uncontrollably. He grinned at the drop in his body temperature. He disconnected his oxygen supply, the radio and thought-guidance leads to his helmet; he unlocked his leg restraints, and his seat straps. He removed the helmet and, as he stood up in the cockpit, he began to laugh.

Yes, the trees hid almost everything. One wingtip and the tail assembly were still exposed, but the shape of the aircraft was altered, destroyed by camouflage. The sky was heavy with snow. A fall would hide the signs of his landing. It would be all right.

The Firefox lurched, as if the starboard landing gear had snapped. Gant clung to the side of the cockpit to steady himself, his ears filled with a terrible, strained cracking noise. He dropped the helmet he had just removed.

A black, crooked line, like a tree growing in hideous fast-motion, moved away across the ice. Branches grew from it. The Firefox lurched again, this time to port, and settled unsurely. Other black trees grew out across the ice around and behind him.

Horrified, he looked over the fuselage. He could see water behind the starboard wing, water behind and in front of the port wing. Water beyond the tail. Huge jagged plates and slabs of ice bobbed and rubbed one another around the Firefox, which now floated on its belly, buoyed up for the moment by the empty fuel tanks in the wings and fuselage. Gant knew that as soon as the engine inlets and tailpipes filled, the aircraft would sink steadily into the lake.

TWO:

Deeper

The tail of the Firefox slid deeper into the water as the tailpipes and inlets flooded and the undercarriage sought the pebbled floor of the lake where it sloped steeply from the bank. The nose of the aircraft jutted into the lower branches of the nearest firs but it, too, was slowly sinking. Gant did not understand. The ice was thin and weak at the neck of the lake, even though the stream that provided the lake's outlet was evidently frozen between its banks. Everything was frozen – yet the Firefox was sinking.

He felt panic mount, rising like a thermometer. He could not control it because he had used all his reserves of energy and self-control to reach the lake with the aircraft intact, and this disaster had struck at the moment of his release, his greatest relief. The panic rose in waves through him, and his hands gripped the side of the cockpit, numb with the pressure he exerted; a mad, dazed ship's captain waiting for the end.

Floor of the lake steep – draining water leaving a pocket of air under the ice, making it thin – engine weight will roll her back into the lake further out – she'll drown, drown . . .

The jagged plates of ice touched, rubbed, moved apart. He could easily make it to the shore, even though the overhead branches were already out of reach. It was the airplane, the Firefox –

There was nothing he could do. His frame shuddered with tension and futility. He was weary, and his limbs seemed very heavy. He had nothing left. Water lapped up the fuselage, very slowly moving higher – the branches over the cockpit were now over the up-jutting nose. The huge weight of the engines and the airframe was slowly dragging the Firefox deeper and further out into the lake. The long nose section thrust from the water like the snout of a creature that had breached the flimsy ice.

The cracks had stopped. They branched perhaps fifty or sixty yards out into the lake behind the aircraft. The loose plates of ice had floated away from the fuselage to gather like a motiveless crowd where the ice remained deceptively firm. To his left, the snow-covered shore of the lake was still within jumping distance.

Gant climbed onto the lip of the cockpit, poising himself, his hands gripping the edge of the cockpit tightly. He looked back down at the still-lit instruments, the fallen helmet, the pilot's couch . . .

The Firefox lurched backwards, out from beneath the shelter of the trees, the water lapping up the fuselage. Now, it was little more than a foot from the edge of the cockpit; another movement, and the first icy ripples would spill into it — fusing, shorting, damaging everything. The panic in his stomach and chest would not subside. There was no nightmare of Vietnam, not in this cold, not with the smoky grey shoreline and the omnipresence of snow. But he was as bereft of purpose as if he were suffering one of his bouts of paralysis.

The aircraft was steady now, tilting backwards on the sloping bed of the lake. Perhaps only for seconds . . . The water was ten inches from the lip of the cockpit . . . the tail was half-submerged, the huge engines already underwater . . .

He dropped, in his apelike crouch, back into the cockpit, his hands nerveless and numb as he tried to make them operate small, delicate switches and buttons. Thought-guidance — shut down . . . . come on . . . weapons-systems — shut-down . . . radio, radar auto-pilot, ECM systems — shut down . . . His hands seemed warmer now, no longer lumps at the ends of his arms but active, moving with a trained, automatic precision and speed. In seconds, he shut down the aircraft, killing it, rendering it lifeless. Then he climbed over the lip of the cockpit. He was still wearing his parachute. Clipped to his life-jacket were his inflatable dinghy and his survival pack. Icy water touched his heel, and he withdrew his foot. Awkwardly, he moved over the cockpit sill, his toes feeling clumsily for the spring-loaded steps. When he found them, and balanced himself, he pulled out the cockpit canopy hand crank from its compartment below the cockpit sill. He cranked down the cockpit canopy until it closed tightly. Then he closed the manual, exterior locks.

A moment of pain, of acute failure, and then he poised and leapt. He landed in soft snow, paining his hand on a buried tree root, rolling over and scrabbling for a hold on frozen glass and icy rocks beneath the snow. His survival pack and the dinghy lay beneath him. Snow filled his mouth and eyes, even his ears, though they were still alive to the terrible scraping lurch that meant the Firefox was moving further out, further under the surface.

Yes. He turned to look. The water had reached the cockpit – thank God he'd remembered to close and lock it – and the nose pointed to the grey sky at a more acute angle than before. He drew his knees up to his chest – the cold of the snow seeping through the pressure suit and the thin underclothing beneath – and dropped his head. He could not move. He felt it was like waiting by a deathbed – but not his father's, for that had been an impatient wait with release and the throwing off of hatred at the end of that tunnel.

It would be no more than a minute now –

He laughed; high and crazy. The noise was like the call of a rook in the thick cold air. He could not prevent it; a cackle of survival and defeat. *He'd certainly hidden the Firefox, hidden it good* –

He could not stop the laughter. Tears rolled down his blanched, cold cheeks, down the creases of his pained face. He cackled like a madman. *He'd really, really hidden it* –

Another grating lurch – some part of him remained surprised that the undercarriage had withstood the pressure upon it – and he looked up to see the cockpit now half-submerged, the water lapping towards the nose of the Firefox.

And the laughter stopped.

The locked and shut down aircraft was twenty yards from him, the black nose jutting, the cockpit half-submerged. Everything – *everything* electronic, every means of communication, was locked beneath the canopy, locked inside the airframe. Radio, radio, *radio* . . .

Gant swallowed, savagely wiped his mouth. The aircraft was steady again, one of the wheels, perhaps, halted against the chock of a boulder or sunk in softer mud. Tantalisingly steady –

There was nothing –

"Nothing, dammit!" he exploded, banging his clenched fists on his thighs. A bird replied in a hoarse voice from one of the trees. "Nothing – ! He could do nothing. He couldn't sit in the Firefox until help came, he couldn't dismantle the radio and rescue it, he couldn't, couldn't, couldn't –

Strangely, he heard the voice of Aubrey then. The soft, self-deprecating, insinuating tones. His final briefing, the fake transistor radio that was a homing receiver which had saved his life, listening as it had done for signals from "Mother One", the submarine that had refuelled the Firefox. It was attached by a single adhesive strip to one corner of the instrument panel.

Receiver – ?

Transmitter, too . . . Aubrey had been reluctant to mention it, hovered over the words like a choosily-feeding pet until he had uttered them. *In case of some* – final *emergency, my dear fellow . . . not likely, of course . . . but, it has an emergency signal facility if you – have to . . . you understand . . . ?*

Gant was on his feet, still nodding at the remembered words as he had nodded when he first heard them. Aubrey didn't want to mention crashing, injury, death, but Gant had understood.

And he had left it in the cockpit!

He slipped and scrambled down the steep bank. He unclipped his survival pack, his parachute harness, the dinghy. The dinghy! – A fringe of ice cracked beneath his weight, and he slid into the icy water. He cried out with shock. He stepped back – pebbles and larger boulders on the bed of the lake, so he moved carefully – and the water retreated. He dragged the dinghy towards him, and inflated it. It boiled and enlarged and groaned, then bobbed on the water. His teeth chattered, his whole body shuddered. A bird croaked, as if in mockery. The nose of the Firefox tilted upwards like a snub, a dismissal of his frantic efforts. He climbed into the dinghy, and paddled furiously towards the aircraft. His head bobbed up at every frantic stroke to study the unmoving nose of the plane. His body temperature continued to drop. His heartbeat raced with tension, with the sense of time lost and almost run out, with the fight to keep the blood warm and circulating.

His hand touched the fuselage, and he withdrew it as if shocked, in case the pressure of fingertips might be enough to thrust it beneath the water. He juggled and bumped the dinghy slowly along the fuselage until it was beneath the cockpit tilted crazily high above him. His hands felt for the spring-loaded steps up the side of the fuselage.

Felt, fumbled, found . . . He tested his chilly weight against the strength of his arms, and then heaved his body out of the dinghy, feet scrabbling – careful, don't kick, don't struggle – until they, too, discovered toe-holds. He hung there for a moment, sensing the steadiness of the airframe. It was holding. He began climbing, hand over hand, feet following with exaggerated caution, slipping more than once.

Lip of the cockpit, smoothness of the canopy . . .

He rested, aware of the airframe now as a see-saw. He waited for it to move. It remained still. The water covered the rear section of the canopy. Water would spill into the cockpit when he opened it. It wouldn't have to matter.

Left-hand side of the instrument panel. He unlocked the canopy, then cranked it slowly open. Water gurgled into the cockpit, splashing down instruments, becoming a pool in the well of the pilot's couch. He eased the canopy open sufficiently to insert his gloved hands, and scrabbled blindly, leaning forward, touching along the instrument panel, across dials and read-outs and displays and buttons and switches, until he felt the edge of the homing device. Like a black cigarette-case, slightly larger than that, same shape . . .

He tugged at it. The adhesive held it. With both hands he heaved and it detached itself from the panel. With a chilly, sodden, shivering triumph, he drew it out and clutched it against his side, hugging it to him like a prize. Still the airframe remained motionless, rock-steady. He began to crank down the canopy once more.

The Firefox shuddered, and the entire airframe lurched away from him towards deeper water. The huge tailplanes sank almost to their tips. The Firefox continued to slide away. With the instinct to preserve himself and the aircraft, he cranked more furiously and grabbed with his other hand at the handhold just below the edge of the cockpit. A tremor ran through him as he heard the homing device slide down the fuselage with a clatter, then drop. He cranked furiously, closing the canopy. He dropped the cranking-handle then, in order to hang on with both hands. He knew the Firefox was going under . . .

He would float away. He looked around frantically for the homing device, and for the dinghy, already ten yards away. Surely he had heard the impact of the plastic on ice, not the slight splash of its falling into the water – but he could not locate it. The water mounted the canopy towards him. The airframe was steadily rolling backwards now. It would stop only when the slope of the lake-bed levelled. The water was only inches away – he would float off.

He released the grip of his right hand, then made to move his left. He unclenched his fingers from the handhold, and tried to move his arm. Water touched his fingers, embraced his thighs. The canopy was almost submerged, the nose was sinking. The tips of the tailpane were still visible, the leading edges of the wings protruded from the dark water. He could not move his left arm.

He had trapped the sleeve of the pressure suit in the canopy when he cranked it shut. As the water reached his waist, he tugged frantically, attempting with all his strength to rip the suit.

Clinging to the canopy of the Firefox, he began to slip beneath the water with the airframe. Waist, chest, neck, mouth. He could not free his sleeve . . .

Above the noise of his blood and breathing, he again heard the bird croak mockingly. Then he disappeared beneath the water.

"There were *two* explosions – two *distinct* explosions . . . you're certain of that?"

Aubrey waited. The underground Operations Room of RAF Scampton had shrunk to a microphone, two revolving tape reels, and the console and its operator controlling the high-speed, scrambled communications between himself and the captain of an AWACS Nimrod aircraft over the Norwegian Finnmark. Beyond the glass, down on the main floor of the room, Buckholz and Curtin stood beside the huge plot-table, staring at the model that represented the Nimrod. Buckholz wore a headset clamped on his short, grey hair. His shoulders were stiff with the tension generated by the transmission and reception delays of Aubrey's conversation.

The tapes rolled swiftly, halted, rewound, then Aubrey heard Squadron Leader Eastoe's voice, mechanical and distant, but clear. "There were two, almost in the same spot, but distinct. A small time and distance gap. At . . ." A slight pause while Eastoe consulted something, then: "Sixty-nine-forty North, twenty-seven-fifty East. That's no more than twenty-two nautical miles from the nearest point on the Soviet border — about the same from the Norwegian side . . ."

Eastoe seemed to have paused once more, rather than to have concluded his message. Aubrey lifted his head. Someone pushed a futuristic model into position on the plot table. It was old-fashioned — on one wall of the Operations Room was a fibre-optic, computer-operated plot map where aircraft, ships and missiles were registered by moving lights — and yet Aubrey found the plot-table comfortably familiar. It had a wartime association. It was out-of-date, super-annuated. He could see, quite clearly, that Gant was deemed by Eastoe to have met his death in a narrow neck of Finland between the Soviet Union and Norway. The model of the Firefox, placed in position, was in the nature of a memorial. Curtin and Buckholz gazed fixedly at the table — except for a brief upward glance by the senior CIA officer. His face was grim. Aubrey, almost furtively and in shame, lowered his head to the tape-reels and the microphones. Eastoe had not added to his statement.

"You conclude that one of the MiG-25s was successful?" he snapped. The tapes spun, then waited. Spun again, rewound, played.

"Yes," Eastoe replied. Aubrey watched Buckholz's shoulders hunch, shrug. Curtin's face was abstracted. The naval officer seemed fascinated by the small black model of the Firefox. The plotters near them hovered like deferential servants, or like the policeman bringing news of a road accident. "They tried to shepherd him, he shook them off, took out the first of them — the second must have pursued at ground level, and they got each other. We couldn't see the MiG-31, of course, so we don't know whether it was damaged earlier. Since the explosions, nothing. The area's filling up with MiGs now, but their activity suggests they can't locate anything." Eastoe's voice paused, then: "Mr. Aubrey — what do you want me to do?"

Aubrey rubbed his chin vigorously, as if conjuring the answer from a lamp. The tape-reels waited for him to speak. Alongside him, the staff of the Operations Room sat behind their consoles and radios and radars and screens. The plotters hovered. The huge wall map gleamed with moving lights. The walls of the Ops. Room displayed other maps crowded with pins and scribbled legends, coloured tapes. Blackboards revealed information regarding the serviceability of aircraft. Large meteorological maps were heavily marked, garlanded with satellite weather photographs. A long row of pale blue headsets, together with a single red telephone, stretched away on either side of him. A multiplicity of technical devices were at his disposal. He dragged his hands through the hair above his ears. His fingers touched the back of his head. He heard old bones and muscles crack and stretch reluctantly. He placed his hands in his lap, hunching forward. He did not know what to say to Eastoe. He did not know how to begin to use the people and equipment that lay at his disposal.

Not once, not once . . . his thoughts murmured hesitantly. Not once, not once –

Until now, he answered himself. Until now. Not once had he doubted, truly doubted, not once had he thought the game lost, the aircraft or the pilot lost . . .

Until now.

Now he believed it. It had been forced upon him. Gant was dead, the aircraft scattered over the landscape like sooty dots on the carpet of snow. Nothing, nothing left of it.

Despair was an unfamiliar companion. A sometime acquaintance, away elsewhere for long periods; older and leaner at each unexpected return. Yet it was despair Aubrey felt. He had failed. The whole operation had failed. Delicate, complex, devious – brilliant and his own, it had failed. Aubrey's despair dressed in a sober suit and carried a briefcase. It was an entirely professional emotion, and bottomless.

He saw an image, then, of civilian air disasters. Newsreel film. Flight-recorders being searched for by the experts who did not concern themselves with the search for the living and the dead. Black boxes. Cockpit voice-recorders, flight recorders. The secret of the dead.

In his mind, he could see a recent piece of newsfilm. The joggling camera registering the walking legs of a man and the two heavy, black, flame-scarred boxes he carried, one on either side of him. Walking legs, black boxes –

He rubbed his eyes. Voice-activated, the tape-reels moved.

"Remain on-station, Eastoe," he ordered, his voice clearing and strengthening as he spoke. "Fly up and down that piece of border until you hear something!"

A pause. Eastoe's reply returned, was rewound, then became audible. "Please repeat, Mr. Aubrey."

Aubrey slapped his forehead. He had not explained. "I wish to be certain," he said. Buckholz, one hand holding the earphone of his headset, looked up towards the glass-fronted gallery where Aubrey was sitting. "If the aircraft has crashed or been destroyed, then there may be nothing. If Gant is alive – if the aircraft is still intact – then you may pick up a signal from his homing device. You have the equipment to activate and receive it."

After a little while, during which Aubrey felt hot and the small sense of excitement that hope had brought deserted him, he turned pale and felt foolish like a gauche new entrant to an ancient and dignified club. Foolish – must try it – foolish, though . . .

"Roger, Mr. Aubrey. If he's there, we'll find him."

"Yes," Aubrey replied abstractedly, unconcerned that the word and its tone would be transmitted. The console operator turned to him. Aubrey flapped his hand dismissively, staring at his lap. Gant was dead. The Firefox was in pieces.

"The AWACS Tupolev is watching us watching him," Eastoe announced. Aubrey hardly heard his voice. "He'll be listening for the same thing. Could he pick up a signal?"

"I hope not," Aubrey murmured in a moment of uncalculated honesty that was full of doubt and foreboding.

The shock of the icy water which engulfed him almost made him open his mouth to scream to expel the lungful of air he had snatched as his face was dragged into the water. His chest seemed too full, inflated under pressure from within. If only he could expel the air, make his body more empty, smaller, the cold would be less intense, less painful. He forced himself to retain the air.

Even a few feet beneath the surface, the water was lightless because of the disturbed silt, as if the ice had closed over the Firefox as soon as it sank. The noise of the undercarriage moving down the steeply-sloping bed of the lake was magnified and distorted into a prolonged groan. The Firefox dragged him by the sleeve deeper beneath the water. His body banged against the metal of the nose as he bobbed and attempted to float. His body's buoyancy tugged at the trapped sleeve of his pressure-suit, turning him almost in a cartwheel, twisting him, slamming him down on his back against the fuselage, then scraping him along the nose of the aircraft.

His lungs seemed fuller. He knew he was beginning to drown. There seemed a simple solution, but he believed it was light-headedness that suggested the idea. He was trapped. He tried to reach his left arm with his right hand. The Firefox continued to roll, and he could not tell whether it was beginning to level out and slow down. He could not reach his trapped sleeve. Without purchase, he could not apply any force to the feeble grip of his right hand on the material of the suit. His hands were numb, anyway, fingers crooked like claws, frozen.

Weariness, and the knowledge that survival and escape had been snatched from him, curtailed his ability to think, to move, to even desire anything. His chest hurt with retained air. His head swirled like the dark water. Just as around him the disturbed mud drifted back towards the bed of the lake, his body sagged down to straddle the nose of the Firefox.

The napalm of his nightmare lit the scene. Freezing and numb though he was, his body still felt hot, burning. From within the bamboo cage in which he had been imprisoned, he witnessed his rescue; the attack upon the Viet-Cong detachment and their hidden village. He saw the little girl with the sadly-wise face running, and he saw her dissolve in the gout of napalm dropped near her. He saw all the others burn like matchsticks, like trees in a forest set alight. He felt himself burn. He saw one of them – he *was* them . . .

The nightmare claimed him. He struggled against it, but his body seemed to have no conception of water and drowning, only of his recurrent dream, only of the napalm. The water around him seemed redly-lit by its flare. Every one of the gooks had burned, the little girl had burned. He had remained untouched physically, safe in his abandoned bamboo cage. Ever since, horror and guilt had caused him to burn, melt, dissolve with the Vietnamese; with the little girl, in her place . . .

His hand embraced his left thigh. He noticed the touch, the clawlike grip. The crablike scrabbling, the tugging at a press-studded flap. His mind was detached and separate from his right hand. His left hand was feelingless, somewhere above him, against the canopy of the cockpit. His lungs were bursting.

He could see only the red burning colour of the water as his right hand closed thumb and forefinger upon the flap on his thigh. Gant did not understand. The flap pulled slowly open like a hesitant mouth. He did not know what his right hand expected. He wanted, more than anything, to empty his lungs, more even than to stop the nightmare because this time he was going to die inside it. His right hand closed on something and withdrew it from the pocket. It felt hard.

The little girl's body, right at the centre of the mass of golden-red fire, dissolved . . . he was on the point of opening his mouth to scream . . . and something detached itself – straw hat or head he had never known, had never dared to look – he wanted only to scream.

His right hand brought up the hard object, close to his face. His right hand needed the evidence, the use of his eyes. But his eyes did not work, dazzled by the light of the flames. Where his hand was, where the object was, it was dark. Thin gleam − ? He could not focus. His head swirled. The flames lessened. His right hand continued to act, reaching forward, ahead of him into the place where the numbing, icy cold seemed to be coming from, where it had already swallowed his left hand, left arm. He tried to watch, to understand −

Empty your lungs, he told himself. *Look −*

See −

He saw the dinghy-knife trailing its safety cord which his right hand had withdrawn from its sheath, he saw it hack at his left hand, left arm, so that he wanted it to stop. Feeling returned to his left arm as it cringed in anticipation of a wound. Then the sleeve was torn, sliced open, and he expected blood but there was none and his arm drifted down towards him, to be clenched against his stomach, its torn sleeve freed from the canopy.

Feebly, he kicked with numb feet, drained and leaden legs. His face was uplifted, but everything seemed dark. He kicked again, leaving the napalm-fire behind him now, afraid at that moment that it was already too late, that he was blacking out and would open his mouth, let the bubbles dribble out as his body slackened . . .

He felt his boots scrabbling on the metal of the Firefox's nose, and pushed upwards. It was only a matter of feet, but in time it seemed endless, because there were gaps of inky, swirling black between his attempts to count . . .

One, one-two . . . black . . . two-two-two . . . black . . . one-two . . .

Black −

Grey −

Black −

Then light.

He roared as he expelled the air, felt his lungs painfully deflate, then draw in cold new air which hurt and made him cough. He swallowed water. His cold arms and legs wouldn't tread water. Breathe . . .

Inhale − hold − exhale . . . inhale − hold − exhale . . . sweeter now. The air tasted. It was sweet, cold, pure. His body hung on the surface of the water, exhausted, as if threatening to slip back beneath it. Life . . . jacket . . .

His hands fumbled on his chest, dabbling there uselessly, it seemed for whole minutes.

Then the life-jacket inflated, bobbing him unresistingly onto his back, holding up his hanging, useless, numb legs, pushing his arms out into a crucifix, keeping his chin out of the icy water. He breathed air gently, savouring it, pushing at the water with gentle movements.

A long time later, it seemed, his feet dragged gratingly against the pebbles of the shore. He was almost sitting in the water. He tried to stand up, could not, fell on his side – the life-jacket turning his face to the grey sky at once – and then turning wearily onto all fours and crawled the last few feet to the steep, snow-covered bank.

And rested, shuddering with cold, hands and feet and knees still in the water, reminded of warmth and function by the sharp pebbles beneath them. The dinghy-knife was still in his right hand, sticking up out of the water.

When his hands began to pain him with their freezing numbness, and his feet were dead from the cold, he clambered upright, and stood, rocking with exhaustion, gauging the height of the steep bank of the lake and his ability to ascend it. He succeeded in climbing by dragging his body behind his arms up the slope, digging the dinghy-knife deep into the frozen soil and heaving against it, digging it in again further up, heaving his body up to its level. It took him ten minutes; the bank at that point was a steep slope perhaps twelve foot high. He lay, when he had inched over the lip of the slope to the bole of the first fir tree, exhausted, panting, his eyes hardly able to focus. For one thing alone he was thankful. He had left the napalm of his nightmare down there behind him, in the lake with the MiG-31.

Later, he ate chocolate. Later still, when feeling had returned to his hands, he was able to rub life into the rest of his body. The pressure-suit was stiffening as it slowly dried. Later, he inspected the area of water at the neck of the lake, realising that his panicky guess had been near the truth. The stream that acted as the lake's outlet was indeed now frozen. But it must have gone on draining the lake before it, too, froze. The draining water had left an airpocket which had kept the ice thin, dangerous.

Later still, after the noise of a low-flying, searching MiG had faded east of the lake, he realised that he should put some distance between hmself and the site of the forced landing. The ice would knit again, form like a cataract over the eye of the water the airplane's weight had opened. The Firefox would be totally hidden by the following dawn. Already, the short Arctic day was beginning to fade.

He had the dinghy-knife, the survival pack, his parachute, and the standard-issue Makarov officer's pistol and two spare magazines. He had no extra clothing, and his body was chilled to the bone. The dinghy had drifted out into the lake, like a marker to indicate the airplane's position. He drew the Makarov, hesitated, steadied his aim, and fired twice. The noise was deafening. Birds protested with cold voices. Slowly the dinghy deflated, began to sink. Gant sighed with relief. No trace.

He was alive. Standard procedure dictated that he remain near the aircraft. In this case, he dare not. If they searched for him – when they failed to find any signs of wreckage they could attribute to the Firefox – then they must not find him near the plane. He had to head . . . north-west, try to make some indentation on the daunting twenty miles or more between his position and the Norwegian border. He had to blindly hope that it was not only the Russians who would be searching for him . . .

The homing device. The transmitter –

In a new moment of panic, he looked around sightlessly. It was nowhere to be seen.

Had he – ? Had it been switched to transmit? He could remember every movement of his right hand as it sought the dinghy-knife and then his trapped sleeve. Now, he had to recall every moment of the few when the slim black plastic case was cradled in his left hand, against his body. Had he done it, automatically? Had he switched it on . . .?

His memory fumbled, struggled with the effort of recalling automatic responses, mere reflex actions.

Eventually . . . yes. Yes, it was switched on. His eyes scanned the ice. The remains of the dinghy had disappeared. He walked clumsily, slowly along the bank – even for the transmitter, he would not allow himself to step onto the treacherous sheet of ice on the lake – searching for what would be no more than a black dot. He did not find it. The landscape was nothing more than black and grey and white.

Finally, he concluded that the transmitter had sunk to the bottom of the lake. If it had dropped onto ice – he was certain he remembered that kind of sound when it fell – it must have slipped off when the ice had been moved or distressed by the underwater eddies created by the moving bulk of the Firefox. It was lost.

Now, distance was his only imperative. He could not stay near the transmitter, near the lake. If he was found, it needed to be miles from here.

His body failed him for a moment, daunted by the prospect of movement, of travel; of survival.

He looked northwards up the lake to where the heavy, crowded trees were little more distinct than a dark, carbon smudge made by someone sketching the scene. The ice was a smooth sheet. He was on the western shore of the lake. He checked his compass and the maps he unstrapped from his thigh. In its clear plastic, it had remained dry during his immersion. The pressure-suit was achingly cold.

He looked in the direction he must travel, towards Norway. Conifers crowding to the water's edge, low hills beyond them. He heard the mocking dissuasion of large, unseen birds. He looked down at the water, still like setting jelly, its temperature dropping. The Firefox was undetectable, invisible. It had to be enough to satisfy him; drive him on.

He picked up his parachute and buckled on the harness. He clipped the survival pack to his now deflated life-jacket, and adjusted its weight for comfort. Then he turned away from the lake and entered the trees.

Air Marshal Kutuzov glanced towards the other end of the compartment and the door which led to the small private office the First Secretary used when aboard the Tupolev. Evidently, the Soviet leader and the Chairman of the KGB intended remaining there for the rest of the flight. Kutuzov glanced at his heavy gold watch. Twenty minutes to the principal military airfield south-east of Moscow. He cleared his throat, patting Vladimirov's leg as he spoke. "Med, I think you have secured the succession for yourself." The old man tapped the shoulder boards on his own uniform. His pale, rheumy eyes twinkled, and he nodded vigorously. "You're learning. And in time – just in time . . ." It was evident that Kutuzov was philosophically drunk.

Vladimirov stared at his own small glass. How many drinks – ? They'd been drinking for less than half an hour. No one gets drunk more quickly than a Russian. What was he drinking to? The American's death? The excessive, almost manic bonhomie of the First Secretary, the cold, glinting appraisals of the still-sober Andropov – both had ceased to irritate or impinge. The vodka had distanced them. He had managed to drown reason and insight like two wasps at the bottom of his glass. Their stings pulled out.

He glanced towards the door of the War Command Centre, then at the door to the First Secretary's office. The Soviet leader had been summoned to the telephone to deal with the diplomatic niceties of airspace intrusions.

Through the vodka, the sense of self-contempt was returning. Vladimirov warned himself against it. And, as if his companion sensed the threatened change of mood, he patted Vladimirov's hand and said: "Be sensible – continue to be sensible, General Vladimirov." The formality of the address was intentional. Vladimirov shook his head in what was a gesture of agreement rather than protest. The alcohol stirred like a solid mass lurching across an empty space.

"I know it – I know it," he murmured. "It's much better to be – oh, what? Nothing? Better to be nothing." As he moved his hands angrily, vodka slopped from his glass onto the shining toes of his knee-boots. He watched the oily droplets flow like mercury across the polish. "I know it."

He stared again at the door to the War Command Centre. Through it officers had appeared periodically in the past half-hour to make their negative, comforting reports. They were like something added to the vodka, doubly calming. Wreckage photographed, pictures being returned for examination; search planes reporting no distress signals, no electronic emissions, no survivors.

Soon, it would be no more than a matter of experts examining the photographs of the wreckage to confirm that the Firefox and the MiG-25F were destroyed at the same moment in the same area. Then later the Finns would give permission for crash investigators and a recovery party to examine the site and bring the wreckage home. Black boxes would be removed, bodies would be wrapped in plastic sacks and brought back. End. Over. Finished.

The First Secretary had cancelled all over-flights of the crash area before taking his call from the Finnish President. All intrusions of foreign airspace could be apologised for because now they had ceased.

"I am offering you no more than a lesson in survival," Kutuzov announced. It was the slurred voice of the vodka. "Because I want *you* to command the air force. *You*." He was patting Vladimirov's knee slowly and heavily to emphasise each word.

"I know that, old friend," Vladimirov replied, nodding. Even to himself, his words sounded indistinct. He mocked himself silently, reproaching and ridiculing himself as bitterly as he could. He swallowed what little remained in his glass. His stomach surged. "I've accepted. I – am a member of the team . . ." He smiled, his lips forming the expression imprecisely. "*How* long before we land?" he added with sudden exasperation.

"Patience. You are now a courtier. You will get used to waiting. It is a talent."

"Courtier . . ." Vladimirov murmured.

"Another drink?"

"No, old friend – I wouldn't be able to keep it down."

"No Russian can – we get drunk too quickly."

"Do you blame us?"

"No."

282

The two men stared into their empty glasses. Vladimirov lifted his to reflect the overhead light. He could see the last oily smear in the glass, see the smudges made by his lips and fingertips. Then he stood up, swaying slightly, tall, grey-haired, drunk, but evidently, so evidently, an officer of distinction. As if he saw his form reflected in a mirror, he mocked his appearance. An impressive outward show, even when he was drunk. Hollow man . . . hollow man.

A young officer opened the door from the War Command Centre. Vladimirov whirled almost too quickly to face him. In his hand he carried a message pad.

Hollow man . . .

Stop it –

It was impossible to drown the wasps, then.

"What is it?" he snapped, his tongue furry, his eyes glistening. The rest of himself retreated somewhere, to wait for a more opportune moment.

"It's the Tupolev, sir – the aircraft commander, Major Antonov. This . . . I don't think he can understand it . . ."

Vladimirov snatched the pad, plucking his half-glasses from his top pocket, wobbling them onto his ears. Sobriety nudged him, having returned from its short absence. Antonov would not be the pilot of the Tupolev AWACS aircraft, but the political officer who theoretically commanded the crew. He was a member of GLAVPUR, the armed forces' political directorate. However, he might still be competent aircrew, even though he was on the Tupolev "Moss" because it flew near all kinds of hostile borders across which its crew might be tempted to take it – *liberating* it and themselves in the process. So, Antonov . . .

At first, Vladimirov did not understand the report. A frequency-agile signal, intermittent . . . they'd picked it up once or twice, got a line on it – the first fix – but not a second clear fix which would give them the exact position. They only knew the signal emanated somewhere along a straight line . . . not near the crash site . . .

Finally, the request for orders; the passing of the buck. Vladimirov waved the young officer out of his path and stepped into the War Command Centre. Immediately, he sensed the familiar and the desired. Yes, it was a clean, well-lit place. It was comfortable here, at the centre; the uniformed centre.

He would have been criminally stupid, he reflected as he crossed the room, to have thrown all this away – and why, and for what? Because the Soviet leader was a boor and a thug? Because the Chairman of the KGB was a psychotic? Because he loathed their company and their intellectual inferiority? Those would have been his reasons; pride and snobbery. Caste.

A clean, well-lit, comfortable place. His place. It would have been criminal to throw it away.

"Put me through to Antonov – over the cabin speaker," he announced calmly, soberly. A moment later, he was given the signal to proceed. "Major Antonov – this mysterious signal of yours . . . what do you suppose it is?"

"Yes, Comrade General," he heard the distant, crackling voice begin, "we don't know what to make of it – any of us."

"When did you first pick it up?"

"Fifteen minutes ago – but we lost it – then found it on a different frequency . . . the third time, only five minutes ago, we managed to get a line on it, but we haven't been able to pick it up since." The tone was apologetic, but it managed to include the entire crew of the Tupolev in any consequent blame.

"Find it again, Major – I beg of you."

"Yes, Comrade General."

Frequency-agile – a signals or communications emission, but without a message or code . . . a somehow-still-operating piece of clever electronics thrown well clear of the crash site . . .? How far – this was too far . . . some Finnish ground installation we don't know about? Unlikely. There had been no Personal Survival Beacon signals from either pilot, so Gant and the Foxbat pilot were both dead . . . neither of them had ejected in time.

Personal Survival Beacon – *Beacon* – secure signal, he *remembered*, secrecy when all the pilot would want was the loudest scream across the widest band. Because of the MiG-31 project, there was secrecy surrounding the aircraft, the pilots, the ground crews, the instruments, the pressure-suits . . . the obsession of the Soviet state, how many times it had enraged him!

The PSB for Firefox test pilots was frequency-agile, and intermittent, to ensure that only those instructed how to listen would ever hear . . . and Gant was wearing dead Voskov's pressure suit!

"It's *Gant!*" he roared. Shoulders and heads twitched with shock. Vladimirov beat his fists against his thighs. "He's *alive!* He's been alive all the *time! You!*" he barked at the officer who had brought him the scribbled transcript of Antonov's message. "Get me the details of the frequency-code for the PSB in a Firefox pressure suit – get it now!" He hurried to the door. Turning, he added: "Transmit it to Antonov as soon as you have it. And tell Antonov he *must* find that signal again and obtain an exact fix. No excuses!"

He went through the door, slamming it behind him, already knowing, without careful analysis, what must be done. The First Secretary and Andropov were emerging into the hospitality room at that moment. Immediately, Vladimirov pointed his long forefinger at Andropov as at a recalcitrant and untrustworthy subordinate.

"I want your Border Guards, Comrade Chairman!" he snapped. "I want a helicopter patrol, three ships, ready to cross into Finland immediately – Gant's been alive all the time!"

The contents of the survival pack from the Firefox were spread around him at the foot of the fir tree. His eyes were gritty with tiredness, and refused to focus for any length of time. Tension and weariness produced bouts of violent yawning. His body shivered almost constantly now, with cold and reaction. He had escaped. He had walked perhaps a little more than three miles in a north-westerly direction, keeping to the cover of the forest. He wanted only to sleep now. The pressure suit creaked and groaned as it froze into stiff, awkward sheets and folds around his body. His toes and fingers were numb. He had to sleep.

He would repack the survival kit except for the sleeping bag, which lay like an orange and blue brick near his left knee. If he got into it, perhaps only for an hour – surely he could afford the time. He hadn't heard the noise of a searching aircraft for perhaps twenty minutes now . . .

He had to sleep. He could not form ideas, make plans. He could not stay awake. There was good overhead cover here. The sleeping-bag, tight around him, would eventually warm him, restore the circulation. He would be able to continue, if only he slept now.

A white Arctic hare watched him from the other side of the fir tree. Its nose twitched as it assessed the intruder. Gant watched it dully, head hanging forward, staring at the small, still animal from beneath his furrowed brow. Even to hold the white hare in focus against the snow required vast concentration.

Automatically, the Makarov pistol came out of its holster, took aim, and fired once. The noise was deafening, frightening in the silence to which he had become totally accustomed. It seemed to invite pursuit, create lurid images of capture. The hare leapt backwards with the force of the 9mm bullet at such close range, its powerful back legs flicking up. Then it lay on its side. A small stain spread from beneath its fur, darkly red. It would supplement the rich cake, the chocolate and biscuits in the rations of the survival pack. He was tired, exaggeratedly saddened by the killing of the hare, and immediately he entertained the emotion it became self-pity; he was utterly weary. He could not, now, gather up, skin, cook the hare.

He began shivering again. Furiously, as if to punish himself, he rubbed his hands on his arms, trying to warm himself. Or scrape away from his skin some guilt or paralysis that clung to it.

An object. Hard. Inside one of the pockets. Left arm. He unzipped the pocket, and withdrew a small orange cylinder. He recognised it at once. His PSB, his distress signal transmitter.

He stared at it, unbelievingly. He had forgotten it, hadn't even attempted to locate it. It would have been activated – without the shadow of a doubt it would have been activated and begun transmitting – the moment it was immersed in the waters of the lake. He looked up at the sky, wildly. Nothing. The search had been called off –

Relief in his mind was a clean image of the grey, darkening sky. Intruding upon that was the white dot of the Tupolev AWACS airplane as he had seen it on his screen. The transmitter in his cupped hand would undoubtedly have the power to beam a signal the thirty or more miles of distance and the forty thousand feet of altitude to the Tupolev. They must have heard it. They knew he was alive, where he was . . .

Panic removed weariness with a rush of adrenalin. He stood up, swayed, then dropped the PSB. He stamped on it, grinding it out of shape, puncturing the skin, smashing the transistors and wiring within. Killing it. The hare lay beyond the distress he had made in the snow, unmoving. He knelt again, scooping the scattered items back into the survival pack. The brick of his folded sleeping-bag, the folded .22 rifle and its half-dozen rounds, the chocolate and biscuits, the compressed rations, the solid tablet stove.

He watched the hare. He couldn't –

He dragged a plastic bag from the pack, scooped up the hare with apologetically gentle hands, and thrust it into the bag, then the package into the survival pack. As he stood up, he kicked fresh snow over the small, darkening smudge of blood.

His tracks would not show because he had been beneath the forest roof for the greater part of his journey. Eventually, he would have to sleep, but now he must strike in a more northerly direction. He slipped the harness of the pack over his shoulders, wearily assuming a fully-upright posture when he had done so. He swayed with tiredness. He looked at his watch. Darkness was still as much as two hours away. Two hours, then, before he could rest.

He groaned aloud. The noise disturbed, magnified the silence of the forest. He studied the map. Ahead of him a country of patchy forest, narrow valleys, dotted lakes. Like Alaska.

He hefted the pack's weight to comfort, shivered with cold and anticipation, listened to the brooding, continuous silence, and turned to face northwards.

He began to walk.

*   *   *

Squadron Leader Alan Eastoe turned the AWACS Nimrod in a slow arc as he completed the southerly leg of his patrol at twenty-five thousand feet above the road which straggled across the Norwegian Finnmark from the Tanafjord to the small town of Karasjok. The road marked the border between Norway and Finland. The aircraft was above the cloud layer as it once more headed north-east, following the wriggling line of the unseen road.

It had been almost two hours since they had reported what Eastoe suspected had been the pursuit and destruction of the unseen MiG-31. He had immediately been ordered by Aubrey to remain on-station and to begin this idiotic patrol in the ridiculous hope of either picking up a signal from Gant's PSB – and they hadn't done that because Gant was dead – or evoking some response from a piece of sophisticated gadgetry that must have been destroyed with the Firefox.

Yet Aubrey needed to be convinced. Thus, they had to keep on attempting to make the Firefox's homing device emit a simple carrier wave on which they could take a bearing. According to Farnborough, the homing device would be capable of responding to their pulsed radio signal for at least eighteen hours. Eastoe did not believe they would ever pick up the carrier wave. No one but an uninformed civilian like Aubrey would have expected to do so. There wasn't a ghost in the machine. The Firefox was just – dead.

Eastoe yawned and adjusted his tinted glasses on the bridge of his nose. At their altitude, the sunlight still gleamed from the surface of the cloud layer below, even below the clouds it would be getting dark.

"Christ, Terry," he murmured, looking towards his co-pilot, tossing his head in dismissal, "bugger this for a ball of chalk. The poor sod's dead – and I'm sorry he's dead – and the plane's a write-off, and I'm sorry about that because I'd like to have seen it, just the once . . . *But*– !"

The co-pilot shook his head, smiling. "You've worked with Aubrey before, skipper . . ." he began.

"Worked *for*, Terry – worked *for* Aubrey. There's all the difference in the world. He's never bloody convinced. I can see him in the Garden, swearing blind the risen Christ *is* only the gardener!" Eastoe laughed, despite his exasperation. He heard a crewman's chuckle in his earphones. "Come on, then, he'd say – just one or perhaps two miracles to prove you are who you say you are – no, perhaps *three* miracles will suffice. Silly old sod!"

"Why worry? In half an hour, we'll have to go off-station to refuel at Bardufoss. He won't order us up again tonight, surely?"

"Don't bet on it," Eastoe grumbled.

Except for their voices, the flight deck of the Nimrod was almost silent. As in all its endurance flying, the aircraft was using only two of its four engines. It was, in every way, a routine, empty day's flying. Yet exasperating to Eastoe – sad, too, because the Yank had almost got away with it, he'd almost pulled it off. Something had gone wrong – damage during the earlier dogfight when the second MiG-31 had been destroyed, probably – and he'd been caught on the hop and finished off. Poor bugger.

"Anything at *all*, John?" he asked, almost wailing into his microphone, addressing himself to the tactical navigator seated before his displays in the first of the major compartments aft of the flight deck. "What's that bloody stupid Russian doing?"

"Who – Pissed-off Pyotr in the Tupolev?"

"That's the one."

"He's running up and down his bit of the border, doing just what we're doing, skipper. He's having about as much luck, by the look of it. No changes of heading, except when he comes to the end of a leg. He's now at – "

"I don't want a bloody fix on him, for Christ's sake! Is there nothing else?"

"Nothing. Not even a Finnish fighter. Keeping their heads down on orders from Helsinki, I should think. Anyway, they've been proven right. Ignore the problem and it'll go away. No MiGs anywhere over Finnish airspace. They've gone home for tea."

"They've got their snaps of the wreckage. They'll be analysing those. Perhaps we should have . . . ?"

"We're approaching optimum distance from the point of the explosions," the routine navigator offered like a grinning tempter. "Are you thinking of having a look, skipper?"

"I'm numb with boredom, but I'm not stupid," Eastoe replied. Why bother? Aubrey would have arranged something with Finnish Intelligence, or an American satellite. If he'd wanted proof of the crash from photographs, he'd have asked for them. Why bother? The same silent answer would be forthcoming. There was nothing to find. The captain of the Tupolev knew that's all there was just as surely as he did himself.

And then, the thought popped into his head. Why not? The Russians had been encroaching into Finnish airspace all afternoon. What if – ?

The colder thought was –

We could be out of range of the bloody homing device. They might have already triggered the carrier wave, but they could be out of range by ten miles, or even a mile, if it was transmitting on very low power.

If he changed course, then the Tupolev would assume he'd found something. But, if he photographed the crash site at low level, then the bluff might work – and the snaps would be useful, more useful than tooling up and down the border.

"Anything, John?"

"Nothing, skipper."

Eastoe glanced at his co-pilot. "Everybody stay alert. I'm just taking a little short-cut here – a little corner off the map. I'd like some souvenir snaps. OK?"

The co-pilot watched Eastoe, then remarked. "You really do like working for these cloak-and-dagger bods, don't you? Deeds of bloody derring-do. When are you going to grow up?"

"Like you?' Eastoe was grinning. "Beats routine patrol. Who'll ever know? Who'll ever make a fuss? We can have our own snaps of the wreckage, and a closer listen for that bloody carrier wave – then, I promise, we'll go home."

"Three or four minutes in Finnish airspace doesn't constitute the crime of the century, Terry," the tactical navigator offered.

"Bob?"

"Yes, skipper?" the routine navigator replied.

"Give me a course for the crash site."

"Roger, skipper."

Eastoe grinned. "Blame me at the court-martial, Terry," he offered.

"You bet."

Eastoe nudged the alteration of course through the rudder. The Nimrod's blunt head swung to starboard. The cloud layer beneath the aircraft was devoid of nationality. Simple, Eastoe thought, feeling the tension stiffening in his frame as they crossed into Finnish airspace.

"Twenty-four kilometres from the crash site – right on course."

"No transmission, skipper."

"ETA – fifteen seconds."

Eastoe dipped the Nimrod's nose. "I'm taking her down slowly to avoid creating *any* suspicion – then we'll turn and come back over the crash site. Everyone ready with their Brownies, please."

The cloud layer rose up to meet the nose of the Nimrod, almost touching it.

"That's it!"

"Christ, what – ?"

"The carrier wave. We're locked on now, transmission steady. It's her all right!"

"I'll alter course for the fix."

The clouds slid around the Nimrod, darkening the flight deck.

"No, it's almost due south of us now – I've got the line . . . first fix, skipper. Just keep on course – don"t alter a bloody thing."

"South?" Eastoe remarked, genuinely surprised. "Not at the crash site. Christ, then he didn't go down . . .?"

"Wait till you find the distance – it could have been thrown upwards of a mile," the co-pilot offered.

"Jeremiah. Come on, John . . ."

"Give me time, skipper – fifty, fifty-one, two, three . . ."

"Do it now – I'll come back for another run if you need it – " Eastoe ordered impatiently.

"Right. Got it." Eastoe hummed tunelessly in the silence. His ears buzzed with anticipation. The tactical navigator would now be drawing his lines on the map, out towards the point where they would intersect and establish the precise position of the homing device. Then they'd know how far away it was – exactly *where* it was.

"It's almost forty kilometres south of us. On what looks like a lake – or *in* the lake."

"His PSB – anything?"

"Nothing."

"If he's in the plane, he'd have it working. So, where the hell is he?"

Gant awoke. Some part of his mind became immediately and completely alert, but he sensed the rest of himself, his thought-processes, his whole personality, struggling to throw off the deep sleep into which he had fallen the moment he climbed into the sleeping bag. Something had woken him – something . . .

He groaned, then clamped his hand over his mouth. Something, something that could already be as close as the Arctic hare had been when he had shot it –

His hand scrabbled within the sleeping bag, emerging with the Makarov pistol. It was almost completely dark. He could see little more than the glimmer of the snow, the boles of the nearest small trees like fence posts. He listened, the remainder of his mind and senses becoming alert, shaking off sleep.

He pressed the cold barrel of the Makarov against his face, leaning against the gun as if for support.

Distantly he could hear the noise of helicopter rotors, the whisper that had penetrated his sleep. He had no doubt that the sound was approaching from the east and moving in his direction. Russians . . . Lights, troops, even dogs . . .

He kicked the sleeping bag from his legs and began to fold it untidily then thrust it into the survival pack. He hoisted the harness, slipping it over his shoulders even as he began running.

THREE:

In Flight

"There!" Aubrey announced immediately he located the coded map reference Eastoe had supplied, his finger tapping at the large-scale map of Finland, which lapped down over the edges of the foldaway table. "There – in a lake, gentlemen. In a *lake!*" There was a note of triumph in his voice.

"The lake would have been frozen – that's why he might have thought he could land safely," Buckholz speculated quietly, tugging at his lower lip and glancing towards Curtin for confirmation. The USN officer nodded.

"He must have gone straight through – or otherwise the Russians would have spotted the Firefox," Curtin murmured, his brow furrowed. It was evident he was considering Gant's chances of survival.

"Agreed. But it's there."

"The homing device is there," Giles Pyott offered. He was still wearing his uniform greatcoat, his brown gloves were held in his right hand. They tapped at the map in a soft rhythm. "But what else, mm? My guess would be wreckage. Gant must have ejected."

"Then why is there no trace of Gant's PSB?" Curtin asked gloomily. "Where is he Colonel Pyott, if he's alive?"

"Mm. Tricky."

"Maybe he switched it off – or destroyed it," Buckholz suggested. "He wouldn't want to get himself picked up by the other side . . . they're a lot closer than we are, and there are a hell of a lot more of them." Despite the offer of such qualified optimism, Buckholz shook his head. "But, maybe he isn't alive. We have to face that possibility."

"But the Firefox – !" Aubrey protested impatiently.

"It could be in two pieces, two hundred, or two million," Curtin answered him. Aubrey's face wrinkled in irritation. "This location is twenty miles from the point where the Foxbat impacted," Curtin continued. "That was up here . . ." He, in turn, tapped the map. It was as if the contoured sheet had become a talisman for them as they gathered around it. Pyott's military cap rested over northern

291

Norway, his gloves now beside it, fingers reaching into the Barents Sea.

"So, it was damaged," Buckholz said. "Maybe on fire – twenty miles is nothing. There's no hope down that road, my friends."

"We really must *know*!" Aubrey snapped in utter exasperation. "We must have a *look*!" As he uttered the words, he was staring up into Pyott's face, like a child expecting assured parental activity.

Giles Pyott smiled thinly. "Kenneth, my dear chap – let's take this one step at a time. In the ten minutes since I got here from MoD, I've taken over his flying station from poor Bradnum, all in the name of this project of yours . . . what else would you have me do?"

"Eastoe must overfly – "

"The lake? What about diplomatic noises from the Finns?" Giles Pyott drew a folding chair to him, flicked it open with a movement of his wrist, and sat down. He placed his hands on his thighs, and waited. Three more chairs were lifted from a dozen or more stacked against one wall of the Scampton Ops. Room, and arranged in a semi-circle in front of Pyott. Aubrey seemed content for the moment, to become the soldier's subordinate. Buckholz was surprised, until he realised that Aubrey was simply playing a waiting game. He expected good things from Pyott, if the colonel from MoD's StratAn Intelligence Committee was given the impression of command, of superior authority.

As if he read the American's thoughts, Pyott smiled and said, "You're flattering me with your undivided attention, Kenneth . . . nevertheless, there are things to be done." Pyott's eyes roamed the Ops. Room. His curled forefinger now rubbed at his small auburn-grey moustache. Scampton was, to all intents and purposes, at their disposal. But, what to do with its resources? Where to begin? "I agree that Eastoe might make a single overflight. I wonder, however, whether photographs will give us enough information? It's getting pretty dark up there by now." Aubrey's face, Pyott noticed, wore an intense, abstracted air, like that of a child furiously engaged in building a sandcastle in utter ignorance of the behaviour of tides. Aubrey was preparing himself to bully, to plead – to ignore the diplomatic in favour of the covert. And yet, his priorities might be the only really important ones in this case . . .

"We need someone to take a really close look," Aubrey remarked quietly.

"Mm. Director Buckholz – Charles – what is your honest feeling? What do we have up there, at this moment?"

"I side with your Squadron Leader Eastoe, Colonel. Gant was picked up visually, pursued, and shot down. We've got wreckage up there, is my best guess." Pyott turned to Curtin who merely nodded in support.

"I'm not disinclined to agree with you . . ." Aubrey made an impatient noise, but remained silent. Pyott continued: "You all know the delicate political situation. Finland agreed – largely because of personal links between Kenneth and the DG of Finnish Intelligence – to this covert overflight by the MiG-31, if its capture was successful. Perhaps they know, or suspect, that has happened. I would expect them to take a very negative line . . . unless you, Charles, can convince your government, as I must convince mine, that pressure should be brought to bear?" Pyott shrugged. "I am suggesting that we hold our fire until we are ordered to proceed by our respective governments. In other words, you and I, Charles, must be very convincing. Now, are we prepared to say, hands on hearts, that the Firefox might still be intact and the pilot alive?" He paused, looked at each of them intently. Almost willing them to answer, Aubrey felt. Then he added: "Well? Time to consider, gentlemen?"

"Not for me," Aubrey declared firmly. "It may very well be true. I, for one, must know for certain." Aubrey glared at Charles Buckholz. "Charles?"

"I don't know – look, you could be right. I hope to God you are. But – it just doesn't look that way to us."

"Will you say that it does – just for the moment?"

"I don't know . . ."

"We can't just write the whole thing off, Charles – !" Aubrey cried, standing up. His chair collapsed behind him, making a disproportionate noise in the Ops. Room. "There has been too much expenditure of planning, time, and lives involved. You must want to be certain, surely? The Russians will want to be, and we may already be behind them in a race we didn't even know we'd entered!"

Buckholz's face was puzzled and a little fearful as he looked up at Aubrey, bent intently over him like a bully. "I – " he began, but Aubrey seized upon his hesitation.

"Once they've seen the pictures they took of the crash site, they'll find the Firefox's remains are missing. We know the plane isn't there. Once they know – and they may know it already – they'll be looking for it. And, if it is intact . . ." He left the threat unelaborated.

Pyott stroked his moustache. "I think Kenneth has a point, Charles," he murmured.

"Maybe," Buckholz replied reluctantly.

Curtin was nodding. "I think we have to, Mr. Buckholz – we have to follow this thing through."

Buckholz shrugged heavily. "Very well. For the moment, I'll lie my head off to Washington. And you'll do the same for London, uh?"

Pyott nodded. "We will."

"We must get our political masters to *order* us to go ahead," Aubrey instructed in a dark, Machiavellian voice, his face at first sombre but breaking into a mischievous smile as he finished speaking.

"OK."

"Let's not waste time. There are secure telephones in the Briefing Room. You can call Grosvenor Square at once, Charles. We'll wait until you've finished your call before we make ours."

Buckholz felt himself dismissed, but not slighted. He motioned to Curtin. "Come on, Gene – let's agree our story before anyone makes a call."

The two Americans disappeared into the Briefing Room, the door of which led off the main Ops. Room. Giles Pyott and Aubrey watched it close behind them.

"Can we do it?' Aubrey asked quickly.

Instead of answering, Pyott stood up and moved to the huge plot table in the centre of the underground room. He brooded over the models and tapes and markings on its surface. "Damn bad show," he murmured, turning to Aubrey, who now stood alongside him. The crash site was represented on the plot table by a model of a MiG-25 and the black, futuristic model of the MiG-31. In deadly, fatal conjunction. Deliberately, Aubrey picked up one of the cuelike rods the plotters used to alter the position of symbols on the table. Awkwardly, he reached out with it and shunted the model of the Firefox southwards, letting it come to rest on the blue spot of a lake. For a moment, Aubrey's movements reminded Pyott of a short, bad croupier.

"There!" he said with intense triumph.

"You're convinced it's in one piece?"

"I'm not convinced it's in a million pieces, Giles – besides, we could still learn a great deal from whatever is left of it – from Gant, were he alive. To know, we must have someone *under* the ice, so to speak."

Pyott rubbed his moustache with a quicker, stronger rhythm. When he faced Aubrey again, he said, "I know what you want of me, Kenneth. There are some people who would suit, up in the Varangerfjord at the moment. Some of our Special Boat Service marines . . . practising landing on an enemy coast from a hunter-killer submarine, that sort of training. Routine stuff. Under the supervision of an old friend of yours – Major Alan Waterford of 22

294

SAS. Perhaps that seems like the workings of an auspicious fate to you, mm?"

"Can we – ?"

Pyott shook his head. "Not until we have clearance – a direct *order* to do something. Washington and Number Ten must give that order. You know that, Kenneth."

"Unfortunately, yes."

"The Finns gave us permission for the covert overflight of their country, and certain reluctant back-up facilities. They are unlikely, without pressure from our masters, to involve themselves any further in this affair. I must argue from StratAn's point of view, you from that of SIS. JIC and the Chiefs of Staff will, in all likelihood, have to persuade Number Ten to continue with the affair. It really depends on Washington's attitude."

Pyott's attention moved from Aubrey to an approaching RAF officer. He had come quickly down the metal steps from the glass-fronted gallery which contained the communications equipment. All that could be seen from the floor of the Ops. Room was a row of bent heads. The Pilot Officer hurried towards them.

"Mr. Aubrey – Colonel Pyott, I think you'd better come quickly. Squadron Leader Estoe wants to speak to Mr. Aubrey urgently."

"What is it?"

"I don't know, sir – the Squadron Leader just said it was very urgent and to get you to the mike at once."

Pyott strode after the RAF officer as soon as the young man turned away. Aubrey scuttled after them both, his eyes glancing across a litter of paper cups, bent backs in blue uniform shirts, scribbled blackboards and weather charts, before he concentrated his gaze on the metal steps as he clattered up them behind Pyott. Eastoe was waiting for him behind the glass, pausing on tape for a scrambled spit of sound that would be Aubrey's speeded-up reply.

Aubrey thrust past Pyott and said to the operator, "Play it for me."

"Mr. Aubrey had better be told at once," Eastoe began, "even through the ground-clutter and the intermittent snow we're picking up signs of helicopter activity, moving west and south-west. Our best guess is three of them, and that they're troop-carriers. They're not interested in our lake, as far as we can tell – their course would take them north-west of it. Our ETA for the lake is four minutes two. If you want us to go, that is. Over."

The tape stopped. Aubrey rubbed his cheeks furiously. It couldn't be – they couldn't have picked up the carrier wave from the homing device, only Eastoe could do that aboard the Nimrod. What, then?

"Eastoe, keep track of them if you can. Do whatever you have to . . ." He merely glanced up at Pyott, whose face was impassive. Aubrey hesitated for a moment, then said firmly, "I'm ordering you to overfly the lake – deceive them as to your object – and obtain the best photographic record you can under the circumstances. And, when you've done that, I want you to take a look at those helicopters. I want to know what they're doing – dammit!" The tape continued to run. Aubrey finally added: "Good luck. Over and out." Only then he did return his gaze to Pyott, whose face was gloomy. His eyes were glazed and inward-looking. Evidently, he was weighing the consequences of Aubrey's precipitation. "I had to," Aubrey explained. "Things are beginning to outrun us. I had to have better information, whatever the fuss."

"I agree," Pyott said. "Even though I don't much like it. Well, we'd better talk to JIC and the Chiefs of Staff – I may have to get down there myself . . ." He crossed to the door of the communications gallery, then turned to Aubrey. "I do hope our American friends are obtaining the most hopeful noises from their President, Kenneth – for all our sakes."

The icicles were like transparent, colourless gloves worn over the dead twigs of the bush behind which Gant crouched. Below him, the noise and movement belonged to a wild hunt: an image of his own pursuit, probably no more than a mile behind him now.

He had heard the noise of dogs. The helicopters – three he was almost certain – had cast about for signs of him, often appearing as they drove westwards above him or close to one of his hiding places. It was as if they knew his position, and were herding him ahead of or between them. He knew one of the helicopters was west or north-west of him now, its troops probably working back towards him . . .

Towards this village, too, this collection of wooden huts below him, beyond which a group of Lapps were penning reindeer. One short, brightly-clothed man was dragged on his stomach behind a galloping bull reindeer, his hands still gripping the lasso. He disappeared within a flurry of hooves and upflung snow, then rolled clear. The images seemed almost to come from within him, as they stirred memory. A rodeo, but now performed by a people as alien to him as the Vietnamese. Short, olive-skinned, some dressed traditionally even to the long-bobbled woollen caps and heel-less shoes, others affecting blue denims and sheepskin jackets.

Alien. People he did not know, whose language he did not speak, therefore could not trust. Reindeer barked and hooted. Men whisked among them like matadors. Great snouted heads tossed. The sight of the round-up chilled him. He had followed the noises, stumbling upon the village, and had become rapt by a sense of the familiar. Then this parody of something American so far north of the Arctic Circle had quickly alienated him.

Torches flickered, lamps gleamed. The lights of a truck and the headlight of a motorized sledge were focused on the corral. Shadows galloped and tossed in the beams. They would be finishing soon, when darkness came. Gant could smell cooking. The Russians, too, would be here soon. It was time for him to move.

He climbed into a stooping crouch. The flying suit creaked with ice. His body was stiff and slow. He needed something warm to wear; a jacket or cloak or tunic, it did not matter. He would steal whatever he found.

In his right hand he held the folding .22 rifle, loaded with the single bullet it would hold. He had buried his parachute, but still wore his life jacket because he needed its harness to hold his survival pack. The Makarov pistol was easy to hand. He moved cautiously down the slope towards the nearest wooden huts. Behind the buildings, the noises of the round-up quietened, becoming no more than a confused babble and a drumming through the frozen earth. He hurried to the wall of the hut, pressing himself against it, reclaiming his breath before moving slowly along the wall to the steamy window from which a flickering lamplight spilled onto the snow. The black holes of his descending footprints were visible in the light. He listened. He could hear nothing except the sounds of the round-up. The Russians could be no more than half a mile behind him now. He shivered with a new awareness of the cold. He had to be warm. He would not be able to spend the night moving unless he was dressed more warmly.

He stood on tiptoe, looking into the long, low room. A huge black stove in the centre, bright rugs scattered, armchairs, a plain wooden table, places laid upon it. Time –

He listened for the noise of the helicopters, but heard nothing. He tested the window. Locked. He moved around the angle of the wall towards what he assumed was the rear of the hut. One window locked, another, another . . .

He eased it open. The smell of cooking was strong. There was no one in the small kitchen. On an old cooker, a huge pot was simmering. The smell was coming from it. Meat. Hot meat in some kind of stew. He dragged his leg tiredly over the sill, sat astride for a moment – where was the cook? – then dropped into the room, dragging the rifle from his shoulder, aiming it towards the door into the main room. He could hear someone now, moving about, the noises of cutlery quite distinct and recognisable. He sidled across the kitchen towards the stove, moving with exaggerted stealth. There was a ladle in the pot. He reached out with his left hand, eyes still on the doorway, and touched the ladle, then removed it, tasting the stew like a chef. The meat's flavour was strong – reindeer, he presumed – but his stomach craved it. He leaned heavily, his head against a clouded mirror, all the time watching the doorway, the ladle moving as silent as he could manage from the pot to his mouth – pot to mouth, pot to mouth . . .

He swallowed greedily again and again, his stomach churning with the sudden, gulped feast. The warmth of it burned through him. He shivered. A pool of melted snow from his boots spread around him.

Then she returned to the kitchen. Small, olive-skinned, a pear-shaped face with a black, surprised little round hole opening in the middle of it as she saw him and understood the rifle. Dark hair, plump figure. Check shirt and denims; again, the familiar – the log-cabin imagery – surprised him for a moment. Then he motioned her into the kitchen with the barrel of the rifle. She came slowly, silently.

"I – mean you no harm," Gant said slowly. "No – harm. Do you understand?"

"Yes," she replied, staring at the rifle. Its barrel dropped as an expression of Gant's surprise.

"You speak English?"

"A little. I – was taught. Who are you?" She studied his flying suit, her face screwed into lines and folds as if she were trying to remember a similar costume.

"My airplane – it crashed."

"Oh." Her face showed she had identified his clothing.

"I – I'm sorry about the food . . ." He gestured towards the stove. His stomach rumbled. The woman almost smiled. "I – I'll leave you . . ."

"Why?"

"I have to."

"We – can help you."

Gant shook his head furiously. "You can't get involved in this," he said.

She moved closer. Evidently, the man represented no real threat to her, despite his intrusion into her home. "Why not? We have a radio." She gestured towards the doorway.

"Christ, radio – " he blurted.

"Yes. Where are you from – the Finnmark?" Her English improved; rusty with disuse, it was now working again. She indicated her mouth, then pointed at him. His accent . . .

"Yes. But, how long?"

298

"Long?"

"Will they come now, at once?" She shook her head. "Then no radio. I must go now. I – " He decided to ask rather than demand. "I need something warm – to wear."

She nodded. "My husband – he will take you on the sledge, when he returns, or tomorrow, to the main road, perhaps." Not alien, somehow familiar and expected. He was warm at last. Tears of weariness and response pricked at his eyes. The promises of aid in the strange, halting English numbed him as certainly as the cold outside.

Could he – ? No. No risks . . .

Quarter of a mile, no more than that now.

"Clothes," he said heavily.

The beam of the searchlight from the descending helicopter swept over the room, fuzzily gleaming for a moment through the steam-clouded window. Then it was gone, bouncing off the slope before it finally disappeared and all that remained was the racket of the rotors. Gant listened. Only one, still time . . .

"Clothes!" he snapped, his voice ugly.

She did not, however, react as if she feared him. She nodded. "Who are they?"

"Russians."

She spat, suddenly and surprisingly. It was the reflex, racial memory of a once-real hatred. She snapped: "We are *Skolt* Lapps – we live here now since we lost our homes in Petsamo. Petsamo belongs to *them* now, since the war. Russians – !"

The rotors roared, then began to wind down. Gant pressed himself against the wall, and squinted through the steam on the window. The rotors died. He heard no dogs, but the noises from the round-up had quietened. Two minutes – ?

He glanced around the room. The woman had gone. He panicked, but as he moved she re-entered the doorway, holding a heavy check jacket and a pair of thick trousers. And walking boots.

"These – I hope they fit you."

He bundled them under his arm, fingers locking inside the boots to hold them. She moved to the outside door. He stared at the puddle that marked his presence, the one or two half-footprints on the polished floorboards. Smiling, she tilted the pot on the stove. Stew sloshed onto the floor. Then she beckoned him.

Cold threatened from the door.

He dropped his bundle, pulled on the jacket for disguise and warmth, then collected the trousers and boots and the rifle. He could hear voices, almost conversational in volume and tone, but he could not hear dogs. On the doorstep, he nodded to her. She touched his shoulder, her expression already settling to a kind of passivity. She was preparing her face.

"They are pretending to be Finns," she whispered. "But their accents are bad. Go now. That way." She pointed back up the slope. She saw the deep black holes of his descent of the slope. She pushed him ahead of her. "I went for a walk, looking for the dog," she said.

He turned to thank her, but she merely shook her head. "Go," she instructed. "The Finnmark is twenty miles away."

He was already climbing the slope, urgency driving out the sense of who had given him the jacket and the clothes he carried under his arm. He was primarily aware of his right hand once more and the rifle it held.

He turned back once, at the crest of the slope, near the bush which had earlier concealed him. The door of the hut was closed. Probably, the woman had begun to be afraid now, to physically shake with reaction, as much at his presence as that of the Russians. Now, she would be deciding she should not have helped him, that her home had been broken into, invaded.

The round-up had ended. Reindeer stamped and shuffled. The MiL helicopter sat like a squat beetle, rotors still, near the corrals. A group of men were talking. Dark clothing and white Arctic camouflage.

Three, four – six . . .

Spreading out, searching. There seemed no resistance from the Lapps. Perhaps they believed the fiction that the soldiers were Finns. He turned his back on the village and trudged into the trees.

Twenty miles, she had said. Twenty.

It was a huge distance, almost huge enough to be a void, something uncrossable.

Vladimirov turned from the window of the Tupolev as Dmitri Priabin entered the War Command Centre ahead of the First Secretary. The young man's face was elated, yet he also appeared to be recovering from a bout of nausea. There was a bright sheen of sweat on his forehead, and his neck was pink above the collar of his uniform. Vladimirov knew, with an inward, cold amusement, that the young officer had survived, that the collar and shoulder insignia of the uniform would soon be changed. Now, they denoted Priabin as a lieutenant. What next? Captain Priabin, or the dizzy heights of a colonelcy? It appeared that the young man's former superior, Kontarsky, was to bear the burden of failure entirely alone. Priabin had first identified Gant, probably by accident more than design, and almost in time to stop him. He had earned the reprieve of promotion.

He had arrived expecting to suffer, and had been rewarded. Vladimirov did not envy him anything except his youth as he hurriedly exited from the room. Then he turned his back on the First Secretary and looked down at the tarmac, where an imposing queue of black limousines was drawn up. Priabin went down the passenger steps and climbed into the back of one of the cars. It drove off towards the administration buildings and the perimeter fence. Presumably, Priabin had some woman to impress with his narrow escape, his unexpected promotion. Vladimirov returned his attention to the War Command Centre.

The Soviet leader had donned his overcoat. His fur hat rested like a pet in one of his gloved hands. His face was stern. He had paused only to listen to the latest report from the commander of the KGB Border Guard units they had despatched into Finnish Lapland. As the voice from the cabin speaker proceeded with the report, the First Secretary nodded occasionally.

Vladimirov watched Andropov. There was a faint gleam of perspiration on his shaven upper lip. Responsibility had passed to himself, as well as to Vladimirov. It was an uneasy and temporary alliance that the air force general did not welcome or trust.

The high-speed transmissions from the command helicopter were received by the AWACS Tupolev, then re-transmitted to Moscow. In the War Command Centre, they were played back at normal speed. Vladimirov could not rid himself of the analogy of some obscure sporting commentary. He listened through the caution, through wanting-to-please, wanting-to-succeed, and tried to assess how close they were to the American.

For he was there. The parachute had been found by one of the dogs, tracks had been followed, a village might, or might not, have given him shelter, clothing, food. He was heading in a north-westerly direction, towards the closest outjutting of the Norwegian frontier. He was, they guessed, less than twenty miles from his objective. The hunters had a night and part of a day, no more.

The transmission ended with a request for orders. Immediately, the First Secretary looked at Andropov and at Vladimirov, and then, having fixed each of them with a blunt, unwavering stare, merely nodded. Men sprang to renewed attention as he left the compartment. They heard his high shoes ring on the frosty metal of the passenger ladder. Vladimirov resisted the impulse to turn his head, and continued to watch Andropov. Suddenly, the Chairman of the KGB gestured him to follow, into the recreation suite.

"Tell the commander to hold for instructions," Vladimirov snapped, following Andropov. He closed the compartment door behind him. Andropov was pouring himself a whisky at the bar.

"Drink?" he asked.

"No, thank you."

Andropov gulped some of the liquor as he turned to Vladimirov. "Well?" he demanded. "What now?"

"From your people?"

"*Our* people!" Andropov snapped.

"I'd forgotten – our people."

"What about this Nimrod aicraft in the area?"

"It must have picked up the helicopters. Obviously, they also wish to know what happened."

"And will they have units like ours in the area too?"

Vladimirov shook his head. "I doubt that. Unfortunately, we have been unable to help giving something of the game away. We need him quickly now. The Nimrod was very low – presumably it collected photographs, which will be analysed. That gives us time. I think enough time."

"Damned forest!" Andropov erupted.

"I agree. It makes things more difficult. We know he was with the Lappes – but he stole food and clothing, no more. He wasn't hiding there. He cannot be more than a mile ahead of our people – once again, they must put down men ahead of his probable track."

"Yes, yes, of course they must – !" Andropov drank the remainder of the whisky, and studied the glass. Vladimirov saw his gaze stray to the bottle on the bar, but he made no move towards it. "Where is the plane, Vladimirov? There's not enough wreckage in those photographs . . . you and I know that, even though the experts will take hours to decide the same thing." Spots of pink glowed on the Chairman's high cheekbones. "We *know* it isn't there – so, where is it? Eh, where is it, this priceless white elephant of ours? We know he didn't eject because of the parachute they found – he landed the plane, Vladimirov. Do you realise that?"

Vladimirov nodded. "Yes. I do. But I do not know where. Only he can tell us that. Had he been one of our pilots, or had it been an American aircraft, he would have stayed near it. In this case, he has been trying to open up the distance between himself and the MiG-31. The British Nimrod, too, wonders where the aircraft is, no doubt. Only Gant knows."

"Then we must have him!"

"We will. His time is running out."

"I wish I could be certain of that."

"Your men are following his tracks, Comrade Chairman! What more do you want? Their footsteps are planted in his. In an hour, perhaps two, he will be ours." Vladimirov smiled. "Then we will both be off the hook, mm?"

Andropov merely glowered in reply. He pondered for a time, then said, "Couldn"t we track back along his journey?"

"Perhaps. But, had it been me, I would have changed direction a dozen times. And, by now, his tracks will have gone, and his scent will have grown cold. Don't worry – Gant has the answer. Soon you will be able to ask him for that answer – personally."

"There's no doubt about these photographs," Buckholz protested vigorously, his finger tapping the glistening enlargements that lay scattered on the plot table of the Scampton Ops. Room. "You use dogs to sniff for explosives – unlikely – or you use them to hunt men. Those are dogs – KGB Border Guard dogs." His large, blunt-fingered hands spread the enlargements in a new pattern, as if he were dealing cards or flinging down items of evidence. "These troops are in Arctic camouflage, but they're not military. These MiL Mi-4s are what the Border Guard favour for personnel and equipment transport. And they don't have any markings at all . . . just the way the Border Guard operates. No, Colonel, what else do you need to see before you make up your mind?"

"Charles," Pyott began defensively, "I realise that Washington is very keen to get on with this job, but – "

"You have to get your government off its butt, Colonel! Time is running out for Gant, and for us."

Aubrey, as a distraction, picked up a sheaf of the photographs that had been transmitted over the wireprint from Eastoe's Nimrod. They were all pale, shining with the ghostly light of the advanced infra-red cameras that had produced them. Men almost in negative in the very last of the daylight and ensuing darkness.

He looked at the prints of the lake. Broken ice near the neck of the lake, but very little of it. A small, shrinking patch of black water. Yet the Firefox had to be underneath the water, beneath the healing ice. The remaining pictures, of the wreckage at the point of explosion, were uninteresting. Aubrey, without study and without expert advice, knew that nothing of the MiG-31 lay there.

Pyott glanced at Aubrey. "Number Ten is being very reluctant over this, Kenneth," he began, seeking an ally.

"Because the Cabinet Defence Committee has always pooh-poohed the Firefox, I wonder? The P.M. isn't bullying them any more, I suppose?" He turned to Buckholz. "Is the President applying the right amount of pressure, Charles?" Buckholz nodded. "Everyone would like to walk away, except for Washington."

"The usual restrictions, of course, Kenneth – if you're caught, we'll deny everything."

"We work with those every day – they're not important. It's *doing*

303

something — and quickly — that *is* important." He stared meaning-fully at Pyott, who held up his hands, wrists pressed together to represent unseen bonds. "Tied they may be, Giles — but *really*!"

"What can I do?" Pyott asked softly.

"Look at them!" Aubrey returned, his hand flapping towards the scattered enlargements. "Gant may be alive — he knows where the body is buried, as do we. If they get to him, *they* will know! We must at least establish what is beneath the ice — *before* we decide our response." He looked at Buckholz, and shook his head. "I don't think there's anything we can do for poor Gant — I can't order military units into the area."

"I know that. So will he. He knows he's on his own."

Aubrey nodded lugubriously, plucking at his lower lip. Then, as suddenly and superficially as a child, his mood changed. He turned on Pyott and said, in an intense whisper, almost hunching over the enlargements on the plot table. "You already have Waterford standing by with a four-man unit at Kirkenes. Their diving equipment is loaded onto a Royal Norwegian Air Force Lynx helicopter. You have the agreement of Commander, Allied Forces Northern Norway, for this flight under the guise of a search-and-rescue mission . . . Giles, *please* make up your mind to act — !"

"I have other people to please apart from yourself, SIS, or even the CIA . . ." Pyott began, then clamped his lips tightly shut. He shook his head. "Unofficially, JIC wishes something done — so do the Chiefs of Staff, but Cabinet opinion is against any exacerbation of the situation. They'll settle for the loss of the two — the *only two* — production prototypes of the Firefox. The expert reasoning is that the Bilyarsk project will have been put back by at least two, even three years by what has happened. The Russians may even scrap the whole, hideously expensive project . . ."

"And if the Firefox is *intact*? And the Russians ask their friendly neighbours, the Finns, for their toy back?" Aubrey demanded with withering irony, his face red with frustration. His hands were clenched at his sides.

"Yes," Pyott admitted. "Yes, I know."

"Washington will carry the day, you know that," Aubrey observed. "Gresham, as P.M., and the rest of the Cabinet will have to sanction whatever the President wishes to happen — however much they dislike the medicine."

"But they have not yet done so — "

"And we have run out of *time*!"

Momentarily, Giles Pyott's cheeks glowed with anger, then he turned on his heel. "Very well," he snapped, "very well."

Aubrey hurried after him as he mounted the ladder to the communications gallery. "Tell Waterford he must check this KGB activity," he called. Pyott stopped and turned.

"No!"

"Yes," Aubrey insisted. "We have to know whether or not Gant is alive – we have to know when, and if, they take him alive. Everything could depend upon it."

Pyott paused, his brow furrowed, his cheeks hot. Then he nodded. He, too, could not escape the conclusions Aubrey offered; could not escape his imprisonment within the situation. Aubrey – the covert world that he and Buckholz represented – was his jailer. He saw himself within a fortress, a castle. The politicians had erected the outer walls; they could be breached, or removed, or their existence could be denied as circumstances dictated. But Pyott knew himself to be imprisoned within the keep of the castle, and the walls of the keep had been made by Aubrey and Buckholz and the MiG-31 and its pilot. The walls were inpenetrable, inescapable. He nodded.

"Very well," he announced angrily. "Very well."

He opened the door to the communications gallery. Aubrey scurried in behind him.

He was floundering through the snow now. They still had not released the dogs, but he could hear them barking close behind him. The snow was deep, almost solid, restraining him, pulling him back. He had abandoned the floor of the shallow valley, keeping to the slope, but even here the snow lay heaped and traplike near bushes and boulders. He slipped often. The effects of the hot food were gone. He was utterly weary.

When he had halted last, he had checked the map. More than three miles from the village, perhaps another sixteen – fifteen now, or a little more? – to the Norwegian border, to villages, to police, to another state where he might be safe. Safe – ?

They wouldn't let him remain. They would take him back.

He stumbled, his wrist hurt as his weight collapsed on it, the .22 rifle ploughed into the snow. Furiously, he shook the barrel; snow fluttered away from it. The sky was black and clear, the stars like gleaming stones. Silver light from a thin paring of new moon lay lightly on the snow. He climbed groggily to his feet and looked behind him. Noise of dogs, and a glimpse of lights. The distant sound of one of the helicopters. He did not know where the choppers were, and it worried him. They buzzed at his imagination like flies, as audible in his head as if they were physically present, their belly-lights streaming along the floor of the valley searching for his footprints. One of them had to be ahead, its platoon already fanned out and sweeping slowly back towards him, in radio contact with the pursuit behind him.

Radio —

He had known, had hidden the fact from himself.

Radio.

It winded him like a blow, the admission of their technology, their ability to communicate. Even now, at that precise moment, he was pinpointed.

He looked up at the black sky with its faint sheen, its glittering stars. At any moment, the choppers would come. The pursuit was too close now not to be able to locate him.

Somewhere along the valley floor, just — *there* . . .

A finger was tracing contours, the twisting course of the valley. A helicopter would bank, turn —

He ran. Ice glittered on a bush, and he brushed savagely against the obstacle. The rifle pumped against his thigh, against the heavy waterproof trousers. His chest hurt with the temperature of the air he was inhaling. The survival pack bumped and strained and dragged at his back. He glanced behind once more —

Lights.

Noise — *ahead* —

Men had been dropped out of earshot, ahead of him, and were working their way back down the valley from the north-west towards him. Pincer.

He stopped running, bent double. He listened. A thin breeze had carried the noises. Shuffling, the clinking of metal, the slither of cross-country skis. The barking of a single dog. Behind him, more dogs, more men, and wobbling flashlight beams. No rotor noise. Nothing. Surprise.

The two groups of Russians were no more than a few hundred yards apart. He began to struggle up the slope, out of the valley. Icy rock betrayed him, a hollow trapped his leg with soft, deep snow. His chest heaved, his back bent under the weight of the survival pack so that his face was inches from the glittering snow. He climbed, feet sinking, body elongating so that he threatened to become stretched out, flat on his stomach. His legs refused to push him faster or further. He used his hands, the .22 clogging with snow as he used it as a stick.

Crest. Dark sky above white snow like a close horizon.

He staggered, pushed up from all-fours to try to stand upright. He gasped for breath, saw the legs, saw the Arctic camouflage, shook his head in weary disbelief, saw the next man perhaps fifty yards away, already turning in his direction, saw, saw —

He cried out in a wild yell of protest and used the rifle like a club, striking at the white form on the crest of the slope. The Russian fell away with a grunt, rolling down the steeper slope on the other side. Gant staggered after the rolling body, as if to strike again, then leapt tiredly over it and charged on down the steep slope.

Trees. A patch of black forest, then the flatness of what might be a frozen lake beyond. The ground levelling out. The trees offering cover, the barrel of his rifle clogged with snow —

He careered on, just keeping his balance. Whistles and the noise of dogs behind him, but no shooting. He ran on, floundering with huge strides towards the trees.

FOUR:

Recovery

The Westland Lynx Mk 86 helicopter, its Royal Norwegian Air Force markings concealed, dropped towards the arrowlike shape of the lake. Alan Waterford, sitting in the co-pilot's seat, watched intently as the ghostly ice moved up towards him, and the surface snow became distressed from the downdraught of the rotors. He ignored the noises from the main fuselage as the four-man Royal Marine SBS team prepared to leave the helicopter. Instead, he watched the ice.

"Hold it there," he ordered the pilot. The downdraught was winnowing the surface snow, but there was no billowing effect. Waterford did not want the surface obscured, the snow boiling around the cockpit like steam, as it would if they dropped any lower. Even so, a few crystals were melting on the perspex. Beyond the smear they made, the ice looked unbroken and innocent as it narrowed towards the neck of the lake where Eastoe's infra-red pictures had revealed a patch of dark, exposed water.

The Lynx steadied at its altitude and began to drift slowly over the ice, the faintest of shadow towed behind it like a cloth. Waterford craned ahead and to one side, searching the surface. As with the photographs, he could see no evidence that an airframe had broken up over the lake. There appeared to be only the one patch of clear water and jostling, broken ice right at the end of the lake.

No undercarriage tracks, but he could not count on them. There could have been a light snow shower, or the wind could have covered them as effectively as fresh snow. Had he landed the plane, or ejected before it ever reached the lake? And if he'd landed, how efficient in saving the airframe and the electronics and the rest of the MiG-31's secrets had the American been in his terror of drowning? Or had he left the cockpit before the plane began to break through the ice?

Behind him, the SBS men, all trained divers, were preparing to discover the answers to his questions. It was too late and too dark to assess fire-damage to the trees on the shore. Gant had to be alive – the Russian activity confirmed that – but had he ejected or landed?

The Lynx moved towards the trees. The patch of dull black water was visible now; ominous. Waterford removed his headset and stood in a crouch. His bulk seemed to fill the cockpit like a malevolent shadow. The pilot, a Norwegian lieutenant, glanced up at him.

"I can't put down this side of the trees – I'm not risking the ice. Tell them they'll have to walk." He grinned.

"They're used to it," Waterford grunted and clambered back into the main cabin of the helicopter. Four men in Arctic camouflage looked up at him. Beneath the white, loose tunics and trousers, they were wearing their wetsuits. Oxygen tanks, cutting equipment, lamps, rifles lay near the closed main door. "You're going to have to walk it," Waterford announced to a concerted groan. "You know what they want, Brooke – evidence that the airframe is intact – don't give it to the buggers unless it's absolutely true. *Any* damage – any at all – has to be spotted. And don't forget the pictures for Auntie Aubrey's album, to go alongside the pressed flowers . . ." He grinned, but it seemed a mirthless exercise of his lips. "Keep your heads down – you are not, repeat not, to be detected under any circumstances. And," he looked at his watch, "Gunnar tells me we have no more than an hour to look for our American friend – even if we don't run into trouble – so that's all the time you've got. And, sergeant?"

"Sir?"

"Make sure you conceal that commpack properly – we won't be the last of our side in and out of here, I'm sure of that, and they'll all want to talk to London as quickly as possible." Waterford indicated one of the packs near the sergeant's feet. "This'll give them satellite direct – don't leave it where a reindeer can piss on it and fuse the bloody thing."

"Certainly not, sir," the sergeant replied. "Commpack not to be left where the reindeer may piss on it – *sir*! One question, sir?"

"Yes, sergeant?"

"Does the Major know the exact height to which a reindeer can piss, sir?"

The Lynx drifted slowly downwards. Waterford, smiling at the tension-releasing laughter in the cabin, glanced at the window in the main door. Snow surrounded them like steam. They were almost down. As he observed the fact, the Lynx touched, bounced as if rubber, settled. Immediately, the rotors began to wind down, their noise more throaty, ugly. The sergeant slid back the main cabin door.

"Out you get – quick as you can," the lieutenant ordered, nodding at Waterford. Packs and equipment were flung out of the door.

Through his camouflage parka, the night temperature chilled Waterford. He felt the tip of his nose harden with the cold. When they had dropped to the ground, he moved to the cabin door.

"Good luck. One hour – and I'm counting." He waved, almost dismissively, and slammed the sliding door closed, locking it. Then he climbed back into the cockpit and regained his seat, rubbing his hands. He slipped on the inertia-reel belt, then his headset. "OK, Gunnar – let's see if we can find this lost American chap, shall we?"

The Lynx jumped into the air almost at once, the rotors whining up, the blades becoming a dish that caught the moonlight. The four SBS men were already trudging briskly into the trees, laden with their equipment. The helicopter banked out over the lake, and headed north-west. The ice diminished behind them.

There was no nightsight on the folding .22 rifle. There were six rounds, each to be fed separately into the breach. It was a weapon of survival – for Arctic hares for the solid tablet stove or any fire he might have been able to light – but not for defence. Never for offence. Gant had no idea how much stopping-power the slim, toylike rifle possessed, and he hesitated to find out. The nearest of the Russians, white-tunicked, white-legginged, Kalashnikov AKM carried across his chest, was moving with great caution from fir-bole to low bush to fir-bole. The dogs had been kept back, still leashed; perhaps moving with the remainder of the unit to encircle the clump of trees in which they knew he was hiding.

Time had run out. His only advantage was that they wanted him alive. They would have definite, incontrovertible orders not to kill him. Maim him they might, but he would be alive when they reached Murmansk or Moscow or wherever.

The frozen lake was behind him, as clean and smooth as white paper, almost phosphorescent in the moonlight. His breath smoked around him like a scarf; he wondered that the approaching Russian had not yet caught sight of it, not heard the noise of his breathing. Forty yards, he guessed. A glimpse of another white shape, flattening itself behind a fir, farther off. The noise of the dogs.

And, omnipresent and above the trees, the rotors of two of the helicopters. He had glimpsed one of them, its outline clear for a moment before he had been blinded by the searching belly-light. Slim, long-tailed MiL-4s. Frost glittered on the dark trunk of the fir at the fuzzy edge of his vision. He had now recovered his night vision after the searchlight, except for a small, bright spot at the centre of the Russian's chest as he sighted along the seemingly inadequate barrel of the rifle. The man bulked large around the retinal image of the searchlight. Gant could not miss at that range.

Still he hesitated, sensing the moment at the eye of the storm; sensing that any move he now made would be his last. Capture was inevitable. So why kill – ?

Then he squeezed the trigger, knowing the true futility of the attack. A sharp little crack like a twig broken, and the white-dressed Russian flung up his arms and fell slowly backwards. Snow drifted down, disturbed by the downdraught, onto Gant's head and shoulders. Beyond the body, which did not move, did not begin to scrabble towards the nearest cover, another white form whisked behind a dark trunk. Gant turned towards the lake, regretting, loathing the gesture of the kill. Through the trees, the shore appeared empty.

Orders shouted, the crackle of a radio somewhere, the din of the dogs. His head turned back towards the body, then once more to the lake. A light was creeping across the ice. Above it, as if walking hesitantly on the beam, a MiL-4 came into view. The ice glared. He heard the noise of dogs released – released, unleashed, loose . . .

He began to run, even though some part of him knew they would be trained not to harm him if he remained still. He could not help himself. He had to run. The dogs were loose.

Yowling behind him, a shot high over his head. Small, low branches whipping at his face, depositing snow in his eyes and mouth and nostrils. He held on to the rifle with both hands, almost heaving the air aside as he ran out of the trees, across the snow-covered, slippery stones of the shore, out onto the surface snow that made the ice tactile, sure-footed. The MiL-4 turned its baleful black face of a cockpit in his direction, and the beam of the searchlight licked across the ice towards him.

No more trees, no more cover, his mind kept repeating, attuned to the frantic beating of his ears, but he could not regret the sky. The trees had hemmed him, formed a prison before he was, indeed, captured. The MiL slipped over him like a huge, moving blanket, whirling up the snow around him, cleaning the ice and making it suddenly treacherous. He staggered, then whirled round.

The leading Alsation was out of the trees, hardly hesitating as it met the stones on the shore and then the smoother ice. He raised the .22, and fired. The dog skidded, sliding on towards him, mouth gaping. He looked up. A face appeared at the open cabin door of the helicopter. It was grinning, savagely. Gant fumblingly ejected the cartridge, thrust a new round into the breech, raised the gun – two more dogs, now on the ice, but he could no longer care even about dogs – and fired. The head ducked back inside the helicopter, but Gant knew he had not hurt it.

He ran on. Skating, slipping, then hurrying through patches of undisturbed snow. Then the MiL slid towards him again, pinning him in the searchlight beam. Whistles, men on the shore . . .

He reloaded the .22, but the dog was on him, its leap driving him backwards, struggling to keep balance. He was winded, but as he doubled over he struck the dog across the head with the rifle. The Alsation twisted away, yelping. The other dog watched, suddenly more wary. Gant stood his ground, watching the men approach behind the dogs, caught for their benefit in the glare of the searchlight. The rotors above him hammered, drowning thought.

He knew he would not move now. It was finished. He was defeated. Or perhaps satisfied at having protested, struggled enough. He had made his gesture. Energy drained away, as if drawn out of him by the light. Both dogs now crouched on the ice, growling, only yards from him. The first troops were forty yards away.

Then the crackling of a loudspeaker from the MiL above him: "Major Gant – please put down your weapons. Major Gant – put down your weapons."

The dogs seemed more alert now. The men hesitated. He held up the rifle slowly, then threw it aside. He drew the Makarov with his left hand, butt first, and dropped it. The white-clad troops hurried towards him. Beyond them, the second and third MiL-4s slid over the trees and out onto the lake. He hunched his shoulders, thrusting his hands into the pockets of the check jacket. He might have been waiting for a bus. One of the two approaching MiLs settled onto the ice and its rotors slowed.

Ten yards. Seven . . .

The dogs were quiet, tongues lolling, suspicious and forgiving.

Fourth MiL, rotors hammering, its fuselage slim and knifelike as it banked savagely. The searchlight blinked off him, loping away across the ice as the helicopter above moved as if startled. Gant looked up. Nose-on, closing and dropping swiftly. The Russian troops looked up, halted, uncertain. The dogs growled.

MiL-4 . . .

Sharp-nosed, not round-nosed as it whipped into full silhouette. Concealed markings, not unmarked like the others. Sharp-nosed, and a white-clad form at the open cabin door, gesturing. The MiL that had hung above him sidled towards the newcomer, much as a dog might have investigated a bitch. The newcomer rose rapidly, hopping over the MiL and closing on his still figure on the ice. The form waved. The helicopter danced closer, then away, enticing him.

The second and third MiLs wound up their rotors, both having landed. The airborne MiL-4 swung nose-on, closing. The form bellowed something. He did not know in what language, but it did not seem to be Russian.

312

Sharp-nosed . . .

Lynx −

The language was English. He moved his feet, lifted his reluctant legs and began to run. The dogs were up, shaking themselves, moving more quickly than himself. The Lynx helicopter danced slowly away, tempting him to reach it, hovering only feet above the ice. The winch had been swung out of the main cabin and its rescue wire trailed like a black snake across the ice.

He slipped, righted himself, plunged on, arms flailing. One of the dogs snapped at him, leaping at his side. He flung his arms at it, fist clenched. The dog rolled and skidded away. Twenty yards, fifteen −

He kicked out at the second dog − the first was recovering, moving again − missed, kicked again, almost losing his balance. The dog watched for its opportunity. Ten yards. Only ten −

Eight, seven, five . . . the wire was almost underfoot, the Lynx rising a little so that he could grasp it without bending, be heaved upwards immediately . . .

The noise of the dogs. Something ripped at his calf, making him stagger. A yard, no more, the face of someone yelling and cursing, firing over his head. The dogs yelping, whining suddenly . . .

He touched the wire −

Then the helicopter was flung away from him. The ice came up, he was winded, the searchlight came back, something pressed down on him, almost smothering him. He smelt onions, felt hot breathing on his cold face. His head cracked against the ice. He groaned. More dogs, renewed barking, as if they expressed his howl of despair.

He watched the Lynx lift away, the cabin door slam shut, the helicopter hop over the nearer of the two MiLs, skitter like a flung stone towards the trees . . .

The Russian soldier who had knocked him over in a flying tackle got slowly, heavily to his feet. Despite his efforts, he seemed satisfied. Other faces crowded around him, dipped into the glare of the searchlight. The light began to hurt, dazzling him as if it were being filtered through a diamond. He closed his eyes and lay back. His calf hurt where the dog had torn at it.

He heard the distant noise of the fleeing Lynx and the rotors of a pursuing MiL. Then nothing except the rotors above him, the shudder of the downdraught, the cloud of snow around him, and the sense that he was dreaming . . .

Dreaming of the Lynx, dreaming that he was being lifted, carried . . . dreaming . . .

Waterford slammed the main cabin door of the Lynx with a curse, heaving at it to expel his rage. He locked it furiously, as if breaking into the environment outside rather than making something secure. Then he staggered as the pilot flung the Lynx into a violent alteration of course. He grabbed a handhold and looked out of the cabin window. The lake streamed beneath them. Craning, he could catch the lights of one of the MiLs, a sullen wash upon the ice. Then they were over trees, and Waterford clambered back into the cockpit, regained his seat and his headset, and strapped himself in. In the co-pilot's mirror, Waterford could see two of the MiLs dropping slowly behind them. The third would be loading Gant aboard and scrambling for home. The Lynx was approaching its top ground-level speed, perhaps forty miles an hour faster than the Russian helicopters.

"We're in Norway," Gunnar announced casually and without any slowing of the Lynx. "They will not follow, I think."

They flashed over car headlights, glaring as they twisted along a north-south road, then the scattered, muffled lights of a small village.

"More important things to do," Waterford muttered, his hands clenched on his thighs as if gripping something tightly. He could hear himself grinding his teeth. To have missed him by a yard – a *yard*! "Oh, *fuck* it!" he raged.

"They've dropped back – shaking sticks at us, I expect, now that we have been seen off the property." Gunnar chuckled. "Are you all right, Major?"

"No."

"You don't like losing?"

"I *hate* losing."

"We were too lucky ever to find them – it could not hold." Gunnar altered course. Two white dots registered on the radar. "Ah. They are heading east, very quickly now. Soon we will lose track of them, they are very low." The dots already appeared to lose sharpness, becoming pale smears. There were other smudges on the screen from the general ground-clutter. The MiLs and the Lynx were all too low for effective radar tracking; which had exaggerated their luck in stumbling onto the Russians.

Only to lose him, Waterford thought. "How long?" he asked.

"A matter of minutes." Cloud was building above the canopy of the cockpit, the sliver of moon threatened. To the east, it might already be snowing on the Russian border. "In a few minutes, we can return to the lake."

"We're all fucked if that plane's in one piece!" Waterford growled.

"Well done, Colonel – well done!"

It was difficult not to smile at Andropov's enthusiasm – smile *with* it, Vladimirov corrected himself. Smile in concert. The War Command Centre was like the scene of a promotion or medal-presentation party, though the guests were not yet drunk. But they had done it – !

"My congratulations, too, Colonel," Vladimirov added into the microphone. He and Andropov watched one another until they heard the Border Guard commander's reply.

"Thank you, Comrade General – thank you."

"What of the other helicopter?" Andropov asked Vladimirov. "It was Norwegian, I presume?"

"The Nimrod knew we were looking. It, too, was looking. *We* found him. Soon, he will tell us what happened to the MiG-31. What he has done with it."

Andropov leaned towards the transmitter once more. The operator seemed to flinch slightly from the proximity of the Chairman of the KGB. "Transfer him to Murmansk with all possible speed, Colonel – then he'll be flown to Moscow . . ." He turned away from the transmitter, and added to Vladimirov: "Midday tomorrow, at the latest. He'll be here by midday." Andropov removed his spectacles and wiped them. His narrow features sagged. "It has been a very long day," he said nonchalantly, "and now I feel tired." He suppressed a yawn.

"I, too." Vladimirov watched the Chairman replace his gold-rimmed spectacles. When he looked up once more, brushing the disturbed wings of hair above his ears, his confidence had returned. Pleasure had been succeeded by calculation. It was evident that the capture of Gant was of some kind of political significance to Andropov. Already, the incident was being prepared as a piece of propaganda, something to be used against the military, or employed to impress the rest of the Politburo. Their temporary, uncomfortable alliance was at an end.

"Of course, General." The remark was a sneer, a comment upon energy, on advancing age. Vladimirov straightened his form, standing three or four inches taller than Andropov. The Chairman turned away. His grey suit could not match the uniform and he realised it.

The Border Guard commander acknowledged his orders, almost unnoticed.

"I'll arrange for a transport aircraft to be standing by. The weather is worsening east of Murmansk, but there will be no delay. A detachment of GRU troops will provide an escort for the American –"

Andropov turned sharply. "Make certain they fulfil their duties, Comrade General," he snapped icily.

Vladimirov's cheeks burned. "Of course."

"Then I will say goodnight," Andropov offered without molification, as a bodyguard placed the Chairman's overcoat over his shoulders and then handed him his fur hat. He tipped his gloves to his forehead in salute to Vladimirov, and then exited from the War Command Centre.

Vladimirov turned to the map-table. On impulse, almost as if reaching for a bottle or a sedative, he said, "Give me the area of the capture again."

Slowly, tantalisingly, the north of Finnish Lapland and the coast of Norway at the northern edge of the projection, appeared then hardened on the table. It was a relatively small area, it had to be . . . the man had not used his parachute, he must have *landed* the MiG –

Or survived a crash-landing.

North to south, no more than fifty or sixty miles, east to west, eighty miles – it could be narrowed down within that area by time, by Gant's condition, by his rate and mode of travel. He *must* have been *with* the aircraft when it grounded.

Where?

His hand stroked the surface of the table, glowing white and green and blue as it moved, catching the colours, fuzzy bright colours . . .

Vladimirov blinked and yawned. He was bone-weary; he needed sleep.

He could sleep, he told himself with an undiminished thrill of satisfaction, until the following midday. Gant knew, Gant would tell them . . .

He stifled another yawn, and blinked the hypnosis of the map and its colours out of his head.

"Stand down all personnel – transfer the transmission monitoring to the operations room here," he instructed quickly, anxious now to get out into the cold night air, to reinvigorate himself with the chill. "And – well done, all of you. Well done."

A chorused murmur of satisfaction and assent vanished behind him as he closed the door of the War Command Centre. In the compartment aft of it lay his cap, uniform greatcoat, and his gloves. How long ago had he laid them down? When he had boarded this aircraft in Moscow, on his way to witness the weapons trial of the production prototype – a million years ago . . . yesterday . . .?

He looked at his watch. Eleven. No, today, still. Early that morning.

He rubbed his eyes and picked up his greatcoat.

Brooke reached out his hand and stroked the metal of the fuselage, just behind the headlike nose and cockpit. It was like stroking some huge, sleeping pet whose body retreated out of the fuzzy glare of his lamp into the dark water. He had swum along the length of the airframe, lifting slowly over the huge wing, gripping the edges of the massive tailpipes as he rounded the tail section, his lamp dancing wildly off the contours of the plane. He had propelled himself forward towards the second great spread wing. His flippers had touched against the metal as he lifted over it, before he returned to the nose section.

It had taken no more than minutes to find the intact airframe. His sergeant had been first down, after he had checked and then hidden the satellite commpack which would carry any transmissions from the site direct to a geostationary communications satellite, and on to London. Almost at once, Sergeant Dawson had been confronted by the blunt, ugly nose of the MiG-31. His lamp had disappeared beneath the new thin coating of ice, for which Brooke was grateful, since their search would be undetectable from the air. He had made the preliminary inspection while Brooke and the two corporals had scouted the shore of the lake, the closest trees and the ice itself for the homing device whose carrier wave Estoe had picked up. They had searched most carefully where the ice had congregated into rougher, jerry-built shapes, presumably from the break-up after the MiG had landed. They had found it jammed between two resoldered plates of ice, after Dawson had returned to the surface and was warming himself with coffee. Brooke had switched it off, and then listened to Dawson's preliminary damage report. The undercarriage door appeared to have been buckled, there was cannon damage in the port wing and in two places along the fuselage where fuel lines might have been ruptured, but the cockpit was closed – some water inside, but not much – and the aircraft appeared to have been fully shut down, presumably by Gant.

Brooke understood the significance of the report. The intact airframe was more dangerous, a hundred times more dangerous, than shards and pieces of wreckage on the floor of the lake. The Bilyarsk project continued to exist. He had dived himself the moment Dawson had finished, instructing one of the corporals – the best among them with an underwater camera – to prepare for a full photographic record.

The aircraft had awed him. Its size, of course, was huge in the partial, weak light of his lamp. More than that, its black paint, its almost total absence of markings, its preying mantis head, its drooping wings, made it alien; most of all, its location beneath the frozen lake was sufficient to make it mesmeric, almost nightmarish as his lamp's beam danced over it.

The corporal grinned behind his facemask as Brooke jumped at

317

the heavily gloved hand on his shoulder. Bubbles, air tanks, facemask, all fitted the scene and the airframe. He nodded, indicating the length of the fuselage, the undercarriage, the wings. Almost at once, the corporal, propelling the large underwater camera steadily in front of him, its flash unit like a blank television screen, began swimming along the airframe. The flash unit fired time after time. Each time, a part of the fuselage glared. Cannon-holes, wing section, tail, tailpipes, belly of the airframe, under-carriage, wing, cockpit . . . the light flashed again and again as each part of the MiG was recorded.

Brooke almost felt betrayal under the ice as he recalled the explosive charges they carried in one of the packs. They had no orders, but the airframe was intact . . . the easiest way to solve the problem, from London's point of view, would be to plant and detonate enough explosive to shatter the airframe, melt the electronics, destroy the hydraulics – kill the aircraft. *That* aircraft, that huge thing in the repeated glare of the flash or in the beam he played almost lovingly over it. He was surprised by his own sentiments; perhaps it was the too-familiar expectation of wreckage whenever he dived. Bodies, twisted metal, charred plates, signals of damage and destruction everywhere. But this – ? It was complete, almost untouched; salvageable.

Impossible. They'd be ordered to destroy it.

The corporal swam towards Brooke, his thumb erect. Brooke slapped his shoulder and the corporal swam towards the surface. His form bumped along the last feet of ice, and then he was only a half-body in the beam of light, legs flapping lazily, moving away to where the shore sloped upwards. Brooke danced his lamp over the MiG once more, and then rose to the surface. He was becoming very cold. He left the aircraft in the darkness in which he had discovered it.

As he waded out of the lake, he saw Waterford, white-clad, waiting for him, and already in conversation with the corporal. Waterford patted the camera equipment much as he touched everything; large, possessive, dangerous contact. Dawson handed the corporal towels and a mug of coffee. Waterford waited for Brooke to remove his facemask. The moment they confronted one another, even before Dawson could take Brooke's air tanks. Waterford said:

"Well? Looks as if he taxi-ied it to the shore and found the ice too thin?" Brooke nodded.

"It seems like it. The stream would have continued to drain the lake for a while before it froze over. It must flow pretty quickly in summer – it's not a deep channel, anyway. It left thin ice and a nice big air-pocket. Oops!"

"The corporal tells me the airframe's factory-fresh. Is that true?" It sounded like an accusation, a laying of blame upon the Royal Marine lieutenant.

Brooke nodded. "Almost. Even the undercart is intact. One of the doors is buckled, but – "

"Christ! That's all we need. So the silly sod landed the bloody thing in one piece, did he?"

Again, Brooke nodded. "He must have done," he said. "Even closed the canopy before he left. God, Major, you should see the thing – !"

"No, thanks!" Then he continued, as much to himself as to Brooke: "I almost had the poor sod . . ." His hand clenched into a grip in front of him, almost touching Brooke's chest. "He was as close to me as you are now. Sheer bloody luck we found him – but they'd found him, too. Some bloody Ivan rugger-tackled him just as he had hold of the wire . . . we could have had him here *now*, for Christ's sake – !" Then, more calmly and even more ominously, he added. "Having been that close to rescue, having looked in my face, into the cabin of the Lynx behind me, he'll go to pieces now – fast. From what I've heard of him, he's half-way off his head already. He's going to last about five minutes when they start to question him." He looked out over the lake. "By tomorrow, the Russians will be crawling over this place like ants. Getting ready to cart the thing home."

"You think so?"

Waterford's face was grim. "I've seen them, lad," he snapped sourly. "In Belfast, in Cyprus, Borneo, the Oman – I've seen how *communicative* people can be when they're put to it." His square, stone-cut features were bleak as he spoke. "Gant, poor sod, won't be able to help himself . . . and I haven't helped him either, arriving like the Seventh Cavalry just *after* they've burned down the fort!" He threw up his hands, and added: "OK, let's tell Aubrey the good news. Dawson, have you hidden that commpack successfully? Will it work for the next lot in?"

"Reindeer permitting, yes, sir," Dawson replied.

"He's going to love this, that podgy little clever-dick – Christ, is he going to love this!"

The rain blew out of the darkness like something alive and impishly malevolent. Aubrey had closed his umbrella because it threatened to turn inside-out in every gust of searching wind, but he held his hat jammed onto his head. Buckholz walked beside him, bareheaded, chilly and soaked, hands thrust in his pockets, head bent against the splashes and gouts of rain. They had been silent for some minutes. Buckholz, numbed by the signals they had received via the satellite link, as he knew Aubrey must be, had no wish to interrupt the silence. The splashing of the rain against the administration building windows as they passed, the faint noises from the Officers' Mess, their clicking or sloshing footsteps, the sudden yells of the wind, all expressed his mood and deadened it at the same time. He was able not to think, not to consider.

Aubrey dabbed at puddles with the ferrule of his umbrella, breaking up their rippling reflections of light. As always to Buckholz, his anger seemed no grander than petulance. Yet it was real and deep. The smaller, older man shivered at the intrusion of rain into his collar, and expelled an angry, exasperated breath. Buckholz thought he might be about to speak, but they continued their patrol in silence. Down in the Ops. Room, Curtin was trying to contact Pyott in London.

They had come to a dead-stop, Buckholz had to admit. They needed fresh orders, a fresh guarantee of support, from Washington and London and Brussels and Oslo, and they had to make fresh approaches to the Finns. But – to what end? For why?

Buckholz brushed away the thoughts, his face cleansed of worried frowns by the splash of rain that met them as they turned the corner of the building, into a gleam of light from a doorway. Buckholz thought it was Bradnum, standing there in his uniform raincoat, but the RAF officer, whoever he was, saw them and turned suddenly back into the building. They passed the main door. Noises from the Mess emerged as warmly as the heat of a fire. They passed on, feet crunching on gravel, no longer clicking or splashing on concrete.

Finally, as if in the grip of a tormenting, unbearable secret he must blurt out, Aubrey turned to Buckholz and said, almost in a gasp: "They have *everything*, Charles – in the palm of . . . oh, dammit, they have *everything*!" Buckholz was prompted, for an instant, to pat Aubrey's shoulder, but desisted. The Englishman would find it patronising, too gauchely American.

"I know, Kenneth – it's one hell of a blow."

"Both prizes, Charles – both of them, lost to us. The airframe is intact and less than forty miles from the Russian border, and the pilot is by now probably in Murmansk, if not on his way to Moscow!" Aubrey leaned towards Buckholz, lowering his voice to an intense whisper as he said, "And they will make him talk, Charles. Believe me, they will. He is alone, you see – their first and sharpest weapon. Before, he was never alone, not for a moment. He had help. Now, he will know he is alone, and that resistance, courage, defiance, all have no meaning. Sooner or later he will tell them where to find the airframe of the Firefox."

"I know you're right, Kenneth . . ."

"And, like me, you can see no way out?"

Buckholz shook his head emphatically, as if to dispel any lingering, foolish hope in Aubrey, who merely nodded once in reply to the gesture.

"No, all I can see is we've painted ourselves into a corner, Kenneth."

"I won't accept that – !"

"You *have* to, Kenneth. I have to talk to Washington again, you to London. And we have to tell them that, in our considered estimation, we've lost both ends of the operation – Gant and the Firefox." Buckholz shrugged expressively. Water ran from his short hair in droplets that gleamed in the light above the main doors of the admin. building. "What else can we say, for God's sake?"

"You want me to order Waterford to set charges and destroy the airframe? Before it's too late to do so?" Aubrey challenged.

"Man, what else in your right mind can you do? You can't let them take it back over the border!"

"If only they didn't have Gant!" Aubrey raged. "We'd then have the advantage of our knowledge. We could spend weeks examining the airframe, the electronics and avionics, the anti-radar, the thought-guidance systems . . . everything. But they *do* have him, and they'll make him talk!" His umbrella stabbed at the puddles that had gathered in the tyre-marks of a heavy vehicle. Stab, stab, stab, destroying the gleaming mirrors, the petrol-rainbowed water.

"The Finns wouldn't let you – "

"It would have to be covert, I agree – "

"Sneaking around Finnish Lapland for weeks – civilian and military scientists . . . *underwater*? Come on, Kenneth, that's a dream and you know it."

"What good are *spies* to us now?" Aubrey asked, his tone that of someone dissociating himself from his lifelong profession.

"Good use enough to blow the airframe to pieces."

"Is that your *only* advice, Charles? It's not very constructive."

"Sorry."

Rain slapped at their faces and raincoats. Buckholz shivered, but Aubrey seemed not to notice.

"I should never have decided on that clever, so *clever* flight across Finland – it should have been Norway – "

"Where they might have been waiting? The flight should have lasted a lot less than an hour and a half, there wasn't a risk – when you drew up the scenario."

"Thank you, Charles – it doesn't help, I'm afraid." The words were murmured. Aubrey walked a little away from the American,

321

his head bent forward, oblivious of the falling rain. Water ran from the brim of his hat. Buckholz recognised the signals of intense concentration. He waited, looking up into the rain. The lights of Lincoln glowed dully on the clouds to the south.

Minutes later, Aubrey turned back to him. His face was determined. Buckholz, knowing the Englishman, recognised Aubrey's refusal to accept defeat.

"Very well. Waterford may lay his charges – he may need an opinion from someone here – but he is not to detonate them. I shall alert Shelley to talk to Edgecliffe and Moscow Station – they're to look out for Gant's arrival. We must know the moment he gets there, where they take him, how long we might have . . ."

"Why – ?"

Aubrey did not seem to hear the question. Instead, he pursued his explanation. "I must talk to Hanni Vitsula in Helsinki." He smiled, briefly and for the first time. "Hanni has no love for Russians since they killed his father, and less love for 'Finlandisation' as a way of life. He will see the problem from our point of view."

"The DG of Finnish Intelligence is a government official, Kenneth, even if he is a friend of yours. What will he do?"

"I don't know – at the moment, we *need* friends, and he's one. Perhaps – oh, I don't know . . . I simply trust to a Finn's long memory. He's from the south-east himself – the part that now lies in Russia, what used to be known as Karelia. He's never been back since he was a child." Aubrey raised his hands, palms outward, and desisted from the explanation, then added: "I don't know what to do, Charles – I'm merely running around in this old, deserted house, opening doors with a bang and whistling to myself in the dark. Who knows what may come of it?"

"You're hopeful something will?" Buckholz asked in surprise.

"No. But I must *try* – !"

Dawn was leaking into the heavily-clouded sky as Gant stepped stiffly out of the large MiL-8 transport helicopter. Light puffs of snow pattered against the fuselage, melting almost at once and drizzling down the olive-drab camouflage paint. Two GRU guards stood on the tarmac of the helicopter base, Kalashnikovs pointed at him, and there were another four behind him in the MiL's main cabin. His hands were handcuffed in front of him. His right arm ached. It had been locked to one of the handholds above his hard seat for the entire journey. His whole body, however, submerged that pain in a general ache. It was difficult to move. His feet seemed numb, the wound the dog had made in his calf pained him, and he staggered as he reached the bottom of the steps. A guard held him upright, not ungently but with care to keep his rifle out of range of Gant's hands.

Then he was surrounded again by his full escort. A truck drew up near the parked MiL. Gant, with almost no interest, watched more guards debouch from it, noticed a staff car and emerging senior officers beyond it – curiosity rather than business had brought them, he thought. Then he raised his head so that he looked beyond the helicopter base down towards the town of Murmansk and the grey Kola fjord which disappeared northwards into the heavy mist and snow towards the Barents Sea. There was the smell of fish on the snowy wind. The hills behind the base were hidden by cloud. The transport airplane which was to transfer him to Moscow would just get off before the weather closed in sufficiently to prevent further flying.

He shook his head, half-amused. He wondered why he bothered about met. conditions. He was in the Soviet Union, and he was alone and he was manacled. It made no difference whether his location was Murmansk or Moscow; they were the same, cells in the same fortress prison.

He was gestured into the back of the military truck, and helped over the lowered tailgate when his legs appeared to fail him. He struggled in and sat down opposite one of the GRU guards, whose rifle was levelled. Everything was constant, and constantly repeated; wrists manacled, rifles levelled, boxlike metal containers – trucks or aircraft did not matter – and this routine would proceed endlessly . . . endlessly . . .

He tried to believe that the routine would never change because, at the end of the journey, at the change of routine, they would begin to ask their questions. He did not wish to consider the abyss of failure that would open up then, in the first hours or even minutes of his interrogation. Thus, the journey possessed him, was everything.

The truck moved off with a jerk the moment the rest of his guards had boarded it. Gant watched the MiL shrink in size as they left it behind. The metal and canvas of the truck pressed close around him. Someone coughed; metal scraped, boot-studs perhaps. Leather creaked. The engine of the truck throbbed. Through the V-shaped gap in the canvas at the back of the truck, he could see belching chimneys and anchored ships and grey water – most of all, he registered the movement of the truck itself.

After some minutes, a brief stop. Red-and-white pole, a guard-room. Then a glimpse of runway, a control tower. Most of all, the renewed movement of the truck. He was still travelling, the journey was everything . . .

There was no destination. Only movement . . .

FIVE:

Restraints

"I have divers – who also happen to be expert soldiers – at Kirkenes, sixty or seventy miles from our lake and our intact airframe . . . pray, what else do I need?" Aubrey asked, waggling his fork in Curtin's direction.

The USN Intelligence officer brushed a hand through his hair and adopted a lugubrious expression, staring down at his plate of bacon and eggs. Eventually, unnerved by the heavy silence around the breakfast table, he murmured a reply, clearing his throat as he did so as if in apology for what he said.

"A hell of a lot else, sir – too much, if you don't object to me saying so. Much too much."

Aubrey snorted, then stabbed his fork at the centre of his remaining egg. Yolk oozed onto the plate. Buckholz glanced at Pyott, who had arrived no more than an hour earlier and evidently had not slept. The Deputy Director of the Covert Action Staff of the CIA searched the English soldier's face for signs of complicity; a willingness to squash Aubrey's ever more unrestrained imagination. Pyott, however, appeared willing to remain silent while Aubrey rambled, prodded, enquired, snapped.

Buckholz sighed audibly. "There's nothing you can do, Kenneth – nothing at all. You're clutching at straws." He spread his hands in front of his chest, a sign of pacification. "It's not realistic, it's not even adult, to scratch at this particular sore the way you're doing. Let's settle for your guy Waterford triggering the charges he's planted . . .?"

Aubrey glared at him, his nostrils pinched and white, his lips bloodless. "Adult? Childish?" he repeated scathingly. "Do you think, when we play our suburban, late-century version of the Great Game, we are *ever* being adult?"

"Kenneth – " Pyott warned quietly.

"It was not *adult* – it was not the behaviour of a *gentleman* – to throw prisoners under interrogation from helicopters, *pour encourager les autres*, in south-east Asia!"

"Kenneth – be quiet!" Pyott snapped. "It was not civilised to sacrifice people for metal, lives for avionics – as you did, as we all have done with this operation." Pyott's face was white, highlighting the dark smudges beneath his eyes. Aubrey appeared abashed, even ashamed.

"Forgive me, Charles – I apologise for that remark," he said.

"It's long ago and far away – another country," Buckholz replied.

"Thank you." Aubrey turned to Pyott immediately. The soldier saw that four hours' sleep had done nothing to improve Aubrey's temper or patience. He was the pestering, gifted child of SIS, and his impatience had become habitual, even incessant. Like the highly intelligent children he somehow suggested, he was solitary, frustrated, intolerantly and urgently alive inside his own mind. He could handle people with suavity and aplomb when he chose, but for the most part he regarded the world as a stumbling-block, no more, placed between himself and his goal. Aubrey was simply – *too* clever.

"Kenneth, you are silently pleading with me," Pyott said with heavy humour. "What is it?"

"I – " Aubrey waved his hands over the table like a hypnotist. "I've seen airframes transported on motorways – in this country. Their wings are folded, or they are absent. What I need is someone to take the wings off this poor butterfly . . ."

Pyott nodded to the Americans, requiring them to answer. Curtin, grinning suddenly and rubbing his hand through his hair once more, said, "You may have seen them here – but you won't get trucks to move far enough and fast enough in Finnish Lapland at this time of year. You don't even have roads they could use, always supposing they *could* move!"

Aubrey's face was taut with disappointed anger. "I see," he managed to utter.

"What you need is a chopper – a very big chopper," Curtin added. Aubrey's face brightened.

"Which one?" He immediately placed a small, gold-bound notebook beside his plate, and touched the tip of a pencil to his tongue. "Pray, what is the name of this marvellous beast?"

"You need the new Sikorsky Skyhook – it could lift fifty thousand pounds in a sling load with no trouble."

"And – this helicopter could transport the airframe?"

"It might take it as much as two hours to get the Firefox back into Norway from the lake. The problem is – the closest one is probably in Germany, as far south as Wiesbaden."

"But it could transport it, in a single lift, all the way out of Finland?"

"Yes."

"Christ, Gene – you're getting as crazy as he is!" Buckholz

exclaimed. "Have you seen the met. forecasts for that area? You'd be real lucky to get the Skyhook *up* there, never mind operating!"

"I'm afraid that's true, Mr. Aubrey," Curtin reluctantly agreed.

"Could it lift it straight out of the lake?" Aubrey persisted.

Curtin nodded. "But, I suggest you have winches as a back-up, to haul that airplane's ass out of the water onto dry land. The Skyhook would like that – and the weather wouldn't help a straight lift, either." He watched Aubrey scribbling furiously in his tiny notebook, and added, as if dictating: "From Waterford's report, it must have run backwards into deep water – you could winch it out, up the slope, along a portable roadway . . ."

"Just a moment!" Pyott snapped. "I'm going to put – a hypothetical case, shall we say? – to the RAF's Field Recovery Unit at Abingdon. I want an *expert* opinion – with apologies to Captain Curtin – on all this speculation." He stood up, dabbing his lips, then dropped his napkin on the table. "I shan't be long," he offered in a cheery voice.

When the door had closed behind him, Buckholz leaned over the table and whispered fiercely at Aubrey: "We know men and machines can do *anything* you want them to – but what about politicians, Kenneth? You haven't gotten a dime's worth of change out of the Finns until yesterday. Even your buddy in Helsinki isn't too crazy about more interference from us – "

"*Or* from the Russians . . ."

"Don't count on that," Buckholz said abruptly.

Ignoring him, Aubrey addressed Curtin. "What else do I need?"

"I agree with Director Buckholz, Mr. Aubrey – you need the politicians to say yes to you. But, if you're asking me, I'd think about maybe even dismantling the airplane and taking it away in pieces – in case you haven't gotten a Skyhook to the lake. You could hide the pieces and go back later . . .?" Curtin shrugged. "So," he continued, "you need technicians, equipment, winches and pulleys, cutting tools, airframe experts, and a hell of a lot more besides, all gathered around your lake, and you need the utmost secrecy and you need *time*."

"How much time?"

"From beginning to end – a lot of days."

"And Gant isn't going to be able to give you that time, Kenneth," Buckholz supplied, staring at his fingertips as he spread them on either side of his cup of coffee. They drummed pointlessly, without discernible rhythm. "Gant hasn't got any time left, so neither do we." He looked up from the table, shaking his head. "This whole conversation's pointless."

"Don't say that — "

"I have to, Kenneth. All right, you're the guy, the main man, the one who dreamed up this crazy scheme — and almost made it work — but it hasn't worked. Blow the damned airframe into little pieces!"

Aubrey stood up. "And that is your considered, your *expert*, opinion, Charles?" he asked.

Buckholz nodded. "That's it."

"Then I beg to disagree." He looked at his plate with an old man's reluctance to leave food uneaten, then shook his head. "I must talk to London — to Helsinki *via* London, to be exact. You gentlemen will excuse me."

He closed the door of the small dining-room in the Mess behind him. A secure line direct to Shelley at Queen Anne's Gate had been installed in the bedroom he had been allocated. He went heavily up the staircase, his mind whirling with the possibilities of his scheme. Pride stung him into desire. He wanted action, activity, organisation, a *scenario*. He would not let the aircraft go; could not bring himself to destroy the airframe. Guilt, too, hounded him now; had awoken him in the short night when he had tried to sleep. Guilt for Fenton, who had been tricked to his brutal murder on the bank of the Moskva after doing good work trail-blazing for Gant; guilt for Pavel Upenskoy, guilt for Baranovich and Semelovsky and Kreshin, all of whom had died at his orders, or had been considered no more than expendable in promoting the success of the operation. It was a heavy toll of good people; best people.

To destroy the airframe now, scatter it over the bed of the frozen lake, would be more criminal than creating the circumstances of those deaths. Gant was lost. Strangely, he did not feel any acute guilt at the American's loss . . . but the others, yes.

He closed the door behind him and crossed to the telephone. He felt the physical sensation of weight between the shoulder-blades, slowing him, wearing him down. He felt he would only rid himself of it if he recovered the Firefox; would only reduce and lighten it if he *tried* for such a recovery.

He dialled Shelley's number.

"Peter?"

"Yes, sir. Good morning."

"What news?"

"As far as we can tell, he hasn't arrived yet . . . sorry."

"Put me through immediately to Hanni Vitsula, Peter, I must talk to him. I'll wait until you call me back."

He replaced the receiver, and rubbed his hands on his thighs. Sitting on the edge of the bed, he recaptured the position his body had adopted when he first woke and made to rise. Hunched, small, lost. Guilt, yes – guilt and pride. Two emotions to move mountains; or bury people beneath mountains.

Stop it, he told himself, sitting upright, hands thrust into his pockets. Prepare yourself for the next step, for this conversation.

The Finns – more precisely, the Finnish Cabinet Defence Committee under the chairmanship of the Prime Minister – had agreed to the overflight of the Firefox and to certain, very limited back-up facilities and incursions of Finnish airspace. Aubrey had been tempted by a new mood in the country, under the new government, to use Finnish airspace rather than order Gant to fly the longer journey down the spine of Norway to rendezvous with the British Airways flight from Stockholm to London. Infra-red invisibility would have been guaranteed by the aircraft's proximity to the civilian airliner for the last crucial stage of its flight across the North Sea. The Finns had agreed because "Finlandisation" had become a term of abuse, an insult to a resurgent mood of independence in the country. But –

But, but, but . . .

Army deserters crossing from the Soviet Union into Finland had been publicised, and not handed back. Granted asylum. Key industrial projects in the Soviet Union designed and built by the Finns had been halted or suspended until more acceptable trade agreements and repayment terms had been agreed. All good signs.

But, but, but –

The telephone rang, startling Aubrey out of his reverie of justification and optimism. He snatched the receiver. "Yes?"

"Director Vitsula," Shelley said, and then he heard, more distantly, the voice of the Director-General of Finnish Intelligence.

"Good morning, Kenneth."

"Good morning, Hanni – "

"What is this business we have to discuss – your aide tells me it is urgent . . . is that so?"

"I'm afraid it is."

"What has changed since last night?"

"Nothing – except our attitude here to what we discovered."

"Yes."

"What is the feeling at present in your Cabinet Defence Committee?"

"Deadlock – I can put it no more hopefully than that."

"What about the Russians?"

"I think they are more angry with them than with your country and the Americans. They do not know about – your little escapade, only about the overflight by the Nimrod, which they permitted, in the event . . . but, there has been a leak in the newspapers here – "

328

"*What?*"

"Only concerning intrusions into our airspace by Soviet fighters – nothing more. But the Prime Minister has made the most serious protest to Moscow concerning the matter."

"Is there any hope there, Hanni?" Aubrey was speaking very loudly now because the Finn's voice seemed more distant.

"Hope for what?"

"A – " Aubrey hesitated, then said: "The matter we talked about last night . . . a fishing expedition."

"Kenneth – I have seen the Foreign Minister and the Prime Minister – nothing, I'm afraid."

"Do they understand?"

"Yes, Kenneth, they understand. They are not unsympathetic. But – troops, vehicles, helicopters – it would be easier to ignore the whole problem, or drop a bomb in the lake . . ."

Aubrey, enraged, snapped: "What is it they want?"

"Ah," Vitsula sighed. In front of his reply, as if coming from the next room, the line crackled and spat. "Reciprocity and access were two of the words being tentatively used, I believe," Vitsula said.

"Would they agree, in that case?" Aubrey snapped.

"I – don't know. It might . . . soften them."

"It's a high price."

"Higher than you think. Access to highest levels, access to the codes, access to the scenarios regarding Scandinavia . . ."

"You mean your people want a full Intelligence partnership with NATO while remaining neutral?" Aubrey asked, taken aback. He rubbed his forehead, wiping slowly and with force at the creases he found, as if they surprised him. "It's *your* price, of course."

"My suggestion, yes."

"In return – ?"

"We would keep our heads down – three wise monkeys."

"For how long?"

"I – don't know. How long must you have?"

"*I* don't know!"

"Then you must think it over. Just one more thing, Kenneth – "

"Yes?"

"Can you assure me – give me your word – that our friends across the border know nothing, nothing at all, of the whereabouts of their property? I must have that assurance, Kenneth, before I do anything more. Are you able to give it?"

Aubrey envisaged Gant's face for an instant, cleared his throat, and said, "Yes. I can give you that assurance. They are in complete ignorance."

"Thank you. When do we talk again?"

329

"Later. I will talk to London and to Washington."

"Good."

"The price is very high."

"So are the risks."

The young KGB colonel, whose shoulder boards and uniform seemed remarkably new, had hurried aboard the Antonov An-26 short-haul transport aircraft with the eagerness of someone meeting a dear relative. Gant watched him clatter up the lowered beaver-tail ramp into the fuselage, his eyes seeking along the row of tip-up seats. Gant was seated on one of them, hands manacled in front of him, a guard on either side, the remaining GRU men positioned on the opposite side of the fuselage.

The young colonel stood in front of the American, hands on his hips, appraising him frankly but without malice. There might have been something akin to admiration in his gaze. Then, almost smiling, he turned to the officer in charge of the guard detachment.

"OK, he's ours now," he said.

As if he had been overheard, KGB men in civilian clothes clambered up the ramp into the aircraft's belly. The cold of the day outside followed them, striking through Gant's check woollen jacket and waterproof trousers. He shook his head, trying to fully wake himself. It had been surprisingly easy to sleep in the noisy main compartment, surrounded by guards. Now he was hungry. The journey was almost over – bath, food at the end of it. He knew why his mind had narrowed and was working at this fiction.

"Major Gant, would you accompany us, please," the young colonel requested. The four civilian-clothed KGB men stood behind him.

Gant stood up, stamping the cramp out of his calves and thighs. The dog-bite in his calf ached. The GRU men were already at their ease. Cigarette smoke was pungent in the cold air. The colonel reached out a steadying hand, but Gant motioned it angrily away. The officer nodded almost respectfully.

Gant moved towards the ramp and the tarmac outside, a KGB man close on either side. Their arms touched him as they moved, and he could smell staleness and smoke on one of the suits, mustiness on an overcoat. The men's faces were pinched and whitened with the cold. Gant shivered as the sleet blew into his face.

The officer was suddenly beside him, one of his guards having dropped back a step.

"I'm Colonel Dmitri Priabin," he explained, the rank still a strange, pleasant taste on his tongue. "I found you," he added, gesturing the American towards a rank of black limousines drawn up on the tarmac. Gant's attention wandered over the military airfield. Familiar, except for the aircraft types and their markings.

"Yeah?" he murmured. "Found?"

Priabin's hand was on the door-handle of the second and largest limousine, a Zil. He nodded. The grin was boyish, the eyes alert, clever, studious. "Almost in time," he explained. "You were on our computer files, of course. But – it was an accident, even then. A *minute* too late, no more than that!" He laughed.

"What happened to your boss?" Gant asked suddenly. Priabin's face frowned, then cleared.

"Colonel Kontarsky is – in disgrace, I'm afraid." His head had turned from side to side, as if checking that his new shoulder boards remained in place. "However, will you please get in the car."

"Where are we going?"

Priabin grinned reprovingly. "Come, come, Major – you know that as well as I. Please . . .?" He opened the door and gestured for Gant to get in. The American clambered into the Zil. The other rear door opened and a KGB man – the one whose overcoat smelt of mothballs and disuse – slid in next to him. Priabin got into the front passenger seat. The KGB man who was scented with harsh tobacco followed Gant into the car. He was pressed between them. No guns had been drawn. Priabin turned to watch the American as the driver accelerated towards the perimeter fence of the airbase. Passes were shown at the guardroom, and then they were turning onto the main road, towards Moscow.

Why hadn't he used his overcoat? Gant wondered irrelevantly, the smell of mothballs and mustiness overpowering now.

"Where did you discover that overcoat, Oleg?" Priabin asked good-humouredly, wrinkling his nose. "It can't have been used for years." Gant grinned crookedly.

"My son took mine before I was up," Oleg grumbled. "You know what kids are like, sir. What's yours is theirs – what's theirs is their own." He tossed his head in mock disgust.

The midday traffic was light on the Volgograd road as they passed through farmland and forest; deceptive countryside, flat and passive like his home state. Only the black car in front and the two black cars behind forced his real context and status upon him. Industrial smoke belched beyond woodland ahead of them, from chimneys scrawled against the grey sky. The sleet slithered on the windscreen as the wipers flicked at it.

"I might make you walk the rest of the way," Priabin said to Oleg, smiling. "Get rid of that smell, at any rate." He returned his attention to Gant. "A pity about the aircraft," he murmured conversationally.

"Sure," Gant replied. "A real crying shame." He converted himself in his own mind to a laconic, simple, truculent figure; as if flexing the first muscles he would use in a contest yet to come. "It caught fire," Gant added.

"Mm. You ejected, then?"

"What else, man? I saw it go." He nodded vigorously. In his mind, from the vantage point of his ejector seat, he saw his Phantom explode in Vietnam. That had been the moment before the quick, breathtaking rush through the trees, the catching jolt as the 'chute caught and held him, the arrival of the party of armed Gooks . . .

He continued nodding. Priabin rubbed his top lip with his forefinger. "Yes," he remarked. "You have certainly seen aircraft destroyed — blow up . . .?" His hands made the expansive final, decisive nod. "What a pity — all that money wasted." Priabin said soothingly. "I hope they believe you," he added quickly.

Gant's eyes narrowed, but his features remained passive. Outside the car, a suburban town in the Moscow *oblast* offered low factory units, chimneys, then wet-black streets and hurrying figures. Scarved or fur-hatted women, a preponderance of black, unfashionable winter overcoats, short fur-lined boots and galoshes. Old-fashioned, poor. Again, the familiar . . .

They halted at traffic lights. He felt the two bodies on either side come to greater alertness. He relaxed, slumping back against the seat. The Zil moved off as the lights changed. Hoardings stared down, alcohol and cheese and chocolate rivalling the flags and the Party portraits for his attention. The town straggled away behind them in the sleet, and an airliner dropped out of the cloudbase towards the Bykovo airport on their right. There was little that was unfamiliar, except the city ahead crowding on its hills like a vast gathering of people waiting for important news. Four days before, when he had entered it from the north-west, from Cheremetievo, he hadn't noticed the hills. Now, the city might have been Italian; a holiday destination that had strayed to some wet, cold northern latitude.

He gave up trying to assimilate the city, change its nature. For him, it was now no larger than Dzerzhinsky Street and the Lubyanka prison behind the dignified façade of KGB headquarters. They passed beneath a railway bridge. Sparks flashed against the sullen sky from a passing train's overhead cage. He was holding on, but only just, only just —

Just keeping out the future. It was beginning to ooze through a hairline crack in the dam he had built with inadequate materials, but he was holding on . . .

Priabin scrutinised him carefully, keenly, as they drove along the wide Volgogradski Prospekt towards the inner ring road, the Garden Ring. He saw the onion domes of a church and a building near it that was large enough, alien enough to Gant, to have been a monastery. He was startled by the outline of a distant bridge over the Moskva as a gap between buildings revealed it to him. Beyond the monastery, against the sky and almost obscured by the sleet, he saw the Krasnoknlinski Bridge. He remembered its lights blurring with sudden tears as Vassily jerked his head back and held him while Pavel beat Fenton's face into an unrecognisable blood-covered dough.

He saw that his hands were shaking when he followed Priabin's keen gaze downwards, towards his lap. He clenched them, ground his teeth, and looked up.

"Yeah," he said suddenly.

Priabin had evidently seen the bridge, for he said; "Well-remembered scenes, mm, Major?" Then he shrugged, and added: "It was clever – ruthless, but clever. I'm afraid it doesn't make you the most popular visitor to Moscow."

Taganskaia Square. They crossed it quickly, using the central lane marked with its broad yellow lines which was free of all but official traffic at any time. Ahead of the cars, Gant saw ugly concrete blocks towering above yellow-stuccoed buildings and monuments and columned arches.

Priabin turned to follow his gaze. A huge hotel block drifted past the Zil's windows. People hurried beneath, dwarfed, hunched into overcoats. There were very few umbrellas. Apart from the buildings, that was the most alien thing he had seen. Most of the people wore hats, or scarves, but there were almost no umbrellas. It *was* an alien place.

Priabin turned back to Gant. Ahead, through the smeared passage of the wipers, the city seemed to hurry like a crowd towards the centre. The streets narrowed, appeared to squeeze closer. The distance from Red Square to the KGB's headquarters was perhaps no more than two minutes' drive.

"Welcome to Moscow, Major Gant," Priabin said, grinning.

The dam broke. Gant was no longer able to fend off, keep off, the future. It broke over him. His hands would not keep still on his lap, however hard he watched them, however much he willed them to stop.

"It's remarkably astute of the Finns, in my opinion," Aubrey observed to Buckholz as they stood at the plot table. Yellow, red and green tape was stretched between pins. The futuristic model of the Firefox remained where he had placed it, squatting on the lake. It ought to be *under* the table, he observed to himself irreverently. "Everyone has their price, especially governments, and the Finns have been very clever at deciding upon theirs – but then, Hanni Vitsula is a clever man."

"Sure," Buckholz grumbled.

"They don't want Russians in Finland, collecting and taking back their most secret warplane – think of the bad publicity that would give this new Finnish government . . . and they certainly wouldn't want to destroy it themselves, and have to own up to the Russians – too much diplomatic flak for anyone's liking there. So, what do they do? Give us the job of cleaning their stables for them, and making us pay an exorbitant price for the privilege of so doing! One really has to admire them."

"Does one?" Buckholz asked reluctantly, sarcastically.

"*I* think so, Charles – oh, don't be such a spoilsport. In the end I don't suppose it will come down to us giving them very much more than we do already. You know that as well as I do. What is it that is really upsetting you? The fact that your President, at the eager prompting of the Chiefs of Staff, the entire Pentagon, the NSA and your own Director, have ordered us to rescue the airframe if we humanly can?"

Aubrey's complacent smile irritated the American, made him unreasonable; even disposed to violence. Washington had given him explicit orders, outlined a specific course of action; pressured London into agreement, into the supply of men and facilities and materials. Buckholz was angry with Aubrey for anticipating, in his insatiable desire for success, the way in which the President's Crisis Management Committee would resolve the matter. An all-night meeting, a morning of computer-discussed scenarios, and the White House had agreed with Aubrey. The attempt must be made, and the Finns made to allow it.

Charles Buckholz felt he now appeared stupid, narrow, defeatist. Aubrey had forced such a view of himself upon him, and he therefore disliked Aubrey intensely at that moment. He disliked Pyott, too, he thought, as the soldier, now attired in a dark suit rather than his uniform, entered the Ops. Room, a sheaf of papers in one hand. To Buckholz's extreme irritation, he proceeded to wave them like a flag above his head as he came towards them.

"Well?" Aubrey asked eagerly. Pyott, on reaching them, seemed disconcerted by Buckholz's sullen expression and glinting eyes. "Oh, don't mind Charles," Aubrey remarked airily. "He's sulking because the President ignored his Jeremiad this morning!" Then he turned to Pyott again. "Is that Abingdon's shopping list?"

"Yes, it is."

334

"Good. And how were JIC and the Chiefs of Staff, not to mention Andrew Gresham, our revered leader?"

"Sullen," Pyott observed maliciously, looking at Buckholz with amusement. "At least, Gresham and the Cabinet Defence Committee are writhing at the pressure the President is putting on them – but wilting, of course. JIC is fence-sitting, and the Chiefs of Staff are promising the moon in the way of assistance!"

Aubrey grinned broadly, almost snatching the sheaf of papers from the taller Pyott. Pyott handed them to him, and brushed at his moustache; a preening gesture, Buckholz thought.

"Kids," he remarked. "You're like kids."

"Charles," Pyott soothed. "Let's not get into that again."

"It's not a game – not even your old imperial Great Game, Giles," the American said heavily, leaning on clenched knuckles on the plot table; a heavy, reluctant figure, someone to be taken seriously. "Kenneth's idea of Christmas, this is," he continued. "And maybe yours." he looked at each of them in turn, intently, then he added: "The President never mentioned Gant, though – uh? Not a gaddamed word!" Buckholz threw his hands up in the air, continuing with great vehemence: "What did he do, uh? Stand in front of the green-tinted window in the Oval Office, put his hand on his heart and tell the Chiefs of Staff and the gathered multitudes that Mitchell Gant was a true American and he'd never talk to the damned Russkies!" Pyott dropped his glance. His eyes seemed to cast about on the plot table for something he had mislaid. Aubrey, too, seemed abashed. "You haven't got a chance – not the ghost of a chance – because they've got him and they're going to make him talk. Today, tomorrow, or maybe if you're lucky the poor dumb bastard will hold out until the day after tomorrow – but eventually, he's going to tell them go look in the lake, comrades. That's where it is. And if he holds out that long, you might just have gotten it out of the lake before they arrive – they won't even have to fish for it!"

Buckholz glared at them, then turned on his heel and walked noisily across the Ops. Room towards the door. He slammed it behind him.

Aubrey stared at the plot table and the coloured tapes marking supply routes and aircraft types and journey times and dropping zones. The sheaf of papers he held tightly in his right hand quivered at the lower edge of eyesight. He could hear his own breathing, nasal but barely under control. Finland appeared so accessible on the plot table. Coloured tape stretched out towards it from the UK, from Norway. The black model of the Firefox sat stolidly on the pinprick of the lake. The quivering sheets in his hand were the foundation, the scenario.

And yet Buckholz was right.

The telephone startled him. He looked at Pyott almost wildly. The soldier crossed the room to the foldaway table on which the secure telephone rested.

"Yes?" he asked, then immediately held out the receiver to Aubrey. It seemed slippery as soon as he touched it. "Shelley."

"Yes, Peter?" he asked anxiously. "Yes . . . yes . . . I see — they're certain, yes, yes, I appreciate they are . . . very well. Yes, the surveillance must be of the best, they may not keep him there . . . yes, Peter. Thank you." He put down the telephone heavily. Pyott, in response to Aubrey's bewildered glance, furiously rubbed at his moustache with a crooked right forefinger. "He's arrived," Aubrey announced in a voice that might, in less serious circumstances, have sounded comically gloomy. "Almost an hour ago, he was driven into Moscow Centre." He glanced up at the large clock on the Ops. Room wall. It was as if he could hear it ticking in the empty silence of the underground room. "Damn it!" he cried, thumping the foldaway table with his fist. "Damn and blast it, it's already *begun*!"

They had taken him directly to Andropov's office. The cobbled courtyard behind the main building had seemed desolate and ice-cold, gleaming with melted sleet. He had glimpsed the old buildings of the Lubyanka as they hurried him from the car. The office of the KGB Chairman seemed like some kind of bribe. Warm, opulently furnished with embroidered sofas and oriental carpets, panelled walls, tall windows looking down on Dzerzhinsky Square and Marx Prospekt. He was given a drink — bourbon, which he disliked but which they might have assumed was to his taste. It burned his chest and stomach, but the sensation, after the chilling cold of the cobbled courtyard, was comforting.

Andropov watched him from behind his large, intricately-carved French desk, hands steepled, face not unkindly. Merely curious. A tall, uniformed man stood at his side, outlined against the artificial whiteness provided by the net curtains. His eyes gleamed even in half-shadow. Gant sat on a delicate antique chair covered with embroidered silk, cradling his drink, while Priabin stood behind him. There was no one else in the room, but the illusion of innocence that the smallness of the company at first provided, soon dissipated. Instead, the status and size of the office, the heavy silence, the furnishings, the intensity of the air force general's gaze and the patent and insatiable curiosity on Andropov's face began to unnerve him.

Vladimirov, standing beside Andropov, was aware of a slow-growing cramp in his left calf. The sense of stiffness reminded him of how motionless he had remained since Gant entered the room; a stillness of body that belied the state of his emotions and thoughts. After a night's sleep and breakfast with his wife and the reading of a treasured letter from their only son regarding his promotion to deputy direction of the power station in Sverdlovsk, he realised that he hated Gant. It was some kind of delayed stress reaction, he concluded. He had suspected it in the staff car as he was being driven to the Centre from his apartment. Suspected it even as he recalled his son's childhood, his poor academic record at school, the fudging that had got him into a technical university, his dislike of the armed forces and his choice of a career in electricity. In Andropov's office, drinking coffee, engaging in the halting small-talk that was all the Chairman could command, he had begun to be more certain. When they had brought in the American – weary, disorientated, fearful – he had known with certainty that he hated him. No admiration, no ex-flyer's fellow-feeling, no *objectivity* at all . . .

Gant had almost ruined him, almost made him fail; almost outwitted him. He had destroyed the other prototype and lost the one he had stolen. He would be made to pay.

Eventually, Andropov cleared his throat with a small, polite sound, smoothed his silk tie, and said, "Major Gant – Major Mitchell Gant . . ." He smiled thinly. "We have – asked you to come here today to tell us what you have done with the prototype MiG-31 which you removed from the secret complex at Bilyarsk early yesterday morning – what have you to say?" The tone was an attempt at silkiness, at a kind of indirect, ironic humour. Priabin sensed that Andropov was unused to the tone, had had little use for it in the past.

"It blew up – I told him," Gant replied sullenly, gesturing over his shoulder at Priabin. Andropov's gaze flickered to the young colonel's face, then back to Gant.

"I see. You, of course, ejected?" Gant nodded. "Where, precisely? Would you describe the incident for us? General Vladimirov is most interested to know what became of the aircraft – aren't you General?"

"Yes," Vladimirov replied in a choked voice. The American's sullen, insulting voice, his pretence to stupidity, further angered him. Even now, he was preparing to play a game with them.

Gant sniffed. "Could I have another drink?" he asked holding out his glass.

"Of course. Colonel – ?"

Priabin brought the bottle, half-filled the crystal tumbler, returned the bottle to the dark, inlaid cabinet against one panelled wall. Then he resumed his stance behind Gant.

Gant swallowed, cleared his throat, and said, "The airplane was breaking up and on fire . . ." Vietnam, he reminded himself. Remember the cockpit, filling with smoke. "The cockpit was full of smoke . . ."

"What caused this damage?" Vladimirov suddenly snapped.

"Cannon fire – the second of the two MiG-25s was on my tail. I tried to shake him off, but my fuel was too low already . . . we flew into a closed valley, he came up first and I thought I'd gotten him . . . I had, then he got me . . . I hit the button and got out of there fast . . . I don't know if he did . . .?" He looked up then, at Andropov. Vladimirov was a tall threatening shadow at his side.

"You lost fuel – why?" Vladimirov asked.

"The second Firefox – must have ruptured my fuel-lines. I was trying to glide her all the way to Bardufoss when your MiG-25s sighted me visually. I was in a corner. I didn't have the fuel to outrun them."

"I ordered them to shepherd you back."

"They almost did – I was lucky, I guess."

Vladimirov was silent for a moment, and then he burst out: "Now I am certain you are lying, Gant!"

"What do you mean, General?" Andropov asked, turning his head to look at Vladimirov.

Vladimirov rounded the desk and moved towards Gant's chair. Gant could see the one clenched fist for a moment before the other hand closed over it, calming it. Then Vladimirov said, "Not you. Never you, Gant. Your life is a mess, you live like a hermit, you couldn't keep a job if you were given one. But, you don't rid the world of yourself, you don't give in to the mounting evidence of failure. And why?" Vladimirov leaned forward, his face level with Gant's eyes. "Why? You are a badly-wrapped parcel, Major, and you are held together only by an unsurpassed egotism. You really do believe you are the finest pilot in the world, perhaps ever. *You* would never be *lucky*! Not you – you could never admit it!"

As Vladimirov turned triumphantly to Andropov, his face reddened with emotion and delight, Gant said, "If I'm so fucking clever, General, then what the hell did I do to get rid of the airplane?" Vladimirov turned back to Gant. "Your guy blew my ass out of the sky."

"*Liar!*' Vladimirov shouted. The fist he had been cradling swung at Gant's head. One of the legs of the delicate French chair snapped like a twig as Gant tumbled onto the carpet. The bourbon spilled, seeping onto the polished floor. Gant's head turned. His dazed

vision encountered Priabin's boots in fuzzy close-up. He waited to
be kicked.

"Can we possibly do it in four days, Giles?" Aubrey asked. Curtin,
whose timetable they were discussing, also looked at the tall soldier.

"With this shopping-list of Curtin's – it might be possible. *If*, and
only if, everything works like clockwork. It won't, of course, but this
is theoretically feasible."

"Very well – what have we got so far?" Aubrey said, more in the
nature of an announcement than an enquiry. He pushed away his
plate – lunch had been served in the Ops. Room, a white cloth laid
over two pushed-together foldaway tables. Buckholz had not joined
them. Aubrey studied the last of the claret in his glass, then
swallowed it. "Giles?"

"Politically, we're OK, with the crucial exception of the Finns.
Their Cabinet still has to decide."

"Yes, yes – " Aubrey interrupted impatiently, waving his hand,
then standing up, thrusting his hands deeply into his pockets as
soon as he had done so. His professional manner angered Pyott.
Aubrey paced alongside the plot table while Pyott continued.

"Washington and London have agreed that the rescue is to be
attempted, and that it continues as a covert operation – deniable
and disownable if and when necessary. Therefore, we report only to
the Cabinet Secretary here, who represents Number Ten and the
JIC, while Charles will report via his Director to the Chief of Staff at
the White House so that the President may be kept in touch."

"Good, good. That gives us a free hand. Now, what about the
substance of the meal?"

"One Hercules has been requisitioned from RAF Lyneham. We
think Kirkenes makes the better HQ. Despite the greater range of
facilities at Bardufoss, it's too far away . . ." Aubrey was bending
over the plot table. Pyott glanced at Curtin, nodded, and they joined
him, Curtin having sipped at his glass of water before rising. Aubrey
gazed at the map as if he coveted it; a stylised portrait of a
conqueror. Pyott waved his hand over the plot table like a conjuror.
"Bardufoss – " he said. "Kirkenes –." He cleared his throat. "We
have the transport, we have the troops to set up a defensive
perimeter, SBS already in Kirkenes. We have a Royal Engineer
detachment – winches, tripods, pulleys, cutting gear . . . RAF
engineers, four of those and appropriate tools. Curtin has our giant
Sikorsky Skyhook fuelling now for its first hop from – where is it,
Gene?"

Curtin grinned at the use of his Christian name; his welcome to
the comfortable circle of conspiracy. "Germany, Giles." His smile did

not diminish. Eventually, Pyott nodded, accepting the familiarity. "We have to finalise the refuelling points – this baby can't travel more than two hundred miles on a full tank of gas . . . that means two, maybe three refuellings before she gets her ass out of Germany, since she's coming up from Wiesbaden. Then there's Denmark, Sweden – we don't anticipate problems with their neutrality – and she's going to come awful slowly up Sweden and across Lapland to the lake. And the met reports are getting worse, Mr. Aubrey, they really are." Curtin looked dubious, uncertain; as if he had blasphemed. Aubrey glared at him.

"And there," Giles Pyott said heavily, looking hard at Aubrey, "is where the best laid plans, et cetera, will stumble and fall. You have no back-up, Kenneth. No fall-back. No second line." He continued to stare at Aubrey.

Eventually, Aubrey shrugged. His face was chastened, and angry. Once more, the image of the frustrated, gifted child came to Pyott. Aubrey really was almost impossible –

"Giles, there can be no fall-back or whatever you wish to call it. The best we could hope for, if the Skyhook does not arrive, is to remove some of the more vital systems from the airframe, then destroy it. Which is why this plan *must* work!"

"Too much hinges on the weather and a single large helicopter, Kenneth. If the ice were thick enough to bear the weight of the Hercules . . ." He brushed at his moustache, a flicking motion. "But, it won't. Waterford's people are certain of that. Even if it landed and the ice held, it wouldn't bear the weight of the Hercules with the dismantled Firefox inside its cargo compartment."

Aubre glanced from Pyott to Curtin, then back to Pyott. "Have you two been rehearsing this?" he asked with evident sarcasm. "I, too, have digested Waterford's reports. I *know* there is no alternative to the Sikorsky. It must arrive. It is *our* job to prepare for its arrival!"

Pyott shrugged, then relented and said to Curtin, "And how have you been getting on?"

"We've had experts study the pictures of the lake, we've spoken to one of your university professors – "

"Gilchrist at King's," Pyott explained casually. "Geologist – actually knows the area."

"What does he say?"

"He pointed out, having seen the pictures, that we might have to do some tree-felling if we want to drag anything out of that lake. Brooke's detailed report on depth of water, slope of the shore, indicated the same thing."

"So – tree-felling. Easy to pick up visually by any overflight."

"I agree. It will have to be made to look – natural . . ."

"How many drops?" Aubrey asked.

"All our people – thirty to forty, including SBS – could go in the first drop, onto the lake. Any non-parachutists will have to be taken in by Lynx helicopter. Equipment can go in a second drop. A lot of what we need is at Bardufoss already . . . our good fortune."

"When?" Aubrey burst out.

"If you get permission from the Finns – if all the pressure being exerted finally makes them bend – tonight."

"Then I must talk to Hanni Vitsula – !" Aubrey exclaimed, hurrying from a lingering glance at the plot table towards the telephone. Immediately he moved, Pyott and Curtin began murmuring rapidly as they leaned over the table. Aubrey dialled the Queen Anne's Gate number, then requested Shelley's extension, having satisfactorily and impatiently identified himself.

"Peter – get me Helsinki at once . . . what? No, nothing. I see – yes, Peter, I realise the importance of the matter, and yes, it does worry me – however, will you please get Director Vitsula on the telephone!" Aubrey realised that Pyott and Curtin were watching him. He could see the model of the Firefox on the table between them, as if they had moved apart solely to reveal it. For a moment, his eyesight became unfocused, the model seemed almost to dissolve as he thought of Gant. The telephone connection clicked and stuttered.

"Kenneth?" he heard Vitsula say at a great distance.

"Yes, Hanni – can you hear me?" It was a ridiculous remark, clashing absurdly with the coloured tapes, with a loaded Hercules transport aircraft and a giant Sikorsky helicopter flying several hundreds of miles north.

"Perfectly, Kenneth – you caught me as I was about to call you."

"You have news?" Pyott and Curtin had stopped murmuring. Both of them were staring in his direction. "Good news, I hope."

"All communications are to be between the two of us."

"I understand – our people have the same idea."

"Good. Then I can tell you that you have – you would call it, I think, a qualified yes."

"Qualified? How?"

"There is a strict time-limit."

"We feel we need a minimum of four days – "

"Then I am sorry, but you do not have it. Forty-eight hours is the offer I am authorised to make. No negotiations."

"Forty-eight hours? Impossible – !"

"Nevertheless, that is the offer. After that, Finnish units will move into the area, seal it off, and inform the Soviet Union of the precise location of their aircraft. I think my government sees some political advantages in this course of action . . ."

"It's still impossible, Hanni," Aubrey almost pleaded.

"It is a fact, however. Perhaps you will consider it more carefully . . .?"

"Forty-eight hours – from when?"

"The clock is already running. Noon today – GMT, of course. It is already less than forty-eight, Kenneth."

They had not hit him again. He had not been kicked. He had lain there for almost a minute, staring at the drying white rim of dampness around the toes of Priabin's boots until the young colonel had helped him to his feet. Vladimirov had stared through the net curtains, out of the tall windows down towards the square for a long time. Then Andropov had ordered a map to be brought in. A secretary spread it on the surface of the large, ornate desk, and then retired. Gant, reseated on a more substantial chair, waited. The broken, delicate French chair had been removed from the room.

Andropov rose and spoke briefly to Vladimirov at the window – the general sucked his bruised knuckles while the Chairman talked – and then sat down once more. Slowly, Vladimirov turned from the window. Light fell on his profile for an instant, and Gant recognised that the man was in no way calmed or mollified. He wondered whether he was the most dangerous, or merely the most obvious, enemy in the room.

"Major Gant," Andropov began, crooking his finger at the American, "there would appear to be some discrepancies in your account – would you show us, please, on this map?"

Gant got up slowly and moved to the desk. The map was a large-scale projection of northern Finland and Norway, and the Kola Peninsula area of the Soviet Union. It was weighted down where it had been unrolled by a gold inkstand and a large paperweight that might have been jade.

"General Vladimirov," Andropov commanded quietly. "You wish to ask the Major some questions?"

"Yes," Vladimirov replied tensely. He remained on the opposite side of the desk from Gant. His long forefinger tapped over the map like a blind man's stick, probing and uncertain. Gant saw only the lake for a moment, then refocused. "Where was the MiG-25 destroyed?"

Gant hesitated, counting the seconds as he had begun to do in the long silence after Priabin had helped him to his feet. Each second of silence was valuable; he had no idea why. It simply postponed . . .

"There, as far as I can remember," he said at last.

Vladimirov's finger tapped the map. "Quite so. Correct. This is the closed valley you described — there is wreckage at this point, here . . ." Gant nodded. Vladimirov did not continue. His finger merely continued to tap at the indicated point on the map. Gant looked up into his face. His eyes gleamed. The general was barely in control of his emotions, but Gant saw clearly the lucid, suspicious intelligence of the man. He might be the most obvious enemy in the room — perhaps he was also the most intelligent? Certainly, he was the most expert . . .

"So?" Gant said in a surly tone. The general's lips twitched. "Wreckage? I told you that."

"Strangely, though, our reconnaissance photographs — which have been examined by experts — indicate no signs of wreckage from the MiG-31. How would you account for that, Major?"

Think, think —

"Uh — it's got to be around there somewhere . . ." In control of his features, he straightened and looked at Vladimirov. "I hit the button, the airplane was on fire, I parted company fom the seat, I saw the airplane explode — how far away it was by that time, I don't know."

"And you landed — ?"

"Less than a mile from the MiG-25's wreckage, I guess . .."

"So you consider that a radius of — oh, what, ten miles? A radius of ten miles around the point would contain the wreckage of the MiG-31?"

"Can't be more than that. It was a couple of seconds, maybe ten — speed was down, and I saw the explosion . . ." He nodded, inwardly envisaging that moment of suspension as the burning Phantom raced away from him and he turned over and over before parting company with the ejector seat — then the Phantom had exploded, a bright orange ball of flame . . . Yes, that was it. Hold onto that. With luck, the reconnaisance photographs were of too narrow a strip. Time, time —

"I see," Vladimirov murmured, fingering his top lip, making little hollow plopping sounds as he tapped it against his teeth. Then he bent to Andropov's intercom, and snapped, "Bring in the exhibit, please."

One of Andropov's bodyguards from the outer office dragged something that looked like a rucksack into the room, then left as Andropov's wave dismissed him. Gant stared at Andropov, who was smiling. Then he looked into Vladimirov's face. The general's mouth was working, as if he were chewing at something indigestible and cold. Finally, Gant looked back towards the pack. Priabin bent

343

to pick it up. His smile was almost radiant. He brought it to the desk and dropped it at Gant's feet.

"Your parachute, I imagine?" Andropov remarked.

"No – !"

"There are not too many of these lying casually unused in the snow of Finnish Lapland. In fact, I should be surprised if there were *any* others. A pity. I believed your story – except that I knew about this, of course."

Gant leaned on the desk. "That's not my 'chute, man! The airplane blew up just after I ejected. I buried my 'chute near the landing point. Where did you find this?"

"Exactly where you had buried it. Not far, in fact, from the village where you borrowed those clothes – which smell of Lapp, I must observe. Dung, grease and sweat . . ."

"*It's not my 'chute!*" Gant shouted.

"It is, Gant," Vladimirov snapped. "You landed that aircraft somewhere – where was it? Where *is* it?"

"No – "

Andropov pressed the buzzer on his intercom. Immediately, two of his personal bodyguards, torsoes large and muscled beneath their suits, stepped into the room. Gant watched them, tensing himself, counting the last futile seconds. Now he knew why he had been counting. It was a record of the time before *this* began, before the pain.

His fists clenched. Priabin's hand was at his holster. The two large men moved swiftly, lightly towards him, almost as if they floated over the carpet. They were close – he tensed –

Stomach, jaw, back, head, legs, side . . .

As he fell, they punched then kicked. Perhaps a dozen blows were struck before he lay stretched on the floor, each a separate, new, agonising pain. It was an assault. Frighteningly fast, terrifyingly damaging. He felt paralysed, unable to move, hardly able to breathe and groan.

Then he was dragged to his feet. His breath disappeared again. He was doubled over in their grasp. Their holds on his forearms and elbows were separate, distinct, new pains. Head hanging, he looked up at Andropov's smiling face. A white handkerchief was held over his mouth and nose, as if they intended suffocating him. But it was loose. It was simply to prevent blood falling on the carpet, the desk.

"He does know, Vladimirov?" he heard the Chairman of the KGB ask quietly.

Vladimirov seemed disappointed that the beating had stopped. "Oh, yes, he knows," he replied. "He knows precisely. He's the only one who does."

"Very well – this must be done quickly – " Gant felt his stomach heave, his body struggle inside the chain-mail of the spreading, burning pain. Andropov pressed his intercom, and snapped, "Tell the Unit to prepare for an important arrival." Then he looked at Gant. There was distaste, probably at the blood staining the white handkerchief. He nodded dismissively. "Take him to the Unit. Tell them to prepare him for interrogation – within the hour!"

Gant was swung around, dragged towards the door. As he passed the young colonel, Priabin was smiling a sad, wise, confident smile. You'll tell, the smile and the eyes announced. Bad luck, but you'll tell . . .

"Kenneth, it's impossible! Forty-eight hours is a strict, complete, *total* impossibility. Please take my word for it." Pyott shook his head sadly.

"But, if we leave tonight . . .?" Aubrey persisted.

Again, Pyott shook his head. "I'm afraid no. *We* could be in position by tomorrow. But, the Sikorsky would not be there and half our supplies would not be there. That would leave us less than twenty-four hours to lift the airframe and get it over the border!"

"Giles, don't be stubborn – "

"You are the one who is being stubborn, Kenneth, for Heaven's sake – ! I lose all patience with you. The discussion is *closed*. It cannot be done in the time available. We must decline the Finnish offer."

"It's there – intact. The prize is still there – "

"Unfortunately," Pyott replied with freezing irony, "we have been scratched from the race."

"Damn you, Giles!" Aubrey breathed, looking around at Curtin and then Buckholz for support. The argument had been in progress for almost an hour. They had skirted the plot table, paced beside it, leaned upon it, as if it were the dock, the judge's seat, the gallery of a court. And ended where they had begun, the Americans siding with Pyott, and Aubrey more and more exasperated.

"I'm sorry you feel like that, Kenneth, but – damn your insufferable self-esteem, your pride. *That's* what is at the root of the matter – *your* success or failure . . ." Aubrey's face was white with rage, with admission. Pyott dropped his gaze and murmured an apology.

Buckholz looked at his watch. Curtin coughed, shuffled his feet, glancing at the plot table where symbols and counters, even torn slips of paper with folded bases to make them stand like cardboard soldiers, indicated their state of readiness. Outside, on the tarmac, the Hercules transport stood awaiting them. It was being loaded with supplies flown in from specialist RAF and army units. Aubrey had been up to see it once; he was gloating when he descended again to the soured atmosphere of the Ops. Room.

Buckholz and Curtin waited. Pyott glanced at the plot table. Nothing more than a box of child's toys, stirring memories but of no use to the adult.

Aubrey hurried to the telephone the moment it began to ring. He snatched up the receiver.

"Yes?" he demanded breathlessly. "Peter — what is it? What — you're certain of it . . . followed the car, saw it drive in . . . no, there can't be any doubt — yes, Peter, thank you." He put down the receiver with great and pointless deliberation. There was, he knew, nothing to consider or think about — nothing to delay his agreement with Pyott that the operation was impossible . . . more impossible now than stealing the aircraft had ever been. He studied each of them in turn.

"Well?" Pyott demanded.

"Well? Well?" Aubrey snapped. "Gant has been transferred to the KGB Unit out on the Mira Prospekt — " He waited for their reaction. He could see that they sensed his depression, but the name meant little or nothing to them. "It is a unit operated for the KGB by the Serbsky Institute. They are going to interrogate Gant under drugs, gentlemen — I'm afraid we do not have forty-eight hours, after all . . . we probably do not have twenty-four, perhaps not even twelve . . ." He sighed, then added: "Gant will not be able to help himself. He will tell them *everything!*"

PART TWO

THE AGENT

> *"This is most strange,*
> *That she whom even now was your best object,*
> *. . . should in this trice of time*
> *Commit a thing so monstrous to dismantle*
> *So many folds of favour. Sure her offence*
> *Must be of such unnatural degree*
> *That monsters it; or your fore-vouched affection*
> *Fall into taint."*
>
> *King Lear,* I:1

SIX:

Echoes In A Tunnel

The dream required the presence of his father. His father had to be made to walk along the Mira Prospekt and be seen from the vantage point of a passing black car. If he could make his father walk in a northerly direction, if he could slow down the moving car to a kerbside crawl, if, if if . . .

It was important to remember the Mira Prospket. Important, too, to remember the room in the moments before the needle, the pause, the unconsciousness. White, clinical, smelling faintly of antiseptic, rubber, ether, furnished with an operating table and hard chair. Most important to remember the faces . . .

Vlad − i − mir − ov −

The Soviet general looked like his father now, but Gant remembered who he was. White coats − doctors . . . Guards, a nurse, others he did not know. He tried to see his father's face, but was forced to allow the shirt-sleeved, shambling figure to wear Vladimirov's features. However, he made him move and glance from side to side like his father. The imaginary car slowed, sliding along the kerb, and Gant peered at the passing faces as they kept pace with his father's intoxicated, shiftless, shameful progress. Nurse, doctor with the needle, other doctor, guard, man in suit − who was he? − Andropov, Priabin − no, no − !

Pavel, Baranovich, Semelovsky, Kreshin, Fenton − his face like red-dyed dough − other faces . . . Gant concentrated. He could see, ahead of them and farther along the Mira Prospekt, against the snow-laden clouds, the huge cosmonaut's monument of a rocket stop its narrowing trail of golden fire. His father was an insect-figure moving towards it, then the car turned off the road, moving at a snail's pace behind the shambling, despicable gait he knew so well. His father was heading through tall iron gates towards the front entrance of a large house hidden from the busy road by tall, thick, dark hedges.

It looked like the house of a dream, but it was real. He recollected the steps, the door opening − nurse's uniform, guards' uniforms − and two flights of marble staircase. His father had disappeared into

349

one of the ground floor rooms, he thought. It did not matter. Each time he retraced his journey, his father reappeared to hold the memories together.

It was important to remember the journey. To remember the black limousine, the pressure of the two bodyguards' frames on either side of him; to remember the Mira Prospekt and to remember the house, the steps, the door, the marble staircase, the columns and doorways and ornamental urns and pots, the old furniture, the white room and its smells, the doctors, guards, Vladimirov. Vital to remember the hard chair, the straps about his wrists and ankles, the needle . . . held up, spurt of colourless fluid, hovering, moving closer, skin pinched up, needle inserted . . .

In his dream, he was sweating profusely with the effort of memory – but he had done it! He had remembered it all while the dream still contained him . . .

Remembered everything, everything that informed him that he was under interrogation, that he was drugged and prepared – probably sodium pentothal followed by benzadrine, or some other two drugs in harness. He was only dreaming now while they waited for the first drug to take effect, he was certain of it . . . then the stimulant would jolt him into wakefulness, dreamy and slow or hyperactive he did not know, but when it happened the questions would begin –

And he had remembered everything! He knew where he was, he knew why he was there. He knew they would ask him questions about – about . . .?

Gant panicked in his dream, felt himself chilled and burned by his fear. He could not remember *why* he was there!

Don't, he told himself, don't . . . *I have to* . . . don't, secret, don't . . .

He had remembered everything – he had remembered enough.

Pinprick – ?

His skin crawled. Pinprick? He was instantly wary . . . something else – quickly, something else, quickly . . . just before the needle, as he looked down at the needle, as his skin was pinched into a little hillock and the needle went in, something else . . .?

Watch, watch *watch* –

They hadn't taken off his watch, he had been staring at it as his eyes snapped shut and he was suddenly in darkness. He had told himself to remember the time, to look when he awoke again. Time –

It was getting light. Murmur of voices that was more than the dream-traffic on the Mira Prospekt. People constructing sentences, discussing, arguing . . . waiting for him to awaken.

Light – his head was lifted, eyelid plucked at, a blurred form

350

moved away, and a fuzzy light was revealed which did not seem to hurt his eyes.

Pinprick again. A few moments, and he was able to see more clearly. Doctors, nurses, uniforms. White room. It's starting, he told himself with great difficulty. He seemed to be trapped in a heavy, translucent oil, his thoughts moving with extreme difficulty. It wasn't like the dream – he had swum easily through the dream, raced with it. Now, his body – he was aware of it quite clearly – was laden, his eyes focused slowly and he could almost feel them moving in his head as he transferred his gaze from face to face. He saw a doctor nod, slowed-down like a failing movie-reel.

He remembered the watch. Focused with exaggerated slowness. Read the time. It did not seem meaningful. Thirty minutes had passed. It did not seem to matter. Father on the street outside, a long gallery on the second floor lined by tall ornamental urns. It did not matter. None of it mattered. He was trapped in his body which was trapped in the translucent oil. He watched the faces around his chair, as dull and unmoving as a fish on the watery side of an aquarium's tank. He stared out at the human faces, unthinking.

Vladimirov watched Gant carefully. The doctor assured him that the man was prepared. He could be interrogated immediately. He was now capable of suggestion. Vladimirov savoured the helplessness of the American strapped in the chair which was itself bolted to the floor of the clinical room. More than the bruising on the face, the swollen lip he had himself inflicted even before the bodyguards had operated upon the American, he enjoyed the man's present helplessness. It satisfied his craving for superiority, his desire for the restoration of his self-esteem. This – *thing* in the chair, drugged and animal-like, could never have succeeded against him. Now, indeed, the thing in the chair was about to tell them everything it knew –

Where he had hidden the MiG-31. After that – his life preserved only for the length of time required to locate the aircraft – he would be disposed of together with the other rubbish that accumulated in such a place; in a Forensic Psychiatry Unit of the KGB.

He turned to the plainclothed KGB officer who had been assigned by Andropov. He and his two fellow-officers were experts in interrogation by the use of drugs. Most of their work was performed at this Unit on the Mira Prospekt. The man probably had a research degree in psychiatric medicine or clinical psychology.

Vladimirov suppressed the contempt he felt for the tall, angular, harmless-seeming man next to him. The man is only doing what you wish of him. He smiled and turned to the tape deck that rested on a metal-legged table behind him. Wires trailed across the floor to speakers arranged on either side of Gant.

"These haven't been edited – I have only the flimsiest acquaintance with them, Comrade General – " the interrogator complained.

"But you approve their use?" Vladimirov asked firmly. "Comrade Colonel Doctor," he added to emphasise the politeness and formality of their circumstances.

The interrogator nodded. "To begin with, yes," he replied. "But the man outside may be of more use. This form of induced regression often has no more than a limited application. We must use it to warm him up, perhaps, make him familiar with the area we want to investigate – but sooner or later, he must be more fully regressed, as himself, not someone else." The interrogator smiled. "He must be debriefed, and believe he is being debriefed." When Vladimirov did not return his pale-lipped smile, he rubbed a long-fingered hand through sparse sandy hair, and added, "We will retrieve what you have lost in his head, Comrade General. Don't worry about it." It was a stiff, formal insult; an assertion of authority, too. Vladimirov nodded thoughtfully by way of reply. The interrogator glanced at Gant, then nodded to one of his senior assistants, who switched on the tape deck. He watched the leader tape move between the reels, then said to Vladimirov, "He speaks Russian sufficiently well to understand this?"

Vladimirov glanced at Gant, as if to assure himself that the American was not eavesdropping, then nodded. "He does."

"Very well, then. Let us see what occurs."

Gant heard the static, the mechanised voices, the clicks and bleeps of communication; recognising them, knowing them as well as he knew his own past. UHF communication between a pilot and his ground control. The sound seemed all around him, enveloping him as if he were wearing a headset, as if *he* were the pilot. He listened, his eyeballs moving slowly, rustily; unfocused. He absorbed the conversation, his awareness pricked and heated and engaged by the brief exchanges. His hands hung heavily at the ends of his wrists, and his body seemed a great way below him. His attention seemed like a little peak rising above dense jungle foliage which nothing could penetrate. He listened. The words enveloped him. He was back in the cockpit of the Firefox.

"I've got him! . . . vapour-trail, climbing through sixty thousand . . . must get into the tail-cone to avoid his infra-red." Whose infra-red – ? "I'll have to slot in quickly behind him . . . climbing past me now . . . contrail still visible . . . seventy thousand now, climbing up past me . . . come on, come on – please confirm orders . . ."

"Kill," Gant heard.

"Two missiles launched . . . he's seen them, the American's seen them, come on – he's got the nose-up, he's into a climb, rolling to the right . . . missed . . . Bilyarsk control, I'm reporting both missiles failed to make contact . . ."

Gant listened. It was *him*, and yet he remembered what was being described . . . *his* violent evasive action . . . it was strange, inexplicable. It was in Russian, it was a Mig-31, yet not him. There was a pressure, almost too strong to resist, which suggested *he* was the pilot, the speaker . . . yet somehow he knew it was the test pilot he had killed, flying the second prototype Firefox. It enfolded him after that moment of lucidity. He was back in the cockpit.

"Missed him again . . .! Wait, he's going into a spin, he's got himself caught in a spin . . . he's losing altitude, going down fast, falling like a leaf . . . I'm diving, right on his tail . . ." Gant heard his own breathing accelerate, become more violent, as if the white room – dimly seen – were hot and airless. His blood pumped wildly, he could hear his heart racing. He sweated. "I'm right on his tail – he can't pull out of the spin – he's going to fall straight into the sea, he can't do anything about it – !" Gant groaned, hearing the noise at a great distance. "Thirty thousand feet now, he's falling like a stone – he's dumped the undercarriage . . . wait, the nose-down's getting steeper, twenty thousand feet now . . . he's levelling out, he's got her back under control . . . I'm right on his tail . . ." Gant was groaning now, stirring his hands and legs against the straps, moving his head slowly, heavily back and forth like a wounded animal. He might have been protesting, repeating *No, no, no* over and over, but he could not be sure of that. He knew the end of the story, the climax. He knew what was going to happen to him as he followed the American down and levelled out behind him, the cold Arctic Ocean below them – he *knew*!"

"Careful, careful . . . I'm on his tail . . . careful . . . he's doing nothing, he's given up . . . nothing – he's beaten and he knows it . . . I've *got* – Gant was minutely, vividly alive to the change of tone, the terror that replaced excitement. He *knew* what would happen . . . he could *see* the other Firefox ahead of him, knew what the American was going to do, knew he hadn't given up . . . "Oh, *God* – !"

Gant, too, screamed out the words, then his head lolled forward as if he had lost consciousness. The tape ran on, hissing with static. Tretsov was dead. Vladimirov was watching Gant with a look almost of awe on his face. He shuddered at the identification of the American with the dead Tretsov. The manner in which the American played Tretsov's role, acted as if he, too, were suddenly going to kill, then die – uncanny. Unnerving. Gant was nobody now, or anybody they cared to suggest. Perhaps he could believe himself anyone at all, anywhere they said?

"Mm," the interrogator said beside him. "Perhaps not quite the effect you wished for . . . but, from his file, I suggest the effect is not without merit."

"How?"

"He has his own nightmares – his delayed stress syndrome. I think he will be sufficiently easy to convince that it was his own nightmare he experienced . . ." He smiled. "When I heard your tape, I projected we might make just such an impression on him." One of his assistants nodded obsequiously as the interrogator glanced at him. "Illness," he continued, "shock. We can work on this now. Very well – bring him around again, to the same level of awareness, no lower . . . and bring in our mimic." He looked at Vladimirov. "I hope the voice is good enough. We have tapes of the Englishman, of course – innocuous material, mostly gathered at long range in outdoor situations. The imitation seems to me sufficient." He smiled again, studying the unconscious Gant and the white-coated doctor bending over him, pointing the needle down towards Gant's bared arm. "He'll probably accept the man whatever he sounds like . . ."

The light, the resolving faces and the familiar voice all came to Gant in the same moment. White room . . . He was sitting up – why had he expected to be lying down? Yes, nurse's uniform, he was in hospital . . . nightmare? He listened to the voice; familiar – changed, somehow foreign-tinted, but familiar. He listened to Kenneth Aubrey as he spoke slowly and soothingly. His eyes concentrated on the only two figures he could see, a nurse and a doctor. They stood directly in front of him . . . Aubrey must be behind him as he murmured gently, confidentially in his ear. Nurse, doctor – where was he? What had happened to him? His body felt dull, heavy, but without pain. What had happened?

The voice explained.

"You're recuperating very quickly, very fully, Mitchell," Aubrey said soothingly. "We're all very pleased with you . . . but time presses us. You're the only one who can help us . . . time is pressing, you must try to remember . . ."

Remember?

There were things to remember, yes . . .

What?

Street, shambling figure, black car –

Who? Where?

Aubrey continued, frightening him, making him cling to the familiar voice. Crash, he thought. Crash? Dead. "You seem to have been suffering from some sort of localised amnesia, Mitchell. Even from delusions . . . You've been very ill, my boy, very ill. But, you're

354

getting better now. If only you could *remember* – if only you could tell us where the aircraft *is!*"

Street, shambling figure, f – ather . . . black car, gates, corridors, white room . . . *remember* –

"Do you remember, Mitchell?" Aubrey asked soothingly.

Gant felt his head nod, as distant a signal as another's head or hand might have made. "Yes," he heard himself reply, but the voice was thick with phlegm, strangely flat. "Yes . . ."

A murmur of voices, then, before Aubrey said, "You remember exactly what happened after you destroyed the second MiG-31 – the second Firefox?" Aubrey's voice was silky, soothing, gentle. Gant nodded again. He remembered. There had been things to remember. These things – ?

Street – black – car – figure ahead – huge sculpture of a rocket's exhaust – street – blank – figure, catch up with the figure, see his face – blank – house – steps – corridor – blank – watch – blank – watch – blank –

It was a series of pictures, but the cartridge of slides had been improperly loaded. There were gaps, frequent large gaps. Blank – car – blank . . . *remember* . . .

"What do you remember, Mitchell?" Aubrey asked once more. "After you destroyed the second Firefox, what happened then? We know that you destroyed the two MiG-25Fs – you remembered that much. Do you still remember?" Gant nodded. "Good. The first one you took out in the clouds, and the second one almost got you . . . but you survived and the aircraft survived . . . What did you do next? What did you do, Mitchell? Time is of the essence. We haven't much time if we're to prevent it falling into their hands. What did you do with it, Mitchell?" The voice insisted. Yet it soothed, too. It was almost hypnotic. There seemed to be a window behind the doctor and the nurse, through which Gant could see . . . what was it? London. Big Ben? Yes, Big Ben. There seemed to be a bright patch of colour at the corner of his vision, perhaps flowers in a vase? He could see Big Ben – he was almost home – he was safe . . .

And Aubrey's voice went on, seductively soft, hypnotic, comforting.

"Where, Mitchell, where? Where did you land the aircraft? You can remember, Mitchell . . . try – please try to remember . . ."

"Ye – ess . . ." he breathed slowly, painfully.

"Good, Mitchell, good. You *can* remember?"

"Yes," he enunciated more clearly. He *was* feeling better. Whatever had happened to him, he was on the mend. His memory had come back. Aubrey would be delighted, they might yet rescue the airframe from the bottom of the lake –

Lake —
No!
"No!" his voice cried an instant after his mind. "No — !"

He was drowning and burning in the lake. His drug-confused memory had jolted awake against his utter terror of drowning. Wrapped in icy water, then in the same instant wrapped in burning fire —

His nightmare engulfed him.

"No — !"

Vladimirov stared at the interrogator, at the mimic bending near Gant, whose earpiece picked up every question suggested by the interrogator and the general, then he stared at the nurse, the doctor bending towards Gant, at Gant himself —

"What's happening?" he asked, then, more loudly: "What the hell's happening to him?"

Vladimirov found himself staring at the slide projected on one of the white walls, the one opposite Gant. A London scene, looking across the Thames towards the Palace of Westminster and Big Ben. Now that Gant was screaming, over and over, that single denying word, the illusion seemed pathetic, totally unreal. Like the flowers someone had placed against the wall. Who would be fooled by such things, even under drugs? Gant was evading him again, evading him —!

He shook off the angry, restraining hand of the senior interrogator and crossed the room. Gant's eyes were staring blankly, his mouth was open like that of a drowning man, but instead of precious air bubbles it was the one word *No!* which emerged, over and over again. Vladimirov looked up, confused.

"What is it?" he shouted. "What is it?"

The interrogator reached Vladimirov's side. The doctor was checking Gant's pulse, his pupil dilation, his respiration. When he had finished, he shrugged, murmuring an apology at the interrogator.

"Put him out."

"No — !" Vladimirov protested. He bent over Gant. "He *knows*! He was about to tell us . . ." The mimic had moved away, removed his earpiece; anxious not to be blamed. "*Do* something!"

"Put him out," the interrogator repeated. "Shut him up! We'll make another attempt later — " He turned to Vladimirov. "It is simply a matter of time. We have stumbled upon something that is interfering with the illusion. There's always a risk of tripping over something in a dark tunnel . . ."

The doctor injected Gant. After a moment, he stopped repeating his one word of protest. His head slumped forward, his body slackened.

356

"How long?" Vladimirov asked, biting his lower lip. "How long?"

"A few hours – this evening. We'll start from a different point. With more careful preparation. Think of it as mining for gold – only the last inches of rock lie between us and the richest seam in the world!" He smiled. "Next time, he"ll tell us."

Dmitri Priabin shivered in his uniform greatcoat as he watched Anna's son playing football on the snow-covered grass of the Gorky Park of Culture and Rest. The bench on which he was seated was rimed with frost which sparkled in the orange sodium lights. Beneath the lights which lined the paths through the park, Maxim and his friends would play until it was fully dark, and then on into the night, if they were allowed. He felt indulgent, despite the cold, though he knew that when Anna arrived she would scold all of them, him most of all for allowing them to get cold and damp and tired. He smiled at the thought, and at the high, childish voices, the imitations of star players' protests and antics. He contented himself with occasional glances towards the gigantic stone porch and architrave that marked the main entrance to the park. Beyond it, traffic roared homewards on the Sadovaya Ring and along the Lenin Prospekt. Workers hurried through the park, one or two of them stopping for a moment to watch the boys' football game; stamping their cold feet, rubbing gloved hands before rushing on into the gathering dusk.

Maxim had new boots – Dynamo First-Class – which Priabin had purchased for the boy's birthday the previous week. The ball also belonged to Maxim. He watched as Anna's son dribbled past two friend-opponents and slid it inside the tall metal rod which marked one goalpost. Maxim pranced, hands in the air, after he had scored. Another boy protested at offside while the very diminutive goalkeeper picked himself out of the snow after his desperate, unavailing dive for the ball. Priabin clapped his gloved hands, laughing, then looked at his watch. Time to go – at least to begin to round them up.

He glanced towards the architrave and the Communist Party symbols carved upon it. Then, from beneath the curving weight of the stone porch, he saw Anna Borisovna Akhmerovna emerge, and he found his breath catching, as it almost always did when he unexpectedly caught sight of her; when it was no more than a few moments before she would be at his side. Hurriedly, with a great show of concern, he stood up and walked through the snow, waving his arms, collecting the teams. All the time, he was aware of her approach, half-amused, half eager, almost to the point of desperation. He still could not properly catch his breath. The boys crowded reluctantly, protestingly around his tall figure. He continued to wave his arms in shepherding gestures, turning eventually to where he knew she had stopped. Red-faced and puffing, he knew he could easily have appeared to be one of the schoolboys. He was taller and heavier, but closer to their age-group than he was to the woman who stood on the frosty path, arms folded, head slightly on one side, appraising the group of which he formed the centrepiece.

"I didn't realise the time . . . you're late, anyway," he protested. Maxim waved shyly, a gesture he could not prevent but which was muted out of deference to his friends and the rough masculinity of their recent activity.

"Who won?" she called.

"I – don't know," he laughed.

"Maxim's team – lucky swines!" one boy explained.

"No luck in it!" Maxim retorted.

Priabin walked towards Anna, feeling his cheeks glow. She was wearing a fur coat and hat and long black leather boots. Her fair hair escaped untidily from the hat. Her face was pale from the cold. Priabin could not bear not to touch her, but contented himself with a peck on her cold cheek and a murmured endearment. Her gloved hand touched the side of his face, briefly; his skin seemed to burn more heatedly afterwards.

"Come on – all of you," she ordered. "Collect your things. Change out of those wet boots before you go anywhere! No, no, coats on first or you'll all catch pneumonia!"

The boys fought for places on the bench. Cold fingers fumbled and tugged at wet, icy bootlaces. Bodies that had wisps of steam about them in the freezing air struggled into overcoats and anoraks and thick jackets. The sons of civil servants, school-teachers, one of them even the son of a Soviet film star. Boys from the same expensive block of apartments as Maxim. From the place where he lived with Anna –

"Come on," he said. "Hot dogs and hamburgers all round – but only if you're quick!" He turned to Anna. "One good thing the Olympics did, from their point of view. We now have Muscovite hot-dog stands . . ." He sniffed the air loudly. "I can smell the onions from here!" he exclaimed. The boys hurried into their shoes and boots and coloured wellingtons. Bobble-caps and scarves, and they were finally ready. Priabin handed Maxim a crumbled heap of rouble notes, and nodded towards the stone porch and the Lenin Prospekt beyond. "Your treat," he said. "And none of you stray away from the stand before we get there!"

Noisily, the party of footballers and would-be diners ran off. Football boots, trailed carelessly, clattered on the frosty path as they ran. The ball bobbed between them before it was retrieved.

"He's not going to take any chances with that ball!" Priabin laughed.

"Like his mother," Anna replied, slipping her arm into that of Priabin. "He can recognise a good thing when he sees it!"

"Bless you," Priabin said awkwardly, blushing. He patted her hand.

She leaned her face against the shoulders of his greatcoat, then said mischievously; "Those new shoulder boards are very hard."

He burst into laughter. The noise of the traffic was louder as they walked towards the archway. Away to their left, across the darkening park, the double line of lights along the banks of the river were fuzzy. An icy mist hung above the Moskva. Priabin shivered. He had remembered their argument the previous evening.

As if she read his thoughts, Anna murmured: "I'm sorry about last night – "

"It doesn't matter."

"I'm still glad about that damned aircraft – I'm still glad it's been stolen, it's *gone!*" she added vehemently, as if making an effort to fully recapture her emotions of the previous night; rekindle their argument.

"I know," he soothed.

"When I think – !" she burst out afresh, but he patted her hand, then grabbed her closer to him.

"I *know* it," he murmured. "I know it."

He detested the vehemence in her blind, unreasoning hatred of the MiG-31 project. It was an intellectual hatred, the worst kind. He had loathed the previous evening and the argument that had seemed to leap out of the empty wine bottle like a jinn. He had been totally unprepared for it. He had informed her of the death of Baranovich at Bilyarsk almost casually, his head light with wine and the meal she had cooked to celebrate his promotion. He had been high on drink, and on his colonelcy. Blind. He hadn't seen the argument coming, hadn't watched her closely enough. Baranovich had been the trigger. As he held her now, he could hear her yelling at him across the dining table.

"*Baranovich is dead?*" she had asked. "*You pass me the information like a bundle of old clothes? Your project – your damnable bloody project has killed Baranovich? His mind was – priceless! And that filthy project killed him!*"

There was much more of it. Priabin crushed Anna's body to him to prevent the workings of memory, feeling her slightness beneath the heavy fur coat. She struggled away from him.

"What is it?" she asked, studying him intently.

He shook his head. "Nothing – nothing now . . ."

"Come on, then. The boys will be getting cold – in spite of their hot dogs!" She reached for his hand, like an elder sister, and pulled him towards the arch and the traffic beyond. He matched his step to hers. The flushed lightness of his mood had disappeared, and he blamed Baranovich, the dead Jew. Anna had met him no more than three or four times. He was not a friend, not even a real acquaintance. Instead, he had become some kind of hero to her; even a symbol.

He shook his head, but the train of thought persisted. It was almost six years earlier, from Anna's account, that her role with the Secretariat of the Ministry of Health had brought her into contact with the Jewish scientist. He had developed a prototype wheelchair for the totally disabled, which used thought-guidance via micro-electronics for its motive power and ability to manoeuvre. Anna had taken up the project with an enthusiasm amounting to missionary zeal. After eighteen months, the project had been scrapped.

Correction, he admitted to himself. He could hear the group of boys around the hot-dog stand now, above the rumble of the traffic. The smell of the onions was heavy, almost nauseating. Correction. The Ministry of Defence had acquired the project for its anticipated military applications; acquired Baranovich, too. The design for the wheelchair which was never built found its way eventually into the MiG-31 as a thought-guided weapons system.

Anna had never forgiven them for that, for creating a means of more efficient destruction out of the prototype for a wheelchair.

Them – ?

Everyone. The military, the civil service, the Politburo – even himself. She had never forgiven anyone.

"Come on, come on," he said with forced enthusiasm as the boys gathered around him, full mouths grinning, feet shuffling, the lights of passing cars playing over the groups. The hot-dog seller stamped and rubbed his hands. Onion-breath smoked from the stand. "Where's your car?" he asked Anna. She gestured down the Lenin Prospekt. "See you at the apartment, then," he said. "Take as many as you can . . . the rest of us will get the metro."

She nodded, and smiled encouragingly. He knew his face was dark with memory. He nodded. "OK – all those for the metro, follow me!" He marched off pompously, making Anna laugh. The boys, except for Maxim and the film star's son, followed in his wake, giggling.

Priabin waved to her without turning round. He envisaged her clearly. Thirty-eight, small-faced, assured, fashionable, ambitious. A senior assistant secretary to the Secretary to the Ministry of Health;

a prominent and successful civil servant. Her income was greater than his.

As they clattered down the steps into the Park Kultury metro station, he thought that last night he had begun to understand her. He started fishing for the fare money in his trouser pockets, hitching up the skirts of his greatcoat to do so, his gloves clamped between his teeth. Yes, he had at last begun to understand.

It was that damned project. It had always been that damned Bilyarsk project. She had wanted revenge for what they had done, for never developing and mass-producing that bloody wheel-chair.

So, she had begun to work for the Americans . . .

He gripped a handful of change and small denomination notes and heaved them out of his pocket.

She had begun to work for the Americans . . .

"We have one chance – just one," Aubrey said with heavy emphasis. "If we can get in before this approaching front brings winter's last fling with it – " He tapped the projected satellite photograph with a pointer. " – then perhaps we can beat the Russians *and* the Finns to the Firefox." Pyott, who was operating the slide projector, flicked backwards and forwards through the satellite pictures as soon a Aubrey paused. They fluttered grey and white on the old man's face as he stood in front of the screen, pointer still raised. Finally, Pyott switched off the projector. Buckholz put on the Ops. Room lights. "Well?" Aubrey asked. "Well, Giles?"

Pyott shook his head and fiddled with his moustache. "This front is producing heavy snow at the moment, and it's bringing a lot more behind it – heavy snow showers, high winds, even the possibility of electrical storms. As you so neatly put it, Kenneth, it's winter's last fling over northern Europe and Scandinavia – I don't know. I really don't know."

"It won't take us forty-eight hours to arrive on the site, Giles – "

"I realise that, Kenneth. But, the Skyhook's already making very slow time. We shall be very, very lucky if it gets there at all."

"The winches we have are capable of moving something as heavy as the Firefox. She'll have to be winched out of the lake."

"And then what do you do with her?"

"The Skyhook *will* arrive."

"And if it doesn't?"

"Then we must salvage what we can and destroy the rest!" Aubrey turned his back on Pyott and crossed to the plot table. Curtin, seated on a folding chair, watched him in silence. Buckholz appeared genuinely distressed and firmly in a dilemma. Aubrey glared at the black model of the MiG-31, at the map of Finland and northern Norway, at the coloured tapes and symbols.

He turned on his three companions. "Come on," he said more pleasantly, "decide. The Finns don't want the aircraft on their territory. If we removed it before the Russians found out, they'd be delighted with us! Their strong language is bluff – *mostly* bluff. We have placed them in an awkward spot. In twenty-four hours, perhaps less, no aircraft will be able to fly in that area, there will be no aerial reconnaissance to interrupt us. There will be no detachment of Finnish troops flown in, either. We would be on our own. *We* – at least our forward detachments – are little more than sixty miles from the lake. We're *nearer* than anyone else! One full Hercules transport could drop all our requirements and our people *at* the spot!"

Aubrey paused. He felt like an orator who had come from the wings towards the podium and discovered an extremely thin, utterly disgruntled audience. Buckholz, instead of looking in his direction, seemed to be looking to Pyott for an answer. Curtin was doing no more than acting out his subordinate rank. Pyott was brushing his moustache as vigorously as if attempting to remove a stain from his features.

"I – " Buckholz began, still not looking at Aubrey. "My government wants this thing cleared up – I don't mind telling you, gentlemen, Washington is becoming just a little impatient . . ." Aubrey watched Buckholz's face. The Deputy Director of the CIA had said nothing of his last lengthy telephone conversation with Langley. This, apparently, was the burden of it. "I've argued the weather, the logistics, the lack of a fall-back operation, the political dangers and pitfalls. The White House still wants action . . ." Now, he turned directly to Aubrey, and added: "I have my orders, Kenneth. I don't like them, but I have to try to carry them out. I don't have any answers, but I sure *want* some!" It was evident that Buckholz had been browbeaten by Washington. He had been ordered to mount some kind of recovery operation, however much he rejected any such idea. Buckholz shrugged. "It has to be done – something has to be done."

"What about Mitchell Gant, Mr. Aubrey?' Curtin asked sharply.

Aubrey glared at him. Then he transferred his gaze to Pyott. "There is the *absolute* time-limit, Giles," he said. "Gant will be unable to hold out for very long against drugs – my God, they could persuade him he was being debriefed by Charles and he'd be likely to believe it! So the Russians, who will also be watching the weather, will move soon. Or they will wait until the weather clears. It's going to be coming from their direction – they'll have it sooner than we will – it might just give us enough time, it might just

362

persuade them to wait – " He cleared his throat of its intended, husky sincerity. "I think it is worth the chance. Don't you?"

Pyott looked up then. His face was clouded by doubts, by a hundred considerations. His features were maplike. He stared at his knuckles as they whitened on the edge of the plot table.

"I agree – that the weather is swinging around the low and moving west across Russia – " he said slowly and at last. "I agree, too, that they will be hampered, even grounded, before we are. I accept that they may, just *may*, wait until it clears before they take their first look . . . *But* – "

Aubrey harried his opponent. "We can withdraw, melt back into the landscape, if we find the Russians there. If we find them arriving *while* we're there, we can do the same . . ." Again, he cleared his throat. "I don't need to remind you that possession of the intact airframe by the Soviet Union – despite the deaths of Baranovich and the others at Bilyarsk – will mean that the Firefox project continues. We shall be where we were last year, before we ever thought of this – this *escapade*!" Aubrey paused for effect. Pyott's face expressed vivid uncertainty. JIC and the Cabinet Office had left the decision, the final decision, to Aubrey and Pyott. "Our people are waiting to embark. Waterford and his SBS people are gathered at Kirkenes . . ." Aubrey soothed "We are only *hours* away – "

"And the Russians may be only minutes away!" Pyott snapped.

"Nothing is happening at the moment," Aubrey countered.

"As you say," Pyott replied with heavy irony. "At the *moment*, nothing is happening."

"Giles!" Aubrey exclaimed. "Giles, for God's sake, *commit*! This aircraft is still the threat it was yesterday and last year. It is invisible to radar, its electronic systems are a generation ahead of ours, it flies twice as fast as our fastest fighter! It is a *threat*! Commit, Giles – one way or the other, *commit*."

In the heavy ensuing silence, Buckholz cleared his throat. Curtin's chair scraped on the floor as he shifted his weight. Pyott stared at his knuckles. Aubrey's left hand made futile, uncertain sweeps over the plot table.

Then Pyott looked up. "Very well – *very well*. Talk to Hanni Vitsula in Helsinki. Tell him we're on our way!"

"Giles!" Aubrey exclaimed with the excitement of a child. "Giles – well done!"

"Kenneth!" Giles Pyott replied in an offended tone. "It is not a matter of congratulation. Damn your scheme and damn that aeroplane!" He stretched his arms wide. "I hope to God we never find out whether or not it holds the balance of terror – and I hope to God we don't find out it's a *dud*!"

"You know as well as I do – "

"Don't lecture me! I know what the anti-radar system would do if it were used on a Cruise missile or an ICBM or a MIRV – I *know* where thought-guided weaponry could take the Russians in five years or less . . . I've *heard* your arguments, I've heard the Pentagon on the subject – I don't need to be reminded!"

"Don't be such a sore loser, Giles," Buckholz grumbled. Pyott turned to the American. "I sometimes think the profession of arms is as morally delectable as the oldest profession itself," he announced freezingly.

"Don't despise we night-soil men, Giles," Aubrey soothed. "Better this way – "

Pyott banged the plot table with his fist. "Let's get on with it, shall we? Charles, you'll be on-site, but Waterford has *military* command – you understand?" Buckholz nodded. "I must stay here – "

"And *I* shall set up HQ in Kirkenes!" Aubrey announced brightly. "Shall we go?"

He seemed to be lying down. He concluded, very slowly, that he must be in bed. The ceiling was chalk-white. It reminded him of other familiar ceilings. People were whispering out of his sight, like mice in a corner of the room . . . it had to be a room, there was a white ceiling and the beginnings of white walls. His head felt very heavy. He could not be bothered to move it to check. There was the ether-smell – it was a hospital room. A bedside light shone in his peripheral vision, and cast a glow on the ceiling. It must be night.

Whispering – ?

Whispering in English, he thought. Why did that matter? What else would they talk in . . .?

He had once known the answer to that question, had known the alternative, strange, indecipherable language they might have spoken . . . but not in a hospital room.

In a bamboo cage –

They poked him with long sticks like goads. Then the little girl had burned, dissolved in napalm fire . . .

He shuddered and groaned. He remembered. Remembered, too, why he was in hospital. His body remembered resentment, even hatred, and he tried to move. His arms were restrained. Or too tired and heavy to lift.

A face appeared above him, floating below the ceiling. A starched cap on dark hair. A nurse. She examined his eyes – a man did, too – and there was more murmuring. . . .

He tried to listen. It seemed to concern him. American – ? His

364

mind formed the word very slowly, as if he were in class, learning to spell a new and difficult word. American . . .

A strong face floated above him. It wobbled – no, someone was shaking his head. He heard the American voice again as soon as the head whisked out of sight.

"Poor bastard. What the hell did he go through, Aubrey?" He heard the words quite distinctly now, though the effort of eavesdropping made him sweat. "My God, those injuries – !"

Injuries? Heavy unmoving arms, the answer came back. Legs he could not feel . . . yes, they prickled with sweat, but he could not move them. He did not try to move his head. Perhaps it did not move. He was stretched out –

He listened, terrified. "The doctors are doing their best for him," the English voice replied. "We have the best surgeons for him . . ."

"And?"

"Who can say? He may walk again – "

Gant gagged on self-pity. It enveloped him, filled his mouth as though he were drowning.

"And he never told them anything . . . not a damn word. Even when they started to break him to pieces, he never told them a damn thing!"

"He's a very brave man," Aubrey replied. Aubrey – yes, it was Aubrey . . . the self-pity welled in his eyes, bubbled in his throat as soon as he opened his mouth. He was drowning in it; only the unwilled and even unwanted pride kept him afloat, like a life-jacket.

His eyes were wet. The ceiling was pale and clear, the glow of the lamp fuzzy, like a light shining down through deep, clear water. The voices appeared to have stopped, as if they wished him to hear no more. Aubrey and an American . . .

He had been asleep. Or they had given him something. Chillingly, he remembered himself screaming. It was the nightmare. The little girl erupting in flame, her form dissolving. Yes, that was it. Yet he remembered water, too, as his mind tried to understand what he had overheard. He remembered water, and drowning – ? It was hard to think of it, difficult to concentrate, but he made the effort because he could not bear to allow any other thoughts to return. Deep water, dark . . . fire down there, too – ? Water, drowning, his left hand trapped, but his right hand moving . . .

A shape retreating into the dark water, like a huge fish. Black. Airframe . . .

He shouted, then. Just once.

"No – !"

Two faces hovered over him. He did not recognise them. The

nurse mopped his forehead, soothed him with clucking noises. He was injured, yes . . .

No –

Yes . . .

Someone was speaking now. To him.

Explaining –

He listened avidly and in terror. "You ejected, Mitchell." It was the American voice. "You ejected from the MiG-31 when it was on fire . . . at least, that's what we conclude from your – your burns . . ." He gasped and swallowed. Burns – ? "It exploded in mid-air. You say you saw that, even in the pain you must have been in. It exploded – "

He moved his head very slowly, wondering whether they would realise it was a negative sign. He did not trust himself to speak. His throat and mouth were full of water which he could not swallow. His father would hit him if he spat in the house . . .

No one seemed to have noticed. The American voice continued. "On the ball to the last . . ." He must have been addressing Aubrey again. Gant strained to hear, holding his breath. "They must have found him unconscious and airlifted him direct to Moscow." Gant tried to remember. He could not remember the ejection from the aircraft or the explosion. Then he could. But that was – was Vietnam, where the cage and the little girl had been . . . he shook his head very slowly. Someone quickly held his face, checked his eyes, and vanished. The voice continued. "And in that condition, they beat up on him until he couldn't take any more. Christ, those people over there – !"

Gant drifted. His father was walking towards a huge golden spire that narrowed towards the top, like the exhaust of a rocket leaving its launch platform. Gant could not explain the fleeting image. He let himself drift. It was better than listening. It was better than the creeping sensations of pain that possessed him in legs and trunk and head and arms.

Pinprick.

He stopped, drifting almost at once and the American voice seemed louder. He did not dare to turn his head. His father disappeared behind a tall dark hedge; vanished.

"We'd better ask him – "

"We must be certain." That was Aubrey. "Yes, we must make certain."

"The problem is – the *real* problem," the American said, "is to make him believe he's safe now. He can stop being brave and silent."

"I agree."

A face overhead. The strong, sandy-haired man. Smiling. The collar tabs of a uniform, model ribbons. Shoulder boards. USAF. An Air Force general. Blue dress uniform. Comforting. He opened his mouth. A bubbling noise came out. He clenched it shut again. The general smiled at him. The American general smiled.

"Mitch – Major Gant . . . Mitch – listen to me, boy. You're safe now. We're going to make you well again. I promise you that. We just need to know one thing – you're certain the aircraft exploded? You are certain? They can't get their hands on it again, can they?" Gant realised the bed near his shoulder was being patted, slowly and gently; reassuringly. "We need to be sure of that."

"We're not tiring him too much, are we, doctor – in his condition?" That was Aubrey, speaking somewhere out of sight.

"Quiet, Aubrey," the general said, then looked back at Gant. "Now, Mitch, how much can you remember? Are you *certain* the Firefox exploded?"

Gant swallowed. He listened. Aubrey was talking, still talking, to the doctor. Concern – ? A tongue clicking like a grasshopper, a low sombre tone.

Then he heard it.

"He's dying, I'm afraid . . . I'm sorry, but there's nothing I can do about it – "

"Shut up!" the general snapped.

"Hurry!" Aubrey replied. "We must be sure!"

Gant was shaking his head more quickly, with a huge and desperate effort of will and muscle. "No," he said.

The general looked very sad. "I'm afraid so, Mitch. It – Christ, it wasn't what they did so much as the burns. When you ejected, boy, it was already too late – but help us now. Tell us the airplane exploded. That's what we need to know. Tell us. Please."

"No – it didn't . . . didn't . . ." Gant sobbed. "I'm not burned. It's not – I couldn't be . . . didn't . . ."

"Didn't what, Mitch? What didn't happen?"

"I – didn't eject –" If he told them, explained to them, they would realise their mistake. They wouldn't say he was dying from burns, not then. They'd realise they'd made a mistake, an awful mistake, if he could prove he landed the airplane . . .

"What? Mitch, what are you saying?"

"I landed – landed . . ."

"Oh my God – ! Aubrey, did you hear that? He landed the airplane!"

"No – !"

"Yes!" Gant cried out. "Yes!"

The general leaned over him. Gant could smell a violet-scented breath-sweetener. The face was concerned. The eyes pleaded. He suddenly looked like the general who had decorated Gant on the flight-deck of the aircraft carrier in the South China Sea — looked just like him or his twin brother. The resemblance comforted Gant, made him want to speak. He smiled. Just as on that previous occasion, he smiled at the general. He had wished he had been able to send the official photographs to his mother — but she was dead . . .

He realised he was in a trough. Like the sea-well beneath the carrier's hull, he was in a trough. The general's face was a moment of calm.

He wouldn't have sent the photograph to his father, not in a lifetime, not in a million years . . .

Father —

Street, monument, dark hedge, front door, corridors, marble staircase, urns, white room, white room white room white —

The finding of his thread appalled him. He tried to shrink from the general whose face bore down on him, enlarging like the opening jaws of a fish —

Fish. Black fish — airframe. Water — drowning. Firefox — lake, sleeve trapped, cut free, airframe intact . . .

He knew he was out of the trough now. He even knew, for the briefest moment, that he was drugged. He knew where he was, he knew he was being deceived, he knew he must say nothing. Then that moment went. He wanted to talk. Had to talk.

"Dying . . . dying . . . dying — dying, dying, dying . . ." Seemed to be all the general was saying, though his lips did not move except to make his smile broader. The words seemed to come out of the air and fill the room. He disbelieved them for a moment then did not know why he disbelieved . . .

Then —

"He's not dying!" Aubrey's voice. "For God's sake, he didn't crash — he didn't eject — the aircraft's still out there somewhere." Aubrey did not come into view. The general's face looked away. His head shook sadly. An earpiece and a wire came out of the general's ear. Gant realised he was deaf. His father had worn an uglier, more obvious one. The general was deaf.

"He's dying, Kenneth . . ." He turned back to Gant. "Tell us the airplane was destroyed."

Deaf — would he hear? Gant reached up — huge effort, sweat bathing his body, but he grabbed the general's uniform and pulled him nearer so that he could hear. He placed his lips near the general's ear, near the earpiece . . .

"Not burned . . . not burned . . ." Something seemed to hurry him, quicken inside him like an increase in adrenalin. He began to babble incoherently, desperately trying to make himself understood. "Not burned . . . drowning . . . drowning – on fire, but water, water . . . not burned . . . landed, not burned . . . water . . ."

The general's earpiece fell from his ear. Gant lay back in abject apology. His body twitched with adrenalin, or something. He felt *too* alive, a collection of jangling nerve-ends. He scrabbled for the earpiece. The general shouted at him, jerked away, but Gant held the earpiece. A long wire snake unreeled in his hand, seemingly alive. There was nothing at the other end of the wire, no box in the general's breast-pocket, like his father had. The wire trailed away out of sight.

Someone shouted, almost a snarl. He did not understand the language. Truth bubbled in his throat as self-pity had done. He gritted his teeth, held the words back, making them into a growl . . .

He did not know why he was stopping himself from speaking. The adrenalin demanded it. His body twitched and jumped with it. If he could tell, say everything, then he could relax. He must tell – must tell . . .

He sat up, jerkily, quickly, mechanically. Sat up in bed. Not bad for a dying man . . .

Not dying – tell – explain – in the lake . . .

"Not – explain!" he said through his teeth, looking around him. "Listen!" he cried.

He saw two figures in one corner of the room. And flowers. And other faces. Nurse, doctor, general, man in suit –

Two generals. Blue and brown –

They stared at each other, the two generals.

"Listen to me!" Gant screamed. He had to tell them now – he had to. He would burst, explode, if he didn't get the words out. He had to tell them. "Listen!"

He moved, tried to put his legs out of the bed but they would not move and he felt himself tumble forward. The floor rushed up at him, blue and white tiles. He dived at it, striking it with all the force of the energy surging through him.

Vladimirov rushed forward, shaking off the interrogator's restraining arm garbed in the USAF uniform, and knelt by the unconscious American. Blood seeped from Gant's forehead where it had struck the tiles. Vladimirov, in his frustrated rage, smeared it over Gant's face and neck like some horrific tribal badge of manhood. Then he turned to look at the interrogator in his American uniform.

"You had him!" he raged. "You had him in the palm of your hand!"

The doctor lifted Gant's body back onto the bed. Then the nurse wiped the smeared blood from his face and dabbed antiseptic on the spreading, livid bruise. Vladimirov stood up and moved away from the bed. Gant was breathing stertorously, his chest heaving up and down as the last effects of the stimulant surged through his body. Uselessly –

"It is a matter of time," the interrogator said, checking the earpiece the doctor had removed from Gant's hands. He had used it to listen to the comments of his aide, seated in another room in front of a bank of monitors where hidden cameras focused on eye-movements, muscular reaction, a hundred other tiny factors. He shook his head ruefully. "A pity – but next time for certain – "

Vladimirov grabbed him by the upper arms. "I *want* that information – I want it tonight!"

"He has to be allowed to rest now. We have to clear his system before we try again."

"I want that information!"

"You'll have it – before morning," the interrogator snapped, shaking off Vladimirov's fierce grip. "Before morning!"

The Hercules transport, bathed in hard white light, sat like a stranded whale at the end of the runway. Beyond it, the lights of Lincoln created a dull, furnace-like glow on the underside of the low clouds. As he stood with Pyott near the RAF Land Rover which would ferry him to the transport aircraft, Aubrey was impatient. The breeze lifted Pyott's grey hair and dishevelled it. It gave a wild, almost prophetic emphasis to the gloomy expression on his features.

Buckholz and Curtin were already on board. The Hercules waited only for Aubrey. The small, routine Ops. Room was behind him. He had left it, and the larger underground room beneath it, with a sense of freedom, of advantages gained, of wilfully having got his own way.

Now, Pyott held him – like the Ancient Mariner, Aubrey thought irreverently, and then said, "Well, Giles, I wasn't on my way to a wedding, but you've nevertheless detained me. What is it you want to say?" His smile was an attempt to jostle Pyott into a more acquiescent mood. The soldier smoothed down his wind-blown hair and returned the smile.

"I want your assurance, Kenneth – " he began.

"Oh, don't be so solemn!" Aubrey chided.

"Kenneth – damn it, you're impossible! I want your assurance, your *solemn word* that if the Skyhook does not arrive before the deadline expires – you will destroy the airframe completely."

"Oh, Giles – "

"Don't, 'Oh, Giles' me, Kenneth. The airframe must not be left intact for anyone else to retrieve. You must salvage the most important systems and then destroy the rest. Now, do I have your word on it?" He paused, then added, "It's too serious for anything less than your word. I know it isn't in your orders – you've persuaded everyone that your precious Skyhook *will* arrive – but, you must make certain the Firefox is not recovered by the Soviet Union. That is imperative."

Aubrey patted Pyott's arm, just at the elbow. "I promise, Giles, that the Firefox will not fall into the wrong hands. Don't worry – you'll give yourself ulcers."

"*You* will give me ulcers, Kenneth."

Aubrey looked across the tarmac. His gamble was beginning. He knew that Pyott was right, that his entire fortune was staked on breaks in the weather and a single helicopter already in difficulties and behind schedule. And, for himself, he was on the point of laying down his cards.

Gant, he thought suddenly, and shivered. He pulled the collar of his overcoat around his neck and ears, but felt no warmer.

"Good luck," Pyott said, holding out his hand.

"What? Oh, yes – " Aubrey returned the handshake. There was no trace of excitement left in his body; nothing now but cold and fear and nerves.

SEVEN:

Felony In Progress

His head hurt. It was heavy and seemed grossly enlarged, a huge melonlike thing. He could not lift it from the pillows. Faint lights washed across the ceiling, but he could not hear the noise of passing traffic. When he breathed in, there was the smell of ether. Hospital. The word filled him with a vague dread. His body seemed jumpily alert, filled with an undefined tension.

Hospital. Ether-smell. He found the thread once more. Street, hedges, steps, door, hall, marble staircase, gallery with ornamental urns, white room, white room –

He stifled a groan. This was not the same room, not the same bed. He had been moved. After . . . after his interrogation under drugs . . .

Gant understood. He raised his heavy arm. The watch was still there. In the darkness, the hands glowed. A little before ten. He let his arm drop, tired of supporting its weight. He was aware of other bodies; aware of muttered or snoring breaths. People were sleeping in the room. He pushed with his hands against the mattress, easing his heavy body half-upright against the bedhead. Slowly, sweating with the effort and stifling his heavy breathing, he turned his head from side to side. A night-light over one of the beds helped him to see the contours and outlines of the small ward in which he had been placed. It was a brief glance. He slid down in the bed again when he saw the male nurse sitting near the double doors. The man was dimly lit by a small anglepoise lamp, and silhouetted against the light entering through small, opaque panes in the doors. He appeared to be reading a book. When he lay flat again he wondered if he had warned the nurse he was conscious, and listened for the scrape of his chair. Eventually satisfied, he closed his eyes and pictured the room.

There were six beds, three of them occupied by sleeping – drugged? – figures. One's head was heavily bandaged, the second was identifiably male, the third, on the far side of the room and away from the weak light, was in deep shadow. The windows of the ward were barred. In a wash of headlights from outside, he had seen

372

the vertical lines of the bars and the wire-reinforced glass beyond them. The male nurse near the only exit from the ward was muscular, probably armed.

Gant listened, but the nurse did not move. So intently was he listening that he heard a page of the book being turned. Then he relaxed, and immediately the small victory of knowing and mapping his surroundings dissipated. He was trapped in the room; parked there until he was again required for interrogation. He knew he had been interrogated twice; he knew they were only waiting until his body recovered sufficiently to be drugged once more; he knew that they could convince him of anything while he was drugged; he knew that at the next interrogation he would tell them what they wanted to know.

He remembered the USAF general in his uniform, he remembered Aubrey's voice. He remembered the scrambled and confused mess his thoughts and awareness had become. He understood the furious, undeniable desire to tell the truth that had come over him, and which they would induce in him again . . .

Burns?

He touched himself carefully. He was wearing a sweatshirt and shorts. His legs did not hurt when he touched them, nor did his arms or face. There was a lump on his temple, but he remembered the tiles rushing up at him. They had saved him from telling.

But he had believed he was dying –

That was the real measure of their power over him, of his inability to continue resisting.

The sweat was cold on his body. His hands lay beside his thighs, reminding him he no longer possessed even trousers. Nothing but a sweatshirt – no shirt, no jacket, no shoes. He was helpless. Like the figures in the other beds, who were probably criminals or even dissidents, he had ceased to exist. Isolation swamped him.

He struggled to escape it by following the thread back into his interrogation. His removal to this silent ward might mean he had told them everything, that they had finished with him while they checked the truth of his story – had he told them?

Slowly, cautiously, he sifted through the wreckage – father, aircraft carrier, burns, Aubrey, the lake, drowning, burning, ejecting . . . the tiles, the tiles . . .

He had been sitting up, screaming for them to listen to him. What had he said? He squeezed his eyes shut, concentrating. What had he said?

He could not stifle the audible sigh of relief when he was certain. Nothing. He had not told them. They did not know.

He listened as the nurse's chair scraped on the linoleum. He heard the footsteps approach. The light over his bed flicked on. Gant controlled his eyelids, his lips. The seconds passed. He tried to breathe normally. The light went out, the footsteps retreated, the chair scraped once more. The nurse grunted as he sat down. Gant heard the book being picked up, re-opened, pages being shuffled.

He was sweating freely once more. It had taken a vast effort of control and made him realise how weak he was. The nurse would have been capable of plucking him upright with one hand and dragging him from the bed without effort. He could never overpower him.

And there was no weapon. His itchy, sweating hands, tense yet without strength, did not constitute a weapon. And there was nothing else. He could never take the nurse's gun away from him, even if he wore one.

He heard the chiming of a clock somewhere, a small, silvery, unreal sound. Ten. He must have been asleep for hours. In all probability they would be coming soon. They were pressed for time. There was an almost frantic sense of urgency about their pursuit of what he knew. There was no reason for it – no one else knew of his whereabouts or the location of the airplane, but they could not seem to stop until it was over.

So they would come, and he would be helpless. Weaponless and helpless.

Mitchell Gant lay in the dark waiting for the doctors and interrogators. The bandaged head of one of the other patients loomed in his thoughts. A mummy, almost. Something, like himself, long dead and forgotten.

He felt himself once more on the point of losing the struggle against his sense of isolation.

Aubrey felt the nose of the Hercules C-130K dip towards the carpet of gleaming cloud he could see through the round porthole in the fuselage. It still lay far below them, stippled and endless. The moon was brilliant, the stars as hard as diamonds. It was difficult to believe that from that black, light-punctured clearness would come weather conditions even worse than they had anticipated when the aircraft took off from Scampton.

He removed the headset, his conversation with Waterford at Kirkenes at an end. As he stared through the porthole, the clouds seemed to drift slowly up to meet them. They were still flying north along the Norwegian coast, inside the Arctic Circle. The pilot was taking the Hercules down as low as he could, to deceive the long-range Russian radars, before turning to an easterly heading which would take them towards Kirkenes. To all intents and purposes, the

Hercules would have dropped out of radar contact west of Bardufoss and be assumed to be a routine transport flight to the Norwegian NATO base.

Aubrey fretted, even though he attempted to allay his mood by losing himself in the mesmeric effect of the clouds. It might have been a white desert landscape with wind-shaped rocks rising from its surface. The self-hypnosis held momentarily, then dissipated. Aubrey transferred his gaze to the whale-ribbed, bare, hard-lit interior of the transport aircraft.

It was almost done, they were almost there. He was for the moment in suspension, unable to do more. It was always the most frustrating, dragging part of an intelligence operation – the flight, the drive, the train journey, whatever it was . . . just before the border was crossed, the building entered, the target sighted. Useless tension, pointless adrenalin. He did not *control* the thing at that moment –

Five huge pallets of equipment were secured in the aft section of the cargo compartment. The team of fifteen men lounged or stretched or checked equipment. Charles Buckholz once more familiarised himself with the cargo manifest, in conversation with the WRAF Air Loadmaster. Curtin was standing at a folding table on which lay a large-scale map. He was talking to the Hercules' co-pilot. Everything had been decided, the briefings had been completed. This was repetition to occupy time, nothing more.

The Hercules would land at Kirkenes and Aubrey, Buckholz and the other members of the team without parachute training would disembark. Waterford and his SBS unit, twenty-five men in total, would then embark and the Hercules would take them and their equipment to the area of the lake. The dropping zone for the parachutists had already been selected; the surface of the lake. Waterford had confirmed its suitability. Once the men had dropped, the Hercules would make a low-level run and the five pallets of equipment would simply be dropped, without parachutes, from the rear cargo doors. At first, Aubrey had considered the method primitive, unsophisticated, potentially dangerous to the valuable equipment – especially the winches. RAF reassurances had failed to convince him, even though he accepted them. It still seemed an *amateurish* manner of accomplishing the drop.

Above the Norwegian border with Finland, Eastoe's AWACS Nimrod was back on-station. It would operate in an airborne, early-warning capacity, a long-range skyplane, observing the Russian border for any and every sign of movement. Also it would provide a back-up communications link with Washington, London, Helsinki and the lake to supplement the direct satellite link established when

Waterford's initial search party had left the commpack at the lake.

He turned away from the scene. Buckholz and the non-parachutists would be flown in by RNAF Lynx helicopters, arriving no more than an hour behind Waterford's party. Aubrey looked at his watch. Ten-thirty. By four-thirty, the whole party would be in place at the lake, where the Firefox lay in twenty-six feet of icy water.

Twenty-six feet. It was hardly submerged. A man standing on the fuselage would have his head above water. Eighty feet in length – the tailfins in perhaps thirty-four feet of dark water – with a wingspan of fifty feet, it had to be winched no more than one hundred and fifty feet before it was ashore. Or, preferably, plucked out of the water like a hooked fish by the Skyhook which had refuelled on the German–Danish border thirty minutes earlier. The figures were temptingly simple, the task easy to achieve. Yet he could not believe in it, in its success.

Gant –

The nose of the Hercules was dipping into the clouds when the operator of the communications console that had been installed for Aubrey's use, turned to him.

"There's a coded signal coming in, sir – from Helsinki." He attended to his headset, nodding as the high-speed frequency-agile message ended. "There's no need to reply, sir. They've signed off."

"Very well – run it."

The operator flicked switches, dabbed at a miniature keyboard set into the console, and hidden tapes whirred. It was Hanni Vitsula's voice.

"Charles!" Aubrey called.

Buckholz arrived as the replayed voice chuckled, then said: "Don't rely on the weather, Kenneth. Forty-eight hours from midnight tonight is our final, repeat final offer. Our forecasts suggest it might be easier to reach the site than you're supposing . . . don't expect us not to arrive. Good luck. Message ends. Out."

Buckholz shook his head ruefully.

"He guesses we're relying on getting ourselves locked in by the weather. Think he'll decide to move in before the deadline?"

Aubrey waved his hand dismissively. "No. But otherwise he means what he says." He slapped his hands on his thighs. "Well, that's it. Your President has gained us the dubious bonus of a few more hours." Through the porthole, Aubrey could see the grey cloud pressing and drizzling against the perspex. "But that's all the time we have."

"Let's just you and me hope the weather turns real sour, uh?"

"Then we will have lost the game, Charles. The Skyhook will never arrive in the weather you're hoping for!"

Dmitri Priabin turned slowly and gently onto his back and sat up. In the soft lamplight, he stared intently at the hollow of Anna's naked back, as if he were studying the contours of a strange and new country. Eventually, he clasped his head, leaned back, and stared at the ceiling. He pursed his lips, pulled dismissive, laconic faces, prevented a sigh, but knew that the time of recrimination had once more arrived. He slipped from the bed and hoped she would not wake.

He sat cross-legged on a padded chair. He could taste the onions from the hot-dog one of the boys had pressed upon him, unable himself to finish it. He belched silently behind his clenched hand. Yes, onions – it recurred more strongly than the wine, than dinner, than the vodka. It was more persistent than the taste of the perfume from her neck and breasts and his tongue and lips.

Onions – recrimination. Both brought back the park and the metro station and other reminders of her treachery that had assailed him at the ticket-counter so that the clerk's face had changed from puzzlement to nerves before he had recollected himself sufficiently to buy the tickets.

Now, recrimination, guilt, fear all returned like some emotional malaria as she slept. It was an illness which never left him, only remained dormant.

He leant forward, resting his chin on his fist, studying her.

He lived on the verge of a precipice. He had done so ever since the momentary looks of guilt and fear he had noticed when he had answered unexpected telephone calls, looks which had vanished as soon as he put down the receiver and shrugged. And, he reminded himself, he always put it down with the sense that he had been speaking to an American who spoke good but very formal Russian.

He had lived on the cliff-edge ever since he began to follow her himself. Ever since he witnessed her make covert contact with a man who might have been her Case Officer. Ever since he had tailed that Case Officer to a known CIA safe house . . .

He had been on the edge for six, almost seven months –

She stirred, alarming him, as if surprised in some deep disloyalty of his own. She turned onto her back but did not wake. Her flattened breasts were revealed as her unconscious hand pushed the bedclothes down. It was a strangely erotic exposure; crudely inviting. He studied her unlined, sleeping face; unlined except where the brow was creased even while she slept. He felt tears prick his eyes, and because he could never bring himself to even begin to tell her that he knew, that he wanted to help . . .

377

Recrimination, palpable as the taste of onions –

As soon as he had moved into her apartment, he had looked for bugs. He had spent the whole of that moving day checking the telephone, pictures, walls, floorboards, cupboards, wardrobes, bed. His relief at finding no traces of surveillance or bugging had overwhelmed him. As soon as he had straightened from pushing back the last corner of fitted carpet, he had had to rush to the bathroom and vomit into the avocado-coloured toilet.

For weeks after that he had been unable to rest until he had checked the files, checked her office, followed her to discover whether anyone else was following her. He had become like a jealous lover, or like the private investigator such a lover might have employed.

Like a spy –

Gradually, he came to believe that it was only he who knew. There was no evidence, no one was gathering information, no one even suspected.

What she supplied was not state secrets, it was little more than high-grade gossip. Details of the Soviet Union's social services, housing programmes, illnesses, alcoholism – the temperature of Soviet society – which would be useful to them in building their total picture of the Soviet state. Promotions inside the Secretariat and the Politburo and the ministries, glimpses of the workings or stumblings of the Soviet economy, matters of that kind –

Almost not like spying at all. Little more than indiscreet gossip, careless talk which was overheard by strangers.

Priabin could make himself believe that. She was not an important agent, hardly an agent at all. Revenge, disgust with the system that preferred weapons to a wheelchair, had made her do it, were her motives. He could understand that. How much the suicide of her husband, in unexplained circumstances years before she met Baranovich and his damned wheelchair, had to do with it, he had no idea. He preferred the motive of revenge. It gave her a certain honest dignity.

Recrimination. He was certain she did not suspect he knew. He blamed, even hated himself for not telling her, for not weaning her away from the addiction, for not saving her. But he dare not risk losing her . . .

He stood up and crossed the room swiftly to kneel by the bed. Very gently, he kissed each flattened breast, each erect nipple. Then he continued to kneel, as if partaking in a further religious ceremony. He could not let her go, but he could not let her be discovered. He must speak to her –

He could never admit his knowledge –

Angrily, he stood up. She stirred and moaned lightly, half-turning away from him. The glow of the lamp fell on the fine down along her arm. He watched, then walked swiftly into the bathroom. He did not switch on the light because he had no wish to see himself in the long, bevelled mirror. Instead, he fumbled in the poor light that came from the open doorway, found a glass and filled it with tepid water.

Recrimination. *He must do something –* !

But, he would lose her –

His mouth was dry and the taste of onions was making him feel nauseous.

Whispering near the door, as it squeaked shut once more. Gant came awake immediately, shocked that he had dozed, making a vast effort to stop his left arm rising from the bed to display his watch. He breathed in, slowly and deeply, and listened.

Dressing change . . . who? He was sufficiently propped up by the pillows to see the two figures at the table without lifting his head. Starched cap, long hair tied back. The male nurse had put down his book. Gant saw him nod, then the woman began moving across the line of sight towards – his bed? – no, the bandaged patient, the mummy. Gant relaxed, and immediately the sense of isolation returned. He did not know how he had slept, or for how long. How had he been capable of sleep?

He could see the nurse's back as she bent over the second bed from his own. She had flicked on the overhead light. The mummified head murmured. It might have been a stifled groan. Gant watched crepe bandage being unrolled, stretched upwards by a slim arm in the muted light. Something glinted, and the arm fell. The mummy murmured again in a frightened tone, as if someone intended him harm. Something glinted, and clicked lightly.

More clicking, like the sound of distant hedge-clippers . . .

Gant felt his body tensing itself without his will. His hands curled and uncurled, his arms lifted slightly, testing their own weight. His body felt compact, less weary. Bruised, though. The drugs had worn off, leaving the pain of his brief, violent beating.

The nurse was murmuring, the mummy seemed to protest. Then her arm stretched again in the light. Then the clicking noise, and something slim and metal gleamed. And, at the moment of realisation, as his thoughts caught up with his body, he heard footsteps coming down the corridor towards the ward, and he moved.

One chance, only one . . .

He flicked the bedclothes away, rolled, wondered for an instant

379

what strength he had, and then rolled across the next door bed, his right hand reaching for her arm, his body closing with hers, knocking the breath out of her. Gleam of the scissors, her frightened mouth and eyes turning to him, the eyes of the mummy and the half-exposed, purple cheek and swollen mouth. Then he dragged the nurse sideways so that they did not topple on the patient, and whirled round –

"Don't – !" he yelled in Russian, feeling her legs buckle but holding the snatched scissors at the girl's throat, the blade imitating a slight downward stabbing motion. "Don't *think* about it!"

The male nurse was on his feet, his hand reaching into his short white coat to where a breast pocket or a shoulder holster would be. Then he was bumped forward as the doors opened behind him. *The doctor* –

Gant recognised the man and fought off the weakness that followed his realisation of how late he had left it. He moved forward with the nurse in front of him, even as the doctor was asking what was happening and breaking off in mid-sentence as he understood.

"Over here!" Gant yelled, pushing the reluctant nurse forward. The doctor snapped on the main strip lights, which flickered and then glared on the scene. There were two plain-clothed guards with him. A stretcher waited behind them; he could see it through a gap where one of the guards still held the door half-open. "Move!" His voice sounded panicky. His legs felt weak, even shuffling at that snail's pace. The scissors gleamed. He pressed the point of them down, touching the girl's throat. It would not take a minute more, perhaps only seconds, before they moved out of shock and drew their guns and killed the girl and took him for interrogation as if nothing had occurred.

The male nurse moved slowly, reluctantly. Three yards separated them now, then only two, but Gant hesitated because the manoeuvre seemed too complicated. He lacked the necessary coordination. The man's eyes were quick and alert, the girl had gone soft and unresisting in his arms. Both of them were beginning to think he was already beaten. In the man's face Gant could already detect his anticipation of what might happen to the girl when he made his move, and his lack of concern.

One of the guards was moving his hand very slowly to the breast of his jacket. The doctor, sensing the approaching moment of violence, had made a single step to one side, away from the doors. Two yards, a yard-and-a-half –

Now – !

His left hand gripped the girl's arm, his arm across her breasts. He spun her away from him, flinging her to the left. Then he kicked at the male nurse with his bare right foot, almost losing his balance, striking at the groin. He had already dropped the scissors to the floor. He grabbed the nurse, hoisted him upright, fumbled in the man's coat, withdrew the Makarov. Awkwardly, he juggled the pistol until it pointed towards the group at the doors.

"Back off!" he snapped. "Out! Move!" He waggled the gun in their direction.

The doctor was flat against the wall. He slid along it and slipped through the doors behind the two guards. Gant turned to the male nurse, who was groaning softly, still clutching his genitals, and prodded him through the doors –

Alarm, hand reaching for it –

Gant moved, bringing the pistol's barrel down on the extended wrist of one of the guards as he reached towards the wall at the side of the door. The man groaned as something cracked. The violence thrilled Gant, made him feel stronger. As the guard slumped against the wall, Gant kicked his legs away and the man sat in a moaning, untidy heap. Gant waggled the gun at the remaining guard and the doctor.

What to do – ?

Guide them – but what about the alarms – ? Guide – alarms . . .

"Move!" he said. "Go on – move! Get out of here!" There did not seem to be any other alarms down the corridor. "Take him – get out." He indicated the guard sitting against the wall, eyes malevolent, one hand clutching the other like a precious, damaged possession. The second guard bent, helped the injured man to his feet, and then the two of them began to hurry down the corridor, the doctor following them, casting occasional glances over his shoulder.

Gant held the nurse against the wall, arm across the man's throat. The girl had not emerged from the ward, but he knew she would sound the alarm the moment the corridor was clear – he knew, too, that the guards were hurrying to the nearest alarm . . . the male nurse understood. His eyes anticipated what he might be able to inflict on Gant before the doctors and interrogators ordered him to desist.

Which way – ?

He gripped the nurse's shoulder, pressing his forearm against the man's windpipe. Which way –? His feet were cold on the linoleum. He was aware of his bare legs.

The alarm sounded above their heads. Someone had triggered every alarm in the building; overlapping, continuous ringing.

"Which way up?" he barked. "Up to the top of the house? Which way?"

He released his grip on the man. The alarm just above their heads was deafening. The nurse hesitated – then shrugged. It was no more than a postponement of his intentions towards the American. He pointed along the corridor, his body adopting a submissive stance. Gant motioned him forward with the pistol. At first, Gant's legs moved reluctantly, and then he was running, his bare feet slapping on the linoleum, the gun clutched in both hands.

At the end of the corridor, the nurse turned left. The ether-smell and the cream walls they had left behind suddenly clashed with ornamental urns and carpets and upright chairs against the panelled walls. A short gallery overlooking the main hall – the clatter of boots on the tiles below – and then they were climbing a steep wooden staircase that twisted back on itself, then climbed again. Gant glimpsed another corridor, wide and panelled. Heavy, unrestored oil paintings retreated along the walls. Snow-bound hunting scenes, a rich, faded carpet, a frowning, heavy Tsarist face, then more stairs. Bare walls, old plain wallpaper swollen with damp. Colder. His feet resented the uncarpeted, dirty floor of the next corridor.

The nurse halted. The gun prodded his back. He half-turned. Gant struck his shoulder with the pistol. The man groaned.

"Where?"

The alarms were all distant now. He heard no sounds of pursuit. He caught the musty, warm smell of animal cages. The nurse went ahead of him down the corridor. He opened a door. Ether-smell, overhead lamps, an operating table. A surgery or another inter-rogation room. They passed into a pharmacy, then into a room from which the animal-straw scent emerged strongly. Monkeys chattered as the lights were switched on – Gant realised the man was leaving a trail of turned-on lights for others to follow, but ignored the danger.

Rats in cages, an operating table, loudspeakers, instruments. Monkeys. In one cage, a cat mewed pitifully. An electrode emerged from its shaved, plastered head. Gant shuddered with the cold of the sight. The room itself was warm, the smell overpowering. Straw and urine and food. A bird chirped somewhere.

"Undress!" Gant ordered. The nurse watched him, weighed him. Gant felt himself swaying on his feet, his breath coming heavily, raggedly. "Undress – clothes on the floor!" Still the man hesitated. "Do it! I don't give a shit whether you live or die, I just want your clothes!"

The man's resolve snapped and he undressed swiftly. At a movement of the pistol, he kicked the little heap of clothes towards Gant. Gant watched him. The cat mewed again. Gant glanced at it, its protruding electrode touching the wire of the cage. Its food was uneaten. The nurse moved. Gant struck out with the barrel of the Makarov, hardly moving his eyes from the cat's gaze. The nurse held his head and stumbled against a cage of white mice, spilling them onto the floor. They scattered and clambered over his underclothed body, making for the room's corners. The nurse lay still, blood seeping from his temple down the side of his face. Hurriedly, Gant climbed into the jeans, then the shirt. He leaned against a table as he put on the shoes that were at least a size too large. Then he unbuttoned the white coat. He brushed dust from the uniform. Still the nurse did not move. A mouse emerged from behind him, sniffed the air and the body, then skittered away beneath one of the tables.

Gant turned swiftly and left the room, switching off the lights. As he closed the door, he heard the monkey-chatter die, heard the scamper of mice-paws. He switched off the pharmacy lights, then the lights of the interrogation room-surgery. As he closed the door behind him, at the moment when he wanted only to pause and recover his breath, someone turned into the corridor. Booted feet. He looked round wildly.

A uniformed KGB man strode towards him. The Kalashnikov in his hands hesitated to draw a bead on a white hospital coat.

"Anything up here?" he asked.

Gant shook his head. "Only the mice," he managed to say.

The guard laughed. "The bloody American's loose," he said. "You know?" Gant nodded. The guard was already reaching into his breast pocket. The packet of cigarettes emerged before Gant could react. "Smoke?" Gant shook his head. He was sufficiently aware to keep his bruised temple out of the guard's direct line of sight. The man struck a match, the cigarette's acrid smoke was pungent in the bare corridor. The man smoked secretively, as if at every moment he expected the appearance of one of his officers. Seconds extended to a half-minute, three-quarters . . .

"I'd better get back down," Gant explained.

"Plenty down there rushing around — say you heard a noise up here . . . thorough search." He grinned, his stony face opening as if a rock had cracked apart. "They like that, officers — " He spat, without malice, more out of habit.

"I'd better go — " Gant said.

The guard shrugged. "I'll take a couple of minutes more," he said.

Gant hesitated. If he left the man here —? The cigarette had not burned halfway to its cardboard tube. Two, three minutes —? The nurse . . .

"You all right?" the guard asked. Gant turned directly to him. Immediately, he realised the guard was staring at his bruised temple

383

and swollen lip. Something slow but certain began to form behind the man's eyes.

"Yes, sure," Gant said, then struck at the man's face. The guard half-stepped, half-fell backwards against the wall. There had seemed no strength in the blow. Gant moved inside the rifle and struck again, and again, his fists beginning to flail at the man because he felt he would be unable to overpower him.

The guard slid down the wall to end in a slumped crouch, rifle between his knees. Gant ran, clattered down the first flight of stairs, glimpsed the ranks of oil paintings again, took the second flight as quickly as he could in the slopping shoes, and reached the gallery overlooking the main hall. He almost collided with a man in uniform. Lieutenant. KGB.

"What is it?" the officer asked. Someone else in uniform emerged from another room. The alarms were loud. Gant shook his head.

"I thought I saw him – " he began.

"Where? Up there?"

"No, coming down this way . . ." it was just a glimpse. I could have been wrong . . ."

"Very well."

There were four people on the gallery now, two in uniform, one in a white coat, one in a suit. Gant did not recognise any of the faces, but knew he could not be certain. He did not know how many people had seen him since his arrival.

"Are you the one he escaped from?" the officer asked.

Gant nodded, shamefaced. "Yes."

"I thought so," the lieutenant sneered, nodding at the livid bruise. "Serves you right. God help you if they don't catch up with him – your mother won't know you!" He turned, motioning to the guard in uniform. "Up these stairs – *he* might have missed him!" Laughing, the officer followed the guards up the stairs.

Gant looked over the gallery, down into the main hall. Two men in white coats were moving up the sweep of the marble staircase to the first floor. Someone who might have been the American general during his interrogation followed behind them. He moved slowly and angrily.

Gant walked swiftly along the gallery, opened a door at the end of it, and found himself at the head of a flight of narrow stairs. He clattered down them, one hand bracing himself against the bare plaster of the wall because he was increasingly afraid to make demands upon his body. It seemed like the fuel leak in the Firefox, the gauges in the red, waiting for the first, hesitant sound of the engines dying. He felt he might suddenly seize up, be unable to move.

The stairs twisted to the right, then descended again. Ground level – ? A narrow corridor, quarry-tiled. He opened the door at the end of it. A room that might once have been a vast kitchen was now dotted with armchairs, a television set, radio, a still-smoking cigarette which had fallen onto the carpet from the ashtray where it had been left. He stepped on it, grinding it into the carpet –

They wouldn't rescue the monkeys and the cat if the place caught fire . . .

He left the room by a door at the far end of it, knocking over a half-full glass of beer as he brushed past a small table, then he crossed a narrow passage. Through frosted glass, moonlight shone; almost impossibly, it was an outside door. A shudder ran through his body. Coats, uniform greatcoats, scarves and hats hung from pegs inside the door. He shuffled through them, found a donkey jacket, snatched at a bright scarf, and tried the outside door.

It opened. He slipped through, closed it softly behind him. The alarms were still loud. Outside alarms –

He judged himself to be at the rear of the house. Blocks of sombre flats marched away from him. Lights from the house spilled onto the gravel that surrounded the building. Here, the dark hedges were replaced by a high stone wall, against which a car was parked. Gant ran to it.

The wind was cold once he moved out of the lee of the house. He shrugged on the coat and wrapped the scarf around his face. He thrust the pistol into his right-hand pocket. He tried each door of the car. All of them were locked.

The door opened behind him. He turned slowly, attempting to deflect suspicion. Two men – no, a third armed man behind them, in uniform. More lights flickered on in the ground floor rooms, throwing their glow at him.

Vladimirov stepped forward, the guard moving swiftly to his side, his rifle raised to his shoulder and aimed directly at Gant. Vladimirov's face was chilled by the wind and half in shadow, but Gant saw his smile of undiluted pleasure. Hopelessly, he tugged at the door handle behind him. Locked.

Two men at one corner of the building, rounding it, slowing, then moving forward. A solitary figure at the other end of the building. The wall behind him, Vladimirov in front –

Vladimirov moved forward, closing on Gant. The guard kept his rifle at his shoulder. His aim did not waver. Two white-coated doctors, emerging from the doorway, shivering with the raw cold. Two plainclothed KGB men followed them.

He turned, then, and mounted the bonnet of the car, feeling the weakness of his legs as he clambered onto the car's roof. The thin metal flexed beneath his weight. A bullet smacked flatly into the walls, inches from his face.

Vladimirov screamed at the guard. "His *legs!* His legs – don't *kill* him!"

He turned to the wall, elated as if by alcohol or drugs. He jumped, scrabbled, his fingers clutching then being skinned by the rough stone as he slid back to the roof of the car.

"Stop him!"

Footsteps running on the gravel. He did not bother to look, knowing there was time for only one more effort. He stood up, swayed – heard footsteps skidding only feet away and heavy shoes striking the metal of the car's bonnet – and jumped.

Clung, heaved, felt the weakness again, heaved once more, his face sliding inch by inch up the stone, then the wind hitting into his face as it cleared the wall. Something touched, then grabbed at his left leg. He lashed out. Two bullets smacked against the stone near his left hand, then he heaved himself astride the wall. Looking down, he blanched at the drop. Two more bullets, the heat of one of the rounds searing his leg below the knee. He swung both legs over the wall, and dropped towards the pavement. A car passed, headlights on. A quiet side street –

He crumpled as he hit the pavement, sitting down hard. He questioned his ankles, waiting for the pain of a sprain or twist. Then he stood up. Looked up. A face appeared. He drew the Makarov and fired at it. The bullet chipped dust from the capping stone. The head disappeared. He glanced up and down the street. Ill-lit canyons opened between blocks of flats. The street lamps were dim and few. He ran across the street, sensing the moment he reached deep shadow.

Sensing, too, the opening of gates, the switching on of engines, the beginnings of pursuit. His leg ached but he thought the flesh only scorched. He had escaped. He did not consider the alien city, not yet – only the concealing night as he ran.

"The Hercules flies south along the airway – my people drop by parachute, the Hercules drops off the Russian radars as if landing at Ivalo, then doubles back below the radar net and makes a low-level pass – booting these five pallets out of the cargo door as it goes . . ." Waterford broke off, and turned from Aubrey to the pilot. "One smoke flare enough of a marker for you?" he asked. The pilot nodded. Waterford returned his gaze to Aubrey. "Buckholz and the non-parachutists will come in on the two Lynx helicopters we've got here." Without even the trace of a smile, he added, "Simple."

Aubrey was nodding, abstractedly. When Waterford had finished speaking, he looked up. "Very well." He glanced at his watch. "You'll be ready for take-off in . . . ?"

"One hour maximum," the pilot answered.

"Good." Aubrey's gaze traversed the interior of the transport aircraft. The SBS men under Waterford's command were now coming abroad, bringing their weapons, packs, skis and diving equipment with them. In conjunction with the WRAF Air Load-master, Brooke and another marine officer were checking the manifest of the equipment the aircraft had brought from Scampton. Aubrey wondered whether or not he should address the marines.

"Sir – " It was the radio operator.

"What is it?"

"London requests immediate signals contact, sir – it's Mr. Shelley. Utmost priority."

"I'll come at once." He crossed the cargo compartment of the Hercules with an agitated swiftness, then seated himself in front of the console. He waited until the operator nodded, and then he began speaking. "Peter – Aubrey here. What is the problem?"

He waited impatiently. He had sanctioned the use of high-speed transmission rather than one-time encoding because of the greater ease and speed of communication, voice to voice. Yet still the conversations seemed endless, punctuated by silences which fearful guesswork attempted to fill. A light indicated that Shelley's voice was now being recorded at high-speed within the console. The operator dabbed at keys, and he heard Shelley's voice; breathless, as if not quite slowed to normal speed on the tape.

"Sir – it's Gant. He's escaped from the Unit on the Mira Prospekt . . ." Shelley seemed to pause, as if for a reply, then appeared to remind himself that he was not at the other end of a telephone line. "We had someone watching the Unit, and they witnessed the alarms, the whole fuss . . . he must have got over the wall at the back, but our man couldn't find hide nor hair of him. But there was complete and utter panic among the KGB. A huge search is underway already . . ."

Shelley faltered rather than stopped. Immediately, Aubrey said: "Peter – wait until I get Charles Buckholz here, please. You're certain there's an extensive search for him?" He turned and raised his voice. "Waterford, get Buckholz – at once, please."

Waterford disappeared immediately through one of the paratroop doors in the side of the fuselage. Buckholz was supervising the loading of the two Lynx helicopters, parked near the Hercules on the ramp of Kirkenes airfield. Aubrey's fingers drummed on the side of the console. It sounded as hollow as an empty drum.

Shelley's voice came back soon after the red light flicked on once more.

"In answer to your question, sir, the British and American embassies are bottled up – no explanation, no official contact, but the cars are outside in force. They're waiting for the lines to go dead any minute now. Our low-grade people still on the streets are ringing in with reports of high-level KGB activity – *saturation* cover, was the term David Edgecliffe used. Shall I hang on now, sir?"

Aubrey turned on the swivel chair. Buckholz, his face half-hidden by the fur trimming of a white parka hood, clambered through the paratroop door, Waterford behind him. He hurried to Aubrey's side.

"He's got out –!" Aubrey blurted. "Damn it, but he's got out of that unit – they're looking for him all over Moscow!" Buckholz grinned and slapped Aubrey's shoulder heavily. But, even before he could speak, Aubrey clicked his fingers – a dull sound in his heavy gloves – and said excitedly, "Saturation cover, the Moscow Head of Station reports – you realise what that means, Charles? Do you *realise*? My *God* . . ."

"What?"

"They don't know – they didn't *break* him –!" He gripped the sleeve of Buckholz's parka, tugging at the material. "If they *knew*, they wouldn't have every available man on the streets of Moscow looking for him – they *need* him!"

"That's just a guess . . . they don't want us to get him back –"

"Squadron Leader!" Aubrey called to the pilot of the Hercules. "Contact Eastoe – I want an up-to-the-minute report on border activity." The pilot nodded and began moving forward towards the flight deck. "I don't believe he's told them, Charles – I don't believe they *know*!"

"It's only a matter of time, Kenneth – he can't survive on the streets for long. Can we get someone to him?"

Aubrey turned to the console. The operator nodded. "Peter, what are the chances of finding him?"

He waited, listening to Buckholz's heavy breathing, his eyes willing the red light to wink off.

Then Shelley was speaking once more. "Edgecliffe's signal was very clear, sir – and I checked at once. Every known contact, every member of the embassy staff outside the building, is already under surveillance. Edgecliffe also reminded me," Shelley's voice hesitated, and then added in a more mumbled tone: "We – used up the best people two days ago – especially Pavel. He's still very angry about losing Pavel – "

"To the devil with Edgecliffe's anger!" The operator flicked at the keyboard to try to overtake Aubrey's unexpected, rushed reply. "Is there no one? Do they have any idea where he might be?" As his questions were transmitted, he turned to Buckholz. "You realise that the time-limit is expanding, Charles? Gant has given us a stay of execution." The pilot appeared from the flight deck, shutting the door behind him. "Any activity?" Aubrey asked.

"No change in the situation."

"See, Charles – they don't know!"

"Where does that leave us? They could pick him up any time. Maybe we ought to pray he gets run over by a bus!"

Shelley's voice anticipated Aubrey's reply. "No information, sir. Moscow Station personnel simply can't move – it's the same for the Americans. We have a few low-grade watchers who Edgecliffe has been using, but no one he could use to give help, even if he knew where to look. He's got out, but that seems to be as far as anyone can go, sir. We can't do anything for him."

Aubrey stood up, punching his right hand into the palm of his left; a dull concussion. He looked almost wildly around the crowded, murmurously noisy interior of the Hercules. Breath smoked. Runway and perimeter lights gleamed beyond the lowered cargo ramp. It was as if Aubrey expected to find a volunteer from among the marines and RAF personnel around him. His eyes rested on Buckholz.

"We must do something, Charles – something to try to keep him out of their hands! Now we have this slim chance – now we might be given all the time we need . . . he mustn't go back into the Unit!"

"I agree – so? What the hell do you expect me to do about it?"

"Think, Charles – *think*!"

"What? Kenneth, what in hell do you *want* me to think?"

Aubrey strutted a few intense, excited steps from Buckholz, then returned to the console. "Peter – do we have anybody . . . anybody we can use?"

He waited in silence, his brow creased, his face intent, until Shelley replied.

"Not a native Russian who's capable of finding him, making contact, shielding him, and none of our officials could get near him. We might be able to locate him, with a great deal of luck, but there's no one we could trust to take care of him – in whichever way you wish –" Shelley added in a softer, almost apologetic voice.

Aubrey wrinkled his nose in disgust. "I'm not having him killed!" he snapped, turning on Buckholz so that he understood his decision.

"Even if you find him, you mean?" Buckholz observed with heavy irony. "Let's face facts, Kenneth. You're hamstrung – our two services are hamstrung in Moscow. We don't know where he is, where he might go . . . and we couldn't reach him to help him if we did!"

Aubrey stretched out his hands imploringly, but his face was flushed with anger. "Then give me someone who *can* help him! Charles, the CIA must have someone – a Russian with the resource, the nerves and the intelligence to help Gant? Give me one of your Category-A Sources, Charles!"

"I can't authorise that, Kenneth."

"To save Gant – to save all this, perhaps . . .?" His arms encompassed the entire contents of the cargo compartment; men, equipment, purpose. "Give me one of your Sources. Someone with freedom of movement. Someone who can travel!"

Buckholz was silent for some time. Aubrey allowed him to pace the cargo compartment, his face thoughtful. His mittened hands rubbed at his cheeks or alternately held his chin. Aubrey instructed Shelley to remain in full contact, and to wait, then he spent the endless minutes of Buckholz's silence furiously reviewing his own extensive knowledge of the CIA's Moscow operations.

They were avid for information, and lavish in their corruption and persuasion of agents. They had dozens of Russians in key positions who supplied them with high-grade information. They were designated Category-A Sources. Any one of them might be young enough, resourceful enough to locate and assist Gant . . . Get him out of Moscow . . .?

But, would Charles agree? Would he endanger one of the CIA's key Sources for the sake of *possibly* finding, *possibly* assisting Gant?

Eventually, Buckholz stood in front of him once more. He nodded, slightly and only once.

"Source *Burgoyne*," he said enigmatically. "I'll have to confirm with Langley . . . Source *Burgoyne* seems the most – expendable." He flinched as he saw the look on Aubrey's face, then snapped: "Like Fenton and Pavel and even Baranovich – you were pretty *wasteful* there, Kenneth."

"Damn you, Charles," Aubrey breathed, but his face was white with admission and a surprising self-disgust. "*Burgoyne* is less important than your other Sources, I suppose?" he asked acidly. "How many Category-A Sources are there at present, Charles?"

"Maybe thirty – scattered through the ministries, the Secretariat, the Supreme Soviet, top industrial concerns, the Narodny Bank –"

"And *Bourgoyne* is one of the least significant, I take it?"

"You got it. I – we've tried to persuade her to request –"

"*Her*?"

"Right. A woman. We've tried to get her to move into more

sensitive areas for years now – she won't. She's useful, but she's not *crucial*, as you put it. You want her or not?"

Aubrey pondered for a moment, then brightened: "Yes, I'll take her. A female companion would avert suspicion, and she must have intelligence and resource or you wouldn't have tried to get her into more useful work. She can travel with some ease. Yes, I'll take her. Does the codename *Burgoyne* suffice to wake the sleeper?"

"It does. Let me talk to Shelley. I'll supply the telephone number. It's then up to you what you do with her. She's a limited asset and no longer our concern – she'll be all yours!" Buckholz grinned crookedly.

Aubrey moved away from the console. Fenton, Pavel, and now Source *Burgoyne* . . .

"What's her name?" he asked without turning around.

"Anna – Anna Akhmerovna. She's a widow. Touching forty. She has almost complete freedom of movement. Just one thing, though. She lives with a KGB officer, if I remember correctly."

Aubrey turned on his heel. "*What – ?*"

"She's the one you're going to get, Kenneth. Langley would never agree to any of the others."

Aubrey turned away. His mind raced, skipping over crevasses and chasms that opened beneath his optimism, threatening to swallow it. If Gant could be saved – ? Edgecliffe could work up a suitable escape route, provide good papers, the woman was good cover . . .

Buckholz completed his instructions to Shelley, then addressed Aubrey. "You still want London, Kenneth?"

"I do!" He faced Buckholz once more. "I'll save him if I can," he murmured. "And her – I'll save her, too!" It was mere bravado and he knew it, as did the American, who merely shrugged.

"I don't think you can win this one, Kenneth. You'll just be losing the Company a useful agent. You'll get *Burgoyne* killed along with Gant."

"No I won't, Charles!"

Buckholz snatched off his mittens angrily, and held up the fingers of his left hand, splayed. He counted them off with his right forefinger, folding them into his palm at each of the names he recited.

"Fenton – Pavel – Baranovich – Semelovsky – Kreshin – Glazunov – the old man at the warehouse, I forget his name . . ."

"Damn you, be quiet!" Again, Aubrey's face was white and his mouth trembled. Appalled, he witnessed the appearance of guilt in his mind. It made his heart race, his stomach turn. Guilt – Shakily, he said, "I will atone, Charles – I'll save Gant *and* your Source *Burgoyne*! Now, let me talk to Shelley – !"

*   *   *

"Yes, Comrade Deputy Chairman — yes, of course. I'll come at once!" Priabin put down the bedside receiver and turned to Anna, his face flushed with an almost boyish pride and self-importance. Anna watched him, watched his innocent pleasure spreading in a broad grin.

"What is it?" she asked sleepily, glancing at the travel clock on her bedside cabinet, propped open in its leather case. Two o'clock. Then she yawned, as if the reminder of the lateness of the hour and her interrupted sleep had wearied her.

"Orders," he said almost blithely, getting out of bed and opening the sliding door of the fitted wardrobe.

"You're going out?"

"I am. Panic stations — " he answered, hoisting his uniform trousers then pulling his shirt from its hanger. He buttoned it hastily, looking down at each button as he did so. He talked as he dressed. "Your friend the American pilot is on the loose — seems they mislaid him . . ." He looked up and grinned. His tie was draped over a chair. He snatched it up and began to knot it.

"What happened?" She was leaning on one elbow, her small breasts invitingly exposed, nipples erect in the coolness of the bedroom. She shivered, then, and rubbed her goose-pimpled arms. Then she stretched. Priabin hunted for his jacket in the wardrobe.

"Some monstrous cock-up, I expect. Deputy Chairmen don't give explanations over the telephone to newly-promoted colonels." He thrust his arms into the jacket, and buttoned it. "Where's my cap?"

"When will you be back?"

He shrugged. "Can't say, love. I'm appointed one of the co-ordinators of the search. They've got saturation cover on the streets as a matter of routine, now they want people like me to sort it out . . ." He stopped smiling. "And people to blame, no doubt, if he gets away. Still, we colonels must bear our appointed loads — " The smile was back. He moved to the bed, bent and kissed her. She folded her arms behind his neck, holding him in the kiss.

"Take care," she murmured.

"I'll watch my back." He grinned. "I suppose you're a little bit on his side, aren't you — with your attitude to the project?"

She shook her head vehemently. "Not if he endangers you," she said.

He winked and crossed to the door. "See you," he said, and opened the door. "I love you." He closed the door behind him. Anna heard the front door of the apartment close quietly a few moments later. Doubtless, he had paused only to collect his holster and greatcoat from the rack in the hall.

She shivered, rubbing her arms again. She swung her legs out of bed, crossed to the door and took down her dressing-gown. Warm and sensible, but silk-lined. She buttoned it quickly.

As she crossed the hall, she listened at Maxim's door. Satisfied he had not awoken, she went into the kitchen. Her anxiety at Priabin's departure was usual, even though disproportionate. To her, every departure was only the prelude to a meeting where he would be ordered to arrest her.

She turned on one of the small strip-lights beneath the kitchen cabinets. It gave the room a hard but confined glow which she could tolerate. It preserved a quality of secretive darkness the room had possessed when she entered it. She switched on the percolator, having checked that enough coffee remained in it.

What was it – ? What had disturbed her so much? It wasn't simply her recurring nightmare of discovery and arrest . . . no. It was something – the arrival of fate as palpably as a knock on the door. Yes, that was it. A sense of fate, renewed by the American's escape. It had been with her ever since Dmitri was transferred to security on the Bilyarsk project. Baranovich's wheelchair had begun her double-life – Dmitri had moved closer to that double-life when he was transferred. Now, leading the hunt for the American, he seemed in some vague and shadowy way to threaten her. There *was* something fateful about the whole affair.

Of course, Dmitri knew. She had known for months. She had learned to live with that terror; it had been like a mad dog in the back garden, gradually tamed and thus ignored. He would not give her away and therefore lose her – not yet, at least, and perhaps not ever.

To go *back*, she thought bitterly, pouring the heated coffee into a thick brown mug. Just to go *back* . . .

The futile recrimination wailed like a lost child in her head. Baranovich, and before that, her husband. Suicide because he had lost his academic post – *samizdat* copies of banned writings in his locked drawer at the university –

She had had to live with the knowledge that he had killed himself to protect her. She had known nothing until the KGB told her, after she had found him dead in the bath, afloat in red water. *Samizdats*, meetings, planned protests, anti-Soviet activities. A dangerous criminal, her loving, gentle, innocent husband? It was impossible to believe; impossible, later, not to realise that he had the courage to face them, to undergo imprisonment. He had killed himself to protect her, to free her from the stigma of being the wife of a prisoner, a *zek* in the Gulag –

Gradually, very, very gradually, she had returned to life and to her career from that dark tunnel where he had left her. And then Baranovich, corrupted forcibly from his idealistic work – his wheelchair – to build a warplane more destructive than anything ever known . . .

That had been the breaking-point. Not her husband's suicide but the destruction of Baranovich's project. She had made her first contact with an American diplomat-agent at the next embassy cocktail party she attended.

And then Dmitri, and Dmitri working to protect that damned, infernal aircraft project, and Dmitri discovering her double-life –

And now hunting the American. It *was* fate. She could not disbelieve it. It was a time of ill-omen –

If only they would let her go, if only she could go back. Her head cried like a lost child – if only . . .

The coffee scalded her mouth as she sipped it, then spilled onto her dressing-gown as the telephone startled her. She put down the mug, staring at her quivering hands. Then she snatched at the receiver hanging on the kitchen wall, as if to protect her sleeping son from its intrusion.

"Yes?" she asked breathlessly.

"*Burgoyne*, is that you," a voice asked in English.

"What – ?" she breathed. "I – I'm afraid I don't understand . . ." She spoke very deliberately in Russian.

"But I do," the voice said. It sounded English – but if it was, then why not an American accent? She felt panic mount in her, filling her throat.

"Who is this, please?" she asked as calmly as she could.

"Listen carefully, *Burgoyne* – my name is Edgecliffe, British Embassy. This line is secure at my end, and I know yours is not tapped – I also know that Colonel Priabin left the apartment ten minutes ago. You're alone, except for your son . . ." The details were as palpably nauseating as hands pawing her, caressing her body beneath the dressing-gown.

"What do you *want*?" Now, at last, she spoke in English.

"Your help. Please listen carefully. You may confirm my identity and instructions with your Case Officer, if you wish. When I have finished. You've been loaned to us, *Burgoyne*, by your present employers, to do a special job."

"What – ?"

"Colonel Priabin, no doubt, has been summoned to the Centre to take charge of some part of the search for the escaped American pilot – we want your help to find him before your lover does . . ." There was a chuckle at the other end of the line. "We're a little limited as far as resources are concerned – we need your help."

"Go to hell!" Suddenly, she was frighteningly angry, hardly able to speak, so full was her throat, so tense was her whole body. "Go to hell, whoever you are!"

"Listen to me, *Burgoyne*!" The Englishman snapped. "I don't have time to play games. You'll do as you're told. Otherwise, well, you know what might happen to you – enough of that, however. It will be up to you to get our American friend out of Moscow, once we've located him. I'll have papers for the two of you, travel permits, everything – and a full scenario in a matter of hours. All you have to do is be ready to move when I tell you."

He fell silent, and into that quiet Anna dropped the small pebble of her voice. "And what if – if Colonel Priabin catches him?"

"Then we won't require your services. You can carry on with your life as before."

"But what do I tell *him* – what about my *son* – ?"

"I'm sure you can discover a sick relative somewhere if you try hard enough. You have many friends, I'm told. Send your son to stay with one of them. Or with your father, perhaps?"

"Just like that – ?"

"Everything is just like that, I'm afraid. You don't have a choice. None at all. You must comply with our wishes – I'm sure you realise that. I won't even bother to assure you that if the KGB recapture the American they will get back their aircraft – the one you loathe so much. Even though that is true, it isn't necessary to persuade you, *Burgoyne*, because you *must* do as we say and you are intelligent enough to realise it."

"But – how? *How*?" Anna asked.

"The details have yet to be decided. Simply prepare yourself for a journey, perhaps by train. Be ready to move as soon as it becomes necessary."

"I *can't* –" she wailed.

"You must. And, who knows? With your connection with Colonel Priabin, our American might be safer with you than anyone else we might have been loaned – mm? Goodbye for the present, *Burgoyne*. I'll be in touch – soon."

The line clicked, then purred. Anna sat for some moments, staring into the receiver, as if the man who owned the voice might emerge from it, oozing smokily out like an appearing jinn. One hot, angry, frightened tear fell on her upturned wrist. Then she lifted her head to the pine-panelled ceiling of the kitchen, and howled like an animal in pain.

It was the absence of pedestrians that worried him most. In the small hours, he might have expected the streets to have emptied, but there had been no crowds and little traffic from the time he had vanished into the dark canyons between the endless blocks of apartments. It had taken him more than two hours to work his way back into the centre of Moscow via side-streets and alleys and lanes and waste ground. And all the time he did so, he knew he was moving slowly but certainly into the mouth of the trawling net the KGB and the police had cast for him.

Sirens, prowling cars, foot patrols, even helicopters. From the Mira Prospekt he had moved east, then north, then west, using the deeper darkness of open spaces, sports complexes, recreation parks, climbing their frosty railings, resting in the deep shadow of trees; fighting his rising panic and sense of isolation like two attackers in the darkness. He passed through Dzerzhinsky Park which contained the Ostankino television tower; the park surrounding the army museum; the zoo park. He kept away from the streets as much as he could; avoided streetlights.

The shops of the Kalinin Prospekt were lit like fishtanks. Above the windows, ranks of unlit offices marched towards Tchaikovsky Street and the American Embassy. Gant knew, though he suppressed the knowledge, that it would be guarded – barred to him. But he needed a destination, an objective. It was the only one he could enlarge in his mind and store with the comforts of safety, help, food, sleep. During his two hours of walking and skulking and scuttling across lit spaces and shrinking into doorways and behind trees, the embassy had become furnished and warmed in his imagination. There was no need to imagine anything after its doors opened. When the door closed behind him, he would be safe. It would be over.

He stared down the Kalinin Prospekt as if studying a minefield. Two foot patrols, two parked police cars, another cruising slowly towards him from the direction of the Kalinin Bridge. It would be a gauntlet he would not survive. He turned right, into the sparsely-lit Malaya Molchanovka Street. Ranks of tall offices and department stores retreated towards Tchaikovsky Street and the bridge on the left. The street was empty, except for the quick darting shape of a cat crossing the road. Gant hurried, hands thrust into the pockets of the short coat, the cap he had found in one of the pockets pulled down over his eyes. He had long abandoned the white coat. His heels were raw from the rubbing of the too-big shoes, and the pain in his calf where the dog had bitten him had resurfaced now that the effect of the drugs and sedatives had disappeared. He stamped out the memory of the frozen lake and the Lynx helicopter only yards from him, waiting to save him.

He heard music coming from a still-lit window as he passed a low apartment block opposite the rear of a cinema. A child cried somewhere, startled from sleep. A car turned the corner from the Kalinin Prospekt behind him, and he forced himself not to run but to turn into the entrance of another apartment block. The outer door was not locked. He pushed his way inside. The foyer smelt of cabbage and greasy cooking. He flattened against the wall and waited.

The car drifted slowly along the street. For a moment, a spotlight played on the entrance, washing over the walls of the foyer. Then it was gone. Quivering, he returned to the street. The police car had turned off. He hurried on, head down, breath smoking around him, feet hurting, legs stiffening.

He reached the corner of Tchaikovsky Street. It was wide and at first glance almost empty. It formed part of the Sadovaya Ring of boulevards around the inner city. It was lined on each broad pavement by trees. A red-and-white striped tent, unexpectedly, occupied one kerb. Flashing yellow lights, a taped-off section, the noise of a compressor. Road works of some kind. He crossed the Kalinin Prospekt, seeing the same foot patrols and parked cars, and began to move cautiously down the boulevard, keeping to the shadows of the trees. The street lighting was good here; betraying. His eyes sought each shadow, trying to dissolve it.

A parked car; he paused. The embassy was number nineteen, less than a hundred yards away, a post-war, ugly building. He could clearly see its façade, safe behind railings and the emblem of the eagle, illuminated by the yellowish street lighting. Just the single car . . .

He repressed the leap of optimism. He must not believe in the single car and its two occupants he could see as shadows through the rear window. He had to *look* − !

Road works. Six men, two leaning on shovels, one leaning on a pneumatic drill, three others using pick-axes in slow, rhythmical movements. He waited, turning his attention to the windows of the buildings, especially the second and third floors. There were smaller, brightly painted houses jammed incongruously between the Stalinist-style apartment blocks, frowned upon by the concrete towers. Gant studied the windows. A car passed, but did not stop, did not even slow down. He looked at his watch, a nervous, hardly aware reaction. Most of the curtains were drawn, most of the lights were off. One or two of the windows were open, even in the cold weather. He watched until his eyes were confused with dots and with dancing, unfocused images of windows, but he saw nothing to make him suspicious.

Excitement began to mount through his chilled body. There would be a marine behind the gates. Once he opened his mouth . . .

397

he needed only one word, his name . . . the startled marine would open the gates and he would be safe . . .

Against belief, it seemed the guard was minimal. Perhaps they expected him to try the British Embassy – ?

He forced himself to study the windows again. Nothing. After ten minutes, nothing. Parked cars too far down the boulevard, only the one near the gates. And the road works –

He looked at the six workmen. The drill was working now, so were the two men with shovels. The other three, the men wielding the pick-axes, had stopped to rest under the spindly legs of the spotlights they had erected. The noise of the drill violated the silence of the street. Each of the three resting men faced in a different direction as he leaned on his pick-handle. Each head moved rhythmically, slowly, traversing an area of the Tchaikovsky Street.

The red-and-white striped tent was twenty yards from the embassy gates. The six men were not workmen. The roadworks were a fake.

Gant swallowed bile and backed away from the shelter of the tree. He had passed a telephone box. In shadow, he hurried back towards it, entering and slamming its door behind him. Immediately, his tension and fear clouded the glass. He fumbled for coins – there were coins in the pockets of the jeans – and dialled the number of the embassy. It sprang out of his memory without effort, a signal of his necessity. He withdrew his finger from the dial and waited. The telephone clicked, then the noise became a loud, continuous tone. He joggled the rest and dialled once more. The same loud, unceasing noise sounded in his ears.

The line to the embassy had been cut off at the switchboard. There was no way to reach them.

He clenched his fist and banged it gently but intensely against the small mirror above the coin box. He swallowed, and shook his head. Illusions of safety dissipated. Then, furiously, he dialled another number, and waited, holding his breath.

The ringing tone –

They'd left the lines to the British Embassy – he would be able to talk to them, he *would* –

"Come on, come on . . ."

The operator on the embassy switchboard – a night-duty man – answered. Asked his name, his business . . . there seemed a note of expectant caution. Gant felt relief fill him, the words hurried into incoherence even before he began speaking –

Then he heard the clicks, three of them.

He stood there, mouth open, not daring to speak. The man on the switchboard insisted, the voice more demanding and, at the same time, more suspicious. Gant heard the man breathing as he waited for a reply. He understood the clicks, and wondered whether the switchboard operator had heard them – must have heard them . . .

The line was tapped. They'd left it open, hoping he would call. A tracer was probably at work now, seeking him.

"Caller?" Gant did not reply. He stared at the mouthpiece. Distantly, he heard the operator say: "I'm sorry, caller . . ." Then the connection was broken. The operator had circumvented the tracer both of them knew had been put on the call. Gant continued to stare at the receiver, then slammed it onto the rest, heaving open the door of the box almost blindly.

He looked down the wide boulevard. Red-and-white striped tent, six men, one parked car. He would never make it. He knew he did not dare to make the attempt.

He felt the wetness in his eyes and rubbed angrily at them. He jammed his hands into his pockets, hunching his body until its shivering stilled. Then he turned his back on the American Embassy.

Gant did not see the shadowy figure slip from beneath one of the trees on the opposite side of Tchaikovsky Street and hurry after him.

EIGHT:

The Strangers

The noise of her anguish had woken Maxim. The eleven-year-old had come into the kitchen, startled and half-awake, rubbing his eyes, his mouth already working with anticipated fears for his mother. Instantly, as quickly as sniffing back her tears and dragging the sleeve of her dressing-gown across her eyes, she had transformed herself once more into the figure he expected and needed. Even his immediate enquiries had been half-hearted. Being allowed to sit with her, drinking fruit juice, had been in itself a comfort, a reassertion of normality. He had gone back to bed satisfied.

Once she was alone in the kitchen, Anna buried her terror in activity. She called her Case Officer at the embassy, and he confirmed her sentence. The image of punishment had occurred to her with bitter humour. When the line suddenly went dead, the humour vanished and she felt chilled and isolated. She had put down the telephone, forcing herself not to consider the implications, not to consider her own danger. Instead, she began to build her fabric of deception. It would have to be an old aunt in Kazan – she didn't even have a telephone, though she lived in comfort, so Dmitri couldn't check on her story, nor could the ministry or her superiors . . .

She ticked off the benefits on her fingers.

Then, Maxim –

Her father, naturally; the boy's grandfather. The father who had assiduously promoted her career and had protected her from censure and suspicion after her husband's suicide. Her father, who had once risen to the position of first secretary of the party organisation of the Moscow Oblast region, and had thus been a member of the Party Central Committee. His retirement to a *dacha* outside Moscow had been honourable, luxurious. He still had the weight, the contacts and friendships to protect Maxim if something went wrong.

She swallowed. Maxim would enjoy a few days in the woods outside the city. The old man had taken up wildlife photography as a hobby. He had even bought Maxim a small Japanese camera for his birthday.

Maxim would enjoy –

She was sobbing. The camera had become inextricably linked in her mind with the Dynamo First-Class football boots that had been Dmitri's present. The two presents, their images so clear in her mind, pained her.

She sniffed loudly after a time, and shook her head as if to clear it of memory and association. Blonde hair flicked over her brow. She tugged it away from her forehead.

If it worked – if, if, if, *if* – she might be away for only a couple of days, perhaps three at the most. If she helped the American successfully, did what they wanted her to do, then she would be back with presents and an explanation that her aunt was a little better and she could stay away no longer . . .

If –

If not, she would have preserved her son from the shipwreck. Her father had protected her; now he could do the same for her son, his grandson. His task would be simple. Narrow and bigoted though his political and social ideas were – a surviving splinter of the Stalinist period who cut and bruised at every encounter with her newer, more liberal ideas – he had always been a kindly, though authoritative father; and an indulgent, fond grandparent. Maxim liked him, they would get on.

"No . . ." she whispered slowly, intensely. It was as if she were already giving her son away. Not if she could help it – not if she could win.

Dmitri's knowledge, her eventual safety from the KGB, her continued function as a Category-A Source for the CIA –

She would face those problems afterwards.

The telephone rang. She glared at it as if it had been a hated voice, then snatched the receiver from the wall.

"Yes – ?" It might be Dmitri, but the second of silence before she heard Edgecliffe's voice told her it was not.

"*Burgoyne*? Listen carefully. The American is still loose in the city. He hasn't been arrested or spotted by the police. We had someone in contact with him, but he shook them off – we presume he thought the man was KGB. We think he's tried our embassy and the American embassy. He realises by now that he can't find a bolt-hole in either place . . ."

"And?" Anna snapped, determined that Edgecliffe should hear nothing but competence, resource – however much that played the Englishman's game.

"The papers are ready – we'll have them delivered before morning. We shall require you to take the American to Leningrad, by train. You and he must manage the station as best you can."

"Leningrad?"

"You'll be met. I'll tell you how and where when we have it finalised. He'll be taken into Finland – What you do will be up to you. Your exit can be arranged – "

"No!"

"I should consider it carefully, if I were you," Edgecliffe warned. "We're offering you a way out."

"A passport to nowhere," she sneered.

"As you wish. Think about it. We will want you to board the Leningrad train this afternoon . . . there'll be clothes for the American, delivered with his papers. Some sort of disguise. Your job will be to get him to Leningrad."

"Your job is to find him first."

Edgecliffe chuckled, an almost pleasant sound. "I realise that. Be ready to leave your apartment the moment I call on you to do so. Once we locate him, he's in your hands. You'll make contact – it's too risky for us to try."

"And if you don't find him today?"

"Then it may be too late – he's running out of time. However, you'll stand by until you hear otherwise. Have you made your arrangements?"

"Don't worry – they'll be made."

"Then expect the papers and another call." He hesitated, then added: "Good luck."

Anna replaced the receiver without replying. She watched as the shadow of the chord stilled against the tiled wall. It formed a tightly-coiled noose before the telephone.

She hoped, fervently hoped to the point of prayer, that Dmitri would catch the American. He had the short remainder of the night, the morning, noon, the afternoon.

Please, please . . .

Priabin stood in front of the large-scale map, rubbing his chin with his left hand. Moscow's main line stations were represented by coloured pins. His right arm was folded across his chest as he pondered his responsibility; the seven principal stations for long-distance routes, and one of the four airports around the city, Cheremetievo in his case. His whole department had been seconded, and he occupied Kontarsky's old office in Moscow Centre, co-ordinating the surveillance. Dmitri Priabin was grateful for the static nature of his participation. At least his men were not walking the streets, combing the parks and open spaces, searching the apartment blocks, the empty houses, the building sites and the shops. Nor were they manning roadblocks in the freezing night.

402

And yet – and this was the splinter in his satisfaction since he had left Anna – it might be his people who let Gant slip. If he got out of the city, it might well be by train. And Gant could bring him down just as effectively as he had ruined Kontarsky.

Surely they had to find Gant soon? It was impossible for the man to roam the city undetected. He was alone, without friends or contacts. The SIS and CIA were bottled up in their apartments, embassies, compounds, safe houses. There was no one to help him, hide him, provide him with papers, protect him. The man was utterly, entirely alone.

His forefinger touched each of the coloured pins in turn, as if for luck. His hand described a circle around the inner city – Leningrad Station, Riga Station, Savolovsky Station, Belorussia, Kiev, Pavolets, Kurskaia.

And the principal airport to Leningrad and Scandinavia at Cheremetievo, north-east of the city –

He looked at his watch. Time to make another tour of the stations and drive out to the airport – yes, he would do that. It was suddenly urgent, necessary to remind his men of the stakes, the risks.

The intercom sounded on his desk.

"Yes?" he asked, depressing the switch.

"General Vladimirov wishes to see you, Comrade Colonel," the secretary informed him. The girl had a heavy cold, and her mood had not been lightened by having to work this extra duty.

"Where?"

"He's here, Comrade Colonel."

"Very well – send the general in at once!"

Priabin took up a position in front of Kontarsky's – *his* desk, almost posed, exuding confidence. He had sensed something overbearing about the general when he had been aboard the First Secretary's Tupolev. Priabin wanted to make a good impression; he did not wish to appear an interloper in that office – some sort of caretaker. His secretary opened the door, nose buried in her handkerchief, much to Vladimirov's evident distaste, and ushered the general in. She slammed the door immediately.

Priabin held out his hand. Vladimirov took it briefly. Priabin studied the older man's eyes. Bloodshot, but intense with purpose. He evidently had not slept for even a small part of the night. Priabin understood that Vladimirov's pride had been insulted and diminished by what the American had done. Only hours before he had been confined and on the point of revealing the truth, yet now he was at large again. To Vladimirov, his ill-luck must have seemed like a continuing taunt.

"General – I'm honoured. What can I do to help you? Please sit down –" Priabin indicated a chair near the desk. Vladimirov shook his head.

"Tell me your arrangements, your dispositions – all of them," he ordered sharply, without preamble of any kind. "Quickly, Colonel – I haven't time to waste!"

The Deputy Chairman had briefed Priabin sufficiently for the authority exuded by Vladimirov not to come as a surprise. However, he was abashed by the peremptory, almost violent expression of it. Vladimirov had been placed in command of the hunt for the American – an unusual step since he was not KGB or even GRU – but that position was a KGB safeguard. Only Vladimirov would fall if the American eluded them – no one in the KGB would suffer. Priabin almost felt sorry for the older man, even as he bridled at his tone.

Swiftly, he explained the disposition of forces, using the map on its easel. Vladimirov stood near him. There was a faint smell of whisky and cachous on his breath. He nodded violently, his rage and impatience barely concealed. When Priabin had finished his outline, Vladimirov studied him with the same piercing glance he had bestowed on the map and its pins.

"So," he remarked at last, "you will simply wait until he makes himself known to one of your men and then arrest him?" The sarcasm was evident and stinging. Vladimirov raised an eyebrow in further emphasis. Priabin felt his face redden and grow hot.

"These – are normal, tried and tested security procedures, Comrade General," he said with heavy slowness.

"It was normal security that allowed the American to escape from the hospital."

"I –"

"I have toured three departments in this building of yours so far," Vladimirov pursued, "and in each of them I have heard variations on the same refrain. *Routine – normal – usual* . . . even from Deputy Chairmen and Directors of Departments and their principal Deputy Directors and Assistant Deputy Directors –" His arms were in the air, expressing exasperated hopelessness. "People who should know better, *much* better, tell me the same things you do! Do you think it is enough, Colonel? Do you think you are doing all you can to apprehend the most important escapee in the whole of the Soviet Union?" Priabin glanced towards the door, whether for signs of help or out of embarrassment he could not be certain. The general raged on. "This organisation of yours has too much experience with *prisoners* and not enough with escapers." His lips parted in a thin, mirthless, arrogant smile. "You're not up to the job, perhaps?" His left eyebrow lifted ironically once more. The expression did nothing to alleviate the heavy anger of the eyes. He turned back to the map. "Well?" he asked. "You've nothing to say? Nothing at all? Not an idea in your head, mm?"

Priabin cleared his throat and composed his reddened features. He was already considering how best, how painlessly, he could manoeuvre the general out of his office.

"I – am sorry you're not satisfied, Comrade General. You are, of course, unfamiliar with our methods . . ."

Vladimirov turned on him. The white light from the table-lamp fell on his cheek, giving it the dead, flat appearance of skin that had undergone plastic surgery. A lock of grey hair fell across the older man's creased forehead. He flicked it back into place.

"Unfamiliar? Aren't jailers very conventional – the same the world over?" he hissed. "Dolts, buffoons with clubs and guns? Well? Have you an idea in your head, or not?"

Priabin stared at the map. A circle of pins, the weave of a net. Other maps in other rooms displayed other pins. A huge trawl-net being dragged across the city. He must surely be netted soon. The Sadovaya Ring, Red Square, the river, the broad avenues and boulevards, the narrow streets, the buildings and monuments – Gant was *alone* out there. He'd walked that city only once in his life before, and that for little more than an hour, on his way to rendezvous with the now-dead agent Pavel Upenskoy.

Priabin clenched his fist; began beating it into the palm of his left hand. Red Square from the Moskva Hotel, past GUM, down to the river – the murder had taken place there, then they'd fled via the metro to the warehouse near the Kirov Street . . . then he'd been driven out of Moscow the next morning in a van. He didn't even *know* the city, not at all – !

His forefinger traced the route that Gant, in his disguise as Orton, must have taken from the Moskva Hotel to his rendezvous near the bridge. Having reached the Pavolets metro station, he traced the route once more.

"Well, what is it, man?" Vladimirov asked impatiently. "Are you awake or half-asleep?"

Priabin turned on the general, grinning. "I think I'm awake, Comrade General!" he said with something akin to elation in his voice. It was at least enough of an idea to get rid of this uncomfortable old man.

"What is it?" Vladimirov's excitement was hungry and dangerous.

"Gant knows very little of Moscow. He must reason someone would be looking for him, he's valuable. If they know he's out, and they probably do, then they'd have people looking for him – low-grade people, unofficials, anyone they could get out of bed on a cold night – ! He might, just *might*, retrace his steps. It's the only piece of knowledge they all share – the route he took to his meeting with Pavel Upenskoy and the others."

Vladimirov looked doubtful. Then he nodded, once. "They might make an assumption – *he* might make it . . ." He stared at Priabin. "Well, where do you begin? Quickly, man – where?"

Priabin flicked the intercom switch. "Bring me the files on Upenskoy's cell – yes, all of them. Every name!" He glanced up. How many were there – Upenskoy, the old man, Boris Glazunov who died under interrogation, Vassily who'd disappeared without trace, one or two others, suspects only . . . it didn't seem much, but it was something. A beginning.

"He'll wait for daylight, if he tries it . . . for the crowds," Priabin explained, once more facing the map. At that moment, he almost believed his own idea, so convincing was his act for the imperious air force general. "Yes, he needs the daylight and the cover of the crowds." He turned as his secretary entered. She deposited the files, sneezed, and left. Vladimirov wiped the cover of one of the files. The name borne by the file was that of Boris Glazunov. Vladimirov opened it eagerly, in desperate, almost pathetic ignorance. It seemed a foolish idea to Priabin, but it appeared to more than satisfy the general. He shook his head gently.

Vladimirov looked up. "Well, help me, man! There are names, addresses, relatives in here, in each of them. Put them all under surveillance. And get me the departments responsible for street surveillance in the areas you pointed out to me – quickly! Don't just stand there, Colonel – earn your salary for once!"

The Hercules had completed its southward run, utilising the airway and a civilian call-sign and flight number. The pilot had requested landing instructions from Ivalo airport and dropped below the Russian radar net. Then, using visual and electronic navigation, and its radar in the mapping mode, it had flown northwards once more, heading for the dropping zone. The SBS unit had departed from the two paratroop doors during the first run over the lake at three and a half thousand feet.

First light was no more than a greyness in the sky, patched with darker cloud. Snow flurried across the windscreen, causing the co-pilot to intermittently operate the wipers.

Every light on the Hercules had been extinguished.

"All clear ramp doors and depressurising," the pilot heard the loadmaster announce over his headset. "Ramp opening, ramp down and locked."

"Roger. Ninety seconds to Initial Point."

"After IP, heading two-one-five, skipper," the navigator informed him.

"Roger – two-one-five."

"IP mark – now."

"Roger . . . turning to two-one-five . . . two-one-five steady." Ahead of the aircraft the dawn attempted to lighten the sky beyond the flurrying snow. The wipers cleared the screen. Stunted and dwarf trees confused the pilot's sense of distance. "Speed coming back to 160 knots." The undulating, snow-blurred outlines of the land seemed to rush just beneath the belly of the aircraft. "Wheels down," the pilot announced. "Flaps down." It was a precaution, in case the aircraft came into contact with the ground. "Lamp on, Diane – "

"OK – ready this end," the loadmaster replied.

"Lake in sight," the co-pilot said.

Ahead of them, beyond the last, straggling trees, the apparently smooth surface of the frozen lake stretched away, narrowing as it did so. Trees crowded down to the shore, like a fence around the ice.

"Got it. Keep the wipers on." Snow rushed at and alongside them. "I've got the smoke marker – "

"Altitude fifteen feet . . . twelve . . . ten . . ."

Stand by – five, four, three, two, one . . . Go!"

The nose of the Hercules tilted up slightly as the five pallets followed each other, sliding off their metal tracks and disappearing through the open ramp. The aircraft seemed to bob up, floating on a slight swell.

"Drop good – all the way, clean and tight. Ground party already beginning to recover . . . ready to close up this end."

"Roger, Diane, stand by for ramp closing."

The Hercules passed southwards over the narrow neck of the lake. A stronger flurry of snow rushed at them, obscuring the pilot's glimpse of tiny, moving figures on the ice. Then the lake was behind them.

"Initial heading – two-two-four."

"Roger – turning on to two-two-four . . . ramp closed."

The Hercules skimmed the stunted trees to the south of the lake. Whenever the flurries of snow revealed the horizon, the lightening sky appeared full of dark, heavier cloud.

Delaying his decision for as long as possible, Gant watched the apartment block of stained, weatherbeaten grey concrete that overlooked the Riga Station on the Mira Prospekt. In the windy, snowy light of dawn, he watched the first overcoated, booted, scarved inhabitants leaving for work. Cheap curtains had been drawn back at a hundred windows; faces had glanced at the day without enthusiasm. The traffic had begun to flow along the wide street. Trains left the station noisily and arrived in increasing numbers from the northern and north-eastern suburbs.

He had returned to the Mira Prospekt almost by the route he had taken to the US Embassy, taking to the streets only when they began to fill with the first flow of workers heading into the inner city. He had made better time once there were hundreds of other pedestrians. He had even risked a short trolley-bus ride, but the sense of closeness of other bodies, the growing claustrophobia of the self-imposed trap, had forced him to walk the remaining distance.

He was there simply because he remembered the address of Boris Glazunov, whom he had impersonated during the truck journey from Moscow to Bilyarsk with Pavel. Boris Glazunov was married – he remembered the details of the papers Pavel had given him. Boris Glazunov had been arrested, but perhaps they would know someone – a name, an address, a codeword, something . . .

He had passed the warehouse near the Kirov Street where he had spent the night after Fenton had been killed. It was locked and empty. The old man, too, must have been arrested. He had hurried away from there, alert and fearful. Glazunov's was the only other address he knew belonging to anyone even remotely connected with the operation to steal the Firefox. He had at least to try.

He was cold, but no longer hungry. He had drunk a bowl of thick soup, eaten bread and a thick-crusted, grey-doughed meat pie from a stall selling hot food to early workers. It was parked near a building site on the Sadovaya Ring. The food gave him indigestion but temporarily rid him of his growing sense of unreality. He could not decide the centre of the unreality. It frightened him. He had learned to be wary, alert, clever, but to what purpose? What could he do? How many days and nights could he spend on the streets, without papers and with a diminishing supply of roubles and kopecks, eating from steaming food-stalls and riding claustrophobic trams and trolley-buses? He could see no end to it – and that was his real fear.

He waited for twenty minutes, until he was certain that the apartment block was not under surveillance, that no one and no cars were halted suspiciously for long periods, that no police or KGB had arrived. The traffic thickened – Party limousines sped past old saloon cars and heavy trucks, using the yellow-painted centre lane. The trains came and went monotonously. People left the apartment block, and its companions lining the Mira Prospekt, in greater and greater numbers.

Eventually, he was stamping his feet in the too-big shoes as much with impatience as cold, and then he crossed the thoroughfare at the nearest pedestrian lights and climbed the steps to the foyer of the apartment block.

"Yes – quickly. You must come at once. The Gargarin apartment block on the Mira Prospekt, near the Kulakov intersection. Please hurry – you must bring your car . . . the American has just entered the apartment block – No, I do not know whether they are waiting for him. It is the apartment of someone who – was arrested, but I do not know what happened to his family . . . but I have just seen a KGB car pull up in front of the block. Yes, someone must have spotted him, someone I did not see. What? They're sitting in the car still . . . I must go in and warn him – Yes, you must hurry. Park in Kulakov Lane. What is your car? Yes, and the number – quickly, please. No, no, they are still sitting in the car – I think that must mean there are people already inside . . . I must hurry. Please reach Kulakov Lane as quickly as you can!"

The wide, grubby foyer of the apartment block possessed a sticky, stained linoleum floor. The walls were badly in need of a fresh coat of cream paint. One of the six lifts did not work. Gant, unnoticed amid the hurrying tenants leaving the building, attempted to envisage Glazunov's papers as they had been handed to him by Pavel. He could see the grainy identification picture which was later replaced by one of himself, he could see the name, see the overlying official stamps, the address . . .

The number, the number –

A hurrying woman bumped into him, seemed to search his face with a scowl on her own features, then hurried away. The tiny incident drained him of energy . . . concentrate –

Apartment – four, four, five – ? Five-four, yes, five-four . . . nine, nine – ! Apartment 549. He stood in front of a set of lift doors. Only odd-numbered floors were served by the lifts on that side of the foyer. For a moment, the foyer appeared entirely empty, except for the concierge – who might or might not have been more than that – reading *Pravda* behind his counter. From the open door behind him, leading to his own quarters, came the smell of percolated coffee. There was also the noise of a radio. Gant half-turned his head as he heard footsteps. High-heeled shoes – boots – and a long, warm coat. Fur hat. The pert daughter of the house, dressed beyond her station. The concierge was also the KGB official and informer. Gant's head snapped back to face the doors of the lift. The foyer was silent, empty. No lifts arrived. The seconds passed. Gant forced himself to remain absolutely still.

Then a lift door opened on the opposite side of the hall. Footsteps, hurry –

He glanced around towards the concierge. He was still reading his paper, uninterested in anyone who passed; apparently uninterested in Gant. Someone called the man, and he turned his head, then went in, shutting the door behind him. The lift door in front of Gant opened. He waited until the lift was empty, entered, and pressed the fifth-floor button. It seemed a tiny but important victory that the concierge had taken no interest in him. He probably thought it was someone coming back for something he'd forgotten, if he thought at all.

People tried to press into the lift on the fifth floor before he could get out. He squeezed through them, not ungrateful for the press of their bodies, their scents and smiles. He did not resent or fear them for that brief moment. Then the door closed and he was alone in the corridor. Linoleum, chipped and stained, on the floor, a succession of brown-painted doors, dirty green paintwork on the walls. It was an infinitely depressing place. He checked his direction, then followed the trail of mounting numbers on the doors. Some of them were missing. Radios played pop music loudly behind many of the doors, as if to drown out something else.

Five-four-nine. He raised his fist, and hesitated. He listened. Radio playing, but not loudly. No other human noises. He looked back down the corridor. No one. Swallowing, breathing deeply, he knocked loudly on Boris Glazunov's door.

At the third knock, as if at a general signal or alarm, a number of things happened. The lift doors sighed open, and Gant turned his head. A young man emerged, saw him –

The door opened. Gant turned. A tall man faced him, a grin already spreading over his face as he evidently recognised the caller. Someone spoke from inside the flat, a man with an authoritative tone. The young man near the lift shouted. His voice seemed full of warning.

Gant's hand remembered the Makarov in the coat pocket, and clenched around its butt. The tall man's grin spread. His hand moved from behind his back, slowly and confidently. He was intent upon the widening fear in Gant's eyes. The young man was running towards him down the corridor shouting, his shoes clattering on the linoleum.

Gant half-turned, half-drew his hand from his pocket. Then the young man, ten yards away, skidded to a stop and yelled his name. A plea rather than a challenge. The tall man had stepped forward through the doorway, his hand now holding a pistol, bringing it up to level on Gant's stomach. Gant squeezed the trigger of the

410

Makarov, firing through the material of the coat pocket. The noise was deafening, ringing down the corridor, pursued by the explosion of the tall man's gun which discharged into the ceiling. Plaster-dust fell on Gant's hair and shoulders.

"Quickly! Gant – quickly!" the young man shouted, grabbing his sleeve. Gant thought the face familiar, distorted by urgency as it was. A second KGB man was emerging from the room at the end of the apartment's hall. Gant fired twice, wildly. The man ducked out of sight. Gant heard a window slide protestingly up, felt chilly air on his face. "Come!"

Gant crossed to the window and the iron fire-escape. The young man climbed out and began to descend. There was frozen snow and ice on the rail and the steps. The young man danced carefully down them as quickly as he could. Gant watched the door of apartment 549 as he climbed over the window sill and felt for the first step. Then he was outside, shaking with cold and reaction.

Familiar – the face behind the two or three days' stubble of dark beard – familiar . . .

He clattered down the first flight, then the second, slipping once, pursuing Vassily –

Vassily – !

He had helped Pavel throw Fenton's body into the river. He had disappeared after the metro journey, near the warehouse. Vassily. Gant looked back up the twisting fire-escape. A face had appeared at the window, a walkie-talkie clamped to its cheek. He saw a pistol, too, and then looked down once more, aware of the treacherous nature of the ice-covered steps.

Relief, the excitement of danger being met and overcome, filled Gant. Vassily bobbed ahead of him, half-a-flight further down. He chased him.

First floor – ground floor. Rear of the building. Lock-up garages, dustbins, football goal painted on a brick wall. He bumped into Vassily, almost breathless.

"Vassily – !"

Vassily grinned. "Come. Quickly . . ."

They ran across the courtyard. Then Vassily jumped at a garage door, clinging to the low roof, kicking his legs, easing himself up and onto the felted roof. Gant followed. He could hear whistles and shouts now, but no noise of vehicles other than the muted roar of traffic on the Mira Prospekt. Vassily crouched as he ran across the roof, then he jumped out of sight. Again, Gant followed.

He dropped into a snowy patch of garden. A dog barked. Vassily was already climbing a fence when Gant caught up with him. Gant heaved himself over the fence and dropped into an icy alleyway.

Vassily ran to the corner of what appeared to be a narrow, quiet street. When Gant reached him, he said, "I hope she is here . . ."

There were a few parked cars. Vassily seemed to be searching for one in particular, reciting numberplates half under his breath. Gant's chest hurt with the effort of drawing in the icy air.

"Is — ?" he began spluttering.

"Yes — there!"

They ran across the street. *She*? Who? Vassily bent to peer at the driver of the car, then nodded. He pushed Gant into the back seat and climbed in after him.

"Get down, both of you!" the driver snapped as she eased the car away from the pavement, then turned left. Gant's face was against Vassily's arm. He could taste the worn leather of his jacket.

"They were — waiting," Gant said as the car turned right, travelling at no more than thirty miles an hour once it had done so.

Vassily's face, close to his own, frowned. He nodded his head vigorously. "Yes. I was not sure. I was watching you. The moment you entered the building, a car pulled up in front. It was KGB, but they did not get out. I knew then that they were waiting for you." A police car passed them, siren flashing, heading in the direction of the Mira Prospekt. "I was almost too late!"

"How long have you been following me?"

"Most of the night."

"Why didn't you make contact?"

"He was ordered not to!" the driver snapped. "He always obeys orders — we all do!" Gant felt the force of the driver's resentment.

"Are we being followed, Comrade?" Vassily asked very formally, surprising Gant. His face was serious, perhaps in awe of the driver.

"No."

Gant felt the car turn sharply left. After a silence, he raised his head, and was shocked to see the cosmonaut's monument, the rocket atop its narrowing trail of golden fire, drifting pass the car windows. He clenched his hands together to stop them shaking. They were near the Unit, heading for it — !

"What is it?"

"Where are we going?" he snapped in a high, fearful voice. They were leaving the monument behind them now.

"We have a place . . ." Vassily assured him.

"A change of clothes for you," the driver said. "A change of appearance. Papers. Everything is to be provided for you." The resentment was deep, angry. The woman disliked, even hated him. Who in hell was she?"

"OK — what then?"

412

"I must get you out of Moscow."

"And Vassily?"

"Vassily is not trusted — not as much as is necessary." Vassily shrugged at her words. He grinned, almost pathetically. "They do not consider he is capable of the task."

"And you are?"

The car had stopped at traffic lights. Gant could see them through the windscreen. The car was almost new, the fawn-coloured fabric of the seats very clean. It was a large saloon. Gant was suspicious. Then the blonde woman turned her head, so that she was in profile as she answered him.

"I have certain qualifications," she announced. "The greatest of which is my capacity to be blackmailed into helping you. I have been told that Vassily is someone who keeps changing addresses, who deals in black-market goods as well as espionage work. He is useful, but not *their* person! I am."

She turned her head as the lights changed. The car drew away, accelerating. They passed the Ostankino television tower, a steel needle against the heavy sky. Gant stared at Vassily, disconcerted, troubled by the woman's resentment. Almost afraid of help now that it had come.

Waterford lifted his head as the noise of the chain-saw ceased. At the far end of the clearing that had been made and was still being enlarged, a tree fell drunkenly forwards with a noise like the concussion of a rifle. Immediately, branches were lopped from it and stacked for later use in general camouflage. At the perimeter of the clearing which reached from the shore of the frozen lake back into the trees in a rough semi-circle, bundles of white netting lay ready for use. Already, much of the camouflage netting had been strung between the trees, forming what might have been the roof of a huge, open-sided marquee.

Two RAF mechanics were laying and checking nylon ropes which stretched from the trees that held the winches down to the shore. They had selected the stoutest trees, capable of taking the strain imposed by the three chain-lever winches which would be used to haul the Firefox out of the lake. The winches were anchored to the trees and additional steel anchor pins had been hammered into the frozen ground — not reaching a sufficient depth in the soil to completely satisfy Waterford or the Senior Engineering Officer from Abingdon. Even the Royal Engineer mechanics who would operate the winches were unconvinced there was a sufficient safety margin. They would only know, however, when they tried.

Waterford returned his attention to the group of marines around

413

him. Six of the SBS unit were seconded as divers, which left the eighteen in front of him in full arctic combat kit. The group was framed by upright or slightly leaning pairs of long cross-country skis and vertical ski-sticks. Each man bore a laden pack on his back. Nine of them also carried radio equipment. They were assigned to work in pairs rather than their more usual threes and fours, and their duties were reconnaissance rather than defence. His early warning system, he thought – which was all they could be with their small numbers.

Their rifles were slung in white canvas sleeves across their chests, below their snow-goggles. The usual mixed bag favoured by an élite force such as SBS – some standard L1A1s, a few 7.62 sniper rifles, one or two of the new, short-stock 5.56 Enfields, and a couple of the very latest 4.7mm Heckler & Koch caseless rifles. Even in their disguising sleeves, they possessed the appearance of plastic planks narrowing at one end. Waterford himself had one, for evaluation on behalf of the army. He thought it ugly, futuristic, and effective, firing its bullets from a solid block of propellant rather than a cartridge case. It had the stopping power and accuracy to penetrate a steel helmet at more than five hundred metres. He appreciated the weapon.

Looking at the rifles, he reminded himself he must stress yet again the reconnaissance nature of their duties. He moved two paces to the unfolded map on its collapsible table. The eighteen SBS marines crowded around him. Their breaths climbed above them like smoke from a chimney. Flurries of snow struck Waterford's face and settled on the map. Angrily, he brushed them away.

"Right, you gung-ho buggers – now you've got yourselves together, I just want to remind you what you're supposed to be doing. I'll keep it simple so you won't have to take notes . . ." He tapped at the map with a gloved forefinger. "You're on recce *not* engagement duties. You have your headings and you know the maximum distance you should go. It's a scouting perimeter, nothing more solid than that. Beyond the trees – beyond three or four kilometres, that is – the country is rolling, with mixed thickets and lots of open areas. Find the best observation posts, and sit tight. Report in only at specified times and keep it brief. We're not playing requests for Grandma and Aunt Glad and the rest of the family this time. Unless, of course, you wake up to find yourself being buggered by a huge, hairy Russian soldier – in which case, don't wait for your allocated time-slot, just yell *Rape!* and get out of there." They laughed. "As far as we know, there's nothing out there. We don't expect trouble, we don't *want* trouble, but we want to know if it's coming. So, make sure your dinky new trannies work, and keep hold of the nice new binoculars MoD issued you, and – good luck. Any questions?"

"Reinforcements, sir?" a lieutenant asked. "I mean, if it comes to it . . .?" He gestured round him.

"I know. You'd like to know there's a Herky Bird full of your mates ready to drop in – well, they'll be at Bardufoss if they're needed. But, just remember this is a nice quiet pub – we don't want a bloody awful punch-up in the lounge bar, if we can possibly help it! OK?" More laughter, then Waterford said, "Anyway, you're the lucky ones – think of this lot having to break all the ice and dig away at the bank until it's a nice shallow incline, then lay runway repair mats. OK, let's confirm your OP sites, shall we? Crosse and Blackwell?"

"Blackburn, sir," one of the marines corrected him amid anticipated and preconditioned laughter at a familiar joke.

"Cross and *Blackburn* – your heading?" Waterford replied, his face expressionless as he stared at the radiating lines on his map that led from the lake to the observation sites he had decided on for the nine pairs of marines. Not so much the thin as the transparent red line, he remarked to himself.

Buckholz turned to look at Waterford, and then returned his attention to Brooke. Evidently, Waterford knew how to handle his men. The laughter that had distracted the CIA's Deputy Director was high-pitched, nervous. The SBS men were, like most élite forces, somewhat too thoroughbred in behaviour when not in action. Buckholz had found that to be true of US Special Forces men in Vietnam. But, they were there to function, not for show . . .

Brooke stood with his air canisters at his feet, a white parka over his wetsuit. Two other divers had joined them, one bringing coffee. Buckholz sipped it now. The snow pattered against the back of his parka and the wind buffeted him.

"This is vital," he reiterated, sensing Brooke's resentment of his inexpert interference. He criticised it in himself. He did not mean to imitate his own grandmother, but he simply could not help it. Brooke had already been down twice through the jagged hole they had broken in the ice. His damage report had been expert, thorough. His inspection of the undercarriage, especially, had been positive in conclusion. then he and two others had removed the charges they had laid when they had first found the Firefox. Now, Buckholz had ordered them to make another check on the undercarriage. "You have to be certain, really, really certain, that those three legs are going to be able to take the strain of the winching. She's got to come out of there by the strength in her legs . . ."

415

"Yes, sir," Brooke said stiffly.

Buckholz grinned. "OK, I know I'm fussing – but humour me, uh?"

Brooke returned his grin. "OK, sir – I'll double-check."

"Good boy.'

"Mr. Buckholz?"

Buckholz turned in the direction of the call. The chain-saw was at work again. Snow flurried into his face. The sky was dark grey, the snow almost constant now, and the wind had increased from around five to more than ten knots. Sure, it was all helping to mask the signs of the air drop and their prints out on the lake, but it was reducing visibility at times to less than thirty yards. From the shore, it was difficult to see across the clearing to the Royal Engineer corporal with the chain-saw. He mistrusted the weather. A small example of its crippling effect had been the three hours of searching required to locate the contents of one burst pack out on the ice. Yes, more than anything it was the weather that made him fuss and triple-check. It held the key. Worst of all, the weather was delaying the Skyhook so much that they couldn't now assume it would arrive by the time they had winched out the Firefox. Buckholz was worried that the one flying crane would never arrive, and they would have to destroy the Firefox where it stood.

Damn the weather.

"What is it?" he called into the gusting wind.

"Mr. Aubrey, sir," the radio operator called. He was bent over the central console of the commpack as he crouched behind a canvas windbreak reinforced by lopped tree-branches. A dish aerial rose to the height of the lowest overhanging branches of the tree canopy on the shoreline.

"OK, tell him I'm coming." He turned back to Brooke, hesitated, then said. "OK, you bums – do your thing." Brooke smiled as the American walked away.

"Mr. Aubrey said it was urgent, sir."

"Sure," Buckholz replied, attempting a grin. "With him, every-thing is. OK – put me through." He shivered. At least in the Lynx helicopter, one of two that had brought in the non-parachutists and which were now tied down and camouflaged on the far side of the lake, it had been crowded but warm. He looked at the coffee-mug in his mittened hand. He hadn't been warm since . . . too old, that was the trouble. Thin blood. Buckholz devoutly wished Aubrey his own present discomfort.

The operator keyed in the voice scrambling code and paused for the light which would signify the console was ready to transmit. Then he sent his call-sign and received an acknowledgement a few seconds later. He nodded to Buckholz, who held the microphone close to his lips, as if about to whisper.

He was assailed by a sense of foreboding, which made him pause before he said: "OK, 'Mother', go ahead. What's on your mind? Over." The conversational, almost jocular tone was deliberate, as if it could fend off what he sensed was approaching bad news. He heard Aubrey's voice through the one earpiece of the headset that he pressed against the side of his head.

"Bad news, I'm afraid, 'Fisherman'. The Skyhook has had to put down at a military airfield in southern Sweden for repairs. I'm assured that the repairs are minor, something to do with the rotors being out of balance. Caused by the bad weather they've been forced to fly through. However, even more important, they can't yet give an accurate estimate of the length of the delay. I'm sorry. Over."

"Hell! Give it to me straight, 'Mother'. Don't bullshit me. I'm a big boy and I can take it. Over."

"At least tomorrow afternoon – that's the earliest they could be with you. Over."

"But they *will* come? Over."

"They must! When do you think you'll be able to begin winching out? Over."

"Some time around midnight tonight. Before first light, the Firefox will be on land. And no Skyhook! Over."

"It will come, 'Fisherman' – it will come. Over."

"If it doesn't arrive by eight, I'm planting the charges and we start ripping out the thought-guidance and anti-radar systems! Over."

"It will arrive, 'Fisherman' – just be patient. Over."

"Get the damn weather changed, will you? Over."

"I'll do what I can, 'Fisherman'. Meanwhile, prayer might be advisable. Over."

"I'll pray. 'Mother' – I'll pray. Out."

Buckholz looked around him. The SBS two-man reconnaissance units were vanishing behind the weather and the trees, on their way out of the camp. He could hardly see the last of them. Brooke had already descended with one of the other divers. In the silence after the chain-saw had ceased, a stunted tree fell with a crack like the beginning of a landslide.

Buckholz looked up. The snow was heavier, the wind colder, stronger.

"Yeah, I'll pray," he said. "I just hope He can hear me above this wind!"

*　　*　　*

He had been like a thief, an intruder, in her apartment. She had had to be careful, almost obsessive, about the things he picked up, touched, used. She was coming back – she had determined on that – and Dmitri would be coming back there, too. There must be no traces of any other man – this American least of all. After each cup of coffee, after the one small whisky, after the lunch she had prepared, she washed cups and glasses and plates and dried them and put them away. The actions prevented discovery and occupied her; distracting her from the growing claustrophobia of her apartment now that it contained the American. His presence was so, so *palpable*, so inescapable.

He spoke little after he had accepted her story. She had no idea what his feelings were towards her, towards his own future. He was tired – for two hours he had dozed in the armchair in which he had first sat down – and his experiences in the Unit on the Mira Prospekt, about which he remained silent, had worn at him. He seemed almost unliving, so passive and withdrawn was he. It was as if he had come to effect her arrest himself, wrench this life away from her.

The suit that Vassily had brought, with his papers, was a good, sober one of foreign cloth and cut. Three-piece. Pads fattened his lean face and half-glasses added age. Once he had shaved and showered and donned his disguise, he appeared almost like one of her senior colleagues in the Secretariat . . . which was what his papers declared he was, a civil servant travelling to Leningrad on ministry business. The bluff was bold, designed to attract attention but deflect scrutiny. The American seemed easy with the disguise, his body adopting a stiffly correct uprightness, seeming to add inches to his height. The dark overcoat would finish the portrait of a bureaucrat.

They left the apartment at four. In the lift, when someone she knew from the floor below her own got in, she murmured to him in businesslike, formal tones, having greeted the neighbour. It was evident from what she said that she was accompanying a colleague; her overnight bag and his small leather suitcase suggested the length of their stay. Gant's brief replies were in practised Russian. He seemed at ease, but she could not be certain. The part he was playing protected him like a carapace.

The taxi, a chequered band along the doors and side panels, was waiting outside the apartment block. The traffic on Kutuzovsky Prospekt was heavy, but sedate. The cars were larger and moved more slowly. The Party limousines seemed almost to queue in the central lane. The driver put their bags in the boot and they slid into the back seat. Gant unfolded a newspaper and pretended to read immediately the door was closed behind him, obscuring his features from the driving mirror.

"Leningrad Station," Anna said.

She thought of Maxim. The dog, and her father, had welcomed him. The dog seemed suspicious of her, as if picking up her mood, and this suspicion seemed to communicate itself to her father. But he did not ask, except after her health and after her KGB lover. A couple of days, she assured him . . .

For her office, she had a heavy cold. For Dmitri, it was a sudden trip to Leningrad – no, by train, the afternoon flight was full and she enjoyed train journeys. What business? Oh, some complicated case of fraud at one of the hospitals, the disappearance of clothing, money . . . no, not a police matter yet, until she had seen the records . . . yes, love to you, love, love . . .

She had almost betrayed something then, over the telephone. Choking back tears, choking back the desire to prolong the call, she had rung off before he became concerned at the strangeness underlying her reassurances.

She had left Gant in the apartment while she delivered Maxim to her father's *dacha*. No one, he said when she returned, had called at the door, no one had rung. When she entered the apartment, it seemed like a stranger's home.

They crossed the river by the Kalinin Bridge and picked up the Sadovaya Ring. Blocks of apartments lined their route. Gant fastidiously concentrated on his newspaper while she stared absently through the window, hand cupping her chin. She determined not to notice the city either to right or left of her, because she would not allow herself even to consider she might be taking some final journey through Moscow. There was the bulk of the Peking Hotel with its pink façade incongruous against the snowfilled sky. If she concentrated on the apartment blocks to the left, even though she saw Gant in profile all the time, their grey, weatherstained concrete and countless, anonymous windows deadened her sense of Moscow. It could be any modern city, anywhere in the world.

They left the Ring at Kirov Street, passing between the twin, guardian-like towers of the Leningrad Hotel and the Ministry of Public Works. Komsomolskaya Square, with its three main-line railway stations, closed around them. The taxi pulled up beneath the portico of the Leningrad Station. She got out first, and Gant paid the fare, and a slender tip which caused the taxi driver to mutter under his breath but which he might have expected from a bureaucrat such as the man who had ridden in his taxi, his nose in his newspaper.

Snow speckled the shoulders of Gant's overcoat. He jammed his

419

fur hat on his head, adjusted his half-glasses, and studied Anna. She saw his keen appraising glance and felt challenged, even insulted, by it. This man, who had done nothing, said little. Then, surprisingly, he smiled briefly.

"OK," he said, handing her her overnight bag. "They'll be checking papers. I'll queue first, you go to the ladies' room or something so that you're further back in the queue. I'll collect the tickets."

She nodded, feeling suddenly undermined and nervous. He had, by taking control of the situation, deflated her little air-pocket of confidence and self-reliance. He gripped her arm as he saw her hands shaking.

"Take it easy," he said, not unkindly, bending his head close to hers. "You've done OK up to now – just take it easy."

She nodded, more vigorously. "I – I'm all right." She changed her grip on her bag, and added, "Very well. But, be careful . . ."

They walked under the portico into the smallest of the square's three stations. Marble pedestals, at shoulder-height, displayed countless ever-vigilant busts of Lenin placing the station concourse under eternal surveillance. The roof of the station arched above them, glass and steel, the ribs of a huge animal. The station was busy with the first commuters. Gant read the Departures board. Anna slipped away from him towards the toilets. Then, walking with an easy confidence, turning his head with the appearance of casual interest, he made for the ticket reservations counter. He picked out uniforms, overcoats, guns, bulky figures questioning arriving passengers. He felt himself moving through a network of invisible alarm beams. Yet it was not as before, it was not like the metro when he had trailed at Pavel's side, trying to keep up, trying to adapt and adjust. He had spent most of the day preparing for this. He had temporarily forgotten Gant.

He arrived at the window and, with the appropriate impatient authority, bent and spoke into the grille set above the swivelling wooden begging-bowl that issued the tickets and snatched the payment for them. He asked for his reserved tickets – yes, his secretary had reserved them that morning. He sounded as if he already anticipated some confusion, some mistake on the part of the ticket clerk, a small balding, grey-faced man in a jacket with a worn collar, and frayed shirt-cuffs. He fumbled with his book of reserved tickets, fumbled out the appropriate ones. There were two styles of first-class on Soviet trains, and Anna had reserved seats at the front of the train, where the best carriages were always placed, the ones with two-seater compartments, heating, air-conditioning, radio – and restaurant service. The most expensive seats; the Party seats.

Gant paid for the tickets with large-denomination notes. They, too, were an element of disguise. Almost new notes. Declarations of privilege.

He turned away from the window, pocketing his change and picking up his suitcase. A leather-coated man watched him, and he tensed. It was really beginning now –

He pretended not to notice the man and headed across the wide concourse towards the platforms. A second man appeared on the point of stopping him, but assessed his clothing and bearing and let him continue. He hardly looked at his face, hardly noticed the features above the well-cut formal suit and behind the glinting half-glasses. Conventionally, they did not expect him to arrive at the station; if he did, they would expect him to sneak, to slip through – not to stroll. He reached the ticket barrier. The long Leningrad express stretched away to where the dark grey sky and the snow cancelled the perspective. He queued. Tickets and papers, of course. The KGB man who informed him was more deferential than he was to the man ahead of him or the woman behind. Gant pursed his lips in affected irritation.

Two people ahead of him. Suddenly, he wanted to know where she was in the queue. The man's papers being inspected with great thoroughness, with absolute leisure. Would his stand up? Where was she?

Stop it.

Where – ? Would they – ? Did they have pictures – ?

Yes, behind them, pinned to the side of the ticket barrier, next to a notice about the penalties for not purchasing the correct ticket for any journey – a silhouette of a figure being grabbed and held by a taller figure, the sense of a struggle, of an arrest –

Stop it.

He dabbed his forehead with his sleeve, pretending to remove his fur hat to disguise the gesture.

The picture taken of him at the motorway barrier, when his papers said he was Glazunov . . . next to that, something they must have obtained from the Centre's Records Directorate computer – himself in USAF uniform, taken perhaps eight or nine years before. He had been much younger then, he told himself, much –

Beneath the pictures, he was described as an enemy agent, spy and saboteur. He was sought with the utmost urgency. People were instructed to be vigilant.

The hairpiece they had given him was an expensive one, one that had been purchased in the West, in all probability. It was, Vassily had said, grinning, better even than Tito's had been. Yet, deliberately, it looked false. His hair was too short from having to wear the

421

helmet with its thought-guidance sensors to be anything but noticeable. A wig which looked like a wig was deemed a bolder call to attention. Were he suspicious, he would not wear an evident hairpiece. His motive would be considered to be vanity.

He replaced his fur hat. The youthful hair showed beneath it, a slightly different shade from his own.

He handed over the tickets, and gave the KGB man his papers, drawing them from his breast pocket. The ticket-collector asked the reason for the second ticket, and Gant turned his head loftily, indicating Anna when he saw her three places behind him. He waved her forward without consulting the KGB man. A man in the queue scowled, resenting authority and privilege. Gant introduced her off-handedly to the KGB man, and she passed over her papers.

To Anna, he paid no attention. To Gant, he was respectful, studying him from beneath narrowed eyelids. He scrutinised the papers for a long time, but did not glance behind him at the photographs. The hairpiece seemed to amuse him but he was nervous of revealing his smile and his contempt. Eventually, he handed back the two sets of papers, and nodded.

"A good journey, Comrade," he said with insolent mock-servility. Gant pretended to study the name displayed beneath the man's picture on the ID card clipped to his breast-pocket – but only for a moment. The man winced visibly.

They passed through the barrier onto the platform. Gant felt his legs weaken, his hands shake. But he did not falter in his stride.

"Are you all right?" Anna asked.

"Yes," he replied without looking at her.

Side by side, in silence, they walked down the long, wide platform, past the newspaper shop, the confectioner's, the gift shop, the buffet. Gant imperiously waved away a porter.

Bullshit, he thought. It's keeping you going, just bullshit. And he wondered who had suggested the disguise and the false identity and how well they knew him. It helped. To play-act arrogance helped. Bullshit –

They reached the designated carriage. Gant looked at his watch. Fifteen minutes before the train left. They found their compartment, claimed their seats. He was grateful for the relative safety of the twin-berth compartment. No one would be able to intrude.

"A magazine or newspaper, Comrade Ossipov?" Anna asked him as he lifted their cases onto the rack. "Some confectionery?"

"No . . . ah, perhaps a magazine. *Soviet Science World*?" he replied, smiling at the pantomime. "Yes."

"Very well, Comrade Ossipov," Anna said, and left the compartment.

He watched her climb onto the platform and make for the newsagent's shop. She looked small and vulnerable as she passed two uniformed KGB men with guns on their shoulders. She had been angry, he remembered – blazingly angry – when she had seen his false papers. Secretariat, like herself. They were forcing her to use her own papers rather than the set they provided, which described her as his wife. She had been insulted and challenged. She'd chosen to travel as his professional colleague. There was some declaration in it, he thought, some assertion of herself, of her personal life.

She disappeared into the shop. Gant began to relax. The hairpiece felt as hot and constricting as the fur hat he had removed. He brushed flecks and creases from his suit. He unfolded the newspaper. He began to allow time to pass more slowly, feeling his whole body relax, inch back from the pitch of tension he had experienced at the ticket barrier. It had worked, had worked, he repeated to himself over and over, like a calming spell. The woman was excellent cover. In the time available, in the extreme situation in which they had found themselves, Aubrey's people in Moscow had done well, very well.

He glanced out of the window, directly after looking at his watch. Four minutes to departure time – she was talking to a man in uniform, a young colonel in the KGB. Fifteen yards from the window. She *knew* him –

Four minutes – she was smiling – three minutes fifty – she was *smiling*!

Gant felt his body constrict into a straitjacket, his fists rest heavily on his knees, his eyes begin to dart about the carriage . . .

Who *was* she – ? What was she *doing*?

Anna leaned up and kissed Dmitri Priabin, aware of Gant's staring face fifteen yards away.

"What a surprise!" she exclaimed.

Holding her arms, as if to restrain her, he grinned. "Duty, my love – duty. I'm here in my official capacity, inspecting the security arrangements. I didn't know whether or not you'd arrived."

She looked pointedly at her watch. "Only a couple of minutes," she murmured.

"*Soviet Science World?*" he asked, looking at the top of one of the magazines under her arm. "Looking for more wheelchair projects? No, I'm sorry," he added when he saw her face darken. "That was cheap." He bent to kiss her, and she responded. She had half-turned and she could see Gant clearly as she pressed against Dmitri's chest. He looked betrayed, frightened. She could not tell him –

She pushed away. "I'd better get on the train, I suppose."

423

"When will you be back?"

"A couple of days."

"You didn't leave a hotel number."

"I'll ring you – tonight."

"What is all this business?" he asked, taking her arm – an image of arrest? – and walking her towards the door of the carriage. She leaned against him, trying to display the innocence of the meeting to Gant. She smiled broadly. She could not tell if Gant relaxed. He continued to watch them very obviously. Had Dmitri seen him – ?

And she realised, with a horrible, sickening force, that the hunter and the hunted were eight yards from each other. She was certain that even she would have recognised Gant beneath that disguise, beneath that ridiculous hairpiece, even from these grainy pictures of him near the ticket barrier . . .

"Oh, some petty fiddling, they think. It's got to be verified before the police are called in."

"No drugs?" he asked in all seriousness.

"No – clothing, sterile supplies, all kinds of silly things – sometimes I think people will steal anything in this country! It may even be a fraud on the part of the suppliers because they're behind with their production schedules – I'm not sure yet. But it has to be investigated." She whirled him round suddenly, and smiled up into his face. "Never mind about that – just say you'll miss me!" A part of her awareness was stunned at the ease with which she lied.

"I will – like hell." He kissed her. She pressed her mouth against his, held his head between her hands, clung to his neck as the kiss continued. It *was* a farewell, to something.

A whistle blew. She pulled away from Priabin. "I must go –"

"Come on, then – on you get!" He was blithe, confident she would be away for no more than two days, enjoying this tiny interlude in the search for Gant. He handed her onto the train, and slammed the door. She leaned out of the window and kissed him again.

The train moved. He stepped back. She waved, blew him a further kiss, which he returned. He grinned like a schoolboy. She waved furiously, already ten yards away.

Hers must be the nearest compartment of the first-class carriage, the others were full, two faces at each window. Who was she travelling with – ? He waved. The train gathered speed, twenty yards away now –

He began running, still waving. He took the first two steps because he wanted to keep her in sight as long as possible – and then the third and fourth steps and all the others because of the face at the window. Strangely, he did not falter in his waving.

424

He was ten yards away, and puffing for breath, when he recognised the face at the window; confirmed the suspicion that had dashed over him like cold water. And saw, too, the horrified, appalled look on Anna's face when he transferred his gaze to her.

And knew, then —

Gant.

Travelling with Anna. Anna, helping him . . .

Gant.

NINE:

En Route

Kirkenes civilian airfield possessed the very temporary appearance of a forward position likely to be abandoned at any moment, crouching uneasily just inside the Norwegian border with the Soviet Union. Its low wooden buildings did not seem entirely explained by its latitude or the Norwegian style of architecture. Instead, they suggested impermanence; the reluctance to invest in Kirkenes – just in case. Aubrey had been allocated a low, barrack-like hut behind the control tower, part of the Fire Section, into which was crammed the communications equipment, the maps, charts, telephones and men he would need to employ. The windows looked out over the iron-grey water of the Korsfjord, and beyond it the peaks of Skogerøya, the Varangerfjord and the Barents Sea. The water was a fitful sight through the slanting snow showers. The main room of the hut smelt strongly of the numerous paraffin stoves that supplemented the main wood-burning stove. The noise of a twenty-eight volt generator outside the hut intruded. Power cables snaked over window sills. The edges of the window panes were foggy. It was a depressing place; an image of exile, or defeat.

Aubrey stared out of the windows at the sleet, attempting to imagine the weather conditions the Skyhook lifting helicopter had encountered on its slow journey from Germany, and the even worse conditions that would prevail if it ever took off again from the airbase in southern Sweden. He had been in communication with the helicopter's US Army pilot, and with the senior engineering officer at the airbase. Repairs to the rotors were proving a slower, more complex, more serious task than had at first been anticipated. Parts were required which the Swedes did not have; parts which, at present, could not be flown in.

The Skyhook was crucial. *No fall-back*, Giles Pyott had said. Everything depending on better weather and a single helicopter . . . If the Firefox was to be removed from the site, they could not dispense with the helicopter. Aubrey knew that he, too, had fallen for the spurious, glamorous excitement of the helicopter lift, just as the politicians had done. There was no way in which the aircraft

426

capable of carrying the dismantled pieces of the airframe, an extra forty-five thousand pounds weight, could land and take off at the lake. They could not have got trucks through – too much snow and no roads.

Now, he knew that the bad weather might last a week. It would worsen for the remainder of that day, and though the following day might begin a little better, it would rapidly close in once more. There might be short breaks, windows in the weather, but they were unpredictable. By the time it finally cleared, the Finns would have cordoned off the entire area and informed the Russians where they could find their precious MiG-31!

Aubrey choked silently on his enraged frustration. He was helpless; bound and gagged. He could do nothing, *nothing*! Unless the Skyhook arrived before the expiry of the deadline, at midnight the following night, then it would all have been wasted, all have been for nothing.

And he would have failed, and he would have to attempt to live with the increasing sense of guilt he felt concerning the people who had died. Aubrey shook his head. He did not want to have to do that. It was an unfamiliar feeling, and it pained him. He had no defences against it.

All he could see ahead of him were the explosive charges clamped to the airframe, the mutilated cockpit instrument panel and systems consoles – then the bang. Snow, earth, metal – then nothing!

Damn, damn, damn, damn –

Guilt thrust itself once more into his consciousness, a weed growing through concrete. Pavel, Semelovsky, Fenton, Baranovich – especially Baranovich. He had killed them all, only to fail to catch the ball they had thrown.

Damn the weather and the helicopter . . .

And damn Kenneth Aubrey!

"Mr. Aubrey?" It was the voice of his radio operator. The communications equipment from the Hercules had been transferred to the hut.

Aubrey turned his head to respond, thankful for the interruption. One of the Norwegian army guards passed the window, face held to one side against the blowing sleet and snow. "What is it?" Aubrey asked.

Curtin was at the top of a pair of step-ladders, leaning against a huge map of the Finnmark, the Kirkenes area, and Finnish Lapland. It was sedatory work, Aubrey thought. Curtin was intently applying red-flagged pins to the map, designating Soviet activity along the border. There were no red flags inside Finland. There had been little movement along the border, and no aerial reconnaissance since the weather had worsened, according to reports from Eastoe in the Nimrod.

"Mr. Shelley from London, sir," the radio operator replied. Aubrey joined him at the console, lowering his overcoated body onto a flimsy-looking swivel chair. He had retained his coat as a vague protest at inactivity, as if to suggest he might be called away at any moment or be engaged in some furious travel. Aubrey had to feel that his own sojourn at Kirkenes was utterly transitory.

"Hello, Peter — what can I do for you?" he said off-handedly.

After a few moments, when the Receive light had winked out and the tape had re-run, he heard Shelley say: "Just to report that they're on the train, both of them. One of our scouts saw them go through the barrier, inspection and everything." He sounded pleased. The rescue of Gant was working like clockwork, and it irritated Aubrey. Shelley would have an easy and notable success with it —

He crushed his anger in the silence. Shelley was waiting for a comment.

"Well done, Peter — is everything else in place?"

"Harris will pick them up at the station outside Leningrad — Kolpino — when they leave the train. He'll have the travel warrants and the visas for them to cross into Finland. Director-General Vitsula has agreed that a team will meet them at the border, just to take the weight off their shoulders when they've got that far. It's looking good on the operations board — fingers crossed, sir."

Aubrey waited beyond the time when the Transmit light indicated that he could speak once more. Shelley's success made him envious. It had been *his* idea to try to rescue Gant and the woman the CIA were prepared to throw away — and now under Shelley's control it looked as though it might work.

And yet, it was the damned aircraft that he really wanted! The Firefox — that was the real prize — the big one, as Charles Buckholz might have described it. The big one . . .

"Well done, Peter," he repeated eventually. "Keep me informed. Harris should do a good job — he's worked for us before. Out."

He stood up and returned to the window, wrapping his overcoat testily and showily about him. Curtin watched him from the top of his step-ladders, tossed his head and grinned, and went back to his map and his pins. A gap in the sleet again showed Aubrey the lower slopes of the lumpy, barren peaks of Skogerøya and the grey, featureless Varangerfjord beyond them. An awful place —

A mirror of failure.

At least Gant would be saved —

And Aubrey admitted that at that moment Gant seemed a poor prize without the aircraft he had stolen.

Dmitri Priabin continued to stare as the last carriage and the guard's van moved around the curve of the line just beyond the end of the platform. Then the train was masked by an oncoming express. Anna and Gant had disappeared.

His thoughts were in a turmoil. He felt paralysed and weakened to such a degree that it was difficult to remain standing; impossible to move – to turn and walk or run to the nearest telephone, the nearest fellow-officer –

That flight of his imagination horrified him. *He had actually thought of telling someone – of reporting it to his superiors – !*

His hands were shaking. Nerves in his forearms made them seem chilly, even beneath his greatcoat. He rubbed his arms to stop them quivering. As he did so, he realised his body was bent. He was leaning forward as if he were about to vomit. He straightened up very slowly, his eyelids still pressed tightly together – warding off what he had witnessed or retaining the dampness behind him. The pain of it, the waves of shock, went on like a series of coronaries, each one worse than the one before. He could not escape the image – *her face, Gant's disguised but recognisable face*, together.

He heard himself breathing very quickly. He sniffed loudly, and wiped surreptitiously at his eyes. He was facing down the length of the platform. And Oleg was coming towards him from the barrier, still wearing the overcoat that smelt of mothballs.

"Damn," he muttered between gritted teeth.

Suddenly, Oleg was an enemy. A KGB man. A spy-catcher. He must know nothing.

"You all right, Colonel?" the older man asked in a not unkindly tone. "You look a bit pale?"

Dmitri tried to smile. It was more like the expression of a wince at sharp pain. "Yes, all right, just indigestion."

"Oh – Comrade Akhmerovna got off all right, then, did she?" Oleg persisted, smiling; almost winking as he continued: "Did you catch a glimpse of the bloke she was with, sir?" The grin was broad, jokey, knowing. Priabin stifled a groan. "Travelling on business, like you said, but with this bloke wearing a hairpiece." He continued to grin at Priabin, expecting a jocular reply. "You might have trouble there, sir," he added. Priabin again provided a slim, pale smile.

"One of her colleagues in the Secretariat, I gather," he said stiffly, and moved away. He had to find somewhere to think, to decide. It was racing beyond him, he was losing control, falling apart – Oleg

429

was making him want to scream – he felt he would explode if he didn't get away from him.

He strode towards the barrier, hearing Oleg's sarcastic: "Sorry I mentioned it, Colonel sir," behind him. *Don't upset the man!* He paused and turned. "It was a very obvious wig," he said with studied lightness. Then he smiled. Oleg returned the expression, nodding and chuckling.

"Wasn't it, though – what a shocker! They always make me laugh, wigs. Don't know why – haven't got much myself – but, wigs – !" He burst into laughter. Priabin joined in for a moment.

"That wind all right, sir?" Oleg asked solicitously.

"Bit better, thanks."

"You got anything?" he asked, fishing in his pocket and bringing out a wrapper of indigestion tablets. "These are good – got them in the *beryozhka* shop. American, they are. Better than those peppermint things they make in Minsk. Try one." He held out the wrapper. There was fluff from his pocket on it. Priabin did not dare risk reaching out his hand. He could envisage fumbling with the wrapper, tearing it, spilling the tablets, arousing Oleg's suspicions.

"Don't do anything for me. It's vodka I need!" he announced as heartily as he could.

"Come on, then, sir –"

Priabin shook his head. "I've taken enough time off – better get on with my tour of inspection." He shrugged. "See you, Oleg."

"A real pity, sir –" he heard Oleg offer.

"What?" he snapped, turning on his heel.

Oleg was holding out the wrapper of indigestion tablets. "These," he said. "They smell of mothballs – taste of 'em, too. Don't blame you refusing."

Priabin smiled. "Bye, Oleg." He strode towards the ticket barrier, passed through it with a nod to the KGB man who must have inspected Gant's papers, glimpsed the poster displaying the pictures of the American pilot, and passed into the station's main concourse. A wig . . . attracting attention to a distraction. See the wig, see the silly vanity, the life-style and personality it suggests – miss the pilot beneath.

The air outside the Leningrad station was cold. It was as if he had walked into a sheet of glass. He breathed deeply, many times. His head would not clear. It was like a night sky against which rockets and other fireworks burst. Crazy, useless schemes, exploding, leaving their fading images on an inward eye. He had no idea what to do.

Except he knew he could not report her. He could not tell his superiors, could not tell Vladimirov, that the woman he lived with,

430

the woman he loved, was aiding Gant in his escape from Moscow. They would arrest her, interrogate her, make her talk – then dispose of her. Into a pine box or into one of the Gulags, it was the same thing in the end. Reporting her would be her death sentence.

"Gant – !" he murmured fiercely, clenching his fists, then pulling on his gloves in a violently expressive manner. "Gant –"

Anna was running a terrible risk. She was in the utmost danger. He clattered down the station steps towards his limousine.

Where?

What to do?

They were going to Leningrad – in all probability, they'd leave the train before it reached the city. Someone would be waiting for them, an Englishman or an American . . .

And then it struck him, jolting him like a blow across the face. *She was leaving – leaving with the American – she was getting out –*

He climbed into the back of the black car and slammed the door behind him.

"The apartment!" he snapped.

The driver turned out into the square. Railway stations all around the square. Images of departure, all fleeing.

He did not know what to do. He knew only that he must not lose her.

The train gathered speed, passing the television tower, its top hidden by low grey cloud. Sleet melted on the window, becoming elongated tadpoles of water. The closest suburban stations all exhibited the same functional, deserted appearance as they headed north-west out of Moscow. The compartment was warm. A loudspeaker softly provided Tchaikovsky. Gant did not know how to begin the conversation he knew he must have with the distraught woman who sat opposite him. She was staring at her hands, which seemed to fight each other in her lap. Her lover, she had replied to his first question. The man she lived with. He had been unable to find another question to ask. Instead, he had stared out of the window as if surprised that the train was still moving, still being allowed to continue its journey.

Finally, as the suburbs flattened into parkland, grey and white beneath the driving snow and low cloud, and then rose again into the old town of Khimki-Kovrino, Gant turned away from the window.

"What will he do?" he asked, staring at his own hands, as if imitating the woman's supplicatory posture. She looked up, startled back to her present surroundings. Her features appeared bruised with emotion.

"What − ?" she replied in Russian. He wondered whether her use of her native language − he had spoken in English − was some way of keeping him at a distance. Or simply security?

"I said, what will he do, the man you live with?" he repeated in Russian.

She shook her head. "I don't know − !"

"He knew it was me," Gant explained unnecessarily. "And he guessed we were together." He cleared his throat. "What would he make of it?"

"He knows about me!" she exclaimed, beating her fists in a quick little tattoo on her thighs. "He already *knows*!"

"Jesus H-Christ . . ." Gant breathed, leaning back in his seat. The small compartment was hot, even though he had removed his formal overcoat and unbuttoned his jacket. He fiddled with the half-glasses on his nose, but did not remove them. "He knows about you . . ." he repeated in English.

"He's known about me for a long time. He's done nothing about it. He −" She looked up, and essayed a smile. "He's very much in love −" She might have been talking of a favourite son and another woman. "It pains him − sometimes he can't sleep − but he protects me. . ."

"Christ −" Gant rubbed his forehead, inspecting his fingers for dampness. Very little. He was surprised. He checked his body. Hot, yes, but no sense of rising panic. The movement of the train, north-west towards Leningrad and the border, lulled his body. The first stop was Kalinin, a hundred miles from Moscow. Perhaps they were safe until then.

He could not panic, he decided. The woman had coped, coped with much more, over a much longer time. While she remained almost calm, so would he.

"Listen," he said, leaning forward, reaching out his fingertips. She withdrew her hand, holding it against her breasts. He sat back. "Listen − think about it. What will he do? What will he think?"

"I − God, I don't know . . ."

"Will he − will he blame the CIA? Will he blame me?"

"What do you mean?"

The daylight outside was failing. It was as dark as late evening already. The tadpoles of melted sleet wriggled across the window. A collective farm lay unused beneath a layer of snow. A tractor huddled near a hedge.

"Does he love you enough to blame everyone else except you for what he saw?" Gant explained with some exasperation. "Is he that blind? Will he blame the CIA, the British, me − ?"

"Instead of me?" Gant nodded. "Perhaps −"

432

"Will he report us to his superiors? Will they stop the train?"

"I – don't think so . . ." Anna's brow creased into deep lines. Gant guessed her age to be around thirty-eight or nine. Older than the young colonel he had seen on the platform. He leaned back and closed his eyes. What had he seen? Seen her trying to reassure him . . . yes. He'd understood that there was no danger, even through his shock. What else – ? The man? Smiling, laughing, holding her –

His *face* when she climbed aboard the train, in the moment before he saw Gant – ?

Love. Something from paintings, almost religious – what was it? Adoration – ? Adoration . . .

And he began to believe that they were safe . . . safe, unless –

"Could he follow us?" Gant asked sharply.

"What?"

"Could he arrange to follow us – *himself*?"

"Why?"

"To kill me."

"Why?"

"He might – just might work it out. If he believes in you, he'll blame me most of all, lady. And he could keep your dark secret and put the clock back to yesterday, if he killed me. I wouldn't even be able to tell tales on you." The Makarov was in the suitcase. Later, he would think about transferring it to his inside pocket.

"Do you think he would do that?"

Gant shrugged. "He might – you know him, not me. You've screwed up what was a nice neat assignment. He could either hate you, or me. There's no one else to attract his interest." Gant leaned back, closing his eyes. His lack of panic surprised him.

Maybe it was the woman's presence? She was a talisman who had, perhaps, become a hostage. He felt safe with her. Adoration . . . yes. Priabin was besotted with the woman, and he could use that to his advantage. Priabin might come after them, but he wouldn't betray her, give her up.

He'd blame the good old US of A and one of its citizens in particular. Yes, he'd want to kill Gant.

Gant could not believe his luck. The car journey after Vassily had helped him, the apartment for most of the day, the disguise and the easy access to the platform and the train – they were all dreamlike, unreal. It had been going too well.

But this – this was real luck.

He found himself thinking aloud: "This is real luck . . ."

Immediately, the woman's face narrowed. She despised him. He could not help that. *Real luck*. He might have had thousands of KGB looking for him, but now, thanks to her, he had only one who was looking in the right place. And, as they say, his lips were sealed.

It was working out. He could make it, with those odds. The papers and the disguise had stood up, would stand up. Harris would be meeting them at a quiet suburban station with a car and new documents. And, if he kept Anna by his side or in front of him like a shield, he had nothing to worry about . . . nothing at all.

"Stop it!" she said intently. He opened his eyes. "Stop it!"

"What — ?"

"You're smiling — you're *enjoying* it!" She was very close to tears. Her teeth nibbled at her full lower lip. Her pale, drawn features seemed inappropriate to the expensive hairstyle, the costly, fashionable clothes.

"All right," he said. "I'm sorry. It was good not to be the one who's really alone for a change. I *am* sorry."

She nodded. "I —" she began.

"Could you go back?"

"I don't know — I thought so, before, before —"

"Take it easy. Maybe the Company will lay off, if all this works out?" He watched her shaking her head. The blonde hair flicked from side to side. On the platform, she had seemed so much in control, so much the stronger partner. But, she was weakened by her own love. She wasn't so much afraid of getting caught as of losing her lover. Well, maybe the Company would release her if she pulled this off . . .? Miracles did sometimes happen.

He looked at his watch. Five hours to Kolpino. They had tickets for the restaurant car. She'd have to make up before she appeared in public —

Gant retreated from concern. It complicated matters. She was, effectively, his hostage, and that was the easiest and most satisfactory way to think of her.

Dmitri Priabin had dismissed his driver when the car dropped him at Anna's apartment. He had hurried from the lift and fumblingly unlocked the door as if half-expecting to find her there. The apartment was, of course, empty.

He tore the expected letter open, glanced at the excuse of business in Leningrad, his eyes highlighting the love that constituted the remainder of the letter. Then he crushed it, threw it across the room, and retrieved it only moments later, thrusting it into his pocket. Without conscious decision, he had packed a suitcase with a civilian outfit — a disguise, he thought — and then he had left the apartment once more, slamming the door hollowly behind him. Maxim was with her father — whatever happened, the boy was safe.

Whatever happened to Anna, whatever was discovered – whatever part he played himself – her father could protect his grandson even if he could not save his daughter.

In one way, then, it would be clean.

He hailed a taxi. Conscious thought seemed to have caught up with bodily activity, and he ordered the driver to take him to Cheremetievo airport.

Flights to Leningrad –

He had to inspect the airport security anyway, it lay under his authority. They would expect to see him.

And what would he do? What was he planning that required the suitcase on the seat beside him? He did not really know. Thought had not yet overtaken reaction, to discover what lay in the future. It, like his body, was content simply to be active. He was hurrying to the airport – he appeared to be pursuing . . .

Who and what was he pursuing?

His hand touched the holster at his hip, providing the answer. The American – Gant. He wanted to kill Gant. He *would* kill Gant! In his death lay safety. Anna would be safe, *he* would be safe.

The driver had a bald, shining head. His ears were red and prominent. The sleet flew at the windscreen, rushing towards the wipers, then sliding jelly-like to either side. It was hypnotic.

Priabin shook his head, waking himself. If there was a flight to Leningrad, he could overtake them. They would leave the train before the terminus, though –

If he got a list of stations where the express stopped, he could work back along the line to the farthest point they could possibly leave the train. There he could board it, and confront them.

Like a cuckolded husband, he could not help thinking, hating the image. He could kill Gant – shot resisting arrest, he could live with Vladimirov's rage, and Anna could disappear into the Leningrad night. He'd spotted Gant, followed him . . .

He should have boarded the train then, *in Moscow* – !

No, no . . .

He's had no plan, then. He'd have blundered in like the cuckold, not the rescuer.

And, when he'd killed Gant, what would the Americans do to Anna? Would they guess who and why and assume she'd been a party to it?

And turn her over to his own organisation?

He sweated, even though the heating of the taxi was primitive. He banged his fist slowly, mesmerically against the leather of his suitcase. Have to hide that at the airport, get on the aircraft at the last moment, mustn't be seen by his own men . . .

435

Any of his personal subordinates posted there? He didn't think so, but was not sure. Have to be careful —

It's awful, he thought. The mess is awful, awful —

He sat back in the corner of his seat, out of the view of the driver's mirror, because he knew his face was pale and cold and utterly confused. He could not see the end of it. He could not believe that he could save Anna. He rubbed one gloved hand over his face, as if trying to remodel his expression by heavy stroking movements.

Each time he thought about his situation, the main priority appeared to be to save Anna. Get her away from the American, get her back safely to Moscow, reinstall her in her apartment. Life could go on, then — from that point.

But, each time he considered the priority and agreed with it, he thought of Gant and the desire to kill him rose like nausea in his chest and throat and it became difficult to consider Anna's safety or his own. Gant's death increasingly thrust itself upon him as a course of action that was inevitable.

"Then, while we do not have the pilot, we must return to our search for the aircraft," Chairman Andropov announced. At his side, Vladimirov did not demur, even though he understood that this was little more than another deflection of blame in his direction. A similar move to his surprise appointment as security co-ordinator of the hunt for the American.

Strangely, he did not resent his assigned role as a scapegoat. Rather, it increased his sense that he was the only man — the only one of all of them — capable of recovering the MiG-31. Even when the First Secretary nodded his agreement with Andropov and looked immediately towards him, Vladimirov felt no resentment and little anxiety. He was prepared, even equable, as he awaited an outburst from the Soviet leader.

It came almost at once, beginning on a low, histrionically calm note.

"Gant must be found," he announced from behind his desk. The Kremlin office had once been used by Stalin. It was not the great anteroom where all visitors were cowed and fearful long before they ever reached the huge desk behind which Stalin had sat, but nevertheless it was a large, high-ceilinged room with a tall marble fireplace and massive, dark furniture. It daunted visitors, and it expressed the Soviet leader's ideas of his own personality and authority. The First Secretary had moved to another floor of the Arsenal building, and the windows of his office and the luxurious apartment beyond it stared across a triangle of grass and trees towards the Senate and the rooms once occupied by V.I. Lenin.

"Yes, First Secretary," Vladimirov replied.

"And so must the aircraft – Gant is only the key to the aircraft. You agree, General Vladimirov?"

"Of course, First Secretary. Of course –" He bit down upon the rising irony in his tone. He rubbed his hands on the carved arms of the huge chair in which he sat before the mahogany desk with its lion's feet.

"Then where *is* the aircraft? Where is it *now*?" The First Secretary got up, pushing back his chair noisily on the parquet flooring. He strode to the window, hands clasped behind his back. He looked out at the failing light, the white trees and grass, the windows of Lenin's office, "*Where is the aircraft?*" he repeated without turning.

Vladimirov did not need to glance at Andropov to realise the satisfaction that would show on his features. To think, *that* man, the *secret policeman*, might become the successor to the grey-haired buffoon at the window. Vladimirov, unable to suppress his contempt, was pleased that neither of them could see his face. But, just to think of it . . .! Andropov was already a member, perhaps the most powerful member, of the inner cabal of the Politburo. He was rumoured to be about to resign as Chairman of the KGB, to become head of the General Secretariat of the Party, thereby broadening his power base. Andropov might one day sit behind that very desk . . .

Andropov would have the Lenin offices opened up again, Vladimirov thought bitterly. They would become offices once more rather than a museum – *his* offices.

"I – have people working on that. We have selected a number of landing-sites, First Secretary; places where the American could have landed the MiG-31." The words were automatic.

"These I should like to see," the First Secretary said turning slowly and over-dramatically to face into the room once more. "And – the American told you nothing under the most intense interrogation?"

Vladimirov gambled. There *was* something there, in those tapes – he was certain of it.

"I'd like you to listen to it – and Chairman Andropov, of course – to the tapes his people made. I'm sure we're missing something there."

He heard the First Secretary sigh with satisfaction. All the man wanted, ever wanted, was his authority recognised. He wanted the scent of subordination strong in every room he entered. It was easy . . .

Careful, Vladimirov warned himself. He stood up slowly as the First Secretary passed him. The two bureaucrats in grey suits preceded him to the door. Their coat-tails were creased with sitting.

He had managed a few hours' sleep late the previous night, a shower and a change of uniform. He followed the two men through the outer offices where the Soviet leader waved secretaries back to their desks. Two bodyguards fell in behind Vladimirov – a prisoner's escort, he thought for an instant, then smiled inwardly.

They used the lift to the ground floor. It was only a single floor's descent, but the lift was modern, air-conditioned and emitted quiet piped music. Guards saluted with uptilted rifles as they passed across the marble floor towards the main doors. The two bodyguards hurried a little way ahead, then issued umbrellas from a rack beside the doors. Vladimirov took an umbrella, but disdained the galoshes the two guards were now fitting over the shoes of the First Secretary and the Chairman. The image of the guards kneeling before the two men was too striking not to be savoured.

They cautiously stepped out into the darkening evening, descending the swept, damp marble steps of the Arsenal like very old men. Birch trees and snow-covered lawns were dyed pale orange by the lights. Vladimirov walked alongside his companions. The Kremlin was a place he did not often visit, and he tilted back his umbrella to gain a clearer view of the palaces and cathedrals within the walls, thereby displaying what the other two might sniggeringly have called his provincialism, his gaucheness.

The place was a monument to absolutism. Even the cathedrals repelled rather than invited. There was little sense of quiet expressed by their façades, nothing of sanctuary. The red towers, topped by their neon Party stars, ringed the buildings; penned them. They were heading towards the largest of the new buildings, the Palace of Congresses, which, together with the Senate, contained most of the government offices within the Kremlin complex. To Vladimirov, it looked like a glass and concrete weed growing up modernistically amid the planted, massive, tropical flowers of the older buildings.

The wind splashed sleet against his shaven cheeks, chilling his skin. Yet he continued to stare, to appraise, until they reached the main doorway of the Palace of Congresses. They passed the guards on duty and entered the main foyer of the glass building. Heavy chandeliers hung from the ceiling. Vladimirov followed the First Secretary and Andropov across the tiled floor – a huge modern mosaic depicting the inevitable triumph of Socialism – towards the reinforced steel doors of a special lift. They descended six floors before the lift sighed to a stop. Guards faced them as they entered a corridor of whitewashed concrete. Steel doors, like the watertight doors of a submarine, confronted them. The bodyguards inserted plastic identity tags into the locks, and the doors opened.

Vladimirov inhaled deeply as he once more prepared to enter what bright, cynical young army officers who had served there called the *Führerbunker*. Beyond what was little more than an airlock, where more identity tags were inserted into computerised locks, examined, and returned, a second steel door opened onto a vast underground room. They stepped into a command centre which mirrored not only that in the Tupolev but also those deep beneath the Moscow Garrison's HQ and his own air force head-quarters south-east of the city. He followed the others across the room, then mounted a metal ladder onto a gantry which overlooked the command centre. A long glassed-in gallery formed the control room of the underground complex.

All this, Vladimirov thought, the means of obliterating most of the earth, is being used for no more than a skirmish, a small fuss on the border. The insight increased his sense of well-being. Officers saluted, operators sat more erect and alert as they entered. Vladimirov immediately directed the Soviet leader's attention to the fibre-optic map against one wall; a smaller version of the huge perspex screen erected on the main floor of the underground centre. It was edge-lit, computer-fed like the map-table aboard the Tupolev, and at that moment it displayed Finnish Lapland. There were patches of light on the screen, dotted like growths of luminous fungus across Lapland.

"We've selected these sites, First Secretary –" Vladimirov began, using a light-pen to pick out each of the small glowing points. "These are the only places where the terrain would allow an aircraft to land." He was confident now. He'd already spent two or three hours in this control room. Its occupants were military personnel – with a sprinkling of KGB and GRU and GLAVPUR people, of course, but soldiers in the main, soldiers first – and he was at home amid the paraphernalia of electronic warfare and computer strategy. He picked out, too, a line of small red dots. "This is the American's route, from the point at which the Chairman's Border Guards picked up his trail." The light-pen's arrow bounced along the row of dots, as if picking out a melody. "He travelled in the same general direction, and we deduce that he was making directly from the point where he left the aircraft to the Norwegian border at its closest point. Paint in the suggested route, in both directions, please."

The red dots became a white line, extending roughly north-west to south-east. It crossed lakes, valleys, minor roads, forest tracks, frozen rivers. In the north-west, it terminated at the border, while to the south-east it halted at the shores of Lake Inari.

"Time is crucial here," Vladimirov continued in the tone of a kindly, expert lecturer of greatly superior intelligence. "We know when the second MiG-25 was destroyed, we know when we first found traces of Gant. We know how fast he was able to travel, and we can begin to deduce distances. This white line is far too extended, of course – therefore, we consider that the MiG-31 must be somewhere in this area . . ." The arrow of the light-pen described a circle. When the arrow bobbed away, off the map, the computer had traced a circle, as if the pen had drawn on the perspex. It was perhaps twenty miles in diameter.

"Very good," the First Secretary announced with evident sarcasm. "Very good – the MiG-31 is in Finnish Lapland!" He turned to Vladimirov. "We *know* that, General – we already know that!" It was obvious that the Soviet leader had simply been waiting for this opportunity to harangue and threaten. Now he had an audience, and it was one that pleased him – the military; the despised and feared military. He would humiliate one of their heroes in front of them, show them their idol's feet of clay. Vladimirov steeled himself to control his features and remain silent. "Find it! *You* find that aircraft, *today*. And you, Andropov," he added in a less hectoring voice, "find the pilot." He turned as if to leave, his bodyguards already opening the door of the control room and making room for him to pass. Then he returned his gaze to Vladimirov. "It must be found," he said. "I do not need to remind you of the consequences if it is not found – today."

He left the control room. Abashed, Andropov immediately wiped his spectacles with his silk handkerchief. There was a sheen of perspiration on his brow. His nostrils were narrow with rage. Vladimirov, feeling the resentment of his body begin to dissipate, realised two things concerning the Chairman of the KGB. He was playing for perhaps higher stakes than Vladimirov himself – and he was uncertain of his allies in the Politburo if he could still be bullied by the present First Secretary. Therefore, Andropov would now become an ally; untrusted and dangerous, but an ally. The Soviet leader had included him in the catalogue of blame should Gant and the MiG-31 not be found.

As if to confirm his thoughts, Andropov moved towards the perspex map, closer to Vladimirov. He smiled, an expression that turned to its habitual ironic shape almost as soon as it formed on his lips.

"If you wish for a more – sympathetic? – audience, I offer myself, General Vladimirov," he said quietly.

Vladimirov nodded. "Accepted, Comrade Chairman."

"Good – now, I understand the logic of your deductions thus far – but, how could he have landed the aircraft? In that terrain – it is snowbound, surely?"

"Yes, it is. However, we think his best chance would have been a forest track or minor road."

"Would *he* have thought of it?"

"I think so. I think he would have felt himself – shall we say – challenged, to do it? He is possessed of a massive certainty of his own worth and talents. He would have tried, I think. He must have tried, because of the parachute. And he was uninjured, which I think means the airframe is virtually undamaged – certainly recoverable, certainly a threat if recovered by the Americans or the British. So, all we have to do, Comrade Chairman, is to find it."

"A forest track or a minor road – still covered with snow –"

"Out of fuel, with little risk of fire, he might have risked landing on snow. Too deep, and I agree he would turn tail-over-nose and break up. But, with the winds and the weather over the past weeks, we think that at least some of these tracks could have had sufficiently little depth of snow to help rather than destroy the MiG."

"And there are two of these tracks within your circle also crossed by the white line predicting his route," Andropov observed. He bent closer to the map, then clicked his fingers. "You're ignoring these lakes," he said. "Might he not have used a frozen lake?"

Vladimirov shook his head. "We discounted them. Our aerial reconnaissance immediately after the loss of the second Foxbat showed nothing. On a lake, he could not have hidden the MiG."

Andropov shrugged. "I see," he said. "Very well. What is the scale of this map?"

"We are talking about a matter of fifty or sixty kilometres from our border, at its closest point, to this road, another fifteen to this one here." The arrow of the light-pen danced like a moth on the surface of the map.

"You have ordered a new aerial reconnaissance?"

Vladimirov shook his head. "All we could do in this weather is high-altitude infra-red, and that airframe is as cold as the landscape around it by now. We won't have photographs. Any search would have to be on the ground. We should have to cross the border – a small party . . ."

"But then, your deductions would have to be correct. They would have to be accurate – extremely accurate for a small party."

"Working back along this white line, into the circle – sufficiently spread out, they could cover a wide area –"

"As long as the weather gets no worse and visibility drops no further – and just so long as the aircraft is not buried under the snow by now!"

Vladimirov shook his head. He enjoyed the Chairman's scepticism.

441

It enlivened the debate and cemented their alliance. "I think it's under the trees somewhere – he taxi-ied it off a road under the trees."

"And left it like a parked car?"

"Just like a parked car."

Andropov looked doubtful. "Is there any other way?" he asked.

"Your experts have been examining the tapes of Gant's interrogations ever since he escaped, in the hope of finding something, some concrete piece of evidence to indicate what he did with the aircraft." Vladimirov's features hardened as he remembered. His hand squeezed the material of Andropov's jacket sleeve. The Chairman seemed not to resent the grip on his arm. "He was about to tell us – on the point of telling, when he knocked himself out. He was within an inch –!" He held up his fingers, almost closed together. "An inch, no more –"

"But, he didn't –"

Vladimirov shook his head. "Your people are good, but they seem unable –"

"I'll have the tapes brought here, together with their report," Andropov promised. "Meanwhile, I suggest a reconnaissance party consisting of Border Guards?" Vladimirov nodded. "I take it their helicopters can fly in the weather they're experiencing up there?"

"Just."

"Then they must be ready to move at once. Where do you suggest they begin?"

The arrow of the light-pen wobbled up the perspex map, alighting above the white line of Gant's suspected journey.

"Here's where they found evidence that he had made camp, slept. All the other traces – parachute found here, village here, capture – are further to the north-west. I suggest we have your party dropped here, and that they work backwards along this line, perhaps making for the closest forest track, here . . ." The arrow buzzed almost dementedly above the line.

Andropov studied the map, then simply said, "Very well – I'll issue orders for a reconnaissance party to prepare for an immediate border crossing – please have the coordinates and any other advice ready for them."

Gant pushed down the window of the compartment. Snow flurried against his face. The drab provincial station on the edge of the town of Chudovo was almost deserted. A handful of passengers gingerly left the train, as if stepping into an alien environment. Boots and galoshes slipped on the snow-covered platform. Lights gleamed through the snow. The train hummed. One or two uniformed guards, railway police, individuals in leather coats or heavy mackintoshes checked papers. There was one more stop and perhaps forty minutes before Kolpino, where they must leave the train to meet Harris. To explain their through tickets to Leningrad, Anna would assume a sudden indisposition, a need for fresh air, a slight fever that might be infectious. The local hospital might be required . . .

It seemed slack and fortuitous to Gant, but he sensed that it would work. A small country station in a suburban town, the staff tired and bored, their unexpected visitors important Party officials. Panache and bluff would convey them from the station to Harris's car with little trouble. A suggestion of food-poisoning, though the restaurant meal had been good, might further the bluff.

It didn't matter, he thought. Priabin had not boarded the train here at Chudovo – and if he was waiting for them in Leningrad, as Anna thought he might, then he was powerless. Gant had as good a hostage as he could have wished for. That thought satisfied him, though it gave him no pleasure. He heard the guard's whistle, saw the swinging lamp the man held winking at the far end of the train, and withdrew his head from the icy air and closed the window. When he turned to Anna, he saw that she had pulled her coat over her shoulders and was shivering.

"Practising – right?" he said. She looked at him vehemently. "Sorry –" He nodded his head towards the window. "No sign of trouble,' he added, sitting down opposite her. The train journey had lulled him; every passing mile had reinforced his sense of having broken through the net tightening around him. Not so for Anna, apparently. The journey might have been one into exile. She was still terrified of what Priabin might do.

She fumbled in her bag, drew out a gold lighter and cigarette case, and lit an American tipped cigarette. The brand was as unconscious as the habit of smoking; a badge, long worn, of success. She blew the smoke towards the ceiling. Her hand was shaking, trembling.

She shook her head, softly and rhythmically, at some inward image or idea. She appeared as if entirely alone in the compartment. It was evident she blamed him, entirely, for her situation; just as her lover would do by now. The thought chilled Gant.

Was there a way out for them? Could they manage, between them, his own death and their safety? He suspected that both she and Priabin would be concentrating their entire energies on finding such a solution.

Killing him would be the easiest way.

The train gathered speed, the last of the station lights flashed past. The darkness of the night pressed at the windows. Snow was caught by the lights of their compartment, beyond the reflection of his features. He stared at himself, his cheeks fattened by the pads, his face changed by the addition of the half-glasses. They might kill him, if they ever got together and considered it –

The door of the compartment slid back. Anna was sitting bolt upright. Gant's eyes flicked up towards the reflection of the newcomer. Civilian clothes, he thought with a sense of relief.

Then he saw the drawn pistol and the distraught and grim features of the man who was holding it. Only then did Gant turn his head.

"Dmitri – !" Anna cried.

Gant felt numb with shock, as if his fears had conjured the man into the compartment. Priabin *had* boarded the train at Chudovo. Priabin with a pistol. The KGB officer who was Anna's lover had reached the end of his particular journey, and he had found his answer. A simple and obvious answer.

Kill Gant.

"Out," Aubrey said, limply handing the microphone to the radio operator. He turned away from the console, and almost bumped into Curtin, who had been standing at his shoulder throughout the conversation with the senior engineering officer at the Swedish airbase. Curtin shrugged, but Aubrey appeared not to notice the gesture. "Damn," he breathed through clenched teeth. The single word seemed invested with a great weight of anger and frustration, even something as dark as defeat.

"It's one hell of a piece of bad luck –" Curtin began, but Aubrey turned on him, glaring.

"Bad luck! *Bad luck?* It is a monumental fall coming after pride, Curtin – that's what it is! It is entirely and utterly my own fault." Curtin made to interrupt, but Aubrey gestured him to silence. "It is *my* fault! I was warned – Giles Pyott warned me, as you did yourself, as Buckholz did. I chose to take no heed. I chose not to listen." He clenched his hands together at his lips. He paced the hut, intent upon recrimination. Eventually, he turned to Curtin and said, "We know that Gant is on the train. In a matter of hours he will be across the border into Finland – it has proceeded with the smooth regularity of clockwork. Harris is at Kolpino to meet them. We know that the aircraft will emerge from the lake within the next few hours – *and we can't do anything to remove it!* We will have salvaged it simply for the *Russians* to collect!"

"You couldn't fight the weather."

"I should never have *ignored* the weather! That was my sin. Pride Eugene, *pride* – !"

444

"Bad luck."

"No − !" He began pacing the room again, murmuring to himself like a child learning by rote. "Thirty-six hours, even then they're not certain − almost twelve hours after the deadline expires − and the weather may not allow them to continue. Pyott told me not to rely on the Skyhook, but I ignored that. Now I have been shown my error!" He did not pause in his pacing. The radio operator huddled over his equipment, ignoring Aubrey's voice. Curtin perched himself on the edge of a folding table, carefully balancing his weight. Aubrey continued with his catalogue of self-blame. He forcibly reminded Curtin of an animal newly caged in a zoo, pacing the boundaries of its prison, seeking a way of escape. "I didn't listen, I didn't damn well *listen* − ! I knew best − nanny knows best. Nothing left now but to rip out the systems we most want and blow the airframe to pieces − and I still want that aircraft." Curtin strained to catch what followed. "I owe it to them . . . but I can't − there's no way!"

Then he turned to Curtin, arms akimbo as if begging for some relief of mind.

"What − ?" Curtin said, spreading his own arms, unable to understand what Aubrey required and reluctant to intrude.

Aubrey's lips worked silently. Then he burst out: "If only the damned plane would *fly*!"

Curtin grinned in embarrassment. "Yeah," he said. "If only."

Aubrey closed his eyes. "If the Firefox could fly . . .." Then he looked up and announced to Curtin: "They would leave me in peace, then, wouldn't they?"

"I don't understand?"

Aubrey disowned his words, his hand sawing through the fuggy, paraffin-smelling air. Then he wiped his lips, as if what he had said amounted to little more than a geriatric dribble of sounds.

"I'm sorry," he said with exaggerated, ingratiating apology. "I forgot myself for a moment." He moved closer to Curtin, placing himself near the heat from the wood-burning stove, rubbing his hands as if cold. He looked directly at Curtin instead of the floorboards of the hut, and said, "Forgive me for asking − but the aircraft could not fly, of course?"

Curtin shook his head. "No . . ." he said. The word was intended to be definite, to end the speculation he could see beginning to cloud Aubrey's pale eyes, but it faded into a neutral, hesitant denial. Aubrey seized upon it.

"You don't seem sure −"

"I am sure."

"Then why not *be* definite!" Aubrey snapped, his face sagging into disappointed folds once more.

"I am, but —"

"But what?"

"I — it's been immersed in water for more than forty-eight hours . . . you've got a smidgeon more than twenty-four hours . . ." Curtin shook his head, almost smiling. "It *is* impossible," he announced. "I'm sure of it."

Aubrey persisted: "As a matter of interest, why did you hesitate?"

"Because — well, because I've heard of Navy planes getting a ducking and making a comeback —" He held up his hands to stop a torrent of questions from Aubrey. "It took weeks, Mr. Aubrey — *weeks*! Well, maybe one week away. I just remembered it had happened, is all. It doesn't help you. *Us.*"

"You mean the aircraft is immediately damaged by immersion in water?"

"Sure, the damage starts at once."

"But the damage is not irreparable?" Aubrey's voice hectored, bullied. Curtin felt interrogated, and resented the small, arrogant Englishman who was too clever for his own good and too self-satisfied ever to admit defeat.

"That depends on how it went in, whether it was all shut down, sealed . . . Hell — !"

"What is the matter?"

"I don't know the answers, for Christ's sake! You're crazy, Mr. Aubrey, sir, crazy." He climbed off the table and stretched luxuriously, as if about to retire. The gesture was intended to infuriate Aubrey and it succeeded.

"Damn you, Curtin — stay where you are and answer my questions!" He pressed close to the American, undeterred by his greater height and bulk. Curtin thought, quite irreverently, that Aubrey was squaring up to him, ready to fight.

"OK, OK — if it passes the time," he murmured, regaining his perch on the table.

"Just answer me this — could the Firefox fly?"

Curtin shrugged, hesitated, and then said, "I don't know — and that's the truth."

"Then, who would know?"

"Why don't you ask the Senior Engineering Officer — what's his name, Moresby? The guy from Abingdon. He's standing right next to the airplane, he knows the state it's in — ask him!"

The radio operator was sitting erect in his seat. "Get me Squadron-Leader Moresby, at once." Then he looked at Curtin and held up his hand, displaying his fingers in sequence as he spoke. "We have the pilot, almost safe . . . We have the runway — the lake . . . We have twenty-four hours . . . The aircraft needs to fly fifty or a hundred miles, no more, to be safe from recapture. Is that asking too much?"

"Much too much – but you don't want that answer, I guess," Curtin murmured.

"Squadron-Leader Moresby, sir –"

"I'm coming, I'm coming –" Aubrey's eyes gleamed, almost fanatically, "I *won't* let it go!" he said. "Not yet, anyway. I *won't*!"

TEN:

"Nessie"

"Don't kill him, Dmitri! Dmitri, *think* – !"

Gant's hand had stopped reaching for his breast pocket. He remembered that he had not transferred the Makarov from his suitcase. Priabin's pistol was pointed directly at him, even though the man was staring into Anna's face. His head had flicked towards her the moment she shouted. Gant remained motionless, an observer of the scene. There was no way in which he could move quickly enough across the compartment, before Priabin had time to shoot him. he forced himself to remain still.

"Anna – ?" Priabin exclaimed in the tone of a child that does not understand a parental order. He was being prevented from doing something he very much wanted to accomplish.

"Don't kill him, Dmitri," Anna repeated, her hand moving slowly towards his gun. He kept it trained on Gant and out of range of her grasp. "How can I escape from this if you kill him?"

Priabin appeared deeply confused. "You? But, you come with me. You'll be safe, then –"

"Do you think they'll allow that? Don't you think they'll know I *allowed* him to be killed? It's a trap, Dmitri – I have to do what they want!"

He held out his left hand, and she caught it with the fierce, clamping grip of a vice. She clung to him, he to her. Then he shook her hand, gently.

"It won't be like that," he said soothingly. Gant saw that he was sweating, and not simply because of the heating in the compartment. He was almost feverish with purpose. And now he was witnessing his schemes begin to dissolve. "It won't *be* like that, Anna!" he reiterated more firmly, attempting to persuade himself.

"It will," she said, "I know it will – you don't know them."

"Believe her," Gant added, and they both looked at him with utter hatred. He quailed. Priabin was a man still in shock and panic, revolving harebrained schemes to save his mistress. The situation eluded Gant. He did not understand how to use it to his advantage. He was certain that the wrong word would act like a spark on the Russian.

448

"Shut up!" Priabin snapped unnecessarily.

Gant squeezed into the corner of his seat, his eyes flicking upwards for an instant to his suitcase. But there was no chance, no hope.

As if room had been made for him, Priabin sat down at the other end of the seat, the gun still aimed at Gant. Gant felt the cold of the window against which his back was pressed seeping through his jacket, between his shoulder-blades.

Priabin spoke to Anna without looking at her. He still held her hand. Anna's fingers were white and bloodless, twisted in his.

"Listen to me, Anna,' he began. "If he tells us where the aircraft is – you know, don't you?" Gant nodded carefully, his face expressionless. "If he tells us, we can pass that information on. We – we could get out of it like that. All they want is to know where the plane is, nothing else – that's their only interest in him. I can say . . . can say that I followed a hunch, or he was reported to me as seen boarding the train, *alone* – we struggled, the gun went off, but he'd told me everything . . .!" He stared at her. "It would work!"

"And they'd be sure as hell to turn you over, Anna," Gant said quietly. He realised he could not remain silent. Ever since he had noticed the bloodless fingers gripping those of Priabin, he had understood that she was not a contestant, rather the prize for which he was fighting with Priabin. If she became persuaded of her lover's case, then she would allow Gant to die. She hated him as much as Priabin did. At his words, Priabin's gun jabbed forward in little threatening movements. The man's eyes were grey, and now as unyielding as slate. His face wore a sheen of perspiration, and his cheeks were flushed. He looked feverish. "Believe me," Gant added, forcing himself to continue, "I know them. They've wasted people on this operation already – he knows that. Even Baranovich." The name was like a stinging blow across her face. "They'll use anybody. He's right – the man's right. They're only taking care of me because I know too much. I mustn't fall into the wrong hands." He attempted to smile at Priabin. "That's why they used you. But, you have to see it through, Anna. I'm sorry, but you have to. If you get me away – then they'll maybe let you off the hook. I'll try to make them do that."

"Don't believe him!" Priabin shouted.

"Dmitri, keep your voice down!" Anna snapped fearfully at him. Her eyes had glanced into the corridor.

"Pull down the blinds," Gant said.

Priabin released Anna's hand. He tugged at the blind above his head, sliding it down behind him. Anna rubbed her white hand. Gant turned, watched Priabin for a moment in the window, looked out at the snow flying past the train, and heard Anna draw down her blind. He turned back to Priabin. He would not jump from the train, not yet. He might just win the game —

"OK," Gant said in English, as before. Priabin's English was better than Anna's. "That's better. I will try to help — but I can't help if I'm dead, can I?" He turned to Priabin. "Look, sonny, I know you want to kill me, and I know why. But *I'm* no volunteer, either, just like her. *I* didn't pull her name out of a hat, so let's get blame out of the way, uh?"

"I'm not going to let you go," Priabin replied immediately. He had wiped the sweat from his forehead. He was calmer now; he held rather than gripped Anna's hand. Yet Gant saw that he was now perhaps more dangerous.

"If you turn me in, I'll tell them where the airplane is — sure, I almost did a dozen times, I guess. But, I'd tell them about Anna, too . . . even if I didn't want to," he hurried on as the pistol in Priabin's hand waggled threateningly. "It would come out, under drugs. Man, you know that! I couldn't keep quiet even if I wanted to."

"So, I kill you."

"And the CIA tips off your bosses, and Anna goes into the bag and maybe you do, too. What in hell are you doing here, anyway? Where's your back-up, who else knows?" Priabin had begun to grip Anna's hand tightly once more. Gant saw her wince, but he did not know if her pain came from the grip or from his words. "Face it, man, you've messed up!"

"No — !"

"Your hide's on the barn door along with hers!"

He wanted to look at his watch. He bent his head slowly, as if weighing his next words. Fifteen minutes before the train stopped at Kolpino, where Harris would be waiting with a rented car. He had fifteen minutes to persuade, or kill, Priabin. And he knew he had no chance of killing him.

"They don't expect her to go over with you to prove how loyal she's been, do they?" Priabin asked in contempt.

Gant shook his head. "They gave her the option," he said. "She turned them down."

Priabin looked at Anna. Her face was pale, frightened. Gant sensed her need to touch the KGB officer, reassure both of them by gentle, continuing physical contact. Priabin scrutinised her face.

"You weren't going?" he asked hoarsely. She shook her head.

"No."

He appeared utterly relieved. The situation, Gant realised, was more complex than he had thought. Part of Priabin behaved like a

450

jealous lover pursuing his mistress and the other man in a triangle he had invented. Probably, he did not realise it himself. But it formed another spark that might ignite him. Gant did not know the truth – did Anna intend to stay?

"Thank God," he breathed. It was touching, and dangerous. "I thought – I thought . . ." Then he seemed to recollect Gant's presence, and broke off, returning his gaze to the American. There was a sharp, quick cleverness in his face now. He was weighing the alternatives.

"That's it, sonny," Gant said. "Think about it. It's all one big trap – a maze. You have to find a way out, just like the rest of us." He smiled carefully. "There's just the three of us. What are we going to do about it?"

"What are the arrangements for this man?" Priabin asked.

"We were to leave the train at Kolpino –" Priabin looked at his watch, and Gant quickly did the same. Twelve minutes. "– the next station. Someone will be waiting for us, with a car."

"Then you're not needed!" Priabin exclaimed. "Don't you see, Anna, you're not needed! You don't have to provide cover for him by travelling all the way to the border – you don"t!"

Gant controlled his features, as she looked at him pleadingly. Priabin had leapt upon the flaw, the escape route for Anna. Now, she would ally herself with him.

"They'd still hand you over," he said.

"No! What are you – one of their Category-A Sources, Anna?" She looked at him, and nodded. "Yes, that's what my Case Officer says."

"Then you're important to them, don't believe you're not. If the American fails to get away, you wouldn't be blamed. If you hand him over to whoever is to meet him, then your part is finished. If he is killed trying to get out of the country, then you cannot be blamed . . ." He hurried on breathlessly, his hand shaking hers in time to the rhythm of his thoughts. Gant felt his stomach become watery. His eyes flicked to the rack and the closed, unattainable suitcase. There was nothing he could do now, but wait.

Ten minutes to Kolpino – but Priabin already knew about the waiting man and the waiting car. He would understand that Gant would be given exit papers for Finland, that he would be hurried out of the Soviet Union to safety. There was nothing Gant could do as Priabin continued talking, his face young and excited, as if he were engaged in nothing more dramatic than watching a football match or opening Christmas presents.

"Stay on the train – leave the American to whoever is meeting him. Understand? Just continue to Leningrad, and then fly straight back to Moscow. You can be there by morning, in work on time, everything . . ."

"And you?" she asked. "What will you do?"

Priabin looked down at his pistol. A heavy Stechkin. "It doesn't matter," he murmured. "I'll be back in Moscow tomorrow."

"He's going to kill me, after waiting until you've averted your pretty eyes," Gant said. "He thinks it's the easy way out."

"No — !"

"Isn't it?" Priabin grinned, but the expression was more akin to a sneer. He knew, now, that he possessed all the high cards in the game. Gant had lost his hostage, his secrecy — soon, his life.

"No. You'll have killed me. They won't like that."

"The Americans?"

"No. Your bosses. Vladimirov, the First Secretary, your Chairman . . . the *really* big boys won't like it!"

"I can live with demotion, with a rotten posting — just like Kontarsky will have to do," Priabin said sullenly.

"She'll still be working for the Americans —"

And Priabin's face unclouded, beamed at Gant. "I've thought of that!" he said, laying down his last and best card. He turned to Anna. Gant quailed. "I've just thought of it — she can become an agent of mine! An agent of — a KGB officer who's just died, or retired, but I knew about her — he would have set you up, Anna, as a double-agent, and you were passed on to me. I went to bed with you as well as made use of you. They'd believe that easily — !"

Anna was horrified. "I would have to go on, and on, and on — forever?" she asked.

"Safe!" he replied.

"But — I'd never be allowed to leave it, to get out?"

"Then why did you do it in the first place?" he snapped in a hard voice. "*Why?*"

Gant glanced at his watch. Six minutes. When the train slowed? Outside the station — ? Would he be able to get to Harris's car before Priabin did? He would be unarmed. But — jump?

"You ask me — ? Why are you a policeman?"

"It's my job."

"I want to get out of it, Dmitri — I don't want to pretend to have been working for the Americans while really working for you!" Her voice was high, her eyes bright with tears. She had released his hand. Both her small hands were clenched into protective fists in front of her breasts. She was shaking her head. She looked much older, almost plain, as she pleaded with Priabin. "I don't care what clever excuses you think up, I don't want to be trapped *forever* — !" She unclenched her right fist and dragged a lock of hair away from

452

her eyes. Then she clenched her hand once more in front of her. She was staring at her lap, not at Priabin. "I don't – *can't* go on with it, Dmitri . . ." Then she looked up. "If only I could go back – you don't know how much I'd give just to go back!"

Priabin appeared to be about to speak, but then he slumped back against the window blind, his eyes staring at Gant.

Gant said quietly, "Come with me to the border, Anna – get me out, and I promise they'll let you go. If you let him kill me, they'll turn you over to his people. His plan won't work because the Company won't let it work. My way, you have a chance – his way, you have none."

"You'll be his hostage, Anna."

"Sure she will. But, there's a way out at the end of it. All you'd do for her is to put her in the bag for the rest of her life – do you want that? *Really* want it?"

Priabin blinked slowly, heavily. His features expressed confusion, indecision. "I can't let you go," he said. Gant thought that he was speaking to Anna, but the remark was addressed to himself. "I can't do that."

Must be no more than three or four minutes, Gant told himself. Stay with this.

"You could go home, resign from the ministry, take a job where you're no use to them. They'll get angry, but they won't be able to stop you. And they won't turn you over just for the hell of it." His voice was soft, the syllables like careful footsteps through a minefield. She looked up at him, attentive, almost beginning to hope. Gant squashed a sense that he might be lying to her, that the Company might indeed turn against her and betray her to the KGB.

"I'll help," he said. "Get me to Finland – keep this guy off my back until we reach the border, and I promise you'll walk away free. Come to Helsinki with me –" he added urgently. Two minutes, was the train already beginning to slow? "Talk to the Company – talk to Charlie Buckholz or to Aubrey . . ." The names confused her, but he pressed on: "Aubrey would be on your side. It wouldn't take long, don't come unless you want to. Just get me to the border alive. That way you have a chance – his way, there isn't a hope in hell you can get away free!"

The train was slowing –

Priabin stared at Gant, then at Anna. When his gaze returned to the American, there was a deep, unsatisfied hatred in his eyes. The pistol was still aimed at the centre of Gant's chest, and the man was still intent upon using it. It depended on Anna. Now they were silent and watching him once more, he had no chance of jumping from the door of the slowing train.

453

The lights of a small town through the snow. White field. The green splash of a signal light at the trackside.

"Well?" he asked.

Anna looked up. She reached for Priabin's hand, and clutched it. Still looking at Gant, she said: "I must do it, Dmitri. I must do as he suggests —"

"No!"

"My darling, I *must*! You've wanted only to help me — we kept it from each other, but all you wanted to do was help me. Now, *please* help me. Help me, my darling. Let him go, and let me go with him. Don't follow us, don't stop us . . . I'll come back, I swear. You know I will. But let him get away, and we can both be free. They *will* do it, won't they?" she asked Gant.

He nodded. "The people I know — they'll let you go. I swear they will."

Station lights, rushing at first, then slowing to walking pace as they passed the window.

"Quickly, Anna," he said, looking at Priabin. The gun was cradled in his lap. His face was miserable, angry and defeated and fearful for her safety.

"Dmitri —"

He nodded, just as the train sighed to a complete stop. "Yes,' he said, then added to Gant: "It had better work, American. It had better work!"

"It will. I swear —"

"Then get your coats and luggage. I'll escort you —"

"No," Gant said.

"Yes. Your excuse for leaving the train here is flimsy, suspicious. With me, you will be asked no questions."

"And afterwards?"

"I'll wait for the next train. I'll wait for you in Leningrad, Anna —"

She rushed into his arms while Gant gathered the coats and luggage. He felt the ache of their passion, the intensity of their relationship. He had walked through the minefield, but until now he had never realised quite how dangerous it had been. And, deep inside himself, he felt something he could only describe as envy.

He owed her. He would, at least, try on her behalf —

"Come on," he said, turning to them, interrupting their kiss, almost embarrassed by it. "Hurry —"

Brooke shone his lamp on the nosewheel strut of the Firefox for what might have been the tenth or twelfth time. He could not help his reaction, avoid the jumpy tension in his body. It reminded him vividly of that period of childhood when he had avoided walking on the cracks in paving stones, always followed the borders of rugs and carpets, always checked and checked again that the light was properly switched off – at first it had needed four checks, then six, then eight . . . He had thought he was mad, until he discovered that half his classmates engaged in the same obsessive routines. Checking the ropes around the three undercarriage legs was now the same kind of thing. He felt almost obsessional. They had to be right. The raising of the aircraft was about to begin, everything depended on these three nylon ropes, on his checking them . . .

He bobbed beside the nosewheel strut. The rope passed several times around it, wound over heavy padding to avoid damage to the undercarriage leg. For that reason, too, the rope was high on the leg. He tugged, quite unnecessarily, at the nylon rope once more, ran the beam of his lamp along it as it stretched away towards the shore.

Yes, he thought, nodding his head – yes.

He turned his back on the aircraft, his lamp's beam running over the MO-MAT that reached down from the shore to the nosewheel. The portable roadway was of fibreglass-reinforced plastic, and lay over the mud and rubble of the lake bed, the incline of the shore itself, and the trampled snow of the cleared site beyond that. The Firefox would be winched along its non-skid surface, moving easily and smoothly, in theory, up onto dry land. The light bounced and wobbled over the waffle-like appearance of the MO-MAT, then Brooke's head bobbed out of the water and he began walking easily up the lessened incline of the shore. As he removed his facemask, he saw Waterford and Buckholz, dressed in white parkas, silhouetted against the lights suspended from the perimeter trees. They were standing together on the MO-MAT, waiting for him.

Snow flew across the glow of the lights as Buckholz waved his hand in Brooke's direction. The SBS lieutenant returned the wave. It was all right – they could begin.

"Yes," he said, nodding. He turned to look at the frozen lake, just as the American and Waterford were doing. "Anything in the latest report from the Nimrod?" he asked. An SBS corporal took his air tanks and facemask, and Brooke climbed into the parka. He did not feel cold.

"Sod all," Waterford replied. "Nothing."

"They still don't have Gant – he's on his way to Leningrad," Buckholz said. "He didn't tell them."

Through the curtains of snow that seemed dragged across the scene at irregular intervals, Brooke located a lump of timber floating in the patch of clear water. It was wrapped in Dayglo tape, and was attached by a thin line to the nose of the Firefox. Beyond it, more difficult to make out but spectrally visible, a huge crucifix of planks

455

and logs, similarly wrapped with luminous tape, represented the position of the aircraft under the ice. He and his divers had measured that outline. Now, all that remained was for the ice marked by the cross to be broken where it had thinly reformed after the plane had sunk. Then the winching operation could begin.

Brooke sensed the excitement in the American beside him. It matched his own. Waterford looked grim, but the expression was habitual. Brooke could not deduce any meaning from it.

Buckholz pressed an R/T handset to the side of his face, watching Brooke as he did so. "OK, diving party. Let's start clearing that ice."

Brooke's SBS divers moved down to the shore. Two of them entered the clear water, walking like penguins down the MO-MAT, then drifting out towards the edge of the ice. They reached the crucifix's tip, and immediately began sawing at the new, thin ice, working outwards from each other around the cross. Two more SBS men moved onto the ice itself, armed with steel spikes and hammers. White light reached out towards them as one of the powerful lamps was adjusted.

Even through the deadened, snow-filled air, he could hear the hammering of steel spikes into the ice. To these, lines would be attached so that sawn-off sections of ice could be towed to the shore. His divers were furiously at work cutting away chunks as the steel spikes were hammered in. He glanced at his watch. Twelve-fifteen. On schedule.

Two plates of ice were dragged by lines across the widening patch of clear water to the shore, then manhandled onto the thicker ice. Twelve-thirty. Lengths of timber floated in clear water now. The cross was losing shape. The sawing and hammering continued.

They had left the ice intact for as long as possible for reasons of security. A Dayglo crucifix, too, would signal their presence, even in bad visibility, to any low-flying aircraft or helicopter. Two hours earlier, they had had cause to consider the delay a wise one. Helicopters had been reported by Eastoe, heading north-west to Finland. Agreed, they were well to the south of them at first and later north-east as they cruised the area of the lake where Gant had been captured for almost an hour. Then they had retraced the route he had taken to that lake. Buckholz's party had waited in darkness and silence for their approach. It never came. The weather had worsened and the helicopters, picked up with difficulty by Eastoe's most sophisticated radar, had changed course and headed south-east to re-cross the border. Immediately, the lights had been switched on and the crucifix laid out on the ice to represent the fuselage and wings of the Firefox. Since then, Eastoe had reported no activity along the border. Presumably the Russians had decided against further helicopter reconnaissance in the weather conditions that now prevailed. It indicated that they did not know where to look, were ignorant of the location of the aircraft.

More plates of ice were dragged out of the water, which now receded to the edge of visibility. Then the scene was further obscured by a curtain of snow. The corporal had thrust a mug of coffee into Brooke's hand which he had accepted almost without noticing. He sipped at it now. Twelve-thirty.

He turned his head. Royal Engineers were checking the nylon lines with the same kind of obsessiveness he had shown in relation to the undercarriage of the Firefox. Some abrasive surfaces were padded with logs of felled timber. The three trees which held the chain-level winches were not equidistant, nor were they in a straight line. Therefore, the winching operation would be complex, and slow, in order to avoid snagging and rubbing against the undercarriage doors and to ensure that the airframe ascended the ramp of the MO-MAT in as straight a line as possible. The officer in charge of the party would be required to monitor the speed and progress of each winch and line – constantly.

Out on the ice, his divers had handed over the task of driving in the remaining steel pins to RAF engineers. They dropped into the dark water, to make a thorough final check for underwater obstacles – they had spent hours clearing rocks and rubble that afternoon – and to take up their monitoring positions. They would be watching the undercarriage for signs of strain or weakness, the ropes for the same – and both for the first movements.

Twelve-forty, Brooke's coffee was cold in the mug, and he threw it away with a flick of his wrist. It dyed the trampled snow at the edge of the MO-MAT's carpet. Two of the shore party were brushing at the waffle-like surface, keeping it as free of snow as possible.

Brooke watched Moresby, the squadron-leader from the Field Recovery Unit at Abingdon and their Senior Engineering Officer, ambling towards them. He nodded to Buckholz and Waterford, taking up the stance of a spectator immediately, hands thrust into his pockets, parka hood pulled around his face, shoulders hunched.

"As soon as we reach the level," he announced as if he had been engaged in a conversation for some time and was now answering one of a series of questions. "I'd expect her stopped – oh, here," he added, waving his arms to indicate the area just behind them where the slope of the shore all but disappeared. "I've had a word with the engineers and they're fairly certain we can hold her on the winches. In fact, I'd like to have a look inside the cockpit as soon as she clears the water."

Buckholz, unabashed, nodded. "OK, Squadron-Leader. Any auto-

457

destruct mechanism is entirely your baby. We'll order the winches to stop just as soon as she's clear of the water."

"Splendid. The anti-radar capability and the thought-guidance systems must be protected by some kind of auto-destruct. Since the bang-seat wasn't used, they may not be armed. But they could, just could, be armed by immersion in water – some of these devices are. So, I think I'd better find out before the aircraft dries off." He smiled perfunctorily, saluted quickly, and ambled off once more.

"It won't be much of a bang," Waterford commented. "They won't have rigged the whole airframe to blow up, much too dangerous. Russian pilots are very thick. Might kill the squadron-leader, of course, and give Aubrey a heart attack when he hears he's lost all the best stuff on board . . ."

"Thank you, Major," Buckholz retorted.

Out on the ice, the last plates were being manhandled onto the firmer ice. The channel of water stretched away into the darkness beyond the lights. Bits of luminous wood floated randomly. The cross had gone. The shore party had begun to return, and his divers were walking out of the water up the slope of the temporary roadway. They were grinning as they removed their facemasks. Brooke nodded, and one of the divers turned and slipped back into the water to take up a monitoring station. Brooke watched the beam of his lamp flicker palely, like the track of some glowing fish, as it moved away towards one of the wings of the submerged Firefox.

"Tell me, Major," Buckholz began, "did Aubrey call this operation 'Nessie' because he thought he wouldn't get the airframe out of the water?" He was smiling as he asked the question.

Waterford tossed his head. "Aubrey's idea of a joke, Mr. Buckholz – just his idea of a joke." He smiled briefly, then added: "Time for me to check with the Apaches out there. Excuse me."

Waterford's huge, solid calm had acted like a barrier, but now that he had moved away Brooke could sense the electricity of the scene, the tension felt by each man. The ice was clear, the lines checked, the divers on-station. Moresby was standing with the party of Royal Engineers at the rear of the scene, upstage. They were checking drills, and walkie-talkies. Then he scoured the ground around each of the trees selected to take one of the winches, checking anchorages and knots. Eventually, he waved a hand towards Buckholz and moved back towards Brooke and the American.

Brooke could smell soup on the snowy air. And coffee. It would be served when – if – their first attempt proved successful and they got the airframe to move. Then, safe in the knowledge that it was possible to move the plane, they would be given a ten-minute break for food and drink. The winching would take much of the night.

Buckholz's head swivelled inside the fur-edged hood of his white parka as he checked with each section of the operation by walkie-talkie and hand-signals. Then he turned to Brooke. His grin was nervous, his face pale with cold and excitement. Brooke grinned and gestured him to begin.

"OK, everyone — let's catch 'Nessie', shall we?" he announced, and immediately turned to watch the winches take up the first of the slack in the nylon ropes.

Buckholz turned his back on the lake and looked towards the three teams manning the winches. As the two men on each winch levered back and forth easily and rhythmically, the nylon ropes tautened. The teams slowed almost immediately at a command from the Royal Engineer officer. The central pair stopped winching altogether at his hand signal only moments later; quickly followed by the pair to the left. The RE captain allowed the right-hand winch to continue as he moved forward to check the relative tension of each rope. A few seconds later, he made a chopping motion with his hand, and the third winch stopped.

Moresby, joining him, spoke briefly, then nodded.

Buckholz heard the captain call: "Numbers One, Two, Three — haul away," and the ropes stretched, creaking slightly in the silence. Buckholz noticed the silence only then, at the first renewed sound of winching. He was aware, too, of the stillness of everyone there, except the six men at the bases of the trees which anchored the winches. Buckholz could sense their effort now; both men on each winch were straining. "All stop!" the captain called out. The lines had lifted from the surface of the MO-MAT. To Buckholz, they appeared overstretched, ready to break. Then he felt the silence again and realised he had thrust his hands into his pockets because they were trembling.

One of the SBS divers slipped into the cleared dark water and swam to the lines in turn, tying an orange marker to each one at the point where it emerged from the water. Moresby, like some parody of a keen-eyed, grasping factory-owner, had walked down to the shore and was studying the diver, as if about to sack or reprimand him. Hands behind his back, head craned forward, back slightly bent.

"Haul away, One, Two and Three!" he called out as the diver turned and swam towards him. The levers of the winches pumped evenly. More quickly, rhythmically, Buckholz felt, as if —

He watched the flags on the lines, almost mocking Moresby's intent, craning stance. Buckholz understood only what he was looking at, hardly considered what it would mean if —

He grinned, and exhaled, seemed to hear a communal sigh in the windy, snow-flown clearing. Moresby straightened up, hands still clasped behind his back, chest and stomach a little thrust out as if continuing to portray the factory-owner whose school history-book image would not desert Buckholz's thoughts.

The orange marker flags, all three of them, had moved off the surface of the water. The Firefox had moved. A facemasked head bobbed above the surface, gave a thumbs-up signal, and disappeared. The Firefox had rolled forward, perhaps no more than a few inches, but the undercarriage had withstood the initial strain of moving.

"One, Two and Three – haul away!" Moresby called over his shoulder, and the captain hand-signalled his three teams to begin in unison. The even rhythm of the levers was barely audible above the wind. Buckholz felt his heart racing, and grinned to himself.

His walkie-talkie bleeped.

"Yes?"

"Mr. Aubrey, sir – sorry, sir, it's Squadron-Leader Moresby he wants . . . sorry, Mr. Buckholz."

"OK, son."

Curiosity made him follow Moresby towards the windbreak which half-concealed the commpack and its operator. The RAF officer detoured to nod his congratulations to the three teams on the winches. The men were bent and heated now, creating the impression of labour as much as speed, effort more than achievement. They would be relieved within ten minutes by fresh teams. Moresby had already picked up the microphone. The look on his face puzzled Buckholz. Something like outrage. Again, he could not help but picture the British factory-owner, this time faced with the prospect of a strike or a Luddite wrecking his machines. He smiled, but the expression vanished a moment later.

"You want to ask me about *what*?" Moresby asked, his face expressing disbelief now that he had spoken. "Are you serious? Correction – you cannot *be* serious! Over." He looked up and saw Buckholz, and immediately waved him into the tiny enclave of the windbreak. The radio operator's glance was vivid with humour and the prospect of a quarrel.

"What is it?" Buckholz asked, and was waved to silence by Moresby, who was once more listening to Aubrey in Kirkenes.

Immediately Aubrey finished speaking, Moresby replied, his face flushed despite the cold. Within the hood of his grey-white parka, he appeared almost apoplectic. "I can't even begin to answer your questions, Mr. Aubrey. I have not worked with you on previous occasions, and I don't understand your sense of humour. What you propose is preposterous! Over."

460

"What the hell's going on?" Buckholz growled.

"He wants me –" Moresby began, then swallowed before he added, "– to tell him whether the aircraft could be prepared to fly again . . . to fly from here, to be exact! Absolutely out of the question –"

"You realise what this means?" Buckholz snapped. "He doesn't ask idle questions. It means the Sikorsky isn't coming, old boy, old buddy – he's just found out and he's clutching at straws. Give me the mike, Squadron-Leader.' Buckholz pressed one earpiece against the side of his head, and said, "Kenneth, this is Charles. Are you certain the Skyhook won't make it? Over."

Immediately, Aubrey replied, "I'm sorry, Charles, but – yes, I'm afraid so. There is no possibility of it arriving before the deadline – until it is well past, in fact. Over."

"So, where did you get this crazy idea from, Kenneth? The squadron-leader here doesn't think much of it."

"Absolute rubbish!" Moresby foamed.

"I realise that," Aubrey snapped. "Very tiresome. Over."

"I think you're as crazy as he does, in case you're interested. Over."

"Charles, there is simply no time to waste. I need a shopping list Curtin can transmit to Bardufoss – if they haven't got what is required, then we may be in trouble. Please put Moresby back on. You listen if you want to . . ." There was the faintest tinge of a dry laughter in Aubrey's tone. It surprised and even angered Buckholz. It made the depth of his reaction to the first movement of the aircraft seem somehow exaggerated and adolescent.

"Listen," he snapped, "we have no one to fly the damn thing!" Then he added waspishly, as if formality was a further element of the ridiculous: "Over!"

"Gant and Source *Bourgoyne* should be crossing the border into Finland within an hour or two. Gant will fly the aircraft." Aubrey sounded self-congratulatory. Buckholz understood why Giles Pyott, out of Aubrey's hearing, referred to him as a gifted, restless, hyperactive child. He *was* brilliant – a brilliant pain in the ass for much of the time.

"You mean you got an airplane that's still at the bottom of a lake and a pilot who's still inside Russia, and that's the groundplan for your idea? You're crazy if you think that will work!"

Moresby snatched at the headset. The radio operator plugged in a second headset and offered it to Buckholz with a grin. "Top rating for this phone-in show, sir," he murmured. Buckholz snorted. It *was* the *laughter* he could not comprehend. From Aubrey in particular . . .

Laughter in the dark. Game-playing. And yet people like Aubrey, even Pyott, made him feel heavy-footed and stolid, somehow colonial and gauche. All of it angered him.

Before Moresby could speak, he snapped. "Get off the air, Kenneth. You're an asshole for ever suggesting such a crazy scheme! If the Skyhook can't make it, we'll dismantle what we can. You get a Chinook from Bardufoss to take us out before the deadline expires. Over."

"Sorry, Charles – I said you could *listen*. Is Moresby still there?"

"I'm here!"

"Good. Now, Squadron-Leader, perhaps you'll be so good as to try to answer my question. Could the aircraft be prepared for a flight of, say – fifteen to twenty minutes' duration, at sub-sonic speed, of course? A distance of a couple of hundred miles? Please think very carefully."

Both Moresby and Buckholz had, by some unspoken common assent, turned their back on the commpack and its operator, and shuffled to the extent of their headset leads; as if to remove themselves from the communicable lunacy of Kenneth Aubrey. Both of them watched the fresh teams at the winches slip quickly into the easy, regular rhythm of the levering. The ropes, at the edge of clear vision out on the dark water, shook off silver drops of light. The marker flags were perhaps a few feet nearer the shore.

A diver's head popped above the water. He removed his facemask and mouthpiece, and they heard him shout: "Port wheels are almost on top of a rock. Stop winching and give me a crowbar!"

"One, Two, and Three – stop winching!"

Brooke, the skirts of his parka gathered up around his body, waded out into the water which moved sluggishly around his legs, and handed the crowbar to his diver. Their conversation was brief. The diver disappeared.

Moresby seemed to recollect Aubrey. "I've already told you that it's impossible, Mr. Aubrey. Please forgive my outburst – didn't mean to sound raped."

"You were, buddy – or you will be," Buckholz growled beside him.

"But it is impossible. I'm concentrating on what kind of auto-destruct may or may not be attached to the thought-guidance systems, the on-board computer and the anti-radar. If we don't locate the auto-destruct, assuming there is one, you won't have anything left that's worth the time and effort already spent. Over."

"I realise that, Moresby. But, please, simply tell me – Captain Curtin is listening, pen poised – what would be needed if the Firefox were to fly again – from that lake?"

The diver's head popped above the surface again. Brooke had

462

waited for him, and took the crowbar. Both of them gave the thumbs-up, and the engineer captain immediately ordered the three teams to recommence winching. Moresby sighed, then with an angry reluctance returned his attention to Aubrey. Buckholz willed him to utterly refute the Englishman as he felt the impact of the news concerning the Skyhook helicopter spread through him. They couldn't get the Firefox out. As simple as that. They were winching it out of the lake only to be unable to do any more than steal a few of its systems and instruments and samples of its airframe materials . . . and photographs. Countless photographs.

Buckholz understood Aubrey's refusal to surrender to the inevitable. But he could not share the man's new, impossible scheme. Which, he reminded himself, Aubrey was conjuring out of thin air just because he left himself without any fall back plan – !

"Hot air blowers," Moresby snapped as if the information was being extracted by physical pain. "Undercover job, drying the airframe. That takes care of the airframe. Now you have a *dry* lump of metal. Do you wish me to go on? Over."

"Please continue, Squadron Leader. All this is most interesting. Over."

Moresby sighed at the sarcasm in Aubrey's voice. Buckholz watched the three orange flags dancing like great butterflies above the dark, soupy water as the ropes strained.

"Engines next, then. Drying out – then you have problems with igniters, and fuel, of course. Number three – hydraulics and pneumatics. They could be OK, after such a short immersion, but everything, repeat *everything*, would have to be thoroughly checked otherwise you could end up without undercarriage, airbrakes, flaps. Four – the electrics. It would depend on what level of operation would be acceptable. Again, everything would have to be thoroughly checked, and any damage would have to be made good. You do have a private pipeline into the Mikoyan production line so that we have easy access to Russian spares, I suppose?" Moresby snorted; a noise not much like laughter but which Buckholz assumed was the air force officer's means of expressing amusement. "Five – instruments . . . the air-driven ones may be OK, since the water may not have got into the instrument heads – but, the electrically-driven gyro ones – I wouldn't even like to speculate on that. Over."

Buckholz sensed that Moresby had flung a great douche of cold water in Aubrey's direction and expected his ploy to work. He imagined Curtin scribbling furiously, shaking his head almost without pause. When he heard Aubrey's voice, however, he realised that he was undaunted.

"What about armaments? Over."

"For Heaven's sake, Aubrey!" Moresby exclaimed. "You'd have to talk to my armourer, but my guess is that you're on to a hiding to nothing on that tack."

"I see. But, thus far, apart from things mechanical and electronic, I would need experts in airframes, engines, hydraulics, control systems, electrics, avionics, instruments and weapons . . . in other words, a full ground-crew who would be experienced in servicing military aircraft. That doesn't seem too tall an order . . . Over?"

"Don't forget the runway, fuel, oxygen, a set of jacks, tools that fit – I simply cannot see any way in which it is feasible. Impossible in less than twenty-four hours, which is what we have. Impossible in three days or more, even at Abingdon – never mind Lapland!"

"Get off the guy's back, Aubrey!" Buckholz snapped. "You haven't got a chance with this. You couldn't even get the stuff he needs here, never mind the men. Forget it. Arrange for that Chinook to pick us up at dusk tomorrow. Jesus – !"

"What"s the matter? Over."

"She – she's on her way up, Aubrey – she's on her way up!"

He had noticed the silence. Now, cheering filled it. The winches paused, the orange marker flags danced. Pearls of water dropped from the taut nylon lines. Cheering.

The nose of the Firefox had slipped above the water, black and snoutlike, ugly and still threatening. Above it, like eyes, the perspex of the cockpit canopy stared at them. It was a sea creature, Aubrey's Nessie, watching them, waiting for them to be foolish enough to enter the water.

"Is she – ?" he heard Aubrey ask in a quiet voice.

"Beautiful," Buckholz said. "Dangerous and beautiful. My God, when Gant first saw *that* – !"

"Now tell me not to try. Over." Aubrey replied sardonically.

"It's still impossible," Moresby interrupted. The winches began again. Inch by inch, the snout and cockpit slipped higher out of the water, sometimes lost in the flurries of snow, sometimes clearer and more deadly in appearance.

"The weather, Kenneth?"

"At dawn, something of a lull is anticipated . . . enough for a Hercules to make a low-level drop. One drop, of *everything* you need. Then the weather will close in again."

"So no one gets out of here?"

"The met reports anticipate another such lull, late in the afternoon. The fronts will allow two windows in the weather, at dawn and around dusk. Over."

"That means less than twelve hours, Aubrey –"

"I realise that, Squadron-Leader. However, you could have

everything you need dropped on the lake at first light. If it doesn't work, I promise you will have my reluctant permission to utterly destroy the aircraft. Over."

Involuntarily, Buckholz's head flicked round so that he was looking at the Firefox. The leading edges of its huge wings were beginning to emerge. Now, it looked like something captured, caught in a net and dragged from its own element into the snowy air; a great manta ray rather than an aircraft. It mounted the slope, moving slowly, very slowly out of the water. Menace. Yes, Buckholz thought, it already exuded menace, even though there was no possibility it could ever fly again.

"I see," Moresby replied.

"It doesn't have a runway and we don't have any way of putting it back on the ice," Buckholz said quickly, aghast at the clear sound of disappointment in his voice. "Over."

"Tractor tug and a great deal more MO-MAT," Moresby snapped. "Over."

"Gentlemen," Aubrey said calmly, all trace of satisfaction carefully excluded from his voice. "How long before the aircraft is ashore? Over."

"Two hours at least. Over."

"Then we have two hours, Squadron-Leader, Charles. I suggest we begin talking in true earnest, don't you? Over."

Before he replied, Buckholz glanced at Firefox. And felt Aubrey's stupidity in having no fall-back, and his illogical, desperate brilliance in daring to assume the airplane could fly out of Lapland. And, he admitted, he too wanted her to fly again. She had to fly –

He glanced at Moresby, who shrugged. Then the air force officer nodded, even smiled. A tight little movement of his lips beneath his clipped moustache. "Very well," he breathed in the tone of an indulgent parent. "Very well."

"OK, Kenneth. Give us a few minutes to round up some people whose opinions we need – then we'll throw it on the porch and see if the cat laps it up!" Buckholz felt a strange, almost boyish exhilaration. In front of him, the wings continued to emerge from the water. The black snout seemed to seek him, the cockpit to stare at him.

Menace.

"Just make sure you don't lose Superpilot at the last fence, uh, Kenneth?"

Vladimirov yawned. It was an exhalation of his tension rather than an expression of weariness. He quickly stifled it. The room was small and cramped, the tape-recorder on the folding table almost its only furniture apart from a number of chairs stacked against one wall. The bare room accommodated himself, Andropov, and their senior interrogator from the KGB Unit on the Mira Prospekt. All three of them leaned their elbows on the table in the attitude of weary gamblers. A sheaf of pages – hurriedly typed and corrected and now overlain with the interrogator's scribble – lay near the recorder. Vladimirov had a pad and a ballpoint pen in front of him. He was no longer concerned to disguise the fact that he doodled occasionally. There were few words on his pad, and little meaning. Andropov's pad was clean, unmarked.

Vladimirov had lost his eagerness to hear Gant's sufferings under drugs, his hallucinations and illusions, his terror at dying and his attempts to persuade them that he was not. He had listened to the two interrogations several times in that cramped and almost foetid room, and he loathed something in himself that had actually anticipated the experience. When they had first arrived he had *wanted* to hear them. Now, he did not.

The tape continued in silence. Gant had hit his head on the floor, silencing himself. Nothing –

Vladimirov had learned nothing from re-hearing Gant screaming for them to listen to him. Even with the volume turned down, it was horrid. He had helped to torture Gant. It was his shame that was being replayed in front of the Chairman of the KGB.

Slowly, he looked up, and shrugged. "Nothing," he murmured.

"Mm. Your opinion?" Andropov snapped at the interrogator, who flinched before he replied deferentially.

"Comrade Chairman," he began. Andropov appeared to be impatient, but could not quite bring himself to wave the deference aside. Instead, he merely pursed his mouth and nodded the man along. "I – am not familiar with the kind of information the general is seeking."

"Was the American about to reveal something or not?"

"You mean – ?"

"From his condition, from the frenzy in his voice and manner at the end of the tape, was he trying to tell you something?" Andropov had begun to doodle on his pad as he talked. Strong bold curves which vanished beneath heavy geometric shapes.

"Yes, Comrade Chairman."

"Then, what was it?"

"I – that I cannot say." The senior interrogator shrugged, brushed his hand through his hair, stared at his notes, shuffled them, looked up once more. He spread his hands. "I – he believed in me as an American general, and he believed that the man he could not see was Aubrey, the British –"

"I know who Aubrey is," Andropov interrupted icily.

"Yes, of course. He — he was attempting to assure us that he was not dying —"

"Because he knew he hadn't burned in the explosion you pretended had occurred on the MiG-31 — yes, yes. We *all* understand that much. Now, what was he going to tell you? Vladimirov, surely there are some clues in what he said, what he couldn't help letting out?" Andropov's pale eyes gleamed behind his gold-rimmed spectacles. Vladimirov felt pressed. The Chairman's perspective was a larger one than his own. He wanted an answer so that he could avoid the First Secretary's censure, because if it was used against him, he might remain no more than a minor figure on the Politburo. However, his desire for an answer was no more urgent than Vladimirov's own. He wanted the MiG-31 more than ever. His insurance would be the recovery of the aircraft.

"Perhaps, but I can't see it. He does not talk — *anywhere* — about landing the aircraft."

"And yet he *must* have landed it?"

"Of course he did!' Vladimirov snapped testily. "Do you think he jumped out without using his parachute?" Almost immediately, he signalled a silent apology. "Yes, he landed it," he said more softly. Then he looked at the interrogator. "Very well. Rewind the tape to the point — oh, where he first claims he wasn't burned . . . find that."

The interrogator looked at his rough transcript and then rewound the tape. He followed the numbers flicking back on the counter, checking it with the column of numerals at the end of each page. Then he stabbed his finger down on the Stop button. He looked at Andropov, who nodded. The tape began to play.

The mimic playing the part of Aubrey cried out immediately: "He's not dying!" Vladimirov leaned forward, head cocked, intent upon the charade, trying to hear something through the illusion, through the familiarity of the dialogue; through his recurring shame. The interrogator in his guise as the American general murmured that Gant was, indeed, dying. Vladimirov remembered, and could clearly envisage Gant's hand crawling as if with a life of its own up the uniform worn by the interrogator. He had pulled out the earpiece through which the interrogator was receiving reports from those monitoring the television cameras focused on the bed. Gant tried to pull the interrogator towards him . . .

"Not burned, not burned . . ." he heard the Americans repeating. He seemed pressed to tell something, to explain, to correct their mistake. Vladimirov could not prevent the pluck of tension and excitement he felt in his tight chest. *Not burned, not burned . . .* What had been happening in his drugged, confused, disorientated head at that moment? What had he wanted to say so desperately?

Andropov's fingers tapped silently on the edge of the table, as if accompanying the words with appropriate music. The interrogator was merely performing a charade of concentration. He did not know what to look for. He had not been a pilot.

"Not burned ... drowning ... drowning – on fire, but water, water ..." Gant continued on the tape, his voice mounting, losing control, trying to convince them that their diagnosis was wrong, that he was not dying of burns. "Not burned ... landed –"

"Stop it!" Vladimirov shouted. The interrogator jumped, then pressed the button. "Very well – you heard that? He said that he *landed* –"

"And where does that get us?" Andropov asked with withering sarcasm. "You already knew that, didn't you?" He smiled thinly. "Now, *where* did he land? Which one of your roads or tracks?"

Vladimirov shrugged. "Begin again," he said.

"... not burned – water ..." Gant said immediately, then there was nothing but the noises of rustling clothes, hesitant footsteps. Vladimirov remembered, then. Gant had slumped back on the bed at that point. A little later, he was to sit up once more, and scream out *Listen!* and *Explain!*

But he had never explained, though they had listened. In his frenzy, his legs had become entangled in the bedclothes and he had toppled out of bed, striking his head and knocking himself unconscious. End of the affair –

Footsteps on the tape – or was it Andropov's drumming fingers? Breathing, murmurs that were indistinct, someone cursing, fumbling with something. Everyone waiting for the moment that had never arrived.

Not burned ... Gant was not burned. He knew that. Vladimirov looked down at his pad. Almost unnoticed, he had torn off the sheet of doodles and had virtually carved words onto the sheet beneath.

He counted. Gant refuted his having been burned five times. He mentioned fire, though – just once. Vladimirov realised he had scribbled each of the words separately, each time they were spoken. Taking Gant's fevered dictation. He had written *water*, too. Gant had said that, apparently, three times. And, *drowning* – twice ...

Burning, drowning, water, fire, landed ...

Vladimirov realised how much depended upon the tapes, the solution, the moment. He *had* to find the answer – !

Water three times, drowning twice, landed once ... His ballpoint pen almost surreptitiously linked the three circled words by trailing lines. *Drowning* and *water* were like balloons floating yet anchored above the word *landed* ...

468

He remembered Andropov asking about the aircraft being landed on a frozen lake –

And then he knew.

Land – water – drowning.

He had broken the code. He knew what Gant had done. He had landed the MiG-31 on a frozen lake, and the ice had given way and he had almost drowned. And there was no trace of the aircraft because the water had frozen over it.

He had discounted the lakes in the designated area because there was no shelter for that black aircraft standing on white snow and ice. But, *under* the ice – !

His hand was shaking. He looked up, to find Andropov watching him intently. Vladimirov hardly heard Gant shouting for attention in the moment before he tumbled to the floor. Andropov gestured for the tape to be switched off, and Vladimirov announced in a quiet, hoarse voice:

"The MiG-31 is at present under the ice of a frozen lake, Comrade Chairman. I am certain of it."

"Explain." Vladimirov did so. Andropov stared at him, his face expressionless. Then, in the ensuing silence, which seemed endless, his features became intently reflective. Andropov was evidently weighing the consequences of his acceptance of the general's theory. Eventually, the Chairman spoke. "I think we should consult the map. Perhaps you would lead on, General Vladimirov." Then he turned to the senior interrogator. "That will be all, Comrade Deputy Director. Thank you." It was evident that the senior interrogator derived little comfort from the flat, noncommital tones.

Vladimirov reached the door. Andropov followed him into the huge underground room. Heads turned to them, then returned to appointed tasks, as they crossed the floor together and climbed the ladder onto the gallery. Expectant faces looked up as they entered the control room of the command centre. Yet no one joined them at the fibre-optic map. Finnish Lapland remained as they had left it, except for a dotted red line that had inched south-east during their absence.

"Well?" Andropov asked, surrendering the consequences to Vladimirov.

The general traced the dotted red line with his finger. The reconnaissance party had made good time, moving on a very narrow front, retracing Gant's journey . . . from a lake, he reminded himself. Where? His finger continued south-eastward, moving swiftly over the road and tracks he had at first nominated. How could he have been so *stupid* – ?

Two lakes, almost in a direct line with the route of the

reconnaissance party; certainly within the tolerances which allowed for slight changes of direction by the American. One of the lakes was rounded, the other longer and narrower. He recalled the scale. Either might have done . . .

And there was a third lake to the north of that pair, and a fourth to the east. Four lakes. The red dotted line was closest to the pair of lakes. His finger tapped the surface of the map.

"There," he said. "First priority — a reconnaissance of those two lakes." He stared at Andropov until the chairman silently nodded his head. Then he said, more loudly, "Major, please check these coordinates, then transmit them to our reconnaissance party. At once!"

A young major in the GRU hurried forward to join them at the map.

ELEVEN:

Crossing The Border

Harris stopped the hired car, switched off the engine, and turned in his seat. For a moment he appeared to study Gant and Anna with a cool objectivity, then he said. "I'll just call in and check with my people in Leningrad. The border is ten miles up the road . . ." He pointed through a windscreen that was already smeared with snow now that the wipers had been switched off. "I don't want us to get caught out by any alarm or increased security. The Finns are waiting for us. They'll have signalled Leningrad in case of trouble. We passed a telephone box on the edge of the village." He smiled. "Best not to park near it – if anyone sees me now, they'll assume I'm a local. Just sit tight. I won't be long."

Harris opened the door. Snow gusted in. He climbed out and slammed the door behind him. Gant turned his head and watched him trudge away, back towards the few scattered lights of the tiny hamlet through which they had passed a minute earlier. Harris had pulled the car off the main road, into a lay-by which was masked by tall bushes heavy with snow.

Harris disappeared from view. Gant turned to Anna.

"Check your papers again," he instructed. He pulled his own documents from his breast pocket, unbuttoning his overcoat to do so. As he opened the travel documents and visas, he wondered once more about Anna. She had accepted the papers Harris had supplied, and the cover story. She had examined the documents periodically during their three-hour car journey from Kolpino, via the outskirts of Leningrad and the industrial city of Vyborg. Yet he sensed that she still in no way associated herself with them. They were like a novel she had picked out for the journey in which she had little interest.

Harris, a British businessman with a Helsinki base and frequent opportunity for business travel inside the Soviet Union, was to pose as a Finn when they reached the border. He possessed a Finnish passport and his visas had been stamped to indicate that he had travelled from Helsinki to Leningrad a few days before. Gant and Anna were to remain as Russians, and as members of the Secretariat. They were accompanying Harris from Leningrad to inspect his facilities on behalf of the Leningrad Party. Harris was in the metallurgical business, and factories and businesses in the area covered by the Leningrad *Oblast* required his products.

The covers were impressive, even unnerving to a border guard. The only suspicious circumstance was the time of arrival at the border and the manner of travel. Yet, Gant knew it would work. He no longer noticed the hairpiece and the half-glasses, and in the same fashion he no longer considered the flaws in Harris's plan.

The journey had helped, of course. The constant moving away and, after Moscow, the openness of the dark, snowbound country-side. Frozen lakes gleaming in scraps of moonlight between heavy snow showers. Moscow had hemmed him. It had been a huge trawl-net laid just for him. Here, he saw no evidence of the hunt and he accepted the innocent-seeming time at its face value. He even dozed in the back of the warm car, head nodding on his chest, waking periodically to glimpse the countryside or the lights of the village or see the snow rushing out of the night towards the windscreen.

But, Anna — ?

It was as if some motive force within her had seized up. She seemed incapable of action or decision. He did not even know, this close to the edge of the Soviet Union, whether she really intended to cross with them. He could imagine her opening the door of the car, even as the red and white pole began to swing up, and start walking back down the road into Russia. Also, he did not know whether Priabin was to be trusted.

At Kolpino, he had looked like a man striving to cling to the wreckage of his life; trying not to display emotions he might normally have considered womanish. He had waved them through the inspection at the station, chatting to them, strutting a little with his superior rank, dropping hints of mystery and important Party business. He had watched them into Harris's hired car, had stood in the falling light of a lamp outside the station, a solitary and enigmatic figure, as they had driven off. Gant, glancing round, had the impression of a small figure with arm aloft. And then his sense of intruding upon some private act had made him turn away. Anna had remained with her head turned to the rear window long after a bend in the road had removed him from sight.

He did not think Priabin would follow them, or betray them at the border, because of Anna's safety. But, he was not quite certain. As they had all three left the train, Gant and he had come face to face for a moment. Priabin had still possessed the grim, almost fanatical look that had been on his features when he first entered their compartment — when he had intended shooting Gant.

Priabin still wanted to kill him.

"You are coming over?" Gant now asked hoarsely, slipping his papers back into his breast pocket. He fiddled with the glasses on his nose, as if working himself back into a portrayal just before going on-stage.

Anna looked up at him. She looked older, even in the semi-darkness. He heard her shallow, quick breathing. He thought she was very minutely shaking her head, but it did not seem to be any kind of denial. He touched her hand as it lay on her lap. The hand jumped like a startled pet, but did not withdraw.

"It's going to be all right – I promise," he said. He had made Harris support his idea, render assurances. Anna could be got back into the Soviet Union without difficulty – via the same route and within a couple of days. Harris knew Aubrey – yes. Did Aubrey have the necessary clout with the CIA – ? Yes, Harris thought so. Yes, he didn't see any reason why she should not be let off the hook for getting Gant back to the West . . .

"A couple of days," he murmured, prompted by his memories of Harris's reassurances. "That's all it'll take, I promise you." He smiled crookedly, sorry that she could not see clearly the reassuring expression. "I'm big for them now – at the moment. I *can* get them to do what I want – get you out of it."

Her head was shaking now. "I can't believe it is going to work." She looked up at him, having taken his hand. "I do not blame you, Mitchell Gant – believe that, at least. You were just . . . the wrong man at the wrong time." She might have been talking of a ruinous love affair, one which had cost her her marriage. That heartfelt tone gave Gant an insight. For her, the relationship with Priabin had been somehow altered, perhaps even destroyed. She could not envisage a satisfactory future unless she restored her relationship with him.

Gant envied and pitied her. And realised the mutuality of their passion. Priabin's hatred, narrowed to himself alone now, was as palpable as if the man had just put his head into the car. The three hours since they had left him would have done nothing to dissipate that hatred. It would have grown, perhaps run out of control like a forest fire.

And Gant knew that Priabin would not give up, would not be content to wait in a Leningrad hotel for her return.

"Listen to me," he said urgently. "You love him, he loves you. What is there to be afraid of? Only people like your Case Officer – nothing more dangerous than that. And the Company will be warned off – ! You won't have to worry . . . and it won't matter how long it takes to get cosy with Dmitri again. You'll have the time to do

473

it. For Christ's sake, Anna, just cross the border with me and I promise you everything will work out!"

He gripped her hand fiercely. It lay dormant in his fist. He dropped it onto her lap, sighed, and slumped back in his seat.

After a long silence, he heard her say softly, almost apologetically, "Very well. I have made up my mind. You are right. I will come with you."

He looked at her carefully. He could see the pale skin and her cheeks seemed dry. Her eyes were in shadow. The touch of her hand did not seem pretended or assumed, and he believed her.

"OK,' he said. "You've made the right choice. I know you have."

"Will he understand?"

"He knew all along —"

"But that was *different* —" It was almost a wail.

"You mean — you weren't helping me, uh?" Gant snapped. "I wasn't the key to his career?"

"He wouldn't think like that."

"Maybe, maybe not. Whichever way you look at it, he owes me. He's a man with a lot of grief to unload, and I gave him all of it. I just hope he sits tight in Leningrad and boozes himself into self-pity. It could be safer for all of us."

"You mean — ?"

"I don't mean anything. Let's just hope, uh?" He was angry that he had voiced his own fears precisely at the moment she had become reconciled to accompanying him. He glanced at his watch, holding its dial close to his face.

Harris had been gone for more than fifteen minutes.

He gripped the door handle.

"I'm going to look for Harris — stay here," he ordered.

"You think — ?" she asked fearfully, as if Priabin threatened her, too. Priabin, yes, he thought. Both of us are afraid of the same man —

"I don't think anything. He could have slipped and broken a leg. I'll be back."

He pressed his fur hat onto his head and squinted into the blowing snow. Anna watched him as he trudged as quickly as he could out of the lay-by and onto the main road. The high bushes hid him.

Anna turned back, and stared at the thick coating of snow that obscured the windscreen. There were lighter, paper-like coverings on the side windows. The car was claustrophobic, small and cell-like. Her fears enlarged within it.

She had coped, so easily and successfully she had always *coped* — ! But not with this.

She rubbed her hands down her face, as if scouring her skin. She was trapped; utterly trapped. Only the American, whom she ought to have hated because he had acted as the catalyst of her ruin, offered her any hope of escape. If they would let her go – *if only they would let her go!*

Gant had said it didn't matter how much time it took to rebuild her relationship with Dmitri. He had promised her the time in which to do it. She could only believe him, because there was no other solution. No other way out.

The door of the car opened. She turned her head and stared into Dmitri's face. Her mouth opened, as if to protest at the appearance of a ghost, and then he had climbed into the rear of the car and was holding her in his arms. She gasped and clung to him. His overcoat was chilly and wet with melting snow. His cheek was cold against her temple, but it soothed her. She held onto him, even when he made as if to push her away, because the world was no larger than the material of his coat, the cold of his cheek, the noise of his laboured breathing in her ear. Then he forced her to sit upright, holding her arms tightly enough to hurt. She studied his face in the darkness of the car. As his eyes adjusted to the gloom, he seemed to be searching her face for some emotion he feared to find.

"Dmitri – where . . .?"

"No time, Anna,' he said breathlessly, placing his gloved forefinger on her mouth. "Listen to me. Come back with me now. Please come back with me now – !" It was an order, but more than that, a plea. As if he saw into a black future, and wished to pull her back from it as from the edge of a cliff.

"What is it?"

"What do you mean? I want you to come with me. Quickly, before Gant returns. Let him cross the border by himself. We can be in Leningrad before morning, in Moscow by noon. Look, Anna, we can explain everything. I – I can explain in some way or other why I had to leave Moscow, why I travelled to Leningrad. No one need know you ever left the city. Come quickly now, before he returns . . ." He was eager to be gone, like a thief leaving a house he had ransacked. She did not understand his urgency. She did not understand why he was there, how he had followed them. There was something in his tone that lay beneath love, and she could not help her mistrust of it.

"Why? Dmitri, what's the matter – tell me . . .?"

Her hands gripped his arms. They appeared to be jockeying for a position whereby one could use a wrestling throw upon the other. She shook her head slightly.

"There's nothing the matter. Now, come with me, Anna – quickly, before he returns –"

She knew, then. The anxiety was clear in his voice. Knew part of it, at least. "Where's Harris, Dmitri? Where is the driver? What will the American find?" She shook his arms.

"It doesn't matter," he said softly.

"Tell me!"

"He's *dead*!"

"You *killed* him?"

"There was a struggle," he answered lamely.

"No there wasn't — !" she almost screamed, outraged more by his lie than by the death of Harris. "You killed him. Don't *lie* to me!"

"Come on —"

"No! Not until you tell me what will happen."

"Anna —"

"No. What will happen?"

"Gant will be arrested at the border — perhaps even shot. Yes, best if he were shot . . ."

"You mean you've told them to expect him — expect *us*?" she asked, appalled, her hand covering her mouth, then both hands clamped upon her ears.

"No. Not yet. I came for you first."

"Dmitri — for God's sake, what are you *doing* — !"

"Saving you — saving us. Harris knew about you, Gant knows about you. He won't give himself up at the border when they try to arrest him — they'll have to kill him. You'll be safe, then."

"No —"

"What matters most — him or us? Anna, if Gant dies no one will know you helped him. He won't be able to tell them —"

"And the CIA?" she asked bitterly. "They will know."

"No they won't! You can tell them he made you turn back, that he went on by himself while you returned to Leningrad . . . he and Harris were killed. It's easy —"

"*Easy*? Killing two people is easy?"

"Anna — forget all this. Just get out of the car, come with me and let him go on by himself. I'll — I won't call the border post, I'll let him go. I promise he'll be safe —"

"I don't believe you — you *want* him to die." She studied his face; even though he moved his head back and away from her, she could distinguish the gleam in his eyes. He did want Gant killed. Like a jealous lover, he wanted his rival dead.

The windows of the car were fogged. The snow was slush-like, beginning to slip down to the sills, because of the warmth inside the car; their anger. She did not know what to do. Dmitri could not protect her from the CIA. She could not let Dmitri kill Gant. Because he was Dmitri, because she could not live with him if she acquiesced . . . she would learn to live with Harris's death, change it from murder into something else. But not Gant. She would have known beforehand, and would never escape it. "I can't let you . . ." she murmured eventually.

"What? You want to *protect* him?" Dmitri raged. "You want to go on being a *spy*, an agent? For the *Americans*?"

"Not for the Americans, not for him – for us. I can't *agree* to his murder, I can't let you murder him! Don't you see? I can't live with that – !"

"I can," he announced with cold solemnity. "I want to."

"Dmitri –"

He shook his head. "You're coming with me, Anna," he said, grabbing her arm. This time the pressure of his grip made her cry out. He pulled at her arm, opening the door with his other hand. "You're coming with me! You'll forget about this, you'll forget about everything . . ."

"No – !"

He grunted and twisted her arm, making her scream. "Come on, Anna," he snarled, threatening her. "Come on."

He twisted her arm further, almost seeming to Anna to be on the point of breaking it. Fire spread from her wrist to her elbow to her shoulder. She cried out again, looking wildly at him, unable to understand his rage, his desire to hurt her. "No – !"

"Come on – !" He pulled her upper body clear of the car. She lay almost horizontally on the seat. He bent and slapped her face. "Come on, come on – !" He wrenched at her arm. She screamed.

Then she felt the pressure, the agony, lessen. The skirt of his overcoat brushed her head, she saw feet slipping and struggling in the trampled snow by the wheel of the car, then something banged heavily against the front passenger door. She heard Gant's voice.

"What the hell is the matter with you?" Gant was breathing heavily, almost grunting out the words. She could hear Dmitri's rough breathing, too. She rolled back into a sitting position. Dmitri's back had wiped away the snow from the passenger window. The freezing air made her shiver violently. She held her injured arm gently, cradling it like a child in her other arm. "That's better," she heard Gant say. "Just take it easy." Then: "You all right, Anna?"

"Yes, yes," she managed to say thickly. Then she groaned as she moved.

"OK?"

"Yes." She got heavily out of the car, still cradling her arm. Dmitri looked at her, horrified. Gant's arm had been across his throat, his pistol at Dmitri's forehead. Now, the American stepped back, motioning her away from Dmitri. She obeyed.

477

"What the hell was happening when I came up?" Gant asked. Then he added: "You know he killed Harris?" She nodded. Addressing Dmitri, he said, "You stupid bastard. What the hell's the matter with you? You could get us all caught!"

"You I *want* caught!" Dmitri snapped back.

"OK, kid, I'm the biggest villain you ever met! That I can understand – but *her*? You're putting her in danger. You think you can just take her back, without guarantees from the Company? You're dumb – *too* dumb." Something else, something more dangerous, occurred to Gant at that moment, and he said, "Are they expecting us? *Are they?*" The pistol jabbed forward, at Dmitri Priabin's stomach.

Anna gasped, then cried out, "No! He hasn't told them yet – I swear he hasn't!"

"I believe you. *You*," he added, addressing Priabin, "what was the plan, uh? Kill Harris so we get into trouble at the border . . . or just me? Anna was going to walk? You'd have left me stranded, and you'd have made sure I got killed." Gant's features twisted in anger and contempt. "Get in the car," he snapped. "Back seat, with the window rolled right down – get in!" Priabin climbed reluctantly into the car and wound down the window. He glared out after the door was closed on him. He avoided looking at Anna. He rubbed his hands together between his knees, as if warming or washing them. Gant pocketed Priabin's heavy Stechkin automatic, keeping his own pistol levelled. "Anna – come here," he said. "Not too close."

She moved closer to Gant. Priabin's eyes blazed as she seemed to touch the American.

"I'm all right," she announced, now rubbing her injured arm. "I'm all right, Dmitri –"

"I'm sorry," he said, shamefaced.

"OK, that's fine, real fine. Now, what do we do with him? If we leave him here, he'll call the Border Guard just as soon as he can. If we take him, he'll turn me in the first chance he gets – and that will mean he screws things up for you, too, Anna."

"No," Priabin protested sullenly.

"Wake up to the fact that I'm the only real chance she has of walking free of this whole mess!" Gant snapped angrily. "You let us across the border and she'll be able to come back to you. Your way – she hasn't a prayer."

Priabin's face gleamed with hatred. He could not accept Anna as a gift of the American. He was not calculating, not operating, in any kind of professional capacity. He wanted to *kill* Gant, but it was because of Anna. He blamed the American for everything. The killing of Gant would be some kind of cleansing ritual; either that, or it would prove his manhood or keep his mistress or ensure their safety. Whatever the reason, the death of Gant was inextricably tangled with any solution he envisaged. Perhaps he wanted Gant dead as much as he wanted Anna safe.

"Dmitri, let us go," Anna pleaded, almost leaning into the car. *"Please* let us go. It has to be this way – I have to be free of them – !"

Gant was shocked at the depth of bitterness in her words. However, he addressed Priabin in a tone of laconic threat. "Well, Dmitri, speak up. You heard the lady. Will you let us go?" Priabin did not reply, did not even look at Gant. Gant said to Anna, "Will he let us go? Can you really believe he won't try to kill me?"

She glanced round at him, as if invited to participate in a betrayal. Then she shook her head. "No," she sobbed.

"Then he's a damn fool!" Gant snapped and strode swiftly to the window of the car. Priabin flinched. Anna made as if to cry out. Gant struck Priabin across the temple with the barrel of the Makarov. The Russian slumped away from the window, across the seat.

"No – !" Anna cried, gripping the sill, stumbling against Gant.

"He's alive! It just gives us time."

"Dmitri –"

"Get into the car and listen to his heartbeat if you don't believe me!"

"No, no, I believe you . . ." She mumbled. "Thank you, thank you."

"Don't waste time. Let me get him out of the car – he won't freeze in this coat." Grunting with effort as he spoke, Gant hauled Priabin out of the car and dragged him to the shelter of a heavy, snow-laden bush. Anna walked beside him, her eyes never leaving Priabin's face. When Gant lowered the unconscious Russian, she knelt by him. Gant watched her stroke the young man's face, gently touch the swelling on his temple. He walked away. The whole attitude of her body, the look on her face, was too much like prayer. "Are you coming?" he asked in an almost fearful tone.

He turned to look at her. She was still kneeling beside the unconscious Priabin. She touched his face slowly, gently. Then she stood up.

"He will be all right?"

"Just a headache."

"There is no other way, is there?"

"No. No sure way except coming with me."

"Will he believe that?" she asked, glancing down at Priabin again.

"I can't answer that."

"I don't believe he will . . ." She shrugged, and walked away from Priabin towards Gant. "But, I have no choice – do I?"

"No, you don"t," he replied softly.

They reached the car and Gant opened the passenger door for her. She climbed in slowly and reluctantly, her face turning immediately to Priabin's body. He slammed the door and walked round to the driver's side. He brushed snow from his hairpiece, from the shoulders and knees of his clothing, then sat heavily in the driver's seat.

Harris had left the keys in the ignition. Gant had checked his pockets when he found the body, thrown into a snow-filled ditch near the telephone box.

"Christ," he breathed, remembering his shock on finding Harris's body and instantly realising who had killed him. "Why the hell did he do it? How could he be so *blind*?" He shook his head, his hands fiercely gripping the steering wheel.

"I don't know – love?" Anna said.

"Crazy –"

"Yes, love." She was nodding to herself, confirming her analysis.

Gant looked at her. "Have you got the nerve to cross the border without Harris? If he's expected along with us, then we'll have to bluff it out – he fell ill in Leningrad, something like that . . . we're angry at being delayed and having to cross the damn border in the middle of the night for talks early tomorrow. Can you do that?"

She nodded. "Yes, I can do that."

"OK. We have ten miles' rehearsal time. We might just make it before that crazy bastard wakes up."

"Do you understand why he did it?"

"It doesn't matter –"

"It does! He's a murderer. I have to find a reason for that."

"OK . . ."

"Harris and you – you were taking me away from him. He didn't believe I would come back . . ." She choked back a strange, crumpled, defeated sound in her throat, but she could not prevent tears from rolling down her pale cheeks. Gant flicked on the windscreen wipers. The view cleared of slush. The wipers squeaked across half-ice. "He didn't believe . . ." she repeated, but the words were submerged. She shook her head violently, as if to clear it. "He didn't . . ." Her voice was awed, and profoundly disappointed.

"And killing me makes everything right, uh?"

"Yes," she replied, staring through the windscreen at the steadily falling snow. "You are to blame. You have to be to blame. If you are to blame for everything that has happened to us, then I am not to blame and Dmitri is not to blame . . . but, especially me. I would be to blame for nothing, nothing at all . . ."

"It doesn't matter." He glanced back at Priabin's unmoving form.

480

"We might just make it, even without Harris," he announced, switching on the engine.

With the assistance of a Norwegian radio operator, Curtin was engaged in a long, wearying, intense conversation with the senior engineering officer, the station commander, and the pilot of the Hercules Aubrey had commandeered, at Bardufoss. Aubrey himself was using the high-speed communications system to talk to Shelley in London.

Aubrey was pleased with himself, with the situation, with the progress they had made. In a little more than two hours, he had put his shoulder to the great wheel of circumstances, and had managed to move it. He was tired, but felt elated. Later, he knew he would collapse, like a cliff sliding slowly into the sea. But not yet, not while things remained to be done.

"I shall be telling Director Vitsula that Gant is required in Oslo immediately for a full debriefing. In fact, he will be brought here. You do *have* the Harrier, Peter?"

Aubrey waited while his message was transmitted via geostationary satellite to Shelley in Century House, overlooking the river. Then the tapes gathered Shelley's reply at high speed, rewound, and spoke.

There was amusement in Shelley's voice, too, as he said, "Yes, sir, we have a Harrier. It is already en route to Oslo, thence to Helsinki to collect Gant. Allied Forces, South Norway, will inform you of the aircraft's arrival. Won't Vitsula think it just a little suspicious that you had a Harrier collect Gant rather than something that *can't* land at the lake?"

There was a pause in the message, but the operator knew that Shelley had not finished.

"There's quite a bit more yet, sir," he informed Aubrey.

"Christ . . ." he heard Shelley breathe in an aside, then clear his throat. "Thank you, Bill. Yes — no, keep running the tape, man!" Then, evidently, he addressed Aubrey directly. The old man was alert, almost trembling. He understood the first drops of rain from an approaching storm. "Sir, message just received from Leningrad Station. Most urgent — the panic button, sir. Harris telephoned in with ten miles to go, and was cut off. They don't think it was the line, sir. Reception was quite good, in spite of the weather, and they swear the line was still open for some seconds after Harris stopped speaking. They even heard the pips demand more money in the slot . . ."

"My *God!*" Aubrey exclaimed, raising his hands in the air. "Oh, my God —"

481

Curtin was watching him from the other side of the hut. He had paused in his conversation. Aubrey absently waved him to continue, as if dismissing him from the room.

Gant – what the devil had happened to Gant?

The radio operator waited for his reply. Looking slightly bemused and a little worried, Curtin continued his conversation with Bardufoss. His technical specifications, the details of what Aubrey had called their shopping list, the ranks and areas of expertise of the men volunteered, the strength and capacity of arms of the Royal Marines – all mocked him now. Curtin's words bore in upon him in the hot, paraffin-smelling silence of the hut. Curtin was discussing Blowpipe missiles, and dismissing the idea. They had not yet decided whether there would be sufficient room on board the Hercules for more than a handful of Royal Marines and their equipment. Aubrey had been prepared to discount the idea of reinforcements because the Russians still had no idea where the Firefox was located. There was less need of defence than of extra equipment. The bales of MO-MAT occupied a great deal of space, as did the tractor tug, and both were crucial.

But now, but now, his thoughts repeated. Where was Gant? Did they have him? He had to *know* – !

He was deeply afraid. He had to talk to Vitsula, he had to have a report of Gant's arrival at the border, his crossing – *if* he arrived, *if* he crossed . . .

He had to. He needed news of Gant much as he might have needed a tranquilliser. Had to have news, had to – at once . . .

"Yes, Peter – I understand. I must talk to Helsinki. Message ends."

He turned away from the console, rubbing his cheeks vigorously with his hands. He realised his palms were damp with nervous perspiration. Curtin had moved on to the subject of air transportable fuel cells and the number required. At Bardufoss, with the Royal Norwegian Air Force's Tactical Supply Squadron, things were still happening. Everything was happening. The Hercules was already being loaded. Met. reports indicated that the dawn window in the appalling weather would occur, and the drop could take place on schedule. Hydraulic and lubricating oils now, and oxygen cylinders . . .

Madness, Aubrey could not help pronouncing to himself. He had taken leave of his senses. To have ever *conceived* of such a scheme – !

The radio operator had signalled Helsinki. Director-General Vitsula of Finnish Intelligence might already be seated before a console, awaiting his message. He must talk to him –

Aubrey knew there was nothing Vitsula could do. The Finns could not, would not cross the border. Gant was on his own until he crossed into Finland.

482

If he was still alive –

He must talk to Helsinki, must pretend, for his own sake, that there was something that could be done, that there were re-assurances that might yet be gained. Mere talk. Filling the accusing silence.

The nose of the Firefox lowered, seemed to droop like the beak of some huge, black, drinking bird, as it moved over the crown of the slope onto the level stretch of MO-MAT. Buckholz, who had been waiting for a sign of eventual success, felt relief begin to invade his chilled body. The winches creaked. He sensed the huge weight of the aircraft as he watched the nosewheel inching forward along the portable runway, dragging the long, streaming fuselage behind it. The nylon lines quivered with strain, and he realised that the three anchor trees that held the chain-winches must be under the same strain. They seemed to protest, sounding like the amplified noises of aching muscles.

Yet he felt relieved; close to success. Moresby's head and shoulders above the cockpit sill were another sign; an imitation pilot, making the Firefox appear to be an aircraft once more. Half an hour ago, it had been different. The undercarriage had become threatened by rocks and rubble on the lake bed. Brooke and his divers had had to inflate huge black buoyancy bags beneath the aircraft's wings to lift the undercarriage clear before it suffered structural damage. Then, when the rocks had been left behind or removed, the divers had had to carefully deflate the bags once more and lower the undercarriage – main wheels first, very slowly and steadily – back to the lake bed. Though everyone had emphasised that it was no more than a hitch, it had affected Buckholz. Once winching re-commenced, he had obsessively watched the nosewheel, measured its progress – waited for it to reach and surmount the crown of the slope.

He turned to look at the winching teams, at the taut ropes and the quivering trees. Then back to the fuselage of the aircraft. Then the winching teams once more; knowing that he was ignoring the real drama of the scene. Moresby was securing the ejector seat, to which any ordinary auto-destruct system would be rigged. He was ensuring that no accident could trigger it. Then he could begin to search the cockpit for any other mechanical or electrical system designed to ensure the destruction of the most secret equipment aboard the aircraft. Buckholz, as a layman, could not believe in the drama of the auto-destruct. For him, it was easier to imagine a rope breaking, a tree giving way, an undercarriage leg buckling, even snapping under the strain imposed by the winches. And Moresby was doing nothing; there was no atmosphere of tension generated from the cockpit. Expertise disguised danger. A bobbing head in a woollen cap, framed by the thrown-back hood of a white parka. Buckholz could not believe that the Firefox would explode.

The tree holding the winch attached to the port undercarriage leg appeared to quiver as he turned once more to look at it. The men on the winch, backs bent, suggested nothing was wrong by their continued, rhythmical movements. The Royal Engineer captain had his back to the tree, hands on his hips, watching the Firefox labour towards him. The nose of the aircraft was fully level now, the two remaining undercarriage wheels poised to roll over the crown of the slope.

The port line was quivering more exaggeratedly than the other two. Its marker flag dancing. Buckholz turned his gaze to the anchor tree. One of the two winchmen had straightened and was about to turn towards his officer. The tree had begun to tilt forward. He glanced at the aircraft. Moresby's head and shoulders, the two rear under-carriage wheels poised to level the fuselage, the two other lines straining, the port line dancing, seeming to slacken . . .

He opened his mouth. His words were cut off by a rifle-like crack. The anchor tree flung down its weight of snow, shuddered again, then the clearing was filled with the noise of tearing roots. Buckholz moved one pace. The engineer captain turned, raising his head as he moved to one side very slowly. The two winchmen had abandoned the winch. Pistol-like cracks. The scene consisted almost solely of sound. Hardly any movement. Monochrome – snow, trees, portable runway, the black aircraft like a creature attempting to return to the water. The roots snapped and broke in a succession of small explosions. The winchmen and the engineer captain flung themselves to either side of the tree as it lurched, then staggered as if entirely free of its roots, and began to fall.

It would miss the Firefox, miss the –

The thought became outdated in the next instant. The two remaining nylon lines began to dance and wave their marker flags as the first one had done. The aircraft was slewing to starboard, turning its nose towards Buckholz. He watched the port line slacken as the tree fell slowly into the clearing. Someone shouted, or perhaps cried out in pain. Everything was slow. Buckholz realised that the tree was moving faster than the men around it. Its dark branches enfolded a man who had hardly begun to run. Buckholz heard his muffled scream. The two lines danced wildly as the Firefox seemed to lurch backwards. He heard the winches groan, sensed the two remaining anchor trees quiver.

The nosewheel was still moving backwards, he was certain of it.

He saw Moresby's head and shoulders, then his upper torso as he stood up in the cockpit, gripping the sill with both mittened hands. Moresby's mouth opened. Some of the overhead netting, caught by the falling tree, ripped and floated downwards like part of a stage backcloth. Snow billowed and fell. Branches were dragged from neighbouring trees, more netting pursued that already torn. The slack line snaked out of the winch and whipped across the clearing. One man fell, another ducked beneath the whiplash. The nylon line slithered to rest across the MO-MAT.

Moresby shouted an order. Buckholz did not hear it. He was aware of Waterford at his shoulder and then the soldier moved towards the Firefox, yelling like Moresby, waving his arms as if to increase his circulation; the two remaining anchor trees shuddered, depositing snow. The engineers were already checking the winches, the trees, the lines; moving as if under water.

Monochrome –

Then terrible colour. Someone screamed, and the noise appeared to conjure up flame. On the far side of the clearing, the camouflage netting had fallen onto the stove that was supplying the relieved winching teams with hot drinks. The nose of the Firefox strained round like the head of a roped bull. The nosewheel had slid sideways, but backwards, too. The groaning anchor trees were slowly releasing the winches, which in turn released the ropes inch by inch. The fire roared up, catching the matting and setting it alight. A man burned, then doused the flames by rolling over and over in the snow, thrashing about in agony.

Only Waterford seemed to be moving towards the scene.

Then others. Other noises, other orders. The flames roared up in a fountain. Men rolled logs forward, behind the two undercarriage wheels, then behind the nosewheel. The undercarriage resisted the attempt to block its retreat to the water. The lines shuddered, their marker flags waving frenziedly. The anchor trees were almost bare of their weight of snow. Above the yelling, Buckholz listened for the first groan, the first pistol-shots of snapping roots. He knew the aircraft was destined to roll backwards into the lake.

Without realising he had moved forward into the chaos of the scene. Flame gouted, a tiny, ineffectual spray of exstinguisher foam reached towards it. Buckholz bent and rolled a log behind the starboard wheel. The nose of the Firefox had turned through perhaps thirty degrees, seeming to fight against the restraint of the remaining lines. The tyre began to mount the log – other logs were jammed against his own. The port wheel, too, was being blocked by logs.

"Get another line on the port leg!" he heard Moresby shouting somewhere above him. As he looked beneath the belly of the Firefox, he saw extinguisher foam arcing through the snowy air towards the fire. Then flame retaliated, licking upwards into the overhead netting that remained. Men ran towards the port side of the aircraft, unreeling a nylon line. He heard Moresby directing his men from the cockpit.

"Get that moved!" Waterford cried out. Buckholz could see the soldier outlined by flame, so close to the fire that he appeared to be burning himself. His body was bent, he was dragging a box-like container. Ammunition — the ammunition supplies were stored at the edge of the clearing. Buckholz could not move. He was kneeling beneath the starboard wing, the tyre trying to surmount the jammed logs acting as chocks. He stared in horrified fascination as the ammunition boxes were slowly — so slowly — dragged clear of the flames. They were doused with foam, the fire was attacked with more foam. The line just above his head quivered, its dance now a shudder, something close to a climax —

He turned to look. The trees were quivering, but did not appear to be tilting forward into the clearing. The crackling of his R/T drew his attention to the babble of orders and responses and reports. The team secured the new line to the port undercarriage leg. The aircraft seemed to sense its imminent restraint, and lurched further, skewing round, lifting the starboard wheel almost over the jam of logs beside Buckholz.

"Here — !" he called. Someone was beside him almost at once. "Hold on here!"

He stood up, gripping the makeshift wooden lever the other man had placed against the pile of logs. Together, they attempted to hold the pressure of the aircraft's weight, trying to keep the logs from rolling away from the wheel. Immediately, Buckholz was gasping for breath and his arms and back and legs ached. A third and fourth man joined them; another crude braking lever was jammed against the logs. It did not seem to ease the pressure on Buckholz's muscles. He grunted as a substitute for protest.

"Then take the bloody risk with *that* tree, Captain!" Moresby yelled in the R/T, and was acknowledged immediately. "Don't slacken the line, you stupid buggers! Pay it out ahead — yes, that's it . . . take the strain, you silly sods, or we'll all be in the bloody shit!" Beneath the language and the apparent panic, there was expertise. "Get the two remaining trees anchored before they give way!" Moresby continued. "Lash each of them to three other trees, nearest ones to them. Come on, before they uproot themselves too!"

"Come on, come *on* —" Buckholz recited, finding the words in his grunting breaths. The man beside him took up the words like a chant. The tyre squeaked in protest against the logs. "Come on, come on, come on –"

The captain ordered his men to attach the winch to the selected tree. Buckholz's leg muscles went into spasm, but they were a great distance from him. The colour of the fire seemed to lessen as it was reflected on the sheen of ice already forming on the aircraft's belly. There was a scorched smell on the snowy wind – netting, canvas, clothing, and something else he did not want to identify . . . *flesh*.

The strain became worse. His mittened hands were welded to the wooden lever, his arms welded to his hands, his shoulders locked above his hurting back and buttocks.

"Come on – get on with it, Captain!" Moresby was yelling again.

"Come on, come on, come on . . ."

"Make sure that bloody fire's out! Look after – who is it, Henderson? – and get the poor sod out from under that bastard tree!" Waterford's orders bellowed over the R/T.

He heard the two remaining winches yield the nylon lines inch by inch, as the anchor trees bent. The tyre that filled his gaze seemed to lift further, almost mounting the logs. Then a rapid noise in the distance, at the edge of the clearing –

"Oh, Jesus – !" he wailed. Rapid clicks, quiet pistol-shots. He was about to warn the men with him to get out of the way, to save themselves, when he realised it was the chain-winch winding the line through to take up the slack as rapidly as possible. Three lines now, almost three, three in a moment or two –

"Come on, come on, come on . . ."

"Fuck this for –"

"Come on!' Moresby yelled. "Have you finished anchoring the other trees?"

Then he saw the line on the port leg snap straight, take up the strain, quiver and become still. He heard the single winch click and click again and again. The nose of the Firefox steadied, as if the animal it had become sensed a superiority of strength in its captors. He exaled a great sigh.

"Is that tree holding?" Moresby shouted.

"For the moment, sir," the engineer captain replied.

"Anchor it to three secondary trees then."

"Sir."

Someone near Buckholz grunted a cheer. In front of him, the tyre had slid back behind the little barricade of logs. It just rested against them now. He raised his eyes. The port and nosewheel lines were shivering into still tension. The trees – did they still quiver and lean

487

or was it the cold sweat in his eyes, the effort he was making, that gave them the appearance of movement? He lowered his gaze to the starboard wheel. The tyre had moved away from the logs.

The cacophony of orders and responses had become muted. Calm. He waited. His body was numb; even the tremor had gone from his muscles. He felt locked into his posture, into his effort. The captain ordered the new winch to begin once more, slowly. The Firefox protested. Its nose swung slowly round, almost balefully, the wheel protesting on the waffle-like surface of the portable runway. He saw the tension in the line from the starboard leg ease. The marker flag stopped dancing and became a rag flicked by the wind. Buckholz waited.

The port winch stopped. He could not feel his hands around the wooden lever, could hardly feel the next man's body against his.

Then he heard Moresby say, "One, Two and Three – haul away!" He groaned. Moresby added: "OK, you lot down there – relax. And thanks. Thanks everyone . . ." Buckholz tried to unclasp his hands. The starboard wheel moved a few more inches from the heap of logs. They rolled after it from the pressure of the lever. Moresby continued talking, requesting a full damage report. Buckholz's back cried out in protest as he straightened up. His legs felt weak. He staggered a few steps, then bent painfully to chafe them back to usefulness. He groaned softly with every breath.

Then, when he could walk, when his feet began to hurt with reawakened blood, he hobbled as swiftly as he could towards the scene of the fire. A canvas sheet covered something. He glanced back into the clearing. There was something else, uncovered by the tree, being lifted and moved out of the aircraft's resumed path.

Two dead, then –

He looked into Waterford's face. It was blackened by smoke, but the man seemed uninjured, unlike the two SBS men beyond him, whose hands and faces were being salved and bandaged. Hot scraps of camouflage netting dropped like windborne flakes of ash from the trees above them. The ground was slushy, slippery with melted snow and foam. Waterford stared at him.

"Two dead?" he said.

Waterford nodded. "Two – and two injured . . . not badly burned." The man's face seemed to become chalky and vulnerable as he added: "Thank God." Then at once he was again his usual persona. "You can help me," he ordered Buckholz. "Make a full damage report. Well, come on –"

Waterford strode off. Buckholz, before following him, watched the taut lines, the inching forward along the MO-MAT of the three undercarriage wheels, all of them now on the level. Moresby was once more seated in the cockpit. Buckholz, on the point of sighing with relief and delayed shock, held his breath. The auto-destruct. They were in as much danger of losing the airframe as ever. Perhaps more. Moresby had been distracted. Time had passed – how much? Minutes . . . perhaps seven minutes. Seven –

His body was trembling from head to foot. He hurried after Waterford on weak legs, as if hurrying away from the aircraft and the danger it now represented.

The whole clearing smelt of burning.

Priabin began to realise he was cold. He seemed to be floating. At least, part of him was floating. A much smaller part, right at the back of his head, was aware that something was wrong. But, there were no answers, only images; dreams, nightmares, visions, pictures, memories. In most of them, he was apologising to Anna.

He apologised for his work, for his colleagues, for his uniform, for his rank, and for things he knew he had never done; actions never taken, crimes not committed.

He sensed she accused him, though she did not appear in most of the pictures or memories or dreams. Not even her voice. But somehow he knew that she was accusing him, and he understood the nature of the charges. No, he had not beaten up those demonstrators in Red Square, no he had not had those people shot for black-marketeering, no he had not had those Jews interrogated and beaten and the one who died had had a weak heart. No, he had not refused that writer a travel visa and passport; no, he had not prevented people from leaving the Soviet Union; no, he had not ensnared those businessmen by using women to sleep with them; no, he had not operated the cameras that filmed them . . .

Some night-bird moved in the bush above his head, throwing down a weight of snow onto his face. He opened his eyes. The snow was in his nose and mouth. He was aware of his entire body, and of its lowered temperature. His fingertips and toes were numb, his arms and legs cold, his torso chilled. He struggled to sit up, and looked around him.

The car had disappeared. He knew no more, for the moment, except that he had expected it to be there. It was a car he had approached, even sat in. His car – ?

His car was further down the road, towards the village . . .

Anna's car.

Harris's body. Harris? How did he know the man's name? He rubbed his arms with gloved hands, slapped at his upper body, then crawled out from the shelter of the bush into the snow that was now falling steadily. The wind appeared to have dropped.

Harris?

Gant —

He remembered. Remembered, too, all the images and visions; the countless apologies to Anna, who had refused to appear in his dreaming, even though she was close at hand. Anna — ?

Gant — Anna.

He knew more; all of it.

He climbed to his feet, and a great weight of ballast appeared to move in his head. He groaned and clutched his temple. The bruise was numb yet tender. He could feel a tiny amount of caked blood, like frost. Anna had gone with Gant. He staggered a few steps. The faint tyre-tracks of the car led out of the lay-by, heading west towards the border.

He knew everything now. Gant and Anna had abandoned him in the lay-by while they made their escape. But the American had made a mistake — he had left Priabin alive. He congratulated himself on Gant's error.

He began to jog, awkwardly at first, his head beginning to pound as soon as he moved. He ran, head down, through the falling snow. Out of the lay-by, onto the deserted main road. He glanced up the road, towards the border. Empty. He bent his head again and began running, chanting over and over in ragged breaths his prayer that Gant had not sabotaged the car he had commandeered from the railway police at Kolpino.

He floundered along the road, arms pumping, chest heaving. He remembered the dreams and realised their significance. Then he slipped and went flying, skidding on his back across the road. The shock woke him as it expelled the breath from his body. He climbed to his feet, brushed down his clothes, and began running again. Not far now, only hundreds of metres, no more.

He passed the telephone box where he had killed Harris. He had intended that. Isolate Gant, he had told himself. Get Anna out then kill Gant — have him killed at the border. Turn back the clock, make it five days earlier, before all this had happened.

He could have done it, but she would not *believe* him — !

He saw one or two early lights in the village ahead. His car was only a short distance now . . . yes, there! He slid the last steps, bumping painfully against the side of the vehicle. He fumbled the keys from his pocket while he wrenched open the driver's door with his other hand. He collapsed heavily into the seat, hesitated, then thrust the key into the ignition.

And turned the key, holding his breath.

The ignition chattered. On the third attempt, the engine fired then stalled. He applied more choke. The engine caught, he revved blue smoke into the snow beyond the rear window. The engine roared healthily.

Just cold.

He eased his foot off the pedal and moved the car slowly out into the middle of the road. The studded tyres bit, and he gradually accelerated. Passing the telephone box, passing the place where the snow was distressed by his skidding body, passing the lay-by. He looked at his watch, but could not estimate how long he had been unconscious. He stabbed the accelerator, and the back of the car swung wildly. He eased his foot from the pedal, turned the wheel swiftly to straighten the car, and drove on.

He had protected Anna because, in part, it preserved his own self-esteem. He was *not* a KGB officer, not *just* a policeman . . . He understood her clearly; even applauded her motives. He always had.

He would have saved her, got her away, but Gant had changed everything. Gant had placed her in danger, Gant had taken her away, she was in the car with him now. She was ready to cross the border with him –

Priabin wiped something from his eyes with the damp sleeve of his overcoat, then concentrated on the snow rushing towards the headlights. He knew he had peeled the onion a layer too deep.

He knew that he had not trusted Anna. From the moment when he had seen Gant on the train and realised how she was to help him escape, he had believed in his heart that she would go with the American. He had not trusted her to stop short of the border, or return if she did cross.

He wiped at his eyes again, savagely. *He had not trusted her!* He had believed she could, she would leave him.

Gant had held up the mirror, had shown him the vile little heart of himself, beneath the layers of love and protection and self-esteem. He loathed his reflected image.

He had to kill Gant. More than anything, he would kill Gant.

"One, Two and Three – stop winching!"

Buckholz heard Moresby's voice over the R/T, and immediately glanced at Waterford beside him. The soldier seemed unimpressed that the Firefox had now been winched safely to the far end of the clearing. Instead, he continued to stare at the ice beneath their feet. They were fifty or sixty yards out onto the lake. The wind flung snow between them and the well-lit clearing. Fortunately, the arc-lamps hadn't been brought down from the trees with the burning camouflage netting.

"Well – what is it you wanted me to see?" Buckholz asked. He

491

wanted coffee, and he needed rest. Reaction had established itself now that their damage report was complete and his work temporarily done. Moresby's danger hardly impinged upon Buckholz's fuddled, slow thoughts. "Well?"

"Look at the bloody ice, man!" Waterford snapped in return.

"What – ?"

"Snow – dammit, snow! Bloody snow!" He waved his arms above his head and kicked at the snow beneath his feet. The weather howled and flew around them in the darkness. Waterford was haloed by the lights from the clearing – where Moresby was working against time, he remembered with difficulty. As Waterford continued in a ranting tone, a break in the wind showed him the aircraft, black and safe, showed him the ragged extension of the clearing along the shore, allowed him to hear the chain-saws at work. "No bloody aircraft is going to be able to take off from this surface." Waterford was saying. "You know how long this lake is. Do you know how much runway that aircraft needs? No? Listen, then – the airspeed won't come up quick enough to give the pilot lift-off with this thickness of snow on the ice. It's as simple as that. So, what are you giong to do about it?"

In the silence, which the wind filled, Buckholz heard Moresby's voice issuing from their R/Ts. "This thing is drying out rapidly, gentlemen..." They had no idea to whom the remark was addressed. Perhaps to all of them. "Icing up. I hope to God that whatever system they've installed, it isn't water-activated. There's nothing in the cockpit or rigged to any of the systems that looks like an auto-destruct.' Moresby paused, but his next words wiped away Buckholz's momentary sense of relief. "But, I'll bet there is an auto-destruct, all the same. You'd all better clear the area. Gunnar –"

"Yes?"

"Any joy?"

"I don't know. I can't find anything in the Pilot's Notes at first look. And there's nothing marked or stencilled on the fuselage so far."

The weather had removed them from Buckholz's sight, but he could envisage them clearly. Gunnar, who spoke good Russian, had been given the task of translating the Pilot's Notes which Moresby had found in the cockpit – a leaflet of fifty pages or more. At the same time, he was translating every stencilled word and instruction on the entire fuselage, searching for a clue to the nature and location of the auto-destruct mechanism.

"That's it, then," Moresby continued. "Everyone clear the area. Five or six hundred feet back should do it. Go and hide in the trees – "

"Jesus," Buckholz breathed. "Is there anything we can do?" he said into the R/T, addressing Moresby.

"You're not helping the situation, Mr. Buckholz," came back the reply. "I suggest you hurry along and see a taxidermist, if you would!" Buckholz heard Gunnar's laughter, and beside him Waterford guffawed.

"Jesus —"

"Even we can walk on frozen water," Waterford said. "But planes can't take off from this thickness of snow. Even if the bloody thing survives its ordeal at Moresby's hands, it can't take off. You think we'll have a nice warm sunny day tomorrow?"

"Don't blame me — !" He was aware of the murmurs from the R/T now. Moresby and his technicians. Gunnar's translations. He knew everyone else would be listening, too. The noise of the chain-saws had stopped.

"I don't. You're just another of Aubrey's trained monkeys, just like me. That silly sod has flipped his lid this time and no mistake!

Without conscious decision, they had begun to walk back towards the clearing. Light blazed out at them as they approached the shore. The trees along the shore had been cleared. MO-MAT would be laid along the shore, and then the tractor tug would tow the Firefox to a point where thicker ice would bear its weight before pulling the aircraft out onto the lake which would become its runway.

Which would not be usable as a runway, he reminded himself.

They trudged along the shore. The snow was blowing horizontally yet, in the clearing itself, there was a sense of quiet, urgent desperation. As he saw Moresby, seated in the cockpit, and the technicians gathered around the fuselage, he realised he had no idea how large an explosion there would be. What would happen? Would it be small enough not to be visible until a little black flag of smoke raised itself above the cockpit? Or would it be large enough to open the nose section of the airframe like an exploded trick cigar? Enough to kill Gunnar and Moresby and the technicians . . .

And himself and Waterford, he thought as they trudged up the MO-MAT towards the aircraft.

There was a film of ice over much of the fuselage and the wing areas. There were great gaps in the camouflage netting which could not be replaced. The fallen tree lay to one side of the clearing, which was empty except for themselves, Moresby's team, and the Firefox. There might have been no chaos only a half-hour earlier. It was as if everything had been no more than a dramatic prelude to the quiet desperation of Moresby's search for the auto-destruct system.

The two bodies had been shrouded in their sleeping bags and removed from the clearing. They lay now like Arctic mummies, waiting for transport to their place of burial; waiting for next-of-kin to be informed. Buckholz shook the thoughts from his head.

Moresby saw them approach, and climbed rapidly out of the cockpit. He waved his arms as if shoo-ing chickens in a yard.

"I told you to fuck off," he said to Buckholz.

"As a kid I used to haunt accident black-spots," Buckholz replied without expression. Moresby looked at him curiously, and then nodded, accepting his presence.

Buckholz looked around the clearing. Stores, the commpack, equipment, had all been removed. It was as if they were about to abandon the Firefox, having spent so much time and effort – and two lives – bringing her out of the lake. "What have you done so far?" he asked.

"There's no magnetic card to activate any auto-destruct," Moresby snapped. "No armed micro-switches – nothing that could be set off other than by the removal of the canopy or the ejection of the bang-seat."

"But – there *has* to be something else?"

"I'd bet on it. Of course there has to be something –"

"Hell."

"Excuse me – I'm needed," Moresby said, and turned away from Buckholz and Waterford. Buckholz let the man go. He had no expertise and could not dissuade Moresby. Instead, he worried about the thickness of snow that had fallen on the ice. Gant had had snow cleared from the ice-floe when he had refuelled. It would have to be done here, with hot-air blowers. He would talk directly to Bardufoss, as soon –

As soon as they knew whether or not there was a clock ticking somewhere, a clock they could neither see nor hear. Was there anything?

Gunnar had covered almost the whole of the fuselage. He had worked around the airframe, reaching the fuselage below the cockpit once more. He had found nothing other than routine fuelling and inspection points, catches, switches, points, bolts, panels.

"Below this small window, it reads: 'In the event of red placard, cordon off airframe and advise Senior Armaments Officer'," Gunnar recited, then began humming and murmuring to himself over the R/T. Then he added: "Yes, that's what it says. There is a red placard showing in the window."

"Let me see," they heard Moresby say.

Involuntarily, Buckholz started forward. Waterford snorted in derision, but followed him.

"What is it?" Buckholz asked as he reached Moresby, who was

494

craning to look through a tiny perspex window set at eye-level below the cockpit.

"Approximately five millimetres of red-painted tin," Moresby answered without turning his head. "It doesn't mean a lot, does it?" He tapped the fuselage alongside the window. "Access panel – be careful, my lad, as you take it off, won't you?"

He stepped back and allowed the technician to reach the panel and gently begin to move the first few screws.

"Is it anything?" Buckholz insisted.

"Who knows? The instruction is pretty clear. You don't cordon off aircraft for no reason, or tell the armaments people it's all theirs. I wonder . . . Come on, lad, get a move on!" The technician had removed three of the flush screws, and he pivoted the access panel. Moresby immediately moved forward brandishing a torch like a weapon. He craned towards the panel, moving the torch's thin beam as carefully as if he were attempting to skewer something with it. Buckholz listened to his commentary over the R/T, having retreated to his former position. "Mm. Two solenoids, a relay – what's that . . .? Wiring, a box with a tag . . . Gunnar, what does it say on the tag – here . . ." Moresby stepped away.

Gunnar wriggled the beam of the torch into the open panel. "It says 'Battery change due on . . .' And it gives the date. Next month."

"Useless!" Moresby snapped. "Let me have another look. What else have we got here? Mm? Small canister, looks a bit like – what? Old flasher unit I had on my Morris, years ago. Top surface has a thin coating of some kind, wires from the base which couple into solenoids and the relay . . . and that's it. Might be to run the pilot's model railway, I suppose . . . Anyone else want a look?"

Moresby passed the torch to one of the technicians, and turned to face Buckholz and Waterford. "Who knows?" he announced with a shrug. "It ought to be important, but I can't see why."

"The red placard?" Buckholz asked.

"If this is the auto-destruct, then it's armed, yes."

"Thanks."

"Pleasure." He turned to his technician. "Well?"

"It doesn't remind me of a flasher unit, sir," the technician offered.

"Brilliant. And what does it remind you of?"

"Looks like the automatic sprinkler device my old Dad fitted in his greenhouses – down Evesham way . . . very pleased with them, he was."

"Fascinating." Moresby flashed the torch back into the open panel, wriggled its light, sighed over the R/T, glanced at the red placard in the window, then back into the hole. "How does your father's sprinkler system work, then?" he asked with studied casualness. They heard his muffled voice continue: "Speak up, laddie, I'm very interested in gardening myself."

Moresby's massive calm and expertise and exaggerated manner had all conspired to lessen the tension which Buckholz felt was beginning to grow in him again.

"You've warned your men to stay at a safe distance?" he muttered to Waterford.

"I have." Waterford had called in nine of the eighteen SBS marines who formed his reconnaissance perimeter, to form a guard around the clearing now that the Firefox had been winched out of the lake.

Buckholz knew they should be starting to arrive within the next fifteen minutes. His concern for their safety deflected his fears for himself. The red placard must mean *something* – !

The technician was explaining his father's greenhouse sprinkler system. Buckholz could not accommodate the seeming irrelevance of the information. ". . . when it dries out turns the sprinkler on . . . when it's wet by the right amount, it turns it off again . . ."

"Mm. Must get one for the lawn," Moresby murmured, his face still pressed to the access panel. Then he stood up, and stretched. "In the absence of anything more technical than the greenhouse sprinkler system donated by Carter and his father, I think we'll wedge the solenoids, just in case. Carry on, Carter. Let's play safe." Immediately, he walked across to Buckholz, rubbing his hands as if washing them inside his gloves. "Hurry up, Carter," he called over his shoulder, "it's getting pretty dry behind that panel."

"Do you think that's it?" Buckholz asked, his nerves and tension making him feel ridiculous.

"I should think so – *bang*," he added with a tight smile. He flicked at his moustache, which creaked with his frozen breath. "I don't know why they wanted a water-activated system. Morbidly security-conscious, though, the Russians."

"So how did it work?" Buckholz was more and more angry. It was an anti-climax, he had been frightened for nothing.

"With the airframe's immersion, the system became operational," Moresby replied, almost with relish. "It was fully armed once it came out of the water. When it dried off completely – bang! At least, I assume that's what would have happened . . ."

He turned. The technician gave him a thumbs-up sign, and Moresby sighed with satifaction.

"Safe?" Buckholz asked.

"Hang about for a bit and see, if you wish. I think so – we'll get

496

down to the real work now. I should get your chaps to cut down a few more trees, Major. It's almost three now." He nodded, and walked away towards the aircraft.

"Christ," Buckholz breathed. "Jesus H. Christ."

"No, but he's not bad for RAF," Waterford murmured, placing the R/T against his lips and turning away from the American.

Hoses, Buckholz reminded himself, masking the fears that he no longer wished to admit to. He felt himself trembling. He had been frightened. Now, he had to find an activity, some occupation.

He wondered whether they had sufficient lengths of hose at Bardufoss to steam a runway across the ice for the Firefox, now that it was no longer in danger of being destroyed.

Then he thought of Gant.

And realised that the pilot might hang by more of a thread than the airframe had done.

The guards were bored, then impressed, then efficient. It had been simple. The barbed wire strung on crossed logs and poles was thickened, whitened and made innocent by clinging snow. It stretched away on either side into the hidden landscape. Snow covered the ploughed swathe of earth that marked the border. Lights shone down on the guard post and customs office, and a look-out tower threw a shadow across the road just beyond the red and white pole.

Priabin had not told them, Gant thought to himself once more. He warmed himself with the knowledge. He stood with his back to the long table where Anna was now showing her papers and answering the few deferential questions offered by the Border Guard captain in command of the crossing-point. Gant could see, beyond the shadow of the tower, the distant red and white pole on the Finnish side. Lights glowed from the windows of the huts like signals. The Finns who were to be meet them would be watching the door of this customs office, waiting for their re-emergence. They would get into the car, the Russian pole would swing up, they would be through. Sixty or seventy yards, and they would be in Finland.

Don't think about it, he told himself, feeling his hands quiver in the pockets of his overcoat. The snow that had gathered on his fur hat had melted, and began to trickle down his neck and beneath the collar of his shirt. Don't think about crossing . . .

If he did dwell on it, his mask would crack in the closing seconds of his performance. It was easy, acting this officious senior diplomat or civil servant. An older man, testy with authority, dry and sharp like a fallen brown holly leaf. These people were half-afraid of him, half-afraid of his power to make telephone calls, speak to superiors, complain, condemn. They had hurried their questions, their examination of his papers. They had not wished to search his luggage. They had accepted his explanation that their Finnish companion, expected to drive them, had fallen ill – *too much drink*, he had snapped with an acid dislike – but *they* had important, vital meetings later that same day . . . planes were grounded in Leningrad, as they knew, thus the car. He was angry at losing sleep, at delay of any kind.

He paced a little now, while Anna answered the brief questions. He clicked his tongue against the roof of his mouth. Nerve, he thought. Hold on –

Act.

He glared at the captain over his half-glasses. The captain caught his look, and immediately surrendered Anna's papers, making the most of a polite bow to her.

"Thank you," Gant said with little grace. "Now, we may go?"

"Of course, sir – please . . ." He opened the door for them. Gant preceded Anna out into the snow and the lights. Stepping into the glare, he almost froze, as if he had been exposed and recognised. Then he walked on to the car. Impatiently, he held the passenger door open for Anna, and she climbed in. Then, merely nodding dismissively in the captain's direction, he rounded the bonnet to the driver's door. The captain himself held it open for him.

"A successful conclusion to your business, sir," he offered.

Gant merely snorted. "I shall be *tired*," he complained.

He bent to climb into the driver's seat. Then he heard the approaching car. Its engine made it clear that it was moving with speed. Stifling a groan, keeping the tremor from his frame, Gant looked up. He saw headlights rounding a bend, dancing towards them. He knew it was Priabin. He hadn't found – hadn't even looked for – the man's car. He should have killed him . . .

He glanced at Anna's face. She knew, too. The captain was alarmed, then alert and decisive. He waved two guards armed with Kalashnikov rifles forward. They positioned themselves in the headlight beams. The car swayed, then slewed halfway across the road as it stopped in a skid. The door opened.

Gant realised the barrier had been raised. He slammed the door. Already, the pole was beginning to descend. He switched on the engine, revved, put the car into gear. The captain bent to warn him, an arm raised to point at the barrier. His head flicked away as they both heard Priabin shouting. In the mirror, Gant saw Priabin running towards them, waving his ID wallet above his head, calling his rank and name and their identities –

He let out the clutch and accelerated. The barrier was coming down. He skidded, but the car slid forward before it started to swing round – the barrier bounced on the roof, shattering the rear window with its impact. He swung the wheel, grinning at Anna, and let the car accelerate as soon as he came out of the skid.

"Stop them!" Priabin yelled. "Stop *him*, stop him!" His ID was thrust under the captain's nose. The man stepped back half a pace, made to salute. The two guards had turned to follow the flight of the car. Priabin bellowed, "The tyres – the tyres!" The guards opened fire. "The woman is a hostage!" Priabin yelled, his words drowned by the first rounds fired from the two rifles. Horribly, one of them was on automatic. "The tyres, *only the tyres*!" he continued to bellow, his voice little more than a screech, hoarse and unheard. The car slid across the road, spun almost to face them, stalled. The two rifles continued firing, both now on single shot. "Stop, *stop*!"

The Finnish barrier was up, a car was revving. Priabin could see its exhaust rising in the glare of the lights. He was running alongside the captain, who had drawn his gun.

Gant was running. He had got out of the car, hesitated for only a moment, and then had begun running towards the other barrier and the car that was moving forward to protect him.

"Shoot him, shoot him – he's the American pilot! *Kill him*!"

Gant was alone. Running alone.

PART THREE

THE AIRCRAFT

". . . the one path of my flight is direct
Through the bones of the living.
No arguments assert my right:
The sun is behind me."

Hawk Roosting
Ted Hughes

TWELVE:

Through The Window

She had swivelled in the passenger seat to stare back through the car's rear window at some excitement on the road behind, just like a child. And it was as if he were gently remonstrating with that child when he turned her in her seat. Except that by turning her he could not prevent harm from coming to her. She was already dead. Gant knew that even as he gently moved her. He knew before he saw the neat blue hole in her forehead, just at the hairline.

He had told her to keep down, had tried to push her back into her seat; but her arm had become limp and unresponding. Anna had turned to look back at Priabin, standing in the middle of the road, waving his arms. Gant had heard one of the two Kalashnikovs on automatic. The bellow of sound had unnerved him more than the concussions of the first bullets; the thuds against the boot and into the rear seat.

He stared at her face for only a moment. Very pale. Her eyes were open. They hardly registered shock, were without pain.

He let her body fall back against the seat and wished he had not done so. She looked very dead the moment he released her. Her head too rapidly flopped onto her shoulder, the hair spilled over her cheek, and there was a snail-track of saliva at the corner of her mouth. He withdrew his hands, holding them against his chest, afraid to touch her again. They were shaking as he bunched them into fists. He groaned.

The Vietnamese girl, burning . . .

He grabbed the door handle. His hand froze for a moment, then flung open the door. Two bullets immediately thudded into it, making the plastic of the panel bulge near his knuckles. He knelt behind the door. The two rifles ceased firing. He straightened, smelling on the freezing air the exhaust from the Finnish car moving towards him. He ran. He heard Priabin shout something; the voice sounded almost demented above the noise of Gant's breathing and heartbeat and squeaking footfalls. He hunched his body against the expected impact of rifle bullets.

Then the Finnish car, a long Mercedes saloon, swung across the

503

road behind him, skidding to a halt. He heard the doors open. He tried to stop and turn, but slipped and fell onto the snowbound road. His buttocks and hands ached. The Vietnamese girl was incinerated in an instant beside the car he had abandoned. Two men were kneeling behind the open doors of the Mercedes, wary yet not expecting trouble. The two border guards had stopped firing, stopping running.

Another man was still moving, charging towards the abandoned car, arms flailing as if he were combating the freezing night and the falling snow. Headlights from the Mercedes glared towards the lights of the abandoned car. The brightness hid Anna; hid Priabin the moment he stopped and ducked his whole body almost frenziedly into the car's interior. Gant closed his eyes. The image of the Vietnamese girl had vanished, but he could clearly discern the blue hole in Anna's forehead. He shook his head, but her surprised, hardly shocked face would not leave him. He breathed in deeply and opened his eyes. A man was extending his hand, offering to help him to his feet.

"Major Gant?" he said.

Immediately, as if the action would help to establish his identity, or remove Anna's image from his retinae, Gant tugged the hairpiece from his own closely-cropped hair.

"Yes," he said.

"Quickly," the Finn instructed, clutching Gant's elbow, forcing him to his feet. Gant's legs were foal-like, awkward. "We must get you away from here — I do not think there will be trouble, but —"

"Yes," Gant repeated dully, brushing down his overcoat and trousers. The other two Finns had also stood up. One of them, the driver, had climbed into the Mercedes. The engine was still running. The incident was over. The two guards had retreated to the customs hut, where their officer stood on the wooden steps, watching through night-glasses. "Yes."

He was ushered to the rear door of the Mercedes. He paused and stared into the other car's headlights. It was as if he had been trapped in a searchlight's eager beam. Beyond the lights, he saw Priabin. He was out of the car, his arms wrapped around Anna's body. Gant could see the splash of fair hair against Priabin's dark clothing. Priabin's face was white, aghast, lost.

Quickly, Gant got into the car, which reversed across the road, turned, and headed back towards the red and white pole on the Finnish side. Gant turned his head, wincing as he realised he was imitating Anna's last living movement, and watched the figure of Priabin diminish, the splash of blond hair against his chest no more than a trick of the light. Priabin did not move, seemed incapable of volition. He simply stared in his lost way after the receding Mercedes.

Then the Finnish border post was behind them, the glow from the overhead lights retreating behind the falling snow. Gant shivered, realising that the car was warm, realising that it was over.

He did not dare to close his eyes. Open, and Anna remained only a tumbled trick of the light against Priabin's chest; closed, and the white face with its blue hole would return. He stared at the back of the Finn in the front passenger seat like a nauseous drunk attempting to defeat the spinning of his head.

Waterford watched the sky. The cloud had thinned, the snow had almost stopped; desultory and innocent, as on a greetings card. The window in the weather had arrived. Out on the lake, a huge cross formed from orange marker tape indicated the dropping point. A single smoke flare betrayed the wind direction. It climbed like a plume from the ice, then bent as it reached the wind, straggled and dissipated. There was no sky above, no colour except grey, but the cloudbase was high enough to allow the Hercules's first run to be at a sufficient altitude for the parachutists to jump safely. The lake was strangely silent against the slow, creeping grey dawn that revealed its far shore, the sombre snowbound country and the pencilled margin of trees.

Then he heard the baritone murmur of the aircraft's four engines. The other heads turned with his, towards the south. He glanced to check the smoke plume, which rose strongly before the wind distressed it like long yellow hair. He turned his face back to the clouds and saw it, at little more than fifteen hundred feet, seeming to drift up from the indistinct horizon, enlarge, then hang above them. The expectant silence around him was all but palpable. The Hercules was a plump, full shape overhead.

Then the parachuting Royal Marines appeared, dots detaching themselves like laid eggs from each side of the bulky fuselage. Parachutes opened, and the black eggs slowed and swayed. Waterford counted them, urging them to be more, wanting to go on counting. Twenty, twenty-one, two, three, four, five, six . . .

And then he reminded himself that not all of them were soldiers. There were also engineers and technicians from the RNAF Tactical Supply Squadron at Bardufoss. They and the pallets of supplies required had limited the number of marines that could be carried. The Hercules would return to Bardufoss at high speed to attempt to take on a second detachment of marines, but Waterford doubted they would be able to drop. The window in the weather would have closed once more before the Hercules could return.

Thirty-two, three . . . already, the first jumpers were drifting against the grey horizon like unseasonal dandelion clocks. The Hercules vanished beyond the limit of visibility at the far end of the lake. The drone of its four engines had become a mild hiss; the noise of a distant saw. The first marine landed on his feet, ran after his billowing, closing 'chute, wrapping it into a bundle as he moved. Then the second landed, rolled, came up grabbing the 'chute to himself. Three, four, five . . .

Perhaps two dozen marines, Waterford thought, assessing the degree of comfort he felt at the figure. Not much. The Hercules would have been tracked on Russian radar. Its run would be too pattern-like, too intended to be mistaken. They would know men and supplies had been dropped into Lapland, and they would know where. The weather window had to be slammed shut against them before they could act on the knowledge, even if its shutting did lock out a second detachment of marines.

Already, every parachutist had landed and was moving quickly off the ice. The air force experts trudged in a hunched, somehow childlike manner, the marines moved more quickly, already identifiable as a group. Everyone was wearing arctic camouflage or long grey-white parkas. They looked like members of an expedition.

Waterford returned the salute of the captain in command of the marines, then turned away from him. The last stragglers, 'chutes bundled untidily beneath their arms, had moved off the ice. Among marines and technicians and experts alike there was a muted, intense murmuring as they climbed the slope of the shore and confronted the Firefox, now at the rear of the clearing beneath the camouflage netting. The noise of the Hercules's return moved towards them from the northern horizon.

Then the aircraft appeared, a flattened, murky, half-real shape at the far end of the lake. The smoke flare had already bent further, like the unstable stem of a heavy-flowered plant. The wind was picking up. There would be no second drop of marines. The clouds, too, already seemed lower and heavier, and the snowflakes blew sideways into Waterford's face, as if the storm were sidling up to him in some surprise ambush. He shook his head. The Hercules moved slowly and steadily up the lake. Then the pallets emerged in turn from the cargo ramp in the rear of the aircraft. Waterford realised that Moresby was standing beside him. It was as if he had taken no interest in the men who had parachuted, only in the lifeless supplies and equipment now to be unloaded.

The tractor tug was bright yellow. Its pallet thudded distantly into the ice, skidded and ran to a halt. A second pallet with tarpaulined equipment emerged, then a third. Then the fourth, bearing great rolls of MO-MAT, a second pallet of rolled portable runway followed it. The Hercules was almost level with them now. The smoke from the flare streamed out horizontally, a few feet above the ground. The trees on the far shore were shrouded in what might have been a freezing fog. Then shapes like great, tyred undercarriage wheels appeared one after the other from the gaping cargo ramp. Waterford thought he glimpsed the figures bundling them out, even the supervising Air Loadmaster at the mouth of the hard-lit tunnel that was the interior of the Hercules. Then the aircraft was gone, lost beyond the trees around the lake, heading south. He saw a vague, dark shape lift into the clouds, which were lower and thicker than before. The Hercules vanished, leaving Waterford with a momentary sense of isolation.

The black fuel cells bounced awkwardly and rolled strangely, like trick balls weighted with sand. Slowly, they came to a halt, giant woods searching for a jack. The air transportable fuel cells had been landed safely; huge rubber containers filled with the various oils and the vital paraffin required if the Firefox was ever to take off from the lake.

The farthest of the pallets, with its bright yellow tractor tug, was already almost obscured by the driving snow. A window – ? Nothing but a glimpse of something through the storm. At least, Waterford thought, the Russians can't do anything. They won't be able to move.

Nor will we –

He watched as men detailed by Moresby moved out onto the ice to recover the pallets and the fuel cells. It would take no more than half an hour to get everything stowed under cover, camouflaged. Just in case –

"You'd better come with me," Waterford said. His voice was pinched in his throat. He growled it clear. "Come on, captain, we've got work to do. Your blokes aren't here to hold spanners for these buggers."

"No, sir. But –"

Waterford turned to face him. The captain was staring at the Firefox, stranded amid trees and beneath camouflage netting; out of its element.

"What?"

"Hell of an aircraft, sir."

"One problem with it – it doesn't fly!"

The Russian major tugged the hood of his camouflage blouse further forward, as if to conceal completely the fur hat with its single red star in the centre. He smiled at his nervous gesture, as if he really had been fearful of their being spotted through the weather from the other side of the lake.

His Border Guard reconnaissance party had heard the distant noise of the Hercules transport while they were breakfasting. He was fairly certain it was one of those big turboprop transport aircraft used by the Norwegians and the rest of NATO. His unit had made good time, even with the poor weather. The moment it cleared they had rested, hoping to make a quick, scrappy meal, then pushed on before the weather closed in again. Of course, once they reached the trees, the weather ceased to matter as much, inconvenient though it was. But the noise of the aircraft, muffled and distant and to the east, alerted them, created fears and prognostications and they had broken camp at once and pushed on with all possible speed. Somehow, each of his men and himself had known that the transport aircraft, even though it had not landed, had business at the two lakes.

The smaller, more westerly of the two had been empty of activity, supplies and people. The plane had made two passes, one at a reasonably high altitude as far as they could discern, the other much lower. The major had his suspicions; they were almost certain enough to report them to Moscow. But, he hesitated. He would be reporting directly to Andropov himself; his ultimate superior, his Chairman. He wanted further evidence before committing himself – yet, he should alert the reconnaissance aircraft, there should be an investigation. However, the weather had closed in again and he knew that no flights would now be possible to investigate the activities of the transport aircraft. But, surely it had been picked up by the border Tupolev AWACS plane and reported? Had the weather closed in too quickly?

His party of twelve men moved behind him on the long cross-country skis across the surface of the smaller lake. Out in the open, the wind was noisy again now; buffeting and yelling around them. The snow drove horizontally across the lake. The clouds were dark and heavy and seemed to hang like a great smothering cushion just above their heads. What was going on at the other lake? What had the transport aircraft been ferrying in? Men, supplies, equipment – why? The questions hurried and blustered in his thoughts, with a cold excitement like that of the wind. He felt on the verge of answers, but would not reach out to grasp them.

They moved off the ice, pausing for a short rest at the edge of the trees. Then they headed across the half-mile that separated the two lakes, climbing slowly and gently through the crowding pines and spruces that were heavy with snow. Birds called from a distance.

Snow dropped with dull concussions from the over-weighted branches of the trees. His men spread out into a curving line of advance with himself at the centre, and began to move more cautiously. He could hear the slither of his skis and those of his sergeants on either side of them. The Kalashnikov rifle in its white canvas sleeve bobbed on his chest.

He crested a ridge, and the trees seemed to straggle more, with brighter snowy spaces between them. The morning was advanced, the light was pale grey. Slowly, he urged his body forward down the slope towards the unseen shore of the larger lake. He felt tense and excited, as if approaching some important promotional interview. He skirted the bole of a fir, glimpsed a stretch of snow-covered ice clear of trees, and came to a halt. He heard the slither of other stopping skis. By hand signals, he urged his men to cover. Rifles were quickly unwrapped and checked, ski-sticks planted like the cross-poles of wigwams for rifle rests. Trees became cover, the hardware of an ambush.

The major raised his binoculars, adjusted their focus, and stared into the flying snow which swept across the lake. Disappointed he could not see the farther shore, he felt he was gazing into a new and unearthly sunrise. He leant against the bole of the tree, a sergeant on the other side of it, and waited. He knew the answers would emerge from that glow, if there was a momentary change or drop in the wind and the snow was moved aside. He was prepared to wait, even though his jumpy, tense body was little more than an impatient net of nerves.

He waited for ten minutes, perhaps twelve. He heard the muffled noises at first. Compressors, a saw, no, two saws, the cracking, thudding fall of trees. The grind and creak of machinery, the whine of drills and what he presumed might be other power tools. He was reminded of his grandfather's hut at the bottom of the garden where the old man enthusiastically concocted gadgets that never worked, or badly repaired household utensils that had been damaged or broken. The tapestry of sounds comforted and excited him, but supplied no answers to his insistent questions. The voices of men, too, were carried faintly towards him by the wind.

Then he saw it. The snow seemed to retreat across the lake like a curtain, and he fine-focused his glasses after raising them quickly to his eyes. He stretched his eyelids, cleared his throat, then saw —

It had to be the MiG-31. It had to be exactly what they had been sent to find. It left him breathless. A black shape at the back of what might have been a stage set. Men half-swallowed by the cockpit or swarming over the tail section and the main fuselage. Great trailing hoses blowing air or supplying something, lay about the aircraft. A wide snail-track of portable runway ran down to the edge of the water — yes, water, where the ice had been broken . . .

"My God," he whispered. "My God, it *was* in the lake! Do you see that, sergeant? It *was* in the lake!"

"Yes, sir. What are they doing to the aircraft, sir?"

"I don't know. They must be dismantling it. Yes, they must be taking it apart, ripping out all the secret stuff, the stuff they want . . ."

The black shape, the men, the noises and the now visible machinery . . . he scanned along the shore. Trees being cleared, more huge rolls of portable runway, a yellow — what was that? — yellow. Small tractor . . . where had he seen those before? Towing aircraft —? Yes, at airports and airfields. One black — football? — almost hidden in the trees, certainly camouflaged from the air, and other, similar shapes behind it. Then the curtain was drawn once more just as he saw the rifles worn by a handful of the men around and in front of the aircraft. Troops, armed troops —

And then it was gone, the noises now the sole indication that they were not alone on the shore of the frozen lake.

There are too many of them, he thought. Then — do I tell Moscow what I fear?

"Sir?" the sergeant began, his voice seeming to possess a weight of insight.

The major nodded. "Yes," he said. "Get Melnik here with the radio — quickly." The sergeant turned and moved off, but the major continued speaking softly, as if answering the sergeant's unspoken question. "Yes, they're going to try to fly that plane out!"

Vladimirov stood before the tall fibre-optic map in the control gallery. His body quivered with excitement. He assessed his appearance as being like that of one of his family's hunting dogs; a luxury his rank and income had enabled him to resurrect from the family's past. The scent of the game, the dog's rippling excitement which the noise of the gun and the fall of the bird would convert to speed, to capture.

Andropov stood next to him, rubbing his spectacles heavily and repeatedly, as if to reassess the information on the map and the transmission from the reconnaissance party. Lights and indicators had been bled into the map, and the projection of Finnish Lapland had been altered. Now, an enlargement of the area of the two lakes almost filled the entire surface. The cleared site the major had seen was marked as was the position of the major's party.

Andropov had not congratulated Vladimirov, but there had been a surprised, almost mocking respect in his pale eyes, before both of

510

them had abandoned their coffee and hurried across the gallery to the map.

As if unable to bear the proximity of the map, the Chairman of the KGB wandered away from Vladimirov. When the general turned to look at him, he realised that Andropov, having replaced his spectacles, was simply looking through the glass down at the main floor of the underground command centre. His gaze was fixed upon the huge map table surrounded by operators; a table displaying the same large-scale images of the two lakes, the position of the major and his party, the location of the MiG-31.

Eventually, as if aware of being observed, Andropov turned to Vladimirov and said, "Do you agree with the major's prognostication, General Vladimirov?" It was a complex, subtle question asked in a direct, neutral tone. It prompted Vladimirov to accept responsibility, it was genuinely undecided, it hovered on the verge of disbelief.

"Yes," Vladimirov said. "I incline to. His descriptions of equipment, of what he saw, even when I questioned him, were too detailed to be misinterpreted. Transportable fuel cells – his black footballs could be nothing else. Compressors and hoses."

"But, could they do it? Could they *possibly* do it?"

Vladimirov shook his head. "I would have thought their attempt likely to end in failure –"

"But not *certain* to end that way?"

"Are *you* prepared to be certain?" Vladimirov countered.

Andropov, as if suddenly made aware of the others in the room, the majority of them military personnel, seemed to scuttle across to Vladimirov's side. To create a fiction of competence, he adjusted his glasses to make a renewed study of the map. Its colours palely mottled his features. Eventually, he turned to Vladimirov and said quietly, "You realise what this means? You realise *everything*?"

"I realise."

"Very well, then. What do we do?" There was no emphasis on the plural, but it was a commitment from Andropov. Out of necessity, Vladimirov concluded. The man had no idea how to deal with the situation. He was no longer seeking a scapegoat; rather, he required a skilled, expert assistant. Vladimirov felt himself burn with purpose, what he would have mocked in a younger officer as crusading zeal. It was at once both ridiculous and gratifying.

"We can do nothing – for the moment," Vladimirov said calmly, glancing through the sheaf of papers that represented the detailed met reports he had requested as soon as the major's report had been relayed to them. Andropov's face was angry, and also he seemed disappointed. "We can only prepare for action – we cannot

act. Unless you wish to bomb the area from high altitude?"
Vladimirov added, smiling. Andropov glowered at him.

Vladimirov pondered the map. He could, hopefully even in this
foul weather, continue to assemble troops ready to move them into
Lapland. In the hours after his first realisation that Gant must have
landed on a frozen lake, and as a preliminary to the location of the
MiG by the reconnaissance party, he had ordered the Leningrad
Military District to place Engineer Troops and *desant* commandos
from one of their advance Airborne Divisions, on alert. Already,
some units were at the assembly point, the military airfield near the
town of Nikel, at the meeting point of the Soviet, Finnish and
Norwegian borders. The facilities at Nikel were adequate, just, for a
swift helicopter assault across the border in the required numbers to
guarantee success. But, the commandos mobilised and at present
at Nikel, were fewer then seventy. They had been intended only as
a guard for the more vital Engineer Troops who would salvage, with
the assistance of a huge MiL flying crane, the MiG-31 from
whichever lake contained it. Now, any salvage operation would
necessitate an armed attack; a rescue by force.

Strangely, perhaps because it so closely paralleled his own embryo
plan, he had recovered swiftly from the shock of discovering that he
had been beaten to the site, beaten to the recovery of the aircraft. He
had clenched his fist the moment he received the news, felt his nails
digging into his palm until the pain became numbness. Then he
realised that the weather had closed upon the lake. They were
isolated. They could not be reached. They were locked in, immobile.
If they intended to fly the aircraft out, they would need another
break in the weather. It was a stalemate . . .

To his advantage. The British and Norwegians and Americans had
done much of his work for him.

Andropov had moved to the door of the room. He was in
conversation with a tall, dark-haired young man with an easy,
confident manner which now seemed harassed and half-afraid.
Vladimirov returned to his map and his thoughts.

To fly the aircraft to Norway, to somewhere like Bardufoss, was a
distance that could be covered in minutes. The aircraft would need
to be no more than half-airworthy for that short hop. Was it
possible? Someone – Aubrey, perhaps? – evidently thought it
was.

They needed a window in the weather. They dare not risk a take-
off with a patched-together aircraft in the kind of weather that now
prevailed. It would kill the pilot, lose them the MiG.

So –

They were waiting for the break that was promised for late that afternoon. He glanced at his watch. Perhaps in seven or eight hours' time.

The site had to be occupied by Soviet troops and the secrets of the MiG protected. If they had been photographed, stripped down, examined, discovered, then –

No one could be allowed to leave with that knowledge, with those secrets. He *had* to put troops into the area, for every possible reason.

It would be close. His helicopters would move just as the weather cleared. According to the met people, they would have the disadvantage. Thirty minutes' delay as the weather cleared from the west.

Now his excitement was intense. He sensed the danger, the knife-edge, and welcomed it. He was combative, certain, aggressive. The prize was tangible. His troops must surround the clearing beside the lake, prevent damage to the airframe, prevent take-off if that was feasible.

Kill –

Andropov approached him, his face grim. Vladimirov allowed a smile of triumph to appear on his lips, then said gruffly, "What is it?"

"I – I have received a report that the American has been allowed to escape. He crossed into Finland hours – *hours* ago!" Andropov was sweating. His forehead shone in the lights. He would be blamed; the KGB had failed.

Vladimirov blenched inwardly at the news. He understood fully now.

Gant.

Vladimirov knew that Gant was the intended pilot of the MiG-31, as he had been before. He could not envisage, even wildly imagine, how he could be transported to the lake. But he knew that that was the intention.

Somehow, when the first Soviet gunships drove down on that clearing, when the first commandos dropped from their transport helicopters, Gant would be there. With a lifting triumph filling his chest and stomach, Vladimirov knew that Gant would die.

The snow had turned to sleet soon after first light, sliding away from the wipers to the edges of the windscreen. The Mercedes had become a cocoon for Gant; warm, moving, self-contained. The Finnish Intelligence officers, though he sensed their curiosity, were respectfully quiet. They supplied him with vodka and coffee, had brought him breakfast at a service station restaurant – coffee, eggs, herring, cheese, rolls, jam. He had resisted at first because of the pungent unexpectedness of the fish so early in the morning, but then his hunger had insisted. Anna retreated; she was no longer present in the warmth and quiet bustle of the restaurant.

The military airfield was north-east of Helsinki. The Mercedes turned in, papers were checked at the guardroom, and then they drove directly out onto the tarmac. Through the windscreen, through the sleet and against the grey cloud scudding low across the runways and hangars, Gant saw a Harrier in RAF camouflage, standing like a fleeting visitor apart from the planes bearing Finnish markings. The aircraft surprised him, now that his next movement, the coming hours, were forced to his attention. He was reluctant to leave the Mercedes and the quiet, respectful, reassuring company of the Finns.

A drab-painted trailer was drawn up near the Harrier. It had been towed into position by a Land Rover. The arrangement of the vehicles and the aircraft disturbed him. It appeared temporary; a beginning.

"Major Gant?" the Finn next to him on the rear seat enquired politely, as if to re-establish some former identity. "Would you please leave the car now and go to the trailer?" The Mercedes drew up a matter of yards from the trailer with its blank windows and dark-grey, wet flanks. "Please, Major Gant —"

He gripped the door handle. All three of them were watching him with a patient curiosity. Already distancing themselves.

"Thanks," he said.

"Our – pleasure," one of them said with an engaging smile. "Good luck, Major."

"Sure."

He got out of the car, hunching his shoulders immediately against the cold sting and splash of the driven sleet. He hurried the few yards of wet concrete to the trailer. The door opened, as if at some electronic signal from himself. He climbed the two steps, wiped his feet on a rough mat, and only then looked up as the door closed behind him.

He recognised neither man in the room. There was a smell of wetness from the olive-green flying suit worn by one of them. He seemed to appraise Gant more quickly, but less expertly, than the one in the fur hat and the leather overcoat. A pilot's helmet lay on a plain wooden table, flanked by two cups.

"Coffee?" the man in the overcoat asked, holding out his hand. "Forgive me – my name is Vitsula. I am a – friend of Kenneth Aubrey. My men were the ones who met you at the border. Oh, this is Flight Lieutenant Thorne of the British Royal Air Force." The pilot nodded. "That is his transport parked next to us." Vitsula smiled. "Coffee?" he repeated.

"Uh – oh, yes. Sure."

Gant remained looming near the doorway, ill at ease. He was assailed by premonitions. Vitsula moved and talked with the ease of seniority. By "friend" he meant counterpart. Hence the trailer. Vitsula was helping Aubrey, but Finland was neutral. No, there wasn't anything to concern him here. No more than a covert exit from Finland in the second seat of the Harrier trainer. He moved towards the table and sat down. Vitsula, pouring coffee from the percolator's jug, nodded in approval.

As he sat down, the Finn said, "You realise, of course, Major, why we must have these precautions? I'm sorry it is cold. The heater is not working." Vitsula sipped at his coffee. "Apparently, you are required – cigarette? No? Ah – required in Oslo, at NATO Southern Norway headquarters. Your people wish to talk to you urgently. I can understand that." He smiled, exhaling the blue, acrid smoke. It filled the cramped trailer at once. "I have been in contact with Kenneth Aubrey – who is in Kirkenes at the moment. They have been trying, very unsuccessfully I gather, to rescue the aircraft."

Gant appeared shocked. "How?"

"By winching it out of the lake where you left it, Major."

"They didn't manage it?"

"Yes, they did. But, they cannot get it out of the area. Their helicopter didn't arrive. The weather – a breakdown."

"Shit," Gant breathed, passing from surprise to disappointment in an instant, almost without registering the implied events of the past days. "It's out, you say?"

"So I am led to believe." He shrugged, blowing a rolling cloud of smoke at the low ceiling. "Do the Russians know its location?"

Gant glanced at the pilot, who nodded.

"Not from me," Gant replied slowly.

"That will be welcome news to my minister," Vitsula sighed. "Very welcome. Excellent, in fact. Yes, excellent. Of course, we shall inform them in due course – we shall have to . . ." He held up his hand as Gant's face darkened and his lips moved. "Kenneth Aubrey and your Mr. Buckholz know all this. It is not my decision. The aircraft will be without certain systems, I imagine, by the time it is handed over. You will not quite have wasted your time, Major." Vitsula stood up. "Excuse me, now, I have arrangements to make. When you have finished your coffee, you may leave at your leisure. Do not concern yourself, Major, at the fate of a machine. You, after all, are alive and safe. That should be enough. Good morning. Good morning, Flight Lieutenant."

Vitsula adjusted the fur hat on his head, opened the door and went out. Gant turned his head from the door towards Thorne.

515

"What the hell's going on?" he snapped in a tight, angry voice. "They've got the damn thing out of the lake?"

"So I'm told."

"Who's Vitsula?"

"Director-General of their intelligence service. The top man."

"Why a Harrier?" Gant snapped. "I know what they do. I've flown our AV-8A. Why a Harrier?" He looked around him, then, and added: "Is this place safe?"

"I think so. Vitsula said it was. I don't think he'd want to listen, anyway."

"To what?"

"What happens next." Thorne was smiling. The smile of a young man, his fingers dipped gently, pleasingly, into the waters of covert work. It was evident on his features that he was enjoying himself immensely.

"What happens next?"

"We take off for Oslo –"

"And when we arrive?"

"Just in case – would you like to get changed? I brought a spare suit. Your bonedome's in the cockpit . . ." Thorne heaved a pressure suit, folded and compressed, onto the wooden table, from the floor of the trailer. "Get in that – then we can talk in the privacy of my aircraft." It was lightly said, with an English confidence, a sense of joking, of game-playing. The tone angered Gant quite unreasonably. Anna came back. Blue hole, surprise. No anger. She should have been angry –

He leant across the wooden table and grabbed Thorne's forearm, gripping it tightly. Thorne's narrow, dark good looks twisted, became pale with dislike.

"Before we fucking go anywhere, friend – tell me what happens when we get there! I don't give a shit if this trailer's bugged by the Kremlin – answer the question!" He squeezed Thorne's arm. The pilot winced, tried to pull his arm away, groaned.

"All right – all right, you bloody crazy Yank! Let go of my arm, damn you!"

Gant released his grip. Thorne immediately applied himself to rubbing his forearm, beneath the suit's sleeve. He kept his face averted. Eventually, when he had ceased rubbing, he looked up.

"You're not going to Oslo. We drop off the radar as if making an approach, then I turn the Harrier north." The confusion on the American's face lessened the threat he posed. Thorne appeared to remember other superiors, more pressing priorities. "Look, I shouldn't be telling you any of this until we're airborne –" he protested.

"Why only then?" Gant snapped. "I could still pull the cord and go out on the bang-seat! Tell me now."

Thorne hesitated. Gant leaned towards him again. Thorne's arm flinched onto his lap like a startled cat. Gant picked up the folded suit and dropped it heavily on the floor.

"All right. But it's your fault if anything goes wrong – !"

"You don't think Vitsula's worked things out? Man, they *all* know everything that's going on. It's just one big *game*. The most dangerous game – people get killed. If Vitsula can't make the right guesses about your airplane, then he won't be in his job for long. Even I can guess . . . but I don't want to. Now, tell me."

Gant stood at one of the small, blacked-out windows. Peering through it, he could see Vitsula had taken his place in the back of the Mercedes. An old turboprop transport lurched upwards towards the cloud. He listened to Thorne's voice as if to something reiterated and already known.

"We turn north – heading up the Gulf of Bothnia into Lapland. Across the Finnmark to Kirkenes. She's almost fully fuelled – we have the range to make it in one hop."

"Aubrey's at Kirkenes," Gant murmured.

"Yes, old man –"

Gant turned from the window, glaring at Thorne. "What the hell does he want me at Kirkenes for?"

Thorne shrugged, seemingly with a renewed awareness of their surroundings.

"I – look, I'm just the cab driver. Get into the suit, Major, and I can brief you fully when we're airborne. I don't know much more anyway –"

"The hell you don't! You know and I know. How does he – how can he possibly believe that airplane can *fly* out of there? It's crazy."

"Maybe. But that's what they want you for." Thorne's face was pleading. "Please, Major – get changed. We have a schedule to keep."

Gant realised that his fists were bunched at his sides. Standing, he was aware of the weariness of his body, the confusion of his thoughts. He wished idly for the movement and warmth of the Mercedes once more. Vitsula knew. Of course he knew.

"What about the Finns?"

"There's a deadline. Midnight tonight."

"For anything Aubrey might want to try?"

"I don't know. But the weather's bad up there. There's a small window – a pantry-window, no more – it's expected this afternoon. Before dark. It's the one chance you have."

517

"They want me to break out, through a weather-window? If I don't make it?"

"I don't know. They'll destroy the airframe, I imagine. You're the only chance anyone's got. I have to get you to Kirkenes. If the window doesn't open, you won't be stranded when the deadline expires. At least, Aubrey will have *you*. If it does open, I'm to drop you in at the lake. If you say you can't fly it out, then I bring you back. And a Chinook, if one can get in, will bring out the best of the stuff they can salvage. Look, Major, I was told to tell you everything. *Tell him everything*, he said. *Be honest with him. Ask him to do it. Tell him we need him.* Now, you know it all." Thorne shrugged, staring at the crumpled, stiff heap that was the pressure suit.

"Aubrey wants me to save his ass for him," Gant growled. "He's painted himself into a corner and can't get out, so he had this great idea — really great idea. Get Gant to fly the airplane out of Finland, just like he did out of Russia." Gant's tone was scathingly ironic. Thorne stared at him as if he had only just realised the identity and recent history of the other occupant of the trailer.

Gant walked to the window, looked out, and then returned to the table. "All right," he said heavily. "Get me there, sonny. Get me to that asshole Aubrey!"

As the Harrier T.Mk4 lifted into the scudding, dark cloud, Vitsula leaned back from straining to look upwards through the windscreen, and sighed. He picked up the telephone from the central armrest compartment, and dabbed at the numbers he required. It was time for him to inform his minister of the departure of Gant. Time to suggest that the first advance units of Finnish troops should set out overland from Ivalo and Rovaniemi to rendezvous at the lake.

He would have to inform his minister of his suspicions concerning Gant's eventual destination, of course. Also, he could not avoid the suspicion that the Russians might know, might suspect, or might yet discover . . .

It was unlikely Finnish troops would arrive by midnight in any strength. If the Russians knew, if there was an attempt to fly out the Firefox — he must consult air force experts as to its feasibility — if Aubrey's people were stranded at the lake by the weather . . .? His minister must be in full possession of the facts before any or all of those things happened.

Yes, he would tell him. He cleared his throat and requested to speak to the minister urgently.

Gunnar rechecked the ropes lashing down the two Lynx helicopters. It was a nervous reaction, checking them again and again. But he

518

could not abandon the tiny clearing, its snow-weighted trees, its stormswept open space, its two huddled, shrouded helicopters. The wind cracked and snapped the shrouds over the two aircraft as if trying to open two parcels with rough, greedy fingers. He worried more than ever now, as the morning wore on. The two Lynxes represented the only means of escape from the lake. They could not be flown in this weather – it would be suicide to try – and they could not fly everyone back. But Gunnar knew that Buckholz would order him, if all else failed, to remove as much as possible of the most secret equipment aboard the Firefox in the two helicopters. He might be asked to fly in impossible conditions. For the moment, he simply had to continually reassure himself that the two Lynxes were safe, lashed down and undamaged.

He let go the taut nylon rope which stretched away to the nearest tree, and thrust his mittened hand back into the pocket of his parka. Reaching the edge of the clearing, he turned back for a last glance. Two grey-white mounds, like igloos. He moved away through the trees, clumping over the snow with broad snowshoes. As he skirted the shore of the lake, he could see it was little less than a blizzard that was raging across the open ice. Snow rushed as solidly as a white wall seen from a speeding train or car. He would skirt the shore, keeping out of the worst of the storm by staying under the trees.

He settled into the slow momentum of his journey. He was cold, and becoming hungry again. Energy was being used up at a ridiculous speed. The storm thumped and cried at his hunched back as he walked with slow, exaggerated footsteps. Gunnar could not believe that a second weather window would bring the American pilot, or allow them time for escape. They were stranded at the lake. By the time the weather improved, the Finns would have arrived and it would all have been for nothing.

There was only one advantage in the weather. Nothing could fly in it – nothing Russian. They couldn't have moved a single helicopter, a single platoon, even if they knew where the Firefox was . . .

He was colder now, and he tried to move more quickly.

A freak of the wind brought him the voices. A piece of good luck he appreciated only when he dismissed the idea that the wind had snatched the sounds from the other side of the lake and flung them in his direction. These voices were close to him. Russian voices.

Cold, he distinguished. *Fed up . . . the Major . . . balls to . . .*

Then no more. He leaned against the bole of a tree. He was shaking, almost gripping the tree for support. His hands spread inside his mittens as if to locate and tear at the bark beneath the snow. Fingers twitching –

Russian voices. Soldiers, grumbling about their location, their duties, their officer. They'd been there for some time, they had a purpose which was already beginning to bore them – surveillance without action, his mind supplied – a major was in command. There might be a dozen, two dozen, three . . .

He turned, his back pressed against the trunk. He saw his breath curdle before it was whipped away by the wind. He was emitting signals as he breathed – where were they? He studied the darkness beneath the trees around him, studied the snow for footprints . . . the big, tennis-racquet patterns of his own were already being covered. Where – ?

He strained to hear, but there was only the wind. Which direction? Over there? Near the shore. Between him and the shore.

He slid around the tree with exaggerated caution. He craned forward, staring towards the rushing white wall beyond the trees. White, white, white. He could see nothing other than the snow. Then someone moved. A white lump raised itself into a hunched back, then settled again. He could hear no words, no sound of voices. Once the lump stopped moving, it could no longer be distinguished from the ground, the trees, the white storm. Gunnar shivered.

What to do, what to do? He was unarmed. He turned his back to the tree once more. Had he already passed any of them? Was he surrounded and didn't yet know it?

It was some moments before he was able to think clearly. Then, minutes later, he moved away from the tree, scuttling as swiftly and cautiously as he could back the way he had come. He heard his own breathing, his heartbeat in his ears, the wind; imagined pursuit. He turned to his right before he reached the clearing, only then realising that they had not discovered the two helicopters, that his trail must not lead anyone to the clearing . . .

He reached the shore. Beyond him, his original tracks had been erased. The Lynxes were safe for the moment. He felt chilled and frightened by the rushing wall of snow, which was closer now. He had crossed the lake to the clearing only an hour before, but now . . .

It was as if he had dived slowly, grotesquely out of the trees into a different and alien element. The wall enveloped him, made him blind and breathless. He pulled his hood around his face, then kept his arms about his head, as if running from a fire. He was buffeted and bullied, flung off-balance seven or eight times. Even when he fell to the ice, or onto small ridges and drifts of snow, he felt the wind dragging or pushing him; inflating his parka like a balloon in order to move him on his back or stomach across the ice. Because of the Russians, because of the distance yet to travel, because of the utter isolation he felt in that wind and flying snow, Gunnar was deeply, acutely frightened. He was lost, completely lost.

He sat on a wind-cleared patch of ice, hunched over his compass. It was only a few hundred metres, metres, hundreds of metres, hundreds – a *few* hundred metres, *only* a *few* hundred metres, to the shore. He got onto all fours, having removed his snowshoes, and began to crawl.

He met a low hard ridge of snow and climbed it until he was half-upright. With a huge effort, the wind charging against his side like an attacker, a bullying ice-hockey opponent, he stood fully up-right –

And ran. Floundering, charging, slipping. Ice-hockey opponent. It reduced the wind to something he knew, something he *could* combat. He blundered on, as if skating the barrier, charged again and again by his opponents. They blundered and bulled into him, but kept going, arms round his head, hood pulled over his numbed face, lips spread in a mirthless grin. Another and another charged him, but he kept going. Slipped, recovered, almost tripped over softer snow, skidded on cleaned ice, knowing he was being blown like a small yacht on a curving course across the lake.

Then the shore. He blundered onto it, and fell. He could hear the very, very distant hum of one of the chain-saws. He had made it. Quickly, before the elation deserted him, he crawled towards the trees on all fours, scampering like a dog through the snow. His hands climbed the trunk of a tree until he was standing pressed against its solidity, its unmoving, snow-coated strength. His body was shuddering with effort. Then he turned his back to it.

Jesus Christ, Jesus, Jesus, Jesus . . .

His mind chanted the word over and over until his breathing slowed and quietened. Then he listened, heard the chain-saws stop, and the crack of a falling tree followed by its dull concussion into the snow. He walked towards the sounds, nodding almost casually to the men clearing the fallen trunk. One of them – his companion pilot? – waved. Gunnar waved back. He hurried, then, along the cleared shoreline but just inside the remaining trees, towards the main clearing and Waterford. He forgot his R/T. Crossing the lake had somehow stripped him of any sense of technology, of being able to do more than speak face to face with anyone.

Waterford was talking to Buckholz. The Firefox was beyond them, as sheltered and camouflaged as it possibly could be in the circumstances. Men swarmed over it, lay upon the airframe, busied themselves beneath it. Gunnar was aware of the nakedness of the clearing, of eyes behind him. He turned to look. Nothing. Only the rushing white wall passing the clearing. Had they seen – ?

Must have seen –

"Major Waterford!" he called, realising only when he spoke how small and ridiculous his voice sounded. It was like an echo of the past minutes. He coughed. "Major Waterford!" he called more strongly, hurrying forward. Waterford turned to him, quickly alert. Even Buckholz's features mirrored the concern he evidently saw on Gunnar's face.

"What is it? What's wrong with the choppers?" Waterford snapped.

"Nothing, nothing," Gunnar blurted out. He could hear Moresby cursing something, above the noise of the wind.

"Then what is it?"

Gunnar was aware of the arm he pointed across the lake, as if it would be seen by the Russians. He snatched it back to his side, but Buckholz and Waterford were already staring into the snow, in the direction he had indicted.

"Russians –"

"*What?*"

"Russian soldiers – I don't know what unit . . . I heard only two voices, saw movement from one man –"

"Where?"

"The other side of the lake –" They had all three turned now to face towards the blind western shore of the lake. "On the shore. They must be –"

"Watching us? Yes." Waterford's face had already absorbed shock, and closed again into grim lines. "How many?"

"I don't know –"

"Did you *look?*"

"I thought I should get back as quickly –"

"Damn! Damn it!"

Buckholz said, "We have to know how many."

"We have to eliminate them," Waterford replied.

"What –"

"Work it out! If there were enough of them, they'd be sitting in our laps by now. No, there aren't very many of them. They're a recce party, keeping tabs on us."

"Where have they come from?"

"Those bloody choppers that crossed the border before the weather closed in! They've backtracked along bloody Gant's hike – and found *us*! They'll have a radio and they'll have told Moscow by now."

522

"Could they have seen us?"

"They must have done! Christ, don't count on them sitting there just because it's snowing and they don't like the weather!" Waterford stared at Buckholz. "Get Moresby and his people working as fast as they can – no, faster than that. If Moscow knows, then they'll be dropping in for tea if that weather-window arrives. Oh, *shit* –"

"And you?"

"I'm going to find out who's over there. Invite them over for a quiet game of bridge. Gunnar, you come with me!"

Gunnar glanced around at the rushing snow, and then nodded silently at Waterford's back. The soldier was already speaking softly and swiftly into his R/T, summoning marines and SBS men. Gunnar hurried after his determined footsteps.

Buckholz moved towards the back of the clearing, into the false shelter of the remaining camouflage netting and the windbreaks. Like a stage, he thought. Lit, peopled, props and furniture set out. Now, they had an audience.

Welding torches flared around that area of the fuselage which had been damaged in the dogfight with the second Firefox; beneath the ruptures in the skin, the fuel-lines had been punctured, bringing the airplane here. Moresby was standing up, waist-deep in the cockpit, a conductor in a white parka directing a noiseless orchestra. His arm movements appeared like semaphore, signalling for help.

They wouldn't do it, Buckholz thought. No way would they do it now, with the Russians knowing everything.

Aubrey watched the storm through the running window. The winds, turned and channelled by the fjords and mountains, flicked the snow towards the hut and away again. For moments, the town of Kirkenes on a headland above the Langfjord which separated it from the airfield, was almost entirely visible. The roots of the peaks on Skogerøya could be seen, as could the creased grey surface of the Korsfjord. Then, for longer, gloomier periods, nothing except the snow lying heavily on the grass, and the gleam of the runway. A yellow snowplough moved across his line of sight, hurling the latest snow aside, preparing for the Harrier's attempt to land.

Aubrey was no longer even certain that Gant would arrive, would share this room with himself and Curtin and the radio operator. He turned from the window, his eye passing over the rucked sheets and blankets of the camp beds on which they had spent some of the long night. He crossed to the table and its heaps of paper. Beneath a rough-hewn paperweight, beside the maps and charts and other implements of their desperation, lay the sheaf of transcribed signals he had received since setting up his headquarters at Kirkenes. He lifted the paperweight in a gingerly fashion. The last two signals, one from Eastoe and the other from Buckholz, were little short of unbearable. Yet he was drawn to re-read them, as if to punish himself for his mistakes and his pride. Mortification by coded transmission.

Eastoe reported troop movements, in extreme weather conditions, along the Soviet border with Finland, near the southern end of Lake Inari. Buckholz confirmed that a reconnaissance party had reached the lake's western shore, and had been identified as Russian. Waterford had taken a party of marines to intercept them. Now, Aubrey waited for the report of that intervention.

No, he told himself. He was not waiting for that. He already knew what would be learned. A party of Russians had discovered the location of the Firefox, had discovered that it had been retrieved from the lake – in effect, had cancelled his every advantage. He and whoever controlled the operation in Moscow were now on level terms. Utterly level terms.

His rage of self-recrimination had passed, leaving him spent and tired. If the window in the weather appeared at all over the lake, then it would appear over those gathering Russian troops at the border no more than thirty minutes later. Thirty minutes . . .

Ridiculous. He was beaten. When Buckholz asked him to make a decision, he would accept defeat with ill-grace and snapping, waspish irony, but he would accept it nevertheless. He would instruct Buckholz to rip out the choicest pieces from the cockpit and airframe and try to get them away in the Lynx helicopters. Yes, he would do that. A Chinook would never get to the lake from Bardufoss before the Russians. His party at the lake would be outnumbered, captured, but probably not harmed. He would order them to display no resistance.

Perhaps he should tell Waterford not to engage the reconnaissance party?

Too late to interfere.

Very well. They must salvage what they could. Something of the MiG-31's secrets, at any rate.

"He's coming in – now!" Curtin announced from the other side of the room. Both he and the operator were wearing headsets. They were listening to the dialogue between Thorne, the Harrier pilot, and Kirkenes Tower. Instinctively, like a man opening his own door sensing that he has been burgled, Aubrey glanced at the window. Skogerøya, barely visible, the town almost hidden. The snow flying –

No! he wanted to say. Don't take any chances now –

But he said nothing, merely nodded at Curtin, who stared strangely at him. Watching the lead of his headset, the American moved towards the window. The radio operator, too, had turned in his seat for a better view. Aubrey put the signals back on the table and banged down the paperweight. Then he joined Curtin.

The Harrier seemed to appear suddenly, a darker dot against the wet greyness of the mountains. It was there, a moment after there had been nothing to see except a few wind-flung gulls. It seemed to rush towards the airfield and its single runway, directly towards them. Behind it, the weather seemed to hurry in pursuit, closing around the mountains and the grey water of the Korsfjord. Aubrey could hear the chatter of voices dimly from the headset clamped over Curtin's ears. He did not wish to listen, and stepped away. He felt his body tense, his hands clench.

The aircraft raced the weather in from the fjord. The dot of the Harrier became something winged, something steady – which then wobbled dangerously, as light and naked as one of the gulls being swept about.

Curtin audibly drew in his breath through his teeth. A high eerie whistling sound full of anxiety. Aubrey wanted to tell him to stop. The noise hurt his ears like fingernails drawn down a blackboard. The Harrier enlarged, racing towards them. The runway stretched out like a grey, wet finger towards the approaching aircraft and its pursuing storm. The wings waggled again, uncertain.

Again, Curtin drew in his breath. The runway lights shone feebly in the gloom. There was nothing except the Harrier, poised against the oncoming darkness. Then it dropped, almost as if falling, towards the end of the runway. It touched, seemed to bounce, then rolled across their line of sight. The weather swept over the aircraft, obscuring it, blanking out the entire scene.

"It's OK, it's OK," Curtin repeated. "He's OK . . . he's slowing, yes, he's OK – *Christ!*" He was grinning.

THIRTEEN:

Outside The Rock Pool

Waterford exhaled audibly through his teeth. Brooke, lying next to him on the crest of the rise, waited for his description of what he could see through the MEL thermal imager.

He continued to traverse the area below them, his face pressed behind the curving grey box of the imager, its rifle-like grip clenched in his mittened hand. Eventually, he appeared satisfied, and rolled onto his back.

"Want a look?"

"You tell me," Brooke replied.

"I count twelve of them . . . you can even see the sap in the trees with this toy. It's warmer than the bark." Brooke grinned. "Shame of it is, you can't see what weapons they're carrying."

They had rounded the southern end of the lake, well wide of the shore, then turned to encounter the rising ground between the two lakes. Waterford and his men were now above and behind the Russians. The surrounding trees were all but stripped of snow. The wind hurled itself between the massed trunks, flinging the snow horizontally before it. It was impossible to obtain any sighting of the Russians without the use of the thermal imager which was capable, on its narrowest field of view, of picking up a human body's emissions of warmth at a range of a thousand metres.

"We're going to have to get closer," Waterford continued with a seeming lack of enthusiasm. "You and me. Brief your men to stay put. I'll wait for you, ducky."

Brooke slipped off into the murky, snow-blown light, crouching just below the crest of the rise as he hurried from tree to tree. The shore of the lake was two hundred yards away. Visibility was little more than fifty – yes, Brooke had already vanished, after pausing to speak to the first two-man SBS unit.

Grenade launcher, he thought. Or mortar. Even an RPG-7 rocket launcher. If they had all or any of those, and they well might, coupled with a laser rangefinder, then at the first sign of trouble they could put the Firefox on the scrap-heap. Their weaponry was more important than their numbers, their knowledge, even the radio with which they had undoubtedly communicated with Moscow.

He waited for seven minutes, then saw Brooke emerge from the snow-haze between the furs, and move towards him in a crouch. He slid into a prostrate position next to Waterford.

"Well?"

"OK. Sergeant Dawson's got our friends on the other imager. His count is thirteen, of course." Brooke smiled. His breath was still hurrying from him. "They're to give us fifteen minutes, no more. Dawson's doing some pinpointing for the others. I told them I wanted the radio operator alive, if possible. OK?"

Waterford nodded. "That's about it. He's more likely to talk than the officer or the sergeants. OK, let's go."

Waterford raised his head, and closed the thermal imager to his face once more. Satisfied, he slung the device at his back and moved the Heckler & Koch caseless rifle to greater accessibility across his chest. He gripped its bulky, almost shapeless form with both hands, climbed over the crest of the rise and began to descend. Brooke moved a few paces behind and to his left. They slipped from tree to tree as quickly and silently as they could. Waterford counted the yards they gained towards the shore, waiting for the moment of visibility. Twice he stopped to check the images revealed through the MEL device. Strange, firelit, patchy ghosts, forms that danced and wavered and changed shape.

He was suspicious of a small group hunched around each other, but not around any central image. No fire, no heater brewing coffee or tea – that was fifty yards away to the left of the group on which he focused. The radio might be there. In the freezing air around each body, each patch of warmth, each heater and cigarette, produced an image. But, in the middle of the group that attracted his attention, there was nothing.

Waterford believed that a grenade launcher or mortar sat, barrel elevated, in the centre of the three shifting flame-shapes he could see through the imager. If such a weapon was there, then it would have to be destroyed; its operators killed.

He motioned Brooke forward, pointing out his exact direction. Then he followed. They had covered perhaps a hundred yards of forward movement. Within another forty or fifty yards at the most, he would be able to see them. They would be able to see him. Ahead, Brooke moved with greater caution, with something almost comic in the way he lifted and placed his feet, held his rifle, hunched his shoulders. A cartoon robber. Waterford followed the same pattern of movement. Then Brooke suddenly stopped and whirled behind the trunk of a fir, rifle almost vertical, hand extended to warn Waterford. Waterford ducked behind the nearest tree.

Lower down the slope, the trees were heavy with snow. The wind was less fierce and insistent. Each time he exhaled, his breath moved upwards for almost a second before it was whipped away. He peered round the trunk. Brooke waved him forward. He scampered the few yards separating them.

"Well?"

"Laughter from the tea-party," Brooke replied. "Didn't you hear it?" Waterford shook his head. "Trick of the wind. Catching the noise, I looked. Saw one figure at least. Off over there." He indicated the gloom to their left and ahead of them with the barrel of his Armalite rifle. Waterford strained to see further into the soft, shifting fuzziness caused by the light and the blowing snow. Something moved, less distinct than the flame-shapes he could see through the imager. He put the MEL against his face. Yes. Two – no, three soldiers, at a brew-up. The thermal image of the heater was clear between them. The mugs of tea or coffee moved like lumps of burning coal. Blue, red, yellow. He swung the imager. A single figure, almost directly ahead, then two more, then the group of three around a cold, empty space, then paler, more distant images. One figure moving, coming closer. Probably the officer.

"To our right," Waterford said. "See anything? There –" He pointed his arm like a sight. Brooke craned forward, then shook his head. "OK let me get closer with 'What the Butler Saw' here, and then you move up behind me when I give the signal." He checked on the moving man, and on the group of three, then stepped from behind the tree. Ninety yards, no more than that now. He crouched and ran, dodging from tree to tree, pausing behind each trunk to listen for noises. Snatch of laughter or jocular abuse from the tea-party, a muffled cough into a mitten. He rechecked the moving man. Closer, pursuing an orderly, steady progress. The officer. Now, pausing at the group, his flame-shape bending over something –

Had to be. Had to be a rocket or grenade launcher, or a mortar. Laser rangefinder. Goodbye, MiG-31. Just in case, Waterford supposed, anything intolerably wrong occurred, they would have the option of preventing the aircraft's removal. Did he hear their voices then, just as he turned to wave Brooke forward – ?

No. Nothing. He pointed the MEL imager back towards the rise, scanning along it, picking up Sergeant Dawson's kneeling, burning shape, using another MEL imager. Dawson would be watching him. He would see the first shots fired. Bright, burning blobs leaving one flame-shape, entering another. Strangely, though, the change in body heat of anyone killed would not show for some time.

Brooke looked and listened. He shook his head.

"Four of them now. No more than seventy yards. Next tree

should do it. Ready?" Brooke nodded. They hurried to another fir, less than ten yards ahead of them. Brooke looked once more, and nodded.

"What is it?" Can you see what they've got there?"

Brooke was silent for a time, staring through the short, stubby barrel of his PPE Pocketscope. The light conditions made its use necessary, though it was most effective as a night sight. He lowered the instrument and said, "It looks like one of their AGS thirty millimetre jobs."

"Effective range, eight hundred metres. Enough. Anything else?"

"Laser rangefinder, I'm pretty sure."

"Right. Let's take them all out. Who knows, we might get the rest of them to surrender if we get the officer as well? You — work round that way. I'll outflank them on the other side. Wait until I start firing before you open up."

"OK."

Brooke moved off immediately, working his way from tree to tree, threading his path inwards and ahead, towards the shore of the lake. When he was little more than a shadow, Waterford raised the MEL imager. Brooke's form burned in bright colours. He swung the instrument. Yes, Brooke was close enough. He moved away from the tree, working to his right for perhaps fifty yards until he was satisfied that he had chosen the optimum position. Immediately he had finished firing, he would make for the position of the radio and its operator. The man was perhaps thirty or forty yards from him. He used the MEL to check. Yes, no more than forty. A straight run. Eight or nine seconds – say ten. How many Russian words can you say in ten seconds?

He checked the group around what he, too, could now see was an AGS 30mm grenade launcher on a tripod, with its round drum, like a heavy case of film, attached to the barrel. The laser rangefinder sat on top of the barrel. Waterford had no doubt that the elevation of the barrel would direct a grenade into the clearing where the Firefox sat.

The officer stood up, addressing a last remark. Someone laughed, a noise above the wind. The officer made to move away. Waterford gripped the ribbed plastic of the rifle's barrel, and fitted the stock against his shoulder. He squinted into the optical sight. He set the selector level for three-round bursts. There were fifty caseless, polygonal rounds in the magazine. He breathed in, held his breath. The officer moved slightly, straightening like an awakened sleeper, hands on hips. One of the others was looking up at him. It was the moment. Waterford squeezed the trigger of the G.11.

The officer leapt across the barrel of the AGS, turning a half-somersault. Waterford felt the very slight kick of the slow recoil. The officer had taken all three rounds of the burst, fired within ninety microseconds. Waterford refocused on the man looking up from the ground, his head not yet swinging to follow the leap of his dead officer over the grenade launcher. He squeezed the trigger once more. The man's face disappeared from the optical sight. He heard Brooke's Armalite open up on automatic, turned, and began running.

The radio operator was half-upright, staring towards the man running at him. Four seconds. He was already bent once more over the radio, his fingers flicking at switches, turning knobs. Waterford skidded to a stop twenty yards from the Russian, flicked the selector switch to automatic, and raised the G.11. The remaining forty-four rounds left the rifle in a brief, enraged burst of noise. The soldier and his radio disappeared in a cloud of snow, the man lifted from his feet and flung away, the radio disintegrating.

In the ringing silence after the rifle emptied itself, Waterford cursed. Twenty yards more, and the man would have been alive. But, he was opening a channel, about to inform Moscow.

"Damn!"

Now, they needed one of the Russians alive.

Brooke's rifle had stopped firing. Already, Dawson would be moving the rest of the SBS team down the slope at the run. Waterford slipped behind a tree trunk and waited. They needed one of them alive – but only one.

"It has begun," Aubrey announced sombrely as he put down the headset and turned to Gant and Curtin. "Waterford reports four taken prisoner, the rest dead. The killing has begun."

"It began days ago!" Gant snapped at him, sitting on one of the camp beds, still dressed in his flying suit. Thorne was lying on another bed, holding a paperback novel above him, reading. He seemed uninterested in Aubrey's announcement, indifferent to the surge and swell of emotion between Aubrey and Gant. "Days ago," Gant repeated. "It killed Anna, too."

Aubrey glared in exasperation. "You have already made your point most eloquently concerning Anna," he remarked acidly.

"The hell with you, Aubrey – the hell with you. Anna's death is as pointless as those poor bastards spying on your people at the lake. Just – dead. Like that." He clicked his fingers. "Just like that. And what the hell for? Why didn't you tell the poor slobs you'd given up on this idea *before* you had them shot? Just so they could know what they were getting killed for!"

"Be quiet, Gant – !"

"The hell I will!" Gant stood up, as if to menace Aubrey. Curtin watched him carefully, analytically, from the other side of the room, near the radio operator's console.

"There is nothing I can do!"

"Then there was no point at all in it."

"I – can't admit that . . ."

"Because you can't live with it."

"I have tried, dammit – I have *tried* . . ." Aubrey turned his back and walked to the window. Skogerøya's mountain roots were visible. Gulls were blown like scraps of paper over the grey water of the fjord. Kirkenes huddled on its headland. Another glimpse through the storm, but not the weather window that was still promised for later in the afternoon. Still promised, still on time. It could, they now said, last for as long as an hour. Aircraft could fly in it. "Pointless," he announced to the room without turning from the window. Then, as if called upon to explain something, he faced Gant.

"I – these events have been uncontrollable, Mitchell." Gant sneered at the use of his first name. "The original operation worked just as planned – yes, even to the unfortunate deaths involved. They were not planned, but they were taken into account. No one was forced to work . . . but these events – the past days – they are happenings outside the rock pool. Do you understand? Intelligence work takes place in a rock pool. In this case, the marine creatures there, in their sealed-off world, have been disturbed, flung violently about by a storm. There is nothing I can do. I am sincerely sorry about the woman's death, but I did not cause it. Yes, yes, she was blackmailed into assisting you, but I intended – just as you promised her – that she would be safe from her own people and from ours afterwards. I would have persuaded Buckholz to set her free. She could have returned to her lover – that foolish, tragic young man who was the real instrument of her death!"

He broke off, as if he disliked the pleading tone of his own voice. He hated the confession he was making, yet it forced itself upon him not so much because of Gant's accusations but because the guilt had returned. It was filling his chest and his thoughts. There was only one justification in the rock pool – success. But, he could not control these events, he had failed to tailor them to the parameters of intelligence work. Soldiers, equipment, a timetable, weather conditions, repairs, the very location of the Firefox – all had conspired to flood the calm rock pool and fling them all into the raging water. He could now only admit defeat, pack and leave.

"I do not need lessons in guilt from you, Major," he said tightly, surprising himself.

531

"I wonder."

"There's nothing more to be done. Acknowledge Waterford's signal." He crossed to the charts on the table, shuffling through them. "Curtin, if you please," he said. "Now," he continued when the US Navy officer had joined him, "the weather-window is such as to prevent the Chinook making it all the way, in and out, from Bardufoss. Therefore, the two Lynx helicopters must be used. We must instruct Moresby to salvage what he can – a list of items from his own descriptions of the on-board systems must be drawn up. Everything must be loaded aboard and flown out the moment the weather clears. They will have perhaps less than half an hour before the first Russians arrive, probably in force . . ." His hand skimmed and dusted at the map as he spoke. It was swift, decisive, false, and he knew it. The imitation of action. The retreat. "Our people, those who can't be got on board the two helicopters, must move out to the nearest crossing-point into Norway – here . . . that's north-west. Waterford can be relied upon to organise everything in that area . . ."

He looked up. Gant's shadow had fallen across the chart. His knuckles were white as he leant on them. His face was bleak and angry; a remote anger, something Aubrey could not lessen or turn aside.

"Yes?" Aubrey asked in a voice that quavered.

"Send me in," Gant said. His eyes did not waver, nor did he blink. There was no colour in his cheeks.

Aubrey shook his head, preparing a smile of quiet, grateful dissent to disarm the American. "No –" he began.

"Send me in."

"Impossible, Mitchell – quite impossible . . ." He essayed the smile. It appeared to have no effect. Thorne had put down his paperback, and was sitting up against the pillows like an interested invalid. Aubrey sensed that Curtin, beside him, was divided in his opinion.

"Send me in."

"I cannot risk *you* – !"

"So now I'm valuable?"

"You always were."

"I doubt it. Send me in in the Harrier. Thorne can fly it – I'll fly it if you want to cut down on possible waste . . . if I can't get that airplane out of there before the Russians, then I come back in the Harrier . . . look, Aubrey, I can *tell* them which pieces to remove, which systems. I'm the only one who can!"

"The senior engineering officer is quite capable of doing –"

"The hell with you, Aubrey!" His fist banged savagely on the table. The paperweight on the sheaf of signals jumped to one side. Gant looked at his watch. "You've got less than two hours to decide. I can be on-site in five or six minutes from take-off. That gives me twenty minutes, maybe more, before the Russians can even move. Tell them to get the airplane ready – find out if they can get it ready. Tell them I'm coming."

"If they wait, they'll have no time to dismantle –"

"Is that what you want from this – bits and pieces? Is that what anyone wants? Washington? London? They want the airplane. They want the balls that comes from pulling this whole thing off. They don't want bits and pieces, they want the whole damn thing!"

"I just can't risk it –"

"You try. You'll find it easier than you think. It isn't your neck. Ask them if the airplane will be ready. Tell them I'm coming."

"It's no more than a machine, Mitchell."

"It always was. It's too late to remember that now." He stared into Aubrey's eyes, and lowered his voice. "Baranovich, Fenton, Semelovsky, Kreshin, Pavel – and Anna," he whispered.

Aubrey's face whitened. From the corner of his eye, he saw Curtin's quick gesture to silence Gant. Gant's face remained unmoved.

"How dare you . . ." Aubrey hissed.

"Do it, Aubrey. Give the word. You said it – we're outside your precious rock pool. Give the word. Get that airplane ready for me to fly."

Aubrey stared into Gant's eyes for a long time. Then, abruptly, he turned on his heel and snapped at the radio reporter. "Get 'Fisherman'," he said. "I want an updated report on the repairs. At once!"

"I'm afraid, Comrade Chairman, that we have to assume that your reconnaissance party was surprised and overcome. Which means, in simple terms, that they know that we know. We are each equally aware of the other." Vladimirov buttoned his greatcoat and descended the steps of the Palace of Congresses. Andropov, in a well-cut woollen overcoat made in Italy, walked beside him. "It's hard to grasp what the weather must be like up there," Vladimirov added, deflecting the conversation.

"Mm?" Andropov murmured, watching the placement of his feet; his expensive shoes were protected by galoshes. Frozen snow crunched beneath Vladimirov's boots. Andropov looked up at the general. "What did you say?"

"The weather – in Lapland," Vladimirov murmured impatiently. He was angry with Andropov, though relieved to escape the claustrophobia of that glassed-in, underground tunnel of a control room for at least a few minutes.

"Oh, yes."

Andropov's mind reached into the political future, towards failure, while his own thoughts anticipated at least a qualified success. The capture or death of the reconnaissance party was of little importance now. The weather conditions prevailing at the lake and along the border controlled everything; defined action, time-tabled events.

The strategy, the tactics, did not satisfy, even interest Andropov. Already, he was attempting to anticipate how anything other than complete success might be used against him, used to thwart his ambitions within the Politburo and beyond it. For Andropov, the weather, more than a limitation, was a prison, a promise of failure.

"The weather-window we are expecting in – less than two hours – " Vladimirov pulled down his sleeve over his gold watch. "– will reach the forward units of the Independent Airborne Force approximately thirty-two minutes after it reaches the lake. With luck, helicopters can be airborne twenty-six or seven minutes after the weather-window reaches the lake. At top speed, their flying time in the conditions would be – no more than twenty minutes." He raised his gloved hands, as if to appreciate the windy blue sky, the swiftly moving high clouds, the raw, clean air. Or the massive, crowding buildings of the Kremlin around them as they walked the concrete paths. "That means they will have less than forty-five minutes of better weather before we arrive –"

"Forty-five minutes," Andropov repeated, deep in thought.

"Gant is not on-site, he can't be. Nothing can get in or out. Probably, he is at Kirkenes – coded signals traffic suggests Aubrey is there, some kind of temporary control centre, I imagine. Gant may take as long as fifteen minutes by helicopter or aircraft to arrive. That leaves thirty minutes or less. The MiG-31 cannot be ready for him the very moment he arrives . . . that lake cannot be utilised as a runway without preparation. Even if the MiG is fuelled, armed and pre-flighted when he arrives, he will have to wait." He stopped and turned to Andropov. Behind the Chairman of the KGB, the Trinity Tower, topped by its huge red star, loomed against the sky. "Do you see? We have him. We have the pilot and the aircraft in our hands."

Andropov adjusted his spectacles. "I seem to have heard that cry all too often before," he replied sharply. "You have a second line of defence, I take it, General?"

"Defence?"

"Against failure." Andropov's narrow face was chilled white.

"I see." Vladimirov felt uncomfortable, almost guilty; as if he had

534

joined some unscrupulous conspiracy against his friends. "Of course," he continued brusquely. "Border squadrons will be airborne. Interceptors from 'Wolfpack' squadrons on the Kola Peninsula will be in the air as soon as the weather breaks sufficiently for them to take off. As a line of defence."

"You still think you can capture the MiG-31 intact?"

"Why not? I don't believe its destruction should be our first objective."

"The Finns will try everything to arrive the moment the deadline expires," Andropov announced tiredly.

"If they get there, and find the aircraft, they will hand it over to us. As long as it remains where it is, it is ours. Obviously."

"As long as it remains where it is."

"We shall have to contrive that it does so," Vladimirov snapped. Lost sleep, concentrated thought, continual tension seemed to overtake him for a moment. He rubbed his forehead. Touching the peak of his cap made him aware of his shoulder boards, his greatcoat, the medal ribbons he wore. They revived him, reasserted his superiority over the ambitious politician beside him. "I have computer predictions of a timetable for repairs, drying out, replacement, preparation . . . all of them suggest that, with limited equipment, they will be hours behind their self-imposed deadline. Andropov, they can't fly the MiG out. It won't be ready."

"So you hope."

"So I believe."

"Mm." Andropov turned away, like a camera scanning the walls and towers and buildings of the Kremlin. The fortified encampment in the wilderness, Vladimirov thought. His mind was filled with contempt for Andropov and what he represented. Protected by their walls, he continued to himself, afraid of the wild tribes outside the palisade. They don't belong –

"I see our revered First Secretary heading this way," Andropov murmured, smiling thinly as Vladimirov's head jerked up and his lips trembled slightly. Then anger at his own weakness darkened the soldier's features. "You can't be above it all, you see," Andropov added.

Vladimirov felt as if the Soviet leader had been watching them from his office window and had pounced, hoping to catch them at some conspiracy, or simply off-balance. His trilby hat was jammed onto his head, his coat with its astrakhan collar was wrapped around him; his bodyguards hurried after him. Both men moved towards the Soviet leader, preparing their minds and faces.

"What is happening?" the First Secretary asked accusingly, looking at each of them in turn. The bodyguards loitered. "I rang the command centre, only to be told that you had gone for a *walk!*"

"It is all decided – everything has been worked out," Andropov replied calmly, indicating Vladimirov. The First Secretary appeared to make an immediate pact with the Chairman of the KGB. His face darkened when he turned to Vladimirov, ready to accuse.

"Well, General – well?"

"Comrade Chairman Andropov and myself have made our decisions, First Secretary. We were on our way to inform you privately."

Andropov's glasses caught the sun, and glinted. It was like a surrogate smile, a small signal of congratulation. "Yes,' he agreed. "We differ in some essentials, however."

"I will tell you what is to happen," the Soviet leader announced, walking on down the path, careful of his footing, waiting for them to fall into step at either side of him. Vladimirov clenched his fists for a moment, then caught up with the older man. Andropov was already to his left.

"We would value your opinion, of course –" Andropov began.

"You will listen to your orders."

"First Secretary, I have to say that you are not –"

The gleam in the First Secretary's eyes silenced Vladimirov. It was more eloquent than the threats which followed. "Orders. Do you really want me to produce the Minister and Deputy Ministers, the Military Council in force, the General Staff, the Commander-in-Chief of Warsaw Pact Forces, members of the Politburo – more than enough to form a quorum – half the Central Committee . . .?" The Soviet leader waved his arms in the air, as if conjuring his supporters. "All of them will tell you that I am right, even before I say anything! What is it you want, Vladimirov? What proof do you require before you realise that this business – all of it – falls under my control? I have *allowed* you to lead. Now, you will follow. Do you understand me?"

Vladimirov stared over the trilby hat, towards the Archangel Cathedral and the great bell-tower of Ivan the Terrible. He fought to control his features; to prevent his lips from twisting in ugly, frightening contempt, to prevent a blush of anger and shame entering his skin. Eventually, without meeting the Soviet leader's gaze, he nodded stiffly. "I understand you, First Secretary."

"Good." Clouds moved swiftly behind the trilby hat, behind the bell-tower and the cathedral's domes. Shadow for a moment or two, then cold sunlight again. "Good."

"What is it you wish to be done?" Vladimirov asked. It was evident that the First Secretary had been in consultation with members of the General Staff and the Military Council. He was certain of himself. He had a scenario prepared. A consensus had been reached.

"You have one attempt – just one – to recapture the MiG-31. If that fails, then the aircraft is to be destroyed where it stands. Do you comprehend?"

Vladimirov nodded miserably. The First Secretary had ensured his backing for such a decision. The wasted billions, the wasted high technology, the wasted lives, did not matter. Safety first. The General Staff and the Council had accepted the wisdom of erasure. Better no one than the Americans. Obviously, he already had given guarantees that the project would be continued, and that continuity of funding was assured. In exchange, the General Staff had agreed that no one be held responsible for the theft of the MiG. A fresh start would be made. The matter would be forgotten.

Vladimirov wondered who had been on his side. The Minister of Defence – Kutuzov, certainly, but who else? He still had some influential allies, otherwise he would never have been granted even one chance to recover the aircraft. Someone would have ordered a small, powerful bomb to be dropped, or a stand-off missile to be fired –

And then he saw the trap, opening up at his feet. Realisation raced like the clouds beyond the domes of the cathedral. He was expected to fail. He would be disregarded, and removed. The First Secretary – perhaps even Andropov, too – would be revenged upon the insubordinate soldier. A warning to others. He dropped his gaze and met the Soviet leader's eyes. And saw that his insight was a true one. This man wanted his head.

Summoning as much bravado as he could, he said, "One chance, First Secretary? Then I shall take it, gladly. We'll capture the aircraft and our friend, the American!"

The MO-MAT creaked with frozen snow as a great bale of it was slowly unrolled along the cleared shoreline. The trees there had been cut down and the bases and roots grubbed out to make an open flat area which stretched away to a point where the ice would bear the weight of the Firefox. The portable runway covered rutted mud, pockmark holes, frozen slush.

Buckholz stood on the shore, his back to the soupy, refreezing water beneath which the aircraft had lain. He could hear the creaking of the MO-MAT, and the noise disturbed him. At that distance, he should not have been able to hear it. The wind must be dropping. He turned his face into it, and his cheeks were numbed almost instantly. But he could hear the MO-MAT, hear distinctly the chain-saws, even hear the voices of the mechanics and engineers

537

who swarmed over the airframe. There should be nothing else but the wind. He pulled back the cuff of his parka, and looked at his watch. According to updated reports, they had another hour.

Runway, he told himself. Runway. He would need Moresby to check that. They needed upwards of four thousand feet of clear ice, and God alone knew what lay out on the lake. He had an image of Gunnar stumbling, tripping and falling against small ridges of drift that had frozen. The aircraft could never achieve its take-off speed, maintain its heading or preserve its undercarriage intact if the obstacles were too numerous, too solid . . .

He moved towards the aircraft. It was like entering a warm and familiar room. Cannon ammunition was being fed into the huge drum aft of the cockpit. Two AA-6 missiles had already been fitted beneath the wings. The ammunition was NATO in origin, but fitted the drum and the calibre of cannon aboard the MiG-31. The two missiles were a bonus, Buckholz admitted. Salvaged from a MiG which had crashed, killing the pilot, on the Varanger-Halvøya while trying to get back to its Kola Peninsula base with an electrical fire on board. The wreckage had been returned, together with the pilot's remains. The missiles had ended up at Bardufoss with the RNAF Tactical Supply Squadron.

Beneath the aircraft lay a crude timber support and a deflated black airbag. They had been used to lift the airframe off the ground to test the undercarriage. To one side, the hot-air blowers lay waiting for re-use. Much of the MiG's airframe was covered by temporary shrouding when operations began, and the air blown around the airframe to dry it. The shrouds remained around the engine intakes. One engineer had only minutes before completed his slow, patient journey around the aircraft with a smaller, more portable blower, drying off every hinge, flap, and lock on the airframe.

The fuselage had been patched where it had been torn by cannon fire. The fuel lines had been repaired. Oxygen had been loaded aboard. The aircraft looked like an expensive model, as far as Buckholz was concerned. Somehow, it no longer seemed designed to fly. Sinister yes, beautiful in a dangerous way. But – a copy. A fake. He could not believe that the avionics, the hydraulics, the instruments, the engine itself, even the flaps and rudders – would operate. More than seven hours after the drop, after work had begun on the Firefox, Buckholz could not believe.

He signalled to Moresby, who seemed reluctantly to detach himself from a conversation with two of his team leaders. Yet the Englishman hurried the short distance between them.

"What is it, Buckholz?" he snapped, glancing back towards the aircraft. "Not just a polite enquiry, I hope?"

"No." He turned to face the snow-swept lake. Visibility, he realised, was improving. He could see the ice, the patches of snow, the ridges, stretching away from the shore. "The runway," he explained.

"Ah, yes. Been thinking about that." Moresby glanced back at the aircraft, and shouted, "I don't want that radio tested until we know we're going for the real thing!" One of the two men to whom he had been talking raised his hand in acknowledgement. "Can't trust the bloody Russians not to be listening, mm? Even if they know, I don't want them knowing any more . . . that way, they might think we haven't got a hope!" His smile was like a wince. "Come on, let's have a look at this runway!"

They walked out onto the ice, hunching against the wind and the intermittent snow.

"Four thousand feet – better give him a little more . . ." Moresby murmured, studying a compass, changing direction almost mechanically. "Swings here . . . Ah, clear ice. Just a spot of paint for the moment." He drew an aerosol from his parka and sprayed red paint onto the ice, a curving arrow in shape. "There – nice touch." Then he began striding in measured steps away from Buckholz, heading north up the lake. Buckholz caught up with him, and they walked together, faces protected from the wind, goggles now in place to cover their eyes.

"How're things?" Buckholz asked eventually. Moresby appeared to be counting. Every hundred paces or so, he sprayed the snow or ice with a blotch of red paint.

"Wife's fine, thank you. Wants to go to Venice this year . . . not keen myself."

"The airplane, dammit!"

"Oh – so-so. Good and bad, yes and no."

"I see."

"It won't be ready in the next hour, nor the next two," Moresby announced. "Except by a miracle."

"Hell – what's wrong?"

Moresby sprayed a patch of clear ice. Then he bent near a ridge of snow, and poked at it. It was only fifteen inches high. "Mm," he murmured. "Some of these will have to be levelled off – hot air, and all that. The rest can be blown off with a downdraught."

"Downdraught?"

"We have two helicopters, old man. If they fly up and down this runway you want, they'll blow most of the snow clear. What's too stubborn to move, we'll have to melt! Come on, let's get on with it."

"What's wrong with the aircraft?"

"Oh . . . Look, Buckholz, let me take you through it, nose to tail, as it were – then you'll see the problem. The problem that is now increased by the fact that the Russians know where we are and what we're doing . . . I really don't think, do you, that a short slow hop into Norway is going to be enough?"

"Maybe not – I just hope . . ."

"Well, you do that, Father, and the rest of us will work. That aircraft *has* to work – it has to be capable of speed, altitude, combat tactics, firepower. Just like when it came from the factory. And that is taking a little longer to achieve!"

"Can you?"

"No. Nowhere near. Look –" He sprayed a ridge with red paint. "That's three thousand feet. The whole airframe is dry . . . the air-driven back-up instruments and systems – they all work . . . hydraulics and flying controls, OK . . . We can't even begin to tinker with the thought-guidance or the anti-radar – we don't know how they work. We've checked the connectors, the switches, the wiring, in case of shorts or damage . . ." They paced on through the flying snow. Visibility stretched suddenly to perhaps seventy or eighty yards, then closed in again just as quickly. Moresby continued: "Patching up the battle damage was relatively easy, so was draining the water from the fuel tanks. The radar and the other avionics in the nose section – well, we've done what we can. Checked it out, replaced just about all the multi-connectors and some wiring that looked a bit dodgy . . . that's about the limit of what we can do here – without the workshop manual!" Moresby smiled, sprayed red paint, paused to kick a low ridge that extended to either side of them, then moved on. "The manual firing systems seem OK. Your man could shoot. However, down at the tail, those decoys are not what the Russians were using, but they might work. *If* they come off the ejector rails OK, and *if* they ignite, of course, they might just give enough of a showing on infra-red to fool a missile – perhaps."

He was silent, then, and eventually Buckholz said, "And yet you won't be ready?"

Moresby sprayed paint and announced, "Four thousand. Where are we?" He stared at the snow and wind. "Mm. Visibility, fifty yards. Let's have a look and see what he's got left before he hits the north shore and the trees!" They walked on for some paces, and then Moresby replied to Buckholz's question. "No, we won't be ready. She has to be fuelled up, for one thing. The radio, the electrics, the engine all have to be tested. We're less than half-way through the full instrument check. I wouldn't give this aircraft a

540

chitty by the end of tomorrow." He paused. "Ah, there we are. Just a bit less than four and a half thousand feet. He'll be lucky."

"How long will it take to strip out the most important equipment from the aircraft?"

"Two hours minimum."

"Then —"

"We're committed, one way or the other. Once the weather clears, your man will have to take off, or else we blow up everything, without salvaging even the anti-radar and the thought-guidance systems. I can't put it any more kindly than that."

Buckholz stared at the trees fringing the curving shore of the lake. It was visible now, a vista that retreated into the snowy haze. The weather was improving. There was less snow, even though the wind did not seem to be dropping.

"Can we clear this runway?"

"Oh, yes – I think so. Not too much trouble, using our two Lynx helicopters. And a hot-air blower for these bloody-minded little ridges. The ice underneath is OK. If he's any good, he could get off . . ." Moresby glanced up at the sky. Cloud, heavy and grey, was revealed above the lessening snow. "But, now that they know, what is he going to meet up there, even if he does get off? I wouldn't give that aircraft any chance in a dogfight with a Spitfire, never mind a MiG-25!"

"Yes, Moresby, I understand that. Yes, yes, it's my decision. Thank you. I'll be in touch."

Aubrey walked away from the console towards Curtin, deliberately ignoring Gant, who was staring out of the window at the returning landscape of mountains and fjords.

"Well, sir?" Curtin asked.

Aubrey wobbled his hand, a signal of dubiousness. "Moresby is keener on salvage than on flight," he said. "What do you have from Eastoe and North Cape?"

"The traffic they've picked up at North Cape indicates at least one troop transport helicopter has crashed on landing. No details, but it happened at Nikel, which seems to be their main assembly point."

"Mm. What estimates of current strength?"

Curtin shrugged. "Now we're really into the guesswork area. Maybe upwards of one hundred commandos . . . that's predicting the time they found out, the weather then and since, the known locations of units of the Independent Airborne Force . . . just about everything. But it's still pretty vague, sir."

"A hundred – I see."

"And gunships. Our people haven't got Blowpipe or any other

541

missile. They're sitting targets for a gunship attack – so's the Firefox."

"I know that – !" Aubrey snapped, then added: "Sorry. Go on."

"Eastoe's reporting movements all the time. It's very difficult for them . . . hence the helicopter crash. That will teach them a little caution, sir, if nothing else. There are troop movements on the ground – hard to make out, but it's safe to assume there are some . . ."

"And nothing has crossed the border as yet – *nothing*?"

Curtin shook his head. "We don't think so . . ."

"But, no one can be certain."

"No."

"Well?"

"It looks like they're settling for one big push – a hundred men or more, perhaps two or three gunships besides the transport helicopters . . ."

"Activity at Kola Peninsula bases?"

"Plenty. No flying – there's no weather for that – yet. The first forward base, at Pechenga, will clear soon after we do, sir. We know what will happen then." Curtin suddenly detached himself from detail, and said, "Mr. Aubrey – they know everything. They *must* know about – him," he added, nodding his head towards Gant, "and they know what we're trying to do at the lake with 'Nessie' . . . it's a race, sir. One we can't win. If all they want to do is destroy the Firefox, they'll have an easy time of it."

"If that's what they want," Aubrey replied, but it was evident that his features expressed his mind's agreement with Curtin's arguments. He glanced towards Gant's back, then into Curtin's face. He shook his head as a signal of doubt rather than denial. "The weather is about to open, Curtin. I have ten minutes, little more, in which to decide. It's – difficult . . ." He pinched his lower lip between thumb and forefinger, cradling his elbow with his free hand. "So difficult," he murmured. "We would have an hour, perhaps less, of sufficiently good weather . . . after that, he could not take off anyway. Half of that time we will be safe – the Russians won't be able to move. Then perhaps another ten or fifteen minutes before their first units arrive. Three-quarters of an hour. And Moresby swears the thing won't be ready . . ." He looked up again. "It is ready, in one sense. Ready for a low-level two hundred mile flight at sub-sonic speed to Bardufoss. He won't guarantee anything more than that. Worse, he cannot tell whether or not the anti-radar is working, or will continue to work, during any sort of flight."

Curtin nodded his agreement. He dropped his voice, and said, "You would be sending him up in an airplane which might break down at any moment, which won't do what he wants, hasn't the speed to run away . . . and may be seen on every radar on the ground and in the air for hundreds of miles around him. That's the gamble, Mr. Aubrey — the *real* gamble!"

"You think I'd be killing him?"

"I do."

"Then I can't ask it of him — can I?"

"No, I don't think you can . . ."

The door of the hut opened. The wind's noise entered, seeming to blow Thorne into the room. As he closed the door, he said, "It's just about possible — now. In two minutes, even better. What do you want, sir?"

The smell of paraffin was heavy in the air. Blue smoke rolled near the low ceiling. Gant had turned from the window. He crossed to the nearest bed and picked up his flying helmet.

"I'm afraid —" Aubrey began.

"Me, too," Gant replied, standing directly in front of Aubrey. His stance was somehow challenging.

"I meant —"

"I know what you meant. It doesn't make any difference."

"Mitchell — listen to me, please. You can't be forced to do this . . . in fact, I'm beginning to believe that you shouldn't even try. Time — time has run out for us. You couldn't survive even if you take off. You know that."

"Maybe." Gant's face was bleak. "I'm not letting them all be wasted, Aubrey. I don't care what it was all for, or whether it really matters a damn — but they're dead and I owe them." He tucked his helmet under his arm. "Wish me luck."

Aubrey nodded, but could not speak. Curtin said, "Good luck, Mitchell. Great good luck."

"Sure."

The door closed behind Gant. Aubrey remained silent. There was a clock on the wall of the hut, an old, bare-faced electric clock with two thick black hands and a spider-leg, red second hand. Aubrey's gaze was drawn to it. The clock of the operation's last phase had begun running. Gant's clock. The second hand passed the figure twelve, beginning a new minute.

An hour, he thought. In an hour, it will all be over. Everything . . .

FOURTEEN:

Whirlpool

The Harrier was an approaching roar which became a misty, uncertain shape against the heavy cloud; a falcon about to stoop. Waterford felt himself able to envisage the scene that confronted the pilot. Whiteness; little more than white-out. A picket-fence of pencilled trees fringing the lake. Contourless, featureless almost.

The shape enlarged, dropping slowly. Roundels, camouflage paint, a grey shark's belly. The undercarriage legs, almost at the wingtips like a child's approximation to their position, hung ready to contact the ice. The fuselage wobbled. Two hundred feet, a hundred and fifty feet . . .

Now, Gant and the pilot would see the faces; begin to see the ridges and bumps of the ice and drifted snow. See Moresby's splashes of red paint.

Waterford saw the wings flick, the descent unsettled by a whipping reminder of the wind. Snow flurried across the ice, flew through the clearing air. Fifty feet. He wondered whether the pilot would abandon the attempt and rise again as if riding a funnel of air until he was at a safe altitude. But the Harrier continued to drop. Hovering, hesitating . . .

An image from his boyhood; the stoop of the falcon, then its violent, brute rise back up from the long grass, the rabbit beneath it kicking feebly, wounded through by the talons. The Harrier's port undercarriage touched an instant before the starboard. Then the nosewheel dropped with an audible thump. Someone – perhaps as many as half a dozen – cheered. Others ran to secure the aircraft through another flurry of snow.

"He's here," Buckholz said to Waterford, unnecessarily; merely expelling tension.

"Who? Superman?" Waterford turned to look at the Firefox, then back towards the lake. Two men were already clambering over the Harrier's cockpit sill. "Yes," he added more quietly. "Poor bloody Superman. How the hell does Aubrey con them?"

"Us, you mean?" Buckholz asked, smiling. Without waiting for an answer, he moved down to the ice, raising his arm to signal to Gant, who was removing his flying helmet.

"Us," Waterford agreed.

Buckholz opened his arms to welcome Gant.

"Buckholz."

"Mitchell — am I pleased to see you, boy!"

"Later." Gant was already looking beyond Buckholz, towards the Firefox. Snow petered out against his flying suit. The wind was a thin, high whine. "Is she ready?" he asked.

"No —"

"Then get her ready, Buckholz!" Gant snapped.

"Wait a minute, Gant —"

"Later." He hurried past Buckholz and Waterford towards the aircraft. Moresby stood protectively in front of it, his technicians and engineers still clambering over the fuselage and wings, and crouching beneath its belly. An auxiliary generator hummed, providing power to test the aircraft's electronic systems. Gant hesitated in front of Moresby, as if the man demanded respect, politeness. "Moresby?" he asked.

"Yes, lad. Now, up with you into the cockpit — tell me what it looks like. You have a lot of work to do in the next half-hour." The tone was light, but Gant saw that Moresby's face was grim and uncertain.

He said, "Buckholz said she isn't ready."

"Yes, sir — had a lot of cars in today."

"How unready?"

"You have to do all the final checks — we have to refuel . . . that shouldn't take long. You're not going far."

"What have you got?"

"Trolley-pump — bit slow, I'm afraid."

"Fill the tanks."

"You only need enough for a short hop to —"

Even as he prepared to climb into the cockpit, Gant pointed his thumb at the clouds. "You know what they'll have waiting up there — fill the tanks."

"You're right, Gant — but, then again, you're wrong. There's no warranty on the vehicle . . ." He paused, seeming to lean his face towards Gant, as if about to confide some secret. Then he said, "I wouldn't guarantee this aircraft for the couple of hundred miles to Bardufoss. Anything could happen —" He raised his hand as Gant appeared about to interrupt. "Listen to me, Gant — please listen carefully. Any kind or amount of damage could have occurred to any or every part of that aircraft while it was submerged. It all looks all right — it all checks out. But — under stress — *combat* conditions . . ." He paused again, calculating the effect of his next words. "*You* may not break up under combat stress, Gant — but I wouldn't say the same was bound to be true of the Firefox. Do you understand?"

Gant glared at him, then turned and mounted the steps. He swung his legs over the sill, and settled into the pilot's seat. After a moment, he looked down at Moresby, his face white and bleak.

"I understand you good, Moresby," he said. "Real good. She could break down, fall to pieces, any time. You don't know, you can't say —" He broke off, seeming to stare at the instrument panel in front of him. His hands reached out towards the control column. "How long are you going to be refuelling her?" he asked eventually in a clipped, professional tone.

"Thirty to forty minutes."

"Then I want her out on the ice — now."

"What — ?"

Gant snapped: "If I'm not sitting there at the end of the runway when they come over, they may never give me the chance. Get her out onto the ice."

"Quite right," Moresby replied, unabashed. "OK — sit tight." Moresby moved away, already raising his voice, summoning and briefing his engineers and technicians.

Gant sat in the pilot's couch. The tremor in his hands subsided. It hadn't been fear. Anticipation. Moresby's warning had had no effect apart from a momentary anger. Now, all he felt was an impatience to be gone. There was an arrogance like that of a bird of prey. The activity around him was no more than the means of returning the aircraft to his control. Anna seemed to have retreated from him, down a long, narrowing perspective. Other figures followed her; the dead and the living alike.

He heard the tractor tug's engine start up. The bright yellow vehicle chugged along the shoreline towards him, creaking and grinding over the MO-MAT. It skirted him almost respectfully, and its towing bar was clamped to the undercarriage leg beneath the Firefox's nose. Gant turned up his thumb, the driver of the tug returned the signal, then exhaust fumes billowed as Gant felt a shudder through the airframe. Reluctantly at first, the Firefox began to move backwards. As the tug manoeuvred him, he used the mirror like a car-driver almost as if he were reversing into a parking place. The Firefox rolled protestingly along the MO-MAT.

Buckholz stood watching the aircraft move. Other people, too, had paused in their tasks. Incongruously, it was moving backwards. For a moment, he had intended protesting the moving of the airplane, before he realised that camouflage was pointless, the trees did not protect against grenades and rockets. Gant would need every second, even half-second of advantage.

Slowly, the aircraft reversed onto the ice, dropping down the shore, pausing, then settling level on the last yards of the portable runway. The tug continued to push her until the Firefox cleared the MO-MAT and turned a reverse half-circle on the ice so that her nose was facing north, up the lake. The snow had almost stopped now and Buckholz could see perhaps for some hundreds of yards before the chill, grey air seemed to solidify into a rough blanket hung across the scene. From the cockpit, he guessed that Gant could see no more than one-third of the total length of ice-runway he would require to take off.

He hurried towards the Firefox. People returned to their work, the marines took up defensive positions beside the aircraft once more. More like a guard of honour than a force to be employed, Buckholz thought.

Around the aircraft, under the supervision of the Royal Engineer captain, men began clearing the packed and drifted snow. A gang of children clearing the front path, or the driveway from the garage to the street for their father's car.

Gant was looking down at him.

"You want the take-off run cleared now?"

"Sooner the better."

"I'll get right on it." Buckholz turned away, then looked back at Gant. "You don't have to do this, you know. Take a risk with this, I mean." Gant did not reply. Buckholz moved back towards him, and touched the side of the fuselage below the cockpit. "Moresby must have told you about the risks involved. I'm just telling you, Mitchell – you don't have to go through with it."

Gant looked down at him. There was something uncomfortably distant and arrogant about his face. "Get those choppers aloft, Buckholz . . ." He paused, then added without grace or warmth: "And – thanks."

"OK – I just don't want you beefing at me when she falls out of the sky like a black brick."

"I promise."

Buckholz waved, and then unclipped his R/T from his parka, "Come in, Gunnar – Gunnar?"

Gunnar's reply crackled in the freezing air. "I hear you, Mr. Buckholz – go ahead."

"Get the brushwork done – man here has to get to work on time," Buckholz said with a faint grin. Then he turned to watch the far shore of the lake, a misty, uneven line. The trees were emerging from the thick air like spars of an old pier. He could hear, quite clearly, the rotors of the two Lynx helicopters starting up, and waited for them to lift out of the grey, dirty haze.

547

Gant watched as Moresby's technicians wheeled the trolley-pump down the shore towards him. Two of the air transportable fuel cells were clumsily rolled forward onto the ice. A hose from the first of them was dragged to the port wing and attached to the fuel filler pipe. Gant waited, almost stirring in his seat with impatience, until the noise of the pump starting up calmed him. Moresby watched the whole operation with an unchanging grimness of expression. Fuel began to flow into the port tanks.

Moresby swiftly crossed the ice to the aircraft and climbed the pilot's steps until his head was above the sill and he was looking down on Gant. He activated the stopwatch on the main instrument panel. Its second hand moved jerkily. Moresby glanced at his own stopwatch, hung around his neck.

"Right," Moresby announced. "We've been working our back-sides off for nearly eight hours now, laddie. Let's see how quickly *you* can get things done, shall we?"

Gant looked into the senior engineering officer's face, and nodded. "OK, Moresby. Let's get started."

"And don't switch on the ignition while we're pumping in fuel, will you?"

"Sure – but if I call for hot refuelling . . .?"

Moresby growled. "*Don't* – if you can avoid it." He raised his eyes, and then added, "Sixteen minutes and twelve, thirteen seconds have elapsed since you took off from Kirkenes. Let's get cracking, shall we, old man? We've been through everything we can . . . you'll know if the read-outs seem different in any way." Moresby glanced down from the pilot's steps and paused in his instructions until the auxiliary power unit had been wheeled up to the aircraft's flank and reconnected to the Firefox. Then he said, "Right – run through the pre-flight check, taxi and pre take-off as far as you can – I'll keep the tally."

Gant hesitated, savouring the moment. Then his hands moved. He switched on the Master Electrics, and immediately heard a whirring noise that slowly mounted in pitch.

"Good. Gyro instruments winding up,' Moresby murmured. "Emergencies pressure normal – check . . . Flying controls. Normal feel and full travel . . .?"

Gant's thumb left the throttles and depressed a spade lever. "Sixty degrees, and indicating," he announced as the flaps lowered.

As he raised the flaps again, the heel of his left hand nudged a lever and the airbrakes extended with a mild thump which gently rocked the airframe. He waited, then. Moresby sensed his uncomfortable impatience. He looked away from Gant as the two Lynx helicopters lifted above the trees on the opposite shore and moved across the ice towards them, perhaps two hundred feet above the lake. Gant, too, had turned his head.

They curtsied and sidled as they hovered near the Firefox, before dropping slowly like fat black spiders at the ends of invisible threads. With Gunnar's helicopter in the leading position, they moved slowly away up the lake. Snow billowed around them in the downdraught, rolling like dust thrown up by a scything, horizontal wind. When it cleared there were ridges of frozen snow amid the smoother, cleaned expanse of ice.

"It's working," Moresby commented.

"Annunciator panel and warning lights – test," Gant prompted.

He pushed switches on the panel. The noise of the helicopters drummed and echoed around the lake. Royal Engineers were already using hot-air hoses and shovels to flatten and disperse the low, sword-edged dunes of frozen snow. He saw that most of them were already marked with something that might have been red paint.

The check lights on the panel glowed in the correct sequence. Eventually, Gant said, "Anti-G control – on . . . and check."

"Now the UHF," Moresby announced. "Select the Soviet Tac-channel. Then we can listen to what our friends are up to. No transmission test yet."

"OK – then what day is it?"

"Thursday."

Gant removed a small card from its holder on the radio control box. He required the sequencing code to lock onto the secure Soviet Tac-channel, since the pattern of frequencies was altered each day.

"Got it," he announced.

He switched on the radio, then slipped the Russian flying helmet onto his head. He plugged in the communications and thought-guidance jackplug at the side of the couch. Then he pressed the selector buttons, keying in the sequencing code, and almost at once the two red dots locked on, stuttering as they followed the changes of frequency. Moresby was looking at him. He concentrated on the crackling lash of voices in his ear. Activity, activity . . . he waited, hardly breathing. The stopwatch informed him that eighteen minutes had passed. Nothing was airborne. Everything was, however, fuelled and ready, awaiting the order to take off. Repeated references to the location of the lake, of tactics, of the pattern of overflights, selected squadron altitudes and search areas . . .

He switched off. "It's OK," he announced. It wasn't. He felt a creeping numbness, a reluctance to go on. They would be waiting for him. Perhaps ten or fifteen aircraft, expecting him to be visible only on infra-red, waiting in specific, clever patterns, as if they held nets between them and would cast for him the moment they saw the heat of his exhaust as he lifted from the lake.

The cloud of snow was retreating. Ridges and drifts were being smoothed and erased. The two Lynx helicopters were distant, unreal black dots at the far end of the lake.

He would have no chance.

There was no other way. He swallowed, and in a dry voice, he said, "Repeat."

"I asked you about the anti-radar and the thought-guidance. We don't know how they work so we can't reassure you as to whether they will work or not. Was there anything on the panel in connection with the anti-radar?"

Gant shook his head. "There was no electrical or mechanical action to be taken." He looked at Moresby. "I don't know —"

The Lynxes were lost again in the cloud that was now moving slowly down the lake towards them.

"Damn," Moresby muttered. Then he punched one mittened hand into the other. "Got it!" He bent his head, placing his lips close to his R/T. "Thorne — Thorne?" His voice was eager and querulous. Gant glanced across at the Harrier. He could see Thorne's hand wave in acknowledgement.

"Yes, sir," he replied punctiliously.

"Be a good chap and see if you can see us, will you?" Moresby asked with affected casualness. "On your radar, naturally."

"But."

"No buts. Just do it, my boy."

"Sir."

"Meanwhile," Moresby said to Gant, "you can check out pressurisation and air conditioning."

"OK," Moresby climbed down the pilot's steps as Gant closed the cockpit. He heard Moresby attach a lead to the landline socket on the fuselage, so that they could communicate. He locked the canopy. He was isolated in the Firefox. He connected his oxygen supply. The oxygen content and pressure were satisfactory. All that remained was to check the warning systems for pressurisation, since cockpit pressure could only be checked at altitude. The lights all glowed comfortingly as soon as he summoned them. He could not check heating and demisting until the engines were ignited and running. Again, he checked the warning lights. They, too, glowed instantly. "All check," he said.

"Good. Now, wait a minute while we unload these missiles, then you can check the thought-guidance system. I'll give you the word . . ." Gant felt the two jolts as the AA-6 missiles were removed from their wing pylons. Then Moresby's face appeared outside the cockpit hood, his thumb erect in front of his features. Gant hesitated, then gave a mental command in Russian to fire a port wing missile. The sequence of lights stuttered across the panel. He counted them, remembered them. It appeared to work.

He opened the canopy. "OK," he said, removing the helmet.

"Right. Get those missiles back on their pylons," Moresby called down to his technicians. "Life-support?"

"OK."

"Thorne here, sir," they both heard from Moresby's R/T. Gant's hand twitched on the sill of the cockpit.

"Yes?" Moresby snapped.

"It's difficult, sir – hard still object on a hard still surface against a cluttered background –"

"But?' Moresby said sombrely.

"I shouldn't be able to pick up anything, should I, sir?"

"No," Gant said heavily.

"I – it's . . . I do have an image on radar, sir. Of the – Firefox. In flight, on the moving target display, I'd expect a strong reading . . . Sorry, sir."

Moresby stared at Gant. "That's it, then." Gant felt a shudder run through his body. "That's sodding it!" Moresby shouted. "The anti-radar's been damaged – it doesn't work! You'll be a sitting duck as soon as you're airborne."

"But –"

"No buts! I can't repair it – I don't know how it works!"

Aubrey turned away from the communications console. Eastoe, already supplying reports on all signs of movement along the border, especially at Nikel, and at the closest Kola Peninsula fighter bases, had relayed to Aubrey Moresby's discovery of the failure of the anti-radar system.

Curtin thought Aubrey looked ashen. He did not know what to say to the Englishman. He was relieved when Aubrey moved away towards the farthest corner of the room. It was as if he wished to hide. But the corner seemed to repulse him, for he backed away from it. When he turned, his face was determined.

"Thorne must get him out of there!" he said, coming back towards the console. He glanced up at the clock. Twenty-three minutes since the weather had begun to clear. The window must be closed to the Russian units at Nikel by now. The interceptor bases on the Kola Peninsula would be free of the foul weather later than Nikel, but there, within minutes, the first helicopters would be airborne, carrying the first wave of commandos. They would take less than twenty minutes at top speed to reach the lake. Less than thirty minutes, then, before there was absolutely no possibility of rescue for Gant. What could they salvage of the aircraft in that time, prior to destroying the airframe . . .?

And getting the people out.

Waterford would have to organise a retreat on foot, to some prearranged point where they could be picked up when the weather cleared. Vital personnel and equipment must come out aboard the two Lynx helicopters –

"He must get him out of there," he repeated, grimacing. "Get 'Fisherman' at once."

The radio operator swivelled in his chair and faced the smaller rack of radio equipment which they used to communicate with the lake. He repeated Buckholz's call-sign, and was answered. Aubrey muttered and paced while Buckholz was summoned to the radio. As soon as he heard the American's voice, Aubrey snatched the microphone with a trembling hand.

" 'Fisherman'." he said. Then realising the futility of codes, he added, "Charles – get Gant out of there at once. Thorne is to bring him back here immediately."

"The anti-radar, you mean?" Buckholz replied. "Look, Kenneth, we have maybe twenty minutes . . . what other way do we have? He *has* to fly the plane out – !"

"Without the anti-radar, he hasn't a chance . . ."

A stray flash of sunlight lit the room. Dust-modes danced, as if mirroring Aubrey's agitation. Then the sunlight disappeared.

"What about the helicopter force?" Buckholz asked.

"No movement yet. Charles, order him to get out of there. Salvage what you can. Get Waterford to organise the loading of the two Lynxes . . . and the withdrawal – Charles, do you hear me?"

Instead of Buckholz's voice, Aubrey heard Gant. His voice was distant. "No way, Aubrey. No way."

"Mitchell, please listen to me . . ."

"I heard. The anti-radar doesn't make any difference."

"You haven't got *time* – !"

Gant was suddenly speaking to someone else – presumably Moresby. Aubrey strained to catch the words. "Hot refuelling . . . the hell it does! Hot refuelling –"

'Jesus!' Curtin breathed. Even the radio operator appeared abashed.

"What – ?" Aubrey began.

"Refuelling while the engines are running. He's going to start the engines while they're still pumping in fuel. One mistake and –"

"Charles – stop him!" Aubrey snapped.

552

"Why?" he heard Gant ask. "Does it matter who blows this airplane up – me, you Buckholz, the Russians?"

"Let me speak to Moresby."

"No. There isn't time – he's busy right now."

The radio operator was scribbling busily. Curtin held one earpiece against his head, nodding as he listened. Then he said, "Three heavy transport helicopters have just taken off from Nikel. They're already across the border. Gant has less than twenty minutes."

"Charles – they're on their way."

"Three smaller helicopters – probably gunships," Curtin reported. "One of them's moving faster than the other two. It's probably unarmed and carrying no passengers. Reconnaissance."

"Charles, give him a direct order. Tell him the mission is aborted!"

"Conditions at the Pechenga airbase should be good enough for flying in no more than seven or eight minutes."

"Charles," Aubrey said levelly, his face white, his lips thin and bloodless, "Gant may no longer have twenty minutes. It is less than one hundred miles from Pechenga to you. A Foxbat could cover that distance in – ?" He glanced at Curtin.

"Maybe another seven, eight minutes at low altitude with half-fuel . . ." He wobbled his hand to indicate the degree of guesswork involved.

"Once any of those front-line airbases is clear, he has no more than seven minutes. Even if he could take off within fifteen minutes, he has no chance of escaping the attention of Soviet aircraft. They will simply be waiting for him. Do you understand me?"

"It's all too late, Kenneth. We don't have the time to strip the airframe of even the most valuable equipment."

"We can't lose Gant –"

"This way there's a chance –"

"There's no chance!"

"I'm not prepared to have him shot in order to stop him, Kenneth."

"ETA of leading gunship at the lake – thirteen minutes."

"And when they see the aircraft on the ice," Aubrey snapped at Curtin, "and a runway strip blown free of snow – what will they do then?"

"Shoot first, talk later?"

"I would imagine so. Charles, please obey my instructions. I demand that Gant be flown out immediately in the Harrier. Then – destroy the airframe!"

"We're getting Eastoe's reports, too. The reconnaissance MiL should be with us in twelve minutes. That's the time we have –"

"No!"

"Dammit, yes! We're going to give it our best shot. Now, I'm busy, Kenneth. Out."

Aubrey was left standing with the microphone in his hand. He stared at it in disbelief, then dropped it as if it contained an electrical charge. He wandered away from the console towards the window.

The clouds were already massing again beyond the mountains, to the north and west. The light was thicker. Snowflakes drifted. The Norwegian army guard passed the window.

Aubrey knew he had failed. His final, desperate throw of the dice had, effectively, cost Gant his life. He had lost both the aircraft and the pilot. Killed people, too — Gant was just the last of his victims. There was nothing he could now do to affect the consequences of his actions. Nothing at all.

"ETA of the reconnaissance helicopter, ten minutes," Curtin recited. "Main force, eleven minutes forty. Weather continuing to clear over Pechenga. It might permit flying in four minutes, perhaps less. Eastoe's picking up infra-red traces more strongly. They're on the runway, is his guess."

They would build a roof of aircraft over the lake, to keep in the Firefox. Without the anti-radar, there was no possibility of escape for Gant.

"What?" he heard Curtin exclaim like a man who has been winded. "Repeat!"

Aubrey turned from the window. "What is it?" he asked tiredly.

Curtin held up his hand for a moment, laid down the headset and looked at Aubrey. His face was lined and defeated. "Just to add to your pleasure," he said, "that was Bardufoss. Their weather is right on the margin, now. In minutes, they guess they'll have to close down. Even if he takes off, he won't be able to land."

"ETA of leading helicopter, six minutes . . . ETA main force, eight minutes."

The commpack operator was relating the information he received to Gant via Moresby's R/T, which was still clipped to the cockpit sill. Gant shrugged, sensing his nervous tension, the urgency in his frame as he gangloaded the ignition switches, reached for the fuel cocks —

And stared in disbelief at the purple light glowing on the main panel, to the left and just below the cockpit coaming.

"For Christ's sake, I thought this aircraft was *checked*!" he exploded.

Ahead of him, visibility was already decreasing. The window in the weather had lasted for less time than had been forecast. The far

554

end of the lake was dimly visible, an irregularity of the thick air rather than a landscape. The two Lynx helicopters had completed their clearance of the ice. They waited silently now, beside the Harrier, as teams with shovels and hot air blowers completed the task.

"It was," Moresby replied grimly. He looked down at the technicians who surrounded the Firefox. "Ramp differential light's on," he called down. "Port engine intake – check it now! Come on, you buggers, the intake ramp's jammed or something! Find out what's wrong."

"How did I miss it?" Gant said, staring at the purple light. "I missed the damn light!"

"So did we all, Gant – so did we all." Moresby leaned out from the pilot's steps, clinging to the cockpit sill, straining to see what his technicians were doing. "Well?" he called. Through the open R/T, Gant listened to Waterford as he proceeded with the disposition of his forces. Brooke and his SBS men were to the south and east of the lake, while the marines who had parachuted in from the Hercules were on the opposite shore, where the Russians had been discovered.

"Nothing, sir – it's jammed all right."

"Why the hell that circuit was only routed through ignition, I don't know!" Moresby snapped in self-recrimination, staring at Gant. Frost had begun to rime his moustache, as if the man had been breathing more heavily. Gant's heartbeat raced. He felt his stomach watery and his chest hollow and shallow, as if there was insufficient space for his heart and lungs. "That bloody APU snarl-up earlier didn't help – nor the bloody rush – come on!"

"ETA of leading helicopter, three minutes fifty."

"Shit," Moresby breathed.

"Sir – we've found it –"

"What is it?"

"ETA – three minutes."

"Piece of sheet metal – looks scorched – it's folded like a bit of cardboard, sir. Wedging the door. Have to be careful with it –"

"Then be bloody careful!" He looked at Gant. "Some debris from one of your military encounters, old man," he said with forced and unfelt lightness. Gant merely nodded.

"Get me an update on the Bardufoss weather," he said into the R/T.

"Sir."

"I hope to God it stays no worse than it is," Moresby murmured. "Because, if you can't get in there, I wouldn't guarantee the vehicle for a longer distance!"

"Two hundred miles – you think I'll be safe two hundred miles away?"

"It's Norway, old man –"

"So?"

Moresby's finger flicked at his moustache. A noise of levering, and scraping, twisting metal, came from aft of them on the port side. Gant shuddered.

"Be bloody careful!" Moresby yelled.

"ETA of leading helicopter, two minutes forty," the radio operator announced.

"Where's that weather update?"

"Coming, sir –"

Gant heard Buckholz's voice over the R/T organising the loading of the two Lynx helicopters with the Norwegian personnel who had been engaged in the operation. Women, children and allies first, he thought with bitter humour. Waterford's constant radio chatter was a muffled background, since he had left his R/T open. He had perhaps forty-five men. The three big MiLs coming behind the leading, unarmed reconnaissance helicopter and flanked by the two gunships, would be carrying perhaps forty or fifty troops each. Fewer than that only if they were bringing heavy equipment or light vehicles. Waterford dare not make the first move, even to protect the Firefox. He had to get the airplane out – ! If he managed to take off, Waterford's men could melt into the landscape, avoiding all contact with Russian troops.

"I have to get her out," he repeated aloud.

"Weather, sir –"

"Yes."

"They're closing Bardufoss in five minutes, sir. Within ten, they say, no one could get in."

"OK," Gant replied in a small, tight voice. He closed his eyes for a moment. When he opened them, he saw Moresby staring at him.

"Where to, laddie? Mm – where will you take her when you get in the air?" It was not sarcasm; rather defeat.

"If I have to – all the way."

"What?"

"You heard me. All the fucking way, man! UK or bust!" He tried to grin.

"I wouldn"t advise that, Gant. Anything, *everything* – could go wrong. *Try* to get into Bardufoss – I really am serious about that . . ."

"ETA of leading helicopter – one minute."

"For Christ's sake, you buggers, hurry it up!" Moresby raged.

"Sir, we're having to be very careful to avoid more damage – it's really wedged in tight."

"Then cut the bloody thing into smaller pieces!"

"You have maybe two minutes or a little more – unless they hold back until the leading helicopter's done some spotting," Gant announced.

"Don't tell me . . ."

"Maybe we can bank on an attempt to capture the airframe more or less intact?"

"You think so?"

"It depends on one thing," Gant replied. "Who's now in command of the operation. If it's still Vladimirov, he'll think he has a chance. If it's politicians – then kiss goodbye to your asses! They'll be blown out from under you."

"It's coming, sir – OK – yes, it's free, sir!"

"ETA, thirty seconds . . ."

"Change to hot refuelling," Gant snapped as Moresby rammed home the circuit breaker and the light on the panel disappeared. "Thank God," he sighed."

"Hot refuelling?"

"Have to now. I want to be ready to move at any moment *I* choose."

"How full do you want the tanks?"

"I've got sixty per cent capacity now." Gant shook his head. "Just keep filling them up."

Gant glanced up, his body slightly cowered in the pilot's couch, his arm half-raised as if to shield his eyes or protect his face. He could hear the noise of the helicopter rotors.

Men had paused, as they crossed the ice towards the two helicopters, and were looking up. Visibility was closing in, heavy as a blanket. The far end of the lake was already obscured. It had begun to snow; big flakes pattering against the cockpit sill, on the shoulders of his pressure suit. He fitted his helmet once more, and plugged in his oxygen supply and the jackplug for the thought-guidance system.

The ugly MiL-24, probably unarmed to increase its speed, appeared like a squat beetle above the clearing. Gant cursed their lack of Blowpipe missiles. Even had they possessed them, he doubted whether Waterford would have opened fire first.

The MiL drifted out over the lake, over the two Lynx helicopters and the unarmed Harrier. Gant could see Thorne's helmet raised to watch it. The gunship floated above the Firefox, as if taunting her.

Moresby's voice instructed his technicians. "Hot refuelling. Let's get one of the fuel cells close to the wing, along with the pump unit. I want everyone clear of the front intakes, and well clear of the tailpipes. An arc of men with extinguishers –" He glanced at Gant, but addressed no words to him. "– on either side of the aircraft. And keep alert!" Then he turned to Gant. "You listen to me over the landline. I'm staying well clear, thanks very much. Keep your engine power as low as you can, but not below generator power level . . ." Gant nodded. "Good."

Gant watched the technicians rolling one of the huge rubber fuel cells towards the aircraft and a beam of the starboard wing. He heard the connections made with the hose nozzle and the tank. Then the technicians retired. Moresby, standing perhaps a dozen yards away, signalled him to start the engines. The noise of the MiL above them pressed down upon him. The helicopter had been there for twenty seconds, perhaps half a minute. The main force was a minute behind it now. When they saw the engines ignite, having seen the fuel cell coupled, they would guess at hot refuelling and know he was speeding up the preparations for take-off. Would they still wait, when that was reported, or would they move in – ?

He could not expect any more time, whoever controlled events. The Firefox was a sitting target they would not be able to resist. He switched on the master start, pressed the start button and turned on the high-pressure cock.

Behind him, halfway down the fuselage, there was the sound of a double explosion; the discharge of a shotgun's two barrels. In the mirror, he saw the two rolls of sooty smoke drift into the air. He heard the whirring of the turbines as they built up. He switched in the fuel booster pump, and eased the throttles forward. The rpm gauges mounted to twenty-eight per cent. He eased the throttles back as far as he dared, and steadied them. Both huge Turmansky turbojets roared steadily. He grinned with relief. Moresby hand-signalled his team to recommence pumping.

"Thank God," Moresby said.

Waterford appeared a little distance from the Firefox, at the edge of the clearing. He raised his planklike rifle, and fired several three-shot bursts at the hovering, shifting MiL. Immediately, the gunship flicked away over the trees. Waterford spoke into Moresby's microphone. "Fucking tourists!" Then he added, "OK, Gant – they'll be back in force in a couple of minutes at the outside. What they do then will depend on what you're doing. Good luck." Immediately, he walked away, re-checking the disposition of his marines.

Gant watched the fuel gauges. When should he tell them to stop? When should he end the risk of hot refuelling? How much spare fuel capacity would he require?

He was oblivious of the scene around him. He scanned the instrument and systems panels, checked the centre console, the left-hand console. He operated the rudder and the flaps. Stiff, sluggish by comparison with before, but they would have to do. Then he heard the commpack operator's voice.

"Weather has cleared sufficiently at Pechenga. Two squadrons of interceptors airborne. ETA – six minutes."

He looked up. Visibility perhaps seven hundred yards, maybe seven fifty. He would be rushing towards a blanket of what might have been fog, except that it was grey-white and falling slowly. The snow was heavier. Only the wind was missing. One of the Lynxes took off, being almost immediately swallowed by cloud. The second Lynx drifted towards the Firefox, to await the rescue of Moresby's technicians.

"OK, that's everyone except your people, Moresby," he heard Buckholz announce. Gant could see him beside the commpack. The rotors of the Lynx died down. "We can leave our four prisoners tied up where they are. Their friends will be along any minute. So – let's go . . .?"

Moresby nodded. "Thank you, Mr. Buckholz. We'll be aboard in a moment or two." Then he addressed Gant. "They've split into two groups – south of us and east, as Waterford suggested. But the gunships are still airborne. They're obviously awaiting orders."

Gant checked the fuel gauges. And shook his head. "Not yet," he said. "I'll tell you when to stop." Moresby's face was tired and angry; even frightened.

"Those bloody gunships," he murmured.

"Gant?" he heard in his earpiece. "Gant – this is Thorne. I've got an idea . . ."

"What?"

"A double take-off – let me take off first . . . it might keep some of them off your back."

"What are the gunships doing?"

"Holding – agreed?"

Gant flicked on the radar. On the scope, amid the clutter from the worsening weather, he could just make out two heavy, glowing blips of light in close formation. Range perhaps two or three miles. There were paler, higher dots beyond them, at the very edge of the screen, but he disregarded them. They were still as much as five minutes away.

"Good idea – but no thanks. They know which is which. You move out now, before they get their orders. Good luck."

There were puffs of snow from beneath the Harrier which became small billows as she rose on the downward-directed thrust of her engine. The Harrier wobbled aloft, lights winking beneath her wingtips and belly; glowing as much as at dusk. The aircraft turned in the air like a clumsy dancer, then the thrust of the engine was vectored to forward flight. The aircraft slipped behind the snow and was gone.

Gunnar in the second Lynx had watched the Harrier's disappearance avidly. Now, he returned his attention to the Firefox. Gant saw the turn of his head. He was the only Norwegian remaining, waiting for the last handful of technicians. Around the lake were perhaps forty-five marines, all of them hidden except for the white-clothed figure of Waterford outside the windbreak which protected the commpack and its operator. He knew they were waiting for the aircraft to take off so that they could disappear into the forest, and make for the Norwegian border in small, quick-moving groups.

The lake was suddenly isolated and lonely. Gant wanted to stop the refuelling that moment, let the technicians go, let Moresby go. Take off −

Two heavy, nearby glows on the radar; other paler dots moving steadily closer above the clouds. In minutes, they would be above him, poised like birds of prey. The encounter was inevitable.

He watched the fuel gauges. He glanced down at Moresby. The two dots on the radar remained motionless.

"Advance units report no contact, General."

Vladimirov listened with his head cocked slightly on one side as the reports began coming in from the airborne troops set down to the south and east of the lake. The British troops must be slowly falling back to the lake itself, with orders not to engage. A quick thrust now − a surprise outflanking movement around the tree-lined southern shore of the lake, and they might yet have the airframe intact −

The two MiL-24 gunships had been ordered to hold their position, despite the reports from the reconnaissance helicopter that Gant had started the MiG-31's engines and the Harrier and one of the Lynx helicopters had departed. There were only moments left. *They must push forward now − !*

The microphone was in his hand, to give the order. His lips had begun to frame the first words. He had summoned saliva into his dry mouth −

The First Secretary's hand fell heavily on his, startling him. He turned from the communications console. The Soviet leader was framed by the fibre-optic map. The scene upon its surface looked like an indictment.

"What are you about to do, General Vladimirov?"

"I − want our troops to push forward to the lake with all speed −" he began.

There was scorn in the heavy face of the First Secretary. "No," he said quietly. Then, more loudly: "No! Your time has run out, General Vladimirov – run out!" There is no time left for you. You – are dismissed!"

The silence in the long gallery was intense, almost audible. Andropov had turned away. No one looked in Vladimirov's direction, although he knew by their stance and lack of movement that they were all listening.

"What do you mean . . .?"

"I mean you are dismissed, Vladimirov – I mean you are to get out."

"But –"

"Go! Give me the microphone –" For a second, they struggled for possession of it like two children quarrelling over a toy. Then Vladimirov wearily, defeatedly released his grip. The First Secretary cleared his throat and said simply, "Gunship commander – you will begin an attack at once. Destroy the runway, destroy the MiG! Do you understand my order? Destroy!"

Buckholz was standing next to Moresby, looking up at him. Beside him was a large briefcase. He appeared like a traveller eager to be gone.

"Mitchell!" he said through Moresby's microphone. "Let's get the hell out of here – all of us!" He waved his arms towards the east for emphasis. Gant checked the radar –

And saw that the two glowing dots, in close formation, had begun to move. At high speed.

He waved his hand in agreement. Immediately, Moresby dashed forward to the fuel cell, and switched off the pump. Then he jerked the landline free with a violent tug. As the pump's nose subsided and the first distant hum of approaching rotors reached them, Gant pulled down the cockpit canopy, checked his straps, switched on his oxygen supply, checked the anti-G device of his pressure suit, and pushed the test button. He checked the gauges. The pump was abandoned, the empty fuel cell, like a huge collapsed black aircraft tyre, beside it. Then he saw Buckholz, Moresby and the technicians scurrying across the ice to the open door of Gunnar's Lynx. They climbed in hurriedly.

Gant checked the temperatures and pressures. The dots on the radar hurried through the mist of ground-clutter towards the scope's centre, closing on him. Runway, he thought. Runway first, airplane second. The Firefox strained against the brakes. He eased the throttles forward once more, paused, caught a glimpse of two helicopters – the Lynx lifting and sliding away towards the western shore of the lake and into the obscuring snow, and the first of the armed MiLs, a hundred yards ahead of him, at the edge of the trees. A gauntlet.

He released the brakes. The Firefox skipped forward, like a dog kept too long on its leash. It raced at the unfolding smooth runway of ice. Visibility, perhaps six hundred yards — snow blowing across the lake once more. He switched on the wipers. He thrust the throttles fully forward, and felt the power of the Turmanskys punch him in the back. The ice rushed beneath the nose of the Firefox. Fire bloomed beneath the stubby wing of the MiL-24, and snow and ice cascaded over the fuselage of the Firefox as he raced on.

The wipers cleared the cockpit screen. In the mirror, he saw the ice open up, but the black snaking branches of the cracks caused by the rocket's impact lagged behind him, out of breath and tired.

Fierce elation. Almost delight. The airspeed indicator read one hundred and twenty knots. He still could not see the far end of the lake. The airframe was shaking as the wheels careered over ridges and bumps. His teeth chattered painfully, his hand shuddered as it gripped the control column. One hundred and forty knots. The aircraft was almost skipping and bouncing as the wheels discovered every tiny indentation in the ice. One ridge that had been missed, he thought — then quashed the idea. It persisted for another moment — just one, and the undercarriage would snap —

One-fifty, one fifty-two —

He began to ease back on the column, beginning to lift the aircraft's nose. In the mirror, he saw the MiL loom up again as it pursued him. Fire billowed from it wing-pods; rockets. They struck the ice behind him, around, ahead. He was showered with fire which burst into boiling snow and ice. Something clattered against the fuselage. A huge crack in the ice to starboard snaked towards him at terrible speed — then he was past it. The scene behind him was completely obscured.

One-sixty knots.

Then he saw the second MiL, directly ahead of him, the end of the lake behind it; the trees like pencil-marks against the white-grey sky. The MiL wasn't moving. Hovering. Helicopter and shore filled his vision.

It was directly in his path. He was airborne, accelerating through one sixty-five knots. The MiL had positioned itself — it had shunted slightly a moment earlier — directly in the path of his climb-out. It enlarged, an enormous black beetle, hanging there.

He hauled back on the column, sweat bathing his body, his lips stretched back over his teeth. The nose of the Firefox rose, began to point at the clouds.

The MiL rushed forward anticipating his action, prepared for suicide. Missiles armed. He pulled the column back almost against his chest. The Firefox seemed to stand erect on its exhaust and stagger into the air as if tearing free of a swamp rather than a frozen lake. The MiL was huge in his vision. He retracted the undercarriage as the helicopter seemed to move its nose in, so that he almost expected a shark-mouth to open and tear at the belly of the Firefox. The aircraft leapt at the low cloud. The MiL had vanished; become no more than a wide dot on his scope. A missile's infra-red trail pursued him for a moment, then fell away, unable to match his rate of climb. It would have been wire-guided, for use against ground targets.

He was at ten thousand feet, climbing at the rate of five hundred feet a second. The airframe quivered and shuddered, like a human body that was chilled and growing rapidly colder, as the storm thrust and battered outside the aircraft. His fingers trembled on the control column. The throttles were all the way forward, through the detent and into reheat. The Mach-meter clicked rapidly upwards. Mach .8, .9, 1.0, Mach 1.2 . . .

Eleven thousand feet. He studied the radar. Three glowing dots were moving towards the scope's centre. He demanded contact time from the computer, and the read-out appeared almost immediately. Twenty seconds. They were at fifty thousand feet, and they could see him on radar –

He would break through the cloud ceiling at twenty-four thousand feet, into a searing blue sky, and he would be under a roof of interceptors. Already other, paler dots were appearing at the edge of the screen. His body was still shaking from the aftermath of the almost-collision. Had he kept the Firefox beneath the MiL, he would have ploughed into the shore and the trees and and exploded . . .

He tried to dismiss the past.

Don't think about it, don't think about it, his mind kept repeating. Don't think about it . . .

He pulled back on the throttles and scanned the instrument panel. No warning lights. Fuel-flow, rpm, radar, avionics, inertial navigator, armaments. The airplane functioned. It *was* an airplane again, not salvage.

Altitude, eighteen thousand feet and climbing. The grey cloud slid and writhed past the cockpit. The bright white blips on the screen were nearer. Ten seconds to contact.

No anti-radar. They can see you, he reminded himself.

Remember that –

The MiGs were too close to outclimb. Stand-off missiles, heat-seeking, would overtake him even if the fighters that launched them could not. Six aircraft, all closing. All of them could see him. Already, they would have reported that fact, and would have deduced the failure of the anti-radar. The adrenalin would begin to flow, now that they knew. They would consider it easy, consider it already accomplished . . .

Hide.

Ground-clutter –

Dive.

Course – Bardufoss.

Twenty-one thousand feet. Contact time six seconds. Feverishly, he punched in the coordinates to the intertial navigator, and began to alter course. Hide – ground-clutter. Deceive the radars. Five seconds, four-and-a-half, three.

He saw the infra-red flare. A missile launched at Mach 3, then a second and a third. He banked savagely, flinging the aircraft into a steep dive, twisting into a roll so that the thicker, heavier grey cloud was now beneath his canopy. Then he completed the roll and the nose of the Firefox was driving through the cloud, the altimeter unrolling, the streaks of the missile exhausts still pursuing him across the screen. The white blips behind them had altered course and were following him down.

He banked savagely again, feelng the G-pressure build until it was painful. The suit he was wearing, not tailored for him or the aircraft, was slow to adapt to the abilities of the Firefox. His head hurt, his vision was hazy for a moment. Ten thousand feet. The missiles were pursuing a different course, dropping away towards the ground because they had lost his infra-red scent. The effects of the savage turn drained away. He eased the aircraft into a steeper dive. The three closest white blips still pursued him.

Five thousand feet. He began to pull out of the dive, slowly and easily. Four thousand feet. Three, and the aircraft was beginning to level out. Two-five, two, one-five, then he was flying level. He flicked on the terrain-following radar, then the autopilot. The inertial navigator altered the aircraft's course immediately, directing it towards Bardufoss. From the read-out, he knew he was already in Norwegian airspace. Somewhere over the Finnmark, inland of the Porsangerfjord.

The Russians, too, were inside Norwegian airspace.

The Firefox twisted, banked, flicked like a dart through the unseen mountains. Gant felt as if he were watching a grey blank screen ahead, through the haze of snow swept aside by the slipstream. There was nothing. Except the sense of the mountains of the Finnmark around him intruding, seeping like a gas. He could not help but feel their solidity, their massive obstruction. They were a maze through which the TFR and the autopilot flung him. He was like a runner off-balance on a treacherous surface. So long as his flight was headlong, arms flailing, he kept upright, leaping from foot to uncertain foot. TFR – autopilot. Keeping him alive. He felt, too, the constant, chilly quivering of the fuselage as it met the impact of the storm outside. It was as if his own body was growing colder and colder; shivering violently.

The three Russian interceptors followed, but they were slowly dropping back. They might have been MiG-25s, or even MiG-27s. They were not the Firefox. They were confused by ground-clutter, they had to trail him at an altitude above the mountains, they had to employ their manual skills. With each change of course, he gained upon them. He glanced at the map strapped to the thigh of his suit. His finger traced his course. Over the mountains east of the Lyngenfjord – flicking through that valley there, wings trembling as the aircraft banked and banked again through the turbulent air, following the valley's turns and twists . . .

A hundred miles from Bardufoss.

The Firefox banked steeply, almost turning into a roll, then changed course again to follow a valley before lifting over an unseen ridge and then dropping lower into another fold of the land. Rock faces on either side crowded upon the slim black fuselage. He could not avoid imagining the landscape or tracing his course on the map. He knew it was reaction; reaction to everything – the MiGs that were dropping further and further behind him, the MiL helicopter that had filled the whole of his vision, the steep climb, even the hours before the take-off.

And it was Bardufoss. If the weather closed in, clamped down with high winds and nil visibility – a blizzard, close to white-out – he would never be able to land.

The thoughts unrolled like the images flicking upon the TFR screen; the blurs and lumps and flashing glimpses of radar-imaged mountains, rock faces, valleys –

The TFR screen went black. Grey. Empty. The aircraft was halfway into a steep turn, following –

No time! Much too late, a row of warning lights had rippled across the autopilot panel. No time –

The Firefox seemed to hang. Grey screen, grey beyond the perspex of the cockpit. Without instructions from the autopilot, the column did not move, the engine note did not change, the angle of bank remained. The two Turmanskys were driving him towards a terrain he could not see. Into it –

He sensed the storm outside the aircraft more vividly. The fuselage seemed to shudder, as if anticipating impact. He imagined the noise of the wind, felt he would be tumbled from the cockpit when the aircraft struck and would hear the wind – before . . .

Still his hands hesitated, clenched almost into claws. *Choose* – He couldn't. The Firefox maintained the steep change of course the autopilot had initiated on the instructions of the TFR. Where – ?

Valley! Lift –

He levelled the aircraft, pushed the throttles forward, cancelled the autopilot by pressing the button on the column, then pulled it towards him. Grey ahead of him, nothing, nothing, nothing . . .

The nose came up, the Firefox climbed. Four thousand feet. Four-and-a-half, five –

He was above the mountains. Sweat ran from beneath his arms. His facemask was fogged. On the radar, the MiGs seemed to have surged forward, away from the bottom of the screen towards its centre. They could see him clearly now; a target upon which to home. Gant shuddered uncontrollably, gripping the column as he levelled the aircraft at six thousand feet. He forced himself to look at the map on his knee, at the tiny printed heights of the peaks. Then he pulled back on the stick once more, lifting to eight thousand feet as quickly as he could. *Now* he was above them; the mountains no longer threatened him.

The MiGs closed. He demanded a read-out from the computer. Contact time, fourteen seconds. He pushed the throttles forward, forcing the Mach-meter past Mach 2; flying blind.

He flicked on the UHF set. He would be over Bardufoss in minutes now. He had to know.

"Bardufoss Approach – this is Firefox. Over." He listened. Checked the frequency. Listened. The UHF set was on, it should be working. "Bardufoss Approach – come in, Bardufoss. This is Firefox. Over."

The MiGs seemed to have halted, dropped back to near the bottom of the screen. He knew they would be listening. It was not a high-security channel. They were waiting. He shivered. They were waiting until he made his approach, slowed down, presented himself to them helplessly as he went in to land.

The UHF set crackled. A distant voice with a Scandinavian accent spoke to him. His hands jumped on the column, as if it had been a Russian voice. But he recognised the word "Bardufoss".

"Repeat, Bardufoss. Say again your message. I wish for landing instructions. Over."

He waited, the aircraft at Mach 2. His positional read-out from the inertial navigator showed him sixty miles from Bardufoss. He was aware of the turbulence outside the aircraft, almost as if it was a warning.

566

". . . is closed, repeat, closed," he heard. "Estimated ceiling fifty feet in heavy snow. Runway visual range twenty yards with eighty degree crosswind gusting to forty-five knots." Then, in something of a more human tone: "I am sorry, Firefox, but a landing at Bardufoss is impossible. We have blizzard conditions . . ."

And they would have heard.

"Thank you, Bardufoss."

"Good —" He cut of the hope, turning at once to the Soviet Tac-channel. Immediately, he heard the Russian chatter, the almost-glee, the agreement, the request for instructions, the decisions, the tactics —

The MiGs surged towards the centre of the screen. He stared numbly at their advance upon him. They were at more than Mach 2, closing rapidly.

He was locked out by the storm. Already, other pursuing Soviet fighters were at the lower edge of his scope. But these three, closing so quickly — missile launch time, seven seconds — knew he was locked out. They were closing for the kill. He hesitated, expecting the leap of bright infra-red dots towards him as they fired their first missiles. *No* —

He moved his hands slowly, almost finding, *finding* —

He groaned aloud. As he lifted his head, he drew the column towards him and thrust the throttles forward. The nose of the Firefox lifted, wobbling in the increasing turbulence. He had ignored it, ignored the weather worsening around him, because he had not wanted to understand, had not wished to admit that Bardufoss would be closed down.

The Mach-meter passed 2, then 2.2, .3, .7 . . . The altimeter mounted through fifteen, then seventeen thousand. The MiGs below him altered course, striving to catch him. The Firefox raced upwards.

He broke out of the turbulent, snow-filled clouds at twenty-six thousand feet, into a searing, eye hurting blue sky. In the mirror, the cloud was massed and unbroken beneath him. The sun was low to the west. He climbed through forty thousand feet. Fifty —

The first of the Soviet fighters broke out of the cloud, a gleaming dot far below; a white blip at the lower edge of the scope. Then another gleaming spot joined it in the mirror, then a lagging third.

Gant levelled the Firefox at seventy thousand feet, and accelerated. The Mach-meter passed 4.5. The gleaming dots faded from the scope. The cloud lay unbroken over the Lofoten Islands. He crossed the Arctic Circle. Almost idly, he listened to the last fading chatter from the UHF. Within minutes, he would change the frequency to the principal NATO secure Tac-channel, so that he could identify himself to RAF Strike Command and obtain clearance to land at Scampton, his original destination. He altered course in order to gain a visual sighting over Shetland, still five hundred miles to the south – eight minutes' flying time. He grinned. He was a blur, a meteor, travelling a thousand miles an hour faster than any other aircraft in the world. He would have crossed the North Sea in another seven minutes; he would be over Shetland. Mach 5.1. Almost four thousand miles an hour.

It was over. He felt exhilarated. The radio chatter faded. He heard – what was it? Rostock? Whatever that meant . . . It didn't matter. Radar clear. Empty. He was alone. The Soviet exchanges faded and were gone.

Anna –

No. He put her carefully aside. The others were paler ghosts. They no longer troubled him. He was alive. He was in the Firefox. He had done it –

He looked down through a tear in the cloud. He was high over the North Sea. He was too high to see the flares burning off on the rigs. More gaps in the cloud. He was suspended above the flat, calm-looking sea. Élite; alone. Alone he had meant to think – alone. Not élite, alone . . .

He would be over Shetland in no more than three minutes. Time to open the Tac-channel – wouldn't be much of an ending, getting shot down . . .

Rostock? Who was Rostock?

Fuel-flow, check. Altimeter, radar, Mach-meter –

Radar – nothing . . .

He felt light-headed. He reached forward to retune the UHF. He was alone; élitely alone. Drifting at four thousand miles an hour.

Rostock – ?

Radar – nothing . . . Glow – ?

He leaned forward. He felt even more light-headed; almost delirious. He screwed up his eyes, trying to focus. Flickering glow on the – panel – ? He was floating. The nose of the Firefox dipped and the aircraft began to dive. He leaned against the control column, gripping the wheel but unaware of the pressure of his body pushing the column forward. He couldn't see clearly, and leaned further towards the panel. His eyesight was misty. He clutched the control column to his chest like a drunken man seeking support. As the nose of the Firefox dipped, the steepness of the dive was controlled only by his one-armed grip on the column and the straps restraining the forward movement of his body beyond a certain point.

Rostock – ?

Vladimirov asked him what it meant. He was being beaten, but he felt nothing. Only numb. Warmly numb. Drugged . . . he remembered his father, shambling into the house on the, the – Mira Prospekt? Yes, yes, Mira Prospekt . . .

He heard voices, speaking Russian. Change channels. He did not understand – who was Rostock?

Glow on the – panel? Glow – ?

He did not understand. The Firefox began to fall out of the sky. Unnoticed, the altimeter unrolled with increasing speed as he slumped towards the panel. The throttles were still set at high cruise power.

He saw dots – blips not glows. Right and left of the screen, converging on him. Rostock – ? His helmet was almost against the panel, and his hanging face opposite the scope. White blips, rushing at him.

Thirty thousand feet, twenty-five, twenty-two . . . The altimeter unrolled unnoticed.

Gant groggily lifted his head, and his hand. He felt along the panel. The Firefox bucked as he adjusted his hold on the column to gain more support. The nose came up slightly, but the stick resisted him fiercely. He believed in it as a solid, unmoving thing to which he could cling. He tried to focus. The radar was filled with closing blips which immediately became a blur. Flickering glow . . .? Rostock, Ro – stock . . .? What did it mean? Glow –

He touched the flicker of light, and tried to count. Tried to remember. It was important, like Rostock. But he could answer this question – he was trained to do it –

He clutched at a switch and threw it with a convulsive jerk of his body. Then he lolled wearily upright, still holding the column, aware now of the restraint of his straps. As his head came above the cockpit coaming, he could see that now the sea had huge, tossing waves. There were fires burning below and around him, flares warning of –

He saw the Vietnamese girl swallowed by fire. He saw Anna with the blue hole in her forehead. His arms ached, seemed close to being pulled from their sockets with the effort required to hold onto the control column.

The girl, Anna – himself . . .

'No – you *bastard* – !'

He fought the column, trying to heave it towards him with a fierce, sudden strength. He dragged the throttles back, then pulled further on the column. It moved more easily. His lungs gulped the emergency oxygen supply. The altimeter unrolled more slowly, the Mach-meter descended. The aircraft began to level out. He continued to fight the column, clutching it back against him. The horizon jolted, wobbled, the waves accelerated less than a thousand feet below. The flames from the oil-rigs rushed beneath him. His head was filled with noises, voices speaking in Russian —

He reset the UHF feverishly. He heard it, then —

Rostock. Spoken in English, an English accent. A babble of English voices.

He raced over an oil-rig, then another, then a third. Snow flurried across the stormy, tossing water, but there were bright gaps in the cloud. Shreds of it struggled to envelop him, but the Firefox kept breaking free of them . . .

His head cleared. He was travelling at less than four hundred miles an hour, at twelve hundred feet, across what remained of the North Sea; towards Shetland.

He continued to gulp down the emergency oxygen supply. The airplane had tried to kill him again. Had betrayed him. The warning light had come on too late for him to recognise its signal. Lack of oxygen had already made him dizzy and light-headed before he noticed it. His heart pounded, his pulse thudded in his ears. His helmet was filled with English voices, themselves full of congratulation. He flicked back to the Soviet channel.

Rostock — they were calling Rostock. Airbase, he remembered. It would have been the nearest front-line airbase on an interception course. East Germany. A couple of squadrons of MiG-25s had been despatched by the élite 16th Frontal Aviation Army to destroy him. The RAF had reached him first. He had been a sitting target. They might even have been just sitting back, watching him dive into the sea. The Firefox had been doing their work for them.

He sat back in the couch. *Bastard.* On either side of him, aircraft appeared. They waggled their wings, coyly displaying their RAF roundels. One of the pilots, the one to starboard, signalled with his thumb. Success, congratulation — something like that. Beyond the Tornado fighter, Gant glimpsed the dark coastline of Shetland rising out of the sea.

Wearily, he returned the UHF to the NATO secure tactical channel. The English voices gabbled for a moment, then one of them silenced the others and attempted to contact him. He glanced to starboard. The pilot of the Tornado was frantically signalling with his hand. He wanted him to answer, to use the radio —

Gant did not care. He was alive. He was safe. There was time enough to answer them. His heartbeat and pulse settled, receding in his awareness. Bastard. The airplane was a bastard.

It was over now.

"Go ahead, flight leader," he said eventually, sitting more upright in the couch. "This is Firefox. Receiving you loud and clear. Go ahead. Over."

"Major Gant? Congratulations, Major — what happened, sir? What happened to you? Over."

"I lived," Gant replied. "Now, get me home."

At twelve hundred feet and at a speed of three hundred and eighty-six miles an hour, the MiG-31, NATO-codenamed the Firefox, drifted towards the Scottish coast escorted by six Tornado fighters of RAF Strike Command. They were the only aircraft registering on his radar.

The grey, stormy sea flowed beneath the belly of the aircraft. A stray gleam of sunlight glowed on the cockpit. Gant, at last, allowed himself a smile of success.

SEA
LEOPARD

for MIKE, *agent and friend*
and in memoriam
ANTHEA JOSEPH
a kind and courageous lady

Acknowledgements

I wish to thank particularly my wife, Jill, for her strict and expert editing of the book, and for her initial suggestion that I attempt this story.

My thanks, also, to GH who acted as captain of the submarine HMS *Proteus*, and to the Royal Navy, without whose assistance, given so freely and willingly, I could not have completed the book. Gratitude, too, to TRJ for coming to my assistance in developing the "Leopard" anti-sonar equipment on which the story hinges.

As usual, I am indebted to various publications, particularly to Breyer & Polmar's *Guide to the Soviet Navy*, Labayle & Couhat's *Combat Fleets of the World*, and *The Soviet War Machine*, edited by Ray Bonds.

Any errors, distortion or licence for dramatic purposes is my responsibility, not that of any of the above.

Craig Thomas,
Lichfield 1980

Principal Characters

Kenneth de Vere AUBREY : Deputy Director, British Intelligence (SIS)

Patrick HYDE : a field agent of SIS

Ethan CLARK, USN : on liaison to the Admiralty

QUIN : an eminent electronic engineer

Tricia QUIN : his daughter

Col. Giles PYOTT, R.A. : a member of the NATO StratAn Committee

Comm. Richard LLOYD, R.N. : captain of the submarine HMS *Proteus*

Lt. Comm. John THURSTON, R.N. : first lieutenant, HMS *Proteus*

Sir Richard CUNNINGHAM : Director of British Intelligence ("C")

Peter SHELLEY : assistant to the Deputy Director, SIS

Sqn. Ldr. Alan EASTOE, R.A.F. : Nimrod pilot

Valery ARDENYEV, Red Navy : O/C Underwater Special Ops. Unit

DOLOHOV : admiral of the Red Banner Northern Fleet

Tamas PETRUNIN : KGB Resident, Soviet embassy in London

Viktor TEPLOV : petty officer to Ardenyev's unit

PLESSEY

The Plessey Company Limited
Millbank Tower, 21-24, Millbank, London SW1 4QP
Telephone: 01-834 9641 Telex 917530

INTER OFFICE MEMO

from: Head of Project L

to: Head of Research

ref: 'LEOPARD'

I quite realise the pressure you must be under
from the Board to achieve results.   You may,
when you report to them, inform them of the
following:-

The broad effect of 'Leopard' is already working.
We have progressed to the point where we can
prevent an enemy sonar signal registering the
presence of a vessel using 'Leopard', and we
can also, after nullifying that signal with the
equipment, return to the enemy a false echo as
if from the sea bed below the submarine.

The remaining problems are related to the
variable quality of the false signal.   I am
confident the improvements can be made.

Registered in England and Wales at Vicarage Lane, Ilford, Essex IG1 4AQ Number 203848

1974   1976

581

PLESSEY

The Plessey Company Limited
Millbank Tower, 21-24, Millbank, London SW1 4QP
Telephone: 01-834 9641   Telex 917530

Commodore D. N. Blackshaw, R.N.,
Senior Projects Officer,
Royal Navy (Projects),
Old Admiralty Building,
Whitehall,
LONDON.

Dear Commodore,

In considering your urgent request to the company
to accelerate the final stages of development of
the field prototype of our 'Leopard' project, I
am advised by the project head, Dr. A. J. Quin,
that it is possible to shorten the time prior to
full sea trials, only by a matter of a few days.
I respect the urgency of the matter, and understand
the kind of mission on which 'Leopard' would be
of inestimable value, but I am afraid that is the
best we can do.

Yours sincerely,

R. M. Bennett

R. M. Bennett,
Deputy Chairman.

Registered in England and Wales at Vicarage Lane, Ilford, Essex IG1 4AQ Number 203848

LEOPARD 42
MOST SECRET

FROM: Peter Shelley

TO: Kenneth Aubrey,
        Deputy Director, SIS

You requested a copy of the accompanying report on the
sea trials of the LEOPARD anti-detection equipment as
soon as possible, together with a summary in layman's
terms.

As you know, a specially equipped Nimrod and a Sea King
helicopter were used in the sea trials with HMS Proteus.
They could not effectively detect or pinpoint the submarine
on any single occasion.

The full report is complex and highly technical, as well
as being liberally sprinkled with service jargon!
However, I have discussed it with the Director of
Technical Services Section, and he has summarised the
sea trials in the following terms:-

   i.   No problems were encountered with the hull sensors;

  ii.   The 'noise generator' unit effectively cancelled
       all external acoustic emissions, and dealt
       successfully with all attempts to detect the
       submarine using sonar;

 iii.   In shallower waters, the unit's delayed response
       system effectively transmitted a sonar echo
       which accurately simulated a 'seabed' response -
       in other words, the vessels seeking out HMS Proteus
       only registered the seabed and not the submarine.
       She was effectively 'invisible', as expected.

DEFENCE DEPARTMENT (NAVY)
UNITED STATES NAVAL INTELLIGENCE

USN (Intelligence) Form TAL 1

Our Ref	Deputy Director
Your Ref	Capt. E. V. Clark, US

page 2 of 2   **Date**

so I don't have to tell you how much of a threat
to the British, to ourselves and to the whole of
NATO the new Soviet sonar buoy carpet in the
Barents Sea represents.   Unless it is fully
mapped, and therefore neutralised as a threat,
the Soviet Navy can close the Barents Sea at any
time, and that would mean the loss of NATO's
northern flank without a shot being fired.

For the reasons I have outlined, it was decided
that the Navy Department ask the British Royal
Navy to investigate and chart this new sonar
carpet, codenamed CHESSBOARD, using the submarine
<u>Proteus</u>, with the new LEOPARD equipment.   The
submarine, if your reports on her sea trials are
accurate, should remain undetected throughout
the time she is in the area of the Barents Sea.

Your brief is liaison and observation, both for
the Navy Department and for NATO.   Don't overstep
your mission orders, but get back to this office
immediate and direct through the embassy if
anything happens you don't like.   Neither the
Director nor myself are really happy about risking
this LEOPARD equipment, if it's as good as they
say.   But, we don't have much choice.

Adml. J. K. Vandenburg, USN,
Deputy Director,
US Navy Intelligence.

SIS
F. TTR 1a
TAPE TRANSCRIPTIONS

FILE REF	SIS/26554/3A - PH/Aubrey
TAPE No	B/163487/82/4/23
DATE	
REFERS	QUIN - DISAPPEARANCE

.......continued

furthermore, none of his personal effects appear
to have been removed from the flat. There was
still mail behind the door, dating back more than
three weeks. There have been no subsequent
sightings.

In conclusion, I think the bird has flown. On
the other hand, I don't believe it was his decision.
There was no pre-planning. Coupled with the
information regarding the 'Trade Mission' arrivals
and departures at the Soviet embassy during the
relevant period, I am certain that Quin was snatched
and is now in Moscow.

I am inclined to believe that his daughter is with
him, since Birmingham Special Branch haven't had a
peep from her since the time of Quin's disappearance.

I have ordered the continuance of 24-hour
surveillance on the flat Quin occupied in Bracknell
and on his estranged wife's home in Sutton Coldfield.

P4

Patrick Hyde

PART ONE

A GAME AT CHESS

ONE:

Bait

The office of Tamas Petrunin, Trade Attaché at the Soviet embassy in London, looked out upon Kensington Palace Gardens, across the lawns of the embassy grounds. The straight lines of bare plane trees marked the boundary between himself and the western city he both despised and coveted. A fierce early spring wind searched for, and found, the remains of last autumn's leaves, and hurried them along the road and beneath the wrought-iron gates into the drive of the embassy, finally scattering them like burnt secret messages and papers over the gravel and the grass. The sky was unrelievedly grey, and had been threatening rain all morning. Tamas Petrunin had leisure to reflect, as he listened angrily to the tape cassette from the duty room and its recorded conversation, that London irritated him particularly at that time of year. *There was no snow*. Wind, and rain – an umbrella threatening to turn inside out carried by an old man passing the gate, unceremoniously jostled by the wind – wind and rain, but little snow. Only sleet in the evening air sometimes, turning instantly to slush in the gutters, like a promise broken. In Moscow, there would be inches of snow, and everyone rotund and animalised in fur coats and hats.

The Scotsman's recorded voice enraged him. Almost always it did. Now nasality and meaning combined to grip his stomach with an indigestion of rage.

"We have been trying to contact you for two days," the authoritative Russian voice insisted. Ruban, the Naval Attaché who worked under the auspices of Petrunin and the KGB at the embassy. "You fully understand how difficult movement outside London is for our people here. Why have you not contacted us on schedule? Now you say the submarine has sailed."

There was an additional nasality, and a promoted, cultivated cough in the Scot's voice when he replied. "I've been in bed with the flu. It's no' my fault. I havena been to work all week. I've been in my bed, y' understand?" The whine was almost rebellious.

"We do not pay you to be ill, MacFarlane."

"I couldna help it. I still feel lousy. I got up to come to the phone.

589

There's fog, too." A small, projected bout of coughing followed the weather bulletin. Petrunin, in spite of his anger, could not suppress a smile.

"When did the submarine sail from Faslane?"

"Three nights ago, early hours."

"What? *Three* nights? What else did you learn?"

"I couldna ask, could I? Just that she sailed three nights ago."

"You are useless to us!" stormed Ruban on the tape behind Petrunin. One of the embassy chauffeurs was walking, leaning against the wind, towards a parked black Mercedes saloon. His black uniform trousers were flapping around his legs, and he was holding his peaked cap firmly on his head.

"I couldna help it – it was no' my fault if I caught the damn flu, was it?"

"Was the equipment on board? Do you know that much for certain?"

"I heard it was."

"You don't *know*?"

"Yes, dammit, it was on board!" The Scot sniffled on the tape. Petrunin pictured him. Pale, rat-faced, unshaven, untrustworthy. Trash. He was poor material with which to start a blaze. Ruban thought so too, by the sound of his voice. Ruban would have to report to Murmansk, via himself, and they would have to decide, on Mac-Farlane's word alone, whether the British submarine *Proteus* was carrying the "Leopard" equipment or not when she slipped out of Faslane into the Atlantic three nights before.

"You're guessing," Ruban said after a pause. "You can't know for certain."

"I'm sure, dammit! Nothing was taken off the ship after she returned from sea trials with this 'Leopard' stuff!" MacFarlane had forgotten his habitual ingratiating manner. "I found out that much. Nothing came off the ship."

"And where is she now?"

"I dinna know." MacFarlane retreated from anger into surliness.

"And that ends your report?"

In the silence that followed, Petrunin moved to his desk and switched off the cassette player. Then he returned to the window of his office, rubbing his chin. In no more than thirty minutes, he would have to summon Ruban, and they would have to make a decision before five or five-thirty as to the nature of the signal they would send to Moscow Centre and to Red Banner Northern Fleet HQ, Murmansk, EYES ONLY Admiral Dolohov. Damn MacFarlane and his attack of influenza.

"Leopard". Was it on board? If so, then the likelihood that *Proteus*

590

was on her way to map the location and extent of the newest Soviet sonar-grid across the Barents Sea from North Cape to Murmansk was transmuted into a virtual certainty. The only way to do that was by means of a submarine indetectable by sonar; which would mean *Proteus* using the "Leopard" equipment. Ethan Clark, the American expert, was in London on liaison work, *Proteus* had sailed on secret orders to an unknown destination as soon as her sea trials were complete. It was a likelihood – was it a certainty?

Petrunin paced the room carefully, keeping to the border of the patterned Turkish carpet, studying his footsteps with apparent intentness, rubbing his chin lightly with thumb and forefinger in a ceaseless motion of his hand. *Proteus* had to reach North Cape in order for the Red Banner Fleet's cock-eyed plan to be put into operation. If she were sailing elsewhere, all the preparations would have been a waste of time and effort.

Petrunin found himself before the window again. The newly-imprisoned leaves seemed to be scurrying aimlessly across the embassy lawns, seeking escape. He shook his head. *Proteus*'s target had to be "Chessboard". The development of "Leopard" had been violently accelerated during the past six months, the sea trials had been conducted with maximum haste; both facts implied an urgent task for the equipment. After all, there were no other "Leopard" units as yet, none fitted to any submarine or surface ship in the Royal Navy. Just this one priceless example of anti-sonar equipment, being used for one special task –

Yes. He nodded vigorously. He would go over it again with Ruban in fifteen minutes or so, but he had decided. They would signal Moscow and Murmansk that *Proteus* was on her way north, making for North Cape. Then it was up to the Red Banner Fleet.

And, he reminded himself, not for the first time that afternoon, there then devolved upon himself the task of finding Quin. Quin, the inventor and developer of "Leopard". Disappeared without trace. Not under protective custody, because British Intelligence, the Directorate of Security and Special Branch were all looking for him. Quin. More important – at least in Petrunin's estimation – than "Leopard" itself. Where was he?

He realised, with a mounting disappointment, that his decision with regard to *Proteus* was no decision at all. Merely a side-issue, a piece of self-indulgence, a war-game for sailors. Quin was what mattered. And Quin could not be found.

It had become routine, watching the house in Sutton Coldfield, in a quiet, residential street between the roads to Lichfield and Brownhills. A pre-war detached house, standing a little back from the road and elevated above its level, partially screened by a stone wall and a dark hedge. Leaded windows, trained ivy like an artificial ageing process climbing wooden trelliswork around the front door, and cherry blossom trees waiting for the spring. The street was still stained from the recent rain, and the slim boles of the trees gleamed green. Routine, boring routine. The young officer of the Special Branch unit attached to the West Midlands constabulary knew the façade of the house in which Quin's divorced wife lived with a familiarity that had become sour and stultifying. She worked part-time in the elegantly refurbished premises of an antique shop a hundred yards away. She was there now. The Special Branch Officer had parked his unmarked Ford Escort so that he had a clear view of the house and the entrance of the shop. He had observed well-dressed women, the occasional couple, a small delivery van, but no sign, none whatsoever, of Quin or of his daughter who had disappeared from her teacher training college in Birmingham at the same time that he had vanished. And there had been no visitors to the house except the milkman, the grocery delivery on a Thursday, the fish van on Wednesdays –

Sugden found himself idly flicking through the leaves of his notebook, rehearsing the boredom of two weeks' surveillance of the quiet street in a quiet suburb, shook his head, and snapped the notebook shut on the seat beside him. He put another cigarette to his lips, lit it, looked at his watch – Mrs. Quin would be coming home for a salad lunch in another half-an-hour – and slid lower in the driving seat, attempting to stretch his legs. He yawned. He and Lane, day and night for two weeks, just in case the missing man contacted the wife he'd left four years before, or in case the daughter turned up.

No chance, he told himself with a spiteful satisfaction that seemed to revenge him on the London superiors who had placed him in his present limbo, no chance at all. It was even duller work than preparing for the visit of the Queen to a Lichfield school a couple of years before, or Princess Margaret's opening of another Lichfield school before that, just after he had joined the Branch in Birmingham. Dull, deadly, dead. Quin and the girl had gone over. Not voluntarily, of course. Kidnapped. Snatched, Sugden yawned again. Quin was building "Leopard" for the Soviet Union by now, watched by his friendly neighbourhood KGB man. Despite wishing to maintain a frosty contempt for his present task and for those who had given him his orders, Sugden smiled to himself. Once Mrs. Quin was inside the house, a quick sandwich and a pint for him in the pub opposite the antique showroom. In the window seat, he could just about see the path up to the Quin house. Well enough, anyway. Certainly he could observe any car that parked near the house, or a pedestrian on the pavement.

He wondered why Quin had left his wife. Perhaps she had left him. They'd moved down to London when he began working for Plessey, and she'd come back to the Midlands after the separation because both of them were from the area and because the girl, Tricia, was enrolled at a training college in Birmingham. She'd repeated her first year twice, the file said, then failed her second year after the decree nisi, and only someone's pull high-up had prevented her from being expelled from the college. Now she'd disappeared along with her father. Another lever for the KGB to use on him, Sugden presumed. Mrs. Quin looked pleasant and capable. Greying blond hair, smartly turned out, could be taken for early forties. Quin, from the look of his picture – on the dash of the Escort – wasn't much of a catch, at least not in looks. The girl was pretty, but student-scruffy rather than making the most of herself. Almost drab, like the female of some brightly-plumaged species of bird.

She came down the path as Sugden rubbed his face and stifled another yawn. Tricia Quin, coming out of her mother's house. The closing of the door alerted him. She took no notice of the car, turned left, and began walking briskly down the hill towards the Lichfield road. Frayed denims, a long cardigan in some sludgy colour beneath a *cagoule*, untidy fair hair. Tricia Quin.

She was almost fifty or sixty yards down the hill before his hand jerked at the door handle, and he got out of the Escort. He could not believe it, though the confirmatory photograph was in his hand. He opened his mouth, fish-slow and silently, and then slammed the door behind him with an angry curse. He appeared stupid, would appear stupid, even when he took the girl in . . .

A rush of thoughts then. Quin might be in the country after all – the girl, how had she got in last night, how had Lane missed her? – comfortable thought, that. Lane's fault – where was Quin? Door opening and closing in the empty house with its For Sale notice, the one he'd suggested using but permission had been denied, too much paperwork to take it over – door closing, the girl further away down the hill, oblivious of him.

Or of the squat-featured, heavy-looking man in the grey double-breasted suit coming down the path of the empty house, a taller, thinner man running behind him. Both of them running, no more than twenty yards away from him now, and perhaps a hundred or so from the girl. KGB, so obvious he wanted to laugh, so sudden their appearance he could not move and was aware only of their numerical superiority.

"Wait a minute –" he managed to say, stepping round the Escort onto the pavement. The one in the grey suit ran with his thick arm extended, palm outwards, to fend him off like a rugby player; the thinner man dodged round the offside of Sugden's car. They were going to get past him, no doubt of it. "Wait!"

He ducked outside the extended hand, felt it heave at his shoulder, then got a hold on the arm behind it, ripping the grey sleeve of the suit immediately. A heavy fist swung at the edge of his vision and caught him on the temple. He was immediately dizzy.

The heavy man said something in Russian. Mrs. Quin was coming out of the shop, Sugden could see her over the roof of the car as the heavy man lurched him against it. The thinner man was galloping down the middle of the road, no athlete but certain to overtake the still unaware girl.

Sugden opened his mouth and bellowed her name. The heavy man struck upwards into Sugden's groin with his knee. Sugden doubled up, retching and groaning, his head turned sideways. The girl had become instantly alert, then had begun to run. The heavy man cursed, and moved away after aiming a foot at Sugden's head and connecting with his shoulder. Both men were running off. Sugden, groaning, his eyes wet with the latest wave of pain, knew he had to concentrate. They would want everything in his report.

Three hundred yards away, still just identifiable, Tricia Quin boarded a cream and blue bus as it pulled away, heading into the centre of Sutton Coldfield. The two Russians were just short of her, and the traffic lights were in the bus's favour. She was gone; they'd lost her, just as he had.

He rolled onto his back, still clutching his genitals, and listened to the tattoo of Mrs. Quin's high heels on the pavement as she ran towards him.

Patrick Hyde hurried through the rooms of the empty house, as if their last, impermanent occupants might yet be overtaken and restrained, just so long as he displayed sufficient haste. Two camp beds in one of the bedrooms, spare linen in the airing cupboard on the landing, food still in cardboard boxes, mostly tinned stuff, the refrigerator half-full, six-packs of lager, bottles of vodka. The two KGB men must have arrived before Birmingham Special Branch began its surveillance. The almost full dustbins at the side of the house suggested they had moved in almost as soon as Quin first disappeared.

Hyde snorted with self-derision and with an anger that included himself, Kenneth Aubrey, the DS, Special Branch, everyone. Quin had simply panicked, hidden himself. Or had he –? He could even be dead, and they might want the girl for some other reason . . .

Quin is alive, and well, and living somewhere in England, he reminded himself.

594

He turned to the police inspector who had followed at his heels through the house. "No sign of them now, sport?" He dropped immediately into a strengthened accent, one he had never himself possessed but which he used always to remind others of his Australian origins – because he knew it irritated them, and it served in some way to dissociate him from their incompetence. The only person secure from its mockery was Kenneth Aubrey. "A right bloody cock-up, mate. Wouldn't you say?"

The police inspector controlled his features. He disliked having to deal with someone from Intelligence rather than from what he would have considered the "proper channels", counter-intelligence. He could see no reason why Hyde, as SIS operative, should be officially functioning inside the United Kingdom, and displaying his superiority so evidently. And a bloody Aussie . . .

"You'd like to speak with Sugden now, I suppose, Mr. Hyde?" he said through thinned lips, hardly opening his teeth to emit the sounds.

Hyde scowled. "Too bloody right, Blue. Where is he?"

The inspector pointed to the lounge window, across at the Quin house. "Mrs. Quin looked after him, then he radioed in. He's still there. The doctor's taken a look at him."

"Bruised balls. He's lucky they were only playing with him. OK, let's have a word with him." The inspector made as if to precede Hyde from the room. He was taller, thicker set, in uniform. Hyde's voice and manner seemed to dismiss all of it. Hyde wagged a finger at him, bringing two points of colour to the policeman's cheekbones. "And *you* called the Branch?"

"Sugden is their man."

"You were instructed to call me – not the Branch, or the DS, or the Home Secretary or Her Majesty the Queen Mum – me. Next time, call me direct. Reverse the charges if you have to, but call me. Quin is mine." Hyde made Quin sound like part of his diet. The inspector seethed in silence, allowing Hyde to leave the room in front of him, just in case the Australian saw his eyes and their clear message. "It's a bloody cock-up!" Hyde called back over his shoulder. "Too much bloody *time* has gone by!"

Hyde banged open the front door and went down the path, the same urgency possessing his slight frame. His denims and pale windcheater over a check shirt did nothing to endear or recommend him to the inspector, who nevertheless dutifully followed him across the road and up the path to Mrs. Quin's door. Hyde rang the bell repeatedly.

"The woman's had a shock, you know," the inspector cautioned.

Hyde turned on him. "She bloody well knew we wanted her

husband and her daughter. Did she ring? No bloody fear. She almost got her precious daughter nobbled by the KGB –"

Mrs. Quin opened the door on its safety-chain. Her hair had freed itself from the restraint of lacquer, and two separate locks fell across her left eye. She brushed at them. Hyde showed her no identification, but she studied the uniformed inspector behind him, then released the chain on the door. Hyde walked past her into the cool, dim hall. Mrs. Quin caught up with him. Her mouth was trembling. The inspector closed the door softly.

"Where is he, Mrs. Quin?"

"In the lounge, lying down." Her tone was apologetic. She offered Sugden's comfort as a token of her good intentions. "Poor man."

"I'll talk to him. Then I'll want to have a word with you, Mrs. Quin."

"Mr. Hyde –" the inspector began.

Hyde turned to look at him. "Too late for that."

Hyde went into the lounge and closed the door behind him. Sugden was lying on a chaise longue, his face still pale, his tie askew, jacket draped over the arm of an easy chair. His face arranged itself into a memory of pain, through which guilt thrust itself like the outbreak of some malady.

"Mr. Hyde –" he began.

"Don't apologise, sonny, it's too late for that." Hyde pulled an armchair in front of the chaise.

"But I am sorry, Mr. Hyde. I just didn't know they were there."

"You cocked it up, son. You didn't expect the girl, you didn't expect the heavy mob – what did you expect?"

Sugden tried to sit up, to make himself feel at less of a disadvantage. Hyde waved him back, and he slumped on the chaise, his hand gently seeking his genitals. He winced. Hyde grinned mirthlessly.

"I don't know."

Hyde took out a notebook and passed it to Sugden. "These are your descriptions of the two men?" Sugden nodded. "They don't ring any bells with me. They could have been brought in for this. The KGB has trouble travelling. They didn't get the girl?" Sugden shook his head vehemently. "Neither did we. When did she arrive?"

"Mrs. Quin didn't say."

"She will. You know what it means, mm?"

"They haven't got Quin?"

"Too true they haven't. Shit, we should have guessed they didn't have him!" Hyde slapped his hands on his thighs. "Why the bloody hell did we assume they did? Too many post-Imperial hang-ups in Whitehall, sport – that's the bloody answer. Quin's gone, we're so incompetent and wet, they must have him. It's what we British deserve." He saw Sugden staring at him, and grinned. The expression seemed to open his face, smooth its hard edges. It surprised Sugden as much as his words had done. "My hobby-horse. I race it around the track once in a while. Trouble is, I fell for it this time."

"You don't think much of us, do you?"

"Too right. Not a lot. You're all a lot more sophisticated than us Aussies, but it doesn't get you anywhere, especially with the KGB. Bloody Russians wouldn't last five minutes in Brisbane." Hyde stood up. "OK, sport, interrogation's over for now. I'm going to have a word with Mum. She has a lot of explaining to do."

He found Mrs. Quin and the inspector sitting in the breakfast kitchen, sipping tea from dark blue and gold cups.

"Mr. Hyde –"

"Very cosy," Hyde sneered, and the inspector coloured. Mrs. Quin looked guilty, and defiant, and Hyde was brought to admire the manner in which she stared into his eyes. She was afraid, but more for her daughter than herself.

"Tea, Mr. Hyde?" she offered.

Hyde felt pressed, even ridiculed, by the scene; by the pine furniture, the split-level cooker, the pale green kitchen units. Only he expressed urgency, was in haste.

"No time." He stood over the woman. The inspector played with his gloves on the table. "Will you check with the bulletin on Miss Quin, Inspector?" The policeman seemed reluctant to leave, but only momentarily. Hyde remained standing after he had left. "You weren't going to tell us, were you, Mrs. Quin?" She shook her head, still holding his gaze. "Why not, for Christ's sake?"

"Tricia asked me not to."

"We'd have looked after her."

"She said you couldn't. I don't know why not. She didn't explain." Her hand shook slightly as she lifted the cup to her lips. They quivered, smudging pink lipstick onto the gold rim of the cup.

"She knows where her father is, doesn't she?" Mrs. Quin nodded, minimising the betrayal. There was nothing in her eyes but concern. She cared for her daughter, it was evident, but regarding her husband she was composed, perhaps indifferent. "Did she say where?"

"No."

"Has she gone back to him now?"

"I don't know." The exchanges had achieved a more satisfying momentum which disguised the emptiness behind the answers. The woman knew little, perhaps nothing.

"Where has she gone?"

"She wasn't supposed to be going out." Mrs. Quin waved her hands limply. They were as inanimate as gloves at the ends of her plump arms. "I don't know where she is." The voice cracked, the mouth quivered.

"She came to put your mind at rest, is that it?" Mrs. Quin nodded. "And she said nothing about your husband – her father?" Mrs. Quin shook her head. Her face was averted from Hyde's eyes now. But she was concealing nothing, except perhaps inadequacies that belonged to her past. She was keeping only herself from him, not information. "She gave no clue?"

"No, Mr. Hyde. Except that he's well, and is in hiding. I think she hoped I would be pleased at the news. I tried to show I was." The confession stuck into their conversation like a fracture through skin.

"She's been with him?"

"Yes."

"Since his disappearance? She disappeared *with* him?"

"Yes, Mr. Hyde. And then she came back here. She's always bounced between us, ever since the divorce." Mrs. Quin tried to smile. "She is a trier, even if she's a failure." Assumed cynicism was an attempt to shut him out, he realised.

"Where might she be now, Mrs. Quin?"

"I have no idea whatsoever. Back with him, I suppose. But I have no idea where that might be."

Hyde breathed out noisily. He looked at the ceiling, his hands on his hips. The texture of their conversation had become thickened, clogged with personalities. There might be clues there as to the girl's character, behaviour, whereabouts, but such enquiries possessed no volition, no urgency. Hyde was impatient for action. The girl was vital now, and he and the KGB both understood that. She'd been shown to them like some tempting prize which would be awarded to the swiftest, the strongest, the most ruthless.

"Thank you, Mrs. Quin. I may be back. I just have to use your telephone –"

Mrs. Quin dismissed him with a slight motion of one hand. The other rubbed at the edge of the pine table, erasing memories. Hyde went out into the hall.

Aubrey had to know. The Deputy Director of SIS had been with the Foreign Secretary when the call from Birmingham had finally been routed through to Queen Anne's Gate. Hyde had left a message, but now Aubrey had to know the extent of their problem, and their hope – or lack of it.

He was dialling the number when the front door opened, and the inspector re-appeared. Hyde ignored him and went on dialling.

"Whoever you're reporting to," the policeman remarked with evident, hostile sarcasm, "you'd better mention the car that just drove past. I'd say it contained the two men who worked Sugden over."

"What –?" The telephone was already ringing in Aubrey's office, even as Hyde examined a residual sense that he had once more blundered into, and through, a private world. Mrs. Quin hadn't deserved the way he had treated her. Yet, had he altered his manner, even though he might not have bludgeoned there would have been little gentleness, almost no sensitivity. He took the receiver from his cheek. "You've got them?"

The inspector shook his head. "Foot down and away, as soon as they saw my lads. The registration number won't be of any use either, I shouldn't wonder –"

"Shit!"

"I beg your pardon!" Aubrey's secretary demanded frostily at the other end of the line.

Ethan Clark, of the US Naval Intelligence Command (ASW/Ocean Surveillance), had been made to feel, throughout the week since he had joined the "Chessboard Counter" team in the Admiralty, very much like an executive of some parent company visiting a recently taken over small firm. He was present in both his USN and NATO capacities, but these men of the Royal Navy – of, more precisely, the Office of Naval Intelligence (Submarine Warfare) – exuded a silent, undemonstrative resentment of him. Which, he well knew, made any doubts and hesitations he had concerning the mission of HMS *Proteus* seem no more to them than American carping. The commodore and his team in this long, low room in the basement of the Old Admiralty Building in Whitehall were dry-land sailors playing a war-game, and thoroughly and blithely enjoying themselves.

Clark supposed it had its basis in a buried sense of inferiority. For years, the contracting Royal Navy had belied its great history, and now, quite suddenly, they had developed "Leopard" and installed it in a nuclear-powered fleet submarine and were engaged in mapping the "Chessboard" sonar grid in the Barents Sea. Their high summer had returned. NATO needed them as never before, and the USN wanted greedily to get its hands, and its development budgets, on the British anti-sonar system.

Nevertheless, he told himself again as he sipped coffee from a plastic cup and observed the British officers waiting for the ritual serving of afternoon tea, "Chessboard" should have waited. NATO and the Navy Department had required of the Royal Navy that they install the only operationally-functioning "Leopard" unit in a submarine, rush their sea trials, then send it racing north to the Arctic Circle. The British had responded like a child doing everything at top speed to show its willingness and its virtue. Even before they had paid Plessey the bill for what they had, and before they had ordered any more "Leopard" units. With that kind of haste, things often got smashed, plates got dropped. Boats had been lost before. It would be a great pity if "Leopard" was lost; a tragedy if anyone else found it.

The long room, with its officers seated at computer terminals in front of their screens, its maps, wires, cables, fold-away tables, was dominated by a huge edge-lit perspex screen which stood upright in the middle of the room. The perspex secreted a multitude of optic fibres which registered the input of the computers that controlled the screen. The lighting at the edges of the perspex allowed the team to use chinagraph for temporary handwork additions to the computer-fed information. At that moment, much as it had done for the last week, the screen displayed a projection of the fjordal north coast of Norway, from North Cape to Murmansk. The coast was green and brown, the sea a deepening shade of blue as it stretched northward. A fine grid of red lights, no larger than dots, was shown off the coast, as if some current in the screen were knitting, or marking a school register. Other lights moved slowly or remained stationary, units of the Red Banner Northern Fleet, ships and submarines. One or two NATO units. The Commodore's team seemed to scuttle round the base of the perspex screen as if propitiating some idol.

The room was now quiet, orderly. An hour before, *Proteus* had come up to periscope depth for one of her periodic, random but pre-determined transmissions. The transmisstion, using RABFITS (Random Bit Frequency Intelligence Transmission System) and via a satellite link, had contained every detail of the mapping work of the submarine since the previous message. This had been fed into the map-board's computers, updating the network of red spots which marked the "Chessboard" sonar grid.

Clark could not but admire, and envy, the "Leopard" equipment. He had been aboard *Proteus* as an observer during some of the sea trials, and he had also been aloft in the RAF Nimrod as the specially equipped plane tried to find the submarine. The Nimrod had been unable to locate, fix or identify the submarine, not even once, either in the Channel, the North Sea, or the north Atlantic. Not even in conjunction with the US-laid sonar carpet in the north Atlantic. No sonar trace, little and poor infra-red, nothing. It worked. Even pitted against surveillance satellites, it worked.

Perhaps, he told himself, his concern arose – like smoke, unformed but dense and obscuring – solely from the fact that when he had lunched with Kenneth Aubrey at his club at the beginning of the week, he'd learned that the man who had developed "Leopard" at

Plessey had gone missing, presumed lost to the Russians. "Leopard" was both useless and unique, if that were so.

"It's going splendidly, Captain Clark, don't you agree?" Clark snapped awake from his unseeing contemplation of the dregs in the plastic cup. Lt. Commander Copeland, the anti-submarine warfare expert on the "Chessboard Counter" team, was standing in front of him, six inches shorter and exhibiting a grin that shaded into smug mockery. The lights of the perspex map were bright behind him. "You don't seem to be too pleased," Copeland suggested with a more pronounced mockery. He waved an arm towards the glowing map. "Everyone else is feeling on top of the world."

"You're really pleased, aren't you, Copeland."

"Your people will be delighted, too, and NATO will be over the moon."

"Sure." Clark shifted his weight on the edge of the desk where he had perched.

"Really, Clark!" Copeland's exasperation was genuine. "Neither the United States nor ourselves have been able to send a ballistic missile boat, or any other sort of submarine for that matter, east of North Cape for two months, ever since the *Ohio* was first traced, shadowed, and escorted from the area." Copeland turned to study the huge map-board. "We're helpless up there until we know how big, how good, and of what kind 'Chessboard' is." He turned back to Clark. "Your Chief of Naval Operations saw that quite clearly, so did Supreme Allied Command, Atlantic. *Proteus* has the most distinguished sponsors." Again, the silent, mocking smile.

"What if we lose her? Then we've lost 'Leopard' for good."

"Lose? Lost? What do you mean? Oh, Quin, I suppose." Copeland shrugged. "If Quin is over on the other side, then 'Leopard' will be useless in a matter of months, don't you agree?" Clark nodded. "Well, then? We must neutralise 'Chessboard' now, while we have the means."

Clark looked up at the board again. A trelliswork of red dots. The carpet of active and passive sonar buoys, and other detection devices, began inside Norwegian territorial waters, less than four miles out, and extended, at present indication, perhaps fifty or more miles north into the Barents Sea. It could be a hundred miles. *Proteus* was moving between North Cape and Kirkenes like a tractor ploughing a field. The work could take weeks. Copeland was right, of course. The northern flank of NATO was imperilled by "Chessboard". The Norwegian coast was prohibited to British or American submarines, the coast of the Soviet Union rendered inaccessible to short-range attack; the Barents Sea finally transformed into a Russian lake.

"Sure. Yes, you're right, Copeland. You're right."

Copeland smiled with evident relief, and looked very young and enthusiastic. "I'm so glad you agree," he said without irony.

"Just one thing," Clark added maliciously, pointing towards the map. "Don't you think there's just too *little* Soviet naval activity up there?" The board's computer was feeding into the map display whatever the North Cape monitoring stations, the surveillance satellites, and air patrols were supplying via SACLANT's huge central computers. "Two 'Kotlin' class destroyers, one 'Sverdlov' class cruiser, two 'Romeo' submarines and one 'Quebec'. They're usually crawling all over the Barents Sea. Where are they?"

"Our information is Murmansk, old man. Perhaps they're taking things easy now they've got 'Chessboard' to do their work for them." The suggestion was in earnest.

"Maybe."

Copeland was about to reply when the door opened and a Wren wheeling a tea-trolley appeared. "Ah, tea," he exclaimed. "Excellent!"

Richard Lloyd, captain of HMS *Proteus*, was suddenly aware, on entering the cramped computer room aft of the main control room and its almost cathedral-like spaciousness, of the claustrophobia that most people imagined was the inevitable lot of the submariner. He did not experience it, merely understood what it must be like for people who never inhabited submarines; or who had served in them forty years before. The computer room was more cramped than ever, since at least half of its available space was now taken up by the "Leopard" equipment.

"Don," he said, nodding. His senior electronic counter-measures officer, Lt. Commander Hayter, had been nominated as trials officer for "Leopard" because of his existing special navigation and electronic warfare qualifications. Lt. Commander Hayter's comprehension of the equipment had relieved Lloyd from all but superficial knowledge of the effects and benefits of "Leopard". Hayter was seated in front of a computer screen, watching the pinpricks of light that emerged from its bland grey surface blankness, then slowly faded. As Lloyd watched, one pinprick brightened while two others were fading. They formed a vague triangle on the screen. Then one was gone while another emerged, glowing brighter. To the left of the screen was another, an acoustical holograph screen which displayed the buoys seemingly in three dimensions, giving them an identity, a shape. Neither Lloyd nor Hayter regarded the holograph display. There was something more obsessive about the silent, brief lights.

"Sir," Hayter acknowledged. "Welcome to the broom cupboard."

"They had submarines smaller than this room in the last war,"

Lloyd observed dismissively. He glanced from the screen to the holograph display, then at the accompanying print-out.

"Weird," Hayter said, as if to himself. "Really weird."

"What?"

"This feeling I have that we don't exist. Not for any practical purpose, that is. Sonar buoys, temperature transducers, hydrophones –" He pointed at the holograph as the shape of a sonar buoy formed in light. "Mile after mile of them, but we just don't exist as far as they're concerned. Like limbo. Yet I ought to feel excited, sailing east." He turned to Lloyd, grinning. "Oughtn't I, skipper?"

"Something's missing from your diet, obviously."

"Much activity?"

"Very little."

"You sound puzzled?"

"Maybe. No, not really. I suppose they're relying on this stuff –" He indicated the two screens. "They must be relying on 'Chessboard'. One or two surface vessels, a few submarines. Something moving well to the north, one of their 'Echo-II' missile boats off to take up station on the eastern seaboard of the States, no doubt. It wouldn't be much interested in us, even if it could spot us. Apart from those few items, nothing in the shop today."

"I can't say I'm sorry."

"You're not running down your pride and joy, are you?" Lloyd nodded in the direction of the main cabinet of the "Leopard" equipment.

"No. But utter reliance on an incredibly complicated system of matching sonar signals, and emission dampers and the like – it's not the same as having a big stick in your hands or a suit of armour on, is it? 'Chessboard' is the most advanced, extensive and thorough submarine detection system ever laid down. We both know that. Like tip-toeing through a minefield, or burgling the Chubb factory –" He smiled. "And here we are, same old faces and same old submarine, but now we're invisible. Mm, I think I feel excited, after all."

"How much of it have we mapped – just a guess? I won't hold you to it."

"My computers don't make rough guesses – just mistakes." Hayter typed on the computer keyboard below the screen. He waited for a few seconds before a message appeared, superimposed on the pinpricks of light, making them more ghostly and unreal than before. "See. Twelve days and a few hours more."

"That means this sonar carpet must extend at least a hundred and fifty to two hundred miles out into the Barents Sea." Lloyd's tone was one of surprise, even though he had half-expected "Chessboard" to be as impressive as he had now learned.

603

"It could be bigger. There's an assumed twelve to fourteen percent error built-in at the moment. That'll get less the more we chart." Hayter turned to Lloyd again. "I'm willing to bet that there's a similar sonar-buoy carpet being laid to stretch south and west from Novaya Zemlya. The Russians, I think, are going to close the Barents completely as far as we're concerned."

Lloyd rubbed his chin. "Could be. Not our worry, old son. Even if we end up doing trips round the Isle of Wight because there's nowhere else we can go. OK, twelve days it is. Don't let the men find out, will you?"

The intercom crackled about Lloyd's head.

"Captain to control room, please." It was the voice of his first lieutenant. Calm and urgent. Lloyd recognised the puzzled imperative in the guarded tone.

"So you think," he said, "that if ever 'Leopard' conked out or was developed by the other side, we'd see the end of NATO's submarine strike power?"

"I wouldn't be at all surprised," Hayter replied without looking at him, and not entirely without seriousness.

"Captain to control room."

Lloyd shook his head at Hayter's back, and left the computer room, passing through the open watertight door into the control room of the *Proteus*. He straightened, stretching the unaccustomed stoop from his shoulders. Artificial light was almost his natural visual medium. The control room – *his* control room – was light, almost airy after the cupboard-under-the-stairs in which Hayter spent much of his time.

Lloyd's first lieutenant, Lt. Commander John Thurston, was standing near the main bank of communications monitors, leaning over one of the operators, a headphone pressed to one ear. He looked up with something akin to relief when he saw Lloyd at his side.

"What is it, John?"

"Listen to this, sir." Thurston pressed the headphone set into Lloyd's hand. The communications petty officer twisted in his chair, watching for his captain's reactions, A brief splash of code, repeated again and again. Lloyd looked questioningly at Thurston.

"One of ours – distress code isn't it?"

"Not one of ours. The computer identified it as a quite low-priority Soviet submarine code, one we broke three months ago. Distress, yes."

"When did you start picking it up?"

"About fifteen minutes ago, sir," the petty officer replied. "It's being transmitted regularly. I fed it into the signals computer, and it came out as a distress call."

"Any ident?"

"Yes, sir," Thurston replied, acclaiming the drama he perceived in the situation by a lengthening of his saturnine face.

"Well?"

"It's a 'Delta'-class ballistic missile submarine. The full works."

"You're sure?"

"Yes, sir."

"What the hell is the matter with her, using a low-grade code? What's her trouble?"

"Massive explosion in the computer room. Most of their ECM systems have gone, and there's gas in the air-purification system. They've shut down almost everything. They're sitting on the bottom."

Lloyd screwed his face up. "They're very descriptive."

"Panic, sir. Sheer bloody panic."

"Any idea where?"

"Yes, sir."

Again, Lloyd looked puzzled. "How did we get a fix?"

"We didn't. They told us where to find them. They're screaming for help. They could begin transmitting in clear any minute now, they're so scared."

"Where are they?"

Thurston, who had evidently prepared the little scene between himself and Lloyd in minute detail, nodded towards the chart table against the aft bulkhead of the control room. Lloyd followed him across.

"Here," Thurston said. "Right here." His finger tapped the chart. He had drawn a livid red cross, dramatic and oversized, on its surface. "Tanafjord."

"What? You must have got it wrong —"

Thurston shook his head. "No, sir. They're wrong to be there, and to be using a broken code to transmit their position. But they're inside Tanafjord. They're in Norwegian waters in a ballistic missile submarine, and they're scared they're going to die!"

"My God," Lloyd breathed. He was silent for a moment, and then he said, "We'll break radio silence for this one. Run up a transmission buoy. We'd better tell the Admiralty – and the sooner the better!"

Admiral of the Red Banner Northern Fleet Dolohov paced the gantry, his footsteps and those of his aides ringing on the metal catwalk. Continually, he stared down into the well of the fleet's central Operations Room beneath Red Banner headquarters in Murmansk. Below him, the huge map table glowed with light. He had just arrived, and the warm lighting of the room, and the pin-point glows in fairy-light colours from the computer-projected map seemed to celebrate and

605

promise. It was a welcome. He paused, placed his hands on the rail of the catwalk, and turned to his aide. He might have been on the bridge of a ship.

"Sergei – status report, if you please."

The younger man smirked with pleasure, real and anticipated. "Sir. The British submarine is in this area –" He clicked his fingers, and a chart was passed to him. It was attached to a clipboard, and over the exposed fold was fixed a transparent plastic sheet. There were faint, reddish smudges on the plastic, one or two firmer images. "The infra-red satellite picked these up, sir. Very, very faint, but there. It must be the *Proteus*." He pointed out one of the brighter images. "This is the cruiser in the area. A clear image, even with the cloud cover. The faint smudges –"

"It works, then? This anti-detection equipment, it really works as well as we have been led to believe?"

The aide considered the possible implications of the question, then said, "The weather satellites promise the break-up of the cloud cover. It will improve our chances of getting a good infra-red trace."

"I didn't mean that, boy!" Dolohov snapped, his pale eyes fierce and alert. "I *understand* that it is hit-and-miss, even with our new geostationary satellite and every unit of the fleet looking for this submarine. I am *delighted* that it works, that the prize will be worth the game."

"I see, sir –" the aide said shamefacedly. "When the submarine moves closer to the Norwegian shelf, into shallower water, we may have a better trace. Not much better, but enough, sir," he added with solemn candour. Dolohov laughed.

"It is a *gamble*, Sergei, a great game!" he explained. "As long as the prize is sufficient, then one accepts the chances of losing the game." He transferred his intent gaze to the map table below. The plotters moved about it busily, yet expectant, knowing that they were as yet simply filling in time, rehearsing.

"Oh, the prize is a good one, sir. It works, only too well. We have had nothing from our sonar carpet, nothing, even though the British have been in the area for two days now."

Dolohov turned back to him, his eyes vacant, his gaze inward. The smile still hovered around his mouth. He nodded, like a very old, semi-senile man. Sergei would not have been surprised had an unregarded spittle appeared on his lips.

Then Dolohov was alert again. "Yes. Satisfactory." He looked down into the well of the huge room, at the map table. The different coloured lights. Cruisers, destroyers, the carrier *Kiev*, submarines, the special salvage vessel *Dioklas* and the submarine rescue ship *Karpaty*, all ready to sail from Pechenga and Poliarnyi, as soon as the word was given. Hours – mere hours – away from the Tanafjord and the distress signal. The thought spoiled his almost complete satisfaction. He turned to Sergei again. "If only we knew the precise moment when the *Proteus* picked up the distress call and her computers broke the code – eh, Sergei? Yes, I know when they transmitted to London, I know that. I would have liked to have known when they picked it up, though. The precise moment. What they thought, and felt, and said. Everything." He laughed. Then he spoke more softly, looking down on the map table once more. "Come, let us begin. Set course for Tanafjord, and sail into our elaborate trap. Come."

TWO:

Contact

The commodore was still closeted with a hastily assembled committee of staff officers, arguing for an investigation by *Proteus* of the distress signals from Tanafjord. In the "Chessboard Counter" room, Clark found himself a lone voice, disregarded and even derided, as he argued against any diversion of the submarine from her mission.

He could not have explained to himself the reasons for his reluctance. The cleanly-shaven, smartly-uniformed young men who surrounded him beneath the huge perspex map-board enraged him with their confidence, their boyish enthusiasm. It was their cheerful dismissal of any doubts on his part that had stung him to contempt and counter argument. He repeated himself again and again, and the baffled, kindly smiles and the frowns of dismissal greeted every statement he made. He knew it was the commodore he needed to convince, yet he once more reiterated the central thrust of his argument in a snapping, irritated tone. He justified his own stubbornness by reminding himself that he was the Navy Department's – America's – only and solely responsible representative.

"Look, you guys –" Lips twisted in derision or disdain. "You already know her type, you might even verify which boat she is. Only ten percent of their ballistic subs are out of Murmansk at any one time. If she's screaming for help, then there may be nothing left to investigate by the time *Proteus* reaches the fjord." He could see the disbelief opening on their faces, livid as blushes. It angered him. "Hell, why would she be in a fjord in shallow water with limited sea room if she was going to play rough? Use a nuke depth bomb on her – it might work out cheaper than sending in 'Leopard'."

"Really, Clark, you're quite the hysterical virgin this morning," Copeland remarked waspishly.

Clark was about to answer when the door opened. He recognised Giles Pyott as soon as he entered the room. Pyott was in army uniform, and the commodore, who entered behind Pyott, was also in uniform. A glassy, urbane, impenetrable officialdom had suddenly settled on the room, the kind of formality that the Pentagon or the Navy Department could never muster or imitate. Thank God, Clark added to his observation. Pyott, grey hair immaculate, part of his pressed, polished uniform, looked pleased and elated. Clark was again reminded of children and their haste to please or to upstage.

"Shall I tell them, Commodore, or will you?"

"Carry on, Colonel Pyott," the commodore demurred, a smile leaking into his face and warping the firm line of his lips.

"Very well." The two men had approached the group beneath the map. Pyott studied it theatrically, glanced at Clark and nodded to him, then spoke to the group of Royal Navy officers. His manner implied that Clark had left the room. "Gentlemen, it has been decided that *Proteus* be ordered to proceed, with utmost caution and all practicable speed, to the area of Tanafjord." A sigh of communal satisfaction, one or two murmurs of congratulation and pleasure; the empty compliments of sycophancy, they appeared to Clark. He was a man in a grey suit with a pocketful of unfamiliar and rather despised credit cards. Not a gentleman, they might have said of him. Worry twisted in his stomach again, and he knew he could not keep silent. "Yes, gentlemen," Pyott – who was from some faceless and important MoD/NATO committee called StratAn – continued, "the first Sea Lord and the Chiefs of Staff assign the gravest import to this intrusion into NATO territorial waters –" Again, the murmur of support. "The government of Norway, when informed, officially requested our assistance. *Proteus* will be instructed by yourselves to carry out a monitoring and surveillance action at the mouth of the Tanafjord." He smiled, at once the headmaster with his junior staff. "I leave the form of the task orders and encoding to you."

"We'll get on with it, Colonel," Pearson, the communications officer, offered, wiping his spectacles. Without them for the moment, he seemed more to suit the dark uniform and the gold cuffs. Returning them to his aquiline nose, he became clerkish again.

"Are you certain of all this, Pyott?"

It was as if Clark had cheered for an opposing team. Pyott turned a lordly glance to the American, who was as tall as he was and more muscular but who did not pose his figure in quite the same seignorial manner.

"I beg your pardon, Captain Clark?" The mention of rank was a reminder of good manners and the proper forms of address. "I don't quite catch the drift of your question." Outsider, the tone cried. Buccaneer. Pyott took in, with a raking glance that went from face to feet and back again, the civilian clothes, the muscular chest and shoulders, the tanned, square features. Clark was evidently a pretender engaged in some dubious masquerade.

"I asked if you were certain? Are their Lordships certain? Are the Chiefs of Staff certain? Is NATO certain?"

"The proper channels, the protocol, all have been observed, Captain Clark," Pyott replied frostily.

"What in hell do they think the Russians are up to in Tanafjord, with a ballistic missile boat?" Clark almost bellowed, goaded by the imperturbable arrogance and self-assurance of the army officer. Like a line of automatons, the operators in front of their screens and terminals snapped to attention in their seats. The group beneath the map seemed to move slightly away from him, as if he had begun to exude a powerful, offensive body odour. "You think they're invading Norway, starting the next war?"

"I do not know," Pyott said icily, his face chalk white. "I do not make assumptions, especially ones that might be dismissive and therefore comforting. That is why *Proteus* must do our investigating for us. Your own Navy Department has been consulted, and has agreed. Brussels is in agreement. *You* are out of step, Clark."

"*Proteus* has 'Leopard' on board. Doesn't that worry you?"

"That fact weighed heavily with everyone at the meeting, and with everyone consulted. It is to our inestimable advantage that *Proteus* is the submarine on station, so to speak –"

"Bullshit! Crap and bullshit, Pyott! You people – you want to play games, you want to *really* try out your shiny new toy. You want to walk close to the cliff. Now I understand –"

"Perhaps we could continue this conversation outside," Pyott remarked through pressed, almost unmoving lips. His face was now livid with anger. The naval officers, including the commodore, had moved away from them, sensitive of the embarrassment they knew Pyott must be experiencing.

"I wouldn't want the time of day from you, Pyott. You're an asshole. A pompous asshole, at that."

Clark brushed past Pyott, who avoided him like an experienced matador. Clark had allowed the situation to escape him. He was angry with himself, angry that it was Pyott he resented more than Pyott's suggestion concerning *Proteus*. As he prepared to slam the door of the "Chessboard Counter" room behind him, he could hear Pyott already reiterating StratAn and NATO's orders concerning *Proteus* to the assembled company. His voice was laconic, controlled, smooth as glass.

It enraged Clark, and he knew he had to talk to Kenneth Aubrey. Something in him, deep as a lust as yet unfocussed, knew that he had to stop this *adventure* with "Leopard" and *Proteus*.

He slammed the door loudly behind him.

Aubrey studied Hyde's face. It was evident the man's challenge with regard to the fact of Quin's disappearance was intended to irritate,

610

and intended also to disguise the Australian's own new doubts.

Aubrey smoothed the last, vestigial wings of grey hair above his ears, and leaned back in his chair. Shelley, his aide, watched Hyde from the tall windows of the office in Queen Anne's Gate.

"You're not sure now, are you?" Hyde repeated.

"Don't jump to conclusions," Aubrey remarked severely. "What you saw was the girl. We know that she is unreliable, something of a failure, a drop-out. Is there any real reason to suppose that she knows where her father is? She wasn't just trying to keep her mother calm?"

"The KGB chased her to the bus stop. Those two blokes were like rape on legs."

"Perhaps Quin won't play ball with them in Moscow without having his daughter with him?" Hyde shook his head vehemently. "Your own source at the Russian embassy gave you quite clear – almost categorical – indications that a snatch squad had stayed overnight, and left again on Aeroflot the day after Quin disappeared. You believed your man then. Why not now?"

"Wait till I see him again. I was led up the garden, taken walkabout if you like. I admit that. But don't *you* go on believing there's nothing we can do. Quin dropped out of sight for his own reasons – he could have had a breakdown, for all we know – and the girl's gone back to him now, or she's on her way back. I *know* the Russians haven't got him yet, but they will have as soon as they get their hands on the girl." Hyde was patting Aubrey's desk, gently and continuously, to underline his words. He looked at Shelley when he had finished speaking, then asked, "You think they've got him?"

Shelley shrugged. Hyde, understanding his influence with Aubrey, wanted him on his side. Shelley plucked at his bottom lip with thumb and forefinger, then he said, "I don't know. There's some room for doubt, I think. It seems too good to be true, after the last few weeks –"

"I will make the assumption – because it is preferable to do so – that the appearance of the girl means that the KGB have not taken Quin to Moscow, Patrick," Aubrey said slowly. Hyde exhaled noisily and relaxed in his leather chair. "I still believe that Quin has gone east –" He held up a liver-spotted, wrinkled hand. "Until there is stronger evidence to the contrary. Therefore –" He smiled slightly, "your first task is to contact your helpful but possibly misleading friend at the Soviet embassy."

Hyde nodded. "Today's pick-up day. He's not likely to stay away after yesterday, whether he's straight or crooked."

"I suppose we might have to consider him planted, or at least re-turned?" Aubrey mused.

"The abortion was a long time ago. Perhaps he's back in favour with his bosses," Hyde suggested.

"Ask him. Then find the girl. Simply that. What about her college, for instance?"

"CID talked to some of her friends last night. Nothing."

"You will go back over the ground. And you will be careful, Patrick, if you are going to begin crossing the path of the gentlemen who were in Sutton Coldfield yesterday. You'd better draw a gun." He waited for Hyde's reaction. The Australian nodded after a lengthy pause. "Good. Don't draw attention to yourself. If your theory is correct, then they might soon begin following you as their best lead to Miss Quin."

"Anything else?"

Aubrey shook his head. "Not for the moment." Then he added, "This girl –" He tapped a file near his right hand. "Unreliable. Unconventional. Is that your impression?"

"Her Mum loves her. If she isn't just a nut-case, then she might be more difficult to find."

"I think we'd better find her, don't you? She's in danger, whether Quin is in the country or not. They want her, apparently."

"How much time is there?"

"I don't know. We have 'Leopard'. It can be manufactured in large numbers, eventually, without Quin. From that point of view, there is a great deal of time. But we are no longer alone. The girl's time, at least, would seem to be running out."

"I'll get on with it, then," Hyde said, getting up. The leather of the chair squeaked as his frame released it. "Pardon," he said with a grin. "You can talk about me when I'm gone. I'll let you know this afternoon what Comrade Vassiliev has to say." He smiled, and left the room.

Aubrey's returned smile vanished as soon as the door closed behind Hyde.

"What do you think, Peter?" he asked.

Shelley rounded Aubrey's desk to face him. Aubrey indicated the Chesterfield, and Shelley sat down, hitching his trousers to preserve their creases as he crossed his long legs. Shelley lit a cigarette, which Aubrey watched with a dry, eager concentration. He had obeyed his physician for more than a year in the matter of smoking. The occasion when the service lift at his flat had not been working for a week, and he had had to walk up three flights of stairs every evening – shortness of breath, body's fragility indicated to him like a sound blow on his shoulder. No more cigarettes, not even the occasional cigar.

"I'm afraid Patrick's right, however irritating that may be." Shelley smiled.

"We have been misled – and principally by his source of information at the Soviet embassy."

"Agreed, sir. But we all accepted Vassiliev after Hyde cleared up the matter of the abortion and the girl in the case was paid off. Vassiliev had walked into our honey-trap, we let Hyde go with him as chief contact. If Vassiliev is forged, then he's an expert job. Of course, he may just have been trying to please Hyde. The swagman's not often fooled. That's why he's so angry now. I can't say that I blame him."

Shelley exhaled, and Aubrey ostentatiously wafted the smoke away from himself by waving his hand. Shelley appeared not to notice the inconvenience to his superior.

"This incident in Sutton wasn't an elaborate charade, for our benefit?"

"I doubt that, sir."

"So do I. The problem is, this 'Leopard' business is so damned important. It really is one of those pieces of military technology the Russians haven't even begun to develop. Or so they tell me at MoD and Plessey. It would put us perhaps years ahead in the anti-submarine warfare game. I really would like to believe that they haven't got Quin. It just seems too good to be true."

"Agreed. But there is such a thing as not looking a gift horse, et cetera, sir –"

"Perhaps. Another thing that worries me – what price the safety of Comrade Vassiliev? If he fed us duff gen at their orders, then they know Hyde will be coming back now with more questions." Aubrey shook his head. "I don't like that idea."

"Bruce the Lifeguard can take care of himself."

"I hope so. Peter, get some Branch people to check around Bracknell again – the avenues we haven't explored or didn't give much credence to. Holiday rentings, cottages, that syndrome. People usually run for the hills not the city if they want to hide. I don't know why that should be."

"Very well, sir."

"And this file –" He tapped Tricia Quin's folder. "Get all the material out of it for Hyde. A list of people and leads. I have the distinct feeling that very little time is available to us, don't you?" Aubrey looked up at Shelley as the young man got to his feet.

"No comment, sir."

"Well?" Lloyd, slumped in his chair, seemed to embrace the small, neat captain's cabin of the *Proteus* as he opened his hands for an answer. Then, as if drawn by some new and sudden gravity, his hands rested on the chart on his desk. Thurston had brought the chart with him from the control room. He and Carr, the navigator, had marked the course of the *Proteus* as far as Tanafjord. Thurston sat opposite Lloyd, Carr standing stockily and red-haired behind the first lieutenant, Hayter leaning against the closed door of the cabin. The air conditioning hummed like a sustained note of expectancy. "Well, John? You two? Any comment?"

Thurston cleared his throat, and in the sidelong movements of his eyes Lloyd saw that these three senior officers had conferred. They were some kind of delegation.

"No," Thurston said at last, "not now we know its position."

"Why not?" Lloyd looked up. "You two are in on this, I presume?"

Carr said, abruptly, "It makes the whole thing messy, sir. I can't understand what MoD thinks it's playing at, ordering us to the mouth of Tanafjord. It smells, sir."

"It does, sir," Hayter confirmed. "A 'Delta'-class sub in a fjord. Why? What good can it do there? It could loose any missile it wanted to from its berth in Murmansk as well as from that fjord. Why was it there in the first place? Shallow water, no sea room. Sir, we both know it's a very unlikely beginning to the next war." Hayter smiled, ingratiating his nerves with his captain.

Lloyd rubbed his face, drawing his features into a rubber mask, then releasing the flesh. It assumed a kind of challenged look. Thurston observed Lloyd's expression with a mild dismay.

"You're suggesting we disobey a highest priority instruction from the Admiralty?"

"No. Let's request confirmation. We could do that –"

"We could." Lloyd looked down at the chart again. "How many hours' sailing, rigged for silent running, taking *all* precautions?"

"A little over thirty-seven," Carr replied. Hayter looked at him in reproach, as if he had changed allegiance or betrayed a secret. "But I think we should request confirmation, skipper."

"Thirty-seven." Lloyd tapped the chart with his forefinger. "Our course alteration is minimal for the first six hours or more. We're to continue our work on 'Chessboard'. For six hours, at least, nothing's changed." He smiled. "In that time, we'll send one signal to MoD, asking for confirmation, and for a fuller definition of our mission status. Does that satisfy you trio of doubting Thomases?"

"I still don't like it," Thurston volunteered.

"You were as excited as hell when we picked up the signal from our Russian friend, John. What's changed?"

"I used to like watching boxing – it never tempted me to take it up as a hobby."

"Don, I want a full tape test and computer check run on 'Leopard' as soon as we alter course."

"You'll get it."

"Are we still getting signals from the Russian boat?"

Thurston nodded. "Sandy's been monitoring them since we got a reply from MoD."

Carr said, "She's broadcasting in clear now. Being careful, of course. But the power's down on the transmission. I think they're using a low-power emergency back-up set, and they're altering the frequency with pre-programmed cards. It's a bloody mess."

"Any more details?"

"No. Code-names, damage indications in some Cyrillic alphabet sequence. Can't decipher that. The letters and numerals could refer to anything."

"What other traffic?"

"Murmansk's been pouring out coded stuff –" Carr shook his head at the light in Lloyd's eyes. "We don't have it broken. Code of the day only, frequency-agile transmissions, the lot. But there's a lot of it. They're panicking all right."

"OK. Sandy, time to fetch Lt. Commander Hackett." Lloyd nodded at the cabin door, and Hayter moved out of his way as the navigator went in search of the engineering officer. When Hayter closed the door again, Lloyd said, "You don't really think MoD are wrong on this one, do you?"

Thurston pulled a melancholy face. "They aren't infallible. I think they like the idea of the game, that's all."

"We're risking this ship, and ourselves, and 'Leopard' on this wild goose chase," Hayter added with a quiet vehemence. "That doesn't seem to have struck their lordships. I think the intelligence yield from this 'monitoring action' won't be worth a candle, anyway."

"I agree with Don."

Lloyd was silent for a time, his hands over his face, the fingers slightly parted as if he were peeping child-like at them or at the chart on his desk. Then he rubbed his eyes, and shrugged himself upright in his chair.

"I'll ask for confirmation from MoD. Meanwhile, we'll rig for silent running – and I *mean* silent from now on." A grin, unexpected and gleaming, cracked the seriousness of his expression. "It isn't for real, you two. We won't be responsible for starting the next war. Nothing is going to happen to us. It's *Norwegian*, the Tanafjord. Cheer up. Just look on it as another sea trial."

Thurston was about to reply, but fell silent as they heard a knock on the cabin door. Lloyd indicated to Hayter that he should open it. The grin was still on Lloyd's face when Carr ushered Hackett into the cabin.

The wind seemed to follow Hyde into the entrance of Lancaster Gate underground station, hurrying pages of a copy of the *New Evening Standard* ahead of him, with chocolate bar wrappers. He hunched against the wind's dusty, grubby touch at his neck. He went through the barrier, and descended past the framed advertisements to the Central Line eastbound platform. A woman's legs, gigantic and advertising tights, invited him from the opposite wall. Lunchtime had swelled the numbers of passengers. Hyde lounged against the wall and observed Vassiliev further down the platform. Even here the wind moved the dust in little eddies or thin, gauzy scarves along the platform. Vassiliev wore a dark overcoat across his shoulders, over a pinstriped suit. He looked English enough despite the high Slavic cheekbones and narrow nose, yet he appeared nervous beneath the clothes and the residential veneer England had given him. Hyde was still unsure of him; whether his crime was one of omission or commission.

The train slid into the arched bunker of the platform. Hyde watched Vassiliev board it, then waited until he was the last still person on the platform, then he got into another carriage as the doors shunted together behind him. He stood watching the retreating platform as the train pulled out. Nothing. There was nothing to be learned from nothing.

He and Vassiliev left the train at Tottenham Court Road, Hyde staying twenty yards behind the Russian, closing with him as they transferred to the Northern Line and then getting into the same carriage of the first northbound train. He studied the carriage and its passengers until they pulled into Euston, then took a seat next to Vassiliev. The Russian embassy official, in making a pronounced movement away from him, squeezing himself against the window, suggested either dislike or nerves. Hyde placed his hand on Vassiliev's arm in a gesture which he knew the man – superficially confident of his heterosexuality but with sexual doubts nagging at him like toothache spoiling good looks and appetite – loathed. The arm jumped beneath his touch.

"Now, sport, you and me have some talking to do, don't we?"

Vassiliev looked out of the window. Mornington Crescent. The name slowed and materialised, like oil adopting a mould. "I – I knew you would question me," he offered.

"Too bloody right, mate! You sold me the wrong stuff, Dmitri – told me Quin was over on your side. Taken away by the bogeymen."

Vassiliev turned at the pressure on his arm and stared at Hyde. Sitting, he was slightly taller than the Australian. His face was thinly imperious for a moment – Hyde, seeing the expression, was strangely chilled – then it subsided quickly into nervousness and apology.

"I am not a member of the KGB, you know that. I am not privy to the things they do. What I told you was a fact. I also heard rumours of who their objective was, I passed these on to you. I can do no more."

Vassiliev glanced away from Hyde, into the lightless tunnel.

"I don't pay you for crap, Dmitri. I don't blackmail you for rubbish. Now, what do you know?"

Vassiliev shook his arm impatiently, and Hyde released it, thrusting his hand into his pocket and slumping more theatrically in his seat, feet on the seat opposite, to the irritation – silent and frightened – of an elderly man.

"I – it is difficult to ask, I can only listen. In the staff restaurant, there is talk of what happened yesterday. I – I am, well, yes, I am almost certain that they are still looking for this Quin –" Hyde listened, every sense aware of the man in the seat next to him. Body temperature coming through the thin sleeve of his windcheater, thigh trembling slightly against Hyde's own, the faint body odour noticeable above the dusty, greasy smells of the carriage and the mothball scent from the old man. The voice, grabbing at sincerity, the breathing somehow artificially fast. The words broken by intelligence rather than emotion; thought-out hesitations. "I have not seen the two men – they were low-grade sleepers, I understand, without accreditation to the embassy –" The officialese flowing now like a broad, uninterrupted stream, but not quite because of habit. Learned, Hyde thought; but he remained silent. Quiver gone from Vassiliev's body. He believed he had acted sufficiently well. "However, there was talk about them, and about the girl – and I'm sure now it is their way of getting to the father –"

"You picked up a lot yesterday and this morning," Hyde remarked laconically.

"I am *trying*," Vassiliev pleaded, turning his face to Hyde. Mirror of helpfulness, of urgent sincerity. The eyes expressionless. "I knew what you would want. I was as surprised – shocked – as you must have been. What else can I tell you?"

Camden Town, slowing down outside the window. Hyde swiftly surveyed the passengers on the platform, those who entered their carriage. He could not believe that they would have let Vassiliev out by himself, without a minder, with such an important role to play. But he could not find his companion. What role was he playing, anyway? Why admit that Quin was still at large?

"I want more detail, more information, Dmitri. That's what you can tell me, and I want it tonight."

"I can't do that!"

Hyde stared into the Russian's face. "Yes, you can. Oh yes, you can. After all, you're my creature, I've got the arm on you. It's not the other way round, is it?" Hyde watched the face. Mouth sloping downwards in admission, cheekbones colouring slightly with a sense of shame, brow perspiring in tiny silver beads – ignore, the temperature in the carriage and the overcoat explained it – the eyes quizzical, blank, then striving for the hunted look Hyde expected. Finding, losing, catching and holding it. Vassiliev was playing with him, at the orders of the London Resident or one of his senior staff. Again, he felt momentarily chilled.

"Yes, I will try," Vassiliev said mournfully.

Highgate. A moment of silence, no one getting on or off the train. Stillness. Then the doors breathing noisily as they closed again. The lights elongating, the words smudged, the darkness of the tunnel, the walls pressing close to the window. Hyde shook off the awareness of himself, the pressing vulnerability. He was being led by the nose, being set up to do their work for them.

"You're sure?" he asked, staring at his feet.

"Of what?" Vassiliev asked, momentarily confused.

"He hasn't been taken over?"

"The man Quin?"

"Yes."

"No. No, they do not have him." East Finchley. Vassiliev began to look uncomfortable, as if he had entered unexplored territory. "They think the girl will lead them to him. I am sure that is what they think." He looked pleadingly at Hyde.

"You were sure they had him three weeks ago."

"I am sure now. Then, I was wrong. There was no *talk*, then. This time, there is gossip." He was looking over Hyde's shoulder as the lighted platform slipped away behind them, then he glanced at his watch. "I must get off – I am sure. Mr. Hyde, I am sure this time!"

"OK, OK."

"Gossip, that is all I bring. You know that. You knew that when you – *found* me."

"Saved your bloody neck, sport – don't forget that."

Vassiliev blushed with dislike. "I do not forget." The train was slowing into Finchley Central. Vassiliev was eager to get up. "Where do we meet tonight, what time?"

Hyde hesitated, then: "The club. Eleven."

"Good – good. Yes, yes, I will be there –" The train had stopped, the doors had slid back. Hyde, shifting his weight, moved his feet and Vassiliev brushed past him, hopping out of the carriage. He immediately lit a cigarette, but Hyde, looking quickly up and down the carriage and the platform, did not consider it a signal. Then Vassiliev hurried into a patch of windy sunlight towards the southbound platform.

Hyde watched him disappear, then settled back in his seat, putting his feet up again. The old man still smelt of mothballs. He closed his eyes. The smell of relatives from England coming out to Wollongong, bringing clothes they hadn't worn for a long time, uncertain of the Australian climate. Big bosoms – Auntie Vi, Auntie Maud, Auntie Ethel – covered by cardigans that smelt of mothballs. He with bare feet and shorts, like an urchin or a school-boy marooned in Australia. Mothballs. And the voices through his bedroom wall, conveying the magic of England, the rain and snow, the television.

Woodside Park. He bolted upright, eyes wide. His spine was cold. The childhood memories, evoked like a cloud of masking ink, faltered and retreated. He was being played. They would be one step behind, or alongside, every moment of the journey.

Aubrey had not enjoyed Ethan Clark's narrative. It was too easy, and perhaps correct, to regard it as tales out of school. He had lunched with the American, as a protégé of various senior CIA officers of long acquaintance, when Clark had first arrived in London the previous week. At numerous points, he had wanted to protest, request Clark to desist, even to leave. Gradually, however, he had become intrigued, then alarmed.

Clark described the "Delta"-class submarine in the Tanafjord, then his voice faltered and he fell silent. Aubrey, his face gilded by weak sunshine from his office window, sat with his eyes closed and in silence. On an inward screen, he could see Quin's face, and knew that his mind had forged some obscure yet inescapable link between the man and his invention. A link of mutual danger?

"What did Giles Pyott say?" he asked at last.

"He didn't listen –"

"What did he *say*?"

Clark choked back his anger. "He said," he began slowly, "that it was none of my damn business and that everyone, including my own Navy Department, agreed with sending *Proteus* in."

"I can hear him saying it, though not quite in those words," Aubrey remarked acidly. "Everyone agrees, through to Brussels?"

"Yes."

Aubrey sat bolt upright. He appeared unconvinced, even unconcerned, then he said, "You've told me about the Russian submarine. Tell me about 'Chessboard'. That *is* important?"

"It is. 'Chessboard' could close the Barents to us unless we map it."

"And 'Leopard'. That is of inestimable value, you assess?"

"While it's unique and while the Russians don't have it, yes."

"I agree. But, what if, as we discussed the other day, Quin, its developer, is with the Russians?"

"Then the sooner we map 'Chessboard', and use 'Leopard' for

whatever else we want to know before the Russians develop it themselves, the better."

"Then I must tell you, Ethan, that it appears that Quin may not be with the Russians after all. How would that affect your thinking?"

Clark was silent with surprise at first, then with concentration. Clouds played shadow-games across Aubrey's carpet, across the man's head. Then he said. "It makes all the difference."

"You do believe this distress signal is genuine?"

"It – seems to be."

"I see. We know the Russians know about 'Leopard'. They must have had someone inside Plessey at some time. They were interested in acquiring Quin's services on a permanent basis. They still are. Perhaps they would like 'Leopard' instead?"

"You can't be serious?"

"I am merely speculating. Would you say that *Proteus* might be endangered by her new orders?"

"It's closer to the Soviet Union."

"Is that why you are so disturbed by all of this?" Aubrey snapped. "Or is it because you don't like Giles Pyott or the people at the Admiralty?" Aubrey's face was fierce, even contemptuous.

"Look, I came to you in good faith –"

"You came to me to moan about your lot!"

"The hell with you, Mr. Aubrey!" Clark made as if to rise.

"Sit down, Ethan!" Aubrey had turned to his desk again. His hands were calm and unmoving as they rested on its edge. "Sit down."

"Sorry –"

"Not at all. You came to me because you do feel *Proteus* might be endangered by her new mission. I did not like her sailing orders in the first place. I wanted her kept at sea undergoing trials, or in safe harbour, until the matter of Quin was resolved. I wished 'Leopard' removed from *Proteus* until such time as Quin was either recovered or known to be lost to us. I was ignored – overruled. It really isn't my field, you know." Aubrey smiled. "The trouble is, MoD is occasionally – and this is one of those occasions – filled with a few too many clots for my liking or reassurance. Giles Pyott is a clever, experienced soldier. He is also a Cavalier rather than a Roundhead. I have always seen myself in the New Model Army rather than Prince Rupert's cavalry. It always seemed much more sensibly organised, and much safer –" Clark, invited to return Aubrey's dazzling, self-deprecatory smile, did so. Apparently, he had been tested, and passed. He bore Aubrey no resentment. "My problem is that I find it hard to distinguish between death rays emitting purple light and anti-sonar systems and sonar carpets laid in the Barents Sea. However, we must turn our hand to the work that presents itself." He studied Clark. "We have one extant 'Leopard' system, in one British submarine, engaged upon a task of singular importance. We have one missing scientist. Until the one stray lamb is returned to the fold, I suggest we don't let the other one loose. Don't you?"

"What can you do?"

"I wonder. I would like to stop *Proteus* – I would like to find Quin. Ethan, I trust your judgment. I trust those intuitions that a man like Pyott would not countenance. You have worked in intelligence, he has not. We are all chronically suspicious, perhaps paranoid. However, you and I and the others like us are all we have. Perhaps all 'Leopard' has. Hm. Go back to the Admiralty, apologise to Giles Pyott – yes, please – and then keep your eyes and ears open. Ring me tonight –"

The intercom's buzz interrupted him. His secretary announced the arrival of some sandwiches and the imminence of a pot of coffee. Aubrey ordered her in. Before the door opened, Clark said swiftly, "What can you do?"

"I don't know, Ethan. Unfortunately, I shall have to do something, or else I shall begin sleeping badly at night. Ah, coffee and sandwiches – splendid!"

"We've got her."

"When?" Dolohov asked as Sergei closed the door of the Ops. Room behind him.

"Only minutes ago. The satellite's had terrible trouble with the cloud cover –"

"Show me. Admiral –" Dolohov nodded to the Ops. Room commander, then almost snatched the folded chart overlain with its sheet of developed infra-red film. Poor, pale smudges, like smeared rust or very old blood.

"The pattern's changed, as you can see." Sergei was leaning over Dolohov's shoulder. His finger tapped the sheet over the chart. "This was her three hours ago – same intermittent smudges, her mapping course, enough for us to tell she was still following the same search pattern. Then here we think there was another trace –" The smear was almost invisible. Dolohov did not move the chart closer to his face. "Then nothing for two hours, then this – then another fifty-four minutes before we got this." It was like the last ember of a dying fire. It was out of the random yet sequential pattern, and it had moved south and east of the other smears.

"You're certain?" Dolohov was looking at the rear admiral.

"We've used sonar in that area, and we got nothing. If it is a submarine, then it is the British ship."

"Excellent! It works, how well it works, mm?"

621

"Too well."

"Come, Admiral – no sour grapes. You have a computer prediction on speed and course?"

"We have one, based on the last three traces. We need at least two more to be at all accurate."

"Show me, man, show me!"

One of the rear admiral's aides scuttled into the control room. Dolohov leaned over the rail of the gantry. As he watched, the rear admiral joined him. Then a curving line appeared on the projection below, from a position far out in the Barents Sea, making south and east towards the Tanafjord. It rendezvoused with the imaginary Soviet submarine trapped in the fjord.

"In excess of thirty hours," the rear admiral murmured, "and no longer than thirty-six. That's the best we can do without another infra-red fix from the satellite. For the moment, she's disappeared again. Possibly cloud again."

"Good man," Dolohov said incongruously. He gripped the rear admiral's shoulder. The man was considerably younger than himself, bespectacled and clerkish. A computer expert, perhaps, an academic; scientist rather than sailor. Nevertheless, at that moment Dolohov felt an unaccustomed affinity with the man. "Good man." He turned to Sergei. "Call Leningrad. Whether they're at the Grechko Academy or the Frunze Naval School, I want Ardenyev and his team informed at once. They will depart for Murmansk immediately."

"Yes, sir."

Dolohov turned back to the rear admiral. "Keep up the good work. If the Red Banner Special Underwater Operations Unit does its job as well as you are doing yours, then nothing can go wrong!" He laughed throatily. "Excellent, excellent! I don't care what success the KGB has now in finding the man Quin – we will be able to present Moscow with Quin's toy. The man himself will have no value, and *we* shall enjoy the sunshine. Excellent, excellent!" His continued laughter caused one of the map table operators to look up.

The strip club was a short walk from Oxford Street, hunched in a narrow side street on the edge of Soho, as if aspiring to membership of that district, or recently expelled from it. Hyde had used it as a meeting place with Vassiliev because clubs of its type attracted the diplomats and officials of East European embassies, especially early on in their tours of duty, and even if Vassiliev had been under surveillance by his own people, such visits would have been regarded as misdemeanours rather than as suspicious or dangerous.

Hyde glanced at the membership ledger, having bribed the door-man. One or two new members that evening, but it told him nothing.

622

They might be Vassiliev's friends, or football fans or businessmen staying overnight in London. Vassiliev's friends would have ensured their membership sometime earlier, if this was an entrapment exercise. Hyde did not consider it was. They wanted him running, moving with apparent freedom. He went down the steps beneath a dim green under-sea light, the mingled odour of sweat, smoke and tawdriness coming up to meet him. The door opened to admit him – he had heard the buzzer sound from the doorman's cubicle as he began his descent.

Disco music thumped against his ears, flat, enervating, unmemorable. Strobe lights played over the heads of the audience. The tiny stage was empty, but there was a narrow bed lit by a silvery, ghostly light at the back of it. Hyde remained by the door. The large man with cropped hair wearing an out-of-style dinner jacket loomed at his shoulder. Hyde suspected he knew his profession and did not confuse him with the Vice Squad or CID. At worst, he would assume him to be Security rather than Intelligence. It did not matter. Rather, it legitimized the club, provided a governmental patron.

There were only a small number of people waiting for the next bout on the stage. Vassiliev – he saw as his eyes accustomed themselves to the peculiar, winking gloom – was in a corner, near the stage, mournfully staring into a glass. There seemed no one who had noticed, or become concerned at, his entrance. He threaded his way between the tables with their grubby cloths and expensive drinks towards Vassiliev. The Russian seemed relieved to see him. If there were other emotions, conflicting ones, then the strobe flicker hid them. Hyde settled in a chair which faced the door, and immediately a waiter appeared at his side. No girls on the floor of the club, no hostesses. A curious puritanism pervaded the place. Untouchable, flaunting, indescribably crude, silicon-enhanced, the women came and went on the stage, separate and inviolable.

Near them, the pianist resumed his seat. The drummer rolled softly, as if communicating with his drums. A bass player leaned tiredly over the neck and shoulders of his instrument. All of them appeared to be awaiting some summons to Ronnie's in Frith Street, two blocks away. Most of the girls stripped to records, anyway. Hyde ordered a beer. It came in a half-pint glass, and there was no change from his pound note. He clicked his tongue and winked at the waiter.

Hyde sipped at his drink. The trio drew attention to the stage with a peremptory call to attention that echoed Oscar Peterson, then slipped into the strait-jacket of "I'm forever blowing bubbles" as a bath was wheeled on.

"Oh, Christ – bath night again," Hyde murmured. "Ivy the Terrible." The subdued chatter of the audience tailed off into a silence that was weary rather than expectant. "Well, Dmitri?"

Vassiliev leaned towards him, eyes flicking over Hyde's shoulder towards the stage, as the pianist imitated a fanfare. Hyde could never decide whether Vassiliev's interest in the girls was genuinely naive and crude, or merely a badge of his manhood, designed to be noticed by those in his company. The KGB regarded homosexuals in only one light – as victims; malleable, male prostitutes. If Vassiliev had any hidden proclivities towards men, then he was wise to hide them.

"You were wrong," he said.

It was the one statement Hyde had not expected to hear. It generated a mass of complex doubts, questions and fears in an instant. The woman on stage was young, breasts extended to unnatural size by injection and implant, face expressionless beneath the make-up. See-through negligée, towel and loofah, bar of soap. The trio vamped the only expectancy in the now darkened room. Hyde watched the stage, picking his way towards the appropriate degree of innocent surprise. "Dmitri, what do you mean I was wrong?"

"They *have* got Quin. They have him, but they want the girl." Vassiliev's sweat gave off the pungency of the body rub he used. It clashed with his after shave, with the girl's scent, the omnipresent cigarette smoke.

"I'm not wrong," Hyde began, but Vassiliev was already nodding eagerly. Hyde felt cold.

"Yes. Look, I risked everything this afternoon. There was no more gossip. I looked in the travel ledger. I went back and checked on the people who came in. They left with a third man – the next day. They flew to Paris in a light aircraft. I have the address, the booking. Three passengers –" He reached into his pocket, but Hyde grabbed his hand – it quivered in his grip, which was slippery against Vassiliev's skin, informing Hyde that his nerves were taking him over. The girl was testing the supposed temperature of the water in the bath, letting the negligée fall open almost to the crutch. None of the audience was watching their corner of the room.

"Three? Three? What proof's that? I don't believe you, Dmitri. I don't think you know," Hyde hissed at the Russian, still gripping the man's hand near his chest. The girl had stepped – with something less than elegance – over the side of the bath. Her negligée was drooping from one shoulder, tented by one enormous breast.

"You must believe me, you must!"

"I don't, Dmitri. Now, what bloody game are you playing?" The girl was obviously going to bath with tassels on her nipples. She slid down into the supposed water. Then Vassiliev's eyes began moving, darting round the room. Hyde forced himself not to turn round. It did not mean there was someone in the room, only that there were others, either nearby or simply giving orders. Hyde gripped his thigh

624

with his free hand, forcing the calm of angered puzzlement into his frame and face and voice. "What bloody game are you playing, mate?" The girl had divested herself of the negligée, but not the tassels. She was stroking herself with the loofah.

"No game, Mr. Hyde, no game!" Vassiliev was leaning towards him like a lover in the hot darkness, but he could not keep his eyes on Hyde's face. Escape, help, answers. He repeated the formula they had taught him. "Three men left in that plane for Paris. Yes, they want the girl, but they have Quin in Moscow – I'm certain of it."

"You don't know who the third man was. It couldn't have been Quin –" Hyde found himself engaged in an attempt to justify the suspicions he had voiced to Aubrey; as if he believed Vassiliev. The girl was on the point of engaging in intercourse with the loofah. Soon she would be dropping the soap. "No," he said, "you're lying, Dmitri. Why should they want you to lie?"

"They? What do you mean?" Too innocent.

"You weren't lying or mistaken at lunchtime. You *knew*, then. Now, you're working for them. Did they ask you how much you told me? Did they?" Hyde's face was close to Vassiliev. He could smell the man's last meal on his breath, and the brandy after dinner. Too much brandy – no, they wouldn't have allowed him more than one or two. "They knew about you all the time, but they didn't let on. Not until they realised you must have told me more than was good for me." He was shaking Vassiliev's hand, in anger and in community. The girl had dropped the soap, which did not slide across the stage. Her enormous breasts were hung over the side of the bath as she attempted to retrieve it. The trio was playing palm court music. The prissy, virginal sweetness of it assailed Hyde. "You were doing all right until you told me you thought they didn't have Quin. And you *know* it!"

"I – must go," Vassiliev said. Now the soap was back in the bath, but lost again. The girl was looking for it on her hands and knees. Snake-charmer music, and she rose to her feet, backside to the audience, buttocks proffered, swaying.

"You're going nowhere. Where are they?"

"Not here, not here!"

"You're coming in, Dmitri."

"No!"

"You have to. We'll take care of you. I can't behave as if I believe you. You're the one in danger now." Vassiliev had thought of it, but had ignored it. He shook his head, as if the idea was only a pain that would move, dissipate. The girl had the loofah again, standing up now, in profile to the room. The loofah was being energetically applied. "Come on," Hyde added.

"No! I can't leave with you, I can't!"

"Why not?"

"I can't!" He was pleading now. They were outside. If he emerged with Hyde, they would know Hyde had not swallowed the tale. The almost religious silence of the room was broken by hoarse cries of encouragement, underscored with what seemed like a communal giggle. The girl's body acknowledged the response to her performance.

"You can!" The gun, the gun – he'd left it at his flat, held it in his hand, almost amused, for a moment before stuffing it under a pile of shirts in a drawer. The gun –

"No, no, no –" Vassiliev was shaking his head vehemently.

"It's your only chance. Come on, the back way." Hyde got up, stood over the Russian, willing him to his feet. Vassiliev rose, and they shuffled through the tables towards the toilets. The door into the concrete, ill-lit corridor sighed shut behind them.

Vassiliev immediately turned to him. "No," he said.

"They concocted this story, right?" Vassiliev nodded, nerveless, directionless now. "Why?"

"I don't know. They told me they had known, that they had fed you the information about Quin through me, deliberately. Then yesterday happened, and while they were deciding what to do about me, we talked. I – I told them everything." A sense of shame, as sharp as a physical pain, crossed his features.

"It's all right, it's all right – was there anyone in the club?" Vassiliev shook his head. There was applause on the other side of the door. "Come on."

Hyde half-pushed Vassiliev towards the emergency exit beyond the toilet. He heaved at the bar, remembered letting in friends by similar doors in Wollongong cinemas just before the start of the main feature, then the door swung open. The windy night cried in the lightless alley. He paused momentarily, and looked at Vassiliev. Then he nodded.

They went through the door almost together, but even so the man with the gun must have been able to distinguish between them. Vassiliev cried out – Hyde hardly heard the brief plopping sound of the silenced gun before the Russian's murmured cry – then he slumped against Hyde, dragging at his clothes, smearing the front of the Australian's shirt with something dark and sticky. Then he fell back, for a moment his face green from the exit sign's light, then all of him was simply a barely distinguishable bundle of clothes on the other side of the alley. Hyde waited for the noise of footsteps above the wind's dry call, or the sound of another stone-into-water plop that would be the last sound he would ever hear.

THREE:

Intruder

The gilded French clock on the marble mantelpiece chimed twelve, a bright, pinging, musical sound. Aubrey paused in his narrative, and he and Sir Richard Cunningham, Director of the Secret Intelligence Service, listened to the sound, watching the blue-numeralled face of the clock. When the chimes had ended, Aubrey stared into his brandy balloon, aware of how out of place his employment of technological and military jargon seemed here, in the study of Cunningham's flat in Eaton Place. Books and paintings – Cunningham had a small Braque and two Picasso etchings in that room – heavy furniture, civilization. A conspiracy to belie the reality of detection systems, anti-sonar, satellites and distress signals in broken codes. Aubrey, for a moment, wished devoutly for a double agent, for the intimacies of a debriefing or an interrogation, for the clear boundary between SIS and MoD. Clark had pushed him across that border.

Cunningham had hardly spoken throughout Aubrey's recital of events, suspicions, fears. He had assiduously filled and refilled Aubrey's glass and his own, refrained from smoking a cigar, and listened, his half-closed eyes regarding his slippered feet crossed at the ankles. The book he had been reading when Lady Cunningham had shown in Aubrey lay on the occasional table at the side of his chair, the Bach to which he had been listening lay still on the turntable. His half-glasses rested on the end of his patrician nose, and his lips were set in a firm, expressionless line. Aubrey felt extremely reluctant to continue.

Then Cunningham spoke. "What, exactly, do you wish to do, Kenneth?"

"Go in there – assess the situation for myself."

"I see. You know how MoD regards us. You know how the navy regards itself. It's tricky. You've no just cause or impediment, after all."

"I realise that, Richard. However, there is a mutuality of interest that might be stressed. Quin –"

"Ah, yes. MoD will tell us that he is our proper concern, one of Her Majesty's submarines more properly their sphere of authority. They will not take kindly to you suggesting they should reverse their decision. Nor will Brussels, nor will Washington. Sure you're not simply acting the old warhorse smelling the battle afar off?"

Aubrey smiled. "I don't think so."

"Mm. Neither do I. Devilish tricky, though. I can quite well see the importance of this anti-sonar system, and of Quin, and of keeping both out of Soviet hands. But we are not the experts, we are not the military. *They* don't seem to believe there is any risk – this man Clark, the American. Trust him?"

"And his judgment."

"Mm. Knew you did." Cunningham spread his hands, wafting them in the air. "I just don't know –"

The telephone rang. Cunningham got up heavily and crossed to it. He listened, then gestured with the receiver towards Aubrey. His face was impassive.

"Yes?" It was Hyde. Aubrey listened to the voice at the other end of the line, his eyes watching Cunningham, deep in thought in his chair.

". . . they obviously didn't want the hassle of killing me – just Vassiliev out of the way. They must have known I would try to take him in if I got suspicious . . ."

"You're all right?" Cunningham looked up at the note of concern in Aubrey's voice.

"Unhurt. I said. What now?"

"You'll see Mrs. Quin tomorrow, and take a trip to the girl's college. Someone must be able at least to *guess* where she might be."

"If you say so –"

"Tomorrow, you will go armed. Good night to you, Hyde."

As Aubrey put down the receiver, Cunningham stared at him. "What is it?"

"Hyde. His contact at the Soviet embassy has just been expertly dispatched in a dark alley. Before he was eliminated, Hyde had discovered that the news of Quin's removal had been deliberately leaked, and yesterday's events in Sutton Coldfield were being hidden behind a smokescreen. The KGB were onto the poor blighter, tried to turn him, realized they'd failed, and shot him."

"Our man is all right?" Aubrey nodded. "They don't have Quin, then. I think we can be certain of it now. There is still no connection between these events and the submarine."

"I agree. Could we not argue a suspension of operations employing 'Leopard' until the Quin matter is settled?"

"We might. The first thing, I suppose, is to get you inside this 'Chessboard' matter. Once there, it will be up to you. *You* will have to find the means to persuade the minister to ask Cabinet to postpone this little adventure. I suggest you go in there for a briefing on this

'Leopard' business, sniff around, and weigh the worth of what's being done. If you can convince me, then we'll go to the minister together, and he can take it from there, if he agrees with us. Satisfied?''

Aubrey pursed his lips, studied his glass, and then nodded. ''Yes, Richard. That will do nicely. I'll make an appointment for tomorrow – perhaps with Giles Pyott.'' His face darkened. ''I'm too old for hunches and intuitions. But Clark is a clear-sighted, intelligent individual with a genuine talent for our work. I'm sorry to say it, but I think there is cause for concern, and I'm *sure* we should recall *Proteus* until we find Quin.''

''Make certain, Kenneth. There are a great many sensitive corns in MoD. Tread softly.''

''Mrs. Quin, you must have some idea where we can find him! I just don't believe you can't help me.''

''Have you ever been divorced, or separated?''

''No.''

''Your parents?''

''No.''

''What happened to some of the girls you've known? Where are they now – just one of them? Tell me what she did yesterday.''

''It isn't the same.''

''It is, Mr. Hyde, believe me, it is. Tricia's coming here was one of her impulses. She spent her childhood making believe that my husband and I were happy when we weren't, and the last three years trying to put Humpty-Dumpty back together again.'' Mrs. Quin sighed, and her brow knitted into deep, thread-like lines. ''I'm sorry for her – sorry for myself, too.''

Hyde sat back in the chair she had shown him to when she allowed him into the lounge. Occasional traffic outside, her day off from the antique shop, the Panda car conspicuous across the street. Trees still leafless, bending and moving with the wind. The gin-hour for lonely or bored suburban housewives. She had given him tea, and seemed not to resent his behaviour of two days before.

''Jesus, Mrs. Quin, it's a bloody mess,'' he sighed, rubbing his hands through his hair. ''Your daughter is in real danger – all right, you already know that, I'm sorry to remind you. Nevertheless, she is. So's your husband. She's with him, or still on her way back to him. The – the other people interested in your husband know that. They know we're interested –''

''Why did he have to involve her?'' the woman suddenly cried, her voice and expression full of blame, even contempt. ''No, that's not fair, I suppose. She involved herself. I know Tricia.''

"I don't. Tell me about her."

"You mean you don't already know?" There was an arch, mocking sharp little smile, a glimpse of white teeth. Today, the hair was firmly lacquered in place, the clothes well chosen, the whole being groomed. "About the pop groups, the drugs –"

"Drugs? Soft or hard?"

"The sort you can smoke, I believe."

"Soft. Occasionally?" Mrs. Quin nodded. "OK – rock bands?"

"Not in your files?" The easy contempt. She had forgotten her alliance with the uniformed inspector, her concern for young Sugden. Neighbours had talked, asked questions, and the police were an embarrassment, a minor disgrace.

"Yes – some references. Some time ago, though?"

"She – the phrase is *slept around*, I believe. With them."

"A groupie?"

"I believe so. Am I entirely stupid to blame her college, and the kind of people they allow into them, and to teach in them, these days?" She evidently had little interest in his opinion.

"Probably," he said. "It's your privilege."

"It ended, anyway. But she never seemed to settle afterwards."

"Who – which group?"

"I don't know any of their names. I believe they were famous."

"Did she travel with them?" A nod. "When?"

"Two summers ago – all over the country, even to the Continent. And an open air festival."

"But you don't know their names?"

"Had I ever known them, I would have forced myself to forget."

"I see. Would her friends in college know anything about all this?"

"I'm sure they would have been regaled with the sordid details."

"Perhaps I should talk to them."

"It's past now – can't you leave it?" A naked plea, the face smoothed young by concern, softened.

Hyde stood up. "If there's anything, anything at all, ring this number. A man called Aubrey. You'd like him." Hyde grinned humourlessly.

"Why didn't he come himself?" The tone knife-like.

"He's too important. Thank you, Mrs. Quin." As they reached the door, he turned to her and added, "I'll get to her first, if I can. You just pray a little, mm?"

"Stop engines!"

The Soviet submarine was back. It had crossed their bows an hour earlier, fifty fathoms above them, moving away to starboard. Lloyd had ordered silent running, the engines moving them very slowly ahead, because the computer identification had been of a "Victor-II"-class attack submarine, nuclear-powered and a hunter-killer. A shark had met another shark. Then the "Victor-II" had altered course again, possibly picking up faint traces of heat emission or prop noise. And she had begun looking, knowing that there was something to find.

The *Proteus* hummed with tension in the new, complete silence. Electronics murmured, those aft sonars required to keep track of the Soviet submarine, someone cleared his throat softly; Lloyd even heard the movement of Carr's sleeve across his chart as he updated the Contact Evaluation Plot at his chart table. The whisper of the hydroplane control wheels as the planesmen worked continuously to keep *Proteus* level and unmoving, constantly balancing the submarine's own attempts to alter position and depth. A juggling act. Easier on the bottom, but they weren't on the bottom.

Lloyd crossed to Thurston, who was standing behind the sonar operator monitoring the approach of the "Victor-II" and whose screen displayed the snail-trail of light that revealed the position of the Russian vessel. Below the screen, red numerals supplied the read-out of bearing and distance. The "Victor-II" was closing.

Submarines had been lost before, Lloyd reminded himself involuntarily. There was no fear and no courage, either. Vessels encountering each other in the dark, crowded sea. Collision or avoidance, attack or retreat. The "Victor-II" was following their scent – heat, prop-wash, hull-noise, the tiny skin-flakings of their passage which "Leopard" could not completely neutralise. The twin hulls that enclosed them like plasterboard walls waited to transmit any sound they might make. Closer. Bearing unaltered. Speed a cautious, stalking twelve-point-seven knots. Time to contact, five minutes.

Lloyd mouthed silently at Thurston, who nodded. The first lieutenant framed his lips to reply in the slightest whisper, after swallowing hard.

"If she doesn't find us, she might just miss us."

"By much?"

"Not much." Lloyd's hand was on the back of the sonar operator's chair. Some transmitted electricity from his captain made the rating twitch. Lloyd moved his hand. He turned to watch the two planesmen, juggling the control wheels like nervous car drivers. As if not in control of the vehicle. *Proteus* remained still, lying in the dark, waiting. Other trails of light – not new, but suddenly noticed and rendered significant by heightened nerves – on the sonar screen. Four other submarines, two destroyers and what might be the carrier *Kiev*, flagship of the Northern Fleet. She was too distant for a positive identification, and Lloyd had tended to discount her appearance in the Barents Sea. This early in the season, she was normally still refitting in Murmansk. And the "Victor-II", brighter than all of them. Contact time, four minutes fifty. Lloyd felt, despite himself, that his hands were beginning to perspire. He opened them. The control room seemed hotter. Illusion.

Bearing unaltered. Speed constant. Cancel. New red numerals appeared on the read-out panel. Speed ten knots. The "Victor-II" was slowing. Contact time three minutes twenty-eight, seven, six –

The sonar operator turned to Lloyd, his face puzzled. The "Victor-II" was stopping, contact time and distance read-outs slowing down, then settling. Stopped. Contact time two minutes thirty-one frozen. The small, cramped space of the control room hot. Thurston was perspiring, a line of beads along his hairline. Lloyd felt the sweat dampening his shirt, running chilly down his sides. The sonar operator's hair cream, a sickly smell of which he was suddenly aware. Stomach light, disturbed.

Stopped. A third of a mile away. Six hundred yards. Close enough for temperature sensors. The movement of bare forearms in the corner of his vision as the planesmen juggled the *Proteus* to stillness. The auto-suggested hum of electronics, like the buzzing of an insect seemed very difficult to discount. The "Victor II" digesting the scraps of information, her captain waiting for an answer from his computer. *Is there an enemy submarine close to us?*

Red numerals flicking off. A bare, dark green panel beneath the sonar screen with its bright blip of light. Then new numbers. Speed four knots, five, six. Contact time two minutes nineteen, eighteen, seventeen, fifteen, twelve, seven – one minute fifty-nine. Bearing unchanged.

Lloyd waited. He could hardly bear to see the "Victor-II" as it moved through the darkness towards them. One minute twenty. Speed ten knots. Distance two hundred yards, a little more, the little more eaten up even as he thought it. Eleven knots, bearing unchanged; as if they knew where *Proteus* was.

Then they listened. Two steam turbines driven by a pressurized water reactor. They would hear them, even though they were little more than idling at eleven knots.

Faces turned to the ceiling. Always that, Lloyd observed. A familiarity of orientation brought with them onto the submarine. It could be below, alongside, anywhere.

The churn of the screws. A slight, almost inaudible thrumming in their own hull. Faces tightening, the sense of fragility obvious. Louder. The illusion of a rising tremor in the eggshell of the hull. Hands sensing it where they rested damply against any part of the hull, any instrument – the planesmen juggling more violently now as

632

the distressed water outside the hull assaulted the *Proteus* – feet feeling it, muscle-spasms in the calves. Louder.

Loudest, going on for what seemed like minutes, the planesmen failing to stop the submarine's bow from dropping, the whole vessel slipping forward into the beginnings of a dive, then arresting the movement, bringing the vessel back to stillness. Retreating noise and vibration. All around them the noise and motion had been, but Lloyd was certain the Soviet submarine had passed below them, slightly to port.

Then it was gone. Thurston mopped his brow enthusiastically, and grinned shakily at Lloyd.

"Close," he murmured.

"Too close." Then the idea came to him, and he voiced it before he considered its effect. "I think she was expecting us – I mean us, this boat and its anti-sonar."

"What?"

Lloyd looked down at the sonar operator, then at the others in the control room. He did not want to explain, not now. The idea, half-formed, frightened him, and he wanted to ignore it.

Thurston waited for his explanation, and Lloyd said, lamely, "That Russian has been following a very poor trail for an hour. As if he knew we were here."

"You're imagining it, skipper."

"As if he knew he was looking for a submarine that wouldn't show up on his sonar," Lloyd added.

"The evidence is in front of you, man. It may not be conclusive, but there is evidence there to suggest *Grishka* encountered the British submarine with its anti-sonar system working. Surely?"

"I will admit that not every trace of heat emission can be explained by temperature differences in the sea – perhaps there are identifiable traces of prop-wash and turbine activity, perhaps the faint gas traces help us –" The rear admiral looked round at his subordinates, then shrugged. "We will pinpoint the British submarine at the position signalled by the *Grishka* and await any satellite confirmation there might be."

"Excellent. She is on course. ETA?"

"On the basis of our supposition, no more than eighteen hours."

Dolohov was about to reply when the door to the control room opened, and a man in civilian clothes – very Western, Dolohov noticed, a sweater, windcheater and corduroy trousers – stood in the doorway. The man came forward into the light, and Dolohov saw that he was grinning. His hair was blown awry. Dolohov returned the smile, and waved away the junior officer accompanying the man.

"Valery – Valery, my boy!" he announced, ignoring the others in the room, embracing the newcomer, kissing him on both cheeks, a greeting that was returned by the younger man.

"Admiral – sir," the younger man acknowledged when held at arm's length by Dolohov. The rear admiral seemed surprised to discover that the civilian, in addition to having a permit of entry to his operations room, was some species of naval officer. The haircut, the acknowledgement of rank. Yet almost like a son to the admiral. A little spurt of envy flared in the rear admiral. This man was not to be treated like a schoolboy slow at his sums, apparently.

"You've come straight here?" Dolohov, even as he asked, was already drawing the younger man towards the window of the control room, already extending his free arm to direct the other's gaze. He was revealing a prized object of desire. The rear admiral bowed frostily as he was casually introduced, resenting the intimacy that had invaded his clinical, sterile control room. "Captain Valery Ardenyev, commanding the Red Banner Special Underwater Operations Unit," Dolohov explained with evident pride, almost with a proprietorial, parental tone, then ignored the rear admiral. "Down there," he said to Ardenyev. "We've marked her with a green light. A colour all to herself."

"You're sure, sir?"

"We think so. She's on course, eighteen hours away from the fjord."

Ardenyev stood looking down at the map table for some time. Dolohov, like a senior priest, allowed him silence and lack of interruption to his meditations, even though there was an impatience about his flinty features that made him appear both older, and much younger.

"The weather's worsening, sir," Ardenyev said finally. "But of course you know that." Ardenyev grinned as he brushed his hair back into place.

"It isn't that bad, Valery," Dolohov replied with a touch of acid.

"Not yet. I'll have to study the reports, and the predictions."

"You have doubts?"

"Not yet, sir. Not yet."

"We've eighteen hours, Valery."

"We have to transfer to the salvage vessel long before that, sir. By helicopter."

Dolohov gripped his arm. "Valery – it will be all right." He was instructing Ardenyev, even the weather. Commanding them both. "It will be. We'll have her." He turned to Sergei, his aide, whose position within the small group of the rear admiral's team seemed an obscure insubordination to Dolohov. "Sergei, get me an up-to-the-

634

minute weather report for our area of interest. And get me *all* the met. predictions for the next twenty-four hours – *now*, Sergei." Then Dolohov turned back to Ardenyev as to a child he had indulged, and who now must become obedient. "It must be done, Valery. It must be done."

"If it's possible, sir, it will be. I promise you that."

The rear admiral, observing the dialogue, conceived the idea that Ardenyev was not without calculation and guile. Dolohov responded by grabbing the younger man's arm, and pressing it with gratitude and what appeared to be affection. The rear admiral recalled gossip concerning the way in which Ardenyev's career had been jealously promoted by the admiral. Some connection with Ardenyev's father, even grandfather, he had heard. For his own part, the rear admiral had risen by loyalty to the Party, and distrusted this Soviet version of what the British called the "old boy network". And he distrusted young naval officers in civilian dress with easy manners and obvious self-confidence. Elitist adventurers.

The rear admiral withdrew to the other side of the control room, to await the updated satellite surveillance information. A small hope that Dolohov was precipitate, even mistaken, he nourished in his stomach like the warmth of a drink.

The college of education was a new one, built in the grounds of a Victorian magnate's former residence in the suburb of Edgbaston. The original house, having fallen into disrepair both before and after the compulsory purchase of the grounds, had disappeared. A tower block hall of residence stood on the site, bearing the same name as the grandiose house that one of Birmingham's Ozymandiases of trade or industry had erected to his own glorification. Two or three small, supposedly exclusive housing developments encroached on the perimeters of the college campus.

Hyde parked his car outside the tower block and sat for a moment considering his forthcoming interview with Tricia Quin's flatmate, Sara Morrison. Birmingham CID had talked to her the day the Quin girl appeared and disappeared, and had described her as unhelpful. Hyde had checked with the interviewing DC, who had amplified his observation by referring to the Morrison girl as a "Lefty cow, anti-police, good background – isn't it usually the case", and wished Hyde the best of luck with her. A moment of futility as dispiriting as weariness overcame Hyde, then he got out of the car and slammed the door.

The sky was overcast, sombre with rain. The downpour that it threatened was postponed only by the strong, gusty wind that swept paper and dust and old leaves across the grass and the concrete walks around the hall of residence; hurried and chafed the few figures he could see. An overriding impression of concrete and glass and greyness, a modern factory complex. He hurried up the steps into the foyer of the tower block.

A porter, uniformed and officious, emerged from a cubicle, wiping his lips. Hyde showed him the CID warrant card which avoided explanations, and asked for Tricia Quin's flat. The porter, evidently unimpressed by the length of Hyde's hair and his casual dress, begrudgingly supplied the number, and the information that Sara Morrison was in the flat at that moment. He had seen her return from a lecture half-an-hour before. Hyde went up in the lift, unamused by the mock-intellectual graffiti that decorated its walls. He gathered, however, that punk rock had achieved the status both of an art form and a political weapon.

A long corridor, blank, veneered doors. The carpet was marked and already worn, the plaster on the walls evincing settlement cracks. He knocked on the door of 405.

The girl who opened the door wore her hair in tight curls. Her face was instantly suspicious rather than intrigued or helpful. A mouth that pulled down into a scowl almost naturally, it seemed. Sallow skin, no make-up, a creased blouse and uniform denims. Her feet were bare.

"Yes?" A middle-class, south-east accent, overlain with the drawl of the fashionable urban. "What d'you want?"

"Sara Morrison?" She nodded. "Could we have a word about Tricia Quin. I believe —" the warrant card was in his hand, his shoulder against the door as she tried to shut it. "I believe she shares this flat with you."

The girl resigned herself to not being able to close the door on him.

"Past tense," she said, her eyes bright with calculation.

"Really?"

"You're Australian."

"Too right." He grinned disarmingly, but the girl did not respond.

"In Birmingham?" she mocked. "An Australian pig, in Birmingham?"

"Could be. It's not only politics that travel long distances. May I come in?"

The girl shrugged and released the door. He opened it on an untidy, cramped room with two single beds against opposite walls. A window in the end wall overlooked the campus carpark. Clothes draped over a functional chair, books spread across a small, cheap desk. Posters on the wall – Mao, Lenin, Sex Pistols, a *Playboy* centrefold with a crudely drawn moustache and glasses and even white teeth blacked out, Castro, Margaret Thatcher used as a dartboard, a Two-Tone band.

636

"What do you want?" the girl demanded belligerently as he observed the door leading off, bathroom and toilet. "She isn't here, you know." Her accent wavered between the glassy superiority of her background and undoubted money, and the urban snarl she felt he deserved.

"I suppose not. Someone would have seen her. The porter for instance?"

"Beria, you mean?"

Hyde laughed. "May I sit down?" The girl swept her clothes off the single chair, and squatted on the edge of her bed, feet drawn up beneath her, signalling indifference. Hyde sat down. The girl studied him.

"A trendy pig."

"We try, darling – we try."

"You fail – or should I have said, try and condemn?" She parted her lips in a mirthless grin, flashing her cleverness in that precise visual signal.

"A hit, I do confess. Can we talk about your erstwhile girl-friend?"

"What is there to say? She isn't here. End of story."

"Not her story. You know she's been seen. Have you seen her?" The girl shook her head, her face betraying nothing. "Sure?"

"I told your thick mate from CID that I hadn't seen her. Don't you believe me?"

"Not if I asked you for the right time. What would I get – the time in Moscow, or Peking?"

"Cuba," Sara Morrison replied without expression.

Hyde looked up at the ennobled poster of Fidel Castro. "He's a bit out of style, isn't he? Even Arthur Scargill's heard of him."

The girl applauded ironically. "Very funny – oh, too witty for words."

"Blimey, thanks, darling," he replied in his broadest accent. "Now we've both tried on backgrounds we never came from." He leaned forward in his chair. Unexpectedly, the girl flinched. He said, "This isn't France or South America, darling. Or Nazi Germany or Kampuchea or the Soviet Union. I could have you down the station, true, but your Daddy would get you out by tea-time, I should think." The girl's face wrinkled into contempt, then smoothed to indifference again, as if she had revealed too much of herself. "Always too busy at the office, was he? Chased other women? Self-made man?"

"Fuck off." The obscenity came almost primly from her lips.

"In a minute. Look, Tricia Quin is in trouble – not with us, before you harangue me again, with some people who you might think you like, but wouldn't if you met them."

After a silence, the girl said, "National security bullshit, I presume."

"Sorry darling, it's the only excuse I have."

"Why can't you fucking well leave her alone!" the girl suddenly yelled at him, her face bright-red with rage. The mood was sudden, manic in its swing.

"I *want* to. She has to be protected."

"Crap."

"Not crap. Listen to me." The girl's hands were bunched into fists in her lap, or twitched open, as if gripping some imagined weapon. There was a violence of rage and guilt and outrage in her that found the body inadequate to express such depths of feeling. "I can't help the situation in which she finds herself. Blame her father, blame national security, blame the bloody arms race if you want to – but I'm the only chance she's got. People want her because they can get to her father through her. They won't mind what they do to her to discover her father's hiding place. And before you say it – yes, I want her father, too. But I don't want to harm him, and I want to help her."

His dismissal passed like a flicker caused by dust in her eyes. Politics in place, attitudes firmly fixed, cemented. She would not tell him. Hyde saw the weapon of threat present itself, and wanted to reject it.

"I don't know where she is – and I wouldn't tell you if I did."

"For Christ's sake, girlie!" Hyde exploded. "Some of the two hundred or so Soviet diplomats with the ill-fitting suits and the poor-diet boils are looking for your girl-friend right now! When they find her, it will be a little bit of slapping about, then the closed fist, then the bucket over the head and the baseball bats, then the cigarette-ends for all I know – they won't have time to talk to her politely, some bigger bastard will be breathing down their necks for results. Even if they wanted to be nice. Your friend could tell them she was a card-carrying member of the Party and they'd pull her fingernails out until she told them what they wanted to know." He was speaking quite calmly during the last sentence, but the girl's face was white with anger and with surprised fear. There was something unselfish as well as disbelieving about her.

"You really believe all that?" she said at last. Her composure, her closed-minded prejudices, had reasserted themselves. "Christ, the perfect functionary!"

"My God, but you're stupid –".

"Tricia's been frightened out of her mind – don't you realise that?" the girl shouted at him. "Before her father disappeared, she was depressed, moody, frightened. Then she left – just like that. She hadn't slept a wink the night before. Doesn't that make *any* impression on you?"

"Was she frightened when you saw her two days ago?"

"Fuck off, clever sod."

Both of them were breathing hard. Only the wind, moaning more loudly round the building, offered a larger perspective than the cramped hothouse of the small room. The girl's face was implacable.

Hyde stood up, then crossed swiftly to her, clamping his hand over her mouth, holding her wrists in his other hand. He pushed her flat on the bed, kneeling beside her.

"You know what's coming now, darling. You've imagined it, talked about it, often enough. You're Blair Peach, love – you're a Black in Detroit, you're Steve Biko. I'm untouchable, darling. It'll be an accident." He could feel spittle on his palm, and sweat, and her eyes were wide with terror. "Everything you've ever thought about the pigs is true. Now you're going to find out."

Then he released her, moved away, sat down. The girl wiped at her mouth, rubbed her wrists. When she found her voice, she coughed out his eternal damnation.

"Sorry," he said. "You would have told me. Your eyes were already regretting your earlier bravado." His voice was calm, casual, unemotional. "We both know that. Tricia would tell them even quicker, even though it was her father."

"For God's sake –" the girl began, but there seemed nothing she could add.

"Yes. You're right again. She came here, didn't she?"

"She bloody didn't!" He knew, with an empty feeling, that it was true. The girl appeared hurt and useless. She'd have helped – lied, hidden Tricia, given her money, taken on the pigs, anything. But Tricia Quin hadn't even asked. Hyde felt sorry. Useless energy and emotion slopped around in Sara Morrison, mere ballast for a pointless journey.

"I'm sorry about that. Tell me where she might be, then?" On an impulse, he added: "Her mother mentioned she hung out with a rock band a couple of summers ago – pot, groupie-ing, the whole naughty bag. Any news on that?"

"Those dinosaurs," the girl remarked, glancing up at the Two-Tone group posturing down at her.

"Them?" he asked, looking up. The girl laughed.

"You remember a band called Heat of the Day?"

"Yes. I liked them."

"You're old enough." The girl had slipped into another skin, represented by half of the posters on the wall, and by the cassette tapes on one of the shelves, next to a huge radio with twin speakers. Something an astronaut might have used to contact the earth from deep space. The girl was now a pop music aficionado, and he someone with parental tastes. Hyde had wondered which way the retreat into shock would take her. It looked more promising than other

639

possible routes, but it would not last long. Eventually, she would be unable to disguise from herself the threat he represented.

"I thought they disbanded."

"They did. You don't read *Melody Maker* any more, obviously."

"Nor *Rolling Stone*. My age." He invited her to smile, but she did not respond. She did not look at him now, merely at her hands in her lap. She might have been drugged, or meditating.

"They're back together – on tour. I remember Tricia was interested."

"How did she get in with them, originally?"

"The lead singer, Jon Alletson, was in school with her brother – the one who emigrated to Canada."

"Would she have gone to them by any chance, would she still be in touch with them?"

Sara's face closed into a shrunken, cunning mask. "I wouldn't know," she said, and Hyde knew the conversation was at an end. In another minute, it would be police brutality, threats of legal action. He stood up. The girl flinched.

"Thanks," he said. "Take care."

He closed the door quietly behind him, hunger nibbling at his stomach, a vague excitement sharp in his chest. Rock supergroup? Friend of her brother? Perhaps the girl knew she was being chased round and round the garden, and had gone to earth where she would be welcomed and wouldn't be looked for, amid the electronic keyboards and yelling guitars and pounding drums, the hysteria and the noise and the cannabis and the young. In that thicket, she would recognise her enemies, from either side, with ease.

It might just be –

Tedium, anger, even anxiety, were all now conspiring to overpower caution. Aubrey felt within himself a surprising violence of reaction to his hour-long tour of the "Chessboard Counter" room and operation. The broaching of *Proteus*'s diversion to the Tanafjord proved the sticking point, broke the camel's back of his discretion. Perhaps, he reasoned with himself, it was the blasé, confident, aloof manner in which the monitoring action on the stricken Russian submarine was explained that so infuriated him. But images of Quin, with their attendant fears, and the pervasive odour of a possible trap, conspired to assist the wearing of his patience. Clark, too, seemed waiting for his cue; expecting Aubrey to make some decisive move, influence events.

And the smoothly running, almost mechanical individuals in the room; the obtrusive freemasonry of serving officers. The sterile hangar of the room; his own sense of himself regarded, at best, as the man from the Pru. He could no longer keep silence, or content himself with brief, accommodating smiles and innocuous questions. The excuse that he merely sought enlightenment regarding Quin's project became transparent in its flimsiness; insupportable. Even so, the vehemence evident to himself, and to Pyott and the others, in his voice when his temper finally broke through, surprised him.

"Giles, what do you hope to gain from this monitoring action?" he snapped. He waved his hand dismissively at the huge map-board.

"Our northern security is in question here, Kenneth," Pyott replied in suprise, his nostrils narrowed to slits, the tip of his nose whitened with suppressed anger at Aubrey's tone. "Surely you can see that?"

"It is a point of view."

"Kenneth, you are not an expert –"

"No, this distress call, now. You don't suspect its genuineness?"

"Good Lord, no."

"What about you, Captain Clark?"

"Not really. I just don't think the matter's important enough to risk 'Leopard'." He looked up at the cluster of lights on the board. They seemed to have one centre, where the wavering arrow of the light indicator being operated by Pyott demonstrated *Proteus*'s position.

"Ah. Now, my immediate reaction, employing my own peculiar expertise, would be to suspect the distress call. I would need proof that it was genuine."

"We've identified the submarine concerned," the commodore explained brusquely. "We have triple checked. I don't think the matter is in doubt." He looked to Pyott for support, and received it in an emphatic shake of the head.

Aubrey was intensely aware of the opposition of the two officers. They represented an opposite pole of interests. Also, they were in some way legitimized by their uniforms. Third Murderer again, he observed to himself.

"I see. It would still be my starting point."

"What would be the object of an elaborate deception, in this case?" Pyott drawled.

" 'Leopard.' "

"Good Lord, you're surely not serious –?"

"How would you react to the recall of *Proteus* until this chap Quin is found?"

"Utter nonsense!"

"The two matters haven't the slightest connection with one another Kenneth."

"Great idea."

"Ah. You would support such a move, Captain Clark?"

"I would." Pyott looked pained by a spasm of indigestion, the commodore appeared betrayed.

"I do really think it's dangerous, risking 'Leopard' in this way without having Quin safe and sound."

"You made that point weeks ago, Kenneth. Try another record."

"Giles, the KGB have started killing, such is their interest in Quin. Am *I* to rate his importance any lower – or that of his project?" Aubrey pointed up at the map, then indicated the rest of the room and its occupants. "Who else is looking into this distress call?"

"It's our show."

"Your work here is important, even if I consider it precipitate. But this present adventure – Giles, what can you possibly gain?"

Aubrey saw the answer in Pyott's eyes before the man spoke.

"Kenneth, I am at liberty to inform you – you, too, Clark – that this present adventure, as you term it, has a highest category security tag on it."

"For a distress call?"

"For *Proteus*'s mission," Pyott explained quietly and fiercely. Aubrey guessed at the nature of the mission, and was appalled. It was what he had suspected he might hear, if he needled Pyott sufficiently, and what he had wished devoutly not to hear. "The mission has been code-named –"

"You mean it's another, and extreme, *sea trial* for the 'Leopard' system, Giles?"

"Why, yes," Pyott admitted, somewhat deflated.

"What in hell –?"

"Excuse me, Captain Clark. Giles, you mean that approval has been given to sail *Proteus* almost into Soviet home waters, merely to prove the efficacy of the anti-sonar system?"

"That's it precisely."

"My God, Giles, it's lunacy. Playing games. You have put the system, the submarine, her crew, at risk, just to score extra marks in the examination. It is nonsense, and furthermore, dangerous nonsense!" He studied Pyott's face, which was colouring with anger, and then the commodore. An identical, undented confidence.

"What is *Proteus*'s ETA in the Tanafjord?"

Pyott smiled thinly. "I see no harm in telling you, Kenneth. Disregarding changes of course and speed, we estimate sixteen to eighteen hours. Some time early tomorrow morning, GMT."

"Giles, what intelligence do you have from the Norwegians?"

"They've backed off, fortunately."

"Aerial surveillance?"

"We have some confirmation – infra-red, naturally. We've more or less pinpointed the Russian boat."

642

"It *is* just an excuse, isn't it, Giles?"

Pyott shrugged, expansively; self-deprecation and dismissal featured jointly in the gesture of his shoulders and hands.

"It is an important – crucial – NATO exercise. A sea trial, as I explained. It cannot be described as an *excuse*."

Aubrey paused for a moment, then he said quietly and distinctly: "Giles – Giles, I am deeply sorry about this, but I must act." His throat seemed tight, and he coughed to clear it before adding, "Everything I have seen today, every instinct in my body, tells me to act." In his turn, he shrugged; a smaller, more apologetic movement. "There is no justifiable reason for this mission which outweighs its inherent risks to men, boat, or security. I have no other choice."

"You'll never obtain authority to override StratAn, MoD *and* NATO."

"I do not need to. This intelligence mission is on the point of going critical. I shall, therefore, invoke an ETNA order. I shall apply to the foreign secretary to make *Proteus*'s mission an SIS operation, and then I shall cancel it and recall the submarine."

Pyott was almost visibly shaking with fury. When Aubrey finished speaking, the silence of the huge room pressed in upon the tight group beneath the map; silence lapping against them like waves.

"Be damned to you, Aubrey," Pyott said at last. "I'll oppose you every inch of the way."

Aubrey regarded him for a moment. There was nothing conciliatory he could say, no palliative he even wished to offer. He said, "It should not take long. I expect to return later this afternoon with the appropriate authority – authority to stop this foolish school prefects' prank!"

FOUR:

Closing

"Kenneth – I'm with the minister now."

"Yes, Richard." Cunningham had called him on a scrambled line direct from the Foreign Office.

"Your request for special status – the ETNA order –"

Aubrey grasped at Cunningham's hesitation. 'C' would have talked to one of the ministers of state, and undoubtedly to the Foreign Secretary directly after lunch. As a Permanent Under-Secretary, the director of the intelligence service could command such immediate access, as might Aubrey himself, whose civil service rank was Deputy Under-Secretary. However, Cunningham had chosen to represent Aubrey's case himself, and alone. It appeared he had failed to convince the politicians.

"Yes, Richard?" Aubrey repeated, prompting his superior.

"The Secretary of State has agreed to your request. The Admiralty has been informed of the decision. 'Chessboard Counter' is, as of three-fifteen this afternoon, an SIS intelligence operation."

Aubrey's sigh of relief must have been audible to Cunningham. "Thank you, Richard," he said. He wanted to know more, disliked having been kept waiting upon events. "I'm sure you were most persuasive."

"I think we might say that the moment was opportune," Cunningham drawled. Aubrey understood. The Secretary of State, for his own reasons, had perceived and employed a means of impressing his authority upon another ministry. "Your authorisation will be waiting for you here. I suggest you come over right away."

They knew, and they resented him. Each and every one of the "Chessboard Counter" team, with the exception of Ethan Clark, met his entry to the underground room with silence and a carved hostility of expression. One tight group stood beneath the map-board, Pyott and the commodore were at the latter's desk, standing as if posed for some official portrait which recaptured the aloofness and distance of ancestral oils; the communications and computer operators had their

644

backs to him not so much in gainful employment, more in some communal snub.

Aubrey went immediately to the desk, shedding his dark overcoat, taking off his hat. Man from the Pru, he reminded himself, and the image amused rather than belittled him.

"Gentlemen – I'm sorry."

"We're not simply going to lie down under this –" Pyott began, waving Aubrey's written authorisation, but Aubrey raised his hand. At the edge of his vision, Clark was moving towards them, triumphantly.

"I'm sorry gentlemen, the time for discussion is past. I regret having usurped your authority, but 'Chessboard Counter' is now my responsibility. And I expect your cooperation." His voice was heavy with interrogation. The commodore appeared, strangely, more reluctant than Pyott. It was the soldier who finally spoke. Clark hovered a few yards away.

"Very well, Aubrey, you shall have our cooperation. The damage you have done today to NATO's security, and to the good relations between the various intelligence branches, is something that will only emerge with time." He paused, his lips smirking. "I shall make every effort to see that this matter is fully and properly investigated."

"I expect nothing less, Giles. When the time is right." Aubrey smiled; challenge and sadness in the expression. Then he turned to Clark. "Captain Clark, our first priority –" His voice invited the American into conference with himself and the two senior officers, "is to recall the *Proteus*."

"That, I'm afraid, is impossible," the commodore remarked bluntly. Aubrey realised he had been mistaken. The posed and still expressions had not expressed resentment, not in Pyott and the commodore. Rather, the closed, secret blankness of card players. They did not consider themselves beaten.

"Why, pray?" Aubrey asked frostily.

"*Proteus* is observing the strictest radio silence until the mission is completed and she has returned to a position off North Cape. Only then will she transmit, and be able to receive."

"Sorry, Kenneth," Pyott added. "I omitted to tell you before. It's quite true what the commodore says – no communications facility exists between ourselves and *Proteus*."

Inwardly, Aubrey was furious, but his face retained an icy control. "I see," he said. "Impossible?"

"Not quite," Clark remarked quietly at Aubrey's shoulder. The old man looked round and up into the American's face. It was gleaming with satisfaction, with the sense of outwitting the two senior British officers. Clark was working out his private grudge.

"Go on," Aubrey prompted.

"*Proteus* has pre-determined listening out times. She could be reached then. With a hydrophonic buoy."

"Dropped from an aircraft, you mean?"

"Yes. One of your Nimrods. Highest priority code, continuous frequency-agile transmission. An unbroken, one-time code. Just tell *Proteus* to get the hell out."

The commodore appeared deflated. Pyott was merely angry, but he kept silent.

"I want to look at the state of play," Aubrey said with gusto, as if he had come into an inheritance and was about to be shown over the property. "Ethan, come along. Giles –?"

Pyott shrugged, and followed. The group of young officers beneath the huge map-board dispersed a little. They sensed that Aubrey had won. They had been betrayed by the American who had opened the judas-gate into the castle. The enemy was amongst them; they had been routed.

Aubrey looked up, then turned to Clark and Pyott: "Well? Where is she?"

"About here." Clark flashed on the light-indicator's arrow. A cluster of lights surrounded it, very bright like falling meteors.

"Those lights are all Soviet vessels, I take it?" Aubrey asked in a quiet voice.

"Right."

"Explain them to me."

Now the arrow dabbed at each of the lights, as Clark talked.

"These positions haven't been updated for three hours – we have another hour before the satellite comes over the horizon and we can pick up transmission of the current picture. This is the carrier *Kiev*, the pride of the fleet. She's changed course three times, the last one took her from here to here –" Southwards. "She *was* heading west. These two are 'Kashin'-class destroyers, they left Pechenga yesterday. These three are ELINT vessels, probably spy-ships rigged as trawlers, but they're not with fishing fleets – they've changed course, here to here –" Southwards and eastwards. "This, according to some very bad satellite photography yesterday is a rescue ship, the *Karpaty*. She left Murmansk a couple of days ago. Why she's in the area, I wouldn't know. It may not even be her, could be another ELINT vessel, but a big one. And these are the submarines – " The arrow dabbed now at spot after spot of light. "Hunter-killers, every one."

"Thank you, Captain Clark." Aubrey turned to Pyott and the commodore, who had now joined them. Behind them, the junior officers formed a knot of silent supporters. "Is it because I am a mere layman that these Soviet naval dispositions frighten me, make me

646

leap to one conclusion, and only one?" He paused, but there was no murmur of reply. He continued: "Gentlemen, it would seem obvious to me that the Soviets have at least surmised that *Proteus* is in the area and making for Tanafjord. This activity is not directed towards the rescue of the crippled submarine. What is intended I do not propose to guess. If anything happens to *Proteus*, I am now required to accept responsibility. If I can prevent it, nothing untoward will happen. Clark, come with me. We apparently require the cooperation of the Chief of Air staff. Commodore, a secure line, if you please."

"Thank God for sanity," Clark whispered. Aubrey turned on him.

"Ethan, it may already be too late. It is now simply a matter of deciding tenses, from what you have shown me. *Proteus* is walking into – *has* walked into – a trap. Pray that the present tense still applies!"

A bright yellow TR7. It was an easy car in which to be tailed, and the two men in the Ford Granada had stuck to him from Edgbaston through the centre of Birmingham – even in the afternoon traffic – and out onto the M6 motorway. Standing in the doorway of the café near the college, the *Melody Maker* tucked under his arm, one hand disguising the burping indigestion that the sausage and chips had given him, he had seen the car parked across the street from his own. It had U-turned and followed him. He had never lost sight of it in his mirror, and they had never lost sight of him.

Thus he passed his turn-off eight miles further back towards Birmingham, and now the signs indicated the next service area. He signalled, and pulled off the M6, up the slope into the car park. He got out of the car without glancing at the Granada sliding into an empty place twenty yards from him, and went into the foyer of the building. He slipped into the toilet, walked the length of it, and exited through the second door, leading out again to the carpark from the side of the building. He approached the corner slowly, peering round it. One of the two men was standing by the Granada, the other was nowhere to be seen. Presumably, he had followed Hyde into the service station.

Hyde waited impatiently. If the second man didn't move almost at once, he would have to go back into the toilet and attempt to shake them later. And now impatience was a nagging toothache. The man by the Granada was smoking, and picking at his teeth with the hand that held the cigarette. Come on, come on –

The man patted his stomach, which was ample, resting over the lip of his waistband. He hesitated, then he drifted towards the shop at the front of the building, moving with angering slowness out of Hyde's line of vision.

Hyde began running then. He reached the TR7, jerked open the

647

door, and slid into the low seat. He had left the keys in the ignition. He started the engine, and squealed in reverse out of his parking space, swinging the car towards the carpark's exit. In the wing mirror, for a moment, the running figure of the fatter man, then the other emerging from the building behind him, yelling. Then he was down the slope and into the entry lane. He pulled out in front of a heavy lorry, and stamped on the accelerator. The next exit from the M6 was two miles away. He would lose them there, then double back to his intended destination. The speedometer registered ninety. He was still breathing hard, but he was grinning.

Hyde turned the TR7 into the most convenient carpark for Hall 5 of the National Exhibition Centre. The fountain in the middle of the artificial lake in front of the huge hotel complex looked cold and stiff, like dead, blowing grass. It had taken him almost an hour to back-track the twelve miles or so to the NEC site. He had not been followed through the suburbs of Coventry, back towards the airport. They might – just might – have assumed that he was heading east, towards the M1.

Streamers bearing slogans. A queue had formed already, sleeping bags were in evidence, denim like a uniform or prison garb, combat jackets blazoned with insignia, out-of-style long hair worn by many. The audience, or part of it at least, for Heat of the Day's concert at the NEC, kick-off at eight o'clock. It was now almost five. Edwin Shirley's trucks were already unloading the sound and light equipment. Policemen.

Hyde showed his CID warrant card, and was allowed through the cordon. He immediately picked out Fat Mary, one of the formerly much-publicised road crew. Many of the faces seemed half-familiar from television documentaries when Heat of the Day were on their pinnacle. They had come back like lost disciples.

"Excuse me – "

"Piss off," the fat girl replied.

"Police, darling." He tiredly waved the warrant card.

"Nobody's carrying."

"I'm not interested. Are the band here?"

"Two hours yet. Want some autographs?" She watched two of the road crew carrying a huge mirror, and bellowed, "For Christ's sake, haven't you got all the mirrors up yet?"

"No autographs. Tell me – is Tricia Quin with them?"

A flicker, like a wasp sting, at the corner of her mouth, then the sullen look returned. "Who?"

"Tricia Quin. She was with you on the Europe tour two years ago. Her brother knew Jon."

"Oh, yes. I remember. No, haven't seen her. It's not *all* the same as before, you know."

"I don't suppose it is. She's not with them, then?" The fat girl shook her head. Her pendulous breasts distorted the claim on her T-shirt that she had attended the University of California. "Perhaps I'll stick around. Collect a few autographs."

"Or a few smokers."

"Who knows, Fat Mary." The girl seemed pleased at the use of her name, the recollection of a former, half-celebrity status. "Keep it in your pocket, not in your mouth. See you." The girl scowled after him.

Tricia Quin, unless he was mistaken – no, he wasn't – was with the band. Two hours seemed an intolerable length of time.

The one-time code message was lengthy, and even the computer's rendering of it into plain seemed to occupy far more time than was usually the case. Even so, when KGB Resident Petrunin possessed the plain-language text, irritation immediately replaced impatience. He felt hampered by his instructions from Moscow Centre at the same time that he wished, fervently, to comply with those orders.

He left the code room in the embassy basement and took the lift to his office. *At any cost – immediately. The girl.* It was almost demeaning that an unavoidable test of competence and loyalty should have as its object an immature girl unable to cope with growing up. And it was infuriating that superior officers as eminent as the Deputy Chairman responsible for the KGB's 2nd Chief Directorate should indulge in some vulgar, glory-seeking race against the Red Banner Northern Fleet to see who could first acquire "Leopard" for the Soviet Union. All those old men belonged to the same class, the same era. *Dolohov appears confident the submarine is sailing into his trap. You have little time.* The girl, the girl –

He locked the door of his office behind him, and flung the high-security document case onto one of the armchairs. He thrust his hands into his pockets, and stood at the window. Lowering clouds, pulled across the sky by a fierce wind. Trees bending.

Damn those clowns in Birmingham, losing Hyde. Correction. Letting Hyde lose them. Hyde was the key, even more so than the girl. And he was at one further remove from Quin, and that was another cause of anger at the unfairness of the task set him. Hyde must know something, must have discovered some clue as to the girl's whereabouts, otherwise he would not have bothered to shake the tail.

What did he know?

The girl student, the mother? Either of them? Something popping into his head as he was driving out of Birmingham? Tamas Petrunin grinned. It was impossible to know. Interesting to speculate. It was

649

what he enjoyed. Guesswork. He rubbed his hands together, and turned his back to the window where the wind rustled tinnily outside the double glazing. Birmingham. He couldn't send anyone to see the girl Morrison, nor the mother. Not so soon after Hyde. And it might not be necessary.

Birmingham. When did he spot the tail car? Petrunin opened the wad of newspapers on his desk. Normally, they would be sent down to junior staff for analysis, but Petrunin often liked to glance through the provincial newspapers for evidence of KGB activity, actual or potential. The *Birmingham Post*. A rather stuffy, empty paper. He flicked through the pages. Nothing. The *Evening Mail*. Nothing. Hyde would not expect to find the girl at a football match.

Then where? Where would he expect to find the girl? Be Hyde, he instructed himself. Talking to the mother and the friend, then suddenly there is something to cling to, some chance of finding the girl. And the need to shake the surveillance he had discovered – *clowns*.

Where?

He returned to the newspapers. The girl now. What did he know about her? He crossed with rapid, bustling steps to a large filing cabinet against the far wall of the office, wood-veneered so that its function did not obtrude upon the room. He opened one drawer and removed the file on Quin's daughter. A narrow, shadowy file. He carried it back to his desk, dumping most of the newspapers on the carpet, leaving open the two Birmingham dailies. Where would Hyde expect to meet the girl?

Movements in Birmingham: he scanned the digest in the file. Clubs, pubs, cinemas, one or two exhibitions, concerts, visits to her mother. Dull stuff.

Social habits: clubs, pubs, cinemas. *Sexual behaviour:* Petrunin scanned the itemised digest. For the last two years, one or two casual, short-lived relationships within the college, a very brief affair with one of her lecturers, then a teacher she met while on teaching practice. Hyde had had Birmingham detectives question all these people. No one had seen her recently. When she ended an affair, she never revisited the scene of the crime. Petrunin savoured the epithet, then grew angry at the truism it contained. It was true that the girl never went back.

Alletson? Oh, the pop singer. The big affair, travelling with the pop group from place to place. Her parents had been worried by that, from all accounts. Soft drugs, promiscuity. A nightmare in Sutton Coldfield. Again, Petrunin grinned. Even Alletson had failed to make any lasting impression upon the girl. A pity.

Psychological Profile: a fine example to us all, he told himself. He skimmed through it. He already knew the girl, as well as she could be

650

known at second hand, and even though her background and past history prompted him to indulge in stereotypes to account for her – she so easily fitted Western and Soviet myths about modern youth and permissive societies – he was certain that there was nothing in the Profile to explain why Hyde had charged off in his little yellow car.

He slapped the file back on his desk. He knew it almost by heart, it had been the merest illusion to assume that the answer would spring from its flimsy sheets. Had she been his own daughter – as he supposed she could have been, in age at least – he would have no real clue as to her whereabouts. As KGB Resident, he could not walk around in her head with ease or certainty. Hyde's head bore more similarity to his own.

Where?

The newspapers. He put the file to one side. Football, cinemas, factories on strike, a Royal visit proposed for later in the year – the appropriateness of the blank crossword – share prices . . .

He folded the morning paper to one side, and returned to the tabloid evening newspaper from the previous day. Grinning beauty queen, footballer with arms raised gladiatorially. Cinemas, clubs, discos, concerts.

The print began to blur. He knew he was not going to find it. Picture of a queue of people, sleeping bags, combat jackets, long hair. He wasn't going to find it. Pop concert at the National Exhibition Centre. Headline to the picture caption, "Who are we all waiting for?"

He flicked over the page, then the next page, before what he thought he had not bothered to read entered his consciousness and immediately caused his heart to thud and his hand to tremble. He creased the pages of the paper turning back to the picture and its caption. Other, smaller pictures underneath, of course. The heroes of yesterday. Heat of the Day. Alletson, the girl's lover. Long hair and soft, almost feminine features. The NEC, Birmingham, concert tonight.

He laughed aloud, congratulating himself. Accident, luck, good fortune, chance never disturbed him. He had placed himself in the way of it. Hyde had stumbled across this in the same kind of way. Something the Morrison girl said, or the mother, or two years ago merely popping into his head.

Whether the girl would be there or not, Hyde would. That was a certainty, and perhaps the only one. In which case, Tamas Petrunin would also be there. He looked at his watch. After five-thirty. He calculated. Just time, if they could get out of the centre of London without delay, to the M1. Just time –

*   *   *

"Is that extra signals traffic co-ordinated?"

"Sir," Sergei answered. The young aide swallowed a mouthful of bread before he answered Dolohov. Then, finding it stuck in his throat, he washed it down with tea. One corner of the Ops. Room control centre had become a preserve, marked off by invisible fences – authority, nerves, tension – from the normal staff. Around a metal chart table, Dolohov, Sergei and Ardenyev sat drinking tea and eating bread and cheese. There was something spartan and disregarded about the food and drink with which Dolohov kept them supplied, as if the three of them were engaged in the field, kept going by survival rations. Sergei began slowly to understand the feverish, self-indulgent manner in which the admiral regarded the operation. The admiral was an old man. He had selected this capture of the British submarine as some kind of suitable valediction to his long and distinguished career. Hence he attended to every detail of it himself, however small and insignificant.

"Just in case," Dolohov explained to Ardenyev, the young man nodding in a half-impatient, half-attentive manner, "in case she receives any signals, or monitors our signals, we'll appear to be making every covert effort to reach, and rescue, our own submarine." He smiled, the mouth opening like a slack pouch in the leathery skin.

"I understand, sir," Ardenyev supplied.

"You're impressed by the British equipment, Valery?"

Ardenyev paused. Sergei felt he was calculating the degree of flattery his answer should contain. "Very. We must have it, sir."

"Yes, yes – but, its effectiveness? It exceeds our expectations, mm?"

"Yes, sir."

"She'll keep on course?" Dolohov asked suddenly.

"I – think so, sir." Ardenyev seemed struck by the idea, as if he had not considered it before. "I think so. She's committed, now, under orders."

"Our activity won't discourage her?"

"I doubt that. The captain of the *Proteus* would have the authority to abort – I just don't think he will. As long as 'Leopard' functions, he'll enjoy the cat-and-mouse of it."

"Exactly my reading of the man – of the situation." Dolohov looked at his watch. "She appears to be maintaining course and speed. We have five hours, or less. Success or failure." Sergei could hear the admiral's breathing. Hoarse gulps of air, as if the sterile atmosphere of the control room offered something more necessary than oxygen. "You'd better get off to Pechenga to join your men, Valery."

652

Ardenyev immediately stood up, an automaton galvanised by the order. Sergei felt the man was simply supplying an impression of instant action such as Dolohov would expect, had waited for.

"Wish me luck, sir."

Dolohov stood up and embraced the young man. "I do, Valery – I wish you luck. Bring me back the British submarine, eh?" He clamped Ardenyev's forearms again with his liver-spotted hands. Ardenyev felt a strength of desperation in the embrace. And of old age refusing to admit the growing dark. He felt sorry, and irritated. He felt himself no more than Dolohov's creature. Later, it would be different, but now it was unpleasant. He would be glad to be aboard the chopper, being flown to the port of Pechenga. "The weather won't prevent you?" It was a command, and a doubt.

Ardenyev shook his head, smiling. "Not if I can help it."

"Report in when you arrive – then wait for my order to transfer to the *Karpaty*."

"Of course, sir."

When he had left the room, Dolohov went on staring at the door which had closed behind him. From the concentration on his face, Sergei understood that the old man was attempting to ignore the voice of one of the rear admiral's team who was reading off the updated weather report from a met satellite for the Tanafjord area. To Sergei, it sounded bad.

Almost as soon as it lifted clear of the main runway at RAF Kinloss on the Moray Firth in Scotland, the Nimrod surveillance aircraft turned north-eastwards, out over the Firth, and was lost in the low cloud. A blue flare beneath the wings, the flashing red light on her belly, the two faint stars at wingtips, and then nothing except the scudding cloud across the cold grey water, and the driving, slanting rain.

It had taken less than two hours to authorize a Nimrod to pursue the *Proteus*, carrying, in addition to her anti-submarine electronics, the encoded instruction to the submarine to return to base with all possible speed. The time was two minutes after six in the evening.

It was almost dark when they arrived. A luxury coach pulled up at one of the rear entrances to Hall 5, and Hyde, standing with the uniformed superintendent responsible for security and order at the rock concert, watched as Heat of the Day descended from it and slipped into the open door to their dressing rooms. Arrogance, self-assurance, denim-masked wealth. Hyde absorbed these impressions even as he studied the figures he did not recognise; managers, road managers, publicity, secretaries. The girl had not been with Alletson, and Hyde's immediate and uncontrollable reaction was one of intense disappointment. After the hours in the carpark and on the platforms of Birmingham International station and inside and outside Hall 5 – all with no sign of the KGB or the Ford Granada, but the more intensely wearing for that – there was an immediate impression of wasted time, of time run out. Of stupidity, too.

But she was there. Denims and a dark donkey jacket too big for her – was it her, certainly the jacket was too big for the present wearer? – slipping out of the coach without pause, walking with and then ahead of the two other women. The white globe of a face for a moment as she looked round, then she was through the lighted door and gone.

"Was she there?" the superintendent asked. His manner was not unfriendly, not unhelpful. Hyde had been scrupulously deferential and polite.

"I don't know." He felt a tightness in his chest. Was it her? Furtive, certainly furtive. Alletson had paused, allowed himself to be recognised, taken the limelight. Declaring he was alone, there was no girl. "I think so."

"The one with the too-big coat?"

"I think so."

"OK. You'd better go and find out. Want one of my chaps to go with you?"

"No. I'll be enough to panic her by myself."

"Suit yourself."

"Thanks for your help."

Hyde crossed the tarmac, rounded the coach, and showed his warrant card to the PC on duty at the door. The superintendent was apprised of Hyde's real capacity, but it was unnecessary for anyone else to know. "Where are the dressing rooms?"

"Down the corridor, turn left. You'll see another bloke dressed just like me. And the press, and the bouncers and the hangers-on. Can't miss it."

"Not your scene, this?"

"I'd rather be at the Villa, yobs and all."

"They playing at home tonight?"

"Too bloody true."

"Shame."

Hyde followed the corridor, and turned the corner into a crowd of pressmen and cameramen, carefully orchestrated outside the closed dressing room doors. Heat of the Day were back in business. Interest had to be stoked, and kept alight. Hyde pushed through the crowd towards the policeman on the door of one of the rooms. He waved his warrant card.

"Which one is Alletson in?"

654

"Who?"

"The short bloke with the wavy hair."

"Uh – that one," the PC supplied, indicating the other door, outside which two bulky men in denims and leather jackets stood, arms folded. Hyde wondered who, precisely, they were guarding. A press or publicity secretary was informing the cameramen that they would be allowed to take their pictures just before the band went onstage. Her announcement was greeted with a chorus of groans. Hyde showed his warrant card to one of the band's security men, who seemed to loom over him.

"Who do you want?" The question was wrong, and revealing. Again, Hyde felt his chest tighten with anticipation. The girl was in there.

"I'm not after his autograph."

"So, what do you want?" Both of them seemed uncertain what to do.

"Just a security check. And I want to talk to Jon about after the concert. Getting away."

"I'll ask him."

"Don't bother. I'll talk to him." He made to reach for the door handle. A large hand closed over his own, and he looked up into a face adopting aggression reluctantly, uncertainly. "Don't be stupid," Hyde said. "It might be big trouble – *will* be big trouble." The two men glanced at one another, then his hand was released.

"Easy, eh?"

"I'll take it easy – don't upset the artiste, right?" Hyde opened the door without knocking. The girl turned in her chair, alert, nervous, instantly aware of what he was and why he was there. Alletson was lying on a camp bed, and the keyboard player, Whiteman, was scribbling with a pencil on stave paper.

"Who the hell are you?" he asked. Alletson's voice provided a more nervous, knowing undertone.

"Trish – what is it?"

The girl simply stared at Hyde as he shut the door behind him. Whiteman, oblivious to the other two and their anxiety, added, "Piss off, we're busy." He glanced contemptuously at the warrant card. "Autographs later," he sneered.

"Miss Patricia Quin, I presume?" Hyde asked. The girl said nothing. Her face, however, was voluble with confession. Alletson got up lithely and stood in front of her.

"What do you want?" he asked.

"The lady in the case."

Alletson took the warrant card, inspected it, then thrust it back into Hyde's hand. "Harassment?" he asked.

"This isn't about smokes or shots, Jon-boy," Hyde drawled. "It isn't really any of your business. You get on rehearsing or composing or something." Whiteman was standing now, just behind Alletson. Long blond hair, his frame bulkier with good living than two years before. He looked healthier.

"Why don't you piss off?"

"Why did they let you in?" Alletson demanded.

"They'd have been silly not to."

"What sort of copper are you?" Whiteman was a Londoner. "You're a bloody Aussie by the sound of it."

"Too true, Blue. I'm the sort that wants to help her. Can I talk to her?"

"Not unless she wants to."

"Stop it, Jon. It won't do any good." Tricia Quin pushed to Alletson's side, and held his arm. "Who are you?"

"My name's Hyde."

"I didn't think it would be Jekyll – he was the goody, wasn't he?" Whiteman sneered.

"He was. Look, Miss Quin, I'll talk to you with your friends here, if you wish, as long as they can keep their mouths shut." He looked steadily at Alletson and Whiteman, then continued. "You are in danger, Miss Quin. It's stopped being a game. You know there are people after you?"

"You are."

"No, not me. Not even my side."

"What's he talking about, Trish?"

"What do you mean?"

"The men in Sutton, at your mother's house?" She nodded, fear flickering in her pale eyes. Cleverness, too. "That wasn't us. Our bloke got kicked in the balls trying to look after you. You need protection – mine. Will you come back with me?"

She shook her head. "No, I won't. I'm safe here."

"I can't risk that, Miss Quin. We want you and your father safe. You could lead the KGB right to him." She was shaking her head violently now. Her fair hair flopped about her pale, small face. She looked vulnerable, afraid but determined.

As if her shaking head was some signal, Alletson stepped up to him and aimed his knee at Hyde's groin. Hyde bucked backwards and the blow struck his thigh. Off-balance as he was, Alletson pushed him against a tall metal locker. Hyde, watching Tricia Quin move towards the door, jarred his head and shoulder against the locker, then slumped into the corner of the dressing room.

"Trish!" Alletson called, but the girl was already out of the door. Two hopeful flash-bulbs exploded. Hyde got shakily to his feet.

"You stupid buggers!" Hyde snapped, rubbing his shoulder. "She's a menace to herself at the moment, as well as to her father. Christ – you stupid buggers!" He opened the door, and yelled to the PC on duty. "Which way did the girl go?" Someone laughed.

"Towards the hall."

"Who is she?" someone asked.

"It'll be pot," someone else answered. "Poor bitch."

Hyde forced his way through the press, jabbed uncomfortably more than once by the lens of a camera, then he was running. At the far end of the corridor, the door into the hall was open. He rubbed his thigh as he ran, his resentment against Alletson growing not because of the pain but because of the girl. Stupid bugger, silly bitch, he chanted to himself, grinding his teeth at the opportunity that had been spoiled. He had had the girl safe, for a moment. It was only a matter of getting her to his car, getting her to Aubrey – *shit*!

In the hall, lighting gantries were being pulleyed up to the ceiling, mirrors were being positioned for the light-show that the band used, and the roadies were still working furiously to rig and test the amplification equipment. Two grubby girls passed him without a glance, pushing one of Whiteman's electronic keyboards. Up the ramp and onto the stage. He was standing just below the stage. Lights, mirrors, amplifiers, instruments – and Tricia Quin picking her way delicately like a cat through the maze of boxes and wires. She must have taken the other turn in the corridor to enter onto the stage itself.

She saw him. Part of her slow and delicate passage across the stage was due to her continual backward glances. She began to move more quickly, upstage towards the far side. Even as he moved, she disappeared into the wings. He pushed past the girls with the keyboard, and ran as quickly as he was able through the maze of cables and boxes – someone yelled at him – and then he was in the semi-darkness of the wings. He paused, listening. Above his heartbeat and breathing, footsteps. Running. He blundered forward again, sensing rationality disappearing and panic encroaching. He suddenly knew that the KGB were out there, and that she was running towards them. He shook his head, cannoning off a wall as he rounded a bend in the corridor.

Lights again. The foyer and main corridor connecting Hall 5 with its companions and with the railway station. A handful of people moving slowly, and one slight figure running. He did not call after her, merely pursued her, his feet pounding, his blood beating in his ears. He felt a sickness of self-recrimination, an anticipation of disaster.

A tunnel of lights down which she fled, a small dark shape. The scene wobbled in his vision. He seemed no nearer to her. The station concourse was at the end of the wide tunnel. She was almost there, sixty or seventy yards away.

Someone turning, moving with her, after her. She was oblivious to whoever it was, didn't even look round for him as she reached the concourse. He began running, impelled by the certainty of disaster now. Someone had recognised her – other men, two of them in overcoats, just come in from the cold of the carpark outside the station, moving to intercept her.

He reached the concourse. The girl had disappeared. Two men had pushed into the small queue for tickets, one of them arguing. He hadn't imagined it. They were stereotypes. The girl must have gone down onto the platform. Two of them, three – where was the other one, the one who had turned in the tunnel, recognised her?

Petrunin. Hyde could not believe it. Standing beneath the announcement board, impatiently watching his men create the wrong kind of disturbance, then turning to the platform ticket machine and banging it because it appeared jammed or empty. No, girl, no girl –

Petrunin, London Resident. KG-bloody-B. Where the hell was the girl? Petrunin. The clever bugger must have worked it out. Tickets being issued, the small queue silenced by embarrassment. Petrunin almost hopping from foot to foot. Train announcement, the next train arriving, Petrunin turning his head from side to side as if regretting something or because he had lost something – and seeing him. Knowing him not so much by his face as by his colour and heaving chest and wary, tense posture.

Hyde ran at the barrier, Petrunin moved to cut him off, slowly drifting, so it seemed, on a collision course. The next train arriving, for Birmingham – special train? He saw the dark, frightened face of the ticket collector, then he vaulted the turnstile, almost stumbling on the far side, hearing the noise of the train. He ran headlong down the flight of steps to the platform, round the corner, skidded, righted himself, flung open the glass doors.

She was almost alone on the platform. He saw her immediately. And she saw him. Policemen, too. Clattering footsteps behind him, but it was all right. Policemen. All round them, policemen. He hadn't lost her. He called to her as she stood looking at him. The nose of the train covered his words as it slowed, then came to a stop.

One of Petrunin's men grabbed him from behind. He turned, lashed out to try to prevent a second man passing him, heading towards the girl. Then they seemed to be drowning in bodies as the special train from Euston debouched hundreds of rock fans onto the platform, every one one of them intent on reaching the exit first. Noise assailed Hyde, and perfume. He was brushed aside, the only certainty the hand holding his collar. He raised his fist, but the crowd trapped it against his chest, pinning it there as in a sling. Petrunin's man had his arm above the heads of the crowd. He was waving a rubber cosh. He struck slowly down. The movement was awkward because he was being relentlessly pushed back towards the exit. Hyde lost sight of the girl, of Petrunin who seemed to have retreated back up the steps, and of the cosh which struck him across the neck and shoulder, numbing him after the spurt of fire through his head. Then the Russian's hand was gone from his collar and he stumbled forward, flung sideways to his knees, then onto his chest. Feet pressed on his back, compressing his lungs. People began surging over him. He was drowning for a moment, then he could not breathe, and then it was dark.

FIVE:

Cripple

"Sir, why the hell is the *Kiev* in the area? There's no major Soviet exercise on, and she couldn't possibly be any help in rescuing those poor dead buggers in the crippled boat – so why do they need an aircraft carrier? What's her game?"

"I don't know, John."

"And the course changes – sir, we remained rigged for silent running for too long. If we'd had the magnetic and acoustic sensors working, and gone to active sonar, we'd have known sooner she was closing on us."

"I know that, John. I know we're the quarry."

"Sir, what in hell are we doing here?"

"Playing MoD's games for them, John. Undergoing our final examination."

"What?"

"I mean it. In this sea-trial, the danger's all the better for MoD for being real."

"Bastards. Sir, we're being gathered into a net. The net is in the Tanafjord, and we're being driven towards it."

"Agreed."

"What do they want?"

"I should have thought that was obvious. What they want is called 'Leopard'. As to what they'll do, you guess."

"What do *we* do?"

"ETA Norwegian territorial waters?"

"Two hours plus some minutes."

"Then we'll run for shelter. We might just get away with it, inside Norwegian waters. We'll hide, John. Hide."

"Ethan, has the Nimrod's position been updated?"

"She's here, Mr. Aubrey, as of five minutes ago."

Aubrey stared up at the huge map-board. The cluster of lights glowed with what he could easily imagine was malevolence. A single white light had been introduced to the board to represent the *Proteus*. Aubrey periodically wished it had not been done. The white dot was in a ring of coloured lights representing the Soviet naval vessels in the immediate area. Far to the south and west of that cluster, a second white light shone like a misplaced or falling star over the fjordal coastline of western Norway, perhaps a hundred miles south of the Arctic Circle.

"Not enough, not far enough," Aubrey murmured. The dot seemed hardly to have moved since the aircraft's previous signal.

"You can't know that, Mr. Aubrey."

"Don't offer me morsels of comfort, Ethan!" Aubrey snapped, turning to the American. Heads turned, and then returned to screens and read-outs. Aubrey had subdued the "Chessboard Counter" team by cajolement and command, and by exploiting their sense of failure. The map-board had completed their change in function as it increasingly betrayed *Proteus*'s danger. They were now a rescue team, busy and helpless.

"Sorry."

Pyott and the commodore had sought another place of residence. Vanquished, they had left the field to Aubrey. Rather, he saw them as children running away from the broken window, the smashed greenhouse.

"My apologies. What's the Nimrod's ETA?"

"A little more than an hour to Hammerfest, then maybe another twenty minutes to the Tanafjord."

Aubrey looked at his watch. "Eight-fifteen. Can we do it, Ethan?"

Clark rubbed his chin. To Aubrey, he looked absurdly young, and much too unworried to be a repository of authoritative answers. And he was tall enough to make Aubrey physically uncomfortable.

"Maybe. Then *Proteus* has to get the hell out."

"Why hasn't Lloyd aborted on his own initiative?"

"Maybe he wants to. Maybe he's running for the coast and keeping his fingers crossed. Who knows?"

"My *God*, what an impossible situation!" Aubrey's face darkened after the quick rage had passed. He leaned confidentially towards the American. "Ethan, I'm worried about Quin. I haven't heard from Hyde. He was at the NEC in Birmingham, some sort of pop concert. He thought – no, he was certain – the girl was with this group. She knows them, once travelled with them." Aubrey's face was drained of colour and expression now. "It is very hard to contemplate, Ethan, but I feel myself staring at the loss of the *Proteus* and of the man responsible for the development of 'Leopard'. It is not a comfortable prospect."

Clark recognized, and admitted to himself, Aubrey's age. Yet he respected the man's intellect and his expertise. Aubrey might, appallingly, be correct in his diagnosis.

"Maybe," was all he could find to say.

"I think we have to consider the possibility that what is happening up there –" he waved a hand at the top of the map-board " – is deliberate." He paused, but Clark said nothing. "We have no proof that there is a Soviet submarine in distress. It has stopped transmitting, and still no Russian vessel has gone in after it. But a great many Russian ships are concentrating in the area we know contains *Proteus*. If they *find* her – and they may be attempting to do just that – then we will have surrendered an almost priceless military advantage to them. If we lose Quin, too, then we will place ourselves in an abject position indeed."

Aubrey tapped at the surface of the commodore's desk, which he had had moved to a position beneath the map-board. As if the gesture was a summons, the telephone rang.

"Shelley, sir."

"Yes, Peter?"

"I've just been informed of a routine surveillance report from the DS team at the Russian embassy –"

"Yes, Peter?" Aubrey found it difficult to catch his breath.

"They think Petrunin left the embassy unofficially around five-thirty this evening."

"Where was he going?"

"I've checked that, sir. His numberplate was spotted heading north, I'm afraid, on the M1."

"Damn!" Aubrey's lips quivered with anger. "Thank you, Peter. You'd better inform Birmingham Special Branch. Get them over to that concert at the NEC – quickly!"

Aubrey put down the telephone.

"I guess I see what you mean," Clark said slowly. "Without even really noticing, we're down to the wire."

"I think we are. The KGB Resident wouldn't charge off unofficially without good cause or strong suspicion. Hyde couldn't have lost his trail. Damn that girl and her father!" He returned his attention to the map. The dot of the Nimrod was crossing the Arctic Circle. *Proteus* was surrounded. The *Kiev* was steaming at full speed to the Tanafjord, and the rescue ship *Karpaty* was on station. There really was no escaping the conclusion, and little chance of avoiding disaster. Aubrey felt very tired, entirely incompetent. "I think we have already lost, Ethan. This may be the view from the canvas, from the loser's corner."

"I hope to God you're wrong about that."

"I don't think I am."

The interference crackled in front of Ardenyev's voice, masking it

662

and giving it, to Dolohov's ears, a peculiarly unreal quality, as if the man were fading, becoming ethereal. Then Dolohov raised his voice, not to be heard but to remove the strange, uninvited perception; the whisper of failure.

"Get aboard the helicopters, Valery! You must transfer to the *Karpaty* now!"

"Sir, I'd really like you to have a word with one of the pilots –" Ardenyev's voice seemed more distant still, the storm smearing his words mockingly.

"No! It is too late for words! The traces are piling up. We're almost there." Dolohov looked round at Sergei, who stood obediently and silently at his elbow as he hunched over the table in front of the telephone amplifier. To Sergei, it seemed that the admiral was losing control, was dangerously elated by events, by the slipping, chasing minutes that passed and the sightings or partial and unconfirmable reports of the British submarine that kept coming in. The old man was racking them up like a score, mere multiplication stimulating his confidence and his arrogance. "We have them, Valery, in the palm of our hand. They're *ours*!"

"Sir, you don't seem to understand. It's a question of whether they can put us down on the deck of the rescue ship –"

"Don't argue with me, boy!" Dolohov thundered, his fist beating a counterpoint to his words on the surface of the table. "You have your orders – the pilots have their orders. You will board the helicopters at once and set course for the rescue ship. Understand?" There was a gap, then, of space and silence in which the storm hissed. "Do you hear me?"

"Yes, sir. Very good, sir. Your orders will be carried out, to the best of my abilities."

Dolohov was suddenly, manically expansive and generous. "Good boy, good boy. Good luck and good hunting. Over and out." The old man flicked off the telephone amplifier and stood up. He moved with some of the robotic jerkiness of arthritis battled and temporarily overcome; or the driven, muscular awkwardness of someone possessed of an unquenchable desire. He slapped his hand on Sergei's shoulder and the young man hoped that his smile did not appear too artificial. Dolohov looked at him, however, with eyes that had little perception in them. Not glazed or dulled, rather fierce and inward-looking. "The end-game, Sergei – the end-game," he murmured in a strange, ugly, caressing voice.

The rear admiral was punctilious, almost smirking, full of a bustle that had previously been absent. "Final positions, Admiral," he offered, indicating the computer print-out sheets in his hand.

"Good, good – come, let me see." He took the rear admiral's arm, ushering him to the window, clutching the sheets with his other hand. Sergei realised that the rear admiral had cast aside all doubts and reservations; whether from self-interest or because he had contracted the admiral's current illness, Sergei could not decide. Probably both. "Where?" They were at the window.

"There," the rear admiral proclaimed, histrionically waving his hand down towards the map-table. "*Kiev, Karpaty* on station waiting for Ardenyev, *Grishka* and the other submarines – see? There, there, there, there, there –" The finger jabbed out at each of the lights below. "The other units of the fleet in back-up positions, or sailing on deception courses." He looked at Dolohov. "It's up to them now. They have their orders. All they need is a positive ident on the British submarine."

Dolohov's face possessed a beatific expression. His eyes were almost closed. Sergei, embarrassed and disturbed, realized that it was a moment of love. The cold, stern, paternal admiral was unrecognizable. Sergei did not know, however, what it was that Dolohov embraced – this challenge, the drama of the moment, the prize, or the winning of the game. Perhaps even the game itself?

"Good, good," the old man murmured again. Then, suddenly, his eyes opened and all his attention was concentrated on the voice of one of the officers behind him in the control room.

"Submarine unit *Frunze* reports a magnetic contact –"

Dolohov was across the room and at the officer's shoulder with the speed and physical grace of a younger man. "Where?" he demanded. "What range?" Then, before the man could answer: "Can they lock on to her course?"

The communications officer listened to his headphones after repeating Dolohov's questions, and the old man could see his head begin to shake. "No, sir – they've lost it. Could have been sea temperature –"

"Rubbish. It was a *magnetic* contact, not infra-red! It was *them*, you idiot!" He turned to the rear admiral. "Order all submarine units to converge on the *Frunze* at once!"

"Admiral, is that –?"

"Do it."

"Very well, Admiral."

Dolohov walked aimlessly yet intently back to the window. He appeared to have little interest in the glowing map below him. The situation had been ingested in its entirety or – here Sergei corrected himself – perhaps it had always been in his head. Sergei half-listened to the rear admiral issuing a stream of orders, half-watched Dolohov, principally being aware of himself as an unimportant cipher, something like a parcel left in one corner of the room.

Then: "Submarine unit *Grishka* reports another magnetic trace –"

"Magnetic trace fading, Captain."
"Thermal trace fading, Captain."
"Planesman – ten degrees down, level at eight hundred feet."
"Sir."
"Steer twelve degrees to starboard."
"Sir."
There was silence in the control room of the *Grishka*. The bow sonars were blank and silent, their sensors absorbed or deflected by the British anti-sonar equipment. The infra-red trace was decaying, was already almost non-existent, illusory. The magnetic anomaly detection equipment was already inducing a frustrated hunching of the shoulders in its operator. The advanced, delicate, heat-sensitive "nose" was sniffing cold ocean water without trace of the British submarine. Every trail was cold, or growing cold.
"Steer fifteen degrees to port."
"Sir."
Guesswork, the captain of the *Grishka* admitted. A blind dog with a cold in its nose seeking an elusive scent. No prop wash even, not a trace of the trail she ought to be leaving in the sea from her movement and her turning propeller. They had picked that up once before, then lost it again.
"Nine knots."
"Sir."
Silence.
"Weak magnetic trace, sir. Bearing green four-oh, range six thousand."
"We're almost on top of her – don't lose it. Steer starboard thirty."
"Starboard thirty, sir."
"No thermal trace, sir."
"Magnetic trace fading again, sir."
"Stand by, torpedo room. Any sign of prop wash?"
"Negative, sir."
"Steer starboard five, speed ten knots."
"Magnetic trace lost, sir."
"Damn!"

"Steer port four-five."
"Port four-five it is, sir."
There was silence then in the control room of the *Proteus*. Whispered orders, like the rustling voices of old men, lacking authority. The sonars which, in their passive mode, were difficult for any enemy

to detect with his electronic sensors, registered the movements of the Russian submarine; demonstrating the proximity of the hunter.

"Computer ident, Number One?"

"A 'Victor-II' class submarine, sir. Our friend is back."

"Range and bearing?"

"Moving away, sir. Speed approximately nine knots, range eight thousand, bearing green one-seven-oh. She's passing behind us."

"Other activity, John?"

" 'Kashin' class destroyer, range eleven thousand. 'Alpha' class attack submarine, range fourteen thousand, bearing red six-five, and closing. *Kiev* at range sixteen thousand, and increasing. The submarine rescue ship is holding station, sir."

"Coffee, sir?"

"What – oh, thanks, chief. ETA Norwegian waters, John?"

"At present course and speed, eleven minutes, sir."

"Speed fourteen knots."

"Prop wash, sir?"

"Correction – twelve knots."

"Twelve knots it is, sir."

"Steer port ten."

The transmissions from the *Grishka* and the other Red Banner units were being received via the aircraft carrier *Kiev*. Dolohov had ordered the abandonment of coded signals in favour of high-speed, frequency-agile transmissions in plain language. Transferred to tape and slowed down, Dolohov then heard them broadcast in the control room. The voices, and the silences between the words, seemed equally to agitate and excite him. Sergei observed his admiral closely, worriedly. He felt like a youthful relative watching a grandparent growing senile before his eyes.

Dolohov's shoulders were hunched as he stared down into the well of the operations room, watching the moving, dancing lights and the flickering, single light that represented the British submarine. It flickered on and off as if there were an electrical fault in the board.

Sergei guessed that Dolohov had begun to entertain doubts; or rather, the doubts he had formerly crushed beneath the heel of certainty had now sprung up again like weeds. It was more than an hour since the first contact signal had been received from the submarine *Frunze*. Since then, the *Grishka* and two other units had reported traces on more than one occasion – *Grishka* three times – but the British submarine still eluded them. Dolohov had been able to ignore his doubts for hours, even days; but now, watching the cat-and-invisible-mouse game on the board below him, he had begun to disbelieve in success. Or so Sergei suspected.

The old man was talking to himself. His voice, in the silence from the loudspeaker, was audible throughout the room.

"Can it be done, can it be done?" He repeated it again and again, a murmured plea or a voiced fear. "Can it? Can it?" The shorter phrase became more final, more full of doubt. "Can it? Can it?" The old man was entirely unaware that he was speaking audibly, and Sergei felt a hot flush of shame invade his features. To be associated with this old man, muttering to himself in this moment of crisis like a geriatric in a hospital, was embarrassing, insulting. Others were listening, everyone in the room –

Then the voice of the monitoring officer on the *Kiev* silenced Dolohov, smearing across his words, erasing them. The admiral's shoulders picked up, his head inclined like a bird's as he listened.

"Submarine unit *Grishka* reports lost contact – "

Dolohov's shoulders slumped again. It was evident he thought he had lost the game.

"The 'Victor-II' is turning to starboard, sir."

"Damn. John, insert our track and that of the 'Victor-II' onto the display screen."

"Track memory is on, sir. Submarine bearing red one-six-eight, range nineteen thousand."

"Do we still have that layer of warmer water below us?"

"Yes, sir."

"Right. Let's make it much more difficult for them. Take us down through it."

"Aye, aye, sir."

Lloyd sensed the dipping of the *Proteus*'s bow. The Russian submarine was on their tail again. They were still three minutes out into international waters, and the "Victor-II" was closing rapidly. Even though he doubted now that an imagined political line on a chart would have any beneficial effect on their circumstances, Lloyd knew of no other move he could make. The display screen traced their track over the seabed, and that of the Russian. A swifter-moving, hazy line of light was dead astern of them now that the Russian captain had altered course.

"Information on the 'Victor-II' becoming unreliable, sir."

"I can see that. The warmer layer's causing ghosting and refracting. Are we through it yet?"

"Yes, sir."

"Level at eighty fathoms, cox'n."

"Eighty fathoms, sir."

"Is that the coast at the edge of the screen, John?"

"No, sir." Thurston was at his side, staring down at the screen. The image of the Russian submarine was faint. The warmer layer of sea water through which they had descended would be confusing the Russian's sensors, hiding the *Proteus*. "It's a small plateau. Our depth makes it look like a mountain."

" 'Victor-II' now bearing green one-seven-oh, range fourteen thousand, and she's in a shallow dive, sir."

Thurston looked into Lloyd's face. "We didn't fool her. She's back with us," he whispered.

"The computer confirms course and bearing, sir."

Lloyd hesitated for only a moment. Then a tight determination clamped on his features. He had accepted the evidence of his sonars and his computers.

"John," he said in a steady voice audible to everyone in the control room, "call the crew to Alert Readiness. The time for playing games with this Russian is over. He's after us, all right."

"Aye, aye, sir."

"Negative contact on magnetic, Captain."

"Maintain present course for one minute, then hard starboard – mark."

"Marked, Captain. One minute."

"Negative contact, sir."

Always the negative. The Russian captain sensed the *Grishka* around him, slipping through the blind darkness of the sea. He sensed the crew closed up to Action Stations, as they had been for more than half an hour on this occasion alone; and three other times he had spoken to the torpedo room, readying them, and calling his men to Action Stations. It could not go on for much longer, he would have to relax them. He was wearing them down. He sensed, especially, the torpedo crew room and the wire-guided, wake-homing torpedoes, one with reduced warhead and the second with the special MIRV warhead, the "Catherine Wheel". Once he ordered their launch, one expert crewman would guide them to their target, relying solely on his own skills. His man was good enough, and the torpedoes would do their job. Yet everything – *everything* – depended on tiny, delicate sensors in the bow of the boat; magnetic sensors, thermal sensors. Somewhere ahead – or below or beside or above or behind – there was a magnetic lump of metal which was emitting heat and which could not be entirely damped and rendered invisible. The British submarine was leaving faint traces, flakings of her skin, faint noises of her breathing. Somewhere in the ocean, those traces lay waiting for him to discover them.

"Coming hard round, Captain."

"Planesman – hold her steady."

"Sir."

Somewhere, out there in the dark, lay the *Proteus*.

"Sir, the 'Victor-II' is coming hard round –"
"I have her. Engine room – plus fifty revolutions."
"Plus fifty, sir."

"Heat trace confirmed and growing stronger, Captain."
"Ten degree quarter – sixty second rate."
The captain of the *Grishka* leaned against the periscope housing. The range of the British submarine was still too great, and though the trace was strengthening it was still elusive. The game might continue for hours yet. He sensed the pressure on him not to fail, but more importantly he was aware of the growing, slightly desperate need for action in himself and his crew. His loyalty was, therefore, to the stifled, tense atmosphere of his control room.

"Torpedo room," he said distinctly, pausing until everyone was alert with attention to his voice, despite their own tasks. "Torpedo room, load manual guidance torpedo, set it for a screw-pattern search. Set maximum range and wait for my order."

There was relief, palpable as cold, fresh air, in the set of every man's shoulders and on every face that he could see. He kept a sudden assault of doubt from his own features.

"Heat trace strengthening, Captain."
"Magnetic trace positive, Captain."
"Sonars negative, Captain."
"Range and bearing?"
"Bearing unchanged, sir. Range thirteen thousand, and decreasing. We're overhauling her, sir."
"Very well." He paused. The low-warhead torpedo was in the tube. He had four of them, and four multiple-warhead "Catherine Wheel" torpedoes. Could he risk the first one at that range? "Torpedo room – fire One! Keep calling."
"Tube One away, sir, and running. Sensor on, lights green. Negative readout."

The Russian captain looked at his first lieutenant standing at the depth indicator panel. He shrugged expressively.

"Torpedo sensors have made contact, Captain."

The wake-homing torpedo began its search immediately it was launched. The wire that connected it with the *Grishka* transmitted to its tiny computer the instructions of the experienced operator in the torpedo room. Its guidance control was tested, and responded, then the speed of the torpedo was altered a number of times in quick succession. On each occasion, the torpedo responded immediately and precisely.

The torpedo crossed the traces of the *Proteus*'s wake one thousand metres from the *Grishka*. Its corkscrewing movement through the sea, which enabled it to search in three rather than in two dimensions, took it across the wake well astern of the British submarine's position. There was, however, sufficient trace of the wake remaining for the torpedo to register it.

The torpedo nosed on through the dark water until it reached the conclusion of its next one thousand metre run, then it began retracing its course, back towards the wake. Once it crossed the wake for the second time, and its sensors registered either a stronger or a weaker trace, then it would be instructed to turn to port or starboard, and to run down the submarine's track until it made contact. Once its path was chosen, and the wake's direction established, contact was unavoidable.

The torpedo crossed the wake and turned to port almost immediately with a flick as lithe as that of some hunting sea creature. Its corkscrewing track evened out as it began tracing its way down the wake of the British submarine.

"Contact continuous, Captain."

"Excellent – keep calling." The captain of the *Grishka* grinned at his first lieutenant.

"Lock on indicated . . . three thousand five hundred metres of run completed, sir . . . four thousand metres completed . . . heat sensor responding and locked on . . . command override on, sir . . . proximity fuse armed and *on*, sir . . . seven thousand metres of run completed . . . TV camera on, light on –"

"Come on, come on," the Russian captain murmured. Too long, too long, he told himself. Should have waited, she's out of range.

"Seven and one half thousand metres of run completed, sir . . . eight thousand metres of run completed."

"Positive contact, sir!"

"Cox'n hard astern!"

"Hard astern, sir."

"Contact identified as a torpedo, sir!"

On the tiny television monitor in the *Grishka*, receiving pictures from the camera in the nose of the torpedo, there was nothing more than a weakly illuminated rush of grey water, almost like a heavy, dull curtain being continually whisked aside. Then there was a blur of darker water, then the grey, whale-like shape of the *Proteus* as the

British submarine began her turn. The torpedo seemed to dip towards the submarine, strangely hesitant, and the proximity fuse detonated the reduced warhead. The television screen at which the captain of the *Grishka* stared went blank, making him wince as if the flash of the explosion had been visible and had startled, even blinded him.

"Target acquired, Captain! Hit, hit, hit!"

"We've got her?"

"Direct hit, Captain!"

There was cheering, which he immediately silenced.

"Torpedo room, load Two. Multiple warhead torpedo, set range at nine thousand. Manual guidance, direct search track."

"Tube Two ready, Captain."

"Fire Two!"

"Planesman, check that roll!"

"– can't hold the turn –"

"Emergency lights – cancel –"

"Can't hold the trim, sir!"

"Trim responding, sir."

"Engines down one-fifty revolutions."

"The dampers aren't controlling the oscillation, sir."

"All stations – immediate damage report." Lloyd wiped a hand across his forehead, his eyes riveted on the forearms of the two planesmen as they struggled to right the trim of the *Proteus*. The muscles flexed and strained, veins standing out, the tattoo of an anchor and chain livid on one of the arms. The whole submarine was oscillating wildly, like a bicycle out of control, a child in the saddle, feet unable to reach the pedals. The lights had come back on. His arm felt nerveless and weak as his thoughts churned like his stomach, over and over, and fused into a circuit. The Russians had fired on them, fired on them . . . Thurston crossed the vibrating control room towards him and lurched against the periscope housing, where he clung unsteadily. "Christ, John – they fired on us!"

Thurston's face confirmed the inadmissible. Enemy action.

"Chief engineer, sir," Lloyd heard over the control room speaker.

"Yes, Chief?"

"Initial damage report suggests external impact, sir. Pressure hull OK, outer plates and aft ballast tanks ruptured. Planes and rudders misaligned, but responding, sir. The vibration we're experiencing is linked to our revs, so there must be prop damage. Or maybe it's the shaft. Or both. The main shaft bearings are heating up."

"Can we still remain under way, Chief?"

"I think so, sir. We'll have to try various rev settings to find an optimum for remaining under way with least vibration and some

671

degree of control. We may be lucky, if the bearings don't get too hot. They're in the orange now, sir."

"Very well, Chief. In your hands."

"Aye, aye, sir."

The multiple-warhead torpedo tracked down the wake of the *Proteus*, following the range and bearing instructions fed into its tiny computer. It, too, was armed with a proximity fuse. The Red Navy's experts had concluded that a reduced warhead, although capable of damaging the *Proteus*, might not have sufficient stopping-power to render the British nuclear submarine immobile, which condition was essential to the success of the operation. Therefore, an experimental multiple-warhead, code-named "Catherine Wheel", had been hurried through its last stages of development and its laboratory and sea trials, to fulfil the preliminary work of the reduced-warhead torpedo that would cripple, but not ensnare, the *Proteus*.

The TV camera switched on at an instruction from the torpedo room operator, and the light came on at the same moment. On the tiny screen, the Russian captain watched the swirling rush of water, and thought he detected the bubbles and general disturbance of the *Proteus*'s wake. He tensed himself, almost as if he had been riding the torpedo like a horse, then the grey-black, whale-backed shape of the submarine emerged from the darkness of the sea. He imagined – saw? – the damage to the rudder and the hydroplanes, and bent his head and cocked it to one side in order to perceive the outline of the stern more easily. Then the warhead detonated, and to his intense disappointment the TV screen went blank. Memory continued the succession of images.

He had seen the "Catherine Wheel" in operation on an old sub during trials. The film had been poor, grainy and cut-about, but the images had been stark, vivid, deadly. When the separate warheads split from the body of the torpedo, they would whirl and spin and weave outwards in a net-like circle. Some of them carried small explosive charges, some barbed hooks of super-strengthened steel, some suction caps or magnets. Twelve in all, each of them trailed a length of toughened steel cable, whipped into a frenzy of whirling movement by the spinning-top effect of the small war-heads. Two, three, four or more of these would make contact with the hull and rudder and hydroplanes of the *Proteus* and, as the submarine moved forward under power, the trailing, whipping steel cables would slash at the hull, be dragged with it, and would fasten and entangle the propellers, twisting tighter and tighter like strangling cords.

It would take no more than seconds, and little more than a minute to halt the submarine, her propeller bound and made immovable by the entangled steel cables.

He closed his eyes, seeing the drama on an inward screen, himself seated in the darkness of the briefing room as the film was shown. He did not hear, did not need to hear the exultant cry from the torpedo room, nor the cheering in his control room. He awoke when his first lieutenant shook his elbow, startling him. The young man was grinning.

"Direct hit, sir. Another direct hit!" he bubbled.

"Good," the captain said slowly. "Well done, everyone." He stood upright. Already, the British submarine would be slowing, her crew terrified by the vibration as the cables tightened against the revolutions of the propeller, strangling it. "Very well. Send up an aerial buoy. Transmit the following message, Lieutenant. Message begins TOLSTOY, followed by target impact co-ordinates. Message ends. Direct to Murmansk, code priority nine."

"Yes, sir!"

"Retrieve the aerial buoy as soon as the transmission ends."

"It's no good, sir," Lloyd heard the voice of the chief engineer saying, "that second impact has either damaged the prop even further, or we're entangled in something." Lloyd was shuddering with the vibration, and the noise of the protesting propeller and shaft was threatening to burst his skull. It was impossible to stand it for much longer. The submarine was slowing, the prop grinding more and more slowly. The Russians had done something, caught them in a net or some similar trap, choking them.

"Very well, Chief." He could not utter the words clearly, only in an old man's quaver because of the shudder in the hull which was worsening with every passing second. He shouted his orders above the noises. They were in a biscuit tin, and someone was beating on the lid with an iron bar. "First Lieutenant." Thurston nodded, holding onto the depth indicator panel, his legs as unreliable as those of a drunk. "John. I want a reading of the bottom as soon as we're over that plateau. If we find a flat bit, set her down!"

"Aye, aye, sir!"

The tension in the control room, even though it remained filled and shaken by the increasing vibration, dispelled for a moment. He'd done what they expected of him, demanded of him. The two planesmen struggled with increasing difficulty, veins proud like small blue snakes on their skin, muscles tight and cramped with the strain. They had to slow down, stop.

"Captain to all crew!" he yelled into his microphone, which jiggled in his hand. "Prepare for bottoming and maintain for silent

673

running!" Silence. A bad joke. The protest of the propeller, the shaft, the bearings drummed in his head.

"Lieutenant, come about and set up another sweep pattern two thousand metres to the east. Sensor control – no relaxation. We *can't* have lost her! She's here somewhere. Keep looking."

"Well done, John." Lloyd tried to lighten the sudden, sombre silence. "Light as a feather." No one smiled. The tension in the control room tightened again like a thong around his temples. The din had ceased, the torture of the prop and shaft was over. Yet the silence itself pressed down on them like a great noise. "All non-essential services off. Stand down non-operational crew and safety men. Get the galley to lay on some food."

"Hayter to Captain."

"Yes, Don?"

"The 'Victor-II' is still sniffing around, but I think she's lost us for the moment."

"Good news, Don."

The lights blinked off, to be replaced by the emergency lighting. The submarine seemed to become quieter, less alive, around him. They were more than twenty fathoms down on a ledge jutting out from the Norwegian coast, and the Russians would now be looking for them, more determined than ever.

PART TWO

SEARCH AND RESCUE

SIX:

Lost

Part of him, immediately he left the warmth of the headquarters building, wanted to respond to the driving sleet and the howling wind and the lights of the port of Pechenga gleaming fitfully like small, brave candles in the white-curtained darkness. He wanted the weather not to be critical, merely something to be endured, even enjoyed. Instead, there was the immediate sense of danger, as if a palpable, armed enemy was closing at his back. He turned up the collar of his heavy jacket, and crossed the gleaming concrete, slippery already, to the waiting car.

His driver was a *michman* – petty officer – from Pechenga base security, and he saluted despite the fact that Ardenyev was not in uniform. His face was cold and washed-out and expressionless in the purpling light of the lamps. Ardenyev had the strange and unsettling impression of death. Then the driver opened the rear door of the Zil staff car, and the momentary feeling evaporated.

The car wound swiftly down from the hump of higher ground on which the Red Banner Fleet's headquarters in Pechenga stood, towards the port and the naval helicopter base. Lights out in the roads, the glare of the arc-lamps from the repair yards, the few commercial and pleasure streets sodium-lit and neon-garish, like the stilled arms of light from a lighthouse.

Ardenyev was disturbed by Dolohov's manic desire for success. The admiral had never been careless of risks before. This adventure with the British submarine obsessed him. He knew the details of the met reports as well as anyone, and yet he ignored them. Ardenyev had, on his own authority, delayed his departure for the rescue ship out in the darkness of the Barents because of the worsening conditions. Delayed, that is, until further postponement would have meant running behind the schedule of the operation; and that he was not prepared to do. Instead, he nursed his conviction that Dolohov was unjustified in ordering them out.

It was cold in the back of the staff car despite the powerful, dusty-smelling heater. Ardenyev rubbed his hands together to warm them. Then the staff car slid under the canopy of white light of the helicopter base and the driver wound down the window to present his pass to the naval guard at the gate. The guard took one swift look at Ardenyev, the cold air blanching his face from the open window, more out of curiosity than to identify him. Then the heavy wire-mesh gates swung open, and the driver wound up the window as they pulled forward. The car turned left, and they were passing hangars and repair shops where warmer light gleamed through open doors. Then a patch of darkness, then the sleet rushing at the windscreen again. Through it, Ardenyev could see the two helicopters, red lights winking at tail and belly. Two MiL-2 light transport helicopters, the only naval helicopters in current service small enough to land on the seemingly fragile, circular helicopter pad of the rescue ship *Karpaty*.

The car stopped almost in the shadow of one of the small helicopters. Snub-nosed, insect-like, frail. Ardenyev thanked the driver abstractedly, and got out of the car. The sudden wind and cold sleet did not drive out the unwelcome, crowding impressions that seemed to have taken possession of his imagination, leading into the rational part of his mind, polluting clear thought. The Zil staff car pulled away behind him.

"You changed your mind then, skipper – decided to come?" came a voice from the door of the MiL. A grinning, cold-pinched face, blown fair hair above a dark naval jersey. Senior Lieutenant Andrei Orlov, Ardenyev's second-in-command and leader of Blue section of the special operations unit. Ardenyev summoned a wave he hoped was optimistic, then looked up at the sky, wrinkling his face.

"The pilot's moaning about the weather, skipper," Orlov added. "It's just having to turn out in this muck, I reckon."

Orlov took Ardenyev's arm, and he swung up into the hollow, ribbed interior of the helicopter. The door slammed shut behind him. Someone groaned with the cold. Young faces, five others besides Orlov. Blue section. Ardenyev nodded at them, business-like. Then he clambered through into the helicopter's cabin. The pilot nodded to him. His face was disgruntled.

"Get your clearance – we're on our way," Ardenyev told him, "just as soon as I get aboard your pal's chopper. Take care." Already, the inertia of the mission had affected him, sweeping him along like a current growing stronger each moment. An easy and familiar adrenalin invested his body. His mind was clear now. He clambered back into the passenger compartment. "OK, you lot?" Each man nodded. Most of them grinned, nerves flickering like small electric shocks in their faces and arms. "Good. See you on the *Karpaty*. Open the door, Andrei."

The door slid back, and Ardenyev dropped lightly to the ground. He crossed the patch of wet, slippery concrete to the next pad, and the door of the second MiL opened with a screech. The senior *michman* who was his deputy leader in Red section hauled him aboard, wiping sleet from his jacket even as he slammed the door shut behind Ardenyev.

"Thought you weren't coming, sir," he offered. His face was bony and angular beneath the cropped hair. Viktor Teplov.

"Thanks Viktor. Lieutenant Orlov thought just the same." He looked round at the other five men, grinning. One or two older faces. Red section was the senior team in the unit. The faces were as they should be. A couple of good youngsters, too. "Everyone keeping warm?"

"With difficulty, sir," Teplov answered.

"Let's get going, then." He clambered through to the passenger seat beside the pilot. "Very well, Lieutenant, shall we proceed?" he said as he strapped himself into the seat.

"You're going to be very lucky, Captain, to get down onto the *Karpaty*. The weather out there is worse than this."

"I have implicit faith in your skills, Lieutenant." He gestured towards the windscreen of the helicopter where two huge wiper blades and the de-icing equipment struggled with the sleet. "Shall we go? I take it you're cleared for take-off?"

"We are. We've been waiting an hour, fully cleared."

"What's the matter, Lieutenant?"

"I've told my superiors – I've told anyone who will listen."

"Told them what?"

"The wind is force four plus. What if we can't get down, just can't make it?"

"The *Kiev*, I suppose. Why?"

"Let's hope it's not too bad for the *Kiev*, then. The range of this chopper means that once we get out there, we haven't enough fuel to get back. You should be in a MiL-8, one of the big boys, all of you. They shouldn't have assigned this –"

"Shouldn't have assigned you, you mean? Two small, light helicopters were requested. The rescue ship contains all our equipment. The *Kiev*'s no good to us. MiL-8s can't land on the *Karpaty*. Now, we can go?"

"All right. Just wanted you to know."

"I'm grateful."

The pilot lieutenant cleared with the tower. Ardenyev settled himself more comfortably in his narrow seat. The two Isotov turbo-shafts began to whine, and above his head the rotor blades quick-ened, cutting through the sleet, swirling until they were transformed into a shimmering dish. The lieutenant altered the angle of the rotor blades, the engine pitch changed to a higher note, and the helicopter moved off its chocks. The pilot paused, checking his instruments, the wheels of the MiL were just in contact with the ground. The pilot's knuckle was white on the stick.

"The wind," the pilot observed gloomily.

"Yes."

The MiL lifted, with seeming reluctance, from the patch of concrete. The sleet whirled round them in the downdraught. A fist of wind swung at them, made contact, knocked them sideways. The pilot shuffled his feet on the rudder bar, juggled the stick and they steadied, drifted, steadied again, and rose above the lights of the helicopter base. A white dish beneath them, darkness above.

"See what I mean?" the pilot offered. "We're right on the edge of possible flying conditions." The wind buffeted them. It seemed a physical strain on the pilot to maintain course. It had seemed a struggle to alter the stick and head the MiL out to sea, as if the helicopter was some reluctant, untamed animal.

"Yes, I see," Ardenyev replied thoughtfully. "Is our fellow traveller with us?"

The pilot looked in his mirror, then spoke into his throat-mike. The other pilot's voice was a pinched, unreal sound.

"He's there."

A shudder ran through the fuselage, as if it had received a powerful blow, some direct hit with a weapon.

Hyde opened his eyes. For a moment, Shelley's features were unfamiliar. Then he recognised Aubrey's aide, and attempted to sit up. Pain shot through his ribs, and his back, and he groaned. Hands pushed him back down on the hard bed. He could feel the thin, hard, uncomfortable blanket beneath his fingers, and he wiggled his toes, eyes very tightly shut for a moment until he opened them in relief.

"You're all right," Shelley said. "God knows how, but you're just bruised pretty badly."

His neck and shoulder ached more than his back and ribs. "One of them hit me," he complained.

"We assumed that was the case. It's why you've been out so long."

"How long?"

"Almost four hours."

"Christ." He covered his face with his hands, as if the light hurt him or he was ashamed. "Jesus, my head."

"I caught the end of the concert. Mine feels much the same."

"Very funny."

"Who was it – Petrunin?"

Hyde's eyes snapped open. "How did you know?"

680

"Routine surveillance report on the embassy. Unauthorised trip north by the Resident. It had to be you and the girl."

"I saw him." Hyde saw Shelley motioning towards another part of the narrow, cream-painted room. A door closed. Shelley's face appeared above his own again, and then he was being helped to sit up. Shelley proffered a mug of tea. Hyde sipped the sweet, scalding liquid, hands clasped round the mug as if to warm them. "I almost had her." They were alone in the room now. "I'm all right?"

Shelley nodded. "You're all right – just a bit crook."

"I feel it. The girl panicked. She's like something high on LSD. Seems to think they're coming out of the woodwork for her."

"She's right."

"That bloody rock band. They got in the way."

"Where do you think she is? Do you think they've got her?"

"I don't know. She could be anywhere." Hyde concentrated. "I got the impression Petrunin had gone back off the platform – the bloke who clobbered me was being pushed towards the steps – the girl was down the other end of the platform. One of them went after her. He might have made it."

"By the time I got here, they'd all disappeared. No one saw the girl."

"Shit."

"I know."

"What does Aubrey want us to do?"

"He's otherwise occupied. He's taken control of the submarine business. He seems to think it's in a hell of a mess."

"He's got the set now, then. It's all a bloody mess."

"Where is she, Patrick? If she isn't at the embassy or one of their safe houses? I've got everything I can screened. They won't be able to get her out – I hope. If they want to, that is. But if she's free, where is she?"

"Why not Heat of the Day? It's where she ran for help and cover in the first place? She might have nowhere else to go."

"The group?"

"Yes."

'Where are they?"

Hyde groaned as he swung his legs off the bed and sat up. He touched his ribs gingerly. "Are they sure nothing's broken?"

"Quite sure."

"Free Trade Hall, Manchester, is their next venue. Where they're staying tonight, I've no idea. Maybe here?"

Shelley shook his head. "Not here. Some country hotel in Cheshire. I'm having it checked out."

"You won't find the girl. She won't stick her neck out again. They could even have hidden her somewhere. She'll go to ground for the duration if the Branch trample all over the garden in their big boots."

"You can't do it by yourself."

Hyde rubbed his neck and shoulder, groaning softly. Then he looked into Shelley's face. "I'll accept discreet cover, but nothing more. The girl doesn't believe me as it is. If I go in mob-handed, she'll never tell us where Dad is. You can see that, can't you?"

"Aubrey wouldn't like it."

"He might. The girl is frightened. She knows one mob is after her, one mob and me on my own. Give me until tomorrow night, and if I can find her and talk to her, she might come in. I won't lose her again."

"Petrunin won't let go of you."

"All right. But the girl's more important. It won't be any good arresting a rock band and sweating the lot of them. She has to be coaxed. She's near panic. Her father must be a mistrusting bastard. She's neurotic about us."

Shelley paced the room, one hand rubbing his chin, the other thrust into the pocket of his overcoat. He glanced at Hyde from time to time. Indecision blossomed on his face. Eventually, he said: "I don't know – I just don't know."

"Look, you work on the assumption that Petrunin has her, and I'll work on the assumption he hasn't. Get back to London and mobilize the troops. I'll go up to Manchester, and sit on my arse and wait. Get me cover, *discreet* cover, from the Branch up there, and then let me try to get to the girl. If she isn't in Manchester, and they won't tell me where she is, then you can take over. OK?"

"All right," Shelley said after another lengthy pause. "All right. We'll do it your way, for the moment."

"At least I'm a familiar face."

"You won't be if you get knocked about any more." He glanced at the telephone on a folding table, next to a black medical bag. "I'll try to talk to Aubrey, though. I want him to be fully informed."

It was a tableau of activity, a frozen still-life of tension, fear close to panic, routine and emergency procedures. In other parts of the submarine, men lay in their bunks or sat on the floor. No one moved unless movement was unavoidable and essential to the survival of the *Proteus*. In the control room, men stood or sat as their functions dictated, and when they moved – which was rarely, and with Lloyd's express permission – it was with an exaggerated, burglar-like stealth. All unnecessary electrics had been switched off, and the control room was made eerie by the emergency lighting. Only Lloyd stalked the control room like a hunter, like an escapee.

682

The sonars, in passive mode, their screens illuminating the faces of their operators from beneath, making arms and chins and cheeks blue or green or red, a ghastly imitation of disco strobe-lights, revealed the *Proteus*'s danger. Under the cloak of "Leopard" the submarine lay on the ledge almost fifty fathoms down, while Soviet submarines moved back and forth around, below and above them like prowling sharks outside a diver's cage. As Lloyd watched over the shoulder of one of the sonar operators, a bright trail on the screen slid slowly to the port like the hand of a clock, mere hundreds of yards from their position. Noise – any noise – would be like blood to that shark, and bring the others.

Lloyd left the screen and stood beneath one of the emergency lights. Once more, he scanned the damage report that his chief engineer had compiled in silence and semi-darkness. They had not dared send a diver outside the hull, outside the cloak of the anti-sonar. Much of it was guesswork, or deduced from the instruments and the computer. The damage was relatively slight, but almost totally disabling. Thurston and the chief engineer had guessed at a low-charge torpedo – wake-homing, as they had known in those last seconds before it struck – which had damaged the propeller blades and the port aft hydroplane. It left the *Proteus* with no effective propulsion, and little ability to maintain course and depth. She needed repairs before she could go anywhere. And in that conclusion, Lloyd perceived the Russian objective.

He was calm. It was partly an act for the benefit of the crew, and yet it was genuine, too. He had not known he would react in this way, in harm's way. It had little to do with the fact that the pressure hull remained undamaged, or with the invisibility bestowed by "Leopard". It was, simply, him. He had no inclination to curse MoD or to blame himself for not aborting the mission hours earlier. The past, even as recently as two hours before, was dead to him. The Russians did not know where they were and, eventually, help must come – diplomatic, military, civilian, mechanical, political.

Thurston left the navigator and Hayter, who was taking a much needed break from monitoring the functioning of "Leopard", and crossed the control room. In his hand he had a notebook and pen. He held it up to Lloyd.

Thurston had written: *What do we do?* Lloyd merely shook his head. Thurston was puzzled, then scribbled furiously on a fresh sheet of the notebook: *We have to tell someone.* Lloyd took a pen from his breast pocket, and borrowed Thurston's notebook. He scribbled: *And tell them where we are?* Thurston – Lloyd could not help being amused by the pantomime they were enacting – wrote: *Must be Nimrod in area by now.*

We can't transmit. Too risky. Lloyd scribbled.

They want "Leopard" – but how? Thurston wrote.
Salvage?

They couldn't, Thurston began writing, then his hand trailed off to the edge of the sheet. Savagely, he crossed out what he had written. Defiantly, he wrote: *Have to find us first*. Lloyd patted his shoulder, then wrote: *Only a few days*.

The sudden noise was deafening, literally terrifying to every man in the control room. It was more than two seconds before the rating at the code-signals console cut the amplification with a hand that dabbed out, as if electrified, at the switch. He stared at Lloyd guiltily, afraid, his youthful face behind his ginger beard blushing. Lloyd tiptoed across to him, his whole body shaking with reaction. The chatter of a high-speed coded signal, incoming. The rating removed his headphones, offering them like a propitiation to Lloyd, something to avert his wrath. Lloyd pressed him, firmly but not unkindly, on the shoulder, and held the headphones to one ear. He nodded, as if deciphering the signal for himself, or hearing an instruction in plain language. The rating flicked switches, and waited. His screen remained blank. Lloyd watched it, looking into a mirror, a crystal ball. Thurston arrived behind him, his breath ragged and only now slowing down. Lloyd felt the tension in the control room of the shrilling chatter of the signal, and the awareness of the Russians beyond the hull, and the knowledge that the signal was continuing. It crawled on his skin like St. Elmo's Fire, or a disturbed nest of ants.

The screen displayed a line of white print. A message buoy. Thurston nudged Lloyd, and mouthed *Nimrod*, and Lloyd nodded. The code identification then appeared, deciphered. *MoD*, then the placing of the security level of the instructions. *ETNA*. Lloyd looked startled. A civilian override by the intelligence service. The comprehension of their danger by some outside authority made him feel weak. They had known, had tried –

The message unreeled on the screen, line by line, then began to repeat itself. *Abort the mission, return to home waters immediate. ETNA. ETNA. Acknowledge, code 6F, soonest. Compliance immediate –*

Compliance impossible. Someone had known, someone in SIS or the Directorate of Security or the CIA, or the Norwegians, the Germans, the Dutch – someone somewhere had known, or suspected, and had tried to warn them, recall them. The knowledge was like a debilitating illness.

There was a Nimrod in the area, on-station. It would, perhaps, wait for an acknowledgement. It would, doubtless, remain on-station to monitor Soviet naval activity. Such would be its orders. It was up there, somewhere.

Signal, Lloyd wrote on Thurston's pad. The rating watched the screen.

684

The message began repeating for the third time. Lloyd reached out, flicked a switch angrily, and the screen darkened. The rating's shoulders hunched as if against a blow from behind.

You can't, Thurston had written by the time Lloyd looked back at the pad. The two men stared at one another, their faces seeming agonised in the dimness of the emergency lights.

Lloyd crossed the control room. Four trails of light, not one of them more than a mile-and-a-half from the ledge on which they lay. Four hunter-killer submarines, waiting for the blood that would spur them, fix the position of *Proteus*. That blood might be any noise, even the sonar shadow of the aerial buoy they would have to send to the surface to contact the Nimrod.

You can't.

Lloyd realized he still had Thurston's pad in his hand. He dare not, in his anger, tear out the sheet or throw down the pad. It would not make a detectable noise. Yet he did not dare.

In how many rooms had he waited, on how many occasions? Clocks. How many clocks? So many of them with large, plain faces and a red sweeping second hand. Arms that clicked onto the next minute. Clocks. The persistence of memory. Even now, there was no clarity to his thoughts, no cleanness. Only the many other occasions on which he had endured the same, endless waiting.

Aubrey sighed. He had not been aware of the number of clocks in the underground room until all the protocol had been observed and Brussels and Washington and MoD had agreed to his assumption of complete authority over the safe return of the *Proteus*. Furious telephone and signal activity, followed by a post-coital lassitude, restlessness. Waiting for the Nimrod's report, waiting then for the first safe occasion when the submarine could send an aerial buoy to the surface and answer their peremptory summons home. Until a certain time had passed – the remainder of that night, perhaps the next day, too – they could make no assumptions. Nor would they be able to prevent dread from flourishing like a noxious weed in each of their minds.

Aubrey knew it, understood the Soviet scheme in its entirety. Daring, almost foolhardy, reckless, extreme. But possible of fulfilment. "Leopard" as the prize. Clark, too, he knew agreed with his insight. He had not asked the American; he had asked no one. He stared at the cup of coffee in his hand, and found its surface grey. His watch peeped like a rising, ominous sun over the curve of his wrist, from beneath his shirt-cuff. He ignored it.

He had never been interested in seconds, in the sweep of the quick hand. Blister or burn operations that relied on that kind of exactitude had never been his forte. Yet he had waited longer, and more often. Back rooms of empty buildings near the Wall, with the rats scampering behind the skirting-board and the peeling wallpaper; or beneath the slowly revolving ceiling-fans, in hotel rooms with geckos chasing insects up the walls or places where, with the fan less effective against even hotter nights, crickets chorused outside; or with windows fugged by the warmth of wood-burning stoves, and wooden walls; and so many embassy basements and signals rooms, and so many rooms like this, in London and a dozen other cities. Memory's persistence, its retained vivacity, wearied and oppressed him.

Shelley's telephone call was, perhaps, the worst moment; the small, personal act of spite or neglect amid a more general ruin. Of course Hyde was correct – he must reach the girl himself, if they were not only to possess her, but to possess her confidence also. Manchester. Aubrey was doubtful that the girl had returned to the pop group; and at the same moment wondered whether his disdain toward their kind of music made him think that. He could not, he found, identify in any way with a modern girl of twenty-plus. An alien species. And Shelley's background was probably wrong. Hyde might know more than either of them.

With great reluctance, Aubrey looked at the clock on the wall opposite his chair. Another minute clicked away. Twelve twenty-four. Another six minutes, with good fortune and communications, before the Nimrod transmitted a status report on Soviet naval activity in the area of the Tanafjord.

And, despite the weariness of the waiting, he felt no desire to receive that report.

"No trace of them? After almost three hours, no trace of them?" Dolohov raged at the rear admiral, who blanched with a suppressed indignation of his own, and the sense of humiliation at once more being berated in front of junior officers, his own and those who had come with Dolohov. "It is not good enough, Admiral. It is very bad. We *knew* it would come to this, we knew it! They found her, crippled her so they say, and now they have lost her. It is not good enough!"

"I – can only repeat, sir, that everyone, every unit on station, is using every means to locate the submarine. We have reduced the search area to a matter of fifty or so square miles of the seabed. The British submarine is inside that square. It is only a matter of time."

Dolohov stared through the window of the control room, down at the map table. A cluster of glowing lights, now merely the decoration for a fir-tree. He dismissed the childhood image, but he could no longer believe in the symbolic importance of those lights. They were strung together for no reason. The rear admiral's voice seemed to whine in his ear, and his own breath whistled in and out of the spaces under his ribcage.

"They could stay down there for weeks, unless the hull has been damaged, which evidently it has not." As he spoke, his exhalations clouded a little circle of glass in front of his face, as if he were attempting to obscure the signals of temporary failure that glowed below him. "It will be wearying for them, but not uncomfortable or dangerous, while we listen for the whispers of their breathing, the sound of their feet." He turned on the rear admiral. "We should not have lost contact when the submarine was hit. *Grishka*'s captain should not have lost contact."

"Admiral, he had poor target acquisition, just a trace of the submarine's wake. The torpedo had to be launched, or held, and he made his decision. I – I happen to think he made the right decision."

"You do?" Dolohov's face was bleak with contempt and affront. Then it altered; not softened, but it became more introspective. His voice was softer when he continued. "Perhaps. Perhaps. If they don't find her soon, then we shall pass from the realm of action into that of diplomacy, achieve an international situation. She is in Norwegian waters, and they will attempt to rescue her. Already, they have made contact. You have no idea what that message contained?"

The rear admiral shook his head. "A one-time code. We would need all their computer cards, and then know which one."

"Very well. It was probably a recall signal. What of the aircraft?"

"A British Nimrod. It will be watching us."

"You see my point, Admiral? Once they understand what we are doing, they will attempt to intervene. There will be evidence, photographs, computer print-outs. It will all serve to complicate matters."

"Yes, sir."

"Temperature sensors, sonar, infra-red – all useless." Dolohov rubbed his chin, staring at the ceiling above his head. In a quiet voice, he said, "Likelihood. Likelihood. If there was some element of *choice* open to the British captain – eh?" He turned to the rear admiral. "If he was able to decide, at least to some extent, his final location, where would it be? A ledge, a cleft, a depression? Feed into the computers every detail of every chart and every sounding we have of your fifty square miles. If necessary, we can send down divers – *before* Ardenyev's team are let loose. Or we can use submersibles with searchlights –" Dolohov was elated again. He controlled, he contributed, he conceived. "Yes, yes. We must be prepared." Then, seeing that the rear admiral had not moved, he motioned him away. "Get on with, it, man, get on with it!"

Twelve twenty-nine. Clark had joined him, together with Copeland, one of the less reluctant members of the "Chessboard Counter" team. He had requested a conversation with Eastoe, the pilot and captain of the Nimrod. The high-speed, frequency-agile transmissions would delay question and answer but not prevent it. When Eastoe spoke, his words would be recorded on the Nimrod, speeded up to a spitting blur of sound transmitted on frequencies that changed more than a hundred times a second, re-recorded in MoD, slowed and amplified for Aubrey. Then his words would take the same few seconds to reach Eastoe in comprehensible form.

"What's she doing now, Ethan?" he asked suddenly. *"Proteus,* I mean?"

"Getting the hell out, if her captain's got any sense," Clark replied gloomily.

"You really think they're onto her, don't you?" Copeland challenged Clark. Clark nodded, his face saturnine with experience, even prescience. "I can't believe that –" Copeland turned to Aubrey and added: "Nor should you, sir. 'Leopard' is undetectable, and they'll have taken no action against her."

"Ah," Aubrey said. "Would they not?" Copeland shook his head vigorously. "I wish I shared your faith, young man."

The communications officer approached them. "Transmission time, Mr. Aubrey." He was punctiliously polite, but there was little respect. As if Aubrey had somehow, by some underhand trick, succeeded to the commodore's job and salary and pension.

"Thank you – we'll come over."

Aubrey ushered Clark and Copeland towards the communications console with its banks of switches and reels of tape. Almost as they arrived, a red light blinked on, and a tape began to whirl at near impossible speed. A spit of noise like static.

"The Nimrod's transmitting," Copeland explained off-handedly.

"Thank you."

The communications console operator typed on the bank of switches like a competent secretary. Another tape began to turn, slowly. After more than a minute-and-a-half it stopped and the operator rewound it. Aubrey was aware of other people gathered behind him, much as men might have gathered around a radio for the cricket scoreboard.

Eastoe's voice, a man Aubrey did not know. Nevertheless, informed of the ETNA order and aware of its significance, Eastoe addressed his words to Aubrey.

Call sign. Identification. Then: "We have concluded a square search of the area, dropping patterns of sonar buoys while surveying the area by means of infra-red and radar. There is a great deal of Soviet naval activity, surface and sub-surface –" Clark scribbled the co-ordinates, even though they were already being fed into the map's computer. "We have identified by sonar at least four hunter-killer submarines in the immediate area, and the VTOL carrier *Kiev* and the rescue ship ident is confirmed. There are other surface units of the Northern Fleet engaged in what appear to be sonar searches of the area. Infra-red and radar is also being extensively and intensively used by all surface and sub-surface vessels –"

"They're looking for her," Clark remarked unnecessarily.

"We conclude an intensive search of a very small area of the seabed, especially inshore. Two Tupolev 'Bear'-Cs function exactly similar to our own, are also on station in the immediate area. All units are aware of us, we conclude. Over."

Aubrey glanced around at Clark, then at Copeland.

"You can speak to Squadron Leader Eastoe now," Copeland informed him.

"I realise that, young man. I am merely considering my reply." Aubrey remarked frostily. He paused. The open channel hummed in the silence.

"Squadron Leader," he began without introduction, "you evidently have no trace of the *Proteus*. Is it your opinion, your considered opinion, that the submarine has received your message and is acting upon it? Over."

The fast tape whirled, and again there was the little asthmatic cough of sound. Then the humming silence again, into which Pyott's drawl dropped theatrically, startling Aubrey.

"Not quite as easy as you thought, Kenneth?"

Aubrey did not turn round. Pyott had entered the room without his noticing. Aubrey sensed a lofty acquiescence in his tone.

"Ah, Giles," he said, "I'm afraid things don't look awfully sunny, just at the moment." Aubrey's own voice was similarly affected, announcing the draw, the honourable compromise. Pyott pushed past Clark and arrived at his shoulder.

"Have they got her?" he asked. Genuine guilt, concern.

"We don't know. I've asked the captain of the Nimrod to make a guess."

Tape whirl, then the slow tape, then Eastoe's unemotional voice.

"My guess is she's on the bottom, not moving." A pause, then, as Eastoe realised that Aubrey could not comment immediately, he continued: "The submarines and surface ships are concentrating in a very, very small area. Either they've lost contact altogether, or they have a pretty good idea where they'll find her. Over."

Immediately, Aubrey said, "In your estimation, is the *Proteus* damaged?"

"You're not serious, Kenneth?" Pyott asked while they waited for Eastoe's reply.

Aubrey looked at him. "The possibility has to be considered. If they are searching a very small area, it may be because they suspect, even know, she can't move out of that area."

"God," Pyott breathed, and his face was slack and grey, much older.

His mouth was slightly open, and he looked very unintelligent.

"I don't think we could raise Him on this set," Clark observed, having overheard Pyott's admission of negligence, culpability. Pyott glanced at the American malevolently. Clark raised his hands, palms outwards. "OK, I'm not crowing, Pyott." Giles Pyott nodded.

Then Eastoe's voice, as naturally, it seemed, as if he was in the room with them. "It's possible, sir." Aubrey's astuteness had won Eastoe's respect, at least for the moment. "The search appears to be concentrated well inshore, but it isn't being extended outside a certain radius. They're refining the search all the time, they're not widening it. I think she's in there somewhere. Over."

Aubrey looked at Clark. "Could they have damaged her, Ethan?"

"It's possible."

"How?"

Clark considered the problem. "Wire-guided torpedo, maybe. If they got a temperature trace – " Hidden fear now made itself apparent on his face. "Wake-homing – yes." He shook his head. Copeland's face was lengthened with realization, complicity in fear. Clark cleared his throat. "If they got some kind of heat trace, and then used a wake-homing torpedo, maybe with a proximity fuse, then the torpedo would follow the *Proteus's* wake like a hound. Yes, it could be done."

"Do we accept that it has been done, and act accordingly?"

"I – guess so," Clark replied.

"No," Copeland said softly.

"What action, Kenneth?" Pyott asked.

"Diplomatic, of course, through the Norwegians. And practical. What other vessels do we have in the area?"

"Not much – and far away. Maybe the closest is a day's sailing from the Tanafjord."

"I see. I wouldn't like to escalate NATO activity in the area, anyway, with the present Soviet concentration of vessels." He paused. "I shall instruct Eastoe to monitor and report continuously. It would seem that, at the moment, the Red Banner Fleet cannot find our elusive submarine. That situation may not exist for much longer. There is a rescue ship in the area – Eastoe must monitor its activities with particular care. Meanwhile, gentlemen, we must consider all possible scenarios for the prevention of the loss of the 'Leopard' equipment to the Russians. Even at the expense of the *Proteus* herself."

Aubrey turned back to the communications console. It was a few seconds before his audience realised the implications of his statement and the uproar prevented him from completing his instructions to Eastoe and the Nimrod.

The sand dunes on the northern side of the airfield at Kinloss appeared momentarily through the lashing rain, and then vanished again. Tendrils of low cloud were pulled and dragged like bundles of worn grey cloth across the higher ground. Glimpses of hills and mountains were just discernible between the heavier squalls. Three RAF Nimrods gleamed in the rain, their nose sections shielded under protective covers, and the only colour in the scene was the brilliant red of a lone Hawk trainer. All four aircraft were lifeless, abandoned like exhibits in some open-air museum.

The controller watched, from the fuggy warmth of the control tower, a khaki-coloured crew bus returning across the concrete, its lights fuzzily globed by the rain, its whole appearance hunched, its roof shining like a snail's shell. Beyond it, two red anti-collision lights winked rhythmically, and a fourth Nimrod was just discernible. A fuel bowser edged cautiously away from it. Because of his headset, the scene had no sound for the controller, not even that of the incessant rain beating on the control tower roof and windows.

"Kinloss tower – Kestrel One-six requesting taxi clearance."

"Roger, Kestrel One-six. You're cleared to the holding point, runway Zero Eight."

Take-off conditions were bordering on the critical. A decision taken on the station would have resulted in the Nimrod's flight being cancelled. The controller disliked the interference of civilians with all the habitual ferocity of the long-serving officer. Eastoe was over the Barents Sea, waiting for this relief Nimrod. This crew were going to take off in distinctly risky conditions at the order of the same civilian, a little old man from the intelligence service. The controller had not been present at the crew's briefing, and the station commander had not seen fit to inform him either of Eastoe's mission or of the origin of their orders from Whitehall. That small resentment flickered through the controller's mind like one of the anti-collision lights out there in the murk.

If he kept quite still, he could line up the nearest Nimrod's fin with a joint in the concrete. He could see the shudders through the airframe as the wind buffeted it. Someone in a nice warm Whitehall office – *ah, tea Miss Smithers, excellent, is it still raining outside?* – giving easy orders with his mouth full of digestive biscuit and risking other people's lives –

The Nimrod Kestrel One-six was almost invisible now, tail-on to him, its winking red lights accompanied by white strobe lights. They alone announced its presence and movement.

"Kestrel One-six – Kinloss tower. You have your clearance."

"Affirmative."

"Roger. One-six. You are cleared for a left-hand turn out above five hundred feet."

The lighting board showed all the lights on the taxiway and the

691

runway to be on. A telephone near him blinked its light, and the duty corporal picked it up, interrupting his making out of the movements slip. The controller lifted one headphone, and caught the information that Flying Officer Harris was sick and would not be reporting for the first shift the next day. He replaced the headphone.

"Kestrel One-six ready to line up."

"Kestrel One-six, you are cleared to line up, runway Zero Eight, for immediate take off. Wind zero-two-zero, gusting thirty-two."

"Roger, Kinloss tower. Kestrel One-six rolling."

The controller picked up his binoculars, and stared into the gloom. At first, there were only the pinpricks of the lights, then a slate-grey and white moving shape began sliding down the corridor of high-intensity lights, the shape resolving itself into the familiar outline of the Nimrod. He imagined the pilot's struggle to hold the aircraft steady against the fierce cross-wind.

The nose wheel began to lift from the runway. The four huge Spey engines began acting like hoses, blasting sheets of water up from the runway beneath them. Fog flickered across the wings as the change in pressure condensed the water vapour. The Nimrod began to disappear almost immediately.

"Kestrel One-six, I'm aborting."

"Roger –"

Too late, he thought, too late.

"I can't hold her – I'm off the left of the runway –"

The controller could see only one indication of the whereabouts and the danger of the Nimrod. The spray of water thrown up had changed colour, dyed with brown earth as the aircraft ploughed across the field alongside the runway.

"The port leg's giving way!"

"No!"

Then there was a silence that seemed interminable, he and the corporal staring frozenly at one another, until he managed to clear his throat and speak.

"Kestrel One-six, do you read, Kestrel One-six."

No flame, no explosion, nothing. The corporal's finger touched the emergency button. He could hear the alarm through his headphones.

"Kestrel One-six –"

A bloom of orange through the rain and murk, like a distant bonfire or a beacon. The windows rattled with the explosion, which he heard dully. Irrelevantly, yet with intense hostility, he heard the voice he had earlier imagined. *Sorry to hear that, Miss Smithers. All dead, I suppose. Is there any more tea?*

It had been so easy, and so pointless. The dull orange glow enlarged and brightened.

SEVEN:

Found

The helicopter dropped through the murk, and there were no longer rags of cloud and a sensation of unreality. The night was empty, blacker than the cloud, and the wind squalled around the cramped cabin with a demented shrieking that Ardenyev simply could not accustom himself to accept or ignore. Only the momentary absence of the snow and sleet reduced the unnerving reality of the wind's strength and velocity, because he could no longer see the wind as a visible, flying whiteness against the dark.

Then he spotted the *Karpaty*, below and to port of them. Blazing with light like a North Sea oil platform, yet tiny and insubstantial, her lights revealing the pinprick flecks of wave-crests against the black sea. Beyond *Karpaty*, outlined like an incomplete puzzle-drawing by her navigation lights, was the bulk of the *Kiev*. Even at her greater distance, she seemed more secure, more a haven than the rescue ship.

The second MiL emerged beside them, dropping into view, an eggshell of faint light.

"Express One to *Karpaty* – Express One to *Karpaty*, over."

The pilot's voice in his headphones startled Ardenyev with the immediacy of their attempt to land on the rescue ship's helipad. He strained his eyes forward, but could not even see the illuminated, circular platform. The *Karpaty* was a blur of lights seen through the still-running tears that streamed across the cockpit canopy and the windscreen of the MiL. The rescue ship was tiny, and they seemed to be making no visible progress towards it.

"*Karpaty* to Express One. We read you, and have you on radar. Range eight point five kilometres. Over."

"Weather conditions, *Karpaty*?"

"Winds oh-five-oh, thirty-five knots, gusting to forty-five. Sea state five to six, waves varying ten to twenty feet. What are your intentions? Over."

The pilot looked across at Ardenyev. He seemed satisfied by the glum, strained silence he observed. Ardenyev considered the shadow of the *Kiev* beyond the lights of the rescue ship. And rejected them.

"Well?" the pilot asked.

"Can you get down?"

"It's on the edge. I don't recommend trying –"

"Express Two to Express One, over."

"Go ahead, Express Two."

"Are we going down?"

"I don't like it."

"We can make it. I'll go in first, if you like. Over."

"You haven't got all night," Ardenyev remarked, looking at his watch. They were running perhaps thirty minutes behind schedule already. A diversion to the *Kiev*, and then a sea transfer back to the *Karpaty* would delay them by perhaps as much as two hours. Dolohov would find that delay unacceptable. The *Proteus* might be located at any moment, and Ardenyev had no wish to be still airborne when that happened. "We're late."

"I fly this crate, not you, Captain. My judgment is all that counts, and my judgment tells me to divert to the carrier." The pilot was calm, irritated with his passenger but unafraid. He assumed his authority would carry the day.

"Hold on, Express One – I'll set down first. When *Karpaty* has filled my tanks, I'll get out of your way." The other pilot sounded to Ardenyev to be less afraid, yet he wondered whether his own pilot might not be right.

"Express Two – I suggest we divert to *Kiev*."

"I'm not putting my bollocks on the chopping-block with Dolohov, Andrei, even if you're prepared to. Just watch my technique!"

Ardenyev's pilot's face was tight with anger, resentment, and something deeper which might have been self-contempt. Ardenyev watched, in a new mood of satisfaction, as the second MiL surged ahead and below them, towards the *Karpaty*. His pilot was playing safe, they would get down now. It meant only that Orlov and Blue Section would be kitting out by the time they arrived, and amused at their superiority.

The second MiL banked, looking uncertain for a moment below them, as if turning towards the surface of the black ocean itself rather than to the Christmas tree of the ship. Then it appeared to steady and level, and began to nervously, cautiously approach the stern of the rescue ship. The helipad was now a white-lit dish, no bigger than a dinner plate from their altitude. The radio chatter between the pilot and the ship flicked back and forth in his headset, suggesting routine, orderliness, expertise.

Ardenyev's pilot brought his MiL almost to the hover, as if they were drifting with the wind's assistance, feather-like. Yet when Ardenyev glanced across at him, the man's knuckles were white. It

694

did not indicate mental or emotional strain, merely made Ardenyev aware of the turbulence outside; its heaving against the fragile canopy of the helicopter. The pressure to move them, overturn them, crush them, was like a great depth of seawater. Once the image made contact with reality, a circuit was formed that alarmed him. The slow-motion below was fraught, dangerous now.

The fly-like MiL drifted towards the helipad. Ardenyev could see tiny figures on the deck, and their bent shapes, their clinging to rails and surfaces, indicated the force of the wind. Its volume seemed to increase outside.

The deck of the rescue ship heaved, and the light seemed to spill like liquid over the ship's side and onto the surface of the water. The whitecaps opened like teeth in a huge black jaw. The sight of the water's distress and power was sudden, making the rescue ship fragile and the helicopter approaching it more insect-like than ever. It was a fly hovering above a motorway, awaiting an encounter with a windscreen.

The helicopter flicked away, much like a gull caught by a gust of wind, and the pilot's voice was high-pitched, his relieved laughter unreal and forced.

"Mishka, get away from there! We'll divert to the *Kiev* and winch them down. You'll never be able to use auto-hover, the deck's pitching too much."

"Don't worry, Grandad," the voice of Orlov's pilot came back. "Just a temporary hitch. Watch this."

The words now seemed to Ardenyev to have an empty bravado which he despised and which frightened him. Yet the rescue ship seemed to have settled again, the whitecapped waves to have subsided, slipping back into the shadows beneath the deck of the *Karpaty*. The MiL began to sidle towards the helipad again. Tiny figures crouched, as if at its approach, ready to secure the helicopter the moment its wheels touched.

The pilot instructed the *Karpaty*'s captain that he would switch to auto-hover just above the deck, which would allow the helicopter to automatically move with the pitching of the ship, so that the deck would always remain at the same level beneath the MiL. Ardenyev saw his own pilot shaking his head.

"What's wrong?"

"What?"

"I said, what's wrong? You're shaking your head."

"The deck's pitching and rolling too much, and I think he's out of the limits for auto-hover and height hold." The pilot shrugged. "Perhaps it isn't from where he is. I don't know." He glanced at Ardenyev as if daring him to comment, or inviting personal insult.

"If there's any real danger, order him to divert – or I will."

Creeping whiteness appeared at the edges of their canopy, like some cataract or a detached retina beginning to float. The sleet had returned. Ardenyev's pilot increased the beat of the wipers, and they watched, oblivious of everything else, even of attempting to interfere, as the MiL below them banked, levelled, sidled forward, moved above the white dish of the helipad. There was a long moment of stillness, accompanied by the breathy whispering of Ardenyev's pilot: "Go on, go on, my son, go on, go on –"

The noise irritated and disturbed Ardenyev. The MiL was above the deck now, and lowering towards it. Stillness. A white-knuckled hand at the corner of his eye, whiteness creeping around the canopy, flying between them and the garishly-lit scene below. The navigation lights of the carrier, outlining a huge, safe bulk, in the distance. Ardenyev held his breath. They were going to make it. When they, too, had landed, Orlov would study his face; there'd better be no trace left of anxiety or doubt, or the young man would burst out laughing –

Dropping slowly like a spider coming down its thread; very slowly. Ardenyev could see himself, years before, watching such a spider in his bedroom, coming slowly down its thread, confident, small, agile, an acrobat. And slowly he had begun to blow upwards, making the spider swing, making it uncertain, vulnerable, that tiny creature who had abseiled from the ceiling with such arrogance. It had crawled, scuttling upside-down, back up its rope of thread, then dropped again with slightly more caution. Blow again. He had blown again.

The MiL hopped away from the deck as if electrocuted. Then it began to drop slowly, more slowly than before, towards the deck as it once more became level. The glimpse of the whitecaps vanished into the night.

The spider had scuttled away, dropped again, but its weight now could not deaden or steady the swing of the thread to which it clung. It had been descending from the lampshade, like a small black god climbing out of the sub. Swinging, unable to control the motion.

Ardenyev's hand touched his throat, feeling for the transmitter switch of his microphone. The spider was swinging across the ceiling above his bed, interestingly, helplessly. The helicopter shifted in a grumble of the wind, and the deck of the *Karpaty* shifted, too. Pitching towards the MiL, which hopped out of its way, then moved back down, drawn by magnetism, it seemed. The deck steadied. The spider swung across the ceiling, flying the landscape of cracks and damp patches, swinging to almost touch the shadows in the corners of the room. And nearing his face all the time as fear or instinct or helplessness made it pay out more of the rope of thread.

Six feet. Stillness now. White knuckles, his own fingers dead as he fumbled with the microphone, tried to think what to say, why he was going to speak. Appalled and fascinated. Five feet, four –

The spider just above his face. Cheeks puffed out, he waited to catch it at the optimum moment, blow it across the bedroom, perhaps at his younger brother's bed and his sleeping form. Cupping his hands round his mouth to direct the breath when he expelled it.

Three feet, two –

"Auto-hover – come on, come on –"

A foot, then two feet, three, four – the deck of the *Karpaty* pitched again, the lights spilling across the angry sea. Five feet – spin, flick, twist upside-down, turning like a top. The MiL staggered with the blow of the helipad, and then the repeated punching of the wind. The spider flew through the air, into shadow, its rope of thread loose, wafting in the air's current he had disturbed.

The MiL hung upside-down for a second or more, then drove back towards the port side of the ship, breaking its rotors then its back on the side of the *Karpaty*, just forward of the helipad. A billow of flame, incandescent and paling the ship's lights, a tiny figure struck like a match falling into the sea, the MiL's wreckage pursuing him into the whitecaps. Flame flickered over the wild water for a second, then the MiL was doused like a torch – and gone.

Ardenyev came to himself, yelling into his microphone that the pilot should abandon his attempt and divert to the carrier. His words were clipped, orderly, syntactically correct, but he was hoarsely yelling them at the top of his voice. He must have begun shouting even before the MiL crashed.

"Shut up, shut up –!"

Ardenyev's mouth remained open, his throat dry and raw. There was nothing. On the pitching deck of the rescue ship, fire-extinguishers were playing over spilled fuel that travelled like lava along the deck and down the side of the ship. Slowly, the flames flickered and disappeared.

"My God," Ardenyev breathed finally. Teplov was at his shoulder.

"All right, sir?"

"No, Viktor, it is not all right," he said in a small voice. "Tell the team that Blue Section have crashed and that we are diverting to the *Kiev*."

"Sir." Teplov offered nothing more in reply. Ardenyev was aware of his departure to the passenger compartment. Ardenyev looked at the pilot.

There was a silence in which each man registered the other's pain, and guilt, then the pilot cleared his throat and spoke into his microphone.

"Express One to *Kiev* – permission to land."

697

"Permission granted." An older voice, senior. A commiseration of rank. The same voice went on to supply wind velocity and the effect of the sea and wind on the pitch of the *Kiev*'s deck. As he acknowledged, the pilot continually shook his head. Then he looked at Ardenyev.

"I was right – for fuck's sake, I was right!"

"We can get down?" The pilot nodded. "Christ –"

"Express One to *Kiev* – message received. We're on our way."

Ardenyev sat in a misery of grief as the MiL increased speed and the *Karpaty* slipped beneath its belly. He was appalled at the deaths of Orlov and the others, *his* men, *his* people, *his* responsibility. And he was shaken and anguished at the ease with which it had happened and with which he had allowed it to happen. Distance, slowness, lights – it had all become innocuous, something for spectators, cardboard danger. He had meant to issue the order to divert, but he had not. He had not believed it would happen. A child stepping from a pavement, behind a milk-float, crushed like an eggshell by the car it had not seen. But the distance between the front gate and the road is so small, it cannot signify danger –

He wiped savagely at his eyes. Through the blur as he blinked, the shadowy bulk of the *Kiev* drew closer, then lights sprang out on her starboard after-deck. The superstructure bulked beyond these lights. Tiny pinprick men moved on the deck, bent and huddled to display the ominous force of the wind. Ardenyev wiped his eyes again. The pilot and the carrier were in constant contact, as if instruction and counter-instruction, speed, distance, altitude, pitch, wind velocity would all render the collision of the two objects safe.

Ardenyev felt Orlov and the others in the burning MiL go away and his own fear for himself emerge, invading his stomach and chest and consciousness. The floor of the cabin under his feet was thin, so thin he could sense the buffeting air streaming beneath it, and anticipate the deck of the *Kiev* rushing up to meet them.

The MiL drifted towards the *Kiev*, so like Express Two just before it collided with the *Karpaty*. The deck did not, to Ardenyev's comprehension, enlarge with proximity. It was a grey strip, angled across the substance of the carrier, all the lower decks between them and the sea.

The pilot turned to him. "You'll winch down while the chopper's on auto-hover."

"Can't you land?" There was a strange relief amid the surprise.

"Yes – but I'm not risking it with you lot on board. You'll winch down. OK?"

Ardenyev nodded. "We haven't got a winchman on board."

"Can you do it?"

"Yes."

"Get back there and get on with it. I'll clear it with the bridge."

Ardenyev paused for a moment, and then forced himself out of his seat and climbed over it into the passenger compartment. The imperatives of Dolohov's orders were insinuating themselves again, until he saw the blank, automaton faces of his team. Stunned into emptiness of mind, except where their own fears peered over their shoulders or crawled like indigestion in their stomachs. A sharp pain of fear, a bilious taste in their throats.

"Viktor, we're winching down. Get the door open." Teplov looked up at him, acknowledging the necessity of the snapped order, resenting it, too. The offices for the dead, their mates, their importance to the operation; all clear in Teplov's eyes. Then he got up and went aft, unlocking the door and sliding it open. The wind howled amongst them as if Teplov had admitted an enemy already triumphing. "Get ready – one at a time." The helicopter lurched, one man getting to his feet was flung back against the fuselage, and his face revealed no pain, only a concentration of fear.

Ardenyev lifted him to his feet and shuffled him to the door. They clung to the straps, watching the lighted deck beneath them edge closer, shifting as the sea willed. The young man looked into Ardenyev's face, and seemed to discover something he could trust there. A habit of obedience, it might have been. He allowed Ardenyev to slip the winch harness beneath his arms, and to guide him to the open door. His hair was blown back from his white forehead, and his hands gripped the edges of the doorway. Ardenyev placed his hand against his back, and nodded to Teplov. The motor of the winch started up, and the man sat down, dangling his legs over the deck. He looked up as it swung away from the chopper, and then suddenly the MiL was moving with the deck, perhaps thirty or forty feet above it, swaying as in a breeze by virtue of the auto-hover matching its movements to the pitch of the carrier's deck.

"Right, off you go." Ardenyev held the man's shoulders for a moment, and then propelled him through the doorway. He spun on the wire for a moment, then straightened and dropped slowly and smoothly towards the deck. Uniformed and oilskinned men waited in the downdraught, arms reaching up to him. His legs were held, he was lowered like a child or cat from a tree, then Teplov was recalling the winch harness. Ardenyev looked at him, and nodded. "Next."

Shadrin, the explosives expert, was at his shoulder in a moment, grinning. "Let's get out of this bloody tin box, skipper," he said. There was a shadow in his eyes, but Ardenyev was thankful for the man's attempt at normality. A small re-establishment of cameraderie, teamwork. Sinkingly, Ardenyev realised that when he got them safely aboard the carrier, he had to rebuild them in his own image; an image in which he felt uncomfortable, even treacherous, at that moment.

He strapped the harness around Shadrin, and slapped him on the shoulder. As Shadrin sat down, then dropped out of the MiL, Ardenyev recollected broiling flames and ignited, spilled fuel and a spider, and prayed that they would locate the British submarine soon. Very soon.

Aerial buoy, Lloyd scribbled on his pad. It rested on the chart table, beneath a dim emergency light. The temperature of the control room seemed higher, and could not be entirely discounted as illusion, which he knew it to be. Silence was humming in his ears.

We can't, Thurston scrawled in ugly, misshapen capitals, and added two exclamation marks for additional emphasis.

You were right – we must.

Lloyd and his first lieutenant stared at one another. The pads between them on the chart table were like scraps of food each of them envied the other. Thurston was now confirmed in Lloyd's original opinion that they must do nothing more than sit and wait out the vessels that searched for them. Lloyd – his calm eroded by the dead, limping passage of time, the slowness of clocks, and the sense that the forces mobilised against them could not indefinitely go on seeking and not finding – had now succumbed to the desire for action.

There was an RAF Nimrod above them – twenty, thirty, forty thousand feet it did not matter – on station, not knowing where they were, what condition they were in. MoD had to be told they needed rescuing, otherwise the Russians would inevitably get to them first. Lloyd was utterly convinced that the Russians wanted "Leopard". He could not envisage how they intended obtaining it, or conceive the recklessness that must have led them to this course of action, but he understood their objective. MoD had to be told; there was no time to be lost.

He scribbled again on a fresh sheet of the pad. *It's an order.* A helpless, obedient malevolence crossed Thurston's features for a moment, then it was gone. His face was blank of all expression as he nodded his acquiescence.

They crossed silently to the bank of sonar screens. Two only in closest proximity, the other submarines farther off, nudging their sensors into other corners of the box in which they had contained the *Proteus*. Lloyd read off distance and bearing. Both of the nearest submarines were, for the moment, moving away from the ledge on which they rested. Lloyd glanced at Thurston, and whispered: "Now."

700

Thurston moved away, and Lloyd found the control room crew, almost every one of them, and Carr the navigator, looking in his direction. He nodded meaningfully, miming the sending up of the aerial buoy. Thurston, at the encoding console, gave the thumbs up – temperature of the control room suddenly jumping – and his hands played over the bank of switches which would release and direct the aerial buoy to the surface. Its journey would take it perhaps a whole minute. Depth figures unreeled on a tiny display unit near Thurston's hand.

Breathing. Ragged, stifled, louder. The control room was full of nervous men trying to control their breathing. Lloyd, his arm draped around the periscope in the centre of the control room, felt hotter, less sure, supremely aware of the aerial buoy bobbing up through the layers of water to the surface.

A small object, a tiny pinprick. Capable of receiving and bouncing back a sonar signal. Something solid that betrayed their location. A flare they had sent up – we're over here, can't you see us?

Lloyd clamped down on the thought, and crossed to Thurston. He gestured for the first lieutenant's pad and then wrote quickly, in block letters, the message he wished encoded and transmitted to the Nimrod. Thurston nodded reluctantly when he read it, and turned in his chair. The console operator beside him began typing at the keyboard, and the code-of-the-day card was automatically fed in. The operator added the transmission instructions – high-speed, frequency-agile. Lloyd watched the depth figures unreeling near Thurston's elbow. The aerial buoy was still twenty fathoms from the surface, almost twenty seconds still to run until it bobbed up into the waves.

Sweating, now. Cold sweat, surprising in the heat of the control room. Lloyd tried to control it, to calm his body. Ten fathoms. Nine –

Someone clearing his throat, the noise of someone else scratching the cotton of his shirt. Six fathoms, five, four. Almost a minute since they had released the aerial buoy. Three fathoms.

Lloyd broke away from the encoding console and crossed to the passive sonars. Pinpricks, distances, bearings. Still moving away. One moving back, one moving back –

Bearing green nine-five, almost amidships, range two thousand yards. Speed eleven point two five knots. Lloyd looked over his shoulder. Thurston saw him, raised his thumb. The aerial buoy was transmitting the message, a split-second blurt of sound, repeated and repeated. They would have to repeat at least fifty times to be any-where near certain their message had been picked up by the Nimrod. Ten seconds, no more.

Speed twelve point three knots, bearing unchanged, range closing.

Lloyd stared in disbelief. Twelve point seven knots and rising. Dead amidships, a Russian submarine. The buoy, or the message, untranslatable but audible to the Russians, had pinpointed them. Lloyd waggled his hand at Thurston, and the first lieutenant ceased the transmission and began recalling the aerial buoy.

Thirteen point six knots. Closing.

Lloyd crossed to Thurston, and indicated in savage mime that he must release the buoy, a chopping motion of his hand, again and again. Thurston paused for a moment, then his hands flickered over the console's keyboard. The figures near his knuckles on the digital read-out slowed, then stopped. The buoy was gone, up to the surface again where it would be swept away from their position by the current. Lloyd wiped his forehead with his handkerchief in undisguised relief, not even beginning to think that they had now only the back-up aerial buoy.

He hurried back to the sonars. Speed fifteen point nine knots, bearing unchanged, closing amidships. Range little more than a thousand yards. He realised he had been standing mopping his brow for almost a minute after they released the buoy. Speed fifteen point seven, fifteen point five.

He sighed audibly, a ragged sound from an old man's asthmatic chest. Speed fourteen knots and dropping, bearing green eight-four. Change of course, uncertainty setting in, scent lost.

Scent lost.

The Russian navy had sea-bed maps they could feed into their computers, superimposing them on their sonars and infra-red. It couldn't last for much longer. "Leopard" would be defeated by likelihood and by the concentration of vessels in their immediate area.

It couldn't last long. Lloyd felt weary, and depressed. It was hard to believe that the Nimrod had heard them, knew where they were and what had happened. No one knew. No one at all.

The decoded message from the *Proteus* unrolled on the screen of the Nimrod's display unit with the kind of stutter given to the pages of a book when they are riffled quickly. Group Captain Eastoe bent over the shoulder of his communications officer, and sensed the man's shoulder adopt the quiver of excitement that was evident in his own body. Like an audience of two, they were experiencing the same emotions, the gamut of surprise, shock, satisfaction, hope, and anxiety that the words had little apparent power to evoke.

When the message began repeating on the screen, Eastoe straightened and rubbed his cheeks with his hands. He yawned, surprising himself, then realised it was a ploy of the mind to gain time; time for consideration. *Proteus* on the seabed, position unknown, immobilised by a reduced warhead torpedo, surrounded by Russian vessels, surface and sub-surface. It did not bear consideration.

"Inform MoD immediately – Flash, code of the day. Poor sods."

"Skipper –" A voice behind him, the Nav/Attack officer in his niche in the fuselage of the Nimrod.

Eastoe crossed to him. Beyond the man's head the porthole-type window revealed the late slow grey dawn beginning outside; only at their altitude, and above the cloud cover. Below them, the *Kiev* and the other surface vessels would be moving through darkness still, and beneath them *Proteus* lay in the permanent darkness of the seabed, where hunter-killers attempted to sniff her out.

"What is it, Bob?"

"Something's happening down there, on the rescue ship."

"You mean in connection with last night's little party?"

"*Karpaty* is changing course, moving closer to the *Kiev*."

"I wonder why. You think one of those two choppers crashed on landing, mm?"

"Yes, skipper, surface wind would have made a landing very dicey. There was that quick infra-red reading, and I'm almost sure only one chopper eventually moved off in the direction of the carrier."

"Then what did they deliver, or try to deliver, to the rescue ship?"

Eastoe considered, staring out of the tiny window, down at the roof of the cloud cover, lightening in its greyness, but thick and solid as the roof of a forest. Eastoe felt a detachment he did not enjoy, and which somehow interfered with his thinking. Being on-station, just watching, for so many hours had deadened the reality of what they could only see by means of radar and sonar and infra-red. Detachment; making thought and decision unimportant, without urgency. "Some sort of team? Experts? People important enough to be ferried out in this weather, anyway. Now you think they're going to transfer to the rescue ship?"

"I do."

"OK, Bob, I'll tell Aubrey. Leave it up to him. We'll be off-duty in a couple of hours, anyway. Someone else's problem, then."

Eastoe went forward again, into the cockpit of the Nimrod.

"Anything, skipper?"

"Signal from *Proteus*," Eastoe replied glumly.

"Bad?"

"She's been hit, Terry."

"Christ – they're all right?"

"At the moment. But she can't move."

"He was taking a chance, sending up a buoy."

"Wouldn't you want someone to know?" Eastoe paused. "Now

who the hell was in those two Russian choppers, and why do they need to get aboard the *Karpaty* so desperately?"

"Skipper –?"

"Doesn't matter. It's Aubrey's problem, not ours." Eastoe got out of his seat again. "Call up Bardufoss – tell them we're off-watch in an hour, and we'll need to refuel. Meanwhile, I'll tell Mr. Aubrey straight away. He might need time to think."

"You saw what happened last night, Captain Ardenyev. I can't guarantee any greater degree of success this morning." The captain of the carrier *Kiev* studied his hands, folded together on the table in his cabin. To Ardenyev he appeared carved, unyielding, even unsympathetic. Yet he was right. A helicopter transfer to the *Karpaty* could not be risked. He even wondered whether his team, Red Section, would board another helicopter. When they reached the *Karpaty* by whatever means, Ardenyev was uncertain of their reaction. The scorched plates, the damaged, twisted rail – he'd seen them through binoculars from the bridge as the grey, pallid light filtered through the heavy cloud – would be too potent, too evident a reminder of their mates, their rivals.

"Then it will have to be by launch, sir."

The captain of the carrier looked up. "I'm not unsympathetic, Captain. I am as concerned for the success of this operation as you are. Which is why I must minimise the risks with regard to your – depleted forces."

Dolohov had signalled the carrier during the night, when he had been informed of the MiL's crash and the loss of Blue Section. His message had been terse, steely, anxious. It had not been humane. He had asked, principally, whether the mission could now be completed. He had not expected a reply in the negative, and Ardenyev had not given him such an answer. Instead, he had assured the admiral that the *Proteus* could still be boarded by Red Section working alone, as soon as they found her.

For Ardenyev, it seemed the only answer he could give, the only possible outcome of his mission. His team wasn't ready, perhaps it never would be. He could only attempt to purge them of fear and shock and grief through action. Desperation might prove effective.

"I understand, sir. I'll assemble my men on the boat deck immediately."

"Very good, Captain. And good luck."

"Sir."

Ten minutes later, Ardenyev was forced to admit that Teplov had done his best with them, and the older men – Shadrin, Petrov and Nikitin – would do, but the two younger members of the team,

Vanilov and Kuzin, were unnaturally pale; cold so that they shivered beneath their immersion suits. It was really their mates who had died, all the younger ones. They seemed hunched and aged, standing amid the others in the companion-way to the aft starboard boat-deck. The movement of the carrier in the waves, slow and sliding and almost rhythmical, seemed to unsettle them even though they were experienced sailors.

"Very well," Ardenyev said, "as soon as we've transferred to *Karpaty*, I'll want a very thorough equipment check. It could take hours, I'll want it done in one. If a signal is picked up from that sub again, we'll be going straight down to her. OK?"

He scrutinised them in turn, not especially selecting the two younger men, but with his eyes upon each face until there was a nod of acquiescence. In one or two gestures, there seemed almost to be a quiet enthusiasm. Not from Vanilov or Kuzin, perhaps, but from Teplov and Shadrin certainly. It would have to do.

He turned to the watertight door, and swung the handle. The wind seemed to howl through the slight gap he had opened. He pushed against a resistance as heavy as a human body, and they were assailed by flying spray. They were below the flight deck, on a narrow, railed ledge on the starboard side of the carrier where two of the ship's four big launches were positioned on their davits. A sailor waved them forward, towards the launch allocated to them and which had been manned in readiness. White-faced, white-handed sailors fussed around the davits, ready to swing the launch out over the water and lower it into the waves.

"Come on, come on," Ardenyev said, hurrying them aboard, clapping each of them on the shoulder as they passed him, climbing the ladder into the launch. Ardenyev followed them, then leapt down again onto the boat-deck as one sailor lost his footing as the deck pitched. He grabbed the man's arm and hoisted him to his feet. He grinned at the sailor, who nodded his thanks. Ardenyev understood how everything except the activities of the moment had gone a long distance from him, and prayed that their mission would begin soon and would have the same numbing, enclosing effect on Red Section. He climbed the ladder again, ducked through the doorway, and joined the officer in charge of the launch, a junior lieutenant, in the wheelhouse.

Karpaty lay a matter of a few hundred yards to starboard of the carrier. In daylight, however gloomy and unreal, the sea raged. Ardenyev was chilled already through his suit from the wash of icy water onto the boat-deck.

"Captain," the young officer acknowledged.

"Lieutenant. We're ready?"

705

"As we'll ever be. I don't think we ought to make the attempt, Captain – to put it bluntly."

"Forget your thoughts, Lieutenant. We're going. Give the orders."

The junior lieutenant appeared reluctant, disliking his own junior status and the obedience it required him to express. He nodded, stiff-lipped, and spoke into his microphone, adjusting the head-phones and the speaker to comfort, or as an expression of disagreement. The launch shifted on its blocks, then began to swing free, moving out over the boat-deck as the davits swung it away from the hull of the carrier. The launch oscillated alarmingly on its davit wires, demonstrating its frailty. Then they began to slide down the side of the *Kiev* the fifty feet or more to the water. The hull of the carrier moved in Ardenyev's vision. It was almost easier to imagine that they were the still point, and that the carrier moved with the wind and swell.

Rivets, rust, sea-life, spillage marking the plates of the hull. Then a grey sheen acquired by distance, then rivets and rust again. A constant chatter of instruction and comment from the lieutenant into his headset, then a shudder as the sea leapt up to meet them. The windscreen of the launch obscured by water for a moment, the hull of the *Kiev* splashed white and grey before the swell let them hang over a trough. The lieutenant spoke rapidly, and the rate of descent increased. Then they were wallowing, and the davit wires came free, and the engine of the launch coughed into life, just as the next peak of the swell broke over the bow and side of the craft, obscuring everything. The screw whined as it was lifted out of the water for an instant, then a trough released them, and the lieutenant ordered full speed and a change of course, towards the rescue ship *Karpaty*.

They butted and rose and dipped their passage across the few hundred yards of sea towards the *Karpaty*. Movement, however violent and uncertain, deadened thought, promised action. The coxswain's hands were white like those of the helicopter pilot the previous night, holding the vessel to her course. Everything was immediate, physical or sensuous.

It took fifteen minutes to make the crossing. Then *Karpaty* was above them, rusty-plated, grey, grubby with use, expressing a kind of toughness that comforted. Less than half the height above them of the carrier, nevertheless the rescue ship was one of the biggest of its type in the fleet. The scorched, blackened plates came into view, the sea working at them as if to scour off the evidence of disaster. The twisted rail, buckled plates at the stern, the damaged helipad, one edge broken as cleanly away as the snapped edge of a biscuit or a dinner plate. Simply missing.

The launch bucked and rode in the swell. The lieutenant was

chattering into his microphone. Ardenyev heard the voice of the tiny, black-clothed, gleaming figure on the port side amidships, beneath the archway of the rescue ship's central gantry, where the cargo deck was located. The boom swung across, and a specially rigged harness was slowly lowered towards them. Teplov appeared, as if by some instinct, at Ardenyev's elbow.

"You first this time, sir," he said. "Just in case."

Ardenyev was about to reply when the lieutenant broke in.

"I have the captain of *Karpaty*, sir. He'd like you aboard without delay. Apparently, one of the submarines has picked up a trace and he's been ordered to alter position."

Teplov grinned. "Come on, sir – get moving."

Patrick Hyde studied the façade of the Free Trade Hall in Manchester. He was sheltering from the rain in a shop doorway in Peter Street, almost directly opposite the home of the Hallé Orchestra, which now displayed, like some unbecomingly young dress on an ageing aunt, the banners and streamers and posters that bellowed the appearance that evening of Heat of the Day. The KGB man on the opposite pavement appeared uninterested in the announcement as he walked down the serpentine, bunching queue of people that stretched almost as far as the Midland Hotel. Hyde did not know whether the man had been detailed to look for the girl or for himself, but he kept the collar of his raincoat turned up and his cap pulled down over his eyes. If one of them was in the immediate vicinity, then he would not be alone.

Two. The other one was coming along the pavement on Hyde's side of Peter Street, walking slowly, conspicuous because he carried no umbrella. Umbrellas handicapped surveillance. There were a couple of young, denimed Special Branch officers in the queue for the rock concert, and plain-clothes police in cars parked at the junction with Watson Street and in the square at the other end of Peter Street. A presence inside the Free Trade Hall, too.

Hyde had spoken to Aubrey – the second KGB man he recognized was drawing level with the doorway in which he sheltered – at the Admiralty and persuaded him that Petrunin and the others should not be approached. Most of them were "unofficials", agents not attached to the Soviet Embassy or to trade missions or cultural organizations. They could not be certain how many there were. Removing Petrunin would be a false security. Free, Petrunin was a focal point. Hyde turned to the window. Transistor radios, stereo equipment, TV sets. The KGB man paused, but his inspection of Hyde was cursory, and he moved on. Petrunin running free would never be far from the action, and those under his control would gather round him, magnetized by his rank. They needed Petrunin and the few they knew from the files in order to identify the others.

Hyde moved out of the doorway. The KGB man inspecting the queue was returning to the main entrance of the Free Trade Hall, the second man was crossing Peter Street to meet him. Hyde nor the police had seen any sign of Petrunin during the morning.

Aubrey had been very clear about the risks, and the responsibility. It rested with Hyde. The girl must be found that day, that night, otherwise alternative methods would have to be employed. The girl would be taken in, regardless, and persuaded to cooperate. Hyde had one chance. Shelley's enquiries at the country hotel where Heat of the Day had stayed the night had proved fruitless. The girl had gone to earth. Shelley was inclined to the opinion that she had abandoned Alletson and the band. Hyde disagreed. There was nowhere else for her to run. Evidently, she was staying clear of her father, desperate not to lead anyone to him.

The two KGB men strolled together towards Watson Street. An Austin Allegro drew level with them, and they bent to the window as it opened, becoming instantly engaged in a voluble conversation with the driver of the car. Then the lights changed, and the green Austin turned into Peter Street. As it passed him, Hyde saw that the driver was Petrunin. There was no one else in the car, which drew in and parked in the square. Petrunin did not get out.

Hyde felt hunger expand as a sharp, griping pain in his stomach. Nerves were making him hungry. He had probably another seven or eight hours to wait. This time, he would not go in until the band was on stage.

He crossed Peter Street to speak to the Special Branch men in the queue. If he was going to wait that long, no one was going in before him.

Aubrey, Clark and Pyott had become, with the passage of the night and morning, an uneasy, indecisive cabal inside the organization of the underground room and the parameters of the rescue operation.

"Kinloss have another Nimrod standing by, with a fresh crew," Pyott argued. "They can be on-station in two or three hours. They won't resent the job, they won't be tired."

Aubrey shook his head. "Get them to contact Eastoe at Bardufoss. He and his crew must go back on-station immediately. I cannot afford to have that area unsighted for that long – no, not even with satellite surveillance. The cloud cover is making things difficult. Eastoe will have to go down to sea level if necessary. I must have *eyes* there, Giles."

"They'll be dog-weary, Mr. Aubrey," Clark offered.

"I have slept for three hours in the last twenty-four, Ethan. We must all make sacrifices." Clark grinned at the waspish remark. "Very well, when the relief Nimrod is on-station, Eastoe and his crew will be recalled – for the moment. Let us discuss ways and means to preserve the security of 'Leopard'. That is our real priority."

"We're to take it you have abandoned any notion of destroying the *Proteus*?" Pyott asked with a mocking lightness.

"That was never my intention – you misconstrued. We may have to expose *Proteus*, however, by ordering Lloyd to destroy the 'Leopard' equipment."

Pyott nodded. "We may have to. We can, however, run it extremely fine. No need as yet. I'm not sure you'd get Lloyd to do it, anyway."

"He would disobey a direct order?" Aubrey asked in surprise.

"For the sake of his vessel and his crew, he would be entitled to do so."

"Very well, Giles. What can we do – before *tomorrow*, when the first NATO vessel arrives in the area? We must do something."

"Diplomacy?"

Aubrey snorted in derision. "I'm afraid the Foreign Office is running its head against a brick wall of denials. The Soviet ambassador has denied all knowledge of the matter. Soviet vessels are engaged in bad-weather exercises in the Barents Sea. He confirmed that, apparently, with Red Banner Fleet headquarters in Murmansk. It will take too long, I'm afraid, to unstick this matter through the proper channels." Aubrey looked drawn, thinner, older. He had slept in a cramped, cupboard-like room off the main operations room, on a thin, hard bed that seemed to imprison him. It had not improved his temper, or his patience. He wondered at his frenetic desire for action, and at the inertia of events which seeemed to be bearing him with them like a great tide. Yet he could not retreat into the dim, cool, shadowed walks of military sang-froid as Pyott did. "It will take too long," he repeated. "Far too long."

"And tomorrow never comes," Clark remarked. "By tomorrow, they may have a fix on *Proteus*, and then you'll find – what'll you find?" He looked at Aubrey. Clark in shirtsleeves and without his tie seemed more American; less sophisticated, stronger. Perhaps a hard-boiled newspaper editor, or a policeman. Yes, without the formality imposed by his suit, he looked more like Patrick Hyde; of the same type or species.

"What will we find, Ethan?"

"My guess is a salvage operation – if they can pinpoint the sub."

"You're serious, aren't you?" Clark nodded. "Why so certain?"

"There's no other way. They have to salvage *Proteus* if they're to save 'Leopard'. At least, I think so."

"And Lloyd may not destroy 'Leopard' now, if we order him to do so – I agree with Giles there. Then we are on the horns of a dilemma, gentlemen."

"Kenneth, we're left relying on 'Leopard' itself. At the moment, it protects *Proteus* and itself. It must continue to do so for at least another twenty-four hours."

"The rescue ship from Tromsø will take longer than that," Aubrey remarked gloomily, staring at his liver-spotted hand caressing the edge of the commodore's desk. "All we will have in the area tomorrow is one American submarine and a Norwegian 'Oslo'-class frigate. The day after, more, I agree. But, too late. We have to have surface ships engaged in any rescue operation, a counter to the Soviet concentration. They will, hopefully, go away when we arrive. I did not want to escalate our presence, but there is no alternative. We have nothing there *now*, that is our problem." His hand slapped the wood of the desk.

"Sorry to be the bad-news boy," Clark said, "but you're ignoring the latest movements of the rescue ship the Soviets have on-station, and those helicopters that arrived last night."

"Yes?" Aubrey snapped impatiently. Then: "Sorry – go on."

"The boarding party?" Pyott queried, and Clark nodded.

"Damnation! What do we *do*? Tell me that. What do we do?"

"Send Eastoe down on the deck to look over the rescue ship and the immediate area – and continue our orisons, I should think," Pyott drawled. Aubrey looked venomously at him, and Pyott blushed slightly with the memory of his culpability. "Sorry," he said softly.

"It's escaping from us," Aubrey sighed. "I feel it. It is too far ahead of us to be overtaken."

Lloyd paused for a moment at the door of the computer room, aft of the control room. Don Hayter's summons – a rating tapping his captain on the arm, beckoning him theatrically – had been peremptory and urgent, and Lloyd's sense of bodily temperature had leapt. Yet he could not bring himself to move through the door, not for a moment. The rating's face had been worried, pale and disturbed in the red lighting. It had seemed, immediately and without embroidery by Lloyd's jumpy imagination, to indicate disaster. Then Hayter saw him, and urgently waved him in. Hayter was bent over one of the "Leopard" screens. The noise he was making tapping a pencil against his teeth shocked Lloyd.

Hayter grabbed Lloyd's arm as he reached the panel, and tapped at the screen with the pencil, underlining the computer-print words the screen displayed. He tapped again and again at one phrase.

FAULT NOT IDENTIFIED.

Then he looked up at Lloyd, who concentrated on reading the rest of the computer's assessment of the situation.

"Leopard" had developed a fault.

"What is it?" Lloyd asked, then repeated his question in a whisper that was not clogged with phlegm. "What is it?"

Hayter shrugged. "It's been happening for four minutes now. We've checked –" He nodded at the rating who had brought Lloyd to the computer room, and the sub-lieutenant who was Hayter's second-in-command. "– everything, so has the computer."

"What – what is the fault doing? What effect is it having?" Lloyd almost wanted to smile at the exaggerated seriousness of Hayter's expression. Lugubrious.

"It's blinking. On, off, on, off. Sometimes, they can see us, sometimes they can't."

"*What*?"

"Whatever the malfunction is, it's intermittent."

"And now – at this moment?"

"Invisible. A moment before you came in, it came back on, full strength, fully operational. Before that, for eleven seconds, nothing, nothing at all."

"Christ."

The sub-lieutenant, Lloyd now perceived, was removing the front panel of the main container housing the "Leopard" equipment, a metal box little bigger or taller than a large filing cabinet.

"We're going to have to do a manual, if the computer can't tell us."

"How long?"

"No idea."

"Could it have happened when we were attacked – the damage to the prop and hydroplanes?"

"Possible. The sensors and dampers at the stern could have been damaged. If they have been – and the fault's outside – then we can't do a bloody thing down here without divers."

"Complete failure?" Hayter nodded. "What about the back-up system?"

Hayter's face became more lugubrious than ever; not a painted clown's downturned mouth but a human expression of concern and fear. His fingers played over the keyboard beneath the display screen, and the message vanished. Then he typed in a new set of instructions, and the response from the computer was almost instantaneous.

MALFUNCTION.

Hayter opened his palms in a gesture of helplessness.

"The back-up system won't cut in."

"It doesn't work at all?"

"At the last check, it worked. Now, it doesn't. I don't understand it.

711

Immediately after the attack, we checked everything through on the computer. It registered no malfunction in either the main or back-up systems. Then we start winking at the Russians, and the computer doesn't know why. At the same moment, the back-up system is u/s. We'll do our best – that's all I can tell you."

The message vanished from the screen before Lloyd had finished reading it. More words came spilling across the screen, line after line in block letters.

MALFUNCTION IN MAIN SYSTEM.   UNIDENTIFIED

"Is it –?"

Hayter nodded. "It's gone again. 'Leopard' isn't working. Anyone who cares to look in our direction can see a British submarine lying on her belly."

Lloyd looked at his watch. The second hand crept across the face like a red spider's leg, ugly, jerking, uncoordinated. Eight, nine, ten, eleven –

"Longer this time," Hayter murmured.

Twelve, thirteen, fourteen –

"Come on, come on, –" Lloyd heard himself saying a long way below his mind. "Come on –"

Sixteen, seventeen –

There were four submarines within a radius of six miles of the *Proteus*. He had been studying the sonars just before he was summoned by Hayter.

Twenty-one, two, three, twenty-four, almost half a minute –

"I think she's gone," Hayter whispered, flicking switches on the console in an almost demented fashion. The movements of his hands appeared in all the more frenzied because of the expressionless lines and planes in which his face seemed to have coalesced. The message on the screen blinked out, then returned with a status report on the back-up system.

MALFUNCTION.

Thirty-two, three, four –

Lloyd could not remove his gaze from the second hand of his watch. Hayter's hands still played across the banks of switches as he attempted to coax life back into "Leopard", or to rouse its back-up system. Complete failure.

MALFUNCTION.

The word seemed to wink on and off the screen at a touch of a key or switch; as if the whole system had failed in each of its thousands of parts and circuits and microprocessers and transistors and coils.

Forty-two. Lloyd knew he ought to be in the control room, knew that they would be picking up changes of course and bearing, changes of speed. Forty-four.

The word vanished from the screen. A status report replaced it. Hayter sighed, perspiration standing out on his forehead, which he wiped with the back of his hand. He grinned shakily.

"We're back in business – for the time being," he said.

"Everything's working?"

"As normal. The main system. Back-up's still dead."

"Get working on the back-up system." Then Lloyd almost ran from the room, down the companion-way to the control room, anticipating what he would see on the sonar screens.

"Skipper, I'm getting a reading from one of our sonar buoys – it's *Proteus*."

"What? Bob, are you certain?"

"Skipper – I picked up a trace. It disappeared after about ten seconds, so I assumed it was a shoal of fish or something of the sort, or a false reading. Then, a couple of minutes later, the same reading on the same bearing, for almost a minute. Now it's gone again."

"What's happening?"

"Could be a malfunction in their equipment?"

"I don't know. Have you got a fix on her position?"

"Not the first time. The second time she came in on two of the buoys. Yes, I've got her."

"Well done. Where is she?"

"What looks like a ledge. Shall I bring the chart through?"

"No. Not until I've decided what message to send to MoD. Have the Russians picked her up?"

"I don't know. Perhaps not –"

"You hope. Keep looking. The moment anything moves closer to *Proteus*'s position, let me know. You're *sure* it's her?"

"What else could it be? I don't understand 'Leopard', even after the briefing, but I know what it's supposed to do. We couldn't see her, now we can. Correction, we *did* see her."

"OK, OK, I believe you. Pass her position to John and tell him to stand by to transmit a Flash signal to Aubrey."

"I'm already standing by, skipper."

"Good. We'll take her down for a look-see first."

Eastoe turned to his co-pilot, and nodded. The cloud cover beneath the nose and wings of the Nimrod gleamed with sunlight, innocent; yet it extended downwards almost to sea level and it was moved by gale-force winds. Their calm was illusory, achieved only by altitude.

"Give me a bearing on the carrier," Eastoe requested into his microphone. Almost immediately, the navigator supplied the coordinates and the course change that would take them over the *Kiev*.

Eastoe dipped the Nimrod's nose towards the clouds. Sunlight, the

713

dense, smoothed roof of the cloud-forest, then a creeping greyness, the first rags and twigs of mist, the darkening of the flight-deck, then the cloud rushing past, swallowing them as they moved into it. The co-pilot switched on the wipers, and water streamed away from their furious beat. Eastoe felt the tremor of the winds through the control column as he watched the altimeter unwind. Down through twenty thousand feet, nineteen, eighteen.

Turbulence buffeted the Nimrod as the aircraft dropped towards the sea. Eastoe sensed for a brief moment the fragility of the airframe around him, imagined the last moments of the Nimrod that had crashed on take-off, remembered the pilot and the crew who had died, and then they broke through the lowest fringes of the cloud, into squalling rain and a headwind. He levelled the Nimrod no more than a hundred and fifty feet above the whitecapped water. The carrier was a fuzzy, bulky shape through the rain, less than a mile ahead of them.

In his headphones, the senior Nav/Attack officer began calling out the readings from his screens and sensors, describing the movements of the surface and sub-surface vessels during the time they were descending. The carrier seemed to leap towards them like a huge stone across the stormy water.

The subs were altering, or had altered, course, and all were closing on the same bearing. The carrier appeared to be lumbering onto a new course. All units closing on the fixed position of the *Proteus*. They'd found her. Maybe foxed for the moment, but they had her now.

Eastoe throttled back the four Rolls-Royce engines, and the Nimrod appeared merely to float above the deck of the *Kiev*. No activity, launches stowed on both the port and starboard boat-decks – the co-pilot calling out confirmation of what Eastoe had seen for himself

and then the rescue ship was ahead as the *Kiev* passed out of sight beneath them. The *Karpaty* was making slow headway and, as Bob called out her course, Eastoe realized that the rescue ship was on a heading that would take her over the *Proteus*.

He realized, too, the significance of the rescue ship. He throttled back once more, and they drifted towards the *Karpaty*.

"See it?" he said.

"Yes, skipper. They're trying to launch a boat from the starboard side, looks like."

The Nimrod crept towards the rescue ship. Tiny figures, moving with what seemed hopeless and defeated slowness around the starboard launch on its davits. Eastoe strained forward in his seat. The co-pilot increased the beat of the wipers. Shiny, oil-skinned crewmen – no, not all of them, surely?

"What in hell –?"

"Divers."

"*Divers*! Shit and hell!"

The Nimrod floated over the dipping bow of the *Karpaty*. A chaos of water flung up over her deck, the surge of an animal as the wave released her into the next trough. Men in shiny, tight-fitting suits, face-masked, oxygen cylinders on their backs. They were pinpricks, tiny matchstick men, but they were divers, climbing into the launch.

"How far is she from the *Proteus*?"

"Less than a mile," he heard the navigator reply as the nose of the aircraft blotted out the scene directly below them.

"I'm going round for another look and some more pictures," Eastoe said, "and then we'd better send Aubrey the bad news – they're going down to the *Proteus*, for God's sake!"

EIGHT:

Seizure

Aubrey stared at the note he had scribbled, the small, neat hand-writing suddenly expressive of powerlessness, and realized that they had lost. "Leopard" had malfunctioned, betraying the position of the *Proteus* to the Russian submarines in the immediate area. The rescue ship *Karpaty* was preparing to launch a small boat on which were a team of divers. They had received photographic proof of that over the wireprint. Opposite his note, Clark had scrawled in his strangely confident, large hand *RB Spec Ops Unit – Ardenyev*. Aubrey presumed it was no more than an informed guess, and it had no significance. The identity of the divers did not matter, only that they existed and were less than a mile from the reported position of the British submarine.

It was dark outside now. Perhaps not quite. A drizzling, gusty dusk. Aubrey had taken a short afternoon walk in St. James's Park, but he had been unable to shake off the claustrophobic, tense gravity of the underground room beneath the Admiralty, and had soon returned to it.

Lost. Found by others. The Russians evidently intended that *Proteus* should be salvaged, perhaps even boarded, and the "Leopard" equipment inspected before it was presumably returned, together with the submarine and her crew. An accident, not quite an international incident, no real cause for alarm, no ultimate harm done. He could hear the platitudes unroll in the days ahead, perceive the diplomatic games that would be played. He knew the Russians would take *Proteus* to one of their closest ports – Pechenga, Poliarnyi, even Murmansk – and there they would effect apologetic repairs, even allowing the American consul from Leningrad or a nominated member of the British embassy staff from Moscow to talk to the crew, make the noises of protest, send their London ambassador to call on the foreign secretary and the PM, heap assurance upon assurance that it was an accident, that all would be well, that this indicated the willingness for peace of the Soviet Union – *look, we are even repairing your submarine, send experts to inspect our work, why are you so suspicious, so belligerent, you will have your submarine back as good as new –*

The diplomatic support for the operation sprang fully-envisaged

716

into Aubrey's awareness, like a childhood or youthful moment of extreme humiliation that haunted him still in old age. It did not matter that it was all a blatant lie; it would work. It would give them enough time to photograph, X-ray, dismantle "Leopard", and learn its secrets.

And, at the same time, they might obtain its designer, Quin, who would help them to build more. In the moment of the loss of "Leopard", Aubrey feared for Hyde's failure and the girl's capture.

"What do we do, Kenneth?" Pyott asked at his shoulder. The channel to Eastoe in the Nimrod was still open, the tapes waiting for his orders. Aubrey waved a hand feebly, and the operator cut the communications link.

Aubrey looked up into Pyott's face, turning slightly in his chair. "I do not know, Giles – I really do not know."

"You have to order Lloyd to destroy 'Leopard' – I mean literally smash it and grind the pieces into powder," Ethan Clark remarked, his face pale and determined. "It's the only way. The guy must know by now that's what they're after, and how close they are to getting it. He has to get rid of 'Leopard'."

"Just like that? I seem to remember the *Pueblo* made a monumental cock-up of a similar procedure some years ago," Pyott observed haughtily. "It won't be easy. 'Leopard' isn't in a throwaway wrapper, Clark."

"You British," Clark sneered. "Man, you're so good at inertia, you make me sick."

"There has to be something else we can do – besides which, 'Leopard' is working again."

"For the moment."

"Gentlemen," Aubrey said heavily, wearily, "let's not squabble amongst ourselves. Ethan, is there anything else we can do?"

"You're not able to rescue *Proteus*, Mr. Aubrey."

"Then perhaps we should warn her what to expect."

Aubrey got up from the chair at the communications console, and crossed the room to the map-board. He seemed, even to himself, to be shrunken and purposeless beneath it. *Proteus* – white light – had been repositioned, closer inshore, and the updated courses and positions of the carrier, the rescue ship, the destroyers and the submarines created a dense mass of light around one thin neck of the Norwegian coast. The sight depressed Aubrey, even as it galvanized him to an action of desperation. He had lost the game, therefore he must damage and make worthless the prize.

"Encode the following," he called across the room, "and transmit it to Eastoe at once, for relay to *Proteus*. Mission aborted, destroy, repeat destroy 'Leopard'. Priority most absolute. Append my signature."

Every man in the room listened to him in silence, and the silence continued after he had finished speaking. A heavy, final silence punctuated only by the clicking of the keys of the encoding machine.

Ardenyev watched Vanilov's feet begin to slip, saw the white face surmounted by the facemask and half-obscured by the bobbing mouthpiece of his breathing apparatus, and felt the wave surge round his own ankles and calves. His hands gripped the rail of the launch, but Vanilov's grabbed for a handhold like clumsy artificial claws he had not learned to operate. Ardenyev reached out and gripped the younger man's elbow, almost as if he were about to twist Vanilov's arm painfully behind his back. He pulled the frightened, off-balanced man to him, hugged him upright, then pushed at his back and buttocks until Vanilov was over the rail of the launch and into it, a look of fearful gratitude on his face. They were all in.

The sea flung itself against the *Karpaty* more ferociously than had been apparent on the carrier, as if encouraged by its success in making the rescue ship bob and duck and sway in the water. Amidships, where they were boarding the launch that would then be swung out on its davits, the sea boiled across the deck as each succeeding wave caught them in the trough behind its predecessor. Ardenyev watched a grey, white-fringed, boiling wall of water rise level with and above the deck, and tightened his grip on the launch's rail and widened his stance. Teplov offered his hand, and Ardenyev shook his head.

"Get below!" he yelled.

The wave smashed against the side of the hull, then flung its broken peak across the deck, drenching Ardenyev. He was deafened and blinded by the water, and he thought the thin, inhuman noise he heard distantly was merely illusion. When he opened his eyes again, there was one yellow-oilskinned figure less than before, gathered around the boat station – and other men were looking blankly and fixedly towards the ship's side. Ardenyev realized, as he shivered and tried to control his chattering teeth, the fragility of their enterprise, even its lunacy; resented to the point of hatred an old man ensconced in the non-climatic, antiseptic surroundings of the Red Banner headquarters in Murmansk. He wanted to open his mouth and yell his anger as the *Karpaty* wallowed her way into the trough behind the wave that had killed one of her crew.

He swung himself up and over the rail, and hurried into the shelter of the launch's cabin, seeking the determination to order the officer in command of the frail little boat to issue his own orders for the launching of the vessel. A tiny yellow blob for a second, out there in the water –?

Ardenyev shook his head, clearing the last of the water from his face and eyes with his hands. The air tanks were heavy on his back. He'd insisted – despite the discomfort and the loss of agility – that they don their full equipment, everything except flippers, in the comparative calm of the *Karpaty*, while the ratings of the rescue ship struggled to load their special equipment into the launch.

The lieutenant in command of the launch watched him, immediately he entered the cabin, with a thin-lipped, colourless expression. His face reflected Ardenyev's thoughts, with its sense of the threadbare rationality of Dolohov's scheme that now made the old man seem mad. Dolohov appeared to have cobbled this operation together in a fit of lunacy.

"Gone again, sir," the *michman* on the launch's sonar called out, and the lieutenant appeared to take this as a final condemnation of what they were doing, the last bitter irony of forces he could hardly comprehend but which controlled him.

Ardenyev crossed the cabin to the sonar. "Show me," he said.

The *michman* indicated a line across the screen with his finger, as if slicing the perspex surface of the sonar. "That bearing," he said. "Range six hundred."

Six hundred metres from them, the British submarine lay on a ledge, less than fifty fathoms down. The invisible Norwegian coast had thrust out a hand, a fingertip, to aid her. Her anti-sonar was flicking on and off like a signalling torch.

"That's it – let's go."

Teplov's head appeared at the door at the rear of the cabin.

"It's all in good shape, sir."

"What about the men?" Teplov paused for a moment, then he nodded slowly. "Good," Ardenyev added. "Make sure everything's secure. Tell them to hang on tight, and be ready to move fast when I give the order." Teplov nodded again, and his head then disappeared as the door closed.

The launch lurched off its blocks, swung fragilely outwards above the deck and then the grey water – they were in another trough between great waves – and the winches with their tiny, yellow-garbed figures working furiously at them, trundled them downwards towards the water. Speed seemed to lend stability and cancel the force of the wind, even still the water as it rushed up towards them. The rusty plates again of the hull, the thin wires above them, then the launch's keel smacking into the water, screw churning, its whine in air disappearing and its power failing to move the launch. Ardenyev grabbed a handhold and braced himself as the launch was lifted towards the grey-white peak of the next wave. It teetered there for a moment, deck awash, windows blind and running with water, the coxswain spinning the wheel feverishly and without apparent effect, then it began falling.

Ardenyev heard someone cry out just after he registered a metallic, screeching slither from beyond the closed door at his back, then he was aware only of the ugly, frightening sensation of being swallowed by a huge, grey-fleshed, open mouth. Then they were in a trough and the rudder and the screw began taking effect and the boat moved with some of its own volition rather than that of the sea. A sense of stability returned to his legs and feet, the illusion of a firm surface, a level world.

The warble of the sonar again, then, as if hearing were just returning.

"She's there again, sir!" the *michman* called out.

"Has she changed position?" Ardenyev asked.

The *michman* calculated swiftly. "No, sir. Bearing now red one-five, range five-seven-eight."

"Helmsman – port one-five."

"Port one-five, sir."

Teplov's face, white and drained and old, appeared at the door again.

"Sir, it's Petrov – his leg. The hose broke loose, sir, wrapped itself around his leg – think it's broken, sir."

"God," Ardenyev breathed, closing his eyes. Six of them now. Dolohov was a fucking lunatic –

"Will you come, sir?"

"It should have been stowed properly!" Ardenyev yelled in his enraged frustration.

The launch teetered, then the bow fell drunkenly down and forward, the noise of the screw disappearing, sinking into the throb of the labouring engine. Six of them had to get themselves, their sleds, hoses and canisters, welding equipment and communications over the side of the launch, below the surface, down to the *Proteus*. There should have been thirteen of them. Impossible now.

"I'll come," he said, suddenly weary and cold.

"One minute ten seconds, eleven, twelve, thirteen –" Lloyd whispered, the lowering of his voice an act of mockery, pointless. "Sixteen, seventeen – twenty."

Hayter and the sub-lieutenant were examining the mass of wiring and circuitry and microprocessors inside the main metal cabinet housing "Leopard". Hayter and the sub-lieutenant were checking the efficiency of each component manually, with multi-meters. The rating was removing the panelling of the second box, kneeling like a safecracker against the metal.

Hayter looked up desperately, shaking his head. "It's no good, sir. We could be doing this for hours yet. Unless it switches itself back on, we're finished. It's no good pretending we're not. Everything here appears to be working, dammit!"

"Get to work on the back-up system, will you?" One minute forty-two seconds. It wasn't going to come on again.

"You know where that's housed. We can't work in there with the space and freedom we've got here. It'll take even longer —"

"Christ, Don — what are you going to do, then?"

"I don't *know*, sir!"

One minute fifty-nine, two minutes of visibility on any and every sonar screen in the area. On the *Kiev*, the rescue ship, the subs, the destroyer, the aircraft overhead. Everyone could see them.

The subs were holding off, not coming in for the kill. But then, they wanted 'Leopard', not blood. And they were jamming every radio frequency they could. *Proteus* couldn't talk or receive. In a corner, beaten, defenceless —

Two minutes ten. Hayter was back at his orisons in front of the exposed innards of 'Leopard', kneeling in what might have been a prayer of desperation. If he could get it functioning again, if it would only switch itself back on, then he would risk the ship by moving her, limping off into another dark corner. At least he'd try to play hide-and-seek with them as long as he could, if only 'Leopard' would work.

Hayter looked at him again, shaking his head. Two minutes twenty-four. It wasn't going to work.

Carr, the navigator, appeared at the door of the cabin. "Sir, sonar's picked up a very small vessel moving away from the rescue ship." As if there had been a public admission of failure, Carr spoke in his normal tone, normal volume. "Ship's launch, we think."

"What does the First Lieutenant think?"

"Divers, sir. Some attempt to inspect our damage."

"Very well." Two minutes fifty. It wasn't going to come on, now. Now it was too late. The rescue ship was less than half-a-mile away. They'd fixed her position by now. Lloyd looked with helpless vehemence at the exposed, purposeless interior of the "Leopard" cabinets. "Tell the First Lieutenant I'm on my way." Carr disappeared. There was no attempt to modify the noise of his footsteps now. It was an admission of defeat, a surrender. "Keep me informed, Don — for Christ's sake keep on trying!"

As he headed for the control room, the image of the opened, useless cabinets remained with him, like a sudden, shocking glimpse of a body undergoing surgery. Hideously expensive, sophisticated almost beyond comprehension, impossible to repair. So much junk —

A team of divers. A threat that somehow diminished even as it presented itself. Perhaps a dozen men, outside the twin hulls of the *Proteus*. His own crew numbered one hundred.

The control room reasserted Lloyd's sense of authority, supplying also a fugitive sense of security. They were almost fifty fathoms down. He must consider moving the *Proteus*, when the critical moment arrived. Thurston looked up from one of the sonar screens, and Lloyd unexpectedly grinned at him.

"Sorry, skipper – nothing. Just the howl of the jamming."

"Make a guess – did *Proteus* pick up Aubrey's order?" Eastoe demanded.

"Doubtful. Almost impossible."

"So Lloyd doesn't know he must destroy the equipment?"

"Don't you think he's done so, skipper? She's been on sonar for over four minutes now."

"That could be the malfunction. Can we contact MoD?"

"No."

"OK everybody. I'm taking her down again, for a look-see. It's almost dark down there. Keep your eyes wide open. Cameras ready. We might as well get any gen we can."

Hyde looked at his watch. A minute before eight. He got out of the unmarked police car parked in Watson Street, then looked back in at the Special Branch inspector before closing the door.

"Half-an-hour. Just keep clear of the place for half an hour, OK?"

"You're taking an unnecessary risk, Mr. Hyde," the policeman offered without inflection. "Yours is a face they know. They'll pick you up on your way in, and bingo –"

"Maybe. And if your lot go in, the girl will panic and either run off or refuse to talk when we've got her. Sorry, sport, we have to take the risk." He looked at his watch again. "Thirty minutes from now, you can come running blowing whistles, anything you like. But not till I've talked to the girl."

"Have it your own way."

"I will. Look –" Hyde felt a sudden need for reassurance, a desire to ameliorate the police resentment of him. "The girl's almost paranoid about us. *We're* the enemy, not the Russians. Christ knows how she came by that idea, but it's what she believes. I have to *talk* her out."

"OK. You've got thirty minutes."

Hyde shut the car door softly. It was almost dark, and the shadows were black pools between the street lamps. Shop windows lighted, and a few pedestrians scuttling ahead of the wind. According to reports, there was one man at the back of the Free Trade Hall – but only one. Hyde thrust his hands into his pockets, and began slouching up the narrow street leading to the rear of the concert hall.

The cars were parked and empty, the street lamps betrayed no pedestrians or loiterers. The weak strains of a country-and-western song came from a slightly open upstairs window of a flat above a shop. The pervasive odour of fish and chips fluttered on the wind, then was gone. It made Hyde feel hungry. He felt small, and alone.

Dim, unlit shop windows. Dust in his eyes. Bookshop, sex shop, barber's. Then Hyde saw him, on the other side of the street, no more than a shadow that moved, perhaps a bored man shifting his weight on tired, aching feet. Hyde stopped, staring into the unlit window of a tiny record shop. Garish LP covers, posters, price cuts daubed in white. The language English but the place no longer Manchester. Some foreign place where he was outnumbered, known, sought. He shivered. If he passed the man, presumably his presence would be noted and reported. They would conclude it was him, even if he hadn't been recognized. On the other hand, if he removed the man from the board, his failure to contact Petrunin – still reported to be sitting in his car in the square – might similarly prove Hyde's presence in the area.

The man had emerged from the doorway of a baker's shop, and was standing on the pavement. As Hyde turned slowly to face him, it was evident that the man was staring directly at him, aware of who he was. Hyde, hands still in the pockets of his corduroy trousers, shoulders hunched, feet apart, was helpless. A Volvo was awkwardly parked, pulled right up bumper-to-bumper against the rear of a Ford Escort directly in front of him. Between him and the man across the street.

One hand of the bulky figure in a raincoat and a hat was moving towards his face, as if to feed himself the tiny R/T set. They hadn't picked up any transmissions all afternoon, Hyde thought, and had discounted R/T. In a moment, two or three paces of time, Petrunin would know that Hyde was about to enter the Free Trade Hall. The hand was moving, Hyde's foot was on the Volvo's bumper, his left foot on the bonnet of the car, the man's hand stopped moving – Hyde could almost see the finger press the transceiver button – one step on the bonnet, then down half-way across the street. The man was surprised, the hand moved away from his face, his other hand fumbled in his raincoat, two strides, one more, collision –

The man staggered back into the darkened doorway of the shop. Old mosaiced threshold, the man's mouth opening in a groan as the ornate, polished brass door-knocker thrust into his back. Hyde, one hand scrabbling at his side, reached for the transceiver in the Russian's hand, and punched at the face that had opened in pain. The

Russian's head ducked to one side as if he had avoided the blow, but the knees were going, and the body sagged. Hyde felt the hand surrender the transceiver, and hit the Russian again, behind the ear. Then he lowered him in his arms on to the mosaic of the threshold. The Russian was breathing as if asleep, on the verge of snoring.

Hyde dropped the transceiver, and was about to grind it beneath his shoe. Then he picked it up and put it into the pocket of his windcheater. If Petrunin tried to contact the man in the doorway, then at least he would know; know, too, that he would have only minutes after that.

He hurried now, shaking from the brief violence, the surge of adrenalin.

There were double gates at the rear of the hall. A uniformed constable opened a small judas-door to him, and closed it behind him. Hyde debated for a moment whether to tell the young policeman of the Russian in the doorway, or the others that might come looking for him, then decided against so doing.

The Edwin Shirley trucks were drawn up in convoy, as if the Free Trade Hall were some cargo terminal. Hyde skirted them, searching in the almost complete darkness for the rear entrance that the Special Branch inspector had pointed out on a plan of the building. He climbed three steps, his hand resting for a moment on a cold metal railing, then tried the door. It had been left unlocked by one of the plainclothes detectives who had been inside the building all day. Hyde went in and closed the door behind him. A lighted passage in need of a fresh coat of cream paint. Dark brown doors. Cramped, uncomfortable, draughty, strip-lighting the only modernism. There was no one in the corridor.

Heat of the Day – Hyde paused to listen, Alletson's high, clear voice riding over keyboards and guitar, part of the suite of pieces "No Way Back" – could be heard mutedly but plainly. He would have to hurry. Normally the band followed the suite with a keyboard display by Whiteman, the other four leaving the stage to him. He had only a few minutes, he realized, becoming aware at the same moment of the small transceiver in his pocket. He opened a dressing-room door. The room was empty and in darkness.

The second room was locked and he saw, looking down, that there was a light on, gleaming beneath the door. Then it went out. He fished for the stiff little rectangle of mica in his back pocket, and inserted it in the door jamb. He paused, listening. The noise of an opening window?

Alletson's voice silent, the slow keyboard section of the suite, building to the ensemble climax. Three, four minutes. A window opening?

He sprang the Yale lock and opened the door. In the light that entered the room from the corridor, he could see a small, slim figure at the dressing-room window, balanced on the sill. He crossed the room in three strides, knocking over a chair, hearing the slight, rustling twang of a guitar he had disturbed, then he had his arms around the figure, keeping his head back from the fingernails that instantly sought his face. He pulled Tricia Quin back into the room, clamping one hand over her mouth, pressing her against him with his other arm. Her body wriggled in his embrace, small, slippery. She backheeled his shins, and he winced with pain but did not let go. He felt the door behind him, raised his elbow, found the light switch, and held her against him after the light came on, but more gently. Eventually, he turned her head so that she could see his face. She stopped wriggling and struggling for a moment, then tried to tear away from him.

"Listen to me," he whispered, "just listen to me without struggling, will you?' His voice was almost petulant rather than threatening, and its tone struck her. Her eyes widened, and he took his hand from her mouth carefully. "OK, will you listen? You'd have broken your bloody neck if you'd jumped from that window."

"We're on the ground floor," she remarked in a superior tone. "What do you want?" She pulled down her T-shirt – a pointing hand in white, black background, the legend *Keep your eyes on the face, sonny* – and then tugged her cardigan straight on her narrow shoulders. She looked vulnerable, intelligent, arrogant, and somehow old-fashioned, out of date. A flower-child who had wandered into the wrong decade. "Well, what do you want? Or was it all for a quick feel in the dark?"

Hyde studied his hands, then looked up. Slowly, slowly, he instructed himself. In his broadest Strine he drawled, "I like 'em with bigger tits, girlie."

Her face narrowed in anger, then she seemed more puzzled than anything else. "You're very persistent, aren't you?"

"And you're very elusive." He stepped forward, hands raised in a signal of harmlessness, and righted the chair he had knocked over. He sat down. "Give me five minutes of your time – just listen to me. I'll try to make you an offer you can't refuse."

"You don't have anything with which to trade, do you?"

"Maybe not. Sit down, anyway."

Tricia Quin slumped untidily, sullenly into a sagging armchair. "All right. Talk."

"I know your mates will be back in a couple of minutes – they're almost finished with 'No Way Back' –" The girl's eyes narrowed with cunning. "So, I'll be brief. There are Russian agents – no don't sneer and don't laugh and don't get clever – outside. The real McCoy. They're interested in contacting your father, and they're sure you know where he is."

"They're just like you."

"No." Hyde bit down on his rising temper. The band murmured beyond the door, close to the climax of the suite. Perhaps no more than a minute. "At this moment, there are a hundred lives at risk under the Barents Sea because of your dad."

"What?"

"The submarine, girlie. Shit, the little old submarine with your old man's wonderful piece of machinery on board, the one everyone wants to know all about." Hyde's voice was scornful, carefully modulated. The band sounded louder, closer to the finish. "Only it isn't working so bloody well at the moment. The Russians have damaged our side's submarine, and your father's bloody expensive equipment isn't working properly. Keeps going on and off like Radio Caroline in the old days."

"I – what am I supposed to do about it?" She was attempting to regain her composure, and she was listening to the sounds from beyond the door.

"Let me talk to your dad – tell him what's what." The girl was already shaking her head. "A telephone number – *you* ring him, I won't watch." Tricia Quin examined the offer for its concealed booby-trap. "No trick," Hyde added.

Alletson walked into their intent silence. Whiteman's tumultuous keyboard playing could be heard through the open door. Alletson's tight-curled hair was wet with perspiration, his damp shirt open to the waist.

"What the hell do you want?" he asked.

"What's up, Jon?" Hyde heard someone in the corridor ask. The lead guitarist, Howarth, pushed into the room carrying two cans of lager. "Who's he?"

"The *secret agent* I told you about." Tricia Quin explained with laden sarcasm. "The *spy*."

"What's he want – you?"

"If you're coming in, close the bloody door," Hyde said lightly, "there's a bloody draught."

Howarth closed the door, and leant against it, still holding the cans of lager. He studied the guitar lying near Hyde's feet with a silent malevolence. Hyde turned on his chair and looked up at Alletson.

"Jon-boy," he said, "tell her to piss off, tell her you don't love her any more, tell her she's a bloody nuisance who could ruin the tour – tell her anything, but persuade her to come with me."

"Why should I do that? She's afraid of you."

726

"You should see the other side, mate. They frighten me." Alletson grinned despite himself. "See, I'm not such a bad bloke after all." He stopped smiling. "I've told her why I have to find her father –"

"You're probably lying." she remarked.

Hyde turned back to her. "I'm not as it happens. Your father's bloody marvellous invention has dropped a hundred blokes in the shit! Now, will you call him and let me tell *him*?"

It was evident the girl was on the point of shaking her head, when Alletson said quietly, "Why not, Trish?" She stared at him, at first in disbelief then with a narrow, bright vehemence, sharp as a knife. "Look, Trish," Alletson persisted, "go and call him; we'll keep James Bondi –" Hyde laughed aloud "– here while you do it. *Ask* your father if he wants to talk to Don Bradman."

The girl screwed up her face in concentration. She looked very young, indecisive; an air of failure, inability, lack of capacity emanated from her. She irritated Hyde as he watched her.

"All right," she said finally, resenting Alletson for making the suggestion, the capitulation, in the first place. Hyde also noticed that in a more obscure way she accepted the role forced upon her. Perhaps she was tired of running, tired of keeping her father's secrets. Alletson had made a decision for her that she could not entirely resent. "Make sure he stays here," she added. Hyde controlled his sudden fear, and made no effort to follow her. She pushed past Howarth, and closed the door behind her.

Hyde studied Alletson. The man was nervous of him now, had accepted that he could do no more to protect Tricia Quin.

"Sorry – about last night," Alletson said eventually.

Hyde shrugged. "I don't blame you, mate," he said, raised palms facing outwards. "Pax. I will help her," he added.

"I told you, Jon, we ought to dump her –" Howarth began but Alletson turned on him.

"Piss off. For old times' sake. It was for old times' sake."

"How's the tour going so far?" Hyde asked pleasantly, wondering whether Tricia Quin had taken the opportunity to bolt again. He did not think she had, but the closed door at Howarth's back troubled him.

"You're interested?" Howarth asked in disbelief.

"I'm old enough to remember your first album."

"Thanks."

"Why is she running?" Alletson asked, looking almost guilty.

"Her father's paranoid about security. She's caught the infection."

"It is all real, then?"

Hyde nodded. "Oh, yes. Silly, but real. The Russians want her dad, or her, or both, because he's invented a purple deathray which will give world dominion to whoever possesses its deadly secret. I'm Flash Gordon, no less."

"That's about what we thought," Alletson admitted, grinning in a puzzled way. Then he looked at his watch. "We're back on. You – you'll take care of her?" Hyde nodded.

Alletson and Howarth left the room, Howarth picking up the acoustic guitar lying on the floor near Hyde's feet before he went. Then Tricia Quin was standing in the open doorway as Whiteman's final keyboard crescendo echoed down the corridor. Her face was white. She looked guilty and afraid.

"OK?"

She nodded. "Yes. Yes, he's very tired. He'll talk to you, but only to you. I think he's got a gun." Her last words were a warning, and an attempt to excuse her own and her father's capitulation. "He's been worried about me."

"He's still safe?"

"Yes."

"Where?"

"I'll tell you when we've left here."

"Luggage?" She shook her head. "Let's go, then." She looked up sharply at the tone of his voice. Hyde had remembered the KGB irregular lying unconscious in a windy shop doorway on mosaic tiles. He hadn't reported in –

His hand patted the pocket of his windcheater in which he had placed the tiny transceiver. As if he had triggered it, it began bleeping. Tricia Quin's face blanched, her hand flew to her mouth. Hyde cursed.

"It's one of their radios," he explained, getting up quickly. His chair clattered over, and she began to back into the corner of the room, as if he had threatened her with violence. The transceiver continued to bleep, its volume seeming to increase. Her eyes darted between Hyde's face and the door she had left defencelessly open. "Come on, let's get moving!" She was opening her mouth, all capitulation forgotten, betrayal seeping into her features. Hyde bellowed at her. "It's no time to change your mind, you stupid, mixed-up cow! Shift your bloody arse!" She reached for her jacket.

He grabbed her arm and propelled her towards the door. The corridor was empty. At the back of his mind, Hyde could see the Russians fitfully on a dim screen; wondering, worrying, beginning to move, guessing, *knowing* –

He could hand her over now to the police, to the Branch, and she would be safe. If he did, they'd spend days trying to find out where Quin was hiding. She'd be in catatonic suspicion, comatosed with her secret. If he went with her, alone –

728

"You're hurting –" she said meekly as he bundled her down the corridor through the door. He released her arm, and paused to listen, holding his hand in front of her face, indicating silence. He could hear her ragged breathing, like the last ineffectual plucking of his mother's lungs at the hot Sydney air in the darkened room. The day she died.

"Shut up!" he whispered fiercely.

"Sorry –"

He strained to hear. Nothing. The dim music from inside, the murmur of a radio in one of the trucks, traffic muted in the distance.

"Come on." He propelled her down the steps, reached for her hand – she allowed him to hold it, it was inanimate and cold in his grip – and they moved swiftly across the yard. The transceiver in his pocket became silent. Moving; fearful, angry, *quick*, closing in –

The same police constable was on the gate, and he acknowledged their appearance with a nod. He did not seem surprised to see the girl.

"Everything all right, sir?"

Tricia Quin seemed reassured by the manner of his addressing Hyde.

"I think so, constable." Nothing in the narrow, dimly-lit street, but he could not see the baker's shop from the gate. They could be there already. Petrunin might already be out of his car, his minions much closer than that. There was little point in the constable being involved. "Nip inside, constable. Now I've got her, we can start sniffing them out."

"Very good, sir. I'll just report in."

"When you get inside." He realized he was still holding the girl's hand, and he squeezed it. "Come on. My car's only round the corner." Probably with someone very unfriendly sitting in it, he added to himself.

A curious but not unfamiliar elation seized him. His chest seemed expanded with some lighter-than-air gas like helium, and his head was very clear. One of his Vick moments, as he had once described them. Everything clear, cold, sharp. The TR7 was behind the Midland Hotel, in the old railway station that had become, without redecoration or conversion, a huge car park. He jiggled her arm, and they began running up the narrow street, away from the rear of the Free Trade Hall and the baker's doorway. Sensuous information flooded in, his brain sifting it swiftly, unerringly.

Light from around the corner – Peter Street. Their footsteps, the girl's padding lighter in flat, crêpe-soled shoes, the rubbing of her arm against her borrowed, too-big jacket, the spillage of music – Brahms – from an upstairs window, the splash of one foot in a puddle, the gun cold and noticeable in the small of his back, thrust into his waistband.

729

The emptiness of the end of the street, no shadow against the lights of Peter Street. He was grateful.

The Midland Hotel was across the bright, traffic-filled street. It was a moment before Hyde remembered that Petrunin's car was parked in the square in front of the hotel.

"OK?" he asked the girl. She was gulping air, but she nodded and tried to smile shakily. "Keep going, then, shall we?"

Pavement. Pedestrian crossing. Normality. Red man, traffic swooping past them and round into the square or into Oxford Street or Moseley Street. Central Library, Midland Hotel. Forget it, don't turn your head, stop searching for them. You either fully pretend or not at all –

Red man. Green man, traffic stopping. Walk. He tugged at her hand. One pace, two, you can hurry a little here, people always do on zebra crossings.

They were almost across the street before he heard the first shout, the answering call, and sensed the acceleration of the pursuit. On the pavement, he turned. A man waved to him, as if to call him back over a matter of a dropped book or wallet, or an unpaid bill. He stepped off the opposite pavement. Petrunin himself. He'd been the closest, most experienced, sharpest mind. He'd guessed, and just strolled round the square from his car, and seen them emerge. Petrunin, who knew him, knew the girl's face, no mistake –

"Is that one of them?" the girl asked, as if facing some extremely difficult task of recollection or recognition.

"That's him." Petrunin was almost smiling. Green man still. Two others, running out into Peter Street from the rear of the Free Trade Hall. Not the man in the doorway, two others who had found him and come running. "Ready?" Hyde asked.

"Yes." Her hand trembled in his.

Red man. Petrunin, three paces onto the zebra crossing, paused so that the others could catch up with him. The sound of an impatient horn, then the blare of another and revving engines. Petrunin skipped back onto the opposite pavement.

"Now!"

They raced down the shadowy side-street alongside the bulk of the Midland Hotel. The illuminated façade of the old railway station was ahead of them, the car park barrier like a border to be crossed into a safe country. Hyde pulled at the girl's arm, urging her on, sensing that she was flagging.

The squeal of brakes behind them, the bellow of a car horn. Petrunin wasn't waiting for the green light. They ran together across the road, up the slope to the barrier. A black face was behind the glass of the booth. Hyde looked behind him. All three men were across

Peter Street and running towards them. Hyde inwardly cursed the bravado of his isolation with the girl. There were police in the square, in Peter Street, Watson Street, in the Free Trade Hall, and he had chosen to run with the girl, making Manchester as alien and dangerous as Prague or Warsaw or Moscow. He slapped notes and change onto the counter of the booth, together with his ticket.

He swallowed saliva, said "I'm in a hurry. Keep the change. Open the barrier when I drive out – yellow TR7. Got it?" Then his hand was in his pocket and he was waving the shorthand of the CID warrant card. The Indian nodded.

Hyde ran on, the girl ahead of him now, but slowing because there seemed no safety amid the cars under the cracked, glassless station roof.

"Where?" she said.

"Over there," he said, pointing.

One or two weak lights revealed the massed, hunched, beetle-like shells of car bonnets and roofs. The girl stared around her wildly. Hyde glanced back. Petrunin and the other two had slowed their pace, almost strolling past the barrier, confident but wary, imitating legitimacy. Seconds between them. Hyde ran out onto the platform with the girl. Dully gleaming, crustaceous cars; silence. The wind soughing thinly in the shell of the station. The three Russians were past the barrier and had paused on the threshold of the station itself. Hyde ducked down, pulling the girl into a crouch, and began weaving awkwardly between parked cars.

He paused, listened, then moved on. They came to the edge of the platform, and he dropped down. He reached up and the girl surrendered to his grasp on her waist. He lifted her down. A row of cars, one of them yellow.

"Mr. Hyde?"

He thought for the moment it was the girl speaking, because of the light, interrogative tone. But it was Petrunin – accent and authority seeping into Hyde's awareness just behind the words. He gestured to the girl to remain silent, and they moved, crouching, along the rear bumpers of cars until they were leaning against the TR7. He heard the girl's ragged breathing again, but not like his mother's now; too alive for that, too much wanting to live. Hyde fished the car keys from his pocket and reached up to unlock the door.

"Mr. Hyde?" Then whispered instructions above the girl's breathing, the shuffle of footsteps as the three men spread out. Petrunin was confident. He hadn't left anyone at the barrier. "Mr. Hyde." A sharper tone, impatient.

Hyde eased open the door of the TR7, and indicated that the girl should climb in. They'd be looking for the yellow car. He crept round to the driver's door, unlocked it, clambered into the low hard seat. He eased the door shut on the footsteps that were coming closer. Steel-tipped heels to the heavy shoes. He slipped the key into the ignition, and pulled out the choke. He looked at Tricia Quin. Hair damp on her forehead, face pale, cheeks quivering.

"Which way?"

"North," she said, hugging herself as if to keep warm; trying to retreat from her danger.

Hyde breathed in deeply, then turned the key. Cough, chatter of the ignition, cough, firing of the engine, drowning a surprised and delighted cry from up on the platform. He thrust the gears into reverse, screeched out of his parking place, heaving on the wheel. The TR7 skidded, almost stalled, and then the car was bucking over the uneven ground.

He reached the end of the platform, and swung the car left, across the hard-packed earth where the tracks had once been, until he mounted the platform ramp at the other side of the station. He had heard no gunfire, nothing after that shout of discovery. The engine whined, the tyres screeched as he roared along the platform, then turned again onto what had been the concourse, heading for the entrance.

One man, stepping out from behind a car, gun levelled. Hesitation, a slight turning of his head – a cry of protest from Petrunin? Then the TR7 was almost on top of him, a spit of flame from the shadowy bulk of the man before he flicked aside like a matador, between two cars. The bullet's path was a groove in the thin metal of the roof, directly above Hyde's head. He screeched the car round and through the entrance to the station, and the barrier was going up, very slowly. Another man was entering the booth alongside the barrier – barrier going up, making a chopping motion as it reached the peak of its swing, beginning to descend almost immediately. The TR7 raced beneath it, bounced over cobbles, and squealed into the road behind the Midland Hotel.

"North," Hyde said loudly when his breath returned and the hotel's bulk was between them and the station. His palms were damp on the steering wheel, and he was perspiring freely. "North."

"Come on, come on!" Ardenyev yelled, his voice already hoarse from its combat with the wind and the sea, his gloved hands seemingly frozen and incapable as he attempted, with Teplov and Nikitin, to drag the largest of the sleds across the deck of the launch to its side.

The trough made them wallow as the helmsman steadied the launch. The young lieutenant watched them through the cabin window, his head flickering back and forth like a tennis spectator, towards them then towards the next peak, looming ahead of them.

"One more, sir!" Teplov bellowed back at him, even though they were not more then three or four feet apart on either side of the sled and its mound of cylinders. Shadrin and Vanilov and Kuzin were already submerged, safe under the water, with the second sled and the welding and cutting gear. Their ten minutes had already begun. There should have been four sleds, more communications equipment, more everything. Petrov was lying on a bunk, his leg broken and splinted in an inflatable plastic bag. Groaning and useless.

The sled tilted on the side of the launch as the next wave reared up in the darkness and opened its jaws. Teplov glanced over his shoulder. Regret was useless, too. Ardenyev strained like someone demented or terrified as Nikitin, attached by a line, flipped over the side of the launch into the water, mask and mouth-piece in place, his ten minutes already beginning. One thought re-emerged from the panic of Ardenyev's mind. Unless they could get onto the *Proteus* within the ten minutes, then they would have to spend hours coming back to the surface to avoid the bends, and no launch would be able to pick them up with ease – perhaps not at all – in this sea and at night. It was a one-way journey.

Nikitin's barely discernible bobbing head was accompanied by a raised hand, and then he swam close to the side of the launch. Ardenyev felt the dead weight of the sled pull towards Nikitin, and saw Teplov's face grey with strain. He yelled at the senior *michman*, who nodded, and went over the side. The wave loomed over the launch, flecked, old, immense. Two black-capped heads bobbed in the water. Slowly, almost out of his control, the sled dipped into the water and sank immediately. Teplov and Nikitin struck down after it.

Then the water, even as he turned his head to look and thought of time once more, lifted him and threw him across the deck of the launch. He glimpsed the lieutenant's appalled face, the rearing nose of the launch, then he was headfirst into the water, spun and tumbled like a leaf or twig in a stream's torrent, whirled down as he fitted his mouthpiece by instinct. His legs were above his head, just discernible; then blackness, and orientation returning. There were lights below him, two pale blobs like the eyes of a deep-ocean fish. He breathed as calmly as he could, then struck down towards the lights.

He tapped Teplov on the shoulder, and signalled with upraised thumb. Teplov's relief sounded withdrawn and almost mechanical through his throat-mike. Teplov slid further back against Nikitin on the seat of the sled, and Ardenyev swung himself into the saddle, holding onto the steering column. Directly in front of him, the tiny sonar screen was switched on, and the bright spot of the British submarine lay below and thirty degrees to port.

"Shadrin?" Ardenyev enquired into his microphone. All formality, all wasted words and energy and air disappeared beneath the surface.

"Skipper?"

"Got her fixed?"

"Yes, skipper."

"Let's go."

Ardenyev dipped the nose of the sled – a light, frail craft now that it was in its own element, not being manhandled across a sloping, slippery deck – towards the ledge on which the *Proteus* lay, not two hundred yards from them. The headlights of the sled picked out the winking, vanishing shoals of fish before they glanced across the silted ledge. Blackness beyond the ledge, but the lights turning the ledge itself almost sand-coloured, almost alive and three-dimensional. The cold seeped through the immersion suit, began to ring in his head like the absence of oxygen. Teplov clung to him, and Nikitin to Teplov. Without Petrov, Ardenyev had decided that the two main sleds would suffice. He hadn't been thinking clearly on the launch, only swiftly, rapping out orders and decisions as if keeping a mounting, insidious sense of failure, of utter futility, at bay with the sound of his voice and the fence of quick thought.

Grey, white numerals, then the blackness of the sea behind. Ardenyev, feeling Teplov's tap on his shoulder in response to what they both had seen, turned the sled slowly in a sweeping curve. He circled slightly above the British submarine like a gull in the wind, and watched as the headlights of Shadrin's sled slipped like a caress across the midships section of the submarine, then up and around her sail.

They'd found her. He looked at his watch. Seven minutes remaining. He pushed the nose of the sled down towards the *Proteus*.

"There she is skipper!"

"Infra-red cameras?"

"Cameras running, skipper."

"Can you see them, Terry?"

"No – wait – *there*?"

"What the hell is that?"

"Looks like a sled. It's going, going over the side. They'll get caught by the wave, no, one of them has – he's going over!"

"All fall down. Can we communicate with MoD yet?"

"No, skipper."

"Then you'd better send the pictures over the wire straight away. Even Aubrey ought to be able to work this one out!"

"I'm sorry, Mr. Aubrey, it could take hours to analyse these pictures." Clark was holding irritation in check, his apology an exercise in calming his breathing and no more.

"There's no way we can communicate with the Nimrod?"

"I'm sorry, sir," Copeland replied lugubriously, shaking his head, folding down his lower lip to complete the mask of apology. "The jamming makes that impossible. Eastoe must have sent these by way of a substitute – and without sub-titles."

"I am in no mood for cheap remarks, young man!" Aubrey snapped wearily.

"Sorry, sir."

Aubrey turned back to Clark. "How many men, would you say?"

They were still clustered round the wireprint machine, and the grainy reproductions of the infra-red photographs that the Nimrod had transmitted, torn off the machine as each frame appeared, were in every hand, or lay scattered on the bench near the machine. The whole room seemed crowded, like boys urging on two unwilling combatants, around Aubrey and Clark.

"This sled?"

"What do you mean, *this* sled?" Aubrey wanted, demanded information, answers to his question upon which he could base a decision. The desire to make a decision, to act, pressed upon him like a manhole-cover which would mask a trap. Failure, complete and abject and humiliating, stared up at him like a nightmare into which he was falling.

"I mean there may be more than one sled. It looks like two, it's a two-man sled all right. Could be three –?" Clark was examining the photograph with a magnifying-glass. It seemed old-fashioned, inappropriate to the advanced technology that was their pressing concern. "Leopard" lying like junk on the floor of the Barents Sea.

"That equipment, then?" Aubrey asked snappily, using his own magnifying-glass, making nothing of the shapes and bulky outlines of the underwater equipment that was strapped and secured on the back of the sled. Yes, he could see it was a two-man sled, there were two men, perhaps one of the grainy dots was another head bobbing in the water –? "You say this man Ardenyev would be in command here?"

"That equipment – welding or cutting gear, oxygen, who knows? And yes, I guess it would be Valery Ardenyev."

Clark was grinning.

"You've met him, then."

"We've been – *observers*, at the same oceanographic conferences, sure."

"What is his field of expertise?"

"Red Banner Special Operations – rescue, salvage, demolition, offence, defence, – you name it, they can do it."

"The launch, Ethan – how many of these sleds could it hold?"

"No more than two, three – why?"

"The numbers involved, my dear fellow." Aubrey was expansive again, confident. Clark was amazed at the brittle, transitory nature of the old man's emotions, whether optimistic or pessimistic. When he encountered the next obstacle, he would fall back into a trough of doubt and anxiety. "Can I assume that they would not attempt salvage – or anything more *intrusive* – with so few people?"

"You might do. Inspection? Maybe."

"Come, Ethan. Give me a best guess. Is this likely to be an inspection?"

"They'll have little time down there, at that depth. Just enough time, maybe."

"Then we have some time available ourselves?"

"To do what?" Clark turned on Aubrey angrily as it seemed self-satisfaction was the object, the sole purpose, of his questions. Feel good, put your mind to rest – and then you don't need to do any more. He almost voiced his thoughts.

"I don't know. We are prevented from making any moves other than diplomatic and political, until tomorrow or the following day. Have we that much time?"

"I don't know. Let's hope Eastoe goes down for another set of pictures when these divers return to the surface. Then we'll know it was only an inspection."

Aubrey's face darkened. He wondered what madcap idea had sprung into Clark's mind, and whether, because he was younger and of the same experience and background, he might not have perceived something of what was in the man Ardenyev's mind. He did not, however, ask Clark his meaning.

"Norway must make another protest about this incursion into her territorial waters," he said, and even to himself it sounded both too little and too late. He avoided looking at Clark as he pushed his way out of the circle of people around them, towards the telephones.

The *Proteus*'s stern lay bathed in the headlights of the two sleds, parked side by side on the ledge. The silt which they and the submarine had disturbed had settled. There was a wide ugly furrow the *Proteus* had gouged before she finally stopped. Beyond it, the damaged stern was grey, twisted, scorched metal, flayed by the coils of steel the MIRV torpedo had released. Ardenyev saw, as he picked his way fly-like in the illumination of the lights, that the fifteen-blade propeller had been thrown out of alignment, or dragged so it became embroiled with the whipping tendrils of steel cable, and that three of the phosphor-bronze, boot-shaped blades had been sheared off. One or two of the others were distorted, but intact. Without the MIRV torpedo, the damage wreaked by the low-warhead hit would not have been sufficient to stop the submarine.

Teplov's shoulder nudged against his as they clung to the port aft hydroplane. A steel cable twisted away from them like a great grey snake slithering towards the silt beneath the submarine. The hydroplane was buckled and torn beneath their hands and flippers, and its skin of metal had begun to unpeel like the layers of an onion, having been damaged and then subjected to the pressure of the water before the *Proteus* slowed and halted. In front of them, the bulk of the submarine retreated into the darkness. Buckled plates, damaged ballast tanks, but there was no evidence that the pressure hull had been ruptured.

"They made a bloody good job of it," Teplov's voice croaked in his earpiece. Ardenyev nodded.

The rudders were misaligned, too, but not badly.

"We can patch it – she'll have to be towed. We don't have time to repair the prop."

It was Teplov's turn to nod. His eyes seemed to be grinning behind his facemask.

"What next?"

"Let's move amidships. Signal the others to start making a din in –" He looked at his watch, "one minute." Ardenyev pushed away from the damaged hydroplane. His watch informed him that four minutes had already passed for himself, and perhaps five for Shadrin, Vanilov and Kuzin. No time to waste. He had six minutes to get aboard. Teplov behind him instructed the others, his voice tinny in the earpiece as Ardenyev glided like a black fish along the whale-like back of the *Proteus*. Each man knew his job; they had performed a hundred time trials in the deep tanks at the Frunze Naval School, and off-shore in the same depth and sea conditions as now pertained. Ardenyev's hands touched the two canisters strapped to his chest, smaller imitations of the two air tanks on his back.

They'd rehearsed it on submerged mock-ups, on the old "Whiskey"-class boat they'd commissioned for practice. After the first month's training the ten minutes had always been sufficient, even with the adrenalin running lower than now. But Ardenyev could not help remembering one severe case of the bends he had suffered by going through the mock-up's escape chamber too quickly, which had incapacitated him, and he could not forget the first full sea trial which had included the use of the MIRV torpedo. The steel cables had ripped open the hull of the old submarine they

737

were using, killing its crew. He and his two teams had been in the launch, waiting to go down, when the wreckage and the released air and the oil had come to the surface.

The great fin-like sail of the *Proteus* loomed out of the darkness. His lamp played on it. Below it, the officers and control room of the submarine. And "Leopard", his target. He hovered, and Teplov joined him. Ardenyev gave him the thumbs-up signal, and the senior *michman* swam down to the base of the sail, his shape becoming indistinct, the light of his lamp feeble, winking on and off, it seemed, as he moved away and sought his own objective. Teplov would begin communicating in morse on the hull of the *Proteus*, offering apology and assistance and reassurance in the name of the Red Banner Fleet, distracting the officers of the submarine and retarding suspicion and activity.

Ardenyev kicked on, moving more swiftly now, dipping down to touch the hull once with his fingertips, then moving off again as soon as he sensed the vibration. The other four were using cutting gear and making as much noise as they could at the stern, a further distraction. Now, everything – the whole operation and its success – depended upon himself. The knowledge satisfied him as he urged his body through the water. He could just make out the forward hydroplanes. A shoal of fish, brief as a torch-signal, were caught in the light of his lamp. He glanced again at his watch. Four minutes fifty since he had reached bottom. Three-and-a-half minutes to decompress slowly enough not to be incapacitated. He kicked on more urgently, gliding over the hull, his lamp playing upon it now with an almost frenzied movement, sweeping back and forth like a small searchlight. The diagram of the submarine was vivid in his mind, as if he possessed vision that allowed him to see beneath the skin of the double hull. He was passing over the officers' wardroom and the crew's quarters beneath them, towards the torpedo room. He reminded himself that the submarine would be silent, alert. He would be making noises almost next door to the wardroom, which would contain the off-duty officers, sitting in silence, nervous of moving. Would they be sufficiently distracted by the tapping, by the noises from the stern thrumming through the hull?

His lamp washed across the hull, then swung back. He had found his objective, the forward escape hatch above the torpedo room. Even here, the British had made it easier for him. A Royal Navy fleet submarine had gone down in the North Sea two years before. The crew had died because the air purification system had suddenly failed, and the rescuers had taken too long to cut their way into the hull. Since that disaster, it had been specified that all nuclear submarines, as well as all the older diesel subs in the Royal Navy, be fitted with two-way hatches that could be opened without difficulty from the outside. The Red Navy had known that when it began to plan the abduction of "Leopard".

He gripped the wheel of the flood control valve and began to twist it, wrenching at it violently, then turning it more easily. He looked at his watch. He had been under for six minutes, some of the others for seven. He had already lost them half a minute. It increased decompression time by the same amount. He began turning the wheel more rapidly. He could not account for the strange loss of time. How much time had he wasted looking at the damage, almost enjoying it, satisfied at the helplessness of the huge submarine? That must have been when he lost the forty seconds he was now behind schedule.

"Viktor?" he whispered into his mouthpiece.

"Sir?"

"How is it?"

"They're demanding to know what we're doing, and how their submarine was damaged?"

"Have you asked to come aboard?"

"Yes, sir. They've refused a liaison officer. I'm giving them the fictitious damage report now."

"I'm going in."

"Good luck, sir."

Ardenyev lifted the hatch slowly, sensing its great weight even under water. A rush of bubbles enveloped him. He would have made a noise already that might have been heard. They'd rehearsed that, too. The other distracting noises had been sufficient to mask his entry – but were they now, when it mattered? He dropped slowly into the chamber, and pulled the hatch down on himself. Then the submarine lurched forward, and his head banged in surreal slow-motion against the side of the compartment. His lamp's light wobbled on the walls around him. He was in a cylinder like the inside of an artillery shell which felt as if it was being slid into the breech of a gun.

The *Proteus* was moving, wriggling like an animal trying to rid itself of fleas. He pressed feet and back against the walls of the cylinder, simply hanging on because the buoyancy within the flooded chamber allowed him no weight, no steadiness. He could imagine, vividly, the control room where the decision has been taken; imagine, also, the hull of the submarine. Teplov might have been flung off – what about the others, the flail of cutting gear, the roll of tanks, the whip of the steel cables around the prop. He could sense the grinding as the submarine's prop struggled to turn against the restraint of the cables, his teeth grinding in his head, his whole head aching with the vibration. They must stop, must –

A glimpse of his watch. Seven minutes and ten, eleven seconds.

Then the lamp banged against his arm painfully. He squeezed himself flatter, taller, bigger, holding himself still. Welding gear, cutting torches, tanks, the whip of cables. He sensed like a medium that one of them, perhaps more, would be dead or injured. All of them were running out of time. Time. That was the calculation; they knew it in the *Proteus*. Twenty fathoms equalled ten minutes' working time, then the excess nitrogen in the blood slowed the body, hampered the mind, began to kill. He was killing them now –

The scraping, the cries of metal as the crippled submarine dipped time and again to the bottom of the ledge, dragging her belly across silt and mud and rock, the grating, thrumming noise and vibration of the captive prop as it tried to turn, the smaller vibration – almost normality – of the small docking propeller being used. It seemed endless, unbearable.

He turned in the chamber, banged against the wall of the cylinder, gripped the lower hatch venting wheel, turned again, banged, was thrown off, his lamp flickering wildly against the flooded metal of his prison, gripped again, braced himself – the vibration and movement slowing now? – and turned a third time. The water began to seep slowly from the hatch into the torpedo room. Three-and-a-half minutes. He had practised the number of turns to allow the pressure to alter at the necessary rate, the precise amount of water to release per second, perhaps two hundred times. But not when it really mattered. He remained gripping the wheel of the lower hatch, the light of his lamp playing on his watch.

Ten, eleven, twelve seconds. Almost eight minutes of time gone, and another three minutes fifteen before the water had drained away and he had safely depressurized. A total of more than eleven minutes. And where were they? Had they hung on? Were they alive?

Slowing, vibration bearable. Scraping on its belly, lurching to starboard, a cry of rent metal, the main prop not being used, docking prop dying away. The *Proteus* was stopping again. He had waited too long. He should have acted earlier, when the noise and vibration were at their height. Now water dripped onto the empty torpedo room floor in the sudden silence as men's hearing returned. Thirty-seven seconds, thirty-eight, nine, forty –

Silence. He stood upright in the chamber. The water was at shoulder-height. He ducked back beneath its surface. Fifty-five seconds. He couldn't wait, *had* to wait. Perhaps the great bulk of the submarine had rolled on one or more of them? Teplov? Nikitin? The others? If they were alive, could they find the *Proteus* again in time in the forest of silt that must now obscure her? They would swim through an unending, almost solid grey curtain of silt, looking for the submarine that was their only hope. It was already too late to begin slowly ascending to the surface. Now he was safely decompressing, no one could enter the torpedo room escape chamber until he had left it. If any of them were still alive. He thought of the whip of a loosened steel cable across an immersion-suited body –

One minute twenty seconds. He was crouching against the floor of the chamber as the water drained slowly into the torpedo room below. Not a trickle, not a drip, but a slow, steady fall, noisy. The wardroom next door, normality returning, things being righted again, objects picked up from the floor, bruises rubbed, hearing returning, awareness of surroundings increasing. *What's that noise? Sprung a leak? Better go and take a look –*

Ardenyev was on his own. He remembered the helicopter going down in flames, then Petrov's broken leg, then the hellish noise and vibration of the *Proteus*. Dolohov, he was able to consider distinctly, might have killed every member of the Special Underwater Operations Unit, *his* unit. For a box of tricks to make a submarine invisible.

Two minutes five. The compartment was less than half full of water. He was squatting in a retreating tide, as he might have done at Tallinn or Odessa as a child, watching the mysterious, fascinating water rush away from him, leaving the froth of foam around him and the stretch of newly exposed wet sand in which shells sat up in little hollows. Two minutes twenty.

Noise, they must hear the noise, no they won't, they're too disorientated, they'll be listening for water, the dangerous water of a leak, a buckled or damaged plate, they'll hear it –

Two minutes thirty-two. Fifty-eight seconds remaining. He pulled at the hatch, and it swung up, emptying the chamber in an instant. His hands had been locked on the wheel, turning it slowly though the forebrain had decided to wait. The pressure of imagination as to what might have happened outside the submarine was greater than any other, pressing down and in on him like the ocean. He dropped through the hatch into the torpedo room, the water already draining away, leaving the cold, clinical place merely damp. Instantly, he felt dizzy, and sick. Too soon, too soon, he told himself. He had never tried to get through decompression at this depth in less than two minutes fifty. He'd been prepared to cope with the dizziness and sickness, the blood pounding in his head, that would have assailed him only half-a-minute early. This was worse, much worse. He staggered against the bulkhead, his vision unable to focus, his surroundings wobbling like a room in a nightmare. The noise in his ears was a hard pounding, beneath which he could almost hear the accelerating blood rushing with a dry whisper. His heart ached. Pain in his head, making thought impossible. His hands were clutched round the two canisters on his chest as if holding some talisman or icon of profound significance and efficacy. His legs were weak, and when he tried to move he lurched forward, almost spilling onto his face like a baby trying to walk for the first time.

He leaned against the bulkhead then, dragging in great lungfuls of the mixture in his air tanks, trying desperately to right his vision, and to focus on the door into the torpedo room. It was closed, but its outline shimmered, and threatened to dissolve. It was no barrier. Around him lay the sleek shapes of the torpedoes. Cold, clinical place, the floor already almost dry, except for the puddle that still lingered at his feet from his immersion suit. He tried to look at his watch, could not focus, strained and blinked and stretched his eyes, pressing the face of the watch almost against his facemask. Three minutes fifty, almost four minutes. He could have – should have – waited. He was further behind now. He snapped the lock on the weighted belt around his waist. It thudded to the floor.

He looked up. Close the hatch, close the hatch. Moving as if still under water, with diver's weighted feet and restraining suit, he reached up and closed the hatch, turning the handle with aching, frosty, weak limbs. If they were alive – he felt tears which were no longer simply another symptom of decompression prick helplessly behind his eyes – then now they could open the outer hatch.

Door opening. Refocus. Slowly refocus. He had been about to focus on the port and starboard air purifiers on either side of the torpedo room when the door began opening. But it still ran like a rain-filled window-pane, the image distorted. A figure that might have been reflected in a fairground mirror came through the door, stopped, yelled something indistinct above the rush and ache in his ears, then came towards him.

Quick, quick, useless instincts prompted. He pushed away from the bulkhead. He could make out the port purifier clearly, then it dissolved behind rain again for a moment, then his vision cleared. He could hear the words, the question and challenge shouted. Another figure came through the open bulkhead door. Two of them. Ardenyev moved through a thicker element than air, and hands grabbed him from behind, causing him to stagger near one of the torpedoes. Slowly, aquatically, he tried to turn and lash out. His other hand cradled one of the two canisters on his chest, and the young face seemed riveted by his hand and what it held. Ardenyev could distinguish expression on the face now – knowledge, realization. The young man enclosed him in a bear-hug, but Ardenyev heaved at the thin, light arms, pushing the man away by his very bulk.

He bent, opening the inspection plate; then his hand was pulled away, and another, larger hand clamped on his own as it held the first canister. The second canister was torn from its strap and rolled across the floor, beneath one of the torpedo trestles. All three of them watched it roll. The two British officers feared it might be a bomb after all.

Ardenyev chopped out with the lamp attached still to his wrist, catching the smaller officer on the side of the head, knocking him aside. He flipped over one of the torpedoes, and subsided to the floor, a vague redness staining the side of his face. Then Ardenyev was hit in the stomach and he doubled up. Another blow against the side of his facemask, then he lunged upwards with his upper torso, catching his attacker in the chest with his head. A soft exhalation of air, the man staggering backwards –

He turned, twisted the canister in both hands, releasing the incapacitating gas, then jammed the canister into the air purifier, closing the inspection plate immediately. Then he was punched in the small of the back, just below his air tanks, then hands were round his shoulders and face, and his mask was coming off. He felt the mouthpiece ripped out of his mouth, and he inhaled the warm, sterile air of the submarine. He staggered across the torpedo room, still held by the second man, lurching against the trestles, his eyes searching the floor for the second canister, oblivious even of the need to re-insert his mouthpiece before the gas passed the length of the submarine down the air ducts and returned to them in the torpedo room.

He dropped to one knee in a feint, then heaved with his shoulders. The second man, the heavier, bearded officer, rolled up and over his neck and shoulders, falling in front of him, winded by the metal floor of the room. Ardenyev scrabbled under a torpedo trestle, his fingers closing over its damp coldness, gripping it. He got to his feet, clutched the canister to his chest, which was heaving with effort, and staggered clumsily across the torpedo room in his flippers, to the starboard air purifier.

Other men were coming in now. He opened the inspection plate, twisted the canister, and jammed it into the purifier, closing the plate after it. He was grabbed, then. The room was full of noise, an alarm sounded somewhere, while he tried to jam his mouthpiece back into his mouth. They wanted to stop him. It was as if the hands that reached for him had only that one minor object, to prevent him regaining the safety of the air mixture in his tanks while the gas moved swiftly through the submarine. He felt himself hit, but his attention could not be spared for his torso, arms and legs, kidneys, stomach, chest. He went on trying to force the mouthpiece back into place.

One breath, two, three, doubling over on the floor, not resisting now, hoping they would assume he was beaten, even unconscious.

Someone turned him over; he saw through slitted lids a hand reach for the mouthpiece and mask again – the mask askew, obscuring much of the scene – then the hand lunged past him, a body toppled down beside him, subsiding with a peculiar, slow-motion grace, mimicking death. He opened his eyes now, knowing he had nothing to fear. Others fell like skittles, ninepins, but in the same seeming slow-motion.

Ardenyev closed his eyes. He alone was conscious on board the British submarine. There was no hurry, no hurry at all. They would be out for an hour, perhaps longer. There were no noises from the escape chamber, and therefore there was no hurry whatsoever. He had captured the *Proteus* and "Leopard", and he was entirely alone. A sad, even vile heroism. He surrendered to the exhaustion that assailed him, as if he, too, had inhaled the incapacitating gas.

NINE:

Retrieval

From their identification papers, Ardenyev knew them to be Thurston, the first lieutenant of the submarine, and Hayter, the officer responsible for "Leopard". Because of their importance, he had allowed them to remain with Lloyd in the control room of the *Proteus* after the remaining officers and ratings had been confined to the wardroom and crew quarters "for security reasons".

Ardenyev had watched Lloyd come round, come to an almost instant wakefulness, and he had immediately warmed to the man and granted him his respect and his wariness. Lloyd would now sabotage "Leopard" in a moment, if he could. Ardenyev stood before the captain of the submarine and his two senior officers at attention, like a junior officer presenting his compliments. It was part of the charade he was now required to play.

"As I was saying, captain," he began again, having been interrupted by an expletive from Thurston, "we very much apologize for the manner in which we were required to board your vessel. However, it is lucky that we did. Your purification system had developed a fault that would almost certainly have proved fatal had we not arrived." He said it without a flicker of amusement or self-mockery. The truth did not matter.

His men, his team were missing, presumed dead. Vanilov, brokenly, had told him he had seen Kuzin catch a whipping, freed tendril of steel cable across his back, and he had seen him flung away into the dark, his body tumbled and twisted in a way that would have been impossible had it been unbroken. Nikitin had fallen beneath the weight of the *Proteus*, forgetting in surprise to loosen his hold on the cutting gear. Stabs of blue flame had come from the cutting-pipes as the silt had boiled round, and swallowed, Nikitin. Shadrin he had not seen at all. Teplov and Vanilov alone had clung to the submarine, been dragged through the water and the boiling mist of silt and mud, rested dazed and exhausted and were slowly being poisoned by nitrogen in the blood until Teplov had crawled back to the stern and found Vanilov and boarded the *Proteus* through the aft escape hatch, into the electric motor room. They had waited in the slowly-draining compartment for five

745

minutes, until it was safe to emerge into the submarine. Dizziness and exhaustion, yes, but not the bends. Teplov had put the neutralizing agent through the aft purifiers, and then come seeking his commanding officer.

Ardenyev felt his left cheek adopt a tic, the last, fading tremors of weariness and shock. These men in front of him had killed three of his men, indirectly killed Blue Section. The knowledge that he would have done precisely the same, threatened as they had felt they were, intruded upon his anger, dimming it. Lloyd, the captain, was watching him carefully, weighing him, the expression on his face like a suspicion that they had met before, or always been intended to meet.

"Fucking piracy, that's what it is," Thurston offered into the silence, and Hayter rumbled his agreement. "How do you explain the guns if you're here to help us?"

Ardenyev smiled innocently. "We understand your concern with security. We would not wish to be blamed for any – *mistakes* you might make, any damage you might cause to sensitive equipment. It is merely a precaution."

"Locking up my crew is just another precaution, I presume?" Lloyd asked sardonically, sitting in a relaxed manner in one of the sonar operators' chairs, which he swung to and fro slowly, almost as if he intended mesmerizing the Russian. A relaxed, diffident, confident child. Ardenyev was pricked by his seeming indifference to the fate of Nikitin and the others.

"Captain, I would understand, even expect, some reaction such as that of Commander Thurston translated into action, either from one of your officers, or some of your men. That would only complicate an already complicated situation. We are here to *help* you –" Here, sincerity seeped into his voice in a measured, precise dose. "– because it is our fault that you are in this situation."

"You admit it, then?"

"What else can we do? The captain and officers of the submarine *Grishka* will be severely disciplined for their provocative action."

"This is unreal –!" Thurston exploded.

"Not at all – is it, captain?" Ardenyev said with a smirk. "It will be the agreed version of events."

"How do you explain the cuts and bruises on two of my officers?" Lloyd enquired. "The air purifiers struck them, I suppose?"

"Falling to the deck, I suppose," Ardenyev replied, "overcome by the lack of oxygen. I came aboard when your signals from inside stopped – you tapped out one word, HELP, before that happened. You don't remember?"

Lloyd shook his head. "No, I don't. Oxygen starvation plays tricks with the memory, obviously."

Ardenyev sighed with pleasure. "I see we understand each other, captain."

"What happens now?"

"From the damage report, there will be some repairs, to your buoyancy and to your hydroplanes. Then you will be towed back to Pechenga, our nearest naval base, for sufficient repairs to allow you to return to Faslane under your own power." He spread his hands innocently in front of him. "It is the least we can do, apart from the sincerest diplomatic apologies, of course. It will take little more than a day or two before you are on your way home." He beamed.

"If your mission is so humanitarian, why is your petty officer carrying a Kalashnikov with the safety-catch in the 'Off' position?" Thurston remarked sourly.

"Security." Ardenyev sighed again. He was tiring of the charade. It was not important. Everyone knew the truth. "Now, I will have to contact the rescue ship *Karpaty* and arrange for divers and equipment to be sent down to us."

"I'm sure you're reasonably familiar with our communications?" Lloyd remarked with forced lightness, as if his situation had come home to him in a more bitter, starker way.

"Thank you, yes." Ardenyev's hand released the butt of the Makarov pistol thrust into the belt of his immersion suit. He tousled his hair in an attempt to retain the mocking, false lightness of his conversation with the British officers. He wanted to clamber back into the fiction of a terrible accident, a life-saving boarding-party, apologetic repairs in Pechenga, as into a child's tree-house. But he could not. Whipping steel cables, boiling flame from a crashed helicopter, accompanied him vividly to the communications console.

As if admitting that the fiction could not be sustained, he drew the Makarov and motioned the three British officers to the far side of the control room before he seated himself in front of the console.

"These pictures were taken forty minutes after the previous set," Aubrey remarked. "You are telling me, Captain Clark" – The excessive politeness seemed designed to stave off any admission of disaster – "that since no divers have resurfaced, they must be on board *Proteus?*"

"Right."

"Why?"

"They couldn't stay down more than ten minutes at that depth. Then they'd come back up slowly, but by now they'd be back on board the launch. Sure, the launch has returned to take station on the port beam of *Karpaty*" – Here Clark nodded in Copeland's direction – " but as far as I can make out, they're loading heavy cutting gear from the rescue ship. And these men on deck. More divers. In full rig, not scuba gear. They're going down. Therefore, you can bet Ardenyev's men are on board."

"But why and how would Lloyd have allowed him on board?" Aubrey asked in exasperation. He was baffled and plagued by the murky high-resolution and light-intensified photographs transmitted from the Nimrod. Clark seemed to be reading tea leaves. The whole matter seemed like a fairy tale.

"He wouldn't need to –"

"The escape hatches," Copeland blurted out. "After *Phaeton* went down a couple of years ago, all the hatches had to open two-way. They'd know that, dammit!"

"Exactly," Clark said drily. "Ardenyev would have let himself in."

"Eastoe reports a change in position of *Proteus*."

"Lloyd trying to get rid of his guests," Clark commented acidly. "Someone's in there, you can bet on it."

"Then none of our messages got through?" Aubrey asked forlornly. " 'Leopard' will not have been destroyed."

"I'm afraid not."

"Clark – what will they do now, for heaven's sake?" Aubrey's eye rested on Giles Pyott's expressionless face with a glance of pure malevolence. Pyott's implacability refuted the accusation of the gaze. Clark cleared his throat, breaking the tension between the soldier and the intelligence agent. Aubrey shrugged.

"Raise her – depending on the damage, or simply take what they want down there. The situation's complicated by the fact that 'Leopard' isn't operational at present. I guess they'll raise her and tow her into port."

"What?" Pyott asked in disbelief. "That would be piracy. The international repercussions would be – enormous."

"You'd declare war?" Clark asked ironically.

"Don't be stupid."

"Then the shit hitting the fan will have been worth it. What will you do? All of you. You won't go to war, *we* won't go to war on your behalf, you won't tell anyone because it's all too embarrassing – so nothing will happen. 'Leopard' will belong to both sides or to none. That'll be the only outcome."

"What can we *do*, Clark?" Aubrey demanded with the impatient emphasis of a frustrated child on a wet day. He was almost shaking with rage and frustration.

"You've been outboxed, Mr. Aubrey."

"Don't be so damned American," Pyott drawled. "So insufferably smug and patronizing."

"Sorry, Colonel Pyott," Clark apologized. He could not mask his grin completely, even though he sensed the gravity of the situation as completely as anyone else in the room beneath the Admiralty. It was so – so *caricatured*, this panic in the dovecote. The new shiny toy was missing.

748

There was an absence of concern for the crew of the *Proteus* that Clark resented on their behalf, even in Aubrey. He also felt, and admitted, a sneaking admiration for the man he felt must have masterminded the boarding of the submarine, Valery Ardenyev. He could remember the man's face and build now, and he could entirely believe in the Russian's ability to successfully surprise and overcome a crew of over one hundred.

Everything depended upon the degree to which *Proteus* was damaged. The nearest NATO units were twenty hours' sailing from the present position of the submarine, except for certain small Norwegian units which the government in Oslo would not deploy in the Barents Sea. They could watch, by radar, sonar and aircraft, but they could not intervene. If it took more than twenty hours to raise and tow the *Proteus*, then the full five acts of the disaster might not be performed. Unless Ardenyev and his men simply unplugged "Leopard" and took it away with them. Clark was inclined to doubt this. The Russians would preserve, at some effort, the bland, apologetic face they had begun to present via the Soviet ambassador in London.

"Can we rescue it – them?" Aubrey asked. "Can we get out of the elephant trap that has been dug for us?" he insisted, worrying at the insuperable problem as at a bone. There had to be some hope within the situation, surely?

"Rescue?" Copeland blurted in disbelief.

"I can't see how," Clark said more carefully as Aubrey glared at the young Royal Navy officer. The map-board loomed over them all, all its lights gleaming and unmoving, except for the plotted course of the Nimrod on-station as it was updated every few minutes. A fly buzzing above the scene, a carrion bird over a kill.

"I don't see why they need to raise the sub," Pyott said. "They're interested in only one thing, surely?"

"Ardenyev's done maybe a half-dozen of these rescues on Russian boats in his career. Board and raise operations. He's an expert at it. They needed him to get on board, sure – but they maybe want his expertise at raising boats, too."

"I must talk to 'C' at once," Aubrey remarked. "Our talking is pointless at the moment. We must establish what the Soviet authorities intend."

Clark shrugged, unoffended that Aubrey doubted his prognosis. His respect for Aubrey had seemed to waver during the past twenty-four hours, like a light revealed and obscured by the movement of clouds. Yet the American, despite the clarity of his own mind, realized he still expected a solution to occur to Aubrey; even a successful solution.

Aubrey made no distinction of security between himself and the "Chessboard Counter" team, and used one of the battery of telephones in the underground room. Cunningham, he knew, was with the Foreign Secretary, having been summoned to a second meeting with the Soviet ambassador. He heard Cunningham at the other end of the line within half a minute of placing the call to the Foreign Office.

"Yes, Kenneth? What news?" Cunningham sounded breathless. Aubrey supposed it stemmed from events rather than exertion.

"Expert opinion – " Aubrey could not suppress an involuntary glance towards Clark and the tight-knit group around and beneath the map-board – "has it here that the Russians may have boarded *Proteus*."

"Good God, that's outrageous!"

"The ambassador hasn't confirmed as much?"

"He's talking of rescue, of course – but not of boarding. Not directly. Not as yet, that is."

"How does he explain the incident?"

There was a chilly chuckle in Cunningham's voice, the laugh of a man succeeding, just, in appreciating a joke against himself. "The captain of the Russian submarine suffered a nervous breakdown. He ordered the firing of the torpedo in question before he could be relieved of his command by the usual heroic young officer, loyal to the Party and the cause of world peace."

"That is perhaps the unkindest cut of all, that they can get away with such a ridiculous tale, knowing we can do nothing to refute it. And nothing to rescue our submarine."

"The Foreign Secretary has informed the PM, Kenneth. She's monitoring the situation. Every effort is being made to pressurize the Soviet Union into leaving the area and leaving *Proteus* to us."

"And –?"

"Very little. They insist, *absolutely insist*, on making amends. For the lunacy of one of their naval officers, as the ambassador put it."

"Washington?"

"The President is gravely concerned –"

"And will do nothing?"

"Is prepared to accept the Russian story at face value, for the sake of international tension, despite what his military advisers tell him. I don't think he quite grasps the importance of 'Leopard'."

"I see. We are getting nowhere?"

"Nowhere. What of this man Quin?"

"Nothing. The girl is the key. I'm waiting for a report from Hyde."

"Would it help if we recovered him, at least?"

"We might then destroy 'Leopard', I suppose."

"The PM will not risk the lives of the crew," Cunningham warned sternly. "The Foreign Secretary and I were informed of that in the most unequivocal manner."

750

"I meant only that we could attempt sabotage, or Lloyd could if Quin was in our hands again."

"Quite. You don't think 'Leopard' had been damaged by Lloyd or his crew?"

"It is possible, but I think unlikely. None of our signals reached the *Proteus*."

"Very well. Kenneth, I think you'd better come over here at once. You may have to brief the Foreign Secretary before he sees the PM again. Leave Pyott in command there."

"Very well. In fifteen minutes."

Aubrey replaced the receiver. The room was quiet with failure. Clark watched him steadily, some of the younger men regarded him with hope. Pyott appeared resigned. It was, he admitted, a complete and utter intelligence disaster – precisely the kind he could not tolerate or accept.

"Giles," he called, and then thought: Where the devil is Hyde?

Quin beckoned like a light at the end of a dark tunnel. A false, beguiling gleam, perhaps, but he had no other point of reference or hope.

Hyde wished he could call Aubrey from the row of telephones with their huge plastic hair-dryer hoods that he could see through the glass doors of the cafeteria. He was afraid, however, of leaving the girl for a moment. He was afraid of letting her out of his sight for any length of time, however short, and afraid, too, that she was beginning to regret her earlier decision. And he was also wary, treading delicately on the fragile, thin-ice crust of the trust she meagrely afforded him, of reminding her that there were other, more faceless, more powerful people behind him. The kind of people her father had fled from originally.

The telephones remained at the edge of his eyesight, in the centre of cognition, as he sipped his coffee and watched her eagerly devouring a plate of thin, overcooked steak and mushrooms and chips. For himself, beans on toast had been as much as he could eat. Tension wore at him, devouring appetite as well as energy. Quin was somewhere in the north of England – the girl had said nothing more than that, and he refrained from pumping her further for fear of recreating the drama of obsessive suspicion in her mind. He behaved, as far as he was able, as a driver who was giving her a lift north. The adrenalin refused to slow in his veins. He was nervous of pursuit – though he had seen no evidence of it – and he was suffering the stimulant effects of their escape from Petrunin.

"How's the tour going?" he asked conversationally.

She looked at him, a forkful of chips poised at her lips, which were shiny with eating. Her face was amused, and somehow obscurely contemptuous.

"I didn't have time to notice."

Hyde shrugged. "I thought you might have heard. I hope they do well."

"You expect me to believe that's all that's on your mind – the profits of an over-thirties rock band?" she sneered, chewing on the mouthful of chips, already slicing again at the thin steak. The cafeteria of the motorway service station was early-hours quiet around them. One or two lorry drivers wading through mountainous plates of food, a carload of caravanners avoiding the traffic of the day by travelling by night, smuggling their way to their holiday destination, the two waitresses leaning at the cash register, grumbling. Just south of Lancaster. Hyde hoped that Quin was somewhere in the Lake District. The sooner he got to him, the better.

He shrugged. "No, I don't think you're that stupid. Just filling in time, trying to lull you into a false sense of security." He grinned in what he hoped was an unsuspicious, engaging manner.

She studied him narrowly. Her plate was empty. "You're odd," she said eventually. "And too bloody clever by half. Don't pull the dumb ocker stunt with me."

She was still in control of their situation, leading him by the hand to her father, only because her father had agreed. She would tell him nothing until the last minute, to retain control.

"Thank you. Tell me, why did your father up and away like that? He wasn't really frightened of us, was he?"

She screwed her face up in thought, then released the skin into clear, youthful planes and curves again. With a bit of make-up, Hyde thought, she wouldn't look bad. They all wear a sneer these days.

"He was frightened of them – people like the ones tonight," she said. "And he didn't believe people like *you* –" An old and easy emphasis lay on the words like a mist. *Pigs, Fascists, cops, the fuzz.* The necessary vocabulary of her age and her education. The silence after the emphatic last word was strained, and she looked down, suddenly younger, more easily embarrassed.

"I see," he said. "We would have looked after him, you know."

"No you wouldn't!" she snapped, looking up again. "They watched him all the time. *Your* people took time off for meals, and the pub, and to go for a piss – *they* didn't! They were there all the time. Dad said there were a *hundred* times he could have been kidnapped while your lot weren't there or weren't looking!" She was leaning forward, whispering intently, a breathy shout. "You wouldn't have taken care of him – he took care of himself."

"I agree we're not as efficient as the KGB," Hyde said evenly. "But he wasn't in any real danger." Immediately, he was sorry he had uttered the words. The girl's features were rich in contempt, and he had no

752

business defending the DS. Quin had been right, in a way. The KGB might have lifted him, any time. "Sorry," he added. "No doubt he was right. Sloppy buggers, some of them." Her face relaxed. "But he's safe now?" Her eyes narrowed, and he added: "Do you want coffee?" She shook her head.

"You?"

"No." He hesitated, then said, "Look, you have to trust me. No, I don't mean because you realize I'm trying to save you and your old man from the baddies – you have to believe I can do it. I'm not tooling around Britain waiting for you to make up your mind."

She thought for a moment, then said, "You'll have to turn off the motorway at the exit for Kendal." She watched his face, and he suppressed any sign of satisfaction.

It was the importance of it, he decided. That explained her almost fanatical care for her father. She was the key, even to herself. Importantly useful for the first time in her parents' lives. Crucial to her father's safety. She clung to her role as much as she clung to her father. "Ready? Let's go, then."

The man near the telephone booth in the car park watched them approach the yellow TR7, get in, and drive off down the slip-road to the M6. There was just time for the brief telephone call to Petrunin before they set off in pursuit. Once clear of Manchester and onto the motorway, Hyde had not driven at more than sixty or sixty-five. If he kept to that speed, there would be enough time to catch him before the next exit. He dialled the number, then pressed the coin into the box. Petrunin's voice sounded hollow and distant.

"I may have some trouble getting away. A slight delay. Keep me informed."

"Trouble?"

"No. I must, however, be careful leaving Manchester. I am known by sight. Don't lose them."

The man left the booth, and ran across the car park to the hired Rover and its two occupants. They were less than a minute behind the yellow TR7.

Lloyd was still angry. The effort to keep his appearance calm, to portray acquiescence to the inevitable, seemed only to make the hidden anger grow, like a damped fire. His father, encouraging the first fire of the autumn by holding the opened copy of *The Times* across the fireplace in the morning room. He smiled inwardly, and the memory calmed him. His stomach and chest felt less tight and hot. It was worse, of course, when the Russian was there – even when Thurston with his impotent raging and coarse vocabulary was in the same room.

There was nothing he could do. With his crew confined to their quarters and one guard on the bulkhead door, and his officers similarly confined to the wardroom, three men had held them captive until a relief, augmented guard had arrived from the rescue ship and the damage repair team with their heavy equipment had begun their work on the stern of the *Proteus*. Ardenyev forced one to admire him, and that rankled like a raging, worsening toothache. The effort of three weary, strained men to drag unconscious bodies through the submarine to monitor the essential, life-supporting systems, to inspect "Leopard", and only then to call for help, surprised him. Enraged him afresh, also.

There was a knock at his cabin door. Presumably the guard.

"Yes?"

Ardenyev was looking tired, yet there was some artificial brightness about his eyes. He was obviously keeping going on stimulants. Lloyd tried to adopt a lofty expression, feeling himself at a disadvantage just because he was lying on his bunk. Yet he could not get up without some admission of subordination. He remained where he lay, hands clasped round his head, eyes on the ceiling.

"Ah, captain. I am about to make an inspection of repairs. I am informed that they are proceeding satisfactorily."

"Very well, Captain Ardenyev. So kind of you to inform me."

"Yes, that is irony. I detect it," Ardenyev replied pleasantly. "I learned much of my English in America, as a student. Their use of irony is much broader, of course, than the English – I beg your pardon, the British."

"You cocky bastard. What the hell are you doing with my ship?"

"Repairing her, captain." Ardenyev seemed disappointed that Lloyd had descended to mere insult. "I am sorry for much of what has happened. I am also sorry that you killed three members of my team. I think that your score is higher than mine at the moment, don't you?"

Lloyd was about to reply angrily, and then he simply shrugged. "Yes. You haven't – ?"

"One body, yes. The youngest man. But that is usually the way, is it not? The others? No doubt they will be awarded posthumous medals. If I deliver your submarine to Pechenga."

"What happened to the fraternal greetings bullshit?"

"For public consumption, captain. That is what our ambassador will be telling your foreign secretary, over and over again. I'm sorry, but your inconvenience will be short-lived and as comfortable as possible. My interest in the affair ends when we dock. Now, if you will excuse me – "

Lloyd returned his gaze to the ceiling, and Ardenyev went out, closing the door behind him. The guard outside Lloyd's door was stony-faced, and his Kalashnikov was held across his chest, stubby metal butt resting lightly against one hip. Ardenyev nodded to him, and passed into the control room. His own team should have been there, he reminded

754

himself, then wished to quash the reminder immediately. The pills, damned pills, juicing up the emotions, making pain easy and evident and tears prick while they kept you awake –

They would have a steering crew brought down from the rescue ship once the repairs were complete. Under his command, they would raise the submarine in preparation for towing to Pechenga. Teplov looked up from monitoring the life-support systems, and merely nodded to him. Vanilov was slumped in a chair, his head on his arms next to a passive sonar screen. Teplov was evidently letting him rest.

Ardenyev went out of the control room and into the tunnel which passed through the reactor housing to the aft section of the *Proteus*. He ignored the windows into the reactor chamber, and passed into the manoeuvring room above the huge diesel generators. Empty. Then the turbine room, similarly empty. The silence of the submarine was evident in the huge aft section, despite the banging and scraping, setting his teeth on edge, that thrummed in the hull; the noises of the repairs under way. Empty, silent, to the imagination beginning to smell musty with disuse. He passed through the bulkhead door into the room housing the electric motors, where the aft escape hatch was located. His replenished tanks waited for him on the floor by the ladder up to the hatch.

He checked the air supply, then strapped the tanks onto his back. He adjusted his facemask, and fitted the mouthpiece. He breathed rapidly, re-checking the air supply. Then he climbed the ladder and opened the hatch. He closed it behind him, and turned the sea-cock to flood the chamber. Water rushed down the walls, covering his feet in a moment, mounting to his ankles and knees swiftly.

When the chamber was flooded and the pressure equalized with the depth and weight of water outside, he reached up and turned the wheel of the outside hatch. He pushed it open, and kicked upwards, drifting out into the sudden blind darkness of the sea, his eyes drawn by pinpricks of white light and the flashes of blue light at the stern of the submarine. He turned, swimming down the grey back of the submarine where streaks of turning, swirling small fish glided and winked in the passing light of his lamp. Slowly, he made out the tiny figures working on the damaged stern, outlined and silhouetted by the flare of their cutting and welding gear and by the arc lamps clamped to the hull.

He crouched on the hull of the *Proteus*, next to the underwater salvage chief from the *Karpaty*, a man he had trained with for the past three months, Lev Balan. Beyond them, the hydroplanes and the rudder were being patched. The force of the seawater against their damaged, thin steel skins as the *Proteus* moved on after being hit by both torpedoes had begun stripping the metal away from the ribbed skeleton of steel beneath. The effect, Ardenyev thought, was like exposing the struts and skeleton of an old biplane, where canvas had been stretched over a wooden frame, and doped. Or one of his old model aeroplanes, the ones that worked on a tightened elastic band. The repairs were crude, but sufficient to prevent further damage, and to make the minimal necessary use of rudder and hydroplanes now possible. The propeller would not be needed, but the evidence of the MIRV torpedo's steel serpents was being removed twenty fathoms down rather than in the submarine pen at Pechenga. The hull around the propeller and even forward of the rudder and hydroplanes was scarred and pocked and buckled by the effect of the whiplash action of the flailing steel cables as they were tightened and enmeshed by the turning of the propeller.

As Ardenyev watched, one length of cable, freed from the prop, drifted down through the light from the arc lamps in slow motion, sliding into the murk beneath the submarine. A slow cloud of silt boiled up, then settled.

"How much longer, Lev?"

"Two, three hours. In another hour we should be able to start attaching the tow lines." Lev Balan was facing him. Within the helmet of the diving suit, his face was vivid with enjoyment and satisfaction. Airlines snaked away behind him, down to the huge portable tanks of air mixture that rested on the ledge near the submarine. "We'll have to come in for a rest before that. Temperature's not comfortable, and my men are tired."

"OK – you make the decision. Is the docking prop damaged?" Balan shook his head. "What about the ballast tanks?"

"When we get her up to towing depth, we might have to adjust the bags. We've repaired one of the tanks, but the others can't be done down here – not if we're sticking to your timetable!" Despite the distortion of the throat-mike, Balan's voice was strong, full of inflection and expression, as if he had learned to adapt his vocal chords to the limitations of underwater communication.

"OK. Keep up the good work."

"Sorry about your boys."

Ardenyev shrugged helplessly. "Don't they call it operational necessity?"

"Some shits do."

"I'll get the galley operating ready for your men."

Ardenyev registered the drama around him once more. Now that his eyes had adapted completely, the arc lamps threw a glow around the scene, so that figures appeared caught in shafting sunlight, the minute sea life like motes and insects in summer air. He patted Balan on the shoulder, and kicked away back towards the hatch. As he travelled just above the hull with an easy motion of his legs and flippers, a curious sensation of ownership made itself apparent. As if the submarine were, in some part, his own, his prize; and some kind of repayment for the deaths of Kuzin, Nikitin and Shadrin.

When he dropped through the inner hatch again, he passed through the compartments of the huge submarine as a prospective purchaser might have strolled through the rooms of a house that had taken his fancy.

Teplov was waiting for him in the control room. Vanilov was sheepishly awake, and seated at the communications console.

"Message from Murmansk. The admiral wants to talk to you, sir," Teplov informed him. Obscure anger crossed Ardenyev's features.

"Weather and sea state up top?"

"It's no better," Teplov answered, "and then again, it's no worse. Forecast is for a slight increase in wind speed and a consequent slight worsening of sea state. The skipper of the *Karpaty* is still in favour of waiting the storm out."

"He doesn't have the choice, Viktor. In three hours' time, we'll be on our way home. Very well, let's talk to Murmansk, and endure the admiral's congratulations."

The feeling of possession and ownership had dissipated. The congratulations of the old man in Murmansk would be empty, meaningless. It wasn't about that, not at all. Not praise, not medals, not promotion. Just about the art of the possible, the art of making possible. And he'd done it, and Dolohov's words would make no difference, and would not bring back the dead.

"I see. Thank you, Giles. I'll tell the minister."

Aubrey put down the telephone, nodded to the Foreign Secretary's Private Secretary, and was ushered into the minister's high ceilinged office. Long gold curtains were drawn against the late night, and lamps glowed in the corners of the room and on the secretary of state's huge mahogany desk. It was a room familiar, yet still evocative, to Aubrey. The Private Secretary, who had been annoyed that Aubrey had paused to take the call from Pyott, and who had also informed him that His Excellency the Soviet ambassador was waiting in another room – protocol first, last and all the time, Aubrey had remarked to himself, hiding his smile – closed the double doors behind him.

Her Majesty's Secretary of State for Foreign and Commonwealth Affairs rose and came forward to take Aubrey's hand. In his features, almost hidden by his tiredness and the strain imposed by events which brought him unpleasantly into collision with the covert realities of the intelligence service, was the omnipresent memory that he had been a junior boy at Aubrey's public school and, though titled and wealthy, had had to fag for the son of a verger who had come from a cathedral preparatory school on a music scholarship. It was as if the politician expected Aubrey, at any moment and with the full effect of surprise, to remind him of the distant past, in company and with the object of humiliation.

"Kenneth. You were delayed?"

"I'm sorry, minister. I had to take a telephone call from Colonel Pyott. The Nimrod has been picking up signals from the *Proteus*, as have North Cape Monitoring." The minister looked immediately relieved, and Aubrey was sorry he had chosen an optimistic syntax for what he wished to convey. "Russian signals, I'm afraid," he hurried on. "We can't break the code, but it is evident that the Soviets are in command of the submarine."

"Damnation!" Cunningham offered from the depth of the chesterfield on which he was sitting. The Foreign Secretary's face dropped into lines of misery.

"The PM must be informed at once," he said, returning to his desk. "Find yourself a seat, Kenneth." He waved a hand loosely, and Aubrey perched himself on a Louis Quinze armchair, intricately carved, hideously patterned. Cunningham looked at Aubrey, and shook his head. The Foreign Secretary picked up one of the battery of telephones on his desk, then hesitated before dialling the number. "Is there anything you can suggest, Kenneth? Anything at all?" He put down the receiver, as if to display optimism.

"Minister – I'm sorry that this incident has had to spill over into legitimate diplomacy. I can only recommend that all diplomatic efforts be maintained. There is nothing else we can do. We must press for details, of course, and demand that one our people in Moscow is in Pechenga when the *Proteus* docks. He must be allowed immediate access, and there must be every attempt to preserve – by complaint, fuss, bother, noise, whatever you will – to preserve the security of 'Leopard'." Aubrey spread his hands on his knees.

"Pechenga?"

"The nearest naval base. Murmansk if you prefer – or wherever?"

"One of your people?"

Cunningham did not reply, but looked towards Aubrey.

"If you wish, minister," Aubrey answered. "But I would prefer someone rather senior on the embassy staff, and someone *legitimate*."

"Very well. I'll put that in motion.'

"I think, however," Aubrey pursued, "that the Russians will delay the travel permits, and that sort of thing, so that by the time our people are on the scene, they will have done whatever they wish and be waving *Proteus* goodbye from the quayside."

"I'm inclined to agree," Cunningham murmured.

"Then there is absolutely nothing we can do!" the Foreign Secretary fumed, slapping his hand repeatedly on the surface of his desk. He looked towards Aubrey as if he were to blame for the situation. Aubrey's features were impassive. "This really is not the way to play the game. The Russians have disobeyed every rule of international behaviour. It really is not good enough." There was a peculiarly old-fashioned inflection to the voice, to accompany the outdated sentiments.

"They are inclined to do that," Aubrey observed mockingly and received a warning glance from Cunningham. "I agree, minister. Obviously, the Kremlin has fully involved itself with, and sanctioned, this covert operation. Because they have done so, they place us at a considerable disadvantage. It is, indeed, a mixing of the legitimate and the covert which is both improper and very difficult to counter. And it has worked. This sort of mixed marriage usually flops badly – like the Bay of Pigs. The Russians seem to have more success than we do."

"You imply that any remedy is strictly the concern of the intelligence service?"

"I have no answer."

"The PM will give her blessing to *any* counter-operation, I'm quite sure of that. Our hands are tied, as you say. We do not even wish to become involved. Our people are in no danger, they will be released within the next couple of days. Our submarine will be repaired. Only 'Leopard' will no longer be our property. Therefore, if you can prevent the loss of 'Leopard', do so. But it must be – and the PM would wish me to stress this, even at the same time as she gives you her blessing – *it must be* an intelligence operation. It will be disowned, it must not endanger the crew of the submarine or any non-intelligence personnel, and it must be done immediately." The Foreign Secretary smiled glumly, though there was a snuff-pinch of pleasure in his gloom because he considered he must have discomforted Aubrey. "Is there anything, anything at all?"

Aubrey cleared his throat. "NATO naval units are too far from the area to intercept. The Soviet government wish to apologize to us by repairing the damage they have inflicted. I have one agent-in-place in the Pechenga district. He is a grocer. I do not have a satellite-mounted laser beam whereby I can secretly and silently destroy half of the Red Banner Fleet – therefore, minister, I am inclined to conclude that there is very little I can effectively do to secure the secrecy of 'Leopard' and the remainder of the sensitive equipment aboard HMS *Proteus*."

"Very well," the secretary of state said tightly, "I will inform the PM of the state of play, and recommend that we have only the diplomatic alternative." Again, he picked up the receiver and placed it to his ear.

"Unless," Aubrey began, amazed at his empty temerity and observing his own words as if spoken by another; and that other a pompous ass without sincerity or resolution. "Unless we can get one man into the naval dockyard at Pechenga or wherever, with a brief to destroy the 'Leopard' equipment before the Soviets have time to inspect it."

Aubrey was intensely aware of the eager, then disbelieving gazes of Cunningham and the Foreign Secretary. But, he told himself, attempting to justify what some obscure part of his mind or imagination had prompted him to utter, the whole capture of *Proteus* was the work of little more than one man, in the final analysis. Why not the reverse, then? The question echoed in his mind, but no answer appeared. Not so much as the first whisper of an answer. He asked himself a second, perhaps more pressing question.

Where the blazes was Hyde, and where the devil was Quin?

Kendal was asleep and windy. At one set of traffic lights, a board advertising ice cream outside a newsagent's shop, where the lights were on within as the proprietor marked up the morning editions for delivery, blew over in a gust, noisily startling the girl who was dozing in the passenger seat. Hyde had watched her face in repose from time to time since they left the M6. Her lips pouted, still greasy from her meal, and her features were pale, small and colourless. Obscurely, he felt responsible for her. She had passed from being the object of a search, the key to a security problem, into a chrysalis stage where she was almost a person, with human rights and human demands upon his time and energies. She hovered, waiting to be born into his emotional world. He did not welcome the change. It complicated matters. It was a pity he seemed to understand her. It would have been easier had she been a replica of her Left-wing, feminist friend Sara, whom he could have comfortably disliked.

He had paused on the outskirts of Kendal and waited, but no cars approached in his mirror or passed him. He relaxed until they passed through Staveley and turned west on the main Windermere road. Headlights followed him out of the village, keeping behind him for almost two miles before turning off down a narrow track. He discovered himself sweating with relief the instant the headlights disappeared. Like a cat being woken by a tension in its owner, the girl stirred and sat up.

"Anything wrong?"

"Nothing. Go back to sleep."

"I'm not tired any more."

"Great. Pity you can't drive."

The girl subsided into a sullen silence. There were people on the streets of Windermere, standing at bus stops, walking with bent heads beneath black hoods of umbrellas in the misty drizzle that clung to the town. The roof of a train gleamed darkly in the lights of the station, which lay below the main road.

By the time they were on the outskirts of Windermere again, the dog-leg of the long ribbon of the lake lay to their left, its further shore tree-clad, wreathed with a chill mist, its steep sides buttressing the low cloud that was just turning from black to grey. It was a slow, wintry, unwelcome dawn as they crossed Trout Beck, heading for Ambleside.

"I reckon Wordsworth lived in Croydon and made it all up," he remarked. "He never said it was always pissing with rain while he was having his visions of nature."

"You have no soul," the girl replied lightly. She seemed to warm herself at humour as at a small fire. He looked at her. She glanced away.

"It's all right," he offered, "I'm not about to pull the car into the side and take advantage of you."

The girl did not reply. A tinge of colour in her cheeks, but no other reaction. He glanced at her from time to time, but she continued to gaze out of the side window, watching the far shore of Windermere slide past, the cramped, heavy firs crowding down to the water like a herd or an army, then giving way to damp, grassy outcrops, almost colourless under the low cloud cover. The land climbed away on his side of the car above the tree-line to bare-sided, long-backed hills, scalily wet and monstrously slumbering. Ambleside was shiny in its hollow between the hills and the grey water.

He pulled into a lay-by overlooking the northern end of the lake, just south of the town, and turned to the girl.

"Where to now, sweetheart? I've driven as far as Ambleside on trust, now where?"

She got out of the car without replying, and walked to the edge of the lay-by. Hyde followed her. She turned and looked up at him. She appeared to be entertaining another bout of distrust, even fear of him. She shook her head, and looked away towards the perspective of the long lake stretching away south. Water and sky merged no more than a couple of miles from them into a non-existence. Hyde found the scene extraordinarily depressing. He touched her shoulder, but she shook his hand away.

"You *have* to trust me," he said.

"I know!" she almost wailed, so that he wondered whether she might not be psychologically disturbed. She certainly seemed neurotically suspicious. "I – can't . . ."

Anger welled up in him. Stupid little bitch. He bellowed at her: "You're wasting my bloody time, girlie! I don't know what's the bloody matter with you, or what the hell the world could have done to make you act like this – but I'm interested in what happens to a hundred blokes at the bottom of the sea relying on your old man's invention!"

In the silence that followed, he heard the water lapping gently out of sight below the verge of the lay-by, some water bird calling, the hum of a generator from somewhere behind them, the noise of the chain-saw from the trees on the far shore, and her quiet sobbing. Then she spoke without turning to him.

761

"You're a bloody shit, you are." Then, as if intending to be both more precise and younger, she added, "A bully."

"Sorry." He began to consider that Mrs. Quin was the strongest member of the family, and felt a preconceived anxiety about the girl's father, and his similarity to his daughter. He found her, at that moment at least, too helpless to be a sympathetic figure.

"It's a cottage, off the road between Ambleside and Coniston. Less than half an hour in the car. I'm ready to take you there now."

The noise of the car startled him, appearing round a bend in the road that had masked its noise until it was almost upon them. His reaction was instinctive, but it revealed also the stretched state of his nerves. Before he assimilated the Renault and its trailing white-and-brown caravan and the two mild faces behind the windscreen, the pistol was in his hand, and beginning to move up and out into a straight-arm firing position. A moment later, it was behind his back again, being thrust back into the waistband of his corduroy trousers. But not before the girl, at least, had witnessed the tiny incident. She appeared terrified, hands picking around her face like pale bats.

"Don't be bloody stupid," he told her, his hands shaking as he thrust them into his pockets, an inward voice cursing his jumpiness. "What do you think it is, a bloody game?"

She hurried past him towards the car.

"What's the time?"

"Eight-thirty."

"The blip's stopped moving and the signal strength is growing. Listen."

"All right, turn it down. That means the car's stopped somewhere, less than a couple of miles up the road."

"Great. Stop at the next phone box, and we can call Petrunin."

"And sit around all day waiting for him to get out of Manchester, I suppose? Marvellous!"

"Don't grumble. With a bit of luck we've got Hyde, the girl, and her father. Ah, there's a phone box. Pull off the road."

"Yes?" Ardenyev prevented an anticipatory grin from appearing on his lips, until Lev Balan nodded and rubbed his hand through his thick dark hair with tiredness and relief. "Great!" Ardenyev hugged Balan, laughing, feeling the man's helmet digging painfully into his ribs as Balan held it under his arm. "Great! We can go?"

"Any time you like. My boys are knackered, by the way – not that it'll worry you." Balan's answering grin was like a weather crack opening in seamed grey rock. Only then did Ardenyev really look at him, and fully perceive the man's weariness.

"Sorry. Tell them – tell them when we get back to Pechenga, we'll have the biggest piss-up they've ever seen. On me!"

"You've done it now. You're on."

"Tow lines, too?" Ardenyev asked eagerly, surprised at his own child-like enthusiasm. Again, Balan nodded, his cigarette now pressed between his lips, in the corner of his mouth. He looked dishevelled, unkempt, and rather disreputable. Insubordinate, too. "Great. What about buoyancy?"

"We've got the bags on. Just sufficient to keep you at snorkel depth for towing. Any fine adjustments we'll make when you take her up. Then we'll do some more fine-tuning in the outer basin at Pechenga, before you dock. Assuming you can drive this bloody thing, of course!"

Ardenyev indicated the skeleton crew of Soviet ratings in the control room. "All volunteers," he said wryly. "They can drive it, I'm quite sure."

"Just in case, I'm on my way back outside – to watch the disaster from there. Good luck."

"And you. See you in Pechenga. Take care."

Balan walked wearily back through the aft section of the *Proteus* to the stern escape chamber. He strapped his auxiliary air tank to his back, requiring it until he could be recoupled to the hoses outside, and climbed through the lower hatch. He flooded the chamber, and opened the upper hatch, climbed the ladder and floated out into the darkness. His legs felt heavy, not merely because of his boots but because of the surpassing weariness that had invested itself in every part of his body. He waddled slowly and clumsily down the whale's back of the submarine, arms waving like some celluloid ghoul, or as if in imitation of one of the cosmonauts space-walking. He was bone-weary, he decided. Another half-hour's working and one of them might have made some small, fatal mistake. Any one of the cables, the jagged edges, the cutters could have injured or killed any of them.

Another underwater cosmonaut, looking ridiculous in a way that never failed to amuse Balan, came towards him from the upright, aircraft's tailplane of the rudder, almost staggering with the resistance of the heavy air hoses. The two men patted each other and clung together like the automatons on a musical box, then Balan turned his back and the hoses were fitted. A moment of breath-holding, then the rush of the air mixture, putting pressure on his ears and face, then the auxiliary tank was in his hands. He looked at it, grinned, and heaved it over the side of the submarine. It floated away down into the darkness.

Balan inspected his work once more. The stern of the *Proteus*, in the hard light of the lamps, was a mess, but it was a mess of which he felt justifiably proud. The rudder and the hydroplanes had been patched with a skin of metal, or their plates twisted back into shape and form by use of the hammer, the rivet-gun, the welding and cutting torches. Scarred, twisted, cracked metal, blackened and buckled. The propeller had not been repaired, merely cleared of the entangling, choking seaweed of the steel cables from the MIRV torpedo. Balan thought the shaft might be out of true, but that was Pechenga's worry not his. Then, masking the operation scars along the side of the hull, where the ballast tanks had been ruptured and the outer hull of the *Proteus* damaged, a lazily flapping, transparent growth idled in the currents moving across the ledge, like the attachment of a giant, translucent jellyfish to the submarine. Buoyancy bags, ready to be inflated when Ardenyev gave the order to blow tanks, they would serve in place of the unrepaired ballast tanks at the stern of the submarine, giving it a workable approximation to its normal buoyancy control.

Balan was proud of what amounted to almost ten hours' work on the British submarine. The work had been as dispassionately carried out as always by himself and his team. Unlike Ardenyev, there was no pleasure at the meaning of the task and its completion. It was merely a job well done, a task completed successfully. The nature of the submarine, its nationality, had no meaning for Balan.

He spoke into his headset. "Right, you lot, clear away. Our gallant, heroic captain is going to take this tub to the top, and I don't want anyone hurt in the process!"

"I heard that," Ardenyev said in his ear, slightly more distant than the laughter that soughed in his helmet from some of his team. "I've been in contact with *Kiev* and *Karpaty*. Ready when you are."

"OK. I'm clearing the slaves from the hull now. I'll get back to you."

Balan took hold of his air hoses in one hand, checking that they did not snag anywhere and trailed away across the ledge to the pumps and the generator. Then he turned clumsily but surely, and began climbing down the light steel ladder that leant against the port hydroplane, attached by small magnets. He lowered his air lines gingerly to one side of him as he climbed tiredly down to the surface of the ledge. The crewman who had attached his lines came after him. They were the last to descend, and when they stood together at the bottom of the ladder, Balan and the other diver hefted the ladder between them, and they trudged through the restless, distressed silt to where the arc lamps had been re-sited near the generators and the sleds on which they had brought down their equipment. The small group of diving-suited figures who composed his team was gathered like nervous spectators beneath the bloom of the lights. Balan joined them, dropping the ladder onto one of the sleds and securing it before he spoke again to Ardenyev.

"OK, chief – you can make your attempt on the world rate of ascent record now. We're safely out of the way!"

"Thanks, Lev. Don't forget our piss-up in Pechenga – if you're not all too tired, that is!"

There was a murmur of protest and abuse at the remark. Balan was almost prepared to admit his tiredness, but there were certain fictions that had to be preserved, whatever the cost; one of them being the indestructibility, the immortality of salvage men.

"We won't forget. You just bring your wallet." The banter was required, expected, all of them were recruiting-poster figures, without separate identity, without reality. Living their own fictions; heroes. Silly, silly –

"I will. OK, here we go."

Balan studied the submarine, partly in shadow now, the light of the arc lamps casting deep gloomy patches over their repair work, rendering it somehow shabby and inadequate. The *Proteus* looked half-built, half-destroyed. He did not attend to Ardenyev's orders, still coming through the headset, presumably for his benefit, until he heard "Blow tanks!" and the submarine – after a moment in which nothing seemed to happen – shifted under the discharge of sea water from her ballast tanks, and then the jellyfish bags began to bloom and roll and fold and inflate. Balan felt the new currents of the submarine's movement and the discharged water. They could feel the hull grinding against the ledge through their boots; the stern of the submarine seemed to be lifting slightly higher than the bow. It would need adjustment. The bow itself was in darkness, where the tow-lines were attached. They'd have to be inspected, too.

Someone cheered in his headset, making him wince. One of the younger men, he supposed. There were sighs of pleasure and relief, though, like a persistent breeze; noises that were their right.

The *Proteus*, still a little bow-heavy, drifted up and away from them, out of the boiling cloud of silt, becoming a great shadow overhead, just beyond the arc lamps, then a dimmer shape, then almost nothing as it ascended the twenty fathoms to the surface. The bags round its stern – like nappies, he thought. Around its bum.

"Come on, you lot. The volume on those bags is going to have to be changed for a starter! Don't waste time, get organized!"

Theatrically, the arc lamps began flicking off, leaving them in a sudden darkness, where their helmet lamps and hand-lamps glowed like aquatic fireflies. Above them, as they began climbing onto their sleds, the *Proteus* stopped at snorkel depth and waited for them.

"Well done, Hyde – excellent work, excellent!" Aubrey was effusive, his tiredness gone in a moment, if only briefly. Hyde had Quin, beyond all reasonable expectation, and at this critical moment. Their first real piece of luck – a change of luck? They needed it. "Well done. Bring him directly to London. You'd better let me arrange for a helicopter from the Cumbria force to pick you up. I want Quin here as soon as possible – What? What do you mean?"

Hyde's voice had dropped to barely more than a whisper, something conspiratorial. Aubrey swivelled in his seat as if in response to its tone, turning his back on the underground room and its occupants. Pyott and Clark, attentive to his enthusiasm at the call that had been put through, now remained some yards away. Clark was making some point about the *Proteus*, his finger tracing across a large-scale cutaway plan of the submarine which Aubrey had had brought down from the second floor of the Admiralty.

"Back-up's here," he heard Clark saying. "Right out of the way –" Then he was attending to Hyde's quiet voice.

"He's in a bad way, Mr Aubrey. Out in the garden now, blowing his nose a lot and upsetting his daughter. Can you hear me all right?"

"Yes, Hyde, yes," Aubrey replied impatiently. "What do you mean, *a bad way*?"

"One of those who can't take isolation, even if he is a loner," Hyde replied flatly, without sympathy. "He's been up here for weeks, almost a week on his own. And when the two of them were here together, I reckon they just wore each other down with mutual nerves. Quin's a neurotic bloke, anyway."

"Spare me the psychology, Hyde."

"You have to understand him," Hyde said in exasperation. "He doesn't want to come back, he's scared stiff of his own shadow, he doesn't seem to care about the *Proteus* – all our fault, apparently."

"That, at least, is true."

"I've spent hours talking to him. I can't get through to him. He'll come back because he's scared not to, and because he thinks the opposition may have followed us here –"

"Have they?"

"No. But now we've found him, he thinks it'll all start up again, and he wants to hide. I don't want him scared off by a helicopter. He'll come back with me, or not at all."

"What about the girl?"

"She's the one who's just about persuaded him to trust me. *I* have to deliver him somewhere safe."

"I didn't mean that. What will you do with her?"

"She'll stay here. Either that, or I'll put her on a train."

"I haven't time to waste, Hyde. Is he fit to work?"

"No."

"Then he'll have to work in an unfit state. Very well. Drive back to Manchester. You and he can fly down from there. I'll arrange it. *You* can hold his hand."

"Yes, Mr. Aubrey."

"And – once again, well done. Keep him happy, promise him anything – but he must be here this evening, and ready to work!"

Aubrey put down the receiver, and stood up, the purposefulness of his movements keeping doubt at bay. He had dozed lightly and fitfully on the narrow camp bed in the adjoining cupboard-like room without windows. The darkness had seemed close and foetid, and the light and noise under the door had drawn him back into the underground operations room. Cold water had restored a semblance of wakefulness, and Hyde's message had completed the work of reinvigoration.

"Well?" Giles Pyott asked, turning from the chart pinned to a board, resting on an easel. "What news?"

"Hyde has found Quin."

"Thank God! Where is he?"

"Lake District – near Coniston Water, I gather."

"He's been there all the time?"

"Apparently. Rented a cottage through an agency."

"Can he get here today?" Clark asked more purposefully.

"He can. Hyde says that the man is in a state close to nervous exhaustion." Aubrey shrugged his shoulders. "I don't know how that complicates matters. Better have a doctor to look at him, I suppose. It really is too bad –"

"Hell, can he *work*?"

"Whether or not, he will work." He indicated the drawing of the *Proteus*. "He has to do something about this, after all. Doesn't he?"

It was almost three before Quin was finally ready to depart. His luggage, which consisted of one small suitcase and an overcoat, had been a means of delaying his departure. He had driven Hyde to the edge of rage again and again, and then capitulated, afraid of the Australian in a more immediate way than of the other figures and dangers that crowded his imagination. Aubrey had telephoned the cottage at noon, and had been frustrated and angered at the further delay. After that, Hyde had handled Quin like unstable explosive; cajolement and masked threat had eventually subdued him.

He stood now at the door of the whitewashed cottage, hesitant while Hyde carried the suitcase to the TR7. Tricia Quin was at his side like a crutch, touching his arm, trying to smile him into complacency. In some obscure and unexpected way, she had strengthened during the day, adopting much of Hyde's attitude and many of his arguments. It was as if she had adopted the plight of the *Proteus* as a charitable cause worthy of contribution; or perhaps she sensed her father needed help, that the greatest danger to his health lay in his present solitary surroundings. Hyde wondered what Quin would have made of the Outback, even the dead centre of Australia. The unnerving silence *was* audible there. The Lake District hummed and buzzed with life, by comparison.

He looked away from Quin and his daughter, towards the stretch of water that was The Tarns, and then at the road and the land falling away, down from Black Fell behind him through the firs towards Coniston Water two miles away. The land pressed in upon the cottage, and Hyde admitted a claustrophobic isolation so different from the Australian hinterland. Perhaps it wasn't surprising Quin couldn't take it after all, staying in that cottage and its garden for a week without seeing another soul after his daughter left. They'd quarrelled about her going to see her mother, apparently. That might have set him off, created his sense of abandonment amid danger.

Hyde shrugged, and opened the boot. The weather was windier now, moving the low cloud but breaking it up, too. Gleams, fitful and unoptimistic, of blue sky; a hazy light through the clouds. It had, at least, stopped drizzling.

The bullet whined away off the yellow boot before the noise of the gunshot reached him. He stared at his hand. The bullet had furrowed across the back of it, exposing the flesh. An open-lipped graze which still had not begun to hurt, matching the furrowed scar on the boot lid. He looked stupidly around him.

A second shot then, chipping pebble-dash from the wall of the cottage two feet or so from Quin's head. His frightened, agape features, the girl's quicker, more alert panic, her hands dragging at her father's arm, the shrouded hills, the distant dark trees – he took in each distinct impression in the moment that he heard the heavy report of the rifle, and then the pain in his hand began, prompting him like a signal. He began running for the door of the cottage.

PART THREE

PLUMBER

TEN:

Rescue?

"What are they waiting for? Why don't they *do* something?" Quin's voice was plaintive, fearful; yet the words sounded strangely irritated, as if the men outside had disappointed him.

"You've seen the bloody cowboy films, haven't you?" Hyde replied, almost snarling, weary of Quin's unabated nerves. "The lynch-mob always waits for dark." The man seemed to possess an infinite capacity to remain on edge, and his emotions rubbed against Hyde's attempts to evolve a solution to their situation like sandpaper against skin.

"Why *are* they waiting?" Tricia Quin asked in a studiedly calm tone, sitting near him on the floor beneath the cottage window.

Hyde turned to her. "Petrunin can't be here yet."

"Who?"

"The bloke who chased us – the big cheese. He's got a face everyone will have a copy of. Must be hard to get out of Manchester. They'll be waiting for orders."

"How many of them do you think there are?"

Hyde watched Quin as he listened to the girl. The man was sitting in a slumped, self-pitying posture with his back against the wall, near the settee with its stained stretch covers. Hyde disliked Quin intensely. The man got on his nerves. He was a pain in the backside. He was going to be useless to Aubrey, even if he delivered him.

"Two, maybe three."

"You don't think they might try something before dark?"

"Why? They'll assume I'm armed, they know I'm a professional, just like them. They're not going to volunteer to get their balls blown off. Your dad's here, and he isn't going anywhere."

She studied her father, then looked away from him.

"What about your people? This man Aubrey?"

"When we don't turn up in Manchester, he'll worry. He knows where we are."

"Will he worry in time?"

"That what I'm worrying about." He smiled, and studied her face. "How are you?"

"I'm all right." She avoided looking at her father.

"What are you going to do?" Quin asked.

"For Christ's sake, stop moaning!"

"It's your fault – you brought them here! This is just what I tried to avoid – what I came here to get away from," Quin persisted. Hyde perceived deep and genuine and abiding fears, disguising themselves in self-pity. He could almost feel sorry for Quin; might have done so, had their situation at that moment been less acute. And had Quin's voice had been less insistent, less whining. "I knew I couldn't be adequately protected, that no one took my fears seriously. And now look what's happened – they're out there, the very people I tried to avoid. And *you* – you brought them here. You've as good as handed me to them on a plate!"

"All right. So they stuck a bleeper under the car. Sorry."

"That won't do us any good."

"Shut up! It's *your* bloody fault we're all stuck here."

"Leave him alone," Tricia Quin pleaded softly.

"All right. Look, once it's dark, I can try to get to a telephone that hasn't had its wires cut. But I'm not walking out there just at the moment. He'll have to sit it out, just like us."

"As long as nothing happens to him."

"It won't. Petrunin's in a corner himself. It's a stalemate. Nothing's going to happen to Dad – unless I break his bloody neck for him!"

Quin scowled like a child sulking. Hyde looked at his watch. Just after three. Patience, patience, he instructed himself. Aubrey has got to catch on soon.

He wondered, without letting the thought tinge the bland expression on his features, whether Petrunin's orders might not have changed because of the capture of the submarine by the Russians. The death of Quin, rather than his capture, might be a satisfactory conclusion to the operation.

It was hard to discard the thought, once he had admitted it. It was unlikely, but possible. Of his own death, he did not think. That, he had considered almost as he closed the cottage door behind him after he had run from the car, would be inevitable whether Petrunin wanted Quin alive or dead. He looked at his hand, wrapped in his handkerchief. His gun made an uncomfortable, pressing lump against the small of his back. It was not entirely a stalemate, it merely gave that impression. Petrunin wanted Quin badly. Petrunin was finished in the UK anyway, after this. When he went, he'd want Quin with him. As soon as it was dark, he'd come for him.

"Ethan, it is not an old man's vanity, or sense of hurt pride – or even senility. I am asking a serious question. Could someone get into

772

Pechenga and destroy 'Leopard' before the Russians can examine or dismantle it?"

"You're crazy, Mr. Aubrey. In twenty-four hours the Russians will have that submarine turned around and on her way. There's no time to do anything."

"I'm not sure about that." Aubrey looked up from the narrow camp bed where he sat perched like a tired, dishevelled prisoner under the hard strip-lighting of the cupboard-like room. Clark leaned against the door, dressed like a golfer in sweater and slacks. Clark's increasing informality of dress during the past days had been a badge of defeat and of defeatism. Aubrey felt tired, directionless; yet at the same time he was possessed by the quick seductive glamour of a counter-operation. "I'm not sure about that," he repeated.

"You don't even know it's Pechenga," Clark persisted.

"Satellite and Nimrod suggest it might be. There are signs of what might be preparations for *Proteus*'s arrival at Pechenga, but not at Murmansk." Aubrey rubbed his hands together in a washing motion. To Clark the activity suggested a pretended, mocking humility. The room was coffin-like, stale and dead, and pressed in on him uncomfortably.

"Maybe. Look, these quick-burn operations always look good on paper. Our intelligence is *nil*, Mr. Aubrey, and there's no time or capacity for back-up. Face facts – the Russians have *Proteus* on their ground, on their terms. They'll give her back."

"I realize that," Aubrey snapped, "but I am not prepared simply to wait until she is handed back like a toy that no longer works."

"Listen, Mr. Aubrey," Clark began angrily, turning from the door, which he had been facing as Aubrey spoke, as if to hide the expression on his face, "I can't give you what you want. I don't know enough about 'Leopard' to be able to tell you how to destroy it effectively without blowing up the damn boat, too! The Russians may have their superman in Ardenyev, but don't put the role onto me. I can't help you."

"Someone at Plessey, then," Aubrey murmured disparagingly.

"You need Quin."

"I realize that. If I get you Quin, can you do the job?"

"What?"

"I said – if I get you Quin, will you do the job? *Can* you do the job?"

"Job?"

"Don't be dense, dear boy. You would have to do it. You are familiar with the whole operation, you are familiar with the equipment, you are in naval intelligence, you have a great deal of field experience. Who else would I consider sending?"

"One man?"

"One particular man, yes."

"And all I have to do is get into Pechenga, board the *Proteus*, destroy the equipment, and get out again with no one any the wiser?" Clark raised his hands in the air. "You've really flipped, Mr. Aubrey. It can't be done."

"It must be attempted."

"I'm not on your staff."

"I'm sure I can arrange your temporary assignment."

"There's no time."

"We must *try!*"

"So where's Quin? Your house of cards falls down without him."

Aubrey's face became saturnine. "I don't know. Hyde should have arrived at Manchester airport by now. He has not done so."

"Then he's in trouble."

"You think so?"

Clark paced the tiny cubicle. "You've spent all your time dreaming up this crazy scheme instead of worrying about realities. Your guy has to be in trouble, and you haven't even given him a thought!"

Aubrey's face registered an expression of rage, directed at Clark. Then, in admission, his look turned inwards. He had been taking an afternoon nap of the intellect. Clark was perfectly correct. He had ignored Hyde, and Hyde must now be in trouble. He clenched his fists in his lap, then got up and opened the door.

"OS map of the Coniston Water area!" he shouted into the underground room, directing the order at every one of its occupants. Pyott looked up, startled, and then reached for a telephone. "Quickly!" He slammed the door and looked steadily at Clark. "You are right. I have been foolishly, dangerously remiss. But if we get Quin here, we shall talk again. You are not off the hook, Ethan!"

"Neither are your guy and Quin."

The *Proteus* reached a moment of equilibrium after her seeming rush from snorkel depth to the surface, and then the motion of the waves began to affect her. Ardenyev watched as the hatch above them slid back. Water dripped on him and Lloyd and the armed guard, and then the platform of the bridge was raised electronically until their heads rose above the fin of the submarine. The *Proteus* rolled gently in the swell of the outer harbour of Pechenga, the adjusted buoyancy bags at the stern maintaining her at the correct depth but impairing her stability.

Ardenyev smiled, and waved an arm towards the low shoreline.

"Welcome to the Soviet Union, Commander Lloyd."

Rain whipped into their faces, and fuzzy lights glowed through the dark late afternoon. Low submarine pens lay ahead of them, beyond the harbour wall with its guard towers and its anti-submarine net. The rain was chilly, mingled with sleet which numbed the side of Lloyd's face as he studied the scene with the hunched shoulders of a prisoner. The rescue ship *Karpaty* made cautious headway, still towing the *Proteus*. He turned to look back aft of the sail. Huge jellyfish bags surrounded the stern of the submarine like splints on a damaged limb. He could make out, through the white-edged spray and the driving rain, the scars and the rough repairs that had been affected beneath the surface by the rescue team. The bow of the *Proteus* was still angled slightly below the horizontal because of the crudity of measurement employed in inflating the bags. A bow-wave surged along the forward deck as Lloyd turned his gaze back towards Pechenga. The *Karpaty* had passed through the gap in the harbour wall where the net had been swung electronically away to allow her access, and *Proteus* was slipping, in an almost lurching, ungainly fashion between the towers on the wall. Lloyd could see faces looking from the towers; they all seemed to be grinning, and an arm waved. The sight created a sense of humiliation in him.

Ardenyev was speaking.

"I'm sorry – you were saying?" he said, indulging his sense of defeat and self-blame. He had made mistakes, fatal ones for "Leopard". Because the situation was so unreal, and its consequences dangerous only for a lump of inoperable equipment in the bowels of his vessel, his mind was more keenly aware of errors of judgment and tactics. He should not have been so slow in realizing their danger, he should not have settled on the bottom. There seemed no limit to the catalogue of blame.

"I intrude upon your self-examination?" Ardenyev asked lightly. "But there is no danger. No cause for alarm."

"That's the most unreal thing of all, isn't it?" Lloyd replied.

Ardenyev ignored the reply. "As I was saying, we will have the submarine docked in two or three hours. Of course, we will not delay you more than is necessary. Your reactor will not be run down, you will be docked in a wet dock – we can manage the repairs quite adequately without a dry dock – and you will be ready to sail in no more than forty-eight hours. That I promise you."

"You would be able to make such a promise, of course," Lloyd replied acidly, "since the damage to my ship was quite precisely calculated, no doubt."

"I'm sorry –?"

"Forget it. It was all an accident, a most unfortunate accident."

"Of course."

The swell was hardly discernible inside the harbour wall. Lloyd was uncomfortably aware, however, of the forward motion of the submarine and of the other vessels in the harbour basin. Pechenga was unsubstantial still, masked by the murk and the flying rain and sleet and remained as unreal as the satellite pictures he had seen of it and of dozens of other Soviet naval ports, but the big ships were real, uncomfortably so. Two "Kara"-class cruisers at anchor, one half-repainted. Three or four destroyers, like a display of toys, small and grey and bristling with aerials and radar dishes and guns. Frigates, a big helicopter cruiser, two intelligence ships festooned with electronic detection and surveillance equipment. A submarine support ship, minesweepers, ocean tugs, tankers. The sight, the numbers, overawed him, ridiculing Portsmouth, Plymouth, Faslane, every naval port and dockyard in the UK. It was like going back into the past, except for the threatening, evident modernity of these vessels, to some great review of the fleet at Spithead between the two world wars, or before the Great War. The harbour at Pechenga, a satellite port for Murmansk, daunted Lloyd. He felt completely and utterly entrapped.

The submarine pens, mere nest-holes in the concrete at this distance, winked with lights ahead of the *Karpaty*. One of those small black holes would swallow his vessel, contain it until people like this Russian on his bridge said they could leave, gave them permission. He shrugged hopelessly.

"You're impressed?" Ardenyev asked.

"As long as they're not all cardboard mock-ups, yes."

"They're not." Lloyd looked at Ardenyev. The man seemed unenthusiastic about the conversation he had begun.

"So familiar as to be boring?" he asked.

"What? Oh, this. I was just thinking what a dull town Pechenga is."

"I see."

"I doubt it." They slid beneath the lee of a cruiser. Crewmen leaned over the rails, looking down at the British submarine, waving their caps, yelling indistinguishable words and greetings. Ardenyev watched them as he might have observed the behaviour of monkeys at a zoo. "The brothels are quite dreadful," he continued. "All right for conscripts, but not for the likes of you and me. A good job you will not be allowed ashore. The casualty rate would be staggering. Quite unacceptable to the Admiralty."

"You seem to have run out of steam," Lloyd remarked.

"What? Oh, perhaps." Ardenyev brushed a hand through his wet hair, and assayed a tired grin. His waving arms indicated the whole bulk of the *Proteus*. "It's over for me. The dull time after excitement. I am feeling sorry for myself. Forgive my bad manners."

They were slowing now. *Karpaty* seemed to lag, and they began to overtake her in a snail-like pursuit, until the *Proteus* herself came to a stop. Tiny figures emerged from the forward hatch and scuttled along the slippery, gleaming deck, casting off the tow-lines swiftly and expertly. A hard-lit submarine pen gaped before them. *Proteus* began to edge towards the open gates of the pen on her intact docking propeller, the "egg-beater" located forward of the main propeller and retracted when not in use. Lloyd shuddered.

"As soon as we dock, I must leave you to make my report," Ardenyev murmured. Lloyd ignored him, watching his vessel slide forward into the maw of the submarine pen. Down the line of pens, men had stopped work to watch. The sterns of Soviet submarines were visible through the open gates of other pens, but Lloyd, after one quick, self-conscious glance, returned his gaze to the bow of the *Proteus*. She stopped again, and men scrambled over the deck, attaching the hawsers whereby she could be winched into the pen. An order was given, the deck was cleared again, and then the winches picked up the slack, measured the bulk of the submarine and began to pull her forward.

Each moment was marked by a further surrender to circumstances. Lloyd felt an emotional pain that was as acute as a physical injury. The hull of the *Proteus* seemed marked like a ruler, measuring off her entry into the pen. Hard lights gleamed in the roof. The pen contained the torpedo tubes, the forward hatch, the forward hydroplanes, then the fin itself. *Proteus* was half-swallowed.

There was cheering from the dockyard workers lining the concrete walks on either side of the water, which sickened and enraged him. Lloyd could see the first teams of men with the props that would support the hull, eager to begin berthing the *Proteus*.

Then Ardenyev's hand was on his shoulder, and he was shouting above the echo of the cheering bouncing back from steel and concrete.

"I'm sorry, my friend! You have lost!"

Lloyd shook his head, not to deny but to admit defeat. *Proteus* was slowing as orders were passed from the officer in charge of the docking procedure to the winch operators. Even the motion of his vessel was out of his control. He felt utterly humiliated. Strangely, there was an air of dejection about Ardenyev, too, amid the coarse cheers and their magnified, inhuman echoes.

A mist was beginning to rise in the dusk. The wind had dropped to an occasional breeze which stirred the tendrils and shrouds of grey. The landscape was subsiding into darkness, the hills already no more than smudges, the trees merely dark, crayon shadings. Hyde saw the mist as a final irony. It cloaked Petrunin now, not any attempt on his part to reach a telephone. Petrunin had arrived too early, just before six, announcing his presence with a deadline for Hyde's surrender. Yet in another sense he was belated. Hyde had already, slowly and reluctantly and with an inward fury, decided he could not leave the girl and her father exposed to capture, and there was no way the three of them could get safely away from the cottage. He had to make the difficult, even repellent assumption that they would be safer, if only because they would be alive and unharmed, in surrender than resistance. Hope springs eternal was a difficult, and unavoidable, consolation. He had admitted to himself that they were successfully trapped even before Petrunin reiterated that simple message through a loud-hailer.

Quin had rendered himself useless, like some piece of electrical equipment that possessed a safety circuit. He had switched himself off like a kettle boiling too long. He was slumped where he had sat for hours, staring at his lap, sulking in silence. Even his danger no longer pricked him to complaint. The girl, moving only occasionally to check on her father's condition, had remained near Hyde. Their conversation had been desultory. Hyde had hardly bothered to alleviate the girl's fears, possessed by his own self-recriminations. The bug on the car, the bloody bug –

Then Petrunin was talking again. "Why not attempt to reach a telephone, Mr. Hyde?" his magnified, mechanical voice queried from behind a knoll a hundred yards or more from the cottage. Hyde was certain he could hear soft laughter from one of the others. "This mist should hide your movements quite successfully." Again the accompanying, sycophantic laughter, coarser now? Hyde could not be certain he was not mocking himself, imagining the amusement. Petrunin was enjoying himself. Was he covering an approach, distracting them? "The problem is, your friends would not be safe while you were away. Can the girl use a gun? Can her father?"

"Fuck off," Hyde replied with a whispered intensity. The girl touched his arm, making him start.

"Give me the gun. Why don't you try to get out?"

"I gave that idea up hours ago, girlie. We're right in the shit, and bloody Lenin out there knows it."

"Won't your people be looking for us?"

"I bloody hope so! But, he knows that, too. He won't wait much longer now."

"Your time is up," Petrunin announced, as if on cue. Hyde grinned mirthlessly. "Please show yourselves at the door. Throw your gun out first, please. We have night-sights. No movements you make will be missed, I assure you."

"The trouble with bloody desk men when they get in the field is they're so bloody gabby." He looked at the shadowy outline of Quin

778

across the room, then at the girl. His hand was clenched around the butt of the Heckler & Koch pistol, and it would take one movement to smash the window and open fire. Useless to try; but in another, more febrile way, satisfying to do so. Bang, bang, he recited to himself, pointing the gun into the room as if taking aim. Bloody bang, bang. And these two would be dead, or wounded. "Nowhere to go, nothing to do," he announced aloud.

"You can't –" the girl began.

"I'm bored with sitting on my bum," he said. "Besides, when the shooting starts, someone else always gets hurt. It's in the rules. Petrunin knows I won't risk your father or you, and I know I won't. Shitty, but true. Now, we have no chance. Later, who knows?" He stood up to one side of the window. It was open at the top, and he raised his voice to a shout. "All right, Trotsky – we're coming out. We've both seen this bloody film before!"

"No cavalry, I'm afraid. Only Apaches," Petrunin called back through the loud-hailer. Hyde tossed his head.

"I'll open the door and chuck my gun out. Then Mr. Quin will come out first."

"Very well. Please do not delay."

Quin was sitting upright now, and seemed to have sidled towards one corner of the room. His white, featureless face seemed to accuse Hyde in the room's dusk. Hyde bumped the edge of the table as he moved towards him.

"No –" Quin said feebly, putting his hands up in front of him, warding off Hyde like an evil presence.

"Sorry, mate. We don't have any choice. They're not going to do *you* any harm now, are they?" He reached down and pulled Quin roughly to his feet, embracing him as the man struggled half-heartedly. There was a mutuality of hatred and blame between them. Hyde sensed it in the tremble of Quin's arms.

He studied Quin's face. The man appeared as if he had been confined in some prison, with no hope of release or escape, for a long time. The prison had been his own mind, of his own making. No, Hyde corrected himself. The KGB had done that, created the stifling sense of the trap closing on him. And perhaps the DS, and even SIS and himself, should have been quicker, smarter, more thorough.

"We may have a chance if we go out now," he said in a soothing, allaying voice. "In here, we have none. You get hurt, Tricia gets hurt. I'm sorry, mate, but it's our only chance."

"I don't *want* to –!" Quin almost wailed. "They'll take me with them. It's not you they want, it's me!"

"I know that. For God's sake, I'm trying to help you!"

"I can't spend the rest of my life in Russia, heaven help me!"

"Better Red than dead," Hyde offered, his shallow sympathy exhausted. Quin's fear and reluctance were now no more than irritants, slowing reaction, muddying thought. Quin would just have to accept his situation. Hyde no longer had time or energy to expend on his psychological condition.

"Now, as the patient said to the dentist as he grabbed his balls, 'we're not going to hurt each other, are we?'. Just wait until I give you the word, then walk slowly out of the door. OK?" Quin slumped in resignation against Hyde. Hyde's mockery was expressed, incongruously, in a comforting tone of voice. "A nice little plane ride across the Channel, then another ride to Moscow. You might even like it there. They'll like you, anyway." He gripped Quin's arms as the man's body protested at his envisaged future. "Nothing bad's going to happen. Just do as they say."

He took Quin by one arm to the door, and opened it, keeping the scientist out of sight. He threw his gun in a high arc towards the knoll, away from his car so that it was easily visible.

"Excellent!" Petrunin confirmed. "No other little toys?"

"I left my bloody death-ray in the car!"

"Very well. Come out, one at a time. Mr. Quin to lead."

"Right, off you go. Just walk straight towards the knoll. Don't deviate, and don't run."

Quin moaned. Immediately, the girl was at his side, holding his other arm. She shouted through the door.

"My father's not well. We're coming out together." Without hesitation, she guided Quin through the open door. Hyde stood framed in the doorway for a moment, then he moved out into the dusk, his feet crunching on the gravel in front of the cottage. He raised his arms in the air, studying the knoll, waiting for the first head to appear. Unreality seized him, and he wanted to laugh. Captured by the KGB, in England! It was laughable, a joke for Queen Anne's Gate for years to come. Perhaps they'd use his urn on Aubrey's mantelpiece to knock their pipes out while they giggled at the story of his demise. As Aubrey would have said, *It really was too bad –*

Petrunin came down the slope of the grassy knoll towards them, a second man following him, carrying a rifle. Quin and Tricia stopped, awaiting him. A third man moved out of the shadow beneath a stand of firs towards Hyde, his rifle bearing on its target. Hyde felt weak, and sick. Petrunin stopped to examine Quin as carefully and as unemotionally as he might have done a consignment that had been delivered to his door. He ignored the girl. The third man had reached Hyde, studied him warily, and then moved in to touch-search him. When he had finished, he spoke to Petrunin.

"He's clean."

780

"Good." Petrunin approached Hyde. He was smiling with confidence and success. He was a bigger, taller man than the Australian, and this increased his confidence almost to a swagger. He paused before Hyde, hands on hips, appraising him.

"I know I don't look like much," Hyde offered, "but it's the public spending cuts. They're going in for smaller spies."

"Aubrey's man, of course? Mm, I don't think you are the cheerful colonial idiot you pretend. Not that it matters. Thank you for leading us to Mr. Quin."

"Not my pleasure."

"Quite. Very well," he said, addressing his two companions, "let us not waste time." He looked at Hyde. "Just a wound, I think," he said with surgical precision and lack of concern. "This incident is already too – significant. We mustn't create an international event from it." He stepped aside. "We don't want him going anywhere. Both legs, I think."

"No –!" the girl shouted, but one of the riflemen knocked her down, swiping the barrel of his gun sideways into her ribs. Hyde remained quite still, tensing himself to accept the pain. He lowered his hands to his sides. The marksman stepped forward – the third man had moved away, Petrunin was still appraising him with an intent curiosity – and raised the gun to his shoulder. Hyde felt the tremble begin in his left leg, and could not control it. Knee, shin, thigh, calf, foot, ankle –

His imagination made the skin on his legs crawl. Hyde tried to concentrate on only one of his legs, letting awareness of the other one become numb. The blood rushed in his ears like a howl of protest.

Then the helicopter. Loud enough at once in the silence to be apparent even to Hyde. Petrunin glanced up at the cool evening sky, then his head whipped round as he located the source of the noise. Red lights beneath a shadowy belly, the racket of the rotors yelling down into the hollow in which the cottage lay.

Hyde's thoughts came out of shock, out of their mesmerized concentration on his still quivering left leg, and prompted him towards Quin and the girl, who were huddled together. The girl was on her feet but almost doubled over with pain and fright. Then a pain wracked him, and he fell to his knees, groaning as if he had been shot. His whole body was trembling, and he could not move, merely grip his stomach and retch drily again and again.

The noise of the helicopter beat down on him, and he heard a voice through a loud-hailer, yelling the same kind of authoritative noises over and over. The helicopter's down-draught distressed his hair, inflated his windcheater, but he could not straighten up. He waited for the sound of firing, but there was none.

Eventually, he rolled over onto his side. He saw scattering figures running, and Quin and his daughter clinging together. Then he heard shots. One of the marksmen – he saw with a fierce delight that it was the one who had been ordered to maim him – crumpled near Quin and Tricia. Other figures moved into, merged with, the trees, and were gone. The police helicopter settled heavily onto the grass below the knoll, comfortingly large, noisily business-like. It was over.

The girl was kneeling over him, one hand pressed against her ribs.

"All right?"

He nodded. "Just scared stiff. You?"

"Bruised."

"How's your father?"

"Mr. Hyde?" A shadow loomed over them. A policeman in denims and a combat jacket.

"Yes."

"Are you hurt?"

"Only my manly pride." Hyde stretched and sat up. He rubbed his hand almost without thinking through the girl's hair. She did not seem to resent his touch.

"We're to get you on a plane at Manchester as soon as we can," the police officer informed him.

"Right. What about my car?"

"One of my men will drive it down."

"I want to see my mother," Tricia Quin announced.

"Your father's to go straight to London, Miss. Mr. Aubrey's instructions," he added by way of explanation to Hyde. "He'll want to see you, no doubt, at the same time."

"Get us to Manchester," Hyde replied. "We'll see, then."

"I'm not going to London."

"OK, OK," Hyde conceded. "I'll take you to see Mummy as soon as we've got your dear old dad on the plane. All right?" The girl nodded firmly. "Christ, why you spend your time worrying so much about them, I don't know!" He looked up at the police officer. "Caught 'em?"

"I doubt it. We haven't the time to waste. Leave that up to the Cumbria constabulary. Come on – let's get moving."

Hyde stood up. The girl immediately held his arm to steady him, unnecessarily.

"You're all bloody solicitation, Tricia," Hyde observed. "No wonder you get hurt all the time. People aren't worth it." She saw that he was looking at her father as he spoke, and a wince of pain crossed her face. Misinterpreting the expression, he added: "Your ribs OK?"

"Yes!" she snapped, and walked away from him. Hyde watched her go, and shrugged. Relief returned in a rush of emotions, and he

782

exhaled noisily. It was over. The cavalry had arrived, with a loud-hailer instead of a bugle. But they had arrived –

They allowed Quin five hours' sleep, under light sedation, before Aubrey had him woken. The doctor had examined him as soon as he had arrived at the Admiralty, and had pronounced him unfit for strain or effort, mental or physical. Aubrey had thanked the doctor and dismissed him. He pondered whether Quin should be prescribed stimulants, and then reluctantly decided against this course. Aubrey suspected drugs, except in their interrogational usefulness. He wanted Quin completely and reliably rational. Quin was the lynch-pin of the scheme that was increasingly obsessing him. It had pre-vented him from taking any sleep himself, it had made him impatient of Quin's rest and impatient during his first conversation with the man, so much so that Ethan Clark had intruded upon their conversa-tion and eventually commandeered it. Aubrey, seething at Quin's weariness, his retreat from reality, his reluctance to consider the plight of his own invention, had left the Admiralty to walk for half an hour on Horse Guards, but the military statues and the nobility of the buildings had made him flee to the more agreeable atmosphere of St James's Park.

The park, across which people hurried at the beginning of a bright, windy day, offered him little solace. From the bridge, he could see, in an almost gilded white clarity, Buckingham Palace in one direction, Whitehall in the other. If he followed the path from the bridge, it would bring him to Birdcage Walk and Queen Anne's Gate and his own office. Shelley would bring him coffee and soothing information of other parts of the world; not Pechenga, not the place on that blown-up aerial photograph propped on an easel. The parade of government officials and office workers passing him composed a race to which he did not belong. His office was barred to him until this business was resolved.

He skirted the lake, back towards Whitehall. The sun was gilding the roofs, providing an unremarked beauty. Aubrey was profoundly doubtful whether Quin would be of the least use to them. He seemed a poor specimen, physically, emotionally. He certainly seemed inadequate to the role in which Aubrey wished to cast him.

One man, who is a grocer. A Harrier jet. The AWACS Nimrod at Farnborough which was used to give *Proteus* her sea trials with the "Leopard" equipment. Eastoe and his crew, returned by now to RAF Kinloss, no more than two hours away by aircraft from Farnborough. And Clark.

And Quin. Miserable, whining, ungrateful, uncaring Quin. Aubrey clenched his hat more firmly, savagely in his hand, mis-shaping its brim with the rage he felt against Quin. It could work, but only with Quin. With Quin as he was, it was doomed.

Pyott and Clark were alone in what had once been the "Chessboard Counter" operations room. Aubrey had stood-down all RN personnel, who would be briefed to run what had become, in his mind, a rescue rather than a destruction operation. He intended that "Leopard" should be repaired and that *Proteus* make her escape, under cover of its anti-sonar, from Pechenga. The scheme seemed utterly unworkable to Clark and Pyott, and it had seemed so to him in the windy light of the park, between the gilded buildings. In this underground room, precisely because Quin had obviously been allowed to rest by Clark, it seemed only a little less ridiculous. An old man's fancy. He had code-named it "Plumber".

Clark's face expressed disappointment, beneath the surface of superiority. He had been proven right; Quin was a broken reed. Yet Clark evidently wished it had been otherwise. There was an undisguised disappointment on Pyott's handsome face as he stood with Clark in what had the appearance of a protective hedge of easels supporting mounted photographs and charts. The bric-à-brac of an operation that would never be allowed to run. The board would never be set up for it, the timetable never decided, the communications and the back-up never arranged. It was already dead.

The knowledge made Aubrey furious.

"I'm sorry, Mr. Aubrey," Clark began, "but that guy's in no condition to cross the street. He's in bad shape, psychologically."

Pyott fiddled with his moustache, as if caricaturing his uniform and rank. "I'm afraid so, Kenneth. Nerves shot to bits, willingness to help nil. Bloody little man –"

"What are these?" Aubrey asked, pointing at the easels in turn. "Did we order these?"

"I did," Pyott admitted, "before we had a good chat with our friend Quin."

"Is this *Proteus*?" Aubrey had stopped in front of one of the grainy, enlarged monochrome pictures. A harbour, the slim, knife-like shape of vessels seen from the air.

"Yes." Clark sounded suddenly revived. He joined Aubrey, Pyott coming to the old man's other shoulder. Aubrey felt hemmed in by younger bone and muscle. "The quality's poor. Satellite picture in poor conditions. Getting dark down there, and the cloud cover obscured most of the shots. This is the inner harbour at Pechenga. That's her." His long, thick finger dabbed towards the top edge of the picture.

"What damage has she sustained?"

"Hard to tell. Look through this." Clark handed Aubrey a magnify-

784

ing glass, and the old man bent to the photograph, moving the lens slowly over the scene, which threatened at any moment to dissolve into a collection of grey, black and white dots. "Those look like buoyancy bags at the stern. Must have been a low-warhead torpedo, maybe two. She's not under power, she's being towed by the rescue ship ahead of her."

Aubrey surrendered the magnifying glass. "How long?" he asked.

Clark shook his head. "Impossible to guess. One day, two. I don't know. No one could tell you from this shot, not even with computer enhancement."

"Show me where on the chart of Pechenga."

The three of them moved, in a tight little wedge, to another easel. Their voices were echoing drily in the empty room. There was a marble, sepulchral atmosphere about it. The huge map-board in the middle of the floor registered, frozen like something unfinished but preserved in ice, the conditions and dispositions at the time the *Proteus* was boarded. Even the dot of the relief Nimrod was frozen on station above the coast of Norway. The board had not been allowed to continue revealing the extent of their defeat.

"Here," Clark said. "These are the submarine pens."

"Well? Well? Is it only Quin we are worried about? *I* will take responsibility for him. We have discussed this operation for most of the night. Is there more than Quin to hold us back?"

"You never give up, do you?" Clark said.

"Would *you* drop out?"

"No."

"Giles?"

"Too risky – no, I'm not sounding like a granny just for the sake of it. Quin is crucial. If Clark can't get the right information, at the *precise* split-second he requires it, then everything could be lost – including Clark." Pyott shook his head, held his features in a gloomy, saturnine cast, to emphasize his words.

Aubrey was exasperated. He had *seen* the *Proteus* now. He had to act.

"You've talked to MoD Air?"

"There's no problem there. A Harrier could get Clark across Finland and into the Pechenga area – yes. You have the authority to send it. The AWACS Nimrod that was rigged up especially for sea trials with *Proteus* is on stand-by at Farnborough. They could accommodate yourself and Quin. Eastoe and his crew are on stand-by to be flown down from Kinloss to Farnborough." Pyott's face now changed to an expression of exasperation; he was angry with Quin for wasting his time and his organizational talents.

"Communications?"

"Yes, we can do that. Between the Nimrod and Clark, with a range of a hundred miles, speaking in a whisper."

Aubrey had passed to the cutaway chart of the submarine. A multitude of hand-written labels had been appended, explaining and exposing each minute section and piece of equipment and function of the *Proteus*. Aubrey, by studying it, would know as much about the most secret of the Royal Navy's submarines in an hour as the Russians would know by the time *Proteus* sailed again from Pechenga.

"Damn," he said softly as the realization sprung itself upon him like a bad dream. "Jamming or interception? Location?"

"Can be overcome," Pyott admitted reluctantly. His enthusiasm had dimmed again, with his own realization. His eyes had strayed towards the door of the room where Aubrey had slept and which now contained a sedated Quin.

"Your equipment, Clark?"

"Portable – just. I could make it, with an infinite amount of luck, without drowning under the weight of what I need – *would need*, Mr. Aubrey. It can't be done without Quin. I can't learn enough in time. He has to be there – in range of my transmitter – all the time, and able to talk me through whatever I find." He jabbed a finger at one section of the hull of the *Proteus*. "Hell, the back-up system's *here*! Not to mention that this stern section, where some of the sensors are, has been damaged by one, maybe two, torpedoes. I can't go climbing over the hull spot-welding alongside Russian dockyard workers! It's crazy."

"If it can't be done, you will abort 'Plumber' and destroy the 'Leopard' equipment with the maximum efficiency," Aubrey said in a tight, controlled voice. "But perhaps it can be done."

"What will you do with Quin? Twist his arm, Kenneth? Threaten to fling him out of the Nimrod if he doesn't answer Clark's questions correctly and without hesitation? I'm afraid that Clark and I agree on this occasion. It would be a complex, expensive, dangerous and ultimately wasteful operation. If Clark must go in, let him go in simply to destroy 'Leopard'. Someone other than Quin could point him in the right direction there."

Aubrey was plucking at his bottom lip, staring at the chart of the submarine, its workings and innards exposed like a biological specimen or drawing. The ringing of the telephone was loud and startling in the room, and Pyott rushed to answer it as if he were afraid that its noise would waken Quin. Immediately he answered, he glanced at Aubrey, and beckoned him to the desk. It was Cunningham.

" 'C'," Pyott whispered as he handed him the receiver.

"Richard?"

"Kenneth – how is our patient?"

"Not good. Uncooperative, unreliable, withdrawn. Chronically suspicious and afraid."

"I see. No use to you, then?"

"Why? Has the operation been cleared?"

"Yes, it has. The Secretary of State has cleared it with the PM. She's enthusiastic, I gather."

"The Prime Minister obviously wasn't made aware of the difficulties," Aubrey said sarcastically. Cunningham had had to clear the proposed operation with the cabinet minister responsible for the SIS, the Foreign Secretary who, in his turn, had consulted the Prime Minister. The recruitment of another national, Clark being American, the incursion into Soviet territory, and the special circumstances pertaining to the submarine, had removed the operation beyond the sphere of the intelligence service acting alone and covertly.

"She has cleared the operation with the President, if it proves feasible in your judgment. NATO ministers will be informed under a Priority Two order. I have been successful on your behalf, but you now seem to imply that I've been wasting my time?"

"I hope not. I *hoped* not. It does seem rather hopeless, Richard."

"A great pity. Then Clark will have to go in just to get rid of 'Leopard'?"

Aubrey listened to the silence at the other end of the line. Behind Cunningham, there was the enthusiasm, the permission, of the politicians. A chance to give the Russian bear a black eye, a bloody nose, without risking more than one life. Turning the tables on the Kremlin. He did not despise or disregard the almost naive way in which his operation had been greeted with enthusiasm in Downing Street and the White House. It was a pity that the seriousness of the operation's parameters and its possible repercussions had required the political sanction of the two leaders. The NATO ministers, with the exception of Norway, would be informed after the event. They did not matter. The naivety, however, gave him cause to doubt the rationale of his scheme. To be praised by laymen is not the expert's desire. Aubrey now suspected his operation's feasibility.

Cunningham seemed to have no desire to add to what he had said, or to repeat his question. Whatever Aubrey now said, he would, with enthusiasm or reluctance, pass on to the Foreign Office and Downing Street.

"No, he will not," Aubrey heard himself say. The expression created an instant sense of lightness, of relief. It was a kind of self-affirmation, and he no longer cared for pros and cons, doubts and likelihoods. It *would* be attempted. "Captain Clark will be briefed to examine and, if possible, repair 'Leopard', and to instruct the commanding officer and crew of the *Proteus* to attempt to escape from the Soviet naval base at Pechenga."

Cunningham merely said, "I'll pass your message on. Good luck, Kenneth."

Aubrey put down the receiver quickly, as if Clark or Pyott might make some attempt to snatch it from him and reverse his instructions. He had spoken clearly, precisely, and with sufficient volume for them to hear him. When he looked at them, Pyott was fiddling with his moustache again, while Clark was perched on the edge of a foldaway table, arms folded across his chest. He was shaking his head. Then, unexpectedly, he grinned.

Pyott said, as Aubrey approached them, "You're taking a grave risk with this young man's life, Kenneth. And perhaps with Quin. Do you think it's worth it?"

"Of course he does," Clark interposed. He was still smiling. "He knows I won't refuse, on any count. Uh, Mr. Aubrey?"

"Perhaps, Ethan, perhaps. I'm sorry you have to enact my romantic escapade, but your President is relying on you, too, I gather."

"That's the last time I vote for the guy."

Aubrey looked at his watch. Nine-fifteen.

"Giles, get Eastoe and his crew moved down to Farnborough immediately. Ethan, get Quin in here again. We have less than three hours. I want to be at Farnborough, and you must be on your way by this afternoon." Pyott was already on the telephone. "Get that Harrier put on immediate stand-by, and get Ethan's equipment details over to MoD Air."

"Very well, Kenneth."

There was no longer a sepulchral atmosphere in the room. Instead, a febrile, nervous excitement seemed to charge the air like static electricity forerunning a storm.

The grocer, Aubrey thought. My immediate task is the grocer. He must meet Clark tonight as near Pechenga as we can get him.

Unexpectedly, it had snowed lightly in the Midlands during the night, and Cannock Chase, where they had stopped at Tricia Quin's request, was still dusted with it. The sky was bright, dabs of white cloud pushed and buffeted across the blue expanse by a gusty, chill wind. Small puddles, some of them in hoofprints, were filmed with ice, like cataracted eyes. They walked slowly, Hyde with his hands in his pockets, relaxed even though he was cold. The girl huddled in her donkey jacket, the one in which she had tried to slip into the NEC unnoticed. She seemed concerned to explain why she had asked him to stop, to have requested him to leave the motorway at Stafford and drive across the Chase until they had passed through a sprawling

788

housing estate on the outskirts of Rugeley and found themselves, suddenly and welcomely, amid firs and grazing land. It was early afternoon, and they were no more than fifteen miles from the girl's mother.

An occasional passing lorry, back on the road across that part of Cannock Chase, caused the girl to raise her voice as she spoke.

"I don't know why I always made their problems mine. They even used to argue whenever we came up here, when I was quite young, and I used to hate that especially."

"Rough," was Hyde's only comment, because he could not think of a suitable reply. He could not join the girl's post-mortem on her parents. His memories of Quin were too recent and too acerbic for him to consider the man either sympathetic or important. He allowed the girl, however, to analyse herself in a careful, half-aware manner. She, at least, had his sympathy.

"I suppose it always sprang from the fact that Dad was much brighter than Mum – much brighter than me, too," she added, smiling slightly, cracking the film of ice over one sunken hoofprint, hearing its sharp little report with evident pleasure, with a weight of association. "He *was* intolerant," she conceded, "and I don't think Mum appreciated what he was doing, after the firm got a bit bigger and she no longer did the bookwork or helped him out. I think they were happy in the early days." She looked at him suddenly, as if he had demurred. "Mum needs to feel useful. I'm like her, I suppose."

"You're a good girl, and you're wasting your time. It's *their* business, not yours. You can't do anything except be a football. Is that what you want?"

Her face was blanched, and not merely by the cold. He had intruded upon her version of reality, casting doubt upon its veracity.

"You're very hard," she said.

"I suppose so." He had enjoyed the drive down the crowded M6 in the borrowed car, after a night's stop which had refreshed him and which the girl had seemed to desperately require the moment her father's plane had left Manchester. Sutton Coldfield for dinner was an amusing prospect. He considered Mrs. Quin's reaction to him as a guest. "Sorry. I'll shut up."

"You don't have to –"

"It's better. It isn't my business."

She paused and looked back. The fern was still brown and stiffly cramped into awkward, broken shapes and lumps by the frost. Bird-song. She wanted to see a deer, the quick flicker of grey, white hindquarters disappearing into the trees. In some unaccountable way, she believed that if she saw deer, things would be improved, would augur well. It would fuse the circuits that existed between present and past. She looked down the perspective of the bridle path, back towards the car park, unaware, while Hyde shivered at her side.

He heard the approach of the small, red and white helicopter first. Its noise intruded, and then it seemed to become a natural and expected part of the pale sky. Tricia Quin knew it would startle the deer, make them more difficult to find, over beyond the line of numbered targets against the high earth bank that composed the rifle range. She looked up, following Hyde's gaze. He was shielding his eyes with one hand. The tiny helicopter in its bright, hire-firm colours swung in the sky as if suspended from an invisible cable, a brightly daubed spider, and then it flicked down towards them.

Hyde's nerves came slowly awake. His other hand came out of his pocket, his body hunched slightly in expectation. The helicopter – a Bell Jetranger he perceived with one detached part of his awareness – was still moving towards them, skimming now just above the line of trees, down the track of the bridle path. The helicopter had hesitated above the car park, then seemed more certain of purpose, as if it had found what it sought. Hyde watched it accelerate towards them, the noise of its single turbo-shaft bellowing down into the track between the trees. Lower, and the trees were distressed by the down-draught and even the stiff, rimy ferns began buckling, attempting and imitating movement they might have possessed before death.

"Run!" he said. The girl's face crumpled into defeat, even agony, as he pushed her off the path towards the nearest trees. "Run!"

She stumbled through frozen grass, through the thin film of snow, through the creaking, dead ferns. Deliberately, he let her widen the distance between them – they wouldn't shoot at her, but he didn't want her killed when they tried to take him out – before he, too, began running.

The first shots were hardly audible above the noise of the rotors. The downdraught plucked at his clothing, his hair and body, as if restraining him. The girl ran without looking back, in utter panic.

ELEVEN:

Flights

The jellyfish bags were gone, except on the port side of the *Proteus*. The starboard ballast tanks had been repaired, and the rudder fin had begun to look like the result of a half-completed, complex grafting operation; spars and struts of metal bone, much now covered with a sheen of new plates. One part of Lloyd, at least, welcomed the surgery. He paced the concrete wharf of the submarine pen, under the hard lights, his guard behind him, taking his midday exercise. The Red Navy had extended the farce even to giving each member of his crew a thorough medical check-up; routine exercise, as much as was permitted by the confines and security necessary to Pechenga as a military installation, had been prescribed. Also permission to use the crew cinema had been granted, alcohol had arrived, in limited and permissible amounts; and fresh food.

Lloyd held his hands behind his back, walking in unconscious imitation of a member of the Royal Family. The diplomat he had requested from Moscow had not arrived, unsurprisingly. Lloyd had made the required formal protests without enthusiasm, realizing their pointlessness. Better news lay in the gossip he and some of the crew had picked up from their guards. Everyone was waiting on the arrival of a Soviet expert, delayed in Novosibirsk by bad weather. He it was who would supervise the examination of "Leopard". It was the one element of optimism in Lloyd's situation.

The fitters and welders were having their lunch, sitting against the thick, slabbed concrete walls of the pen. They looked a species of prisoner themselves, wearing blue fatigue overalls, lounging in desultory conversation, eating hunks of thick dark bread and pickles and cold meat – in one instance, a cold potato. They watched him with an evident curiosity, but only as something belonging to the foreign submarine on which they were working and which was the real focus of their interest.

Lloyd stopped to gaze back down the two hundred and fifty feet of the *Proteus*'s length. Nuclear-powered Fleet submarines possessed a menace not unlike that of the shark. They were long, shiny-sleek, but portly, massive. Three and a half thousand tons of vessel, well over twice the size of a Second World War ancestor. Backed like a whale, but a killer whale. It hurt Lloyd's pride as her captain to have watched, before the hooter sounded deafeningly in the pen to announce the lunch break, Russian fitters clambering and crawling over her; Lilliputians performing surgery on a helpless Gulliver. He turned away, looking over the gates of the pen, into the tunnel which led to the harbour. One o'clock. In the circle of light he could discern a Soviet destroyer moving almost primly across his field of vision. The view was like that through a periscope, and he wished, with clenched fists and an impotent rage, that it had been.

Pechenga harbour lowered under heavy grey cloud, and he resented the weather as an additional camouflage that aided the Red Navy.

He turned to look back at his submarine once more, and Ardenyev was standing in front of him, hands on his hips, a smile on his face. The smile, Lloyd saw, was calculated to encourage, to repel dislike rather than to sneer or mock. With a gesture, Ardenyev waved the guard away. The man retired. The stubby Kalashnikov still thrust against his hip, barrel outwards. The guard swaggered. A Soviet marine, entirely satisfied with the guard-prisoner relationship between them. Young, conscripted, dim. Ardenyev's amused eyes seemed to make the comment. Yet the wave of Ardenyev's hand had been that of the conjurer, the illusionist. *There is nothing to fear, there are no guards, we are friends, abracadabra –*

Lloyd suddenly both liked the man and resented him.

"Come to gloat?" he asked. For a moment, Ardenyev absorbed the word, then shook his head.

"No." There was a small satchel over his shoulder, which he now swung forward, and opened. "I have food, and wine," he said. "I hoped you would share lunch with me. I am sorry that I cannot invite you to the officers' mess, or to the only decent restaurant in Pechenga. It is not possible. Shall we sit down?" Ardenyev indicated two bollards, and immediately sat down himself. Reluctantly, Lloyd joined him, hitching his dark trousers to preserve their creases, brushing at the material as if removing a persistent spot. Then he looked up.

"What's for lunch?"

"Caviar, of course. Smoked fish. Georgian wine. Pancakes." He opened the plastic containers one by one, laying them like offerings at Lloyd's feet. He cut slices of bread from a narrow loaf. "Help yourself," he said. "No butter, I'm afraid. Even Red Navy officers' messes sometimes go without butter."

Lloyd ate hungrily, oblivious of the greedy eyes of the nearest fitters. He drank mouthfuls of the rough wine to unstick the bread from his palate, swigging it from the bottle Ardenyev uncorked for him.

Finally, he said, "Your people seem to be taking their time."

"Our workers are the best in the world," Ardenyev answered with a grin.

"I mean on the inside of the hull."

"Oh." Ardenyev studied Lloyd for a moment, then shrugged. "You have heard rumours, it is obvious. Even Red Navy marines cannot keep anything to themselves." He chewed on a slice of loaf liberally smothered with black caviar. "Unfortunately, our leading expert in naval electronic counter-measures – the man designated to, shall we say, have a little peep at your pet – is delayed, in Siberia." He laughed. "No, not by his politics, merely by the weather. He was supposed to fly from his laboratory in Novosibirsk three days ago. He is snowed in."

"You're being very frank."

"Can you see the point of being otherwise?" Ardenyev asked pleasantly.

"It was a clever plan," Lloyd offered.

"Ah, you are trying to debrief me. Well, I don't mind what you collect on this operation. It has worked. We're not likely to use it again, are we?" His eyes were amused, bright. Lloyd could not help but respond to the man's charm. "It was clever, yes. It needed a great deal of luck, of course – but it worked."

"If your Siberian snowman arrives."

"Ah, yes, Comrade Professor Academician Panov. I have no doubt you will also be meeting Admiral of the Red Banner Fleet Dolohov at the same time. He is bound to come and see his prize."

"You sound disrespectful."

"Do I? Ah, perhaps I only feel annoyance at the fact that an old man with delusions of grandeur could dream up such a clever scheme in his dotage." He laughed, recovering his good humour. "Drink up. I have another bottle."

"They intend removing it, then?"

"What?"

"I'm obliged not to mention sensitive equipment. May I preserve protocol? Their Lordships will be most anxious to know – on my return – that I gave nothing away." Lloyd, too, was smiling by the time he finished his statement.

"Ah, of course." Ardenyev rubbed his nose. There were tiny raisins of caviar at one corner of his mouth. His tongue flicked out and removed them. "No. I doubt it will be necessary. I am not certain, of course. I have done my bit, the balls and bootstraps part of the operation."

"I'm sorry about your men."

Ardenyev looked at Lloyd. "I see that you are. It was not your fault. I would have done the same, in your place. Let us blame our separate masters, and leave it at that."

"When will they let us go?"

Ardenyev looked swiftly down the length of the *Proteus*, taking in the repairs, the fitters slowly getting up – the hooter had blasted across Lloyd's question, so that he had had to shout it, making it seem a desperate plea rather than a cool enquiry – the new plates, the buckled hull plates, the stripped rudder, the skeletal hydroplane below them in the water.

"Twenty-four hours, assuming it stops snowing in Novosibirsk," Ardenyev said, turning back to Lloyd.

Four days, Aubrey thought. It is four days – less than one hundred hours – since I became involved in this business. I have slept for perhaps fifteen of those hours. I have been out of that damned room beneath the Admiralty for even fewer hours. And now I am consigning myself to another box, something even more uncomfortable, something much more evidently tomb-like.

He took the crewman's hand, and allowed himself to be helped up the last steps of the passenger ladder into the fuselage of the AWACS Nimrod. He did not feel, despite his reflections on age, mortality, sleep and habitat, either tired or weary. True, the adrenalin was sufficient only to forestall such things rather than to invigorate him, but he was grateful, as he ducked his head through the crew door near the tail fin and directly adjacent to the huge RAF roundel on the fuselage. Then the bright, quick-clouding windy day was exchanged for a hollow, metallic interior. And Eastoe was waiting for Quin and himself.

"Here you are, Mr. Aubrey. You and Mr. Quin here, if you please." He indicated two seats, facing one another across a communications console from which thick wires and cables trailed away down the fuselage floor, in a channel that might have been a gutter in an abattoir, the way in which it riveted Quin's fearful gaze. Other swivel chairs, bolted to the floor and the curving sides of the fuselage, stretched away down the untidy, crowded interior of the Nimrod towards the flight deck. For Quin's benefit, Eastoe added as Aubrey seated himself, "You're wired into *all* our communications equipment, sir, and the principal sensors. We'll do a full test with Clark when we're airborne. Your equipment operates through this central console –"

"Yes, yes," Quin said impatiently, like someone interested only in the toilet facilities provided. Eastoe's face darkened. His patience was

794

evidently running out. The door swung shut on a gleam of sunlight, and a hand clamped home the locks. Quin appeared physically startled, as if suddenly awoken, and he protested, "I can be of no use to you!" His voice was high-pitched. He held his hands out in front of him, demonstrating their uncontrollable quiver. "I am no use to you!"

"Quin!" Aubrey barked. "Quin, sit down! Now! None of us is here to be self-indulgent, especially you. We all have a task to perform. Kindly see to it that you do yours, when the time comes."

Eastoe studied both civilians like a strange, newly-encountered species. There was an easy, adopted contempt around his mouth which Aubrey had met before in military officers. Pyott was an expert at it, when he chose. No doubt even Lloyd in his confinement was employing the sneer *militaire*. Aubrey almost smiled. The French, of course, had always been world champions. He remembered the young de Gaulle of London-exile days, when Aubrey had been at SOE. The nose had helped, of course.

Aubrey thrust aside the memory, almost with reluctance, and confronted Quin and the RAF Squadron Leader who, he well knew, considered his scheme to rescue *Proteus* wildly incapable of success. Quin slumped into his seat, swivelling in it instantly like a sulking child; there was a moment of debated defiance which only reached his hands as he clenched them into weak fists. He rubbed a nervy hand through his wiry, thinning hair which stood more comically on end as a result of the gesture. The inventor of "Leopard"; the machinery made of silicons, plastics, metal, the man constructed of straw. It was easy to feel contempt, hard to dismiss that emotion. For Eastoe, it was evidently impossible to remove that attitude from his calculations. Aubrey spent no time in conjecture as to Eastoe's more personal feelings towards him because of the crashed Nimrod and its dead aircrew.

"Squadron Leader Eastoe," Aubrey said levelly, "how long before we are ready to take off?"

Eastoe looked at his watch. "Fifteen minutes."

"You will make that ten, if you please," Aubrey said, treading with a delicate but grinding motion of his heel on all forms of civilian-military protocol. Eastoe's eyes widened in surprise. "As I said, Squadron Leader. Ten minutes. Please see to it."

"Mr. Aubrey, I'm the skipper of this –"

"No, you are not. You are its pilot. In matters of flying, I shall consult you, even defer to you. But I am in command here. Please be certain you understand that fact."

Eastoe bit his lip, and choked back a retort. Instead, he nodded his head like a marionette, and went forward to the flight deck. Aubrey, controlling the tremor of weakness he felt in his frame, sat down again opposite Quin, who was looking at him with a new kind of fearful respect.

Aubrey calculated his next remarks, then observed: "It was MoD who originally cocked-up this operation," he said casually, confidentially. "I do not intend to let them do so again. Damn fools, playing war-games with 'Leopard'. It simply showed little or no respect for – or *understanding* of – your development."

Aubrey watched Quin's ego inflate. He had suspected a balloon of self-admiration in the man, and was not disappointed; except in the arcane sense that Quin was so readily comprehensible, so transparent in his inner self. Whether the ego would keep him going, make him sufficiently malleable and for long enough, remained to be seen. Quin had talked to no one except his daughter for weeks. He required the conversation and the admiration of intelligent men; of men rather than women, Aubrey suspected. A deal of chauvinism there, too; Mrs. Quin would have been useful in the early days, but not a sufficient audience for the man's intellect and achievements. It cast a new light on why Quin had allowed the take-over of his small firm by the Plessey giant. It had enlarged his audience of admirers.

"You understand?" Quin asked, almost in surprise.

"Of course. Don't you think I get tired of dealing with these people, too?" Aubrey relaxed, offering Quin a cigarette. The man's right forefinger was stained brown. Quin reached for the cigarette case, taking one of the untipped cigarettes. He used his own lighter, and inhaled deeply, exhaled loudly. Confidence was altering his posture in his seat. He did not slump now, he relaxed.

"I see," Quin said. "I advised them against using 'Leopard' so early, and relying on it so totally. They wouldn't listen." There was self-pity there, just below the surface of the words.

"Arrogant," Aubrey murmured. "They're all so arrogant. This time, however, they do as *we* say, Quin, my dear fellow. They do exactly as we instruct them."

It was six minutes later – Quin had just stubbed out his second cigarette – when the Nimrod reached the end of the taxiway, turned, then roared down the main Farnborough runway, lifting into the patchily cloudy sky, the ground shrinking away from them at a surprising speed. As the buildings and aircraft had sped past his porthole-like window, Aubrey had reminded himself of the delicacy, the weakness of his control over Quin. Laving him with the oil of flattery; no grounds for confidence there, he remarked to himself, watching the man as his hands gripped the arms of his seat and he sat with closed eyes. No grounds for confidence at all.

*   *   *

The Harrier was a T.4 two-seater trainer, and it was unarmed because of the load it would have to carry and the extra fuel tanks, each of one hundred gallons, beneath its wings. There were no circumstances in which it would require cannon, bombs or missiles, for its mission would be aborted unless it could avoid all contact with Soviet aircraft or ground defences. Despite being a training aircraft, however, it was fitted with the latest type of laser range-finding equipment in the nose.

Ethan Clark was able to move only with difficulty in the pressure suit with which he had been supplied, because of the immersion suit he already wore beneath it. It made him waddle awkwardly, flying helmet under his arm, giving him the appearance of a circus clown imitating a pilot. The pilot of the Harrier, an experienced Squadron Leader whose response to his mission was shading to the cautious side of excitement, walked in front of him across the tarmac of Wittering RAF base, in Lincolnshire. Clark's packs of communications equipment, explosives, sensors, meters, spares and tools had been stowed beneath the wings in two pods where bombs might normally have hung.

Clark had been transported by helicopter to Wittering, and he had briefed the pilot, in the presence of the station commandant and Giles Pyott, who had provided the MoD authority appropriate to the commandeering of an aircraft and a pilot. Now Pyott strode alongside him, the wind plucking at his thick grey hair, his bearing upright, his form cloaked in the camel-coloured British warm.

The pilot clambered up the ladder, and swung himself into the cockpit, looking down immediately from behind the face panel of his helmet as Clark paused before his ascent. Pyott extended his hand at once, and Clark took his cool, tough grip.

"Good luck, Clark," Pyott said stiffly, as if avoiding the real subject of a conversation that was both necessary and important.

"Thanks, Colonel." Clark grinned, despite the gravity of the moment. "Here goes nothing, as they say."

"If you can't make it – if you can't *repair*, you *must* abort," Pyott warned solemnly. "Remember that. No heroics over and above the required minimum."

"I appreciate your concern, Colonel."

"Right. Get on with you. I think we're keeping your pilot waiting."
Clark glanced up. "Sure."

He released Pyott's grip, and began clambering awkwardly up the ladder. It was difficult to swing his unaccustomed weight and bulk over the lip of the cockpit, and hot and strenuous work to ease himself into the narrow rear seat. Eventually, he achieved a degree of comfort, strapped himself in and adjusted his flying helmet. The pilot reached up, and closed the cockpit cover. Instantly, nerves raised his temperature, and he felt a film of perspiration on his forehead. He looked down, and the ladder was being carried away by a member of the ground crew. Pyott was striding after it like a schoolmaster harrying someone for a breach of school rules, his walking-stick accompanying his strides like a younger limb. Clark had never noticed Pyott's limp before.

When he reached the grass margin of the taxiway, Giles Pyott turned, almost posing with the little knot of the ground crew.

"Fingers in your ears, sir," a flight sergeant informed him.

"What? Oh, yes."

Pyott did as instructed. The Harrier was using the runway in a standard take off, instead of its unique vertical lift, because of the extra weight of fuel that it carried. Lights winked at wingtips and belly, suddenly brighter as a heavy cloud was pulled across the early afternoon sun by the wind. Then the aircraft was rolling, slowly for a moment, then with an accelerating rush, passing them – Pyott could see the helmeted blob that was Clark's head, turned towards him – and racing on down the runway. The heat of its single twenty-one and a half thousand pound thrust Pegasus 103 turbofan engine distorted its outline like a heat haze might have done, so that the aircraft appeared to have passed behind a veil, become removed from them. It sat back almost like an animal for an instant, then sprang at the sky and its low, scudding cloud and patches of gleaming brightness. The runway was still gauzy, but the Harrier was a sharply outlined silhouette as it rose then banked to the east.

Pyott took his hands from his ears, realizing that the ground crew had already begun making their way towards the hangar area, leaving him a somewhat foolishly isolated figure in an overcoat, a retired officer out for a constitutional who had strolled by mistake into a military installation. He turned on his heel, and followed the others, his imperative now to return to the room beneath the Admiralty.

The Harrier had already climbed into the lowest of the cloud and was lost from sight.

The safety offered by the trees had come to seem a kind of privileged imprisonment, the further they ran. Hyde had seen figures, three of them, drop out of the helicopter into the buffet of the rotors' down-draught in the moment he had paused at the first trees, and knew they were cut off from the car. By now, someone would have driven it out of the car park and hidden it and removed the distributor. The trees masked them – they heard the helicopter roaming in search of them every few minutes – but they bordered a long, higher stretch of barren heathland where summer fires of a drought year had exposed

798

the land even further. Dull, patchy with snow and fern, treeless, exposed. A minefield as far as they were concerned.

When they first stopped, he had held the frightened, shivering girl against him, but even before her breathing calmed and she had drawn any comfort from the embrace, he was asking her urgently, "How well do you know the area? Can you see it in your mind's eye? Where's the nearest road? How far? Can you run? What's the shape of this plantation? What *do* you know? *Anything*?"

Roads? No, she didn't know, she couldn't explain the shape of Cannock Chase, she'd never seen a map of it –

A childhood place, he understood even as he fumed silently. She remembered it as a series of snapshots, the sight of deer, high blue skies above whitened landscapes, the fall and rise of the land only as a viewer who wished the ability to paint would perceive and remember. Useless to them now.

They followed the edge of the plantation north for almost two miles, further and further from the road and the car park and the town of Rugeley. Then the girl announced that she did not know that part of the Chase. They were north-east of the rifle range, but it was hidden from them by the trees.

"The road from Stafford to Lichfield," the girl said, her face screwed up in thought, her chest still heaving with the effort of their last run.

"What?" he said.

"It runs through the Chase." She looked up into the dark trees, as if for inspiration. She was painfully trying to remember turns in the road, bearings from her childhood, signposts. "Past Shugborough Hall – Wolseley Bridge, turn right . . ." She shook her head while he slapped his hands against his thighs in exasperation. Then she was looking at him, a sense of failure evident in her eyes. She added, hesitantly, "I think if we continue north, we'll hit the main road."

"Trees all the way?" he snapped, unable to restrain the sense of entrapment that glided out of the dark trees and accompanied them at every step. They were like her precious deer, confined to the trees.

She shrugged hopelessly. "I don't know."

"Oh, Christ!" She looked at if he had struck her. He added, in a tone that aspired to more gentleness, "Any wardens', gamekeepers' houses around here?" Again, she shook her head.

Beyond the trees, the afternoon was bright, dazzling off the last paper-thin sheet of snow on the higher, open ground. The chilly wind soughed through the upper branches of the firs. To the north and west, the direction of the weather, there was heavier cloud. It was a weekday afternoon, and they had seen no other people since they left the car park, which had contained just one other car. Once, they had heard a dog bark, but they had seen neither it nor its owner. A distant vehicle's engine had sawn into the silence at another point, but again they had not seen it. Hyde had never realized before how isolated he could feel in a part of the cramped island that had become his home.

"I'm ready," Tricia Quin offered.

"OK, let's go."

Their feet crackled on fallen twigs, or crunched through the long winter's frosty humus and leaf litter. An eerie, dark green, under-water light filtered through the firs, slanting on the grey and damp-green trunks. Hyde had time to think that he could not imagine how it had ever been a magic place for the girl, before he dragged her without sound off the narrow, foot-pressed, deer-run track they were following, behind the mossy trunk of a fir. Deep ravines in the bark, its hardness against his cheek, his hand over the girl's mouth, his breath hushing her before he released her; the movement of an insect over the terrain of the bark, almost so close as to be out of focus. He held the girl against him, pulled into his body. She was shivering, and her head was cocked, listening. Her breath came and went, plucking at the air lightly yet fervently; an old lady dying. He dismissed the inappropriate image.

She reached her face up to him in a parody of intimacy, and whispered in his ear, "What is it? I can't even hear the helicopter."

He tossed his head, to indicate the track and the trees in the direction they had come.

"I heard something. I don't know what. Let's hope it's an old lady out for a brisk stroll." The girl tried to smile, nudging herself closer against him. He felt her body still. He listened.

Footstep. Crack, dry and flat as snapping a seaweed pod. Then silence, then another crack. Twigs. Footstep. The timing was wrong for an old lady, a young man, even a child. Wrong for anyone simply out for a walk, taking exercise. Sounds too careful, too slow, too spaced to be anything else than cautious, careful, alert. Stalking.

His heart began to interfere with his hearing as he stifled his breathing and the adrenalin began to surge. He should have moved further off the track. It was *their* tracks that were being followed, easy to do for a trained man, too much leaf-mould underfoot not to imprison the evidence of their passage, along with the deer prints, the hoof prints, the dogs' pawmarks, the ridged patterns of stout walking shoes.

Crack, then a soft cursing breath. Close, close. He pushed the girl slightly away and reached behind him, feeling the butt of the gun against his palm. She watched him, uninitiated into that kind of adulthood, looking very childlike and inadequate and requiring him to be responsible for her.

She pressed against the fir's trunk beside him. The tree was old enough, wide enough in the trunk, to mask them both. He nudged her when he could not bear the waiting any longer and substituted nerves for knowledge, and she shuffled two small paces around the trunk. He remained where he was, his hand still twisted, as if held by a bully, behind his back.

Breathing, heavier than the girl's, the sense of the weight of a heavy male body transferring from one foot to another, the glimmer of a hand holding something dark, the beginnings of a profile. Then they were staring at one another, each holding a gun, no more than seven yards apart, each knowing the stalemate for what it was, each understanding the other's marksmanship in the extended arms, the crouch of the body into a smaller target. Understanding completely and quickly, so that neither fired.

A heavy man in an anorak and dark slacks. Walking boots, the slacks tucked into heavy woollen socks. A Makarov pistol, because a rifle couldn't be hidden.

The man's eyes flickered, but did not look up, as the noise of the helicopter became apparent to both of them. A slow, confident smile spread on the man's face. Not long now. The stalemate would be broken. Hyde concentrated on watching the man's eyes and his hands. Perspiration trickled from beneath his arms, and his mouth was dry. His hand was beginning to quiver with the tension, beginning to make the gun unsteady. The noise of the helicopter grew louder, and the trees began to rustle in the down-draught. He could not kill without being killed, there was no advantage, not a microsecond of it –

A noise in the undergrowth, a small, sharp stamping pattern. The brushing aside of whippy low branches and twigs. High, springing steps. Then the deer was on them.

Hyde it was who fired, because it had to be another pursuer, even though the subconscious was already rejecting the idea. The Russian fired too, because he had been startled out of the confidence that it was a friend, another gun against Hyde. Tricia Quin screamed long before reaction-time should have allowed her to do so, as if she had foreseen the animal's death. The small, grey deer tumbled and skidded with cartoon-like, unsteady legs, its coat badged with dark new markings, then it was between them, veering off, then falling slowly, wobbling as when new-born, onto the crisp, rotting humus, where it kicked once, twice –

Reaction-time, reaction-time, Hyde screamed at himself, even as a wrench of pain and guilt hurt his chest. He swung his pistol, the

Russian doing the same, a mirror-image. Reaction-time, reaction-time; he hadn't totally ignored the deer, kicking for a third, fourth time, then shuddering behind the Russian –

Hyde's gun roared, the split-second before that of the Russian. The man was knocked off balance, and his bullet whined past Hyde's left shoulder, buzzing insect-like into the trees. The man lay still instantly, unlike the deer which went on thrashing and twitching and seemed to be making the noise that in reality was coming from the girl, a high, helpless, violated scream.

He ran to the deer, placed the gun against its temple – the dark helpless eye watching him for a moment, the red tongue lolling – and pulled the trigger to shut out the girl's screams which went on even after the report of his gun died away.

"Shut up," he yelled at her, waving the gun as if in threat. "Shut up! Run, you stupid bitch – run!" He ran towards her, the noise of the helicopter deafening just above the treetops, and she fled from him.

Thirty thousand feet below them, through breaks in the carpet of white cloud, Aubrey could make out the chain of rocks that were the Lofoten islands off the north-west coast of Norway. Clark was perhaps a hundred miles away from them at that point, to the south and east, near Bodø, linking up with the RAF Victor in order to perform a mid-air refuelling of the Harrier. Until that point, both the Nimrod and the Harrier had maintained strict radio silence. Now, however Aubrey could no longer delay the testing of the communications equipment that would link Clark and Quin together when the American reached the *Proteus*.

Quin was sweating nervously again, and a swift despisal of the man passed through Aubrey's mind, leaving him satisfied. The emotion removed doubt, even as it pandered to Aubrey's sense of authority in the situation he had created. The man was also chain-smoking and Aubrey, with the righteousness of someone forced by health to give up the habit, disliked Quin all the more intensely for the clouds of bluish smoke that hung perpetually around their heads, despite the air-conditioning of the Nimrod.

"Very well, Flight Lieutenant," Aubrey instructed the radio operator assigned to monitor the communications console Quin would be using, "call up our friend for us, would you?" Aubrey could sense the dislike and irritation he created in the RAF officers who were crewing the Nimrod. However, having begun with Eastoe in a testy, authoritarian manner, he could not now relax into more congenial behaviour.

"Sir," the young officer murmured. He flicked a bank of switches, opening the channel. There was no call-sign. Clark's receiver would be alive with static in his earpiece. He would need no other signal. The maximum range of the transceivers was a little over one hundred miles, their range curtailed by the need to encode the conversation in high-speed transmission form. A tiny cassette tape in Clark's more portable equipment recorded his words, speeded them up, then they were transmitted to this console between Aubrey and Quin. As with the larger equipment in the room beneath the Admiralty, tapes in Quin's receiver slowed down the message, then replayed it as it had been spoken – whispered, Aubrey thought – by the American. And the reverse procedure would occur when Quin, or himself, spoke to Clark. Clumsy, with an unavoidable, built-in delay, but the only way the signals could not be intercepted, understood, and Clark's precise location thereby exposed.

"Yes?" Clark replied through a whistle of static, his voice distant and tired, almost foreboding in its disembodiment. Clark was a long way away, and alone.

"Testing," Aubrey said, leaning forward. He spoke very quietly.

"Can't hear you," Clark replied. There had been a delay, as if old habits of call-sign and acknowledgement waited to pop into Clark's mind.

"This is a test," the flight lieutenant said in a louder voice.

"That's too loud. Clark, I want you to speak quietly." The RAF radio operator evidently found the whole business amateurish and quite unacceptable. Even Aubrey found the conversation amusing, yet fraught with weaknesses. He would have liked to have taken refuge in established routines of communication, in batteries of call-signs and their endless repetition, in jargon and technicalities. Except that this communications network was simply about being able to communicate in a whisper over a distance of one hundred miles, Clark lying on his back or his stomach in a dark, cramped space, out of breath and perspiring inside an immersion suit, working on a piece of incredibly complex equipment he did not understand, trying to locate a fault and repair it. Call-signs would not help him, even though they seemed, by their absence at that moment, to possess the power of spells and charms. "What?" Aubrey said, craning forward towards the console. "I didn't catch that." There was an open sneer on the flight lieutenant's face. "Yes, I heard you clearly. Now, I'll hand you over to Mr. Quin, and you can run through that technical vocabulary you worked out with him. Random order, please, groups of six."

Aubrey sat back, a deal of smugness of manner directed at the radio operator. Quin looked like a nervous, first-time broadcaster or interviewee. He cleared his throat and shuffled in his seat, a clipboard covered with his strange, minuscule, spidery writing in front of him. Then he swiftly wiped his spectacles and began reading – Aubrey motioned him to lower his voice.

For five minutes, as the Nimrod continued northwards towards North Cape and her eventual station inside Norwegian airspace off the coast near Kirkenes, Clark and Quin exchanged a complex vocabulary of technical terminology. Aubrey remembered occasions of impending French or Latin tests, and the last minute, feverish recital of vocab by himself and other boys, before the master walked in and all text books had to be put away. The dialogue had a comforting, lulling quality. When Quin indicated they had finished, he opened his eyes. Quin appeared drained, and Aubrey quailed at the prospect of keeping him up to the mark.

"Thank you, Clark. That will do. Maximum communication, minimum n ɔise. Good luck. Out."

Aubrey cut the channel, and nodded his satisfaction to Quin and the flight lieutenant. Out of the tiny round window, he could see the herringbone pattern of a ship sailing north through the Andfjord, inshore of one of the Vesteralen islands. The Nimrod was perhaps little more than half an hour from North Cape, and the same time again from their taking up station on the Soviet border. In an hour, they would be committed. "Plumber" would really be running, then.

Clark flicked off the transceiver, and shook his head as if he doubted the reality of the voices he had heard. The Harrier was seemingly about to settle onto the carpet of white cloud beneath them, and the tanker, the old Victor bomber, was a dot ahead and to starboard of them. Below the cloud, where the weather had let in small, almost circular viewing ports, the grey water and the slabbed, cut, knife-carved coastline were already retreating into evening, north of the Arctic Circle. Half an hour before, he had looked down between clouds and seen the vast sheet of the Svartisen glacier, looking like a huge, intact slab of marble fallen on the land, tinged by the sun into pinks and greens and blues.

The Harrier moved forward, overtaking the Victor tanker. The pilot changed his position until the tanker was slightly to port, then the probe that had needed to be specially fitted aligned with the long trailing fuel line from the wing of the Victor and its trumpet-bell mouth into which the pilot had to juggle the Harrier's probe. Bee and flower. Clark considered another, more human image, and smiled. Not like that. This was all too mechanical, and without passion.

The Victor's fuselage glowed silver in the sunlight from the west. The RAF roundel was evident on her side as the Harrier slid across the cloud carpet, and there seemed no motion except the slow, dance-like movements of possible combatants as the two aircraft matched speeds and height. The probe nudged forward towards the cone, the fuel-line lying on the air in a gentle, graceful curve. The probe nudged the cone, making it wobble, and then the Harrier dropped back slightly. Too high, too much to the left. Again, the probe slid forward towards the flower-mouth of the cone. Clark watched its insertion, felt the small, sharp jerk as it locked, then saw the glimmer of the three green locking lights on the instrument panel. The fuel began to surge down the fuel line.

Six and a half minutes later – it had become noticeably more evening-like, even at that altitude – the refuelling was complete, and the probe withdrew, the cone slipping forward and away as the speed of the two aircraft no longer matched. The gleaming, part-shadowed fuselage of the tanker slid up and away from them, the fuel-line retreating like a garden hose being reeled in. In a few more moments, the Victor had lost its silhouetted identity and was little more than a gleaming dot. The cloud brushed against the belly of the Harrier.

"Ready?" the pilot asked in his headset.

"Yes."

"Hang on, then. This is where it gets hairy. Don't look if you've got a weak stomach." The pilot chuckled.

"I can stand it."

Even before he finished speaking, the nose of the Harrier dipped into the cloud, and white turned grey and featureless and dark immediately. Clark felt the altitude of the Harrier alter steeply as she dived through the clouds, descending from thirty-five thousand feet.

They emerged into a twilit world, and the pilot levelled the Harrier and switched on the terrain-following radar and the auto-pilot which would together flick and twist them through the mountainous Norwegian hinterland. Clark watched as the dark water of the Skerstad-fjord rose to meet them, then flashed beneath the belly of the aircraft. The pilot was flying the Harrier at five hundred miles an hour. The tiny lights of fishing hamlets flickered along the shore, and then were gone. Small boats returning from the day's fishing, the main north-south highway, then the dark, high, sharp peaks of the mountain range engulfed them. Clark winced, despite his experience, as the tiny insect of the Harrier flicked between two peaks, then followed the snail-like track of a narrow fjord, a smear of lighter grey in the gloom.

The aircraft lifted over the back of a line of hills, then dipped down to follow the terrain again. A huge glacier seemed to emerge suddenly from the darkness, gleaming with a ghostly, threatening light. The Harrier banked, and slipped as buoyantly and easily along its face as a helicopter might have done. Clark had never flown in one of the US Marine Harriers, built under licence by McDonnell Douglas, and it was the only means of comparison he could apply; a demented, speeded-up helicopter. Then the glacier was behind them, one eastern tip of it falling into a small, crater-like lake.

"Sweden," the pilot announced.

"Nice view," Clark replied drily.

"Want to go back for your stomach?"

"I'm OK." Clark noticed the change in his own voice, the subconscious attempt to discourage conversation. He had moved into another phase of "Plumber". Already, he was alone, already it was another, different border they had crossed.

There were lakes as the terrain slowly became less mountainous, the peaks less sharp against the still lighter clouds and the few patches of stars. Grey, almost black water, the jagged lilies of ice floes everywhere. A rounded space of mirror-like water, a few dotted lights, then two companion stretches which the Harrier skimmed across like a stone. Then a long ribbon of lake, almost like a river because he could not perceive, at that altitude, either end of it, which the Harrier followed as it thrust into the centre of Swedish Lapland.

A village, like one dim street lamp at their speed, even the momentary flicker of headlights, then the Harrier banked to port, and altered course, following the single road north through that part of Sweden, the Norbotten, towards the Finnish border. The sheer rock faces closed in again, and the darkness seemed complete, except where the swift glow-worms of hamlets and isolated farms and the occasional gleams of car or lorry headlights exposed the whiteness of snow in the narrow valleys through which the road wound. Then, lower country, and a gleaming, humped plain of whiteness stretched before and beneath the aircraft.

"Finland," the pilot announced, but added nothing else.

Clark attempted repose, sensing like a man with a severely limited water supply, the waste of adrenalin his tension betokened. The shadow of the aircraft raced over the snow less than a hundred feet below them as the Harrier skimmed under the radar net. Bodø radar would have reported a loss of contact immediately they had finished refuelling, and the matter would not have been taken further. Neither neutral country, Sweden nor Finland, had been required to know of the passage of the Harrier, nor would they have sanctioned its incursion into their airspace.

A herd of reindeer, startled by the roar of the engine, scattered at the gallop beneath them. Then the darkness of trees, then whiteness again. The cloud cover above the cockpit was broken, mere rags now, and the moon gleamed. They were so close to the ground, it was like impossibly fast skiing rather than flying. It was a mere seventy minutes since they had ended their refuelling, and their flight was more than half completed. Clark glanced to port and starboard, and considered the packs in the two underwing pods. Right hand good, left hand bad, he told himself with a smile that did not come easily. Right-hand pack, repair equipment, meters, spares. Left-hand pack, explosives, detonators, the end of "Leopard". He believed that it was the left-hand pack that he would be forced to use. He did not consider his own fate. He would be arrested as a spy, naturally. Prison, interrogation, exchange for a Russian agent. It was a pattern of events that was predictable and not to be considered. The trick was, not to get caught, even when walking – swimming – into a Russian naval base; don't get caught.

The quick, easy toughness amused and comforted him. There was always a persistent sense of unreality about field operations, until the clock started ticking and the adrenalin became uncontrollable, and he knew, from experience and from training, that there was no alternative but to exist within that spacious immortality. It was the state of mind the CIA called "concussive readiness". It was the state of mind of the successful field agent.

Lake Inari, the sacred lake of Finnish Lapland, began to flow beneath them, illuminated by moonlight, the town of Ivalo a smear of light, then a mild haze, then nothing. The occasional lights of boats, the carpet of ice-dotted water persisting for mile after mile, an unrelieved, gleaming expanse where only the few black humps and spots of islands relieved its unreflecting mirror.

Before they reached the north-eastern shore of Inari, the Harrier banked to starboard, altering course to the east and crossing the border into Norway, a tongue of NATO thrusting southwards from Kirkenes and the coast between Finland and the Soviet Union. A tidier, smoother landscape – though he wondered whether that was not simply illusion – well-dotted with lights, then within a mile they were skimming the treetops of well-forested country, and there was a sullen, hazy glow to starboard.

The pilot throttled back, and the blur of the landscape became a dark flowing movement. Clark could not see the trees themselves, not even small clearings in the forest, but the landscape now possessed a life of its own. It was no longer a relief map over which they passed, or a three-dimensional papier-mâché model.

The lights to starboard were from the watch-towers and the rows of lights along the wire of the border fence separating Norway from the Soviet Union. Clark swallowed, then breathed consciously at a relaxed pace, spacing the intervals between each inhalation and exhalation exactly and precisely. Right hand good, left hand bad, his mind recited again.

He saw the lights of a string of hamlets along the one good road north to Kirkenes. Kirkenes itself was a dim glow on the horizon ahead of them. Then the Harrier flicked to starboard, altering course eastwards to run along the Norwegian border. Pechenga was eight miles beyond the border. Eight miles, and they were perhaps now twelve miles from the border as it swung north to the coast. The Harrier was at little more than one third speed and well below the radar net. Four miles per minute. Three minutes. No, already two minutes fifty. The landscape seemed to take on more vivacity, as if he were studying it in order to remember it. The ribbon of a road, dark patches of trees, vague lights, sheets of white snow. Lumpy, softened white hills. Then the sullen, ribbon-like glow, enlarging to a string of lights, decorating the darkness beyond. A gap in the trees, after a narrow strip of water no more than a pool at that speed, where the two fences and the lights marched north and south, and then the glow was behind them, fading.

He was inside the Soviet Union.

The pilot flicked off the auto-pilot and the terrain-following radar, and assumed manual control of the Harrier. The plane's airspeed dropped. Pechenga was a bright, hazy globe of light ahead. The Soviet Union. Fortress Russia. Clark had never taken part in a penetration operation before.

"Ready? It's coming up to port."

He saw the water of a lake and an uninhabited landscape of woods and open stretches of snow. The Harrier slowed even further, almost to a hover, above a tiny white space between the trees. The image of a helicopter came to Clark again. The sound of the Pegasus engine faded, and the pilot modulated the air brake. Then he increased the engine's thrust once more, directing it downwards through the four nozzles beneath the fuselage, putting the Harrier into a hover.

Snow blew up round the canopy, and the dark seemed to grow above them by some freak of fertilization. More snow, obscuring the canopy, then the final wobble, the dying-away of the engine, and the heaviness of the aircraft settling into the snow and slush.

"Right. You're on your own. Don't waste time."

"See anything?"

"No."

Clark opened the canopy. Snow powdered his upturned face. He hefted himself upright, and then swung his body awkwardly over the high sill of the fuselage, beginning his burglary of the Soviet Union. He looked around him, the sudden chill of the early night and the wind making his teeth chatter. He scanned the area of trees around the clearing three times, then he saw the pale, easily missed wink of a torch signalling.

"Right. He's there," he said to the pilot.

"Good luck."

"Thanks." He placed his feet firmly in the foot-holds on the side of the fuselage, and climbed down. He moved beneath the port wing and snapped open the clips on the underwing pod. He lifted out the pack – left hand bad – and laid it on the snow. Then he unloaded the starboard pack.

He picked up the two packs and moved away from the Harrier, dragging the heavy packs through the snow, which was deeper outside the half-melted circle caused by the downthrust of the Pegasus engine. When he looked up, a small, bulky figure was hurrying towards him. There was the inevitable, electric moment of doubt, was it the right man, was it the KGB, almost bound to be the KGB? Then the man spoke.

"Welcome, my friend –"

The remainder of what he said, Clark could see his lips moving, was drowned by the increasing whine of the engine. Clark, still gripping the man's hand tightly, turned to watch as the Harrier rose above the level of the trees, lurched forward, then smoothly accelerated. He was inside the Soviet Union, a couple of miles from the naval base of Pechenga, and on his own, except for the help of a grocer. It was difficult not to feel a sense of hopelessness nibbling at the feeling of concussion which he required if he was to succeed.

The grocer picked up one of the packs, and hefted it onto his back.

"Come," he said. "Come."

Leper. The girl wanted to get up, talk to the two people passing twenty yards away below them, but he held her down, his hand now almost out of habit over her mouth. Fortunately, they didn't have a dog with them. The man wore an anorak and carried a camera, swinging by its strap, and the woman was wearing a fur coat that looked almost like camouflage, white with dark patches. Hyde listened to them talking, watched the man put his arm around the woman because she remarked on the cold of the evening, watched them, too, look up at the fading light and the gathering clouds; finally recognized that they were heading back towards the car park.

Two reasons. He didn't know them and therefore he distrusted them, and also he could not risk enlisting anyone on their behalf. He'd killed now. Anyone who came into contact with him was thereby endangered. Leper.

He released the girl, and she shuffled away from him, rubbing her arms, touching her mouth where his hand had been clamped.

"Why?" she almost wailed. "Why not?"

"Because you could get them killed, or us killed. Take your pick." The wetness of the ferns was soaking into him. He was hungry, his stomach hollow and rumbling. He was thirsty. He scooped up a thin film of half-melted snow, and pressed it into his mouth. Then he rubbed his wet hand over his face in an attempt to revive himself. The girl looked no fresher than he felt.

"They were out for a walk," she said sullenly.

"Maybe. Look, just let it rest, will you? We're on our own, and that's all there is to it."

"Why – *why* are they chasing us?" the girl asked, her face recovering earlier anxieties, past terrors.

Hyde studied her in disbelief. "What?"

"My father's safe – why do they want us?"

"Oh, Christ – don't you understand the simplest moves in the game?" Hyde shook his head. "Perhaps you don't. Obviously, Petrunin has had new orders. You're as valuable to them now as you were before. If they have you, they can trade you off for your dad. See?"

"How? You've got him, for Christ's sake!"

"He's not in prison. If he knew they had you, he'd take the first chance of walking out to join you. On a plane to Moscow."

The girl appeared about to ask another question, then she fell silent, watching her hands as if they belonged to someone else while they picked at the stiff, rimed grass.

"You ready?"

She looked helplessly, tiredly at him, then got slowly to her feet. "Yes."

"Come on, then."

After the death of the deer and the Russian, they had worked their way east across the Chase, assuming that other men on foot, and the helicopter, would pursue them north, towards the Stafford road. The helicopter, blinded by the shroud of firs through which they ran, drifted away northwards, its noise following it like a declining wail. They saw no other Russians.

Hyde waited until this moment, when it was almost dark and the thin, half-melted sheen of snow had begun to gleam like silver, before attempting to make the car park and the road where they had first stopped. The rifle range was behind them now, to the north.

They trod carefully down the slope of dead ferns, then began to ascend slowly along a tiny deer-track through the tightly growing, restraining heather. Almost dark. Perhaps they could risk this open slope –

The shout was alarming, but almost as unnoticed, except by Hyde's subconscious, as the bark of a dog. The girl looked round slowly, but only because he had stopped. A second shout brought him out of his lassitude. A figure on a rise, perhaps two hundred yards away, waving what might have been a stick. Rifles now. No easy-to-hide handguns. They had put them less than equal with him. His body protested at the effort required of it. The girl bumped into him, staggering as though ill or blind. He took her hand. A second figure rose over the edge of the rise, outlined against the pale last gleam of the day. Cloud pressed down on the open bowl of dead heather in which he had allowed them to be trapped.

The helicopter. Almost too dark to see them, too dark for them to make it out until it blurted over the rise and bore down on them, its noise deafening by its suddenness. He did not have to tell the girl to run. The deer track was not wide enough for both of them and he floundered through wet, calf-high heather keeping pace with her.

Shots, deadened by the noise of the rotors and the racing of his blood. Wild shooting. The helicopter overshot them, and began to bank round.

"Over there!"

The land folded into a deeper hollow. Deer scattered out of it as they approached it, startled by the helicopter. A hallucinatory moment as the grey, small, lithe, panicking forms were all around them, and Hyde remembered the pain-clouded eye into which he had looked that afternoon before he squeezed the trigger; then the deer were gone and the hollow was dark and wound away in a narrow trench which they followed. It led northwards, back towards the higher ground and the rifle range, but he had no alternative but to follow it. They ducked down, keeping below the level of the ground, then the trench petered out and they were left almost at the top of the rise.

Hyde threw himself flat and looked over the lip of the ground. Nothing. The light had gone. In no more than a few minutes, there was nothing. The noise of the helicopter was a furious, enraged buzzing on the edge of hearing, as if already miles away.

Couldn't be –? He turned onto his back, and groaned. Worse than he thought. He had imagined a flesh wound, a scratch, but it was throbbing. His whole arm was throbbing. He tried to sit up, and then lay back, another groan escaping him.

"What is it?"

"Nothing –"

"What's the matter?"

She touched his shoulder, and immediately the pain was intense, almost unbearable, and then he could not decipher her expression or even see the white blob of her face any longer. It rushed away from him at great speed, down a dark tunnel.

TWELVE:

Access

"On station." Eastoe's communications with Aubrey were now of a single, close-lipped, unhelpful kind, the RAF officer providing only a grudging assistance. Aubrey, knowing it would not interfere with the pilot's efficiency, was prepared to allow the man his mood.

The Nimrod had begun flying a box pattern over an inshore area of the Barents Sea which would take her to within a few miles of the Soviet border at the end of each eastward leg of the pattern. Travelling westward, the Nimrod would pass up the Varangerfjord, then turn north across the block of land jutting into the Barents Sea known as Varangerhalvöya, then turn onto her eastward leg which would again take her out over the Barents. A rigid rectangle of airspace, at any point of which the Nimrod was no more than seventy miles from Clark's transceiver in Pechenga.

Aubrey glanced once more through the window in the fuselage. A red, winking light to port of the Nimrod, a little behind and below. A Northrop F-5 of the Royal Norwegian Air Force, one of three somewhat outdated fighter aircraft that provided their screen. The arrangement had been considered necessary by MoD Air, and by the Norwegians, but Aubrey considered it mere window-dressing. He did not anticipate problems with Soviet aircraft, and if there were any such problems, the F-5s would be immediately recalled to the military airfield at Kirkenes.

"Thank you, Squadron Leader," Aubrey replied to Eastoe. "Would you come forward to the flight deck, Mr. Aubrey?" Eastoe added, and Aubrey was immediately struck by the conspiratorial edge to the voice. He removed his headphones and stood up, not looking at Quin.

He moved down the aircraft gingerly, an old man moving down a bus or a train, hands ready to grab or fumble for support. He paused between the two pilots' chairs, and Eastoe turned to him. His face was grave, that of a messenger with bad news to impart; some battle lost.

"What is it, Squadron Leader?"

"This." He handed Aubrey a sheet torn from a message pad. "It's for you, Eyes Only. No good letting Quin hear the bad news."

The message was from Shelley, and it informed Aubrey – who felt his heart clutched by a cold, inescapable hand – that Hyde and the girl had disappeared somewhere between Manchester and Birmingham, without trace. Shelley had organized the search which was now proceeding. Aubrey looked up from the sheet, and found Eastoe's gaze intently fastened on him, as if demanding some human frailty from him by way of reaction.

"Thank you, Squadron Leader," Aubrey said stiffly. "You were quite right to keep this from Mr. Quin. You will continue to do so."

"Makes things a bit awkward, mm?" Eastoe sneered. "Any reply?"

"Nothing I could say would make the slightest difference," Aubrey snapped, and turned on his heel, retracing his steps down the tunnel of the aircraft, composing his features and silencing the flurry of thoughts and images in his mind. Now all that mattered was that Quin functioned like a machine, when the time came.

He regained his seat. Quin seemed uninterested in his reappearance. Aubrey studied him.

Quin, under scrutiny, became quickly and cunningly alert. His posture was totally self-defensive. Then he attempted to achieve the academic trick of distracting attention by vigorously polishing his spectacles. Aubrey's features wrinkled in impatience, and this seemed to further embolden Quin.

"Your man hasn't called in, not since he left the aircraft," he said.

Aubrey was incensed. "His name is Clark," he remarked icily.

"But, the time factor?" Quin persisted. Aubrey realized that the man's silence for the last hour had led to a consolidation of truculent fear. He had, as it were, husbanded his bloody-mindedness until they arrived on station. Every minute that Clark had not reported in satisfied Quin that there would be a premature, and not long delayed, end to his confinement aboard the Nimrod. Clark, in fact, because of the short range of his transceiver, had not signalled them since the test. The Harrier pilot, making for Bardufoss to refuel had sent one brief, coded signal to inform Aubrey that Clark had landed safely and without trouble. That had been forty minutes before.

Aubrey looked at his watch. Eight-thirty. He knew that in two, at most three, hours, he would cancel the operation. "Plumber" would be over unless they heard from Clark within that time. He would have been caught, or killed. Aubrey composed himself to wait, wishing that he could do it somewhere where he did not have to confront Quin across a silent communications console in the skeletal, untidy fuselage of a Nimrod. It was, he considered, rather too much like sitting inside a television set. At least, its screens and wiring and circuitry and sensors gave much the same impression as did the innards of his set, whenever the engineer from the rental company had to come to his flat to effect a repair.

But it was Quin, more than anyone, who angered and threw him into doubt. Clark had to depend upon this pompous, cowardly, indifferent man, and it seemed unfair.

Abandon that line of thought, Aubrey instructed himself. You will have to make the man helpful, when the time comes. He felt the Nimrod, at twenty thousand feet, make its turn onto the eastward leg of its flight pattern, out over the Barents and towards the Soviet border. Somewhere to the north of them, perhaps no more than twenty or thirty miles away, was the location of the attack on the *Proteus* and the ledge where she had rested until the Russians had raised her to the surface.

He found his fingers had adopted a drumming, impatient pattern of movement against one side of the console. Guiltily, he stopped the noise immediately. Quin seemed wreathed in self-satisfaction. He had evidently decided that Clark would fail, even had failed, to penetrate Pechenga. He was like a man sheltering from the rain. The shower would stop, soon, and he could make his way home.

"What about the air tanks?"

"Those I have stored for you with a friend. No, not one of us, but he can be trusted. It is lucky I had them still. I have not been asked to make a – what do you say, reconnaissance – ?" Clark nodded, smiling. "Yes, a reconnaissance of the harbour for a long time. My old wetsuit – perished, alas. But the tanks are good, my friend, I assure you."

"And I believe you."

They were seated in the small, cramped room above the grocer's shop. The Pechenga agent-in-place for SIS was a short, rotund man with a stubble on his jaw. His eyes were small and black, like raisins folded into the sallow dough of his flesh. When he smiled, he showed remarkably white dentures. Clark trusted his ordinariness as much as his thoroughness. His name was Pasvik. Once, generations before, his family had been Norwegian. Whether that had been before the war, before the first war, before the Revolution, even Pasvik did not know.

Pasvik owned the grocery shop himself. His father had acquired the contract for supplying eggs and flour to the naval base, for use in preparing officers' meals. It was his patronage, his "By Appointment" that had enabled him to retain control of his shop, collect the naval intelligence London required and used, and which gave him freedom of movement and access. Also, it provided him with what Clark suspected was a thriving black-market business involving smuggling from Scandinavia and supplying to the naval base and Pechenga's Party officials modest but lucrative luxury goods. Pasvik had made only passing mention of these activities, as if he felt they qualified his status as an accredited agent of London, but for the American it only increased his awareness of the man's intelligence and nerve.

Clark studied the large-scale map that Pasvik had laid on the wooden table between them. A large brandy glass stood near Clark's right hand. The odour of the liquor mingled with the smell of bacon and flour and washing powder – one of the modest luxuries, Clark supposed, since he had seen the brand-name Persil on one shelf of the store-room behind the shop.

Much of the map was originally blank, but the censored, sensitive areas of the town and the naval base had been pencilled in, and labelled, by Pasvik. Pechenga lay at the neck of a narrow inlet in the coast where the river Pechenga reached the Barents Sea. It was a thriving northern fishing port as well as an important subsidiary base to Murmansk, headquarters of the Soviet Union's most important fleet. The fishing harbour lay on the northern outskirts of the town – Clark had smelt it on the wind, even locked in the back of Pasvik's delivery van – while the naval base, as if hiding behind the civilian port, seemed from the map to be entrenched across the neck of the inlet, behind its massive harbour wall. The submarine pens, his mission target, were arrayed and dug in along the southern flank of the base, farthest from the fishing harbour.

It was evident to Clark that Pasvik regarded himself with some reluctance but without evasion as expendable in the cause of "Plumber". Clark, however, realized that he could not efficiently exploit the man to the degree of endangering his life, and was pleased at that fact. Pasvik making a late, night-time delivery to the base would be a transparent pretext, and the van would undoubtedly be searched. Clark would have to go in by water, not with the groceries.

"We could easily do it," Pasvik said hesitantly, as if he had read Clark's thoughts. Clark shook his head.

"Uh-uh. That's the obvious way to get caught. The water is the only way."

Only then did Pasvik display his full fear and pleasure, in the same instant that exposed his dentures, creased up the dough around his eyes, and brought beads of perspiration to his forehead. These he wiped away with a red handkerchief.

"Thank you," he said.

"No problem. This," he added, dabbing his finger on the map, "the net?" Pasvik nodded. "Here, too?"

"Yes. You will need to go over, or beneath, two nets."

"Mines?"

Pasvik pulled a leather-bound, slim notebook from his pocket. It seemed misplaced about his person. It required an executive's breast-pocket, in a grey suit. Pasvik laughed at the expression on Clark's face.

"One of a consignment that I kept for myself," he explained. "They are very popular with junior officers." He opened the book. "This, you understand, is a digest of gossip and observation collected over some years." He fished in the breast pocket of his shirt, and hitched a pair of wire-framed spectacles over his ears. Then he cleared his throat. "The mines are of different types – proximity detonated, trip-wired, acoustic, magnetic. They are set at various depths, and the pattern is very complicated. I do not have any details. Indiscretion in Red Navy officers goes only so far, you understand?"

"The mines I don't worry too much about. Except the contact stuff. Are they marked? Do you have any idea of their shape and size?"

"Ah, there I can help you, I think." He showed a page of the notebook to Clark. The sleeve of the old dressing-gown that he had borrowed from Pasvik brushed the brandy glass, spilling what remained of the drink across the map in a tobacco-coloured stain.

"Damn!" Clark exclaimed, soaking up the liquid with the sleeve of his dressing-gown. "Sorry." Some of the neatly written labelling on the map had smudged.

"No matter."

Clark studied the drawing. A small mine, probably, activated by direct contact with the horns. To deter and destroy small vessels venturing into the restricted waters of the inner harbour, even to kill a swimmer. He handed the notebook back to Pasvik. The stained map absorbed his attention like an omen.

"OK. Where's the *Proteus*?"

"Here are the submarine pens. This one, as far as I can make out. Gossip, as you will imagine, has been rife." He tapped at one of the numbered pens. There were two dozen of them, and *Proteus* was supposedly in the fifth one, measuring from the eastern end of the pens. "Many of them are empty, of course."

"Where will you be?" Clark asked.

"Ah – here," Pasvik replied, "you see, in a direct line. It is, or was, a favourite picnic spot in summer." He sighed.

Clark looked at his watch. "Nine-forty. Time to get going?"

"Yes."

"Will you be stopped on the road?"

"Yes, but it's not likely I will be searched. Not going in the direction of the fishing harbour. Anyone who knows me will assume I am making a pick-up of some smuggled goods from a freighter. On the way back, they may be more nosey. So I will have some of the old favourites – stockings, perfume, chocolate, cigarettes, even sex books from Sweden – in the back of the van. I make a habit of free gifts, once in a while. You are ready?"

Clark found Pasvik studying him. The raisin eyes were deep in their folds, but bright with assessment and observation. Eventually, Pasvik nodded and stood up. "You will make it," he announced, "of that I am reasonably sure."

"Thanks."

Clark took off the dressing-gown and laid it on Pasvik's narrow, uncomfortable-looking bed. Then he donned the immersion suit again, heaving it up and around his body, finally pulling on the headcap.

"Another brandy?"

"No, thanks."

As they went down the bare wooden stairs to the store-room and the small, noisome yard where Pasvik had parked his van, the grocer said, "So, Mr. Aubrey is not very far away at this moment, up in the sky, mm?"

"He is. At least, he ought to be. I'll signal him before I take to the water."

"I can do that."

"Better me than you." In the darkness, Clark patted the side of his head, then the tiny throat-mike beneath his chin. "This stuff has got to work. I don't want to find out it doesn't after I get aboard the *Proteus*."

Pasvik unbolted the door and they went out into a wind that skulked and whipped around the yard. Clark looked up at the sky. A few light grey clouds, huge patches of stars. The clouds seemed hardly to be moving. Almost a full moon, which he regretted. However, the improvement in the weather would mean a less choppy surface in the harbour, and he might need to conserve the air in Pasvik's tanks. Pasvik, he noticed as the man crossed to the van and opened the rear doors, moved with a leg-swinging shuffle. Presumably the limp explained why he no longer carried out immersion-suited surveillance of the harbour.

Clark climbed into the rear of the van, and the doors slammed shut on him. He squatted in a tight, low crouch behind stacked wooden crates, near the partition separating the rear of the van from the driver. He watched as Pasvik clambered into the driving seat, slammed his door, and then turned to him.

"OK?"

"OK."

Pasvik started the engine, and ground the car into gear. A moment later, they were turning out of the narrow lane behind the row of shops into a poorly lit street on which a few cars and one or two

817

lorries were the only traffic. Clark felt tension jump like sickness into his throat, and he swallowed hard. He squeezed his arms around his knees, which were drawn up under his chin. His two packs – right hand good, left hand bad – were near his feet. Without conscious thought, he reached out and unsealed one of the packs. He reached into one of the small side pockets and withdrew a polythene-wrapped package, undid the elastic bands, and removed the gun. A small, light .22 Heckler & Koch pistol with a ten-round magazine, effective stopping range less than thirty metres. He unzipped the neck of his immersion suit and placed the re-wrapped pistol inside. If he ever needed the gun, he was close to being finished.

The grocery van trailed a tarpaulin-shrouded lorry along the northbound road, through a dingy, industrialized suburb of Pechenga. Pasvik seemed to have no desire for conversation. Perhaps, Clark admitted, he thought talk would make his passenger more edgy. Pechenga was little more than a ghost town after dark. There were few pedestrians, fewer vehicles. The town seemed subdued, even oppressed, by the security that surrounded the naval installation. The place had a wartime look, a besieged, blacked-out, curfewed feeling and appearance which depressed and yet aggravated his awareness.

There was a haze of light to be seen over the low factory roofs from the naval base, a glow like that from the border lights as he had seen them from the Harrier. Then he felt the van slowing. The brake lights of the lorry in front of them were bright red. There was a squeal of air brakes.

"A checkpoint – outside the civilian harbour. Get down," Pasvik instructed him. "Cover yourself with the tarpaulin."

White light haloed the bulk of the lorry. Clark could hear voices, and the noise of heavy military boots, though he could see no one. He slid into a prone position, and tugged the tarpaulin over him, which smelt of cabbage and meal. Once underneath, he unzipped the neck of his immersion suit once more, though he was able consciously to prevent himself from unwrapping the gun. Nevertheless, through the polythene his finger half-curled around the trigger. His thumb rested against the safety catch. He could not prevent finger and thumb taking what seemed a necessary hold upon the pistol.

A voice, very close. Clark's Russian was good, but he reacted more to the interrogative tone. A guard leaning his head into the driver's window. Pasvik's voice seemed jocular, confiding in reply.

"Hello, Pasvik. Out and about again?"

Pasvik smiled, showing his dentures, opening his hands on the wheel in a shrugging gesture.

"You know how business is, Grigory."

"Keep your voice down, Pasvik – the officer'll hear you."

"Then you'll be in trouble, eh, my friend?"

"You want me to search your van, have everything out on the road, now and on the way back – eh, Pasvik?"

"Don't be irritable, my friend."

"Look, I've told you – I'm not your friend. Just keep your voice down."

"You want to see my papers?"

"Yes – quick, here's my officer. Bastard." Grigory uttered the last word almost under his breath.

"What's going on here?" the officer enquired above the noise of the lorry moving off and pulling into the docks. Beyond his short dapper figure Pasvik could see the outlines of cranes, the silhouettes of cargo and fishing vessels. "Are this man's papers in order?"

"Yes, sir."

The officer took them from Grigory, perused them in a showy, self-satisfied, cursory manner, then handed them back. He turned on his heel and strutted away. Grigory pulled a scowling face behind his back, then thrust the papers back at Pasvik. He bent near to the window again.

"I want some more," he whispered.

"More what?"

"Those books."

"You sell them off again, eh, Grigory?"

"No!" Grigory's face changed colour.

"I'll see what I can do. Stop me on the way back, get in the back of the van then. I'll leave some for you, under the tarpaulin. OK?"

"OK. I'm off duty at midnight, though."

"I'll be back before then."

Grigory stepped back, and waved Pasvik on. The red and white pole between the two guard huts swung up, and Pasvik drove the van into the civilian harbour. In his mirror, Pasvik could see the officer speaking to Grigory. The posture of his body and the bend of his head indicated a reprimand rather than an enquiry as to Pasvik's business. He would have to be careful when Grigory collected his sex books from the back of the van on the return journey. Perhaps he needed something for the officer, too?

He drove out of the string of white lights along the main thoroughfare of the docks, turning into a narrow, unlit alley between two long, low warehouses. Then he turned out onto a poorly illuminated wharf, driving slowly past the bulk of a Swedish freighter. Music from the ship, a drunk singing. A head peering over the side. Two armed guards patrolling, leaning towards each other in conversation, stultified by routine and uneventfulness. Pasvik stopped the car in the shadow of a warehouse, beneath the dark skeleton of a dockside crane.

"Very well, my friend. You can get out now."

Pasvik slipped out of the van, and opened the rear doors. The two guards, unconcerned at the noise of his engine, were walking away from him, into and then out of a pool of light. Clark sat on the edge of the van, stretching. Then he hefted the two packs onto the concrete of the wharf.

"Thanks," he said.

"You have everything in your mind?"

Clark nodded. "Yes. What about the tanks?"

"One moment." Pasvik limped off swiftly, towards the door of the warehouse. He appeared to possess a key, for Clark heard the door squeak open, then the intervening moments before the door squeaked again were filled with the singing of the Swedish drunk, who had become utterly maudlin. Clark heard, as the door closed again, the reassuring metallic bump as the tanks struck the concrete. Then Pasvik came scuttling out of the shadows, hefting the two air tanks over his shoulder. He placed them, like game retrieved, at Clark's feet. The American inspected and tested them. The hiss of air satisfied him. Both gauges registered full.

"Good."

"The patrol will be back in five minutes. By that time, I must be aboard the freighter and you must be in the water. Come."

Pasvik helped Clark strap the tanks to his back, lifting the mouth-piece and its twin hoses gently over his head like a ceremonial garland. Then they carried the packs across the wharf, slipping quickly through the one dim patch of light into the shadow of the freighter. Pasvik make a lugubrious face at the singing, still audible from above. The water was still and oily below them, against the side of the ship. Clark could smell fish on the windy air. He unwound short lengths of nylon rope from each pack, and clipped them onto his weighted belt. As he did so, he felt he was imprisoning himself. An anticipation of utter weariness overcame him for a moment, and then he shrugged it off. He would make it, even with that weight being towed or pushed, since the packs would become buoyant in the water.

"OK," he said, about to slip the mouthpiece of his air supply between his lips. "Thanks."

"Don't forget the landmarks I described – don't forget the patrol boats – don't forget the contact mines, some of them are small enough, sensitive enough . . ." Pasvik halted his litany when Clark held up his hand.

"OK, OK." Clark grinned. "I'll take care, Mom."

Pasvik stifled a delighted laugh. "Goodbye, my friend. Good luck."

He lifted one of the packs as Clark moved to the iron ladder set in the side of the wharf, leading down to the water. Clark, holding the other pack, began to climb down, his back to the freighter's hull. Then he paused, his head just above the level of the concrete, and Pasvik handed him the second pack. Clark appeared almost to over-balance, then he stumbled the last few steps and slid into the water. Pasvik peered down at him. Clark waved, adjusted his mouthpiece and facemask, then began swimming out and around the bow of the freighter, pushing the two packs ahead of him, slowly and awkwardly.

Pasvik watched until the swimming man was hidden by the hull of the Swedish ship, then softly whistled and shook his head. Then he slapped his hands together, shrugging Clark away, and headed for the boarding ladder up to the deck of the freighter.

Clark swam easily, using his legs and fins, his arms around the two packs, guiding them through the water. Their buoyancy made them lighter, easier to handle in the water. After a few minutes, he trod water, and opened the channel of his transceiver. The ether hummed in his ear.

"All is well," he said.

Aubrey's voice, slowed down from the spit of sound in his ear-piece, replied a few moments later. "Good luck."

Clark switched off, and began swimming again. Ahead of him, there was a rippling necklace of lights along the harbour wall, with one dark gap like a missing stone in the middle. The water was still calm, its surface only riffled like pages quickly turned by the wind. He headed for the dark gap in the lights, keeping the flash of the small lighthouse to his left, and the steering lights of a small cargo ship to his right. It was a matter of some seven or eight hundred yards – or so he had estimated from the map – to the harbour wall. He moved with an almost lazy stroke of his legs, using the buoyant packs like a child might use water wings. The mouthpiece of the air supply rested on the packs just in front of his face.

It was twenty minutes before he reached the choppier water of the inlet beyond the fish and cargo harbour. Suddenly, as he passed between the lights, the water confronted him instead of allowing him easy passage. The packs began to bob and move as if attempting to escape him. He checked his compass, took a sighting on the lights above the twin guard towers at the entrance to the naval installation, and rested for a few moments, accustoming his body and his breathing to the choppy sea. Then he swam on.

The wall of the harbour curved away from him, as if enclosing him, then it rose in height and the lights along it were brighter and closer together. He was paralleling the wall of the Pechenga naval base.

His awareness, despite his experience and his desire that it should not be so, began to retreat into the confines of his immediate surroundings and experience – the packs behind him like brakes moving sluggishly through the water, the choppy little wavelets dashing against his facemask, his arms moving out in front and then behind, even the tight cap of his suit seemed to contain his senses as well as his mind. Thus the patrol boat was a light before it was a noise, and a light he could not explain for a moment. And it was close, far too close.

A searchlight swept across the surface of the water. The boat, little larger than a motor yacht, was a hydrofoil. Clark, catching the high-bowed outline behind the searchlight as he was startled out of his dreamlike state, saw its forward and aft gun turrets, its depth charge racks. It was paralleling his course, moving along the harbour wall. Even though startled, he continued to observe the patrol boat move lazily across his vision. The searchlight swept back and forth, moved closer to the wall, swept back and forth again, moved closer . . .

Clark panicked into acute consciousness. He fumbled with the two packs, hauling them into his embrace. He ripped clumsily at the valve on the first one – the light moved towards him again – and failed to turn it at the first attempt, and his hand hovered towards the valve on the second pack – the light swung away, then began to swing back, the patrol boat was sliding past him sixty metres away – then he turned feverishly at the first valve, hearing above the panic of his breathing and blood in his ears, the hiss of air. The bag sank lower in the water, and he grabbed at the second valve, telling himself ineffectually to slow down – the light moved forward, closer, like lava flowing over the wrinkled water, almost illuminating the pack that remained afloat – he twisted the valve, heard the air, watched the light swing away, then back, then begin its arc that would reach his head. The pack slipped beneath the water, and he flicked himself into a dive – the light slid across the distressed water where he had been, hesitated, then moved on.

Clark thrust the mouthpiece between his teeth, bit on it as he inhaled, and drove downwards against the restraint of the two packs from which he had not released sufficient air. They pulled like parachute brakes against his movement. The twin diesel engines of the patrol boat thrummed through the black water. He looked up. Yes, he could see the light dancing across the surface, as if it still searched for him. Slowly, it faded. The vibration and hollow noise of the boat's engines moved away. He allowed the buoyancy of the two packs to slowly pull him back to the surface. When his head came out of the water, he saw the patrol boat some hundreds of yards away, its searchlight playing at the foot of the harbour wall.

He lay in the water, the packs bobbing just beneath the surface on either side of him, until his breathing and his heart rate had returned to normal. Then he embraced each of the packs in turn, pressing the button on each small cylinder of oxygen, refloating the packs on the surface. Having to drag them through the water would have exhausted him long before he reached the *Proteus*.

He swam on, still resting his frame on the packs as he clutched them to him. Ten minutes later, he reached the entrance to the harbour. The guard towers on either wall, apart from beacon lights, carried powerful searchlights which swept back and forth across the dark opening between them and swept, too, the water of the harbour and the basin beyond it. He trod water, absorbing the pattern of movement of the searchlights. He saw the silhouettes of armed guards, the barrels of anti-aircraft cannon pointing to the night sky. He felt cold, the chill of water seeping through his immersion suit. Thought seemed to come slowly, but not because of the cold; rather, because he already knew the dangers and the risks. There was no necessity to discover or analyse them. The submarine net stretched across the entrance to the harbour, perhaps fifteen feet above the water. He would have to climb it.

He edged with furtive strokes of his fins around the base of the harbour wall, touching its barnacled sliminess with his hand, reaching the steel net directly beneath one of the guard towers. The packs had begun to resist him, he imagined, as if they had lost their buoyancy. He let them drift behind him as he clung to the mesh, watching the lights. Thirty seconds. He lowered his arm as his watch confirmed the gap of darkness between the passage of each light across the harbour entrance for the second time. He had thirty seconds in which to climb the net, mount it like a rider, drag his packs after him, and climb down again to the water. He could not wait for the chance of the net being opened on its boom to admit a vessel.

The light of the searchlight on the opposite wall slid down the concrete and swung away into the harbour. His fins hung round his neck, and his mouthpiece dangled between their strange necklace. He felt clumsy, burdened. He reached up, and began climbing. The heavy steel cords of the submarine net did not even vibrate with his effort.

Seven, eight, nine, ten, eleven –

The seconds began racing away from him. His mind was blind and indifferent to the progress of the light, hearing only the moving numbers in his head. The numbers ran ahead of him, as his breathing did. *Thirteen, fourteen.* He felt the weight of the packs thrum lightly through the steel net.

Top. One leg, *sixteen,* other leg, packs holding him back, *seventeen,* swing the other leg over against the restraint of the two packs, *eighteen*, his stomach was stretched and pressed painfully along the steel boom, *nineteen*, stand up, *twenty*, five seconds behind already, lift the packs, lift the first one over, drop it, *twenty-three*, hold on, hold on, as the inertia of the pack tried to pull him from the net, arms full of pain as he resisted the pack's weight, *twenty-five*, other pack now, easier, drop it, hang on, pain again, *twenty-seven*, go now, go –

He scuttled down the net, feeling it vibrate now, his breath ragged, his body as tense as a spring, as vulnerable as an insect's. He was aware of the light on the opposite side of the entrance swinging back now, a hazy blur at the corner of his vision. *Thirty-one*. The light slid down the net, opening the shadow beneath the harbour wall, slipping across the small blur of bubbles his entrance into the water had made.

Clark clung to the net, forcing the mouthpiece back between his teeth, trying to calm his breathing, feeling the packs tugging him lazily back towards the surface. He held on to the net with one hand, and reduced their buoyancy with the other, his hand completing the task robotically. They bobbed beside him in the darkness, nudging him as if to remind him of their presence, or to ingratiate themselves because they had almost betrayed him.

He clung to the net until the searchlight's wavering globe of light had passed over his head another four times. Then he further adjusted the buoyancy of the packs so that they began to pull at him, drag him down. He fitted his fins, and let go of the net, moving smoothly down into the darkness.

The mines, now. Magnetic, electronic contact. Pasvik had been unable to provide the pattern. MoD had had some detail, but not enough. There did not seem to be channels through the minefield, since the mines would all be armed or disarmed by remote signal. If a Soviet vessel entered the harbour, the mines would be switched off. Simple. Effective. Clark reasoned that he must dive deep, almost to the bottom, to avoid the contact mines which would be set off by a touch, and which would have been laid at varying depths. He swam down, levelling off when his depth gauge registered a hundred feet. Time closed in on him immediately as decompression became a determining factor. He flicked on his lamp. The packs idled alongside him as he trod water. Compass direction checked, together with the time and the depth, he began swimming, moving rapidly now, ignoring the sense of isolation in his system like an antidote to adrenalin, and which assailed him for the first time since he had left the cockpit of the Harrier. The weak glow of the lamp illuminated the dull silver of fish and the strange forest of cables growing up from the harbour bed below. Above him, invisible, the mines sat at their determined depths. He jogged one cable, then another, and occasionally the packs snagged against them, operating like brakes. He had guessed correctly. He was too deep for the mines themselves.

He swung the lamp from side to side, however, in a precautionary swathe. The mine that came suddenly out of the darkness still surprised him. He flicked aside, remembering the two packs only as he did so. He stopped himself. The chill disappeared from his body. He flicked the light of his lamp behind him. One of the packs rubbed against the cable. It seemed to be sliding upwards towards the mine's old-fashioned, deadly horns. A small contact mine, almost too small to do any damage, but enough to pull a human frame into shreds. He moved slowly. The mine seemed to bob and weave like a fighting animal watching him. The water distressed it and wafted around the pack, moving it upwards. It was only inches from the mine.

He reached forward, trying to keep the light of the lamp steady. The mine bobbed, the pack imitated it. Inches. He reached forward, hardly moving his fins, feeling his body sinking away from the mine and the pack. He could not tread water any more violently. He reached forward along the short line which attached him to the pack. Touch. The buoyant pack crumpled then reshaped as he touched it. Inches. He swept at it, banging his hand down past the horns of the mine onto the pack. It bobbed away like a struck ball, and he reeled it in on its line, clutching it to him like a child who had avoided a road accident, feeling weakness envelope his body.

Eventually, he moved on, holding the packs closer to him by their lines, making slower progress but gradually sensing some kind of courage return. He ran up against the inner net, separating the outer basin of the harbour from the submarine pens, almost before he saw it in the light of his lamp. He clung to it with a kind of desperate relief which surprised him. He realized how much his nerves had been strained already. He released the net eventually, dropping down towards the bottom, dragging the unwilling packs with him. His lamp searched ahead of him. The mud and silt, its lightest elements disturbed and lifted by his movement, drifted up to meet him and almost obscured what he sought. The net ended some four or five feet from the bottom. He gripped it and slid under, pulling the packs after him.

He swam on immediately he had checked his bearings and the time. The mine cables were fewer, as if he had moved above the tree-line for these growths. Soon, they straggled out. The water became slightly warmer, and it appeared lighter. He checked his watch, then ascended twenty feet. Here, he waited, then climbed another twenty feet, waited again. Nerves began to plague him now, the need for action, for arrival, nudging at him, irritating him.

His head bobbed above the surface. The packs lay below him at the end of their lines. The row of concrete pens was in front of him. He counted. Fifth along. Lights, noise – no, no noise, just plenty of light. The gates of the pen were closed.

Proteus was in there. He had got to within fifty yards of his destination.

Pasvik the grocer studied the harbour through his night-glasses. He squatted on a blanket which protected his buttocks from the cold of the damp ground. Beneath the blanket he had spread a ground sheet. He had a hamper of food beside him, and he had his back to a tall, old tree.

He moved the glasses up, and the dim, night images blurred and smeared until they were lit with the glow of the submarine pens. He refocused, and he could see, with some degree of clarity, the lights in the fifth pen and a shadowy bulk beyond them that must be the British submarine behind the high gates. Good.

He lowered the glasses. No one would come up here in this weather, but he had a spare blanket to throw over the small dish aerials he had set up alongside him. Clark would be unable to communicate with the Nimrod from within the concrete pen without his messages, and those of the Nimrod, being relayed through the two aerials situated on a small knoll overlooking the harbour of Pechenga, the one with narrow beam facility directed towards Clark, the other, capable of handling broad-beam signals, directed towards the Nimrod.

Pasvik had no fear as he sat there, waiting for the first transmission. He was patient, warmly dressed, and he was engaged in a flatteringly important piece of espionage. However, a dim and long-past regret seemed to move sluggishly in his awareness like a tide coming slowly in. He realized it would be his companion while he remained on the knoll, hidden by the trees. He voiced it.

"Ah, Ivan, Ivan," he murmured, "remember the times we used to come here, eh? Remember?"

A chill, gusty wind plucked his sighs away and scattered them over the darkness of the harbour.

Clark bobbed in the water beneath the repaired propeller of the *Proteus*. He was exhausted after climbing the gate into the pen, exhausted in a subtler, more insidious way by the tension of waiting, of absorbing the routine of the guards patrolling the pen, of choosing his moment to slip over the gate and down into the water. The good fortune that no one appeared to be working on the submarine did little to erase his weariness.

Despite their buoyancy, the packs were like leaden weights beneath the surface. His arms ached from them and from the deadweight of his own body. Now he had to climb the stern of the *Proteus*, to the aft escape hatch. He did not even want to try, could not entertain the idea of beginning. His air tanks and weighted belt he had left on the bottom of the pen. Yet it was the weight of the packs that unnerved him.

The repairs appeared almost complete. There were a number of scarred and buckled hull plates, but the propeller possessed new blades, the rudder fin and the hydroplanes gleamed with new metal. He looked up. The hull of the *Proteus* loomed above him. He groaned inwardly. His feet, flipperless again, rested on a rung beneath the surface, his hands had hold of another rung of the inspection track up the rudder. Tiny, separate *pitons* in the rock-face of the hull. He looked around him. A guard, bored and dulled by routine, turned at the end of his patrol, and walked back out of sight along the pen. Clark heaved his body out of the water and into the irregular rhythm of his ascent. His wet feet slipped, his hands wanted to let go, but he climbed up the rudder, level with the huge fifteen-bladed propeller, until he could clamber onto the hull, dragging the two packs behind him. There, he paused. Along the smoothness of the hull, on the whale's back, was the impression of the escape hatch, a circle cut in grey, shiny dough with a shaping knife. It was sixty feet from where he crouched.

He raised himself, pressing back against the high fin of the rudder, in its shadow to escape the white lights glaring down from the roof of the pen. The guard he had seen, on the starboard side of the *Proteus*, was half-way along its length, back to him. The other guard, on the port side, had almost reached the extent of his patrol, in the dimness of the other end of the pen. He would not make it to the hatch, open and close it after him, before that guard turned and was able to see him. He waited, the tension wearing at him immediately and violently. He felt inadequate to the demands made upon his physical strength, his nervous system.

A voice called out, and he believed for a long moment that a third guard, one he had not spotted, had seen him and was addressing him. But the voice was distant. He watched, heart pounding, as the port guard moved out of sight behind the bulk of the *Proteus*, presumably having been hailed by his companion on the starboard side. It was his chance, perhaps his only one. He weighed the two packs, one in either hand. An obstacle race. He remembered basic training from long ago; fatigues and punishment and discipline like a thin crust of ice over sadism. He gritted his teeth. He'd run up sand dunes carrying two packs then.

Then he began running, hunched up with fear and the weight of the packs, his feet threatening to slide on the smooth metal of the hull. Fifty feet, forty, thirty –

The packs began to slither on the hull, restraining him. His breath began to be difficult to draw, his heart made a hideous noise. Then he slid like a baseball player for the plate, legs extended and reached the hatch. Feverishly, he turned the wheel, unlocking it. Two turns, three, four. His head bobbed up and down like that of a feeding bird. No one. He raised the hatch, and slid into a sitting position on its edge. His feet fumbled for the ladder, and he climbed into the hatch, packs pushed in first and almost dragging him with them; then he closed the hatch behind him, allowing his breath to roar and wheeze in the sudden and complete darkness. He slipped from the ladder and landed on the lower hatch of the chamber. He rubbed his arms, and his body remained doubled over as if in supplication. It was another five minutes before he could bring himself to move again. He unsealed one of the packs – right hand good – and rummaged in one of its pockets. He removed a bundle, and flicked on his lamp to inspect it. Blue, faded blue overalls. He stood up, unrolling the bundle, taking out the socks and boots and putting them on. Then he donned the overalls. His immersion suit was still damp, but the effect might look like sweat, with luck. He patted the breast pocket, feeling the ID there. If the repair and maintenance crew had a specially issued ID for this pen and this job, he still would not be blown as soon as he was challenged. Not with that ID.

He stowed the two packs in the chamber, deflating the second one, securing them to the ladder in the wall. If someone used the hatch, they would be found. He, however, dared not be seen carrying them inside the submarine. His watch showed twelve-fifty. He switched out the lamp, and stowed it with the packs. He would be back within an hour. They should be safe.

Cautiously, he turned the wheel of the lower hatch, then lifted it a couple of inches. He peered into the room housing the electric motors. It appeared empty. He pulled back the hatch and stepped onto the ladder – imagining for a moment Ardenyev or someone like him making his entry in the same manner – closing the hatch behind him and locking it.

He looked around the engine room, rubbing his hands tiredly through his short hair, untidying his appearance. He looked at his hands. They possessed that wrinkled, white, underwater deadness. He thrust them into his pockets as he stared down at the main turbine shaft running across the length of the room. There appeared to be little or no sign of damage. *Proteus* was almost ready to go. She could be taken out of Pechenga and into the Barents Sea on her turbines, even on the electric motors whose bulk surrounded him now. If "Leopard" worked –

He cautiously opened the bulkhead door into the turbine room. Empty. The submarine was silent around him, huge, cathedral-like, unmanned. Clark presumed the ratings were being kept in their accommodation under guard, and the officers in the wardroom. Lloyd would be in the control room, more likely in his cabin, also guarded. He looked down at his creased overalls. A uniform would have been an impossible disguise to have transported in one of the packs. A pity.

He entered the manoeuvring room, aft of the nuclear reactor. For a moment he thought it, too, was empty. Then a figure appeared from behind one section of the computer housing. He was short, almost bald, and dressed in a white laboratory coat. He carried a clipboard, and when he saw Clark, adjusted his glasses and studied him.

"What do you want?"

"Who are you?" Clark replied in Russian. There was an instant, well-learned wariness behind the thick spectacles. Clark continued, "What are you doing here?"

The man was already proffering the clipboard, but then resisted the craven instinct. He did not recognize Clark, and would, presumably, have known which ones to be wary of. Clark appeared officer-like, perhaps, but he did not suggest KGB. He lacked swagger, the birth-right.

"Who are you?" the man in the white coat insisted.

Clark reached into his breast pocket. Aubrey had insisted, pressing it upon him like a talisman. A red ID card. Clark tried to remove it insolently, and waved it briefly at the other man.

"OK?" he said. "Or do you want my birth certificate as well?" He laughed as coarsely as he could. "Don't say you don't think I have one."

"I wasn't going to –" the man said. Clark took the clipboard. He understood enough to realize that the technician was from a naval laboratory or testing centre. He riffled the sheets of graph paper. He was checking to make certain that none of the machinery in the manoeuvring room was essential to, or part of, "Leopard". Perhaps – Clark suppressed a grin here – he was even trying to locate the back-up system. He handed the clipboard back to the technician.

"I don't understand all that bullshit, Comrade Doctor," he said in a belligerently unintelligent voice. The technician succeeded in quashing the sneer that tried to appear on his face. "See you."

Clark, hands in pockets, tried a swaggering, lazy, confident slouch out of the manoeuvring room into the tunnel through the reactor. Pausing only for a moment to register that the reactor had not been shut down, he opened the door into the control room. As he had expected, it was not empty. There was no sign of Lloyd or any of the British officers, but white-coated men and a handful of armed guards had occupied the control room, like terrorists in a foreign embassy. Undoubtedly, every piece of machinery and equipment was being tested and examined during the hours when the crew were confined to their quarters. *Proteus* would be a known, familiar thing by the time they had finished. A dog-eared book, a faded woman lacking all mystery. They would possess every secret, half-secret and secure piece of design, knowledge and equipment she had to yield. The computers would be drained, the sonars analysed, the inertial navigation system studied, the communications systems and codes learned by rote.

Clark did not believe that Aubrey had envisaged how much and how valuable would be the information gained from the temporary imprisonment of the *Proteus*. However, Aubrey was right to believe that "Leopard" was the cherry on the cake. This was the present, "Leopard" was the future. He slouched his way across the control room. No one paid him more attention than to look up, and glance down once more. He had acquired the swagger. *Exaggerate it*, Aubrey had said, fingering the red ID card. *However ridiculous and opera buffa you think it is, it will work. You are an immortal.* And then Aubrey had smiled, cat-like and with venom. The red ID card claimed he was a KGB officer.

Clark stepped out of the control room into the corridor. There was a single guard opposite a door, no more than a few yards from him. The guard turned to him. Clark waved the red ID and the guard relaxed at once. He was a young, conscripted marine.

"I want a word with our gallant British captain," Clark drawled. "See we're not disturbed, OK?" The marine nodded. He had probably never met a KGB man of any rank in his life. He had an entire and trusting awe of the red card. Aubrey had been right. Clark opened the door without knocking, and closed it behind him.

Lloyd had been reading, and had dropped off to sleep with the light above his bunk left on. He awoke, startled, fuzzy-eyed.

"Who are you –?" The book resting on his chest slipped to the floor as he stood up. Clark bolted the door, then leaned against it. "Who are you?" Lloyd repeated, more irate than disturbed.

"The Seventh Cavalry," Clark said softly, then put his finger to his lips.

"What? You're an American –" Lloyd studied Clark, his manner, features and dress. His face went from shock to hope to suspicion. "What is this?" he asked with surprising bitterness. To Clark, the man looked tired, dull, captive.

"No trick." Clark sat on the end of Lloyd's bunk. The captain of the *Proteus* hunched away from him. Clark said, in a louder voice and in very accented English, "Just a few simple question about your sailing orders." Lloyd looked as if Clark had proved something to his satisfaction. "I'm here –" Clark grinned, despite himself, "– to repair 'Leopard' and help you get out of here."

Lloyd appeared dumbfounded. "Rubbish –" he began.

"No kidding. Look, I can spend hours trying to convince you who I am. How about one simple thing, to prove my credentials?" He paused, but Lloyd remained blank-faced. "Your daughter has a pet tortoiseshell cat called Penelope and a white rabbit called Dylan."

Lloyd's mouth dropped open, then he smiled and tears prompted by relief and remembered domesticity welled in his eyes. He took Clark's hand. "Who are you?" he asked.

"Ethan Clark, Navy Intelligence."

"Assigned to 'Chessboard Counter'?"

"Right."

"We didn't meet."

"I don't think it matters – uh?"

"No. How the devil can you repair 'Leopard'? Alone? In these surroundings?"

"First, I talk and you listen. Then you tell me everything that happened and everything your people think might have gone wrong. OK?"

"OK. You begin, then."

"Just a moment." Clark raised his voice, and again produced the heavy accent. "Your sailing orders. We already know a great deal. Just fill in a few details, OK?" He smiled and tossed his head in the direction of the locked door. "Now listen," he said.

"We will be with you before first light, Valery. I want *you* to conduct me around your prize." Dolohov was in a mood that Ardenyev could not match and which did not interest him. Behind him, through the glass doors into the mess, Balan and Teplov and the others were raucously into a round of obscene songs and another crate of vodka. The drink and the noise whirled in his head, separating him as surely as static would have done from the admiral's voice.

"Yes, sir," he said as enthusiastically as he could.

"Panov's weather has improved. He's reached Moscow. He'll be here in a few hours' time. Then we'll fly up to you by chopper." The old man might have been a relative reciting his holiday travel arrangements. Ardenyev almost giggled at the thought, and the image it evoked. Old thin legs wrapped in a travelling-blanket, back bent under the weight of a suitcase, and the admiral's mind full of

831

worries about the toilets, obtaining food in transit and would he be there to meet him with the car. "What's all that noise?"

"A – small party, sir."

"Excellent, excellent. Polish vodka, I presume."

"Yes, sir." The old man's voice sounded boringly full of reminiscence. Ardenyev hoped it was not so.

"Good, good." Dolohov sounded offended. Ardenyev cursed the casualness of his tone of voice, his lack of control. Even when half-drunk, he should be able to pretend respect. "Make sure you're sober by the time I arrive, Valery. Understand?" The question was a slap across the face.

"Yes, sir."

"See you in, say, seven hours' time? Enjoy your party."

The receiver purred in Ardenyev's ear. His mood was suddenly, inexplicably deflated. He felt sober and dry-mouthed. He looked at his watch. One o'clock. Dolohov and his scientist from Novosibirsk would be here by eight. Shrugging, he pushed open the door to the officers' mess, to be greeted by a roar of welcome and insult.

The two packs were still in the aft escape chamber. He removed his overalls, rolled them into a bundle, and stowed them in the pack containing the explosives. This he took with him as he climbed back through the hatch into the room below. He hid the pack in a steel cupboard containing repair equipment. Then, he once more closed himself into the darkness of the chamber. He flicked on his lamp, and checked the second pack. He removed a tool-kit already clipped to a belt, and two bulky packages which he strapped to his thighs. He had an image, for a moment, of his ridiculous appearance if he were seen and caught on top of the hull of the *Proteus*, and then it vanished in a rush of nerves and tension. He had trembled, and the pool of light cast on the floor of the chamber wobbled.

He turned the wheel of the hatch, and lifted it. The hard light of the pen poured in and he felt exposed and vulnerable. His legs felt weak, despite the reviving swallow of rum Lloyd had given him, and the coffee he had ordered from the galley in his KGB persona. He waited, but the nerves did not seem to abate. He cursed them silently. He wanted to drop from the ladder to the floor of the chamber. He held on, grinding his teeth audibly, his eyes squeezed tight shut. It was like a malarial illness. His whole body was shaking, revolting against the idea of leaving the dark in order to climb into the spotlit brightness of the submarine pen.

Then the mood passed. The illness retreated, and he was able to swallow the phlegm in his throat, and to feel strength returning to his legs. He lifted the hatch once more, and raised his head above it. The curve of the *Proteus*'s hull prevented him from being able to see either of the guards, and he waited. Two minutes later, the port guard appeared, his head bobbing along the horizon of the hull. He was smoking a cigarette. Clark waited until he had turned in his patrol, with hardly a glance at the submarine, and the starboard guard had come into view, making for the seaward end of the pen. Still only two of them. He was able to diminish what opposed and endangered him to these two men. two against one, that's all it was. He felt calmed.

He waited, but without the bout of nerves returning, until the two men had passed out of sight, and returned. Each patrol, from the point opposite the escape hatch back towards the bow of the submarine and returning to the escape hatch, took three minutes and a few seconds. The time, however, when they both had their backs to him was less, since they were not on identical courses. Two and a half minutes of running or working time.

He watched them, heads down, one of them whistling tunelessly and the other slouching with both hands in his pockets, Kalashnikov slung over his shoulder, until they passed out of his vision towards the bow of the *Proteus*. Then he climbed out of the hatch onto the smooth curve of the hull, crouching like a sprinter on his blocks for a moment as he looked over his shoulder. Neither man had turned, and he straightened and ran for the rudder fin sixty feet away.

He hid in its shadow, hardly breathing more rapidly than normal, then climbed swiftly down the *pitons* in its smoothed, repaired surface to the water. He held one of the propeller blades and trod water gently.

Lloyd had given him Hayter's assessment of the damage to "Leopard". The submarine officer had said, in simpler and clearer terms, what had sprung instantly to Quin's mind when he heard the estimate of damage the submarine must have sustained. Clark, by seeing for himself the repairs and hearing Lloyd's account of his experiences and his conversations with Ardenyev, agreed with Hayter and Quin. At least one, and possibly as many as three or four, of the hull sensors must have been damaged. In themselves, Clark knew with a heavy sensation in his stomach, they would not account for the manner and degree of "Leopard's" malfunction, but without their being repaired the equipment would never work effectively. Before investigating the back-up system which had never cut in, Clark had to inspect and repair the sensors on the outer hull.

When Lloyd had described his conversations with Valery Ardenyev, Clark had sat listening with a faint smile on his lips. He had known it, all along. It had to be Ardenyev. Even the wine and the caviar would have been in character, just as would killing Lloyd if it had proven necessary.

Clark watched the two guards approach the seaward end of the pen once more. The whistler was now being echoed by his companion, who provided a shrill descant or counter-melody as the fit took him. They laughed at their musical antics frequently, the noise having a hollow quality under the bright roof. Lloyd had confirmed that work on *Proteus* had stopped early the previous evening, as a delaying tactic. The repair crew might return at any moment, just as the man from Novosibirsk might also arrive in minutes or hours. Clark felt the weakness pass through him once more, like the debilitation of a stomach infection, and he realized that it was Lloyd's report of Panov's expected arrival, learned from Ardenyev, that had struck him more forcibly than anything else. It all hinged on the weather in Siberia; everything. It was that random, uncontrollable element that had thrown him.

One of the guards began telling a joke. The two men loitered at the seaward end of the pen, giggling at each other across the stretch of imprisoned water. Clark ducked further into the shadow of the propeller, only his head out of the water. Clark's impatience began to mount. Then some vestigial fear of a *michman* or even an officer arriving seemed to prompt the storyteller, and they began to move again, the storyteller's voice rising in volume as the bulk of the *Proteus* interposed itself between himself and his audience of one.

Clark ducked beneath the surface of the water, and switched on his lamp. Its weak beam would probably not be noticed, reflecting through the water, unless someone looked very hard. The two guards wouldn't. He swam along the hull, only a few feet below the surface, holding in his mind as clearly as a slide projected upon a screen a diagram of the hull showing the locations of the numerous sensor-plates. His left hand smoothed its way along the hull, and his lamp flickered and wavered over the metal. Eventually, as his breath began to sing in his head and his eardrums seemed to be swelling to fill his head and mouth, he touched against one of them. A shallow tear-drop dome of thin metal protected the sensor beneath. It was intact, undamaged.

He rose to the surface, breathed in deeply three times, then ducked beneath the surface again. He began to locate the sensors more quickly now, as if he had found the thread that would lead him through the maze. Surprisingly, and to his relief, the wafer-thin titanium domes over the sensors seemed to have withstood damage from both the torpedoes. Beneath each dome lay either sonar or magnetic or thermal signal detectors and, within the domes, baffles like those in a stereo loudspeaker guided and channelled any signals, whether from enemy sonar or other detection equipment, into a transducer. The signals were then fed via fibre optics into ''Leopard'', where they were analysed, reverse phased and then returned to the transducer. The process was virtually instantaneous. The effect of this was to nullify or deflect any enemy's detection transmissions. The signals returned to the enemy vessel unaltered, thereby confirming that they had not registered or been deflected off another vessel. In addition, some of the hull sensors worked to damp the noise emissions from the *Proteus*'s propellers and hydroplanes, rendering the submarine ninety-eight percent immune to detection. Clark had to assume that some sensors, at least, would be damaged.

Four of them undamaged, then five. It had taken him almost thirty minutes, working on the starboard side of the hull and avoiding the patrol of the guard, who now had a tiny transistor radio clasped to his ear. Clark had heard a sliver of pop music once as he ducked beneath the surface. When the man had gone again, Clark dived and swam down, following the curve of the hull until he surfaced on the port side. Checking the sensors on that side took him twenty minutes. He worked with greater and greater confidence and speed. He moved towards the stern of the submarine, where the damage was more evident to the lamp and to his fingertips. Then he found the first damaged sensor-cowl. The titanium skin had been torn away, whether during the attack or the subsequent repairs he could not guess, and beneath it the delicate transducer had been torn, smashed, rendered useless. In the light of his lamp, he saw the tangled mess of wiring within; it looked like a ruined eye. He cursed, bobbed to the surface, exhaled and drew a new breath, then flipped down towards the bottom, his lamp flickering over the rust-stained, oil-smeared concrete until he saw, to his left, the huddled bulk of his air tanks.

He strapped on the weighted belt, then the tanks, and began swimming back towards the surface. As soon as the short helical antenna clamped to the side of his head broke surface, he spoke into the throat microphone. He described the damage to the hull sensor and its location, and only moments later Quin began speaking excitedly in his ear, sounding very distant and obscured by static.

"You'll have to replace the transducer unit, of course – that will be quickest. You have three of those units with you. As to the cowl, you'll have to do without that. It should be OK. The domes are normally water filled."

Clark acknowledged the instructions, and swam down again to the damaged sensor. Immediately, he began to clear the mass of loose wiring and circuitry and fragmented glass and metal out of the hole, which was no more than a foot in diameter at its widest point. A small shell-hole.

The cleared depression in the hull looked merely empty, of no purpose. He released the locking ring and prised the transducer from its seat. Once he had to surface and request Quin to repeat part of the procedure, but he worked swiftly and with a keen and sharp satisfaction. The new unit plugged directly into the box of the signal converter. It took him no more than ten minutes to complete the task. He swam back to the stern of the *Proteus* and rose slowly and cautiously to the surface, once more in the shadow of the propeller.

The guard was looking at him, looking directly at him. He had to be able to see him.

Clark waited, his hand holding the zipper of his immersion suit, ready to reach for the Heckler & Koch .22. Then the guard blew out his cheeks and spat into the water. The noise was sufficient for Clark to grip the handle of the small pistol tightly, and almost draw it from his suit. The guard seemed to watch the small blob of spittle intently, then he began his desultory walk back to the other end of the pen. He had been staring absently at some point on the hull, some part of the stern, and had not seen Clark's head bob to the surface. Clark zipped up his suit once more, as quickly as his nerveless hands would allow, then he removed the air tanks from his back. They clanged softly, like a sounding bell, against one of the propeller blades, and he held his breath. There was no sound from the guards, and he hooked the webbing of the tanks over one of the propeller blades so that they hung below the surface.

He looked up, then at his watch. Two-fifty-seven. Shaking away the tiredness that seemed to have insinuated itself behind his eyes while he studied his watch – an intent, staring moment which seemed hypnotic, sleep-inducing – he began climbing the hull again, ascending the rudder fin until he could see both guards, backs to him. He had perhaps a minute before the port side guard reached the limit of his patrol. He scuttled out along the hull, unreeling a fine nylon line from around his waist. He had to check every sensor on the stern of the hull in full view. One head had only to turn, one figure emerge from the sail of the *Proteus*, one officer or *michman* come into the pen to check on the guards, Panov to arrive, eager to inspect "Leopard" –

He placed the magnetic pad at the end of the nylon line against the hull, jerked hard on the line, then abseiled down the curving hull, watching the port side guard continually. The sensor was beneath one of his feet, then level with his eyes. He ran one hand over the titanium tear-drop. Undamaged. He looked at the guard, almost out of sight behind the swelling midships section of the submarine, then clambered back up the line to the top of the hull. One.

He saw the starboard guard little more than half-way up the pen, his feet jigging unconsciously to the noise coming from the tiny radio. He swung down on the starboard side until he was level with the tear-drop dome. It was loose, and he cursed silently. He pulled a screwdriver from his kit, and prised at the thin titanium. Beneath it, the sensor appeared undamaged. He juggled his lamp in his hand, and switched it on. He checked, feeling the arm that gripped the line begin to quiver with nerves – guards nearly at the end of the pen, moving into the shadows beyond the hard lights – and his body heating with the tension. Undamaged – yes, undamaged. He loosened his grip on the lamp, and it dangled from his wrist again on its thick strap. He made to replace the screwdriver in his belt, and it slipped from his fingers – the guard was out of sight behind the swell of the midships, and in the shadow – and slid down the hull with a rattling noise that sounded deafening in the intent silence. It plopped like a large fish into the water. They must have heard it. He clambered, feet slipping, then able to grip, body hunched, almost jerking upwards on the line as if he were a fish and was hooked, waiting for the challenge, the shout of recognition at any moment.

He flattened himself on the hull, bunching the nylon line beneath his body, feeling his whole frame quivering. Another malarial attack. He could not stop himself shaking.

"Progress report," he heard in his earpiece. The port guard was in sight again, meandering down the pen towards him. Then the starboard guard came into sight, chewing and cocking his head into the tinny noises of the transistor radio at his ear. "Progress report", Aubrey requested again in his ear, this time with more asperity. Clark wanted to howl into his throat mike for the crazy old man to shut up.

The guard passed beneath him on the port side, then the starboard guard was level with him again. The radio made tiny, scratchy noises. A Western pop station, beamed in from Norway or Sweden.

"Lend us your fucking radio," the port guard called across to his companion in a not unamiable manner. "Bored stiff."

"I'm not," his companion replied, facing him. "You bloody Ukrainians are all the same – scroungers."

"Clark – progress report." *Shut up, shut up –*

"Fuck off." Clark craned his neck. The port guard, the taller of the two with the cropped haircut and the stooping shoulders, had unslung his rifle, and was pointing it at the man on the starboard side. "Hand over your radio, or I'll fire," he demanded.

The man on the starboard side laughed. He wore spectacles and a thin, weak moustache and looked no more than fifteen. He, too, unslung his rifle, and pointed it across the water with one hand, the other still pressing the radio to his ear. "Bang, bang," he said, hooting with laughter when he had done so.

"Piss off."

"Progress report, Clark. Clark?" *Shut up, shut up –*

Clark knew what would happen next, and knew it would be audible. Sharp, painful bleeps of sound, like morse dashes, to attract his attention, then a continuous tone like that of a telephone that has been disconnected because the subscriber has moved. Both guards looked up. Clark squeezed himself flatter against the top of the hull, praying for the curvature to be sufficient, to hide him like high ground or a horizon.

"What's that?"

"Dunno. Fucking radio. Our lot trying to jam it." The starboard guard laughed again, a thin high cackle as if his voice had not yet broken.

"Race you to the other end, you skinny, underfed Ukrainian!"

"What about –?"

"Ready, set – *go*!"

The noise of their boots echoed off the concrete walls and roof of the pen. The tone stopped, and then began again in his head. Clark whispered intently into his throat-mike.

"For Chrissake, get off my back, Aubrey!" He went on quivering, his body seeming to jump with the detonations of their footsteps bouncing off the roof, until Aubrey replied.

"Clark – what is wrong?"

"I'm lying on the fucking hull, man, with two goons training for the Olympics right below me. I can't *talk* to you!"

A few seconds later – he could hear a thin, breathless cheer from the far end of the pen as the taller guard won the race – Aubrey replied stiffly and formally, "Very well. Report as soon as you can."

"OK, OK."

"And again?" the shorter guard called angrily.

"You're on. Ten roubles on this one?"

"Twenty, you Ukrainian bullshitter!"

"Ready, set – *go*! Hey, you jumped the gun, you cheating sod!"

Then the bootsteps rained down from the roof again as they charged towards the seaward end of the pen. Clark lay icily still now, his tension expended with his anger, his sense of time oblivious to anything but the slow passage of seconds on the watch-face he held in front of his eyes.

The starboard guard won, by virtue of a flying start, and crowed and pranced. His companion, now his deadly rival, challenged him to a return. They regained their breath, watched each other like combatants for a fortune in prize money, crouched into sprinting starts, and then began running on the call of the taller man. Clark got to his knees. Their row would bring someone, soon. He scuttled along the hull, careless of the noise he made, fixed the pad, and lowered himself feverishly down the nylon rope, checked the undamaged sensor, climbed the rope again, imagined the ragged breathing of the two runners, waited until he could hear them arguing with out-of-breath shouts, and swung down the port side of the hull. He was elated by the clownish behaviour and the stupidity of the two young guards; almost reckless with confidence. Undamaged. He climbed the line again.

They were still arguing, their voices coming from the far end of the pen. He could dimly discern them, shadows in shadow. He moved back along the hull, lowered himself on the port side again – the two men had moved slightly to starboard of the bow of the submarine – and checked another sensor. The titanium blister was dented, but undisturbed. Then the starboard side, his luck beginning to extend beyond the point at which it was simply acceptable and becoming instead a source of anxiety, where he checked two more sensors. He was almost level with the rudder fin again, almost finished –

Another voice, a snarling petty-officer voice, and silence from the two guards. Berating, angry, loud. Their parentage was stripped from them, then their maturity, then their manhood. Layers of the onion, until they would be left with nothing but total humiliation and punishment duties. They would be replaced, the new guards would be fearfully alert, punctilious in their patrols. The crushing reprimand went on and on.

Clark lowered himself down the port side of the hull again. The plates were scarred, as if the metal had been lashed with a giant whip. He knew what he would find. A weal like a furrow lay along one hull plate, and whatever had caused it had crushed the wafer-thin titanium in upon the sensor beneath it. He reached into his belt, moving with feverish haste now as the *michman*'s voice rose again, perhaps towards a peroration. He drew a smaller, stubbier screwdriver and jabbed it into the slot on the locking ring and heaved. It moved, and then turned. He lifted it clear and snapped it into a hook on his belt. As he prised out the transducer he could see the damage clearly. Shattered fragments fell from the transducer and rattled and slid down the hull to the water.

Bare wires. The sheathing was cut through, and half the wiring was severed. Dangling from the end was an ABS multi-pin plug. Half of it. Half a smashed multi-pin plug. He registered it with helpless fury. Silence. The *michman* had finished. Christ –

A door slammed, and then there was silence again, a heavy, ringing silence. He was alone in the pen for perhaps a few minutes at most. Perspiration drenched him. He wiped the back of one hand over his face.

"I got problems," he announced. "Stern sensor fourteen – one of the sonar signal nullifiers. The wiring behind the transducer's a hell of a mess.''

He continued to lever at the wiring with the screwdriver while he waited for Quin to reply.

''What extent is the damage?''

The rest of the transducer slid away with a noise like the claws of a crab on metal. Then it plopped into the water. Clark hefted his lamp and shone it into the hole.

''Bad. Most of the wiring has been sheared; but there's worse. The connector's smashed.''

''Can you check beyond the breaks?''

''Maybe.''

''Can you see the socket and the box?''

''Yes.''

Clark peered into the hole. He tidied the sheared and twisted wiring to one side and looked again. The wires reached the fibre optics converter box on the underside of the outer hull.

''Remove it complete,'' Quin instructed. ''Fit a new one. And Clark – ''

''Yes?''

''There is a second plug, for the fibre optics. A bayonet fitting. Be careful. The first has forty pins, and it fits only one way.''

''Right.''

Clark looked at his watch. One minute since the door had slammed. He reached in, pressing his cheek against the hull, feeling the activity within the submarine as a slight vibration. His fingers flexed in the narrow space, snagged and cut on the exposed, shorn wires, and then his fingertips had hold of the upper section of the box. He pulled. Nothing happened. He pulled again, surprise on his face. The converter box would not budge.

''It's jammed,'' he said. ''Jammed.''

The door slammed. Marching boots, double time, the voice of the *michman* savagely drilling the two replacement guards. Clark clung to the nylon line and the converter box and prayed for the fifty-fifty chance to work in his favour.

The boots clattered down the starboard side of the *Proteus*. He had a moment or two yet –

''Have you got it? Can you see what's wrong?'' Quin was frightened.

Clark heaved at it, curling his fingers round the edge of the converter box. Nothing moved. One finger touched the clip – *clips, strap*, he'd forgotten the clips and the strap securing the box – he flipped open the catch with his thumb, felt it loosen, and then gripped the box again. He gritted his teeth and strained. His arm shot out of the hole

840

and he wriggled on the nylon line, holding on to the dangling wires and the box as the velocity with which he had jerked them free threatened to make him drop them. The *michman*'s voice snapped out orders to the new guards. In a moment, they would appear on the port side –

He ripped open one of the two thick packs and drew out a replacement converter box already wired to the transducer. He fed the complete unit into the hole as carefully as he could. He pushed it forward. Then he let go of the rope, dangling by its tight, cutting hold on his armpits, and shone his lamp. The *michman* had stopped shouting. He was watching the two guards doubling on the spot. Push – no, slight adjustment – push, get it into the clips – push home, feel for the strap ends, yes – hook them over, clamp the catch. He fitted the fibre optics plug, then fastened the transducer into place, and fitted the locking ring to holding it. The *michman* had ordered them to stop doubling.

Clark's arms felt lifeless and weak. He heaved at the nylon line, but his body hardly moved. His feet scrabbled on the smooth hull. The *michman* ordered the second new guard to follow him. It was like a yelled order to Clark. He clambered back up the line. Fifty feet to the hatch. Seconds only.

He ran. He heaved open the hatch, not caring any longer whether or not he had been seen, and tumbled into darkness, the hatch thudding softly shut on its rubber seals behind him. He lay breathless and aching and uncaring in the safe, warm darkness of the escape chamber, every part of his body exhausted.

"Well done, Quin," Aubrey offered, and watched the slow bloom of self-satisfaction on the man's face. He was difficult to like, but Aubrey had ceased to despise him. Quin was back in the land of the living, as it were. Flattery, cajolement, even threat had all played a part in his rehabilitation. Finally, however, Aubrey had seen the danger to his invention, his project, overcome and prompt Quin. The man would not surrender "Leopard" without some effort on his part.

"Thank you," Quin returned. Then his face darkened, and he shook his head. "It's almost impossible, " he added. "I don't know whether Clark has the necessary concentration to keep this up –"

"I understand the strain he must be under," Aubrey said, "but there's no other way."

"I'm – I'm sorry – stupid behaviour earlier – apologies –" Each word seemed wrenched from Quin, under duress. Aubrey respected the effort it was costing the cold, egotistical man to offer an explanation of himself.

"Quite all right."

"It's just that, well, now I don't want them to get their hands on it, you see —"

"Quite."

"It is the only thing of importance to me, you see." He looked down at his hands. "Shouldn't say that, but I'm afraid it's true." He looked up again, his eyes fierce. "Damn them, they mustn't have it!"

"Mr. Aubrey?" There was something trying to force itself like a broken bone through Eastoe's frosty reserve.

"Yes, Squadron Leader?"

"We have some blips on the radar. Four of them."

"Yes?"

"Coming up rapidly from one of the airfields on the Kola Peninsular. Not missiles, the trace is wrong for that. Four aircraft."

"I see. Range?"

"Not more than thirty miles. They'll be with us in three minutes or even less."

"With us? I don't understand."

"They've already crossed into Norwegian airspace, Mr. Aubrey. They didn't even hesitate."

THIRTEEN:

Concealment

They were MiG-23s, code-named Flogger-B, single-seat, all-weather interceptors. Four of them. Even Aubrey could recognize them, in a moment of silhouette that removed him more than forty years to basic aircraft recognition tests at the beginning of the war. A vivid streak of lightning to the north, and the brassy light illuminating the night sky, outlined the nearest of the MiGs. Slim, grey, red-starred on its flank. One wing-tip rose as the aircraft banked slightly, and Aubrey could see the air-to-air missiles beneath the swing wing in its swept-back position.

Immediately, Eastoe was talking to him. "Mr. Aubrey, they're MiG-23s, interceptors. The flight leader demands to know our mission and the reason for our invasion of sensitive airspace."

"What is their intention, would you say?" Quin was staring out of the window of the Nimrod, watching the slim, shark-like silhouette that had begun to shadow them.

"Shoo us away."

"What course of action do you –?"

"Just a minute, Mr. Aubrey. I've got the Norwegian flight leader calling me. Do you want to listen into this?"

"I don't think so," Aubrey replied wearily. "I am sure I already know what he wishes to say."

"Very well."

The headset went dead, and Aubrey removed it. It clamped his temples and ears, and seemed to cramp and confine thought. He did not like wearing it. Quin did not seem disappointed at Aubrey's decision.

There was another flash of lightning, streaking like bright rain down a window towards the sea. The blare of unreal light revealed the closest of the Northrop F-5s turning to port, away from the Nimrod. Their Norwegian fighter escort had been recalled to Kirkenes. Norway's unwritten agreement, as a member of NATO, with the Soviet Union was that no military exercises or provocative military manoeuvres were undertaken within a hundred miles of the Soviet border. Evidently, the Russians had registered a protest, and their protest had been accepted.

Aubrey replaced his headset. "Has our Norwegian escort gone?"

"Yes, Mr. Aubrey. We're on our own."

"Very well. Our signals cannot be intercepted, nor their origin traced so far as Clark is concerned?"

"No. Mr. Aubrey, how long do we need to hang around?"

"For some hours yet."

"Very well." Eastoe sounded grim, but determined. "We'll do what we can. I'll try not to get shepherded out of range."

"If you would."

Aubrey stared at the console on the table between himself and Quin. The hull sensors had been inspected and repaired, yet the achievement of that task had been the completion of the easy and least dangerous element. Clark now had to inspect and, if necessary, repair the back-up system of "Leopard". Aubrey suddenly felt alone, and incompetent.

Eastoe spoke again in his ear. "They're demanding we leave the area. They'll see us off the property."

"You are on our eastbound leg at the moment?"

"Yes. But that won't fool them. They'll have been watching us on radar for a long time. They know we're flying a box pattern."

"But, for the moment, we're secure?"

"Yes –"

The window seemed filled with the belly of the MiG-23. The sight was gone in a moment, and might have begun to seem illusory, except that the nose of the Nimrod tilted violently as Eastoe put the aircraft into a dive.

"Shit –" the co-pilot's voice cried in Aubrey's ear. The Nimrod levelled, and steadied.

"They're not in the mood to waste time," Eastoe commented. "You saw that?"

Aubrey remembered the underbelly, almost white like that of a great hunting fish, and even the red-painted missiles beneath the wing.

"Yes," he said. "What happened?" He ignored Quin's worried face, the man was frightened but there was a determination in him now, replacing the former cunning that had sought only escape.

"One of them buzzed us – and I mean buzzed. Crazy bastard!"

Aubrey paused for a moment. "The aircraft is in your hands, Squadron Leader. All I ask is that we never pass out of range of Clark's transceiver. The rest is up to you."

"*Thank you*, Mr. Aubrey."

The MiG – perhaps the one that had buzzed them – was back on their port wing, slightly above and behind. Shadowing them. It was, Aubrey considered, as unpredictable as a wild creature.

Tricia staggered under Hyde's weight, slipped, and fell against the long, high bank. Her breath roared in her ears, but she could feel it in her chest – ragged, loud, heaving. Hyde, unconscious, rolled away from her, slid until he lay at her feet looking sightlessly up at her and was still. Tricia was simply and utterly relieved that she was no longer bearing his weight against one side and across the back of her neck where she had placed his arm. She loathed and hated Hyde at that moment, and even feared him; as if he might wake and attack her himself. She blamed him totally, for every fragment and element of her predicament.

Her body was bathed in perspiration, and her limbs were shaking with weakness. Hyde continued groaning, like a murmured protest at his pain.

"Oh – shut up," she whispered fiercely. "Shut up." The repetition was bitten off, as if she admitted he was not to blame.

She had helped Hyde, often supporting his unconscious weight when he slipped once more from pain into stillness, as they moved north, then west. There had been no effective pursuit. The helicopter had lost sight of them after she had half-dragged, half-shouldered him away from the rise where he had first passed out, into a small copse of trees. A tiny dell, where the dead ferns were long and curving, like the roofs of native huts, had concealed them. Terrified, she had heard legs brushing through heather and ferns, voices near and more distant, the crackle of R/Ts. She had kept her hand over Hyde's mouth, in case he babbled in delirium.

The wound had been ugly, and she knew nothing of medicine or nursing. It had bled a great deal. It seemed that the bullet had not lodged in Hyde's shoulder or chest because there was a small hole near his shoulder blade and a larger hole near his collar-bone. She had seen sufficient television wounds to assume that the bullet had passed straight through. Her knowledge of anatomy was sketchy, and she watched anxiously for blood to appear around his lips. When it did not, she assumed the lungs were undamaged. She did not know what other bones, muscles or organs might reside in the area of the wound. She bound the wound with a torn length of Hyde's own shirt.

Now, under the looming shadow of the long, high bank, she knew she could go no further. Hyde's weight had become intolerable. She could bully him no more, support him no longer. She was hungry, and cold, and impatient of Hyde's helplessness. His repeated groans of pain enraged her.

She knelt by him because he would not quieten. She shook his head carefully, as if it fitted only loosely, her fingers holding his chin. His eyes flickered, but then closed again, as if he wished to exclude

her and what she represented. She shook his head more violently. A
great weariness possessed her, and she sat instead of squatting on her
haunches.

"For God's sake, wake up," she pleaded.

"Uuh," he grunted. She looked at him. His eyes were open.

"You're awake."

"Oh, *Christ!*" he cried in a broken voice, his breath sobbing. "My
bloody shoulder." He groaned again.

"You're not delirious?"

"My bloody shoulder won't let me. Where – where are we?"

"Behind the rifle ranges. Are we going to stay here?"

"I'm not going anywhere." Hyde looked at the stars. "I can't go
anywhere, Tricia."

"I know."

"Have a quick look around. See if you can find some dense undergrowth, a ditch, a trench, a hole in the bank, anything. If we can get
under cover, we –" He groaned again.

"Where are the police?" she asked plaintively.

"Searching Cheshire probably," he replied, coughing. She looked
anxiously for signs of blood as he wiped his lips. There were none.
"Trouble is, we're in Staffordshire. They'll get round to us. I hope."

"They must be looking, surely?"

"I bloody well hope so, darling. I pay my rates and taxes so they can
pull me out of holes like this. I'll be writing to my bloody Pom MP if
they don't turn up."

She almost laughed at the pronounced accent and the sentiments it
expressed. Something lifted from her; not her weariness, but something of her isolation. Hyde sounded more like a human being, less
like a liability.

"I'll look," she said, and got up. He turned his head slowly and
watched her. He felt tears in his eyes which might simply have been
the result of pain and weariness. He did not understand them, and for
a few moments he could not prevent them. The pain in his shoulder
subsided now that he was resting, but he felt his body could make no
further effort, not even to defend itself or the girl. He needed to hide.

The girl came back quickly, almost running.

"No –" he protested, sensing her pursued.

"What? No, it's all right, I've found a hollow, scooped out of the
bank. It's almost masked by a bush. Can you come?"

He sat up, rocked, then steadied himself. "Give us a hand, mate."

She tottered, but pulled him to his feet. She hitched his arm across
her aching shoulders again, and dragged him along the gully behind
the bank, which loomed thirty feet or more above them.

It was less than fifty yards, but she was staggering with tiredness when they reached the bush growing out of the bank. Hyde felt its stiff, resisting branches, the sharp ends and points of old thorns. It had spread and flourished for many years, but he could see behind its present leaflessness the outline of a hole in the bank.

"How far in does it go, do you think?" she said, shivering as she realized she would have to investigate.

"It's all right. No bears left, and no wolves. And no bloody snakes like we've got in Aussie biting your arse when you climb in. Go on, then." He sounded genuinely impatient.

She heaved and struggled with the branches of the leafless bush, then went head-first into the hole. "It smells," he heard her call hollowly.

His cackle degenerated into a cough. "It's those bloody rabbits from Watership Down," he said. "How big is it?"

Her head emerged. "Just big enough for two, if you don't mind a crush."

"You'll have to push me in," he said.

She climbed out, snagging her jacket on thorns, then she helped get him to the bush, lifted some of the whippier branches aside like a curtain, then got her shoulder beneath his buttocks.

"Ready?"

"Yes."

She heaved, and he disappeared into the hole.

"Are you all right?"

"Yes," he answered faintly. "Rearrange the bush when you climb in."

She squeezed into the hole, then turned with difficulty, putting her foot into his back at one point, and reached out, tugging and pulling the bushes back into place as well as she could. Then she slithered backwards until she was bunched up against him.

"Wait a minute," she said, and fumbled in the pockets of the donkey jacket. She rattled the box of matches, fumbled with it, then struck one. "There you are."

Hyde's face looked grey and ill, but he managed to say, "Now I get you alone at last, some bloody Russian puts a contraceptive through my shoulder."

"Yes," she said thoughtfully, already finding the light of the match much too bright and wanting to close her eyes. She shook it out and dropped it. "Are you all – right?" she asked faintly. The darkness closed satisfyingly around her. She was not certain whether his reply was positive or negative, and she did not really think it mattered. She heard him groan once before she fell asleep.

Clark closed the tiny hatch into the space between the outer and the pressure hulls, leaving his helical aerial attached to the surface of the outer hull. The darkness was sudden and intense after the hard lighting from the roof of the pen. He could not stand upright, but bent his head and hunched his back as he waited for his breathing to return to normal, or to an approximation of normality.

He had emerged from the aft escape chamber knowing that the new guards on either side of the submarine would be self-consciously, fearfully alert for any and every unexpected noise and movement. Their peripheral vision would be enhanced by the threats of the senior *michman*, and they had been on duty for only twenty minutes. Yet he had to risk it.

When he recovered in the escape chamber, his arms full of cramp and pain, his whole body exhausted with the effort of abseiling down the hull and climbing it again, he first collected the second pack – left hand bad – from the electric motor room and took it into the chamber. He would have to take both complete packs with him. He was on the point of incarcerating himself between the twin hulls of the *Proteus* until he either repaired the back-up system or was forced to abort and plant the explosives which would melt it into a lump of useless metal.

The hatch fitted to the *Proteus* which allowed access to the inner hull where the blister containing the back-up system was fitted lay thirty feet from the aft escape hatch. He had eased open the hatch a matter of inches, listening with his whole body. When the guards' footsteps moved out of range, precise and regular and unconcerned as clockwork, he opened it fully, climbed out, closed it again, and moved along the hull. He had opened the other hatch, and lowered the first pack in. Then he had closed it and returned, waiting until the next patrol of the pen took the two guards towards the bow before moving the second pack along the top of the hull, dragging it after him as he slithered on his belly, into the space between the hulls.

In the darkness now, the two packs rested at his feet. He was aware, as his breathing calmed, of the way in which the pressure hull curved away on either side of him. He was on a narrow ledge, a metal bridge across a chasm, and he must never forget the fact.

He paused for another moment, his bearings uncertain then assured, and then he hefted the two packs until they no longer dragged on the pressure hull before moving forward. He pushed his feet forward, disregarding the lamp for the moment because his hands were full and because it seemed necessary to establish some sense of mastery over his new and alien environment. Behind him, he paid out the wire from his transceiver to the aerial outside the hull. He felt the hull slope slightly upwards, in ridged steps. Unlike the smooth outer hull, the pressure hull of the *Proteus* did not follow

848

exactly the same outline or shape. His shoulders bent lower as the two hulls narrowed the distance between themselves. Another three steps, and he dropped lightly to his knees. The outer hull seemed to press down upon him in a moment of claustrophobia, and the pressure hull beneath his knees and toes seemed thin, uncertain, narrow. The chasm waited for him on either side.

He switched on the lamp. Ahead of him, where the space between the hulls narrowed like a thin, deep shaft where a miner would have had to work on his back or his stomach to dig the coal, he could see, like the pit-props appropriate to the analogy his mind had discovered, the stanchions growing like grey metal trees between the two hulls, separating and binding them. He moved the torch around him, pressing back the thick, blind darkness. It smelt old, and damp, and empty. The sounds thrumming lightly and occasionally through the pressure hull, the murmur of machinery and air-pumps and filters and voices and electrics and ovens and toilets, seemed completely removed from him and not of human origin.

The outer hull sloped away like the roof of a dome to either side, falling sheer out of sight. He could see the lip where the pressure hull followed its shape on either side. The ledge seemed narrow and fragile. He flicked the torch's thin beam deliberately forward again. A hump like a turtle shell or the scaled back of an armadillo hunched in the shadows beyond the stanchion trees. The sight of it relieved him. He fixed the packs to his belt by their clips once more, and lay flat. He began pushing the packs in front of him, slithering awkwardly forward, alarmed by the noise he seemed to be making.

He began to weave through the stanchions, thrusting and pushing the packs in turn ahead of him, then using his elbows and knees to moved his body forward behind them. Whenever he flicked on the lamp – needing its light now as reassurance as well as a guide – the grey humped back of the turtle shell remained ahead of him in the shadows at the edge of the pool of light.

Push. The left-hand pack was fumbled round the next stanchion. Push. The right-hand pack moved. He then moved his body forward. His cheek rested for a moment against the cold, wet-seeming metal of the stanchion, then he pushed the left-hand pack forward again. His lamp clanged against the pressure hull. He cursed the noise, momentarily distracted, and the left-hand pack slid away from him. He felt it tug at his body, urging it sideways. The pack slithered into the chasm. His right hand grabbed the stanchion, and his arm was almost jerked from its socket. He suppressed a cry of pain and held on, reeling in the heavy pack with his left hand. He gripped it to him, shaking.

When he had swallowed the fear in his mouth, and his legs had seemed to recover some of their strength, he moved on, passing the last of the stanchions, slithering more quickly the last few feet to the shell of grey metal, the tumour on the pressure hull.

He was able to kneel, just, with his back arched like a frightened cat's, and shine his lamp over the surface. His first task was to remove it. He placed the packs carefully beyond it, where he would not disturb them accidentally, and began removing the bolts from the sealing gasket of the grey carapace. He was aware that he was above the ceiling of the turbine room, crouching in shadow, alone and even ridiculous, taking his first steps to cure an illness he was unlikely to be able to diagnose. Below him, from what he had seen when aboard the *Proteus*, it was likely that engineers and technicians from the naval base would be inspecting the giant turbines. He had to presume that they were there, assume that the slightest carelessness with regard to noise would betray his presence to them.

"I'm in the tunnel," he said softly, aware of the point on the relief map which Pasvik had pointed out and where he now hid. Pasvik was in the bushes with his dish aerials, the one fragile link between himself and Quin aboard the Nimrod.

"Good." Aubrey's voice.

"Beginning to remove the cowling," he said.

He reached into a pocket of his immersion suit and removed a rubber suction cap. He fixed it to the lamp, and pressed the other side against the outer hull. He jiggled the lamp, but it remained fixed. The pool of light fell upon the grey metal shell.

He loosened the final screw, pocketed it, and lifted the carapace away. Inside it were the carbon fibre braces to withstand pressure at depth. Beneath the carapace were a number of further box-like housings with neoprene seals. He half turned a spring-loaded catch, then lifted the first of the inner covers. What he saw, as he had suspected from the diagram but which still surprised and daunted him, resembled a dug-out, exposed telephone junction box he had once seen beneath the sidewalk of Pennsylvania Avenue in Washington. The telephone engineers had exposed a mass of bright, spiderish wiring, incomprehensible, baffling. He shook his head, and began to learn the nature of what he looked at, remembering Quin's voice guiding him through the wiring diagrams and the "Leopard" manual. Printed circuit boards, a sickly grey-white and green where the copper was coated with anti-corrosion varnish; on the boards, resistors with bright bands of colour in the lamplight, capacitors in tubes of various sizes, some sheathed in coloured plastic, some like sucked cough lozenges. He nodded to himself. His eyes recognized the number of small boxes set out as regularly and rigidly as units of some eighteenth-century army drawn up for battle. Pins like defences protruded from the boxes, glinting gold. Microprocessors.

It was no longer mysterious. Merely a collection of components. He breathed easily, with satisfaction. He was now the telephone engineer, not the passer-by. The sheer mass of wiring, however, prevented complacency; all colour coded, lashed into ropes with fine cords. Each circuit board had a serial number, which he would read to Quin or Quin would instruct him to test, and each component, however tiny it might be, fitted in its place in company with a reference number.

His finger traced across the bulk of large power transformers, mounted on blocks of metal and used to dissipate heat from the system. Then his eye began to register the miniature switches labelled *Self-Test Facility* and the multi-pin sockets labelled *Input Tester Socket Type 27 P3D*. They were his heart of the matter, all he really needed to recognize.

He hefted the carapace away from him, together with the inner cover, and placed them gingerly on the pressure hull beyond his packs, steadying until he considered neither of them would slip into the chasm. Then he removed his special test kit from the pack, and clipped it to his belt. A bead of wetness ran down his cheek, then dropped from his jaw. It would take hours, just the checking. The thought made his hands almost nerveless and caused a cramp in his arched back and neck.

"OK," he said in a whisper.

Quin was back almost immediately, the eagerness evident in his voice. "Begin with the Opto-Electric Converter," he said. "You can identify that?"

Clark studied the exposed boards. "Yes, got it."

"Good. Switch SW One off, and SW Two on."

"Right."

"Rotate SW One to Test."

"Yes."

"Look at the two rows of LEDs – describe the sequence of lights to me."

Clark watched the two rows of light emitting diodes. The top row lit up one by one, accompanied by a low hum. As the last one illuminated, the first light of the lower row lit up, followed by its companions, the top row of lights going out immediately. When the second row was complete it, too, went out, and the first light of the top row lit up once more, repeating the sequence.

When Clark had reached the end of the sequence in his description, Quin interrupted him.

"Switch off. Everything's working properly there. The transducers, the wiring, the fibre-optics and the connectors are all working as they should."

"Uh," Clark grunted, disappointed in a childish, impatient way. Nothing wrong. He sighed.

The Nimrod banked sharply to starboard. Eastoe was trying to come round onto the northern leg, across Varangerhalvöya, and two of the MiG-23s had crossed the nose of the aircraft as soon as he began to change course. Aubrey gripped the sides of his seat fiercely, but he did not allow any expression to appear on his face. He could hear the Russian flight leader, speaking in correct, unemotional English, demanding that Eastoe continue on his former course, west along the Norwegian coast towards North Cape. Eastoe remained silent.

The Nimrod, however declared his intention. It dipped violently as the two MiGs banked up and away, flicking with the agility of flies across the darkness, illuminated by a flash of lightning only when they were already more than a mile away, and beginning a turn to bring them back alongside the Nimrod. Eastoe levelled the big aircraft below the flight level of the Russian interceptors.

"Everyone all right – *you*, Mr. Aubrey?"

"Thank you, yes. No more than unsettled." The console in front of Aubrey crackled, and what might have been a voice tried unsuccessfully to communicate something to them. Quin had turned up the volume to maximum, and was leaning forward.

"What did you say, Clark? Clark, I can't hear you."

"What's the matter?" Aubrey snapped fearfully. "What's happening?" Quin shook his head and shrugged. "Eastoe – we can't hear Clark."

"I'm at the limit, Mr. Aubrey. Over a hundred miles out. I'm sorry, but I'm trying to shave the corner off the northbound leg. You'll have to bear with me." There was no satisfaction in the voice. Eastoe had suspended his personal feud with Aubrey.

"Very well." The storm filled the empty ether that was being amplified by the console. A MiG popped into Aubrey's vision, below and almost beneath the port wing of the Nimrod. It had bobbed there like a cork tossed on rough water. There was only the one. Aubrey bent his head and stared through the starboard window opposite him. He could see two more of the Russian interceptors. They were close in, as if juggling for position in order to refuel from the Nimrod. Dangerously close.

Drawn to what he suspected was happening, Aubrey left his seat and crossed to the starboard side of the Nimrod. The aircraft was sliding into a turn, banking slightly and nose-down so that the metal floor had tilted like the floor of some disorientating fairground tunnel. The closest MiG was edging into the Nimrod like a smaller animal ingratiating himself. Its speed had matched the Nimrod's and Aubrey could already see the helmeted head of the pilot within the bubble of the canopy. The flying was skilful even as it was threatening and dangerous. The Nimrod was being headed off, a sheep being directed by a sheepdog. A collision appeared inevitable as their paths converged. Aubrey could do nothing except watch with an appalled fascination. His old frail body trembled with its sense of mortality.

He dimly heard the Nimrod's four Spey engines increase their power, and he felt the nose tilt upwards suddenly. He hung onto a bracket like a straphanger in a tube train, his body wanting to lurch towards the tail of the aircraft. The MiG-23 appeared, then whisked away from the window, like a fly that had been swatted. Even as the Nimrod climbed it began to bank to starboard, pushing Aubrey against the fuselage and his face into the double window port. He felt the glass against his cheek, and his arm aching from its hold on the bracket. The MiG was below them, the other Russian interceptor above, at a distance that implied respect or nerves. Aubrey felt himself hanging over the chasm of thirty thousand feet, imagined the rocks and the landscape below them.

He heard Clark's voice bellow behind him, reporting a stage of his inspection. Then two hands moved his small, frail body, and he was able to let go his hold on the bracket. He looked round into the face of the young flight lieutenant who was in charge of communications.

"Please don't leave your seat again, Mr. Aubrey."

Aubrey shrugged his clothing to greater tidiness on his form. "I'm sorry," he said. "What did Clark want, Quin?" Aubrey sat down heavily.

Quin shook his head. "Nothing so far," he said.

"He is performing the check correctly?"

"He is."

A livid flash of lightning in the distance. The storm was behind and to the north of them now.

"Mr. Aubrey?" It was Eastoe in his headphones.

"Yes?"

"I'm sorry, Mr. Aubrey. I'm not going to be allowed to fly the eastbound leg. They won't stand for that."

"What can you do?" Aubrey asked in utter exasperation.

"Fly a north-south course, over and over – if we can get away with it."

"You're not hopeful."

"No, I'm not. Our time here is strictly limited, I'm afraid. They're determined to get rid of us, one way or another."

"Section completed. All readings positive," Clark's voice announced ominously from the console.

"Damn," Aubrey whispered. "Damn."

They were all drunk now, yelling, bellowing, fighting drunk. Falling down and laughing drunk, too. Disrespectful, abusive, coarse, uproarious. Ardenyev enjoyed the noise, the swirl and shudder of the vodka in his veins and head, while one still sober, cold part of his awareness perceived where their laughter and taunts were leading, and anticipated with nothing more than a shudder of self-consciousness the nature of leadership and what he would now have to do to fulfil their expectations and to maintain his grip on their affection and respect.

And also, he concluded, the drinking party had to end with buffoonery, with the game of the ego and the shallowly physical prowess they required to perform their duties. After the death of Blue Section and the others of his own team, the three survivors had been absorbed and ingested as they drank and ate into the cameraderie of the men from the rescue ship *Karpaty*. Balan had understood the necessity of the merger. So Balan's challenge now to him to demonstrate how he boarded the *Proteus* was that of a shrewd drunk. His men wanted it, a boast and valediction. *He* had survived, become more than ever a necessary figurehead, even to the salvage men. In the absence of an athlete, a football star, an actress, he had to submit himself to their fuddled worship, their drunken amusement.

He was drunk, though. He knew that as soon as he stood up, and swayed as if the vodka had punched him in the temple. Teplov was watching him, he could see, as if weighing whether he should let his officer proceed. Viktor Teplov appeared sober, as ever.

Ardenyev looked up, the two images of the wall and the ceiling of the officers' mess coming together, as if he had correctly, though slowly, adjusted a pair of binoculars. He held the new and single image with an effort of concentration. Teplov nodded at the fuzzy corner of his vision. He was prepared to extricate his officer from whatever situation he found himself in.

"Come on, then!" Lev Balan roared, pointing up at the air-conditioning grille. "From that one, right round the room to that one!" His arm swept round the officers' mess, now deserted save for their own noisy group. The two grilles were on opposite walls. Ardenyev was being challenged to clamber and push his way through the duct until he could emerge with honour. Two of Balan's team were busy, balancing with difficulty on chairs, unscrewing the two grilles. Ardenyev looked at Balan, and then at Teplov, and Vanilov. All that remained of the Special Underwater Operations

Unit. Teplov had the face of a stoical peasant in which his eyes gleamed with memory and with a strange amusement, perhaps even with approval. Vanilov looked as if he had drunk too much to forget. He wanted Ardenyev to prove something, perhaps only to be the adult coming into his child's bedroom, easing away the threatening shadows that had gathered around the cot.

"OK. You're on. Two hundred roubles it is."

"One hundred –!" Balan protested.

"Two."

"All right, two. That means a time limit. OK?"

Ardenyev hesitated for a moment, then he nodded. Balan's man stepped down off his chair, the grille in his hand. Ardenyev flicked the remainder of his drink into his open mouth, feeling it burn the back of his throat, then he reached up and took hold of the rough plaster edges of the square hole where the grille had been. He felt mouse droppings under his fingers.

"One minute," Balan called. "You've got one minute to get at least your head out of that other hole. Five, four, three, two, one – go!"

The cheering was deafening. Ardenyev pushed himself up level with the hole, ducked his head into it, and then heaved himself half into the duct, which bent immediately to the left. His shoulders rubbed against the plaster, and he found he had to angle his body in order to be able to move at all. The cheering behind him was muffled by the bulk of his body and by the plaster wall and the metal. He kicked, and his legs followed him into the duct. Immediately, Balan's voice came from behind him, counting.

"Eleven, twelve, thirteen . . ."

Ardenyev shook his head to clear it. Then he began scrambling, leaning to his left, his body rubbing along the metal channel. The cheering was dim and wordless now, falling away into silence. He reached the corner of the room. The duct was a severe right-angle. He squeezed his head and shoulders around the angle, then tried to bring his thighs and knees after his upper torso. He found himself wedged immovably. He struggled as if panicking, and sweat broke out all over his body. He cursed in a yell, and then lay still. Balan's head appeared further down the duct, in a shadowy patch of light. There was a noise that no longer interested Ardenyev coming from behind him.

"Forty-seven, forty-eight, forty-nine . . ."

"Piss off!" Ardenyev yelled, not even attempting to move again. "I'm bloody stuck!"

Balan's head disappeared with a shriek of laughter. Teplov's head appeared in its place. At the same moment, a huge cheer went up as the minute ran out. "All right, sir?"

"Yes, thank you, Viktor."

"Bloody silly game, sir."

"Yes, Viktor."

"I'll come in the other side and give you a shove, sir."

"Thank you, Viktor."

Ardenyev smiled, then relaxed. It didn't matter. Nothing did. The air conditioning duct enclosed him more surely and tightly than the aft escape chamber of the *Proteus*, but there was similarity of darkness and confinement that pressed itself upon him. He allowed a congratulatory sense of memory its place in his fuddled awareness. He'd done it, he'd done it –

No one else, he told himself. No one else could have done it. Then, more sharply, he thought, if I could, someone else could. Most of the team, the dead team –

His thoughts had swung towards a maudlin, drunken horizon. He heard Teplov moving along the duct behind him, grunting with effort. He giggled drunkenly. Anyone could have done it, he affirmed in a mood of quick and sudden self-deprecation as he imagined those who had died. It wasn't anything. Then, through a connection of which he was not aware, he wondered, Why is that Nimrod hanging around? What is it doing?

Teplov's hand tapped his calf. He called back to the *michman*: "What's that Nimrod doing up there, Viktor?"

"Beg pardon, sir?"

"That Nimrod – they were talking about it earlier."

"Oh, that one," Teplov said indulgently. "I wouldn't know, sir."

If I could do it, he thought, anyone could. That Nimrod –

He was aware of himself, stretched out on the pressure hull, held there by the mesh of nerves that covered his body. He had heard the footsteps clattering along the hull from the stern. The boots had stamped to a halt directly over the hatch through which he had entered the space between the two hulls. He had immediately switched off the lamp, as if the outer hull had been no more opaque than a curtain, and he had turned onto his back. He seemed to himself to be less vulnerable, facing the direction of the noises. Evidence, evidence? he asked himself repeatedly. Why? Why now? Noise, suspicion, *evidence*?

He stared up at the outer hull as if he could really see it, almost as if he could see the armed man whose boots had clattered up on him. He listened. Tiny noises now, almost mouse-like. The irresolute shuffling of feet, the claw-like scratching of nails and metal heel-tips. The darkness pressed in, unwelcome, bringing its unexpected and disturbing claustrophobia with it. He reached up and flicked on the lamp. It shone in his eyes. He inspected his watch. Six o'clock, almost. He had been working on the back-up system for over two hours. And he had found nothing. Every circuit, every resistor, every capacitor and microprocessor and wire and pin *worked* –

There was nothing wrong with it, at least not with the sixty-five percent of the back-up system that he had checked. There was something less, or something more mysteriously, wrong with the complex lump of junk near his head than was the matter with the Nimrod. Sure, Aubrey kept reassuring him, but the communications black-outs and the poor reception and the constant re-requests and repeats of instructions told him everything.

The boots shuffled, then moved, on the hull. They were over his face now, only a couple of feet from stamping on it.

The Nimrod was at the fringes of, and at times beyond, the communications range. Which meant that the aircraft had company, Soviet company. MiGs were shadowing the Nimrod, maybe even playing shepherd games with her –

As he rehearsed the conclusion once more, a chill coldness seized him. They suspected, even knew, about him. The boots on the hull, and the silence which he had noticed from the turbine room beneath him. They were listening, too. Everyone was listening for him, waiting for the mouse behind the wainscot to move again. He held his breath, one part of his mind explaining with a weary patience that he was behaving ridiculously, the remainder of his consciousness believing that the hull above him and beneath his back and head and legs was no more than a sounding-board, a corridor of whispers eager to betray his whereabouts.

The boots moved away, forward along the hull towards the sail. Almost immediately, Lloyd was speaking in a voice muffled by the pocket of his immersion suit, through the tiny R/T Clark had left with him. Relief overcame Clark, and he felt the renewed perspiration cool almost at once on his skin, making his flesh shudder.

He removed the R/T from his pocket and pressed it to his cheek.

"Yes?"

"I've seen Hayter and Thurston. They know what to do."

"Good."

"Any luck?"

"None."

"It's six now."

"I know."

"Is it still on?"

"Eight o'clock, on the button."

"I heard my guard and another talking. The man from Novosibirsk has arrived in Murmansk."

"Damn. Is he on his way?"

"I don't know."

"OK – I'll call you."

Clark replaced the R/T set in his breast pocket, and zipped the pocket closed with a real and savage anger. He rolled onto his stomach, and the turtle without its shell was humped on the edge of the pool of light from the lamp, still baffling him, still apparently undamaged.

"You heard that?" he whispered. There were noises now from the turbine room. He had imagined the silence.

"Yes," Aubrey replied. His voice was gauzy and faint, a smear of distant sound. Flying on the limit again.

"What trouble are you in?"

"None."

"Tell me."

"Four MiG-23s. They're keeping us as far away from Soviet airspace as possible –" The voice blacked out, then Clark heard an additional smear of sound some seconds later which he could not decipher. Then two more spits of sound which the cassette recorder slowed down and replayed. He could understand neither of them. The cool part of his brain suggested a storm might be adding to the difficulties, but the remainder of his awareness was raging with the same kind of helpless, impotent fury his body felt. He was shaking as he knelt in front of the "Leopard" back-up system. He was in a mood to break, damage, throw. The rational part of him understood, and mocked at, the emotions he felt and his desire for their expression, and gradually he calmed himself. Then, suddenly, Aubrey was speaking again, clearly.

"Can you hear me now?"

"Yes."

"Eastoe has dodged them, ducked inside," Aubrey said. Clark could even pick out the irony of the old man's tone. "Quin suggests it will take only hours to dismantle 'Leopard', if that is what they intend, and the same amount of time for a full analysis, with the resources they have available. Once they begin the work, they will be searching for the back-up system. You must not be where you are when that happens. 'Leopard' must not be intact when this expert steps aboard. Do I make myself clear?"

"Yes."

"It will take an hour from Murmansk by helicopter."

"All right, all right. I'm moving on – what next?"

"Very well. You have *both* packs with you?"

Clark looked up and into the gloom beyond the lamplight. "Yes," he replied with a sense of defeat. "Both of them."

858

"Keep me informed."

"Clark?" It was Quin's voice now, not so irritating, not so pessimistic as that of Aubrey. Quin allowed the fiction of success to be entertained. "You should move on to the spectrum analyser, noise generator and phase reverser unit."

"Right."

"You need the special test kit."

"Sure." Clark unclipped it from his belt. A dial, various scales, a rotary switch, buttons, a small grille. Quin had to instruct every step of the way; every switch, every light, every reading. "All right, I'm ready." He studied the exposed maze of wiring, microprocessors and circuits in front of him. For a moment, his mind was a blank and the system before him was a puzzle to which he had no clue. Then, sighing, he shrugged off his numbing reluctance, and reached out and waited for Quin's instructions.

It was six o-five.

"It's almost six, Admiral – perhaps we can now be leaving for Pechenga. Too much time has already been wasted."

"Comrade Academician, you say it will take a matter of no more than three or four hours to complete your work on 'Leopard'. What is your hurry? You waited at the airport in Novosibirsk for almost three days." Dolohov was expansive, and mocking. He was almost drunk, Panov decided, and had abandoned most of his dignity. Panov did not like the military, especially the older representatives, the officer caste. As a man who was an honoured member of another élite, one without the stain of imitating those that existed before the Revolution, Panov disliked, even loathed, the upper echelons of the military.

Panov glanced again at his gold Swiss watch. He had purchased it in Paris, while attending a scientific congress, and that had added to its potency as a reminder of his identity. The large-faced clock on the wall behind Dolohov, which Panov would hardly have admitted to his wife's kitchen in Novosibirsk, jerked its hand past another minute. The drunken old fool remained in his chair.

"Admiral – I must insist that we leave for Pechenga at once. My colleagues will be waiting for me. I must study their preliminary findings before I can specify what needs to be done." Panov stopped at this point, feeling the asperity in his tone raising his voice beyond the point of acceptable masculinity. He despised his own too-high voice. The admiral growled and huffed like a bear.

"I see. You insist?"

Panov cleared his throat. "I do."

Dolohov reached across his desk and flicked the switch of his intercom.

"Get my car to the door at once, and warn the tower I shall want an immediate take-off." He switched off, and stood up, his arms extended in a bear-like embrace. The image made Panov suppress a shudder, and smooth dislike from his bland features. "Come, Comrade Academician Panov – your carriage awaits." Then Dolohov laughed. Panov had to endure a large hand slapping him on the shoulder, and the log-like fall of an arm across his neck, as he was ushered to the door. Dolohov's voice was like a caress when he added: "Don't you think *I* am anxious to see our prize, too?" Then he laughed again.

The hand of the clock on the wall clicked again. Six o-five.

Clark moved the rotary switch on the test kit for the final time, the needle on the dial flickered away from zero, and he cursed as he unclipped the kit's leads from the last of the test pins on the power supply units. Each and every one of them worked, gave a positive reading, had nothing wrong with them.

"OK, that's it," he said, glancing at his watch. Seven-o-two. Another hour had passed, and he was still at the moment before beginning. Everything he had done during the past three hours had been necessary, and pointless.

"Very well, Clark, you'd better run a check on the power lines, from TP Seventeen, Eighteen and Twenty-Four, using the cable adaptor with the yellow sleeve, marked BFP 6016 –"

"I got that," Clark snapped, wiping his forehead, then letting his hand stray to his eyes. He rubbed at them. They felt gritty with tiredness and concentration. He squeezed them shut and opened them again. He wanted another perspective. "Hold it, I want to talk to Lloyd again."

He took the R/T from his pocket, and pressed its call button.

"Yes?" Lloyd said quietly a moment later. Clark pressed the R/T to his cheek.

"What's happening?"

"I've just been on my rounds." Lloyd almost chuckled. There was a crackling, electric excitement in the man. He had swung away from the helpless depression of the prisoner. Now he was the schoolboy escapee. "I managed to brief one of my chief petty officers while I was doing it."

"What about the gates?"

"There's a minimal guard outside, always has been. The repair crew won't be here before eight. The gates can be opened by two men, one to throw the switches, the other to guard him. I'll detail men as soon as we free the wardroom. Then they can smash the switches so the gates can't be closed again."

"I agree."

"Clark – can you give me 'Leopard'? I can't risk my men and my vessel unless you do."

"Can you kill the first guard, Lloyd, the one outside your door?" Clark snapped back at him. "Because if you can't, then *Proteus* goes nowhere!" Clark, in the silence which followed, imagined Lloyd reaching under his pillow for the tiny Astra pistol he had left with him. Everything depended on Lloyd being able to kill the guard outside his cabin, retrieve the man's Kalashnikov, and release his officers from the wardroom along the corridor from his cabin.

"I – think I can," Lloyd replied eventually. "I'll have to, won't I?"

"And I have to repair 'Leopard', don't I?"

"Very well. Rumour has it that Panov, the scientist, is expected at any moment. The technicians on board have been informed to that effect. No later than eight o'clock."

"It's all coming right down to the wire, uh?" When Lloyd did not reply, Clark merely added, "I'll call you." He replaced the R/T in his pocket. Even as he did so, he heard Aubrey's voice in his ear.

"Clark, you must begin preparing to abort 'Leopard'. It will take you at least thirty to forty minutes to place the charges. You must begin at once."

"No, dammit!"

"Clark, do as you are ordered."

"Mr. Quin gave me a job to do – maybe after that."

"*Now!*"

"Not a chance."

Rapidly, he fitted the cable adaptor to the first of the power lines Quin had designated. Positive. He cursed under his breath. Then the second. Positive. Then the third. Positive. He sighed loudly, in anger and frustration.

"Fit the charges, Clark – please begin at once," Aubrey commanded with icy malice.

Ardenyev watched the MiL-8 transport helicopter sag down towards the landing pad. The down-draught, exceeding the wind's force, stirred the dust on the concrete. Behind it, the sky was beginning to lighten, a thin-grey blue streak above the hills, almost illusory beyond the hard white lighting of the helicopter base. Ardenyev glanced at his watch. Seven-ten. The admiral and Panov were almost an hour early. Viktor Teplov – face-saving, loyal Teplov – had picked up the information somewhere that Dolohov was on his way, and revived his officer with coffee and one large vodka, which Ardenyev had felt was like swallowing hot oil. Then he had commandeered a staff car and driver and accompanied Ardenyev to the helicopter base.

The MiL-8 hovered like an ungainly wasp, then dropped onto its wheels. Immediately, ducking ground crew placed the chocks against the wheels, even as the noise of the rotors descended through the scale and the rotor dish dissolved from its shimmering, circular form into flashes of darker grey in the rush of air. Then they were individual blades, then the door opened as the rotors sagged into stillness. Dolohov's foot was on the ladder as soon as it was pushed into place for him. He descended with a light, firm step, inheriting a kingdom. Men snapped to attention, saluting. A smaller, more rotund figure in a fur-collared coat stepped more gingerly down behind him. Panov. Dolohov waited for the scientist, then ushered him towards Ardenyev.

Ardenyev sucked spit from his cheeks and moistened his dry throat. He saluted crisply, then Dolohov extended his hand and shook Ardenyev's warmly.

"May I introduce Captain Valery Ardenyev," he said, turning to Panov. The scientist appeared intrigued, his face pale, almost tinged with blue, in the cold lighting. He shook Ardenyev's hand limply.

"Ah – our hero of the Soviet Union," he said with evident irony. Dolohov's face clouded with the insult to Ardenyev.

"Thank you, Comrade Academician Professor Panov," Ardenyev replied woodenly. He was enjoying fulfilling Panov's prejudices, meeting one of his stereotypes. "It was nothing."

Dolohov appeared bemused. "Shall we go?" he remarked. "Directly to the submarine pen, I think?"

"If you please," Panov said primly.

"This way, admiral – professor. The car is waiting."

"I'm sorry you lost so many men," Dolohov murmured confidentially as they walked towards the car. Panov, who was intended to overhear the remark, appeared at a loss, even embarrassed.

"So am I, sir – so am I." Teplov came to attention, then opened the rear door of the Zil. Ardenyev smiled wearily. "A ten-minute drive, sir, and you'll be able to see her. HMS *Proteus*, pride of the fleet!"

Dolohov laughed uproariously, slapping Ardenyev on the back before getting into the car.

FOURTEEN:

Running

Hyde woke, and reacted instantly to the cold air that had insinuated itself into their burrow. It was damp. He knew there was a fog or heavy mist outside, even though he could not see beyond the bush. There was greyness there, which might have been the dawn. He felt his shoulder protest with a sharp pain as he tried to rub his cold arms, and he stifled his groan as he remembered what had roused him. The running feet of deer along the track behind the rifle range, past the bush and the entrance into their hole. He looked immediately at the girl. She was soundly asleep.

He listened. And tested his shoulder, moving fingers and wrist and elbow and forearm. Slightly better. He touched the crude, dirty bandage. Dry and stiff. He investigated his resources. His body felt small, shrunken, empty and weak. But not leaden, as the previous night. His head felt more solid, too, less like a gathering of threads or misty tendrils. There was some clarity of thought, some speed of comprehension. He would have to do as he was. He was all he had, all they had.

The hoofbeats of the three or four deer who had fled past their hiding place died away, swallowed by what he was now convinced was a heavy mist. He listened to the silence, slow and thick outside the hole. He stretched his legs carefully, not disturbing the girl, felt the expected cramp, eased it away, rotated his pelvis as well as he could while hunched in a seated position. His back ached. He flexed his fingers once more, aware of the small of his back where the gun had been. Having completed his inventory, he pronounced himself incapable, with a slight smile. Some stubbornness had returned during the few hours' sleep he had had.

Noises. Slow, regular, cautious footsteps outside. He reached up and pressed his palm flat against the roof of the hole. The sand was damp. He levered himself out of his sitting position, and stepped over the girl's drawn-up knees. Her head rested on her chest, and her blonde hair, dirty and hanging in stiff, greasy tails, was draped like strands of cloth over her knees. He leaned forward, then slid towards the entrance to the hole. The branches of the bush became clear, as if he had focused an inward lens on them, and beyond them the heavy mist was grey and impenetrable. One chance. Don't wake up, darling –

The figure of a man emerged from the mist, bent low to study the track, the slim, pencil-like barrel of the rifle he carried protruding beyond the bulk of his form. He was little more than a dark shadow in the first light seeping into the mist. Then he saw the bush, and might have been staring into Hyde's eyes, though he registered no sign of having seen him. The gun moved away from his body, and Hyde recognized it, with a chill of danger and a strange greediness, as a Kalashnikov. Stubby, with a folding steel stock and plastic grip and the curving thirty-round ammunition box beneath the magazine. It was infinitely desirable, and deadly. The small R/T set clipped to the pocket of the man's anorak was similarly desirable and dangerous. Hyde coveted them both.

He held his breath as he felt one of the girl's feet touch his shin. Don't let her wake up, not now –

The man moved closer to the bush, the Kalashnikov prodding out in front of his body. Hyde flexed his fingers, keeping his head as close to the lip of the hole as he could, watching the man intently. The girl's foot stirred again, and Hyde prayed she would not make a noise in the last moments of her sleep. He felt her foot shiver. The cold was beginning to wake her. The stubby barrel of the rifle moved among the leafless branches, disturbing them, brushing them to one side. He squashed himself flat against the damp sand. He felt, through her foot, the girl's whole body stir, then he heard her yawn. Immediately the man's head snapped up, alert, cocked on one side as he listened, attempting to gauge the direction of the sound, waiting for its repetition. His eyes glanced over the bank, the rifle's barrel wavered in the bush, pointing above the hole. The girl groaned with stiffness. Hyde reached out, grabbed the stubby rifle, one hand on the barrel the other on the magazine. The man jerked backwards in surprise and defence, and Hyde pushed with his feet and used the man's response to pull him out of the hole and through the bush. He cried out with the sudden, searing pain in his arm and shoulder, but he held on, twisting the barrel of the rifle away from him, rolling down the sand to the track, pulling the man off balance.

The man almost toppled, then jerked at the rifle. Hyde had to release the grip of his left hand because the pain was so intense, but he had rolled almost to the man's feet. He kicked out, using his grip on the rifle as a pivot, and the man overbalanced as Hyde's shins caught him at the back of the legs. The Russian held on to the rifle, and Hyde felt the heat before he heard the sound of the explosion as a round was fired. Hyde used the rifle like a stick, an old man assisting himself to rise from a deep armchair, and as the man made to turn onto his

side and get up, Hyde kicked him in the side of the head. The grip on
the Kalashnikov did not loosen. Hyde, enraged and elated, kicked the
man once more in the temple, with all the force he could muster. The
man rolled away, his head seemingly loose on his shoulders, and lay
still. Hyde could see the man's chest pumping. He reached down for
the R/T, and a hand grabbed at the rifle again as Hyde held it still by
the barrel. The man's eyes were glazed and intent. Hyde staggered
away, taking the rifle with him. He had no strength, he should have
killed the man with one of the kicks, it was pathetic –

The man was sitting up. He heard Tricia Quin gasp audibly. He
fumbled the rifle until it pointed at the man, who was withdrawing
his hand from his anorak and the hand contained a pistol, heavy and
black and coming to a bead. Hyde fired, twice. The noise of the shots
seemed more efficiently swallowed by the mist than the cries of rooks
startled by the gunfire. The man's pistol discharged into the earth,
and he twitched like a wired rabbit. Hyde, angry and in haste, moved
to the body. He swore. One bullet had passed through the R/T set,
smashing it. Tricia Quin's appalled groan was superfluous, irrelevant.

Hyde knelt by the man's body, searching it quickly with one hand.
He had had to lay the rifle down. His left arm was on fire, and useless
to him. He hunched it into his side, as if he could protect it or lessen its
pain by doing so. He unzipped the anorak. No papers. The man didn't
even look Slavic. He could have been anybody. He patted the pockets
of the anorak. Yes –

Triumphantly, he produced a flask of something, and a wrapped
package of sandwiches.

"Food!" he announced. "Bloody food!"

The girl's face was washed clean of resentment and fear and revulsion. She grabbed the package eagerly. The sandwiches had some
kind of sausage in them. She swallowed a lump of bread and sausage
greedily, then tried to speak through the food.

"What –?" was all he heard.

Hyde looked around him. "Help me get this poor sod into the hole.
It might hide him for a bit. Come on – stop stuffing your face, girlie!"

Tricia put the sandwiches reverently, and with much regret, on the
track, roughly rewrapped. He took hold of one arm, she the other,
averting her eyes from the man's face, which stared up into the mist
in a bolting, surprised way. They dragged the body to the bank,
hoisted it – Tricia would not put her shoulder or body beneath the
weight of the man – and Hyde with a cry of pain and effort tumbled
the body into the hole.

"His foot," the girl said as Hyde stood trembling from his exertions.
Hyde looked up. The man's walking boot was protruding over the lip
of the hole.

"You see to it."

Reluctantly, the girl reached up, and pushed. The man's knee seemed locked by an instant rigor mortis. The girl obtained a purchase for her feet, and heaved. The foot did not move. She cried with exasperation, and wriggled and thrust until the foot disappeared.

"Bloody, bloody *thing*!" There was a crack from inside the hole. She covered her mouth, appalled. She turned accusing eyes on Hyde.

"We can all be shitty when we try hard," he said, eating one of the sandwiches. Then he added, "OK, pick the rest of them up –" He thrust the Makarov pistol into his waistband, and hefted the rifle in his good hand. The girl pocketed the sandwiches, looking furtively sidelong at him as she ate a second one. "Come on, then." He looked around him. "Bad luck and good luck. No one's going to find us in this."

They walked up the track behind the bank. The girl looked guiltily back once, still chewing the last lump of the second sandwich.

Clark ground his teeth in frustration, and clenched his hands into claws again and again as if to rid them of a severe cramp. The sight of what he had done enraged and depressed him. The plastic charges were taped and moulded to the back-up system, lying across the wiring and the circuitry like slugs, the detonator wires like the strands of a net that had dredged up the equipment from beneath the sea. He had done as Aubrey asked – commanded – and then he had requested Quin to set him another task, like an over-eager schoolboy. More power lines, and still nothing.

"Clark?" For a moment, he was tempted to curse Aubrey aloud. Part of him, however, admitted the correctness of Aubrey's decision.

"Yes?"

"It's time for you to rig the main 'Leopard' system. Good luck." There was no sense of possible argument or disobedience. Aubrey assumed he would behave like the automaton he was intended to be.

The bleeper on the R/T in his pocket sounded. He pulled the set out and pressed the transmit button. "Yes?"

"Clark? I think Panov's about to make an appearance. The technical team are streaming out of the *Proteus*, lining up like a guard of honour. I've just seen them."

"Where are you?"

"Hurry, Clark. You do not have much time –" Aubrey said in his ear.

"The officers' bathroom."

"Your guard?"

"Clark, listen to me –"

"Outside."

866

"Mood?"

"Pretty sloppy. He's waiting for his relief at eight."

"Clerk, you will abort 'Plumber' immediately and proceed to destroy 'Leopard'. Do you understand me?"

"Well?" Lloyd asked with a nervous edge to his voice.

"Get as close to him as you can, preferably the side of his head or under the jaw, and squeeze the trigger *twice*."

"Clark, you will rescind that instruction to Lloyd −"

"What about 'Leopard'?" Lloyd asked.

"I'll give you 'Leopard' in working order!" Clark snapped. "Where is Thurston, where's Hayter?"

"The First Lieutenant's in the cabin next to mine, Hayter's in the wardroom with the others."

"Then −"

"Clark −!"

"Time for Quin to earn his money!" Clark almost shouted, with nerves and relief and the adrenalin that suddenly coursed through his system. "Help me get this fucking back-up working, Quin!"

"Clark − *Clark*!"

"Go or no go?" Lloyd asked.

"Go − *GO*! Kill the bastard!"

"I'll be in touch."

"Clark − you are insane. You will never get out of Pechenga without 'Leopard'. You have not, you *cannot* repair it. You have just sentenced Commander Lloyd and his crew to imprisonment, possibly even death. You are *insane*." The last word was hissed in Clark's ear, serpentine and venomous.

Clark felt a heady, dangerous relief, and a pressing, violent anxiety. "For Chrissake, Quin − help me get this fucking thing to work! *Help me!*"

Aubrey stared at Quin. He could not believe in what Clark had put in motion, could not apprehend the violent and dangerous half-motives that had prompted him. In its final stage, the *Proteus* business was escaping him again, running on its own headlong flight unhindered by reason or caution or good sense. In a split-second over which he had had no control, Clark had made the decision not to abort. Now, everyone would face the consequences of that decision.

"Quin? *Quin*?" he snapped at his companion. The scientist tossed his head as if startled from sleep.

"What?"

"Can you help him?"

Quin shrugged. "We've tried everything we can. There's nothing wrong −"

"There must be, dammit!"

"I don't know what it is!" Quin almost wailed.

Aubrey leaned towards him. "That bloody American has set the seal on this affair, Quin. Lloyd will either kill his guard, or be killed. If the former, then they will kill others, picking up weapons at each death, until they can open the gates and sail *Proteus* out of Pechenga. Without 'Leopard' in an operational condition, they will be a target for every naval unit in the port. I would not wish to assume that the Russians will be prepared to let her sail away scot free! What can you do? Think of something!"

Quin began flipping through the "Leopard" manual, most of which he had written himself. Aubrey recognized an unseeing, desperate gesture. Quin *knew* the manual, nothing would come from it. The man's hands were shaking. He had collided with a brute reality. Aubrey shook his head with weariness. Tiredness, the sense of being utterly spent, seemed the only feeling left to him. Clark had renegued on reason, on authority. He could understand how it had happened. The American had simply refused to acknowledge defeat.

He heard Eastoe's voice tinnily in the headphones resting around his neck. He placed the set over his head. The microphone bobbed in front of his mouth.

"Yes, Squadron Leader?" He had not meant his voice to sound so waspish and dismissive.

"Mr. Aubrey. We're out of range again. I can try to get back, but I won't be able to hold station for very much longer. I can give you a couple of minutes, perhaps."

Aubrey wanted to rage at the pilot, but he acknowledged the weariness in the man's voice. The MiGs – there was one on the port wing again, turning silver in the beginning of the day – were making patterned flying impossible. Slowly, inexorably, the Nimrod was being shepherded away from the Soviet border.

"Do what you can, Squadron Leader. We're in your hands."

"Very well, Mr. Aubrey. I'll give you as long as I can."

The nose of the Nimrod dipped, and then when Eastoe judged he had lost sufficient height, the aircraft banked savagely, rolling away towards the east and the sun. The porthole in the fuselage became a blaze of gold, blinding Aubrey. He felt as old and thin and stretched as a ghost. Transparent in the sudden light.

"Quin, come on, man – suggest something. We don't have much time."

Quin groaned aloud, and rubbed his face with his hands, washing off his present circumstances. He looked blearily at Aubrey, and shook his head.

"There is nothing."

"There must be. Some faulty system, something you disagreed with Plessey about, something you've always suspected or disliked about the system – anything!" Aubrey spread his hands around the communications console, which hissed at him. It was as if he were about to jettison it as useless cargo. A MiG, gold-bright, popped into his view, just off the port wing. Craning his neck, Aubrey could see the grey sea, the misted coast below them. The MiG ducked beneath the Nimrod, and Aubrey saw it bob like a cork into the starboard porthole opposite him. "Something – *please?*"

The console crackled. Clark's voice was faint. The coast and sea below moved, and Aubrey could hear the Spey engines more loudly. Eastoe was running for the border with the Soviet Union in a straight, desperate line.

"You must help –"

"For Chrissake, Quin – say something!" Clark bellowed from the receiver.

Quin's face was an agony of doubt.

"Come on, Quin, come on, come on," Aubrey heard himself repeating.

"I can hear shooting!" Clark yelled. Aubrey knew it was a lie, but a clever one. And perhaps it only described events that had already occurred. Lloyd dead, a guard dead, two guards, three?

"Change-over – automatic change-over," Quin murmured.

"What's that?" Clark snapped.

The MiG on the starboard wing – two of them now, one above the other, moving on a course to head off the Nimrod. There was a slim shadow taking and changing shape on the port wing. One of the MiGs was above them, appearing almost as if it might be lowering itself onto the wing, to snap it in half. Eastoe dropped the nose of the Nimrod again, dropping towards the sea and the rocky coast that seemed to lurch up to meet them. The port wing and the starboard window were swept clean for a moment. Aubrey felt Eastoe begin to turn the aircraft. He'd given up. They were on their way back, and out of range.

"The automatic change-over from the main system to the back-up. I argued time and again, with the Admiralty. No trust in completely automatic systems. They insisted –"

"Tell him!"

Quin leant towards the console. "Clark," he began, "you must check the automatic change-over on the power supply from the main system to the back-up. Locate the power supply box . . ."

Aubrey ceased to listen. The Nimrod had completed its turn, through the brief blinding sunlight on the porthole, and was now heading west once more. Eastoe had dropped the aircraft's speed, but it was a matter of mere minutes until they would no longer be able to talk to Clark.

And, in Pechenga, with whatever outcome, the killing had undoubtedly begun.

One of the MiGs bobbed back into view, off the port wing. The Russian interceptor appeared to be flying a little further off, as if its pilot, too, knew that the game was up.

Lloyd hesitated for a moment, on the threshold of the bathroom, straddling the body of the guard who had only had time to half-turn before the small Astra, pressed against his side, had exploded twice. Lloyd had had to take him into an embrace, feel the man's final shudder against him, and lower him to the deck. One guard only in the corridor. Lloyd had been surprised at the small, muffled sound the gun had made when pressed into the spare flesh the man was carrying. It was as if the pistol had been fitted with a silencer.

He saw the guard outside the wardroom door at the end of the corridor, and hoped, as he studied the man's movements and saw the Kalashnikov turn in the guard's hands and draw a bead on himself, that Thurston would not blunder into the line of fire out of the cabin next door to his own. Then he prayed his hands would move more swiftly to bring the small pistol up to the level of the guard's trunk. He could not believe that he would move more quickly than the trained marine, but some realization that the clock was ticking away precious seconds only for him, came to him as he fired. He had moved inches faster, reaction had been milliseconds quicker, because he had an imperative the Russian did not share. The guard thudded back against the wardroom door, and slid down, feet out, to a sitting position with his head lolling. The pistol now made much more noise, and would have attracted attention.

"Come on, come on!" he yelled, banging on Thurston's door as he passed it. Then he was stooping to retrieve the Kalashnikov, which felt immediately bulky and menacing in his grip. He flung open the wardroom door. Surprised faces, half a dozen of them, mostly unshaven, were grouped around the table above mugs of steaming coffee. Thurston was behind him now. He passed the Astra back to his first lieutenant. "Get the others out – now!" he snapped, feeling the dangerous, elating adrenalin running wildly through his body.

Seven twenty-one. Clark had recognized, almost subliminally, the two shots, then the third after a slight delay. He imagined that the same small Astra pistol had made all three reports, but he could not quite believe it, until Lloyd's voice could be heard plainly, coming from the R/T which was clipped to the breast of his immersion suit,

870

ordering his officers to remain in the wardroom until the control room had been recaptured. Then there was the awful, cloth-ripping stutter of the Kalashnikov on automatic – Clark presumed feverishly that it was the one Lloyd had taken from the wardroom guard. It was. Lloyd yelled at Hayter to recover the gun of the man he had just killed. Clark nodded to himself. Lloyd would go on now until he became exhausted or until someone shot him. He was high on escape, even on death.

Clark lifted the lid of the power supply box, as Quin had instructed him. LIFT HERE ONLY. He had unclamped the lid, and obeyed its command, stencilled in yellow.

"Clark?"

"Yes. The box is open," he told Quin. Communications were already weakening as the Nimrod moved towards the fringes of reception. Aubrey had told him what was happening, then patched in Eastoe. The pilot did not enjoy admitting his weariness, his loss of nerve, his failure, but he had done so. The Nimrod was shot, finished. It was on its way home. Eastoe had dropped the airspeed as much as he could, but they were gradually moving out of range, taking Quin with his manual, his diagrams and his knowledge with them. He had, at the Nimrod's present speed, no more than five minutes. Seven twenty-two.

"Switch SW-Eight-R should be off." Clark followed Quin's instruction. Lloyd's breathing was audible to him in the confined, lamplit darkness from the R/T against the submarine captain's chest. Running –? Cries, yells –? *Come on, Quin –*

"OK."

"Press the yellow button marked PRESS TO TEST. Have you got that?" A faint, weak voice, like a man dying in the next room.

"OK?"

Firing.

"Lloyd, what's happening?" He knew he should not have called, that it might be fatal to distract Lloyd now. Yet the sounds tormented him, made his body writhe with an uncontrollable tension and anxiety.

Firing.

Quin said something he did not catch. He prayed it was only his inattention. ". . . through top . . . cover?"

"Repeat, please," he requested loudly, holding his breath. Lloyd's breathing roared on his chest like an illness he had contracted.

" . . . contacts move . . . clear top . . .?"

"Repeat, repeat!" Clark shouted, almost as a relief for the hours of whispering and silence he had endured and partly because he was panicking. The irreversible had begun. Lloyd had killed, the officers were armed with two Russian Kalashnikovs and were in the control room of the *Proteus*. He had begun it – *he* had. "Repeat. I say again, repeat your message." The words were formal, the voice running out of control.

"Right. Hold them over there – no, get them off my ship, *now*!" Lloyd's elation, his success, drummed in the cramped space between the two hulls. "Clark?"

"Yes?"

"What's wrong?" Even in his excitement, Lloyd was responsive to tone, to nuance.

"Nothing."

"We have the control room in our hands again."

"Good –" Clark paused. There was a spit of sound, but when the tape had been slowed, there was only the ether, mocking him. A gauzy, sad, distant voice mumbled behind it. *Christ, what have I done?* "Outside?"

"Thurston's taking a look. I've despatched three men, two of them armed, to the control booth for the gates. A couple of minutes now – ?" The statement ended as a question. Another spit of sound, Clark's heart pounding as he waited for it to replay more slowly in his earpiece, Quin's voice broken and racked by the interference.

"Can you see . . . through top . . . moving?"

Contacts, *contacts*, he recalled. Can you see the contacts moving through the clear top of the cover?

"Got you!" Then, immediately, he cried, "They're not moving!"

"Clark, what the devil's wrong?"

"I *can't* –!" Clark cried despairingly. "I don't know what's wrong!"

"For God's sake . . ." Lloyd breathed. "Oh my God!" Clark stared desperately at the contacts, which remained unmoving. Then he jabbed his finger on the test button again and again.

Spit of sound in his ear. What is wrong? What is the matter?

"Examine the relays," he heard Quin say quite clearly in a calm, detached voice. Then the interference rushed in to fill the small silence after he had spoken.

Relays, relays –

"What do I do?" Lloyd asked peremptorily, a sense of betrayal in his voice.

"Open the fucking gates!" Clark snarled. "You got nowhere else to go!" Relays, relays –

One of them is unclamped, *one of them is unclamped*!

"Chief – get the men to their stations, immediately. Engine room?"

"Sir, we're clear down here."

"Run up electric power. Well done, Chief!"

"Thank you, sir."

"Sandy, clear the ship of all Soviet personnel – all of them, mind you."

"One of them is unclamped!" Clark yelled into his throat-mike, as if he expected Quin to be able to hear him in an identical freak reception spot.

"What?" Lloyd asked.

"You do your thing, Lloyd – let me do mine!"

"Is it go?"

"It was go a long time past! Let's get out of here!"

"What about 'Leopard'?"

"I'll give you 'Leopard', dammit!"

"What about you? You can't be outside the pressure hull when we dive."

"You worry about your business, I'll worry about mine."

"Very well. Thurston's opening the gates now."

"Get with it."

Faulty fitting, he told himself. The relay, one single fucking relay, lying there on the base of the case. His fingers trembled as he reached down to it, touched it almost reverently, fearfully. His fingers stroked, embraced, lifted it. The vibration caused by the torpedo damage had shaken it out of place, disabling the back-up system, preventing the automatic change-over from working.

There was another spit of sound in his ear, but he ignored the slowed-down, true-speed voice of the storm and the air. Quin was invisible, inaudible somewhere behind it, but he no longer mattered.

Clark pressed home the detached relay, flipped over the retaining clamp, then removed his fingers from it. They came away clammily. The electric motors of the *Proteus* thrummed through the pressure hull.

His back ached. He groaned with the sudden awareness of it and of his cramped and twisted body and the rivulets of perspiration running down his sides and back.

Lloyd's stream of orders continued, murmuring on his chest like the steady ticking of his heart, slower and calmer and younger than his heart felt.

"Slow astern."

"Slow astern, sir." Thurston's voice was distant, but Clark could still hear it repeating the captain's instructions. They'd got the gates to the pen open, they'd cast off their moorings at bow and stern. How many men had they lost, just doing that?

"Clark?"

"Yes."

"Have you finished?"

"Yes. I hope to God, yes."

"Get back in here – now."

"Aye, aye, sir."

Clark turned, still on his knees. He could hear a siren through the outer hull of the *Proteus*. "Leopard" had to work –

He turned to look at the back-up system – the grey carapace lay behind it. He tore at the wiring and at the wads of explosive, huddling them into his chest then thrusting them back into the pack in pure elation. Then he lifted the grey metal casing, fitted it, fidgeted in his pocket for the screws, fixed them one at a time, feeling the submarine moving slowly backwards on her batteries, out of the pen. Yes, yes.

Pack, pack – left hand bad. The other could stay. Whatever happened, he would not be coming back. He took hold of the pack, and turned once more to make his way back to the hatch following the wire of his aerial. He shunted the pack and his lamp in front of him, hurrying now, winding through the tree-like stanchions like an obstacle course.

The *Proteus* lurched forward, as if freed from some constraint.

Clark slipped, and began to slide into the abyss, into the dark. His lamp slid away, wobbling its light back at him for a moment before leaving him in entire darkness, his body weighted by the pack in his right hand – left hand bad – beginning to pursue the fallen lamp. He crooked an arm round one of the stanchion trees, heaving his body into stillness, into a quiver that was devoid of downward movement. He felt sick. He felt exhausted.

"Clark – Clark, where are you, man?"

Clark groaned. He swung the pack until it rested on the level top of the pressure hull, then grabbed the stanchion with his right hand, changing the agonizing hold of his crooked arm for a two-handed grip. He heaved at his leaden body, feeling the revolutions of the motors rise in speed. *Proteus* must be almost out of the pen.

He pulled himself up, aided by scrabbling feet and knees, and lumbered along the top of the pressure hull, reached the hatch and thrust it open. He hefted the explosives through, and let them roll away down the outer hull. Then he clambered after them, closing the hatch and locking it behind him.

The stern of the submarine had already passed into the concrete tunnel leading to the harbour. On her docking prop, *Proteus* was sliding through the tunnel, out to sea.

He watched as the sail of the submarine slid into the shadow of the tunnel. Above the bellow of the siren, he could hear shooting in the distance, like the pinging of flies against a windscreen. Then he ran crouching along the hull, almost slipping twice, until he reached the aft escape hatch, lifted it, stepped onto the ladder inside the chamber, closed the hatch and locked it. Then he felt his legs go watery and he stumbled to the bottom of the escape chamber, bent double with effort and relief.

"Prepare to dive," he heard Lloyd saying, then: "Clark? Clark, where are you?"

"Inside."

"Thank God. Well, does it work?"

"Switch on, and pray."

"You don't sound too hopeful –"

"Switch the damn thing on!" Clark bellowed with rage and relief and tiredness.

Valery Ardenyev instinctively placed himself in front of Dolohov and Panov. The scene in the pen had no precise focus, nor did it possess a great deal of movement – certainly not sufficient to suggest panic – yet Ardenyev knew what was happening. One guard was firing, the technicians who must have been lining up like an honour guard to await Panov's arrival were shuffling like a herd smelling the first smoke of the grass fire. Also, there was someone clambering up the side of the *Proteus*'s sail, making his way back into the submarine. Ardenyev had the immediate sense that events were already minutes old, even though the white-coated group of figures seemed only now to be reacting to them. Yes. The gates were wide open, and there were two uniformed bodies lying dead on the concrete, alongside the *Proteus*.

He heard Dolohov say, in a strangled old voice, "No –!", and then he ushered them back through the door by which they had entered the pen, pushing them against the officers who had accompanied them, then had stood deferentially aside so that the three of them might be the first of the party to see the captured British vessel.

"Close the door – give the alarm!" he snapped, then he was pushing through the jostle of technicians towards the submarine.

The *Proteus* slid away from him. As he passed the huddled bodies he believed he recognized the face of the guard on Lloyd's cabin, the man who had patrolled behind the British officer when he had brought Lloyd lunch and told him about Panov.

He ran faster. The *Proteus* shuddered against the side of the pen, then was free. The bow was still moving away from him as he raced to overtake it. He could not believe the panic appearance of the break-out. There had to have been help, and hope. Lloyd or someone else had been given a gun. He *knew* 'Leopard' must have been repaired. Lloyd would not have risked lives, and his submarine, without knowing he could rely on the protection of the anti-sonar equipment.

The bow was behind him now. He ran closer to the hull. It rose smoothly above him. He was half-way down the pen, the only moving figure. There was rifle fire behind him, pointless but noisy. The *pitons* of a ladder climbed away from him. He reached for the lowest one, felt his feet lifted and dragged, his stride extending to great lunar bounds as his arms protested. Then he was pressing himself against the side of the submarine, watching the concrete wall of the tunnel approaching. He might have been half-jammed into the door of a metro train, watching the end of the platform racing at him.

He clambered up the hull, feet slipping, hands sweaty, onto its upper section. He climbed the last few *pitons* and stood on top of the hull as it slid into the tunnel. He ran to the forward escape hatch, unlocked it, lifted it, and clambered down into the chamber, closing the hatch behind him.

"Did he hear you, man? Did he?"

Quin shook his head. "I don't know," he admitted. "I really don't know."

Aubrey looked at his watch. Seven twenty-seven. They were out of range. The link between Clark and the Nimrod had been broken as certainly as if Pasvik had been shot, and his dish aerials smashed. There was nothing more to be done. As if he saw clearly into Aubrey's mind, Eastoe's voice sounded in the headset.

"That's it, Mr. Aubrey. Sorry."

"Thank you for your efforts, Squadron Leader," Aubrey replied.

Aubrey looked through the porthole, out beyond the sun-tipped port wing. Ahead of the Nimrod, the sky was darker, and the land below them was tumbled and cracked in shadow. Cloud and mist wound like white, unsubstantial rivers through the peaks and the fjords. The MiG-23 on the port wing waggled its body like an athletic silver insect, dipping its wings in turn, and then it dropped away and out of sight. The Nimrod was more than a hundred and fifty miles from the Soviet border, making for North Cape.

Aubrey groaned with disappointment.

"I'm sorry," Quin said.

"Do you think he would have found anything?"

"There seemed no other place to look –" Quin shook his head and stared at the still-open manual in front of him. He closed the wire-bound book. "I don't know. I could think of nothing else."

Behind them, *Proteus* and her crew would be breaking out – to what purpose? With what reprisals? There was blood now, instead of diplomacy or an intelligence game. People had been killed, Soviet citizens. It did not bear consideration. Aubrey surrendered instead to his utter and complete weariness of mind and body; a comforting numbness.

Seven twenty-nine.

Then the signal, in clear, that he no longer believed to be possible.

"Mr. Aubrey?"

"Yes?"

"A signal from *Proteus*, in clear."

"No –"

"It reads – 'At one stride comes the dark' – end of message. Do you understand it? Shall I ask for a repeat?"

"No thank you, Squadron Leader. Let us go home."

"Very well, sir."

A beatific smile wreathed Aubrey's features, inflating his grey cheeks, forming his lips, screwing up his eyes. Coleridge's *Ancient Mariner*. "At one stride comes the dark". The signal he had told Clark to make in a moment of amusement, a moment of looking for the right, witty, portentous thing for Clark to say if and when he repaired "Leopard". Somehow, he had done it.

"What is it?" Quin asked.

"It's all right. It's all right," Aubrey repeated, opening his eyes, slouching back in his seat, almost asleep already. "Clark has done it."

"Thank God," Quin breathed.

The man's daughter, Aubrey thought, his body immediately chilled. Tricia Quin and Hyde. What of them? Alive, or dead? If the latter, how would he tell Quin?

"Admiral, we have no units capable of detecting and stopping the British submarine – not in the inner harbour," the officer commanding the defences of Pechenga explained to Dolohov, nervously standing to attention before the older, more senior man. Inwardly, he wished himself a great distance from the defence control room, set beneath thick concrete and lit by strip-lighting, but he struggled to preserve a form of dignity and an impassive expression on his face. Dolohov was evidently beside himself with rage.

"Nothing? *Nothing*?" Turning, Dolohov waved at the sheet of perspex marked in a grid, displaying coloured lights and chinagraph markings. The two anti-submarine nets were bright red strings of beads, the mines, represented by colours according to type, were like the knots in a fine skein, ready to be drawn about the *Proteus*. Beyond the first net, the units of the Red Banner Fleet at present in Pechenga appeared as a host of bright lights.

"Everything is cold, Admiral – reactors, diesels, turbines all need time to run up to operational readiness. We have been caught flat-footed –" He cut off his explanation as Dolohov turned to him again.

"Where is she? *Where is the submarine?*" he bellowed.

"She disappeared from our screens two minutes ago – here." The defences commandant hurried to the perspex screen in the centre of the operations room and gathered up a pointer that rested against its base. The perspex flexed and dimpled as he tapped with enthusiasm at it. A chinagraphed dotted line ran from the fifth of the submarine pens to a point marked with a circled cross, in the inner harbour. "We think she was already turning at this point –" A junior officer beside the perspex screen nodded in agreement.

"What do you intend to do about it?"

"There are two patrol boats in the inner harbour now – the mines, of course, are all activated. However, the inertial navigator memory aboard the submarine may have tracked their course when they entered the harbour, if it had been left on. Even so, it is unlikely they will be able to avoid the mines with any degree of success –"

"Switch them off! Switch off all your mines, at once!"

"But, Admiral –"

"Do as I order! That submarine must be stopped, not destroyed. We cannot take the risk of doing permanent or irreparable damage to her." Dolohov paused. The political consequences would be enormous, and possibly violent, he considered. In making that judgment, he gave no thought to London or Washington or Brussels, only to the Kremlin. His political masters would not forgive the international repercussions of the destruction of the British submarine in Soviet territorial waters. That had been made clear to him, from the outset.

The commandant nodded to one of his juniors, and the order was given. Almost immediately, the fine skein of lights blinked off, leaving great areas of the perspex screen blank and grey. Every mine in the inner harbour and in the outer basin was now disarmed. The fleet vessels which had before glowed in tiny pockets of greyness, their safe anchorages clear of the mines, now beamed out in isolation; single, unmoving lights. Dolohov hated the blank areas of the screen, like areas on a map still to be explored.

"Now," he said heavily, "I want every unit in the outer basin to be prepared. You have a minelayer in port?"

"Yes, Admiral."

"With low power mines?"

"Yes, Admiral."

"Then they must be instructed to sow fresh mines along the seaward side of the inner net. Proximity fuses, or magnetic. But they *must* be of sufficient strength only to cripple, not destroy. Understand?"

"The inner net, Admiral, will not be opened?" The man evidently did not understand.

"You will lay the mines, by aircraft if you have to, and you will do it at once," Dolohov said with a passionate calmness. "The British captain has torpedoes, wire-guided with television cameras. He can blow a hole in the inner net. If there are mines waiting for him when he escapes through his own hole, he will go to the bottom, or be slowed down, or be forced to the surface. Now do you understand?"

"Yes, Admiral. I will issue the orders at once."

"Good." Dolohov thought once, and briefly, of the fact that Ardenyev was aboard the *Proteus*, and then dismissed his image in favour of self-congratulation. In the midst of his fierce rage and disappointment, there was room for satisfaction. He had anticipated what the British captain would do to escape, and he might already have made the move that would frustrate his efforts.

He studied the perspex screen intently.

"Torpedo room – stand by."

"Aye, aye, sir. Standing by."

Lloyd studied the sonar screen in front of him. As its arm circled the screen, washing the light-pattern behind it, the bright spots and lines of the submarine net appeared on the screen. It was, as Clark had originally outlined, the only way out – through both nets.

"Range?" he said.

"Eight hundred, sir."

"Torpedo room – load number one tube."

"Number one tube loaded, sir."

The Tigerfish wire-guided torpedo was ready to be fired. Lloyd looked at his watch. Four minutes and thirty-six seconds since they had cleared the pen. Speed was the essence, Clark had said. Just like killing the two guards, he reminded himself with a sick feeling in the pit of the stomach. Speed, surprise. And the gamble that Pechenga would switch off and disarm its minefield in order to preserve "Leopard".

"Range seven-fifty, sir."

"Torpedo room – fire one!"

"One away, sir."

Lloyd crossed the control room to where Thurston was studying the tiny, blank television screen set alongside the fire control console's other screens and panels of lights. The screen flickered on. Both men ignored the voice over the intercom calling the range and speed and functions of the wire-guided Tigerfish. They seemed mesmerized by the stir and rush and billow of grey water illuminated weakly by the light on the torpedo. Lloyd's wrist with its curling, dark hairs was at the edge of his eyesight. He saw, conjointly with the image on the screen, the second hand ticking round, moving up the face of the watch, a red spider-leg.

The flash of something, like a curtain or a net though it might only have been an illusion created by the moving water. Then the screen blanked out as the torpedo operator registered the correct and chosen proximity to target and detonated the warhead of the Tigerfish. The shock-wave was a dim, rumbling shudder along the outer hull a few moments later. Lloyd grinned at Thurston.

"Let's see if you can find the hole, John, mm?"

"Aye, aye, sir."

The mist had lifted, remaining in small, thin pockets only in hollows and folds of the ground. The sun had resolved itself into a hard, bright circle, and the sky was palely blue. Hyde was sweating with effort and the rise in temperature as he pulled the girl up the steep bank behind him. When they stood together on the top of the bank, Hyde could see the Chase sloping away from them. He pulled the girl down beside him, and they lay on the wet, dead ferns, staring down through the silver-boled, bare birches towards the tiny figures making their way with laborious effort up towards them. The rifle ranges were behind them, the line of huge, numbered targets perhaps six hundred yards away.

Three of them – no, four. Somehow, Hyde knew there were no others. He checked the magazine, weighing it. Perhaps ten rounds left of the thirty it had originally contained. He thrust the folding double-strut stock against his good shoulder, and looked through the tangent rear sight and the protected post foresight. The action gave him confidence. The mist had been their patron, then their betrayer. Now, the clear air and the bright, warming sun were on their side. Hyde held the high ground. The effective range of the AK-47 was three hundred metres. The four men were at twice that range. He was required to wait.

"You all right?"

"Yes."

The situation became increasingly unreal the more he considered it, the closer the Russians drew. He was in the middle of Staffordshire, these men were either accredited diplomats of the Soviet embassy or they were casuals called out from the woodwork to assist Petrunin. They were the ones on alien ground, and only now that he looked down on them, armed with one of their rifles and with the mist evaporated, could he perceive the situation in those terms. He had already won. The men down there pushed other men under buses, poisoned them with tiny metal pellets in the tips of umbrellas, pushed them onto the live rail of the underground. Maybe in the north of Scotland they could go on playing this hunting game, but not here. In a minute, a portly matron would appear, exercising a small dog, or someone from the Forestry Commission would pass them in a Land Rover.

Stop it, stop it, he instructed himself. It was still four to one, and the police would be out in force on the M6, but not necessarily on Cannock Chase. Perhaps four hundred yards now. The four men had spread out, but until they reached the trees on the slope below they had no cover. They moved more cautiously now, probably afraid.

"Not long now," he offered to Tricia Quin.

"What isn't? What won't be?" she asked in a sullen, tired voice. "Christ, I'm tired and scared and hungry."

"That's two of us." He opened his squinting eye, and removed the gaze of his other eye from the sights of the Kalashnikov. He studied her. She had become girlish again, and his attitude to her hardened. The rest of it, anything warmer, belonged in the burrow where they had hidden and in his disordered imagination as he half slept. Now, he could not say that he even liked her particularly. She, evidently, disliked him. Their former attitudes had re-emerged, as if they both understood that they were already on the other side of their experience. "We've got the advantage now."

She shook her head, staring at the rifle. It alienated her from him. He accepted her distance. She was about to climb back into the feckless skin which he had forced her to shed. She already resented the sloughing of her past self for the last few days.

He looked back. Still the four men, clambering through the wet ferns and the dead heather. A Land Rover passed along a distant, open track behind them, and he grinned. He put down the rifle and cupped his hands.

"Petrunin! Can you hear me, Petrunin?" he bellowed. The men stopped immediately.

"Yes," came the faint reply. Petrunin remained just out of effective range of the Kalashnikov. And he knew he was out of range.

"I've won, you stupid joker!"

"Not yet."

"Admit it. You're finished. You'd better start making arrangements to fly out before they catch you. You're finished in England, mate!"

The four men remained standing, looking like an irresolute group of hikers. Just over three hundred yards away. There was nothing they could do, no way in which they could move forward into the trees without coming into range. Stalemate. Stand off.

"I think not. We are four to one." Petrunin's voice was faint, unthreatening. The Forestry Commission Land Rover had turned into a wide, sunlit ride, and was moving away. The normality it represented did not, however, diminish. Petrunin was bluffing, his words empty.

"Piss off!" Hyde yelled with a quick, sharp delight. "You're beaten and you know it! Go home to Mother –"

881

The girl's gasp was inaudible, the beginning of her scream merely scratched at his attention, far below the volume of his own voice, but the slump of her body at the corner of his vision attracted him, caused him to turn, his hands reaching instinctively for the rifle. It was kicked away from him, and then a second kick thudded into his wounded shoulder as it came between the walking boot and the side of his head. Tricia Quin, he had time to see, had been struck by the man's rifle stock on the temple, and her head was bleeding. He heard himself scream with pain, his whole body enveloped in the fire which ran from his shoulder. He raised one hand feebly as the man kicked again, then drove the wooden stock of his AKM rifle down at Hyde's face, an action as unemotional as stepping on an insect. Hyde attempted to roll away, but the stock of the rifle caught him between the shoulder blades, winding him, forcing all the air from his lungs so that he felt transfixed to the ground.

He went on rolling, and the man who must have doubled around behind them before they had reached the top of the slope came after him, rifle still pointed stock-first towards the Australian. There was a set, fixed smile on the man's face. The man wasn't going to shoot him, he was going to beat and club him to death. Petrunin and the others would already have started running, reaching the bottom of the slope, beginning now perhaps to labour up it to the top, through the birch trees.

Hyde kicked out, struck the rifle but not the man, who stepped nimbly aside and then came forward again. Hyde tried to get to his knees, aware of himself offering his back and neck for more blows, for execution. He could not catch his breath, which made a hollow, indigestible noise in his throat. The rifle swung to one side, then the stock swung back. Hyde fell away from it, and kicked out, catching the man on the shin, making him exclaim with the unexpected pain. The rifle stock sought his head. He pushed himself half upright on one arm, and dived inside the intended blow. His head snapped up into the man's groin, making the man's breath explode, his body weakly tumble backwards. Hyde grabbed the man's legs, squeezing them together, aware of his back exposed to the next blow. Broken back, his imagination yelled at him. Broken back, lifelong cripple in a chair. He heaved at the man's thighs against his shoulder, and they tottered in that supplicatory embrace until the ground dipped and the Russian lost his balance and fell onto his back. Hyde clambered along the man's body, aware of the shadow of the rifle and the man's arm moving to his right, holding his belt, then his shirt, then his throat as if he might have been ascending a sheer slope. He raised himself above the man, blocking the swing of the rifle with his shoulder and back, pressing down as he levered himself up on the man's windpipe.

882

Then he released his grip, bunched his fist, and punched the man in the throat. The man's tongue came out, his eyes rolled, and there was a choking, gagging sound from his open mouth. His body writhed as if at some separate pain.

Hyde scrambled back to the lip of the slope, dragging the man's AKM behind him by its strap. He fumbled it into his hands, and flicked the mechanism to automatic. He knelt, unable to climb to his feet, and squeezed the trigger. The noise deafened him. Bark flashed from the scarred birches, ferns whipped aside, one man fell just as he emerged from the trees, twenty yards from Hyde; a second man was halted, then turned away.

Hyde released the trigger, and inhaled. His breath sobbed and rattled, but it entered his lungs, expanded them, made him cough. He swallowed phlegm, and crouched down, breathing quickly as if to reassure himself that the mechanism of his lungs now operated efficiently. When he could, he yelled at the hidden Petrunin.

"Tough shit, mate! Nice try!"

Silence. He waited. The man behind him was making a hideous noise that somehow parodied snoring, or noisy eating. Otherwise, silence. He looked at the girl, and thought he could see her breasts rising and falling in a regular rhythm. He hoped it was not an illusion, but he could not, as yet, summon the strength or the detachment to investigate. Silence.

Eventually, he raised his head. Beyond the trees, three tiny figures were moving away. One of the dots supported a second dot. The one in the lead, striding ahead, Hyde took to be Petrunin, his mind already filled with images of his skin-saving passage out of the country. A small airfield in Kent, after he had arranged to be picked up by car and driven down the M1. Hop across the Channel, then Aeroflot to Moscow direct.

Hyde lay back exhausted, staring up at the bright sun in the almost cloudless, pale sky. He began laughing, weakly at first, then uncontrollably, until his eyes watered and his back and ribs were sore and his shoulder ached.

He heard a noise, and sat up. The girl was wiping her head with a dirty handkerchief, pulling grimacing faces, seeming surprised at the blood that stained the handkerchief. Hyde wiped his eyes, and lay back again. The sky was empty, except for the sun. He waited – he decided he would wait until he heard a dog bark, and then raise his head and check whether it was indeed a portly matron out exercising a runt-sized, pink-bowed dog in a tartan overcoat.

Clark looked up at the ceiling of the wardroom pantry with an involuntary reaction. A forkful of scrambled eggs remained poised an inch or so from his lips. The cook had disliked his insistence on eating in the pantry rather than the wardroom proper, but the rating now seemed almost pleased at his company. What was it Copeland had said? *They'll have to be careful, like small boys scrambling under a barbed wire fence into an orchard. Lloyd could get his trousers caught.* Clark smiled. Evidently, they had found the hole they had blown in the net, but not its exact centre. The starboard side of the *Proteus* had dragged for perhaps a hundred feet or more against some obstacle, some bent and twisted and sharp-edged remnant of the net, and then the fin had clanged dully against the net, jolting the submarine, which had then altered its attitude and slipped beneath the obstruction.

Clark registered the scrambled egg on his fork, and opened his mouth. He chewed and swallowed. The food was good, and it entirely absorbed his attention and his energies. He picked up his mug of coffee, and washed down the mouthful of egg. He was eating quickly and greedily and with an almost sublime satisfaction. The responsibility was no longer his. "Leopard" worked. Immediately, his concussive readiness had drained from him while he lay slumped in the aft escape chamber, and he had gone into a doped and simple-minded superficiality of awareness and sensation. He realized how dirty he was, how much he smelt inside the immersion suit, how hungry and thirsty he was, how tired he was. A junior officer had escorted him to the wardroom. By that time, food had become the absolute priority, after removing his immersion suit. They gave him the disguise of his overalls to wear until he had taken a shower.

What was happening, in the control room and outside the submarine, was of no interest to him. He could not, any longer, have recited the instructions he had given Lloyd when he first boarded the *Proteus*. Some tape in his mind had been wiped. He could not have seen the loose relay in the back-up system now, without having it pointed out to him.

"Like some more, sir?" the cook offered, holding the saucepan out towards him.

Clark grinned, and patted his stomach. "That'll do, I think, don't you? Very good."

"Thank you, sir. More coffee, sir?"

"Please."

The senior rating brought the jug of coffee towards the table where Clark sat. Then he seemed to wobble sideways, and lurch against the stove. A stream of dark coffee flew from the jug, cascading down one of the walls – at least, Clark knew that would be what the coffee would do, but the lights went out before he could observe it happen, and he was flung off his chair and bundled into one corner of the pantry. His head banged sickeningly against some jutting piece of kitchen furniture, and he rolled away from it, groaning. He sat up, rubbing his head, his ears ringing with the concussion and the noise that had accompanied the shudder of the submarine, as the emergency lights flickered on, then the main lights came back almost immediately after.

"All right?" he asked.

The cook was wiping coffee from his apron, and rubbing his arm. He still had the empty jug in his hand.

"What happened, sir?"

The *Proteus* was maintaining course and speed, as far as Clark could apprehend.

"Mine." Someone in Pechenga was thinking fast. He got to his knees, head aching, and the second mine threw him forward as the submarine rolled to starboard with the impact of the explosion. Darkness, slithering, the clatter of utensils, the groan of the hull, the terrible ringing in his ears, the thud of the cook's body on top of him, winding him, then the lights coming back on. He felt the *Proteus* right herself through his fingertips and the rest of his prone body. Over the intercom, Lloyd requested an all-stations damage report immediately. The senior rating rolled off Clark and apologized.

"OK, OK. I think I'll just go see what's happening." The cook appeared disappointed at his departure. "You OK?"

"Yes, thank you, sir."

Clark left the wardroom pantry, his body tensed, awaiting a further explosion. He entered the control room at the end of the short corridor from the living quarters, and immediately sensed the mood of congratulation. *Proteus* had not been seriously, hamperingly damaged.

"Contact at green three-six closing, sir." Someone had got the Soviet ships moving in double-quick time.

"Increase speed – nine knots," he heard Lloyd say.

"Nine knots, sir."

"Net at two thousand yards."

"Contact at red seven-zero also moving. Range one thousand."

"Contact at green eight-two closing, sir."

The hornet's nest had been poked with a stick. Clark realized that the Russians needed less luck in the confined space of the harbour than they needed out in the Barents Sea, and then they had found a crippled *Proteus*.

"Contact at red seven-zero making for the net, sir."

"Contact at green three-six closing, sir. Range seven hundred."

Lloyd saw Clark from the corner of his eye. Clark waved to him, and grinned. Lloyd returned his attention at once to the bank of sonar screens in front of him. Moved by an impulse to see the equipment he had repaired actually functioning, Clark crossed the control room softly, and exited through the aft door. The "Leopard" room was directly behind the control room.

As he closed the door, he heard Lloyd speak to the torpedo room after ordering a further increase in speed.

"Torpedo room – load number two tube."

They would make it. Just, but they would make it.

The door to the small, cramped "Leopard" room was open. Clark, as he reached the doorway, was instantly aware of the rating lying on the floor, and the officer slumped against one of the cabinets containing the main system. And he recognized the dark-jerseyed man who turned towards the noise he had made, knocking on the door-frame in the moment before he had taken in the scene in the room.

Valery Ardenyev. It *was* him. Clark knew he had killed Hayter and the rating.

Seven forty-three. He saw the clock above Ardenyev's head as he took his first step into the room and the Russian turned to him, a smile of recognition on his face. Ardenyev's hand moved out, and threw the switch he had been searching for before Clark disturbed him. As the switch moved, Clark knew that "Leopard" had been de-activated. The *Proteus* moved through the outer harbour of Pechenga, registering on every sonar screen of every Soviet ship and submarine.

"I knew it had to be you," Clark said in a surprisingly conversational tone, warily skirting the rating's body near the door. Ardenyev had apparently killed both of them without a weapon.

"I didn't reach the same conclusion about you." Ardenyev's back was to the control console of the "Leopard" equipment, protecting the switch he had thrown. "Perhaps I should have done." The Russian shrugged, then grinned. "It won't take long. I only have to keep this stuff –" He tossed his head to indicate "Leopard", "– out of action for a few minutes."

"Sure." Clark shook his head, smiling. "You're beaten. We're on our way out, you're alone on an enemy submarine. What chance do you have?"

"Every chance, my friend. That's the Soviet Union a few hundred yards behind you –"

Clark sprang at Ardenyev, who stepped neatly and swiftly to one side, bringing his forearm round sharply across Clark's back. The American grunted and collapsed across the console, his hand reaching instinctively for the switch above him. Ardenyev chopped the heel of his hand across Clark's wrist, deadening it, making the hand hang limply from his forearm. Then Ardenyev punched Clark in the kidneys, making him fall backwards and away from the control console, doubling him up on the floor. Ardenyev leaned casually against the console, watching Clark get groggily to his knees, winded.

"You're tired, my friend," Ardenyev observed.

Mistily, Clark saw the red second hand of the clock moving jerkily downwards. Fourteen seconds since Ardenyev had thrown the switch. He staggered, then tried to lean his weight against the Russian and hold onto him. Ardenyev rammed his knee into Clark's groin, and then punched him in the face. Clark fell backwards again, groaning. He did not want to get up, and did not feel he had the strength to do so. The clock just above Ardenyev's head obsessed him. Twenty-two seconds. *Proteus* must almost have reached the net.

He seemed to feel the submarine hesitate, and saw the attentiveness on Ardenyev's face. He heard a noise scrape down the hull. The net –

The mine exploded beneath the hull, rocking the submarine, blinking out the lights. In the darkness, Clark struggled to his feet and groped for the Russian, feeling his woollen jersey, grabbing it, striking his hand at where the Russian's face would be. He felt the edge of his hand catch the man's nose, below the bridge, felt Ardenyev's breath expelled hotly against his cheek as he cried out in pain, and grabbed the Russian to him in the dark. The room settled around them.

Ardenyev thrust himself and Clark against one of the cabinets. A sharp handle dug into Clark's back, but he hooked his leg behind Ardenyev's calf and pushed. The lights came on as they rolled on the floor together. Clark drove his head down into the Russian's face, but the man did not let go of his neck. Clark felt his throat constrict, and he could no longer breathe. He tried to pull away from the grip, but it did not lessen. Blood ran into Ardenyev's mouth and over his chin, but he held on. The fin of the submarine scraped beneath the holed outer net, the submarine jerked like a hooked fish, shuddering, and then *Proteus* was free.

Clark's thoughts clouded. Ardenyev was interested only in killing him. Nothing else mattered. He beat at Ardenyev's face and neck and shoulders, his punches weak and unaimed and desperate. Consciousness became more and more fugged and insubstantial, then Ardenyev's grip on his throat seemed to slacken. Clark pulled away, and the hands fell back onto Ardenyev's chest, lying there, curled like sleeping animals.

Clark looked at his own hands, covered with blood, bruised, shaking. In one of them he held something that only slowly resolved in his watery vision until he was able to recognize it as the R/T set from his overalls pocket, the one he had used to communicate with Lloyd. He leaned down over Ardenyev's chest, listening. He avoided looking at the man's battered face. He had slapped the R/T set against Ardenyev's face and head time after time with all his remaining strength, as if the movement of his arm would pump air into his lungs.

Ardenyev was dead.

Clark clambered up the cabinet, then lurched to the control console, flicking the switch back to "On". "Leopard" was activated. It was seven forty-five. "Leopard" had been switched off for almost two minutes. Long enough for *Proteus* to have been spotted, not long enough for her to be attacked.

He sensed the increased speed of the *Proteus* through the deck, as she headed for the open sea. He avoided looking at Ardenyev's body. He dropped the blood-slippery R/T to the floor and hunched over the console, wanting to vomit with weakness and disgust and relief. He rubbed at his throat with one hand, easing its soreness. He closed his eyes. Now, he wanted only to sleep, for a long time.